Praise for *The Runaway Soul*

"*The Runaway Soul* shudders with a present-tense urgency, a desire to exhaust the meaning from an event, to fathom the heart of loved ones, to lay the dead finally to rest. . . . All these doomed characters glow with life, and with sexuality, whether adulterous, incestuous, homosexual, thwarted or ecstatic."
—Michael Dirda, *Washington Post Book World*

"To read *The Runaway Soul* is to uncover a tome authored by a refugee from some now-obscure devastation, who survived in his wilderness of place and mind by writing to himself about himself: deliriously, brilliantly, ceaselessly."
—Harold Jaffe, *Los Angeles Times*

"Moving. . . . A monstrous, ambitious, bold and puzzling novel. . . . Mr. Brodkey is clearly. . . a brilliant writer."
—D. M. Thomas, *New York Times Book Review*

"Reminiscent of both William and Henry James, [*The Runaway Soul*] is some kind of poetic masterpiece in its psychological depiction of the pragmatic American temperament."
—Laurence Donovan, *Miami Herald*

"A Victorian novel with a lot of sex . . . convincing and poetic. . . . Brodkey treats his unbearably flawed characters with tenderness, and a surprisingly old-fashioned touch."
—Jane Mendelsohn, *Voice Literary Supplement*

"Provocative. . . . Pulsing with sensory imagery and with flashes of insight . . . . The sheer wizardry of words tumbling on the page, the turbulent torrent of memories and desires, contribute to an intriguing meditation on existence."
—*Publishers Weekly*

THE RUNAWAY SOUL

Also by Harold Brodkey

First Love and Other Stories (1958)

Women and Angels (1985)

Stories in an Almost Classical Mode (1988)

THE RUNAWAY SOUL

HAROLD BRODKEY

HarperPerennial
A Division of HarperCollins*Publishers*

The author would like to thank the National Endowment for the Arts and the John Simon Guggenheim Memorial Foundation for their support.

Portions of this book have appeared in a different form in The New Yorker.

A hardcover edition of this book was published in 1991 by Farrar, Straus & Giroux. It is here reprinted by arrangement with Farrar, Straus & Giroux.

HarperCollins books may be purchased for educational, business, or sales promotional use. For information please write: Special Markets Department, HarperCollins Publishers, Inc., 10 East 53rd Street, New York, NY 10022.

First HarperPerennial edition published 1992.

Library of Congress Cataloging-in-Publication Data

Brodkey, Harold.
The runaway soul : a novel / Harold Brodkey. — 1st HarperPerennial ed.
p. cm.
ISBN 0-06-097504-0 (pbk.)
I. Title.
PS3552.R6224R86 1992
813′.54—dc20 92-52626

---

92 93 94 95 96 RRD 10 9 8 7 6 5 4 3 2 1

For Ellen

and Andrew, Roger, Jonathan,

Bill, Robert, and Harold

Contents

NATURAL HISTORY

LIFE ON THE MISSISSIPPI

THE INHABITED UNIVERSE

THE RUNAWAY SOUL

UNNATURAL HISTORY

SAINT NONIE

HOMOSEXUALITY, *or Two Men on a Train*

NATURAL HISTORY

1930

I was slapped and hurried along in the private applause of birth—I think I remember this. Well, I imagine it anyway—the blind boy's rose-and-milk-and-gray-walled (and salty) aquarium, the aquarium overthrown, the uproar in the woman-barn . . . the fantastic sloppiness of one's coming into existence, one's early election, one's senses in the radiant and raw stuff of howlingly sore and unexplained registry in the new everywhere, immensely unknown, disbelief and shakenness, the awful contamination of actual light. I think I remember the breath crouched in me and then leaping out yowlingly: this uncancellable sort of beginning.

The other birth—of a mind shaped like a person—all that skull buzz and mumble—a mind starting up, a mind that wants so much to know the truth that it makes the effort and takes the shape of a boy—and comes into existence: only a first draft at first, sketchy, watercolored, clichéd—cardboard air, a symbolic wrist, a painted eyebrow—a tattered, half-real boy as proud as a mind: an apple-eater in an unspecific light: two differently born creatures, one guy. Imagine the twists of suspense in being in two different autobiographical narratives at the same time. Think of all the myths of single meanings . . . of there being a single line of one's own history.

And then to be born in two sharply divergent ways, if I humor the hypothesis of two births, if I admit I sense MYSELF as a consciousness, a more or less consciously *alphabetical* gesticulating shadow—but real-seeming—and real, as real as real, but as only partly filled in, not to others but to myself, two days old, two years old, five years old, fourteen, fifty, sixty . . . Well, imagine a shadow-consciousness imagining itself a sleeping fourteen-year-old boy, real in St. Louis County in the month of May. That would be 1944. A boy, ill once, who in his delirium felt himself to be triply born, quadruply born, to be a son of illness, nutty with delirium (and near death), and a son of luck and recovering to be a body and a mind, a difficultly born descendant of Adam born once more . . .

LIFE
ON THE
MISSISSIPPI

1944:
6:12 a.m.

Sometimes waking feels *piggish*: you know? Rooting and snuffling and snouting around? Do you think dreams are elegant? I do. I think they are—sometimes.

Anyway, sometimes it seems a shame to leave one's dreams. Maybe it's because real life is hard. I don't, as a rule, have strong opinions about those matters any more than, when I first awake, I know quite who I am or where I am; I don't remember what I am *supposed to look like.* The unfixity—well, I was adopted into a new family when I was two. Waking up was weird then. I don't remember waking with confident expectations about the color of the hair I had; in life, my hair has changed color often—I was white-blond until I was five, dirty blond for a year, then reddish-blond ever more reddish; and then I had brown hair, dark in midwinter, reddish in spring, blondish (again) in high summer, and so on. And people talked about this, so I erratically knew it was so while it was happening. As a question it was something like a kite attached to me—*Wiley's hair* as a subject of conversation and of reality. His aura, sort of. My mother, ill in 1944, lately makes scenes about how I look like *something the cat dragged in* and shame her by not being *sane*, clean, semi-Godly, sensible, the rest of it; she wants me to be kempt, groomed, whatever the term is.

Hi, I say snidely to the pillow, to wakefulness . . . to the morning.

The tone of snotty self-address is adolescent, upperish-middle-class . . . wartime. I can place social class and physical setting, the era and me—I mean my age and size, my physical condition in terms of sports.

A suburban fourteen-year-old in wartime 1944, Middle Western and large.

—Who are you, Kiddo?

—That's for me to know and you to find out . . .

—Ha-ha. You're as funny as a crutch . . .

I'm Wiley *Silenowicz* . . . I am real, a fate for others . . . I *am* real . . . God, *what a mess.*

In one sense, waking is like leaping from a boxcar into roadside gravel, into the realities of your own waking breath. The night's long jostling in the runaway actions of dreams (which insisted they were plausible) fadingly echoes in the unstable, living-in-a-weedy-ditch-among-old-fading-pictures shaky moment waking up (in bed) when I hear my own breath. My monkey flesh . . . flibbertigibbet electricities . . . *me* . . . I'm here *classically*—in the physics sense: life-size—in the almost always unreportable actual scale of the world. Not a dreamer, I have lasted to this age, this moment. I am colossal in the mistaken sense in which consciousness tends to feel itself and its reality first as an image of all that is real—this is in the remaining and drenching sense in which it was the universe for my dreams and the landscapes and the inhabitants and machinery in them.

But now one has a side, daylit, leaning and lit at the edge of the unknown future, at the very edge of an unknown logic—a day with others in it—every one of them independent of my mind and ungoverned by my consciousness. The not quite daylit world. Science was different in 1944, not so scientific, not so widely popular. In my morning confusion, I am a Jew suspended for a moment in no real order of things. Boy, did I love everything. It's odd to have the beginning of not being young, of my being *flesh and blood* in my pajamas. I feel battered by waves of the barely albino pallor of the air. The vague lightedness of the air: objects in the room had dim outlines, not clear ones; and the air outside the window screens is translucent. Inside the room the darkness is more complete, although, as I said, things are visible at their edges. My outward senses, like butterflies newly out of the chrysalis, do a slow monochromatic fluttering. I am deeply patterned for the moment by the night's introspection.

I have to take a leak. The I-have-landed-on-a-new-planet thing, the realities of the room ticklingly hardening, the all-that-is-here, the slow, pale—half-dark—roses of the actuality of sight, the thing that *nightlong* was not *lifelong* although it seemed it while it was happening: this stuff means my nighttime gullibility aches and fades. Here is a real windowsill. The upper edges of real trees, the real leaves there, lightly scratch at the window screens. The sounds in the variably shuffling Middle Western air joins with the sound of my breath in the pillow: I pay attention to one and it predominates and drowns the other. Then I switch. I am the-voice-that-matters and I have risen to the day—fascist —image-drenched—fantastically nursed. The sensually factual present tense after so many chapters of images (from the flesh-pool), so many episodes of dreaming—in it are no figures from my dreams. The onetime seemingly actual people have been erased, massacred, obliterated . . . *Waking is pitiful*—my father used to say (S.L.)—it is *naked* and *republican* for me now; the *weight* of tousled hair on my new skull is grown-up hair after the years of having a child's fine hair *up there*. I stare, a fourteen-year-old boy, at my own wakefulness. I am no longer a dreaming tyrant who can command and match the light. I am geographically placed here with my head at the foot of the bed, where air from the windows in two walls flows . . . It is May. In St. Louis, Missouri. The window facing me as I lie here looks down into a walk-trisected, flower-bedded, U-shaped courtyard. We live on the third floor. The courtyard is empty in dim light. My skull, boulderishly heavy, is farther from my feet than I remembered—I have grown more than twelve inches in two years. I have gained thirty pounds in that time . . . If I loved you, this is the creature who would love you.

When I sleep, I breathe outside the mysterious circle of my attention. I breathe on another planet, far from the stories in front of me. I start in now on a male flirtation with my breath. In a blurry alertness, a sort of embarrassment, I feel my new skinny neck—my Adam's apple . . . my height: my toes down there: gosh . . . And I breathe.

Actually, to be tall *does* feel like a ladder that I escape on . . . perhaps this is unforgivable. I had not been confident that, if I slept, I would wake. I am conscious of being erect sexually—my father sleeps in the other bed in the room. Then I remember that my father is dead . . . *Daddy's dead.* The breath-scraped, ribby, itchy sexual heat and then the weird memory-thing of my father's dying four days ago, a thing which has its own heat, shakes me like two currents of steam pushing in different parts of a machine.

Then I am weirdly still. Then I shake. Then I am weirdly still.

I stretch out my arm and hand to touch the wire-mesh screen on the window. My fingertips. My rustling consciousness is stilled, light-tropic—a broken-domed, lightly hissing observatory—an aspect of light itself. In this broken-domed thing I perch in the hawkish miracle of attention. Part of what I like about girls—and my mother—is that they say, *Don't go crazy and embarrass me.* I stay sane to show off to them that it's okay to like me. In the at-the-moment-ill-lit actual congresses of the consecutive physical world, tiny particles in me, tiny Noah's arks, carry me between now and darkness. In a kind of Goddishly faintly rolling, somewhat roiling now, silent, more or less quiet, and more and more lit, the smell, the morning smell has a blasphemously moral thing to it—freshness, I suppose. It stinks of *God*, kind of—stinks as in stinking, dirty Jew, rotten goy. I ask the Powers of Prediction—they're in me, mounted in such a way they can see things approaching from farther away than my toes can feel things—Will the war eat me up? Will all the Jews be killed? Am I all right even if my Dad is dead? Do I have to die, too? Do I have to die soon?

I apologize to myself in the real air now for having dreamed *night-long: I'm sorry I was stupid* . . . The inconsecutive, lovely wildness of the mind in the huge present tense of the morning now, the morning head and my bony spine form material low wild angel stuff with death and a sexual fall in it. The mind pokes up blackly, snaggingly—*witlessly*—I have a queer sense of personal defect—and I take my hand from the screen and tuck it into the warmth under my chin—Samuel Silenowicz, Samuel Leonard (S.L.) Silenowicz, my dad (by adoption) is dead . . . Is absent from the drifting, thuggish real. The mind's cater-wauling whisper is: *THERE'S A WAR ON: LEAVE ME ALONE.* I snuffle at the air: an electrical feat of consciousness: a snout-tic . . . Then Venetian blind passages of grief and some self-concern and wake-up peerings—water wiggles of perception, glints, flashes, and semi-mechanical off-and-ons of trying things: if I don't blink, I see spots; if I roll over onto my side, the bed will creak; if I touch it in a certain way, the window sash will grunt. Look, look-a-here, look for yourself, see, rays of absurdly pale light out the window are touching fat, gray, low clouds and some leaves in the treetops.

The pale light—the false dawn—a diffuse grayness—do I want to live? Blind emperor-boy, *Gestapo agent* in his nosiness, so Gestapoish *cock-a-doodle*, the whisperingly breathing fourteen-year-old boy, I am alive so far— *So what?* I more or less want to die with this curious pain of actuality; but that is almost clearly part of the border of how wanting-to-live defines itself in me.

In a glamour of obscure distortion, I remember my face as *his* face from glances in the mirror—a little scared—as those glances were—with the *reason-to-live* stuff, the *reason-to-die* stuff in the silent mirror. This becomes embarrassed *amusement*, taut-nerved, fattened with uncertain and *embarrassed* recollection: imbecile. My temper: what I look like . . . *who gives a fuck* . . . is contentiously male. In the liquor of the blind-sightedness of recall of one's circumstances first thing in the morning when one awakes, I remember that, on the average, *he* (I am) is odd-looking but okay. My looks are not a torment to me.

The Masturbation

In the strange-for-me new privacy in the room, my (maybe) okay face first and then a lot more of me, but not all of me, takes on the temperature (the temperament) of heated and mercurial permission, deadened with caution and reluctance: *Sir-Kamikaze-Fleet-of-Carbon-Compounds Little-Cutie-Little-Cutie-Wants-to-Die-Love-All-Used-Up* does this other stuff.

At the touch of my hand on me, in the tremble of relief, of sensation, I promptly entered a territory of sexual *hallucination* . . . masturbation is a plenum of hallucination; my solitude fills promptly with hallucinatory fullness—love is now naked in the world. Isn't it deathless here now, for a while? Aren't we all gathered here—anyone I want? Hallucination—and sexual will—clobber me with softly ravenous wingbeats. The heft of things and the cawing of nerves (here, where gesture is soliloquy) becomes a tautening balloon of sensation. No one has told me how sexual reality tugs and pushes at a sane sense of things. I find out for myself. The morning drama and the insanity of pleasure and the overripe silliness of pulls-pushes, yanks-presumes—I move without moving. *Hallelujah*—semi-*Wowee* . . . The moment, unbridled, boy-bridal, is loathsome, racked: exaggerated, and grotesque—and okay. Disgust, fear, bitterness, horror, boredom, pleasure—it's of a puzzling enormous interest to me.

In the act, my skin feels like warm cloth on me—a privacy of heat like being rolled up inside a smouldering mattress, in the stuffing. Tickled, sweaty, blotched with heat—*IT'S HOT, I'M GETTING HOT*—I feel self-contempt; and I stop. Self-contempt cools me.

But I remember—and am oddly unsettled—that the rhythms and touch had been blowsily explosive. I refeel some of the sensations scatteredly. And piercingly.

Then I remember being a little kid and my wet bathing suit coming off me, the bareness and hurtful readiness of the self back then—ignorantly alight; and my dad, too, but unignorant, him.

Pleasure now, in some almost childish sense, means that a childhood sense of something odd is *rectified.*

Then, in a trance of exaggerations I begin again—*giant breasts on a giant woman, giant prick*, I have *giant hands*—as if I were nostalgically in or half in the scale in which childhood is set. I ache. God, this is foolish. Other boys seem to me to be professional, expert and well instructed—and practiced—in this stuff and in being boys generally whereas I am unprofessional . . . uncertain and capricious, goadedly unsteady . . . *personal* . . . (this was tied to the age I was).

I had tried to remember, but pleasure is not knowable by memory with anything like its passionate convincingness when it is directly gained and present. Reality has a monopoly of *real* pleasure. A lad and his lamp. The alluring, imaginarily dimensioned dementia of meaning tucked into the animal bribe with its hint of favorable apocalypse: I have to fight it off, this sense that the conclusion is ALL. Masturbation is nutty with idealism, with hallucinations, with self-induced finalities.

The boy has big red convulsed zeroes and pallid ones that moo or mow at him: mad doorways: this is his sense of *sexuality* for the moment. It is so interesting that, as he denies it, some of the stitches of the self break at odd seams. It is a *killing* sense: it strains him and it feels like it is shortening his life.

I proceed in a sensible or *greeting-death* way, a little shocked, a little resistant . . . Bits of throbbing and twitching sweetness—motionful, honied—storylike *pricklings.* I can see where advertisements come from. Odd and loony with lapses and collapses, I avoid the jerking dance of coming—I lie here and let it die away. Nothing can undo your life. I am in a lurching and shoving, half-breathless gauntlet-labyrinth of mind and body in the morning. I am in a state of sensationalism and puzzle-ridden semi-discontinuous attention.

The not-stayingness of pleasure hurts oracularly—and intimately. Heats and oils, exudations and flares of consoling and BRILLIANT renderings of *pleasure* become a momentarily irreversible knowledge that pleasure exists ON ITS OWN TERMS. This chimpanzee reality and the light, I have been in love with these Tarzan doings, these animal carryings-on, since I discovered them two years before; it is almost true in sex that easiness and lies rule the world. Some people are good at this stuff. Some are against it. Christ, the beauty of what some people know. I am homemade flesh, I am sincere—I am a sincere jerk-off. I miss my father.

I turn over and move; my hands are under me on the linen sheet; I move in A KIND OF anxiously flinching recklessness—in a pathos-tinctured heat of the body . . . As in the bony hand of a girl. Of a boy.

The sensations, good, bad, dry, moist, effective, ineffective, irritating, inside a clouded mass of hallucinations, and then, at the edge, neural and a thing of the flesh, and then outside and watching but half-painted with the oddity of the aching intoxication of onwardness—as if one were in love with time and the future—actually the boy was—and with the foolish shamefulness of such a complex state calculatedly brought about and yet partly accidental, the increasing number of more and more serious seizures and the abrupt passages of decline as a kind of meaning (of refused sobriety), I laugh at myself and this *stuff* (pleasure and absurdity), I laugh out loud but under my breath, I laugh at the world's history as it is known by boys.

Sarcastic, mocking, and dizzied, *hoo-ha*—okay?—holding myself and fucking my hands and the bed, I keep my mind on this matter long enough and completely enough that length and completeness are felt as dimensionally sexual things—maybe the only sexual things—the half-witless, the neurally witty, biologically universal thing of *the whole thing* . . . my scandalous attention to it . . . I love this . . . *I love this bed—ha-ha* . . . Love can be extorted. I laugh some more, *hotly*, under my breath the scandal of close attention in a state of whitelit, repetitive shock, pausing only to spit, childishly, on the palms and fingers of my hands which I promptly reinsert and I start being tender with little motions of my fingers while I inhibitedly fuck in the face of death and of youth—I mutter, *Oh you DARLING*—and hallucinate *rhythmically* . . . in a junior or juvenile brute romanticism . . . I wouldn't want anyone to see me like this. Who, seeing me, would forgive me? Who would join me? Who would like me? Whooo-ahhhhhh-eeeee: the world is dangerous . . . The unsystematic twists of the lips and blurredly mad eyes and the pantomimic jerkings, the sporadically blabbery pseudo-boneless writhing of sensation—*OH FUCK* and *OH YOU DARLING* and *KAZOW, KAZOWIE*. And OHHHHHHHHHHHhhhhhhhh. How strangely worded *A Book of Fucks* would be. Whatever is gathered in the body, the sibling—the congressional—the running mind feels as gathered force which spurts, not in orgasm, but still in unexpectedly *sensible* ways in further spasms.

It spurts like light and seems to be thought-and-vision giving answers now, musical answers, substitute compensations and apings to improve one's sense of THE REAL.

The *mental* spurtings of light are a kind of explanation of the world, realer than a dream, but it is wakefulness of a sort. And this is only a corner of the world although it feels like a center. But nothing is more beautiful or commanding than this light. It is dreamlike and real both. I thought I saw why it was that male virginity was not widely praised except in special instances. This self-enclosed stuff involves an irreversible alteration, a mysteriously and tentatively ripening sense of a glory—a personal beauty of that sort. Fear and attention sheathe me in a weirdness of sexual discretion, however. The unease is pretty complete. I think it is scandalous. I think it is scandalous to be a real person alone in a room. I think this is a *scandalous* attention to pay to anything.

The boy's head, as if in a kind of a pointless accident—as with a land mine—jerks upward in a baffling noise of breath, torn *spinally* by sexual sensation, large and jolting, and accompanied by a beautiful whitish light spread out in neural marvelousness. The bleached solar pleasure, if one persists in searching out this disappearing and then reflaring light, one *comes*. One is a gateway away from the world in an almost silent furnace. An explanatory light. To pause in astounded denial of *this shit*—to resist its power is independence that causes a kind of nervous, thin-fibered throbbing, also some laughter at the soul's throbbing now, the soul's *readiness* (to die), the will's unwillingness to die. How can it be that one is sheltered by that shelterless stuff? Nature—and any easy idea of God—is a swindle.

Among boys, practicing this stuff is a virtue. The shaking escapee's is in a spasm of denial that spreads through his spine, buttocks, neck, the insteps of his feet. The tuneless physical hilarity and its shadow of *deep* (and yet minimal) omnipotence has a matching but confusing element of an *omnipotence* of modesty, of shame—I guessed this was *normal*. I wondered about it—*normalcy* . . . the category of the really human or maybe not . . . (This is part of the retreat from the *nowhere* which is a somewhere briefly of as-if-explanatory light.)

It is a game like hopscotch to catch bits of sensation in memory and to advance in knowledge of the sensations while backing off from them. It is like some weird sport that isn't a famous sport. *MY BIG FEET* and skinny legs brace themselves; and then, stringent and vigorous jerks and tics of the torso, of the torso muscles and of the muscles at the backs of the thighs, and in the muscles of the behind are sex, the memory of the recent sex, and me backing off from sex—dick and hands and mind.

All ordinary shocks—as of swallowing—are amplified and are clownish in the actual light now. Alternate and quieter attention gapes, semi-scientific, quick-witted (in a way), at the novelties of illumination in the morning. My mornings are partly a matter of engineering my *masculine* citizenship. But I don't want to be forceful, fully grown, opinionated yet. I don't want to be known and *final.* Voluptuarial—polyphonic—boyish knowledges: almost a first movement of a piece—after a fallen childhood.

Genital size and one's courage and one's right to *breed*; and the piercingness, the quality of okayness, of duty—the *pain* in this thing of being a recruit (for natural increase), I stare at it now, I guess, helplessly. I am almost lunatic with mourning, the foredoomed obscenity of this essentially nameless state—*my adolescence in St. Louis* . . . I hate being dumb. The after-echo of two departed physical realities—of my father and of sex—have the hilarity of presence, of after-echoes. I want to survive my grief. Shrewdness in a neurally tense moment is because I feel how prompt madness and disorder might be if I don't do something such as be shrewd. They appear anyway, madness and disorder. I am poignantly addled. I can hear fragments of all my weeping in childhood and since. I reexperience, almost as if in synopsis, what seems like all the pain I ever suffered plus the recent grief. I seem to remember tensely every moment of difficulty that I ever had. It seems that way in the pangs of agony. One has such a grotesque need of consolation that one *understands* the semi-masturbation retroactively. In the agony, presences flicker, and I contort and constrainingly, and partly surrenderingly, hug my fatally bent self, groaning a little, murmuring under my breath: *It's okay, Kiddo* . . . *It's okay* . . . *canoodling* around . . . *It's all too much for you* . . . *Big deal* . . . All of it, all *seems* MASTURBATORY . . . The grief is slowed, elevated, private, kind of inspired in its recurrent flare-ups of heat, then in its chilled rushing fall. I realize I have made A MISTAKE in waking up, in having a second father . . .

The grief is a muddle of electricity, joltingly without a conviction even of a limitedly favorable meaning in my world.

The clasping, warm agony, the visceral heat, do not explain themselves . . . I am tired of being young. The last is a familiar reality. The phosphorescent heat of the grief and the mirror soul have elements of an aesthetic arrangement to them. Some bandit-deserter-like element of the soul goes running away into shadowy territory saying, *This is the way to evade grief.* The moment: its whole name is *What-my-life-is. Hey, Wiley, bullshit causes cancer* . . .

It hurts to remember the size of my dad's hands. *You have to get up, Kiddo* . . . Dad in the past said that.

I want to be unawed and unpersuaded by grief (or sex). I am a kicking captive, sort of, of grief . . . I want to enter that state that Daddy used to describe as *Can't complain* . . .

It's sad inside me . . . the willfulness and the intensity of feeling. If I looked in the mirror at this point, I might think, *I don't want to be shallow but I don't want to feel this much either* . . . I suddenly imagine my own face here a sharp dark-whitish blur of emblematic and compromised presence. Not real. I am very still. Oh, the tight-balled grief . . . I have a rictus-smile. On my palely sweating face. I'm ashamed of my dad's death. I feel shame that death exists. I feel amazingly lost and wrong—muscularly and electrically jangled. This grief—I am adopted. It burns, the thing of being awake and real: it burns. Daddy sometimes said when I was in pain about something, *JESUS GOD, LOOK AT YOU*; and I would blush and try to be deadpan.

The blaze of supreme heat behind my eyes: juiceless and hot, ironic, *lunatic*—the lostness—one's flammable breathing edged hoarsely with upset at absence, loss—a noticeable sound: one knows oneself this way from before . . . *Peekaboo, Bad Times; whoop-de-doo* . . .

The fear of the wild world, this partly obliterated world (by grief, the continuums of grief, of griefs of all kinds) I am cheatingly ashen and sweet, tense-nerved, stinking—and secret. I don't like the force there is in grief. I stare blindly in the weirdly lit lightlessness, the whitening real moment. One piece of pinkish light is on the window screen. I smile wryly. The tastes I had that year were foul and rough—tender and sincere—childish and hidden—but wartime-*fashionable*, all in all. I don't know about others but *I* want to be able to be a brave soldier. I compare my reserves of strength and my state now. I oppose the anguish, if that is what it is, to my morning strength and my chances of living through the day and lasting to tomorrow. I don't really know about tomorrow or if I'll make it until then and be sane, I don't even know about the next few minutes, but I'm not going mad in this grief just now.

This part is over and I'm safe for a while . . .

A Brief History of Being Loved (and Unloved)

The faint early morning illumination is shimmying in the room's emptiness when the boy-bride of grief sits up. I swing my legs over the side of the bed. It's a thing of *being alive* AFTERWARDS . . . very stark and clownish. Daddy asked me not to say Kaddish for him: *Fuck the Jews . . . My heart is bad . . . I have to go bye-bye because the Old Ticker won't work no more . . . it's all iffy-andy-butty for me . . .* His big-deal, baritone, snorting voice. *Come on, Willsy-Wiley-poop, be* PHILOSOPHICAL. Or *DON'T BE PHILOSOPHICAL*, which meant the same thing: *Be human, let me talk . . . Bear up. Let my mood dominate . . .*

He used to complain, *I wasn't saying something for the ages, for God's sake. Don't pay so much attention to what I say . . . Understand me. Have a heart, be human. Let me have the last word, do you mind:* BE PHILOSOPHICAL . . . Or: *Don't be philosophical . . . Just listen to me . . .*

He didn't want me to like famous philosophy . . .

Let it go. Let it go. Be of good cheer, smile and show your dimples. Have a good time—is that all right with you? It's all right with me. Let's have a little peace, is that all right with you? It's all right with me. He said, *Every man is a great philosopher. Every man has* GREAT THOUGHTS: *that's what it is in America . . .* Dear Dad the dear doodad. *Don't stand near the window: you'll drive all the girls* MAD *. . . Be nice . . . Keep it up for a while . . .* (Being nice . . .)

I was a little kid, undiapered, standing on a bureau. I felt the light on my short legs . . . Daddy was wounded in the First World War . . .

a good-looking blond rajah of a man: Lila said that of him. My mother. By adoption. Daddy said of the First World War, *That war was filth . . . And life went on afterward anyway.* He said to me, in an odd tone, when I was little, *You like being reckless no matter who it kills: you're the Wild Man of Borneo.* I don't know what age I was. He said it when I was a lot of different ages . . . *You look like the Wild Man of Borneo* (from third grade to sixth grade). *You are one hell of an ugly kid—you are goddamned ugly: they call you Mutt-puss at school? The Hunchback of Notre Dame? We should put you in the movies: you could be the child Wallace Beery. I am famous for my sense of humor. Don't pay any attention to me . . .*

He said things over and over, but he said them differently each time. It wasn't me being nuts that I thought he was cold-and-sad, or affectionate or *really* affectionate (which was *very* different from affectionate—*like night from day*) but all in the same words when he spoke. Sometimes this made me laugh when I was little—especially when he meant the opposite of what he said—*Oh ho ho ho,* I'd go helplessly when he said, *You are one hell of an ugly kid,* and kissed me and said, *You are a hell of a tearing beauty of an adopted kid, you know, even if you are retarded.* He did think I was retarded for a long time. Sometimes he was *deranged* and as if *shell-shocked . . .* Male. Sometimes other people upset him, but sometimes it was me. He could say stuff like the above and mean it was sad that a kid's looks mattered when kids' looks wouldn't matter if this were a better world and people were really kind. Or he was addressing himself to the merit in plain boys, sometimes to the conceit of pretty boys . . . Or of smart ones. In the same words—not the same voice. It was the voice of idle grief, of him feeling sorry for himself, of him feeling sorry for me: *You're some ugly kid.* Or it might be a tearing rage—God and Christ, the range of the different ways; he didn't like me when he didn't like me; and the split ways, as when he didn't like what I looked like but he still liked me—or not, as the case might be, as the case was. I would just sort of throb sometimes with the mad, I guess grammatical and inflectional, the emotional *excitement* of talking to him. I would go deaf, just looking right at him, hearing, in advance, some wild thing coming from him: *Are you a sparrow on a branch? Are you a sparrow or a branch?* That was nonsense. *Are you as happy as a bird coasting up in the air so high?* Ironic and vaguely dirty lyricism cleaned up for the kid who was of a different species—morally—from him.

Staring at him, I often kind of half thought I knew what he was saying, and partly I did know, and partly I didn't pay real attention—just as he often said. It was too hard. But if I did pay attention, it seemed clear to me that what he was saying wasn't what he wanted to say. After all, there's the stuff he better not say to a kid; and there's the stuff he can't say, that he isn't able to say; and there's the stuff he just won't say to me that he maybe says to Momma, or to women. I don't know.

You can see how well or poorly he thinks he's doing when he talks. I got into the trick of playacting comprehension even when he wasn't comprehensible (to me) because I hated it when he looked sad. Also, I learned he didn't like my opinions of what he said. I was supposed to appreciate everything. It was like a game: I had to guess what he wanted me to feel and then I feel that but I don't ask for too many instructions or footnotes or anything like that. And if he didn't really want me to know what he was saying when he was talking dirty or about lousiness, how much should I show patient incomprehension or hint I might understand some of it—some of what he is hiding from me? *We are all dressed up as father and son but what we are is two blond guys out on a binge . . .* How much does he want me to understand?

He has an aimed-at meaning and half-aimed-at meaning and the unwitting (giveaway) meaning: You can't get it right: I can't. Being a good listener and a good son is impossible if you're not a blood son, and maybe not then: someone has to like you anyway before they like anything at all that you do in the way of listening . . .

He had a tone of voice that went: *Do you wander in the desert of the details of a face . . . the musical (and unmusical) detailing of a voice . . . the arc of manner and of mannerism . . . Is it beyond you . . . Well, here is a smile and here is a glance of the eyes and here is a hug and here is a kiss to go with it . . .* He said the last thing.

My soul's vocabulary is a mess of his musics—natural or not . . . And much of me is an immediate meaninglessness of shocked attention. A kid with its father.

Half the old women in the neighborhood have a crush on you. Well, I am four years old and pretty *(You was famous for your coloring.* A number of people said that to me later. [*Oh,*] *Where did your pretty coloring GO?).*

Then, when I'm ugly, Dad is odd—and *ugly* in another sense—when he goes on saying, *Half the old women in the neighborhood have a crush on you . . . God, you're a mutt-in-the-manger: let's hope it's a phase—you believe in prayer? Maybe you ought to pray, Kiddo. Have a little pity . . . after all, we adopted you because you was good-looking—and you changed!*

Daddy was making *a song and dance* of *his* feelings . . .

Daddy comes from a Jewish tradition—one that has existed since the seventeenth century—of being Jewish by being not Jewish. By believing in evil and in such notions as that God is embodied in this or that man, Jewish, and sometimes the devil, similarly . . . And in Christ. He hated piety—except in really sweet priests and ministers. He said it was vaudeville. He said of himself that he was modern, sensible, a man of breeding, sometimes deranged, shell-shocked. He believed in lying—Daddy was that sort of *Wild Man of Borneo. I'm not a smarty-pants but I'm no fool, Kiddo . . .*

He *liked* to lie . . . He liked impostures . . .

When I was six—just before I turned ugly—Daddy when he dressed me would brush my hair with his hands and shape my curls while I leaned against him. It was at such a moment that he would say, *Half the old women in the neighborhood have a crush on you.*

It was also a sort of *real* information about something unclear to me.

Lila said, *I don't know who lies more, S.L. or my sister . . . It's six of one, half a dozen of the other . . . My sister Beth is a* REAL *liar.*

When I was nine and Daddy called me *Ugly Little Dog* and *The Hunchback,* I used to walk tensely with my head down between my shoulders, partly ready for a fight; and he would put his balding blond head at an angle measuringly and he would say, *You're an ugly mongrel . . . Well, arf-arf . . . Ain't we arf-witted? What do you think . . .*

If I was standing straight and was neatly dressed and peaceable and was holding his hand, and if he said the same thing and *wasn't looking at me,* it had a different meaning, it had to do with me being dressed up and an impostor in love's chambers: he sometimes said, *You look like Wiley Silenowicz but you're not him: I think you're an impostor . . . Little Stone Elf: how's your sense of humor . . .* I believe I did resemble certain squat, scowling, mass-produced garden sculptures of that period, sculptures of gnomes.

Lila said to him, *Be careful, S.L., little pitchers carry grudges, S.L.*

Do you have a grudge against me, are you a mean little elf—or are you a friend to me—what sort of good child are you?

I don't know yet . . .

Ape-Child, the one and only Tarzan of St. Louis, Missouri . . . the Jewish Wild Man of Borneo.

(Momma said of S.L.: *One thing I'll say for S.L., he may have misled me by saying he was sweet and a lover, and he led me on to think he was rich, but he always was ready for a* GOOD *joke together—it may not sound like much, but I* HATE *a man who has no humor, I can't stand a gloomy man—I have enough troubles of my own . . .*)

His humor sometimes had a desperate insistence, a lunatic tic quality.

My mother and father imitated each other in talk. They did variations on almost anything the other ever said, vocabulary or grammar. They imitated their friends and movie stars and comics. They imitated enviable neighbors. They *add* and *mix* and *blend*—they use stuff from parts of their lives I never saw or knew. What they knew was so far from me as a total thing that it moved in them at moments like some strange beast of farsightedness caged in me that was also a human blindness toward a child . . .

And it becomes a wiggle of their eyebrows and a movement of their nostrils; and then that stuff that I had no personal idea of comes near me in their glance . . . like the hippos that stink in the zoo . . . or the slither of snakes in a dream, in the zooish heat of attention like an encompassing embrace—which is how I felt it for a while . . .

They say personal things to me, but it may not be their own remark: they may be jealous of some person they know who loves a child more than they love theirs. They may conceal this with a slow mocking blink—Daddy winks a lot . . . Momma does, too, more excitingly.

A hidden sense of other *romantic* lives may cause their voices to mean stuff oddly if either of them says, *Half the old women in the neighborhood have a crush on you already . . . Put your pants on . . .* Or: *Don't stand there near the window half-undressed, you'll drive the girls in the neighborhood over the edge.*

Sometimes it's a love speech, but I don't get it that that is what it is right away. It can feel indirect even with them looking at me . . . Sometimes maybe it's a recitation, a joke, an incarnation—an evocation of the past when they made that remark and it was nice maybe . . . You know?

The air, the light, the clothes I wore, the ways I was *deaf*, a Wild Man of Borneo immune to *civilized* speech; sometimes Daddy's emotion is a jealousy of me and sometimes he is jealous about me. He speaks in longing, or in a glum, sweet, teasing tone, or like someone in a movie, and it is about *him* getting older more than it is about me. *Listen, Pisherkin, you know about the nature of girls?* Does it concern the nature of girls? Of old women? My dad's genital chronicles? I remember looking outside to see the mob of crazed neighborhood admirers, but no one was there, just a woman from across the street who did sometimes tell me she liked me but who wasn't looking in our window that day. She was weeding a bed of tulips and not looking toward our house.

Was he grieving, saying that thing, grieving a little, a lot? Do we have a *family* language—him and me? Them and me . . . yes and no. It depends on what my mind and heart and soul have some linguistic grip on . . . Immediate, intimate love—and personal and emotional—usefulness, *family* meaning, that sort of family meaning does have something to do with stuff being said a thousand times—the skill in saying something anyway, that comes with practice, the knowledge, so that each time adds to and constrains what-is-meant until you get so expert that when you leave home, you float off in haze of local linguistic expertise, never quite to be repeated outside the house.

S.L. says, *I don't want to do anything for the first time ever again: I'm no beginner; no thank you. It's not good news for me to start over at anything . . . I'll tell you what it is: I don't want to be a* DUMB *beginner. I'd like to think my life meant something . . . I'd learned a thing or two—is that all right with you? I like having had a little practice. I like having a little experience under my belt . . . I'll tell you about me: I'm an old cowhand . . .*

He said, when he was ill, *I'm the sort of man likes two-toned shoes; if I got to wear one-toned shoes, I wear me some spats . . . I'm a dandy, a jim dandy . . . You know what that is? I'm a Yankee Doodle Dandy, stuck a feather in my cap and called it macaroni. Well, what can you do? I was a pretty man—you know how it is? If you don't I'm not a-goin' to tell ya. I'm no William Shakespeare—or his daughter . . . ha-ha-ha.* This thing about the daughter had to do with all the best-selling women novelists of that time and with Lila's having such a large, if unstable, vocabulary.

The mind longs for clarity, but clarity in relation to reality is peculiarly forced, often. I like it that it's hard to guess at what he intends when he speaks. I like it *in a sad way* that so much of what he did is *over my head. We're almost rich . . . You know how it is . . . You will never have the luck of being one thing or the other.* His friendly and complicitous sarcasm . . . *You want to play keep-away with your kiss, you and that come-hither coloring—shame on you—dost thou knowest about gathering rosebuds, you little Cupid. Come on now, give me a kiss . . .* How could I know what he really meant?

Or when he spoke like that in a totally other pitch of voice—sarcastically—either when I was ugly or when I hadn't been paying attention to him for a while—at certain points in listening to him—face-to-face (or in memory)—I go into a kingfisher's or a dive-bomber's dive, staringly but skimmingly and erratically over a glare of his face and of the sounds and music of the voice and then of the light in the room and of a hundred times when he talked: I dive and race along in order to have a context for what he says, a wheel of translation, whatever . . .

I hear so variably, so untamedly, that it is scary—the abrupt floppy carrying off of a meaning—or the drill bit boring into what he is saying—or the deafness and my giving up, my escape from him and from *love in the world.* The varieties, all of them changeable, of being unloved, and of the thing of being Jewish and of the thing of having money, and of being American, and then the thing of the *politics* of listening . . . I am *afraid* of how rambunctious reality really is and how limited the reach is of *my* wit . . . my interpretations and translations of my father are.

Sometimes—*always?*—he is talking in rivalry, to see who loves better, him or someone else, him and everyone else, which one is the better man, which one do I like best . . .

He is rivalrous toward silence—toward books—toward movies. Some people he's enjoined (or constrained) to look up to, and the fates of the kids of those people he is careful of; but he wants to be better than them and to make up for the "respect" he unwillingly feels. Or he goads me with how wonderful some other kid is . . . Boy, it's dangerous to be somebody's kid. Isn't it *dangerous* to be his child? Anybody's child?

And not just because of him but because of what people do to you because of him . . . Or Mom . . . Mom and Dad do things to me because of other people—it is an odd light in their actions. Also, Lila's mother liked Lila a lot and was jealous of me, or was friendly to me because of Lila and S.L., and I disliked her for it so much, for not caring about me *directly,* that I wouldn't go to her funeral when, at last, in her eighties, she died.

Both my parents liked to say that where there was smoke, there was fire.

My dad had images for feelings. *You're as nice as a dog and twice as clean.* And: *I defended you yesterday. Beth said you wasn't fit to sleep with hogs, and I said you was.* And: *You're the one I want to kiss: come on over here and be my merry sunshine for a change . . . And don't ask me for any change; keep your greed to yourself, tonight, Darlingkins . . .*

I am in a wild woods of memory. Voices speak and hands and expressions and movements of the lips fly around. I-am-lost-here. Memories in a bunch never happened that way. In relation to *driving the girls in the neighborhood mad*: I have to catch on in order to be their son, but I don't have to catch on all the way. It might be creepy if I did that. Anyway, am I their son? Sometimes, in the years when it was agreed I was startlingly ugly, *My God, look at you,* either of my parents might say, but so might even kind strangers say it: I would pray at night, *Keep me ugly, Dear God: make me a little uglier, if it's all right with You*—it was for the freedom, the semi-invisibility of it—but they, my parents, my parents by adoption, long for me to be a *knockout, a killer-diller*—as in the old days (when I was little). *You was such a beauty* . . . they say to me . . .

It was a more interesting story for me, Momma said.

It makes me no never mind, Daddy said—but he didn't mean it . . .

Each idea of things in him is a specialized focus of his eyes, I think . . . I peer at him, this year, some other year. In me is a Grand Army's worth of specially focussed *eyes,* each with a different kind of gaze—my inner mind has odd legs and strange wings for travel—its slow shovelling, its scratching . . . its weird hands . . . the weird efficacy. Its rebelliousness. I use it. I remember Dad saying stuff when I was ten but by then it is not just him: it is the whole world and my fate—sort of—that is speaking; he and Mom brim and leak over with stuff different from what I know of public and schoolish prose and from the kinds of English in newspaper stories and in the books I read. But I hear them accordingly, in line with that stuff and in line with the past. They thought I was a *scandal* . . . weirdly shameful: a smart aleck, a traitor, treacherous kid, a snot, a moral engine gone wrong, a rogue machine of pissy moods, wrong actions, vandal acts, stupid dialogues . . . a humor of independence . . . The neighbors liked me sometimes when they didn't like my parents. Or if I was in trouble, I was someone that some of the neighbors HATED—do you know how it is when you're ten? People say I was good for the Jews, bad for the Jews . . . good for my sister, bad for my sister . . . good for the neighborhood, bad . . . People spoke of this stuff that concerned me in tones with or without lyricism, and mean as shit or nice-nice—the bloodbath of the measurements—*You're not practical,* Daddy said; *you're a standout as a' impractical man.*

Then I am fourteen and Daddy says, *Half the old women in the neighborhood have a crush on you.* The immediate history may be of him glancing at my eyes and knowing I'm thinking dirty or romantically and me noticing what he is doing and him noticing my noticing. Maybe his attention is drawn to my being taller than he is; and he is *vastly* irritated by that . . . Or amused and sad. Then it might be like he is reproducing the tone of a children's book, one where a little kid is in the jungle and meets Mr. Elephant and now he is the kid and I am Mr. Whatever. If I slouch so that our faces are on the same plane, I can see how *Daddy's* eyes and lips and throat and tongue go wading out and then dive in and swim into syllables of what he says . . . stuff which I can't see at all, after I've gotten to be six feet, if I don't slouch. He is used to talking to me. I am used to hearing him when I was a different size, so that I hear him with a weird temporal echo as if I were in a well and his voice reverberates but not meaningfully except in terms of the distance between us. I am so used to his voice and his speech that it is almost as if he were breathing in a legible way and then that shrinks me or pushes me back to *Fourth Grade*, say, when he breathes dramatically or restrainedly or with a systematic intelligence in front of me in a way that is, or that merely seems to be, familiar . . . to be similar to stuff in the past that I knew in one way and now have to know in another.

When I am older, his talk might, indeed, be anything, even a tone, a zone of silence. This morning, grief-stricken—or at any rate struck down in some ways by grief at being solitary in my room—Daddy slept in my room the last four years of his life—I *think about things* and I decide I *can't* remember voices and what is said in a real way. I deny the confusion: I won't admit it comes from reality: for a few seconds, I remember only in a school way, usefully: bookishly: *accusingly* . . .

To remember in a real way is too emotional—too *rending*. I don't want to live as someone who loved his father a lot. Maybe I don't want to live at all. I am something of a prima donna of being reckless (Daddy's view). Momma's theory is that I died when my real mother died and that I was brought back to life but then I still had a yearning to be with my real mom and to give up, and so I am not to be trusted in life-and-death matters since, she feels, I prefer recklessness to caution, and death to politic kinds of living. A *Drang* to recklessness . . . A Nazi policy is the *Drang nach Osten*, the *pull-to-the-east*. Dawn is real now outside. Any grief I feel is linked to the primal grief at the disappearance, actually the death of my real mother and my near-death then; my dying and my reunion with her or my punishment of her or my weakness—reunion wanted and unwanted but reunion *anyway*. I'm saying a wild limitlessness of infant grief underlies my sadness when it occurs . . . I'm *up shit creek without a paddle*. I tend to try to suffer limitedly, without remembering. I remember oddly; I go around voices and real moments and remember my dreams and opinions and conclusions about people, not letting myself be partly eaten by the beloved darkness or whatever the fuck it is that makes life into pure shit. I try to live . . .

Everyone likes you, Daddy said, although he is just as likely to say, *No one likes you, no matter what* YOU *think*. I'm not supposed to say anything back *because you don't know how to talk, Wiley, and you hurt people, you don't know what a man's real feelings are, you aren't good with people, Pooperkins.*

When Poppa talks, I'm expected to listen, to be purely a listener and not to answer back. I'm not to be *fresh* or *conceited* or simple—or *simpleminded.* I'm supposed to pay attention to his wittily ironic and deep complexities of meaning and intention. He says, *I like the strong, silent type in men, myself.* I'm *supposed* to admire him. One of the reasons he lies so often is so I *will* admire him . . .

Momma has said she doesn't like *blind* men—blindness in men—but she has also said that she likes a man she can depend on, one who is *blind to my faults.* And, I think, blind to the world for the sake of loving her. She said once—she was drunk—*I would have put Samson's eyes out: I'm that type; when he was blind, if you ask me, he was a real man.* If Daddy is saying stuff about old women and young women and me, he is *taking many, many, many things into account; he is trying to hold his own with a growing boy.*

He is *living up to the situation.* But, also, I saw he was saying stuff about his philosophical powers of penetration: *Look-how-I-have-managed-to-show-*MEANING*—see-what-an-artist-I-am . . . I-am-an-artist-of-real-life.*

He is being *a dream of a father* (when he says that stuff, nice stuff to me). He is challenging me to have grown-up (complex) values about masculine performance in real life—and in my family existence with him. He is telling me to be *careful* (with women) without really expecting I will be . . . I might kill him with my carryings-on, my carelessness. I might ruin my life . . . I might kill myself . . . I might kill some girl (of the neighborhood) or an old woman (he said that). He also said, Daddy did, of one old woman: *To flirt with someone like that, you might as well take an ax to her and hit her in the head, Wiley: it's not good for her now that you're a big guy.* He was lying . . . It was an intelligent woman he was talking about and not one who was sexually fond of men. I don't think he was merely wrong.

He sang part of a song called "Only a Gigolo." He said, *Don't be a fool* and *Don't be a gigolo; don't be someone people can wrap around their little fingers.* He says stuff in ways that please him because what he is saying is and is not *quite* true and is attractive in his eyes in that mixed-truth-and-whatnot form. It is dreamlike to speak anyway, with anyone, but it is especially dreamlike for two men to talk to one another, I think, and even more so if it is your *father* you are talking to.

It is a myth, a dream to speak to your adoptive father . . .

Him on sex: BEHAVE-or-you-will-die . . .

Yeah but then I think, *You die anyway.*

He laughs and laughs, a dying man; he laughs carefully as a matter of fact, and then he says, looking me in the eye: *But you don't want to be someone who dies too soon, Wiseguy . . .*

Daddy likes to soothe people: the power to soothe soothes him. And it soothes me to soothe him by being soothed by how he talks . . . Ping-Pong and yo-yo, all the echoing stuff in the soothing line of intention . . .

If it is true that he knows what life is like for me, then he speaks to encourage me, to keep me alive and less suicidal—or more cheerfully suicidal—and not too blatantly, patently unhappy, ill, confused, silent. He was famous (locally) for his looks. By real-life standards he has a *good* sense of humor. Daddy, when he says, *Don't stand near the window: you'll drive the young girls mad,* he is using his sense of humor. He is of various sizes; it is in different periods and styles: pudgy-waisted or thin-waisted, almost wasp-waisted. And he isn't always only talking *ordinarily*—he is talking as a *great* philosopher—a visionary lecher. With a sense of humor. A girl across the courtyard, who is older than me—seventeen—and strictly brought up—she's a *strict Catholic,* Daddy has said ruminatively—she's a girl I lied to about my age for a while . . . She undresses and dresses in front of windows that face those of my bedroom. Sometimes, half-dressed, she stands near the window. I have wakened from naps and seen her across the courtyard in her window looking toward me in my clothes twisted in my sleep, at me motionless on my bed. One time she did that, she was naked . . . I remember the astounded excitement in my LOINS—you know?

Is she after me or you? Or do you think she just likes windows? Daddy asked.

Across the street lives a publicly lesbian teacher who is much admired locally . . . seriously admired . . . a woman with white hair—fine-faced, proud and *just*—famous locally for being just and for being pretty—she has made speeches about being a lesbian and about women's needs and about the nature of freedom for a woman. Daddy has a crush on her, on that *just* and good-looking woman, although I think she has made it clear that he gives her the creeps. I mean he knows that he gives her the creeps. That bothers him, and so he pursues her to try to get a better grade from her. He waves to her. Sometimes she waves back. She remembers me from third grade. She has her ups and downs about *me.* Now that I am a half-grown male or whatever, she is distant with me, but she was good to me the year I had her as a teacher. Distant? Now she smiles tensely and talks to me weirdly-*weirdly*—and once she said, *Are you driving all the girls mad?* Was it from a song they all remembered from the 1920s? I fainted in a way when that happened. I stood there but I went dead inside and was obtuse and was white-minded and didn't know where I was for a few seconds. Daddy used to say of *her* that she drove all the young girls and old ladies mad. There is a *tradition* of him saying that thing: he said it about Nonie and men. He said of Nonie, his daughter by blood, my sister by adoption, that she drove all the *boys* and *old men* mad—he did it to comfort her and make her laugh; she would laugh in a lost, contemptuous, confused, kind of bitter way. He meant so many things when he said that to her or me that it made my head spin. But its relation to *truth*—Nonie did drive some guys mad, a number of them—that part of it was *shocking*. It shocked *me* anyway.

In a real moment, I hear oddly. When I lie still and just remember, I forget how in real moments I have purposes, shyness, hopes, pretensions, dogmas, looks, a daily state, an age, a mood, and so on. I know that some of what my Dad says has to do with the local rules about talking to kids—he obeys that . . . He gets perverse toward that and disobeys it. He forgets, too. He is perverse and bad and daring and forgetful at times when he speaks. I want to understand. Is there a normal way for a father and son to talk to each other? Is this a side issue? Is it important? I don't assume I know which meanings are *typical*.

I'm good at schoolwork by local standards. From the point of view of *the man in the moon*—a luminous owl—*they* (my momma and poppa) are legitimately—intimately—like figures in a dream I am having even if, in a real moment, they are actually there and are talking to me and I am not daydreaming, which I do a lot, but really am making an effort to listen to them. Perhaps this is what is meant when I am said still to be *a baby*.

A baby, if I remember rightly, is a figure of edification and fun; my helplessness supplied a purpose for others; I was an example of innocent consciousness. Daddy: *You were someone we took care of night and day—it was fun then, Wiley: don't misunderstand me: but it was fun, it was nice when you was sick* . . . Now (Momma says) I, the one-time baby, tend to look like I have on makeup (healthy and all that). Daddy says, *You have* GOOD *color in your face* . . . Momma says, *Why waste such coloring on a boy?* S.L. said, *You look like you're rouged and powdered like a kid playing dress-up: actually, you look like you were lying down somewhere and some goddamned undertaker slapped makeup on you.* I say to him in my head: *I saw* YOU *in your funeral-parlor cosmetics.*

Momma lately has been saying that something or other, whatever she's just said or quoted is *the-final-truth-*NOW*-the-subject-is-closed*. She's bluffing. There's longing in the bluff. It's strange to me how little of what goes on will translate honestly into confession. I am very factual, but I don't know what my life is like. I didn't know my life was like this—this stuff I've just described. I sing popular songs with really a *lot*—a whole lot—of feeling—to show how I feel about hard matters such as this one. I use a lot of very, very *cool* deadness—and I do a lot of joking around—when I sing. Or when I'm with other guys.

But that stuff doesn't contain my sense of real reality even a little —not even *up to a point*. And this hurts—so much I want literally to die. Maybe I'm worthless; maybe I'm half-worthless—who knows? Maybe I have *a perverted mentality*. Inside me, the foreshortened visual dialects there are trying to hold a whole lawn and its insects and odors and light in place. And a person. School papers are called *themes* at my school —I write them out longhand in the hall at school, surrounded by other kids, and I talk as I work . . . The other voices keep my mind quieted, my lies straight . . . I get my classroom pitch from the voices around me. I can steal their voices. Did my parents do that? Is that part of what I should understand when they talk to me?

S.L. says that I am *Mr. Too-Big-for-His-Britches, Little Sir Know-It-All*. When I am *thoughtful*, he says, *Gone off somewhere? We're here; where are you? You're in never-never land.*

It's true it is like leaving him alone somewhere when I sort of go off somewhere into my head to think . . . When I write for a teacher, it is as if my sense of things (and my senses) and my sense of the world were held in common with her (or him) and not with S.L. anymore. I write for the school paper which is run by a young English teacher who genuinely hates the English teacher I think is the smartest English teacher and is the person in the school system who knows the most about worldly things. The politics about good language and what it is and who speaks it and who doesn't leaves out my parents. And there are more politics, further politics, with my parents about this. When I write for the school paper and claim I have written what someone said, that boastfully kills my memory of what really went on. I mean the piece becomes what I think *really* went on. It becomes the chief or guiding memory—authoritative. When my parents talk they believe themselves that way for a while. And the real scene waits behind . . . If I keep a real memory alive the whole time I'm thinking about what I'm writing, I can't write or talk at all, and then I am truly miserable . . . *Lost*. And the stuff I write then sickens me. It doesn't sound at all like *what is real around here*. It seems to me I have to give up waking life and the real stuff that goes on between me and my friends and my parents, and that I have to give up my mind if I write stuff that is acceptable to any of my teachers . . . To a sponsor of truth plus or minus a few doubts. My inner speech, which seems honest to me some of the time, well, when I *look* at it, it seems like an intense and compressed jumble, really . . . a jumbled lunatic *Allness*, echo-y, knotted, private, *snotty*. It maybe *dimly* has a real sense of bodies and of an actual schoolday and of my parents in real moments . . . But that is a source of grief. It is like I'm talking in a hot, closed closet, no one knows we're there, me and whoever I'm with, the part of myself, or myself as The Reporter, it's nearly complete darkness in there behind the closed door. And your sense of your body and hers or his isn't all that clear—*Is this your leg or is it my leg, ha-ha?* Stifled in that airlessness, you can't see lips moving or eyes or the rest of it. Sometimes I hardly know which of several things I'm saying I am really saying—I lose track. It's really unclear—maybe it's just unusually freed talk. *Talking to you is like reading a book*, I said to myself once—the rank communicativeness head-to-head but in only one head in the dark was no metronome tick-tick of noticed time—only words.

The mind-become-a-boy is islanded in stillness—but it is as if in a library—he waits: half waits: half lives. Christ, that lousy waiting—do you remember all the waiting in childhood? The world a savage and loony waiting room? And you wait. But not for older kids. Not grown-ups.

The boy—draped by reality willy-nilly in veins, muscle, heart; colon, knees, uncertain voice; date of birth and perverse will foreign to whoever speaks; draped in blinking and in mood—is *a real boy*, (pardon me) meaty, autonomous, caught in an attendant mass of realities.

A meaty boy dressed in Polite Fictions—shared conventions, manners from a fictional sense of childhood and of life—draped in ghostliness and flesh—would such a boy resemble the androgynous nudes on the ceiling of the Sistine Chapel? Ah, I don't know . . . I've never seen my life in any of its phases as a single image—like one in a picture.

Sometimes in silences and wordless shouts of emergency and wordless sinkings of the belly, I feel my whole life . . . suddenly . . . I feel it as fault-ridden from the inside out . . . I feel my soul then as a kind of flayed creature . . . Ah, is it too involved to go on about it this way? The question is whether I am to be believed, and if I am like my father and my mother when I talk, when I speak on the page. One must estimate whether the music of what I say is essentially honest. See, Daddy was not entirely to be believed or listened to literally, ever.

I Move Toward the Bathroom . . .

I move toward the bathroom, barefootedly. Quietly, I carry my clothes. It is genetically *weird* to be adopted. From deep inside yourself, what you are is stuff that is visiting, not entirely, not even all-in-all, but enough that you feel like an intruder even in grief, even when it's your own grief . . . He's not my real father . . . The grief is like a barely moving but very strong wind—an enveloping force generated by absence—S.L.'s a whirlwind that is also *a hole*—I make my way along, anxious to be out of the house: I want to avoid my mother and sister . . . I don't want to be part of their dealing with their father's and their husband's death . . . S.L.'s death.

In the john—white tile, white walls, white towels—in the mirror is the boy: skinny . . . an odd, *sudden*, temporary thing, me-this-month, my share of the physical world *at the present time*: a partly moneyless boy—in the moments—shoulders like lathes . . . broken lathes, wooden, youthful . . . youthfully girlish . . . a fitful sweetness of semi-acceptability (of appearance) . . . a scowl in the eyebrows in a deadened looking-in-the-mirror face.

Getting dressed: it took three minutes, jeans, T-shirt, cut-off jeans underneath the outer jeans—shorts; you take off the jeans and you're in shorts—no socks, sneakers. The child-boy is *six feet two*. Facts are intimacies . . . The way I look . . . The universe reeks and spins . . .

Dressed, I sit, I dump: *Baby, baby . . . I'm here shitting and you're dead* . . . The boy's tensely biological breathing in the tiled room—I never imagined myself the hero of anything—that's the hot truth. Hot *scoop*, hot poppalopping poop . . . YOU'RE ASKING FOR DEATH, SHITFACE

. . . Wipe, ee-yi, ee-yi, oh . . . Cold water on the fizz-face. Teeth silently (almost dryly) brushed: *Get your teeth into that one* . . . Uncombed, on tiptoe . . . What's real is not a school subject . . . Reality is not a school subject . . . Which is why people don't like school. I hate bathroom taps . . . I can't identify my own feelings: they don't have labels on them: *this seething whatever* . . . *love* for the dead man? The film of sweat means bad news or what? I touch my cooling skin. The drip of the tap: plumbers don't come in wartime . . . the hurried and blurred noise of a dripping tap as I sneak out of the john.

Jass: *Do you like being a Jew? Do you go to a special school and learn how to be a Jew?*

No. I'm allergic . . . I go into convulsions, I explained. *A dead mother . . . She was religious. She disappeared one day and she never came back . . . I was little and I couldn't believe it . . . I thought she would return. Now, sometimes, it seems she returns . . . Or is on the way; then it's a nightmare: then nothing is real. It's all a dream. If I get too strong a sense of her. So I don't study Jewish things. So far as I know, I really don't care about her but it's a thing in me whether I like it or not, this thing about her . . . So I can't go near certain feelings . . . I kind of have to go around so that I don't trigger that other stuff. So I'm not a real Jew as she was . . . I'm a real Jew the way I am.*

The kitchen is dark. The drawn-back spring of the thumb—(this is a memory when grief is partly impossible for you)—the click and click and then the hiss of the angling and rebounding marbles rolling on the powdered dirt . . . astronomical revision: striped, clear, or bubble-dotted crystalline glass spheres rolling . . . In front of my playmates . . .

Then: *Come home with me now* . . . And he grabbed me, Daddy in suit and vest, watch chain, spats . . . Gold-rimmed glasses. *I'm winning: it's bad if I leave.* He says, *Be kind to me now, don't play games. I come home at night—I want a little peace and quiet; I want you . . . you could give me a little happiness, it wouldn't ruin your life, it wouldn't break your heart.* The other children are at an increasing distance, he has abducted me so ruthlessly . . . so relentlessly . . . *I go through a lot so you can have a home—so you can play marbles. Shut up, shut up . . . Don't embarrass me—I want to see you, you should be flattered I like you. Come home—play with* ME . . . *Leave the white trash alone.* He likes to repeat things: *Leave the white trash alone. Can't you enjoy yourself with me—do you mind making that little effort? Don't give me any back talk: be nice: you argue too much—over every little thing. Give your head a break: save your eyes—you want to have ugly eyes: you're getting ugly eyes. You answer back too much.* Christ.

Now I go out the kitchen door . . . He's dead . . . The outdoor air sighs and seems to tick, swelling around me, and then it curls into the soft *yah* of a wind . . . The binding order of difficult logic has to do only with what is *real* . . . A friend told me, *I know how much you loved your father* . . . Did I? I remember being punished by confinement in my room for not hugging S.L.—*I want to be with my friends, I like them better than I like you.* I see the dancing motes of dust in sunlit air at twilight in the room I was imprisoned in—family-given cubicle. The electric hush, the unsteady hush of my mind *running* there . . . The world is realer than consciousness . . . which is like a little brother, smaller than the world, consciousness is. The nearly horizontal sunlight is extraordinarily white, is wobbly. But near me on the brick is an unexpected yellow patch, the yellow of the interior of a peach. Or yellow silk. Bright yellow, partly hardened and glinty, partly soft and powdery.

I am on the third floor, on a metal porch with a concrete floor; the back porches are a single unit of girders and pipes painted black. The steps are metal and they echo; they have raised places on them to prevent slipping. I climb out into the gray air of twilight-like grayness of just-at-dawn in full view of the dimly lit sky, pale. The sky sees me and my disobedience. The air. I swing out on one of the posts—that is, I grab the post—Jass Nolloquot, a friend (of sorts), sometimes says, *Let's play let's-die games, Wiley*: and I step out into the air, I wade out into space, three floors up—Jass taught me this—and, legs pumping, I swing around the pole, out, out—I am in bitter, brilliant, charcoal-diluted-milky lightless light and then I am back in the truer grayness again.

I descend the outside of the railing, on the outside of the porch; I stoop and lower myself until my legs are around the pipe on the second floor. I get my hands—abradedly—onto the floor of the upper porch; then I get one underneath to grip the pipe and, in imitation of Jass, I raise my other hand up and out like a rodeo rider and say silently to myself, *Yippe-i-ay*—and *Fuck* IT*!* and I slide down, heart pounding.

Then I swing out into the almost light. And then I descend again. Jass did it and another guy, Jimbo, jumped from the second floor without being hurt: I go down to the first level and jump eight feet, onto gravel, in the umbral abracadabra of an early wind in this cusp of a moment. What are the procedures of mercy?

The River

If one might try the different language of a different self, one might write that the Friday of the week of my father's funeral, I sneaked out of the apartment we were living in on Kingsland and Kingsbury Avenues and went downstairs in one of the intricately complicated physical-password ways that I used in that year of my early adolescence to certify my courage and my willingness to live, to find if they existed; and, having already been medicated, so to speak, by being outdoors, having been enlarged and soothed inwardly by the gray air, the outdoor silence, and the immediacy the nerves take on outdoors (as if for physical emergency), treated by the sensual registry—the volitional freedom abridges, cheats, shortchanges THE GRIEF *by denying* STILLNESS, IMPRISONMENT, THE TOMB *for oneself. The amazing and companionable thing of dying partway, too, of making one's life be still . . . I am in the next moment, outdoors—in University City—in the pretty air, the gray semi-opacity, semi-translucency without color, lightly-dark-and-moist, physically undead, unburied, unimprisoned, the self observes after my monkey descent, the earth, and the sun, and the light between them, in triple conjunction, in swift motion that seemed slow, formed first a silver-whitish tiara-shaped glow at the eastern horizon, and then—a fret of nearly unimaginable fire . . . It was a freakish moment. Along the alley, from the east, came long, horizontal rays of white light—actually white and black mixed as if the rays were zebralike. A peculiar fusillade of glare, of revolving rays—both black and white—these revealed and illuminated the nearby world so oddly—in such strong black-and-white, with such shadows everywhere and such glare, that the revealed alley with its familiar garages*

and ashpits was as if lit by a flashbulb—or a magnesium flare in a battle. It was in worse concealment than it had been in the dark in being whitely redrawn by glare and outlined so spinily.

In that immensely striped moment I was catapulted (silently) inside myself toward a kind of further unburial inwardly, a self-conscious thing . . . While outwardly I cleared my throat and spit—a gross maleness—to acknowledge my flight (and freedom) from parlor caution in the moist, open air. The night-renewed spaces of the giant room . . . The early-morning out-of-doors had no strong suggestion of death—or of life; it was merely an un-Jewish semi-pagan arena of odd light, a kind of crimped, glaring-blaring light—hardly useful. Squinting, one accepted one's place as if in a mechanical model of planets, an orrery, and went whirling and clanking off among the spheres in those ellipses gilded on one side of a demonstration of gravitationally orbital order in relation to the weight of certain fires set into the cold of outer space and warming and lightening the atmosphere around here now.

In a way, this was the other half of the uncompleted masturbation. The physical world—of the out-of-doors . . . was at climax . . . one of many for it . . . An almost human skin of dew was everywhere—on metal, on macadam, on brick—and on the light-struck and shadowy black-tar pavement of the alley, small drops, themselves, glaring mightily as they dried.

And the freshness of the air, the near-silence, the amendment of suburban life, the immediacy (the nerves and senses were without porches) so set one's self up in one's heaviness and near-motionlessness of grief that, without warning, one's physical self and temper felt the combat between grief and being suitable for entering the morning as irreconcilable. One grieved or lived. Going into the basement, getting one's bike . . . do you know what it is to CHEAT *on grief? To double-cross the dead? To refuse old love? The great inner hounds are baying with moodedness. All sorts of inner selfhoods are clutching at stillness. Parts of me are sitting on cushions, are motionless with grief . . . One moves in heavy and resistant air, in one's mood, one's own emanation. One can't escape and move in ordinary glare-torn, dew-wet air, half-grief-stricken. I mean the grief takes its place among the committees of the self, the congress of voting and squabbling selves, dealing and bullying, vetoing, bribing . . . And it tries to regain the tyranny it lost, to reestablish the monarchy of death (and whatnot) among the committees. And some nodule (or seed or pit) of self-and-will which is allied to light—in spirit and in actual composition—the flying knot of identity-in-the-motions, one is now this particle, now this wave—is presidential;*

I live, heavily, reluctantly, with a stone in my belly and a certain overwhelming and crippling shadow in my spirit, a lament, and a huge, huge private force of regret, but one isn't chained, overwhelmed, or entirely crippled. One limpingly flies along. One does not grieve openly for oneself—parentless twice now, with affections frayed, toyed with, born and torn. I slowly force the observatory to observe the real moment, the present moment with its absence in it; but I am not absent from it. And the silent birds within, the boys, the children, child-selves and school-selves, sport-selves and the like, look, they look and see the alley, the tar-paved aisle that goes past the garages and ashpits—and the glare, black-and-white, and made of revolving and perceptibly demarcated, powdery rays. The fire of the glare and the unfire of the shadows pick out bits of vines, of flowering shrubs, to make black-and-white flags under a wide gray sky without glare in it; the glare doesn't penetrate it; it is a glareless roof for the revolving spikes and rods which change as the earth tilts—which turn into a flood of whitish light beginning to be tinted palely as normal light is, which fatten and revolve and thicken and spread into a flood in the more and more lit alley, the walls and trees and ashpits, which are ignited with glare and shadow in noiseless confrontation with light—

while the birdsong, morning song, begins, and creatures fly in gray air, or lower, where they are rent by black-and-white glare; and patches of blue begin to appear, and swathes of yellow, yellowish light; the seemingly purposeless richness of the real—

continues incrementally, maybe a little madly, almost limitlessly. Certainly theatrically. I'm not just an audience, I'm a tenant here . . . I'm a tenant under this sky. The American sky.

Then, all at once, the stuff is just light and shadow. I stop staring and go into the basement to get my bike; but by then, you see, I don't lean up against the whitewashed wall of the basement to see if I'm going mad with pain as I had earlier in the week. I manage to live on, without remission, to carry my bike up to the alley, up whitewashed concrete stairs cut into the earth; I get on my bike a little clumsily; I swerve and sweep off . . . a little cautiously . . . since I am aware I am not in great, or tyrannical, command of myself; I am not in full command of myself; I haven't a life-and-death say with myself, my selves, time-and-mind, time-and-flesh, whatever it is that I am.

Time itself proposes consciousness simply in the nature of its own being—in the way it is no longer itself but is itself still, split and riddled and whole, subject to will in some ways, given to fluctuation . . . I have this raw theory, quite stupid I know; but everything is a sort of flowering and receding whirlwind of nervous time at the edge of a future; everything, including me, a sort of clumsy calculating machine exploring the nature of event, of time, and of time unoccurred-as-yet, of the future. I am interested in the future, in the prettiness of morning light. Past milky stretches of morning mist, I bike. Past buildings with no lights in them, no movement in or near them. The still mostly grayish sky holds huge clouds that are partly white. Whole blocks lie in shadow. I bike over shadows that are decomposed and light-speckled whales of receding dark—and among some, cast by apartment houses, that were as big as tinted but partly bodiless whales and dinosaurs. Through those temporary selves I pass sensibly—and like something in an image as well.

Past the lawns in a suburbanscape, grassy tablecloths, miles of repetitive, and not entirely convincing, gentryhood, a great number of front doors, not to speak of windows, I go; and then out Delmar Boulevard, a wide, empty stretch of concrete at this hour, to North and South Boulevard where countryside begins, woods and farms: the end of one NORMAL *and the beginning of another. In those days, where the ground was good (for farming) farmhouses and fields and farm buildings appeared with such frequency that domestic windows and farm women and farmers watched you everywhere along the road . . . a loose extension of a network upholding respectability, a theory about virtue.*

And unfertile land, wasteland, marshland, or rocky upland, was eyeless, windowless. One biked there with suspicion. And curiosity.

All in all, in both sorts of countryside, not much history ruled here. There were tales of Indian torture and of European land-grabbing and of slave raids and the like; but none of that went very far back, two centuries, three at most. Despite the tilled fields and the painted houses, you could sense the raw prairie . . . the real sky—I mean as it had been when it had been above emptiness. There were no traces of a countryside magistracy, no mansions, no castles. There was no split between free farmers and tenantry, no five dark centuries of saints and wolves—nothing redolent of the rise and fall of empires, nothing like that was here. Everything here was owned differently: grabbed-and-done—this landscape, this odd wished-for Eden—pale, glare-pierced—a pale, stuttering attempt, almost a sandbox attempt, a first version of Eden carried out this far with the wastelands and failed farms, woods, and abandoned fields and barns. I mean Eden with decrepit parts, evidence of social tactics that did not work, weedy stretches. Districts of seeming darkness, the opposite of Eden: Snakevilles, nihilism-domes of shadow entirely unlike the watched countryside, where the light often was actually brighter than here, since these darker places had more trees, untopped, unpruned; and often these places were set in dales or little valleys shaded by ridges so that there was less light and thinner light to start with. At this hour.

In those places one was watched differently. The darker places had people in them. I had a sense of different emotions, different ideas in eyes alert differently. People walked differently near the shadowy and not-well-painted farmhouses set in hollows, dampish and with lightning-struck trees, with acreages of shadowy farmland.

Biking, I got a strange taste in my mouth, my mind, really, of the strange, complex, brilliant, bitter invention of respectability and disreputability. Of poverty and some money. Of different kinds of money. Of luck, ill-luck, of character in this form.

The tide of respectability, or the pool of it, and ponds and spreading lakes of the doctrine of it really, were shallow in the countryside in some parts . . .

And, then, the dirty water and scummy foam of this shadowy other reality, local, poor, strange-looking, warehouse-barns set in crooked and blasted fields; and a loony kid here and a moron there, or mean-looking kids, angry, maybe, staring at me, while a bony dog barks and a malicious farm woman with a big face and wearing dirty clothes yells from a twisted mouth at a conceitedly proud, ignoring her, mean sort of tall, thin farmer, in farmer clothes, walking away from her across a muddy yard toward a barn.

Then you come to another sunny district—puritanical little gardens, garden beds, dry-looking rural lawns, clean ditches alongside the road, and fewer trees, and those are topped or pruned or solitary in wide spaces. Nothing is hidden. A single tractor moves at the far end of a dipping and swelling field. A moronic boy sits in a kitchen chair with a doll and near him a sad woman is peeling potatoes over a washtub . . . And nearby is a birdbath and in its raised quartz-and-mica-sparkling concrete basin are sparrows splashing, chirping, flirting in the early morning.

The highways, all of them back home then, were two-lane—some concrete, some blacktop. In Illinois, a few were made of brick or cobblestone still. I was biking in the Missouri countryside.

Where I biked, in each hamlet that I went through, the street changed into a highway when the houses stopped being so close together. The hamlet trees vanished. The road continued baldly, the major highway, narrowly among the fields. The sunlight ticklingly held its poses but not for long but altered. Shadows formed a closer tie to what cast them. The shadows shrank steadily and the glare ebbed—this was the open highway—until the shadows were like loose sacks tied to branches or eaves or tractors, or were like sheets of dark paper on weeds.

But they—the shadows—were faintly glittery in the morning light, shaped bags of less-lit portions of the air, speckled with light often; or, in the gloomier sections of the countryside, punctuated by a somberness of deeper shadow among the multitude of trees. There they gave an effect of sadness.

No one threw rocks or got into a rattletrap truck and chased me. It was as if the sun and I shared a laboring sense of things—I was in motion this early, too.

The time-inflected distances were logical in this part of the world but the specklings in the shadows were as if shadow could not bear to be shadow which was not logical. In half-okayness, one risks a kind of formality of self—one is logical among the logics of the sunlit and time-inflected distances . . . This is very tiring. The heat of the increasingly heated air was registered by committees of skin and sight, hair and lips and throat. The reports were of effort and of sweat—of the sweaty and hard-breathing condition and the comparative safety or danger of a section of the narrow highway among the fields. The heart strained beatingly and blood pushed and brushed in me. Alternately pinkish and livid, I biked along. I biked forty miles, a little more than an hour and a half's ride. Then, at some points on the highway, far into St. Paul's County, I could smell the Missouri River. The road was on high land, safe from some floods, not all. I am aiming toward some land we'd owned from around when I was three or four until I was eight years old, land and a house, where we'd lived part of each summer. Back then. Now, in wartime, in 1944 when it looks like we can win the war if we don't slacken, the old trucks that carried eggs and produce to market rattle along. Often, they had chain drive; and there weren't many of them. And young men never drove them. Cars, well, engineers and pilots and servicemen on leave, and salesmen: there was gas rationing and no civilian cars were produced. Very few women drove, and almost none alone; and those were in Cadillacs. It was shabby in St. Paul's County: the dissolution of a onetime promising rural world was well advanced there. The rush of the cars as they went by in that landscape, well, you could tell, sort of, who was country and who was city, and who had some sort of automotive sophistication and who hadn't. You could tell about the frame of mind, almost the religion and social standing of the father of the driver: a Catholic speeder with a policeman father . . . A middle brother in a Lutheran family with a lot of money . . . It was partly a joke to think that, but partly it wasn't. It was a different traffic from that in U. City. Knowing this was part of being a hick.

I mean the unabstraction, not of a field but of THAT FIELD OVER

THERE, *the old-time country ballast, or morbid conservatism, about destinies (not what they were worth to the people who lived them, but what they were). With drivers you could tell if the farmers had young sons in their trucks or if they didn't by how they behaved toward you on your bike. You could almost tell who had younger brothers they didn't like. And who had something to lose, privileges back then. (Breeding.) You could tell who was wild and who was getting heated up to compete. You can daydream as you bike about being a great baseball player—normal but famous—you can project this mental light of daydream on the landscape like my shadow on the ditch and then on the field or down the side of the steeply banked causeway. The narrow highway is crossing a bit of flood plain. Your mind can enter the shadow world and close out the real one. Illogic of that sort can do nothing but be imaginary. It does not dare ally itself with the real.*

Daydreaming and not daydreaming form a wild pendulum-swinging in me. The drivers, well, the drivers, some of them, cut it so fine that the whoosh of the wind of their passage woke me. I'd see them leering, it seemed, behind glass in those other shadowy, fictional foot-on-the-accelerator stories of their own lives that they were working on on this road. I was scared, exhilarated, partly murdered over and over. My bike would start to keel or heel or leap or twist or swoop. I would be blown into next week—*a phrase from back then and part of almost all the rural tall tales when I was a kid and part of all rural descriptions of mental states of love and luck, of revelation and of wakefulness. Me-myself-and-I on the bike were blown off the road almost half a dozen times. We went careering noisily, boundingly (bounced on rocks and tree roots) down the shoulder or bank into a field of weeds or into the clutter of tree trunks and the crazed almost churchy-Gothic light in the woods there. Angry, crazed—dangerous—some hoboes in the woods . . . Well, get your ass in gear and get out of there, hoo-haw . . . You do what you can to save yourself among the highway loonies . . . Dirty old . . . Often okay . . . Sometimes not. Alone in the woods, in the diminution of communal voices.*

And back on the road, on an adrenaline sine curve, one admired the people who made hand signals, who made room for me, a kid. Near the river some of the land was really flat, and the plowed and planted fields were darkish in color, a real brown, and the stuff coming up was really green, or strongly yellowish-green, planted so geometrically that the planting looked like notation of some kind, an idea spelled out stalk by stalk, row after row; that tickled the eye and the mind.

The changeable day, clear early, became cloudy in mid-morning.

The clouds came in from the west. The air turned humid and close. It was greenish-lurid under the clouds, then greenish-dark, then occasional low clouds spat and sprinkled rain. Thinly, then heavily. I left the road and stood with my bike under a tree lower than the ones beside it until the rain thinned. The day lightened but clouds remained in the sky; some were partly dark, some were very white. Part of the sky was blue . . . The clouds in their motion darkened again. The temperature shifted and shifted again; it was hotter; and clear sky appeared again among questionable clouds. I did wind sprints. Because my father had had heart trouble, I was uneasy about the possibility of my having a stroke at an early age. My father had had his first stroke when he was thirty-nine. I had no sense of what the odds were physically for me as his son-sort-of —no sense of what was normal in the (male) physical world, anyway: health stuff in newspapers and magazines wasn't all that common back then. It was all talk instead. Health gossip. I wasn't S.L.'s son genetically, but how many of his moods had affected me? How many of his tastes? So, I did wind sprints, a little soldierlike, in a weird military spirit (in wartime); but I was also some sort of madman giddy freak who came to his senses now and then and stared, worriedly, out the jumbled doorways of his senses, at the alluvial fields and woods, the cars, the people in them. The sensations of pseudo-athletic breathlessness and the dizziness of too much exercise, and the projection of an imagined purity of grief, of the feeling of belonging to a family . . . various ideals, simplified, glory-riddled . . . came and went. A mean-looking sergeant passed by too close in a 1938 Ford, his meaty features masked by shadow behind his windshield. I wanted to think about death—and life, my dad and me . . . Well, I didn't know how to think . . . Life around me did a lot of my thinking for me. If I tried to think, it was like I was standing somewhere, to one side, above the subject, the schooled sense of it as a topic, with worry as my chief personal sense of the subject. Then it was sort of as if I was suspended in blue air—trying to dive into the subject but not getting there. It was a little like diving dumbly through blue air in a dream but nothing happens.

Or you do get somewhere, into a green sub-sky radiance, the substrata of the nearest part of the subject. One is surrounded, immersed, in a cold shock of another medium foreign to the self and where one could not stay. The air ran out; my courage gave out; and a kind of mental flailing took over; and I went back to real air—the alternately okay and then humid air—not sure where I'd been. But I knew the subject wasn't virgin *for me now, since I'd gotten into it, so to speak.*

Sometimes, as I rode, I dove in again—into, so to speak, what I had thought before. Nothing of this was lastingly clear. There was a sense of drowning. Of Come on, it's a joke . . . *Coming back to the surface, seeing the road, feeling the sprinklings of rain, dodging the Fords and Chevies, smelling the dried-recently or moist air—I would ask myself,* What do you think about death, Wiley? *to encourage myself to* THINK. THINKING *meant to me to put something into words. And sometimes something in me would, as it were, put up its hands, or blurt out something—*Ugh, it's dirty *(death was)—not sensibly, so far as I knew, more like a fool in a classroom than sensibly.*

Still, I tried. I have a kind of harsh courage that I can call up by being not good or sensible but careless—like a naked soldier in a machine-gun fusillade: or ALL WET, *with thought, with dreaming, a surprised bather. Twistedly wretched and obstinate. A hick-rube, a local yokel—in regard to death. To grief. This isn't a bad way to be. As far as other kids are concerned—in the eyes of other kids—this doesn't make you obscene. But it had made my dad sad.*

He'd said, You don't have good judgment: you're not smarter than me . . . You're not smarter than ANYONE I know.

Thinking is a shadow fruit, shadows and weirdness in an electric orchard, blossoming with mirage after mirage, crumblingly real, then shadow paintings, mock photographs in black-and-white, then a mere sickly sense, an exposed underpainting, the overlay lost.

You have no common sense . . . What's the point of the way you are? . . . you'll lose what little common sense you have. You like being the way you are? It's you against the world—you like it like that?

Looniness and INTELLIGENT REFLECTION *and sensible scale and discipline: but in stuff unusable for school, the terrible pain of the nerves, in sliding from the subject: the awful abrasiveness of failure. I breathe hard. A half-loony whicker of nerves. An image from baseball:* You're OUT, you're OUT, you're OUT . . .

You ride on . . .

A quick glimpse through a band of dark-trunked trees of the river. Then a clear view of it across a flat, muddy field lower than the road, a field of weedy riverside corn planted in wandering, careless rows. A mighty but dowdy river back then, undammed, with visible shoals, sandbars, mud islands.

Off to the right, below the highway but higher than the field of corn, is a falling-down house, a fancy house on a knoll with a two-story side porch set between two columns, and not far from the house, under some small trees, a collapsing pergola.

Also visible (your eyes move around) is a brown unpainted barn, and then an unpainted wooden tavern with a number of neon signs already turned on, one saying FISH *and another saying* BEER *and one announcing a local brand called* OILYCOCK LAGER. *In front of the tavern is a stretch of dried mud—the parking lot. Behind it is a short jetty in an inlet. Overall the place didn't have an honest look now. When we had owned this place, there had been a different barn, one painted white, with a green roof: it had been down near the river—I'd heard it had been washed away in a flood—and we'd had no tavern, no signs, no parking lot, just trees and grass and farm fields. We'd often parked on grass.*

I hid my bike in a copse near the road, in the muck under a fallen locust; I covered it with fallen branches. I took off my jeans so I was in the cut-off jeans I'd put on underneath at home. I left the long jeans with the bike under the branches and I made my way through the woods walking in a stream in my sneakers—the stream which wound down (through often tall banks) to the inlet. Ignoring the flies and mosquitoes—the bugs—I walked along, stung-legged, wet-legged, odd-mooded, now with the sky visible, now with it hidden. At the mouth of the stream, where it emptied into the inlet, under willows, lay a very large, ungainly river dinghy. It was greenish and heavy, made of thick and heavy pieces of wood, scarred and scratched, peeling, and warped, moored to a ring in the trunk of a willow. Dilapidated and poor. I step into the sloshing water in the boat. In that water are warped, unpainted oars; I lift one and figure, sadly, they are too big for me to row with but I can use one as a pole in the muddy bottom of the shallows. We'd owned this boat once. I untied it. The boat moves slowly in smelly water. I was uneasy, then afraid. Then the fear was tremendous in me and only laziness and self-doubt kept me from giving up . . . I could see how some men wore out young. As S.L. had.

The clay of the banks, the yellow marl, had dirty red and loose-edged brown stripes and ovals in it. Past decrepit and mournful willows, I poled, tense with adventure. At the spreading mouth of the inlet, only a little current is present, guarded by a sandbank, shoals, and an island of reeds a hundred and fifty yards off shore. The ripples of the currents of a sensible river move here—it is not as it is in my head later in New York, years later, ostensibly present in the dry mind, a slop of fluids and electric traces. A real river is not uncertainly mounted in space but is actually there.

I poled out into the shoaled water where real current was possible, but it was possible the water would be calm. It looked calm. At the edge of the reeds, which rose maybe sixteen feet into the air, I tied the dinghy to a log, half buried in the mud. And I climbed out of the boat into the muddy water; I feel my lower legs moistly muddied in the water . . . my bare feet are in the gooey mud of the bottom . . . river molluscs cut my feet and river shrimp tickle my ankles. My feet and lower legs are as if murmuring with sensation. My gym shoes, their laces tied, are around my neck. The quick pulsations of fear and the alternating and, maybe, ruling bravery, or recklessness, and the thing of how it felt to be really alone for a change, the expansion of the mind then—as if your own mind became a mother or a brother there with you for the day, going along with you for the day's stuff—and to be alone in this wobbly state of bravery with no audience, I had come here for this but hadn't remembered from before what it was really like . . . The reeds towered over my head, and the mud flats and the muck of shallow river water smelled. To be frank, it was really creepy. As I said, the Missouri was undammed then, was a loosened and natural river, a naturally occurring, shoally, sloppy, weird thing, wet and wide, flat-surfaced, twisty with currents, big, unsafe.

Among the reeds, the water was combed and rendered into glass, stilled. I waded into the reeds, which walled in the eye. They themselves had tickling odors as the water did, the stifling air, and the muck did, too. So did I, I smelled, too, by now, the motionful wader in the stilled water, smelled with nerves, and heat, with grief, and of the river. One's mind moves in the endowment of silence—and in that quietness feels how hot it was in that odd grove and how it really stank there. The thin shimmer of dankness that rose gassily among the reeds in the shadow-strips and light and the odor—and bars and blobs of light and the thin shadows and the smell; it was sticky . . . the bugs bit. In a way, it was like being indoors, in the reed-columned roofless room—or in reed-walled, wet corridors. I walked testingly observant for sinkholes and snapping turtles. In the striped brightness, the stippling on my arms of brightly lit tiny blond hairs and the precise shadows they cast were ordinary nature which meant me: a hunh *of loud breathing: a raw madness . . . different from home: not a domestic madness: my breath moves differently; I feel my ribs inside my skin; my degree of strength—physical strength—is a constant issue here of life and death, or life and injury, and not of politeness and murder, as at home, or whatever it is there. The rawness of being a self is kind of raucous here. A nervous, crowlike cawing, an intruder thing is what my identity feels like. I don't know. I turned over* in my head *(and partly in my chest and throat) the idea of swimming out into the river—a* fifty-fifty chance *of drowning—"fifty-fifty" was rhetorical: I didn't know what the odds were. After a few minutes, I felt myself running out of courage—I had minded my dad's not being entirely courageous about his own dying. I had forgotten that that was so about courage, that it ran out, that it was subject to being used up: it burned in the friction of the moments and went out. I maybe partly understood* a little *about the ways my father had gotten tired of life, of courage. What he had meant when he said he was tired, what he'd meant when he'd said my mother—or I or my sister, Nonie (his real daughter, not adopted)—had ground him down, worn him out, had used up his courage. He said those things; those were his phrases. The reeds rustled in a passing wind. He sometimes used words like* guts, courage, class, a fighting heart, a Fighter's Heart *(like Man o' War's or Jack Dempsey's). He said that pushing yourself to your limit, and so on, destroyed your heart; don't do it, he said. I didn't want to commit suicide, but I was accustomed to turning things over to* chance, *to my darker self—selves—and seeing what the vote was, seeing what happened. I did want to die . . . but maybe not entirely.*

I made myself be brave again. I knew from the odor kind of freshening itself and becoming a kind of sweet stink and then not so much a stink at all but merely clinging and wet and riverine, and from a difference in the heat, a lessening of it, and a sound like a rumble growing louder, that I was approaching, in the bed of reeds, a limit of the privacy and that I was coming to the unobstructed river. I wasn't sure what I was coming to. I should have said I had some warning before I came out of the rustling discontinuum of reeds at the rim of a great, immediate circle of wide, hurrying, gray-colored water. And sky. A scene of peculiar radiance, that immense showy grayness: a brute enormity, an enormous scene of water, an everywhere of hurrying water and of reflections . . . giant reflections: in places, a gigantic expanse of river that rippled and that was inset with vast reflections of clouds moving on the hurrying water. The reflections shifted curlingly.

Impressed and dubious toward the natural glory and its plainness and its dangerousness, I trailed a hand in the light-struck, unstable, hurrying surface as if to restore a sensory narrowness of perception, but I felt the water moving and wrapping itself around me, my fingers, and the palms and backs of my hands and my wrists; and the merciless transience, insatiable-throated and sulphurous-muddy, on my hands or in them, my wrists were half-clasped by it; the stench-ridden, flowing and unobliging, gliding pliability and wet suffocation of the water. The reality held me and then dragged me out into the middle of the river and then, oh, two hundred feet into the air. Aerially, I felt the, uh, goddamned, remorseless replacement of everything, the air, the water, every moment, by itself, itself a moment later; so that everything is in a different moment but it's not the same everything, it's only the same everything in an unfocussed way, somehow, because it's a moment later. Have you noticed it's a different moment all the time? The marvelously undulant atoms and electrons and this mysterious other motion—or the same one—but it's like blinks and flights of attention . . . in gallopingly fluid cantos, stanzas: the motions of things. You FEEL *the air on your lips rhyme itself from a few seconds ago. The earlier state has skedaddled away. And this moment, this n-o-w, is not clearly formed, it's not still; hardly alit; it hasn't alit; it's fluttering; but it's still n-o-w, but it's* a different now, *loosely or wildly different.*

A river-borne tree trunk, dipping and twirling, sodden, with some roots and leafy branches on it still, went by thirty feet away from me. It would have broken my back if it had hit me. So I thought of the drowning of everything in being newly everything all the time and still, continuingly, drowning in being attached somehow—a mysterious spine of twirling, bodiless vertebrae . . . I saw stuff arrive at the surface of the river near the hurrying water around my thin legs, real stuff, but I felt the moment doing stuff, and I felt the stuff of moments doing stuff in me as well, becoming everything or taking it's place eerily, coming and going; and I became recalcitrant; I became slowed pools of watchfulness in motion and watching everything be in motion, eddying without surface or bottom or banks. And the reflections, the thoughts *were like clocks, and had tides and were slowed and recalcitrant pools as well . . . And what was watching ticked, too, and moved and swept along and was swept or stood still and flowered and died and kept going in some way or other.*

But it was too hard—and too immodest—to do this. Instead, I felt *time to be held in my silently blowing-bellows-like taut lungs—and in my hair and in the belly wall and in my toes in the mud underwater, but I was separate, too, so that I was a* committee *of times and hours and of timelessness anchored and unanchored chronographically in ways taught in school, a ribbed and breathing steeple made of whirring clocks, whirring clocks for eyes and stiller ones for the inner eyes, and clocks, also, of my breathing and, differently, of my memory of breathing if I looked at myself breathing a moment ago . . . And then I gave up the timelessness; and life seemed an* AMBITION*—oh, something like the nature of time itself with its direction fixed—to be known in-my-blood now as a spirit of individual chaos humming or whistling along* ambitiously *in a universal tick-tock and bustle. So that I was, oh, sort of, time in a bag* *and forked at the crotch—the bag was time, too, and was blowing along and the mind was rolling along, one member of a congress of sightednesses, all of them awhistle with time.*

I felt, maybe stupidly, the humming and whistling inside my lips and of my lips—breaths, atoms—atoms?—and the molecules of my breath, oxygen-drained and monoxide-ridden or whatever—but all of us, me, and all of me, and the river, flying along mysteriously, ticking and breathing, into being and being in this flowering surf and eerie tide.

*The wish to continue the world, to have it continue as an I-am-*alive *reality in itself, in no degree or jot or iota separate from what couldn't be named as me (there was no place apart from it for me to name it from), was crudely different now—everything in its reality, bustling, hurtling, ticking, hymning and humming along . . . in fraught* ambition*—like my own breathing throat and its ambition to continue to breathe . . . Or a molecule or atom or electron existing . . . But more pervasive and single and not exactly different as muscle and blood and tendons were from each other—and trachea and neck bones and hair on the nape from hair on my crotch. I didn't think I was a prophet or that I had been given a message, or, rather, I did wonder about that, but I doubted that it would matter to a lot of people, what I'd thought or what had happened here—I doubted that I was a big-time prophet . . . I couldn't think this was a historical moment.*

I did think, pretentiously, Well, try to be important, Wiley. *I thought that what was weirdest about time being everywhere was that if it was everywhere, if it was universal, then God was biographical and had a history, whether I could understand it or not.*

I felt a radiance spread in me equal, in minor terms, of a maybe only mildly successful orgasm during masturbation, but not from trying to think about that last thing, but from the kind of meaning earlier, more a sense of meaning than a meaning formulated. Then, this sense of meaning in the bustling and hurried universe, this sense of a sense available to ME, *I located (a certain actual image of it) in my mildly convulsed throat with its various labors of supporting the skull and of angling and twisting to aim the eyes and ears while it worked away at carrying blood and air in this heat. A throat. A throat. Then that faded into a mob of* clocks *that stare at each other and overlap and tug and flower in a great brouhaha. It is very like music. I have an inward shout of* GOD WHAT AM I TO DO ABOUT THIS? *I wasn't told what to do about it. I thought,* Well, shove it up your ass, Wiley . . . *I waited, not with a lot of hope; but I wasn't told anything. Shyly prophetic—since no project was given me—I told myself to* back off, quiet down, button up: *it would* mean too much trouble, it would cause too much trouble to argue or believe what I myself thought—to lay claim to meaning. But it seemed to me that I saw in the shadows on the water, and in the ones in the depths and those cast by the ripples, a dot or an egg, sort of a mirroring thing, that I did believe and would hold onto as belief. People had said to me, Don't ever believe yourself, Wiley.

In the nowhere inside my head—that unperpetual everywhere—the nowhere-but-there in my head kept claiming an apartness from time—but it now had a belief that what was truly out there was a papery and rustling and crumpling NOW with an unresolved arriving as well as a steadily observable moving off of it, both the old moment and the new moment, not in sequence, but eccentrically or syncopatedly overlapped, the complexly shaped n-o-w; and that this was so in me as well, and was so of my thoughts and ideas. I did believe this—but not all parts of me believed it—my mind itself, my very mind, kept insisting on being apart from the motion.

Well, I still had my hand in the water, and then I bent my head back and opened my eyes to the air—sort of waiting for a sign, you know?—but the touch of the water on my hand touched me flickeringly; and then I was high, high up again; and it seemed to me that moments don't move physically quite; it's spiritual; anyway, they simply fail to pause in place even while they seem to present themselves in an almost knowable courtesy, as if they did pause.

But they are unroofed, unfloored, even if stiffly (or stilly) present. Please-forgive-me, the air whispered . . . And the part of the mind cut off from the regular mind, the part of the mind that thought this said Please forgive me to the other part, which didn't think it and never accepted it, the divinely unstable—and ferocious and devouring—and illusory stillness-of-other-motion of the motion of the moments.

Dreamlike! Dreamlike! The nearer air and the farther air and a further air of a notion, and somehow the sky flittering and receding (when you look at it), the separate pieces of the softly oozing everywhere in its unresting flowering. This dwarfed me: mad, madding, maddening NATURE—and time in it . . . Big deal . . . I got mixed up: I was studying Virgil and Horace in school, and Abraham (Abe) Lincoln in history, and physics and geometry and English; and in English class, Thomas Hardy and George Eliot and Notions of Fate in the English Countryside. I was actually studying what teachers said those writers said they saw . . . I figured I wasn't having a vision. I was trying to join some kind of band of people who didn't have dead fathers and who had opinions about the countryside.

I felt the humming and buzzing in my ears and legs as well as in my lips and lungs, and I felt it in my certitudes and grief, in my errors . . . the humming of time everywhere.

In and above and around and under the shaking river—and my mind blinkingly dreaming—real time and me, I'm made of time. I take on an immediacy; I take my hand out of the water; I hear my mother's and my sister's and my father's voices: You're a fool. You sound like a fool. You were always a fool . . . I have no time for your crazy ideas . . . *They and I say in separate tones,* Leave me alone.

I say it out loud to the sky . . . I say out loud, Leave me alone. I don't believe it . . . I don't believe it is this simple . . .

I don't know if I do believe it or not . . . I don't want to think about it anymore: *Incomprehensibly linked (not end-to-end but overlapping) and unstoppable moments—never a nothingness, never stillness—a universe of such restlessness that it explains everything—but if it explains* EVERYTHING, *what good is it?*

Come off it. What's the Big Idea? Don't make me laugh.

The shuddering plenum, is it true? Don't listen to yourself. Stay sane.

You can't have a nothingness in which everything buzzingly moves, can you? I think it is possible that GOD *never retreats from the birth of consciousness onward, from being surrounded by, immersed in, the restless ambition of everything, all the trash tyrants hooting and hollering and going* boo *and whistling and singing along.*

This moment was like being blown up but not killed, partly explained instead and filled with a radiance of sorts. But it seems fatal.

Leaning hayricks of revolving and variedly colored rays of sunlight —oblique, slanted—come through lit-up holes in the cloud cover and touch the gray, current-tickled surface of the water. Weird bird shadows move skimmingly on the lit and shadowed melted lid of the currents. The shadows slippingly skid, without sound, across the visible patterns of movements of the water. Birds, a water hawk—a river eagle, maybe —and three fish crows—bird eyes, bird feathers, whatever—chirring and sudden—their reflections are legible, are recognizably of a species. Motored with appetite and directed by habit and in the lovely and grotesque oppressions of both, they appear and vanish and then reappear as they move in the sky. They are never more than partly visible. But their reflections are legible.

HELP ME.

The eerie truth and lopsided song is that the gross outer shells of the world twist and gleam and darken, and I believe in nothing, not in them, not in me. Only in death and in youth for the time being. Unconcluded truth shifts in me in the varying light. Breath moves a bit kissingly in the rolling passages of the minutes . . . It is okay to be wrong. It's part of who I am the way the shape or the movement of wings is part of a family of birds. The eyelid thing of blinking and thinking in the middle of a stinking river. Proof is different from this.

Light and clouds and the shadows on the water, the birds overhead, their cries and skimming reflections, the boy, the reeds, the shore, the truth, the error—all of it exists here in the many-winged flutter and mutter in the moment. It flies to nowhere. It moves motionlessly into unexistencehood in actual moments where I am still, like a phonograph needle, noticing the deviations that become the course of argument of the thoughtlight in my mind. It becomes memory—usefulness—a flag, a cloudy thought. I stand in the struggling flowing rot of the river. I think (or feel) this stuff months before being willing to argue it with Remsen (a friend at school who sometimes sucks me off) and years, decades before I will be willing to write about it. Illusions of God, delusions—hallucination—confusion on confusion. I will say to Remsen: I'm not brave enough to be crazy.

We don't know enough about the world to speak of it conclusively so far.

I will say to Remsen, We don't know enough to be dogmatic, you asshole . . .

But that's in the future . . .

A sense of motionlessness as proof of sanity in a peculiarly scheduled world immaculately freshened every moment isn't where I was before. To know which lies work isn't necessarily to have a sense of reality. But to know that ideas of timelessness don't work visibly, but you have to use them, really, that is faith of a sort, a shrewd sort maybe.

Does a moment have motiony walls? A real moment?

The exquisite flutter of the present tense . . . the real . . . it is the real that is spread in front of me . . . The present tense is where I live . . . It's the only place where life is . . .

In the hope of affixing a modesty of meaning to the slowed rampage of mind, I, uh, took my dicker out. I would be reminded of the real every time I peed. But in this state—in solitude—screened by the reeds—I, when the thing was abruptly erect, I, being afflicted with emotion—the hateful joy and even more hateful fear in a thought—and hoping for common sense and peace, I jacked off. It was willful and fantastic, the pumping and whatnot in the riverscape . . . The boy on the river, head back, coloring and breath and posture absorbed in this, felt the sexual progression as pure time. Some guys I know are interested only in final motions, climaxes . . . Only climaxes matter.

In the rottedly placid (moo-cow) *afterwards, the grays of the muscles of the water look mutedly pale, white—almost spermlike—in the vaporous air. Browns in the air and flickering bits of blue. Motionful reality I see is the only moral reality, of course. The only existent one . . . Unwilled by us. This one where beauty is . . . the existent moment. But perhaps this one has no truth to it except scientific truth.*

After the dissatisfactions and sport of masturbation, cleaning myself in the smelly water, I feel demons move in me: my fear of being alone has a new shape.

Then the fear of the strength of the water and of being unfooted in the wet current drove me walking and thrashing with my hands, nervously back to the shallows in the center of the reeds . . . I took off my wet shirt and pants, stumbling in the muck; and putting my clothes around my neck, I waded naked for a bit and swam a little in half-shallow water there, trying to control my cowardice. My nerves.

But when I started to swim with my clothes and shoes damply knotted around my neck, I came to the point of real terror. I could put my hands down and touch the muck or kick it if I swam the crawl, but that terrified me further. I was immersed in the muddy water.

Quickly and, I guess contemptibly, I stood up; and the air on my muddily wet, skinny flesh unmanned me further; my fear became uncontrollable. I stumblingly walked back through the reeds to the other side facing the shore. The deep fluster of fear battered me; and the stink of the river kind of forbade thought. Cowardly and harried, in a brainy restlessness of terror, I said to myself in words, You know, in your heart, it is without exception motion. You've always known it. There is no timelessness.

The fear during the attempt to swim, the ordinariness of the ejaculation, the being naked and scared now, make it minor—the thought —and make me minor, too. But as if to spite me, the sense of enclosure on this side of the reeds hints at the spreading air over my head—and the sensation is of motion again, undilute, ubiquitous.

"Shut up, shut up, shut up," *I say out loud.* "SHUT UP!"

The cowardly boy in the reeds wanted to have good ideas, *ideas that would make him famous. This didn't seem like that sort of idea . . . It seemed merely true. Still, he said out loud,* "Well, I don't know . . ." *Then:* "Well, shut up about it. Don't be a martyr . . ."

If time is everything, then everything is not geometric or symmet-

rical. I want to be a liar. In this framework, death happens one person at a time. Everyone disappears but we each die. Death and time do not reduce to abstractions . . . Into life and consciousness and out again—to be personal about it, to be personal about the direction of things—maybe we—and everything else—were formed in the image of motion—like real light of any kind . . . Maybe the Bible meant to say this but got rewritten locally.

I think of people as bunchings and bouquets of velocities; and then I try to take the thought back but the actuality sticks. What if each thing in the universe were a hypothesis about velocity—a manifestation of a hypothesis in an actuality of present-tense moments. A person is a knot of velocities of different kinds and has an overall velocity, while the velocities of the smaller parts continue in currents and branchings, magnetisms, collisions—sighs and brilliancies or dullness. It is a kind of free-for-all of free will in the magnitudes of time.

No. That can't be it. That's just words. Duration is swell. The direction from creation to now is Try Again. The persistence of modification. Denying that may be the conceited origin of lying and the chief joy of living—I will not try again. To be snotty is to be honorable . . . The bitter source of violence is prideful staleness.

It seems a denial of the actual smile of God to say God doesn't change. But it seems a denial of everything sensible. I am the brother of everything in the universe in the sense of being, oh, a tormented sibling to it, simultaneous with others and sequential with some others, too . . . The argument is that imperfection is great . . . Very great. But how can that be?

An eerie peace comes from my being not so bad by comparison in an unconcluded universe of unfinal experience and unfinal prophets so far. But that's not humble . . . It's humble to say everything is over . . .

Be humble, Wiley . . .

Be humble? I AM *humble. Big deal.*

Still, I believe the world is hardly chaos but it is in motion.

As a child hiding in a closet, I heard the house move, heard the moments come and go, heard distant footsteps . . . People are so fucking temperamental that if they can't speak for the entire universe, they throw tantrums and say they'd rather live in hell. They'd rather live in hell than think clearly, my dad always said. He also said that thinking clearly led to hell.

Some people think that the more you control, the more truth you have in you. Okay. That makes animal sense.

Why shouldn't I believe myself?

Don't you dare, Wiley. Don't do it. Just don't. Be smart. What I came here to do is think about death—I probably had better do it . . .

Good old Death, common and universal—your basic COMPENDIUM *of endings would have the title* DEATH—DEATHS*—whatever . . . But real* DEATH *will be indicated by a red asterisk signifying endings that preclude recurrence . . . that doesn't mean there is no transformation, or transportation . . . Oh, what* TERRIFIC *solitude and fright . . . How mournfully unknowable. Each of us will die in a way specific-to-us . . . Death is undergone singly—it is* KNOWABLE ONLY *as specific to one person . . . to each of us. All our data comes from that. It is so much not general, even if thousands die at the same time, that the thing is that it is not knowable as a general thing; this is the chief moral fact of it and not paid much attention to; and is maybe the chief explanation of generalities having so much attraction, because they push the singular specificity of your own death around, so that you feel it as a theory and not as the whistle and whisper—and kiss—and shove and inevitability in your own actual minutes.*

Of the openmouthed quality of time and of all its edges, its cliffs, DEATH . . . DEATH *is the first thing not lived through. It is not possible to say yes in it or at the edge of it to anything and have it really involve you in any further continuation of the moments . . . not a yes that means anything in the human sense of presence anyway.*

Approaching one's absence from things is not like entering on a blink—it's really solitary. It isn't shared. It is an ultimate loneliness, you being separated from everything, you going into the earth while the universe goes on playing.

It may be like a slowly forming diving bell of goodbye. Really, what a final discipline of evasion. Pain and lunacy pushed you right into it. What a correction of failure, of any failure of a sense of reality. Really, what justice. I supposed it was justice in the light of a world that was a mixed-up storm of motion.

By its singularity in each person, it gives, I feel, someone who dies a terminal okay to take on the terrifying and awesome originality of admission of just how singular they are as creatures of consciousness. It is a correction of all the generalities one uses to avoid death—to as-if-know things and all things through false generalities. Death makes someone a genius whatever he was before. I bet we die, each one of us, an isolated genius, semi-lightless. It happens to everyone and some can bear it—that's bravery—and some cannot: and that's scary . . . Well, so what?

It's a universal event sooner or later but not simultaneously (so far), but it is an untransferable single thing for each of us, no matter the violence of the denials we resort to in order not to think this and no matter how simultaneously universal it ever is.

The difference in how many moments you get matters.

I doubt that people can comfortably move from thoughts of it as the name of a universal category to what it is inside them, inside each person, in the only real form it has. The pain of the existence of death does not undo all pretty truths. I stand naked in the river. DEATH *was always here and we had pretty truths anyway. Do I believe what I am saying? Consciousness in real moments is partly mutual, so then that stops when you die. Every part of your consciousness is humanly yours and singular and perhaps clear . . . But so what? Clarity in death may not be so great. It seems to me no one can think of death* honestly *as an abstraction or as it is in someone else: you can only stumble onto the edge of it in someone else, and then the onward rush or creep of time deposits you in the middle of the singular death in yourself . . . You can't see anything else but that.*

*The boy says, helplessly, to himself blurredly—then he repeats it, in careful syllables—*People can lie all they want but I am not sure that justice does not exist.

What I know about real death (inflicting it, observing it in the flesh or in plants) has (a tang, a quality, a merit) a thing of (ignorant, wartime) MALE PROFESSIONALISM. *Death has a great weight of primary emergency in a real moment. The two human forces that are, in a way, absolute, absolute for consciousness, are giving birth and killing things. From the point of view of a woman. Fucking and killing that would be, from the point of view of a man.*

A good laugh, a little tenderness and kindness: they're like little sparrows: anything can scare them away, *S.L. said.* But fucking and killing: even leaves do it—*with the help of the wind and of certain principles of growth and the placement of the sun.*

Then, with solemn stupidity, or sparrowlike and mischievously, I try to think in conventional, general patterns: Death is the real case that offends fantasy.

Particles have to move and be time itself down to the least constituent of themselves or they can't exist as particular particles separate from other particles, which, of course, they do exist as, at least some of the time, in some circumstances, so far as I know. This branch of science isn't popular with people . . .

There is no unmoving mass yet that we know of. If there were and it had no date, then okay, but if it had a date, then it has direction, and direction, even when it changes, is an identity (with a boundary).

Big deal.

I'm trying to be reasonable: I'm showing off while standing still in the river; birds and distant observers take me to be a naked piling in the river. Or a giant egret. Or a log upendedly stuck in the mud. But when I move, they can guess at me better, that I am a wader, a skinny boy in a river. My eyes move. My chest moves blurredly with my breathing. I move a little into and out of a blurredness of attention. And I put my wet shirt and wet pants on with difficulty and with a lot of acrobatics, nearly falling into the water. I splash to get my balance when I slide in the muck. Or slip to one side. I am distended achingly with a kind of nervousness . . . It comes from trying to think. I'm glad I don't try to think all the time. Thinking means one is akin to expanding wakefulness. I have a dim, quivering inkling that my first mother, my real mother, called Divinity *The Nothing-omitted.*

I cannot possibly be original. The universe, the universes, shadows in the water, me and love and war, death and murder, me and days, me and holy and unholy things. Me and facts. A tickling eddy (like a girl's cunt and clitoris and legs maybe) pressed with no tact against my wet waist . . . My father, who had his own ideas, said once when he was drugged that it was all a lot of trash—everything wants to own you. And I am as if in the open mouth of a moment and its huge and thrashing flight. I am scared of the consequences of things . . .

OH YOU—YOU'RE a phenomenon—you're A GENIUS . . . I DON'T THINK SO . . . Somebody's making a fool of himself here. Daddy said it . . . Daddy said I was too consistent to be interesting. He said, *Don't be boring . . . Don't hang yourself on your own petard—spit it out . . . Spit out what you can't chew. Don't talk to hear the sound of your voice . . . Learn to be happy: be a happy gentleman.* Daddy said it.

In the present tense, in the great drafty corridors of the real, in the actuality of the wet timeyness of the unsteady river and of me, and the dry but vaporous-cloud-occupied sky overhead, I feel myself to be truly, guiltily, a boy burning with stupid consciousness and error—in persistent metamorphosis—numbly amnesiac.

What did I just think? Repeat it . . . I can't . . .

Thinking has in it a lot of the faithless fascism of dreams.

Someday I will reproduce what I thought on the river, I thought then. Meanwhile, I last dutifully into the next flying noticeability of a flutteringly present moment, aware that this is at the beginning of an arc of giving up the argument for now.

I go from moment to moment, I do that for the sake of love—of people and of this world—and out of fear of the terrible sense of singularity I bet people have and that I will have when I die. When I leave this world. Sure, death is attractive: want to be *a genius*—go die . . . I go to the NEXT and THE NEXT in the blink-scarred continuum of my life.

Daddy said he wanted to die . . . He said it was time for him to get off the shitter and give someone else a turn at drenching the world in shit. I.e., time for others to have thoughts of how much of life was shit—and of how a person was like a threshing machine making acres and acres of corn and orchards full of apples into turds . . . Into shit. He believed intelligent, good people had all the same thoughts—and should have the same thoughts. But I am afraid to have his thoughts in me . . .

A fading of the light draws my eyes to an oval patch of darkness on the water and a floating ovoid of darkness in the air, an interrupted shadowiness—to the west—and it comes nearer—and then is here, a spotty, brief rain, airy pitter-patter on the water in a diffusedly almost lightless air. Discontinuous chains of drops going slantedly up and down and moving along on the water like a float in a parade, going on also in that other direction, which is to say, toward my death . . . thinly bouncing, travelling rain—thinly-welling-so-many-ways rain.

Help me . . .

I'm more deeply scared, emptier, too, in the immediate air of that rain than even when I swam a moment ago. And it's even worse in the drying air when the smell and sight of the lines of rain is hardly more than a thousand yards off, if that. And beads of scalding light on some of the eddies where the rain has stopped rack me with warnings of the approach of a seizure of the opposite of despair. I have a sweaty sense of truth . . . I have a sweaty flesh and a flesh of light. I stood in the light of right-after-a-rain. In the afterwards here. The parts of me I am aware of are motionful clouds of matter, brothers and cousins of one another and of light and of the water. This is just for now that I feel this . . . I promise not to believe myself . . . I swear, cross my heart and hope to die—in the singularity of my own death—that I do not believe I know the truth. I sweat with nervous grief in fear that I might know a little bit of truth, enough to fuck up my life, let alone the next step IN THE BEAUTY *of the inexplicable one-way flow in the direction of my death, of the death of everything, and which is my fate, my territory, my garden, my frontier. I feel nerves at the bottom of my belly and in my now shaking thighs, and in my nose chokingly, and in my lips.*

BE TOUGH, SHITHEAD. BELIEVE SOMETHING ELSE . . .

My angled head . . . My father said, I know who you are, Charlie, by what you look like: you're a real cutie, you are, Wileykins.

I have no idea of what he really saw when he looked at me, when I was little, or in the middle part, or lately. Cutie here. *Daddy said,* Tell me, are there any more at home like you . . . You're enough and you're too much . . . You're enough and a little over for any one household to manage.

Madness blows and whistles, sunlight rains every which way among the lazy and more or less corkscrewingly erect vapors here after the rain, and the rain itself is visible downriver. Help me . . . Vapors rise from the river and the clouds move and the rearoused birds skim in the sunlight over the water, and I see them as so many dimensions of 'duration' *that I am afraid I am truly lost and will maybe never escape again back to certainty. I slide from madness to madness . . . I want to be ordinary . . . I want my father back . . . Do you hear me?*

I don't want him back, but I don't want to carry the weight all my life of agreeing it's time for him to die.

Yes, I do want that weight.

Madness partly ends with the lesser madness of announcing it is time to stop and you take steps *to stop, not really knowing if you can or not. The snail house and bunches of twig shadows and the nest of flying paths—my head, if I might say this—the boy shuts down his head, my head, with dramatically only partial* SUCCESS. Get back to the boat . . . Get back to the SHORE . . .

But it is, truly, partly over anyway. He scrambles splashingly in the water, a haunted and falling boy, feeling, in terms of perception, that he is made of an infinite regression of eyelids and of eyes—of quanta*— only some of which ever obey his will at any one time; and he jokingly* *calls himself* COWARD, COWARD, MOO-COW COWARD. *He says to himself, jokingly,* The GREAT EYELID is not subject to me. The principles of The Great Eyelid are beyond me.

But he hears GOD *delusionally as The-Breath-and-Motors-of-Time stalking him along his path in the reeds, and storming along as* A GREAT HA-HA *of final force in him and everywhere, both wildly and peacefully.*

The boy blinkingly hurries through the reeds, strangely accurate about the direction of escape. Jesus, God—and Moses, *he says—the reality of matter sailing along is truth—that is, reality is true or it stops being real. But truth gets to waver. Matter in its courses in time is so true, that is, the world is so real, that even breath and death are not more final than real truth is. But one is helpless in this mess. In a scramble of breath, death, and truth—and of the river-wide, gray-tinged flutter of the present tense—the boy climbs scaredly into the dinghy.*

Dad says, It's all a lot of crap . . .

And: Whatever you do, don't be a prophet: that's a real can of worms . . . That's really a terrible thing to do with yourself.

Worms of light flying in the membrane-wrapped, blood-tinged direction. In one's consciousness—When you're dead, real worms feed in your brain.

S.L. said, Do you think of heaven when you're on the crapper?

I don't know. I haven't noticed yet . . . Do you?

Sure. You know my heart may give out in a crap—*the sphincter is a real sphinx*—I think about heaven, sure.

(Lila said, Don't take it wrong, Wiley, but S.L. was a more interesting person than you are.)

I thought when I heard him say that, that that was a fine thing to say, elegiac, lyrical, accusing, funny . . . I thought it was majestic.

(Me, I am a mess of changes of subject, but he, he had a lot of real experiences.)

What are the mind's motions when the brain changes the subject? What is the point of decision? How does the attention turn aside? What is its neck, its pivot? What is the mind's neck? What is a motion of the mind? Attention is the most racingly swift part of me—is it faster than light? Maybe my thing like light is the queer, inhuman, swift shuffle—the glides and swoops—of attention: maybe they're rivalries and mirrorings of light . . . mysteries . . . I-see-you . . . I-am-seen . . . The mind is fretfully unstoppable, having been stirred up. The boy poling in the muck, standing up in the dinghy, half falls three times, twice inside the boat and once nearly toppling over the side: this emergency *ends the prayer, already hardly remembered, ends it with a sense of failure.*

Chagrin—derisory and gnawing—and chomping—a sense of loss in the peculiar air and light, raw with time—says I am wrong in whatever I do. I have an ancestry of people who died . . . I have a flesh of light and I have sweaty flesh and I'm always in error . . . Big deal . . .

A slopping pitcher of darkness is in my breast now.

Now this stuff is over, too.

THE INHABITED UNIVERSE

My (New) Mother's Voice: The Other Narrator: 1932

(Chapter 1:) Water flows and knocks and bubbles on the walls of the house. And watery rivulets and glassy and engraved and noisy curtains of water fall from the eaves. Along with the loud, wet rubble of general splashing goes a sense of the immense motions of the world—really, though, it is the railroad and the Mississippi, locomotives and the weight of a river a mile and a half wide. They shake the limestone bluff on which this neighborhood is set.

The house is on a pale rumbling footing as Daddy gently washes my face with a cold washrag and I turn my head from side to side—the blurring of that motion being part of an orchestral piece of guest voices and rain and a wooden house . . . It is daytime but it sounds like a night orchestra—*sometimes* the beauty of confusion is as strange and obvious as water.

We saw about adoption in the movies . . . Still, it's a big thing to do nowadays—Momma talking biographically. *I've always lived well. I have my own teeth. You have to know the kind of woman I am. The people that take care 'a our house at the river? The farm woman? We bought her her teeth. She's younger than I am. One of her sons has TB—it isn't worth her while to get out of bed in the morning if you ask me. I don't want that kind of life for myself and mine—that's the first thing to take in consideration . . . I started out sweet but, I don't know, one day I turned the other cheek for the last time, and lo and behold, I turned into the other sort of girl that you see before you. I don't know;*

why do you suppose it is people do what they do? If I had time I could think about it but if you want to know what my life is like, it's first one thing, then another, and, to be frank, I'm busy, I'm so busy I'm rushed right off my feet—where am I going to get the time to think? I have to think on the fly. Rush, rush, rush. I wouldn't know where my head was if it wasn't fastened to my shoulders. I don't know. I make my bed, and it's like a dream; I lie on it; I'm a serious person but sometimes it feels like a game. Maybe it's whatchamacallit—psychology. You like Eugene O'Neill? A little excitement is good for what ails you . . . You know what I remember? The horses. The horses outside all day long and in the middle of the night—it was strange late at night—a horse outside making those loud steps and then doing that thing, that braying, not braying, one of the horse cries, I don't know what you call it, a whistle and a little shriek and a hunh-hunh-hunh in the nose, a snuff-snuff . . . And the smell. They ran away sometimes—what a noise that was, the banging, people screaming; people got hurt; we had a lot of cripples. I sound like an old fogey . . . I remember running downstairs and along the walk and inside next door because they had the telephone already, they were on the line, and we weren't, and there was a telephone call for me, a boy. He was in love with me . . . He wasn't the only one; I was a devil. People were nice about sharing their telephones if you had a nice smile . . . well, that's water under the bridge. I was fifteen; I'm thirty now. [She was thirty-five.] *The world was nicer then, boom-boom. It's funny, all the things that are gone: the old trees and the noise—and the smells . . . Before you could say Jack Robinson: gone . . . Don't spread it around how old I am. I'll tell you how spoiled I was: in the War, my mother and my father gave me a Cadillac convertible and a fur coat and pearls to scare off the poor boys. Well, war is hell.* [She was joking; she grew serious.] *The suffering takes the heart out of you. So I was off and running with a bang . . . ha-ha . . . and a heavy heart . . . But you know how it is, once you're off to the races, you don't turn back. Who wants to die of boredom? I was the cutest thing around—you know how it is—you know what* They *say: Too soon old, too late smart? My father was a nice man. I was his pet. Marie Dressler came to town to sell war bonds. I was introduced to her but she didn't say I should be in the movies. She said,* Watch out for this one . . . This one is trouble . . . *Ha-ha. I just loved her; I always loved funny-looking women who could make you laugh. I was some looker. Well, what can you do. I got married. I married a good-looking man; I don't like winters. The twenties were good; a good time was had by all. It was a different world from before the War but even so, it was a scandal to be in the forefront—I'll be frank: I was a flapper . . . I was something, let me tell you, me and my big dark eyes, I had pearls down to my knees and the shortest skirts in Illinois. I had the figure of many men's dreams—a nice Jewish girl gone native . . . Ha-ha. I had the kind of bust that was popular then—twenty-three skiddoo . . . It was only a few years ago. I will say for myself, I knew my way around. I'm no What's-her-name, Madame Curie, but I'm a fish people take into consideration in a little pond. You don't think I'm conceited, do you? I wouldn't mind being conceited: who's going to stop me in the middle of the Depression? I look like something the cat dragged in today. Well, it's a short life but a merry one. I have opinions; I'm not a dumb bunny—using your head is the shortest distance between two points I always say: ha-ha. I listen to no one; I'm an independent. And I don't want anyone—and his brother—telling me what to do . . .*

In the river sunlight, in the front room, Momma laughs—is she doing it for company? When I am near her, I can tell from her breathing, her nervous momentum, the color of her skin, the lines of her neck, what her mood is, her degree of social lackadaisicalness-cum-tension-and-whatnot. I can see the launched-arrows-the-battle-is-joined-smiles of hers as they go flying into the air. I feel, in a childish way, the angles of intensity in her, the sulky life-is-without-meaning effort she is making; whew, it is powerful for me, what she is doing . . .

(Chapter 2:) *You ask me what's fun: I enjoy myself now and then. I've been known to flirt with one or two people in my time. But charity work is my be-all and my end-all. You know the song, "Let Me Call You Sweetheart"? I'm the sweetheart of Sigma Chi: the world is my sweetheart. I try to do good. It isn't fun to try to help a poor family: people go crazy; people get beaten to death—I don't mean only at home. You go with a little girl who's along to buy a tombstone for her drunkard father who was killed by the bootleggers and see how you feel. Believe me, you learn a thing or two. I helped get a boy who was raped to the hospital . . . His embarrassment could give him gangrene. I don't faint easily; I'm practical. Still, you have to ask yourself, with the world going to hell in a handbasket, what do you want to do with your life . . . I think things were better before the war; life is a lot simpler in a town where people don't go to the movies. Here, I'll tell you a secret: I'm not a snob—but I am a cynic . . .*

*

Youngish, superior, thin-legged, neat-footed Momma in white stockings, in a white linen dress, with her arms bare and a lot of ivory bracelets, Momma shakes her dark hair: *I get it styled and set in St. Louis; I'll be damned before I let myself look like a farm woman . . . You like my little ring? I call it a go-to-a-St.-Louis-store-wait-on-me-and-keep-a-civil-tongue-in-your-head-ring . . . You have to have the soul of a slave driver if you want to get anything done in this world. I like to put on the dog now and then—I do it for Visiting Firemen; it's a duty; you know how it is. You want to take a look at us? It's better than a movie—so, take a look at us while the looking is good. We're the official sight for sore eyes in this burg. People pack lunches and drive miles these days to have a good laugh: no one's got any money: we're on the lists of things to see; we're good for a laugh now and then. I'm a high-stepper in a little town—oh my, I really have to laugh. Well, I don't like post-mortems but I'm Lila-she's-modern-she-wants-her-own-way-she's-a-born-troublemaker-so-go-run-and-hide-maybe-*[a whisper here]*she's-a-bitch. Well, I was always the fiery type. I've been called a spitfire more than once. But give me credit—I'm a sport . . . I take too many aspirin, I smoke too much than is good for me but I give other people their due; I take my turn; I don't take more than my share. S.L. says if you stay up past your time, the cows will come home to roost . . . I know what he means: we had a good party last year; we had a dance in the backyard with black men playing jazz: the Japanese lanterns caught fire, the heel broke on my shoe, my brother Mose stole my pearls and wore them around his head—he isn't good-looking at the best of times: he has a real potato face—I have to admit a good time was had by all. A little screaming, a little running around helps a party. In Alton, you can work up a real sweat if you want to give people a good time. And have one yourself. So, wave your arms and shake your boobies—pardon me—and spill things right and left on your dress—people loosened up; I practically ran from house to house telling people,* Come at once, it's a good party *. . . It makes a good story but don't believe me . . . Believe me, it was uphill work. Try and see if you can get small-town people to have a good time. People are stubborn. I could have shot everyone there, I realized the next day I could shoot everyone I knew and the world would never notice the difference . . . I've forgotten my point . . . But it's a bad bad feeling to feel your life doesn't matter: my life didn't mean anything, Moira. I'm not a scenery lover. A muddy river to look at isn't my idea of heaven either. I'm not a woman who can feel something and then do nothing about it. Ask me no questions; tell me no lies. I have my am-*

bitions; I aim to be the wildest thing around; but when all is said and done, I lack confidence. I have to go step by step. I know my limitations.

She sighed, sighed again, deeply; and she coughed a bit. The river at the foot of the bluff imparted a smell to the rain even where we were . . . As a rule, Momma is an uneasy sleeper: troubled by message-bearing dreams. I am a heavy sleeper.

I take myself seriously . . . Don't laugh at me . . . People live like animals but I say no thank you to that. Well, keep your powder dry—this isn't a real good time to be lords of the manor. People say I'm pretty but that doesn't give meaning. I would of liked to be a scientist. Or a nurse. But my mother didn't approve. To tell you the truth, I never liked school—and the school I went to wasn't so good . . . St. Louis has more Jews but I haven't the confidence at the moment. A lot can be said for a small town—people know you have brothers. I have an interesting life all-in-all but there's no rest for the wicked; I always say you might as well get hung for a sheep as a goat but I don't mean it. I would like to be a nun—there's more than one way to skin a cat. Nuns are smart. I get along with Catholics. I think Protestants are very, very smart people—scary. What can I say? I used to think a woman was a fool not to become a streetwalker—respectability is a fine kettle of fish; it doesn't come cheap. You know, there's not a lot I can say around here that isn't a case of I'm-going-too-far.

(Chapter 3:) Momma's nervous stylishness of assault was a curious amalgam of playing with daydreams and melodrama, not always playing, of course.

As a child, I assumed the whole story was known to someone in its entirety; and back, then, in 1932, I was hardly aware that the story was not over; and when I *heard* the soft darkness in the voices among the cones of orange light and in the fluttering rainshadows at the as-yet-unknown further edge of the future, I did not at all know what that meant.

Lila in the rainlight says daringly, *I'm an example of someone who wants her own way.* She is a heroine for the moment of a disobedient species. The presence in her voice of actually unknown possibility in the moments marks it as her real voice—I mean it is not a toneless medium my memory uses to constrain what I imagine her saying; it is not a voice solely in my own head. If I hear her in such a way that I know *there-is-*

no-knowing-what-she-will-do-next (her phrase), then I am listening to her and not merely paying attention to my ideas of her and of a woman's speech—one must make allowances for a mother's lying and careful speech and imagine the person behind the speech, the woman who talks to other grown-ups her own age.

The gray electrical hush of the mind listening, running, hears her among the sounds of the rain and the other voices, hears the sounds, the inflections of her voice, the riding-on-the-breath thing—hears meaning happening in her voice as it goes along. I don't want the darkness of the future to be subtracted from her actual voice. But I need the comfort of knowing how it all comes out—I give up an omissive and needful and silly omniscience for the sake of presence but then I believe falsely that the story is over. Know-it-all, aide-de-camp Memory has to be nice to my mother or I won't pay attention to it.

In some ways, even back then, I like Lila best . . . I hear her the most easily. She is on duty at her party.

One thing I'll say for myself, if I have to toot my own horn, I know how to toot it—I know how to toot my horn—shaking her foot at the end of the prettily silk-stockinged leg crossed over a knee: the foot in the air moves with as-if-desperate female decision. The lunatic color of an actual voice, its music of intention—at a party—its meaning is gripping. Her voice, her face are not opinion or example; they are real; she looks amused in the watery light. One hears her breath and one's own—the weird mental echo of wonder. I am looking at *her*—in this crazy light. The other mother I had is dead. Lila Silenowicz's body and her dress, her face, her partyishly combed hair on a rainy day: I am hidden and listening and not fully seeing her from inside myself. Nothing here can be proved with finality. Her voice overrides the electrical hush of my mind: *Sometimes I like to lie*, she says. The watery and show-off musics of young Momma at a party. *I'll answer your question, Moira, I'll say first that I'm aware that not everyone concerned, and ones who it is not their business, too, do not approve of what S.L. and I have done. So what I want to ask is, we've always paid our way, and we've done our share of good around here, believe me, and I will say it, although I shouldn't, who gives us credit? Who gives us the credit we deserve? Who says our character's above reproach in the ways that count? Who comes right out and says we're good people? Ask yourself why don't people applaud when a woman like me takes a sick child into her house.*

A real echo fattens the watery music of her company voice.

It is Momma talking.

We went to six adoption agencies, religious, unreligious, Jewish,

Gentile—we even went to the Catholic one. No one would give us a child; they didn't approve of S.L.—don't ask me why. Maybe they didn't like me, but I had pull and they were afraid to tell me I wasn't to their taste. I made scenes; they couldn't stop me from getting a child—maybe they thought we had too much on the ball. We weren't like a picture book, or maybe we were, the wrong picture book. I can joke now; I was upset then. Who knows what they thought? I'm not home enough. I'm not homely enough, if you ask me. S.L.'s too opinionated . . . he didn't finish college. Who knows why people think the things they think? The world is full of crazy people and the worst are the bureaucrats—they want us all dead, if you ask me—well, they're only human. People want everyone to be like them; they have to feel important—I don't want to take that away from anybody. God knows, I always voted Democratic. But most people don't care about people's feelings; we just didn't make a good impression. But, if you ask me, they were very small people who judged us. Jealous people. The rain hisses steadily. *Who knows? Maybe they didn't mean any harm, but they upset S.L., who blamed me. He always blames me—I've had more than my share of blame, believe me—and he left me because of those fools—those mean fools, I'll be honest; the story's out and around; he left me and Nonie; he went to live with some woman, some trashy woman; she's left town now: it's always that kind. I admit I took in a crippled child so S.L. would see I had a good heart. The child hasn't turned out to be crippled but who'd have known that then? Give me credit. I'll tell you the real truth, even if it does toot my own horn. I always wanted that child; I could tell he was unusual. People said it wasn't right to ask his mother for him but she died. Listen, even then people said it wouldn't work out, he's a different blood, blood can be too different even in a little child; they thought I wouldn't be a good parent for a child. I had Nonie; she was thirteen, and no one admired her; S.L. wouldn't stay with me for her sake. We'd had two little boys who'd died, infants: they died—that does something to a man: I was good and scared: no one gave me credit, but I was trying. Maybe I should've stayed home more—who knows about fault? Casting the first stone is not my idea of a smart thing to do. I don't look very far ahead, I don't approve of worrying something to death before I do it; with me, it's a case of strike while the iron is hot—I have to, or I won't do anything. I'm decisive, I'm the executive type, I make up my mind and I move, I move at once or I won't move at all. I live with the consequences: I know myself: I'm good at human nature.*

Listen, what was I saying? I'll tell you something—I expect the worst, but that doesn't keep me from doing my best. I'd seen that child with his mother, I knew it would work with S.L. When S.L. came to see me—"Just once," he said—to see the child I'd taken, come and see, I said; I knew what made him tick; a woman has to use her wits; the child was so sad and even looked a little like him and the child was barely alive—S.L. never had real charity, you know; he helped people but he would get tired of them. S.L. was selfish, but he needed to do charity, he was proud, and there I was, there it was. Listen: Wiley was very pretty but he was half-dead; he was a cripple, all marked up from a beating; the woman taking care of him was a drunk; his mother was dying; it isn't a pretty story, but what is? I'm a realist.

You had to feel sorry for that child. And S.L. did. He stayed. I'm not a fool. I don't think you can tell you did the right thing. I was very good-looking, and I like to get my own way what's wrong with that? We bought this house; it cost too much money; all these houses are overpriced; people want to live on the bluff; that's one thing, and these places have good workmanship, that's another, but if it makes you happy, that's something else, then something's cheap, no matter what it costs: it's a bargain if it makes life worthwhile; then it's a big bargain, I'll tell you: I know. I wanted a nursemaid and a nice house, I knew I wasn't good with children—I can make myself cry if I go on about that. But I don't like to cry, I'm not a crier, not many people ever will see me cry, no matter what happens to me. My mother pays for the nurse. We live very well but we owe a lot of money, we owe a lot of people: we're typical that way. Anne Marie is wonderful to us; we'd be nowhere, we'd be nothing, without her. I know about some things. We have to put on the dog for Anne Marie, because she doesn't want to work for pennypinchers, she doesn't want to give her life away for a song—I don't blame her. She's a wonderful person, even if she does lack imagination. We do a lot of entertaining—some women won't do that anymore; I do it every day; I run myself ragged. I'm the one who knows people. I had some wonderful opportunities while S.L. and I were separated: I'm probably a fool to say it, but some people think I'm an outstanding person. I'm not a piker.

Well, I'm not as vain as I sound. But I am vain. I have my little conceits. S.L.'s not a calculating person but don't worry: I can be smart enough for two. Never underrate a woman like me. But the thing about being good-looking is that you can face things; it's not easy to get people to keep investing in you if you're a woman. I admit I can't do things on my own: I'm not the type. S.L.'s a help. Anne Marie helps. Some days, I'm not afraid of anything. I have to encourage S.L. to spend money; you have to keep your nerve: if we look good, then it's easier to make money. He can make good money if he keeps his head; I have a good business head, I'm a good wife for him—not if you're talking about the—you know, the Ideal, but who's ideal? I'm a good wife if you're being realistic about what he can get on the open market. We're good people; we're good citizens—are you a well-wisher?—I know you are—if you're a well-wisher, wish me luck . . . I've got my sights set high . . . That's absolutely all I can say for the time being . . .

Something in me booms and bangs—a childish heart: it's louder in a child's chest than a grown-up's heart is in a grown-up.

Momma says, *Remember Eve in the Bible? Well, I'm Madame Trouble myself in my own little way. I'm trouble just like her, me too, if I do say so myself. I don't like the Bible. I don't think it's good to women. I think women are better than men—I'm Mrs. What's-his-name who stole the fire, but I did it, not him—Old Thingamajig—a vulture ate his gall bladder—well, I've got a little gall bladder trouble myself—Madame-Troublemaker-on-a-rock . . . I have big ideas; want to hear some big ideas? Want me to put on fresh lipstick and tell you a few of my big ideas? I intend to have a good time in my thirties like I had in my twenties . . . Don't wish me luck if you're one of the ones who disapproves of what I do: just don't talk cheap about what I do . . . Money's not* MY *life's blood—I'll always get by. I'm someone who gets things done. If you sneer at me, I'll sneer right back at you; I'll say ha-ha and then some—the world won't come to an end if I say I'm optimistic now that we've stepped in . . . I'll tell you something: I will never say to him,* Watch out, you might kill somebody—*I think that's the wrong training for a Jew.* She breathes. It is almost a ha-ha.

Momma. She has a breathtakingly illiterate, numbed look she has when she lyingly tells some of the truth: this other narrator has her own techniques and her own soul—runaway or not.

The Real World Addresses the Baby Boy

Back, ten, fifteen, twenty minutes—I had a faulty sense of time in 1932, to say the least—S.L., upstairs in my room, said, "Pretty world, isn't it a pretty world?" S.L. said that. "Pretty world, pretty, pretty little boy: cat got your tongue?" And he lifted me out of my crib bed: "Look, it's raining but we have company, nice people, they've come to see you. And look who's here, you're here."

The child who lived on after his mother's death is awake—and is in his father's arms—against his father's chest—in gray rainshadowed air.

The popping noise of summer rain, the spatter, the spattered fire of voices downstairs (my memory has its own light; it has its own air inside the air of the room). A child big-eyed and mute, the watery ooze of rain, mirror-inset (a mirror is on the wall), sickly, unambitious child and a present moment and the seeming curtains around it that make itself. The warmth of Daddy's flesh, his presence, and his voice: "Are you okay? Are you fine? Are you sitting on top of the world?"

The child's smile is speech—is child speech . . . I was never innocent—except by comparison to others.

Social voices rattle, mumble—cry out. "Look at him, he has secrets—look in his eyes . . . aren't those secrets, what I see there? I see secrets and pretty eyes . . . Tell me, little charmer, do you speaka-da-English?—smile once for yes, twice for no . . . Don't give a kiss to anyone but me."

All-in-all *is a chaos* as is an all. The all is a *true* abyss of nothingness, all-there-is bound into a single meaning is like a burial of me, too. I prefer an all that is an All-but-me, little bandit of Mother-loss, Father-blaming.

"Us philosophers," Daddy said: "We don't mind the rain . . . We like this a-here . . ." He seats me on the potty. . . . "*We are here today* . . . We're here: we lived . . ."

My mother has not been the same person . . . The other one sometimes wore sensible shoes . . . Each mother has different laughs that depend on her moody purposes. The other one was steadier in appearance: she inhabits parts of me but I have no guarantee of further, or future, presence of that sort . . . A feeling comes from the flow of sounds from downstairs among the flow of moments up here. The sounds are like flying birds that draw shadows across my face.

The marshland downriver stank in the rain . . . I smell it . . . The wind in the waterscape tickles my skin—fine drops of water come through the mesh of the screen . . . Daddy jokes about the rain: "There's a lot of water out there . . . all-in-all . . . A flood everywhere just like in the Bible . . . what do you think of that? And we're safe in our ark—and it isn't even Arkansas . . ."

A universal water . . . all-in-all . . .

What I think can't matter to an All . . . Time itself can't matter to it. You can't set boundaries, even of interest, to an All . . . Or you can but then you are in a desert of an extended vocabulary of will—the force of fear . . . The mind is conceited. It cannot bear itself as an uninterrupted pulse of time for a while . . .

An All and A Nothingness are related in a grand way as in a legendary marriage of some famous king and a famous queen—the *Immense* is without kinship—only cunningly—only surrenderingly can it come near us . . .

The river was green that day . . . What day? The green of not-an-example-of-itself over a thousand days but gray and lurid with the rainstorm, gray and dateless. We can see it from the hall, through a bedroom, out a bedroom window.

Perhaps to be invented and misremembered is to be timeless and *fine*—but I believe otherwise . . . Here is the blue and sagging *light* from the stained glass window on the landing of the stairs, Daddy's noisy descent of the confusion that stairs are to me still . . . It is, as I said, after a nap, and the wet, frail light, and the mind hunting for a sense of things like an immense, scuttering, obstinate spider but a pale one, an ill-informed one—attempting to know the actuality—well, it's 1932 but I didn't know that then either—actually, I knew some things clearly . . . I already clearly knew that pain existed.

Downstairs. The party . . . The rooms: orange light, electric light, cones of orange light, some cones going up, some going down . . . But it is daytime.

"Hello. Hello."

"Isn't he *adorable?*"

In that separate air, the sounds are painted whispers, intricately intimate although they come from far away—downstairs—at a great distance from me: they are almost like a fiction. I am independent from the immediacy of pressure they have when they are real, in their intentions—in their being beyond me . . .

I am not entirely well yet . . . I half like being here. I see out the window over the flesh (of Dad's shoulder) the rain outside strike a cobblestoned street. Puddles, pocked and echoing . . . In them dark water leaps up, fish-mouth-like, and scares me slightly—again in mistaken immediacy.

"Hello, hello, *hello.* I'll just sit here with my precious freight."

Someone, a woman, says, "Oh . . . oh . . . oh . . . He is precious. He is *adorable.*"

S.L. in tones like rocks stirred by hand in a partly water-filled porcelain basin says, "The rain has the right idea: it falls on the adorable and the not-so-adorable alike . . ."

The mute child, a field of attention unwincingly in an increasingly imperial wish to live, has the noticeable heat of childhood, therefore guided, as if formally, focussed, restrained, mannerly—perhaps brilliantly so.

The facts of spectacle include the frail facial shadowing of S.L. in the window glass near us. A multitude of grown-ups are shadow-tumults vaguely near us. Three smaller tumults, girls, more visible to me, sit cross-legged on the floor: a separate sect. Outside the window, occupying a damp niche of dripping leaves in the implicit roll call of the rain, is a colored cloud, small, ticking. The child shakes his head so that distractions run out. The child cannot see any real thing but only the attributes of the moment—of a moment—I say it; *he* didn't know it was true.

I don't know how to see. S.L. extends above me as if he were in leaf. I am on his lap.

The man near me—I have momentarily forgotten it is S.L.—he says to me, "You like looking out the window?" His voice pours and splashes over me inundatingly. "You don't want to talk yet? What are you looking at? You looking at a robin? That's a robin come to see you."

A woman I do not know is a tall ghost with a tall-ghost voice: "I think it's a cardinal, S.L. It's an all-red bird."

S.L.—I remember him now—said, "I'm not that crazy about birds, Katherine—to tell you the truth. Here's the way I feel about birds; what I feel about birds is little ones are sparrows—unless they're robins. What my system is, pleasure calls, it's a matter of opinion so long as you have a good American attitude, isn't that right? Of course, if I said that bird was a red eagle, I could understand your feelings . . . I'm not a man cares a lot about large birds—" Mockery, friendly-dangerous—scandalous translation of flirtation . . . "If a little bird has color in it, it's a robin—that there's MY system: Let Littlekins here go to college, he'll get it all straightened out."

Ghosts are present in the rainy air. Fear is present—and people who are lost to me—and memories, and nightmare with its immense plausibility. An abundance of moments of failed vision, failed one way or another, as I stare now, becomes a single smudged anatomy of inability, of a generalized and uncomprehending stare. I remember. I remember not seeing very well. I'm a pressured rationalist. I consider the smudged sight as me nuzzling and sniffing ocularly around the boundaries of myself: those are the living and smelly powers of sight I had. I no longer knew that my blindness, my inability, was, in part, from the confusion of my names and lives. But perhaps it was real ignorance, not the result of that story. I mean I am always somewhat ignorant about cause in a real moment as I go along. *Tick-tock.* Tick-tock. In those days, that day, no explanations at all of the world around me worked for a while. One way and another, I was blinded; I was unsighted.

The bounteously upward-bounding bunch of shapes—the woman—has a thing, a sack, a purse: "S.L., *honey,* it was ALL red, the bird outside."

"Spare me, Katherine: I say a robin a day keeps the doctor away."

His jocularity somewhat meanly, somewhat generously announces what he does is a provision of charity toward a woman like her. *She has a giant set of everything: she is not BONY, she is not STARK. It's enough to make you polite*—someone not stark. She has a kind of triumphantly endured ready enmity—a sense of her being disliked and of her self fighting back.

A dictionary was fetched. Or a volume of a picture encyclopedia opened to *Birds*—a party moment *(People don't know what else to do with themselves).*

I knew very little about pictures except in the nervous kingdoms of my dreams. Picture books, in their deathly stillness, did not yet entertain me. They were, indeed, often unrecognizable, such books, the volume itself and what was in it divorced from movement, unless the movements of someone's hands and voice are present; then it is the hands and not the book that I recognize; but the book itself is dead or strange to me in its inertness. Images have to do with absence, and I do not have a happy connection to absence. Absence does not always turn out well, you know? One sees pictures in dreams and I do not have a happy connection to my dreams. I am afraid of unedited knowledge. I was completely wakeful, limited in that way, rational entirely in a sense.

But some pictures, without inhabitants or a center, without real light, or a pretense at real light, were yet nervous and trembling explanations, representations—among other things—of affection toward me. Toward my mind. Looking at the room, then at the pictures, my consciousness glided among the radiant logics of the diagrams. I felt their meaning as presence—ghost breath among the indecipherable lines of a drawing. I was a child overly awake with the ghost presence of meaning whispering to him as if I were asleep somehow in the same moment. That promise, or hint, of answers was a stillness to be entered; it invited me to approach it, to enter, to become familiar with it. Then an answer begins and is like a dream but it is undreamed and real; it is ordinary perception, unsure and, so, perhaps only dreamed after all. But it is a clarity and if it seems to work, it seems to be made of lucky, mad guesses at a dreamed-of law, a law of recurrence—a useful surrealism of intellect. It is quotable and lasting (sometimes), and private and docile. My periods of madness after my mother's death continue to instruct me. Perhaps they forbid me certain things—faithlessness, easy faith, too easy mistakenness. Back then, mine was a perverse sanity, skeptical, aware that it was singular and inept—who here knows as little as I do? Or is as uncertain? I had thought the house I lived in was different from this one. I had thought my father had a different face from this one. My errors are the shape of my name, are how I know things. My name is *Wiley* now and not Aaron. I have been wrong. I am often wrong. I am uncertain with each step my mind or my body takes. But I am here now.

And then to speak of the old pain and its fearsomeness, the dissolution of the self in grief, in the unanswerability of grief, that echoes in my being unable to answer anyone at all. I was shaped in the weeks and months when no one answered my cries. I cannot answer to myself now. The merest touch of language burns my lips. At bottom my memory is the memory of failure and absence. The pain was so great it was, boringly, like a stone on the chest crushing my breath. In the return of well-being,

I found that some errors hardly mattered if I avoided words such as '*mother*' and '*house*' or, after a while, any words, all words, since syllables echo with doubleness, tripleness, example, and the specific now and with their being specific as a gesture of a particular voice; comprehension of them in any direction echoes with an entirety of the partly buried but always-ready grief. So, I am mute.

The matter of my identity includes my having no memories of any mother but Lila and of no house but this one and of no father but S.L. And of no sadness. Everything from before is folded into what is here.

When everything or anything of mind and body—my mind, my body—moved at all, when it stirred from motionlessness, what it did was leap through a doubled medium of wakefulness and sleep-in-the-moment, a medium doubled further by the fires of loss and despair that I must avoid. Infant's madness, death of a kind—the death of everything for a while. The wakefulness and then the false explanation of the true explanation and the confusions and oversimplifications of the senses (as in dreams) frankly have a faintly heroic aspect—childish-Promethean—a bit timid, appealing. But a peculiar and doubtful and doubted sense that things worked, prayers worked, pain *was* eased, after all, was here. And no memory of an actual moment in childhood escapes that sense, that tone.

Meanwhile, from the time my memory starts up again, I remember people talking about it, my sleep, the way I slept. I never actually slept as other children did. I was locked up, smothered, clubbed with sleep: "Nothing can wake you—maybe you're too polite to your dreams . . ." Sometimes I woke and was nowhere and it took the efforts of the entire household to persuade me I was somewhere; sleep then for me was so thick-walled, so odd, so convincing to me as a place and as a separate existence with no clear, reliable path back to the world I had left when I had fallen asleep in a mysterious longing for that other place of the solitary mind, even at that age, mind containing all-there-was, so far as I knew.

The way things were named in dreams was very odd for me, since *I* didn't speak in waking life. *Tree* and *corn* and *flowers* and *talk*—I had no sense of language being fixed. Language was as riotous a matter of presence and surprise as people and their faces and their odors were.

And as time itself was, days arriving and departing; and it, language—what the people around me said—depended on the *household* and on the hour of the day and who was there: the number of men in the room. I never mistook the people who woke me for the selves they'd had before I slept. I knew it was someone new who came to release me.

I hoped they would be somewhat as they had been. I knew that I saw them newly—educatedly. They were new and different for the child who was himself newly another person after his sleep and now in this different order of life, in waking. The moving, wobbly air, how time trembles and breathes there. And in what I do, in what I know. Someone new woke me who was as new as I was. And this was to begin what was called a new day. This was a return to my waking senses: *Are you back? Are you yourself yet? Hi, Little Pisher . . .*

Waking life each morning seemed to occur on a fresh layer of moral sediment, a silt of new history deposited in the night and obscuring what had been in existence before. The day offered a new flooring for the senses—and for the intellect (such as it was).

So, I am all eye blinks and rattling ears in a particular way. "He's not like everyone." In how light exists in me in this real moment, I am, all unknowingly, as in everything I do, an example of a skeptic consoled—this is visible to some members of my audience back then; I have that beauty, at least at times—the beauty of an *example* of a consolation that succeeded.

I sometimes experience an actual moment as if it were a brief interruption of actual sleep and is so tinged by sleep that all the consolations and knittings-up of sleep are somehow mixed into the waking moment no matter how skeptically and with what widened, staring eyes I regard it—perhaps in a comic way to an adult, a cheering and comic way—I am partly guessing, partly remembering.

"Look he's daydreaming—he's such a dreamer," S.L. says further. And he says further yet: "This is a dream of a child."

With especial attentiveness and fear (in tonalities particular to me in form and mixture) the day's child watches the woman's hands push, shuffle, catch at pages, and straighten one particular one. I can say now that she must have been quite irritatedly interested in correcting S.L. Such feelings as I had were wrapped in the suggestions, the suggestiveness of intimacy of attention that includes in its hot focus a knowledgeable sense of moods and of intention. Suggestion, suggestiveness: and the postures of her hands: the rustling pages and the motions of her fingers had a dreamlike authority: that suggestiveness was as real to me as bread. And on the pages, the myriad strange colors and the black-and-whites of diagrams, not much like nature, seemed more accurately to be real in terms of thought, in being color and a little blurred and light and dark black-and-white, than real things were in themselves as they appeared to me off in a corner of the room or nearby or out the window. The drawings were gifted with hovering and moving presences, as I was, as certain words were for me, or as people were when I silently looked at them in that room. That is to say that the pictures began to address me with the actuality of dimensional *real* creatures—like dogs or a cat awake and stalking in and compelling attention because it can spill surprises, worry and pleasure, jealousy, merriment, or astonishment on you, as the voice of your mother can.

Animals are not common even in my unremembered dreams—I would bet on that—even of my dreams back then; but perhaps I would lose. I never had a sense of the unreality of animals. I think I expected or wondered whether the few animals in my dreams would appear on those pages, these pages, and then emerge, furry-footed, feather-winged, actually here in the presence of Daddy's breath, the ghost-woman's, my own. My absurd safety at this time, at this very moment, inflects my eyes, strengthens my sight, enables me to bear this reality—some of it. My safety? I am safer from unwanted surprises than I am even in the, after all, awkward passages of my dreams at their most flattering. I am awake and extraordinarily safe from suffering and intrusion, more than if I were in hiding. I can afford to risk seeing. Then one *sees* suddenly . . . One sees that there is a step, from the less true—the falsified, a model—to the real. The real is a skiing and rainy blur. In dreams, mine, the creatures are sometimes plausible shadows, not fully sensed, but as if fully sensed in laboring wakefulness—isn't that confusing? But that was lied about: they were not dimensional examples of purpose toward me, full of their own purposes and tones; they were dreamed about and named in the dream by the mood, by my sense of the mood: a mood is everything I know about this, whatever *this* is.

The drawings in the book and the names the adults speak hold other information, hold things I might know if I thought to ask someone, but I don't speak. In a single moment, a name is an obligation to have an identity in terms of someone else's sense of language and reality in a room. The creatures in the book, dimly seen, known to be charts or pictures, have the character of explanation and then of *animals-and-birds.* My name, as I watched the pages in the book, is precipitously, alternately, an untrue and then a real thing, a focus of moral indignation—a human child's truth. I think the pictures should move more slowly and should be clearly of what they are of. That is my name when it is real: my name has to do with information about the world that I want given to me and with my being balked in that regard. My name contains a right to comfort so far as I knew then. It contains a need for others to be gentle toward my mind.

A rush of feeling, then a silence of feeling, announce the clarification of the intentions of the large bodies around me. An explanation—a guess—a doorway, dreamed, undreamed—appears. In a second, it is known. The picture holds the hand of an expectation in me that my seeing something in real air in a way now will be aimed and guided by the picture. Love and fear say the picture is a more ideal presence than the thing is. I press one hand on a picture of a cardinal. More ideal? It depends on where one is in one's wakefulness. Stilled. Safe. I want to see the real bird again but it is gone. The light on the pages of the book makes a glare, through which, at last, I see a representation, half-drowned, almost as in recollection of the bird I saw; but it is drowned in my surprised discovery of how it works. This drowned discovery is like when one's fingers find a pebble in the crooked marvel of refraction of clear water—the refraction of the light being puzzling but regular in the clarity of that other mostly transparent medium.

Daddy says, "Look at the little *shikker* [drunk]; look at the scholarly little *pisher*; he's a scholar and a gentleman and a cabalist right off the bat: he has a real *Yiddisher Kopf*: look at him."

Daddy and the others thought I was slow-witted, damaged by my mother's death, perhaps even deranged. And Daddy used Yiddish as another, wittier, sourer form of country-and-Western, as another rural American dialect, poetic, a medium of sentiment and irony about life around here and about such topics as children damaged in passing by the deaths of others.

The pisser is peering around in the clarity which is the distillate of his immediate education. I am peering in a leopard light where rain-shadows run and glide and jerk on the wall and on the curved page, on the curved picture on it, and on my leg where no birds are. Nothing here is like the thing pictured. The quick shadows of raindrops fly and prowl and leap around me, and shadows weight the bottoms of the raindrops on the windows. The narrowing—and stabbing—of the excitement of explanations organizes the body in a way that is rigidly voluptuous. Shadows and raindrops, pictures and representations, the casting and catching of comprehensions of a sort, I slap gently, I swat or pat the picture, the shadows on my leg, the sounds of the slapping forming imperfect rhymes in the noise of the party and continuingly novel, this rhyming accompanies me as I breathe and look. The shapely blot, the logical presence of my recognition of things, is ecstatically new now—is real, in me. Life is summoned, embodied oddly—a onetime, *post facto*, huddle-bird, a creaturally red thing, is now a handsome and flashy armada of photographically crimson birds astreak and afloat in a shivering trickle of greater and lesser existence in the kid.

S.L. Takes the Baby Aside

And outside the window, in the air, gray, slanting strings of rain belly here and there, pushed by the wind. The window is open. Damp air touches me. A gray bird perches, preens, walks, and coos on the windowsill. I see it as red. My transactions with the visible dream me. Here, for a moment, all things and all people sleep and they dream me. And I am free and I move among the qualities of the room as in a dream in the semi-dark of today's rain, in the foreign light. I cannot list all the constant mercies and subtle courtesies that underlie the foundations of my sight. Rain-ribbons, shadows lie and wriggle on the shadow-striped glare-porcelain of S.L.'s face. I stare. Below the everted basins of his cheeks lie the tumbled, partly shadowed, further ribbons of his lips. I ride inside my face as in a car, and I study him in a rush of childish attention. Affection. Did he save me? The party of travellers in the room share the shelter here with me. Fear, temper, adversity, bankruptcy, and death are here, but diminished, so in a sense they are not here, although they are. No one dies at a party. Some things are not likely or suitable in given moments. *Now you know me*, the picture says. *Now you are reasonably safe and you know me . . .* I lean against S.L.'s shapely ribs. The powers gathered at the transparent passage of the window beat at my face, and thump, and they aureole the window frame and people in front of it.

"Look at Cutie Pie here; he's got eyes like gymnasiums." Large, hollowed, echoing? "Hey, you playing basketball in there?" Looking up—some nearby grown-ups are talking to him, to us; I don't understand:

Daddy is talking for all of them perhaps: "He may be a little slow but he's ours—that's enough for us—"

Lila asked, "Do you think *that* child's unhappy?"

Summer rain tumbles weightily outside. S.L.'s face, S.L.'s nose and eyes, as edited and proposed by the glare, have the spectacular wobble of real life inside that other, further, spectacular wobble of being young. He is young and in a particular mood. S.L. and I live here. His face is not smudged in a summary of a bunch of moments. My memory gives him to me in this way now and then, real, and not a moody average of a thousand times in a number of years. This is not blurry S.L. in the mask of my opinions of him. I mean now and when I was older; he is not that caged person, he is free and a little scary but humanly *familiar* although in a partly shocking, booming sense . . . SPECTACULARLY lonely and shiny, physically confident, and with a confiding manner, publicly young—a known lecher, S.L., full-grown but not final, *brilliantly* male, phallic, supple-waisted, beaming-faced, then deadpan (in a post-1920s small-town, practiced, provincial way)—a sort of hero, Dapper Dan, Valentino, Mr. Romance—guys in high school called someone like him *a cocksman*—and high popular art began to call someone like him *a stud*—well, that was in him along with a leery good fellowship—an ironic straining and calculated vivacity among people. An I-am-a-good-guy . . .

That's Daddy—not just at a party but a lot of the time—and at a party he might be rebellious. See, some of the later S.L. is mixed into him, shadowy and porous—and cavernous with shadow creatures moving in the hugeness of the cavern—of S.L.-later-in-life. In his life now, S.L. is young and monied, blond and moody.

He had been a soldier in the First World War; he has a lot of opinions—where are we in the web of jealousy? He talks, this one does, in a variety of tones mysteriously and excitingly and soon-to-disappear, disappear first from his repertoire and not just in moments of anger and boredom, of dark-mooded thoughtfulness, but even from the face of the earth . . . He will speak in the tones of an older man . . . DADDY!

He never had an *always*-talks, not in a given week, not in a year; but in the years that I knew him when I name the year, he is differently blond, different-voiced. He is a different mix of moral styles. He smokes a pipe this year. He has on a sleeveless sweater like one he saw in a photograph of the Prince of Wales that was in *Esquire*. He carries his large stutteringly movie-star-like head at an angle. He has abducted me from the party; we are in the back hall, at the back stairs, refugees from the party noise, and the smoke. It is possible Daddy is avoiding someone in particular.

I say now that he felt then delighted and lucid fear—and mournful fear—party fear; dry-toned, tumbling-breathed feelings . . . And he was also sort of locally soigné—the last was his and Mom's word. His heartbeat, against which I, a little itchingly, was held, was loudly rhythmic; and over it, his breathing is like the whispery-almost-rumbling sound when I drive in the car with him on the spans of a high bridge over the river.

Emotion and nerves. The nearby rain-glare of a little window. My small-ribbed chest, my erect neck, my wide-eyed watchfulness observes his festive nervousness off and on, the amiable party strut of his giant's voice and his masculine manner. The glow of special behavior—male —social—private—the mockery, the private affection—my spine trickles with hot, hotly jumping, popping sensations. S.L. whispers, emptily and hotly mocking: "It's always fair weather when friends get together, i'n't that right, Pisher? You got honest hands? I like honest hands." He smells of brandy and aspirin, cinnamon Sen-sen (breath freshener), and of cookies, and of coffee. And of fear.

S.L. said, *I'm a kisser and a sniffer . . . You like the smell of apples? Do they remind you of trouble?* Brains and sin.

The violent thing of personal beauty in America shapes his temper, his life, his sense of the world. The tones of his speech. His neck thickens—and pulses—with some of the mechanical and nervous stuff of speech:

Is this something? Isn't this something? I hope you know enough you're flattered, Pooperdooperkins: all these people coming out in the rain to see you, to get a look at YOU*—we're showing you to the sons-of-bitch doubters: smile and show your dimples . . . Are you a little piece of golden sunshine in the rain? "Sunshine—you are my sunshine," he sang the last part. You know about Old King Cole and the four and twenty blackbirds? Four and twenty blackbirds baked in a pie? Pecked out your eyes? Someone's eyes . . . You're blinding me, Angelpuss . . . Are you a nebbish who don't know the tango? People are conceited, Pisherkins. It's all funny business—you want me to tell you everyone's secrets? It's all funny business . . . Little pitchers got big ears? Look who's here, Cupid himself, hello, hello, and more hello, you, hello, you be nice to me, I do favors. You don't know who your friends are when the chips are down . . . I'm the man to have in your corner when the shooting starts. They hung a Jew in Alabama: they won't hang you. You want tuh* *have a good time? Is that right up your alley, Pardner, a good time? It's up* MY *alley . . . I aim to feel good on general principles . . . A good time was had by all: why not? I'm not religious but I have one or two qualities a reg'lar fella can like . . . Lincoln spoke Yiddish, did you know that? Lincoln freed the slaves but he didn't free me—I get time off for good behavior: once I learn to behave—how do you like them potatoes? My mother didn't raise me for all this horseshit—I'll tell you about me: I'm all for mother love and the tariff. I'm a good-time Charlie named Sam. Yum-yum . . . Booop-booooop-be-booooop . . . I'm sick and tired of all the shits . . . It's raining cats and dogs, Pisher: arf, arf, bow-wow, meow, meow. I'm a fan of yours; how about that? What do you to say to them little green apples? Hon . . . honey . . . honey lamb . . . Isn't this just the cwaziest weather? Your momma's got the best breasts in Illinois but a woman might as well be bald as have a smart mouth—who knows what's right and wrong in that case? I ask you. Well, it makes me no never mind as girls used to say down South; don't make a face. I got my weak moments, so what? Get me when my guard is down, you draw blood: that's no reason to tell a man like me to go jump in the lake. We got nervous nellies—tightwads—the small-fry—today. I'm not the world's best talker. A man don't like to talk, Pisher. Lila is the family talker; she's hell's own talker. Christ, the g.d. rain. A man spends a lot of time talking to himself, you know that, Pisher. It's a sad world. But you, you got a man talkin' to you. Are you just a lot of fuss and feathers or are you an honest soldier? Are you true blue and a yard wide? I'm a jolly good fella; I'm no dentist. Tell me honestly, you like people? You like me? You're really something, those big, big googly eyes . . . I'm a philosopher, you know; I don't ask for trouble. Pisherkin: kiss me, I'm the last of the Red Hot Poppas. Women, slow and fast, they hound you to death . . . They kill you. I fuck too much—I admit it. It's not all roses, believe me.*

I don't know how to punctuate his speech, the way his tones played among his intentions. He nuzzled me: *You little heartbreaker . . . I like women . . . I don't know; I'm in over my head a lot of the time—You want me to be careful, I'll be careful for your sake—as careful as I know how to be.* He gazed at some woman outlined in the flare of his mind. *I'm a big muck-a-muck. I like Abe Lincoln but would Abe Lincoln like me—and that is the question: was he a big-hearted Joe like me? Would he go for a sexy Jew from North Carolina? Tra-la tra-la. Smile and show your dimples: You have to be nice: that's the rule—that and you have to throw in a good five-cent cigar every other Tuesday—is that a good deal or is it not? You want to know what goes on in the back room?*

Well, I'll tell you: it's simple, it's ABC, it's sweat-of-the-brow and a little dirty talk . . . Tell me the truth: you have honest feelings? You pulling the wool over my eyes? What would you like to know about me? I'll tell you what you want to know. Are you a good boy? Are you always good? Are you bad, badder, WORST *. . . Well, join the Rotarians just like yours truly. Your little face kills me . . .* Daddy has an odd quality of waiting and of thinking as if he can not often for long detach himself from the predicament of waiting.

I can tell you everything everyone at this goddamned party will say: How are you? I'm okay . . . You look well, dear . . . Then: *We're the center of the universe: look around you: it's all there, even on every side: go ahead and look. The Cardinals don't look too good but they got the Deans.* Dizzy and DAFFY. *I look like Valentino the sheik except I ain't dark. Valentino's dead. He was a dark Eyetie. Calling Mr. Moto . . . Calling Sherlock Holmes . . . knows all, sees all, tells all . . . No more moonshine. No more ether—and reefers. There's money in those things, real money. Someone's been running trucks a stuff all night on route 917. This is a free country but not if you want to eat. I like bank robbers: they got the right idea. Some men have the life. Their own armies. Of hooligans and goons. Well, all's well that ends well. Be an officer and a gentleman if it kills ya . . . Learn to keep your mouth shut . . . Me, I'm Mahatma K. Gandhi and Woodrow Wilson and I got things on my mind . . . I'm Samuel Leonard Silenowicz and I come to give you Louisiana . . . You ever notice women like tenors . . . Isn't that a can a shit . . . If the shoe fits . . . Kiddo, let's strike it rich: I'm going to be rich like Rockefeller. Hot-cha big-shot. I'm the man on horseback. Did you know The Great Depression ain't so great? Believe in me, Kiddo: I'm a great, great man . . . What do you think of them coconuts? I'm a real hellraising go-getter; you're living now with better people than you are used to . . . I want you to be a Champion Little Boy. I ain't no wolf in sheep's clothing.* Abruptly he howled like a wolf. *Not funny? I guess you had to of been there. You want a graham cracker? You know what they say in Merrie Olde England? They don't say "shut up" . . . They know better; they say, "Hold your tongue."* He stuck out his tongue and then he took it between the fingers of one hand. He laughed and stopped and said, *It's a great life if you don't weaken. You think Old Fatty's the fairest one of all?* Anne Marie. My nurse. *Y'all, ninety-nine and forty-four one hundreds-th(uh)s percent pure? Should I ask the man who owns one? I'm a corny son-of-a-bitch, right? I yam Popeye the Sailor Man. Well, let's go back to the mob scene in there. Have pity. Walk softly but carry a big stick . . . I hate to think how many newspapers I read, how many movies I've seen. I'll give you the shirt off my back, you go easy on me . . . Why is it a man's supposed to have no nerves? Look at me: I'm wringing wet; it's the humidity. You got to have the stamina of a champion. We got to go face a houseful of know-it-alls? I can't help my feelings. I ain't cardboard. Kiss me: I pay my taxes . . . Happiness is in your own backyard: I'm an angel just like you, you know that, don't you? Want a white man's kiss? Hear my heart going pitty-pat? Lover, I'm not as dumb as I look— You think I'm too pretty to be a husband? That's what all the girls say, Punkin.* He whispers: *A man like me can't live without love . . . Slow and steady wins the race—you want a slow and steady Poppa? Kiss me . . . I'm the Wise Man of Borneo . . . When your heart gets broken, it's too late. I don't know—you and me; the chair I like is the yellow chair in the front room . . . You like the yellow chair? Pooperkins, you know what yellow is? Let's us go and sit in that yellow chair . . . Or let's not and say we did.*

His voice, his motions, the party noises down the hall and at the other end of the house flutteringly move on me like beetles: they crawl, mutter, buzz, bite, and fly around in the moving shadows in the unlit back hall, in the shadowy motions of the shadows cast in here by the rain-dotted air outside the little window and the back door. We move on the strong momentum of his and my breath—I'm a *child*, almost a toy. How hot the grown-ups' bodies are in their clothes, how hot their clothes were, his were, how steamy the flesh was inside his clothes. The curious crinklings of response in the flesh to the changeable intentions of the man, think of the childish self as an eye and eyelid that opens and closes, perhaps on revealed emotion toward him.

The Laugh the Child Laughed at the Party in an Imperfect World

S.L. carries me through the skinny channel of the back hall and out into the spread-out space of the front hall where, at first, the rain-darkness is like a deep hole with a screened door. Through the screen of the door, one sees the streaked, busied air.

"Let's go out, let's have us a little *airea purea*; let's just take this blue jobby; we'll just play a little truant here . . ." He's been playing truant. The yellow chair is forgotten. The wooden house shivers with voices; and S.L. closes the screen door and we are in the rain: the coarse blond hairs of his arms that hold me grow wet and flat while above our heads a blue umbrella opens and rides and thumps, oscillant and scary; and on S.L.'s eyes, on his forehead, on his hair glides the color blue.

He breathes a few times in the watery coherence of the moment under the lightly thundering-tinking blue spoon-bowl. My now melodramatically gentle *father* and the paternal-erotic heat of his throat, stubbled and shaking with breath: "Enough? Ready for the den of thieves?" A lively melancholy fills him, or seems to. Daddy kissed my slightly twisted, exposed, rain-dampened face. "*Women* are hard . . . But would you rather share a house with an elephant?" he asked in an optimistic tone. "Let's see if we can round up a few laughs." The me of my-face-when-I-was-a-child hears the screen door slam—rattle, ting. "Life's a struggle and I'm a quitter, Poopchick, how about that? How about a kiss?" I shake my head. He's a grown man; it isn't necessary to spare him anything. "Are you ignorant?" Daddy whispers to the child.

H. L. Whitters observes us. Leon Cohen observes us. Also watching are Carol Forz, Rosemary Williams, low-kneed, wide-bottomed Margaret Karlson, and many others. Daddy carries me into and partway through the room; raindrops burn coldly on the shaking trumpet lily of my thigh; the oddities of vision become me smiling oddly; a wet pain of astonishment on the childish face in the loosened tide of shadows in the room, among the shoals of heads, chairbacks, shoulders, and the minnow-shadows of the raindrops darting. He carries me at an angle across the room—he makes noises—people laugh or smile—we go around and in front of people. He is locally famous for his jokes, his carrying-on at parties. He is an agent of counterchagrin, a blond, thin man with a pretentiously romantic face. I-don't-know-what is slithering in the sad obliquity of his eyes. He rises on tiptoe; he walks. Daddy is parading. "Aren't we divine, us two?" he says out loud in some kind of odd voice, and people laugh. His inexpert pantomime and the planets of people's faces, thumbed, squeezed, colored protrusions, form a parlor astronomy. S.L.'s eyes bulge a little. I see us in the mirror. His *high* bitterness, his friendliness are obstinately impertinent. Also he is dapper, and has a quality of intensity—and of folly. He's good at this; he doesn't look down on people. He has said to me, "A pretty man has a deeper self." Some men are looking at him disgustedly—or naïvely, jealousy halted by a sense of his foolishness. Daddy has the impractical imposture of his assumption of a unanimity of pleasure, a funny, laughable edginess of that. He is aiming toward getting a general beauty of mood to declare itself. This disarms some of his critics. His face doesn't have a whole hell of a lot of innocence in it; he is a man who arouses emotion as if he were a woman, a child, a famous athlete. Beauty is not *serious* . . . MONEY IS SERIOUS . . . He does not have a large fortune. Or an army. Someone who causes feeling is not usually allowed to cause it as he wants. S.L. lifts me over his head;

he moves his entire body beneath me; I'm on his shoulders. His head is between my legs. The air near the ceiling is like starched cotton in its irregular shininess. It's warm here. Echoingly musical wasps of near suffocation are in my nose and throat. And in my ears. It is hot up here. I see slantingly down. People's hair. Their heads and noses. I see out one of the windows of the room the false dusk of the rain. He says, "You-all up there, you all-happy-go-lucky-upsy-daisy? Okay? Here we go."

S.L. mimics a clown carrying a child: bowing and deadpan, he is doing a clog dance. Then he does a funny half-baked Charleston. He clowns in this ornate way in and out close to the legs of people—some laugh and exclaim—Daddy and I, our oddity, our ordinariness, we are flushed with heat in the humid room. We have hot and transparent stares; we are a spectacle. I imagine seeing us.

"We seem to be nice people!" S.L. says self-consciously . . . It is something performers do in vaudeville and on the radio and in some movies, announce the virtue of themselves and their audience. I'm above faces doused in watching us. S.L. walks wide-legged. I wobble. S.L. trots in a quaint manner and *announces to all and sundry*, "A laugh a minute keeps the doctor away." In S.L. is a recurrent awareness of the compression between young girls' legs and of the weight of buttocks and of sexual curiosity in people, that extreme if odd poetry, or whatever. He is proud that he has a grown man's arms. Such knowledge, such awareness, is carelessly unlyrical, all-in-all. His charity purifies this. His heated, clumsy gait is pretty odd. I think performers' envies are soothed and dead in them when they're performing, since no one present is more alive than they are for a while. The watchers wait to be alive if they're drawn to the performance. They wait for our performance to end or they interrupt us. S.L. has a clumsy version of the sorrowful sexual presumption of a famous and heroic performer, the stagy ideality. The parading child is mostly solemn. Or so I say. What Daddy does for me encloses me in a contradictorily wide-awake, present-tense oblivion, a semi-place. The comparative ease with which children die and are hurt makes them less valuable than grown-ups, except sentimentally. I am sentimentally valuable. "Carry me next!" Cousin Trish cries out to S.L. No selfishness is necessary in you toward a performer.

"Don't be fooled. This is no fun. Don't jump to conclusions," he says. He's being ironic. He jumps from side to side—but not to a conclusion and says so: "I jump from side to side but I have no conclusions," he says. I hang on. The floor shakes. One woman in the room laughs on a high, repeated note. S.L. says, "I'm Esel the ass; I've come from Tennessee with water on my ass; don't wriggle too much, I'll fall on my ass . . . Look who's laughing NOW . . ." He's not professional at this, he's human. Daddy reaches up and holds me, one hand over my stomach, one on my rump as he jumps.

I am unbelievingly, unbelievably jostled. I laugh—doubtingly, flutingly; then, when he doesn't stop, I plummet into hysterical, real hilarity and then into hilarious silent gasping. The irregular and ecstatic gasping sound I make eccentrically commands interested attention—Daddy says, "He's a fine orphan . . ." A portable item of theatre . . . a lucky happenstance of theatre.

("It's lucky that child is easy to amuse," Lila will say.)

"Summer rain dee rain dee rain. And you and you and you," Dad says—his voice emerges from below me, from between my legs. I gasp silently from the top of the flesh-and-bone tree where I am—I laugh helplessly—it is a major and unargumentative helplessness among the erratic scrawls, the racing vandalism of rain-shadows.

S.L. walks rapidly, tilting from side to side. "We're hogs of good times . . ." Harbingers? "Here come the gigglers; forgive our dust—you ever seen two gigglers like us! Pay no attention; we aim to please." I tilt back and forth metronomically. The nearing noise of unwindowed rain on the screened side porch becomes assault by dainty, tickling transparencies that fly everywhere, a tickling haze of particles of rain. Bits of wet fly into my mouth. I move into further laughter when he makes me fall, and he catches and jiggles and juggles me. I'm outsprawled in the air in his arms in my laughter. God. I laughed and laughed and did not scream. The blessed thin-throated child. The surrender to coerced (and blunt) gaiety of this sort—to this mirth-at-home—is a matter of importance to the rescued and speechless child. The sustained stutter of sound-riddled and often silent merriment are part of the child's this-way-amended sense of life. Daddy, my companion, roars piteously, a joke; and he laughs in manful and perhaps semi-*helpless* accompaniment. The child's unpoliced splurts and silent convulsions make S.L. squint. I remember my amusement-astonishment. It was painful, the clutch of the hypnotic novelty and rapture. S.L. is impassionedly breathing the limitless broken rain. The tingling screens. I see through the screens our soaked yews. And the damp reek of rain odors and my prolonged spasms. I had a partly amused existence.

A stuffed Scottie is on a chair; S.L. holds it up to me. I grab it—a laugh racks me. I clutch it, the smelly effigy that shepherds me in naps. S.L. puts me on a chair and puts on me a garish and damaged turkey-feather warbonnet . . . a too large crown-of-battle, beads and feathers, with a long tail of feathers . . .

I imagine the open and plundered and bony look of the child . . . S.L. and a staring, feathered boy with a stuffed Scottie under his arm . . .

Bonneted, mounted on the galloping man inside the droning semi-dark of the rainlight, I endure it, shocked, that S.L.'s fleshy shoulders whop me with each step he takes and that the tail of the warbonnet jerks and slaps me stingingly again and again and again. The often amended moment is felt as beauty. "Not everybody has a good time like you, Pisher . . ." S.L.'s head and hair are in the grip of my trembling thighs. S.L.'s skull knocks against my body. The film of glare from the electric lights near the ceiling is as glittery as flies' wings. The trick of comprehension is beyond me. I have stopped laughing and am simply frozenly mirthful. Daddy is jumping, hopscotch fashion. I am akin to drunks and other shouters. I suppose this is a form of comedy. I am changed from the child my dead mother knew. I'm S.L.'s heir now. I am at home here near the unstill gloss of the mad natural flowers of light on the walls: American light, American childhood: American happiness . . . I say this but I suspect myself of being wrong in this matter . . . Yet the room is as convincingly for me the direct presence of good as a conviction of the direct sight of truth would be. Daddy's hair is bunched and disordered by my grip. I like being his child. We pass a dirt-speckled ceiling light fixture. I bounce among my own skull lights. I am partly unconscious with jostled, overexcited, hurtful sweetness. Pleasure is not stupider or less remarkable than pain or grief is, is it? I felt the moment as one of glamour. I think it had glamour. The child cries out oddly in the stifling moment. On my father's shoulders I was swallowed by the leopard light. It was ocher-and-black. I remember I was costumed in the hot blur of union. I don't want to confer an unwise amount of awe on amusement but I was profoundly amused—gigantically pleased. My bare thighs scratch along (from the rear) his cheeks. I expect serious amusement to recur in my life. The climate of sensation is inflamed with an oddly slanted OPTIMISM. What soreness of soul is here I cannot say. But I say it is reasonable to be like this. I remember his stale breath alongside my knees. My anomalous descent and nauseated ecstasy mean *I-don't-know* is pretty much who I am unless his mind, his breath are fitted onto me in the immediate vicinity of the world.

I love you, you Pitiable Frenzy . . . your character of violence and of intrusion and sympathy. I love you.

*

"Will you remember me? Will you remember my hair? I'm going bald, Sweetiekins. I have nice hair—will you remember that I was blond?" The blond Jew whispers to me some biographical information: "I'll tell you about me: I won't wear another man's shoes or kiss another man's woman, but I'll tell another man's jokes." He said, "I'm the father to another man's child."

Nonie

An eerie gray-white light appears at the window and displaces the rainy shadows there briefly, and then a segmented noise, a thunder, splits my head open; and my eyes go rolling and banging everywhere.

My parents' daughter, Nonie, enters the room. She is not quite a child, not really small—I assumed for a long time that being victimized was a matter of size. Nonie is pudgy. A pink weight of haunch settles on the couch, pushes me: a haunch touches Daddy, his daughter's. She stares; her eyes are set in the small bones of a pretty and oval face, clay-bright. She's thirteen but seems younger. In this light a lynx mask of yellow glass rides askew on the upper part of her face.

She greets people in the room with high-pressured, uncentered, and impersonal and loud friendliness, cheerleaderish but in an eccentric way and juvenile: "Oh, hi . . . Hi . . . Oh, hi."

Each time she says "Hi" she adopts and discards a strenuously open look, a display of bright health of mind (and body), and a demand that she be seen as highly normal, a very high—or even the highest—form of normal; and as pleasing: she's bringing brightness into the room; she's a happy girl, a friendly greeter. She smiles—and smiles—she resmiles to the full width of her face each time she looks at someone.

Her skin is clammy. She wraps one arm over and then under my legs. She's S.L. and Lila's real daughter. She's breastless, barely literate, unmenstrual. She flunks school; she's been put back a year and a half: she takes after S.L.'s family—*They're not bright; they've done all right in the world, though; they're Southerners, Carolina-nice types* (Lila).

Nonie, in answer to someone, says, "I'm eleven now."

It was Lila's notion that it would be smart to lie about Nonie's age: *People think they know a child's age, but they forget—believe me, you can get away with it.* Nonie had been worried about being cheated of something she couldn't guess at by this notion of Lila's. Daddy said, *That lie hurts no one, and if it makes you feel good—why not?* That is, he'd as soon she lied and freed him from the embarrassment of her loathing for school and her being behind by a grade and a half.

S.L. whispers to her, "Do up your shirt, Honey—you have too many buttons undone."

Anger at being corrected makes her go rigid. The veins in her temples show and tremble. Her mouth dies with hurt, then stiffens into toughness, a sinuous obstinacy. She is engaged in surviving the cruelty to her in any correction or disapproval shown her—any at all.

Nonie's griefs, her determined jollity, her victories over tragedy are part of a comedy. Perhaps not.

A self-conscious woman asks Nonie with bitterness, "How is school? The teachers still like the boys best—as always? As ever?"

Nonie's eyes grow nobly unfixed. At moments, they glance fixedly, however, at the grown woman's breasts. Nonie's pink-yellow face, Nonie's legs-tied-together, coquettish, scratching-at-you, I-have-to-pee voice: "I can't stay awake in school; it's dull—I don't know who can like that stuff. It's all dumb and foolish. You know what it is. They don't like Jews at my school, either. They show movies, but their movies put me to sleep. Daddy has to carry me home sometimes from real movies, even. I guess I just like to sleep—that's all."

An interview with the host and hostess's daughter—a celebrity, on this occasion.

Nonie's an athlete. She is someone of monosyllabic calculations, and of a quick shieldedness of those calculations, and then she has a knowingness in action, and there is the absurd, enormous elegance of her childish coloring—shades of peach and roan—all in all, she is a particular sort of creature; she would like a boy's education: the femaleness of school is what evades her.

Daddy says, "When she sleeps, she really sleeps. This is someone who likes to sleep. She's my Sleeping Beauty."

"I'm the best sleeper Daddy knows."

"She's sensitive, whether she looks it or not." This is Lila preparing to explain Nonie's style as coming from feminine sensitivity.

Nonie immediately scowls, comprehending, athletically, at once, elements of oppression and chance in her life, even if obscure, in what Lila said. And then, she, Nonie, in a weirdly biting voice from inside her warm weight, says, "You be quiet."

At once, a number of women simultaneously break into speech:

"I envy that girl her skin."

"She's so pretty I can't believe it."

Nonie's forearms are damp. She observes the women concealing her outburst, her public display of temper. A terse boy, and quick and shielded—but she's not a boy—she reaches for, she grabs, the child: me. From behind me then she stares at Lila, at the guests. It's noticeable that this one's undaunted: her mixture of the defiant and the conventional, the conventional being a general principle of defense, of justice rather than manners, a claim that she's typical, she's good—it is a matter of personal style.

A nearer flare of lightning theatrically whitens, then blackens our front lawn. Nonie states in an immoderate voice, "I don't mind the lightning!"

The child on her lap is a pillow, a muffling device, a fleshy shield against electrical bolts and the storm if God rips off our roof soon. Nature does not have Nonie's survival at its heart as its first principle but it has her bravery, her comedy in it. Her survival as her first principle is part of nature as I know it. She feels her own life as the moral given, and large—larger than any other moral given. She's less subsidiary in her view of the drama than anyone else; everyone is servant to her vastness —the vastness of her mind, her consciousness of things, her sense of things; it's Nonie's world; she knows what it's like to be in it; she's been a child in it now for a long time, she's lived this long, she's experienced (in her own view, she's expert) and not innocent, not stupid. I say this as a description of her moral style and of the sort of protection she craves.

She's maybe the spirit of darkness, and of nothing-special to boot. If I love my accidental sister enough, perhaps the world of darkness and of nothing-special will be given to me, too.

Perhaps I will see my parents and myself straightforwardly.

Her breath is unquiet and present. She is small compared to Daddy, tiny-boned—not so much lately, but it used to be he called her a little bird and told her to take shelter under his arm and he would hide her from the rain and thunder and so on. He used to say, "*Can you tweet like a little bird, can you whistle like a little bird, can you do it for me, can you sing like a little bird for your dad?*"

Like a canary, or like a child, fastidious and frail, she is sensitive to the presence of *Evil,* the possibility of Evil, the approach of nightmare, the nightmare asphyxiation of her pride—the terrible onslaught of the horror of that—and she registers the approach, the presence of Evil, and is discolored by it when it approaches, as now in the lightning. If I try to be her, to know her, I sense the darkness and enraged exasperation of her mind—it is an unlimited exasperation. Her mind cries, It's wrong. The lightning is. It's an impropriety and Evil; she will be upended. She directs Evil away from her. She's fierce. Maybe she's sort of the way everyone is, maybe she is the spirit of not being a subsidiary character which is in everyone who is proud—maybe she is the spirit named *I-am-the-chief-story, I-am-the-BEST-point-of-view.*

She is a spirit caroming like a swarm of molecules in a quickening hysteria of the application of heat. The passage of lightning toward her, the streaks become sheets of light at the windows; the great white skyey burning becomes weird light flung whirling through our windows and filling the room with interrogatory glare that pinions her in the stormy attention of the sky—perhaps Nonie is Evil Incarnate—perhaps Nonie is being visited by judgment. She squints. I feel she is Evil in the way she puts her life, her feelings above mine—mine and everyone's. Maybe she is the Angry and Indomitable Secular. She says, "I love Wiley so much. Lightning doesn't strike the same person twice. I used to be afraid of lightning. I'm not a conceited person, I'm a nice person—the lightning isn't interested in me. I had science in school—it's really silly. People think very silly things all the time—not me—" She laughs. She says, "I know what a lightning rod is—I can't explain science but science is good."

The things Nonie said stood in relation to what she felt and knew, the way a calculated poem, an artificial thing in relation to secret matters, might. She had an air as of anything-could-be-said-but-it-had-to-be-sane—but she wasn't honest about that; Nonie was the Primal Sanity, sort of—or Lunacy attempting to pass itself off as sane. Anything she accepted as a standard for herself she became priestess of, sort of; her interpretations were a little startling: she had no patience for other people's motives, or perhaps even for their existence. She had an air of jollity and discipline and yet of undisciplined threat: *Don't doubt me, don't question me.* This wasn't exactly boyish but was an inversion of a heated, womanly, and sensual thing of you-want-to-question-a-woman-and-know-all-my-secrets-I-know-all-about-it-and-I-will-be-evasive: well, she was not evasive so much as a real liar, and violent . . .

So it wasn't amusing to ask explanations of Nonie. She did have some gift for being an example of skepticism; she was as cynical, then, as a ten-year-old boy waiting for puberty—and knowing all about it but not from experience, and so feeling cheated while she waited perhaps forever. Her temper came from her being proud, which was an aspect of her prettiness, and there was a sweetness she sometimes had—a spring-and-tall-grasses kind of sweetness, maybe temporary, but piercing all the same, when she felt experienced in things and not cheated.

"A lightning rod carries the lightning to the ground and dumps it there. See, I know," Nonie said. "I'm not afraid." A much-privileged, much-spared girl, an American girl—that was her tone. "Lightning is stupid, thunder is stupid. Thunder is the noise—thunder is a stupid noise." She quotes—and adopts and adapts—then she owns the thought, the thought is hers, the priestess's; she alters it, she announces it: it's a law.

Doubt is criminal, an impropriety: AN EVIL THING.

From the doorway to the sunroom—from which come voices and radio noises—a cousin of Nonie's (and mine) stares at the clayey girl. "Nonie, we're listening to the radio—do you want to come be with us?" Then: "With me?"

Nonie's face, as it often is for me, is as if lit by the overhead light in her bedroom or bathroom. That is, I don't see her freshly. I remember her face when it was clearest to me, when it had a star's illumination. Hers is an important face to me.

That is to say, to me Nonie is as if undressing and washing while sitting in the front room. But the hovering cone of whiteness for those acts is nowhere in the rainlit room—it is just that I know her that way; I have some knowledge of the variety of sounds of her clothes; her smell; her roughly bitten, torn fingernails. Is everyone like her? All the voices so far? Mine, too? Is it the relationship—the motion of her life—alongside mine—for a while—in this odd way, the particularities of that? Am I wrong about everything?

"I'm busy; I'm with Daddy and Wiley now," Nonie says.

The cousin's face is hurt and doting, an upright fish, shiny in the air, long, smooth, scaly with rain-shadows. Nora Cynthia "Nonie" Silenowicz.

Nonie is a specialist in fearlessness: this catches her up until much of her life is cast in the boastfulness and fatefulness of an epic: she is a girl Achilles. But now a *televisiony light* (a term from later on) appears at the window: the light extends into the room silently and then recedes without a sound, rapidly. Visible outside is a corridor of wet trees, and then they are rain-blurred and half-hidden, obscure—obscure again. Nonie's head is yanked. Her face hardens and gets thin. Then it fattens and is yanked again. The thunder comes bowling jerkily into the room. The thunder gets loud and then louder and then passes credibility. It is so loud my sense of separation from it is erased; I am inside it, swallowed. After I return to myself from my sojourn in the noise, my mind and lots of the parts of my body go on being startled for a while.

Daddy says, "What did you think of that?"

Nonie angrily recites, "Sticks and stones—STICKS AND STONES."

That is, the lightning is defamation, and no such defamation can touch her—she is from a good family.

The lightning tried to expel her from the *Iliad* into a different poem, not sunny, one mostly about the spirit and squalor, defeat and complaint, one with only one hero, not her, someone pure, not Nonie.

"It's time Wiley had a little rest. Nonie, will you take him upstairs? S.L., do you want to go chaperon the fearless duo?"

Damp rises from a blue, oval rug.

Some pee trickles down Nonie's leg.

Our housekeeper, my nurse—Anne Marie—she has been keeping trays of little sandwiches filled—has a dish towel over her arm. She moves toward Nonie. She dabs—she knows what to do. She says, "The Devil's banging skulls." She's partly sorrowful, duplicitous. She has a German accent. She doesn't like Nonie—she wants to scare her. Maybe not.

A lightning flash moves in tree branches outside the front door—its flare touches us in here. What it is this time is that the light balls up not far from our lawn, a cloud of glare runs toward us, it's around us: in the glare, walls and windows visibly quiver; and there's a ringing and hum from the rush and flow in house gutters and on the walls—the sounds of water streaming sharper in the moment of eerie light.

Nonie yells, "IT'S BAD." Then she's quiet and she pees some more.

Daddy says, "You're not a child, you're not scared." He says it sweetly—the untruth, the consolation. The hint. "It's some storm, I'll tell the world." Then he says, "Anne Marie, no Devil business: Devil business is monkey business—this neighborhood's too expensive for Old Nick; we get only nice people and Republicans around here; that's what we have and that's enough to keep the Devil away from our door."

He doesn't touch Nonie; he smiles (to show that this isn't an emergency for his emotions yet); complications of voice and intent make rosebushes, thornbushes, and paths, a park, a site of something made into a public sweetness. Anne Marie mops Nonie.

Daddy's a guard, a reinforcement, a plural: he's reinforcements, he's so big. He shepherds us—we're on the stairs. Anne Marie, the towel, me, the pale, reciting girl, saying, "I'm not frightened—sticks and stones can break my bones—" The ammoniac smell, her spraddled legs as she walks.

In an eerie balloon of white light, her face seems to sail outward: bleached pottery with black lips.

The air smells burned.

"The Devil stinks," Daddy says, partly during, partly after the thunder. Then: "That's why he can't live around here."

He now admits, sort of idly, that the Devil exists—at least, as far as Nonie is concerned.

Outside the white-sashed mid-stairs window are waving branches, swooshing and askew. It's semi-dark in the deluge out there. The wind dies, the branches droop, are bent in affecting, water-weighted postures, and the rain takes on a hard, harsh, cracking sound. Everything is moist and odorous.

"Don't let it get you down, honey," Daddy says.

She stares toward the window, where a nervous river of skinny light runs in the domelike, temporarily lighted sky.

She shouts, "YOU DON'T KNOW WHAT TO DO." She has an athlete's comprehension of danger, of tactics. A series of blurred ripples of weird light are rising and sinking in wet clouds. Something hisses in my ears —it's abominable: it's her breath—her fearful breath.

I see Nonie in you, in you, in you.

I see her in me.

Crimes against Nonie exist.

Skating past this, arguing with it, hiding it restlessly, querulously—powerfully—lazily—Daddy says, holding her shoulder, "Well, it's not the end of the world, but it's a real siege. God, it never rains but it pours."

In Nonie is an inverted rapture of exploding pulse: giant doors boom and slam in her. It is a godawful filth: she feels it as that: "I HATE THE GODDAMNED LIGHTNING . . . I HATE THE GODDAMNED LIGHTNING . . . MAKE IT STOP . . . DADDY." Then: "THE LIGHTNING WANTS YOU, DADDY . . . GO OUTSIDE AND LET THE LIGHTNING GET YOU . . . DADDY . . . THE LIGHTNING'S MAD AT YOU . . . DADDY."

He won't obey her today—with company here: his obeying her never has calmed her for long. He's not very brave in her cause anymore anyway. But he laughs courageously: he's brave in another way, denying her and the whole outdoors while knowing her temper, her gift for outrage. And while the rain goes on, while the storm continues outside the house.

A glare, milky, has the effect that we and the stairs are completely without shadow. That flattens the planes and curves of our faces and irons out the folds of wood and of carpet. Nonie shouts, "YOU BASTARD. I KNOW YOU. I KNOW WHAT IT IS. YOU BASTARD."

"Nonie, sweetie. God. Oh, Nonie—goddamn it—what's the matter? Sweetie, what's wrong?"

"IT'S IN THE HOUSE, YOU GO STAND ON THE LAWN, YOU GO LET IT BURN YOU, LET IT BURN YOU UP, DADDY."

I hold Nonie's hands. Her bones are loose in nets of muscle. The noise of tambourining leaves disappears in a bass halloo. A rod of wood is swiftly rolled shakingly along my spine. Nonie's mouth opens; she's forced to swallow noise.

When you see someone at an absolute physical limit, it does suggest the passing over a line toward deity.

Or something dirty, in another sort of story entirely; but in real life, happening inside the same moment, so that, as a child, you blink and see and don't see.

Big-bodied Daddy and Anne Marie—the big-bodied characters here—haul and hustle Nonie along the upstairs hall; she's howling and growling. Nonie breaks loose, Nonie is leaning at the waist, sideways, a little backward in the half-dark, in the noise. We have company in the house downstairs. Now we push her. Now we have her in the bathroom. Anne Marie has gotten Nonie's pants half off and in the flexing and wriggling of Nonie's buttocks, big and pink-gray-brown in the muddy light, is the proof of the abject sincerity of her terror, even though her finely shaped head is stiffly erect—terror is discouraged by assertions of the nothingness of the humiliation.

I see Nonie everywhere I look.

A point of white light across a bedroom at a window speeds and blooms. Faces float. The rending and clatter spread Nonie's face: it's painful to see—people sometimes remark, *That girl's painfully pretty*.

She says in a really crazed way, "THE LIGHTNING DOESN'T WANT ME—IT WANTS YOU, YOU MEAN PIECE OF CRAP."

Daddy's cheeks are scored with effort, with dry tiredness. Daddy says, "Nonie, Nonie, stop it—what is it? Tell me. Listen to me. What are you scared of? It's only some rain and a little noise and some electricity like a—a flashlight—in the sky."

She stares at him: the complexities of his logic are walled spirals which she is too canny to admire even in her state of crazed, involuntary terror. "GO AWAY. I DON'T WANT YOU NEXT TO ME. IT WANTS YOU. YOU GO. LEAVE ME ALONE."

Daddy gets tired of the slyness and temper and selfishness in this sort of *woman's heroism*, so to speak. He holds her arm firmly and gives her a very little shake: "You try to get hold of yourself, Nonie. You be a lady, now."

Nonie doesn't listen; she almost never listens: she eavesdrops face-to-face. It's her tactic to believe women are what's moral: the unreligious part: a measure (they're soft flesh—solace and amusement; they make up for God's being what He is). The woman says, *I'm more than God—Daddy, go meet your death and Maker and say How-ja-do.*

And: *Do you love me? Are you my father?*

Daddy is tired of both those things. Daddy looks into her eyes; he has a jutting, determined posture of his face, a set of postures that slide finally into an obliquity of address: he often speaks before her and not to her, which seems a witch's triumph that she has—it's an odd privilege or rank with him that she has—but now he's talking to her, except, ultimately, he's sure of her because she's a female: "Listen to me. No one's hurting you."

"I KNOW WHO I AM." That is, she knows what's going on and she would like to call on certain facts of biography and of social reality: *I'm Nora Silenowicz, aged thirteen; I live at home with my parents: home is 4 Vista Drive; you leave me alone. Don't you know who I am? I just told you—are you too dumb to catch on? I'm not exactly a big-brain type of person, I'm not real booky, but I get the point and you don't seem to. I'm not a creep. I love sports, do you? Don't get too funny. Just maybe my family can handle you. We can get you thrown in prison.*

"HELP ME, DADDY, I'M A GOOD GIRL."

"I know you are, sweetie."

She yells, "OH, AH, YAH-AH"; that is, she argues for a moment sheerly as a girl yelling—if she was that noisy and that upset, then something was wrong; you were supposed to help her—this was a serious argument, an earnest one.

Her eyes are screwed into being maybe three-quarters shut, and yet they're peering; she's not totally defeated; her eyes have nutty angles of vision; they're also twitching and angry; but they function still; they have a childish obstinacy of function. In her terror, this terror.

"I DON'T HATE MYSELF, DADDY!" she screams.

She's been in treatment with psychologists—they try to help her be happy.

Her warm thighs, stickily pressed together, tremble syncopatedly.

Daddy says, "Nonie, it's like a knife in my goddamned heart. My heart is breaking. Oh, Honey, can't you get hold of yourself?"

He's not thinking, he's being uncalculating, it's on purpose: he's being warm; he's not judging or guessing or seeing through her—it's an effort. His face gets a little pudgy, cloudlike with warm *foolishness*—it's for her sake, for everyone's. She sees, she partly grasps it—*Be-foolish-for-me*—his story isn't congruent with hers, with Nonie's story. She stares at him. Daddy says, "Here, Honey, want some love out of my pocket? I have a whole lot of love right here. Just put your hand in and dig it out. It's all just waiting for you."

Love rests on illusion, they say—that's one of Lila's remarks. *I can face it,* Lila said; *can you?*

Nonie's jumping around, wincing, agonized.

"YOU GO TO HELL. YOU HAVE TO GO TO HELL." It's not clear what she means, why he has to, for her sake or because of his vices, or his having failed her, or in order to save her, or what. She shouts, "THE DEVIL WANTS YOU RIGHT NOW."

Anne Marie tells me, "Don't look, *Liebchen.*" The sin, the being an animal, a little animal, and ashamed and disliked by everyone—well, don't look, except medically: to exorcise or to quarantine or to help.

Anne Marie is pious.

Daddy's sad look of affection says that Nonie is crazy now. Nonie, alert, shouts, "I'M A GOOD GIRL, I'M NICE!" She shouts it accusingly.

Knots of nerves in her skull skitter shrilly: in the prepubescent, pudgy, pink-thighed girl are facts of nightmare trafficked in, compromised—compromised but not a joke. Her intensity is the size of the warning, of the emergency. Such meaning won't condense, won't distill. She shouts: the effect she wants is to reproduce in you what's in her: but in a family *what does she mean by that?*

"I know it," he says; "I know it, Honey." What does he mean?

Her consciousness dives and races along; it's not big, her consciousness; it's mostly eyesight and speed—see how she squints and wiggles: ferocity of endeavor is her emblem. She flies along, flat-out and pure—without pain in this sense: pure indomitability—and complaint: that's a system. She shouts, "I HAVE GOOD INSTINCTS, DADDY." Is she advertising herself? No; yes. But she also means, *Listen to me.* And: *I will win*—or is it: *I will win if you help me*?

She's in a rush.

Is it English she speaks, Nonie-dialect? In this tribe, you have to have a split and blobbing tongue. Other people say the same words as Nonie, but they mean something else, so it's not the same words.

Nonie shouts, "I'M A GOOD GIRL."

Hugging me, whispering in my ear; we're on the porch: another time: it is four o'clock, a summer day: perhaps it is another city—*"I'm a good girl,"* someone *pure—a good girl*—the meaning-of-this in the sunshine is that something pure doesn't hurt you; she's pure, and whatever she does to you, whatever you think about it, you're not hurt.

The whisper in my ear partly means her feelings weren't hurt by Katie Rogers or by Ida Nicholson Gray—a grown-up—or by Momma; and that Nonie *hates* Ida and Momma and Katie because they make the world impure one way or another. She's not like them: she's blameless, she's perfect—if you don't agree, she has a right to hurt you for hurting her . . . Perhaps she is daydreaming, pretending. She vaguely intends to make you wise in regard to her purity.

"I'm nice." She's pure and unhurt and unhurtable, she means. Nonie pinches me—a hieroglyph, an ideogram, an idiocy, a poem on this subject: if I cry out, I'm not pure, I'm hurt; she has hurt me because I distrusted her; and the proof of my treachery is that I am hurt. She will hug and stroke me, and make me pure now. She's redeeming me. She's recruiting me. Purity is smoothness, invulnerability (inviolability), and conceit toward others. Also, it is sweetness—in some cases, in me for instance, it is turning the other cheek. In her, purity is satisfaction, is satisfied appetite.

She kisses me, she kisses the kid and holds him at arm's length and won't let me move successfully—getting what you want, and no one can get even with you for it, or be jealous, that's purity, that's being good—and middle-class. You are a person who's pure, and, therefore, are unpunished for what you do. If I want something from Nonie, if I wriggle and try to escape, I—*I* am impure by definition: it's an appetite in me: see her startled and seeing-through-me eyes as I do this, her fluttering scorn that I expect something of her. We're on the porch; Anne Marie is at work in the kitchen depending on what city and what year of my childhood this is . . . Nonie looks at me that way (with moral scorn). *Being fond of people is a good discipline*, Lila's said more than once. Lila has said, *S.L. lies to Nonie, and you know what they say the outcome of lies is. What does he expect to happen? She has to figure out everything for herself. A young girl's life is terrible one way or the other, but no one pays attention. Well, she won't listen to me—I'm not to her tastes lately. It's a phase.* NO: it was lifelong. *If she wants a stay-at-home, plain-Jane mother—and she won't settle for what the cat dragged in (which is me)—then I guess she'll just have to suffer, take it or leave it. I'm the only mother she has.*

"You," she says, "you always want someone to do your dirty work for you—well, I'm the only mother *you* have, too . . ."

We have a local form of childhood, Nonie and I.

A dog scampers sidelong, crazy-jawed, across the lawn. "Look at that crazy dog," Nonie says. Nonie likes praise that is extreme, that is enthusiasm plus a loud silence in regard to any qualifications of the praise: *It was great, it was really great, it was perfect, you're perfect, you know that, you're just absolutely perfect.*

"You're perfectly lovely," she says to the child, and regards him. "Want a glass of milk? I think that dog belongs to poor people."

Poor people are cowards and bullies toward people like us—everyone knows that.

Ipso dipso facto ficto.

Daddy wants Nonie to be happy: *Stay away from grown-ups, Darling; you can't tell about them; sometimes they like to make you feel bad.*

Nonie says, *Momma's like that.*

Nonie is well-bred, high-strung (Momma says). *She doesn't get along with popular children; she can't hold her own with them; no one likes being overshadowed. Wiley, listen to me; I give good advice: no one likes to be outshone—they'll kill you if it bothers them enough.*

Nonie likes nervous, soft-mannered kids with some social glamour: she'll pick a girl or a boy with a noticeably behindhand, peripheral social beauty. *Doesn't she know any better? Nonie only likes people who can't possibly like her once they get to know her. Once their luck changes, they turn on her, and she deserves it, she asks for it, and the fat is in the fire and I have to pay the piper.* Momma often sighs; she has a repertoire of good sighs—very different kinds. This one is pigeony, cooish. *Doesn't Nonie know who she is?*

Nonie learns little from the passive kids she likes; she imitates them badly. Momma says, *We have an ordinary middle-class household.* A portrait. Nonie doesn't like to listen to what anyone says—she evades the intentions of speech; she eavesdrops face-to-face as a general rule. She's maybe *ordinary* morally—Momma has said that's the best possible claim for Nonie: *She's ordinary and like everyone else, so good-and-normal it hurts.*

(*I'm shouting in a vacuum; no one listens to me,* Momma said. *Only Wiley—sometimes.*)

Nonie's happiness is universally desired by theoreticians, by decent people. *Universally.*

When she's *crushed,* if she's *shattered*—Momma's words and Nonie's—Nonie says, in an agonized and angry tone, "I'M ALL RIGHT." That may mean she's given up or is about to. When she is defeated, she says, if asked, "I'm fine, thank you," and blinks and turns away if she doesn't want you to notice—she makes you be quiet, though. You notice, but you have to be quiet.

If she's hurt badly enough, honesty sets in.

Then something in her widens—her consciousness maybe—and she's private and soft, even if a little shrill in pitch but sometimes not even that: she's vulnerable, out of control: not evil: defeated—gentle: not lyingly—maybe as an emblem or result of *Evil,* but she seems to be good then . . .

When I'm drawn to Nonie when she's in that state, in some version of it, she sometimes turns on me to show I'm a sucker and she's stronger, she's getting strong again.

When she's defeated or hurt, half-nice or the whole thing, she is sexual, private, human, not shrewd—knowing about it in her, feeling it in her, the sound of it while it's happening near me, the feeling in my head of being near a secret part of Nonie, her weird self in this moment, I like her a lot. She knows it. She holds my hand moistly. Her hurt causes a ripe propriety of soul and demeanor in her. This is one reason she's so interested in hurt, because of what happens to her then—the sort of grace that comes to her. Similarly, she wants to see *the finest part* of someone. A theory. Her physical sense of the world, of herself, is stronger than her mental sense of herself and of things, despite the way her hands don't know the feel of the world as well as her wits do. She lives between the round folds of her thighs; she is physically aware, she is caught in the fleshy constrictions and awarenesses of the inside of her mouth and throat—she drinks water with elaborate and, to me, ornamental gluttony. Flesh overlaps flesh and forms pockets, companionable, not clanking but noisy in a way for her. And then there's the reality of her toes down there. The physical is familiar to her, a place of automatic diversion. Hurt is always partly physical; it infiltrates her flesh, the pockets—places of registry of herself—in real life, waking life. The *inside-the-oyster pearl and pink* hind end, in your clothes or naked, is the *exposed heart of flesh*—the key to attentiveness: to confession; one is driven to touch the finest part: a thrill.

Look: here's something: she's fallen asleep while hugging me. I step, I move, tinily, into another realm of observation: sleep covers her pink face with a smooth look like doors; Nonie is ELSEWHERE. Her eyelids are skin with no fleshy stuff under them—but animal noses twitch and sniff at dead eyes there. Little snores, bleached delphiniums of breath rise from her mouth, stalks and bells above the small vortex at her lips. The insuck. Giant girl—her ribs are muffled spans, the handles of ladles, big, big spoons, faintly vibrant. All this lies against me: she's hugging me. She is—ELSEWHERE. She is in the mysterious horn of sleep, running inside a rolling egg. I struggle to get free, I push at her arms, I tug, I rub and wiggle against her—chest—I put my mouth on her chin and I bite her. I suck her breath, the bits of private air, the private delphiniums, scratchy grasses. Suddenly she awakes—she looks at me.

It's Nonie. Nonie's eyes.

A form of speech—do you *understand?* This *is* like any look, this is in every look that she gave me—we have years in which we don't look into each other's eyes: it's pointless; but it's not like that yet.

Her being wakeful, like every quality of THIS GIRL, has a foreign tonality, often silvery and thin—elf traits; ghost droppings; animal acts; leaf noises in a wood which can't be identified, which signify an unknown life. Her breath doesn't have the weight of Daddy's or Momma's speechy murmurousness, of their pale groans or sighs that tip suddenly like seesaws into shadows, into the nighttime and me eavesdropping without the hope of understanding anything. Nonie's face is complex because Nonie's here—hands, pink body, moods: these multiply and are the opposite of isolation, are implication, a tangle of possibilities, snakes or shrews in a thicket, cottonmouth or a hunting cat, the proximity of Evil from the beginning. Her presence is rhetorical in a spare language. The five public senses are façades breathing mood, an architecture of seduction, of menace. This isn't play, this isn't just play, it's real: *Hey, were you lonely? Did you dream of a playmate?* Look, this is a dream come true, this is for real. *I'm the boss—I'm the older sister . . . A deal. Is it a deal?* Her hug, her clayey arms, her tenderness, her ribs, her head opening onto her tickling, finely pretty hair, her affection are a limited speech, opening onto a large-scale babble: common sense. Her eyes and mine are as if in a piazza. The locked gazes form a piazza of apparent and mutual consciousness; awareness is echoing and returned, amplified—a proper blackmail: her size and physical power—Nonie's being Nonie here—the world has a sudden fluttering tenderness, foulness, Nonie-style. I have no choice: the child's drowning. His face is parkland, grass, airy vistas; or a flock of pigeons; or a house; or bells, slim fires; secrets expressed as films of wordlessness—a landscape of altered and fluctuating noises of response, attachment; a listening: perhaps the child is noticeably male for Nonie, a weight of foreignness, a genetic glistening. She moves; she grips me in the unfinished, barely begun web of her arms—a species of passion? Ho! Or minor rape—I turn and twist, I subside against her puffed chest; she lifts her prisoner—*Her Prisoner.* We go sit creakingly in a white wicker chair among the columns and screens of a wooden porch. We are in a drifting light; the chair creaks, a plunging elephant; Nonie swings her legs: a game: I drop through her legs: I yell: Nonie grips me between her thighs, then between her calves—I grunt—I lean backward, and the bones of her ankles bongle-thang my ribs. I drop to the floor. I'm free—she grips my wrist—her hair hangs ticklingly, brightly. Is she bored? It's hot; a fly is caught in the girl's other hand, a curled fist; the buzzing is constant, it grows louder, swifter—I twitch. Nonie says, *"Die, fly—die-ee-ee."* Her fist is at my ear, shaken, a gourd, an instruction: I hear an insect skeleton snap. Nonie puts the snapped bug on my shoulder. *"I'm your mother; you have to do what I say; wear this"*—funeral epaulet—*"You have to wear that."* I push it off. Her lips touch my nose, she bites me swiftly, in a flush of rosied hate, an eagerness. I stiffen; my soft fists clench; I hunch over and she stops; she lifts me; we go down some steps to the grass; we sit on the grass in silence, among midges and yellow discs: *"Those are butter."* Then Nonie pushes my face toward the dandelions: *"Lick the butter, Wileykins."* I twist my head, wriggle, get free: I stare at her. She leans closer to me—I bat her nose —she places her firm, fat leg over my folded legs to hold me while she makes a dandelion wreath. *"You're just a wild man, you're just so bad we don't know what to do with you."* I don't have to listen to her. I don't have to hear the tones. I don't have to know hers to be now an exploratory malice. No one else here speaks to me with This Immediacy of Evil. The promise of having a separate soul, responsibility, my own life lies in Evil—which is secret. *"You're a bad little prince."* And: "Here." She bestows the diadem, and then, after a while, yanks it over my eyes—I am inside the wreath, inside the act: I don't know what's happened, what's happening. Here is yellow light, here are yellow shadows. I sit. I'm naked in this part of the day; the child is naked, dusted with faithful suburban light.

"What a pretty pair of children!"

I'm hugged; my head is forced to a weird angle.

Locked into her affections, the prey of some sentience of hers about what is real, I fight. See the kid push at her unfurry, slidy, technically fond arms. She pulls me close: "Wiley adores me. See, he *loves* me."

"Don't hurt her feelings, Kiddo. Stay with Nonie."

"You've made a conquest, Wiley. She's crazy about you."

The mysterious potencies of what I am, which include the way I look, lie like cut flowers in the baskets of her head, her chest. Jesus: the mad and silent child (*"He's a beauty; he's a real winner"*). The child's somberness and force are lunatic, noiseless. Here come her arms: I'm between her legs: her eyes, nostrils, mouth—and mine—apertures, heat, childhood.

I saw her beat a dog to death. Like a farm woman. A heroine.

This is the way I am: I play dumb, or sleepy, or watchful. If I'm too knowing, someone says, *He's mischiev-i-ous*, or, *He's a tease; he's teasing her: he's teasing you, hon.* Her eyes do a Nonie thing: curiosity, pain are mixed: curiosity starts as part of a deficiency; it is an extension of an ache. Nonie will squeeze me so hard that I go airless and briefly shameless, limp; she will lie on me while I struggle to breathe and to get free until my struggling tapers off, and then we gasp, almost in unison. Is this an uncorrected foulness or is this a merely human thing? Her face is reluctant, obtuse. She has a smell of wakefulness, a stench. Is this A TORTURE? I'm clutched in her smelly arms near her childlike breath. Nonie interprets the world for me and to me: she supplies the terms of my sense of things . . . of my language.

I see her everywhere.

I have a sense of union with her, an odd form of transport, a childhood pleasure. I am not free of being her—or of being near her, whatever I do. "Are you happy?" she asks me in a dry, earnest, menacing way. "I want us to be happy."

Nonie says, "I want everyone to be happy—I want everyone to be happy so they'll be nice."

She is politically serious when she says this. Her politics govern many of the ways in which we are lovers.

I feel the wind at my ear. Nonie's over there in the sunlight on the tennis court under the blue sky, with two dibbie clouds in it and two sour crows ashriek. Her shoulders are hiked up; she holds her racquet stiffly; she crouches; her legs swell and bend and she runs sidlingly: *Look at the dear thing run—she's quite a good* little *competitor.* She had the rapid postures of physical concentration that are possible for her when she *competes,* when she is *revved up,* when she is playing with her full will. But she's not good enough—the sports talk is *Poor Thing, she's dying on her feet, Nonie's being just slaughtered out there, she's in over her head . . .*

Sweat lies in the folds of her skin. The intricate wind guides and deflects, raises and stymies and presses on the flight of the ball. *Nonie is not in her league here*—this is a serious matter.

Look: the Silenowiczes don't have and can't get—they'll try, but they can't do it—a similar commitment to Wiley as they have to Nonie as a conduit of genetics, let's say, traits of theirs passed along, a family line expanded and multiplied—as they do, willy-nilly, to Nonie. It is possible that they "love" me more, far more, than they do their daughter or each other or anyone else, "love" here as feeling—amusement and also wanting-to-be-with—but not love as the power and full strangeness of alliance, of competition, of serious blackness. The Silenowiczes were told again and again and again and again that they can't care what becomes of me as someone can who is of the same blood. Blood? Do we have to see some blood soon? Whose child am I? I am there for the sake of these people's happiness, so to speak, not for the sake of their or my or my real mother's lineage—they are not loyal to what's found in me: why the hell should they be? They love me passionately—*Our life was you, our whole life, off and on, and for a while you liked that.* No matter how feelingly they care, I will never exist in certain ways for them—and nothing is compensated for: it is a convenience to say this balances that: it has nothing to do with it to say that otherwise the child would not have lived—*perhaps.* I had my audience early; they were attached to what I meant to them—in actual moments, always a *now,* a romance. I am expendable to them in a way a son of theirs could not have been—my lovers: not my family. I don't know that a family sense is much different: it's less clear, certainly. I have no family sense. This gives a glitter to everything I know—and feel.

Nonie is closed in, as it were, on three sides, or two, and open only on one, and I am open all around.

Nonie has sweaty, slightly spread legs; her thighs, her crotch—she's aware of heat in them.

Wiley, I don't ever want to think you're jealous of her.

I can't *as a general rule* locate my cruelty toward others; it tends to lie in my acting on acknowledgments of superiority in me. *If I'm smarter than you, why don't you* LISTEN *to me?* I tend to display virtues rather than to take on obligations—a child, a younger one, adopted, piratic, unrooted.

The sunlight: the tennis court: the girls on it . . . I ran out on the court. "GET HIM AWAY! I DON'T WANT HIM NOW! GET HIM AWAY FROM ME!"

"Wiley, don't do that!"

I hit Nonie a number of times in childhood—never with male embarrassment or a boy's regret or that vile remorse of what-have-I-done. I felt satisfaction, a sense of order—a sense of symmetry sated by a feeling of decency at hitting her—*this is a truth*: I admit it. Nonie sometimes disgusts me. Often. Always—a little . . . No: only sometimes . . . Nonie, when she strikes at someone, feels it to be JUSTICE. I'm below and behind and ahead and high above her in a dark space, a black sky—without team spirit, contemplating her sense of JUSTICE.

She runs inside the airy globe of my sight at this minute. She is on the tennis court. She will never know about this representation of herself as something in nature both immediate and recalled, as physical and real in present moments, one after the other. "Whee!" she says. Her speech does not represent the life in her except as a contradiction of what she hides inside herself. She shouts, even so. I dislike or hate her because she hit me on the arm with her tennis racquet while Daddy dragged me off the tennis court. I must sit here and watch her play. The pockets of her flesh move me. The ball in one flight has ninety-nine positions of ghost readiness and then an arc of accusation: *You better hit me*—an accusation means itself plus, unspoken, *Hit me*, since everyone fights back or falls to one side. Nonie hears time's soon-to-be-changed sportive accusation and test questions and score in her head. *She hears*, she sees and hears and feels the flight-of-the-ball—the ghost tails, cherubic ghost heads of the arcing ball, fill her sight—her foresight, her powers of prediction. Look: Without enmity, she has no edge; she's not solid in her game; she's cloudy, overweight—strange. *Do you forgive her? Why can't you forgive her?* She's slowed in the weird geometric set pieces of her emotions and of her faith in things, as in a dream in which motion is recalcitrant and her screaming is interdicted and her only safety is in rescue by something outside the machinery of this particular episode. By justice, or luck in a disguise. Let her fight back. Let me. Her sense of the court, the battleground—my sense of ecstasy—form an unshiny, heat-struck outdoors rhythm. Is it the game, the remembered game? She speeds, quickened, deadened in consciousness, narrowed to the game: she escapes me. I want her, Nonie, for my own purposes: my feelings want her to sit still now.

She proceeds in the unforgiving indignation of her art in sports. Her mind is on top of—a healthy body. Her dearest treasure, her weapon, her soul, her prize of competition and rivalry, is her body below: her mind is no trophy: it's hers: her admiration is loathsomely allied to the compromises of that body: her mind rises on the flailing arms, pivoting torso, chuffing and then braced and then scuttling legs, like a perched dragonfly on a brick colossus, in a space of great ice, great cold. Inside a sheltered dome, a brainpan mosaicked with visions, the motto, the point is lodged: *Wiley can't hurt me, things can't hurt me.* A victory is to the girl's wakefulness as a dream is to her consciousness asleep. Life is explained in an intensely theatrical (a directed) light.

4–2, Lisa—it's not credible that Nonie should lose, and be without meaning. She will be an ordinariness—a matter only of sentimental report.

Nonie is trying. But Lisa finds it apparently easy to tip Nonie into a rubbish heap of miscalculations, the frenzied clumsiness of someone who does not matter as a force but who will not give in yet. Such contradiction between will and result lays bare the presence of meaning—usually unwanted. Unprepared for. *So this is what is to end up badly . . . Help, help . . .*

Daddy says under his breath, "Our girl ain't lookin' too good. Well, there's other things in life besides winning."

In the text I have failed to supply here—*Nonie's Book of Pity for Herself, Nonie's Sadness, Nonie's Charities Toward Her Will, Her Life*—among the victories she does not gain, Nonie's mind is described as an agency of discipline beating with mad persistence at a single point, beating herself into a single point, then that single point against the adamancy of being eighth-rate, against odds and defeat, perpetually turning its sharpest side outward.

All her truths are *secret*—all. When she killed the dog, the boys and the other girl egged each other on to strike; one boy was dogmatic, exasperated: "*It's probably DISEASED.*" Nonie, mostly silent, spoke twice, as if she were the leader. "Here we go." Then, during the execution: "*It just has to be done.*" She struck firmly with a half-clutched half-brick; her eyelids were lowered partway, they fluttered; she peered and didn't look, both; her nose was wrinkled at first. A rope had been wound around and around the dog's legs and then around a tree trunk and then under the dog's belly and over its ribs and its back haunches and around its neck so that its head was held, loosely, against the rough hide of the tree skin. The sounds of breath—the dog didn't bark—the sounds of the blows: a childhood thing. The squish of the pelt: struck bone. As if politely, Nonie struck the dog on its ribs first, far from the center points of the senses, but she saw that was a girl thing, as in *Watch out for its eyes*—or *ears*. She's concentrating; she's goddess-like. Her temperament, her uncertain temperament, rests uneasily in these areas of life and death from which girls are *unfairly* excluded, excluded from open and from secret discussions of this stuff. She held her neck stiffly, her head back as if to mimic and understand the musculature and terror and courage of the dog: she goes berserk over ideas of good-and-evil, of justice, of I-like-it-and-I-don't-like-it—the permitted idioms—sometimes with phony innocence, or ignorance, girlish, useful, a cover story for a bloodied agent. She struck at the forehead, at the squelchy fur and bone. She struck at the jellied eye and called out "*Oh,*" and then she boasted, "*I hit it* IN THE EYE . . ." Nonie, when she was young, was afraid of being buried alive. Nonie advances in her classroom-and-chapel study of DEATH: the real thing—not a word, not a word for a state of quiet, for an intervention in life's time, but for a finality of one's will, one's citizenship, one's role in the epic of the world.

The kid, *he* plays unmeanly—well, I'm adopted—he plays gently: *he's a Jew, he's not very Jewy* (*ha-ha*): I'm welcome here: *he's a little king.*

Do you hate her, Wiley?

Yes. I'm sorry.

"I'm so normal it's awful. I'm not like Wiley."

Go slow, pace yourself, turn yourself inside out.

I-went-for-the-kill—I-went-for-the-killing-shot, but-I-just-didn't-have-it.

Lisa's mouth is set; it shakes from time to time; her eyes hold intention, unnegotiably—she is prepared for winning—she is defeating *Our Little Sister of Tennis.* Nonie says, "I got too eager; I was just too hot to trot. Coach Bill says you have to be a tiger, not a pig. I got silly in the second set. You have to know that a game takes a long time, you have to just be patient and stick to your game strategy—and your strategy will stick by you . . ." A strategy unfolds—it is a form of obtuseness toward others, it is a cancellation of accident, it magnifies parts of oneself. She holds me between her legs and tightens the barrette in her hair. "I learned my lesson. I'm just going to be a ti-ti-tiger, like Coach Bill says, and never a pig. Hold still, Wileykins."

Her sense of her own knowledge gives her a sense of beauty—something that represents what she knows . . . A representation of truth is *beautiful, just perfectly beautiful.* When she feels knowledgeable, she is nearly beautiful; her intelligence about the world shows as such in her posture and in her face. Not in her words: "*I know how to win—you have to have spirit and you just keep hitting the ball back more times than the other person.*" Nonie liked unarguability in speech; that is, for her the world of the mind, no matter how public it is, is not in the open air where things are contested—it's in houses, it's more like the talk in houses: it's more certain—it's subject to control by a woman. (Momma said, *You never liked her from the beginning—I'm glad you never went after me.*)

Bits of the real day cling to her. She holds me between her legs, and my jealousy included a blaze of longing to experience the world that seemed to live, fresh but logical, grand, adumbrated, in Nonie's speeches: it was real to me, that ecstatically calculated world: I thought she knew a lot; I thought she went from our house into that reality; I thought her talk adequately, directly, honestly spoke of that world: and I wanted it—that world, that power of entering it—that clarity about it. Nonie liked a certain flatness of speech which was like driving a ball: she swatted the Local World in her talk. Jealousy is an openness of attention. A brilliant disorder of attention. Of deduction. Nonie half knows what to say if she wants *me* to listen. Nonie's courage is not experimental: it's acquisitive. Grief, for her, is a thing of being poisoned and helpless, boiled in humiliation. A fever of *it's unbearable—it's unbelievable it's so bad.* Her eyes get funny. She wants to shrink the world to a matter of inherited laws, set rivalries, modes of peace and of alliance—a burst of girl's common sense, above all of privilege separate from character and from freshly interpreted adventure. Separate from one's own pained learning. *("His people are trash, but you'd never know it to look at him.")* What do I inherit? An underdog has the simpler will of existent hurt, of no victory so far, no victory as yet. Nonie has won twice on her way up the ladder in a tournament: she's never won a tournament—but she tries. She gets to the quarterfinals. Why do we have to take *her* seriously? Do I distort what is there? I mean, when I see? When I feel? When I speak? We go outside in the dark after dinner onto the back lawn—she wants to dance. She's not a holy or mad angel of movement, she's not God's pantomiming sweetie; she sways, she's bunches of limber sticks; she's been taught; her physical intelligence produces pale musicality: glides, sweet turns. She is slenderly visible in the local dark—perhaps everyone will come to desire her now. The kid dances, too—well, he runs, he spins, he does interpretations of what she does, of the prettiness of what she does. He is mad. He is a mad angel of movement. He does half-cartwheels, roll-overs, runs and leaps, somersaults.

"Look at Angel Pie—ain't he wonderful?"

"Wiley, *you're in the way.*" She kicks at the child.

"Nonie, don't do that. It's ugly. Kids are a pain in the ass—you know that—but you just put up with him now."

Nonie tore up handfuls of grass, she dropped grass on the kid in rapid quantities; she threw or dropped handfuls of dirt until he couldn't see or breathe: he's stained: he stops: she pushes him: she trips him: his shin is bleeding: "*I'm not sorry; he interferes.*" She won't dance or be present if he dances. *"I don't blame her. The littlest ones always get all the credit—when they're young, like that, they're all heart, and he's learned he's adorable; he makes himself look adorable compared to her."* The child stands quietly. Nonie is in a state of displeasure, suspicion—extreme, and with funny admixtures of thwarted pleasure, terrible pleasure, frustration, longing; she has silenced him; she wants to dance again; she dances formally on the site of his nutty exhibition to test her powers and to erase his performance. *"Don't, Nonie—that's silly, what you're doing,"* Lila says. Nonie turns to me. *"You're silly, you're terrible, you need lessons. You ought to be like me. I'd be ashamed to be like you. You're a little sissy."* And: "*Lessons would be wasted on you. He's too crazy, Momma. You should be worried about him.*" A girl's mode of argument. One time, she ran at him and hit him while he was in midair: "*Nonie! Wiley! Okay, we'll have none of this. No dancing if you can't be peaceful.*"

I didn't speak yet, but I looked at her with contempt on the dark lawn—a version of disdain, anyway. She tried to grab me from S.L.'s arms when he lifted me. He held me away from her. "*I'm not mad at him, Daddy,*" she said. *"Let me hold him."* She dribbled at the mouth with the vigor of her insistence that her anger, her blows, her jealousy were not serious, not an issue. Momma said, "*If you ask me, children go too far—it doesn't make any sense.*"

Daddy said, "*They're all little wonders—I've read that they are.*"

In the matter of emotions, here's a sample: Nonie likes Katie Rogers. Sometimes if Katie is available Nonie snoots me: it hurts, it burns. *"Momma, I have to go see Katie—she wants me to come over and be with her."* Nonie is infatuated; and tough about having attention paid to her as someone afflicted with intense (and okay) feelings, as the wooer of the other girl; then, too, she makes a point of demeaning whomever she woos. *"She's just someone I like, she's not special, she's not an a-ath-alete."* And overpraising her: "*She's so nice, she comes from a very distinguished family, she's just so A-1 smart, it scares me.*" And she practices outgrowing that-which-infuriates-her: "*Momma, Katie's not real smart—she doesn't know anything about clothes.*" She tries to make whomever she woos into an immediate servant, a dependent, someone to be used: "*Katie, you're my hostess. I get to go first in everything, I pick the game. You better do as I say. I don't like people who don't act right. Be careful or you'll make me laugh at you.*" Momma says that everyone does a version of this: she calls it breaking-your-spirit, or breaking-you-in, or trying-to-get-hold-of-you-by-putting-a-ring-in-your-nose or a ring-a-ring-in-your-*heart. Getting you where they want you.* Momma says Nonie's stupid in *how she goes about it.*

Nonie believes that servants and dependents don't have to compete: winning is Nonie's job, she's the flag, the young woman. She says often to Anne Marie, "YOU BE QUIET AND JUST HELP ME." *You don't have to think, you don't have to live: I do.*

I do the living around here . . .

Her bravery carries so bureaucratic a charge of emotion about herself that it is serviceable in attracting the devotion of some frightened and uneasy and uncomfortably cautious people. Not Lila, though, or S.L. She is rarely in their terms in a state of grace. In a sense, no one loves her—or ever did or ever will.

But in another sense, there will always be people who care about her . . .

She charges the net, a pudgy, pink-thighed girl, small muscles taut. The other girl is amazingly thin but thick-thighed; she is freckle-cheeked, and she wears glasses that cloud over. She's already at the net, where she jerkily intercepts Nonie's floppy drive with a sort of half-remarkable *lurch* and interposition. Her tightly gripped racquet shudders but stays mostly forward. The ball's flight reverses abruptly, arrhythmically—Nonie raises her racquet; the ball is sailing past. I look at Nonie's face, the scene goes so fast that I only think I see Nonie's face, Nonie's racquet. The ball bangs on the side of Nonie's racquet, Nonie's racquet comes down and strikes the wrist of the big-thighed girl at the net. Nonie's tender-boned wrist and hand, with the puffed fingertips and pink and puffy palm, some fingers roughened, and the bitten fingernails, is a familiar sight, a commonplace memory of mine.

The court—the tennis court: if I put in sunlight, real light, not painted, not any construct of the mind, but drenching light, hot and much larger than me, and then if I grant peculiarities of curvature and of vividness to the air, if I stick to the real light of that real day, I see a child's foot in a child's sandals: *mine*: and Daddy's bulgy shadow as a semi-cavern in the drenching light—my white-hatted head is near his ribs: both girls are at the net: I see the ghost-tail, ghost-cherub face of the ball go past Nonie . . . A pause . . . Nonie's racquet moves . . . That's all I see.

And the big-legged girl screams—I see then but that's because I hear the very loud scream: her head goes back, her eyes bulge . . . What has happened? What has been done to her? Nonie's motion was that of trying to slam the ball—nothing held back—the motion was full.

Was Lisa's wrist broken? Bruised? Was it a bone bruise?

It is a local and seedy reality, the afternoon's blast of heat and light, the real air lionlike and aroar.

The big-legged girl screamed, "YOU HIT ME!" Then she stared at Nonie. She yelled, "YOU DID THAT ON PURPOSE—YOU'RE TERRIBLE." A sort of convulsion took her as she tried to speak, tried to fit a name to her thought. "NONIE!" she said in a deep, racked voice. Lisa chopped at Nonie, slung her racquet sideways—at Nonie—she wanted to hit Nonie. Then she clutched her own wrist. I can rerun this part of the memory. The girl wears white, white clothes like a boy's undershirt and little, full white pants. *She's overdoing it to get Nonie in trouble.* Nonie rears back, away from the whirling racquet; she moves *minimally*, staringly—too much evidence lies in that calm movement: the dreamily contemptuous movement of evasion. The scene grows gray-toned as if at twilight—half clear, half uncertain. Lisa sinks—her legs out straight; she holds her hurt wrist like a dog's paw. She howls, sort of: she howls and yells, "*Help me; it hurts.*" She stares at Nonie; her look has the aim and anger of how much she wants Nonie harmed. Her head sinks forward. No one screams or anything. The event is left unsettled—we're peaceful here.

Nonie: "*I didn't hit her—*" A blunder can't be called a hit—it's to be considered a *miss.*

What's in Lisa's eyes is more negotiable now than what was in them before.

The moral reality of women, the moral reality of men . . .

It is somehow part of the substance, the very quality of my mind, to conceive of goodness as absolute, unchanging, as solid and philosophical, and of *evil* as cloudy, interpretable, changeable, capable of redemption, worldly, temporal. But that is the mind's doing. That conception hardly matches actuality or my own thought but is a shadowy thing, an absolutist notion of the matter . . . traditional . . . since goodness is temporal, too, is as cloudy, interpretable, changeable, as ridden by storyness. After all, time exists with such entirety that what the conscious mind mostly does is calculate-and-remember chiefly in regard to the future—near and far future—what is approaching us is what we keep in mind. But not exactly. We do it in terms of laws, with a sense of predestination, of fixity—we make it one thing with memory—but I think that is nerves . . .

Do I think that goodness is a set of laws negotiating the decisions of this moment relieving, diminishing the element of gambling? One argues about what goodness is—as a final thing . . . And no one is reasonable about this. I mean, for instance, whether all the laws are known or not, or if we are still guessing. And if we are behindhand in figuring out a little about the recent past so that we might half know what to do next, that is, if we can't guess, we argue about that. The future is oddest and we are most unreasonable in real life when we believe all the laws are known, known by us almost, and then accepted, and the future is foretold, grinned at, sort of, when one is *good*—or bad if you believe bad is good in this world, if you think practical evil rules this world . . .

But if we say goodness is real, is changeable, is freedom itself, is not fixed and unchanging, then no one listens, perhaps. What will I think of Nonie when I am on my deathbed? Doesn't it depend on how my life turns out? When I was a child I was *good* in relation to her, but I have been a man for a long time now.

What the conscious mind does meantime is remember itself at earlier moments in regard to the future: that is what I think. I mean it tends to prefer its earlier decisions about physical reality to *physical reality* now, and not only now but to physical reality long ago: it imprisons it in laws. The bodily real is too hard to remember. Too embarrassing. It teaches a different morality . . . it has too many forms of moral responsibility . . .

So that the mind's testimony is as if mostly at a court-martial of itself at which it lies triumphantly and cleverly—and wickedly—in favor of itself—and its moralities, most of which are Utopian lies with only the thinnest tie to real events and to actual moments and the lives of others. The mind does an odd and conceited thing of perverting and tampering with its own sense of justice, its own perspectives in order to claim Perfect Justice, Complete Innocence . . . I don't know which. It is enraged and caught—in a punished way—when it gives in to truth and to the real . . . I, Wiley, think my mind is trained primarily by my dreams—and by things that imitate my dreams—and by the structures and purposes—fascist, Fascist, separated from the real, focussed on me and what I know and on what happens to me—those structures of my dreams . . .

I think that my mind, besides remembering itself, remembers other minds and bans the world—the world and the wind and the actuality of eyes. The sadness of the mind at not being an animal is a complex thing.

Are we evil? I suppose so . . . if we live . . .

But that isn't the end of it . . .

That isn't all we are. And we aren't it purely or at least not often. It can't be a simple story—can it? Look around you. I mean it is an open gamble for each of us, isn't that so? That we are bad, that isn't the end of the story, whatever it is . . . The story . . . I am not quite my mind. My body has a mindly quality—and a mind or consciousness of its own and an ability to calculate. My mind, even as a shadow self among shadow selves—as in a law court of shadows or as in a royal court of shadow selves in a dream—or as in a real moment as in a racing courtroom—it is aware of an outside-that-stuff—an outside the aching circle of thought, of theory . . . of myself, then of myself bodily, then of the shadow book of the mind: my mind has a weirdly freed almost-bodily sense of things, perhaps an illusion, perhaps an act of intellect. Thinkers speak of a model-of-the-world that exists in the mind; some psychologists speak of what-is-NOT-I; I think of an *outside the mind* . . . I am trained primarily, after all, in actuality, I say—in the exigencies of nightmare and, perhaps, of happiness. I am not at home in the exigencies of the mind's demanding-and-eternal type of happiness or its clear-cut sense of nightmare. I have my life still. I am *chiefly* aware of those things as they occur in actual life where I study willy-nilly and *blindly* meanings and *Meaning*-that-cannot-be-fully-interpreted. In real life, too many real people, too many real moments, too many acts, real acts, are involved for the full interpretation of anything. Thinking about one's life has to be like giving up on a final determination of π.

If the subject is degrees of evil, I tend to look in immediate moments—as into a closet in a house where I have lived for a long time. I see it in who says what to who and in what words they use with what expression and inflection. I see it in what I thought and did at a given time then, in a story, more generally among my ideas than convention allows . . . My sense of it is determined by my ideas of what reality is, or was, and, in some ways, still is. Moments are explained over and over in my dreams but not as real moments, merely as plausible and willed synopses, quicker and with fewer dimensions and other elements than real life has.

But in my thoughts, it is different; there, moments require practical explanations: in my thoughts, nothing I know in actuality is more certain than a legal truth is—which is uncertain; but precedent and real-life evidence and guesswork and partial laws are useful; no final explanation arrives: only a kind of judgment set within both a patriotism and a policing thing of force—a vast, towering, not entirely honest machinery—it seems to involve even the sky and clouds or, at least, my sight of them, not the shadow world alone, and not the physical world without my mind, the legal truths.

I don't like lies. False witness. Ugly intentions. I saw when I was young that I could not, without taking sides, foolishly—meanly—judge Nonie as someone unlike me or so much unlike other people that she ought to be exiled or ought to be shot . . . She was someone who went *too* far. Who was stupid and aggressive, dangerously self-willed—maybe sometimes . . . But automatically taking sides *against her* was unfair, wasn't it? I remember the taste of fear in my mouth—a scaly snake. Because of Nonie. Still, she has some obvious rights—merely as an element of reality. (If I say *truth* is not cruel, I mean the brief statements of law people think are true are not truths except as political devices that help them live. They are semi-true as Political Reality, not as emotions can be true, not as one's own experiences are true . . .)

Lisa's mother is shouting at Nonie. Daddy says, "Here, here . . . Let's close the books on this one." We don't examine in any detail the actions of girls. A notion of a definition of evil as a state of will and hurt in a girl, a sister, is a joke.

The limits of thought in real life—even of highly specialized thought—are funny, ha-ha, and weird, and scary . . .

"Don't ask me—I wasn't looking. But Nonie's all right—she wouldn't harm a fly."

Hey, what happened, what was that, did you see it?

I saw something—it looked bad.

I must've missed it—did you see it? What was that all about?

In front of the grown-ups, Nonie symbolically shouts, "*Oh, Lisa! Don't say such things about me!*" She swacks her racquet against her own leg as if dismay and despair power her arm. The sound makes Lisa wince—a reminder, a threat, a tic of the reality that has Nonie in it.

Girls grow up to sexual reality from their side, not starting from the reality of men—from our kinds of good and evil. We specialize in kinds of good and evil by sex and by individual souls. No one human being deals with all kinds of good and bad stuff. Nonie had daydreams of violence, of willful assertion that included a lot of people—is it the false innocence of women, their permitted (and unexamined) violence of soul and act that make many men envy women so passionately? Is it that the only way *not* to be a frontier scout—and ALONE—leads to the imitation and love of women?

That pale and careless and unjudged power of theirs?

I'm a lot kinder in talking about myself than I am when I talk about Nonie. Sight has shadowy areas where wide and untrained vision spreads out from the narrower, schooled registry of conscious inspection. Coherence is a serious and censorious matter—but it is not part of the ordinary nature of things: *Hey, it's all in your head, buddy-boy. I guess that's how* YOU *see things, like a crazy man . . .*

We'll wait and see who's right; we'll see how it comes out.

I am a confessed dream self, a translator of night murmurs into public statements—somewhat. I peer out of my dream of knowledge at her—at Nonie; I'm in a burrow of assumed comprehension.

Take me, for example, at age thirteen—the age Nonie was at the time the lightning affected her so much. I was a party to my puberty, quarrelsome, sometimes cruel, un-Edenish expelled—was I so different from her? I was male—and tall—she wasn't those things—do I mind her aggression? I was known to have a temper, to be *grudging*—not all the time . . . I'm a lot kinder in talking about *myself* but I can begin to see her.

I was considered more often than not to be oddly *good* in spirit . . . rabbinical: philosophic: scientific . . .

Well, put that aside. I had a wish, an ambition to be *bad*, to be *ordinary*, to enter *the real world*— these are not my terms, my words, but those of boys and girls in other scenes, on porches in varying lights, and in living rooms and rumpus rooms and *rathskellers*, and in the woods and fields: confessions, boasts, seductions . . . The football coach told me, *You're okay in a pinch. You're rough* . . .

But he kicked me off the team for not being *serious enough*. He gave me a talk, a semi-talking-to; a burly man, with blue eyes and wavy grayish-gold-rust hair: he said, *Now don't talk, don't talk back, don't change things around—you're tricky* . . .

The rest of this talking-to was a somewhat defensive, somewhat offensive attack on himself and then on everything that was ordinary or unblessèd compared to the purity of sports and of the will then, and then he attacked sports to show he was fair-minded, and then came a paean of praise for competition and victory and single-mindedness, and finally a gently and maybe frighteningly kind-and-*rough* dismissal of me.

But my mother—Lila—said I was relentless—but she liked getting her own way particularly in relation to me—and she tried to train me to give in to her—she said I was relentless especially in relation to Nonie—and sometimes when I was obstinate toward her, toward Lila, she led me to understand—rightly or wrongly—that I was *admirably* set in my ways, male, humorless . . . cute . . . and to be outwitted . . .

She felt I was asking for it . . .

Nonie's slanders were different, perhaps in kind and spirit, from my *roughness* . . . She said of Lisa, for instance, that she was a bedwetter, which wasn't true . . . I doubt that I ever *lied* in order to do harm to someone through lies: but I tell the truth to do harm sometimes . . .

Lila said, *It's terrible when you tell the truth—it makes me sick when you tell Nonie you don't love her, you can't stand her . . . I never saw such battles between any two people. I'm a battler myself but the two of you, my God, my God . . . Goodness, it scared me, the two of you going at it, hammer and* TONGS, *it scared me out of a year's growth . . . And you, you were always, I don't know what, but even as a little child, you came out better than I thought you would . . .*

Then—in a strange, drugged, sad voice—*I preferred you, which was a terrible thing to do to my own daughter . . . Listen, Wiley—* And a funny look overspread her face: *You have funny weapons: you had a very strange mother:* *LISTEN TO ME: YOU AND NONIE WASN'T SO DIFFERENT: SHE'S NOT SO DIFFERENT FROM ME: I DON'T KNOW WHAT YOU SEE* [*IN THINGS*] *BUT IF YOU ASK ME A LOT OF WHAT YOU SEE IS CRAZY* . . .

Nonie was born in the 1920s and had her adolescence in the 1930s, and to whatever extent she was Momma's and Daddy's creation—and of the movies and schools—and of ancient beliefs and whatever—she carried the marks of that period, of events in the world then: she flickers with those moments, those distant men, those famous women, the ones of that time . . .

The opinions of the moment (a phrase of Lila's) . . .

Is she a symbol? Is she a set of choices that she made and that we made, too, but with differences because we're separate people with different endowments and different fates—because we live and have lived in moments different from hers? Is she sort of all of us—me too? Is she herself in no language except that of actual seconds in a real day . . . in reality?

You use what you are the way she uses her wits, Wiley . . . What do you expect? You're the same as she is but you hide it better . . . It makes me sick, the two of you not getting along: why can't we have peace and common sense—and some family love?

Lila differentiated between me and Nonie this way: *You're the killer; she's just a troublemaker—she's only a woman. You make some sacrifices for people; she never does. When you stop and think about things, you're not so selfish. You mean well sometimes—she doesn't care—she doesn't care about anyone . . . Neither one of you is generous. I don't like her as much as I like you—you're more likable. She's not interesting; I think you're interesting, Wiley . . .* (It's a family secret how it matters which one is interesting and to whom and when . . .) *It's not livable around her—I like being with you.*

Well, then she's *the killer*, isn't she? And I'm the sucker—isn't that so?

The thing about being interesting to Lila is that then her forbearance and her wish to cheat you and sometimes smash you—those become built-in. In the real world, back then, and still, I often forget who I am, that I have any worldly attributes—I turn pale and transparent in my own mind, changeable. I am a lot of characters in my own mind, maybe unconvincingly. Still, if someone's watching and listening to you, you get a chance to live through a day with roughly the same baggage of identity as when you started the day, as when you first woke up in the albino air. But, still, there is more to it than this.

When memory tries to draw on this stuff, it tends not to use actual moments because in them the stuff of futurity—which is in every actual moment—makes memory stagger and stammer around as the mind did at the time in the face of, in the light of what you can't know about what will happen next and in the face of what then happens next.

The abrupt truth of reality remembered is ignorance all over again.

This absence of finality can make me hunger for finality, make me murderous or apocalyptic, crazed, overly rational, religious and set in my ways—suicidal . . . Pointlessness for me then is waiting for the point to be made, the blade to appear, and I'm humiliated or scared or empty or all of those then, or I manage to be gallant on the chopping block, at the sight of the materializing act—enmity, judgment, the point—and my opinion of it then, at the last minute . . .

I think I mean that, symbols aside, Nonie and I are merely two people, not nature and an unnatural will to educated truce, we are not the spirits of good and evil: we are sister and brother—adopted brother. Nonie's face in my memory never has the sharp and incredible loveliness and ferocity of her presence when the presence of the future was in her—that is, in one of the actual moments of the past with the presence in it of thoughts of the future and of that urgency . . . Do you remember what it was like when no certainty existed about what would happen, and, so, no certainty existed about what her character was—this is so even in an in-between moment, in a lull after and before her acts offer their clouded testimony . . . her blurred and complicated acts. Her face when everything is in play, and we don't know what will turn out to have been good and bad *in the long run*, has a vibrating brilliance of reality that it can't have in memory when the story is over and only inquiry and questions remain. In memory, I get only a general face, a face without the future in it—not the real thing.

But sometimes I get a real moment going with the real blur of her real face in it, and then I'm so flabbergasted by the shrewd intensity of her *reality*—and of my own reality, too—dragged along into the continuums of the shared light of those times—when our lives were conjoined—dragged into the reality that she was so good at (as an older child) and because her style said she was good at it—that I lose control; and sequences and good sense disappear in the miracle and blare of such recall.

Then, almost, I see her unedited face at the edge of her unknown future when she was eleven, thirteen, twenty, twenty-nine, thirty-three, and dead—then, in the last case, it is not her real face, it is memory, it is her future as thought, as memory, saying the future is over for her . . . But that mixture of ages, the mixture of faces in one face, and me actually there looking at it, is uncomfortably without meaning, without distance inside my own life and head. The actuality of seeing her face again in one real moment at the edge of the void of real time to come is so hard to bear that it blinds me for hours at a time—*it kills me*. Daddy used to say, *Be a gentleman and a scholar even if it kills you*. He wasn't kidding. He *meant* it . . . my God. Why should I want to see Nonie, good old Nonie, my prime knowledge of evil, NONIE, at the cost of hours of my life sickened and shocked, astounded by *reality?*

This cost makes her invisible, unexaminable, immune to judgment—*ordinary*. Well, why not? Is it such hell to be *ordinary?* Is it worth it, is she worth an actual and unexpurgated moment of judgment? *She had character, she made up for what she actually was* . . . See, I am quoting Momma, but even as I write, I see the pinkish skin of Nonie's lower abdomen and upper thigh, big—so it's when I was small—and I seem to smell her. I know it's fragmentary. The height, the air, the dimensionality of continuance hold mysteries, the future, the not-mastered thought . . . Can I approach that flesh knowing I won't survive, innocently or uninfluenced, this time, either? Pride is never in such abeyance as that, is it?

Did Nonie feel real pain? Of course. Nonie was often miserable psychically. And she had bad monthly cramps and that affected her feelings, too. She was dramatic over scratches, cuts, her periods, and being snubbed. She never got significantly hurt physically that I can recall. She had her appendix out—never mind.

Did she feel pain to *match* the pain she caused? Or was it that any pain she felt triggered her demand for justice? She burned to death—maybe that hurt. If I think of her as a forty-two-year-old woman burning to death, I'm moved not to tears (except for all of us in one form or another caught in moments in apocalyptic or ordinary incineration) but I am moved to fear and doubt . . .

Mostly, it's hard for me to care what happened to her—including her death in the flames. Do you love your sister? Do I? Probably. It's enjoined. And she was there. But I still don't care much what happened to her. If I love her or forgive her or whatever, it doesn't mean I want her to come back—I don't want to be with her. Any forgiveness going, she always used for her purposes. I can't go through that anymore—you know how it is in real life, don't you?

To say it, a third way, differently—to define it as (a narrative hypothesis) a relative absolute, powers and illusions and emotions and one's strength of command are really different when you picture them tinged with the openness and logic of an as yet unknown future. Men and women and children are kind of beautiful naturally but scarily then. And fear . . . I mean the famous fear and trembling—is it toward God? It is more toward life than toward Godlessness . . . Is it a sickness, a weakness, a neurotic thing? Is it just us moving humanly in a real moment at the edge of a human future? Do you have to imagine a Utopianly improved or an apocalyptically ended future to control your fear and trembling?

And up-until-now is not a pure thing. If this moment is after a defeat at her hands, I don't have honest access to *my* future except in repentance or unease and caution toward her. And if it is after a victory over her, then it is as a perpetrator that I find my identity in being grown up . . . necessarily oblivious of the harm I do . . . as I proceed into the future with some kind of guilt or other, which is insufferable for others in a lot of ways and for me, too, of course.

The trembling then . . . The taste of life in my mouth . . . The taste of actual seconds as they pass . . . is it an unforgivable, and inescapable, motion?

Momma said, *I always stood by her—she's my daughter*—an extension-of-Momma-into-Futurity—*it wouldn't look good if I didn't . . . And I'll be honest: I'm glad she's a fighter; I'm a realist; I was a good mother to her—no one ever advised me honestly about this.*

About standing by a *real* child? In her temper? And abilities? And disabilities? In her flawed reality? About violence and pain and reality? About how to help a real child survive? About forgiveness? In real life? In the rush of things in the real world? About the toughness necessary to get your own way?

You know what it was like when Nonie woke up to what was going on somewhere? Nonie was always someone who had to keep up with you, she always helped herself to whatever was there to be had . . .

Nonie fought with *her* weapons to have what she wanted, to have a share of the world, to have what she saw others having; and this was a daily thing, merely that; and a truth about everyone . . . Over and over, Momma came back to saying, *It is normal, all of this, all that Nonie is . . .*

But if, then, Nonie, *abstractly*, was *normal* or *typical* or *okay*—she needed no defense—she didn't need Momma . . . She could find a home anywhere in the world, Nonie could, then . . . And, so, Momma couldn't manage, usually, to stick to any consistent degree of abstraction about Nonie then unless she sort of gave Nonie up to wickedness or to being really *successful* or to being another self of Momma's . . . Is that what *being successful* means? That you become an image of that sort, purely, but in an unclean way, for everyone? For a lot of people? I mean, is abstraction about one's self possible only if someone is really successful and is invisible in that? Is that what *being successful* means? If you become a celebrated writer who represents *The Normal?*

I mean, Momma and all of us had to be illogical and dumb if we wanted to protect Nonie and not be liars and accomplices, if we wanted to be unlike her. And Nonie had to sail along without an honestly known or honestly felt past and with only an idealized—or typical—future, one with the usual meanings, if she didn't want to know or think about this.

So it was as if *her* life was at the center of abstract meaning; and *her* language and errors and stupidities were clever after all. She was freed from moral common sense so completely I thought it was moral bliss to be *ordinary* . . . I wanted to live in that moral anarchy, too. The recipe for this citizenship, Nonie's system, was that in it you never have more than one moment—or than one *type* of moment—and it is rigorously typical, no matter what. And it fills one sentence, maybe two, but they're the same old sentences—it all is typical—it is always a *now*, always an *always*, always *a game in progress*; and always in it she is innocent enough and she knows the game and the most real moral truth . . .

The greater the degree of abstraction, then, if you go along this way, the more moments are subsumed in it without your noticing that the real moments have disappeared: that it is costing you your life that you are doing this, that this is being done. The more any one actual moment is excluded, the more anyone's life loses its features, its particularity . . . perhaps its truth. But the easier it is for you to come to convenient judgments about yourself.

Momma stayed in individual moments without Nonie's history and with only Nonie's general future in them: *The way I talk is warning enough to the wise. A friend would understand me.*

A *friend* would know what category of *uselessness* to put Nonie in just from the tones, the obliquities, the ways Momma talked about her, she meant.

It was as if the truth was hidden at a slant among falling beams of revolving light among the leaves and bugs—beams and rays and ovals of glare—in a truly old, full-grown woods . . .

But then what did it mean when Momma seemed to speak with directness: *You have a future—no wonder Nonie hates you . . . unless she marries a rich man . . . unless she gets what she wants . . .* Was that about a Jewish girl's fear-and-trembling that she wasn't in the male line? Was there a simple meaning there after all, unhidden, and as obvious as a ravine into which an entirely new army of everyone—nearly everyone—would fall? Or when Momma said, *S.L. likes to think everyone's an angel, so he gets lied to, he gets hurt a lot, but I like people just as they are: I can take it.* Is that explanation enough?

S.L. said Momma didn't know anything; she invented the nastiest ideas possible in order to scare people and get her own way and to drive everybody mad. But sometimes he listened to her. Sometimes I did, too.

Momma would say to me, *Why do you hate her so? She's not a criminal.*

I said, *She's no good at all*—that's what I said. I *thought* she was, in the end, of a criminal order of being, among the genera of worthlessness. Further degrees of Evil had to do with psychotic boldness. But I wasn't sure of this; I wasn't sure I wasn't being petty and selfish. I mostly refused to let myself think about it. When I didn't think, I carried feeling, or mood, a mooded conclusion about her: I felt that Nonie was as "*ruthless*" (domestically) as her standing at a given time permitted, that she was a point at which Evil bubbled into the world as a kind of truth of an individual soul and particular will and as part of the overall concatenation of events . . . In some ways I thought her An Ordinary Nazi but well this side of Nazism morally because of where we lived, but I thought her to be worse than most murderers in books. I didn't always mind that, though. I just behaved in certain limited ways because of feeling like that. Sometimes I minded it. I did and I didn't want her punished—I mostly wanted to have the world near me, around me, to be different. Sometimes Momma and Daddy both said, *You're some kind of terrible snob who's bad for people . . .* Sometimes they said, *You're the nicest person of all, you're too sweet for your own good.* Often I minded it that they were real.

Daddy tried to calm Lisa's mother: *This is a terrible thing to happen. We're a friendly neighborhood.*

I guess the measure that establishes limits is not clear since it has to do with *pain* in degrees and in nature and is, in a very creepy way, statistically and metaphysically considered even if people aren't statisticians and philosophers—on the face of it, although, in truth, clumsily or not, they are.

I fainted . . . The thought of pain makes me ill.

A threatened lawsuit—over a tennis game? *You-must-be-insane—you're-talking-like-a-crazy-person. A lunatic.*

The sight of Lisa's pain, the reality, means what? *These things happen all the time.* Bruises and abrasions and defeat bloom in our garden.

It's too terrible—I can't think about it. Let's keep this in proportion; no one broke any bones. Everything is peaceful . . . We're all one big happy family . . .

The family is made up of some essential universality of Nonieness having to do with us and them . . . And with blood . . .

I don't mean the family is this as a gist or essence. I mean the reality, the thing itself, in real moments . . .

Nonie: "*I didn't do . . . anyTHING. I didn't do anything. I didn't do anything bad, I didn't do anything you should think was bad.*"

A partial analysis of Nonie's speech: The first *I-didn't-do-anyTHING* is a correction of *suspicions* that anything meaningful occurred. The second *I-didn't-do-anything* means that nothing substantive occurred through the agency of her act. The third denies that her act occurred in any reality in which jealousy, violence, and mental or physical pain exist commonly enough to be used as a measure for *every little thing* even assuming it can be. Nonie refused that, insisted that it was not so, and that no suspicion should now or ever attach to her at all in regard to pain, ill will, cruel and limitless impulse, calculation, calculations of *will*—and so on.

Nonie was clearer, in a way, than Momma was. Nonie claimed the right to be seen as someone who lived entirely in sunlight. Her acts were not worth discussing, were not to be discussed. No questions about her ought sensibly to exist. The simplicity of her vocabulary maybe was *stupidity,* as Lila said, but it was also a style and a tactic, a conscious anesthesia of her mind and soul and everyone else's, a way of separating her life from *any* universe of harm and from any real responsibility for the consequences of her will.

When I was young, much of the time the future so prevailed with me that nothing else had that much authority as explanation, as comfort (and unease), as the source of reason, and as a measure of (practical) goodness, the future with me in it and stronger than I was. Nothing mattered as much as the future, a common future, a firm and unarguable continuing, an ongoing persistence of more or less joined destinies . . . A protection of that. So, goodness arose from that, from what lasted in real moments and involved more than one person.

I might have liked the tactics Nonie used but they were hers. I thought *she* ruined them. I could not see that Nonie was wise but I did think she was clever and shrewd . . . The future is in my bones then and now—it has never stopped being a measure of goodness although, God knows, I am not young anymore.

A falsity is futurity lied about as *solved.*

I feel it like a doom, my hatred and amusement and pity for Nonie. I pitied Nonie's way of trying to handle the sneaky—furtive and gorgeous—ghost-dwindle and ascent to futurity. Conventional meanings are comforts. They're classics—you're a fool to use them and a fool not to. *It's all okay. Nonie's nothing much.* I cannot ever fully grasp how Nonie, in her pride, was willing to cast off the imperatives of intelligence, an honest view of the past and a real worry about the future, and how she proceeded with such assurance—and such velocity—anyway . . . She needs me . . . The way she did it, she lived in a Now become paramount in pleasure and excruciating pain, those things as they were present, flat-out, up-front, sans perspective. Nonie's calculations were based on notions of people in a sort of present-tense landscape and on notions of *what-works* and *what-will-work* as a sure thing there . . .

Am I so different?

I think the cheated-on past, the lied-about future will harm us more than we have to be hurt, but I think it is hard to measure. I think the degrees of this matter—and motives, and terms, and extents of accomplishment and judgments about lesser and greater and more dangerous crimes. It's easier just to choose sides and to do everything because you're on one side but then the world suffers, doesn't it?

Pudgy Nonie makes you choose sides just in the obvious way she presents herself—it's hard to be rude to her but if you're not, you're her accomplice. We must go into the future as those who have hurt her or as her friends. She went out every day to play with other children and she forced herself on them. She forced them to accept or *deny* her. It is a matter of degree . . .

Similarly, she went into people's houses even when those people were uncomfortable with her.

She was pushy, obtuse, talkative: *I didn't do any . . .* THING. She was without moral self-consciousness. She was actual and unself-conscious.

Momma said, *What can I do?*

Nonie's fine eyes are ripe and guarded—they are hard-surfaced with denied guilt. Often, they have the bloom of tantrum. She was always pretty in some way or another. She slept long hours. In her dreams, she dealt with the future—and with her past. In wakefulness, she was active, very active . . . often snubbed . . . Then she'd go to bed . . . In the waking hours she was often in bed sleeping. Momma went around using phrases for Nonie like "*More-normal-than-normal.*" Nonie had clear skin and *good sleep habits.* Momma kept Nonie's image obscure. Momma had a funny, cruel, partly sentimental grip on the actuality of pain all-the-time for everyone and on what it cost her to be *a mother*—she was different from Nonie in other ways as well. It hurt Momma to be a mother at all and especially to be one to Nonie. She wanted Nonie's too openly cheerful-cheerleader smile and Hollywood-starlet-in-the-sunshine-with-ermine-on-her-bedroom-slippers-while-she-reads-comic-books-like-you-and-me style modified to show that Nonie knew she was expensive for the world, for women, for Momma . . . for everyone. Momma said, *People around here are not absolute fools.* Momma said, *Nonie won't listen to reason: Nonie doesn't know what reason is . . . It could hit her over the head, a good reason, and she wouldn't even feel it . . .* Momma said, fairly often, that the presence of pain was too much for sensitive Nonie.

And then, because Nonie and her real-life manner existed, Momma said, *Nonie's a fool, but in some ways she's a realist. Many people like her. She gets along in the world.*

Momma went in and out of any number of opinions about Nonie.

Nonie said to her, *You make me laugh. You're a riot.*

And Nonie said to Lila, *You make things up. No one likes you.*

(Nonie was *steadier* in her moods and purposes and dislikes than Lila was in hers . . .)

Lila-makes-things-up: that meant Lila no longer had a real life or mind but was abstract, *a mother*, and dead and ghostly otherwise. Nonie often said she herself had no gift for *what-was-made-up.* Nonie couldn't watch the movers from a window, for instance—she'd have to go outside and touch the side of the truck, the metal hot from the sun. Watching children play, she'd twitch, she'd start to play, too, on the sidelines, and not only with truncated and imaginary (or little) gestures of play, either: she'd do what the children she was watching were doing: the whole game, all-out, but alone and strangely—I mean because of its odd reality, its echo-yness as well . . .

I'm a better person than you, she said to Lila often. That meant, in part, that Lila wasn't cheerful-likable—*being likable* had to with feeling good in the way Nonie sometimes felt good: a rapid shallows, a brooklike flow of will as a being regarded as *innocent* by a docile company—as someone good in an unvarying progress of goodness in an unchanging and certain world. Until she was challenged—then the world changed nature and *being likable* became a claim of righteousness among the issues, the challenges, and the wars.

Nonie's sense of *the normal,* her idyll of the world, was melodramatically single in intent, and unambiguously set on her own projects, her own life—she insisted on this to what was a dangerous, and even imbecile, extent, Lila thought. This insistence lay in Nonie's face, its expressions, her voice, its shrill, birds-tied-together tone: *I am happy, I am justified in being happy, people who disagree with me are really wrong, I am really truly right.*

Nonie was really *right.*

Do what I say or I will hate you . . .

Physically, Nonie seemed terrible to me. Nothing in her posture or style or face showed any sense that life would proceed moment by moment in the future and would have to be lived by us as humanly and as anarchically as the past had been, or that there was just us as bulwarks against despair and against the isolation in our souls. I think Nonie imagined an entirely new, entirely happy future that would be truly as she wanted it, as in an ad.

Momma said once, *I think ads destroyed her mind.*

As part of this insane newness for us that Nonie kept insisting had come into existence along about the same time as her life—well, Nonie felt it put her teeth on edge to call Lila Mother. She said *you* and she said *she.* Or she used a sentimental but commanding tone when she said *MOTHER—it stuck out a mile.*

She's only guessing, like the rest of us, Momma said, referring to Nonie's certainties and tactics and renamings and sporty—and cultist—taciturnities. It was clear day-by-day that Nonie made mistakes and was limited in her systems even when she was having successes. But it sometimes seemed she was right. It was hard to keep track of in moment-to-moment stuff concerning her. It was easier to think her judgment was better—was saner or "more normal" than it was, than our less cheerful and more wobbly judgments were. As Lila said, *A lot of the time it takes too much energy to hate her or anyone* (to keep in mind that someone is foul and a blot on the world and is wrong but insistent in judgment). *So you can get away with a lot—having a lot of gall is a good tactic.*

Nonie was the quickest of anyone to pick up traces of other people's abysmal cruelties, those in-the-cause-of-good, too. Nonie caught what seemed to me to be *every* over-the-line murderousness or cold-bloodedness that came along in her presence; and she did it faster than anyone—or so it seemed to me. It occurred to me that she was sensitive to it, attuned to it—valuable in that way and dangerous that way, too . . .

So you can see how, in the light of this, and considering her disdain for futurity and the past, she would understand her being pretty—when she became pretty—better in a lot of ways than other pretty women (or men do) their being pretty. And you can guess at some of the mistakes she made. I never knew anyone who lived so consciously, so thoroughly, what it was to be pretty. Nonie was startlingly complete within her own system. She became pretty when she was sixteen. *Breathtaking for a while,* Momma said, *but it won't last; she's got nothing to back it up. She's not serious about it*—treating it as grounds for charity toward others, for instance, or as something that involved her in the negotiable opinions of others in a more earnest way than in childhood. Nonie said Momma was jealous of her, and hateful and mean, as Momma had always been to her (Nonie said). Thin and fine-mouthed and erect and quick to smile, Nonie, pretty in the way she was, in an open, friendly style, took credit for her looks and began to sound both naïve and shrewd: *I don't have any flaws. I'm* perfect—this year." Nonie's joke. About irony: an idea is not, in actuality, an ideal thing even if it is treated as if it were just that. 'Realism,' which, since it doesn't predicate romance or anything subtle, is a form of modesty: *I'm sweet sixteen and I'm very stuck-up.* That was modest in a way. Whenever she said she was 'stuck-up,' she meant she wanted to have her own way, all the way, because she was pretty and young, and such things were temporary—although not for her: she turned it into an *always* in her usual reasoning. But you were supposed to see her wanting her own way as a modest (and sometimes tragic) request—as in a queen in a history book or in an ancient play. Her legs and voice and eyes weren't good, but her overall appearance was, and *not too many people notice flaws for a while,* Lila said.

She likes to hear herself talk, Nonie said of Lila. *It doesn't mean anything, what she says; it's all made-up stuff; it's beside the point.*

Nonie said to me, "If I had good legs and a better nose—and a better hairline—I'd go to Hollywood . . ."

And, still, her eyes gave off intermittent signals of her incredible obduracy, signals of darkness, not such bad darkness when she was a sixteen-year-old. *It's been a long wait: women need to get their own way,* Lila said; *Nonie is at the crossroads, she has a chance—so we'll see. Maybe she'll turn out to be a nice person if she gets what she wants—she's a fighter.*

Nonie said, *I like having really nice skin—I'm like a rose—and I have very pretty* eyes.

She knew what was happening to her—even if she didn't understand, she knew. But when she claimed credit for her looks it was a trick on you—a demand not to be a victim and a request for intellectual credit for her prettiness: as if she had thought it up and worked it out and gotten it down on paper, on flesh, and on actual moments as they tooted along.

You could see it in her face—slightly concussed but a little fibrous and calculating, hard-minded, a resistance to everything outside herself.

So that the faults she saw in others were her own faults, the secrets hers . . . She had no time for your real faults, usually . . . She was alert, and anxious not to lose out, and curiously wrong, insanely wrong, sometimes, about things: "Looks are the only thing that matter in THIS world . . ."

Still, she was sad. *I see things in perspective,* she said. That is, she preferred her sense of consequences to that of anyone else. I didn't know her well anymore. Her life was such a hash of flirtation and anger and clothes and parties and distaste and appetite for sex in her version and on her terms that I couldn't disentangle the individual words she had for things, one from another, or recognize the intention of the paragraphs, the soliloquies of her utterance as a very pretty girl. I think that women, and competing with them (and hurting them), all that was more important to her than stuff about boys and men or than anything boys or men did. Men pleased her mostly by being *real gentlemen.* She was secretive about her violences and her crushes on women and her real moodiness, a stringent moodiness now. *People know me. I have an even temper,* Nonie said. *People know I'm likable.* To Momma's dismay, Nonie drank a lot—she passed out in public a few times. She was self-willed but she was secretive about being like that. She tried to make it a matter of rules, of respectability and breeding, being self-willed: *I know how to respect myself . . .*

Nonie held her head in such a way when she was dressed up that it looked as if she were in sunlight and wind. And it worked: a lot of people who didn't like her thought she *was* likable, somewhere, to others. I never saw Nonie lose her nerve. Not once. I was interested enough in her at this time to watch her off and on.

Lila feels that hate is to be expected as a general rule and that Nonie lays down her fortifications and tactics steadily and from early on in any given circumstance.

Nonie says, I like everyone. I think well of everyone.

She didn't expect a future in which anyone would keep track of her statements and her acts and, except with her sons later, she had no such future.

Lila: "Sympathy's not so wonderful. It's what you get when you're down and out and no one's scared of you anymore. I'd rather be hated." *Like Nonie*—nervy, brave, hated? "I have to hand it to her: in many ways, she is a freer person than I am . . ."

Nonie: *I'm not good around sickness and sick people—they only care about themselves. If you can't love somebody, just keep your mouth shut—that's what I always say . . .*

Nonie could not genuinely give sympathy. She wanted it but she was too angry to give it; Momma had foxed her in this area—Nonie's asking for it seriously meant Nonie was really defeated; and Nonie *couldn't* do that, at least not too often. She *couldn't* ask for real sympathy. And she was too jealous of it and too embattled and too enamored of what other people might have in the way of it for her ever to relax about it—or give it; it was an incredible issue with her. It made her raw and sore and gave her little rest.

With sympathy ruled out, when someone was weakened you couldn't love them. Nonie thought she was *like everyone*: she had evidence that some people were like her, so everyone—*everyone nice*—was. (If you weren't like her, you weren't nice.) She firmly, crazedly believed *love-among-the-healthy* didn't involve sympathy at all but only envy and acquisition—of each other, of each other's rank, of each other's belongings. The sick can't have or get first-rate love—*real love*—so you should shut up about your flaws and admire the leading woman. And since you don't love someone sick, you should shut up about sympathy except as a matter of lying socially.

Nonie: *I like love but I'm not sloppy.*

In a world of original sin, Lila felt that love, romantic love or family love or both, was a lot of *madness* since lovers attack you. She felt she had the right to be disgusted when loved, to feel grabbed at—she used cruelty to breathe, to live. But she felt love, she felt suffocated, she felt cruelty—she was a feeling-riddled narcissist, hugely proud and clearly strange. But Nonie would have nothing to do with any of that; everything was spoken of as if sunlit (as I said); all endings were happy endings (unless she was saddened); *real love* was a sort of splendor of games, a local equality-of-scrapping—with Nonie on top. Hearty, athletic sentiment: straightforward secrecy; propaganda; festivities in the present moment of being the *center-of-a-story*: Nonie in love, this was Nonie in love: *I'm in love with love, [but] I'm hard to please when it comes to men.*

She wasn't strange at all but, Christ, I didn't want to know her—but I was used to her. It was an entire metaphysics in its way, her attitudes and her victories in the moment, nearby or actually present, but as if present, and her prettiness and her being a trap for anyone who went near her . . . I mean there was no trade-off, there were only Nonie's rules, Nonie's victories, Nonie's view of how one was likable or else *a drip*, an enemy to be punished.

Lila: "Nonie learned a lot of wrong things from me—maybe everything's a mistake—what do you think of that philosophy?"

In her truthful and superior mode, she told Nonie, "For a number of reasons, don't attract too much attention. You can't afford it."

Insult and curse. And Nonie lived by such advice but she denied that she did: "I don't listen to you. You're jealous. I will never listen to you, and you can save your breath. Oh, it's terrible—I have to have you for a mother."

"She can't think. She doesn't know what she's doing."

"I do, too—you're the fool—"

Nonie did not ever admit she was *gambling* . . . Part of why she was so dictatorial, so tyrannical, was that she believed there was one truth—one only—and she wanted to be the one who had it in her care: she was the chief enforcement officer, the prophetess—the columnist—the executor-executioner of the one truth . . .

She argued with Lila so often that I remember almost nothing else. Sometimes their arguments seemed to be a fixed matter—it was fixed that they would argue; and the methodologies on each side were fixed or habitual often and not reinvented, except at times, they did, both of them, or one of them, go off on a new tack—in arguing, I mean.

Nonie said to Lila, "You're too psychological—I like *some*

psychology—but too much is just sickening, and if anyone asks me that's what I'll tell them. I hate it when it gets sloppy and lets sloppy people off the hook . . ."

Lila said, "Nonie, you don't make a good impression if anyone thinks about it . . ."

A remark of Nonie's, one that she made several hundred times: "Nothing ever happened to me; I had a happy life. Nothing ever went wrong. My parents loved me. There's nothing to me, I guess. I'm just a smile and a good game of tennis—that's what my husband says. And maybe Hank"—her husband—"can tell you I'm good when the lights are out—that's what he tells *me*. But he's a *liar*; he likes to flatter me—he thinks I'm sweet."

Hank never made a lot of money, and Nonie kept *scrapping* all her life—she stayed active in the world in her style; she persisted in her methods; she drank more; she became more combative; she was an adult form of the various younger Nonies but drunker, meaner, more righteous, more self-assured. No one knew why she had ended up on the social level she did . . . She chose it, in a way, or it chose her, and she gave in: "I have a wonderful life, I am a truly *HAPPY* woman," she would say, drunkenly, angrily, spitting a little at me . . .

But she burned to death.

Hank never disagreed with her in public. He took her side wholeheartedly, whole-spiritedly—in every moment I saw them together, in all the fracases, litigations, feuds, innumerable quarrels and wars that she spoke of, that I knew about, he shared her views utterly, totally. He was fat and sly-looking and had a face with a particular expression on it: a sort of numbed self-congratulation and childish hurt on very small features; but the overall velocity or motion was set among the details of eyes and mouth and eyebrows and forehead that indicated slyness—slyness, self-congratulation, and hurt . . . A hurt sweetness.

He had no quarrels of his own that I knew of, no real energy, no real life, no actual history of slyness apart from her: only a history of maybe extreme complicity with Nonie . . . A certain simplicity was in that—I don't know. The talk was that he was limitlessly scared of her, but when I say *the talk* I mean seven or eight people who enjoyed bringing the subject up with me because they were fighting with her, with him and her, or they had the temerity to do it because they were scared of her and wanted to talk to *her brother*.

I was *scared*—morally—to talk about her or to judge her, and I often would tell an anecdote of my early childhood when my best friend—this was in second grade—had disliked her and said she was *a witch* . . .

The other men who had liked her had not been like Hank or had not been so openly like that that I had seen it although I could imagine that that was much of what life offered her: I mean, what she wound up with: she had a foresense of it. Some of the men who had liked her a lot had been remarkable. After her death, Hank didn't remarry. He worked as a clerk in a drugstore after she burned up. Before, he had been in real estate but had been considered lazy and detached. Inept. His mother said Nonie had sucked out all his blood and replaced it with *her poison* but Lila had said before she died that Nonie had a mother-in-law-and-a-half *and could use a little help* . . .

Before he and Nonie married, Hank had been "popular" and had been thought "clever" and "brave." It's funny to judge other people's lives—it's damned odd even to sum them up . . . Books and stories really have a lot of moral nerve. Nonie seemed to me, when I was younger, she seemed to me to have choices, a good many of them, and I was startled and uneasy at the life she, in part, chose.

I did not exactly judge it.

If I turn to what other people said of her choices, it is because they did judge. Lila said, *She doesn't know what she's doing but she won't listen* . . .

She herself said only, over and over, *I want to be happy* . . . And: *What I know of the Good Life is how to be happy and I've been happy and very very very lucky all of my life.*

A cousin of Hank's told me, "He let her down—he was no good at anything—she's a terrible person—but she never had a chance married to him . . . He just dragged her into a pit—she never had a chance . . ."

Nonie's cousin and mine, the one at the party who was in the sunroom, said, "Hank was a good soldier and a smart boy, and she cracked him like a nut and ate him for breakfast. Hank never had a chance in hell."

Here is a terrible story, not necessarily to be believed: *Twice, I left infant sons in the house when I went out, and both died; Nonie was with them. It's the worst thing in my life. It's the only thing I can't bear. The second time was just terrible, just terrible. I did it to show I wasn't frightened. The doctors never knew what caused either death. I know it could be anything; you think I don't know how terrible it is that I think what I think? I'm only saying I know what I know. What was strange was that Nonie wasn't upset—not at all. A mother knows. She did something. I know—she said when I came home,* Momma, nothing happened. *I screamed at her when I found out. We didn't get along after that. Maybe she was just being foolish. Maybe she did nothing, but it was something that bothered her—I don't hate her, Wiley. She never admits anything. I took you in right away—I dared myself. I wasn't going to stop living, I wasn't going to let everything I had be wrecked, and let people feel sorry for me, right and left. I know I imagine things, but I'm not a fool. Maybe I ruined her because of the way* I THINK ABOUT THIS. I THINK AND I THINK. *Maybe she hates me because I'm wrong about her —or maybe because I guess—how can I know? Why does she hate everyone so much? Because no one's as bad as she is? She wants to think we're all as bad as she is—worse than she is. Why does she talk like such a fool? She's not a fool. She tried to be so clever. Why did nothing ever work out for her? Something's wrong with her. You know, she's like a baby in many ways. It's so she won't have to think about anything seriously. I'll tell you something. I will never know. I will never believe anything she says as long as I live. She's mean—she's really mean. But I was a bad mother; my own mother told me so; I know I let myself off the hook when I think these things about the babies. I get so miserable. I know I may have been unfair to her and done something terrible to her. S.L. always said I sacrificed Nonie to my own convenience. I know I build everything up. I did her a wrong to suspect her. But no one pays attention; so she gets away with it . . . I know whatever happened was my fault—but I want to know what happened and I never will . . .*

Did you accuse her, Lila? Did Nonie yell back at you?

Did you and Nonie accuse each other, Lila?

Someone else's life: the knotty dramas, the sense of meaning—with (or without) catharsis . . . And the pile-up of moments, the kinds of forgetfulness—of *burial* . . . Of forgiveness. Absolution. Forbearance . . . Lila saying with astonishment, *Then Nonie forgot about it . . .*

Then Nonie forgot about it because it was such a nightmare for her, Momma? Or because she persuaded herself none of it was true?

Did she get over it because it was over?

Did Nonie have moments when she began her belief that she had to fight to live, that she was fighting for her life? Did she pray for forgiveness? Turn into an athletic girl so that she would run and run and sleep and sleep?

Lila couldn't keep the guilt and grief to herself: Lila had a restless soul—an explorer's sense of things . . . (This is what *I* think.) If I am to playact Lila in a drama, I address myself: *You like to talk, you like to say you know you're not a good person, but you have to set yourself so that your guilt never is the question—you can't exist without protection . . .*

How old was Nonie when the first death occurred? Seven? Eight? Ten?

I mean if Lila saw the act as accident—as a twitch of a blind and malign universe, an empty chance materializing in a given moment as a fate to be overcome—would Nonie match her movements, twist them, be a version of Lila and of Lila's *predicament* . . . Lila's grief . . . Lila's attempt to live? Nonie's right to live, to command her own life, includes what acts?

Was Lila a great-souled dealer in truth who saw and saw and saw and who showed the truth on her face? Would Nonie have already begun to be unaware of it in herself—of the chemical feelings of the act, of whatever *truth* it was that Lila saw—if Lila saw the truth? Would Nonie have said, *I did nothing . . . I did nothing bad . . .* Would she be immersed in that pattern of definition . . . ?

Is that what social class and lineage and faith and "normalcy" are, is that what each one of those things is, a set form of absolution—an almost automatic absolution up to quite a farfetched point?

And what if it was true that she had done nothing, that only her feelings were at fault, if one wants to speak of *fault* in this matter, in matters such as this? What did she and Lila see in each other's faces—complicity? Horror? Disbelief? Relief? Shock? Love on one hand and *not-love* on the other?

Mutual hatred? Dismay at the world? Utter innocence? Immediate innocence? Innocence in the end, *all-in-all, because-what-can-you-do-but-live-and-let-live?*

Imagine it is factually true, that Nonie was in the house *twice* alone when an infant, or a near-infant, died . . . Imagine Momma refusing to believe *the worst of Nonie* the first time . . . And then . . . And then . . .

Or are you too modest to imagine or know or to have a sense of reality?

No, no. Imagine the first time: Would Nonie have confessed? Even if nothing particularly bad was true? Boasted? Boasted madly? Would she have said, *It's not my fault,* or blamed Lila: *You did it, you just want me to be blamed . . .* Did she say, *Momma, help me?*

I mean the oddity of what people say and then of what we think they said . . . And this is in the real rooms, the actual hallways, the dailiness of the stairs of that house . . . This is in actual moments . . .

I was not there. Was Nonie so fierce and strange back then that she would have been set in secrecy—and the claim of *normalcy*—that soon, even as a little kid?

I wanted her to be as tough as a boy . . . I knew what the world was . . . I brought her up to take things for herself: I wanted her to have the freedom my mother never gave me . . . I was A TOY *for* MY *mother . . .*

Did Nonie say, *I was only trying to help . . .*

Or: *I was* playing *with him*?

What is it that they knew, that they understood, and misunderstood and imagined?

Did Nonie invent herself as normal so fast that it happened in the course of an hour? So early in her childhood?

Lila said, *I never got over it . . . I'm not over it now . . . S.L. blamed me . . .*

Of course. Of course.

Lila said, *It could have been a mistake the doctor made . . . And children get poisoned from bad milk . . . Life is life, Wiley . . . I was never childish.*

But since Nonie didn't die, or crack up then, at least not openly—and Lila did—*I had to go to a sanitarium, I had to get away from both of them*—Nonie and S.L.—*and from my mother, who kept blaming me for not being a better Jew . . .* Whatever happened must have happened over time in a ghostly way as well, Lila dreaming about it, crying, or not crying, Lila turning into the Lila I knew and whom I am inclined to take as an absolute being, as someone who was chiefly one thing all her life when, of course, she changed all the time, not back and forth but onwardly, cumulatively—accumulatingly . . . And with all her own reality wadded up behind that sort of greeting-card smile, that imagined fixity of motherhood . . . Or whatever it was I was inclined to ascribe to her in easy moments . . .

Take the circumstance of *innocence*: I mean how that circumstance can seem a horror beyond all bearing . . . Imagine yourself suddenly stricken with a kind of burningness of guiltiness—you are cut off from everyone . . . But not from your own child—not if she is guilty, too. One might slip into a reality of being horrible . . . I *think* Lila believed that God disliked her, Lila, individually . . .

Nonie felt she, Nonie, was lucky, and that her mother was doomed . . .

But again, the real house, the afternoon light, a cloudy day: Nonie, let us suppose, imagine, hypothecate, is fully innocent—even in her thoughts. Her mother's suspicion, then, over a period of actual days and weeks, and her father's disbelief, and other people's curiosity and their minds, their eerily self-protective notions, would have defined the world in such a way that Nonie might have begun a lifetime of resisting all of them . . .

So that then my lifetime became, has become, a systematic and emotional and spiritual attempt not to be Nonie's brother . . .

It is not *exactly* anyone's fault.

And the negation—of not being her true brother in a spiritual sense—might seem like a positive thing (but with drawbacks since it is human: it isn't divine and in *Heaven* and without flaw).

Then she and I, Nonie and I, are parallel systems, or almost parallel ones, and we are linked and perhaps trivial and like a good many other people: and hardly tragic . . . . Perhaps we are but it seems boastful to think so . . . But if you do things, then there is a result; consequences change people—it is just common sense . . . Then how much freedom can be allowed in a well-run state of things?

If I assume, instead, that Nonie was playing with her own feelings and with the complicities there are in solitude in a house—in one's being alone and the queen of the silence there—and if I then assume that murder as a moral absolute, a bodily one, is present as a realistically absolutist correctness in the sense of making the world truthful and orderly, and that this is always, epically, naturally, endemically, epidemically so—then I can't see that Lila's story, her anecdotal recounting, could have much truth about what happened.

Only some truth.

I mean her claim of innocence, of any absence of collusion with Nonie, of any absence of confusion, is too great . . . And the moments of knowledge, and of tacit, almost overt acknowledgment between the two of them, have vanished from Lila's memory—or from her speaking of the matter as a poet might in a way one would want to accept as bringing light to a thing of darkness . . .

Or, rather, they are sort of there in odd tangential ways . . .

If you're my friend, you'll know what I mean . . . .

I knew Lila to be a cynic about government—about love—about men and maleness . . . *Who is going to govern the ones who govern?* she said of any ideal proposal or any ideal notion of human existence.

I'm a liberal, but you know me, I go too far, but I don't ever go too far when it's serious . . . It's all a sleight-of-hand, you know . . .

I mean her accusation of Nonie could have been ideological—a suspicion—a jealous suspicion—a deduction . . .

Also, I don't know that I am separate enough from her and her ideas and from Nonie and her life to speak without complicity with one or the other of them—with Lila, a mother of sorts, or with an anti-Lila, a mode of escape—complicity not necessarily with her actions but with the idea under the ideas under the ideas that governed her actions in actual moments . . .

Our almost genetic attachment through negations and acceptances and mirrorings and reversals.

I know this about Lila: she didn't want to know what happened in these two instances . . . She didn't blame herself . . . And for her curiosity to work, well, it didn't work, not ever, unless she was *the worst person* —the smartest, meanest, toughest person, and yet good overall, or after all, or *when the chips are down, I did some good in this world*—so that there was no greater omniscience, no greater potency or strength of judgment than her accepting the bottommost level and yet not being really bad: she was secular but she was like God, sort of: I mean like her idea of God: she knew the worst, she was the ultimate arbiter, the ultimate authority, she knew the truth—it was her pride . . . She wouldn't vote ultimately for evil, no matter what—not if the issue came to her in a certain overt form . . .

Hell, I can't make it clear. You have to guess at it—from your own experience.

And Nonie, by the time she died, by the time Nonie died in the fire, in the time I knew her, a lot of the above, a lot of what Lila said, was something Nonie could have said by the end of her life, such as *When the chips are down, I did some good in this world.*

And Nonie believed that she was the toughest person . . . the ultimate authority wherever she was even if she had to do harm to prove she was the ultimate authority . . .

One notion I have, not my favorite and not necessarily the most likely, is that Nonie did *something* and suffered afterwards, not morally, but from *fear*, in a luminously dark way . . . I try to make it all childish with her denying any real question of guilt but saying something later; perhaps she almost truthfully confessed but she wouldn't remember clearly: *He wasn't a good breather*—something like that, not really knowing what she was confessing to but looking for an explanation of the fear and so on . . . And Lila, since she would be blamed for having reared Nonie in such a way that this had happened—and, also, since she would be blamed for having left Nonie alone with the baby—whispered and then perhaps shouted at the child, *Shut up, shut up, shut up* . . .

And forgave her.

But did not forget.

People have feelings. I'm not a bad person. Nonie was better for a while after we took you in; everyone nursed you, even me—me the least. I wasn't so good with babies—do you understand what I'm saying?—and Nonie was better for a while—a lot better. You were in such bad shape it didn't matter; no one would laugh at me—if things went wrong; at first, back then, no one could say I wasn't charitable. Bad-Lila-not-so-bad, isn't that it? Isn't that a good style for me? Maybe the first baby irritated her and she teased it too roughly, and it had a defect and would have died anyway, but it happened then. And the other was—I don't know what—an accident. Nonie's so proud, it's as good as murdering her to disapprove of her. Do you know what being realistic is? It means taking risks . . .

Moral risks.

You, she said, *you're no angel* . . .

Do I blame myself for my real mother's death—oh, not in my head, not anywhere in me that my will can reach—but down among the shadow truths? I have been told by three or four women that my real mother died of a bungled abortion: *She had you: she didn't want another child* . . . Lila, even when she was dying, said, *Nothing was simple* . . . *My whole life long* . . . *If you wanted something simple, you had to make it that way: simple costs money* . . . *I expect you to blame me: but I want to ask you a favor—I want to ask you to tell me now that you forgive me* . . .

Am I complaining that such people as Nonie exist? I do not see how existence can exist without Nonies. Without my being somewhat like her. Then, am I complaining about existence? Making a confession about my childhood? About myself? Am I describing the texture of the air of an actual moment?

You went after her—she suffered from you more than you did from her—although I suppose one can't keep track, one can't keep count . . . *The way things happen.*

Am I complaining about the obscure omnipresence of *evil*? Perhaps. I am not aware mostly that I am complaining that she behaved too much in a fashion so openly true to the life in her—so true to herself—that much of the time I knew myself in certain ways too soon because it was in relation to her.

Childishly stripped of innocence—but given life. Perhaps I am not complaining. Perhaps I am trying to say that human diversity is not a minor matter and that it has to do not just with efficacy and Babel and such matters but with moral reality . . .

I think that we are all like Nonie—but not exactly—and part of me is in reaction to her—culture and belief and will . . . And that good and evil—and fear—and reality have this other element, these elements of existence, this elemental existence, this eternal and sneaky presence all the time, in and for all of us . . . Lila said once—she was in some weird, upward-mounting, joyous-mouthed mood—*I'll tell you how I feel: anyone who doesn't live in this household is a LIAR* . . .

I.e., if you are not here with us, you are lying . . .

Am I saying, then, that Nonie was complex enough to be known differently as a fact or facet of *nature* and not simply an accident of my adoption—a family accident—an aberration?

Yes.

But then, in the flickering eyeliddedness of thought—of private judgment—the answer is no . . .

I start in innocence, and shallowly . . . I have been drawn in to saying these things . . . The shadows deepen around me in this garden . . . No: not quite, not quite that. In the shadowy afternoon, one says only that Nonie was not complex enough in regard to me: she was bad to me too often . . .

But then I am swept along in the current of associations, the slant-footed abruptness of simultaneities, or seeming simultaneities in the strange motions of the moments where I am drenched with the conviction that there is no point in lying about what people are . . . Why make yet more mysteries and lay up a store of future bad actions when there are real mysteries enough whatever we do? Without the false ones of sentimental maundering about what people are and what innocence is (a device, a technique, not an actuality except as a comparative matter)? Why not be *sensible* about these matters?

Guilt is not simple . . . Blame, therefore, ought never to be simple . . . Stories are not simple at all if they contain any truth in them . . . any truth in them whatsoever . . .

Was Nonie innocent—in the beginning? One learns innocence as a charm against one's own helplessness as an infant. One is helpless as an infant without innocence . . . And there is a *comparative* innocence to be considered . . . an ignorant, myth-ridden, comparative powerlessness—toyed with, experimented with . . .

There is how you feel.

Then there is what others judge you to be.

And innocence clung to becomes a social matter, a form of rent one pays; it is like a sticker on one's forehead allowing one to enter the house in a certain privileged way . . .

But then character, and the shape of character, the shape of one's social class, of one's social rank, take on a peculiar and singular shape: one's mark . . . Lila said, drugged and ill, *Nonie has the mark of Cain on her* . . .

Who doesn't?

It's true that I am a pacifist—in part. I became one. It's true that Lila used her hands for nothing—she didn't cook or sew or touch people . . . or slap anyone . . .

Nonie: *I'm not a booky Jew. I'm a tennis player.*

Momma's and Nonie's wit—and bitterness—toward moral chivalry and the world of intellect made them partisans of common sense.

I don't read; I'm practical.

And: *Nonie had a pet. She let it die, too.*

To punish herself, Momma?

Me, I don't care for Nonie; I think everything's better since she's dead. But if I posit her as deciding-to-live, if I posit EVERYONE as causing moments of horror and defeat in numbers of other people as Nonie did, and if I believe that the grounds of faith, and forgiveness, are only human and need not be fine or pure, then I'm left with a resigned and filthy kinship to her.

The two of you, peas in a pod, after all. Well, who's an angel?

Momma said that.

She said, *I'm not as bad as Nonie is . . . Goddamn it, I am not . . .*

But I am, sometimes, goddamn it, sometimes I am.

I remember when Nonie was *fifteen going on sixteen,* how she practiced in front of the mirror and taught herself to look, and in a way be, virginal, and to have a frightening unrough aspect of never-doing-any-harm.

It was a very specific look and in the style of a given era . . .

The underneath is poking out—it's peeking out—it's part of how she's pretty: she's a two-souled, complicated, duplicitous, and punishing and mindless *lover*, a *fearless* lover, a peerless infatuate, fully and finally and quickly enraged: a young, *normal* girl . . . But how can you love anything if you're unwilling to be frightened?

And: *She was bound and determined to be fearless as long as she could . . . I don't understand Nonie*, Momma says. *What no one tells a parent would fill a book . . .*

What children do when they're alone is as strange as what absolute rulers do on their thrones. Imagine a single overriding heartbeat that commands the universe of a house.

The maid we had was sick that day. When I came home, the infant was in the crib, fat and still—it had no marks on its little self: I can talk about it but I can't think about it—it's the one thing I can't think about. Maybe I took some of it out on you, Wiley: you never looked like you could die. I came home, and Nonie was in the hall, and she said, "Momma, nothing happened. I'm sleepy."

The death of an infant.

If only one had died and not *two*.

Maybe Nonie could bear some *guilt*. But then the second time, innocent or not, the unpracticed mind went haywire in her.

Or she had been insensately brave—a monster of bravery, a girl Achilles, a strong-hearted girl loose in the world. Unkind. Murderous—secretive early, and dishonest, and brave early.

I know what Daddy said: *Well, we'll manage, we'll fix things up; it's not the end of the world.*

And Lila: *I advise you, no one will pay attention if we just drop the subject.*

The reality-turned-into-a-subject, into a moment-regarded-in-various-ways, is partly a device. Nonie is a wronged girl, a wronged soul. I mean, in truth, and then, in sarcasm, it is not true. Nonie is sensitive, mistreated—this is said or claimed as the ground for moral charity: is it moral charity? She is a spoiled and affluent girl. She is lordly, cheerful, obtuse—enraged. Enraged, she insists on her own happiness. She is forgetful—she's without a future . . . *People have to live . . . We live day by day . . . We do the best we can . . .*

Nonie has no drama, no story at all: she has only triumphs—and *Normality* . . . Is that possible in all the moments of childhood as a real part of life? If it is not possible, then what does she do to her mind in order to believe that it is not only possible but that it happened to her?

If you ask me, it hurts too much to think; I'd rather be natural.

We are playing one time and she says, *I don't like your face—here, wear this pillow . . . It's just a game . . . don't cry . . .*

Active, bright-cheeked, wooden-faced Nonie. Unredeemed, nervous, shrill-voiced *little Jew,* a lying lynx mask of yellow glass blurs her eyes. A piece of futurity, a child, she carries in her a large part of Lila and of S.L.: *We love her. We love her plenty—till the cows come home . . . Up to a point, and then I have to draw the line.*

It was taken seriously when she got upset about my disdain for her and she shouted: LISTEN TO ME—HE NEVER TAKES MY SIDE, HE DOESN'T ACT LIKE MY BROTHER, HE DOESN'T CARE WHAT HAPPENS TO ME.

When she was younger, Nonie was right in there, among one's emotions, one's reasons. She looks a little sneaky, a little scared, a little triumphant, but she's there, she matters. She looks sad, too, and enraged: she wants to matter more than she does. Lila says, *She's my daughter—I'm stuck. Well, I'm not going to throw her out the window . . . Or my life, neither.* She sees Nonie as becoming finer if she, Nonie, can learn to be less autonomous, *if she would only learn to listen*—she would be more obedient then: swindleable sometimes: listening is giving in.

"Wiley, would you do something for me? Would you do *anything* for me?" Nonie asked me that . . .

The more Nonie "loves," the more secret and "passionate" in request she becomes, the more she has an aura of request . . . She asks and extorts: *Take-my-filth; I have your virtues because I love you.* A kind of competition: its one-sidedness makes it a romance—dreamlike in wakeful hours. "Love" as competition. As ambition. "Love" is here. *Nonie doesn't know how to love.* What is anyone's life, what is *my* life worth if it is at *Nonie's* disposal, her willful disposal, if at any point, her argument, her emergencies are as she defines them?

When Nonie looks shiny and well tended, she gets more admiration; it is perceptible that her value increases—she is what-she-is plus the efforts of those who tend her. Nonie, pink haunches, bitten fingernails, when she's Nonie-who-doesn't-have-to-lift-a-finger, when she's an angel and *perfect,* grades us loudly on how well we nurture her because we are responsible then for how virtuous she can risk being. *I need this-or-that: make Wiley help me.*

Daddy said, *Lincoln freed the slaves, Hon.*

If her eyes are canny when she leans back in a chair and stares over at us, past her slightly bulbous torso, and uses her clearly compromised innocence to make us *kiss her ass*, her claims of innocence, her privileges as a child, then what have we become?

Daddy says, in fake ruralese, *Don't get too big for your britches, sweetie, or the goblins'll git you good if you don't watch out.*

Nonie says, "Daddy's jealous of me, too!"

She's perceptive in her way.

If you generalize too intently from yourself and your experiences, if you make your tics into universals, you claim the more than somewhat *royal* privileges of madness . . .

Momma says to Nonie, "You're too pudgy to have such a swelled head—*dearest* . . ."

"IT'S PURE JEALOUSY!" Nonie says. "I'm not wrong—*you are!*"

Does Nonie become . . . *pure* . . . when she plays tennis? She says she's not bored then—she feels good: that's a state of piety for her.

Human politics, if controlled, seem to her, to me, a kind of beauty. They become a kind of beauty—the future opened and mutual like that—but it's a little rough.

Lila says, *I like the last laugh as well as anyone.*

Daddy: *He who gets the last laugh better laugh quietly, or the goblins'll git him, I betcha.*

Nonie's your enemy if you laugh at her.

Never-Tease-Nonie is your nickname, Daddy said to her. *Be a good sport.*

"I'm not going to be a good sport. I have my self-respect to think about."

Nonie has her self-respect often. Maybe.

We expect policemen to die for Nonie but they may not want to if they know her. It's better for her if people think of her as A Daughter, A Girl, A Woman, rather than if they look very hard at her.

I don't get to dislike Nonie—she is a *sister*—but isn't it unfair to treat human love as if you had less choice toward it than you have toward dislike directed at you? I mean, if it *has* to be assigned to this one and that one, whereas dislike is freed, is part of your free will, isn't love insulted? Can't I love where I choose? In life, it's disgusting to treat Nonie as if she were pious or reliable, as Anne Marie is. If I'm supposed to love her because she's in trouble, that's no good—if you give Nonie special rights because of an emergency, she'll create fake emergencies. Emergency is a social form for her, a device of hers.

When it's clear to Nonie that she's not innocent enough for Daddy, that he will not die to preserve or enhance her life, she becomes frantic.

She suffers then. He is not a mystery to her, or foreign, and so she finds him to be just at times. She knows him and she wants him to love her, and she gets angry and unpersuaded about everything, maybe *strange-in-the-head* if he makes it too clear that her habits and systems have worn him out.

Here she is, reading the comics aloud as if to show how well she reads and how naïve she is, while Daddy reads his paper in a chair near her. She lies on the floor and chants the words—she's playing with images of innocence: she is nine and cold, eleven and cool and malign, thirteen and moody—Daddy recognizes her courtship: he embraces her thoughtlessly, heatedly; and she laughs at him and is appalled and observant in her coquetry of guilt and shameless virginity—a virginity she will improve on when she sets to work on it, when she's sixteen. She tests her power over him in his heat—she does it by rebuking his heat. Momma laments, *Why isn't she smarter? Why can't she learn how to handle him? It would make my life so much easier if she was only a little smarter.* Lila means Daddy's bored and wants to have *interests-in-life.* Why can't Nonie be his interest in life? But he doesn't like Nonie's using her body's power (and his blood in her) and the past in order to command him. He ignores her even when listening to her . . . He tries to enjoy her, he does the best he can, but he gets bored, he gives up . . . He lies about this . . . Daddy says to her, *It's worth every cent I have just to see you happy.* When he's angry, he says to her, *You're so greedy I don't think you'd spare ten cents to save my life.*

Once when he was angry he accused me: *Would you give ten cents to spare your sister's life?*

Would *I*? No.

We are not guilty all the time of everything and neither was she. People are good or half good or a quarter good and it changes all the time. The addition can come to a different total *all* the time. Consider the blind political reality of people who want to be good but who are, also, *realistic*? How much is explained by that? *Listen* (as my mother used to say): What does guilt consist of? What is a fair trial like? We begin our lives, formatively, among the necessary lies told to children. And we have children's wishes then and, to some extent, always—this is part of human *goodness* or is associated with it . . . families and truths . . . those lies, that care (such as it is), and the rest of the like matters. One half knows one is being lied to but the lies are the truth, too, they are the truth of one's childhood.

And the lies are told us by people who are fully alive in their lives, and their lives are going on, and they are not subordinate to us in the drama then or in any story in an actual moment but, instead, they are in the physical and moral and emotional scale, *giants* compared to us. Twelve people on a jury had twelve versions of that and have grown up differently and have changed differently—and to various degrees, their sense of goodness and of right and wrong and the ways they are, also, *realistic* . . . In the shadow biography I have, I was born and two years later my real mother died and I was adopted by the Silenowiczes of Alton, Illinois. *We can all agree with that. Go on.* Respectable people, upper-middle-class—not much like me. *Yes and no* . . . Some people disliked them; some people loved them . . . *No one is perfect* . . . If no one is perfect, the flaw, the flawed elements in each of us, are they criminal? Do they smack of crime? Should we, do you think, think of the human as containing *Original Sin?* If so, then in a world of *Original Sin*, what is a family, actually?

Perhaps I should have asked this first . . .

This sense of how one begins to know things . . . Of how one begins to live.

THE RUNAWAY SOUL

Ora: New York: 1956

With Ora in New York—in 1956—far from Nonie in Alton in 1932 and the early specifics of pain—I am in the invented unreason of love with the past left behind like an acquaintance who has moved away and who writes and calls irregularly. I am twenty-six; one's youthful self is burning in the heavyish wind of one's momentum—one is aflame a bit, in a way, in the narrow streets of Manhattan among the car fumes and in the sight of others and their judgments.

At this time my life felt dreamed to me, dreamed by others as well as by me, while being clearly, achingly, brightly real, a shiny and civilized actual life, shopwindow-mirrored, and daily experience here near the dreamed-of skyline and in real air.

Tonight Ora wept in her sleep. I was awake and lying beside her, nude, reading a book I didn't like, making theories about why it was bad, drawing contingent conclusions about its notions and its technical lacks . . . And I was thinking about fame as a branch of politics and about prowess at making money as a branch of good sense and about determining opinions and setting ranks for things as they come into existence in the culture as a curious branch of ambition. And what flashed into my mind for a tiny portion of a moment was that it was Nonie who was weeping. I knew it wasn't Nonie. I knew by then in my life that my mind played games, that my mind, my memory—even my prick—my eyesight, my speech and dexterity at games—each of my attributes had a degree of independence from my direct will. My self, mysterious and busy, manages to function almost as a junior commander—at least, mine did. I repeat: I was twenty-six years old.

It seemed that one's basic self was Nonie-esque, or Ora's was; and Ora and I had graduated, not quite to selflessness, but to something in regard to one another; and she might grieve for any of a number of reasons . . . But for that graduation, that nakedness of dependence, she might grieve over that, particularly . . .

It was rational, but it wasn't any sort of solid thing of a sensible sort, the queer presence of Nonie in that intimate moment; her brief presence was more a bodiless film, a definition of the human (and of possibility and of despair)—it defined us as imperfect.

Or as not-angels.

It seemed an important negation, semi-hallucinatory, scary—that Nonie was in my head. *My* independence seemed slight, at least in the rush of the 'truth' if I can call it that—of exigencies of breathing and of sanity, so-called, in the real world. I cannot readily believe that I am alive. Or that I am real to others. I am startled that I have lived long enough that how I feel about things is a grown-up matter. I never expected to last to this age. Ora, weeping in her sleep, is lying partly on top of me, asleep, and not a small woman, and saltily weeping. Ora, almost every night really, that year, sleeps on top of me. Was it that Nonie-in-me persecuted Ora? Did Ora pay because of my past with Nonie? For a brief, escaped, maybe ludicrous and pointless fragment of time, I saw Ora as Nonie-esque herself—not entirely—but would I have loved her otherwise? It is Ora weeping—unheartbrokenly—*industriously* . . . Ruminatively. When I say Ora slept-on-top-of-me, I mean, really, her torso rested, most of it, not on the mattress but on me—on my ribs, my legs. Ora is five seven or so, a biggish young woman, and big-boned. She is boldly bony. And a good sleeper. I was reading (as I said) and she was deep inside her body beside me, asleep. She stirred, and then, in her sleep, she moved a silken-skinned, fine-limbed arm over me—my ribs, my chest, my neck. Dreaming flutters in her veins, in her fingers. The ache of someone else's reality being near me hustles me into feeling my own ignorance—it is my ignorance that seems solid to me, to be my bones and reliable, to be like the banks for a creek that rushes by me in the dark. My ignorance seems untime-ridden but it is time-ridden . . . It was my degree of ignorance-that-night that heard Nonie crying in Ora.

Knowledge in an actual moment shivers and shimmers—and changes. Are you decisive? Knowledge has a feel: moist and dark, a slippery darkness, or eellike, or like a ghost—or an unsteady light . . . The contingent rebelliousness of the light of opinion: everyone attacks my opinions. The absurd adventure of paying attention to what one thinks, that means having a career, that means being a grown-up in a scale of would-be masterful agency and urgency—a childhood sense—but this refers to one's present size and one's present circumstances.

The knowledge comes to a child as if in a vacant lot in a permanent twilight, probably uncertainly wondering what happens if one is right, wondering at the metallic electricities of the mind, wondering if one is crazy.

I never saw Nonie cry. I wanted to look inside Ora's head to see what she felt—if her crying in her sleep *was* related to something in Nonie. Was she like Nonie? I wanted to know with some certainty what her lying on top of me signified. And her tears. My knees ached with my sense of vulnerability at my being ignorant and susceptible to accusations of ignorance . . . *Do I love her?* This goes to my knees; my knees get shaky. I don't know enough to answer . . . In the end, I don't know much . . .

The week before, I had been reading *The Great Gatsby* again, a young man's book. Young Fitzgerald, in his twenties then, had written of glamour. Ignorance was not glamourous or was it? And Ora's leg, which was lying like a drugged boa constrictor without scales or menace, on top of mine, moved. I was prickly with restlessness at our closeness —the remembered text in the mind and the one I was reading that night more erratically like the sight of trees in an orchard in winter when one is running down a row of them, between two rows of trees, actually, twigs and wintry light like the alphabet and words. And this other moving, shifting thing of the flesh, of our bodies, hers and mine in contradistinction . . . Her leg lifted a bit and climbed and swung itself over my farther knee and the lower thigh counting from the central Rome of my face. Her sleeping, warm-skinned leg lay across both my legs, pinning me. Absurd. Was this the association with Nonie? I laughed a little. Ora was socially unlike Nonie. Ora's father owned a house in New York in the Village and a shabby plantation with a run-down house and half a dozen tenants' cabins on it—this was on the Eastern Shore of Maryland. One of her grandmothers had a large place on an island near Cuttyhunk. And the other a handsome little place on the top of a ridge in Connecticut. Sometimes her smell—actually, the array of her odors suggested, or even were, those of places and things such as those places, places where she had lived—dim rose-garden odors or budded oak-leaf smells or an odor of something like locust bark and a lawn—the smells of different parts of her body. Odors from her grandmothers' houses—of sheets aired in the sun and salt air and I don't know what, woods and a quarry pond—and me in "love" and caught between intimate things and large things: now the odor of nipples—of armpits—of abdominal skin . . . Her lower self was delicately semi-squeezed by her bent behind in its ladyish amplitude against me; she shifted her weight in her sleep, pressing heavily on one cupped wing of my pelvis behind the surface of skin and muscle. She was arched, one leg still on the mattress and one arm and most of the rest on me.

Distant states of *intimacy* and an accompanying world of discourse and opinion, inward shouts, inner exclamations, interior whispers—and accompaniment inside my head—as mysterious in me as in her. Further motions hide a certain shabby interest.

The nerves, the mouthy eyes (eating the sight of her) relay to noisy surfaces in the mind, decoded, half-interpreted sexual thoughts which echo as if they were inside tunnels of comparison or in mineshafts of associations. She moved thoroughly on top of me, her odors, heats, bones, flesh, body orifices, protrusions. And mine. One notices this stuff. I grunted with the reality. Naked and slightly odorous—and more than a little available sexually in her sleep—she breathed; her muscles, the exudations . . . her odor . . . An almost farfetched suppleness possessed her in her sleep.

Her sleep is altered by what we are to one another.

Naked Ora. Naked Wiley. But then she wept—in her tampered-with sleep.

"Ora! Ora!" I whispered and then I spoke more loudly. I was unsure what I was feeling. "Love"—intimacy—as a slightly foreign consternation, a little boring, perhaps; hallucinations are approaching, real to the flesh, *perhaps*, but are they welcome just now? Like a general observing the topography of a place, I observed her from above although I was mostly under her, but an aerial view is what I had, as if I were floating in the dark air outside the sphere of light around me and her in the bed. She was faintly on her side but her shoulders and cunt were flatly on top of me. Sexual hallucination hummed quietly in me—or imagination, if you prefer. Her arm that extended over my chest touched the bed on the other side of me: that arm rested on the side of its wrist. Her hand was bent ineffectually and curled upward into the air. And her breasts and ribs, the odd skin-covered motioniness of that warm and complexly vibrating and slightly oozy-tissued and somewhat hottish group of structures pressed against my own chest—my half-athletic, pectoralled, sometimes-praised chest . . . I mean some kids at college had commented on it. But I was saying her torso on me was warm, or even hot. There was her futilely cupped and sleeping hand; and here was her hair—long, straight, dark hair—some of it in my mouth and on my eyelids and tangled in my eyelashes and tickling my ears . . . Her head rested on my neck—and partly on my chin and lower cheek. I bent my lips sideways to kiss her hair and forehead experimentally. In those days, I often prayed usually for the will and stamina to see to it that an outcome to events did not come about only through my weaknesses. Now I prayed more questioningly: *Is this going to turn out okay?* For me, for her—for long-term designs of history or Deity toward meaning. *Give me a sign—if you can bear to. What does she want?* (Ora.) Partly that meant what-did-she-intend . . . Her breath, her mouth—are a giant, fluttering moth—are an infant thing.

Me as waker and her sleeping, I was aware, tremendously, of the tremendous opposition between our states—it is almost as if we had two different kinds of flesh. Or money and fame as *wakefulness* and flesh as *sleep* . . . And then the thought past the one of *Dear God, I don't understand my life,* to the sense that *truth* and a book were all very well but reality was real. This wasn't as simpleminded as it sounds since I'd been advised, perhaps dishonestly, of one's *greatness,* so to speak . . .

I am here in the moment; her breath flicks—on my skin—it is Ora's breath. Her breast moves wobblingly with her breath. Her left nipple presses and recedes beneath my right nipple. *Is this love? Is this true love? Am I lucky? Are we part of* A REAL LOVE STORY? Her breath in the odd silence of the room has in it that further odd quality of sleep—of innocence . . . I am less suspicious of her than when she is awake. The peculiar unevenness of her uneven breaths in the shatteringly empty silence of her inattention, it was as if one exploded rhythmically in a confused dreaming about her when one was awake. Her body is a softish, anatomical coral reef in which bits of dream flittered . . . Not innocent? Adult and meritorious in the world? Her sleep is a form of truce, an unconscious scrimshaw of breath, semi-peaceful, an artifact of a false peacetime.

I am a bony young man. Her distance—from me, inside her sleep—marks an actual vulnerability: *I am not afraid of death, Wiley.* She has said that but I know she is afraid of death . . . I know she is afraid of it sometimes—does her fearfulness stop entirely when she sleeps? The factual part of the moment allowed me no observation of this fearlessness in Ora. The sun, the season, the climate of the moment, Ora with her faint veining of peace and then the graining of restlessness-in-sleep and of past stuff between us and then on, by association, to Nonie are an obscurity that becomes an insanity of tickling her, half waking her. I push her off me. Me breathing through my nose and only half noticing this idle, unwicked, uncivil contact with her body, her dreams. I am fastidious as a villain. Unmasculine. Unable to live. My own *sane,* separate, somewhat desperate, but unpersuaded breathing is unlike hers . . . I wait for her to wake . . . The twin elements of plausibility and of wish are loosened in her . . . This thing of being merely real—whether I am or not—is like holding onto a dock when you are swimming at night, say. To understand, to see, to feel, as (now) half-asleep with obscure impulses and concerns about personal meaning is to feel privately, uncorrectly that *I love her*: it balloons in a vacuum of no comparison with her feelings, in a vacuum of her not being there. Its quality as feeling is thicker but less actual than feelings I have when she is awake.

She and I as embodiments of romantic or sexual love: well, I am unpersuaded of our fatedness; but as revealed now, tonight, in the reality of this intimate moment, in the light of this intimacy we have, I am persuaded of life's offering me a momentarily *happy ending* which is remarkable.

Or not a *happy ending* but an episode of *Reward* (with some penalties built in).

What, as I blinked and breathed, was real in bed—on the white sheet alongside the partly-wakened brown-skinned (dark-complexioned, tanned) Ora, her weight, her breath touching me—and she was already shifting her weight onto me again—was not that the moment announced itself as *supposedly* happy, or happy (or as something in between), it had announced itself as redolent of, or stained with, Nonie-in-the-past: or as if rectifying the past. Ora is weeping in her sleep a second time, and her leg is on top of my leg and her head is on my chest and neck again. The nature of the self now—one's self as *Dearly Beloved*, one's first child—does not permit a sacrament of escape. One is anxious to have one's experiences. This is not an idolatry of the real so much as it is an attempt to locate (or just to peek at) earthly meaning. A breast squunched against an abruptly self-consciously flexed pectoral, her nipple moving on my skin—as does her sleeper's breath . . . a continuing *somber* hilarity . . . really a seriousness, her hair, youthful and rich, she is part of me, my hand strokes the fine hair of her upper legs, touches the magically darker, wounding reality of her hairy cleft, moistly sweaty, oiled . . . ready . . . I do see that I am, for a while, here with this extraordinarily beautiful woman whom I distrust.

I pushed her away. I built a barrier of pillows, all the while breathing with sexual lightness, that approximately earnest unlaughing giggle of sexual authority that contradicted the tonality of not-fucking and which suggested the different—and other—hilarity of the act which one is holding back from.

Her prompt encroachment on the pillows—was it heat? companionship? that drew her? She proceeds with unalert wit: a sea anemone, a dreaming octopus of a woman, Ora in her odd sleep.

She does not subside into semi-indifference. God, here comes her hand, right across the intervening space to where my balls lie on my thigh; the bulbous flicker of sexual reaction becomes male sexual availability, often a complicated matter. Manhattan is the place for this sort of sexuality—sexuality is subject to place . . . She and I, she dreamed and I hallucinated in incomplete agreement—and in rebellion to ordinary, unsexual life. Or we dreamed in tandem. We give each other clues—with our breath—about what we feel; we engage in mutual education terrifyingly; she is almost awake; we frightenedly share a widened sensorium now, a widened sense, binocular—two-souled, unspecifically gendered, not well-trained . . . What sort of *joining* did we have? An eerie sexual contagion. An uneasy rivalry of different consciousnesses? The affection-riddled reality of proximity? As on a school playground?

The overlap (and dependency) of the moment—conscious man, semi-conscious woman—was weird enough that some adviser in me warned, *Don't look, don't look.* I was at some limit of mine of sexual bearability—like an apprentice surgeon watching an operation in a hospital and wanting to join in there, in the bright, hideous light, the liquescent reality, the insult, the trespass, the intrusion.

Are you real, Wiley? You're inhuman . . . Before birth, in the symmetry of electric dramas between child and mother, the vast nervous respond of her around me, it was a question, a reality, whether I was human or not. The nervous resolution of uneasy appetite, the wobbling and ebbing of breath and of the body's state, the sudden warming in desire, the increase of it, of response—it is a breathingly murmurous rhyme of companionship . . . The eeriness of being dreamed is part of the "joke" that when she wakes I will be here in my body, not banished like a figure in a dream.

And I am not constrained by the plausibility requirements of her sleep. By the structures of riddling storytelling of her dreams. I am independent and strange to her mind—I am goddamned real.

Sleep on. Sleep on, Ora.

This one night was after I had started to become famous—no, I had begun to be known, merely known. Her theft of my autonomous heat to feed the *plausibility* requirements of hallucinatory romance in her semi-dreams or in her dreams—in those weird gardens, the theft of me—for her life—in her mind—why should this become apparent to me as a dare on her part? The reality of the fernlike murmuring and dispersions and malproportions of the metrics of her breath as a sleeper, contrarily, tames me. The half-melted walls of my independence reflect the ridiculous rhyming of the murmurously sensual grammar I have with earlier events in my life: the unlikely uncrude music of a mammal's tie to an ocean, salty and pulsing—a somewhat shared blood and heat—to something beyond that ocean and heat—I was afraid of it—of us . . . of her. I was disdainful and warm . . . a comic snob . . . and at home in it all—or half-at-home in it with her. I was not afraid and did not feel odd. Partly erected and in a kind of muttery-buttery heat, I hear Ora breathe—and think how in this affair, her mouth and body are half mine—they are shared with me. I can do what I like—in a way.

When she wakes a bit more, I will have to deal with the presence of her will. The thing of our being like Holland, with great walls closing us off sacramentally from the wills and true histories of others in the world.

Her body and mouth and sleep are half my own mouth and body and sleep—I breathe loudly, I sort of sigh, to locate and identify, to reclaim myself. It is a marsh; one practices a husbandry toward a reedy commingling of land, sea, sky, in a fen, an unclear place. I have my own, independent footing, entangled. It is as if I, or we, drowned, in a way, at times in this morass. Now we breathe each other's stale air—our mouths are close—and anyone's sense of the separation of our wills, of our having separate destinies, is mistaken. But we are jealous of each other. We are separate.

Her dreams, her body and its cleft, are literally inset with my pulse when I come yet closer to her where she lies atop the pillows. The tempo of her dreams, of the scenes she is dreaming, comes from my breath. My pulse is embodied in the night stuff of her dreaming. A sense of her dreams and of her body and *our affair* tears me, tore me; I felt a moist wholeness and a burning woundedness and sweaty pride and a near-hemorrhage of the ordinariness and specialization of being young; I felt an agonized tingling of the flesh. My no longer independent and not now hidden soul tears since my soul, in some ways, in a lot of ways, my soul prefers her to me. I jerked still closer to her on my side, and I poked her with my forefinger. And I kissed her. And I partly *poked* her near her crotch with the begging-and-threatening thing. I poked her with my knee, too. The fact of my wakefulness, *my* factual state, humanly, recognizably, is not like hers. She sat up in bed: abruptly. The mattress throbbed and shuddered with her, with our private motions. Beautiful Ora. Beauty is dimensional and has duration. And it flowers and recedes;

it alters with time, quickly, in each second, actually; it is not an empty factor. It is not merely another element in someone.

I said submergedly, oppressed: "You out of your mind? You're out of your mind again; you're playing octopus—Ora, I can't sleep or read if you do that . . ."

I sometimes can say things the first time I attempt to say them . . . Ora can't do that. She uses slight variations of inflection and of her eyes to attach the things she's said before to her present use of them in a somewhat New England–executively-intellectual way; and she doesn't really say things for the first time. She goes from earlier speeches to later ones.

She is half-asleep. I have startled her into a kind of automatonlike life. She gives an example of the rehearsed form of her saying something she has said nine, ten, eleven times before: "I was alone too much as a child, I don't ever want to be alone again." Then to me, to *me*, she said, as if I had said something other than the stuff I had said, "DON'T DO WHAT?"

"You're lying on top of me in your sleep again . . ."

Not automatically, she said, "I trust you . . ."

That is one of a number of things she says to me *sincerely* and which is not entirely true.

I can feel in her—as I could when she slept and encroached on me and I observed her exploringly and driftingly—I can feel in her a profound emptiness, depths, depths of willed blankness, a power of The Nothing. In the relentless firmness of her flesh, emptiness is a kind of waiting beauty, part of a tactical will of readiness for adventure—adventures with men and with women and with ideas—of a sort that I cannot have . . .

Ignorance as the changeable bones of one's powers of observation and a kind of faith in me equals her thing of being empty and young: a stonelike ruthlessness: cold-nerved will: she'd had a kind of schooling in will as a personage—a social-class thing. I love her. I have a strong will. Behind the insolence of her beauty is the extraordinary inhumility of the enormous waiting of her kinds of ambition—ambition of such a far-flung and far-off, not uncommon but unexpected kind, that it is insulting toward me and toward blighted-lipped intellectual women and others except when she relents; and this is tinged with an inherited (a finely taught) ability-to-rule.

What she is is mirrored motionfully in me, so we are similar oddly although different in gender—I am stained by maleness—a thief of her, a reflection. What we are is lovers.

But our being together rests on her will: she is an oldest child. I feel I am unfit for a human tie and I rely on her judgment that I am fit for this one.

But beyond that was something unexpected: MY insolence, MY arrogance—an odd, not entirely ignorant *commandingness,* mine from the start: *This is the one I want . . .* Or: *This is the one I wanted . . . And here she is . . .*

One time, when she was sad—her mother had made her sad—and I had made things worse—I'd said, *Just tell your mother to fuck off, Ora*—she said, "Why bother to live?"

She hadn't meant it except to convey a dull hint about the slurry of the stuff she felt. I repeated her remark to her—with a cold inflection, deadpan, meaning I was the reason, and she said, "Oh, I'd live for you if I could—I will live for you." Back then I said, "No. Don't do that. I wasn't saying it to change you—I don't manipulate people."

But I'd stolen that remark of hers, not as a serious question but as an idiom for sadness. I stole great areas of my life from her, as, before her, I had stolen things and mannerisms from others; I stole my ambition and my willingness to live mostly from her lately.

So now, *late at night,* having waked her, I said, "Why bother to live?"

It wasn't clear even to me what my teasing her meant or if I wanted so badly to be understood and welcomed that I simply used that remark as a warm joke-thing, rebuking her and welcoming her, teasing her into response.

She hated male ego. And male clumsiness. But, being well-bred as such things go in America, she was not clearly jealous of men—well, maybe of men who were successful and *potent* without her help. With a kind of ribald mockery and genteel patience, she made room for what she disliked in me (as a man), made room in certain ways and to a certain degree—and this was a big part of what she called *LOVE.* I couldn't have said this back then, at least not in this way, but I knew this, knew it in the tissues of my body, and I didn't think it *was LOVE.* I knew it as a chemical smokiness of the soul. I was sure she knew it too. Before she could make room for me, I started to laugh in the almost nonstop, occasionally maniac-manic hilarity I felt at being-with-her—some of that was disappointment. I often laugh when I am nonplussed at reality. I am old for my age in some ways and a child in other ways.

This laugh was weird and baritone—musically elaborate and compelling—sexual, I realized halfway through.

She said, "What is it? Why are you laughing?" She was sexually stirred by it . . . Stirred? As by a flickering spoon.

In the complicitous, semi-dissolved, complicated antagonism then, I asked, "Are we *normal*, Ora?" Still laughing, faking the laughter a little, pushing it along, prolonging it—part of it was real—it was sort of pruned and displayed—I wanted to be *earnest*, but, ever since college, I was helplessly ironic toward earnestness. It seemed dirty . . . too sexual. Bullying.

"No: we're not normal, we're lucky," she said in her ruling-class way, a ruling-the-world, thin-flanked, maybe gorgeous dowager-to-be . . . modern . . . aware of the sexual currents now—now pretty much awake, huge-eyed; more maneuverable than I was, maybe faster.

Maybe falser. I hear the thud of the rough fuzzy boardlikeness of her breath rasp in her throat—sexuality does that. To her. She disapproves of sexual games—*foreign la-di-da*—and costumes and the like feeling (or thinking) the sexual thing had enough draw or magnetism or gravity or strong or weak-and-dancing force and that, for her, true sex, the truer sexuality, lay in the social identity and beggarlike recession, or retreat, or abdication into simplicity—she longed for no tools or specificity of daydream knowledge or hallucination . . . Perhaps, too, this was a safety thing or a test thing: an experiment—one derived from experience of sexual props and the banishment of feelings and then the authority given the director. She is the older child in her family: *Do it in the body—or don't do it,* she has said—theoretically, discussing sexual theory. I had proposed nothing. I am fascinated and *stirred* by people who dress their lives and their moments in specifically sexual costume—but that includes someone dressing in simplicity and directness, like Ora. For us, her and me, she goes first in certain matters, into them, not as commanding officer, but as scout, as someone of experience and fine nerve endings and whose judgment is part of our judgment overall and is often the deciding judgment: we are each free, however, to be a, or the, *commanding officer* . . . We work this out as we go along: this was a common form of affair at college with exceptions among the very rich and also among very defensive kids where judgment rested in one of the pair and not in both. Soundlessly, like her bumping into furniture in a dark room, or avoiding it—she goes first in darkened places because she sees better in the dark than I do and she senses objects with a batlike high-pitched murmurous breathing that she does with a treble edging, or piping, to it; she doesn't always go first; sometimes she's frightened and I go first;

but one of our (twenty-eight thousand, two hundred and four) arrangements is that she gets to choose when she goes first in the dark and when she follows; and this moment, now, in bed, late, when she has just waked, counts as a moment in the dark; and she stirs, warm-flanked, as powerful a presence as a lioness or horse—or cow as in cowlike Hera, the Queen God, in Homer—in bed.

I can hear her soundlessly bumping into the thoughts that she is furnished inwardly with about sexuality and us; and—I can *hear* her mind—she chooses to take the lead.

I hear her mind existing buzzingly, circling and moving on, humming and thinking in the rigidly undeniable forward (in some sense *forward*) motion of the moment which nothing in me can ignore just now; and around which are gathered the seemingly unwandering, stone thoughts, or the shadows of such piers and finalities—it is as if she, partly pagan and cowlike like Hera the Queen, is also a dairymaid or child-girl, but anyway she is calculating in a cathedral—stained glass, fine arches and trefoils, the final form of a woods seen as an absolute thing in stone . . . It is unsuitable for the wandering, libidinous thought and for sexual heat, indeed.

I sense it. Or invent it while sensing something. My own sexuality is crudded up some or hidden or is defended in a labyrinth or by a combination lock; and hers unlocks it; or creates steps for it to emerge, sweet-stinking monster thing, semi-ancient, sloppy, whatever.

Or hers rolls on the cathedral-bedroom floor and I watch it and see my own body lying there; and it rises and comes over and enters my watchful body here. "Hi there," I whisper in her ear. I say it so inaudibly she can't really know what I am saying but she knows in some way. The breath of the syllable, the shape or form of the colloquium, tickles her —as if a wind ruffled her.

Maybe our minds nuzzle each other on some astral plane . . . Maybe I ought to say she nuzzled at my mind and woke me . . . I am —if you can pardon me for this—often taken as an acceptable sexual presence: for some people a final one . . . People stare at me in certain ways sometimes. Much of this is delusion, sexual hallucination, semi-absurd stuff, and some is not: part of what I look like is that I am the one who has had my life.

Well, many of her thoughts, the ones that hold pride of place in her, come from books; and some from talk; but a lot is family—family talk, I guess—her dowager grandmothers, her father and mother, her talkative aunts and firm-voiced uncles—the idea of family and of runaways, or an orphan, of a Jew: she has said of herself that she is a woman of opinion.

But mostly, and *oddly*, it seems to me that she and I, because we're young, because we're together, are, thoughts and all, primarily *nothing-so-far*, nothingness, uncostumed, solid-bodied, clever *nothingness* . . . uncertainty and will . . . a freshness of will . . . orchardy nothingness. I reflect her emptiness. A little dirtied on both sides. Also, nerves, hopes, experiences with each other: a little leapy, leapish—like young panthers —what-have-you—wild, a little wild sometimes.

She says now, as she said before, "You are unsafe, you are an unsafe person," but she is conflating me with darkness, with male will, with the sexual history of the species, and with her dreams before she woke up and with various things in her anyway and which do not relate to dreams.

I twitch, flinch, stiffen in potency of a degree—which I appreciate and am kinged by (as in the last row of a checkerboard)—and am unsteady on, as if on one stilt: this is inside the curious bubble of the reality of having a human potency, somewhat *democratically*—i.e., more gamblingly, less willed than if I were costumed, angrily brutal for real as playacting, and assertive on my own and without her.

That it is, in that sense, a free erection—as in a *free* country—and joint—and *nice*—but, of course, corrupt and based on various deals and inequities, that erects me further—I feel the moments pushing, in a linked way, in a kind of heat of linkage, or with an almost hot, or flame-heated linkage of what might be called *sexual effects*—the power, say, of her eyes now that they are open and then of the exposed breasts as vulnerability and pride and the thing between her legs like the top of the skull of a small cat and stirring catlike: it is a peninsular half-motion in which everything stirs: the wind of the passage of time lifts us, blows, moves—caresses us as if we were dozing on a train and a stranger or all the strangers there were very lightly kissing and stroking and gazing. I feel my height, my looks (such as they are), my inner strength (such as *it* is), my sexual opinions, my sexual rhythms and views on coming, my sexual depths as having been chosen by this weird wind of invisible and *foreign* attention to perform—to perform *sexually* . . .

The foreignness is, of course, in me, too . . . I am at some peninsular edge of myself: I blow and circle inwardly and, both, wait to perform and want to *see* and *feel*, as the audience, the performance here.

Her eyes—eyelashes, bony sockets, the warm, faintly oily gaze—meet mine which are—masked as far as my knowing what their gaze is: it is *moyen* sharp, their gaze, felt from inside—an erectile structure of sight touching a kind of broadcast-receiving thing or sound-receptor thing in her face, in her warmish eyes.

She says breathingly, "You are unsafe for children . . ." A not uncommon remark in my experience, a flirtatious remark, a lie, sexual flattery: something she's said to other men; something other women have said to me. She smiles in the light in the bedroom, drowning out the presence of remembered other eyes.

Her smile is an accomplishment—unhurried, tense, actorly-amused.

A lot of men have been infatuated with her—in love with her. Older men: some of them famous . . . Younger men. Able ones. She says to me when someone reveals to me part of her past with some man or other: *I was an object for him—a teenage trophy* . . . She never admits to having been a collector; but she has moods of confession, a bit movielike, of having been an adventurer-adventuress, an explorer of the jungle and a kind of girl Tarzan in these matters among others.

She has very handsome, unfragile hands—not a raccoon touch at all and not boyish: her eyes and neck and hands are those of a woman as young as some movie stars are who seem to be without age and without social background or social limits.

She is a hairless, large teddy bear and *as-if-great* movie comedienne and sexually liberated and partly commanding Scandinavian (or German) movie beauty—her hands have the curious authority of that unanimal thing: their touch—it is so odd—on my legs, on my abdomen, on my chest—suggest not an animal thing but a gift of jewelry—in a jungle—or a commanding companionship: the smallish hands of an intelligent man with some sort of anal-and-oral fixation: it is like that for a moment.

Then, feeling my breath, my eyes, my glance moving from her to the wall of the bedroom in a kind of embarrassment at her sexual nature and her sexual experiences which led to my having that kind of sense of her touch and after I look back in the oddity of our *friendly* (not melodramatic) sexuality, she becomes *demure-but-forthright,* as animal as a movie star who has that style and with hands like Scandinavian birds, coldly (or coolly) exotic.

This is a feeling, a sense-thing having shape as a name and as an opinion.

She takes being fucked very seriously—as a compliment and as a really vile insult, both those things; and the two jointly and mostly both present most of the time give off a peculiar radiance of flirtation, of foreplay, and not as a joke but as a form of potency or of potent *beauty*

. . . Or truth . . . And she is very alert to how you take it—her fucking with you, you as *the-fucker-of-record*—and she can't express all she feels about this except as posture, and the postures radiate that double-thing, a vibration back-and-forth, so she can't exactly be honest: she is honest first one way and then the other; and in the alternations she calculates within the cathedral—so to speak.

She says *flatteringly*, "Christ-who-is-God, we are unsafe people, you and I, Wiley . . . We have to be careful, we have to behave . . . We have to be careful to behave with each other . . ."

She likes to lay down the law. She likes to lecture. She has the soul of a headmistress in some ways. Her father, a man who talked well—he talked as a man who had gone to the famous private schools and college he had gone to would talk if he meant to be known for his talk; he had a social-class tone; and he was also sort of movie-earthy, sort of like an ex-journalist and lobbyist, someone who had partly given up his social-class stuff, he said, *We have no religion in our family anymore; we have only a persistent belief* . . . A persistence of—*a belief in something: a lot of that is belief in ourselves: we do pretty well in the world—and we have for a number of generations now . . . My ancestors were ministers for two hundred years and then they saw the light and became rich—that's Calvinism for you . . . I would say my daughter suffers from the profound nihilism of a readiness to live at any price—do you understand me? She includes suicide as an adventure . . . And a broken heart . . . We have many many traditions we've gotten rid of; we have some traditions we've kept; we can't be nobodies even if we tried . . . We have abilities, they run in our family, not in all of us, I must say. We have some recognition from the world . . . We ourselves do not care about family or possessions . . . We are merely people who have had our kind of history, our place in history . . .*

Her family? She is unfamilied in a sense. Very familied obviously. She takes no orders from them at all. In her emptiness pulses the extreme isolation of her quite extreme beauty—you don't have to believe me about its being so extreme: you can wait and see how you feel about it. The history of her looks is a history of events that is told in *her* tones only—the history of her physical reality. She has the corresponding fortress nature you might expect of blasphemy and of distance—nihilism, education, strength and readiness—nihilism of a kind as an extreme beauty—*People don't act very well*, she has told me—not nihilism then as a fashion.

But I can't have her be nihilistic if I depend on *her* . . .

God oh God God oh God God . . .

She said, "Don't you like being close? I hate sleeping alone—(*uh, eh*: she made little glottal sounds)—my dreams worry me . . ."

She has said that she dislikes being praised because praise is often a way people have of laying unfair responsibility on you. We don't praise each other, she and I. Instead, I, for instance, fail to believe in her torment—that's a form of praise. And she believes in our happiness and that I am human—that's a form of praise. She says, "I was dreaming, I was dreaming of Joe Stalin and Casanova and a cockroach—of Mozart: he was sort of cockroachy—I don't like him. I was afraid of Stalin. Lillian Hellman shot Charles de Gaulle with a gun she had hidden up her tush . . ." Ora unfocusses her eyes while she recites, or invents, her dream, while she lays herself, drolly, carefully, on top of me again. I start to laugh. I grip her arms. She is not particularly coherent when she is unrehearsed—as in telling a dream. In telling a recent dream, she will often drift into telling an old one for which she has since come up with some coherent language. She resees her dream as she tries to recount it, and it fails to exist; it dissolves as memory; it is like drowning in an empty and somewhat cruel coherence. She can't help changing the dream to suit the linguistic circumstances of her talking about it so that she does not drown in coherence but manages to display it instead, a little dishonestly. She cheats. I believe you pay an often terrible price for lying—that she will pay a terrible price for her blasphemies. I wish I intimidated her into honesty. I feel I am being used by her. I don't much mind. I don't really mind. I'm beginning to mind.

And, so, unclearly, I shove her, limb by limb, off me.

Laughing a little, unwillingly, she submits.

She says, "Don't be angry with me because of my dream . . ." A New England comedienne, she makes a droll face; she has no sense of shame in making a *humble* spectacle of herself . . . She says, "If you weren't so fascinated by me, you'd disapprove of me less . . . Luckily I'm strong . . . I'm the strong, patient type . . ."

I rolled away from her and lay at the edge of the bed, on my side.

She said—vaguely—"Well, it's probably cathartic . . ."

"I like a woman who uses big words," I said.

"Words excite me, too," she says slowly, without excitement. "Can't we lie closer together?"

"Sure . . . Uh . . . Why not?"

She turns on her side and begins to glide—somehow—over the sheets toward me . . . All at once she is there. I halt her with a finger to her left boob—*boobie*, she calls it, softish, a little bomb-shaped. I move the pointing finger to her breastbone, between her breasts. Her fearlessness has always impressed me.

"You don't like me," she says.

"You don't like me," I say. "It's just that I'm available . . ."

"That's not true," she said. "You are so unavailable, it's horrible . . . Oh, fuck it, I don't know how to talk to you about things you don't face . . ."

"That I don't face? You're the mad lover of illusions . . ." I move my *face* closer to her *face*; "I am facing *you*," I say. We are *face*-to-*face* in bed in the *nothingness* of our half-explanations—our half-comprehensions. Our weird semi-ignorance, sweet but scary—I become differently erect, yet once more; *it* touches her down there . . . The moment is like gliding out into a dark gulf of air in a dream and not knowing if you have wings, not knowing what the dream is and what sort of creature you are, what the rules are for you in this episode . . .

Neither of us is quite blocking the other's will—so that part *is* dreamlike. The foreignness of my dreams, from her point of view, and of hers for me, similarly—the fact that the actual smell or tang of her love was unfamiliar to me and mine was strange to her (and so had a pungent and addictive quality of novelty) and the recurrence of the thing of permitted will are something hugely smothering—the as-if-feathered breast of a swan? A Venus-thing? From childhood when bodies and their powers were in a different scale, one has a sense of bodies being giant —this is at once fated and homelike . . . It is also very strange.

Oh, you gigantic ripe emptiness. You. "You ripe girl," I say: I am a relatively sophisticated talker.

"You turn it on, Wiley . . . It is part of what I like about you," she says.

It is a quasi-warm terror here. What is immanent here—the sexual stuff—eats you as a whale might in a story. Or a monster in a mythological tale . . . Abduction and jealousy: they might interrupt or result from the thing itself; rage, madness, coldness, metamorphosis . . .

Soothed jealousy. Quieted rage. Almost-placated madness. Shredded, defeated sexlessness. Or us stolen by perversity of desires, someone's intervention, or the past might intervene, or the thought of money (it nearly always interrupts me inwardly for a few moments), the memory of infidelity—the fragility of closeness—all the ways there are of being stolen, as in old novels and in movies, by ideas, other lovers, illness, fear of life, fear of each other, death, self-sacrifice . . . The somewhat scary do-jigger here of some kinds of stuff not happening after all is itself a momentary blurred story . . .

Ora's thoughts, her fears, maybe, were different. Ambitions—in the realm of *desires* and stuff having to do with *envy* since childhood, her rules as a woman, her sexual methods—"I break all the laws," she's said. And intellectual defiance of meanings other than her own? A fear amounting to a French Revolution against masochism—in herself and others? I am stupid and sentimental and not sophisticated in the ways she was —and not as "interesting" as a sexual rebel—all in all, I am tense and I doubt that we are *Great Lovers* . . .

I could only partly see myself as her rebellious (and Faustian) choice of a lover, as *the-one-who-fucks-you*, the you being Ora, but I figured I should see myself as that; but when I did, it excited me in a certain hard-edged way; and she looked smug; and the sex got odd.

She was aware that we punished people with the fact of us—I 'understood' that only nervously. She wanted us to hide—to avoid people. To inhabit a silence. Us to be pure as *lovers*, purified, redeemed by silence. I kind of poisoned myself with emotional and sexual cowardice toward that . . .

I thought we needed to be defined by others and that it was her *mistakenness*, her pride, that saw us that way. I half felt this. I went along with her; I agreed with her, too—it depended on the time of day and on what day it was and how her position had been modified as the days passed; I distrusted her. Face-to-face with her I am embedded with listening sections of myself—listening to her for more information—looking into her smile for an augury as into a disembowelled lamb—it was a gift like winning a medal at a fair (as the fattest pig) to gain her deadpan smile in a moment like this one. It was very different for me before sex if she wasn't dead-faced. It wasn't really surrender on her part to be with me. She wasn't always intent on us. She had a sleepy look but inside that look was a far-off element of alertness, of worldliness, as though she had been redefined by her cold fortress dreams and the hot fortress air of herself away and garrisoned by thoughts and wit and by the ghostly remnants of her dreams here in the approaches to sex.

I imagine her dreams as self-willed, hiddenly fascist piety of poverty as a woman in a male-dominated world. I have a thing I do of recognizing that in her so that she isn't alone in her feeling like that. I don't want to play at taking advantage of her, but that costs me something in terms of sexual presence and makes me, oddly, violent-in-spirit—reformist . . . Not tender so much as companionable. Tenderness has to do with apology—I haven't wronged her yet . . . I try not to resemble what other parts of life are knowably like for her and which displease her. I want her to give herself—to give herself to me and yet to create me—not as a sign of God but just *personally*. I don't want her to dream of something else. I don't want a dreamed-of Wiley laboring alongside me in her sense of things, every touch, the correcting shadow in every sexual movement, every sexual motion.

She makes a weird sexual offer that I love—and which scares her. She has said I love her traits and my ideas about her and not her; she says that's fine; and she makes a sexual offer of not letting others vote on us, our rights, our merits as a couple of fuckers or whatever; she keeps others at bay in regard to my flaws and her excellences; she ignores, at times, others' weirdly political, forceful wishes. But freedom from generalized sex, the idea of which is derived from bad novels and grubby movies, isn't included; but we were not to be punished for that stuff if we did it: this is part of the sexual offer.

She has a wish not to be unlucky in love; and I love that in her . . .

Like other young people we knew (but people from her social stratum more than from the next level down), she believes that lives contain vast reaches of 'universal' luck—there is some sort of competition because of this. A competition actually to have such luck and to live in a state of absolute blessing, Americanly, shrewdly, sagely, passionately . . .

One's ideals and then one's place in history and one's tragedies and one's great good luck—such glory . . . and it reflects from her limbs and enters my life through my knowing her, you know?

What is *not* present—and so *is* present for me as a definition of her sexual offer—are her dark rages, suicidal depressions, mockeries-of-others, tremendous snobberies toward others, a dark preference for the lowest classes—she hid this from me mostly, protected me, protected the image of her I had; I mean 99 and ½ percent of the time.

But I knew about it, sort of. She does not claim to be a *good* person. I do not think she is a *good* person. (She has said of me, *You're an optimist, Wiley . . .*)

She says, "You have a mocking look on your face . . . You shouldn't laugh at us, Wiley."

My intelligence is unlike hers and that worries her: she is rivalrous—of course . . .

"Why should people like us expect to have good luck . . . Ora?" I asked.

"We make our own luck," she says. In a bold tone. Maybe in a semi-right-wing, superior-person way.

A come-on that is also a sincere thing?

Our ideas at the moment, hers and mine, have to do with our sexual wakefulness, to what we are inside the throbbing of sexual hallucination by way of a maybe collegiate sophistication of *sexual realism*—may I call it that? We are each being sexually realistic while hallucinating. Sexual realism raced through me like a hot-bodied and scarily thin-boned and nervous-furred little animal; it magically ate me and circled through me and let me alone, somehow, at the same time. There was Ora, young and beautiful (truly), her heart pumping like an uncelestial clock—biologically—she is eccentrically real: *Ora*; and I am the perpetrator there with her—not her first love; the one she loved just now (if *love* is the word), if she loved just now.

Let me say that she loved ironically and carefully and with a wry discipline and she didn't expect me to notice . . . she expected me to hallucinate and daydream *a perfect degree of love* or of *torment* or of whatever I wanted. She made a stylish point of the strangeness of her loving me at all . . . Gentile love—God, nature, and man being what they were—yet being loved by *a woman like her*, by her really: she is bravely, willfully, spiritually trend-ridden in a certain way.

Her experience, her inexperience at love as I understood it, scared me. But I have one vote among two; she may be right; I may be wrong.

It was too real, too personal, too troubled by breath and by the *nothingness* that lies inside opinions to be comfortable. The nothingness that waits for you in adult life is not infantile but is the child, or the father, of the nothing of the loneliness of a child in a crib waiting to be lifted out.

The emotional reality of a slave crew on a mad ship of breath and desire is pretty much an actuality. Certain movie ads and certain covers of cheap romances in paperback excited her unduly and justly.

I said out loud, to excite her, "Are we a slave crew on a mad ship of breath and desire, Ora?" The cheapness and the understanding (so-to-speak) of how the cheapness of the world aroused her now and loosened her legs and drew oil into her cunt: I could see that all this was reasonable, biologically and metaphysically: I could feel the sexual response in her.

And she could see (in my *eyes*, say, or in my *shoulders*) what I felt, or all or some of it, since, I'm pretty sure, in those days we would wake simultaneously in the middle of ordinary moments and sexual ones to a kind of grieving resignation at being there with a degree now of comprehension of the other person.

A realization that neither of us had been stolen or abducted or metamorphosed but was there giving birth to the other's feelings moment by moment, and that neither of us had absconded, this was a major thing, maybe the most major . . . In the middle of the night in Manhattan.

Because of this, we were, I think, political and courtly although naked and a bit heated rather than theatrical. My sexual tastes are untheatrical. Her sexual tastes are decidedly theatrical—camera-and-memory-tropic. She offers me the welcoming committee of her selves, in a rather dry and ironic way, passionate but restrained (for my sake), moistly oiled and vaguely watchful and yet sleepy: this is a power in her as far as I was concerned.

I was wowed, awed, cowed, flattened, flattered, bemused—*triumphant*—erected in another form (yet another one). For one thing, it was her whole life that was there. This wasn't rape. Or her doing some daydreaming. It was the *totality* of mindly welcoming, the *degree* of physical welcome. One sighs with an immensity of relief. I wanted to resist her power over me though . . . I wanted to be cheap that way. But in a glance—in her eyes—and I mean eyeballs, for God's sake, irises, pupils, eyelashes, eyelids, and eyebrows—I *saw* that she was as resentful or even more so at our having become lovers-in-the-way-we-were-lovers-now than I was—and that was a shock. The cheapness of refusal—of the rape by the truth of something—we could, neither of us, breathe with the expansiveness of refusal in us . . . "Ha-ha," I said.

And then, strangling on my life, I drew breath, laughing seductively, to attract her and to free us of resentment. She closed her eyes: I am the one who has the more beautiful feelings here. The irony is nearby, the fear, the resentment, so to speak, but I was erect—it changes more than a puppet does along the line of action of the sexual story—and I began poking her, trying to gain entry, poked gently, and then used fingers, managing to wedge myself half in the entry, then with a muscular thing-amajig in her and in me, I was half in, half out, then with a silent whoosh I was halfway in her, as such things go, and I said, "Whoo," and "Ah," and "Whoa, Nelly . . ." A joke.

I did this naïvely, on purpose, an unwittingly hypnotized, half-*beautiful*, unwitting boy: a sweetly violent trespass, a lie, a context for the other, sincere in a way. A literary conceit maybe—an image she maybe accepted.

It wasn't at all clear what she specifically welcomed. We had been doing this stuff for four years and had worked out some things and were rehearsed and were still startled by the novelty, the edge of darkness of the future here, the darkness of what might happen. She welcomed *all* of me despite a lot of things. No, that's not true. She judged; she had reservations. But she went way beyond any kind of bargaining or holding back of anyone I had known sexually. A *more* if it is more enough feels like an *all.* It does. But I hate being grateful to a lover. To be welcomed is a little like being barefoot in mud, almost: creepy and tickling and natural and wonderful—and a relief from existing in another state.

It is a little hard for me to believe when it is happening that it is happening.

I am a shade ethereal—a little bit disgusting . . . gross . . . much more interested in fucking than in seduction . . . and this shows right away . . . And she sometimes finds that, feels that, to be, sees that as, *truly disgusting.* She isn't sexual; she is seductive—which, considering the nature (and finickiness) of erections is an extremely valuable and important—and *sexual*—thing to be.

But she responds in this part of the fuck. I see that she sees (in my chest, in my eyes, in my motions, in the motions and major convulsions and state of a degree of hardness and of a specific kind of hardness of my prick) the foreignness of my sensations and of my reactions to those sensations—she is at the border of my fluttery and so far semi-docile hallucinations and she almost sees them in me.

When I reject them in favor of my sense of her and of my being present to her and with her, she worries: my being like that is a threat in that I demand presence of her at this stage and she would rather that I daydreamed and was alone and did not see her. No-retreat-on-my-part, my not drifting into reaction or into thought and private association, means she is not free. *My* fear, *my* defiance, *my* eerie fearlessness, it is hard to say this in a just way, but Ora deeply disliked my taking charge of things and my giving orders in this tacit fashion. She likes fucking to proceed as it's supposed to—kind of horribly but cathartically. This was no mild resentment on her part. It was nothing to joke about. She truly loved her own mind—her own senses—her own thoughts. *Loved*: was deeply attached to, like a child to a horse it owned. And maybe there were horse elements in her—a horse, a house, a property of immense extent. Who knows what range her mind has in these moments? On her horse, her high horse (of beauty and mind), she was not jealous of stony and earthy realities or of me in my fucking but I pulled her away from that into awareness. She was aware of me, of us; I was aware of her—I pushed her into this sort of consciousness. And I hurtled into it. I feel ripeness at the mere thought of her own thoughts, her reality *consciously* releasing the Midas treasury of the sexual stuff of her rhythms (such as they were), all the stuff between her legs and the punctuation stuff of the sexual dramas of her nipples—then all of it really—breasts, judgment, cunt, eyes and lips and legs . . . fucking, consciously fucking.

Of course, the obstinate (sly?) fucker was conscious, too. She was fucking someone she thought a blind, conniving, tyrannical, wise fool —a good fool? Maybe. A good-at-it fool? I doubt it. I don't know. A good-enough-at-it fool maybe. But a Machiavellian fool, weird-thoughted. Her views of me.

I felt heroic—in a way—and odd-footed, an insect or a cripple—I had the feeling she felt as something flying around oddly like light inside her skull and absolutely (and Jewishly and mirroringly) known by her—and pathetically in regard to—what? Ego? Evil? Social logic as she knew it? Sexual and personal reality?

In these days, when she self-consciously readied herself inside the act of fucking—when she settled into it—I often thought that what I felt, my sense of pleasure, my sense of *homecoming* was that it was as if she asked me what I wanted and I could answer in pantomime, almost doing it, but doing it socially, so to speak, or as a performance—she accepted me to some degree of reality in a kind of intimacy of that stuff, a lessened antagonism.

She accepted one's being lost in genetic egoism . . . In one's abilities . . . In what one represents in that natural madness of generation . . .

Language and dreams. Dreams are too self-centered for language. And what is the point of carting dreams into reality? Dreams represent enormous experiments in grammar based on no one else being present —on the unreal, time-skewed grammar of no listeners; only the speaker is there. Real presence wakes you. The skull behind the face and under the hair is the white bone of a moon sadly out-of-place or not out-of-place in the real-life logic of what one *feels* in a fuck. The oddity of being a creature, the oddity of the homecoming thing, and the intimacy in her crotch—front gate and grassy lawn and porch in the genital grasp—they are also terrifyingly present, magnified and obvious, on her wide-cheekboned, short-strong-nosed face. Her deep-socketed-eyed, warm-mouthed, genuinely beautiful face. And her adventures. One time, I walked into a barn in the countryside and was blinded in the shadow after the sunlight and something came swooping and fluttering toward me, beaked, eyed, striped, and huge. I never really *saw* it: I *felt* it. So I see her face—and her—and her interest and contempt . . . contempt for death, for pricks, for complaints. She lives. Bravely? With audacity really? Her face is partly turned aside. She has the neck and the posture of someone grown-up. Contempt, interest, love—fear and love. She clings to me without touching me except inside the cunt. We are touching only in there and only slidingly just now. In this moment in me is a *premonition*, a *prediction* of the sexual *more-to-come*—and of my tiring of her. Some kisses came next. Her hands moved to my shoulders. Then to my butt. Then she put her arms around me, her fingers palping my back. Me, I touch her—but lightly—she is too startled inside the balances in the power thing just now for me to want to touch her heavily. Then, oh, then, there are enormous awards, *enormous*, maybe poisoned with ego, there is her beauty and the beauty of the sensations and of the psychological reality of homecoming.

So many people have strutted for her, blackmailed her, pursued her throughout her past (and still, or rather, at that time, too) that it is not purely a private thing to be with her. The element of choice here goes very deeply—genetically. We don't want children yet but we are breeding stock. This is part of the odd semi-professional sensual grammar and sexual vocabulary of lovers—lovers now dirtily joined—alone, the two of us, with each other in the queered circle of intimacy. We were as if in a hotel room or a room in a *pensione*—she doesn't smile when I say—when we are already fucking—"Want to fuck?"

She doesn't always find me *seductive* through my humor—she preferred seduction to anything—but she accepted this.

I became impossibly overweening and temperamental—excited, overexcited—overbrimming—spermatically: and opposed to all her opinions. So that Ora, who contemptuously loathed and dismissed selfishness in me, is faced with this opposition to her having so many opinions. I am so set in my course of sensation—and of sensational *will*—that I feel myself as having a face of bronze bones and heavy, marbled eyes and canvas skin, eyes of willed nothingness heavily willful. I am on top of her, phallically overbrimming.

It is rottenly delightful. Then, briefly, I become human again. I fill with a sense of her. I am reasonable in a New York bedroom; and I heave in this other, pedalling-slowly way—but I am so densely compact with sexual will that I am a hell-figure—this is maybe a sexual hallucination and maybe a scary truth . . . I feel I am able to kill merely by falling on someone. But that she can bear this, that I think she can, is one reason I care for her.

But she has not been able to bear this in me as well lately, now that I have the rank of being *known* while she, in her career as a *woman* (or whatever), is mostly an adjunct. I think she is generally addled with stick-to-it-iveness in regard to things, to sex which is good, and to her "career" —her becoming a legendarily important woman. *Stick-to-it-iveness* was a word she said she got from her "horrid" grandmother—the bitchy, very rich one. During a fuck, Ora has a thing of lapsing openly from the sexuality in the stop part of the stop-and-go of excitement, in the blinking part of the blinking advance, which shocks me. Essentially shrewdness is sexually grating—it depends on how it's combined with letting go. She is not ethereal or transcendent during this but it was a form of shrewd idealism, what she was, it was her form of being a *real* person.

I say, "Okay, Ora?" And she nods. I am in a phase more all-the-way, more out of reach, more unreasonable and violent-in-spirit than the phase is that she is in.

"I have what *I* want, Wiley—go ahead . . . It's okay . . ."

"Move your hips on me, Ora," I say; my voice, like my face overall, feels far away from her, a million miles away; she is at the mouth of a tunnel, *over there*, so to speak.

She says—oddly—"I guess you'll never understand that I am the kind of woman I am." And she kisses me. But she doesn't move her hips.

And then, just as I am saying, "So what?" she moves her hips semi-violently and not seductively, but graspingly along the prick—angering me, soothing me, blindingly making me stare.

I don't know if I liked it or not. We often have agreed not to be alert and just to fuck (blindly) but that agreement doesn't hold all that often, or perhaps ever; it just means we don't do postmortems at all; and often, off and on, we are alert, although we then often pretend we are not alert. But, sometimes, we just admit it and go along with it, jolting each other out of it from time to time, into unalertness.

I have as general principles these *rules*: All our fucks are imperfect. All our fucks are merely human.

But, see, I *knew* when I was in her in that phase and I pushed and pulled back, half out, gasping, I knew two things: that I was averse to struggle as sexual shenanigans (or as sincerity) and that what I was silenced her wit. Witless, she was violent, too—like the rest of us. This silenced her and built up a debt of a kind of anger owed me for distressing her.

Which was like, but not as great as, my debt to her. Sexually, I mean.

Her pride was such, her independence was such that the smallest triumph for me was like stuffing her mouth with sand or with dead leaves. She knew this better than I did, and the knowledge of this made her clumsy—with me—sexually often, more often than not.

I say now, "Ora, one of these days, you will kill me." Reversing the "truth" of my killing her. The reversed fearsome image is exciting for her. She quivered with an excitedly, eager, somehow muddy, muddied, passivity—on-the-edge-of-attack—a hasty masochism, with assault held back; this self-offering has in it some penalty half-invoked now of future revenge for this—maybe in the near future: this is the dimensionality of the reality of the mood as I see it, her kind of hinted-at and partly performed clutch at me to balance what I do to her. The imagery of her touching me through the prick, the prick of the Jew, is scary, the vain boy who thinks he is so smart . . . The long-legged blond boy with his odd, blinded eyes and the queer variations of sightedness in him instead . . . Fucking with her, fucking her, being fucked by her: it doesn't matter which; I enter her fully then.

It is all the way in. It is clasped and held. Then she loosens. I don't know why this means so much to me. I don't know why it isn't written about more—the ways women fuck. Someone—a lot of people—have lied to me about women. Not just Ora but her, too, sometimes.

I say it again—"You will kill me—this will kill me. This is killing me."

"Too many words for a fuck, Wiley," she says.

"Don't tell me what to do . . ." I say that.

On some dark level—on a thrusting level—the idea of bossing me around pleases her.

She, Ora, grows silent, purposefully depriving me of the sounds she might make to show me what she is feeling. I feel a superstitious reverence at this genital stage of feeling a lot. The homecoming-and-intimacy thing, I *feel* it poignantly. And Ora's silence is *poignant*. I am as if pierced by a sense of her depth of will and oddity of mood, the furtherness of her temper.

She is moving nicely. Killingly. I am responding—writhing a little, breathing hard. I like truth. The two bodies, the two souls naked at the skin, just behind it; and you hear each other's presence . . . The sexual bells and ding-dings and lights and sweats in reality are not as interesting to me in her as the other thing of sexually being present.

I gripped her haunches and moved her in a different rhythm from the ones she had erratically been doing. Once or twice, in quarrels, she has accused me of being intrinsically infinitely bossy but of hiding it behind an ideal of something or other, but when I am bossy she often —sufferingly—accedes.

Ora was much more conscious of herself than she was of me—that wasn't a sign of no-love—it was just what you should expect as natural. But it indicated what kind of love we had. She wasn't mad with focus on me.

For a moment—whether I'm bossy or not—for a moment there was some weirdly profound, easily fractured simultaneity of mutual listening. I'd call it a ripeness. Then it stopped. It felt as if she took it away, but it could be that it burned itself out. She offered her body more or less coolly for a few seconds and less like stuff in the movies and more like suddenly unchaining her spine and her muscles and just being there, moist, dark—honest—earthen and outside any story she knew, any hallucination . . . any wish . . . any fantasy. But not mutually: with separate destinies. A rival's gift. Then she slides away from that; I know there are pleasures for her unlike any that I feel.

She has often said to me that she liked a man who talked during sex. Jealously—I was jealous of her odd pleasures—I said—as we fucked—"Are you a realist, Ora?"

"Oh yes. That's. What peo[ple]. Find so hard. To bear. About me." Then: "No one. Ever. Liked me. But you. Wiley . . ."

These are sexual remarks for her. She is not exactly in alignment with me but she is not off alone inside herself.

I say, "I don't like you either . . . I'm just caught . . . I'm a butterfly broken on your wheel . . ." I *love* sexual power so much when it's mine that I get silly with having it.

We are thrusting or oozing around.

"Oh you like me now . . . It's our time now . . ." she says in a highish, peculiar voice. Our youth.

She *inflicts* a kind of romance on our sexual do-jiggery—a kind of romance which is foreign to me. I remind myself she may be right—sexually.

I say to her, "Oh my yum-yum, oh my fuckable woman, oh fuckables . . . fuckables . . ." She has said she likes jokes—and some disrespect—some forms of it . . . I wouldn't be able to tell the difference whether she really does or not, but we grow closer in the strange oddity of this real and half-real stuff.

She was maybe a masochist looking for a master, for a while, and I was maybe a master not interested in mastery but in long-term collusion, but what I was sure of was that she wanted no defeats at all, not even glancing ones, and that she would fight back to the death—that is, it was a whole cycle, a whole history for her, now and to come. I live differently from that. And to defeat me was obscene, was a delirium for her, truly, a satisfying *vileness*, a form of violence—which she often abjured. She often policed herself. But she longed for it, maybe only as the other shoe that had to drop, but also, I think, as justice and as the triumph of devilry—of her view of life; and she'd let go and just do it—triumph over me one way or the other. The fantasy in that actuality was in the social thing of *my* superiority over her which she rectified—the romance lay in that fantasy . . . I thought it was fancy stuff . . .

That and the further fantasy of her *giving* sexual fulfillment to me, me being *the other* for her—Ora as a great whore. My God.

"Go ahead; fuck me as you like—I'm strong," she said.

The reality-illusion, the stage-setting, the home-away-from-home (or tenting-out-tonight-thing) or whatever it was we had—the paper city of a fuck—rustled then with *harsh* performance—romantic-harsh—I gripped her like a pirate in a poem or a movie, a little realer than that maybe—she stiffened in a real way—but also as a daydreaming actress —or girl; it was sort of *things collapse, things-get-out-of-hand* . . . girl apocalyptic; the performance reality of not-respectable. Will, cunt, and sensibility—soul and phallus and cunt . . . and rhythmic—and gestural—disreputability.

My sense of what was going on came from sexing around before now (with other people) and from sports and so some of it concerned guys. But I am in her cooze; and this stuff comes complete with a sense of two genders and of her committing suicide, of lovelessness, of the real risk of violent meaninglessness after all—or not risk, inevitability—lives-down-the-drain, death—the-death-of-this-and-that, murder, sexual murder, cancer, death overall, the death of the soul. Well, she has a *violent* recklessness toward all of that—a drunken bravado and a cold attitude toward it—toward the shit women have to accept—and toward the shit men have to accept—and this animated her and she did this other rending—maybe heartbreaking—thing of kissing me sloppily and saying, "I am ready to die . . ."

It wasn't stupid of her. But it was partly fake inside the game of what she is doing with someone who is not a gangster. It isn't fake inside the further reality of what she might do . . .

Or what I might do if I am as dangerous as she thinks I am.

I warn her: "Ora, don't test me . . . I'm ill-bred . . . I haven't got that kind of class . . . I can't feed myself with shadows—with fantasies . . ."

She never believes me—not quite. It is her fate to love me as someone superior but with her family being *finally* superior and deaf-and-superior to what I say.

"I don't have fantasies, Wiley," she said in a deepish voice.

"No. You just have . . . ideas. . . . Big ideas . . ."

Then to be nice but also to mock her *Big Ideas,* I pull her hair a little then, and she says—not playfully—"No! No!" She doesn't like that. Or my tone. Maybe she has more depths of *feeling* than I have . . .

I feel—judging from the lovely oiliness and soft grippingness of her cunt as I move in her and do such other things as grip her hair—that she cannot listen to me very often. It hurts her to hear me unless I speak on some sociable to-be-possibly-heard-by-her way. That now it was pure fantasy-elaboration-of-hallucination pushed into reality by my prick and my male smells—and the oddities of male temper—in me—reminding her of men she'd known: and she heard that and moved among her memories of that and of them, so that I took on the full properties of my size and age and of who I was in these moments. Nowadays in New York, then, I become largely invisible to her—off and on—and an enemy: the invisible man, no-lunged, silent, audible only when and if his speech diverged into clichés dealing with this stuff in a way palatable to her. The invisible man among the others. Unless I was wrapped in bandages, in pitiability. And she was armored against that. I mean she "loved" me—and she refused most of me. My ideas, my voice, my body—prick and balls—

My individuality. My character.

"Don't think . . . don't think tonight," she said—she is sweaty-faced, a nice girl—or woman . . . in mid-fuck.

I hate her for the abrupt simplification of herself that she did just now. The solo sonata effect, not the duo and *tutti* thing—all of nature joining in.

"Fuck off, Sweetie," I say. Not each word in the same key . . . instead, each is tied to motions. She is amused, not challenged or angry—I always felt it was *kind* of her to be amused; it was a radiance in her—as if I were, somehow, a lucky sexual fate for her . . . romantic and amusing now.

(It was vainglorious of her to be so egotistic but who gives a fuck? The idiom means a fuck is not important.)

She is changeable and she makes a funny noise. I *think* she wants more violence. I hesitate—since she will pull back if I do something or if I do nothing . . . She wants to prove herself to herself. She wants me to be guilty toward her. But I don't want to be that. I don't want to be ashamed. Those satisfactions. That dirtiness. The shuddery and shivering and mostly unlikable and violently-to-be-hated voice of violent masculinity—I was merely an unideal example of it in a way, and I was her destiny for a while.

That she has no clear twinship: that irritated her even while she was loosened by it and even a little awed by it . . .

So, I arouse zones of silence in her, unsettlingly—not exactly *sexually*. She watched the veins in my forehead and neck—I could see her checking my breathing and my rhythms in the fuck and my pulse—she is seeing-through-me; she was some kind of peering-eyed, infinitely proud, *dirtied* CRITIC—at a distance. CHRIST, I loved her. Maybe not enough. Maybe I didn't love her at all . . . Maybe I was in my soul (and asshole) queer . . . Promiscuous. How do you *really* know? I was sensible of her unhappiness—her unhappinesses—in her pleasure (if it was pleasure, if she wasn't faking)—as the elements of a fire of almost sentimental unsentimentality in her, a version of reckless murderousness, something un-Hamlet-y, ungrateful, active and dangerous. I doubt that her body ever lied much.

She whispered, "It is to the death . . ."

God knows what I thought she meant, but fear grabbed my balls. Ora liked women who had a crush on her, lately a monocled Polish *countess*, one, and, two, an American heiress, and, three, a movie woman, a wife mostly—to a producer.

"You're wonderful, Wiley," she said oozingly—a little phonily.

"Christ, I'm not!" I got truly weird. "It's an accident—let's be nice, Ora . . ." This was along with fuck motions, in and out . . . The syllables were broken . . .

"Oh shut up," she said like a heroine in a comic movie and bouncing on the bed. "Don't keep on giving lessons . . . I know—about—the real world . . ." It was in an affectionate tone.

She grinned, smally—sweatily seductive . . . Then all at once, again, and in a way, I was generally content. But I let the mood in me be one of contempt—this helped hurry orgasm; it was to get to my orgasm. It was the pirate captain fucking dispensable Ora . . . It was Captain Sin Cold Ruthlessness fucking poor ordinary Ora . . .

Bleak, black, blank power—hatred-of-a-sort . . . It's okay . . . She often said she could handle all that stuff.

"Fuck, Ora, fuck . . ."

She did it in some sincerity but not a bone-shaking huge amount —her body had become silent—by that I mean detached from its own circuits of orgasm; it wouldn't have an orgasm. She wouldn't. She moved in a kind of dreadfully dutiful way, a foolish, freed, generous way, "lesbian" and dear, unsatisfying, and yet okay, if you didn't go crazy with longing for what she wasn't doing. In the peculiarly arctic silence, her perhaps involuntary withdrawal from orgasm—I may be disgusting or too sensitive or any number of things—*love* of this sort—if it is love—and because of some wry cheapness of cruelty and forgiveness and some considerable fatuity here—it seems like a ruling-class fuck to me.

I approached orgasm. Taut and faintly hulking shoulders and tautly backwards-curved spine—and she bore me along and she bore with me with extraordinary Gentile cruelty-companionship: she-loved-a-fool. That kind of thing, a fool who yet was superior to her in some way she established, took care of, and accepted and got even with: she was in a romance of that sort. I don't know how much she really minded anything. Private dramas did not bore her. She minded boredom more than she minded death. Boredom, meaninglessness, emptiness tortured her.

I paused and wiped sweat out of my eyes and off my forehead. I sat up while I was in her. While I stayed in her. Still, it is not clear to me what I want sexually.

"I don't want to come," I said—maybe to mock her, maybe to get her into a mood of mutuality, maybe to apologize for not having handled things better.

So I came. Two movements. Three. A jazz piece. A riff on convulsions, genital convulsions. She backed off and let me alone while I came. But it felt like a punishment, her doing that.

I said crossly, "You fuck like a mother . . ." A woman with other people she cared about more.

"Don't be cruel—my mother is a dolt." Ora didn't precisely mean stupidity so much as, in a rather high-handed social sense, she meant someone who'd failed to be legendary—to have a biography written about her. "I have sold my soul to you." Then she corrected it: "For you . . ."

I thought I was in condition to hear her . . . I could see what she was saying . . . She was saying she was more thoroughly orphaned than I was . . . She hadn't had much (or any) interest in being a *daughter* . . . This orphan of ladies' freedom in the half-dark. Our breath creaky—like the springs of the bed—the fluster of us settling back and holding each other's hands after a fuck. Us having affrighted death. We lay on our sides, looking at each other for a moment; and then I turned away, wanting to be alone. Or at a remove anyway from her particular courage and insolence toward life, toward death, toward reality.

I had a postcoital sense of a madness underlying and creating her beauty . . . A fan fluttering in front of her eyes. She had this other rank, a form of modesty in her, a boast of identity. To avoid horror—and she was not open about her feelings about horror but she accepted horrible social situations—she advocated romance-and-sex as a red-hot given. She lied about her sexual interests enough that her sexual heat was, in part, a device that was a serious modification of chatter blending with serious talk. It was not to be loved or trusted. (How you judge a fuck determines the next part of the story.) Her display of desire was in favor of your being willfully selfish. A semi-demi-abandoned display of male will—some fantastic hallucinations—is that bliss? Luck? Pain? Betrayal? I muttered out loud, "That was an unjudgeable fuck, Ora . . ." A sudden reality of *love*, falsified, dramatized, and the reality of our odors—we stank of the cunt-fish and of sour lemon sperm and of sweat and rut—made the acceptance of lies and of betrayal, betrayal of the self, and so on (as breeding stock) factually okay. She might be childlike, childlike-adult-cold about it, *despairing* but undefeated, but the honor we had came from me, the man, not from her, and I betrayed it every time I spoke and upheld it in my lying there, in my wobblingly accepting the fuck as sufficient. I didn't bargain or defend myself or attack her . . . This was my sexual honor, to do this . . . She sighed. She was beyond rules. I don't mean she behaved dishonorably. I mean she indulged herself in honor, sweetly, tragically, while being realistic after a fuck—well, after my orgasm. She was carefully sexual while being carefully not sexual. Ora's eyes, famous since she was a child for beauty, are discreet, maybe a bit argumentative, I notice coldly, postcoitally. In the slipperiness of life after a fuck, she had a slidy directness; she lived out her hypotheses about love. She showed her ability to bear risk-and-mess . . . She was sighingly good-tempered. Patient. But in an operatic way that suggested madness, drunken love, scenes of lust, but earlier. And people getting hurt—an overrich category of experience. One was aware that another woman would be very different and that she was very different each time.

I 'loved' her too much to play certain games, and not enough to be careless and without thought or concern. I loved her changeably. I was sorry I loved her. I was pleased. I was a little desperate at being caught in this tie to her.

Each of her breaths is betraying me if I am my ideals. She is who she is and each flicker of my thought as a writer who was *clear*-minded betrays her.

So, my selves agree in committee, even now, let's consider a female hero to claim ours is real love.

I do not want a life of struggle with her. I would like to have areas of firm agreement with her.

"Men are fools," she said. Then: "We're lucky to have each other —do you know that?"

She, too, wants areas of firm agreement between us but other areas, not the ones I care about.

She had submitted to fate, to reality, and she wished I would—to myself, however as fate and as reality—and to her as love. To the pressures she submitted to, including those from other people, men and women —so that we might be twins . . .

"I wish you would try to be like me," I said. "Just a little. Fit in. All that jazz."

She hadn't ever submitted to a social group or to a man ever, or a woman, a mentor. Perhaps she hadn't ever adopted personal or professional discipline except as a beauty, some of the discipline of being beautiful. We met as bandits in that sense. She put up with life, with reality, is what it was that she did. She adopted current fashions in thinking about life. She had her own twist, or view, in reacting to things. She was Radcliffe-Harvard, Maine, upper-level New York (but not the best level because of her father's mésalliance). She was isolated by her beauty and her independence of spirit but not by originality or independence of mind or of soul. The terms, the way in which we were together and alike were up for discussion: who fit in, who wandered free, who was perversely himself, or herself. Those are specific dramas.

She put up with things. Each thing that happened, if she chose to, she put up with it. Me and that now and then the servants went mad, literally, in her rich grandmother's house—she had a brute of an extremely socially powerful grandmother whose social standing was considerably higher than her granddaughter's. And Ora had a grandmother who was fairly sweet and very pretty, someone who read a good deal and who talked well, someone socially-successful-in-that-way.

So Ora, if you adjusted to her—whatever that means—you adjusted to this heaving and changeable grab bag, to bone-snapping surprise, to surprises in who she was; and not only that, who-she-was with an air of having always been it even if she hadn't been it at all the night before. She put up with passes from men accompanied by threats and often violent scufflings and with semi-rape attempts from relatives. She bore with married men, sad, desperate, well-to-do, or poor, or very rich and stunningly famous, and with older sons who wrestled with her doomfully, tiptoed into her room at night or after lunch and had to be shoved out or tricked or partly given into or who shoved her off the sailboat in the middle of the cold green waves in Penobscot Bay. Or she pushed them off. And so on.

But it was not simple moral reality you adjusted to in her if you did adjust or if you could. Slander and weird remarks by jealous women and enamored ones. Blackmail and betrayal as commonplaces in ritzy surroundings and chic ones. Her careful social lying about certain of these matters, darkening them if she wanted or lightening them as *normal* among smart people or whatever, kind of set off with a frame of foil my own games of semi-innocent hickdom and boy-from-out-West (sort of) and orphan-who-has-found-a-(glamourous-)home-at-last. She was not exactly a femme fatale so much as a young woman of sufficient beauty and intelligence and background that she was a young woman of romantic and social and lustful fatality purposefully and now going straight—so to speak—now being a nice girl in any of a number of various ways, on top of the past, as reformation, or as a variant always present in the past. Or not being a nice girl—she tried various things. Time goaded her, as it does everyone. People would exclaim sometimes, *But she really* IS *beautiful!* She had kept her nerve this long. In the oddity of her moments, her unamused ironic acceptance was a toughness that she had.

Being sold fairly often had made her sensitive to being a commodity that people dealt in—sold by guys to other guys, by her parents or half sold by them and her social grandmother and by her favorite aunt and her least favorite aunt and by her godmother—and then her weaseling out of it or storming out of it, she felt herself as *failed* but superiorly knowledgeable. Failed but lucky and of high caliber. To be listened to—except when she wanted privacy and was busy imitating or even usurping me, being me: she walked like me at times. Her sense of failure—and her truly mad pride—covered the more or less *accepted* thing that she, her parents, her friends, at any given moment, and me perhaps, would ignore, would even *favor* some celebrity's assault on her, some ex-general's hots, some semi-billionaire's wish to whatever, some politician's or some famous actor's pinching her breast, her bottom, following her into the john . . . But if I meddled, as I did, from the start, *when she asked,* she blamed me for being possessive—and for ruining her life: she did it patiently, argumentatively. One could imagine the steamy sense of possibilities in her head—or in her breast.

Then her sudden uncringing telling-everyone-off stuff—*her* telling the truth in a way—her being the editor of the lifey text or the long-lost narrator—her refusal (usually) to be sold, her half-agreeableness toward it at her own say-so at times that had nothing to do with me, this gave her a moral-amoral, ethical and personal tone—one of hatred, of rage-ready-to-go-off, and of a kind of sexual grief, a sexual tearfulness, as in being in the hands of a cruel owner.

But then the queerly pitched laughter of her *not* expecting sympathy, her attitudes toward her weird notoriety (which lasted most of her life): that's *normalcy* for her although she does not give it that name.

But it and certain lying romanticizations, romancings about things, tincture what she does, not all the time, but much of the time when time itself is spread out, like a corridor, say, and isn't an intimate boxcar thing, although this stuff in her is present then, too: *normalcy* known with terrific honesty and ease as a crazedness, as peculiarity and as *a* peculiarity of hers, as *uniqueness*—Ora is unique in her hurts and in the ways her being hurt is socially sought after by this or that person for this or that reason. This gave her the conviction that she was talented—a Lady van Gogh. This *beauty*—self-willed, insistently alive—bridged the rush of such oddity in herself with the further eeriness of her persisting in being a *beauty*—a somewhat more portable and self-governing thing than being a talent is—beauty considerable and persisted in and envied: she *accepted* the stories of that, the enmities and people getting even and the praise and the romance, and that made art unnecessary.

She was maybe on the make in regard to what-was-envied—she moved solely among things-that-were-envied—and this aspect of her was not paled or hidden but was nervily flaunted as a kind of okay personal elitism. Her education at the hands of people infatuated with her left her with an avidity (echoing theirs) which was her special rank, her special arrogance, a special pathos in the human flavor of her.

And to accept the consequences of this in herself: that, too, was part of her. She did that—accepted what results—or did so except when she collapsed. And this acceptance allowed her to choose her life up to a point. Was the world universally infatuated with her? No. It wasn't a unison sort of thing. But you had to defy the world if you wanted to be with her—but it wasn't considered *chic* to admit this. Her circumstances limited her powers to choose her life while creating those powers, choose her life or her men or her women, but she could sort of choose anyway.

She had powers which were like rights. Rights of story and rights of revenge. People banded together to assail her, to make her an outcast. And not a power. Often, even in New York, when she came into a room, into a party, a silence would commence. Men and women would choose their reaction—would embark on certain trajectories of partisanship or of rivalry or of pursuit or of who-knows-what. She had an American velocity; she was a young woman of affairs. She was no one's *type*. She wasn't owned or constrained that way. Her beauty was her own. Nothing of what I was could constrain her or own her; I was an act of willfulness on her part; I said this to her once and she said it was true of me with her, or more so, "because life is even harder on a man than it is on a woman, Wiley," she said.

So then, what she and I did sexually had tag ends to it that smacked of being leftovers from her intense—and glamourous—experience. And mine. And it smacked of her having comparatively free will. She said more than once that she and I had more free will than a lot of people did—or I said it and she took the remark on; it became primally hers.

Her sense of sin and of right and wrong, of *Faustian* sinning in our being in love, so to speak, against the will of the heavens and the dictates of intelligence—Faustianly not sinning—and with reasonably giant social difficulties down below—this included her belief that she sinned in her free-willed and betrayal-laden submission to mastery in me—not a real one, but the one she imagined romantically, not steadily, but romantically and unsteadily. This was not a conventional sin. It was an Ora-sin. She was in a sub-Ora, sub-love way, Longing's daughter interested in *dirty* submission, but you couldn't count on that. She was hugely exercised, like a fighter, for *real love* . . . "You know a lot, Wiley, but you can't really win an argument with me." *Real love*—i.e., final love, death, death as the last and ultimate and greatest act and which made you *a genius* . . . She was kind of self-consciously at the edge of being *a genius*—she toughly played at it often with a tone of realism, changeably . . . She wasn't realistic about *that* . . . I don't know the sources for her terms for love as she imagined or saw that subject. I don't know the whispery forms of her ideas or the extent of her mind or the scope of her feelings. But she believed that love was not specific and changeable but that unchanging LOVE had entered our lives, the real and only thing, the mythical thing.

I have a mythical sense of her that quivers and moves. But a real sight of her face means that all her face is not clearly visible. So much value was compacted in her for me that I wonder how does all that I knew her to be come to be compacted into value, period, or does it dissolve it, value being a dream thing and imaginary? Her mind, her will, her decencies, her face, her mood, her nuttinesses of a low kind, she was often startlingly unkind to others. Often. She was startlingly charitable, too. She would support the pride of the defeated . . . not mine but poor people's. She was clear about their value. Her willingness to die for love—die in certain ways—in a certain exuberant exhaustion—with me, with love, to get the whole bloody, elaborately awful-and-wonderful mess over and done with, she was impressive.

Do you love whoever creates you? Do they have to be *nice* about it?

Some people are regarded so romantically when they are young that the knowledge of childhood romance is part of how they look—ideas and hallucinations in a real past of love . . .

The fall or tumble of her—uh—glorious hair around her stunningly boned, rather wisely warm face—the effect of her face burned in you. You could not duplicate or portray the bones or the eyes or mouth, the life in them, in her, or her mind. Anyway, she was ready for self-pity and temperament in herself and others and for faulty sex and for a degree of violence as a measure of a man's appreciation of her. Or a woman's. She was remarkable—but worriedly: with a sense of failure—with a sense of scandal. With a small laugh, or with almost any mannerism, she made it clear that she was under the threat of her own boredom and that she had a history of flight. She was infinitely conceited, infinitely and despicably *A Beauty*.

She said that, in a bizarre way, I was that, too.

She accepted the scandal of what she was, not all the time though. When we talked late at night, she compared herself to darkness. "I'm like the night." The wind was mumbling outside. "I'm dark. I know you will hurt me . . . I'm a grown-up. I know what you want . . ." She liked aristocratic English lady writers. In her bad moods, she knew herself as deformity and fault, ordinariness, un-Christian, as pagan meatiness-and-death; and then again, at bottom—*au fond*, she said—repicturing herself as a mightiness, a meaty mightiness of majesty, I guess—"I am not conceited, Wiley, but I am really of high caliber." Then she said again, "I'm grown-up." This is not the time to say this but in boredom with her life as it had been, after the first year with me, she wanted me to be the *Beauty* and herself to Wiley.

She passed herself off as plain: "I lived before you came along, Wiley. I had my books. I had my philosophy. I had my interest in the theater. I believed in the death of God. I was not jealous of artists then."

"Is that a quote?"

She liked extreme theater but she quoted speeches from middlebrows and from movies that had impressed her when she was thirteen.

The postcoital whatever—the white mist of *sadness*, bored, fleshless, fancifully exact, terrestrial and classroomy, *sadness* so-called—brought doubt.

"You don't ask for the whole kit-and-caboodle when you have oodles," she told me. "My godmother said that."

Her godmother had been a Creole temptress from the Dominican Republic with a right-wing political leaning and a large circle of Washington acquaintances—including the last few presidents and their families.

She was married to the chief of the Washington bureau of *The Newsman*, probably then the most politically important magazine in the country. When Ora and I started living together, Kiki, the godmother, had said it was okay. She was fat and clever, very good-looking, an insomniac rumored to be insane off and on. Ora said so.

Later her husband had a stroke when he was sixty; and she nursed him for a year; and then she had a heart attack and committed suicide, leaving her husband who said he understood what she had done and why she'd done it. She was a coldly and powerfully entertaining madwoman, quite sane socially. An alcoholic.

Ora was a victim to my degree of fame—take this on my say-so—this was a half-polite form of anti-Semitism. It wasn't entirely unpleasant—she established it in the rough social equations of people-she-knew (who accepted delusions with Christian patience) that I was a sexual powerhouse beauty—as a man—the one who had hunted Ora down and now Ora was stuck with him and behaved well toward him in order to keep him. You know? The modish male, daring and potent, potently aggressive, competitive—whatever? Her fantasy lover? The man whose sexual-hallucinations-as-sexual-reality she dealt in? Well, that was one of the sexual stories she told. I don't know why she chose it except that she figured it would travel well. People who know what lies will work feel they have a strong sense of reality. *Why you?* Guys—and some women—would say that to me and start a fight with me over Ora and my reputation and my work and who knows what-all? My rank includes this stuff.

The sexual stuff: orgasm—when I came in her, she was freed and free so long as she didn't come, free to be my victim while having her own will and so on. The issue arose in some circles whether she had stolen *me* and she half acceded to that story, too . . . She liked having that said of her.

She lies in bed postcoitally, the hardworking thief, her long neck at an angle and her extraordinary face starring in the moment's dramatic quietness. You can see her power as a real thing—the power of a freaky, social monster, the looks, the naked thighs, the amazed temperament—the mind, her experiences, education, dreams, deductions—you can see the sometimes upsetting power in her.

Her astounding, intelligent, sturdy, enticing lips: she said, "I'm bad mad Ora but I feel peaceful now . . . I'm on my best behavior—I'm on parole . . ." Perhaps the vast snake-dragon Medusa-deathgiving stuff in her said more stuff silently: *I love him, I am submissive, he's the* master, *he's the beauty* . . . Partly a game and partly an analysis of male-dominated reality out there and up close.

See, it is a game. A matter of style. And of will. Love as the will and style of a beauty interested in love has what merit? "I must be nice in some ways: no one ever calls me a cunt. A lot of people said I was a bitch: I said no a lot," she giggled. It was sort of a giggle.

A castrater, people said of her.

"I was never part of men's fantasies—of anyone's fantasies," she said proudly. Such tremendous untruthfulness—and inaccuracy—was not an issue with her. In the contractions and fadings and arrivals of the moment, her pride, her impotence-causing gorgeousness, her self-presentation hold hints of her being whorelike at times and of her having a genteel nursing streak now; she is trickily self-abnegating. She offers a human tie, expensive, helpful, dangerous.

"Jesus, what a world," I say. "Beauty in a democratic age—wow . . ."

"I'm not beautiful . . . You're in a state of illusion because you love me . . . Power and position and rank are more important, Wiley . . ." Sweet gorgeous nice girl in love for a while, free from male voices, more or less, the confessions: *I'm not happy with my wife . . . my mother . . . my life . . . my daughters . . . I'm a premature ejaculator . . . I won't take a minute of your time—ha-ha . . .*

Ora's suitors . . .

The daily surround, or hourly, of such drama gave her incredible merit as someone who reflected part of the society. She was like some slowly turning, very powerful, slowly focussing mechanism with a power of entry and a giant capacity for attention. Her strength was quite real. She was, herself, an entire corner of the world—oldish people invariably liked her and came alive talking to her.

She says, "I know what people think of me. But people like me—I'm no good—I'm a terrible person, Wiley. People are okay . . . I like people . . . I'm not a hermit . . ."

I echo with the reality of her and with the reality of our tie. She is not similarly scoured postcoitally. By association I echo with the reality of women. I have to stop loving her if I want to love her sensibly. If we are to live together, live and breathe. Of course, nature arranged just that very thing. I loved her best by going in and out of focus, by having moods and distraction, by failing her, by seeing her postcoitally—I'm being ironic—but it was also true so long as it was love. Acrobatics. A set of contortions.

"God, life is hard," I say, not really meaninglessly, but maybe repetitive and meaningless in her view.

Ora turns those knowledgeable eyes of hers on me, eyes which are pure pools of life shadowed by death-at-bay-for-the-moment—and she says, "You fucking son of a bitch, you really don't have a lot to complain about—do you know that?"

I can't make an absolute image of love or believe that an absolute love exists.

It's the tug and yank of the recurrence of love which makes it so oppressive. After sex, a politic shrewdness and an embarrassment with private images arrives in my case. I feel the force of her in the world, the bowsprit quality, the phallic or spiritually phallic do-jigger, but I see her as a pain in the neck and our tie as wrong for us both. I mind that. But I mind it only sadly. I am constrained by the ways men have rested their lives on her and then rebelled against that and revelled and spat and wallowed in knowing her, and were silent and cautious, and so on. I don't want to be part of that in regard to her.

The thing about the absolute and the artists who made art out of it is that the only structure they have which generates emotion is the structure of the awesomeness of the absolute and then the curiously moving pain and comedy of the mind wandering as it inevitably does in real moments, in the immensities of the real; and I prefer the structures of actual emotion and the reality of moments.

The false absolutes of false laws don't jolt me with their humanness. Jealousy is a universal thing and perhaps sex is, too, but then sexual or romantic or erotic jealousy have to be specified. I mean to say that jealousy, when all is said and done, is a way of thinking about the role of the other in one's life rather than about the other. You go on thinking mainly about yourself the whole time you are jealous. But if you think about the other person, that doesn't clearly happen; it's not the chief thing.

But I'll tell you this: the absence of the universal jealousy has a sense of monstrousness about it—and of monstrous cruelty—as if you were sublimely confident or blessed and had great faith or some such thing. I don't know that this is forgivable—this form of warfare with the entire rest of the world.

What I do know is that you can feel love without jealousy being the chief or major or fundamental part of it.

I have no readiness for nightmare. My arm beneath my head on the pillow is asleep; it tingles. My skin is goose-pimpled. I thought that a guy with Ora has this reflection of himself from her and it's as if history had already singled him out to be famous-in-a-way.

This is not illusory magnification. And it is not all there is to love, either.

It gave maybe a strange shape to my life for me to be with her. The little breathy currents of a thought, postcoital, in their cleaned-up-of-life form included the thought that this semi-comprehension, too, was momentary.

She has turned her head and is watching me.

"Don't peek," I say. Then, insultingly—but this is a tradition of asking for trouble between us because I am fragile after sex and take the offensive rather than shatter as if I were made of glass—I say, "You're the mud I roll in . . ." A joke. Of a kind.

"Wiley, you ever notice the whiteness-of-things? The way they have an outline even in the dark?" She refuses the bait.

"No," I say, although I have. "Why do you ask?"

She sniffs and doesn't answer. She may know I am being odd toward her. She has slept with two of her analysts, one of whom attempted suicide when she told him she thought he was disgusting. She'd been eighteen then. Kiki told me this.

Kiki said, *Be kind . . . She has been very hurt . . .*

"Your life insults me," I say to Ora. (Hidden in that is a compliment: that I am not equal to being near her life.)

"Your life insults me too," she said adroitly. Then she said, erasing that: "I know the world, Wiley—I'm not sentimental, I assure you . . ."

"I didn't know it would be like this," I said idly.

"Don't laugh at us, Wiley. This is once in a lifetime. No one else will love you the way I do . . ."

"Others have. Others will."

"Christ, you're a bastard. Why are you talking like this tonight?"

"Because you were getting noble . . . ."

"Oh, shut up, shut up, shut up—you can't always be right."

We understand each other, sort of.

I take her in my arms in the postcoital scoured whiteness of acknowledging that my powers in the world are at the moment greater than hers.

She says, "Love proves the world has value."

Her body in my arms adopts a reality of a pose of living, breathing death that I did when I was child and my dad held me in his arms.

My boss—I work for a television network to pay the rent—has told me he will get rid of me if he can't have Ora. My literary editor says he is infatuated with Ora although I am reasonably certain he is mostly queer. A friend of mine wants Ora to work for him: he wants to control for hours and hours of the week the woman I am close to. People approach me to see if I will double-cross her. They measure what they are against what she is in this way. Ora has a bunch of phrases she tosses around: "So be it," she says now. "THIS is the stuff dreams are made of. It matters. We *love* each other—and love is rare. To hell with God and Mammon—*go to hell, God and Mammon . . .* Other people are such shits . . ."

Even if you don't do the Gestapolike mutual interrogations of each other, holes open up, shadowy pits, fear in what she says. I am always a little afraid because of her. I say, "Am I your top hat, Ora?" People choosing their men for a board game, for Monopoly.

Her breath seemed to say she felt what I felt; she often faked such agreement. I often did, too. Do you ever fake that stuff? I said to her, "Wouldn't it be nice if we were utterly truthful?"

"I am happy for the first time in my life, Wiley . . . Leave us alone. For the first time I can see that might be partway just. So leave it *all* alone . . ."

"Okay but no one can leave things alone for long." Then: "What if we're wrong about each other?"

"Are you losing your nerve?"

It requires death finally if you really want to know about your life, perhaps. You can try to know about it even if it kills you.

She went on, "I'm not crazy, Wiley."

But she is; we all are; she has an extreme soul; she's a madwoman really; she's young, self-willed, valuable and kind of morally awful off and on but practical.

She is quite a jealous person. We were in some sort of parallel synchronicity, Ora and I, but it wasn't clear if it mattered a lot—a state of an abeyance of major pain, not totally, and a thing of being not lonely but incompletely so. It wasn't clear what the merit was. It felt meritorious though, a truly weird mixture of pity and envy and desire and nerve—an acceptance—and a slightly mythical charity toward people but toward her especially and she toward me, and a charitable but heated contempt for life itself, maybe . . .

She says, "Our passion is like a naked dahlia, Wiley . . ."

"What the fuck does that mean?"

"Oh, *you* know what that means."

"I don't."

"Then you're even more of a Jewish puritan than I thought—don't act insulted: that was not an anti-Semitic remark."

"Why would I say it was, Ora?" I said snakily-nobly . . . wearily.

"You did last time . . . You know it shows on your face—that you love me . . ."

The intelligent justice and profound sadness and oddly toned (labored over as unjeering, willfully sincere) merriment of her eyes and the silliness and calculation in her, these things are persuasive in her; they make her persuasive to me. Her bluff.

"What is love?"

"I am physically for you what the smell of a baby's skin is for a woman who likes babies."

"Is you is or is you ain't my baby, Ora?"

She shakes her head and says, "I'm hard as nails, Wiley."

Part of me loves her.

One time she wrote a play titled *To Hell with Olivia.* In it a sensitive Irish guy is in love with this coarse, earth-mother type named Olivia who gives in to his whining and they go to bed; when he can't get it up, he pushes at her head to make her go down on him to get him going; she wrestles very strenuously and carries on in words—it's not quite a good play—and she says, *Do it or don't, it wasn't my idea, it's no skin off my nose* . . . It wasn't her responsibility; and the boy says, *You're hard, Olivia, you're hard.*

I didn't like the play overall but as far as the lines went I felt I'd never seen anything so truthful written by a woman before and I was scared, pretty much, of Ora.

Of character opening off of her looks and life and mind of that sort.

Her father told me, *We were always an ugly family and then Ora came along . . . She's a swan.* Hissing and trumpeting and of enormous wingspan, and an inhabitant, in a sense, of *Swann's Way,* a book about jealousy and will and social-human cruelty in France. My father-in-law said Ora came from a line of powerful women, social duchesses, city-ruling. A shadow hovered in Ora, of feelings narrowed and specialized, of a specialized American life, its choices, its moral style, with a frame of the humane, kind of, and of being a beauty: *Oh my God look at her, she is really beautiful—she hasn't lost HER nerve . . .*

Part of me doesn't love her. And never will. One loves the pattern, the model, more than the specific example, the picture in the catalogue and not always the thing sent to you—at least you don't care in the same way. You can, I think, hold the Platonic idea in the present-tense woman willfully. Ora was faintly worn, faintly soured. She said of her nerves once: *They're like dirty piano wires now; I wish they were clean as when I was young.* I met her when I was a sophomore at Harvard and was trying to get free of a girl who, to punish me (as a moral and ethnic duty) and also just to see what would happen, to see if I had any ranking with with other girls, insisted she would let me alone and not hound me in front of other people if I would let her introduce me to Ora. At first sight, I was blistered and blinded and overcome—for a lot of seconds. I thought confusedly, *Oh Christ, this is the one.* And: *I'd put up with a lot of shit if I could live with her for a while* . . . When feeling ran cold, that meant I'd hang on in return for now. And: *Jesus, is this ever the wrong one for me, but who gives a fuck, I want this one . . .* Love at first sight takes various tones. A lot of other people felt that way too, not about the tones, about her—Ora.

It wasn't special to like her. She and I almost ran off together the night we met; we stared at each other, talked, went off to be unobserved—people had gathered flatly around us to watch—and we talked alone, outside, for hours, but she decided against me; I had too many opinions, was too young, too poor—and Jewish; she sort of said she'd already had her Jew—and she put me on her list instead. She got around to me two years later. I thought I'd live monkishly. A bachelor of uncertain tastes. But when she came after me, I gave up all my ambitions, intellectual and military—I'd wanted to go into the army—and I thought I'd try her. I'd never been drawn to anyone as I was to her—electrically, harshly, wearingly. But so were a dozen other people. Dozens. It was vulgar and hardly unique to be drawn to her. She said I had my followers too. That had been four and a half years ago.

She was superb at physically taking care of herself, doing her nails, her hair, bathing, tending her feet. Expert. Expertly knowing how to breathe, how to sleep. She never complained of hangovers, never seemed to run out of strength. The soft tissues of her breasts and cunt were scandalously independent; unmeek, they seemed to generate irony and amused complaint: she defended herself. Every moment. Oddly. If she didn't defend herself with notions of her being pathetic or being evil-and-scary, then in an ordinary busy way, but finally in a kind of scarifying truthfulness, why she was busy, who you were, her state of mind, whatever . . .

But if she put that aside and you kissed HER you found that the inside of her mouth was sweet and not clutching or acidy with nerves. She accepted it, who she was—she almost accepted it . . . A pummelled and frighteningly outsprawled and life-loosened girl, of extreme intelligence and quasi-extreme wildness, mostly practical and physically very adroit and well-informed . . . A low-level artist of will and discipline. Of character. An incredible searchlight of feminine in this form played on the world—or as an observatory observed it; the information was doled out by Mother Ora who was socially of that caste, of the segment of that caste that knows it deals in information. Newspaper people, history writers, people who want to eke out their upbringings. Socially well-placed women with troubled sons, women with a great deal of money and often of wit and style, twice, according to the stories, sought out Ora for their sons, to save them. It was just her—she had to steal some underpants to go to Nahant for one of those things. She was able. She was clumsily expert at a lot of different kinds of politics. She had unbitten fingernails. She said when I first knew her, *I don't ever want to be pitiable . . . I plan to kill myself when the juice is gone.* She said, *Some people think I'm an interesting person.* The drugs she experimented with did not capture her. Or wreck her. Certain books of ideas, books self-flagellant and conceited, she carried with her everywhere; and if you thought she was a snob for liking the writers she liked in her sophomore year, Aristophanes, Vita Sackville-West, Ortega y Gasset, and Jane Austen, snappish and comic, elitist and comic further, romantic and comic yet further, she would say, *Go fuck yourself . . . I don't discuss literature on first dates . . .*

And then her programmatic submissiveness to some of the women writers of her own time, the tinkling awfulness of the styles, the opinions, the spun sugar of will or the iron of it, the rage, the hideous vaginal gothicisms, the unreliable intelligence was very like that of guys with the clunky styles, and staggeringly stale opinions, and pocketknife things of will, the rage, and hideous phallic lament or triumph. She was impressed by Hemingway but she thought his stuff was jejeune.

And all the time, the glow of what the girl was, the uneven and troubled radiance, stained and irregular, her hands, her tempers, her sudden amusement, the way the dirtiness and the stupidity touched her.

And then all she already knew.

I said, "God your life is interesting. I tried to go to an analyst: he was interested in me until he asked me about money, and when I said I had none, I was on a scholarship, he started telling me I was normal . . ."

I was grateful that my nerves held up when I was with her.

"You had an analyst who told YOU YOU WERE NORMALLL . . . OH MY GOD, OH MY GOD, OH MY GOD . . ." She laughed then in a strange tone.

I never saw her burn her mouth on coffee. She was physically hyperconscious. She couldn't keep track of all she knew; and she'd become bemused. She knew I was infatuated with her. Then she said, I 'loved' her—she saw or at least named the stuff differently after a while. Our madness and reclusiveness as a couple were her idea, were part of her style ab ovo—prep-school lovers going off to be alone, being social but belonging to the affair: in our case, at first because I wasn't from a prep school, we did that more and less both; and then we heavily did it. At some parties we went to, she slept in the middle of everyone. She more flatly rejected professors and the like—despite a new sweetness in her face, she still looked like fate, or fatedness, to a lot of people.

She said, "You and I are twins."

"No we're not. I wish we were. But we aren't."

Imaginary twinship is how she got past self-centeredness—she believed that solipsism was the truth of things. But she was aware of people: she said, "In the country of the blind, the one-eyed woman is king . . ."

She couldn't always hold a job—people were hard on her. She usually picked one man, married, but he only occasionally protected her.

A person is, of course, limited and is caught up in the unyielding motions of everything, including her own. Stubbornly wronging, often wrong, awash in the mornings—in heartbeat, in desire—she chooses to be loneliness enlarged and partly eased echoingly.

She leans over and fiddles with my mouth with her fingertips. For a moment I have a queer glamour of being ministered to. She declared herself mine in this bossy way—she did it in public and in private. I was grateful but not always pleased. I was amused by her, however. She is jealous of everything she doesn't cause.

"What do you dream of, Ora?"

"I dream of peace and of catastrophe. You're not so different from other men." I was man enough, ordinary enough, extraordinary enough in a regular way, that I could be with her. She said, "Your eyes—you never come forward inside your eyes, you always stay back—in the bandit territories. You know you like to hurt people, Wiley. You're too self-righteous to be honest. You will hurt me in some way that will last me the rest of my life . . . But it's all right; I'm very strong. It's worth it not to be alone . . . for once."

A love speech . . . from a narcissistic solipsist? I don't know. My mood was lightening. Privileges and all, she's human. My heart clenches, then pounds in the elevation of my luck. When we first started to be together, I'd said that I would risk being hurt or humiliated by her or others and that I would risk harming her, bearing *that* guilt. I would do it in order to be with her . . . for a while. "Fancy-shmancy Harvard speeches," I say now, as she said four and a half years back.

She said, "Don't laugh at us anymore just now, Wiley."

I know from the fuck, as she does in a different vocabulary in her, how we feel. This isn't final. The extraordinary self-violation, self-squandering of love that goes on, my flesh gropes along in the swirling boxcar-rustling arrival and surround of the multiplicity of slightly sequential arriving and fading in these lucky and troubled circumstances.

Her breath testifies, terrifies, soothes, confesses, and lies. Her nighttime relentlessness of personality—I mean, the absence of fear in her when we are alone at night, toward me, toward us (I am always a little frightened about us and of her—and of an individual moment and how it might slide this way or that for me)—the evidence of the fuck offering a temporary modification of the infatuate's terror—this has worn beauty.

Ora says suddenly, "You know, Wiley, guilt is a cliché."

I say, "Touché . . . Yeah, I know. Is it?"

She says, "I think you ought to admit I am mostly a sincere person. You know something? You're not typical . . . You're not a Wandering Jew—not really. You're not like other men. Are you worried about the Jews?" Because of the Holocaust.

"No . . . Not right now . . . Not at the moment." I am in a way. I'm haunted by ghosts. A phrase gets into my mind—*They're all dead*—and won't leave for a while.

She says, a little Radcliffe-ishly, "The Catholics are right: despair is really a no-win cul-de-sac. Why do you want to be *good* . . . It's not possible." She offers this, at this hour: "You're like Julius Caesar."

I say, "You like names becoming historical words . . . I like some act or ritual or quality of person that indicates, I don't know, *grace* . . . I'd feel better then . . . I feel all right now but I'd feel better—especially if tough times are coming . . ."

"I don't know. I'm not afraid," she says. "Now a name that people would use for all time, Wiley, I don't know—maybe it would indicate love."

Our vague blind sociability at this hour suddenly opens, for me, into deep fear: a pit of meaning but part of the meaning is my own meaninglessness and error so far, so far during my life; I say, "What do you know about it? I try to be strong for you. I show off for you. I lie to you all the time about how strong I am. Let's go to sleep."

"Okay."

"It's not good to be tired in New York among the MONSTERS. You don't understand; you never get tired . . ."

"That's because I'm not ruthless. What are you really after? I think you're a Napoleon type. After all, all I am is someone who is going to be destroyed by you . . ."

"Ah, your destiny . . ."

"Well, it matters . . ."

"I told you, Ora. I told you my great secret: when I was a child, people said I was a genius and that it would push people around."

"Oh I love minds. I love the human mind. Just hush up. Really, you come from a small town after all. I'm a thinker, Wiley. I'm prepared. I don't think your mind is so strange."

It's strange about city darkness; it is made of specks of light and smears of shadow and then deeper darkness, and then of dots and dashes of quiet grayness, some of them bunched; and all of it together forms a shadow-riddled whitish late-night iridescence, phosphorescence, luminescence.

She went on with emphasis at first, "I AM a thinker, and I think a lot of what a man is is he is not a woman. I understand you," she said.

"I understand that boasting at bedtime is a little like a lullaby you sing yourself . . . Or it's maybe like hugging your pillow . . . I understand nothing," I say.

"You're putting on weight. You're pretty, still. We can't understand things, Wiley . . . People can't . . . We do what we have to do—we obey categorical imperatives. I think you're sentimental about understanding stuff. The world is everything that is and is not the case—if it is the case then we know it is not the case," she said collegiately, quietly-hugely. A statement can be like a pole for a pole vaulter. From some mental position, some authoritative and watched aeriality, she said, "I don't know what you want . . . You don't know either . . ." Then: "I don't want to know now anything." She is only dimly visible. "You think other women are as good as I am but they are not. I am more peaceful now than I have ever been . . . Even as a child I hated sleeping alone in a bed." Hers is an assertive, creating-life beauty.

"Oh, don't be so *human*, Ora," I say. "It's an uphill battle living with the way I see things." Then: "It is strange about even small distances—how they dilute stuff. If I am right next to you, I can't remember much or see much beyond you, past you."

"You're the only person who knows how sweet I am," she says somberly. Then she laughs in an odd way—a smallish but drawn-out lengthways laugh . . .

The reality of being empty, of being defiled by grown-up life—by love among other things—the distillation and concentration of love is the heart of long-term fucking, perhaps too of the efforts on one's part to rule one's life. To understand one's choices, even that one has made choices, and the connections and parallels, the threads and gimmicks of the foreseen: all that happens in a certain, somewhat literary, French tone, in emptiness. She, Ora, *fights* to see that we love, that I do . . . I really don't know why: I know it is a human and not an absolute thing.

It scares me . . . makes me uneasy . . . makes me ironic and *superior* . . .

"What is one to do about one's lostness-in-the-world? Lie about it? I suppose you have to when you have children—all the little reasons crawling around the floor and yelling their heads off . . ."

"Are you going to sleep?" she asked.

"I am going Nowhere," I said. "Bye-bye: will you miss me?"

"Yes . . . Do you want a cover over you?" Ora asked.

"When I get cold. But soon your hip will creep over me, then your arm, the big hot stones of fire-baked arms and legs . . ."

"Am I too heavy? A shallow girl like me? Oh, I'm shallow as a puddle . . . Why should I be *heavy*," she shook her head with no-understanding and as if with self-loathing, comically. It is a joke . . .

"Ha-ha," I say.

She says then, putting her head on my chest, "Tell me the truth: is my skull too big?"

"No. Yes-after-a-while . . . See how untrusting—and nervous—we are."

"Oh, Wiley, tell me what you're thinking: do you see the future? Is everything all right?"

"No. Let's just guess. It would be so nice to be real. Ora, I'm too apologetic—and embarrassed—to be anything much."

"You're real."

"Thanks . . . The measure for love that I use is middle-class; it is the limits we set to how much we let ourselves hurt each other and when we knock ourselves out not to hurt the other guy . . ." Now there is a thing in speech that someone has to see through what you're saying. They have to do the opposite of what you say you want—otherwise, they can never see what you're talking about. I could feel myself unconsciously but I observed it now a little after the fact daring her to test our tie. "I shouldn't have said that . . . If I were more like my sister, if I were more like Nonie, I'd lie so you'd react in another way . . . She's more suitable for these kinds of moments than I am . . . She's sort of freed to try them out." I am not Nonie. I said it out loud. "But I am not Nonie . . ."

Ora stirs where she lies next to me and on me; a tension is in her body; I sigh and think, *What next* . . .

Nonie in Love

Pain, the murder at waking: the murder of dreams (and the obliteration of the populace in dreams) that waking is: a cough, a fever: a sudden emotion making itself known as unbearable: Nonie said to me once, "You never get hurt. You're not human. You don't have feelings. You don't know *anything* . . ."

She said of herself, "I'm a strong person, things just roll off my back, I guess: look at me, I'm just bright and shiny and raring to go—"

The body remembers pain. A stick, a belt, a person. An effectual taunt. In duration pain can seem to represent an aspect of eternity. One's own pain. Someone else's. I'm not sure what difference someone else's pain *ought* to make in the moral scales of determining what you do—so many people, so much pain. Because of the statistics, this isn't something that should be put to a vote, probably.

But my own pain—I remember the first time my arm was twisted: *Tell me the truth and I'll let you go* . . .

The shock, the disbelief at the sensation didn't keep me from calculating whether I could afford to give in: *Owwwwww* . . . *I'll tell you the truth* . . . The unfortunate self-revelation then, the unmasking of this technique, this other plane of reality when you've lost, lost out, is this part of *normalcy*? Is fear? When I was very little, I fell down a flight of stairs, and I remember the pain and shock and the curious absence of fear . . . *Oh, you little idiot, did you hurt yourself?* I remember my strangulated and agonized silence, I had knocked the air out of myself and I couldn't breathe or speak. The immediate memory of wheeling and cartwheeling walls and ceilings as I fell, the nausea, the devastation of my breath and mind, the dissolution of the ordinary reality of my strength in pain, and, still, I wasn't afraid.

Do you want to kill yourself? Have you no sense? I think I did feel fear for someone else before I learned it for myself. I think it was my nurse, Anne Marie. Did you ever wake early and move silently and come on someone who was close to you and who had been awake all night, in a bad state, and was wounded, scarred, *at the last gasp*? I felt fear then. Did you fall silent? Did you feel like a child on a battlefield?

Often, when I was a child and I was hurt, Daddy would say, in sympathy, *You're breaking my heart . . . I can't go on until you feel better . . . Will you help me feel better,* PISHER*?* Sometimes it's fine with me then—truly—if his heart breaks . . . I don't care what becomes of him. I don't love him. The abstract and as-if-*universal* darkness of hurt, the sharp wretchedness, the delirium of defeat, make it hard to go on; it is like walking in fire; and Dad says, *It's not fair to punish me like this. I'd prefer it if you hit me in the head with a coal shovel, Pisherkins. Just learn to keep on going. It's time for you to learn to live to fight another day . . .*

It's scary how it matters who loves whom and what love is in someone and how that burns and stings and stinks and tears you and then how it doesn't matter. Ma said, perhaps on this matter: "*Nonie is of the world, worldly* . . . Well, we all have to learn to grin and bear it . . ."

S.L. said, "We'll fix it, we'll fix it . . . The U.S.A. is the land of hope and good medicine." He was a Utopian. "It's the home of the cure . . ."

Momma said, "S.L. is impatient with the least little unhappiness . . ." Momma said of that, as she said of a number of things, "I tell you that can be *A NIGHTMARE*."

Do you treat your soul like a child? Do you guard it from the sight of blood? From the knowledge of unkindness?

The point at which my speech could goad a grown-up or a child my own age to violence was one of the things I studied in my childhood . . . I tested and observed and tried out various things.

In the first second of falling, Katie didn't believe she was falling, that it was happening. She didn't know what she should believe. Katie withheld her belief. Katie had no factual sense that she was falling. She didn't think it was plausible. She asked, *Am I falling?* She didn't answer herself; she saw that she was—the trees suddenly moved in such a way that she knew she was falling through the air. She hoped she was dreaming . . . This is how it had happened to me; I change it and apply it to her. I saw her fall down her front steps. I don't really know what she felt . . . She saw that time had gone funny . . . I mean she knew it was real because it didn't rearrange itself to seem plausible. It just went on. She —or I—when I fell, I thought, *Oh, oh.* I had no certainty yet that I would come to irreversible harm. I mourned the day's dreamlike and racing and skidding peaceableness, the world's upside-down and spinning beauty as I turned over as I fell. I mourned my lost safety. The light darkened for me. In the nostalgic and sickened nowhere that the moment is for me, now, she's bouncing on the steps and grass: her shoulders and back strike and slide. Her head jounces, too. The grass tears and slides beneath me and gives off its own disturbed, odorously lamenting odor. It's real.

I don't know how to rescue myself. I am in the middle of a nowhere. The sky glides pivotingly and I start to feel the coldness of shock . . . I can bear real pain only for a while.

For a while in her life, until now Katie has mostly loved unhurtable, uncheapenable God, her Father, more than she loved the dirtied Jesus. But it will be different now. When her shoulder hit the step near the grass and went out of its socket, she passed into a state of cold patience, a marvel: faith and resignation and numb endurance. In a planeless space of hurt.

Don't hurt me . . . Don't hurt me anymore . . .

"NO! NO!" she said aloud as she fell.

In her monstrous momentum, Katie bounced and slid on tearing grass and on firm-edged stone steps; she was flung up and over; the blood when she skidded, *the breath knocked out of her* and the rigor of shocked suffocation and the supplication for air, well, when I was older, I could almost bear it. Something in the soul is criminal—and perhaps because of its own fright—or pain—knows a lot about these things from early on in one's life and comes to terms of a kind with them—do you know?

One time when I fell, I fell from a tree; I fell fourteen feet, and in that short section of a minute, I felt myself to be stretched, a wire of inner noise and to have an Animal Impracticality of Shape—my arms and legs were too long and would be hurt—and I would be violated—and insulted by the injury.

The first moment of pain is partly guessed at and is only partly known; it is partly unfelt because of shock—and a kind of horror: *Why is this happening to me? Why are you doing this to me?* . . . whoever *you* are . . .

The concrete of the driveway rattles my cheekbone and numbs and stuns my skull.

So far in my life when I've been hurt, I've yelled or shouted or grunted; I haven't yet in my life screamed with pain—do you know?

One time, skin-diving, I saw in a rough-edged cavernlike hole in a reef a moray eel, its mouth wide open second after second. It looked to me as if it was insane with combat and with constant, quite awful *pain.*

And the sound of a bone breaking . . . *I told you never to throw the baseball bat, I told you someone would get hurt* . . .

Hurt flesh, you can't promise it that sleep will be unwounding. Sleep is wounding over and over. I don't love her and I never will love her. I forgive her but I don't love her. I'm just not interested, I'm sorry. I'm a coward. I've been hurt enough.

A local accident: her mother had not wanted Katie ever to feel pain—*You'd think she'd know better,* Lila said of someone else; but, really, she didn't *know* better at all . . .

Thud, thud—the sound of fists on flesh . . . I remember that. Do you love those who torment you? Do you get even? Do you live in a haze of agony? Do you find hate to be useful? Do you hate often? A lot of people? I'm not actually curious about these things. When S.L. died and, off and on, I couldn't get my breath, I said to myself, *Oh my God, it really* IS *like A Blow* . . . Momma believed, I think, that the truest awareness of the world was to be found in a sadist who knew what he or she was doing . . . This isn't something I face often. I remember putting dark thoughts aside when I was a child, especially when Mom said, *Well, put a good face on it, company is coming.*

Pain and felicity and being trained to handle and endure pain so that you can have some real power over your own life, and trespasses and intrusions and being politic—aren't they part of every childhood?

Daddy said, *A good time isn't a kick in the pants* . . .

Pain: cheap windup clocks clanging and jerking in my breath, and an electric buzzing and chiming in my mind from my alarmingly, seemingly swollen backbone . . .

You goddamned well better know what you're doing to me or I'm going to educate you in my existence (as someone-who-does-harm). But forgive and forget, we have to learn to take the bitter with the sweet, we only have one life.

Leave me alone . . .

Pain? It was like silk, dirty and scummy silk, and then it got bite-y—like bite-y, dirty, scummy SILK . . . Ora said this. *I never want to be* THAT *wide awake again. I wouldn't fight cancer: I'd kill myself before I'd live with that pain.*

I steal a lot of what I consciously think. I have taken a lot of what I consciously think from things she said during the time we were together. *I never want to be that far from my dreams again . . . I have no interest in that part of life . . . The one thing I'm not is a masochist . . . I don't like pain. I'm probably not a moral person because I wouldn't go through a lot just to keep things going or to serve my country—I don't care if things go on or not. I want you to know this about me . . . I am brave, strong, and true, and I am willing to die, but I don't like pain: you'd better know this about me.*

And now the creep Wiley will have his name inscribed in THE BOOK OF AMERICAN PAIN.

Lila said, This is a democracy. We all get our turn in the sun, we get our turn at winning and then we get the other, the pie in our face . . .

Things I didn't think about when I was young included a cousin's suicide in an insane asylum and never admitted to except in a low, secret voice—I mean the texture of feeling in her before she did it—and an uncle's heart attack while his wife was yelling at him—this was also a family secret—and a neighbor's death while waiting for an ambulance to come . . .

Except when showing off with other kids who wanted to talk about and maybe think about such things, I never thought how bad it was inside some people when they were going through a terrible moment . . . I had friends who had said that was *middle-class* and stupid, to think about such things, to be afraid that such things existed.

I hate it when someone says, *No, no, you're not hurt . . .* when I am hurt. I hate it when someone plays with my feelings, causing me stupid pain, and they're not really licensed to do that. I hate when people say of your pain that it's minor; it doesn't count; it's all in the game. And it's major and it does count and it's no game I volunteered for. I hate that amateur self-absolution.

Lila said, *I have to hand it to Nonie for one thing—she lives in the real world.*

I read in a book that devils were interesting and angels were boring as shit—and I agreed until I thought about devils and pain, and I thought, *Oh oh, the hell with that jazz.*

I'LL BE CRAZY IN JUST ONE MORE MINUTE IF YOU DON'T SHUT UP

. . . YOU'RE DRIVING ME CRAZY. I DON'T KNOW IF I'M COMING OR GOING AND I DON'T WANT TO TALK ABOUT CHILDISH THINGS RIGHT NOW DO YOU MIND? BAD THINGS HAPPEN AND THAT'S THAT.

Momma said to me once, *You know that thing where they say, "My strength is as the strength of ten because my soul is pure"—do you suppose there's any truth in that?* She said more than once, *Pain is a terrible thing.* And: *Pain is just disgusting.* And: *It is very hard to be with someone in pain, Wiley, unless they're brave.*

A lot of people I knew, young and old—everyone really, at least now and then—was finally merciless in any of several styles.

I figure I can kill. Mostly I'm a pacifist, but I can stop caring about self-restraint. Ora's mother asked me with resignation when she first met me, *Are you a psychopath? Of any kind?*

I said, *Do you think Ora would pick a psychopath?*

She said, *Just tell me if you are or not.*

Ora did like psychopaths; she'd told me: ex-cons, crazed, great ex-generals, loon-lesbians of a great order of accomplishment, mean theater directors . . . So long as they had *glamour.* She liked *glamourous* psychopaths and always had, she said.

I said to her mother, *I'm very middle-class—I've never really hit anyone. You can look into my eyes and see. See what's there: I'll hold still.*

Ora's mother, Millie, a heavy drinker, said, *I'm nearsighted. Just answer my questions. I'm her mother and I don't know you.*

Irritated, I said, *I don't know. We'll have to wait and find out. I would say that I doubted that I was a psychopath.*

I am not certain what terrifies me in real life. I think I have an *inherent* chemical suitability for bearing horror, a genetic thing of anticipatory or a priori shock or anesthesia but not numbness. It permits concentration. I used to be able to help at accidents. *Don't get your father angry—you don't know what it will lead to* . . . When S.L. became angry, purple came and went in his face. His lips darkened and his eyes swelled up and looked at stuff without fondness or caring. Mom used to send me to talk to him then. I would be tense and excited but not scared and sad. My Uncle Henry had cold, snobbish malice and dismissal at his disposal—he was the richest person in the family. All the guys and women I know have some sweaty reality of temper or other. S.L. said of my real mother, angrily, *She was some kind of religious nut and a whore who slept with killers and rednecks . . . She liked laughing at people—she got what she deserved—you're well out of it, knowing that fat bitch of a whore . . .*

Lila said to me: *Don't hold it against him. You never know with him who he's going to be jealous of next.* And he apologized later, too.

S.L. often said he was ashamed. He would sit on my bed at night and he would say, *Give me a hug, Pooperkins: make everything all right for me, will you? How about it, how about telling your old man all is forgiven: he's a real good guy: he pays the bills: he's a good guy and he loves you, Pooper; so you want to tell him what a sweetheart he is?*

If I wanted to hurt him then, I would push him away and not let him hold me and I would say—in one tone or another—*I like Momma better than I like you . . .*

Often I did, in part because it seemed to me that she did less harm in the world, that she hurt people less.

If he wanted to fight back with me when I was unforgiving, he would indirectly call me a baby: *Well, maybe you'll outgrow all the horseshit,* he would say; *and maybe you won't.*

Sometimes you get sick and you give up.

Lila said before she died, *I would have been nicer but I thought I was having a good time the way I was.*

The Nazis: about the local ones and the ones in Europe, she said, *It takes only one fool to burn your house down.* And: *I don't want to be insulted. I don't think it's smart to live in a small town at this time.* She made a joke in front of company about this: *In St. Louis, the houses are brick. I take* The Three Little Piggies *seriously. Well, that's the long and the short of it. I've got a new project: tell the truth and shame the devil—you think that will work?*

Nonie Continued: Welcome: At the Net: University City: 1934

In University City, Katie Rogers lived in a large brick cottage on a street, a cul-de-sac, of such cottages, each one imaginatively droll, with high sweeping gable fronts and lower gabled front porches in brick and whitestone. And each had an unusually tall, fairly droll brick chimney, with decorative white brick crosses and lozenges set in patterns here and there or had twisted bricks at the corners. Each cottage had small leaded windows with black shutters with brass fastenings—a real street of a hundred of these windows, one street over from ours—actually, half the street, and on one side of the street only, facing larger Queen Anne brick houses.

Katie's house was set high on a plump round of lawn, through which a curving reach of sixteen brick- and whitestone-walled steps were cut from the front porch down to the concrete driveway which led to the garage in the basement of the *adorable* cottage. The driveway, too, was partly underground and had brick stone-topped walls of different heights on either side and beds of daffodils on top of both walls.

Likelihood changes when people freely shop and read advertisements often. Unreality becomes real: fairy tales are told and are acted out and influence the architecture.

"I DIDN'T DO *ANYTHING*! I DIDN'T DO IT, PEOPLE SHOULDN'T BELIEVE *HER*—PEOPLE BELIEVE THINGS ABOUT ME BECAUSE I'M AN ATH-A-LETE AND I PLAY TO WIN. PEOPLE SHOULDN'T BELIEVE *BAD* THINGS . . . KATIE IS NO GOOD! LISTEN TO ME, SHE WETS HER PANTS, SHE LIKES TO DRINK LIQUOR —I KNOW ABOUT HER, MOMMA, LISTEN TO ME!"

"What a tumble she took . . . My God, I don't want to think about it . . ." Then: "Well, it isn't life or death, thank God."

Nonie said, "IT IS TOO LIFE AND DEATH . . ."

Daddy said, "Don't make a mountain out of a molehill: no one was killed, she took a real tumble is all it is . . . We're lucky it's not worse . . . It's only good sense to know it coulda been *worse*. Everyone got off easy this time."

Margy, Katie's mother, is combative and pious, not dressy, and she goes from sad discipline to surprised interest and amusement. Sometimes she seems as if she has been thrown into a pit of innerness. She is mostly present but dutifully, patiently. She has frizzy hair and good features. She has a nice, tuneless, flat voice. She took her daughter out of parochial school and put her in the pretty-much-Protestant public school. I have heard people say her husband is better educated than she is, and better looking; but he married her and they're Catholic; so he sticks to her. Lila has said, *He plays around; he's cute; but I don't like him*.

It may be because of her mother's voice or because she is tense and somewhat pious but Katie blinks her eyes as often as if she were in a noisy factory. Katie was *interesting-looking*—tall for her age and freckled, big-legged and blurting, soft-eyed. Katie has longish, wavy hair often braided with escaped and often shiny red-brown filaments in the light. Her presence is actually honeylike for me—I taste it . . .

I played with the two of them, Katie and Nonie. Sometimes we played in hidden places, such as the porch of some people down the street who were away on a trip. The porch had a low brick wall around most of it; and if you sat down you were out of sight of the street. The porch was unswept. Some twigs and dried leaves here and there mean the people are away.

In the corner of the porch, out of sight behind the low wall, we sat cross-legged on the cold concrete and the girls spoke in low voices or in whispers. Bribed, kissed, hugged, cajoled—ordered by Nonie, smiled at by Katie—I joined in their games—mostly silently . . . Sometimes idly and hardly interested, sometimes incontinently interrupting, I was the child if they played house, and one or the other of them was the wife, and the other was the husband. I was sometimes the patient when they played doctor and nurse. Katie undresses me: nifty *Catholic* fingers, her soapy odors, the half-nutty glare she had when she was playing these games; and the tremor she had, as it were of unease or fear or interest at the no-clear-boundaries of unwatched games.

Nonie, the ship's doctor, makes a play incision in my stomach—with a twig. My short pants are around my ankles. My shirt is unbuttoned. I am largely undressed except for my socks and shoes behind the brick wall of the porch, a smallish, blond child, a month or two short of being four years old. Katie kisses my stomach to make it well after the operation. She is the mother of the ship's surgeon and a queen—something like that. The two of them bent their varicolored, bright-skinned girls' heads over me down there; and they studied my balls—they handled and turned over and lightly pinched the little, pale beans. I remember the girls stroking them with bits of dead leaf. And using twigs like pick-up-sticks and even like tongs. They used their fingers delicately, and I remember their breath on my small stomach and the wind above my head at the height of the wall and the concrete on my bared ass. I remember laughing and the girls telling me to hush.

Or we played more safely, and they sang lullabies, and I pretended to sleep. I would softly cry out "Wah-wah" like a real baby. Sometimes the wind circled downward and nipped and bit at me like a puppy.

In dreams when I am naked on a suburban street I feel I will die in some final way if anyone sees me. I will congeal with exposure and embarrassment and will burst and not live anymore, but in real life I didn't always much care.

Katie, big-eared, unshrewd, gets angry if Nonie teases her. Nonie waits miserably-angrily for Katie to telephone her sometimes. In street games in which a lot of the kids join, Katie is a *tearing* (Catholic) *maniac*, people say. Katie's moods are like river birds scuttering in her, ticklish to see . . . for me. She screams easily in large games, breathes tensely in smaller ones.

She screams when Nonie boosts me onto a tree branch to hide and then she gets Katie to come near; and when Katie comes near I say *boo* and Katie screams and screams.

Katie says, *"I have a stupid silly face, I KNOW it."* The freckles and large, emotionally simplified, farsighted, eerily vague eyes.

"She gets to go to heaven—that's very consoling. I feel worse for atheist kids." Dad said that of her after she fell. He often spoke of hellfire and of goblins and of demons and pitchforks. Of hell he said, "It's noisy down there." He was haunted by it, the idea, the possible reality of the sizzling clutch of a demon, the wretched whisper and scream of eternal pain. "The goblins'll git yah if yah don't witch out." And: "In hell, bad folks'll sizzle and grunt like pork sausage." He was mostly interested in women who were Catholics and in ex-Fundamentalists who had a fear of hell. He'd say to me, "You in a rush to go to hell?" I was playing with a cigar of his that I'd taken from his pocket—the cellophane, the

band, the smell of the thing. "Give it back, Little Pretty Eyes. Hanging's too good for a cigar thief . . ."

(Lila said after his funeral, "My heart breaks for him now, that poor son of a bitch. I knew him backwards and forwards and I don't hold it against him one bit what he was.")

Katie's a pet of Wiley's, he likes her freckles, Momma said. I lolled against Katie's barely started new breasts childishly. Katie was *nice.* In high school I had a teacher who said the word nice was an abomination and *conveyed no information whatsoever* but it did. Katie spoke differently from Nonie but Nonie then talked like Katie for a while: *Fant-TAS-TICKLE . . . Grub-grub . . . OOooh, that's worse than WHALE DOOO-DOOO! Yuh-yuh-UGHhhhhh.*

Katie fell-in-love with trees, sports, sunsets, children, movies, famous people—and insisted blankly that you had to, too. Of a certain boy she liked, she said, "Oh, he's just so cuuuuuuute I ca-hint stannnnnnnnnn(d) ITTTTT . . . I will probuhhhhhhhblee die-eeeeee . . ." It was his bike she mostly liked—and his style riding it, it turned out.

Enthusiastic—mannerly—huge (in proportion to me). It is possible that Momma, angry with Nonie and trying to win an argument with her, said, *I'd rather have Katie for a daughter than YOU.* But rivalry doesn't always need an outside trigger to get it going more violently.

Katie's flapping sundress the day she fell, it flapped like a flag as she fell. Her shoulder blade was thrown out. *Fantastickle, grub-grub.* If you see someone fall, in those seconds, in some of those seconds, the figure is not that of a person—it is that of someone who is unlucky . . . and you withdraw. I do, I become a bystander figure . . . I try to regulate my sympathies. It is not one of us, it is someone who has lost her safety who is falling.

Lila says, *I can't feel sorry for everyone—I haven't that kind of time—I'm serious when I feel sorry for someone . . . Now, S.L. feels sorry as a general rule; he does a little here and a little there; and then he thinks he's Mahatma Gandhi; but it's a big show with him. He likes to pretend he's the Biggest Cheese in the World and just like Gandhi.*

A pretty girl, a lovely person . . . a child. Those were terms for sympathy. They set, or calibrated, one's dismay. *A fine person, never did any harm to anyone.*

(If I asked S.L. or Lila a question about what they were saying, each, either was likely to say, *Hush, the grown-ups are talking.*)

It is hard to know what to think about someone else's pain. After she fell, she was there on the concrete of her driveway. She held out her hand—her thumb is askew. Her nose was swollen and torn. Her forearms begin to darken a purple-and-green and shuddery ochre and were beginning to swell. Her shoulder is out of its socket. She is not so deep in shock that she fails to be upset at how she looks.

Don't let the pain break your spirit . . .

Katie, six months ago, hurt a boy (who was teasing her) by hitting him in the forehead with a roller skate.

It was what Ma would call *A seven days' wonder . . .* No one particularly cared about it.

(Lila has said to S.L. about one thing and another: *You ought to fight back, S.L. Taking it lying down isn't going to improve your standing.*)

In the first moment of falling, when you're the faller, you enter a wide and glassy moment—or I did—a moment of the conviction of the oncoming of real pain. It's a different circumstance of will. You keep yourself from screaming or you don't—Daddy used to say, *Being a coward makes a lot of sense some ways.* It's been my .perience that my blood does run cold when the accident starts, maybe in preparation for the chill of shock. I fall into the raw mouth of air and pursue comfort—first in a calculation of the event as *This probably won't kill me . . . Daddy's near . . . He'll get me to the hospital . . . There'll be blood . . .* Then the first thud and the conviction of pain around a central wooden mass of shock, your body still conscious in ugly surprise. Then maybe you lose your head for a while in the pain. My head sits above the plunging, roaring body and is silent and inert. Maybe I am crying. I pass out in blinks; the chagrin is raw. I trusted a dead tree branch. In a way, the onset of pain is a little bit like falling asleep: here is the *sudden* other landscape, or world, or planet, or headscape, here is the ruined other light; now I will never be, oh, a good shortstop, or beautiful . . . I will never be a worthwhile person now. The dread *ruinousness* of the state . . . the thread snapping and you are in darkness . . . You are in the pain continuum.

A slap, a fall, serious grief, the collapse of love, a bad humiliation, I think: *Oh yes, here it is.*

I was never of divine substance, never so clever or so privileged as to escape this stuff for very long. The feeling of my face and of my hair in the air at such times—well, once blood fell from a cut on my forehead and clotted on my eyelids, and in my eyelashes. The self-conscious belief, overall, in a suburban neighborhood that the place is idyllic or *Elysian*, that no one needs to suffer, trembles and collapses.

Momma, Momma, I hurt myself . . .

Be brave. Try to be brave.

Momma, Momma, I look disgusting . . .

One time when I was hurt S.L. looked up at the sky and muttered, *What the hell is going on?*

Katie, as she fell, called out, "Nonie!" I have thought about this, and I can see that it can be argued she called out to Nonie to save her. Maybe Katie stepped backward and fell *accidentally* . . . Nonie was saying something bad and Katie stepped back . . . MAYBE THE DEVIL WAS RUNNING THINGS AT THAT MOMENT—it was Pure Accident that means. Maybe Nonie forgot the steps were there when she pushed Katie—if she pushed Katie. Maybe Nonie, goaded, did it unconsciously. Maybe Katie felt *guilty* and *was looking to have an accident* (a local thing that was said often). The movement of Nonie's hands was perhaps a flutter and not a push and Katie misread it, especially if both girls were in an unruly bonfire of temper toward each other—*little fishwives* (a phrase of Daddy's). They were shouting at each other. Under some circumstances, *THINGS CHANGE. YOU DON'T BLAME PEOPLE THEN* . . .

The memory of the ugly phosphorescence of the realization that you have been hurt triggers the sympathy, but if you want to help, you must not let yourself be upset—by the damaged nose, the skewed thumb, the blood in the eye socket. Do you live in a luminously *intended* universe some of the time?

(Daddy, being unkind, has said of Margy Rogers—as he has of other women—that she sees the Devil in every man's butt-end.)

When Margy ran out of her house to go to Katie, her face was lit with a kind of narrowness of brilliance of doctrinal resistance . . . An immediate agony—and exaltation—of revision. Daddy often accused women (and children) of being *important*. For a long time I didn't know why he thought that was *an accusation*.

He said, *Everyone has to be important: that's what's wrong with the world: a little humble cooperation would make the world a better place.* But he taught me that holding some doctrine or other unreasonably *was* a matter of honor.

Nonie hit me with a brick once . . . And she threw a knife with the blade aimed and cut me just over the eye. The motions of her temper are a given language. Not uncommon.

Margy in her shorts, navy-blue. The muscles and visible skin of her throat ticked and flinched. Shock, nausea and chills, then screaming and the bile; and the awful shame at being hurt—in the sunlight, Katie and Margy in shorts holding her daughter. She begins by saying, "How did you let this happen?" but then she mostly shuts up. In a practical sense, this was one of the human limits of kindness. Nonie may have been innocent, *but it was Nonie*. Nonie, up high on the lawn, said, "I can't stand the sight of blood—" She was going to faint. She was asking for help. I felt that her making a claim to be the primary survivor here was a form of guilt—the wish to be the one whose survival matters more, or most, suggests what the reality was like before this moment. The *Deal with me first: save* ME means the other person was never real. I think Margy knew from her past when she had been the guilty one, knew the terms of guilt; that thirst for fame, the attitudinizing thing in self-justification. That asking for one's own suffering to come *first*. Innocence takes its turn . . . I think . . . I don't know. I am alive. I don't *know*.

The sly thing that the mind is. The *demon*-twists of one's pretensions.

A neighbor—Melissa Van Maytree—was running across her lawn with a white enamelled tin box with a red cross on it in her hand. (The box held gauze bandages, a scissors, an enamelled white tin circular thing around a central hole—adhesive tape—a bottle of iodine with a rubber eyedropper . . . Mercurochrome . . . a mercury thermometer, a dimestore one, with red mercury.) The box was rattling-chittering. Melissa, forty years old, ran, smart-eyed, clumsy-footed, horrified, worried-looking, calm enough; she was accusing-and-important. Margy Rogers is kneeling in the driveway holding Katie. Nonie at the top of the steps is faint. Nonie *can't bear* the sight of blood. The time she hit my eye with the thrown knife, she passed out. Margy said to Nonie, "Why are you looking at us like that?" Katie, the bloodied girl, hair disarranged, long legs sprawled and bare, her damaged hand rests against Margy's blouse. Lila said later, *I stand by Nonie just the way Margy stands by Katie* . . . The ways the girls were mothered are part of the story.

Nonie wibble-wobbles on the steep, rounded height of the lawn. She is about to faint.

"GO AWAY!" Margy shouts at her in a kind of dementedly demanding madness of wanting to have the power to comfort her kid. The danger to Nonie and the comfort for Katie are like light and shadow. Does the world have sense and reason? For two opposed people? I cannot imagine an embodiment of mercy in real time that is not a darkly sympathetic thing of immense exclusiveness: *Go to hell, all the rest of you: I intend to save my child. Help me to save my child.* A universal mercifulness would be a different world from this one, surely.

Nonie is no longer really a child; still, she is a child of sunlight. How pretty she is. It was an accident. No one is to blame. I have no filmed record of Nonie's face that day—her eyes, her lips, the flesh around her lips . . . the muscles of her neck. A *confession* of malice is often a boast—so in what ways, to what degree is it true if it is meant to hurt and scare you? The hysteria, the politics of a real thing, the *dirtied* unsacredness of being merely a human observer, the thing of *just-because-something-is-there-for-one-moment-doesn't-mean-it's-always-there* . . . And: *Just-because-someone-does-something-once-doesn't-mean-they're-guilty-of-everything* . . . make judgment very difficult.

You don't have to go on tiptoe.

Do you want to be friends?

Not if you're going to hurt me.

Boys are rougher than girls. Being a boy makes it that a wound is almost a cousin to me. One carries guilt with some difficulty. One stumbles. Were the games we played very bad? The mind hardens and is trained against memory and openness; a stupid but shy mindlessness rules you. A potently forceful mindlessness means you're dirty-souled and awful and ashamed and watchful; *guilty* often means that soon you will be more guilty. When I was guilty, I laughed a lot and was wild and behaved *crazily* in various risky ways and thought erratically if I thought at all. Otherwise, guilt isn't a transparency. But to imagine events as having no traces is wrong. Take having a bath. People after they bathe, after something as minor and common as that, are different, aren't they? For a while? This is just common sense, isn't it? Say that Jimbo and I horse around and my back gets broken because of him . . . Or say that Ora Perkins and I destroy each other . . .

The intensity of self-forgiveness in some people defines them for me. Like Momma's *sophisticated* and angry degrees of being uncontrite. She goes mad a lot, though. Momma used to say to me, *I believe Safe-and-Sound has the last laugh*.

Nonie in the sun is about to faint. She tries to escape. She walks blinkingly across the lawn toward the sidewalk. Shadows are on the grass cast by the trees around us. She is a tomboy. Heaven, luck, Katie, Nonie, Nonie's nerve; her beliefs; the crude scattershot art of screaming—of Margy Rogers—her lack of *skill* in the science of democratic accusation . . . Nonie did faint . . . on the grass; she fell and then sat up—it wasn't a full faint: her eyes remained open. She was dead-white. She breathed funny: she was elsewhere.

Margy Rogers on the concrete driveway shouts up at the stricken Nonie: "YOU MURDEROUS LITTLE WHORE, GET OUT OF HERE!" Margy yelled to Melissa: "GET THAT STUPID BITCH OUT OF HERE BEFORE I KILL HER—"

Nonie said, "I DIDN'T DO *ANYTHING*!"

My sister did not seem truly overwhelmed by the unfairness in reality toward her. She reached toward me—for me to go to her and be at her side. I didn't go to Nonie and stand by her . . . or in front of her . . . I have a stake in this event.

Nonie shouts at Margy, "YOU SAID A BAD THING TO ME!"

Melissa Van Maytree then made a pushing motion in the air and said, "Go HOME—get to your HOUSE— Go—"

Nonie ran then.

She ran unsteadily. She ran in a partly draggy way—not in a fifteen-year-old fleet-of-foot way. Nonie ran home. The door opened and Momma was there. She didn't hold out her arms . . . Nonie didn't fall into her arms . . . Nonie didn't touch her and she didn't touch Nonie. Nonie said, "I feel terrible . . . I'm going to faint." Momma said, "What is it? Come in . . . Lie on the couch." Then Momma closed the door.

I stayed outside. I'd followed Nonie home, sort of to make sure she got there, but I stayed outside.

Later Melissa Van Maytree's oldest son hosed the driveway off.

Momma said later, *I apologized until I was blue in the face, but that wasn't enough for Margy . . . She wanted me to have Nonie's head examined.*

Margy said to Momma, "Your stupid animal of a daughter should go rot in A PENITENTIARY."

Momma said, "Don't talk like that about my daughter." She told me later, "What's the point of examining who did what? I'll tell you a secret about when you look into things, Wiley. When the chips are down, no one is innocent *enough*. It will be Margy Rogers's standing against mine . . . That's what will decide . . . that's what things get down to, in the end. My daughter can't have done such a thing . . . How do people live, Wiley? Tell me, I'd like to know. There's no sense in it. Do you know that it's my reputation that keeps the two of *you* out of reform school when you get into trouble?"

Lila said, *Nonie's no angel but she's no devil either. S.L. says Nonie couldn't live with herself if she did the things I say she does. And I say she didn't do this on purpose* . . . She said, listening to herself, thinking,

Let's be nice people for a while—do you mind? Is that okay with you? Let's shame the naysayers. Don't be a fool and shame us—don't you go shooting off your mouth . . . you don't know how dangerous people can be. I'm tired of trouble. I'd like a little peace and quiet—and common sense, do you mind?

Lila said, *I have never heard a story told with any justice—to both sides.*

Momma and Daddy, Momma more, used to go to the cemetery once a month to visit the dead babies. But at other times Momma put the thought of them aside—she said so: *I have to live.* Sometimes, after going to the cemetery, Daddy wouldn't come home for a day or so—he would blame us, Momma mostly, but all of us, and God and accident. When he came home (this was especially when I was mute and small and somewhat helpless), he would ask ME to hug him.

Daddy said, *Be a Valentine . . . and don't fight with me. Be a good boy—be like a sweet sister—show me your lovely eyes. Tell me, pretty maiden, are there any more at home like you . . .*

Nonie said to me, *You don't know anything . . . You're a baby; you shut your trap . . .*

Momma said to me, *You stay out of it. Shut your trap, do you hear me? Take Nonie's side, no questions asked. Accidents happen. Nonie's not the one who's going to get blamed for this if I have any say in the matter. You want to live in the same house with her you'd better take her side loyally. Don't be stupid . . . A word to the wise.*

When Momma called someone stupid, it was that person's future *doom* she had in mind.

(Momma used to say to me, "You have too many *preconceptions . . .*")

Nonie had "loved" Katie. What girls do with each other is complicated. When they suffered over each other, did they wish for each other's death? Blasphemously-daringly? The little kids in our neighborhood often played *mean* games . . .

Katie's blood hopped like worms or greenish-bluish-reddish half-grasshoppers—pulsingly . . . The day after her fall her bandages were stained with dried blood and smelled of it as well.

(The *mean* games the kids played included *Cops and Robbers*—killing others righteously and imaginary beatings and imaginary handcuffings—and imaginary or real *Torture*—and *Cowboys and Indians*—really a variant of *Torture*—and *Galley Slaves Being Whipped to Go Faster*—really a third and more culturally profound variant—and various dirty games using knives ((secretly, since knives were forbidden us)) or bricks or stones to deal blows with.)

Both my mother and my father said to me, *Do me a favor—learn to have a little sense . . .*

Be middle-class, fearful, and instructed . . .

Everyone should have ideals, but listen to me, learn what's what. Learn how to take care of yourself and learn how to get along in the world—no one is fair who doesn't have to be . . .

Lila: *Ask me the truth about anything, I'll tell you it's a matter of opinion . . . Some people's opinions are better than other people's. Well, what can you do . . . A person can say what she likes, you can talk until you're blue in the face but a lot of time what's true is what works . . . Well, there's no rest for the wicked. You think you remember everything but you don't. Some people remember nothing—then it's just a lot of talk. They just like hearing themselves talk. A lot of people do more than talk. I'm the one who sees things through. I'm Mrs. Stick-to-it-iveness. Sometimes I think my middle name is Madame Galley Slave. It's a burden, you take my word for that . . . I used to be the Queen of the May but I'm getting old. I have a brain and I use it. You want the real story? Well, the real story is it doesn't matter in the long run . . . The Rogerses moved to California and they probably had a wonderful time out there. And Nonie didn't like it in this neighborhood once she and Katie were on the outs. You think anyone knows what's what? I'm a learner—you can't say that about everyone. I fly by the seat of my pants but I get to Capistrano a lot sooner than a lot of people do. So I say judge me not. To tell you the truth about me, I can be hell on wheels. Well, what can you do—that's not an empty boast—I'm useful in the world. I know I drive myself too hard. Well, so be it. I'll start taking things lying down when I'm in my grave . . .*

A sequel: Momma had a run-in with a bus. She said to me about it, *I can't tell you exactly what was on my mind but something was on my mind . . . The important thing you have to take into consideration is that I'm a nice woman. That's the sort of person I am. I was driving along, and with no warning, it was all boom-bam: you have no idea . . . I hit a bus. And when the smoke cleared, we were all catty-cornered in the middle of the street.* Midland. The bus and my mother's Buick . . .

People always liked the way I looked, if I do say so myself, but when we moved to St. Louis it wasn't so easy—as it had been. The bus driver yelled at me. The passengers did, too . . . Horrible noise—it was HOR-

RIBLE. *God's honest truth: I didn't know what was happening . . . I ruined a good faille suit: I got so wet, dress shields and all . . . I'm being too personal. I was very nervous: the smell of gas scared me. No one was bleeding. I didn't know if I was coming or going. I have always been nervous. My own mother thought I was too nervous for anyone to stand. People think I have an easy life. They say I'm spoiled. What it is is I'm good-looking. Let them try my life and see if they like it. Let them try and cut the mustard . . . My mother minded it that I was so American, so she said I was too nervous. She said I'd be calmer if I lit the candles on Friday night. I tried it. Don't ask me if it worked or not—I no longer remember. The bus driver was angry—very angry; did I say it was a county bus? Not one of the big city ones . . . Oh no: I wasn't that crazy . . . The bus driver thought I was a rich woman . . . I don't know what he thought. I was getting older. I had on a veil and a nice little hat. If you ask me, he didn't like the way I looked. He didn't like my type: I wasn't his type . . . I drove out of a side street and I sideswiped his bus. I wasn't looking; I didn't signal . . . I admit it. I looked; I saw him; I had the right-of-way. I'm pretty and I was in a pretty car and I thought he would give me the right-of-way—men did—if they weren't stuck-up. But he ran into me instead. And he leaned out his window and he yelled at me . . . God, did you ever hear of such meanness?*

He said I drove the car into the side of his bus but he drove into me, and he called me names, bad names, FILTHY *names—he was the worst sort of person, no one should ever say such things to a woman—he was scum . . . I'll bet a lot of people knew it.*

I suppose he thought he would be blamed and that he was going to be fired. It was an accident—that's what you say when you're willing to compromise. I had a big car, a Buick, but it wasn't as big as the bus. I knew why he yelled those filthy things and didn't give me the right-of-way: I was too old and he thought I was rich.

Listen: I've spent my life making things easy for people: he could have remembered I was a woman. What was in my mind was to kick him—I have my little ways . . . that would make people laugh at him. I did that once in Alton—kicked a man. He'd yelled at me on the street—I'd bumped into him . . . He'd chased me around a parking lot. I was twenty-two years old. He was big and ugly and everybody laughed at him when I kicked him: everybody. I brushed against him, he dropped a package is all it was. Everyone knew me in Alton, they laughed at him and said he'd been beaten up by a woman, but the people on the bus, all of them, they yelled and screamed, they yelled and screamed at me. No one yelled at the driver. I was in my highest heels, I had on a tight skirt—I was in my best bib and tucker, if you really want to know—and still there was no sympathy. Well, let me tell you, you can say let bygones be bygones but I knew my way around, I know when politics get bad: those people didn't know me and they didn't like me, not one bit—they didn't like what they thought I had; and I hiked up my skirt and I ran for dear life . . .

I was six or so. We lived on a street called Amherst—all the streets in University City were named after universities. Or colleges. I was playing spaceship with a boy my age and a girl and an older boy—Joey Brooks, Marilyn Berger, Martin McCauley. Joey was facing the street and I was doing something with a ray gun and he said, "Is that YOUR MOTHER?"

Up the street, westward, in the maw of afternoon light among the leafed-out dappled enormousness of trees that seemed so large to me when I was small was a running figure. The street was dead-end at its other end, chained—the chain ran between stone piers—and at each end of the block in the street was a triangular park where the street widened into two roads, one for leaving, one for coming in. The houses were staid compared to the woodland fairy-tale cottages on Katie Rogers's block. In my memory I see the bus and car, although it's odd, I am standing so close to them—I must have dreamed that or imagined it—I was standing a tenth of a mile away on a lawn, and in that setting, in the distance, under the great, leafy, light-and-shadow structures of the trees, was a running figure dressed mostly in black, and veiled, or with a blackened face, and running swingingly . . . In furs and high heels.

If I reenter the memory, I do, actually, shrink—I mean in my consciousness—and the color of the macadam of the street changes: a lot of orangey pebbles are in it. The light itself has an odd quality—the pollution then was different: St. Louis suffered from fogs, from so many coal fires, in so many houses; and anyway, the light is thickened and a bit oily: a whitish-yellow, buttery, dulled light, but thick, and then the green, and then the reddish-brownish-bluish brick of the houses and the blue-gray slate or shingle roofs. Birdsong and the temperature of the air—my sweaty skin—my neck rising from a childhood shirt—my bare legs.

Dandelions in the grass . . . The cracked pavement of the sidewalk . . . My mother, my mother by adoption, Lila; what I remember is the sight, first at a distance; and then came a sense of the motion on the street, nightmarish, the dressed-up thirty-five-year-old woman (really thirty-eight), trimly curvaceous and overly glamourous in her fur neckpiece—foxes, with glass eyes, biting their tails—and a little gravy-boat-shaped hat with a long black-green feather floating behind and a flying veil with darker dots on it than the regular netting, and black gloves, and bracelets . . . She was so truly a pretty woman that children and older children and adolescents gathered, or leaned toward each other, to watch her run past . . . On other occasions, they used to come and sit on our lawn and wait to see her leave the house; she used to say jokingly, I'm the prettiest woman for miles around . . . The orthodontist, the doctor, the insurance agent we used had crushes on her. She could get things—favors—special treatment.

That woman in perspective, running in a pretty-straightforward-but-sideways-slipping kind of way down the middle of the suburban street under the trees, shifting her fur piece as she ran and not stumbling much in her three-inch heels and panting and with her purse and she had on pearls—it is my mother.

I dreamed about it for years—the monstrosity of it, the monstrous shock of it. In the language of the age I was, I murmured, "Aw-ow," a little groaning whistle kind of thing—it meant what "Oh-my-God" would mean twenty years later if a kid said it. Joey had identified her before I did. He'd had to say, *That's your mother, Wiley, isn't it?* before I really saw who it was. I think I thought at first that with Lila's sense of emergency and of daily horror she was running to tell us that Martians were landing on Delmar Boulevard or that a flood was coming down Midland—or that a monster was loose on the next block of Amherst and was on its way to eat us . . . I assumed she was running in order to save us, the children, some of us, me. I didn't know what she was saving us from—crooks, fires, hoboes, kids from poor neighborhoods in a raid . . . Revolution . . . Invasion from Europe . . . Something bad. "No," I said. Then I called out, "Momma!" and I started running toward her.

I called out, "Momma! Momma!" and Lila was startled and she stumbled: she hadn't been looking for me. It wasn't Martians or dinosaurs awakened and coming out of the sewer. I ran to her and then I ran alongside her. We ran another fifty yards mostly in silence—she said, "Don't ask me questions . . . I . . . can't . . . talk . . . and . . . run . . ." And: "Go . . . and . . . hide . . ." and perhaps a little more.

I didn't leave her, but ran alongside . . . I kept up and even was a little ahead at times. And Momma scrambled up our stone steps—she got through the front door—(in dreams I often can't get into our house)—I don't remember her getting out her key—and we were inside, in the shadows, in the darkened hallway . . . The house was kept dark much of the time to preserve the fabrics and the paintings . . .

And she said, "Oh God . . . my heart is pounding to beat the band . . ."

Then we hid, she and I, behind the couch: she was all dressed up still except for her shoes; and as her breath slowed, she got her hat off and then the fur neckpiece which she laid on the floor and she got the jacket of her black faille suit off. She was crouched in white blouse and pearls, one stocking foot forward, one skirted knee up. Men walked heavily up onto our porch talking in loud voices—a detective and the bus driver: perhaps some of the passengers or uniformed policemen: I could not see them. I saw only the black, limp fabric back of the couch tacked to the wooden frame. I heard voices, loud, threatening, and determined.

I was surprised they came after me, I knew they would (often the degree of inconsistency indicated her lack of calculation—or it meant she wanted to seem uncalculated in order to express, somehow, how upset she had been: she is breathing loudly next to me in her fancy clothes, the furs on the floor, behind the couch)—*for all I knew, it was the Ku Klux Klan . . . It was the Nazis. I have a good memory usually, I have a good memory, period. I'd put the brakes on, I didn't run into the bus on purpose: but the brakes on the car were bad: what good did that do me with that mob? It was a lynch mob . . .* The terms of her fear—of social unease . . . *Why were they blaming me? I was shaken up . . . The police took his side: union people . . . It would have been different if I'd been a nice old lady . . . They came to the house and I told them a piece of my mind . . . No, you're right: I hid—were you there, too? You know what I'm like: I have no feeling about busses. If I'd been in a housedress and had no makeup on and had a child with me, they wouldn't have acted like that . . . The way I was dressed laughed at them—well, what can you do? Often people are nice but do me a favor: don't count on it. Maybe no one is ever nice . . . How should I know? I'm not a liar, I had only one life, I had only my life, I'm not the kind of liar who says I know what everything means and what everyone does . . . I know my limits . . . I never heard of a son listening to his mother before except in a rich family when she has the money. You like my stories? You like how I talk? Well, what I don't know would fill a book . . . It fills all the books—ha-ha, ha-ha. You like stories? I'll tell you a story: I'll tell you this: I did it on purpose: that bus driver was a son of a bitch, that mean-eyed hairy fat man yelling at me, cutting me off: he made me feel old and I didn't give a goddamn. If it's the end of the world, I'm sorry. But I'll tell you this, too: it was an accident that it happened . . . I didn't know I'd do anything . . . And when it came* *near, I didn't make up my mind: my hands slipped . . . You think I know this for a fact? You think I knew what was happening then? Everyone knows by the time they're five years old not to say they did it on purpose—so you never do anything on purpose . . . You make a little accident: it's a kind of joke. But it gets to be not a joke . . . It goes too far—the whole thing was a mistake: not the whole thing, but that's what you say. I'm the executive type: but still . . . But still . . . I'm not sure what I know and what I don't know: I trust to luck—and I use my head. You don't trust me, find another nice woman to tell you a long story . . . I may not be whaddyacallit, ideal, but I'm what there is. I'm telling the story. Maybe I'm crazy, after all—the brakes were bad—I'm not playing games; I'm telling you the truth now. Bad brakes are illegal. When people act like they know what they're doing, it's very—you know—*SMART*: it's a way to get to be the head of things. You get attention—a little attention goes a long way—there is such a thing as enough attention is too much attention, do I make myself clear? I was wrong, I expected sympathy, I was dressed like Kay Francis— Who knows how that is going to work? You can't keep track of everything. A woman who keeps her nerves is an interesting person . . . People often want to know me better because they want to know who's better, me or them: button, button, who's got the nerve . . . Well, try me and see . . . It's human . . . But that's not the question. The question is, I wasn't wrong . . . People made it up that I was worse than I was . . . But what else is new? About the long haul I can't complain . . . On the whole I got what I deserved—I'm not the religious type. I grieve every day of my life over what I've lost, but I'm not going to sigh over the way things are . . . Ask me no questions, tell me no lies . . . I know what's what, and believe you me, one thing you can count on is I'm not asking for it . . . I was never the type to play dumb-fluttery, fidgety—I had big breasts before my operation and I didn't like to be touched: even women touch you—what I hate most in the world is being grabbed at. I've never been a crawler . . . I've never been a hail-fellow-well-met. I always lived the other way: if you're someone who's outstanding—I'm not saying I am but a lot of people have been impressed by me one way or the other—you get a lot of attention, people want to see you in jail, they want to see you in the loony bin: it's only fair. Well, I lived with that all my life: give people what they want and don't give them what they want. You know why S.L. and I gave parties until we ran out of money? We didn't want to be hated. People thought we were a cute couple. Well, there are cute couples and there are cute couples . . . Now people think I'm smart because of you, but I was always smart . . . All in all, about those*

Rogerses, I'm not going to say I'm sorry I stuck up for Nonie. You liked the Rogerses, but they were no great shakes . . . She couldn't work her way out of a paper bag; and he was a corporation toady. I'm not sorry . . . I've forgotten more than they ever knew . . . I didn't keep on educating myself . . . I stopped short, but I always was a learner . . . But life is fun if you can get away with things . . . That comes to an end . . . I would like to have been right—that's what makes a woman interesting—to be the one who was right . . . Oh well, with two l's, *I'm the original I-don't-care-girl . . . No one was ever interested in what Nonie had to say. A woman gets more chances to think than a man does: is that why you like to talk to me? But Nonie never took a chance to think . . . I didn't want to hurt the people on the bus and I didn't hurt anyone . . . Maybe they were shaken up . . . They yelled before they were hurt . . . And if they were hurt, what's so bad about that? I'm a grown-up. I go too far. So what? You want to shoot me for that? You want to hang me? I wanted to be a nurse when I was young but that wasn't a nice thing to be. I do charity work. I pull my weight in the world. When I was little Momma always knew something about me I didn't know, that I'd left out, that I should have known—that scared me. I showed her: I became the I-don't-care girl . . . What are you going to blame me for? For what I thought? For what I didn't think? That I was helpless? That I was too calculating? Oh please, spare me . . . I'm a sick woman. How much bullshit am I supposed to take? What's the point of confessing when you don't know what you did? I'm too old to be clever. I'm tired of being clever. I didn't want to slow down: I hit a bus: the brakes were bad—I don't know what-all—who does? And who cares? I came in last in the horse race, but I came in first for a long time. My mother said I lost two infants because I was a bad person, a bad Jew. I forgive her—but I never will, never forgive her. You don't get over things, but you pick yourself up, dust yourself off, and you go on again. I sit here some days and I think—when I feel good enough to think—some days I feel like thinking—don't laugh—what God wanted, what it would have been like to have a better time. I don't blame Momma—she went through hell in her life—I'm not a blamer: I'm not like you: I make do. In the end all you know is you know what you know—and what can you do? One minute it hasn't happened, then it has, and who are you then? You tell me how you're supposed to deal with that . . . Listen, you think I didn't talk to scholars? I was pretty and I had my share of those men, and I met smart women, too. You think I don't know what the problem is? God is this, God is that, but then nothing else counts, nothing else matters. So you have things God isn't—can you follow me? Tell me what you think. Wait: I'll lose my thread—you talk too much as it is . . . What I think is, God doesn't know what is coming next—God is here, not there. We have minds so we can help.* Is it like a tidal wave, Momma? The onrush of time and of consciousness? *I feel it like burning water although I don't like to say so—I'm not that type of woman . . . That bus driver was some kind of religious fanatic and he called me a dirty whore. I was pretty and I had good clothes on—he didn't think women should drive cars—everyone has a voice whether you allow it or not . . . And then it was all happening: and it just went on happening —tell me who to blame for that? Nonie wasn't Hitler—you think it's all one thing? I never thought like that. Tell me what to blame her for and I will judge her. I'm not a woman who gives up but on some issues I have to say I pass. Try to love her, Wiley . . . She's a fool . . . I blame her for being a fool. What happened happened . . . An accident is an accident—once it becomes an accident, no matter what you do first or second . . . That girl, what's-her-name, was calling Nonie names, she called her a dirty Jew, and Nonie told her to go fly a kite, and the girl took a step backward. She wasn't a nice girl no matter what you thought . . . You liked her is all—and Nonie liked her for a while—but I'm not going to be stupid about it just because the two of you were. Nonie didn't touch that girl in harsh feelings: and if she did, who gives a damn? I'll go to hell, she'll go to hell, we'll all go to hell—will you be satisfied then? I'm not like you, Wiley, I stand by my own. Going, going, gone . . . That's not me. You want another mother: go ahead: I'll be dead in a little while . . .* Two days . . . *I know a dozen women who will take you in. You want a mother this minute: I'm the one you have. You know what I like about me: I'm on my deathbed and I haven't lost my nerve, Wiley. You know what's wrong with me? I'm all used up—I can't handle things anymore . . . I'm not going to sit in judgment until I know the true story, and even then who knows what I'll think.* I *never expected to get to heaven in a Chevrolet. I know who I am, I was just what the doctor ordered for a while. I'm still a regular devil, you want to smile at me now and hold my hand? You got a soft spot for me now that you're bigger and I'm at my wit's end? Are you thinking of something else?* In the rebelliousness of attention . . . *You want to go love someone else, go ahead . . . I've had enough . . . I'm tired of my own head. I am someone who requires mercy and I go where I can get it . . . I don't know if I'm coming or going—if you ask me, enough is enough. IS THAT OKAY WITH YOU, POOPERKINS, THEN IT'S OKAY WITH ME. I'll tell you about dying, I go a little crazy from time to time. I know my way around: I can't say I ever wanted to hurt anyone but sooner or later although it hurts me to say it, I can't say I was an angel and didn't want not to hurt someone . . . I do what I have to do . . . I like to sink my teeth into a good fight now and then . . . I don't mind showing what I'm made of. S.L. says I take on all comers. Well, I believe women get the raw end —frankly, I tried to change the world—and I don't care who knows it. I'm ready . . . Put up your dukes . . . hahaha. I never wanted to be one of those women who was too sensitive to live: take my advice and stay away from that type. I'll be honest with you: I don't trust myself: I think I have the killer instinct—I don't always trust myself . . . I could kill somebody, I play for keeps, you know . . . Just don't get in my way . . . S.L. used to say to me,* You have no conscience: you're the Queen of Hell . . . *And I'll tell you the truth, I was flattered. I don't know about me . . . All I ask of you, S.L. honey, sweetheart—Wiley—is pay attention when I talk . . . I'm something of a bluffer. I like seeing what I can get away with. A lot of things I wanted to do, I wanted to do just for the hell of it. What I regret is that I played for small-town stakes. When he got mad, S.L. was worse than I can ever be: he wants you dead then and there . . . He wasn't like that all the time: if you picked the right time and a good place, he'd cave in like an angel, he'd give in like an angel —he could be soft as a little bunny rabbit. When you look at me like that, Wiley, you think you're being polite but it's like you're putting me in my grave. Momma thought we shoulda stayed religious Jews and prayed all the time and never known one little thing about how we thought and lived, just been dizzy and conceited, but that was never me . . . I am what I am, said Popeye the Sailorman. Go away now and let me sleep . . . I like to talk but enough's enough, it's as good as a feast . . . I'm all out of breath. Hold my hand; I want to take a nap . . .*

The Talmudists, who proposed a contraction of God—called *zimzum* (I think)—to allow in the abandoned space the world to exist with its inhabitants condemned, after Eden, to moral choice—separately from the omniscience of Omnipresent *God*—also proposed never listening to women. Or rarely. What my mother hinted at was her sense that thought was the track or wake of the truth but wasn't the whole truth but was as strange, as ambiguous, as subject to interpretation as a Biblical text was for the Jews—and for others.

She meant even one's thoughts about driving—even one's thoughts before making an error or committing what others called a crime.

She didn't mean there was no crime: she was very practical. She merely meant it was a difficult matter for humans. I *think* she was proposing that at the edge of the present the ideal ceases to exist; no contraction of the human or the divine makes room for it in the present.

And if the present is real and not a dream—and she never proclaimed what it was, real or dreamed, less than thought or more than thought, never so far as *I* know—but *if* it is what is most truly real and is what most immediately has to be dealt with by a parent, say, or by an ambitious woman and by every man (that was how she had been brought up and she rebelled but she permitted, I believe, the thought in herself, and in others, that she had been wrong to rebel), by *a person,* then that is God *if* GOD is *real* . . . If, that is, some final meaning or point exists, some finally intelligent thought or other—as in the moment of revelation in a dream episode, then it doesn't dismiss reality or the present: it must rise from it as from the mouth of a tunnel but one going upward (so to speak).

If I take Mom to be a major novelist and someone to be listened to and a narrative artist whose work is to be analyzed and whose life is to be studied or at least like that for me, then, among all the other problems of dealing with that, among the problems of *my* dealing with that (an outsider can, of course, see into the psychological twists and turns with less fuss than I can; it doesn't matter as much to an outsider—unless the outsider has taken the story over and changed it and made it apply to his or her life) is the almost simple fact that she took *the real* to have two levels of reality—male and female, for one—but also one of uncertain voting about the nature of things in the onrush of reality and another one of more solidified sense that only a fool would trust.

And she hid this from me most of the time. For all her truth-telling, she was an absolutist sort of mother—or semi-mother. She let me, and others, peek at reality; her flirtatiousness was of someone peeked at and who allowed it, a wicked Susannah with the elders but a serious one with the juniors; she constructed a central lie, let's say, of *respectability* and of *respectability* in an Anglo-Saxon mode somewhat (and not piety), but she lied about reality—both about the crimes there, the pains, the assertions of will, the blindness and the rest of it, and about the limits that the crimes perhaps did not go past.

She lied about the degree to which we were not in Eden and the degree of absolute innocence she, and we, had.

That we were not in *Eden* was balanced partly—but strenuously, rigorously and vigorously, stringently—by snobbery about who we were, about the social level we had reached (largely through her efforts): her snobbery was social and personal, sometimes intellectual or at least was about the mind, and often, nearly always, it was *sexual.* An accusation she made often (of others) was: *Who would* FIND *someone like that*

ATTRACTIVE? But, you see, then, Nonie and I, S.L. too, we *were* in Eden, part-time, when she allowed it. And, sometimes, we were sent out by assassins from a castle to deal with *reality*. It was very complicated, really. She nearly always defined my role and the real morality possible for me—young, then less young, then a boy, then an adolescent—as *simple*—she often used images to say so: *Just go ahead and fire when ready, Gridley*, a thing from the Spanish-American War in her girlhood, meant you didn't have to think, but she often said, *You don't have to think, you're a boy, there'll always be some woman to think for you, if you're smart*—but that was not only ambiguous and teasing and part of her superiority as a commanding officer (a commanding person), it advertised her own merits as a commander: she had given us each *A Golden Age*.

And that, too, was an image, for us having some bit or piece of a heart's desire, lied about or true.

But, further, because of emotions and the silence at night sometimes in a suburb, and food-on-the-table, and clean clothes, nice clothes, it was more genuinely *true* . . . sentimentally and actually a truth . . . than perhaps one might expect. This confused her, too—our true, local queen. She struggled to accept this image-ridden, tilty, oddly actual reality.

And attached to that but undermining that was what she, as a woman, always saw as less simple, as not simple at all, as never simple, but which, as a realist she admitted, sometimes out loud, and often claimed for herself: it was *what you owed yourself*. But that became complicated if you were clear and put it into round sums.

The lies; the reality . . . If I try to see over reaches of time, it is a bit like looking across the black water of a bay at night; and I see very little if I haven't studied the view first—if I haven't seen a diagram of a cardinal across the black water of a bay at night. And if I have been instructed, then I see the distant lights of conclusion, of a destination (if I were travelling). Or I see where other lives are being lived at that moment. But I see in a ghostly way, with the lights and shapes and salt odors of the water veiling and yet explaining my actual reality standing on a pier, say, while the distant sight fits the pattern that informed me of possible meaning.

Or I can say it materializes, to some extent, the reality of what I see, as good sense: a view across a bay at night. A notion of my mother . . .

The other narrator. But the first narrator, or the second, me, if I look nearby, I see dark water—the dark, meek surface of the quiet bay and the faintly illuminated dark air; and then, if I think of its stirred, maybe wild depths, the primary sense I have might be of the strong restlessness of the salt water and a kind of amazed fear that something might exist that was without surfaces or levels—that was without limits.

And it is a thought about what-I-see in the distance. Or about my mother's gestural narrations. Daddy said once, looking at an open fire, that fire was a whore. He meant it had a natural promiscuity, a disdain for family meanings and for personal affections. If I were making up a story I might hint in it coolly and falsely that I had always lived in a way that I understood. I might say I *always* understood that a mother was not a whore—a mother might have *fires without number* in her, a hundred whoredoms, social and sexual, but she had ties or, really, realities that were not that—that were, at least in my case, after my real mother died, contractual and personal. Of course, for me, that is the pattern I then see everywhere in the nervous kingdoms of my observations.

But the heat of attention—the wars of the world—the *look-at-me*'s of others and one's own doing that—the selfishnesses, the dark water, the meanings, the blunders, the kinds of self-assurance there are and the truths of a kind about this that emerge urge that as many as possible of the lies should stop.

Momma, perhaps drugged and remembering the past, sliding into the past, into an old self, into a costume version of it, a little dusty, not very dusty, said: *Don't push me too far. Believe me, there are many, many things to like about America but the part I like best is that people are allowed to defend themselves—take me for granted and just watch my dust. I* LIKE *going too far. If I have to pay the piper, I'll pay . . . I don't give a hot damn: I'll pay through the nose—to hell with everyone: I'd rather be a hellcat than a doormat . . . Want to try my temper and see?*

This is the mid-ground where faces and eyes are not censored for children. Or for the neighbors.

I learned—and you'll learn—you have a few lessons to learn yet, whatever you may think. THE WOLF IS AT THE DOOR*—try that on once in a while. And believe you me, the wolf is* OFTEN *inside the door: try* THAT *and see. Be an angel and see where that gets you. I'll tell you something, Little Lord Goes-to-Harvard-*[and-]*has-a-profile-for-a-change, you're aren't civilized, S.L., you don't know what you're doing . . .*

It hurts to hear her. In childhood games of *Torture*, who would you ever trust enough to tell what you were afraid of most? Even my gentlest friends experimented to see if they could own me with their knowledge of me. People try different things. They say, *Don't do that or I will hit you* . . . Or: *I won't let you listen to the radio* . . . Or: *You won't have dinner* . . . Or: *I won't like you anymore* . . . Or: *I will lock you in a closet and put out your eyes* . . . You build certain walls in yourself—defiances—violences of the mind and body, violences (and coldnesses) of temper, snubbings, withheld love, public scenes. You know each other, children I mean, by your courage in regard to your parents. The kids who gave in, who were thoroughly owned, were *a separate sect*. Us rougher kids who did not give in, we lied to each other when we played *Torture*: we would pretend to be afraid of rats or spiders rather than of blows on the backside if that was what shook us up the most. I don't remember a *tough* kid ever, even under pressure of extreme infatuation—or in some cases of actual torture, tied up and the executioner using soldering irons and the rest of it—admitting to what he or she was genuinely most afraid of back then.

Lila said, *You were always afraid of the truth. If you're going to get hurt over and over by the same things, don't come to me for comfort. Learn to take care of yourself. I let you run in the streets like an I-don't-know-what* . . . *You're the Wild Man of Borneo. I want you to learn how things work, Wiley—do you hear me? I don't want you to listen to fools. I don't want you to listen to anybody. Learn for yourself. Don't be a scaredy-cat. If you ever want to* WIN *at anything, keep your eyes and ears open* AND LEARN. *Don't come to me complaining—and don't tell me too much good news either: I can be as jealous as the next man. Crow to me too much and I'll give you a swift kick in the tush. Be a realist. Choose your bed: lie in it. I may not be ending up as the champion of the world but I give good advice. Whatever it costs you, be a realist, not a dreamer. If you're a holier-than-thou, you'll end on the cross. I'll tell you a secret: learn to win. Take a lesson from me. I fight fair. Being finicky is no use. A lot of good it ever did anyone to be finicky. You have to try things out. You have to learn* . . . *Oh, you'll never listen to me* . . . *Listen, Smarty-pants, I'm not the type who gives advice—not to a boy. Why throw good money after bad? You have a mind of your own—you have to have your own say: well, go ahead: so, catch on or the caboose will run over you good and proper. You're wrong more often than you're right. Well, go ahead: don't expect me not to notice. Don't expect to fool me. The Rogerses got mean and this is a nice place to live and their meanness cost them the ball game. Listen, if you have clean hands, it's because I don't run away from things and I protected you. My hands aren't clean and sometimes I'm heartsick. Listen to me: do one or two bad things and you're still innocent enough for most people's tastes. For my taste. Live a real life and watch out. I think if you want things to turn out okay you better put yourself in the right* toute suite. *That doesn't mean you hold back: that means you know how to live. Nobody goes around confessing the truth. You want to stand out of the crowd as a fool, that's how to do it.* THERE IS A GOD. THERE IS JUSTICE. *There could be justice. Probably. What do I know? Margy Rogers called Nonie a little whore, she said she'd kill her, she said she'd kill her herself but she wouldn't want to get her hands dirty with Jew blood . . . That cost her the ball game; she had to leave the neighborhood . . . The nice people wouldn't put up with that . . . She went over the line. Why should I respect what she feels? If she talks like that she can go straight to hell. I can forgive her but Nonie won't. If you don't know where the line should be drawn, that's your Achilles heel. The Rogerses had to move . . . Well, I'm not a fool. I won after all. I guess I do the right thing now and then. When the chips are down. See, the guilty run away. Not always—just sometimes. Sometimes they pick your bones—it's not a hard and fast rule. But* THEY *left the field of battle*—HAVE I MADE MY POINT? *What bothers me is that no one thanks me. There's no reward, Wiley; that's hard to live with; but that never stopped me . . . Nothing's ever stopped me yet . . . There are a lot of lost stories in my case . . . I want a cigarette . . . I'll settle for a piece of candy . . .* At times in the past, when Lila wanted a favor from Nonie—or me—she had courted us, her daughter, her adopted son . . . She said now, *I don't count on gratitude: do it because you like me. You want me to put on makeup and a good dress? You want the whole song and dance? I'll go back to being sweet—in a minute.* She had a sweet-eyed look, greasy and funny and steamy and with mean, glowing, ache-y eyes. *You like stories? I'll tell you a story. You think monkeys are the smartest people? Well, try me. It's a bad day. I'm blue, Wiley—that's better than being black and blue, Pisher . . . See, my sweet voice is back . . . You know what?* I *never saw the truth about a mother in a book . . . How are you going to be a mother to a real girl? I never saw anything about it in a book. Wiley, I'm tired. I'm so tired, I could die . . . Do you like my little joke? I'm not scared to die; I'm scared of meeting your real mother in hell. In heaven—who knows? Who knows anything? But, Wiley, how do you help a child? How do you know what the right thing is? I was never one to take orders about things. Do you make a little saint out of a child? Do you give them a gun and tell them to go be a Nazi roughneck? Do you tell them nothing? That isn't very friendly. I'd like to know what the middle ground is. How do you teach a nice self-respect? Well, I for one don't know. Do you daydream about heaven on earth, Pisher? I don't.*

You have eyes just like an owl . . . You're not pretty anymore . . . I'll tell you this, Wiley. I'm not scared of anything. I taught myself and I learned it: there's nothing I won't do if I have to. Then: *Too much around here is said to be my fault . . . Enough is enough . . . A friend would understand me . . . We all have to learn how to keep going as long as we can—but not me, I get to stop now . . .*

I can't write an ordinarily moral book.

Wiley in Love: 1956: The Second Ora: Twenty Minutes Later

"When you were young," she asks in the darkened bedroom in New York a few minutes later, "did you know I would come along in your life? Did you imagine someone like me?"

"No. Not at all. No one like you."

"You never daydreamed of someone and now you see it was me all along?"

"No. I don't think I daydreamed about anyone I didn't know . . . I never daydreamed about movie stars, for instance."

"Who did you sleep with first?"

Pause. "I don't know . . ."

"You don't know?"

"How do you define *sleep with*? Who I first put it in? Whose vagina I first put it in? How many inches did it have to be in before you'd count it?"

"Oh God, you're so complicated. Put it all the way in . . . the girl . . ." Pause. "Was it a girl?"

Pause. "You have the energy for this at two in the morning?" She didn't reply. "A gruelling interrogation in the dark and nightmares afterward and you being sullen in the morning—then the sexual daydreams—you want to do this? And the jealousy? Toward what I did and who I did it to and who I was in the years before I knew you? When we have an agreement not to pry in each other's lives?"

"I asked one question—"

"You want to get going on the differences in me and you? We have an agreement—you and I—we don't speak of the past."

"I'm only a little interested . . . I'm not letter-of-the-law—you know?"

"The rules are off?"

"I'm not grilling you—whatever you may think."

"Ora—"

"I'm not interested in family, in your family past: I'm not asking family stuff . . ."

"Don't you have any fear that this stuff may go off in our faces?"

"I'm afraid of you. I trust myself. I know my feelings can be counted on."

I said, "It's true you have no interest in family—what if I married you for your family?"

"You didn't. I hate genealogy. It's all lies. But I am interested in your past . . ."

"But isn't my sexual past unbearable to you?"

"It is *unbearable*," she said, using the same word but as a change of subject.

"You don't even ask if your sexual past is unb—"

"You son of a bitch." She took the ashtray off the bedside table and hurled it into the dark, not at me, at the wall; and in the dark, it clattered and rang, banged, and skidded barkingly on the shadowed wall and then was silent.

"—bearable to me." Then: "Sleep and late-night talk and you in your feelings are all—"

"Yes?" she said as if she'd thrown nothing.

"—part of some category of suicide."

She said sturdily, "I am a coward who is also a very, very brave person."

"Helen Thwaite"—a woman writer of quite high-ranked family (Boston), a good-looking woman, bossy, interesting, untamed; she'd taken a liking to me and to my work; her own work was about herself; she'd done a very successful novel which had in it two chapters of a second husband maddened and torturing his wife with questions about her past. It was shabbier, plainer, more horrifying, more unendurable than any good book on such a subject was—"says I am *un homme fatal* and you are a woman of great good sense but absolutely untalkable to; and neither you nor I know what we are doing; but it's all right because we're blessed."

"I should have been named something like Rachel—I'm an impossible person—I'm old-fashioned, Wiley. I think Helen Thwaite is a mad old egomaniac who's full of shit."

"God . . . You're so wide awake. You really want to talk about forbidden and daring things at two-ten in the morning?"

Without a pause: "Yes."

"Well, maybe. But if it's going to be forbidden subjects, let's talk about your family and not about my fucking around—tell me about your family."

Pause. Her breathing and then a faint ahem and then her voice indicated she was making a deal. "My grandmother, Bomma, didn't like my mother and insulted her at mealtimes. In Maine. This was Mount Desert. Bomma had fifteen people at any meal, sometimes twenty-five, even forty—people did that in Maine then. You were just plain folks even if you were social but you were plain in a large-scale way. So, this was in Maine—in front of everybody—the cook and the maids and the men who served. Some of the kids helped serve. My mother was very pretty. She tried, Wiley. She was remarkable-looking. She might have been a little nervous—a little drunk. Bomma was mean to her."

"What did she say?"

"I don't remember. My mother ran out on the porch—it was a very large porch—it went all the way around the house—it was a large house, thirty rooms, forty—and she looked at the ocean and she cried: she was very hurt. I went to her. I didn't like her but I am the same as she is. Blood is thicker than water. I was darker than my blond cousins . . ." Pause. "My father insulted everybody. He thought they were dumb—and he said so. They *were* dumb. I didn't fit in. Not ever. I was *always* miserable . . ."

To know the fakery in the speech, one would have to know that Ora was being *nice*; one would have to know how *nice* she was being; the dark side of Ora and what her unniceness is, its degrees, its effect at various times, and what it includes, how far it goes: the comparison, the unhurtingness, but the hurt at not being really told anything: one has to know Ora to know what is going on.

"Jack"—John Lorrimer "Jack" Perkins, her father—"said it was interesting the two lines of people *you* come from, the café-society part, the gangster connections there, then his family, crooks to start with, in with the Vanderbilts—then becoming reputable—with their seats on the board, the vestry, whatever it is, of Trinity Parish, and with all their charities, looking down on your mother and her father, when, on that other side, and it is a *little* funny, one of your great-grandfathers robbed his regiment in the Civil War and founded a fortune on that robbery, and your grandfather got away from him and married a woman he thought was well-bred and one of her grandfathers was a crooked lawyer who started a college but not a good one—it's not much, Jack said, as a family history but it's American. And it's better to be descended from true stories than from false ones. Jack said the crooks who founded the Republican Party in New York State looked down on the crooks who came later—well, why not? Jack said the Republican Party was a party that lasted for seventy years." Jack sounded to me a little like, oh, a newspaper columnist, someone who makes wiseacre sentences when *he* talked. Intelligence shows the era that formed it. "Then your aunt on your mother's side married that Hindu poet, Mahoti . . . And hated gangsters and became a Communist and slept around for the sake of the party—so that's quite a spread . . . It is American . . . All the stuff about club memberships and getting thrown out of this and that—cabal, club, whatever—and slights and feuds—and well-run weddings and vulgar weddings and the scandals and the bad investments and the good investments and the good marriages—you understand things differently, America differently when you look at it from the point of view of family. It was always a sort of lower-middle-class mess in America is what Jack said. But that was fine if you had money and sense—enough money to feel special. Jack said his father had been about to be appointed secretary of state when he quarreled with John Hay *and* with Mark Hanna, with one over principle and with the other over a secret share of some boodle that was due him, and he lost both arguments—he lost out totally . . . Is any of it true?"

"Jack's stories are good," she said. "But frankly, Wiley, I'd rather talk about sex. I think my family's awful. Jack tells good stories but they're not exactly *true* . . . That's what you want to know—postcoitally? Is there truth in what my father tells you? He may have told true stories once but he's gotten ahead in the world—and he wants to impress you."

"I think what I love about you, in part, is that you don't want to come from an ideal line. You never do this *my perfect father, my darling mother* bit. Well, he's usually drunk. They're usually drunk . . . I suppose you get sophisticated that way?"

Silence.

She said, "He likes to fool people—it makes him feel good—he has to do it: it's politics *and* psychology. You know about will and reality—have you read Ortega y Gasset?"

"Some."

"He's very good." Then: "Jack does have some family standing, although he threw most of it away when he married my mother—you know?" Then: "Politically, Jack is very serious—sometimes. On the whole. He was very far left—now he's very far right—he's a logical cuss . . . I suppose it is some lost psychological truth. The terms alter but the basic setup doesn't. And, anyway, Jack is first and foremost a certain sort of *very able* liar. Lying is second nature to him—mother's milk—meat and drink. When you want to irritate him, what you do is say something outrageously truthful: it's like slapping him in the mouth with a dead fish to do that. Sometimes he likes it."

"I think so, too . . . Now tell me about your mom."

"Millie."

"Millicent 'Millie' Burywood Osterwald Hoffenburg Perkins."

"She is very healthy; she's never sick; she's very, very Republican; she has no taste in clothes; everyone agrees she's fabulous-looking; and everyone thinks she's a jackass. We sometimes have a lot of people over, and they talk politics and money, and no one will talk to her, she's so silly. She told someone last winter, 'That Ike Eisenhower is a drunken liar.' Well, that person just moved away from her. Jack tells her she's a jackass. She says she knows what's what. They still have sex. Do families in life ever act like families in the movies? Millie is unreliable—she was never a good mother: everyone says so. I say so. She's cold. Cold, cold, cold. She makes up stories and she believes them—she has entire imaginary feuds with people. I hate the way she waits for three-thirty to take her first drink. Have you seen that?"

Sitting, checking her watch, and then getting up from her chair and standing by the liquor cabinet and counting as if in a comic recitative. She was very like a soubrette in musical comedy.

"Are *her* stories mostly untrue?"

"You never know with her. She can be malicious, Wiley."

"What do you dislike most about your mother?"

"The way she talks to animals when she's drunk . . ."

"God . . . I've seen *that*."

"She doesn't like people . . ."

"Is that what you dislike, or does that stand for something else? I'm not trying to be clever . . ."

"Yes you are."

"Well, is this literally what you dislike—or is it a symbol?"

"It is what I dislike. I don't know. I like her wit; maybe it's witty her talking to animals in baby talk. I hate it when she makes speeches about politics at dinner and she calls politicians names and she *sneers* . . . I just can't stand it when she says someone is a *pantywaist*."

"Do you prefer that to tragedy?"

"I don't know. I think I prefer tragedy to that. I hate it when she talks to the animals, Wiley . . . She talks to bugs, even."

"But she's drunk, Ora—and people don't want to talk to her."

"It's not something she does with any feeling. She doesn't like animals. She killed a thrush once at pistol practice, with Jack and me."

"I sort of like the pistol practice after dinner."

"Momma and I don't like each other . . . What do you like least about your mother?"

"Which one?"

"Lila."

"She's dead. Her death . . ." Then: "I wish she were alive—she'd be something for Millie to have to deal with."

"I think Momma and I loathe each other . . . Millie feels I laugh at her, my politics are so different from hers. I do laugh at her. Of course. My mother is a cold rat. Was Lila noble? Did she have a noble soul?"

"Yes. No. I don't know. I don't think so. What do you mean by *noble soul*? I respect your sense of reality. I haven't really thought about this, Ora."

"My sense of reality is spotty, Wiley. But somebody loved you; you manage quite well."

"So do you. But there's Millie . . ."

"Jack helped. And in some ways I'm special, Wiley. I wish we never saw my family. If you and I love one another, we don't need anyone—" Then: "You want my family . . ."

"Not really. It would be odd to have a father-in-law with connections to the F.B.I. And the C.I.A."

"Why?"

"I don't know."

"You play him off against Uncle Peter . . ." Her Aunt Hilda's third husband: a rich one, a vice president of the U.S. Resources Group, a big corporation.

"You know, Ora, I don't feel I really know you. Why do you say from time to time that you miss your mother and want to see her?"

"I never had a mother."

"But you miss her."

"I do." Then: "You like my family—you worry about them."

"That isn't necessarily liking . . . I'd hoped you'd have sweet parents—lovable—poor and noble and with clean houses."

I'm a snob and the Perkinses' houses, the farm in Maryland and the house in Philadelphia, were run-down.

I said, "I do and I don't like them." Then: "Millie's a terrible housekeeper and Jack is *dirty*—like a little boy."

"He is actually a dirty boy at heart . . . His parents wouldn't let him go to Annapolis."

"I suppose that follows. If he didn't get to wear dress whites, he gets to be unclean."

Ora said, "He's a dowager's son . . ." Then: "You're a Jewish snob."

"I know. But the houses *are* dirty . . ."

"I always clean up for us." She did. She and the servants would set to and would make some part of the large houses habitable. "For you. For me."

"A taut-nerved, middle-class Jew—and an impossible daughter. Jack told me it always irritated the shit out of Millie, you doing that, cleaning up the house—you've done it, bossily, since you were ten years old, Jack says."

"Jack likes to talk. I don't want to talk about my family. Did you masturbate a lot when you were young?"

"You are really odd. Your enunciation, your profile, your mind—you're odd."

"I'm a bit Hollywood," she said.

"Created by studio heads? Self-chosen? Nothing created by heredity?"

"You guessed it," she said admiringly. "You understand: I'm not something made by heredity."

"You don't seem like Jack's daughter—he's physically ugly, sloppy-faced . . . And then there's him saying, *We weren't as rich as the Joneses"*—Edith Wharton's people—*"but we were in a position to make them fidget a bit.* Ora, how come you're not like that?"

"The past is the past." Then: "I hate *all* those people—they laughed at my mother. Who the fuck were they, anyway? A bunch of sexless creeps with crooks for ancestors. I'm Faustian . . ."

"Oh? Well, why not? Why, when we met, did you say, *My people are poor: they're nowhere people from nowheresville . . ."*

Silence. Then: "Well, it's true . . ."

"They're dirt farmers?"

"They're not that nowhere." She was being foolish—she grew haughty to cover up.

I knew she was making conversation. This wasn't real talk exactly—it was an imitation of book talk, talk in a book. But what her purpose was in doing this was obscure to me.

"When we're older we won't have the energy to amuse each other in the middle of the night . . . courtship energy," I said. She was silent. "Ora . . ."

"I'm a comedian—a buffoon . . . I always was." Then: "I'm more undercover than you are." She said it whisperingly and she lifted the sheet I had drawn over us and she looked underneath at our naked bodies there—it wasn't a strongly dirty action.

I ignored the risqué do-jigger. "Have you ever succeeded in seeing yourself as no one?"

"When I'm sick. When I run a fever . . ."

"With a high temperature you become a girl of the people?"

She blinked. Then: "*One touch of nature,* Wiley."

"I suppose that's true . . ." Did she *want* an interrogation?

Did she want to come?

Did she want me to come again? What did she WANT?

"I'm mere flesh and bones anyway," she said. "Ashes to ashes, dust to dust—God, that always gives me a chill . . ." Then: "I have been bored for the last time. I have you . . ."

"Bored by Jack, too?"

"He's not as boring as some men. But *he* bores *me.*" Then: "Jack is a compulsive Protestant liar." She said this coldly. "He is a brilliant man but he is A Disappointed Man . . . That's why he won't let you go once he starts to talk . . . he's *the Old Man of the Mountain.*"

"I thought it was his ego as a seducer—he's *the Great Charmer* of the family . . . Isn't he? Men often want to have the power of beautiful women without their saying that is what they want. They want to command lives and deaths—in the real world. He's the master of adult corruptions—not all adult corruptions—but it's funny how Hitlerlike most people are. In some ways. One night I said to him, 'Tell me about your disappointments'—he'd been saying he was a disappointed man. It was quite a list: he was not a figure in world diplomacy; he was not one of the richest men in the world. He was not an inventor of any importance; he was not one of the members of the shadow cabinet; women disappointed him—sexuality had—modern comedy was not good, modern death; your mother; *you* disappointed him; the American navy and American foreign policy and the history and current state of American intelligence operations and of American intelligence, the mind of the country, had disappointed him; and his parents had disappointed him; the last machine lathe he stole from his corporation was lousy: a lousy piece of equipment: so was the Colt .45—the Luger: now THERE was a gun. The culture and politics and sociology and social shenanigans of his time were repulsive: automobile design; American education; American manners;

movies: it was most impressive—and a little funny—this off-the-cuff immense lament, reverse Hitlerian and then Hitlerlike, wanting a complete reform and complete power to carry it out."

"He gets a lot of it from Schopenhauer."

"There was more: American journalism; contemporary conceptions of power; Hitler was a shabby squirt—even modern corruption disappointed him. 'I am like Candide: I cultivate my garden,' he said in that accent he gets at one in the morning."

"I know. It's Choate."

"But he went to Exeter."

"But his accent comes from Choate—he likes the Choate accent better. He doesn't use it often—he likes you."

I imitated it: " 'No good, all of it, it's *all* no good . . .' I'm too nasal . . ."

"Yes . . ."

"I like him, too. A lot . . . really."

"He's sly, Wiley—don't trust him, promise me—he wants to be *dangerous*—he's very proud."

"And you?"

"I'm not proud . . . I would die rather than be like Jack."

"I would rather die than be like S.L.—but if I were like him I would die anyway . . . You are dangerous. You have a terrible inner temper. It's not smart to disappoint you . . ."

"Wiley . . ."

"Does he imitate Bogart, too? Sort of educated-Washington Bogart?"

"Yes . . ."

"But *Bogart*?"

"He picked it up . . . Bogart came from Good People . . ."

"Jack told me even crime disappointed him."

"I like it best when he talks about the Middle Ages . . . He would like to have faith and be a baron . . . He likes the idea of Heaven and Hell. He says Catholics are the best cannon fodder—everything they do gets forgiven . . ."

"*Everything*?"

"Everything."

"Wow. Yeah. Yes. I keep forgetting that. Does your dad ever listen, or does he just do monologues?"

"He just does monologues. Doesn't he let you talk?"

"Only if I insist on it. Then we do alternate monologues."

"Well, that's it, then. He talks to you more than he does to me now. Don't ever trust him, Wiley . . . He does things. He breaks up things that concern me. Bomma never thought he was any good—she didn't trust him."

She just wanted to talk? She was frightened of something? She'd cheated on me?

"He seems very tricky; he makes up quotes. He changes the dates of historical events, even quite famous ones, such as the order of Civil War battles—then, if I correct him, he says he wanted to know if I was paying attention and if I knew my history. I'll never get used to his way of arguing—is it a ruthlessness? Is swapping lies useful? Truth can't win with him. I catch him out over and over. It doesn't faze him. He has great assurance.

"He's such a spider . . . He's ruined my life, Wiley."

Well, she was up to something—she was giving me something I wanted, booklike talk about well-to-do Americans.

"So you're crippled and not pleased with your life?"

She made a face. "He *nearly* ruined me . . . ," she said correctingly.

"You know what he told me: *Find out who keeps the little black book*—that is, who the procurer is for the others in the group—and *find out who disburses the spendable cash*—that's all we need to know. So you're saying his lack of idealism ruined you, *nearly* ruined you?"

"Bogart and Jack went to the same school in New York. Jack used to tell a story about how he hurt Bogart's feelings in first grade . . ."

"God . . . humiliations and a lot of hide-and-seek—is that grown-up life?"

"I don't really understand you but that sort of life, the sort you're talking about, no one does it anymore—it's out of date."

"It must have been grotesque. Jack keeps talking about decadence but what else is there for people who have to die?"

I still didn't know what she wanted.

Jack, after a day of drinking, late at night, and he and I are in his library and he is still drinking: "People like you and me, my dear putative son-in-law, are part of an army of the *comfortably* dispossessed—we have no time for heaven or for hell, not in America—just *shrewdness* . . . SHREWDNESS is all. You heard it first from me. In America, character is independence—not fate. I am a positivist of grace. Can you follow me? You Jews have good things but you don't know much about grace . . . As I read the Bible, you are concerned with *the Blessing*—which is a very different thing. Calvin had a number of interesting points—a number of interesting things to say . . . I bet you haven't read your Calvin—or your Luther."

"I have. I don't understand much of it—I had some *cultural* difficulty with it."

"Did you? Did you now? Well," and he leaned forward combatively: he did a great many imitations. "What, with the *cultural* difficulty, DID you see?"

"Protestants have a quite sophisticated sense of reality."

"Unh . . . Oh, you saw that, did you? Protestants do have quite a sophisticated sense of reality. What I learned as a boy is people in nice houses throw stones, and that a daily manner—and the right style—mean more than God, are God, are God embodied—if you accept the notion of *grace*—if your life and your notions are shared by enough of the right people—by enough of the people to get elected. It is all interesting to a Protestant. Christian belief conveys certain difficulties inherent in life—in sex and breeding, for instance. I'm not Christian: I'm *pagan*. But I know where my life, and my written English, is buttered. I know the Christian past it emerges out of . . ."

"From . . ."

"I speak American English . . . Out of . . . Language and class; do you know about language and class?"

"Know how much, sir?"

"About Christian belief—post-Christian intensity? What we have—and this is something the scholars miss—is the search for a way to *return* to belief—do you understand? Thought and reason—and a sales pitch—are you following?"

"Belief is immanent, not present?"

"Yes. Protestants understand how to be truly temporary."

"In modern circumstances of truth and untruth—truth and truth and untruth and untruth—the Protestants are ahead of the rest of the world."

"That's not bad. I will confess to you—you are a little priestly: you will admit you are a little priestly? My class of men, able or disabled—ha-ha—are compulsive, clever, and resigned—capable of constant lying . . . Slanted truth . . . But I like you. I really do. You're not empty. I don't mind your being Jewish."

"Ora minds my staying up late, drinking . . ."

"Ora is well educated but she can't talk like a man." His eyes were moist with alcohol, lies, and slanted truths. And his body, all of it, was tense and quivering with will and exhaustion averted, a sort of ambitious reality of moment-to-moment existence as a mechanism of devilry—as a voice, so to speak, of *hell*.

He never kept his physical distance from you for long. He slid forward on the chair, leaned over, touched my leg, then my arm. I could feel the quiver—the truth element of it—the thing of its being true as a gesture in a moment in time but not all that true, but rather a thing of a moment of feeling and of physical existence beyond churchly summary and to be worked out and observed over time . . . His dishonesty, his trickiness had an unabsolute quality. No part of what he did was determined. There was nothing contractual or fixed in it. It dismissed eternity and moral consequences while engaging in a skirmish with them. It was *contingent*—a way of owning my attention: a command to me that might be worded as *Hold my affection* and *Think about me.*

He said something kind of opposite to that: "I'm a faithful cuss—and son of a cuss. I've stayed with the same woman . . . I stuck around while my children grew up . . . That's the meat-and-bones of it." He meant, I think, that his character, his affection were not absolute but were contractual after all but that that was *tragic* for A MAN.

Or tragically unsatisfying. "Most of my heart's desire, most of a real man's character, most of reality is of a forbidden nature—and doomed," he said in a Tristan sort of way. "Have you noticed that every single one, every single one of the Seven Deadly Sins is a social virtue if you want to amount to a hill of beans in the world: pride . . . anger . . . gluttony . . . lust . . . covetousness . . . despair . . . and the other one. Intemperance? A man is underground—is an underground soul—he is background for everyone else . . . But I believe men throb with the rhythm of the universe."

"Are you writing a book, sir?"

"Yes. Yes, I am. Human nature as we know it in our class"—gazing at me—"came into existence in this country around 1850 as the social possibility of antislavery developed and industrial modernization. And it lasted until 1932. You should know about this . . . It should be taught in school—the betrayals by weak-minded imbeciles of their class: every attempt at class principles has gone down to defeat through betrayal. We have betrayed what they are most anxious to imitate—fools, fools, fools. Hah.

"Boys will be boys," he said in a savage tone. "Prep school was a school for fools . . . Ambition, position, pride—I am an American realist—except that I like words; it runs in my family—words do. Well, you can't buy the world with a little masculine *naughtiness* . . . A naughty nastiness won't do—not when it's THE WORLD . . . Ora can wait . . . Men have to talk . . . Have to learn . . . Nodding, nothing matters if you don't understand power. Emerson *is* Schopenhauer. The question is power. We add and subtract from that question at our peril. Our peril!

Do you know what those words mean? Our lives, our bodies, our souls of honor are at stake. It suits us to play around? Then hellfires gape. I have accomplissed, -plished, a little in my time, and I know one or two things; I know this subject—I know *men.* You think I lie like any man of affairs, but I tell you I make the stories I tell more pointed than men who are more famous than me, than I, do."

He was about fifty; he was taut-bodied, fully present—not shyly present. Nasty and dirty, short-leggedly strutty even when sitting down, just in how he shifted around, he was of a rarefied nature mentally with an agonized sense of truth—of one truth, one truth only, one truth ultimately—not Jesus, or not admittedly, but through Christian minds and Christian speech, through the hardworking famous minds, mostly English and German, of the last two centuries.

But physically he was utterly a rushed, half-drowned relativist, crowding you in his thrashing, maybe powerful strokes, the powerful strokes of a semi-champion swimmer.

"I am not a fool. I am not *always* a fool. I am conscious I was shaped by my mother's notions in 1920 of her parents' gentilities and privileges—their beliefs were Victorian; the dominance of the Anglo-Saxons after the fall of Napoleon: that was an active part of their politics . . . And of our religion. We needed the willfulness of the Germans. We distrusted the French. The Vanderbilts were always backing the French . . . My mother cordially *loathed* the Vanderbilts, the Morgans—and the Rockefellers: *the awful Rockefellers,* she called them—but not to their faces. Oh no. Never to the faces. She always said the 'geniuses' who matter are usually of family." Then: "Tell me: why am I not *a great man*?"

"But you are, sir . . ."

"Outside this house! In the books!" he said.

Ora is the child of his wished-for, dreamed-of greatness. The existence, nonexistence of his life historically fathered her mind. She talks in the middle of the night practicing her greatness.

"The final eschatological truth testified to Calvinistically is or isn't the question," Jack said. Jack wasn't a good reasoner or speaker to the point that he could make his rhetoric cohere or persuade. Its influence on anyone was slanted as the truth was in it. He said so: "To understand me, you have to be prejudiced in my favor. I come from a social class of privilege and duty; but in order to serve my country I have had to become an honorary dishonorable citizen of another class, one of ability and of high occupation, and I can't always live with it, Wiley. No, I never saw battle: I am of the order of aides-de-camp: but I have been disgusted. Disgusted. Don't misunderstand me: I give orders. But I'm a sissy—but I know it's *us or them* . . . I can fight. In the end we are tested by war, real war, but, my friend, also by the infighting of civilization . . . Don't go: it does Ora good to have to wait. Youth's a stuff that lasts forever—didn't you know that? It lasts forever for a while . . . Where was I? How much money you have counts—it adds up. Intelligence and the ability to talk are for parlors. Power. Power. Power . . . that's what a man cares about . . ."

"But then the best jazz musicians are low since they have no power—"

"They have the power to corrupt—"

"And the worst highbrow musicians are high—no matter how limited their understanding of music is because they command people and money."

"Music doesn't matter, my boy."

"Not even in an analogy?"

"Not even in an analogy."

"But if it's power—and not any other issue—and not a choice of pleasures—that is the question, then it's a very specific question for you that I want to go now to be with Ora. You want to demonstrate your power(s)."

"My daughter is probably as frigid as her mother," he said, with a guileful and wild-and-demonically-well-bred-and-crashing-through-barriers and licensed look. Ora has said to me that her father listens outside the bedroom doors. One time I saw his eye and part of his face at the slightly open door to his bedroom when I was on my way to the bathroom after Ora and I had screwed. He said, "How much reality can you bear?"

"It depends what kind it is and why one should bear it. I have the power to walk out of here, right?"

He said, "Tell me about Ora and your carryings-on: I ask it as a dirty old man who thinks you're a very, very interesting person, a fine person." He gazed at me naïvely, as if he could be exploited.

I said, "You always thought Ora was frigid—like her mother?"

"Those good-looking women: bitches all." Then: "In some eyes, some measures"—some hierarchies—"you rank higher than *I* do—you get things I can't get—although you're not as high as I am in terms of club memberships—and for certain dinners where things are decided for the whole country." He spoke with some satisfaction and with some worry. He said, "I admire the way you handle yourself." I had risen to my feet; I was going to leave the room. He was affectionate, ironic, testing—

desperate, uncaring: it was relativism in action, Junior Einstein (in a Protestant sense), the plotting relativist, a Protestant of family, or some such thing and me. He said, "You want to talk about Einstein? I have written a refutation of his Theory . . ." His sequence of moves wasn't incoherent in relation to traditional meaning if you don't romanticize traditional meaning. His fondness, his treachery, his will, and so on. He was convinced that *tone* was sufficient for worldly meaning. He said just then, "I have a very low view of worldly meaning but I am a pagan . . ." His masculine and almost youthful emotion was part of a daydream of historical importance. He offered no legitimate or coherent meaning among the grammatical structures of his speech. He used kinds of meaning, things from the media that he thought I'd know, he used these as toys. His thick, liquor-loose lips smackingly enunciating his quite educated ideas (if they were, properly speaking, *ideas*), he was correctly and incorrectly naked in discourse . . . His social class had versions of this kind of discourse in it. His ironic, impotence-potency, the despairing but ironic impudence—the wickedness—his having a degree of affection for his contingent and changeable wish for *my* affection—all were an ironic imprisonment in a clothed-and-naked state of intelligent-discourse-*as-we-know-it-in-my-[social-]class: do you know what I mean?* Ora had said of him to me, "He asked me to sleep with him in return for his paying for my college." And: "I don't know if he meant it." But she didn't, she said, and he paid anyway. "I offered to pay him back and I will. He wanted me to marry a rich man and repay him. But he never spent the money on me I needed if I was going to marry a *rich* man. I never had the right clothes. And none of *those* boys ever liked *him*. He wasn't important enough . . . Or rich enough," she said, veering in her sympathies at the end.

He said, "I am the opposite of an absolute believer but I am a *Pilgrim's Progress* sort of fellow, lost in my times among the vanities and corruptions of the world and placed quite high toward my fellow passengers on the ship of fools; but low to the point I would want to sell my soul in rage at what my intelligence could have done in an era less low than this one . . ."

His life was so demeaning that it was worth it to him to sell his soul for a chance at being of public use. Ora said, *It's convenient for him to attack the era . . . It IS a low era, however.*

Ora said, "I breathe Jack's air when I am near him . . . He has a good mind." His mind succeeded in organizing the forms for her with which her mind saw things.

"A little cheap, his mind," I said. "I mean I understand why you run away from him, why you say, *We have to get away from here.*"

Time and again, we left the farm or the big house in Philadelphia like gangsters escaping. Like kids eloping again and again.

At dinner, he watched us. Me more than Ora, and I would glance at Ora, and, depending on her eyelids—she signaled with her eyes—I would go with Jack after dinner, after pistol practice, or without such practice, to talk, under the conditions he established. Or I would refuse, in a prep-school manner—my version of it—a nasal imitation—or as a rebel, or whatever, in a different accent. When Jack and I talked, he inevitably set the lamp so that it shone in my face.

Ora was, within this frame of things (her father and his childhood, his infancy, his youth, his early years as a man), a daughter who mostly refused her father's world: its hierarchies, its bitter dustiness. "It destroyed him, Wiley." She "loved" him, enjoyed him, avoided him. She named him second-rate and she said he'd *failed*, and she named herself as the real hero-heroine and as his avenger; she would be famous and restore his pride. I don't know if she meant it. He named himself as a failure but when she named him as it, she took the irony out of it and made it a glamourous thing—desirable. Not always. It depended. And the important consolation and justification he found in his social placement she dismissed with the peculiar violence of the blood child: *What a stupidity* and *What a waste of life* . . .

But the shining, if eccentric, literacy of the man (whether or not he lied about the degree of it), the occasionally darkly charming and often threatening love of authority in him, the blasé ruthlessness, the scale of his will, the extent of his willingness to get what he wanted, the emotional harshness and the near illiteracy of feelings (compared to books and to some people, not many), the sly wit and seductiveness of his sorts of forgiveness and of semi-forgiveness if you forgave his considerably graver and more directly rewarding crimes—(Ora pointed out epigrammatically and rehearsedly that he never forgave crimes more profitable than his own—"Jack is a democrat," she said seriously—"especially when it comes to money and to getting away with things.")—did he shape her? Is part of him in her, too? Now, at two in the morning? We have all had unideal parents . . .

He spoke of such matters as everything being permitted in the death of God—he said this was according to Nietzsche (and I said, *And*

Dostoyevsky)—but that that had always been so in defense of God and of one's class. He spoke of such matters differently in the course of an evening's drinking, depending on the time of night and on what had been happening in his life and what his purposes were at the moment and how Ora had acted recently (in front of him and to him) and according to national and international politics and his mood concerning recent events: he would say, oh, at ten o'clock, after some flop of an international conference on the tariff and Ora's recent deafness when he spoke to her, "After all, we need to know that act B can be taken to preserve value A . . . Why do you look doubtful?"

"We need to know what act B is and under what circumstances it is likely to occur, in a human sense, in real time, and moment by moment; and we need to know a good deal about value A."

In an odd voice—*disappointed*—Jack said, "Well, we can see you're not a man of action."

"No. I'm mostly not Nonie."

"What is that?"

"I don't know . . . I'm not a man of action, I agree."

"A man of reaction?"

I looked at him with gratitude: "Yes . . . Yes . . . I need to be that way . . . Morally . . ."

"A priori absolution?"

It is difficult to write honestly about men you have learned from, taken a large part from of what you have become. It is hard not to act superior in retrospect, in the amendments of a memoir.

Ora, in college, after the war, turned me down three times over a space of three years, and then, in the fourth year, she came after me, more or less full tilt and ironically-comically—I mean really not kidding around, so that it was flattering and really Very Very Confusing.

"Do you want me or not?" she said in an earnest and yet devil-may-care and *complicated* way.

"Give me twenty-four hours to think it over—okay?"

"Well, telephone either way. Don't be a shit. Don't be a shit who's too cowardly to call to say no. I always said no to YOUR face."

I called her in an hour and twenty minutes and said, "Well, how about *maybe*?"

She laughed. "It isn't funny; but I'm a madwoman—so what the hell?"

Why did she want me? Well, others had failed to interest her—and some had failed to be held by her. I think that, for a lot of people, it is true that we hold on to the interest of someone who interests us—you want to make someone happy, you mostly can. She got around to me. How come *I* was on the list of such a woman?

I was in style, sort of—male target of the month . . . sort of. Off and on, for a number of years. How did it happen that I was in style? I was male but not entirely obtuse—not pure momentum and endurance. I practiced a nothingness of the self, *negative capability*, a form of educational readiness, an at-least-halfway-honest openness to idea for a while. This involves a humility toward one's past and considerable risk toward one's future—one uproots oneself and is unmoored . . . And probably unroofed, unfloored as well. But the lack of immediate purpose, the sense of indulgence of one's deepest curiosities—this opens you to others and you listen to ideas, expressed in those other lives, that other flesh, if I might say that—I am truly not a Platonist or am, at best, an incomplete one—and you have little flashes, flushes, of inspiration, not always valuable but still something; and you are inferior to people who start their careers young or who are hotly ambitious, now, while you're doing this; but you're open, as well, to new perceptions . . . whatever *that* is worth; and, well, what the fuck, *I* had the impression that I was considered "good-looking" but not "handsome"—or I was considered "the handsomest boy" but still "not handsome" if you know what I mean. *Possible*: is that a useful term? If I went to see a girl in a rooming house or in a dorm, a lot of people might be gathered to see me arrive, to watch me with her. People said things such as *You're ugly* and *You're funny-looking*. Or they muttered about how good-looking I was. In the mirror and in photographs, it wasn't clear, it never is, what evidence is being presented. I knew very little about her—some gossip. I hadn't done any of the social climber's homework—or any of the lecher's homework either. Which is odd, since I did want to be shrewd. Shrewd, clever, and practical. Licentious, corrupt, and amusing. I suppose I thought it was shrewder in regard to her not to be shrewd at all. She said, "You are violent and absurd and *sweet*."

You would have to feel the last word as a kind of definition of a dilution or weakness of appeal—of course, she might be lying—it *was* a negotiation.

Naïvely I said, with a certain lopsided smile, bulkily leaning over her—a posture I had put together during a year I spent in Europe being *an American type, Jewish*—"And shrewd?"

"Oh, you're a devil. You're shrewd . . . But let's don't talk about those things—let's not be lovers of that sort."

"Um? What sort?" She raised her eyebrows. I said, "Who just play psychoanalysis and talk about themselves?"

"You guessed it . . ."

"Why? What would you like to play? Us to play—as lovers?"

"Oh, let's just be sensible lovers."

"Are you sure, Ora? Are you of that opinion about us?"

Often when I shifted the level of discourse, or pulled up the hem of my secrecy, so to speak, and showed my more or less actual legs, again so to speak, she shifted, too, but dilutingly, educatively—perhaps evasively. "I have faults, Wiley—and one is that I'm too sure of things." She is a year older than I am. "*You* aren't naïve," she said. "That's such a relief."

"Am I sophisticated?"

"*You're* a full-fledged nut," she said. Then: "You're a young man with a vision . . . I think that's really pretty nifty . . . I'm a very serious girl . . ."

I could not believe in my or her significant relation to our pasts. Ora said in the early days of our sleeping together, before either of us began to be silent and amazed—before we began to listen with odd parts of our bodies to what was going on in the room and in the eyes and breath of the other—"My background is *bad*, Wiley . . . My people don't have enough money to matter . . . We don't have *real* power . . . I intend to be the first one in my family to be *big*."

I said to her, "At this time I do not want to believe that your identity or mine matters much if we are willing to accept what comes in the way of hurt."

"It's pig-in-a-poke—you think?" she said. "I'm a mere bag of emptiness—from nowhere—from the gutter actually, if you want to be exact about it."

I believed her, but not with much knowledge of such contexts as Helen Thwaite, say, had, by whose standards Ora *was* ill-born. I believed Ora literally and yet I assumed that what she said was part of a "pose." I tend to believe people face-to-face and then I think later about what they said (and did), but face-to-face I believe people literally and I answer them literally: "You have risen from the gutter very nicely."

Her looks. And manner. And mind.

Ora said, "You're new . . . You're infatuated with me . . . You overrate me. You're new blood; life is better for you—it's fresher in your nostrils."

She was an uninhibited cliché user and quoter whose quotes and whose cliches weren't always familiar to me and she gave no ascriptions or footnotes: she believed in Universal Common Knowledge. "No giants live in our society now . . . It is a mass society, Wiley, and it is good only for people with elbow."

Later, when I met Jack and Millie, I half saw a little of why Ora had said what she said. "But your parents have *some* money," I said.

Ora said, "Wiley, when J. P. Morgan died, Rockefeller said, *Think of all he did, and he wasn't even rich.*"

"Oh . . ."

It was a certain familiarity with summits—maybe a false familiarity—well, who cares . . .

Then, still later, when I complained of *The-Eat-Shit-Initiation-Rites* in New York for a new writer under the men and women who were overseers, or thought they were, of admission to *the Temporary Pantheon . . . the local branch of the Fraternity of National and International Brilliance* (they thought they oversaw *SERIOUS Success*), she said, "You're lucky . . . It's a good thing to have happen to a person. You're not honest about it. Lovers should be honest with each other, Wiley, otherwise what's the point of living?"

"Living or loving?"

"Living. If love is no fun. And fame is worthless, Wiley?"

"I'll try to be more honest . . . I am trying," I said. I meant in the social-class way she meant—as one of the rulers of the world (sort of)—and also as an artist. Or *would-be*.

I said, "But what is happening right now is not giving me an identity to crow with, Ora—it's taking my identity and throwing it away."

She looked at me sort of obliquely, her head at a backward slant. "You are a very good liar . . . You had daydreams . . ." She said the last accusingly.

"No. I didn't, not the ones you mean. Even after I wanted you, I never daydreamed about you. See, I have this thing: you're not supposed to borrow real people or real lives and use them in your head—unless you pay royalties to them. I partly mean this, I partly mean what I say, Ora, I don't like to lie; it uses up my head's spaces, its peace—I don't lie very often. When I was a kid, my family told me I was a very poor liar . . . lousy."

"I know. I know," she said, pursing her lips and bringing her head forward. "I know. You're a poor liar. But even partly . . ." That I partly meant it—maybe she meant: she picked that out to respond to: "You're ambitious—I'm someone who sees things and I see you; I know about you: I face things—where you're concerned."

I sighed with a kind of pleasure. Life during courtship is sometimes sweet, even Edenic. I said, "It's hard for me with women, or girls, who are too nice." Who saw none of the things Ora saw. Who would not have known what to make of Lila. But even as I blushed I heard the maybe-*insult.*

"Oh, I know. I hate those Goody-Goody Two-shoes," Ora said sternly. She talked, some of the time when she talked, without self-correction, no matter what she said, a good-looking woman with no apology in her. Strong-nerved. She really wasn't a flirt in the sense of being delicate about it. She was more like a climate putting itself over to you, turning itself over to you as the rainmaker or the sun-evoker.

Or she was like a robber chieftain welcoming you for a while . . . With some humor in it. She said, "After all, it's your *style* to be honest." Then: "Do you think style is just the way people handle emptiness or are you one of those people who thinks style is the soul of things?"

"No. I think style is usually just the way someone gets past the pain of amateurishness. I learned that from Guy . . ."

Guy was someone I knew in college, a young man, rich, with a great deal of manner (or style) who had been and still was, sort of, a friend, and, at odd times, not often, a *lover.* I mean, it's hard to explain. He didn't attract me. I am not drawn specifically to that stuff. I didn't like him enough. I liked him some. I was drawn some. I wanted to be fair to his feelings; I was nosy . . . I don't know. Feelings don't name themselves in me . . . There's just sort of a heat, a bubbling . . . I had to force myself to shake his hand, to kiss him—on the cheek. But other stuff happened now and then. I liked him somewhat and it was also true that he repelled me. He, too, wanted to be famous—like Jack Perkins; he had the same notions of hierarchy as Ora—fame or celebrity, entering history that way, was the main or highest thing, at once real and luxurious and *ideal* in that you existed as an image in the shadow world, racingly. Ora and Guy looked a bit alike. Their mothers looked alike. Ora, when she met Guy, said to me, *Clearly you have a type and we're it.* I was not as clearly established as what I was as they were as what they were. I didn't know if I had a type. I didn't know what I wanted sexually—or professionally.

Neither of them was welcome at all among *Serious People.* They were both sour about *Serious People*—they used really quite a lot of invective toward them. One other thing constrained me toward Guy: he was unreliable as a friend—he was jolly and rather cavalier about it. *I'm no good,* he would say. But in his favor was that he wasn't shocked by me. Or, if he was, he kept quiet about it. In private, alone with myself, I was not able to accept my life: he accepted it for me.

But he never had the rank with me as someone it was important to have my life accepted by that Ora did.

"Rank" was Jack Perkins's word.

Guy was *nouveau riche*, he said (that is, third-generation rich), and *queer* (that was the word he used then) and suicidal (he said so), but he was handsome and very rich; people chased him. He was a figure of scandal and glamour. Ora had been a much more out-and-out figure of scandal since she was fourteen and wore black fingernail polish and came home to Jack and Millie with a tight-eyed, nervous ex-convict she'd picked up at a gas station. They were somewhat alike, those two: I figured I'd been influenced by Lila. Guy, too, was famous for his looks although not to the extent that Ora was. I thought Guy's looks were unappealing.

The mystery, though, was simple, as it did not chiefly concern Lila: Guy and Ora looked like my real mother: I didn't entirely know this. But the sight of them and the presence of either of them placated, pacified something in me in the hard years that college was for me. My first mother at some fantastic degree of social luck . . .

It is always impossible for me to see Ora without caring what becomes of her. In a way, I was as concerned with her as their fans are with singers. Love: a kind of love: kinds of love . . . But after I knew her for a while, a good deal of emotion came from knowing her and was separate from the resemblance thing, or was linked to it only strangely, painfully really.

"I'll tell you something about me," she said. "Two things," she said, not correcting herself: simply continuing. But she was correcting herself and talking directly to me—this does not happen all that often. I was making every effort to listen. I mean, we were giving birth to one another in a factual sense of mutual identification, of a sliding address on streets of words—and of personal manner—in a world of names and events. One did this without self-interest or real purpose (or calculation) except to bring it about. And to get laid by someone you cared about. Ora called it my Pygmalion game and said all men did it to all women up and down (the social scale) and that it was a bore. Ora was sort of the leading expert on heterosexuality at Harvard and Radcliffe at this time.

"I don't talk like a Hemingway woman and my life is not set up for pain . . . I hate pain," she said. Then: "I'm not a jealous person, and I'm very, very strong. That's the fourth thing . . ."

Johnno Fynner, the poet, homosexual (like Guy, whom Johnno disliked), ex-Catholic, and opinionated—to a lot of the would-be talkers and writers among the students, Johnno was sort of king. So was I, though—but differently. But Johnno liked being King. At one time I told him something I thought about a writer, and he said nothing; he was deadpan.

"Well, agree or disagree," I said, and he shrugged. It was witty, how he did the shrug. "Bah, you're an ass," I said.

"*Cum grano salis*, cutie pie," Johnno said.

Ora's Aunt Hilda—a hostess of the tenth rank or thereabouts; actually, that's not true; she slept with celebrated men and women, or had, and could fill her house with names of the third rank—said to me, with a snarl—she was a drunk—"So what's it like to know Ora sleeps with you to punish her mother?"

"It's not bad," I said. "Her mother isn't someone I worry about a lot." I didn't care at first if Ora's 'reasons' for being with me were lousy or not. What good reasons are there?

Ora's mother and aunt—Hilda's nickname was *Betticent*—had no use for me. Betticent had an unrequited obsession concerning Ora. Millicent and Betticent were both "good-looking failed artists." Jack said, "Betticent was the worst poet of the 1920s. But she could be cute. Millie was a soubrette: she had potential but no one picked up on it."

Betticent was one of the worst people I have ever known who was not an outright criminal. She lent money to her poor friends and made them crawl. Betticent had a collection of paintings of scenes of bloodshed, mostly animals getting killed, but one was of a woman being mauled by a bobcat. Betticent's mother, Ora's grandmother, said to me, *Have you met Betticent? Well, we're not like her, you know.* Betticent said, a couple of times, that I was a bowl of ripe fruit—that's pretty sickening in itself—but she would add to it: *Whenever you open your Harvard mouth something momentous comes out.* Johnno didn't like Ora; he said to me, "You play a Puritan-and-repentance game—save yourself, John Alden." He said it to me with an air of wit. I didn't get the point. I figured you had to grow up Irish Catholic in Boston to really get it. I rarely penetrated the secrets of his conversation once he started drinking on any given occasion.

To get back to Ora and me: When she said that thing about style, she meant she was afraid of what I thought of her in the light of the real life examples of style, locally—at Harvard. That stuff about style that she said was special to her in that it had to do with my rights and privileges within the particular hierarchy she recognized in regard to ambition and to being somebody in the world. In the early days, partway into the affair, Ora began to speak of us as having one soul. If someone wants there to be one soul between the two of you, it's not going to work out for very long. Someone's soul is going to disappear. I muttered, "You're waiting for a son . . ."

"Don't be Freudian," she said. "Please . . ."

Brotherhood across the lines of gender and a surcease of the roughness of heterosexuality in a not entirely amateur courtship setup and freedom from the goad to breed and from a lot of the rivalries in real life (but called all-the-rivalries in the Eden-shit), I think she was a fabulous tactician-technician of some sorts of amateur stuff in real life. She would not have been ashamed to the point of becoming physically fatally ill if she had been unsocial, unsmart, unwomanly. She was a femme fatale, sort of. Mean, malevolent Betticent, drunk, said Ora was *a failed femme fatale.* Ora as a femme fatale . . . Well, think of it in relation to actual men—and to women such as Betticent . . . God. Two men, older, said, in front of me, things they wanted to do to Ora, the mildest of which was to imprison her. She has to go on living and breathing every moment of more or less twenty-four-hour days. She has to talk to people, kiss them, fend them off, lure them, whatever.

"I'm looking for *the golden mean,*" she said often. Darkly.

I think she felt she had the right to show jealousy. We were living together the first time she read Proust's novel, with its stuff on jealousy and love. The oaks on her parents' place rustled in the country wind. She sat on a side porch and read, a box of Kleenex beside her: she cried and cried and read and read. She said, "He writes well . . . He's deep."

Jealousy

In spasms of it, she would be insane—she would spit out vituperation toward her father. She threw towels at me. She cried. She was partly a *collagiste* as a personality—she was jealous more in the way of a man. I knew from the start that a lot of what she was was recognizable from my having read certain books, certain magazines, from my having gone to the same college. I knew some of the same people she knew.

Her voice was a *brilliant* mélange of breeding and intellect (as intellect was considered at Harvard, short of the minds of the *College Fellows*)—and a further mélange of education and social-class energy, rich, deep, and full, a little formal, unexpected in someone so young—and in someone who looked like that, as she did. She often had a rich person's grave summer manner—youthful tomboyish seriousness-of-intent, a bit important, collegiate if you like.

But she bellowed when she was jealous. She wept and twisted and turned. Or she was cold and stiff-backed and shadowy-eyed and noble —and more than sort of unclean.

Her voice was so hideous with will, so tin-can-ish, that it was like a license plate she wore identifying her as not-what-you'd-expect—as capable of murder or of killing: those hours of pistol practice—and the rest of it. A lady of a curious type—not girlish or demure or guilty and hardly safe for you and clearly *capable de tout*—her phrase. She said it was "typically Anglo-Saxon to say that in French—if you don't learn about such things when you're young, you never learn them—it's *all* in the details."

"Hey, Ora, you going off the deep end again?"

"I am someone who is hobbled to the golden mean!" She was famous at college for her bitcheries. A professor, known for his sadism, courted her and went too far, I guess, and Ora was heard to say, "You stay away from me, you ratty little girl-torturer, stay away from me or I will have you run out of town on a rail."

She said to me, "I am capable of anything and I am glad of it."

People took her side—not because she represented virtue and judgment, but because she was in her temper, well, nobly squalid: they rooted for bad stuff. She was a part-time kleptomaniac—mostly only when she was jealous and needed consolation. She was given to slandering girls who galled her—or even just sweet-faced girls with freckles. She hauled off and slapped a woman who was insulting her and pawing her. A number of women adored her as a female hero.

She had a particular loathing for ungenerosity of any kind. If a guy she was with left too small a tip for a nice waitress—or a sad one—Ora would throw it in his face and say, "You fucking tightwad," and she would empty her purse on the table.

She was often drunk. Often jealous and maniac. Premenstrual . . . Always, however, UNASHAMED. She had a gold-and-jasper cigarette holder. After sex, she'd load up her holder; she might go barefoot, smoking with her holder, to the john or to the kitchen, or she might go naked, but in high heels, clickety-clacking, smoking, bobbling. She might have an air of tragic self-importance and satiety or of impatient fear of punishment. "I'm the whore of Babylon," she said. "You're innocent by comparison . . . Not psychologically, though." Then: "I'm not really the whore of Babylon . . ."

The energy, the élan of her showiness made you realize how unshowy a lot of girls were. How careful even if their voices were snotty or full-of-display—how careful in a world of violence—and of mean-throated social opinions. Or how smart and shadowy they were and how bitter or how funny . . . Or how capable of love they were. Ora was sort of a super-brat of beauty, but ladylike and well read—and impossible. She was ninety-percent audacity. I indirectly got a shivery sense of how different women were one from another and how they hid that—and of a *type*—beautiful, or would-be beautiful, or some equivalent, equivocably beautiful and mad, mad in rebellion—and *courage*: she was courageously noticeable: she was, I said, but Johnno stole it, Madame Charge-of-the-Light-Brigade. Courage, or nerve, not symmetry, is beauty. Men, women, professors, homosexuals. She was snottily interested in ads and snottily and defiantly affected by them: she wanted sort of to actualize those fantasies of pleasure—or of horror—and then she'd begin to go numb and just watch what happened, seeing some of it, blanking out quite a lot. Ora was showy, determined, and yet indeterminative, a drinker, a pagan-feminist mistress of despair, saltily not Christian, physical as hell, suicidal and resigned, unresigned, murderous and nuts . . . indomitable.

Johnno called me a "man-moth" in a poem: he stole it from another poem by a poet, a woman. Ora would eye me and semi-grin and say, "*Man-moth* . . ." Johnno came to dinner one night and when he came in the door, he kissed my hand and said, "Oh, hi," to Ora.

Older writers who chased her, more famous than me and Johnno put together, irritated and angered her. She was jealous of their reputations and sexually unyielding toward them. One of the most famous critics of the time, Cory de Haddon (who had slept with Betticent, who claimed she had to bite him so hard to get him to come she cracked a tooth), pursued Ora at a dinner party and telephoned and sent her books. Ora told him, *Lose twenty pounds and try me again—or wait until I write a book.*

She also told him to save his energies for the untalented women writers who slept with him to get blurbs: she went really far; she was really temperamental.

I often said to her, as I did that other night, the one I'm writing about, "I *like* your realism, Ora."

Did I want her to flirt with Cory de Haddon so that he would write about me? Yeah. But not enough to ask her to. Or to begin even slightly to maneuver toward it. I figured we would never recover from it, she and I. I mean, consider my need for her to be around to calm that infant sense of irrecoverable loss—that sense of loss was now revoked. Consider the hours of the day and my moodiness. Consider my jealousy of her. My self-destructiveness. My ambition. Ora said to me once, faintly excited by the wickedness, "You want to sell me to him . . ."

"No. But suit yourself."

Opt for happiness, such as it is, or not, is what I meant.

It is my opinion that what her face registered then was startled love for me: it startled her—it heated my blood. She had often accused me in her life of whoring her, of not caring what she felt about herself. She burned with an appetite of contradictory lust for privacy, evasiveness, but she was mostly, even essentially, an exhibitionist.

"The two of us are just narcissists who like each other . . ."

"I'm an exhibitionist, too," she said. A doubting one who made flaunting entrances at parties and then more or less caved in uninsolently, or semi-insolently; but she didn't pad in, or sidle in, as I sometimes still did . . . when I wasn't carried along in her style.

The energy with which she was *Ora Perkins* moved me. The energy with which she made trouble for herself was half an elegance of contempt for the world and how it treated her—her mother—and poor people—this was so although she was a right-winger at bottom. She was half made of a curious sort of longing for and absorption in a kind of honey of *common* notoriety—not the sort that kills but the sort that leads to your being mentioned in common talk . . . *Life after all.* "I'm not dead meat," she says on the night in New York, not averted-eyed but looking at the wall, daring it to show shock. "As sure as shootin'," she said in her extraordinarily fine voice. And she added, shamelessly, "Ultimately I'm okay . . . past all argument . . ." Then: "Your sex is never *Wham, bam, thankee ma'am . . .*"

"The greasy slide . . . the Hour of Equipment . . . the Hour of Enchanted Equipment . . . Excerpts from the *Kama Sutra.*"

"Putting thoughts into words is very odd," she said.

She was going to try it. Her mind was set but it worked well even so. The structures of her belief were not open; she wouldn't change them because of argument—or for a book . . . Or for a man. A certain amount of polish was finish: she was finished. She said, "Love for you and me is a kind of miracle." I guessed in the dark that ideas and thoughts, partly unmediated, were in play now. She was set up, like a tent for a mood in this odd place, this odd *climate*—she was as strange to me as a pyramid in some ways. (Mostly, this is being written in the tones of the language I had available to me at the times I am writing about.)

She assumed people had the same fixity in them that she did . . . and similar uncertainties. She seemed to know to what extent she was eccentric (and now this is a tone of feeling I had but not the language I had at my disposal), a soul bold and striding, the amount and direction and digressions of time that a soul is, swimming and flying, running and walking, breasting time—and catching its breath: one says, *My soul is catching its breath*—the interrogated and strained soul, interrogated by life; she moves toward fame, or toward forgetfulness; a set of magic syllables in a famous name or someone forgotten and relegated to oblivion. She saw herself as that more clearly than I saw myself as that.

She had a kind of virgin's rage, also a whore girl's amusement—after all, to be invited somewhere for your looks is to be whored—she had a bloodied and maybe unappeasable bitterness, and she was semi-almost-satisfied and patient with me, with us, with the world: she controlled the universe with her style—with her daring—not with prayer. Her moments of giving in or of being overwhelmed, her moments of stylelessness, so to speak, were a kind of prayerless prayerfulness: a grudging submission. It really was a circus of ideas with her, and then it was her body, cleft and buttocks, breasts and waist, her hands and neck, and then her face. It was a little like being in a dirty French movie of backstage life to be with her. She saw meaning in thinking of us, her and me, as clowns, serious clowns, among semi-criminals—others. And our being sexual she saw as purity and as a theme of insistent pre-nostalgia, so to speak. I forget what else she saw in us. The formal elements she had taken from her instruction, schooled and familied, in the world, she had folded into a confessional tone of considerable sad go-to-hell audacity—vivacity, too—and odd, almost heartless moments, of obstinate charity, toward herself first, then toward others. Talking in bed in the semi-dark—"semi" because so much light came through the windows, the city late at night, and from the moon—well, for me, it was Ora talking to me, her beauty there, her voice in play, and her not laughing at things; and her being a bitch, her keeping the bitchery retracted, her making us a thing of joy (if I might say that), it was really something. That glorious, thickish, glossy skin of hers, and the profundity of her eyes: her sweetly honied stench of rebellion—and of horror, the horror that afflicts women as an immanence—and her powers of creation—of moments, of feelings, she was serious and not serious, lost and found. In love? Well, it all had some reference to style—not a style of the first rank in the history of the world. She spoke almost entirely in referential language, referring to things in a slantedly educated, social-class, social-group way—not reverential but jocular *at a slant* of near-reverence, this side of her violence of rebellion, lyingly twice over despite whatever truthfulness was there, so a lot of her was *really* hidden. She wanted to manage life, to get even with it, to keep up, to be a fox and not a fool. It touched and maddened me, scared me, struck me as large-souled, wonderful really, in a real room, what she was. I thought so, anyway . . .

A way of putting it is that she didn't mean much of what she said but she always meant something by it; and much of what she meant showed although not simply or directly. She was enough of a personage that her meaning something meant more than that she meant something: it had a public resonance. You were being tested. This had become different in spirit—and principle—lately, recently, in the last two years, when *the world* held it to be the case that I was of more public importance than she was. Then she upheld her meaning as the Great Right . . . Or as the Great Light . . . the light of intimacy, the light of two people as opposed to the single nature of thoughtlight. She never chattered: that's only half a virtue, not to chatter. She always had a purpose, she was *always* a presence, she shared her strength with you; but there was no real peace because of the testing and the actuality of her character and the nature of affection in real time, at least of my affection. She treated me as if we were two bandits with a semi-forbidden sexual tie between us—semi-forbidden, not really workable; but maybe you could work it out in some sort of joint blasphemy (that was also a sacrament, a secular one, besieged). It was like that: that was how it seemed to me: her sexual anger, her sexual power, in this part of things, was tremendous . . . TREMENDOUS. In real life, it seems pushy of someone—and bold—to come and go, in presence and in focus, into overt truth of self-display and of will and then out again. She was like that but mostly she kept things at a slant—which was maddening, too. "I can't win," she said in the semi-dark; "but I don't give a fuck . . . I'm strong." She was the single most beautiful person I had known until then, and, by far, the most envious individual I had known. I wondered if it might be the source of her health (and a form of privilege) to be avid. Everyone I knew showed envy. I was aware of it in myself. Envy. Ambition. A certain will-to-live. A constant thing, or a thing constantly recurring, inevitable, a part of waking—perhaps even the core of things.

I figured, kind of cloudedly, that as long as she felt she would envy someone their having me, she would be interested in holding on to me. But I offered her a deal: "Let's not make each other jealous—" We worked at it. She rewarded me for that: it freed her for a while—and that freed me.

I had bouts of integrity, of being myself and letting her stay or go as she chose. I was cool-nerved at times. She settled her butt on the bed that night. I said to Johnno, who was vituperative about my feelings for her, that Ora mattered to me as an American war would. She overshadowed everything in my life: "I'm not proud of it," I said. "It's not like loving a cripple or someone very noble—or someone useful . . ."

But he was not mollified.

So far Ora and I had been together for a thousand and a half days. I had begun to model myself on her largely—or on her in reverse—or on what she knew about men and my contradiction of that and my identification of myself as contradicting that. This was weird and intrusive—I had entered quite deeply into her life, and I was a force there—and, although I wasn't the only force in her life, it was as if I had eaten her up in some dreadful mythical procedure. I wasn't in style Lila's son anymore or S.L.'s (or my real parents Max and Ceil's): I was a guy who lived with Ora Perkins. She knew she had, in part, educated me into being *Wiley-Silenowicz-Now.* This was capricious and arbitrary—maybe it was ordinary. It felt like a regular fate, one that happened to other men.

It wasn't symmetrically two-sided. When, because of my writing, I became a young-man-of-talent—in the eyes of some people—she modelled herself on me differently from before. She wanted that stuff. She became me at times, as if it were a common thing to be someone who wasn't you. She'd done this with other people, I think, roommates and grown-ups, analysts and guys and women—and people in her family—but so powerful was the initial image, or so valuable to her, the initial pattern of her life, that none of the other stuff led her into art or, really, into orphanhood. She hadn't really left home; and she didn't leave now into caring for me or caring about me or, in some ways, being me.

A *collagiste.* She used junk in people, stuff she saw as being successful. She took over things I said. I said to some people that New York was "raw envy acting as if it were intelligence . . ." Then: "God, maybe it *is* intelligence." And a few days later she'd made it, "*What I like about New York is that here, at least, people know envy* IS *intelligence . . . It's the core of New York seriousness . . . It's the core of upper-level* SALESMANSHIP."

But then not long after that she said it mostly in my words: "New York is envy acting as intelligence . . ." And so on.

When I laughed at her she said strangely, "But I didn't say that *New York was self-pity at a critical pitch.*" As if she hadn't borrowed anything if she hadn't borrowed that.

"But *I* didn't say that—I got that from Patrizia di Gustino, who got it from Bernie Kellow—maybe he got it from her: you never know . . ."

"Yes, yes, you told me."

"Yeah, but, Ora, you didn't say *that* either." Sometimes she is flattered when I try to bring her remarks into a coherence she associates with the biographies of famous women.

"I did now," she said. "To you . . . And you aren't blaming me." I had, and have, no idea what she was getting at. I was blaming her, wasn't I? I wasn't asking her advice on real existence, was I?

"I won't use it," I said confusedly. I am a blunderer and rather easily outwitted: a large, dumb young man. With some abilities.

Ora has a strong sense of how real other people's lives (and minds) are to them. I'm stupid for a while in my life (and mind) but I'm not *entirely* helpless in the long run.

"Men *always* steal from women, Wiley."

Her speech had a brittle effect of echo, maybe even a faint staleness, of earlier success.

But this was balanced by the excitement of her presence and of her bold manner, by my interest in what she intended now. It was a curious and workable balance. Love—you know? Maybe it was.

She said in the dark, in bed that night, "You keep your amateur standing by making up your own speeches as you go along—that's an interesting way to be."

"Amateur morally? Uncollusive?"

She sighed: she didn't associate it, my doing that, I mean, with any merit in the use of language. By repeating her remarks, she gained almost a laboratory sense of language, *her* language, her purposes, people and their sense of their own reality. Then she bronzed that, made it absolute. But her remarks trembled with the differences in their meaning each time anyway, different from other times. The same remark made by her dressed in some way and then naked saying it to me, and then her making it again dressed and saying it to someone else, not to me—her being sexually not really available or slidingly—she regularly gathered such data: I watched her: she knew a great deal. She was weirdly a forward edge to my own mind. She was a master-mistress of echoes and of measurement of social echoes. She was a laboratory technician of social and sexual arousal-of-interest—of well-being because existence took on a certain tone. She credited herself for this. Johnno Fynner had a phrase: "repulsive and terrific heroisms." He used phrases for a while but when they came to a certain pitch of use in his life, he dropped them—this was in general.

And he spoke of "all the horsepower in you getting out of hand and you become a runaway . . . The art *is* life, *boyo*."

Ora said, "I like him . . . he is truly interesting . . . I'm a talent scout . . . Well," she sighed, "but because of you liking me, he'll never forgive me. Not now. He would have liked me otherwise." He never did like her; he died without *liking* her; he imitated her though. He thought it unjust that she had the powers of attraction she had and the kinds of merit she had. He "liked" wretched, mostly plain, "witty" women. Or pretty ones wildly having sexual careers. He wanted it to be the case that only one sort of person had merit.

Ora's rank: *the most beautiful creature I ever saw . . .* Or as *really beautiful . . .* And independent: you can see the glamour of it—and the youthfulness. Then, this year—the year of the night I am writing about, she had chiefly the rank of who-Wiley-was-living-with. A New York rank of that kind.

It was a kind of filthy thing, not something she was likely to accept. It was kind of like a series of scorpions people dropped on us.

I could tell from the responses of her body to me that she didn't sleep around or fool around with other people much in order to get even for this stuff—not yet. As I would have. And occasionally did. We'd had no arrangement that included being faithful to one another, but she wanted to change that lately—as I said. She said to Bern (or Bernie) Kellow—a stylish magazine publisher we saw—that she wasn't free enough of worrying about what I felt toward her to fool around. I think she found actual sex puzzling. So did Johnno Fynner—but differently. One night when he was drunk and importunate—and I was drunk and confident and easy and had been amused—a lot, I had laughed a lot—by him and some of his friends two evenings in a row, I sort of leaned back and let him start on me down there, but he had no feelings in his mouth. It was creepy.

Or even in the moments of friendly (but nerve-ridden, still amused) *drama*, unzipping and so on. Not even longing: I mean, it was all meaning, meaning short of words, this side of being worded by him, this side of his attempt to put it into words, and the longing was to understand—and to be humbled and to be conceited and beautiful. I mean nothing was there but his sorts of hallucinations. Nothing was there for me but Johnno—and a curiously deadened power of my bodily realities, my measurements, my youth—I don't know how to say this: a strangely breath-riddled *coffined* reality—one in a coffin and on display, spider-bitten, scorpion-destroyed—well, sort of.

I think I mean no sense of the present tense was there—only a sense of dreams and, I guess, their painless time, *their* pain of longing—the strange cardboard flutter of the presence of dream-longing in a guy's head and face and neck—Johnno's—and the pain and rage in abeyance—as in Ora and me in that other way—the way life is in a wildly demon-riddled, angel-wing-thrust-at-courtship truce, or whatever it was . . . *Say it again*: The way life is. *He* would never believe me about anything—hell, and fuck it, even my body was a dream for him. He is a nearly pathic narcissist who in his sense of things writes everyone's dialogue for them—he is more and more isolated—as in a control booth. "You love me," he insists.

"No, I don't . . . You gonna suck it . . . or not?" Then: "The deal is clear, Johnno."

But it wasn't . . .

Ora, at least, let me mostly be someone who had some separate will of response and language from hers. She was not as formula-ridden as Johnno was. She was braver than most women, too. Maybe foolish. Johnno was made of metal, he was so dense with a loathing of time and of himself maybe, and of *the-way-life-is*. He so loathed time that he made himself into a kind of metal. He accepted real time as itself a rapist of boys, him being a boy. He had brick hutments of words he hid his metal self in—sort of. Of course, I did love him . . . But in this way which was as invisible (and lost to him) as some collapsed bridge in a distant continent—or in a legend. His mouth was like metal. He was a hero—he was heroic—but the agony in him was poisonous—poison ivy or a pit of scorpions or of snakes—all those images—and ones of *festering wounds*—and of beggary, beggary pulling you down into a gutter or into a dirty alley. The agony was extreme and not neutral or powerless—the agony in him. I don't mean only that it was contagious, unless it is understood contagion rests on an ambition in the germs or viruses . . . I mean they want to live. Ora wasn't like that. Or, rather, the agony was self-consciously obliterated in her by her having a hell of a *cheap good time*—or an *arty* one—or one that represented *what the world has to offer*. The agony in her showed less. It was moderated by blankness—by a stylelessness of consciousness . . . A differently conceited beggary—sunnier. She wasn't as ambitious as Johnno. He, like me, stood often in a rain of words. Of consciousness. It was the will-to-affect. The will to be pierced and to affect. It was purer in him than it was in me. His happiness was of the most curious, spiritual, and somehow semi-lower-class kind—a conceited and proud and vanity-ridden grovelling. Ora's varied wildly but her happiness was mostly like an elbow nudging her suspicious knowledge of things. Mine? Mine was like, oh, I've said this in my life: *a startled bird*. Ora was sexually real. Or almost real. Johnno was not. For neither of them was sex a source of light—so far as I know, painlessness was the source of light for them—the source of life as opposed to mere rush and maddened velocity. One time, drinking with Johnno, I accepted it that things were the way they were for me—I hadn't done that ever before, or if I had, it had been childish, or young. After that, it happened for me with Ora, and with books, and even with Guy, but with him in silent, unimportant moments—as when we were painting a house, say, for a friend. The first time, with Johnno (that I accepted my life), I accepted it *in drunkenness* and *for a while*: self-pity, rage, conceit, luck, moments of happiness, predestination, and the moments of flickers of free will, all of it. The drunkenness was simply an excuse for the vanity of believing myself for once. "I am entirely a fool and I am not entirely a fool," I said. "Dawn . . . see, that's dawn . . . It's dawn . . . Dawn is the model of painlessness after terror." I spoke much more elaborately when I was drunk. Johnno wrote a poem sequence on this idea. I can claim to know a little, but the truth is that I can't know, with any statistical finality, what is or is not true sexually for other people. Or morally. I was glad Johnno stole, or used, the idea . . . I was free to breathe . . . I theorize and guess at other people. His mouth wasn't always like metal, but it mostly was. Sexual charity is like murder, of him, of them—of you, too: you get *hung*, they get hung up on the emptiness; you are hung, bedecked with the cruelty of no response to them—a curious definition. I don't know. Johnno's lips were almost lips—but not quite. Sex was almost a source of light mentally, but not quite. Johnno became intent on his own further claims to justice—to justification. He really did rule the universe—as he saw it. Its laws, its rules . . . You couldn't survive it, either of you, his absolute sense of how things worked—he swept you onward toward sin-and-friendship—sacraments he ruled—and into his personal doctrines of getting ahead in the world—the team—and his notions of love—as if you were a Catholic housewife. Or a bricklayer. It seemed a terrible sort of onrushing cruelty that he opened himself and you to, that he broached.

Fynner said, "*You are a genius and a hick . . . Like Cézanne.*" His cocksucking was as if he was stropping my prick with the inner mechanisms of his mouth. *"It's too bad you're beautiful, it's too bad I love you . . ."* Now, in America, in my day, few people talked, women either; and such statements were startling—even more so if you weren't dreaming, if it wasn't dreamlike.

"Hey," I said, after a time lapse—sort of like a double, triple, quadruple take of a comedian in a movie. "Say that stuff again, will you?"

He froze—I think because I was real. "*All you want to do is paint apples,*" he said with contempt. I was *interesting*-looking: as I said, people would come into the dining hall at college who didn't belong there and they would stare at me and then leave. Johnno said that flattering stuff about me and I heard in my head my father's voice saying, *What do you think of them there apples?* and *As sure as God made little green apples.* And I didn't know what any of this meant except that I was arguing with my father and being nice to him somehow, long after his death, in what I did—or passively allowed—with Johnno.

Later, when I refused to accept the event in the romantic terms he proposed for it—madly, loonily, autocratically proposed, I thought—I said to Johnno, "As sure as God made little green apples, you just want to talk about it, I'm just a notch you want to cut in your belt, you want to make it all words and collusion. But I—I can't do it."

"You're a know-it-all—"

"What's wrong with that? You think you're omniscient. You're only talking about yourself . . . You call me a know-it-all when I say no."

Johnno said, "You're an incredible bastard."

"You're just being Catholic. Look, I don't know: I CAN'T do it . . . I don't want to, but the point is, Johnno, I CAN'T."

The odd thing was how merciless he became: "Of course you can: you're lying." Any offer of truce I made, he treated as the vestibule to my defeat. It's possible that this was the way he negotiated things. It's possible that he wanted me to hit him—the way he was pushy, the faces he made, the abrasive, comically effeminate, goading voice he used. Hit him and comfort him—in some eerie and vague combination or variation. Or perhaps even more, not to comfort him.

He had a fevered quality of wanting something I could not guess—unless I was a sort of criminal negligence in underpants—or something. It's probable that the likable thing to do was to grind-him-under-my-heel and then live with the consequences, more or less lifelong. My mother used to say, *I'm not a mind reader* . . . But she was. People *are* mind readers. A written page of gestures, of colors of the voice, skin colors and features in motion, uttered in that sense, statement, muttered aside, assertive vocatives, questions, trick things, tales, sales pitches . . .

Johnno held his body very stiffly—with a Catholic heaven-and-hell *elegance*—not of money, but artful in a private way. He improvised weird scenes, wild ones for you and him, and friends of his, in art and in life . . . sketches. He used the actual light in real restaurants, and he used the light in your mind—in mine anyway—to pose you in, and him, so that, if you will bear with me, he got a poem, or a possible poem, or a phrase, out of his turning you into a sense of you as a *handsome* young man (in some maybe mostly Irish way), or even a handsome-young-man-who-lived-with-Ora-Perkins-who-was-a-beauty, so that all the associations, the corridors, the big stores or malls in your head opened up of you being treated a little the way some women were and of how you'd treated women when you were young, or still—and of him, Johnno, as *A Grand Figure*—a master of ceremonies of knowledge and of life in this way—and you couldn't get this in any other way. I couldn't. You had to pay for this. In various living-breathing ways. He held back. He doled stuff out. He went crazy—typhoonesque—and then you were in Kansas or in Oz. It wasn't so different with Ora. I was envied as I had never thought I would be. I had a somber grinlessness, a kind of singing grimness of being young and male that was like a triumphant grin. I felt it burning in the lower quadrant, but almost the center, of my face. The whispers, the weird mixture of anonymity and of notoriety. One is rewarded. And used by others. Or one exploits *them*. One is pawed and indulged. Worshipped, actually. Although not all that much. Remarks about Ora and me as Beauty and the Beast. It is lousy and amazing . . . and all that. X loves me because *Y* does. I was modest—in a way. I lay on the grass in Cambridge Common one day, in my pink Brooks Brothers shirt (of that era), and I looked at the sky and I wished I was tall. I don't know how many seconds passed before it occurred to me that I *was* tall—and had been by then for years. I was living inside some sort of marvel of luck that was not clear to me or even entirely present, truthfully, or half-accurately, in my consciousness, in actual moments. Later, with Ora, I was known for writing with a brute straightforwardness of the acceptability of life, ipso facto, a priori, religion or no religion.

Or, rather, my work was technically admired, as a display of voice and lyricism. A falsified persona, not despairing. *An Artist.* Does *love* (being loved) make you narcissistic? Praise and love? Death and destruction and love? Does it confer value on you arbitrarily? Undeservedly? A cruel endorsement . . . Huge white clouds, the whitish Manhattan light . . . Thoughts change from moment to moment. *Try to know less and be happier* . . . I had usually been less sad than my mother. So what had she meant? It is some sort of scary, frighteningly slidy, superior-inferior condition. All is turnabout and fair play—among independent wills. The "superior" one is outwitted and slain, dried and made into a trophy, driven crazy. Time-ruined . . . Penalized in the sequences of popular tastes—styles change . . . Moments go by . . . go bye-bye . . . *Everyone* is richer, smarter, handsomer, happier. But one is the one—the one the host and hostess wait to see . . . The heat of special attention . . . Ora . . . Oh God . . .

In 1956, that night, ah: it's warm—it's late spring—the adopted and quivering and troubled child—he's spoiled; he's here—what does it mean? *Dear God, I promise not to enjoy this too much and not to become smug, but let it go on for a while. Help me to be smart enough to see that it goes on for a while longer . . . Please . . .*

"We're spoiled. And smug, Ora . . ."

"*You're* spoiled. And smug," she said.

Ora wasn't trying to be famous. She'd stopped. She wasn't fucking around (so far as I know). That stuff was in suspension. She wasn't writing movies with monocle-wearing countesses or liberated semi-princess girl-Jews with intelligent eyes who disliked me or who liked me and pawed me when she wasn't looking. She wasn't painting or designing clothes. Those things were in suspension. Real feeling? Feeling real enough to her? For us? I wanted her to work. We needed the money. I was afraid of what free time would do to her.

She said, "Wiley, I just want to stay home for a while—I just want to have my feelings." She said a little shyly and a little boldly, "I want to specialize in my feelings, Wiley, for a little while." Then: "I want to be an artist like you."

I didn't want her to. I didn't want a mirror of me. And what was that stuff worth, her feelings and me? Was I so great? Were we so lucky, really? And if I was enviable in the ways she was, then why was she imitating me? Well, I got drunk soberly on the thing that it was worth a good deal, a great deal to be me—or at least it sort of was. But I'd given it up to become *Ora-and-me*. "Real feelings," she said, "are special." *Real feelings?* I didn't think she would stay interested in this stuff or in me for long or that it was innocent, what we were. It was all work. And mirrors.

And luck . . .

luck . . .

luck . . .

luck . . .

Or God's will . . . Or an American accident . . .

Anyway, we didn't have enough money for sincere affection. We *had* to work at things. Ora's sincere and uncertain but proud affection —reliably proud, testingly proud, expensively proud—her proud obsessions—were an art. My overexcitement was a kind of lunatic freedom. Her freedom lay in her being the better *artist* in this sense. She wasn't a better *artist* as far as art went.

I said, "I wish you'd work. I feel stronger if we have two incomes than if we have only me bringing home the bacon . . . I have to be too flexible, too politic—I can't think. So I don't want you to be merely a girlfriend."

"Welcome to the real world, Wiley," she said. "I love you. You. You. You know, it's the first time for me . . ."

"I keep pointing out to you we've been together four years now . . ."

It hurt: it was a daily pain, an hourly one—the value, the not-value of our lives, of us in this way, the pressure in actual moments.

"Are you thinking of Sam's movie?" I then asked her. A guy we knew had directed a movie in which he used stuff from our apartment, he'd used our lives, some of our mannerisms.

Ora said, "I want to leave New York."

"I don't know, Ora . . . I bet what we have is realer here—I bet that we are *realer* in New York pressure . . ."

"Oh, confess you have secret reasons . . ."

"Maybe I'm just being ambitious? Or nosy? Or self-destructive . . . so I can get away from you and be promiscuous?"

I kissed her beautiful nose in the dark, its tip.

"Things are exciting here," I said. "Ora . . ."

"I'm not your slave," she said.

She and Johnno and Guy and a few other people (Bern Kellow, for one, and the woman who worked for me part-time) said that from time to time—suggesting a mental submission, with limits.

"I don't want a slave," I said bewilderedly. "I would like to become so famous I could make people be coherent my way when they talked to me." Then: "Now that you're not working, are you enjoying your feelings, Ora?"

"Miserably," she said.

"Oh no!" I exclaimed. I don't know the exact second I recognized her joke—maybe even before I exclaimed.

She laughed. She said, "Oh, it's so wonderful not to be tired of someone . . ."

"We aren't tired of each other but maybe we're wearing down . . ."

"God, don't talk like that!"

"Sorry . . . Well, we aren't free of being concerned about each other's opinions . . ."

"People don't stay in New York who have real feelings. You go somewhere else if you want to be sincerely together with someone. It's asking for trouble to stay in New York. It's like a jungle of appetites here, Wiley."

"Do you, as a general rule, root for the underdog? Are you unfair to people you don't look down on? Is that what's wrong with New York, Ora?"

"Here, everyone is in a mood . . ."

"The city as a huge storm of will and uncertainty—epigrams and albatrosses: you know how I know I love you? I would interpose myself and take the death blow from a robber. I admit I get more hot and bothered with arousal when we're not in the city. Here, love is a convenience—sort of . . . but twilight is quite carnal."

"You're showing off," she said. Then: "I like that."

Kellow and Higgins. They both objected to my style as a writer—yet they admired my work, they said. They objected to me—yet they spoiled me and courted my company. Years later they confessed they'd "loved" me. Or did. I mean still. I couldn't listen. I had longed so for them to *like* me . . . I mean I couldn't bear the realer story. Kellow was considerably older than I was and much more sophisticated. He owned three magazines and was a tyrant and was also a complete charmer—charitable, energetic, a small-boned bully-arriviste, well-informed, cagey, the complete instructor, the completely coldhearted and interesting companion-and-instructor—the doting hyena-cobra and an exposed cold heart (in New York). He had a kind of dragonfly-and-lion-beetle way of talking: a little flutter; and he would alight; and then he would carry the subject off to a burrow, a dark one.

Once he caught sight of Ora—and of, uh, ah, oh, *our* love—he was, for all his wriggling, power, money, and extreme cleverness, almost mine to do with as I wanted—especially since I asked him for nothing, preferring to observe his fascination and his reactions, preferring that to making any profit from any of this or to cementing the friendship through obligations on both sides. Preferring being with Ora to submitting to the obvious history.

Of course, that tempted him.

He had an awesome amount of personal authority—it came from having made people famous and from having guessed *the temper of the times* and from having made a good-sized fortune and so on.

He said, "New York is not a place for true love." And he looked at me sharply. *"True love is not how you get your picture taken."* I think I understood a little of what he was saying—of how you had to be emotionally available to the machineries, the apparatus of becoming someone in public consciousness. He said, "Not true love that lasts very long."

His wife said, "Oh, true love doesn't last . . . Psychoanalysis lasts . . . And money, sometimes money lasts."

And so on . . .

He was not like Johnno. Neither was Higgins who was a *nouveau* old-line Wasp—the first generation of such pretension, up from small-town-hood. A Johnny-come-lately Sensitive Gentleman, so utterly dishonest, so tricky that it was a form of dearness that was dear even while it set your teeth on edge. He asked for charity all the time—as a form of his own Christian humility. "Love is one-sided," he said. "One person suffers. One person is bored." He was much too selfish to be interested in anyone's loving him—Ora pointed this out. He was my literary adviser and could talk really well: the beginning of a story, he said, no matter how much light you try to cast in the first sentence, is really no more for a reader than light under a door in a dark hallway.

I like men who talk . . . I'm scared of men who have too much real power . . . presidents and army generals and billionaires . . . I dislike being an accomplice . . . and being emotionally slain or owned: employed, I guess that is.

Ora said I loved both men but was hopelessly evasive and suspicious—and a know-it-all. She said I believed them more than I believed her, but that's not true, at least about emotional matters. Or about metaphysical issues. Or aesthetics. I did not let them talk about Ora. Or whether ours was *true love*—hers and mine.

"You despise your friends," she said.

Those two. "Well, what I'm interested in feels to me to be beyond stuff those two know about. And they fight dirty," I said to her. "It would be odd if someone like me knew what true love was—or experienced it."

"We're very lucky, Will." A nickname. She (and Johnno) didn't like the name Wiley. It wasn't romantic.

"I'm independent—I'm lost," I said.

"Hush, hush, you want me to make us some cocoa?"

"A lot of what we feel for each other is fairly real. At least that."

"It would be realer out of New York . . . New York is for people who are really not able to be serious, Wiley, about anything much except seeming to be central while boring everybody to death."

"Yes? We're better than everyone?"

"We don't do things because they're subject matter, Wiley . . ."

"No? We do them because they arise in the soul?"

"Yes."

"The soul is bent by ambitions—whatever they are."

"How do you know about the soul?"

In Ora's presence, everything was real. She watched me to see if I *loved* her still, I watched her to see what she felt now—it was amusing in a dark, full sense.

"Are the halls of self-consciousness like the halls of Montezuma?"

That was from Johnno. "I didn't say that right. The soul is the totality of what one is—what one has done—of what has been done to one and what one has done in return. But the soul can be used—puritanically, promiscuously: it hardly matters that being Puritan and being promiscuous are so much alike in the moments. It is almost an irresistible pleasure to lower oneself, one's soul, and to become the propagator of the fame of one's name. A kind of swindler . . . The wit of success . . ."

Ora, a little drunk, or drunkenly dryly sober, and a little cross, said, "They do a big P.R. number here about their *feelings*, but it's all *a creepy lie*. I'd like to leave: I'd rather live in the country—or in Hollywood or Paris—I'd rather live in *New Jersey*." Her family, being New York State and Massachusetts and Connecticut and Maryland, was contemptuous toward New Jersey.

I was sure of myself in some ways—maybe not realistically.

"And us?" I asked.

"You and I are mostly real, Wiley."

"Yeah . . . sure . . ."

"DON'T BE *CLEVER*! DON'T BE A FOOL OF THAT SORT—NOT NOW—I CAN'T STAND IT. You thought ahead—you planned it all—coming to New York—us—all the things that have happened here." Including her liking me more after a while than she had in the beginning. "You told me what would happen and it happened."

I had a dim memory of predicting these things.

"Ora, I'm not that smart. Maybe you plan things out . . . I don't. It was a gamble. I thought you might be entertained in New York. I thought we might have an 'exciting' time. I knew I could go on being reasonable from time to time with you and I figured you'd like that."

"But you don't know how *your* unconscious mind twists things so that the prophecies come out crazily, Wiley."

"Life always surprises me, Ora . . . You can't predict the whole thing, the flavor or whatever, of a real thing."

"My analysts said *they* could."

She said now in the dark, "I can't have a career"—she was a little drunk, more than a little sober—she sounded faintly like Millie: "You have to sleep your way up. It's better if you're droll-looking—droll-looking and crippled—it's a lot better. People don't have to crush you. But if you're real, they try to hurt you and you fight back. They don't want to learn from you. And that's that . . . That's the end of that . . . It's quite, quite, quite awful. In our lifetime, what we have are people who are clever amateurs . . . It's the Decline of the West." She had shifted to quoting from her father.

I said clumsily, "In a lot of careers, Ora, like logging and exploring and medical research, you know when what you're looking for will kill people, but in most work, if you fake it, everyone is safer in a way, even if the world falls apart. Real work can kill everyone else." She looked blank. I often left out data or words that would explain things to her. I thought I was obvious and dumb when I talked. I said, "People get hurt. So you hold back . . ."

Her eyelids silently twittered. Her eyes gleamed. You ever see swallows in a canyon, hunting? Her eyes flickered. Then she got it, got something—

"It's about being dangerous—the dangerous young—and envy—rivalry—the myths of the species."

She said, "I don't have the slightest Jewish streak . . . I have *no* guilt . . . No guilt at all . . ."

"I hate the word *guilt*: I always hear *gilt,* as in gold-leafed and airless. How about responsibility? You feel responsibility?"

"The dullest word of tongue or pen," she said, quoting someone, quoting a joke. "I'm ruthless, Wiley." She was in earnest and yet roguish . . . she managed it. "Listen, Wiley"—she put her hand on my arm: she really *liked* talking in bed—"listen hard," she said as if we really had been making real sense as in a very good book.

"The Lady John Wayne," I said.

"I am a very very very *moral* person . . . But I don't expect to be understood . . . They can all go to hell." Then she muttered like a movie star (very audibly, very well recorded, very central—I didn't see enough movies to know if it was Ingrid Bergman or Edwige Feuillère she was influenced by here), "The maimed, the scarred, the freakish aren't going to be kind to us. And they do the work. Everyone else is just fucking the time away. But what can those other people *know* that we know, Wiley?" The ones who didn't have looks, the competent ones? "I don't want to be wrong but I don't think they count." She was talking about someone's loving her best? Putting her first in this area, too. Me doing it. "I believe in what John Adams said: *Things are run by the rich, the well-born, and the able* . . . I grew up tough . . . I never worry about Jack and Millie."

I only partly knew what she was saying and that filled me with despair. "Oh God, Ora, you're not any of the things you just said. You're such a liar it scares the piss out of me . . ."

"It scares you that I put love before politics, Wiley, but I know that in the end politics is everything. Love comes and goes. *'It is like an untamed bird . . .'* " That was from *Carmen*. "But our love is mythological," she said obstinately.

"I see what you mean," I said earnestly—to make her laugh. "I see that," I tried again. "That's what scares the piss out of me."

"Ha-ha," she said then.

"I want a drinky," she said.

"Go ahead."

Ora drank before we went to parties when she was getting dressed and putting together how she would look. She drank a lot, a vast, huge, *legendary* amount during parties and dinner parties. And then among the eyes, the lives, and the voices of other people, fuelled but not visibly drunk, she would become deeply silent and amused and often almost sweet-tempered. She would talk in the sense of holding forth—but never that I knew of in New York City.

"I'm glad we don't do la-di-da stuff in bed." She had risen from the bed and was pouring herself a drink from the bottle on her vanity table. "I don't like that la-di-da stuff," she said.

She meant I didn't ask her to compete with whores or with more sexual women.

In the dark, I see her flesh, her body: the semi-stilled waves of flesh . . .

She had *private* reasons of the sort that are generalized during analysis . . . the *emptiness* and *misery* that are not here—well, some *is* here. "I am cerebral, Wiley—it's a flaw," she said as she came back to bed, sipping at her uniced Scotch in a plain glass. "I'm honest, Wiley . . . Liars *implode*." Jack's word. "I hate imploded liars." With alcohol, she spoke to me with fewer, or with different, pretenses—taking more risks. And then, an amazing thing—and clear, all things considered—it was from one of her college papers: she quoted it now: "What would be the point of permanent but inconsistent *social* reason? It must be to be human." An argument in favor of frivolity. She sat on the edge of the bed. "A gentleman never talks about being not corrupt," she said. "Anyway, real Americans aren't gentlemen . . . I don't like gentlemen. I love you—and I believe in *America*." Some of that was from Jack. She said, "I could never be a Stalinist or a Trotskyite . . . But some of those people are fun to be with."

Her looks. Her courage. *To see her at the dinner table was to see Marxism die . . .*

"Oh God, I shouldn't be drinking—I've been naughty . . . I feel sick." She went into the john and closed the door. "Don't come in," she said through the door. She ran the water, obscuring the sounds. After a while, she came out, wet-faced, washed, not looking tired. "You still love me, Willsy?"

"Sure. Less, but, sure, I still love you."

She said, "Love me simply." She meant it.

"I can't." Then: "You didn't let me nurse you . . ." Then: "Sure, simple is as simple does. You too. Love *me* simply."

"Uh," she said. Then: "I don't believe in justice," she said. "Not for women . . . Those ideas of even-steven? They're not for women. People hold those ideas for the publicity."

She wasn't the *prettiest* or *loveliest* woman or the most charming—but she was oddly logical and bold within her tactical cowardice and her illogic—she was the most seriously beautiful person—perhaps the most naughtily alert.

A thief, a usurper of my life. A pallor of intense shadow. She has a deep and deeply physical soul—a soul like a gulf, a cleft in the dark . . . She half hated it, this thing of being of interest to me. An affair. A belated fling. She said, "You're pretty in the dark—you look sensitive when I can't see you; would you give up what you look like if you could write like Milton?"

I was smart-alecky and I said, "No."

She sighed and said, "I wouldn't either . . . But some days I would . . . Oh, it's too sad; I'm so trivial: I can't bear myself . . . I wish I'd been an orphan . . . Like you . . . Like Moses. Would you be willing to be awful-looking if you could be a Moses?"

"And give you up?"

"Bullshit in the bulrushes," she said in a delicately willed, foolish voice. Then, in a stronger voice: "Yes," she said.

"No."

A long silence. She put her drink down and lay across me, perpendicular to me. My arms went over her breasts. She stared at the ceiling. Finally, she said, "What would you do if you could write like Shakespeare?"

"What would I pay for it? I don't know. What would I do for fifty million dollars?"

"I wouldn't do anything for fifty million dollars," she said.

Of course, she'd had the choice.

So, in a way, had I.

A silence then.

I looked at her fine-boned, heavy-skinned, powerfully affecting profile—in the dark. Really, *beauty* in someone is a trial of your ego. "I could forgive you for affecting me . . . If I could write like Shakespeare—if I knew that I could . . . I would do it easily if it was a sure thing I wrote like him. After all, knowing that, if you could know it, would be pretty damn *cheering*."

"Yeah, I see your point," she said, lying on me.

"But how can you tell it's not illusion? Would you give up your face to be Shakespeare?"

"In a minute. Less than a minute."

"And lose me?"

" 'Love is not love which alters when it alteration finds.' "

"Come on, stick to the rules."

"What rules? I would still have an interesting face, whatever it was, if I wrote like that."

"Oh . . . I see . . . But I'm used to your present face."

Ora's face—the sedate and educated and yet large and *naughty* mouth, softish and smart-ass mouth, luminous with health and mind? with intelligence? And her amazing eyes, suffering and empty and deep at the same time, with an unfortunate *hurrah* element: *Come on, let's not be suicidal.* I 'loved' her in part. I really had no idea if she was a serious person. She was a person.

I said, "I can't daydream like this . . . I can't be a Marxist either . . . We can't be Shakespeare."

"Well, don't say that to a Trotskyite celebrity writer who's no good," she said, suddenly becoming my instructor. "Agreed?" She had been a Trotskyite one time for almost a year—but no one had believed her. She said, "I hate myself, Wiley . . ."

"I'm sorry."

"Don't be . . . I have you."

"Ora, I have my notions of love—they're not yours—yours are based on the power of jeal—"

"Jealousy can make YOU crazy—fast enough." She said it darkly—she was, abruptly, at the edge of a sea of rage, more memory than directed at me.

"I don't believe jealousy is the sign of love. Proust lied. Unless everything is love."

"Oh, you're so competitive," she said.

"What do you mean?"

"You want to have a better love life than Proust did . . ."

"Well, he wasn't *happy*, Ora . . . He died *young*."

We are naked . . . The night sky in the window is visible in the mirror of her vanity table. If I stood, I could see up and down Madison Avenue.

Ora looked a little, oh, quiet and improper, lovely and a little drunk, startlingly alight and not young in a way.

"It's all *degrading*," I said. "It's more sensible to be a woman . . . I believe that famous athletes, dictators, actors want to duplicate what you are—want to have your kinds of knowledge of life in this world. People talking to you—your parents, grandparents, teachers, analysts . . ." Then swallowing (and choking a little), with a slight pause: "The men before me . . . I'm a little crazy. I'm still drunk. You are The Library at Alexandria."

"It was burned down, Willsy . . ."

"Yes, it was . . . That's the point. You can't trust me. Rightly or wrongly, I see you as a symbol—a real person who is a symbol—one of a number of examples—people study people like you: what our part of New York is about is unhappy people who become the equivalent of a beautiful woman."

"I'm not beautiful . . . You're just in love with me." Then: "You're beautiful . . . Bern Kellow calls you *the smart Farley Granger*."

"That's affectionate meanness—he thinks Granger is revolting. He sees me as your lover—lucky in having the life and body—" Of someone who loved a woman. "He can't see beyond that. I don't have that life, that body, but how blessèd it feels to fool him—the imposture. I mind the hatred and mischief . . . in him . . . toward us. *And* the affection. I wish he weren't such a poisonous little monkey."

"You've had a *sweet* youth," she said, not unenviously.

"Me?" A sweet, honied youth? "That's interesting . . . Like a treat I gave myself?" She said nothing. "I know I'm in good shape lately—I can breathe. I can smell odors. I can see colors."

Suddenly she said, "I'm inferior goods . . . I'm terrible . . . I'm a cheap cunt."

"Are you going to confess something?"

"You saved me . . . Promise me you'll go and save me some more."

"Christ, Ora: you're funny. You're so snotty and then you're some kind of masochist crawling around like I was the Pope or King Freud or A Clever Daddy."

She said, "You're this subtle and cowardly hick . . . And powerful—now with a heart-on—" I did. I called it *heart-on* and not *hard-on*. "And so it's hard to be near you."

"Are you humble—and loose up between the legs—or between the ears—my darling, believe me, you're-one-of-the-wonders-of-the-world."

"Thank you, Wiley. I know you love me . . . You're blind. Love is blind—you know, you're not everyone."

"You always argue . . . Do you feel a lot of fear of what would happen if you ever really listened to me, if you ever really talked to me like it mattered?"

"It matters. Yes. Oh God. Truth is so sexy. It turns me to jolly jelly. I can't bear how much it matters to me," she said, draping herself looseningly over my thigh. "If I listen to you, I will break in two—like my heart."

"Yah-tuh-tee-yah-tuh-tee . . ."

"It's true: my heart is broken . . ."

"And jealousy is the tie between us. Stop playing with my feelings: I'm a violent orphan, Ora."

"Ah . . . ah . . . ah," she said. Pause. Then she giggled quietly.

"You're always huffy toward my prick—like you've known better ones . . ."

"I have," she said daringly.

Pause. "I am choked up with rage . . . I could kill you for that . . . Christ: are we happy? Well, if we are, it's in this way. Is it good enough, Ora?"

"You're getting even, aren't you?"

"Ask me no questions, tell me no lies, I tell you none," I said, seeing Lila—and Nonie—briefly, phantasmally, in the dark.

"Now we have sexual desire, somewhat painful . . . sore-pricked," I said. Then ironically: "And a few eensy-weensy seconds of melodramatic breath," I said as I turned her over mostly on me but partly to one side. "Every time I touch you, my touch kind of *burningly* churns inside me, inside itself and then in me . . . What does any of it mean? Does my violence interest you?"

"No. But I can be patient with what you are."

I was balked and scared, both, by the sexual reality—the feeling in a real moment of lives—*permissions*—and so on.

I said, "You're my ghost lover and I'm your virgin male . . . You're so *clean* . . . I am spiritually almost like a virgin." Here, as I spoke, masculine ambition centered on her being the darker one of us, the more violent actually, the one more free, the one with nothing of the virgin in her.

I held my cock in the hope she would admire it.

She said satirically, looking at it idly, "One in every pot? Like Herbert Hoover? *À la?*" Then, moving her head, she kisses my reasonably muscular abdomen. Not the cock.

"God, not Herbert Hoover."

She touched the cock with her hand.

"Oh, it's so pathetic trying to live, oh, oh," I said, *amused*. We're breathing not quite in unison.

She says, "I don't follow that—that description is out of kilter . . ."

"I can't concentrate," I said. "I want to explode and die . . . I'm sorry for the CLICHÉ."

"That's all right; you're caught in your persona. Producing what-becomes-cliché is the mark of an important writer." She was quoting a professor we'd had in college.

She stopped and said, "I want a cigarette." She just looked at me, though.

"There you are," I said, "an unsymbolic version of beauty." I didn't hit her. "I'm scared: you play with things and you play at things . . ."

She turned away from me and took a cigarette from a pack on the table and she lit it, and she turned back, holding the ashtray near her breasts, and I moved away from her, covering my crotch and pubic hair against bits of ash, fiery coals.

She said, "I like to veil myself with smoke." Then: "I am a deeply serious person: I never play at anything . . . I'm like some men that way . . . Why do you have that look?"

"It's so startling: *the real thing*. You were grovelling a minute ago."

"I have a fat tushy," she said.

"Not really . . ."

"I have enough for a spare if part of me got shot off," she said. A rehearsed line: I'd heard it from her twice before.

An odd hopefulness mixed with a particular grimness of a to-be-carried-out action—a sexual grimness at the slapstick deadline—filled me; but I can sometimes—I could at that age—if I want to, slide into my other feelings as a young man and feel my skin and the reality of my erection in the moment, the moments—and the amount of sincerity, sort of a dominating flavor in the reality with its tinge of *American luck* and awful realities of *happiness*-and-sadness here—again in an American version in the middle of the night.

A plane of discourse.

She said, "It's so wonderful knowing a man I can *talk* to."

Quick: let me know the name of these moments. The sincerity was like a gaping, gulping mud rut pulling at me—the variable sincerity—I am not a man sad enough to matter in the history of the language. But in the expenditure of nerves, you yet keep your nerve while you throw your life away. The sincerity caught me. The sense of drowning and of flying upward both. Our eyes met in the confusion of the passage of time and the actuality of feelings.

She put out her cigarette. I moved toward her then—one hand covering my pubic hair and part of my prick against the vanished cigarette. "Ah," I said, touching her breast.

The warm, oddish reality of an actual breast affronts me and empties me of affront. She waits this out, my pulse and eyelid—and breath—thing, the dit-dit-dit of these. My reactions to her breasts, mine, don't interest her much, almost-peace, an odd, taut immanence, sexual. This closeness or intimacy is not two-sided.

I said, "Your breasts bore you?" Actually, I was a dullard in this part of sex.

"I'm a sick person in some ways," she said gravely, fondly. "I've never been someone people thought was normal."

"Aw, Ora, fuck—I don't want to go to bed with a *sick* girl."

At first she scowled. Then she laughed—semi-delightedly. "You don't like badly damaged, crazed women, do you? In the end, you idealize me?"

"I'm a sissy . . ."

"Don't say that!"

"Then don't say you're sick . . . Let's think highly of each other—what do you say to that?"

She said mysteriously, "I can see where that game would interest you . . . Yes. Anyway, it's true."

"What's true?" She said nothing. "Ora, let's shut up."

"I like to talk, but okay, if you want . . ."

"Ora, I hate the master-slave thing." But it did establish the erection yet more tautly.

"Oh, don't be critical now—you're very self-absorbed, Wiley. Don't glare at me; if the shoe fits . . ."

"The shoe fits the tit." I tried my hand on it. "Ora, you don't like being a sexual object . . . You're weird," I said, laying my face facedown on her right breast.

"Oh, I get sloppy . . . But I'm a powerful person, Wiley. Jack is right about me: I'm hard to take." She held my head inside her arms. She took one arm away and lit another cigarette and puffed on it and ashes fell into my hair.

"Let's fuck again," I said, sighingly moving my head away.

She said, "I hate that: can't you say something romantic?"

She began to dispose herself for entry.

"No," I said, getting up on my knees, straightening my hair with both hands.

"I get to say yes," she said dryly. "And smile: oh goody, let's fuck. I like more imagination than that. It's not attractive, Wiley. You cause me constant pain—you're a terrible person. But I can stand it: I am very, very strong."

I snorted against her skin and licked her vaguely. "You sound like a mother . . ."

"Men marry their mothers first—then their daughters. Don't get mad if I laugh—I'm ticklish." Then she roared . . . With a kind of amused pain. I am a talentless licker . . . I tickled her then with my fingers and tongue, nose, ears, and hair . . .

She said, "DON'T! I'LL COME!" Then: "STOPPPPPPITTTTTTT, I HAVE TO PEEEEEEEEEEEEEEEEEEEEEEEEEEEEEEEEEEEEEEE . . ."

I stopped. When I stopped, she said, "It *is* VERY low-level eroticism to *tickle* a woman, Wiley." She said it sadly. She was disappointed in me, truly.

"Don't break my *heart*, Ora," I said.

She said, "Now I do have to pee." She got up and walked, wavery-whitish, only half-visible, beautiful—into the john. She left the door open. "You don't really love me: you're in love with me is all. That's a lesser thing. I have a bigger soul than you—you're very petty . . . I love you more than you love me."

"Ora, don't break my heart." Then: "My mother told me always nurse the pride of the fuckee . . ."

She washed afterward and flushed.

She said as she neared the bed, "I'm a boring person . . ."

"I'm only slightly *famous*." Then: "I don't want to fuck a boring woman who loves me more than I love her."

"I'm a good fuck . . ."

"We're white and middle-class, Ora."

"So? I don't believe all of that racial shit . . . Only some of it."

"All right, Ora, time to shut up; time to fuck."

"Oh, be romantic . . ."

"NO!" Then: as I put two fingers in her somewhat slowly: "Leave us alone . . . You're readier than I am." I rose up on my knees. I looked at her for a second or two—*romantically*, I hoped . . . *romantically-ironically*—tempestuously, coolly . . . I don't know. I said, "This is a romantic gaze . . ."

She said, "It is not. It's creepy and dirty. You're cruel."

In the fuck proper, I wouldn't be able to see her. Even now I didn't exactly see her. The sight of her—the beauty—was the ground, or base, for hallucination. And wonder. Sexual self-congratulation. Sexual conviction. And will. I doubted that it was the same for her, seeing me erect, but maybe it was, or similar. Her face was odd with what I took to be the change of consciousness when one fills with sexual realities. She is more alert, more watchful, more guarded than I am—less successful in a way in these moments than I am.

"Lie down," I whispered. But she already was. I walked kneelingly on the bed and bracketed her thighs with my legs, touching her thighs. I was on my knees above her. I saw her. She was in that state of slapstick grimness before sexual acts in the dark but smiling-bodied: readied. She "loved" the atmosphere, the reality of the agreement-in-her-favor *before a fuck*. Or so *I* think . . . She loves to test and wreck things—everyone but me says she is nightmarishly difficult . . . I say she's smart and restless.

One's life has this much meaning. These kinds of meaning, opinions, actions mutually permitted. At least to this extent. I expect this carries over person to person, country to country.

She said, "If we had only this one time, what would you say to me? How would you look at me?"

"Ora, you have no sense . . . That is not an artful request."

"It was, too . . . You don't know everything . . . DARLING."

"I KNOW MORE ABOUT SEX THAN YOU DO."

"Not statistically . . ." She had been to bed with more people than I had. And more seriously. I pushed the knobberhead against her lower lips, in a little. Maybe barely. I put my hands on her ribs. She was *amused* . . . a little. This stuff among the sour and corrupt velocities of the self . . . Shadows slickly inundate her face.

The sexual stuff at my crotch begins to pulsate. *Don't let's hurt each other* is what I feel. But that's not a simple thing given the appeal of strength and the licenses in sweetly-grandly or earnestly or meanly living down there—in nature. She hadn't much interest in fighting for anything, really—I mean in that moment. She died when she was fifty-eight. Pancreatic cancer. She refused all treatment. She was married then to a man I didn't much, or entirely, like. He told me she shouted and wept and screamed after she took the suicide pills. But she wouldn't tell him what she had taken. Then she told him, *I changed my mind: I want to start over . . .*

She protested and yelled until she died . . . SHE KILLED HERSELF NOISILY.

They are all dead.

She said now, "We're an aphrodisiac couple . . ."

Almost my best friend at that time was the actor-playwright Bertrand Millier, who had become famous at the age of twenty. He was handsome, intelligent, well paid, and, as I said, famous. He treated me like an older brother. He was insanely likable. I'd go backstage and some big-time movie star would be there. Bert would be saying, "My prick is too small for this part." He had a thing about that. He'd say, "This is Wiley Silenowicz: he's not insane; he has hair on his chest." He was enormous genitally, but he had been seduced when he was fourteen by his mother, then by some of her drunken friends, and he had some sexual doubt or unreality thing. I don't know if men had been included or not. One time we were talking and I was showing off what I could drum up in myself to say, and he said abruptly, "I would rather go insane than go on living." He tried to make trouble for me and Ora: he pimped for her—unsuccessfully. Finally, we came to blows—sort of. He went nuts for ten years.

In bed I kissed the side of Ora's face. She was slightly twisted under me. I twisted a little to get the head a tiny bit farther into her. My breath was like a *tee-hee.* To hide that—I never wanted Ora to know my real secrets—about what I really felt—I said: "My mother always said it wasn't worth going through the *contortions.*"

Ora said nothing at first. Then she said, "Let's turn out the light and fuck on the window ledge." The window had a deep sill and rose up and was high in the high room and a little narrow. We walked over to it, our arms around each other. At the window, below us, was a tide of lights. Some noises rose. City noises . . . I helped dispose her on the windowsill. Standing, I fitted it partly into her. The city—*our city,* New York, Manhattan—buzzed below us and it shone with lights. As always, at the moment of fitting it in, I felt slowed, solemn, freed, and giddy. "I love you," she whispered. The words were slightly far away compared to the somewhat grand conversation of the bodies beginning their lovemaking in a sort of white shyness of sensation and of expectation and of somewhat experienced carefulness. I was shy and not sorry to be present and doing this thing.

A moment.

I am slightly ashamed of my lovemaking—it's stodgy, I guess, and opinionated, obstinate, a little conceited. I will say I haven't ever been laughed at in bed. Never? I'm not sure about never. How strange. I expected it for years—I had a sense of that vulnerability . . . of that possibility in people, for me. The window ledge was her way of adding imagination, fantasy to my stodginess. Well, why not? I suppose for physical reasons I found her presence and the moment to be a marvel and yet ordinary, but with a degree of unreality such that a hallucination when masturbating—something that much in a mind, in a single mind—was, in some ways, more real, more plausible to one's consciousness, less strange, less dreamlike . . . less frightening than the feeling-filled linkage of the crotch things of two people with the hallucinatory element present anyway. It all rocked with time, with comparisons to other times, with luck. Something loosened in me and I found it hard to believe that reality was really occurring in the flood of the ungeometric fragility of inward sensation. I don't want to call it that: it had no label: a heat, a heated thing: soothing: soothed. Sly . . . The second one . . . The phallic tinge of my life goes along with an increase-in-strength, a validation, along with this secret, other way. Ora has enticed the future and it is here. She is in the form of a doorway goddess of approval—semi-approval in reality—a doorway to the future, the future in shadowy form.

A hint of exhaustion-to-come, masculine shame: a cliff edge of performance, in a way; a window ledge. I felt biggened: grown-up-ish, okayed—a little. The semi-educated semi-hick's slides and little, semi-tactful pushes, *lunges,* my breaths, her *uhs,* the sliding around, the reangling, the near-socketing, and her legs widespread like a weird book, her grunting, more or less hospitably—bluffing: this isn't so great—and then a note of grudging surrender and of admiration for me—showing imagination, I think, or for my obeying her wish—but if I push hard and test her physically and grimace like a bronze athlete, that admiration changes to the real thing, her thing of *I-want-you-dead-and-in-chains-you-bastard-but*—that feeling ameliorated by inverse sexual grace of some sort—by my own strength and by her mercifulness—*I-will-keep-you-alive-for-once-and-for-all-but-for-this-moment-you-and-I-are-not-to-be-trusted.*

Ora then opened her inner muscles so that I felt almost nothing, so that I was small in comparison to her. I mean the sex became a mixture of perverse combat and measurement and of comfort for herself. It was not innocent and it was not malevolent; it was innocently malevolent.

If Ora opens too wide inside and if I slap her, she tightens: I did that once. This thing she does, if I feel it in relation to moments in their fluid rush, in ongoing time, is dialogue, is preparing the next moment in which I will act in relation to this thing she does. And then she will react to that. So, it's major stuff in this scale of things. I squeeze her thighs. She tightens some and loosens again. She doesn't admire me. She hates me, kind of, or not kind of but really. But it's not some general hatred, it's Ora fucking someone she maybe likes—if you follow me—

and what she rides sexually then—I mean you can feel it, I can feel it —is my guilt, my early death, my despicability compared to her, to feminine stuff, oh, her comparative decency, her humanity—whatever. She is not necessarily reasonable, but not necessarily at fault either. It depends on what happens—and on what the world is. If she can't blame me for a lot, really, of obviously awful things, such as drunkenness or violence, she can't live: what room is there for her if she is not better than I am in a lot of ways? She thinks she is worthless if she is not important. It is all kind of slidy in a dirtied lyrical thing of make-believe and this-is-trouble—it's okay. This weirdity of stuff is love enough—maybe. It's not *so* bad . . .

This is, sort of, the conversationally *moral* element, or part of it, the give-and-take sentimentality, and with the sentimentality inverted. Ora's size and my having to keep my knees bent makes the fucking this way kind of hard. The nihilism: she somewhat likes it. She'll settle for it—she's a big shot. That inflects the reality and irreality, the hallucinatory part and the slidyness with the uninert terror of the contortions and the oddity of fucking for her sake. It is almost as absolute a terror for me as I know . . . A meaninglessness. From Nonie? From Nonie-in-us? In her? In me? And pleasure is laced through it. The terror is not of castration of the flesh but of the irreversibility in the quality of one's soul because of what one is doing here and what she is doing. Who *wants* to be born again in the same form as before? What one does because of what she does, moment by moment, moment after moment, is what one is—it is my character in a sexual event with her. The working sexual definition of who I am sexually with her has to do with irreparable flickers of associative memory and with losses in my past life. For God's sake—rough or not-rough in my view or not—to persist without blaming her is forgiveness of a sort. This is forgiveness of a sort, an abandonment of blame and an access to rough comedy, sexual comedy, mean comedy—it's not clear. But it seemed to me that for all her and my sturdiness—a kind of sturdiness each of us had in the moment—we were being laughed at in our sexual frothing—right into death.

It was both lighter and heavier than I had, when young, expected fucking to be. The second time is not passion, or is a different sort of passion. The terror was of caring, was of caring too much and going hurtling along, a noble beast, or an ignoble beast caring too much—for sex, for pleasure, for myself, for her. The wheels of the moments might then stick and one would go headlong into some then-to-be-obsessed-over-forever moment of loss of this *rough* forgiveness of the past. The fuck was like a board game with different things happening every moment, but the odds had been prepared, had been tampered with. And it was like a board game in that we were not exploring—and hurtling—along, with willful blindness and in an agony that it was real. It was like a game in the various ways it was not happening even while it was happening—emotionally as well as in the way it touched on sexual depths and offered promise of release, of rising to the surface after the weight of the water and the breathlessness. In the act, you're sort of painting a portrait of yourself, and of her, slapping paint on genital effigies—no: that metaphor is impossible, since the genital is the brush. The hell with it. It is happening and it doesn't mean all that much no matter what depths it reaches—it is special, it is self-conscious and passionate, some, one is oneself, and one is something one has created. It is folly and swindling play and it is *as serious as anything* even if you think of it as merely biologically general. Some of it, much of it, has a thing, a quality of not meaning anything—are you brave enough for that? It doesn't mean there is no meaning anywhere or even that this is mostly no meaning. It means nothing even if you name it meaninglessness; and meaning lurks and recurs even if you say it doesn't. Craven dust fucks craven dust. But then in the event's happening comes a flash of its meaning something. Sincerity is coming round again. We aren't in a story of no meaning. Yes we are. We are too chic to be sincere. But here is the blushing and ecstatic *fool*, physical and without time or knowledge for thought, the generous-souled harmdoer, the mean-eyed harmdoer. Who knows what all the shit that is in play here is? Rattle, buck, quiver, seesaw, subside—and variation. What would we do if all this meant something truly? If the realities of being together overwhelm us? Ora, stage-managing, directing, creating us, actress-fucker, playwright-fuckee, said to me—tacitly, silently—that I was too fastidious . . . too careful . . . *Ham it up . . . Be cruder, crueler, madder—be without calculation . . . Don't keep accounts . . . Don't keep track of things so that you can give an account to yourself later . . .* Do you remember a kind of ecstatic beginner's rhapsodic brutality of romance, changeable, overexcited, unreliable, human? After childhood? In my version of it—in my being taken over by it—in my submitting to it—in my dressing myself in it (as in a red union suit)—what happened, what she spied on, was that I jerked my hips in an ugly rhythm of assertion and of brute, sly-nostrilled pride. The Minotaur-beast is a runaway. The minus tower in her. Me. *Dis.* Dis dick . . . disdain . . . Hey, *dis, dese . . . dem* . . . Me. My dick and my gruntings ripsaw away. In the webbings of muscle of the not-a-goddess, the not-much-of-a-girl: in the *beautiful mess*—her term for herself. Except that her will was like the prow of a liner with a huge curving wake of the possibilities of fullness—in the webbings of muscle. That she loosened. And a slap—in the slapstick of the moment—or a threat would tighten her? Is this a peculiar curvature of love? Her reality extended mine—my feelings in my back and in the back of my shoulders—can you call those feelings?—the small of my back, then my butt (as it was then), and the abdomen and thighs, upper and lower, and in my mind and in my eyes and in my feet, which were braced—my reality continued on in a kind of hammock of responsive, responsively further extents of me and my body, mirrored and contained in her, permitted and impregnated by her with life, by her body and mind, her wriggling feet, her butt, her cleverness. I'm holding her. Oh, what a sea of effects. Of causes. Of things . . . Oh, what a rapidly flowing river. Of moments . . . I was violently shocked by the ugliness and her lack of simplicity, the lack of demure sweetness and of devotion—by her not being in a state of grace—and I was at home: shocked: scandalized: continuous in a great span of seconds.

Then she moved us to another place—another plane—she put up a hand; she had very beautiful, ladylike hands, strong, quite large—like a ballerina's—and she placed one hand on my stomach as if to slow me, as if I were strong enough and vile enough and big enough to hurt and stun her. Although her pride was that I wasn't. And, so far, I hadn't. And I was so flattered, I whispered her name, "*Oh, Ora . . .*" Something I rarely did.

It wasn't that I was so grand sexually. I am acceptable sexually (which is actually quite a lot), but I make a point of it, of being that, and that doubles the acceptability for some people, that it is something known, and that one *tries* to be it. Often, then, I am a little bored sexually—that redoubles it . . . Only a little bored . . . "You are the handsomest man in the world"—she says that; it is a metaphor of a kind. She was collecting herself, finding herself, in an inconsecutive way, among the consecutions of our invention of our sexual tone back and forth, and in the faith that in the sequences of moments something might happen and all the moments (all our moments) were unbetrayed so far and would be unbetrayed still at the end, sort of.

The slightest twist of body, depending on the tone of the motion, of torture or of distaste-cum-salt—all of it was vital, was of vital importance for the Meaning—such as it was—or for the Grand Meaninglessness of the Bribery, the Animal Swindle. When you ride a wave, once you catch the wave, once you are in the rush and watery dominion, the whoosh, in the eerie green and bluishly rushing thrill, any part of you that you bend might upset your trajectory and then you might be ground on pebbles and cut up and bruised and forced to swallow water. You might drown . . . If you escape, and you have to sit on the sand above the waterline, exiled from the water, until you recover, you might not want to ride the waves here anymore. So it is risky. You can lose it *all*—all the past, all the rest of your life. You can win through to a momentum, a coolness, and lose everything else that might be here. In a way, you can't do much: tenderness forces you to avoid the statistically evil danger of hurting each other. To bore a body that you want to like you is one of the worst feelings there is. Unless it all doesn't matter from the start. Strong-bodied, strong-nerved, sensitive to the rush of the waves, one way or other, trickily barely managing, thrilled, Ora and the guy—the guy is me.

The way we were doing it—the ironic thing and the physical effort and the showiness and the sincerity—from time to time—and that stuff being shown (rather than the physical mattering most)—well, in body-surfing, you land on the beach and you're okay and you think back over your recent ride so you can have it in near-consciousness, so to speak (but the memory is all rushed and a lot of what happened is hidden from you inside the sense of wondering pleasure), you have bits of a conscious sense of ordinary reality and of the thrilling part, the ride in the fairly large-scale surf, and then of being young and bare-fleshed and borne along by the melting green locomotive. Something unhallucinatory, something graspable, the shine of faint sweat on Ora's face, the faint fakeries of the posture in the first place—I'm not comfortably a showy fucker. I'm hammy. Ora said, *Oh, you beautiful man* . . . But, see, it was *proof* of a kind of wrongness—which was okay—it went with the thing of the *sex* being softly and oozingly mechanical and breath-driven, and unmechanical, and fitting and suitable, and loving and stupid—and not stupid—and grand really only, *sublime*, a little—as when you were small and were on a swing and went too high and suddenly the sky was there and light and infinite air and a separation from the world which was infinite, infinite—for a second. That was her judgment—her view. I am guessing at it. It's the body parts and then the motions of them. And of the minds. Glittery, amazed, semi-opaque—like eyes. Two wills, changeable, and then the applause, thunk, thunk, of abdomens. And the permissions, I suppose. The glimmering lights of birth are echoed here, are repeated in a kind of semi-inverted animal talk.

The downward pressure of the weight of her stomach, when I put my arms around her upper waist and lifted her a little, lifted her into an arch—and she held herself weightily at first before she caught on and let the arch willfully, tremblingly, be incontrovertible reality, the sensation now (in the animal conversation), made the prick seem to me to be my realer self with that weight or angle resting on its movements. In "love," one was a *lover* not a shadow self. Most of the feeling self was heroically entombed in doing this stuff . . . And genital will, genital sensation ruled. Sensation animated one's back or was animate, scurrying up and down one's back—you know . . . The animalled everything, furred, skinned, restless, real? The Kid Fucker, the jerk jerker moved a bit, only a bit. "The yo-yo labyrinth," I said. She didn't hear me, didn't pay attention, didn't decipher it, didn't like it—whatever.

She wasn't scared of sex exactly—not as I was. Not in the ways I was. And I'm not scared of *it* so much as I am scared of it-with-certain-people-at-certain-times-and-of-what-will-happen-to-me-then. But she disliked a lot of things about it. I recognized that she was sexually uneasy; enraged, I think, at giving in to anything so unabsolute, so unabsolutist, except as romantic crap—she wanted an absolute fuck, *a fuck to remember, Honey*. But you can't ever remember the sensations . . . She wanted an "I see rainbows, oh, oh, oh . . ." She said that now.

"Cut the bullshit and just fuck, Ora, okay?"

You don't have to say things out loud: it's the heave of the buttocks, in a certain tonality of the breath, the things you'd say if you said them.

Of course, in some ways, I know too much. So I try to fuck without losing heart. Or steam. Whatever. I was embarrassed that her body responded to the remark and that I didn't know what to do with that response.

Instead I spoke: "A lad in a warm dark suffocating cave FINDS A LAMP . . . AND RUBS IT . . . RUB-A-DUB-DUB . . . THE LAMP IS IN THE LAP OF MY GODDAMNED WHORE-AUNTIE-LAMBIE-PIE . . . POEM . . ."

I don't know why it was an aunt—ants are laborers; and in faggot talk aunts are older lovers, bald, with paunches. I talked and was doing it; and the talk was the way you hallucinate when you jerk off—this was because of something in me that was maybe unmasculine—no doubt—and it was trying to share with her the thing of my progress toward coming and not the fake thing of the window ledge and her absolutist, and autobiographical, notions of a sexual event flattering in being tremendous and, therefore, worthy of her and giving her life meaning. And so on . . .

I was doing it. In a less kidlike and college way than a few years before. My head was next to hers, to *Ora's*; my cheek was against the side of her hair, Ora's hair, a few silly bits of her hair were in my mouth. The central hallucinating button of the point of decision in the self moved in my throat airlessly.

I still loved her. We both knew it. She was willing. We fucked on.

Of the patterns a fuck can take, some—most—are not possible for me. I was mostly interested sexually in sincerity and truth—a thing of caring what became of the other person. This mounting to the level of self-sacrifice due chiefly to infatuation and the excitement of thinking that if one was okay in bed while fucking, one's life would be okay—and the world would change: she took those things for granted, and the crap they were punishingly opposed to, she accepted that, too. She'd had men be infatuated with her since she was three years old. Our minds hadn't married each other (and never would). Our fates were entwined, though. Our eyes, the way we use our eyes, that is, see each other, they're married.

I don't know why but I said, "Ora, feel sorry for me."

She said, "I can't feel sorry for you, Wiley." Then: "After all, you have me . . ." Then: "Hee-hee . . ."

"Hee-hee," I said, moving a little in her.

I guess it was a little interlude *as a vaudeville* . . . Or as a vaudeville rehearsal—a stage-lighting rehearsal, so that we could do it differently in a second or two.

She said, "It's your sad eyes . . . It's that you don't hate anyone."

"It's not that you're *bearably* jealous, is it?" That I was someone she could *reasonably* love and not someone who made her wild.

"Huh—uh—huh— Oh, fuck me," she said. Then: "This is bliss." She said it because it wasn't bliss . . . It was in a way, but not seriously so.

"Ora, shut up. Does your back hurt?"

"I'd rather fuck in the bed," she said graciously.

Then dirtily, she said, "Or on the floor . . . We haven't done it on the floor since Santa Fe."

We sort of half fell out of the window thing or from the sill or whatever to the carpet.

We landed on our feet. She was at once twice as oily as before and more palpitant inside and I was gasping and pumping while we were standing, bent-legged—I mean I was bent-legged, and anxious to use this warmth in her for myself, in the odd light of the mind then. One knew her, sort of. I knew who she was, not by sight so much, but by the other weirdly set-up sexual senses, those and what my memory gave me as a sense of her—a cold white heart . . .

And I was mostly a large *whitely* pointing finger.

Us fucking there with more and more lifeless limbs, we'd fall in another minute. We waddled toward the bed. "White folks havin' us a goooood tyime," I said. I moved her. Her legs had a peculiar limpness. I didn't want to come out and lose erectility or whatever and then have to reenter. I don't know. Hope, irony, youthful sophistication of a kind, a lot of willing ignorance, a *lot* of folly, a fresh and resilient heart, a body agreeable to the demands made on it mostly for Ora's sake. The body in that agreeable stage, that phase of being *able* to be agreeable for the sake of your feelings about a woman.

"We're not great in the sack . . . I'm sorry this is an uninspired one . . . Uh-unh . . . nnnn . . ."

"Uninspired is all right," she said. She was settling in to being the socket. We more or less got into bed—without enmity. We fell in. And then we cautiously straightened out, some. A jumble of stubborn bones. Me holding on to her, her holding me in her was a truceful arrangement, and, moreover, in me and in her were further truceful arrangements in the flesh, inside and out—particularly her flesh inside her. I mean arrangements, certain alignments and orderlinesses of disorderly (pulsing) permissions, for the entry of motions and the added pulse of arterial excitements—exclamations—that were not hers—you know? What an incomplete, grease-slimed wonder of sexual welcome. Sexual reality's real foreignness is the way it borders on humanly *absolute* forgiveness while harboring an absolute criminality of will—or stupidity, a stupidity of will—do you forgive someone you're trespassing on? A foreignness to the mind, to words, to moments when you're not fucking, when you're at a distance from the fleshly forms of things, you're in mid-fuck, then, *that year*, shocked and senseless to some things in the processes of sensation, an entire mass of boredly cruel excitement, your own self like the act, like Ora, tinged with mystery, with the mysteries of selfishness, loneliness, domineeringness, and cleverness. The bull . . . And the bullshitter. The boyfriend-and-killer and the murderously healthy girl. The kids in the bed, the long-legged, flesh-bearing, tubular-plump-pricked, warm-cunted, bobbling-breasted kids in the bed. Maybe it's a joke. Maybe it's not a joke. God, I don't know . . . I do it . . . *fuck-a-dee-fuck-fuck* . . . Anyway, the thing that I was envied for then happened in the fuck: people had a sense of this as a possibility for me, with me, if no clear knowledge of it: Ora hinted at it in how she dressed—and smiled—it was there—at other times. Of how we were together for a while in our worth and worthlessness—her conceit came from this: that in bed she would ready herself—she was immensely strong physically—she was as strong as men who were a little smaller than she was or who were her size and weak. Her mother and father had seen to it she did boyish things and tough sports, raise and lower sails on their boat, stuff like that—she would brace herself and I would feel the cross-girdering of webs in her of will and education, physically reasonable, but unreasonably so—I mean it was *passionately* reasonable—the female musculature—and the privileges of such extreme health—enlisted in this; and I would enter onto a dreadful freedom of personal being, a kind of forbidden sprawl, a devil's pose—this was with her connivance—a pose in rhythmic motion, a motionful pose—and this was, maybe, a commanding truth, not entirely fake, this freedom-in-a-biological-prison. Stuff in sex can't be repeated, so you can't be sure of anything in it in terms of knowing about it for hard, cold statement. The commandant male, commanded, commandeered—by this and that—in his male pumping in the readied girl and he is on her—imagine the strategic *and* tactical complexity for her, inner, outer, the various geographies, or don't. He did—I did—imagine it, *then and there*: IT IS IN HER. *I am in her.* All boundaries crossed . . . All? Why is it exciting to know what you are doing? Maybe only for me—maybe it's not exciting to everyone. Really an awful lot of people were in love with me that year—it must have been because Ora liked this stuff. That recommended me to the deepish hallucinatory pulse. You briefly enter some supernal realm of intimacy—oh, not final, but you're inside the oyster—so to speak. And it's of great value. But do you want to belong to it? I mean as your emblem? As the thing that is the center of your getting from day to day? When the woman is as independent in spirit as Ora is? Would you prefer a dependent woman pulling you down into lifelong meaning as the center of *her* life when you fuck? I don't see that there can be a clear decision judging one thing as clearly more desirable than the other. The two of us, largish, exercised, and muscular in different ways, the male limbs bulking in the foreground of my mind since they were mine, her reality is mostly the jellied bed for containing this odd swarming stupidly charming blossoming—or whatever it is—sweet Eros. Sweet stinging vanity and harbinger. Of illumination. And its own wordless death. You harvest exhaustion and the parenting of yourself—we are the metaphorical real children of our fuck. The crimes of parenthood await us. We did it to ourselves. Squish, squuush. Pushhhhh. Sweatily breathe . . . "I *love you, Ora* . . ." My sense of something stupid in us, of some horror or other, slows me in affection.

She disconnects our agreement of sexual freedom in mid-fuck. I pause and breathe with an attempt at some discretion of the lungs and throat. I am still in her. She says, "I will poison you if you ever leave me, Wiley."

"We're fucking, not talking, Ora," I say in a crudded-up voice.

Fucking, we could, I thought, second by second, transpose cruelty and privilege into mere contingent conceit, mutual and laughable, somewhat ironic. Fidelity then would be blasphemous. To confuse the stuff we did with anything sacramental was ironic no matter how unironic and scary it felt.

I suppose it sounds odd, but she would writhe outwardly and flex inwardly *dizziedly* under male self-love and sexual conceit and the self-protective irony and the rest of it of the guy—I mean in ways that would be stilled if she was the direct object—the star at the center of the sensation of light here—the real center of this part of the act—she could do that if I was not flawed by having too many perceptions. Well, I hated it that she knew so much about me. She felt the same way toward me. I refused to believe her—about me, about us. I wanted us to be different, to be simple folk in a country tale . . . I did and did not wish this . . .

I could not believe yet how much psychic and sexual and physical reality she could stand and actually needed . . . It was a lot. I never had a simple coed comprehension of the physical-emotional-spiritual realities of our fucks. It was always *just-Ora-and-me* and not in a frame of psychoanalysis or of movies or of *the-fucking-of-our-era-around-us*.

Everyone important in this book so far (but me) will die fairly young. These aren't long-lived examples of the real. Oh well . . . That's what I'm interested in because of my adoptive parents, I guess . . . *A short life but a happy one* . . . People who embody that.

In the moments of fucking, us awake in these partly dreamed, partly disowned hallucinatory *moments*, the reality of will and daydreaming in the real world becomes, again, chiefly, the thing of us checking up on each other, of *feeling* the degree of feeling for the other in each of us (that funny complicity in the funny business of fucking). In the back-and-forth shenanigans of just about all the meaning one finds in sex (if one finds meaning in it, impure meaning but convincing even when it's laughed at)—well, in that current of stuff, I was aware of Ora's body, of her cunt, of the pleasures or, in the labors, of the almost boredoms of the moment, and of the bodily reality of her *abdomen* and of her noises—of the angle and shapes of noises in her throat as intelligibly loving; the body stuff, too, but I was not aware anatomically or sensually of her as a whole but of her love as love-as-jealousy-eased-here—love as jealousy-eased 'love,' a category—in this moment, by these means. The jealousy in her did not need to be of me or of her as she might have been. It could be of others, of their tales of perfect fucks, of ripping clothes off each other and of the ecstasy they had known—blah, blah, blah. It was of movies. Of happiness or completeness in sex as promised by stories and charlatans and evil troublemakers (so to speak). I didn't have to be great here. I mostly Just Had to Be Here. And then something-*sexual*-had-to-happen . . . Authentically . . . It saddened me that this was what life gave her and, through her, us. But the sadness defined the okayness—which was a happiness. What she felt was socially wittier than if she'd felt the other stuff—dependency, say. It was wittier than other forms of love. Shapelier. It was more intelligent, I thought.

I associate it with and with being a more likable form of *IT WANTS TO HURT ME . . . GO LET THE LIGHTNING GET YOU GO STAND ON THE LAWN WHERE IT CAN GET YOU*. I associate it with its being not that—willfully.

Ora *loved* ME in a complicated and complicatedly honorable and *corrupt* and, in a sense, self-protective, annealing, selfish way—well, what the fuck is new about that? Real love—is it fit for a book? I mean, books are so self-important about exaggerated purity—about abstractions. Will readers be *interested* in 'love' that's daily and partly lied about by the participants and yet is so shockingly real to them that it shocks them? Will readers give up? Maybe it's not real love . . . I'm just guessing, after all. How would I know whether love was real or not? It's just my opinion, after all.

Men have a sexual thumb, an organ of grasp of the sexual universe. Women have a living, breathing receptacle setup that opens onto still other receptacles closer to their hearts and throats. The drama continues in them while we sort of die off. So the drama, or melodrama, in the early stages is different. The universe, the future, time and all its currents and its remorselessness, the souls of other creatures nest in them, land in them . . . in a dream-and-real funnel. I don't find envy simple . . . Hell, sometimes I even envy myself. Sometimes when I'm in her, I envy myself as I was in the past or as I would be in some other, more hotly sexed cunt. Or as I am here—that it won't last. That it's not just me. I envy different lovemaking—other pleasures. Hers. Anyone's. I envy the absence of pleasure. Whatever. But above all, me now doing this and being somewhat lucky and this being finite. I don't know how to say it: I wanted to receive my own attentions, not because I was vain, but because *I* wanted to know what I was envious of: I wanted to part the bony curtains and see into her head . . . I wanted to understand this male thing.

Some universal and original thing is involved here in me actively as it is in the private receptacles in her. A debt and then another debt and then an underdebt and linkages to stuff widens out the cavern, the moment, the mushy on-movingness of the actions. And the leakages! She licks the side of my face: cubbishly? Nothingness makes its way laboringly through me and in seconds out of me into minor and major gasps of actual air in eerily pious–almost impious existence. I am transformed into being darkly concerned with *her*, and her at a great and honorable distance, her as audience and *mother* and as lover unstably enough that through depressions of clouded no-light and bursts of neural light something in me begins to turn toward ordinary light *longingly*: not quite the dark and light actually in the room, but a foreseen afterwards light. A light yet to be invented. An old light newly appreciated. A sanity of light to be newly found, found again, found for the first time. I don't dare die. Among notions of *expensive* harm done to the selves of the past—to two amorous warriors of a sort—(or in the afterward or in the course of the fuck itself as it takes place) is a scorekeeping thing of an expensive avoidance of any final harm to each other tonight. She thought such care or holding back was merely avoidance, was merely holding back . . . But she was cautious and unbelieving as well.

I should say here that her certainties were bluffs, but were bluffs based on her experience and on her certifications and on her code as a woman, known through keeping a (stupid) diary and through seeing an analyst (analysts) and through talking to women, through reading and comparing, and through dreaming: these things that I have listed were the source of the alphabet and the vocabulary and the syntax of her code—such as it was.

She believed in letting men go *fuck themselves*. But she refused to harm me. She has the nature of someone who is an athlete of sorts—a rock in a way—"*Are you the Rock of Gibraltar?*" I say in the fuck, moving her to the edge of the bed. She has said at other times, *Oh me, I'm the Rock of Gibraltar*.

If I balance her—or half balance her—on the bed edge and then stay on the bed, I mean that if she is sliding off the bed except for me holding her on to me, she will, in her uncertainty, start to laugh, and perhaps she will partly respond in a naïve way merely because I control her balance, such as it is, her physical balance at that moment of oily and sweat-tinged and slightly smelly in-and-out carryings-on in a broken, personal rhythm.

All this can be written complainingly. But that would be a lie.

By respond, I mean not according to her own code and will but to me, freshly, startledly, inventingly. It will be just us. Ora is truly good-looking and she has a habit or mannerism or tactic or strategy of fucking with a loosened cunt after a certain point . . . She does what she wants to do; the man can go fuck himself (as I said). I consider this an unresponse, an emptiness, a curse almost maternally laid on the lover, her lover, me, her emptiness enclosing his whatevers . . . My voyage here.

At the edge of the bed, me pushing her legs up—which she doesn't like much—and me clasping them—she starts to laugh—a little—and to say, "Wiley . . . Wiley!"

She is undefeatable, indomitable . . . Whatever . . . *So* she is careless about interim defeat . . . A little careless about it. It isn't only that. She is someone who denies she is good-looking—or luckily born or educated. She says she is *sexy*: and self-made. I half know what she means by this—the place of the will; and then the shadow self and one's shadow history; and one's using that inside reality separately from time-and-the-real, so it seems a cleverness, a matter of breeding, almost that. Her looks in physical reality are not those of a toy, but they become a toy for her mind—as well as a fleshly reality—this way. She is genuinely disturbingly *beautiful*, really beautiful—which means she is not anyone's toy. I mean she is not sexlessly beautiful—and, so, she is ashamed, and fearlessly afraid—if you know what I mean—but her chief sexual quality is one of patience rewarded, of waiting, of waiting and of strength and of impatience rewarded. A kind of exploding huntress thing . . . But her pride in her sexual adventures is of her being finally *sexless* in them—not subservient to God, nature, or the prick—she doesn't use these terms in describing herself; this is me describing her. But she has to be the dominant judge of her own life-silencing efforts in the shadow realm. She silences her parents, her doctors, their theories. Her lovers and would-be lovers. She silences all the fuckers. Ora learns slowly—and mightily—if at all. But she learns, although in a sense she *never* has to learn. She has said (and *I* agreed with her), *I know too much, more than is good for me.* She is almost a matron that way, in that sense. *A woman too smart to fuck*—she has said that of people screwing with her and her screwing with people. A long time before me she found a road to freedom-of-a-sort, a calculation, of being *sexier* than her mother and grandmothers and her aunts, perhaps not really, but in her own view; and that amounted to something quite serious: a temporary but truly profound ability as a strong-bodied, very young, extraordinary-looking, and fairly brainy and nervy girl to live among men in the real world, in *their* world, and even, in part, to see what they saw—at least she looked in the same direction. In a certain era, in a certain part of the world, she was *important* in ways that *I* was not and could never be. Her sense of personal greatness was, if you will forgive me, Napoleonic; it was that of a prep-school boy from a noted family . . . un-Jesuslike, unfeminine . . . Bold . . . Knowledgeable . . . Legendary early (I think) and not without reason in what she did . . . Although it sounds odd, looks are something politically settled; and in that frame they do vary. Every face varies every hour: so do one's postures in relation to one's looks. And so do people's tastes. Of the people I have known, Ora was the one whose looks were most generally granted, including movie stars (who, in those days, were said to have looks that lacked distinction or which were too public)—but the judgments by people of Ora always held provisos of her lacking this or that —I disliked the shape of her breasts, for instance . . . I am reasonable often. She never acknowledged me *physically*—at least directly—once a fuck started. Ahead of time, some. In words now and then, although not often. Mostly whatever she expressed along these lines verbally was expressed as negation: *Thank God you don't have a fat ass . . . I will never, never fuck a man with a fat ass.* (I don't believe she ever did.) And: *Thank God you don't have silly looks.* That is, she reflected back part of her fate. She had a physical reaction to me, though, and she lived with me and behaved in a certain way—that all ended partway into a fuck. If I understood her tales of her past, she tended to accept the attentions only of men or boys who were in certain categories of *the enviable*—family and looks, or family looks, or leader of a social crew, a social crowd, or known for their looks but as a personality as well, sweet looks or harsh looks or the looks of a hero. *They wouldn't punish me all the time—I thought* (she has said this). *They would know who they were, I thought . . . I only did that because I was ignorant . . . I was getting on my feet as a person.*

It seemed to me her life was interesting, glamourous, and had its dramas. But, then, in a fuck she cannot very often *be* physical and have her life. She cannot throw her life away truly. If she did, then she cannot save herself. She would have to trust the guy and accept her own woundedness. She tends to love-and-despise the guy and to worry about her woundedness. The mind charts the course of the shadow event mostly. Physical common sense is hard to come by. Hence the showiness of the window embrasure and then the edge of the bed. And the reflection of me as reflecting her luck. She can respond to that, not to the body of the man she is with—me—this is so in this year of her youth . . .

Of her life.

I don't see this as *a fault* in her but as part of the expense of knowing *her*. I minded it at moments in the fuck—minded it to the point of feeling the heart had been ripped out of my breast—minded it that she was not otherwise, less glorious, more uneasy, more likely to respond—but enough other stuff went on in me, in her, between us that what was there seemed sufficient most of the time, although, to be honest, always at the edge of a general bankruptcy of all of it, luck and blessing and no luck, and reality and hallucination, our *romance*.

But, again, she swivelled (her soul) and posited, or created, *this-sort-of-romance-at-the-edge-of-the-cliff* (of her being left or her being found to be unsatisfactory or of the fuck itself not working or her being left out) as romance because of other women's having romances. Maybe that was it—I think that was it. It was a created thing. She created and invented it—the way a great-grandfather of hers invented some part of the flush mechanism of industrial boilers—maybe it was toilets and her family lied—and then he marketed his invention. She was an industrious-creative-rebellious-independent-individual-and *inventive* American girl of a high degree of social privilege—an American lay.

Literal stuff was hard for her—it made her mind tremble—halfway beyond willfulness. "We are fucking at the edge of the bed," she said aloud. One could feel it in her body—the naming, the adventurousness—the trembling of mindshadows half rounded into actual breasts and real haunches. The cautious, even small-minded, distancing from the things here was shaved into a sense of herself *here*: one could feel the next day's terse or coded phone calls in her—the confidences to her friends, her role in converting this to legend of a sort, foolishly, unfoolishly.

Or telephone calls not made but only imagined: a kind of fidelity in that.

I was not particularly faithful or reliable in our years together, although I was careful of her ego and, on the whole, respectful of her capacity to feel pain.

So we watch each other *to see what we can see*—my father used to say that—and to see what the day has brought us, what the world has done to us, what our moments amount to, and what we have done to ourselves. We watch silences and tensions in the body. And techniques. We distrust techniques—*la-di-da* is what she calls them. We watch in the light of her *inventive*, Anglo-Saxonish, anti-Napoleon-Napoleonness, her *storytelling*. And we watch me. We watch each other fucking.

This is between moments of inspiration and of sincerity, when we watch something else entirely. It is cruel to notice some things—I mean it is cruel to speak about them. To notice in words is to remember differently. Without surprise.

It is part of an old game between her and me, this stuff. I say to myself as I fuck—I say to myself in fuck-rhythm—*Can the truth be cruel?* Isn't truth a relief?

"Get me away from the edge of the bed, oh, oh God, tee-hee, stop it, STOP IT I DON'T LIKE IT . . ."

"Tighten on me, Ora, tighten on me . . ."

She wouldn't. Or couldn't. She could be bought—half bought—but not coerced. She had a weird shyness, a strength, a code, a notion, a realistic idea about defeat for her and *the phallus.* She punitively, or helplessly, widened inside. She couldn't grip it (the phallus) and respond to it and be intense and *loving* or obscene. Passion for her came from giving in to the power to hurt—in the other—to my standing-in-the-world—so it was a giving in to being hurt even in avoiding hurt for the moment, within reason. So, she *loved* my butt—and the nape of my neck . . . And my lips somewhat, the not-hurtful things. I'm big enough phallically that some people do what she did and widen helplessly. Maybe that is really common. Really, she loved my prick, too—as she would a child, who, if I loved it, she would compete with it and she would vie for its attention and then she would treat it harshly if she was second to it in my regard.

But she hated the prick's autonomy when it was really set in its course; its full readiness she turned into a comment on herself.

More than that, she had a thing which, while she knew about pricks and noticed them in men's clothes, she had to erase in order to care about the man in the grand way she did care—death-y, death-filled, generous, and final . . . And perhaps not very real. The rod of hallucinatory absolutism . . . The immediacy of bodily caring was not part of her repertoire toward others except as an extension of herself. One could call this *narcissism* but why bother? One could call it anything one wanted. Anglo-Saxon individuality and pride. She manicured my hands—and my *feet*—humbly, for instance. She fitted herself into how *I* looked. She never asked me to react to her visually—her outfits or her walk or her as an icon in naughty dress. We were a couple of a neutral sort. She never lost herself, or not very far, in our being with each other visually or naughtily—she lied about this all the time—but with us it was physical intimacy, ours, I mean, and then the world, and the friction of that ignited us, or me, and then for her, it was in the contemplation of her own fate, her fatedness, in being here with me, it was in that that she lost herself.

On the edge of the bed, she cried out, "I love you, Wiley!" But she didn't tighten on me . . . Was it a compromise?

"You don't love my body or my prick," I said, letting her slide to the floor—slowly but a little fast so that she was jolted. She tensed all over—but not inside the cunt. The temptation was to slap her, but if we had gotten really violent, it would have horrified me and I would have left her—not because of moral stuff—just in terms of our souls and our desires and what the story was likely to be if we met head-on in that way. I mean, the sexual issue would have been resolved in a way I would have despised and exploited. Instead, a different story had been set up; it had fastened the screws of romance in place. The issue for us was how much was she under her own control—I mean, since her own will let her be uncontrolled? And how naughty was I, ultimately? How much was this stuff hidden from her? I can't be uncontrolled—or controlled by someone else; she would be hurt in more than one way. Fatality is everywhere—of course. The abundance of fatalities makes me odd in these matters. She lied about this to herself—much of what we were was covered over, but I think she knew quite a bit about it on her own terms.

"Goddamn you! You son of a bitch! I LOVE YOU!" said the strong-muscled, superbly supple, healthy *bitch* in her disorder THUMPING onto the rug—but well within the tones and echoes of *anecdote* . . . of daydream—as we fucked on. But also at the edge suddenly—of feeling things *now*—of a different order of deep, even profound readiness as for getting pregnant—or as for being hit and hated and, then, for her and my dying in all or in part (as young people of a certain sort)—for having the power to tempt, to allure, to upset, upend, and to arouse, and no real conviction, for twenty years so far, of being *deeply* attached to safety—or perhaps never. It was and it was not smart to *satisfy* anyone more than she did by presence and patience, good temper, strength and inventiveness. It was clear that she needed to—for her own sake or social well-being or whatever.

But perhaps the profundity of the joke in her—the giggling flesh in her cunt and in her mouth and in her jiggled breasts and in the trembling muscles of her abdomen and thighs—had to do with the nonsexual nature of where we stopped in this trajectory or trek or whatever. She sometimes hinted at her *mushily* wallowingly falling into the next step of resignation, or ugly patience, with an extorted and aching satisfaction—a scream of the abandonment of the flesh to the somehow dirty satisfactions of the will.

Innocence? An innocence? So that one might feel in one's haunches—one's back, one's balls and shaft and (forgive me) hard-headed prick—not just an anxiousness to come but a truly terrible and fierce, even overwhelming sadness and *pity*—as if the other stuff had happened:

as if, peeked at, it was still real—a hateful pity and charity—at what she had experienced or might experience with other men, including her father and grandfathers and male cousins—and, which, in my being a Jew, she had expected to find a tradition or some familiarity of expectation of this stuff, male stuff . . . I don't know. *I* heaved her up . . . I held her lengthways in my arms. On this journey at the center of the night, I got her back on the bed, past the edge of the bed. "This is Anecdotesville, Ohio, Ora," I muttered.

"Smart-ass . . . Oh, you smart-ass," she mumbled, odd-eyed—glaucomaish, cheaply blissed—i.e., interested, not satisfied, but satisfied enough for a while—to love me for a while, to be unwilling to be unfaithful or too horrible. One of her *immense* charms for me was that she never minded not getting what *I* said—she did not often accuse me of being crazy.

On the edge of the bed but facing the other way, not slanting down to the floor or over the edge but merely at the edge, she was on her back. I had my arm under her legs. I stood on the floor and she was on the bed. She said, "Oh, I never did this . . . This is pure *Kama Sutra*, Wiley."

Again, one could *see*—feel—bargains in her, the boldness, the reluctances—and in oneself as well—edges like the edge of the bed or the edge of some sort of inverted smile.

I think it was assumed between us that I could destroy her—if I wanted—even if she resisted. She had caught herself in some sort of trap—like a wolverine or a vixen—and I had some sort of *inner* (or outer) advantage.

That this must be acted out in the dark—and with me as oddly juvenile—and her as if she were aging—is part of what is unspoken between us at other times and perhaps not even remembered. Or I don't remember it . . . the Perseus or some other thing where the boy slays the woman-thing.

The not *acting-on-it* somehow is yet an acting it out anyway. I parted her upreared legs by ducking my head and shoulders between them. She grunted the way a girl with a different sort of soul might cry out . . . Or might be silent. I got my body between her legs. Each of my arms held one of her legs. I reentered her—mock-brutally—movieishly maybe? It was just a little real—so it wasn't friendly and it wasn't just a reference to entry. It was real.

But, see, the trespass then explained her loosening—explained a thousand times over her systems of defenses. The shaft had gone a little mashed-potato-y but she was so mushy and loose it was like putting it in a greased-up laundry bag. You didn't even have to say, *Your body is mine* . . . Or: *Give me your body.* She had, in some primal Christian way, with her soul quivering like a huge mouth in a fairy tale or a death-grin of the flesh (with a flutter of a wicked departure of the spirit toward knowledge like a glossolaliac mumbling of a tongue), already accepted the 'practical' necessity of these emotions in a fuck. She is phallic in the way she is unphallic—*that* FEELS like a mistake in her calculations. And while her body welcomed me with a sigh and a further spreading of the grin—so to speak—it was as if she wept with the release of despair as in infancy: she oozed and gushed namelessly. I didn't keep count of the ways. She didn't tighten on me except mentally with her satisfactory *readiness,* so that then if I said, "*Tighten on me, Ora,*" she would, she did; and I said it; but then she loosened again with a waitfulness of *say-it-again* or *go a little further* that altered the scene and drove it toward being systematized—toward a kind of escape for her in its being that, if that indeed was the case—but it was me who was her lover, it's me in that role so far: an acceptance—almost bridal . . . almost romantic . . . wells up in her, although she is scowling when I become laboratoryish about entering and going in and out watchfully, thoughtfully—it is sexual thought, though. I exclude her leatherishly, her expectations—she cries out . . .

And I laugh—more or less naturally: just a sort of grunted thing almost of *I'm busy* as I seat it or go partway in and adopt a jiggling rhythm—phallic ragtime—but not steady, a kind of stop-and-start streaminess: "OOh—whee . . . ahhhh . . . uhhhh . . ."

"I'm all topsy-turvy," she said, mingling romantic *satisfaction* with complaint and doubt to get my attention.

I grin and persist, aware of my *standing* here.

Then, in a sort of amused and mean way, and wary, and weary of her but too young to be really weary, I say—I mumbled, as an aside, "Shut up, Ora . . . You *matron.*"

That means I like her.

"Don't be cruel, Wiley," she says, and she loosens.

"Christ," I mutter, and pat and lightly slap her haunches until she tentatively, tremblingly tightens—coerced by curiosity and good sportsmanship as much as by sexual impulse, if you ask me—and, see, this within the tight cuntal clasp—and clapping (sexual, and horrible, and final) of her historical abandonment to *the truths* of what it meant to *satisfy the wills and longings* of able and wellborn and monied men and boys and now me, and who knows what others as well—and within the liquidy, deathily sticky sexual rhythms (such as they were) of her flesh and her pleasure (such as it was) is the incalculably cruel thing of the *extraordinary* trespass in her of my unsharable and slightly far-off (in my head, in my balls, in the small of my back) pleasures, taken from her and burning or reflectant (like Christmas tree ornaments in front of a fire) in relation to the *extraordinary* and *abominable* pelvic lovelinesses of her, of us, of love, of lovemaking, pelvic loneliness still present—still we are of different construction, she and I—the whole thing *abominable* with sexual smells and secrecy and a sense of maybe having gone too far even if we did stop short and of youth and too much looseness in her and too much *playing around* in me and a wild, and wildly racking oiliness and the jerk of far-away (loosened) inward motions, the fisher-woman's jerking net, in which my fatherliness is trapped, and the surface motions—ah, what a joke: the pelvic *loveliness,* pelvic *loneliness,* the not inconsiderable loveliness of the marvelous head and marvelous hands and wonderful shoulders and marvelous voice and wonderful mind and too big but yet admirable butt and the lovely, lovely, miraculous *ladyish* musculature and the marvelous inventiveness toward daily life—all of it—rolling downhill—while I ascend toward orgasm again.

And one's own, so to speak, *upper-class* and dirty will, that she permits here, the abominations of jealousy and knowledge, calm choice, resignation, fury, and semi-addiction—now *love*—the *reality* of fucking, the bicycling flight or whatever, the claptrap for young lives—it's *permitted*—

And her judgment of us as *enviable* carries us along. And her judgments of reality. And my own harsh ineluctable tendency to deduction. And my sense of things, unworded, hard to hold, yet present in my *flesh*—the evil and the retreat from evil in me—it's ACCEPTABLE—I insist on it; she decides to agree—and the thing of pleasure elicited, cajoled —the prick, the lonely body, and the farfetched and far-flung mind—she okays it, she does—soul and heart, if you will let me say this: we are at home—failures, penetrations, successes, cowardices . . . I don't think she ever let me forget what it was like to be a man in a world of rivals, men, women, and her—and in that world her being my most reliable *friend,* who would kill me if I left her. Or if I humiliated her too much or too often.

Or if sex did. The sense I had as I fucked—in *that* posture (i.e., bent-legged, rodeo-showy, chest visible: she had begun to say the year before that I had *a beautiful chest*), the prick going in and out of the magic (greasy) shopping bag—was of the world of social ambitions and of aesthetic ones as a readiness for rage that could be utilized in sex or transposed, more commonly, whatever un-Bohemian provincials thought, into *conceit,* either of surrender to despair (at the world) or of one's having, as a form of that, literally a furious rage to live now, to exist, mentally, phallically, willfully, famously—as if one were already entirely or merely largely and famously dead . . . or as a caution-haunted life-thing, full of trails and hints, half-scenes—a hallucination or a dream.

This was womanly in a certain way . . . like living inside the dreams of a woman. One was *entombed* most of the time or buried and then was briefly free—like a vampire . . . I cannot make it clear. It was not clear to me that among the rivalries and the, er, *revelries*, among choices—wittily (within terms of what was given for Ora and me)—I ascended, we climbed, she sank, we fought, we scrambled, we failed. I hurried toward orgasm—to give her raw pearls, pearls in a raw and milky state . . . my adorable swine . . .

"Don't ever write about us," she said, grunting and working away at the sex.

One could feel her refusing to be *destroyed* (an idea she used often: her own destruction), even while a sad, wild conviction of a readiness in me to be destroyed, or a resignation, or tropism, or inclination grew strong: as if a door were banging on a cabinet made of flesh: the banging door is flesh, too, in this sensation. One's best fate might consist of using oneself up.

I couldn't open myself to her . . . in front of her.

She had to guess at my secrets. Her body—her cunt—had become eyes of some kind, small fingers, guessing. Did I trust her? Was I a coward? A queer? Her refusal to be destroyed was maybe the main reason I lived with her. Is that an odd thing to "love" a woman for?

Imagine a universe of hotly breathing Nonies, all of them having different traits, though: they're not exactly like her. Or imagine a man troubled with hallucinations in his bottommost vocabulary of what life is.

"Hold me tighter with your *cunt*, Ora, *if you love me* . . . One if by land, two if by sea . . . HELP ME . . ."

And she did—for one, two, three strokes . . . part of a fourth—

"Is that all?"

She grunts, "Do what you want, Wiley . . . I'm okay . . ." Then: "*That's all.*"

How much more can one ask of her? She refuses to be destroyed. Jealousy . . . and love . . . do not cow her. She has refused so far to murder me. Or anyone. Physically. Mentally and spiritually she has harmed a dozen people. A hundred. Who hasn't? She was aware of it, though. What I want from her would be the same as melting and recasting the skeletal structures of her mind where the bones are speed of attention and of memory and are, in a way, made of light—and of words—and odd, mirror bits of the soul.

"DO YOU LOVE ME!" she calls out, cutting into the private part of the fuck.

"Yes," I muttered disgruntledly, sticking it farther in than it really could go, socketing it blinkingly, wondering why there isn't more phallic feeling and why there is so much feeling in my chest and butt—and in my harshly breathing mouth and in my mind and in my somewhat agonized soul—oh, I want to *come*—and is all this her taste, her doing somehow?

Her legs are on my shoulders and are sliding off. I am, forgive me if you can, deadpan, knowing I am fine-faced in a somewhat electric way. "This is a silly kingdom," I say in a muttery voice, knowing her to have literary interests and a weakness toward language. I pinch her vaginal lips—I hold them on me—I don't hurt her. I don't mean to hurt her—maybe I don't care.

She said—wildly—"You are a titan . . ." Or a *tight 'un*: I don't know. She is, except in the cunt, tight: stingy: careful-breasted: not entirely present—scribbling in some light-racing diary.

"You are *titan[t]ic*," she said, maybe the word, maybe saying *tight-and-antic*. Then—incomprehensibly—"Give in, give in . . ."

It is confused but it is not incomprehensible.

Her ass having tightened, but not the jerking and as-if-hysterically-giggling cunt (but with the ass tightened, the cunt is tightened somewhat), I am partially content, contented, while being left in a state of somewhat mysterious dissatisfaction. She shields her face: she suspects me of extreme violence—so did my mother and sister.

I proceed secretively—an adolescent, more than an adolescent . . .

"You're more beautiful as a woman than I am, Wiley," she whispers.

I hate to talk when I am near coming. I want to observe this thing.

Still, I say to her: "Fuck-talk butters no parsnips, as my mother said." I push her farther onto the bed—I feel guilty—and I lie on top of her—on all of her (as she did on me in her sleep: a sexual anecdote)—in a sort of sexually romantic silence in which I *feel* the arterial pulse of the fineness of the sexual courtesies, if that is what they are, and not idiocies, or sensual gaucheries, as an alliance and a fixity of residual loneliness only to this extent and which she cannot resolve and in which I bridge my shadowiness unfinally with the diffused white glare of the sensations near orgasm. She and I bodily, and as if cuntedly—both of us—and both of us phallic—are uttering a maybe *fine*-enough soliloquy (for us) as if it were a speech in a dialogue or as if we *were* speaking to each other, but it is only me; she is carrying me aloft . . . Pegasus . . . Bucephalus, in night penury, real beggary. Someone has made us, me, adventurously *rich*—

But I am already too old for a story in which the beggar, all at once, plans to steal and rule the world. But it was recognizably *love-of-a-kind* that I felt. The reason for not talking is that it draws the attention away. If you focus, you still are surrounded by shadows—and haunted by a lot of shit . . . The young man's sweaty face is against her. His back is sweaty and his butt and his legs as he goes on plugging away, moving scramblingly up a slope of exploding magnesium-flaring, white, glarelike bursts of sensation. Here is a sanctity of contract and a humility foreign to law. Earlier conceit is insulted here. *Beggary* and *penury* are attached to getting to orgasm. It is a kinship to light—this simplicity of unattached and penniless being. This residual and present thing. I start to grunt—very softly.

"Go ahead . . . Do what you like," she says as she said earlier.

The buttock sweeps and the ass-swoops and the flesh pausing for the light, and so one can listen, and the lurching rhythms, dreadful, foolish, at the edge of orgasm, effectual gatheringly for no clear reason—and the listening—in loneliness, the loneliness was intruded upon (unwisely) by Ora's breath—it veiled the lucubrations of the as-if-too-conscious or brainy obelisk—I rose up on my braced hands. The fluid grace of sensation shifts oddly—intelligently—as if in speech: a remarkable capacity: this-for-this love-speech, the now meager muscular shuffle—a shift of rhetoric—in recognition of the dominance of elicited feeling, too imperial to be ignored, suffocating any counterfeit blather, but axiomatic, unarguable in some ordinary and yet exotic and bossy way. The grating pleasure of the second time. The emptied and instructed wish for presence survives the moment-of-silence.

Then it weakens in the democratic rush of fragments, portions of the soul and body in pre-orgasm, a flash of more than private value. I resist. I stiffen. One tries to preserve the walls—the old sense of things. She does that, too. I grow giddily cold. And burned at the edges high in some stratosphere. Ora did not follow me here. And when she breathed, it intruded. It distracted me. Me, in my self-change; she offered herself as a tail for me in my self-change in the amphibious moment—a dawn thing, dawn transportation . . . absurdly immense and unreal, artificial, inner light is a pivoting within a peculiar cowardice: one is on top—is up there—but one is upended, bleeding light—one is bleeding with light—heartlessly. The second silence is very large—is full of dismissal—I am very young. The slide and glop of Ora's companionship—her presence—and a potency of sexual-hallucinatory-neural-quicksilver-*milk*, milky stuff at the end of the world in an informative spasm. Alliance, complicity. Patience with the airy space of moonish-mindlight: one has no need of gender now. The mid-body, which is literally full of shit and which has its courage and its odor—now a bright, awful stench—sweatily convulses with physical emanations of the odd, inner, tremendous, and shuddering and sailing-off, or shattering light, in what I suppose is the pagan caliber of the moment. *Love* such as it was with us . . . *"Ora, tighten on me . . ."* She didn't, though. Perhaps I didn't speak it out loud. Unmoored. Unrooted. The orphan at genesis feels breath, silence, the turnings inward coerced by the welling spasm, the weird foreshivers of the crotch-wing; the not-quite-pigeon-body prick throbs. Then the repetitive flight and explosion, marvelously hot, shapeless, ungrasping, the dismasted weird uncurtaining in terms of light and heated quicksilver milk as an explanation of the beginning of the world. "Go ahead," she whispers as in the fuck before this one. The sexual event brought me here. An orbital and veering solar heat, a partly emptied, largely unemptied solar expenditure in lunar light among linked shadows forming signs in spasms of linked, extraordinarily piercing, piercingly wonderful comprehensibilities—not comprehensible in language. *See, I told you*, the wicked self whispers. *See what is here?* Everyone knows about this. But differently. Knows differently. My heart's rhythm was like a goose cackle, a rhythmic thing, in the labor of the second spasm among the scary whirr of nerves and the contractions and puckers of muscles and electric and chemical *horse-whinnies* inside oneself, oddly —more or less laughably here—then the phallic *shovel* unearths quicksilver and throws it in some sort of lateral and downward and yet upward and prayerful fountainingness, and well, the flesh is drenched in it and jerks squirtingly into phosphorescence, neurally aflame, indescribably present—the clench and pound and the being pried open for the hemorrhage of light, the eerily delighted fatality of the spurting. Spurting hot quicksilver light irreversibly. I am young. I am with *her*. On her. In her. It is not a symbol, this giddy-gaudy, good, goody-goody American stuff. The truce between good-looking murderers. This sweat on the cheeks of my face . . . and on my buttocks . . . *I AM NOT DEAD IN THIS LIGHT* . . . It isn't her flesh that I do this for, but it is with its help that I do it. The third spasm, rockingly silver, pumps and swings back and forth, tearingly existent in me . . . Hi . . . Ah . . . Ora said once (upon a time), *What can you do to me, Wiley? I'm not a virgin, I'm an unhappy young woman . . . Let's live together* . . . So we did. In the real world as opposed to the drawn world in a story, assuming I could write one, I cannot ask her anything really truthful about this stuff, since she does not know these inmost terms. She said in her flesh, *I am used to cold guys . . . male selfishness at orgasm. This weight of lunacy . . .* The fourth spasm is weak. It is accompanied by slyness—an impudent daring—the *insolence* of conscious half-emergence, of hope. Now I notice that she coos a little . . . This *pretty* mindlessness . . . *Love, a comedy . . .* Some sense of that in her. My apish buffoonery—murderous. I see the healthily pale, dramatically boned face, dark-eyed, colossally present below me. Ora has said, *You were never* SERIOUSLY *hurt, Wiley*. Carelessly, filthily, resigned-to-being-sneered-at, one is brave—and experienced in tonight's orgasm —and one rides its subsiding—this stuff as *happiness*—uh uh uh . . . —and is more and more aware. One exits, one enters through veils of fading event. Her body watched me. It's loony—the undry, not austere *not-turning-away* THING of a pretty body if the person is interested in you, death, genius really, fluttering on the flagpole. The lash-inflected small poem of eyes erotically unpromising now: reality. I am here among a separate order of meanings in a field of her breath.

I am in her arms. I am in her, shakingly still. The vein in the prick trembles. ORA'S eyes are unfocussed, giving me privacy. I alight more steadily. She focusses and whispers—senselessly—"Stop noticing things." Then: "I'm here . . . Go ahead . . ."

"YOU'RE NICE!" the young man says fatuously. "I'm done." I thought she could tell.

Her mouth: the murderously ad hoc absolution of its expression—beauty, criminality, and forgiveness—I understand certain movies now. She has a large soul—it is awing and jolting to share your life again, to live in this, the only world.

May I go on?

I lie here, softening in her, occasionally achingly restiffening in less wonder and dryingly—so to speak—with quick *shoves*, or strokes, of recent memory of parts of the hallucinatory sacrament, the addictive 'innocence' of hallucination.

I said, "Thanks, honey."

After a while, she said, "You will hurt me someday, Wiley."

"Physically? Mentally?" Then, before she could answer, I said, "Let's not talk—it's so late . . ."

"I am not talking," she said in her maddening-refusal-of-all-coercion way. "This isn't real talk." Then: "You're not as innocent as you think you are."

I said to her, "*I* think we'll go on together a little bit longer, huh?"

She said nothing. But some flexure of her body—her odor—spoke. It produced her and her body's definition of me in terms of her body's sense of the moment.

"Don't look at us, Wiley," she whispered.

I said, "Ora, am I hateful?"

"No," she said.

"Am I heartless?"

"I can live with it." She said, "That was a purple one, a royal one, Wiley . . ."

And it was over.

The Moments As They Follow

THE MOMENTS DO FOLLOW—the moments—a line of elephants, of rooms, of the cars of a railroad train as vast as the universe, an invisible but palpable train of an all materializing and vanishing, the great hidden railroad of time—ha-ha—and, if something is around it, part of an all that includes the train—dark or lighted air, a landscape of a wholly other sort—then that, too, stirs in the passage of time . . . *In the following moments*—in the line of childlike exfoliations of chambered now's—one breathes—and perhaps, in the actions—fluxions—articulations of subsidence—of nerves, of blood—in the slow wonder of waking from the sexual event, one finds oneself on this strange planet of *The Afterwards*, place of Naked Cannibal Moments—in which, maybe to my horror, familiarity stirs: every morning is echoed here, wakefulness, waking . . . Ulysses blundering through the surf of the island toward the shore—a hobo jumping from a freight car—the innocent and dawnlike pallor of objects, dimly outlined by the distant light that keeps our window from being dark as it would be in the country on a moonless night—what is one to do next? What is this *afterwards*? Is this truer than before? The extent to which moments differ is a mark of reality. Why isn't every moment largely the same? Feelings here are attenuated and dry—a little—and some odd, somewhat aboriginal tribunal is sitting here—naked elders in the pretty and yet grim afterlight, in immediate sexual memory—ah, oh, uh, ah, the light! the light! SUSPICIOUS OF LOVE—OF LIFE, for that matter—restless as if in the holy and secular procession of the moments, or no, the ritual and casual and relentless and capricious procedures of the moments as they were in their courses of existence, near-existence in this direction and in that—nearing me, the nodule becoming the slow breath of a wing of a nervous recognition of the immense and infinite and petty procedures—in which my skin proceeded—a sewn kayak thing in this eerie, as if bubbling, goading, tickling current—this everywhere current going in the utterly inspired, inspiring direction of my death, in the direction of the death of everything, the moment with its somewhat treacherously snakelike heading toward a ferociously harsh, apocalyptic meaning—the moment! I am goaded and borne, pushed and touched everywhere, occupied and racked by a mere sense of the moment, submerged in that sense, filled with different orders of it—a committee of clashingly different orders of senses of passing time—I am drowning in reality; I choke dryly on my airlessness even while I breathe directly after the odd, semi-hallucinatory seconds of orgasm; I choke in an inward despair at being real, us being real—it is like being born—into my life: this being my life: one is entangled with this and that nursing procedure—to be close to Ora, this was like wearing or having a skin that is mine now—tattooed? Well, shaped. I would never succeed in entirely removing these moments—a costume I felt and never saw.

I lit a cigarette (back then in the 1950s) and, in the restless currents of meaning, substituted actual motion. I got up and said, "Got to piss," and I went, naked as I was, through the shadows into the small bathroom, above Sixty-eighth Street, the lights, the late night below, the whalelike rush of something, a truck, a van. The acerbic smoke, the cold tile, the faintly slide-y bathroom rug mean that I am here—in this order of factuality—and I pause, in the shadows: I am thin-bodied still, not as thin as at birth or when I was fourteen, but thin: the line of connection is recognizably present for me of some of my outward selves in other moments, ones that have occurred; and the longing—the anger at longing and the passionate wish not to long for things but to have them and to be at rest, ashore, asleep, in love, not in love, whatever—is a longing for an absolute, the single absolute thing, the sentence, the one statement, the word, the syllable, the breath of the intention to speak in which the novel, this one, and the moments, and their reality, are encapsulated, are held as purely—well, as sensibly—as a seed in a cotyledon or as a baby in a womb or as my eye in its socket or as, supposedly, I am, in various theologies, held in the eye and mind of God.

But God is here, on Madison Avenue, as fretfully and violently as at Sinai, a majesty that chooses to bother with gender and armies and perhaps with time, time being *ITS will*—unblasphemously. I am as if in the beard of the ungendered God, whom I see as male like me but then as womanly and engendering a sexual rush.

A love as momentary as the other. I sort of half prayed as I pissed, my arm on the tile wall supporting my bent head, my nose near the tile, my back bent sideways: *Let me say something, let me feel something, utterly and singly and simply true . . .* free of time, let me love simply . . .

But even as I thought it, as the now brazen, now dimly thunderous, now tinkling piss sounded among the walls, I was in a different place, I was on something like a rocky slope . . . I do not know where I am . . . I do not know if I love her . . . if I will go on loving her. Time, the reality of time in its peculiar deathward motion and eddying and flow, is so full of choices that one chooses, with a dry will, choicelessness: *The world is . . . My psyche is . . . Love is . . . something or other, fixed: a fixed pattern.*

But it is not as when I was a child: formulas and quotes quiet nothing. The hiss of time—not entirely audible—a goose and vortex in the sea whir, and a flowering rush—and *suddenly* (it wasn't exactly sudden) I am in possession of my *professional* senses: I am on the slope now of a kind of sobriety—or at least of my waking senses—that my mind, *wandering*—bedouin, skeptical, violent—saw in the dark the downward shapes of the front of my body in this posture and the line of piss in the shadows and the unlit, eviscerated moon of the toilet bowl.

Holy, holy, holy be thy name. The toneless music of the moments—and that of the piss—in the shadows—the toneless music of the shadows themselves—and me supporting myself on my arm—my happiness—I considered my *happiness*—and the *lion* of presence lying in the john. God's lion, the tiles—lying, lying, fabulating and in me the whir of pigeons, of bugs, of leaves, of windy gusts of dead leaves, of dust, the curious motion-ignoring stillness—emotions in their motions . . .

Spirals and alightings, subsidings, heavy displays of substance as they sink underwater in both a willed stillness and a kind of fixity of some parts of one's fate—as in having feet *if* one does have feet—one calls out—as if calling out were a jetty and words were stones to build a further levee or dike—were a breath of holiness, that is to say, if holiness were not time—"ORA, YOU DIDN'T TIGHTEN ON ME." How curious speech is: one means, Be sensible, let's be sensible, let's be sensible and immortal—and absolutist.

How one longs to be right in some universe-wide way. One prays, *Dear God, show me just Your Little Finger . . . I am not asking for anything that will alter history.* And then lonely and upset—coerced and owned by restlessness and duty—coerced and owned by reality—and sexually not emptied—and one feels *her* footprints, the cunt sense, the sexual stuff all over oneself and in oneself, and one's mind is half-owned by her—and by an unbreathing sense that she had intruded on the orgasm, she had not tightened—the young man jerked off—quickly: readied and sore. I jerked off: with this reason—in order not to be jealous, in order to be at peace enough that I would not assail her—that she might find me *interesting*, mysterious, other, unlike what she expects.

I want to own myself.

I find myself in this odd trolling and dim and dumb cast for a half-lost self—is that it?—the earlier man, the one who fell into the hallucinations I have wakened from, been expelled from? The one who entered the garden is not the one who left it, angels with flaming swords at the gates. Flaming and sore-pricked, flamingly genitalled, sorely, I thought of some dirty *representations* of sex—absolute notions of sexiness: books, pictures. I did not think of her (*Ora*) but of fucking in this or that famous poem and infamous one.

Something left over rose in the blood at once. Shame and insolence, the oddly fluttering privilege in me (of being young), the not-yet-sufficiently-dulled radiance—the strained, onrushing stain of invidious individuality—as if individuality were a denial of death—or more as if embracing death and lifelessness and not procreation and the generations—not my life with her . . . The bad and rebellious—but favored—son, I, came *a little bit.* At my own will—God and Ora be damned. Time can go to hell. I came *a little bit.* Only. And it hurt. Squeeze. Peer in the dark. Drop the cigarette in the toilet bowl, in the urine, the sperm. Flick one's thumb . . . Breathe. Notice the odors—of the city through the open window—the tile—the stuff in the toilet bowl—my own rut-tishness. What is stirring in my bowels distends and hurts me: *Let the law rule* . . . The blasphemy was private and is not meant to shock anyone now: the toilet paper was a strange commentary on the Torah—not blasphemous. We proceed among the procedures of time—to clean my thumb finally, and the back of the toilet seat. The flush produces a local vortex. Ah, God, the mind needs a laboratory limitation of factors.

The everything world.

She is in bed, smoking drowsily. Opulently limitless she seems to me—a figure at a small distance, through light and a doorjamb—and then I am past the doorjamb; and the figure is changing in scale, the aristocratic amusement of flesh which in its breasts and ribs, in their appearance, in their posture, is *aristocratic* . . . in a tone of victorious *amusement*, of challenging-you guiltlessness—the secular knowledge of the inward postmortems in you—the slidingness of life. She is the other body there—thighs, lower legs. She has turned on a lamp. She isn't middle-class. Or working-class. Or Upper-Bohemian . . .

My sense of her stability—of *her* timelessness—of her having emerged from the ruck of the sublunary rush and boiling outward and inwardly toward some purpose—is strong and childlike. Perhaps I am enclosed in her presence.

I am as if at a crossroads—of worshipping her, or *it*—the grace or blessing perhaps—or some improvement on life—or of—and this is stronger in me—a sense of going back to work, under the moon, and in the middle of the night, because she is enclosed in time, too, and encloses it, and because her emotions bubble and foam, and because we are alike and individuated, both: we are both those things.

And the bed is our raft; and so are our wills our rafts.

The brushwork, the carving, the sewing, the hewing, the captaincies, the crewing, the hoeing and hemming and hawing—I clear my throat a lot—it doesn't matter how I long to be still and to feel the lion of God in the room and the breath of God mysteriously in me—the trembling and frightened audacity of the chorale of more than molecules in this sense—I chose the human long ago: I want her to live. Her form of masturbating afterward is to disapprove of me and then to forgive me—the fuckee fucks back—or Ora does, anyway—but so have the others I have known—one struggles with this knowledge, which is not an omniscience and is not tied to an omnipotence or to an absolute rightness of any sort. To see her is to see time embodied in a certain way—that is all. She will attack me not sexually as I do her—the parallelisms, the parallel arms, never quite match but they have some eerie equivalency which I adopt as 'love'—she will attack me as a pretentiously male soul and liar—as someone who lies to himself. She said across the intervening space, in the dark—she is in the light and naked and smoking—and I am in the dark and naked and approaching the bed—"If I could be an artist, I would be a good one, not a moralist." She would be it better than I am it. But she is afraid of me lately, and she says quickly—and a quick, drowsy voice is obviously dishonest, you know—"You are my life."

"Love talk in the middle of the night," I said, now near the bed and looking down at her—navel and belly, breasts and fingers—the site of the naval battle—or Jericho, where the walls fell. The winds and trumpets of God—of time—of madness—of sanity, which is an unholy and shrewd thing—blow and whistle and hum around us, shocking now her, now me. "Time to get to work? Build bridges. Sleep." What do I say when I say *sleep*? She partly knows what I am saying, but this speech is like sexual event in that it is comprehensible only as it occurs, and then it goads and shocks you in memory. I am at work; it is love talk of a kind. I am getting in bed, under the sheet—then I throw the sheet off me—I am not yet ready to give in to fear or sorrow or restlessness or despair.

But I am not quite ready to go on either: and I loathe memory: how odd that the two things exist in the same moment—*TOWARD AFFECTION AGAIN* and toward one's knowledge of things, if I will now, or ever will again, feel in a way to be thought of as precoital.

Naked, reaching for another cigarette, I say, "Who knows, Ora? Who knows?"

"You have a handsome behind," she says *treacherously*. I.e., I am a human sacrifice—treasure—a child—sexually persuasive (to a degree).

We have betrayed the stuff before, both of us; what went on before now has been double-crossed so often it has been a thousand-and-million-times-doubly-crossed: this, too, is an uneasy seesawing balance thing. I say, in a cold way, "Ora in love . . . Ora has known love . . ." In a way, I'd like to goad her into an absolute statement that just blasted me into rock-solid surefootedness.

Perhaps absolute nihilism would do.

She said in a suddenly anguished voice—too loudly, in a way, for sincerity: I mean, the sincere way to say it would have been different from the way she did say it—she shouted like a rich girl, showing how lively she was in a tantrum of power, a tantrum of a leader who loved me: "DON'T INSULT ME!" Then, with a kind of acid anger, "Don't insult what we have! God, you are the only person I would ever murder. You are the occasion for the worst sin." Then: "I forgot: Jews don't sin—do they?"

"Women after a fuck fuck what they can. Fuck up what they can." I am showing off. Throwing an idea as if I were a fleet-footed girl with a bunch of golden apples to distract my pursuer with. "I don't know. Jews are weird. I don't like smoking . . . It tastes like shit."

"I like the veiling," she said. "I like reaching for the package and pulling one out—of course, you've got one . . . Well, I'm not Freudian: I don't believe any of that . . . I never dreamed that I had horns."

"Ora, after a dream, when you wake up, do you feel you abandoned everyone in the dream? They're obliterated—massacred—and you're, you know, you sort of go to Washington to rule the world in daylight? Is it a little like that? Do you consider it a massacre to wake up?"

"I don't dramatize things the way you do. I'm not a Jew . . . I'm not a Jewish writer."

"Thou speakest with, uh, hatred, jealousy, pity—and with a queer allegiance to your father . . . Jack . . ."

"Thank you, I guess. I don't really know what you're saying." She is fighting in some broad-striding way—as among corpses in front of Ilium—or as if in a surf—and it *feels* as if she is fighting partly for us and not just against me, not just against me for her own sake—not for the sake of her father's ego—she has betrayed him—I betray my work and many of the ideas I painstakingly tried to hold in college (in order to try to be *distinguished*): she is fighting the way things are for us in real time. She says, as if ignoring what I just said and what she just said, "I am, though, actually . . . A Jew. I am your twin, Wiley . . . I am like a pencil in your pocket."

"Since when?" I turn real attention on her. It really is in no way true. She barely makes room for my notions: she certainly doesn't share them—or hold them.

"Since I stopped being crazier than you are," she says jocularly, senselessly—really advocating senselessness or illogic, an organic thing of absolutes in abeyance inside a sacrament of convention-*cum*-incoherence, but not really in abeyance. It's hard to explain the ripening of wakeful attention after an orgasm in someone else—the second one that she knows about, the third one actually. She may have known what I did in the dark in the bathroom. What she says is not senseless to her: it has whole landscapes of meaning, anyway: "I don't like dreaming anymore—do you want me to massage your neck?"

"No more dreaming? You?" Again, it isn't literally true. It is in some way true. The massage: often I can't sleep—at all—when we stay awake as late as this. When I am as much alive or try so hard as I tried tonight. No more dreaming and a massage for my sleeplessness is like a sunny and shadow-speckled thing of saying she will *allow* for a while a thing of me being real to her. That is as intrusive as a fuck, as the prick entering her, or more intrusive even than that. In a curious way—since she doesn't actually flinch; her eyelids merely go up and down rapidly —it is as if she gives birth to me, to an actuality, to a moment. But it may not be a moment in which she asks anything of me. If I did it, I would be asking her to give me something: herself, probably. She is asking me to stay with her . . . And, more awingly, to be not too unhappy. I.e., she is asking me not to write or feel as my real self. But she is not entirely doing that . . . Of course, it depends now on whether she asks me to pay for something or to do something specific. But even that might be all right if what she asks for is much less in value than what she is offering. The hugeness of what she is offering is quite clear in life: she is moving beyond ideals and beyond ideal (or shrewd) requirements. She doesn't want me to be flighty and turn on the fuck. Or on her. She has upped the ante. Maybe. I possibly am filled with an emotional perception that is entirely a misunderstanding, that is merely wishful. I am maybe a fool in the end, and that may be all I am. I say to her, "You are much more ruthless than I am—I am afraid of you, Ora." This is a step backward from where she is. I tug her along this rocky slope.

"You should be," she said. "But you're the ruthless one."

"Christ, Ora, do you know how hard I work to be acceptable to you—to be lovable to you? I work my ass off to make things work." Then I said, not sulking exactly, but nobly (I thought), "I want my dreams for myself . . ."

She is not simply heterosexual. She is not simply anything.

"*Pish-tosh*," she said in a social voice. "You're just afraid of what we have." Then she said, going further yet—through curtains and over mountains into a kind of madness that what-is-male in me hates: "I want you to dream me." Hates and is awed by. Is orbitally affected by. I don't know what my face and breath and neck are doing. She knows, assumes, adjusts her thoughts, measures, and says then, "You don't understand people, Wiley. Wisdom isn't the point."

"I know that." I have said to her other nights that it isn't wise to talk about love: *That isn't wise . . . Ora*.

Now she says, "You don't understand love . . . I told you: I'm strong."

"That's the bloody fucking truth . . . Well, fuck all that."

"You don't have to work so hard . . . I'm here. I wish you wouldn't say *fuck* in that way . . . *I'm* not that Anglo-Saxon." Then: "Speak for yourself . . ."

"I am. I do. You're not Anglo-Saxon?" I said under her clumsy massage. "God, it is impossible to trust you."

"Wiley, that hurts . . . That's a brutal thing to say."

"What a bully you are! What bullies women are . . . You see to it that I can't trust you past a certain point."

"It's not good to take anybody for granted, Wiley. It doesn't suit you to be petty." She wasn't sure whether I was laughing at her or not.

"Fuck, fuck, fuck," I said. Then: "Fuck with its diminishing-everyone sections and with its transcendent sections."

That aroused her curiosity and her envy—or rivalry. She wasn't sure she'd noticed those things. "You want to fuck again, Wiley?" she said.

"No. Don't make me feel small, Ora. I'm pooped."

She said, "I don't know how you stand yourself—the way you see things . . ."

I said, "I see what I see—I am what I am— It does suit me to be petty."

"You ought to listen to me more than you do, Wiley. I know a lot . . . I love you—a woman of my caliber doesn't get to say that all that often—not in *this* life, Wiley."

"I listen to you a lot," I said. Then: "We're two dirty kids," I said.

"We're not *dirty*—I've been around a lot and I know," she said.

After a while, I got past the blow of jealousy and guessed a little of what she meant; and hating and distrusting her strength—in the ripening of attention and deciding not to fight with her or to leave her—it was that tricky, that tightropeish. I said, "Good night, Ora," meaning she'd been dumb. A radio program involving a woman acting dumb had ended with the guy saying, "Good night, Gracie," to the woman.

She said in the dark, "You've never been unloved . . . Don't be ruthless . . . Admit you're spoiled."

"No."

"I have been destroyed by you, Wiley."

"Good night, Ora." Then: "Thanks." Then: "Are we going to talk about your destiny now or are we going to go to sleep?"

In the dark came her voice: "You *are* real to me—God, are you ever; yes, you're real to me."

"*Sometimes,*" I said.

She said, "You're fortunate."

"I am a fortunate man . . . You're a beautiful and intelligent woman—sometimes." She gasped with hurt. "Not all that fortunate but fortunate . . ."

But she breathed for a second or two, and when she spoke, she didn't discuss *her* hurt: "I want you to be happy . . . That was a good fuck, Wiley, and you know it . . . *Please* be happy: life is very short: I want you to be very happy now at least for a little while." Then she said, as if she were doing a college paper—this kind of talk sometimes held my attention more steadily, more comprehensively than emotional talk —"*I* love talking during sex . . . That was quite a *coup de theatre*."

"Go to sleep."

"*You, too. Geh Schlafen*. I'm not selfish with you, Wiley."

We held hands in the dark. The throb of blood in us was a throb of mutual but not equal amusement—an unbalanced humor in the dark: that is what we had.

Then, in this fashion, *next*, she fell asleep. She falls asleep in bed with me. Her soul blows away like smoke; her breath has the sound of a dry leaf on a marble floor . . . A faint echoing tiny noise marks where she is and is not.

And I know this because I am awake in a burned state of exhausted hope and of half-exhausted half-terror—nervousness. I am almost placidly bitter, as steady as an old scar—as frail in the odd light as the shadow I cast as moonlight. The hallucinations in sleep, splendid, splenetic, monarchical-*fascist*—my dreams, the ones now approaching me, the ones in me as I lie here awake and long for simplicity—for a finality of conclusion about emotions—scare me. In my somewhat amused tiredness, I start to *concentrate*—a little—the observatory that I am, hissing, dimly rustling, oddly sighted, on what are partly involuntary flashes of sexual memory—bits, inconsecutive, *goading*—advertisinglike really. A reason to live on—for the next time. To remember sexual stuff in real life, in the actuality of fragmentary recall, is to be distracted and convinced, persuaded, lured, lured again by bits of heat. The cruelty of being stung by the bitterly acid-sweet, semi-frenziedly hot dart and glide of recent sensation, remembered bits of it, once more, silver-and-dark reciprocal responses, reciprocal motions, greasy, slick-sweaty, light-infested . . . the *in-and-out*—the whole vast terrible weight of unwitting and goading pornographic recall as soon as Ora was asleep is like being pinched or pushed harshly (in wrestling or semi-horror) into desire—into offering oneself or into trying for triumph that way. It is not nice. The sense of the sexual stuff as a journey and the work and good sense (and wicked sense) that go into it, the labor and repetition are omitted in these flashes of mind but do exist as an intellectual sense around and about the recalled and as-if-spied-on reality that they had been omitted.

And the dark-woods aspect, the forest thing of the electric foliage, the terror and all the choices, those are omitted: the lure, in its brevities, in its fantastic and witty brevities and omissions, is semi-absolute, breathes and hints of the absolute, or of *an* absolute thing. The thing that will happen is not like the thought now—not like the memory . . . Not like sensations, foreshortened, intense, pointless-seeming, omitted, or oddly and editedly recurrent.

Her leg crawls over mine. As I said, I hated her nighttime relentlessness. Her arm is flung over my neck. I move it down to my reputedly *handsome* chest. It is work to have a human tie—it is like a horse or dog I keep, this thing with her. Or a lawn I mow. The way she slept, the dream aspects of her *perfect* rule over sleep, she breathed then with great satisfaction. I began to cry inwardly . . . It was not consciously willed . . . it is something that happens to me: a return of something in the past—as if all strong feelings, once I am tired (and nearly ill), are linked. *I* didn't mean much by it—the part of me that returned then—the ghostly other self now embodied in me and now so ghostly—that inward grief, that tiresome, tireless, infantile weeping is more comment and music and accompaniment, is more an aspect of helplessness-in-a-sense than it is a summons to action.

I can turn it into a ruling code. What, oh what, is the right thing to do? I need a sign. What are my rights in terms of being mistaken in this matter? What error, how much error am I allowed? Explain this to me. Make a heaven. Make a hell. Set up laws. Govern me. Only do not say, *Do as I tell you.* No. Don't do that.

Villains—such as Ora, Jack's daughter—and Nonie's brother, me—like the innocent (if innocence is understood, always, as comparative)—exercise their sense of happiness—of less pain, which is what one sees and feels as the stirring of others around me. I need comfort. There is only truth. I light a cigarette. It is shaped like an image of one truth. A foolish image. There is one truth, but I will never know it.

Soon I will deny that anyone can know it.

I smoke and, mildly hallucinated from the tobacco, I see a gendered and splendidly psychological sun rise over a palace. Then this widens and widens until gender is lost and my complaints of vertigo at the omnipresence of time, of motion, that, too, goes, and the blowsy women of my sleepiness begin to welcome me. And I put out my cigarette . . . And the peculiar and often wrongheaded nourishment there is in night—the fatality of gender and a fascist conquest of time begin again, memories, and quests, sleep masked as sleeplessness . . . feelings, thoughts, hypotheses . . . the past and the future . . . and the meaning of it all, for the time being, pending further life, further knowledge of the truth.

UNNATURAL HISTORY

David Coppermeadow

S.L. FELL ILL IN THE SUMMER OF 1939.

If I look into that sentence (or behind that sentence, so to speak) I find I might say at some length that S.L. fell ill in the summer of 1939 not in the sense of a fever, but he had a stroke while he was driving to Chicago in a year-old tan Chevrolet two-door coach—that was the name of the body style back then: it was cheaper than a coupe; it was the cheapest car he had ever owned.

I don't know what the pain was like. People told me later it had been extreme but that he had managed in spite of the pain to drive on and ask directions to a Veterans Hospital and to drive there; and he had collapsed only on the steps in front of the doors of the hospital—which had not opened for the day.

He was unconscious for weeks, I was told . . . I never saw the hospital records. Tan was his favorite color in suits and ties and in cars the year he *fell ill* . . .

He wasn't just driving to Chicago—he'd left Lila. And us, the kids. For good, he'd said. He was through. Lila told us this in a certain tone of voice, private-but-public, tearful, defiant, indomitable, domitable. Human and personal. And like Irene Dunne. She did it for a few select listeners: *S.L.'s left me . . . It isn't a joke this time.*

Daddy told Nonie in the spring of that year when she was to graduate from high school that he hadn't the money to send her to college. She would have to get a scholarship or work her way through. But as she herself said, she was not scholarship material and she did not want to work in front of other girls who did not have to work, whose fathers had sent them to school in a haze of luxury, husband-hunting. Daddy told her she was a pretty girl and didn't need college and it would be best if she went to work. He said that daydreams didn't enter into it; her grades weren't high (they were very poor) and he was strained to *the uttermost* (his phrase); the world was *going to hell in a handbasket*—war was coming; the American Nazis made his life difficult as a small-town Croesus-entrepreneur—with no money. The Depression had not lifted. She could help him by going to work. He was at his wit's end as it was without finding more sums to send her to college on a fool's errand.

He had said, always, that he would find the money for Nonie to go to school. He had given her no warning that the promise was rescinded—Lila said that he had sneaked into this out of cowardice toward Nonie and the situation.

Lila tried to help Nonie; she told S.L. to go rob a bank if he had to: a real man did whatever was necessary for his family: he had given Nonie his word.

And Nonie, in a different voice, with much greater intensity, begged him, then commanded him, to do just that, to steal the money. It was almost funny, the somewhat pretty-but-fierce way in which she meant it.

He said to her, "I'm not going to wreck myself for your sake . . . You have to go to work . . . No one wants to give you money to go to college . . . Not Grandma, not Casey"—his sister who was rich, Nonie's aunt. He grew cruel trying to end the scene and her tears: he'd tried to raise the money for her, he said, "but everyone I go to says the same thing: Don't try to make a silk purse from a sow's ear."

Nonie's high-colored face went white—we knew, I knew by then, I was nine, that S.L. was often snobbish, often cruel, and that he often lied—that he had done genuinely shameful things whatever his pretensions with us were and that he was not a model of rationality or of judgment.

And that he was perpetually embarrassed. Or close to being embarrassed. Or enraged. He intended for her to forgive him.

She said, "I'll become a streetwalker . . . I hate you . . . I'll marry a rich man and I hope you starve."

She wasn't restrained when she said it. She yelled and screamed and sobbed when she fought with him. She said to him, "You lied to me, you're no good, everyone will have the last laugh over me now."

"A girl like you shouldn't have enemies," Daddy said. "A sweetheart like you, Little Miss Sweetie Pie." Ironic. Tricky. You know?

We were all more grown-up than we had been.

Lila said, "Unhappiness is not funny—she trusted you, S.L. You broke her heart . . . You lead her to expect you'll take care of things and you let her down . . . Now you see what it's like to be taken care of by you; see what you've done to me? Well, what do you expect of her? What do you expect her to do? What can she do when you're the way you are?"

"Christ!" Then: "Have some mercy on me," he said dryly. "And let's have some silence."

Lila refused. She and Nonie both refused to let the issue go. No silence supervened—at all. They cornered him—Lila accused him of having no feelings for anyone but himself, and he began to shout, purple-faced, thunderous. He had considerable power. When he shouted back at her, she flinched. She shouted at Nonie, too.

But he hadn't enough say-so to silence them. Nonie, like David, advanced on him; Nonie called him names; she said, "You're weak and stupid and a liar." Daddy got a look that I associate with nightmares—the hurt-cum-anger, the being past most, or all, caring: the approach of limitlessness. "You have destroyed my life, Daddy," Nonie said.

I saw *the logic* then of him *feeling* he had nothing further to destroy in her. "I never expected to hear such talk from a daughter," he said. "Maybe you're not *my* daughter—maybe you're trash like your mother's family—did you ever think of that?"

Then she slapped him.

He looked at her with disgust—disgust-and-rage, disgust-and-hurt; but he didn't hit her back—he said, "You're no good . . ." He said it simply.

And she said it back to him, "YOU'RE no good . . ." With mounting hysteria.

He was still holding his face. He said to the air: "She's no good . . . It's all no good. I'm through with her . . ."

The yelling continued in conversational tones—the pain, the weird strain of debacle, of failure. Nonie would shout, "I HATE HIM. HE'S A FOOL!"

He would be sitting there.

In the kitchen, Nonie palely went down on her knees to hug me sweatily and murmur, "I think I am going to die . . . I won't give in, I won't . . ." I was somewhat, a tiny bit, on her side: parents shouldn't break promises . . . Of course, I had an interest in that issue. But neither she nor Momma in scenes that went on for days could drive him now to try again to raise the money and he didn't care that I felt the issue mattered. Oh, he was hurt. Daddy would come in the side door of the house and tiptoe to the door of my room and beckon to me to come to him; and sometimes I went; but if I went, he would hug me too hard and he smelled of nerves and of sadness—and of cigars; and he would drag me back into my room no matter how I protested or kicked and onto *my* bed; and he would imprison me and lie down; he would lie there and hold me near the thudding of his heart against my will; and he would complain about the women—and about me and promises—and he would whisper fragments of poetry about *late and soon, getting and spending.*

And he would say, "It is the end of the world, Wileykins . . . They have *gouged* me high and dry, they have wrung me for a loop, they have no love or respect in them."

But he was monstrous with being in the wrong. And I couldn't bear to be held like that. I couldn't bear to be near him. "You shouldn't have told Nonie those things."

"Don't you start . . ."

"You said she was your pet and she should never worry."

"Give me a hug," he said. "Don't talk like a woman."

I was silent and waited to get away from him. He would hold me too tightly, too watchfully for me to be able to get away easily; but I would not submit.

And by then he knew better than to go too far in trying to break my will . . . The school was interested in me; and so was my real father.

S.L. said man-to-man: "You don't care about money. You never ask me for money. Wiley, they are killing me . . . Be nice to me." My real father sent money which paid for me by then. I would wiggle out of Daddy's grasp and run from the room, from the house, until the middle of the night, even waking him if he was asleep: they hurt him as much as they could in order to win. Nonie would yell (at Lila and S.L. both but particularly at Daddy), "WHAT AM I GOING TO DO NOW?"

I slept with a pillow over my head in order not to hear the nighttime scenes. But the night he left, I heard the side door *slam* . . . How dark it was. The slammed door echoing; it echoes still, the sound of the wood, hollow wood in a ten-year-old house, the rattle of the metal doorknob, the hardware. I feel the dark. And my heart pound. Far off, the trunk lid of the Chevy bangs—a peculiar, compressive sound; and then the metal, the air sound, appears—in my ear, in my head—and then the rubber and metal clang and the tinkling whistle, the dim cling-clang of the chrome ornaments that go with the basic sound are there. Then the car door—then silence—then the motor's lurching whine and the eventual throb moving in the peculiar cavern under the house which is the garage and out into the air behind the house and then on the driveway that runs alongside the house; it passes under my bedroom window—a close-by rustling that stirs the window screen—and then among the night sounds of the tree-lined street, the buzz and drone of distances: *Say good-bye to your father, Dear . . .*

Or your dear father . . . if he is dear . . .

How strange the world is. I feel it when I am forced to acknowledge the newness of circumstances. A newness almost unidentifiable in the general almost-familiarity of your own breathing, but still scary and unidentifiable in the other way of the horror of being alone; then your own breath begins to seem strange to you.

Lila said, "Don't tell anyone he's gone. Be a help, not a hindrance."

A day or two later, she said, "Do me a favor and clean up after yourself." She was sort of excited and bossy. And defiant. She couldn't help blaming Nonie for having driven S.L. away.

Nonie was angry—pale-nerved and wild-nerved, maybe horrified, but unsorry, a bit burning-eyed, finally and ultimately and forever now obstinate: a realist.

Lila said to her, "Don't show off—let's see what you're made of, we'll see what your mettle is." Nonie found a job and went to work every day and was steady and reliable. Lila took a job two weeks later—she "got friendly" with some man who liked her and she became an insurance agent, working for him—but she was *temperamental* and did not always go into work, and she was often late: she was moody and important. She said the men all wanted to sleep with a woman "at least once just to show they got their money's worth." She was incredibly bitter and would not tell me why. Her mettle was not as good as Nonie's in some ways.

She did say, "I'm not the best-looking woman in the world, but I have a little oomph and they take it for granted that if I want their business, they can have me if they want me. Well, they've got another think coming, I'll tell the world. The way they carry on, you'd think I had no say, no feelings, no opinions . . . no connections. S.L.'s gone but I'm not alone in the world. Wiley, how far do you think a mother should go to make a big sale of insurance?"

Her commission would come in over a period of years, she said. "It isn't laughable, but what is it worth to earn two hundred and fifty dollars a year in commissions from my business with them? Is it worth my self-respect? I like to do what I want to do." She'd be lying on the couch in the front room in the silent house with no lights on, to save money on electricity, and she'd be talking about this stuff.

Nonie, walking a little like a hunchback—Nonie kept to herself, wounded in her moneylessness; and she read novels about girls who rose in the world on their own efforts, read mouthing the words; and she played the radio and spoke about the money that radio stars earned. Her posture was bad, Momma kept saying; it had always been good. *Don't lose your nerve now*, Momma would say. Nonie mostly ignored me and Momma. She did not become engaged to any of the men interested in her. "She kept her nerve that way, anyway," Momma said. "I don't know if I'm coming or going . . . Do you know if I'm coming or going, Pisher?"

Nonie boasted how good she was at office work—at office politics—she was, too. She was soon promoted and given a raise and encouraged to stay, but other people were eager to employ her and she switched jobs for a still better salary. She didn't exactly make wisecracks but she sort of did. She went to night school to learn to better her office skills—she studied psychology and English Composition.

I wasn't good or loyal—I stayed away from the house; I stayed at friends' houses. At home, our home, the women of my family, flayed, exposed, horrified me; and I helped some but did not really *chip in* . . . ; and I wasn't really loving or kind. I said, "You were too hard on Daddy."

Five weeks after Daddy left, when no message had come from him, Lila announced to the world (around us; the world in which everyone already said S.L. had gone) that he had left her and that he intended to be horrible and tough and not do it in a clean way. He had just disappeared—which was embarrassing.

A number of family meetings were held, and Momma told me—in the kitchen, where we were each eating coffee cake she'd made—she could bake but not cook—"It's all decided: I divorce him and get around and take a look and choose someone a little more reliable and I marry *HIM*. Meanwhile, Momma and my brothers will give me an allowance."

I wasn't included in the family conferences—I resented that. My real father came to see me and said I could come live with him. Lila did not object, but my real brother did. I did too—somewhat. Enough is enough—in the way of changes in one's family.

At any rate, my father-by-blood sent money for my expenses and he telephoned me and he came to see me six or seven times to try to persuade me to come live with him. I did not want to leave my school or to entrust myself to him. Precociously under the circumstances, I negotiated a treaty with Lila: she was not to boss me around anymore or I would leave and take Max's money for myself—she mostly or entirely embezzled it for herself now.

I delivered papers and mowed lawns. I tutored—young as I was. Some relatives and one or two local professors (*who want to make experiments on you to see if you're crazy or not,* Nonie said) offered to take me in. If I would convert, the choice was much wider. The local Jesuits made a firm effort to recruit me—*young as I was.* "I bet you'd like being a Catholic," Nonie said. "Why don't you try it and see."

My real father Max's older brother offered to take me if I would become Orthodox (Jewish). These matters confused, bothered, upset me. I became aware of a curious measure I used; I measured people by how much pain they saw in me without letting up or offering some sort of consolation. Or mercy. Rough mercy was better than nothing but it wasn't desirable. Momma's divorce lawyer proposed to her—or so she said . . . She was something of a fabulist at this point.

She said the lawyer wore too much cologne and kissed like a log and had no idea how to treat women. But he had a Cadillac, and I thought he was a good bet for her; and we could have been a family again. And I could drive the Cadillac.

Momma said she could not make up her mind to accept the lawyer. "Nonie and I don't like each other: and you, I know nothing about boys . . . S.L. runs off and gets the best of it. I need to be alone. If you ask me, she travels fastest who travels alone."

But it was possible she had mostly made it all up about the lawyer; she was weird-mooded, and as if hopeful. But she was brutal, too, at this time. "I don't want a stupid daughter and an ugly son hanging around my neck . . . If I have to go out and shake my rear end and look for someone to marry, I don't want you two watching me."

I 'understood' she was tired of some things and not flexible and not very interested. She asked me to do the housework, and Nonie made scenes insisting that I do the housework, but I was working, too, and bringing in, when you count the money my real dad sent, more money than either of the women were: and I got the impression they were trying things out, they were seeing if they could swindle me: they had no real reason to do it; and nothing having to do with honor was involved—it was personal, as in seeing whose eyes turned away first when you stared at each other.

"Nonie puts the least in the kitty: she keeps almost everything she makes for herself. Make her do the work!" I insisted on this.

"Shut up! Shut up! Shut *up*!" Lila said. "I'll get a maid." And she did. We were broke but we had a maid.

*

In the loose federation the three of us had so suddenly become, in such a ménage, the role of an adoptee is a curious one. So is being male. You are a pet—and an enemy—a stranger and an insider and an excuse for things. You are not perhaps a person quite—or perhaps that was a problem of mine and not a problem arising in the situation. Or perhaps one should not generalize at all. The women quarrelled often—but they were more like each other than either was like me—I was an outsider—a distraction—a possible ally—a duty for Lila, not for Nonie—but not a duty Lila accepted. Lila said to her once, "You never even hand him an aspirin, how do you expect him to like you?"

But Nonie was obdurate—and stare-y.

I heard her say over the phone to some girl she was talking to: "He can get away easiest of any of us: he's got a good escape hatch." Then, in a weird tone: "He doesn't have to marry anyone." Lila, maybe everyone just about, was after her to marry anyone just then—to get her out of her circumstances.

But she didn't.

Lila said—moodily—"I'd like to be alone just once in my life."

Or Momma, undoing her brassiere and unzipping the side of her dress, and turning her back to me as she steps out of her dress and puts a robe on over her slip, she says in the darkening air, "Where are the breasts of yesteryear?"

She attempts to get me to do things—she is like an older brother trying to see how dumb I am.

Sometimes I feel sorry for her.

She said to Nonie in a harshly jolly tone, "You and I ought to marry Swedish men—cold men are the most interesting." About business lunches making her fat: "Look at me; I look like a pig—and not a pretty pig either."

It's hard to live among the things that people say.

Momma—depressed—said to Nonie, "Why don't you be pathetic and get someone to take you in . . . I'll tell you the truth, I'll tell the world, I can't do it all." Then, screaming (Momma is unwell): "YOU'RE NOT SO BADLY OFF . . . I'M THE ONE WHOSE LIFE IS NO GOOD ANYMORE."

We went on being locally semi-upper-middle-class, though—"Other families do it, so can we."

The sounds of Lila's voice are a softish clicking of sparrow wings and sparrow-chirping, a linear flock of cries. Sparrows—dry-bodied, dry-toned, quick. She is brownish in tone nowadays. The feel of the fabric of the chair I sit in through the tired fabric of my clothes . . . The taste of the air in the room . . . The smell of dusk . . . the restlessness of the soul at sadness . . . Momma's need to rule—even if over a kingdom of sadness: Momma said, "It's all for one and one for all."

"No thanks . . . I have my life to live." Nonie said that, actually.

Momma put me and Nonie up for grabs—who would take us in? It is possible she refused offers for me. She said to me, "You help me look respectable." I gave her an excuse, she said, to say no.

But no one locally wanted Nonie to live with them—not even Grandma: "I connt do nuttin mit a yung guhl . . ."

Lila, lying on the couch, in deeper darkness among the shorter dusks as winter came, said, "They like her just fine but they can live without her . . . She's not worth the price of admission. I'm an old cowhand; I'll tell you, I'm at the end of my rope."

Nonie said she would tell us what she looked for in the man she would marry: she wanted a young man who was blond, easygoing, a good businessman who knew how to have a good time, whose family had a big colonial house—with pillars and a circular driveway with azaleas along it.

Lila said, "I want to live in an apartment hotel with good service for a change and I want a smart operator for a husband for a change—I've earned it. If you ask me, I'm ready to meet my ideal."

The women came home a little sweaty, work-stained, scared, in their *good clothes*: "What am I going to do? . . . oh God . . . I can't stand up anymore." Collapsing in a chair, telling some incoherent tale . . . and you attempt to cheer them up. At times the house stank of fear and of disorder. A peripheral dwelling at the edge of a lighted space . . . Offstage, they were onstage still, in their sadness. Momma did commerce in Nonie's *chances* as if they were business futures. Some of this was parody, some was a mysterious cruelty in an *infinite* maternal *comedy*. Momma was tired of the world and she was pushing Nonie into it.

Some of it was affection—some of it was deeper than affection: a passionate and sightless attachment, one that included all the events around us but which excluded me. It gave me gooseflesh—a sense of a dark universe that the women were in. Tempers and favors and rank as they were set in the company of those two women had a peculiar tang or sourness now for me.

I was used sometimes as a guinea pig for IQ tests at the nearby university. One man there, a professor, used to put his hand on my shoulder while he prepared to say, *Get ready, get set, go,* watching his stopwatch. I tried to describe the steadying quality of his touch to Lila; and she said, covering her eyes with her arm—she was lying on the couch *as per usual* (her phrase), "That's called squiring you—I like it too . . . in small doses."

The professor did not think I was a likely child for the Silenowiczes or for Lila now. Lila said, "I need the money you bring in." But it was not a cold or insulting—or blood-chilling—remark the way she said it, dryly, sadly—realistically. She let me peek at the truth. "All right," I said. "Just don't try to talk me into other things and you have to let me do what I want about bedtime and it's okay."

"Okay," she said.

"It's a deal," I said.

She said later, "I never saw a child as independent as you are."

But she rented me out to the professor by the weekend—for tests and whatnot. "Is it all right if I don't pack for you, *Macher*?" Operator, that means.

But she liked me, sort of.

I went to the professor's house. It was brick, Georgian, with green shutters. He had a smallish, nervous wife. They were *polite*—they had two children—voices and eyes, favoritisms, veered here and there. Lila had said, *You'll find that it's like everyplace else in the world: it's real—nothing is ideal.*

Lila called up late Saturday night and screamed at them crazily over the telephone. She *was* crazy off and on nowadays. The professor, pale and distressed, said to me, "Your mother is a difficult woman . . . Please don't be embarrassed," he said. "She wants you to come home tonight."

I telephoned her and Lila started in on a tirade about child-stealers. "You'd better come home where you belong."

"Why, Momma?"

"I'm not going to give you any compliments . . . You want compliments? Well, I need to see your pretty eyes in this empty house. Your sister is driving me crazy: she wants to kill me."

Sometimes her words evoked scenes—these were just words.

What is inside the head takes refuge in formulas—capsule things to carry into a present-tense moment. It's all nonsense, though, if you examine it. When I got home Momma was wearing lipstick: "I'm trying to look glamourous for you . . . Are you *embarrassed*? Maybe *I'm embarrassed*: did you ever think of that?" (By my life among people who then talked about her.)

"I don't know what you expect me to understand, Momma."

"I expect nothing from you . . . Just turn on the radio and sit where I can see your baby blues. I need some friendly eyes . . . My nerves aren't good . . . I don't want to be alone."

Of the professor and his wife, Lila said, "They weren't exactly heroes, were they? Did it get to them, how smart you were, did they catch on you're impossible? I'll tell you a secret: people want to kill you. Stay still . . . The thing is not to care . . . I'm the I-don't-care girl . . . You and me, we don't care anymore. Don't get a swelled head just because you and I are such swell people with such a sophisticated outlook. I can't live without you. I don't need you around for company . . . It's not my peace of mind . . . It's your real mother's ghost: she gives me no peace. I need the money your father sends you."

At the edge of every statement is what it means further than itself—and what it doesn't mean. Around us is what she denies: my real mother's ghost gives her peace, it is Lila's peace of mind, she can't live without me. It's not just money. And so on. I mean you *know* when it's just money—the voice is different then. She said, "You're not so bad—I didn't know I liked you. I'm like Garbo—I vunt tuh beee uhlohnnnnnn . . . But you're okay . . ."

She had never cooked for me; but she cooked meals for me after that. She was a terrible cook, though. Neither she nor I liked her cooking. It was a symbol. (The local idiom was to say it was a symbol, *though*.)

Momma was seeing a guy who had liked her when she was a girl: "What it is is it's Memory Lane." Then: "Ben is not an interesting man." A childless widower, he wanted a son. He'd be good to me. Nonie was seeing a rich homosexual guy who'd told her about his being homosexual. He was very rich, Momma said, but Nonie would never sacrifice herself for us—she wouldn't marry him to help us. Nonie said to me, "We'll give him you . . . He can have you." She didn't mean it: she never let me meet him, even. She said it to Momma but she let Momma meet him.

In the moments then . . . among the actual breaths . . . nothing that concerned the women was sufficiently in my range *then* that I can speak of it now with *full* knowledge.

"What I want I can't have anymore," Momma said on the phone to someone. "I'm spoiled. Ask me no questions, tell me no lies."

Even though she spoke to me in the ways she did, Momma hid the world from me as she knew it—her world, if I can call it that.

I stayed away from the house for days at a time—among boys and sometimes girls and their families, their mothers, women who were unlike my mother and sister. One cannot take the time to remember every moment of a period of a number of weeks: it would take longer than a number of weeks. I wanted to be difficult and bad, ordinary, and free . . . Sly . . . And athletic.

At a certain date after eleven weeks, a Veterans Hospital not far from Chicago called Lila. Someone there telephoned to say that S.L. was ill; he'd had a stroke in his car while he was driving to Chicago—and so on. Lila told me this: *No one knew who he was, he was in a coma for three months, but he came out of it and he asked for us.*

That story has certain problems of plausibility. Such a long coma causes brain damage. Daddy had a wallet and a car registration and a driver's license with him. It is likelier (but not necessarily true) that in the car he began to feel very ill, and he checked into the hospital, and while he was there he had a stroke and went into a coma and came out of it knowing he was an invalid; and then he went on day after day, seriously afflicted with grief—or perhaps for a day or two. *He had a time of it,* Lila said. *He changed his mind* . . . He most likely, after a while, now that he would be an invalid or a semi-invalid the rest of his life, chose to let the hospital call us. Or someone did without asking him. I believe all the stories . . . I believe what anyone—everyone—says to me. I imagine him lying in bed and giving up the project of being ill by himself.

He said to me when he came home that he'd missed me: but I had been unhappy with him before he left; so what exactly had he missed? He had often complained, "You're too smart for me—you have no heart." He'd often said he didn't like me. He said to a couple of men who came to see him when he was at home with us that he told the hospital he had no family and that the hospital on its own had called us and that he would never forgive the hospital—it was a dry, male joke-not-a-joke. He told his brother on the telephone to California that he had been unable to speak all that time (or most of the time he'd been in the hospital) and that he had not wanted to see anyone. He told Nonie the hospital had found out about us among his papers and had refused to give him any more free treatment but had sent him back to Lila, whom he hated. It is hard to know why one decides certain things or why one decides to say certain things. It is hard to remember coherently or sensibly. It doesn't much matter now. The dragonfly flights of memorial glimpses of this and that in the past change things around anyway.

*

More family conferences to see if he ought to come back—if we ought to allow him to return . . . *We'll all just be nurses* . . . conferences in the house and on the phone. Lila said, "They all have their axes to grind, I don't know what the good-sense thing to do is or if there is one." Momma said to me, "You're a know-it-all—tell me what *you* think?"

I shook my head. I refused to think.

She said, "It's not a good idea to say yes—it's the end of my life, but if I say no, I have to be someone who said no to him now when his back is against the wall."

She became odd-faced. Shadows haunted the sockets of her eyes. She was shadowy-mouthed. Meanwhile, Nonie said she would rather be left out of the discussion, too. She told me she was against S.L.'s coming back to us. "The bad stuff will start all over again." She wanted me to agree with her. In the days of *thinking-about-what-to-do* Lila got more difficult, *catty* with people, outspoken (that is to say, rude), and obstinate and *hard to talk to*. "What starting over is there? What starting over is there at my age? S.L. will pull himself together and he'll go to work part-time; we'll make a go of it; we'll make a comeback—I understand him. Listen, I made my bed and I'll lie in it . . . I don't want to get to know another man . . . If he's no good, I'll walk out. He likes me well enough: I'm not easy to get along with . . . He would have come back if he hadn't gone into a coma. I don't want to start over. I started with him and I'll finish with him. That's the way I am." And: "No one can tell me what to do. I'm going to start over, but with him . . . We're turning over a new leaf . . . S.L.'s not going to die like a dog in the gutter. I'm tired of thinking. These are my last words on the subject."

Nonie said, "She just wants to torture him and the rest of us. She hasn't got any nerve left."

Nonie said, "Well, I can't live in a house with a sick man and make goo-goo eyes at boys I want to get to marry me . . . No one thinks about me."

Momma said, "At my age, I know I'm making a mistake but"—she coughed—"*but* I *want* to make it . . . and who's going to stop me, I'd like to know. What I want to know is who's against me and who will help me now. What about you, Wiley? People say someone your age shouldn't stay in a house with a sick man . . . Will you stand by me?"

Her eyes: they were not unfamiliar to me. The defeat—the absence of merriment—the presence of dark amusement—a universe of half-calculated carelessness . . . you have only a second to prevent yourself from being moved. I kissed her eyelids. "Count me in," I said. I was pretty young. I said it in a storylike voice—like it was all foregone. "I'll try to help." I pretty much meant it.

My face—a doggish, twisted, nervous boy's somewhat tough face—"You don't have the face of my dreams, Pisher," she said that now with a faint smile. And closed her eyes. She put her still-pretty arm over her deep-sunken, deep-shadowed eyes, and from behind her arm, she said, "Well, it doesn't matter."

"Tell our fortune," she said.

The cards said we were doing the wrong thing.

I laid the cards out and said, "We're doing the right thing."

She said, "I know . . . I tell you what my secret is: I don't love anyone." She eyed the darkness in the corners of the room. "I don't know what anything means . . . Well, maybe my luck will change . . . I'm flying blind, I'm flying by the seat of my pants. Well, so be it."

An ambulance brought Daddy home—from Chicago. Gray-faced, skinny with illness, scared-looking in a kind of squirrellike way unlike himself before he was ill, friendly and querulous, emotional. Lila in the kitchen said, as if to herself, "My God, he's a beaten man."

I slept on a couch in the dining room. Dad slept in my room.

Lila said to others, "Well, it is and it isn't a second honeymoon, but I will say this, the subject is reopened. My plate is full. I always say, Let the devil take the hindmost . . . See no evil, do no evil, speak no evil—just get on with what you have to do."

She was negotiating decency—absolution—death—an ad hoc morality . . . in the face of illness and mortality.

She said to me late at night when the house was quiet, "I'm making up my life as I go along." She said, "I don't know what to do." Curtains were blowing at the open window. I didn't feel I liked or loved my parents much anymore or that I needed them—and if I did, it hardly mattered. I was scared, though, not just of having another family—my third, after all—but of the accumulated sadness—the meaninglessness. I thought we should fight death in each other and in ourselves and that we should fight other things, our own human nature, for example, and the way accident and bad things, so to speak, chewed everything up, and that it was more "important," more "vital," to do something kind than it was to be smart or reasonable or sensible.

I "decided" to be "indomitable," like Ulysses, and not to care about being poor and caught up in this mess but to be *a good child* to the best of my ability—a son and all that—and to believe in simple things and to be cheerful and loyal and okay. I foresaw my own freedom in that—a weird intellectual freedom that had to do with will: I would do this thing, stay with the Silenowiczes, and *behave*, and then I could think about what I really wanted to do. But I wouldn't be haunted by my own darkness, at least. I'd be good to Dad. Uncomplicatedly good.

Lila saw it differently, understood me differently. "We have to be suckers because it would be worse to be the other thing." But she looked terrible: it really was killing her. "I can't help the way I look, Wiley: my life is over now."

For the umpteenth time I decided not to remember things but just to go along from day to day.

Daddy said, "You're going to stay and be a help? Can't bear to miss the show, is that it, Pooperkins? *Forgive and forget? make no claims: be a gentleman even if it kills you?*" He was trying to be noble; he was trying to be skeptical; he was trying to remind me of the past; he was being a lot of things and it came out like that.

He looked terrible; he was really ill, really ill and scared. Terrified and angry, bitterly scared in that style—and it showed.

"Take my advice: leave: don't stay here—I'm not good for anything, I'm good for nothing now." Dimly: "Ha-ha . . ." He said, "I can't protect you from anything . . . I can't protect you from *her*."

I know it sounds mad but it *felt like* a pressure from God, an arrogantly experienced wind of death that kept me there and kept me from having seizures or nonstop nightmares: there are a lot of ways to escape a bad situation. One is by going right up to it and standing next to it, or in the center of it, until you either die or feel its *normalcy*, by which I mean its forbearance, the possibilities of living with it that are in it for you.

Daddy said again, "You're going to stay and be a help? *Can't bear to miss the show, Pooperkins? Forgive and forget? a gentleman if it kills you?*" Decisions, in real life, of course, are never quite final; you set yourself to be stubborn—you act it out, the finality. But it's touch and go whether you keep on. Daddy coughs and blacks out, and you hold him until his fear subsides and he begins to peer through his semiconsciousness at the air. I loved him some. Each occasion of seeing him brought, in its train, *messages*, omens: bits of affection: old dismissals-of-him as well. My sense of the world was refreshed in my losing touch with it.

Now when I daydreamed it was with new clusters of intensity of actual reference to what was lost. Meanings formed and were clear for a while—like clouds in the sky, their shadows on the ground.

And other children made a place for me—for a while I did not have to defend myself. I had this rank, this *laissez-passer*, this other role, so to speak: the kid with the really ill father. A day, a school day, to enter a school day—that *next* huge trembling block of time—was to enter an immediacy tailored to my being a sick man's son. One can forget and run in the playground at recess. But then when I stopped running, I felt my heart in him; I held my hand to my chest and wondered if my heart was weak like Daddy's—I gasped as he did . . . I felt close to him after a while and not human—not like other kids . . . at all.

The other oddity was that I judged S.L.—when I was nine years old. See, he and Lila needed me there to arouse interest, pity, compassion in doctors. The child's presence, his loyalty, inspired loyalty. Sometimes, walking home in the wintry light, I wished I knew less, but to choose to continue walking toward home, the thing of refusing to choose anymore, was to be filled with breath. It was the opposite of suffocation. It was not like being adrift in airlessness. One did this stuff for *them* in order not to have worse memories about oneself. It was okay.

I hung around the house a lot the first months S.L. was home. I cut school. The school protested, but I kept on. At first S.L. was upset by illicit presence: "I want no sacrifices from you, I want no sacrifices from *a child*." I couldn't help *feeling* (seeing) that he didn't *like* me although he *cared-about-me*.

I was a tough, frog-faced, tense-nerved nine-year-old.

But also, in the seconds, I could feel his breathing change when I entered his room. And when I drew near him, I could see in his eyes a changing condition, a lessening of solitude. Part of it was because I was dumb to have stayed: we both knew this—and that it made room for him. This efflorescence of stupidity. The specific feelings of a specific boy. He straightened his hair with his hands. He'd get up, even, and brush his thinning hair—I was important company, ugly and young and stupid or not.

Some days he might ignore me . . .

Some, even though he was lying down, he would put his arm around my waist and say, "Don't talk . . . Just sit here and look at the light in the window with me." Once or twice he said, "I can't stand the things you say, you know that? Here, have a piece of licorice: someone brought me licorice: it's bad for you: have some." He said, "I like watching the light . . . I have become a simple man, Pooperkins."

It wasn't true but it was okay. The yews, the light in the yews alongside the house, outside the bedroom window, the light on the grass, on our backyard fence: we watched the late-afternoon light as if it were a show, Daddy and I.

Daddy said—over and over—"I can't do nothing for no one—not a thing—not for a single human soul. Stay if you want—but you're a fool . . ."

I could feel his heart lift . . . his heartbeat straighten out . . . in his relief at being in the presence of a fool.

So what? I have nothing else to do as interesting as this. I told him that once. He said it wasn't a kind thing to say. Then that it was. Then that he didn't want to think about it.

One is no longer shy. One is abrupt, little-boyish, crude, and stupid—not one's real self: perhaps this is one's real self now, the self you offer someone in companionship.

Daddy said, "Maybe that's the point of having nothing. You get to enjoy the company of a fool . . . Then the next thing you know you even like being with yourself. Remember that . . ."

It was more complicated than I can show here.

Various relatives gave *moral support* and a number of others sent money. Momma preferred the relatives who sent money. Grave remedies were considered, including a set of operations that would last several years. The project was dropped: it was too expensive, too uncertain, he was too old, the wrong body type, the wrong mental sort. He was not worth it . . . something like that.

I paid no attention.

My parents loved me a lot—really a lot—not simply but really a lot, noisily, you might say, then, for a while.

Nonie still said nothing kind to me—not ever—not once—not even then.

But she was different in manner . . . faintly respectful or in fear of me . . . a little.

Love

Love? A Calvinist sense of the merely human in oneself and one other person, or in a family, a Calvinist sense touched by willful grace here and there, in more than one person, touched by some obstinacy, some persistence in identity and attachment which is a sort of piety: touched off, set off, lit and fired by the presence of stupidity or faith—stupidity-with-a-purpose—stupidity of a certain kind for the sake of a family?

"Well," Lila said, sincere and yet ironic and laughing at me, "let's put a good face on things . . . let's all pull together—let's make a home and see what happens." She said to me, "Are you listening? You ready to put your best bib and tucker on? You have your good manners ready? Will you be a bright spot in a dark, dark world for the rest of us?"

Nonie said to her, "Leave my feelings alone . . . I want to be young, I want to have these years for myself. I have to get married and try to save what I can."

Momma said, "She never lifts a finger to help anyone . . . and she never will. She wants to save herself is all it is with her. What it is is silly . . . Well, that's not always the worst thing in the world to be."

But sometimes it is . . .

Momma said to me, "Oh, you, you're a boy—you can make sacrifices, you can let things go for a little while and you can pick up right where you left off—you'll still have a life."

Momma was bluffing. And Nonie was amiable—and patient—but *merciless.* I assumed a similar mercilessness could be applied to her. One might bluff with Momma. One might have, with either of them, an equivalent concern for oneself.

Some of Lila's remarks at this time:

I'm no one's sweetie pie anymore—

Nobody wants you when you're old and gray—if you're the realistic type.

Life is a battle, we have our own little war, we're a hospital unit.

Thank God, God put the spirit of toughness in us, we don't lie down and play dead . . . We put up a good front.

A percentage of what she did was *always* sincere.

In 1940, Daddy changed. He had been difficult all along, mostly difficult—frightened and surrenderish, overexcited, and sometimes determined to act as if he were well. Daddy, acting as if his illness had been imaginary all along, or had been a dream, became more or less *wild,* vengeful toward Lila—and death. He blamed her. In order to argue with her, he was *vengeful* toward health, even toward daylight at times. He and Nonie joined forces.

And Momma, showing off, was a heroine-commander—she was very commander-in-chiefish—I don't mean noble: she gave in to anger and to despair. The daily reality in the house was like being in a firing line. "We're in the trenches," she said. "It's a terrible thing . . . We're under bombardment from indecency—I can't go on . . . I want you to go on, Wiley."

Daddy fell ill again and died and was resuscitated, sort of. Nonie went to live with relatives in North Carolina. Once she was out of the house and we spoke maybe every six weeks on the phone, I tried to ask her for advice if Momma and Daddy fought—or if I was sad. I won't say I missed her. Yes, I will say it. Perhaps, too, I imagined missing her as a proper thing to do.

On the telephone, long-distance, if I spoke about the family, Nonie would cry out, "Don't talk to me about that: I can't stand to hear about those things . . . I can't stand the way you talk about things anyway: I want things to be nice. Other girls don't have sick fathers. If I smile and have a good time, people wonder if I have regular feelings about my *father*. I don't want boys to wonder about me."

Lila said, "There's too much life-and-death around here for her . . . For me, too."

Nonie would ask how we were eating. Momma had said that getting food on the table would kill her—we had a maid who cooked three times a week; and three nights, we had cold cuts or Chinese food that one of us went to the restaurant and ordered and brought home in little white cartons with metal handles. One night a week, Momma cooked and I washed up. But it wasn't *the cooking* she meant. Momma said she couldn't go on selling insurance and "nursing" Daddy and "keeping my looks at my age when I don't have an easy life. I don't have a friendly life, let me tell you, it isn't *decent* to ask so much of one person—I'm not a saint."

Daddy, who felt terror (and shame) at being ill, said to me, "Did they stick you with the latrine detail? Well, you always were a fool, weren't you?" Momma refused to nurse him; he refused (or had refused) to talk to her. I never knew the details of that story (although I can imagine them). I took over the stuff of taking care of him mostly; and he helped; mostly he took care of himself once he recovered from the second serious episode.

But it got weirder. Momma told me that the way men treated her, that the thing of being a woman without a man around to protect her—she didn't explain in what way—sickened her as it had Nonie. "That's the real reason I sent her away, where people will look after her rights."

Anyway, Momma quit her job—or was partly fired—she stayed home and had, she said, *a nervous breakdown*—a long and complex tantrum or spell of longing for life to be other than it was.

Momma said she couldn't stand being a charity case but she became one full-time. She said she was breaking in two. She said to Dad, "This is your doing, S.L., this is the life you gave me." She said to me, though, that she did this, was unkind to S.L., at the doctors' urging; she said she was supposed to "shame" S.L. into trying harder to live, to live a more active life. "The doctors want you to put up a fight, S.L.; it's not good medicine for you to be a *coward*." Daddy called her Madame Goebbels-Poison-Mouth and said she was killing him; and she said he was killing her—and me. He never again forgave her, or if he did, it was in such dark ironic ways I didn't like to see it; and I don't want to think about it now, my dad's ironic mercy. Momma said, "I don't understand Original Sin . . . If everyone has it, it can't be very original."

She would gouge charity out of everyone she could—clothes, invitations (to get out of the house and away from Dad)—to prove she wasn't helpless or ground down into mere piety by illness, comparative poverty, growing older, despair. Sometimes it seemed to me that a dozen unlikely truths were visible every day at home. Lila said she could not survive if she wasn't herself, did I want her to die, and Daddy said he could not live if he wasn't himself, did I want him to die, and each said to the other, *Look what you're doing to the boy—do you want* HIM *to go crazy?* It seemed to me that self-preservation was lousy, a lousy thing to do. I don't know. It was hard to think up some meaning that would accept all three of us.

But without such a meaning the days were impossible. Kindness was impossible. Sanity was impossible. The accusations: *Are you trying to kill me?* And: *You are dragging us all down . . .* And: *You* ARE *ugly; you've brought us to A Pretty Pass—this is the end, I guess . . .* made the house a rough place. Dreams and omens, views and moods, feelings, there is a buildup, an accumulation, of events and of opinions in odd ways, but no central truth makes itself known by miracle, not even an *I will save myself.* Maybe that was because Nonie exemplified the latter. Teachers came to the house to plead with the Silenowiczes to release me; but, in some moods, Lila believed I had put the teachers up to that, egged them on, tricked them, and Daddy would half go along with her in some kind of quick alliance about that . . . Anyway she *believed* in having me around. You can look from face to face in our living room and see nothing but people being people: you can see the failure of every idea. You can listen to the breathing and see how human people are. It got so it made me laugh—in a way—the fifteen bad minutes on a humid rainy day of hysterical and overtly shrill and even screaming and genuine horror in one or both of them, my parents. In school, for Current Events, I argued the *probable* reality of death camps given Nazi statements and "human nature" and lies and carelessness about consequences . . . carelessness and blindness . . .

And then, if you're stubborn, *things calm down* and we go back into truce—into being good and noble or ordinarily patient, long-suffering, tolerant for a while. I was there: the suffering was blurred . . . changeable. I was a kid. Lila said, "No one's to blame: we tried, we're trying: listen, I'm not slow to cast a stone; but I don't see that that's called for here. I wish S.L. would try harder . . . He's the world's worst patient: that's where Nonie gets her selfishness: the two of them are the most selfish people you can ever know—well, monkey see, monkey do." (She explained *Hitler* that way, too: "He's a success—that impresses people —you know what happens—monkey see, monkey do . . . *Well, what do you expect?*" She could do a lot of variations with catchall phrases.)

She said, "I don't think being sick gives S.L. the right to lord it over me. I know he's under a strain, but we're all under a strain and enough's enough. I blame no one but I'll tell you this: I don't know HOW MUCH LONGER I CAN GO ON—AND THAT'S THE TRUTH." She said, "Even in suffering, people are just people." She was ill herself by then, gall bladder and the first hints that she might have cancer.

S.L., unhappy, tense, and bitter, said to me, "Is that woman handing out a lot more shit than usual? Why do you listen to her? Don't you know anything? Do you know about learning to come in out of the rain?" He said flatly: "You should save yourself from her. DON'T BE A SISSY . . ."

He couldn't sleep if I wasn't in the house. Sometimes he said, "Save yourself from me" and sometimes he said, "Don't save yourself from ME . . ." Gosh, it was creepy.

"Try not to think about it," Momma said. "Hang on to your health."

Sometimes Momma would be downright cruel to S.L. "He lorded it over me long enough . . . He's good for nothing now." She said that to him—in the third person like that, wearily, dramatically.

If she saw me listening, she said to me, "Curiosity killed the cat; you know that, don't you?" In my dreams, curiosity, an adolescent boy, killed and dismembered a dog.

My parents had an edge of mercilessness, not always unconsciously or drivenly, sometimes semiconsciously, sometimes consciously fully—with wild breaths and chemistries akimbo, fully conscious, merciless.

I didn't have to be honest about it with myself. I saw that they cared about each other in some way, that, off and on, they preferred this stuff to a merely medical fate.

The bad time worsened. They resented it that I was alive . . . By then, in a sense, they were permitting so many things in themselves—indulgences in wartime or because life was hard—that they slid easily into disliking me at times just because I was there. It was habitual for them to go too far.

But if I yelled or protested quietly, their states worsened, accelerated by guilt almost. Anyway, I brought money into the house but nothing was spent on me—not for doctors or clothes or anything. No schoolbooks, no notebooks. Sometimes not even milk for me. Momma said, with a wrinkled face and a look of honesty, "I can't bear it. I can't take care of anyone. We all have to be in the same boat OR I WILL GO MAD." Scary egalitarianism.

But human.

Nothing in my life announced that I could endure much of this or that I might live through it and on after it for a while in some kind of regular life.

It is very strange to have no books, no lessons, no notepaper or pencils or stamps, nothing but ragged clothes and haircuts you get for nothing as charity, crewcuts, and you're still sort of semi-upper-middle-class. We had a spectrum of poverties, a continuum of deprivations in the house. The moments of self-control became fewer and fewer. My father had little time or strength for nobility. My mother had no hope and no wish to exemplify lies. I had no innocence about any of this after a while. I tried to get the two of them to be simpler and less violent for my sake, so I could be innocent—I may have sounded like Nonie.

Momma, quite mad by then, loony, said, "You want us to make sacrifices for you: go live somewhere else." She never said that to Nonie. I could escape in that way. I tried to leave at that point; I moved in with some people who lived a block away and I stopped off at home every day. Lila, though, came after me and stood in the rain on the sidewalk in front of the house on Water Place where I was staying and screamed at the house, at the doors and the windows of the house where the people lived I had taken shelter with: "Wiley, your dying father loves you and needs you, you bastard!" People said she was crazy—that it was the strain and that she was that age . . . And that I should go away to school. Dad said she had always been crazy, that now everyone could see what she was like. The circumstances of our lives—as I said—made me laugh.

I asked Nonie for help—this was on the telephone to Carolina.

Nonie said, "I'm young, don't ask me to interfere . . . You're their pet now: you won out—do what you like."

Lila said to me: "I know what you're doing: you're laying up grievances so you can leave us in the lurch—you're just like Nonie, that's what you're like: when you're good and ready, you'll take off and have your life. And we'll die here like dogs."

The thought had occurred to me that if things got bad enough and I left, I would go on remembering, but if I stayed, I might not remember actively *once the worst was over*—one of Mom's phrases. S.L. said, "Life is shit." The shattered condition of his heart drained his face of color, and not only that, of the power to be absent in thought or attention from a present moment in relation to his condition, his illness . . . He wasn't there with you—with me—mostly he would talk only to me, see only me (Lila said) at this time—but when I was with him I was in the presence of my father-by-adoption, who wanted me there, but it was all contradictory, contradictory madly: he was entirely (and intently and fearfully) present—to his own danger, his own state—really like a man on a tightrope or like a man being tortured—and yet, even if he was in a sense performing his death-and-life trick in front of me, at the same time, his face, even with its hiddenness gone in performing, his face seemed partly erased, gone from me anyway . . .

Momma got weirder and weirder: she would confront me when I came into the house and she would be half-dressed, her breasts out like wild milk-and-eyes, and she would say, "Tell me how you live through this . . . Tell me how you stay alive."

If I burst out laughing, she might, she often did, sober up—if I can say that.

It was almost like seeing a moment—I know a moment is not a thing—but an eyelid room, a room with eyelid-walls that blinked, and a semi-airy stage and a tree-thing-almost-a-letter-of-the-alphabet with me perched in it and Mom on the ground and a rush of wind *seen* as thin, curling lines—a restless brevity which, having alit, had not alit at all: so grace and patience came and went in my parents in certain moments and took the place of self-concern and mood and then were replaced by this other stuff but always unstably. You never knew what flicker or flight or obstinacy or cruelty would shift the balance, the mood, the shiny or dull-colored distortions. Daddy said it was all *disgusting*—"but you make a game out of it, Pisher." He said I was a kid and was okay—sometimes. It was, actually, male forgiveness—*alit* and *not alit*—a shifting as of light or as of breath or as of ribs, a distraction, a generosity—a form of love in a given moment . . . a specific moment. Love? Things were often okay in their way. I remember Momma coming into the living room, where Dad and I were listening to the radio, and saying, "Well, is this the best you have to offer a good-looking woman on a rainy night? I suppose it will have to do. Make room on the couch for me, will you?"

I guess it's odd to be sentimental about a time of horror and my father's love and my mother's half-baked charm, but in a world of Original Sin (maybe) was hidden this almost erotic and weird *justice*—and it wasn't entirely pitched beyond one's hearing—not anymore, although one was a child still in many ways.

Daddy said to me, "Sometimes I'm sweet." He said, "Sometimes everyone is sweet."

Meanings

Because of how things changed, walking into our house, then into the apartment we moved to, was like starting *in medias res* every day. The past kept being rewritten. It came to this new total—or so the two of them, Momma and S.L., would insist.

Lila maybe was contemplating sleeping with a local corporation head grown rich in wartime, and moving out of the house. Or she was fighting with some woman who was trying to place her in a lower social category than she felt she had been in before S.L. became ill. Or she had won or changed her mind and was having *a little case of shell shock, battle fatigue, tonight.* You never knew. She and S.L. might be getting along. Reality *is* duration—*in medias res* becomes an evening. Three hundred and sixty-five evenings become a year. Things that last longer are not realer even to the mind. But they become what is largely and as-if-*intuitively* known. I was ten and eleven. Then I was twelve and big—I was long-legged and skinny in a wartime crewcut the barber humiliatingly did not charge me for unless I insisted. The stuff at home had gone on for three years. My feet are big and they bump on things. I keep forgetting I have big feet and that I have grown. It is spring . . . The windows are open. On my way home I saw limp spears of forsythia in the almost longitudinal rays of late-afternoon Midwestern spring sunlight. The aging drapes—heavy, pale blue-gray silk damask things—are blowing as are, in a more active wind-tossed fashion, the white muslin undercurtains. Daddy is visible in the front room. Has he been sneaking coffee in the kitchen? And Momma is on the phone . . . with her sister? Her mother? A friend? The corporation-president lover, or almost lover, or whatever he was? No one will ever explain to me what went on. I know what I know at various ages and almost, it seems, by accident—in the almost unbearable paradoxicality of accident turned into a geometry of accidents, into likelihood and logic-in-real-life.

I mean the *logic* starts at a certain point and then extends through certain phenomena in a disciplined way. Momma's eyes: now that I was tall, I looked down into them and saw that they were like darkened theaters, with things going on in the dark in them; and then the lights would go on in a way; a performance would begin; but not a lot would be explained even then. But I knew this much—in part, only because I was tall . . . And spoiled, she said.

Sometimes I thought about things in such a way that the *truth* was transposed; and instead of realizing that I saw things from a different angle, I would think Ma had changed, that in the past—this is in regard to her eyes—a performance would begin but the lights wouldn't go on and nothing would be explained—but it had been my age, the absence of genital information, may I say that?, and not just her secrecy that made things seem so entirely unexplained.

Nowadays Daddy might mutter about her: "That bitch," and I could half tell, depending on whether I was in a steady mood or was upset or not, whether he was angry or was signalling a broken heart.

If I didn't know who he was talking about, he might get angry with me because his medical state burned him and altered his temper or because he was okay and just masculinely sneery at me for my general obtusity, my obtuseness, my being dumb in a lot of ways.

And I would burn with rejection—or I would laugh. You don't usually disturb a broken heart—or try to cure it—especially if it is also the actual failing heart of a man ill with genuine heart trouble—but by this time Daddy would let me address his broken heart. And this was odd and private, since it was like, in a sick way, I guess, a guy entrusting his son with his car—it was sort of like that. But it was his feelings. But it would be in his eyes: a special area of permission—of car keys and ignition—kind of—and of that sort of distrust and resignation—and a veiling, politic and clever, over that of *indulging-the-kid*.

He might enunciate an aphorism, "Gentlemen don't snitch, gentlemen don't tell tales out of school." He meant about him having come to like me.

He might say, "Flirt with me like a nice fella."

Or: "Give us a hug . . ."

I often felt in him the murderously ribald thundering of his conviction, in a male-ish big-shot way, that this was love . . . worthwhile love.

But love as meaning. Not piously. But like among the troops, you know? Catch-as-catch-can? Male flibbertigibbet or shed-time and off-duty stuff? He seemed to assume that the truth about his feelings and about his life when I was not there would do him no credit with me, and yet he would discuss some of those things if I remembered to have the air—and some of the reality—of being the other half of a duo, a pair of guys sitting in a bar in an agreed-on-and-loyal-and-yet-sly way with principles-of-despising-women-as-dishonest—us as dirty but loyal pals, mutually. This was if I hadn't forgotten him during the day and had not, oh, gotten involved at school or something, or in sports, or in daydreaming. This stuff had evolved with him and me over the years.

When Momma's nagging (or *ragging*, her term) got him *off his duff and on his feet* with a forbidden unlit cigar in his mouth and him looking like a pale parody of his well self, he would talk to me in certain ways then. Sometimes he would complain, sort of as if giving sort of a footnote: "The fibrillations are bad. I'm taking it slow . . . That bitch is asking me to go make money again . . . I'm not in the mood for any bullshit . . . I've had a bad day, *Sonny Boy* . . . *Pisherkins* . . ." The thing for me with him, when I was twelve and had gotten big, was to recognize with masculine discretion the presence of a not-final, not overwhelming-all-else love.

This didn't necessarily extend in two directions to cover my feelings so far as he was concerned, unless he was in a mood to be just either out of a sense of strength or out of a sense of weakness.

We are inarticulate about a lot of things—no: it was agreed between us that I would not judge or even think about a lot of things: mannerliness was one such thing, mannerliness such as it was for us, with all the stresses and the ailments changing daily and sometimes hourly; and *understanding* and *forbearance* were his subjects, not mine; and how to be a lot of things such as masculine without being *rough*: I didn't judge that or think about it but more or less trusted Dad's taste in the matter.

Of course, a lot of this made you attractive to other people. To be shaped like this, to be the tall, gawky kid who was living through this made you a kid attractive to some people. A lot of the irony was that I was inarticulate some anyway, in ways that hurt, that burned and stung and tore me apart: embarrassment took the place of guilt and of irony. I thought the universe was dirty. It was okay but it was dirty. It was not to be understood—not truthfully understood—but a lot of theories were floating around, a lot of pieties: and a lot of rhetoric. You could read the rhetoric of battles daily. Or I could think about my dad and break the cheeks of heaven and make them weep and so on, none of it was untrue entirely; but none of it was even almost entirely true either.

Sometimes you could just emanate pain—I could—or he could—and the universe did crack open and weep in the sense that the other guy died for you in a way and was quiet about it and did not add to your woeful bitterness or the burning thing by showing you they don't care about you. One of us stood for *them*. For fate. The other guy's a *they; they* come first . . . Or whatever. This patriotism, this stuff goes on, this sympathy, past the sharpest perceptions, past the dullest ones; and it comes out on the other side of vengeance and of rivalry. The moment ticks; but there is this other stillness in it—of yourself and this stuff as meaning for you, willed though, a kind of secular or pragmatic idea. The actual moments of happiness then: *they can happen at the worst times*: I don't know what that means; but it was *a truth* . . . We had a considerable amount of decency in the house off and on and for days on end—for months sometimes. It just wasn't there forever—you know? It wasn't ever forever.

People will be people, and some of that was tarted up, made use of; some of it was faked, lied about, cleaned up, made visible, oddly edited . . . promoted, shown provocatively. Speaking now in the realm of opinion, I can't say I ever in my life saw anything lovelier, really, than S.L. sometimes in the horror when he was ill and he decided to dilute the horror—for me. He could be warm, smart, kind, gentle, ironic, knowing, not phony either—he was better than any father in any movie at those times. "What's a little death between friends," he would say, getting his breath after a kind of phony asthma attack, his breathing having failed during a bad dream. I would be holding him in my arms. His manner had a swing and neatness. And huge sophistication—huge to me, much more than I would have believed possible. A touch of genius; humane, though. It wasn't impersonation—or just impersonation. It was a display of knowledge and of ability and of a not entirely ironic courage and, I guess, forgiveness, toward life—*Look what you get in the way of surprising things: an example of personal nobility like me in my illness.* But he didn't persevere in that stuff very long. Not usually. Mostly he didn't keep it up—he didn't want to. He couldn't.

It doesn't matter.

I kept Dad company—that was mostly what I did instead of growing up. People said I did a good job; I kept him from being lonely. I didn't know if I was dead or ill, though—by osmosis, contagion, a fever of reflection of him.

Lila said, "You've done well . . . You came up smelling like a rose again." I was admired as A Good Son. Admired quite a lot. I didn't act crazily. But, see, time doesn't stop. You can't really have a trauma and freeze things at a moment of praise. Or maybe you can, but I don't think so, judging from my experiences.

At the moment she was speaking, Lila felt that people admired me more for being a son than they did her for being the wife she was, the wife who had stuck by S.L. for years now and whose life now seemed over. She said this to me. She said, "Why are you laughing? You got silly when you got tall—you know that?"

"The something laugh that bespeaks the empty mind . . . the vacant mind. I have a teacher who says that," I said. You have to *remember* that time goes on, moment by moment.

"Yes? Well, that's how you laugh . . . Like a vacant lot—ha-ha . . . A lot of weeds . . . Stop laughing before you make us both sick. Ha-ha."

I used to go into these spells of nutty laughter—almost on purpose: it was like being drunk on purpose: I laughed soberly-drunkenly on and on. We laughed drunkenly differently, Lila and I: Daddy wasn't supposed to laugh because it endangered his heart. He could smile and do a male kind of *tee-hee,* though. Lila is laughing in the complicated way of a movie star who remains photogenic with an open laugh—a woman who has learned to laugh photogenically but persuasively.

Laughing, she said, "I know you: I know what you're up to."

"Yeah? What? What am I up to, Momma? What am I doing?" You have an appetite for information about yourself.

"Never mind . . . Never you mind . . . You think you can get away with it but I'm on to you."

"Momma, tell me, what am I getting away with?"

Our situation, simply in itself, kept drawing my attention to the actuality of truth and lies, love and not-love in the moments of them doing their routines, the swooping and silent thing of the approach and of the arrival of a moment, of a mood enclosing us; departure and setting us free, or expelling us, already beginning to occur. The lightest, moistest kiss. "Tell me, will we live another week? What do you see for us in the Christmas season?"

"I don't know. We'll do something. Stick around and you'll find out what happens."

"That's the one interesting thing *you* ever say."

The proposal of curiosity as a reason to live, she meant.

To this subject of love and action as meaning in Calvin's world of Original Sin in which I am not sure a virtue can be named, at least for very long, the blessing of time, as I saw it back then, was that it permitted projects such as getting along with someone, and from those projects, as you went along, you and others derived some pleasure, some happiness; and at the usually unclear end, the fading into a result or of the result or the fading away of the result—and on to the next thing—something good came of all of it which continued or which could be passed on, maybe: that was how you measured and judged. Those were the grounds on which you made decisions.

When you were steady . . .

The blessing of time . . . I guess that's a funny thing to say.

"Lies" keep breaking into moods—they become truths; one lyingly imagines that time is not a component of life, but then evil results. In a grown man's smile or in a grown woman's nerved-up laughter, as in those things in a child, one sees outbursts of visible truth—for a while . . . In the racing courtroom of the world. It may not be a final truth: it doesn't last or necessarily recur—but it sometimes did recur—in the queasy instability of circumstances.

It is a queer truth you see in a period of brief conclusions, a form of stillness that is not final but which is important to you. In such a zone of stillness, one was sentenced to awe and to some happiness and to some silencing of complaint, which like the seeming message of a particularly fine piece of music formed a complex form of lived truth, unwordedly . . . Music and dance have little ultimately to do with lying—not all the truth of the sounds, of the inflections, of the inflected movements, can be false. Like a child on a beach putting shells in a box, I feel actual time day by day in my youth, omnivorous, omnipotent, ubiquitous time all around me and in me, in my breath and eyes; and in it, the children of time, if I might say that, are the grains of sand of the beach, are the shells, are my fingernails, my eyelashes. These are properly if temporarily arranged, in silence, in the noise of waves and seashore wind, seashells, tidal detritus in a box on a beach near the sounds of the waves; and if the box is shaken, it becomes someone telling the truth—for a while—the truth as can readily be seen—even if the truth is only *the child is shaking a box of shells on the beach and I can hear it inside the sound of the waves*—whether this stuff is okay as truth or not, it has a beauty which may creep into one's face. Or one's manner. Then the other thing will recur—stuff as in childhood, the *Let-me-see-your-face* other truth of things.

Then the ugliness—the devil's stuff recurs, too—when Daddy says, "You got a smug look, you know that: your face sickens me," and he lies down and turns his face to the wall. "I am bored and scared and you are scum—I am tired of scum." ("And he's a man who never kept his word in his whole life," Lila, who was listening in the hall, said later.)

"I am tired of fakes and of fake shit and of you . . . The world is shit and I want to die."

Lila said he couldn't bear it, not being the main attraction in the house, the attraction in the center ring, and that he used his (ill) health to be the center of everything; and that if he wasn't the center, he wanted to quit. "He was always a quitter," she said.

It was dying he used mostly, not ill health, just ill health; and it wasn't fake: he *was* dying.

He did the other, too, but he also made his dying into—well, I have to live with this—he made his dying into sincere criticism of the world, of Lila, of Nonie, and of me . . . Maybe not sincere. How do you know? Sincere not as doctrine but in regard to him living. S.L. said that we were ugly people, him too, we had made him ugly, we were ugly in our souls; he said that life was ugly—then, sometimes, if I said, "What about me? Do I have a chance?" he'd change what he said; but sometimes he didn't; and he said, "You have no chance, no chances."

His second stroke, when I was ten—that one was in the middle of the night. I guess he and Lila had been doing stuff. Maybe just quarrelling, but maybe other stuff—you can only think this later when you're older. Lila said to me when we were waiting at the hospital in the middle of the night, waiting for the moment of S.L.'s death, "I'll tell you something sad: truth can kill you." And: "It isn't always good for people . . . S.L. has had to face things people shouldn't have to face." She said, "A lot of people have dropped us . . . They blame me. Well, what can I say? I did it all with my little hatchet—well, Wiley, you'll see; no one lets you get away with anything. They get even for everything—even for favors."

Favors . . . and condescension. Dependence and gratitude. My twelfth birthday came two months after Dad's third stroke. Dad lived on then, too. He lived on for a little while more. I was surprised I'd made it to twelve. This family stuff went on. When I was ten, Lila, in tones of the collapse of hope: "You never know what you can live without until you try . . . You never know what you can live with, either . . . until you have to."

Well, this is what it was like at home. There was no one I wanted to talk to about it.

Time Poems

I was a snotty kid as a ten-year-old, grim and a little joyless as a competitor. It sure was different when I got bigger—and better—at sports: *You're getting a little bit of a sense of humor,* Momma said. *That's interesting to people, you know.*

When I laughed, it was always a little crazily . . . a little like trying to sing. I was lost to myself, I couldn't locate reality too well for a while—then as I got better, I didn't really get much better; I dragged around; the sky seemed darker than before; dusk seemed grimmer and grayer; sunlight had no power to dispel vagueness or to warm me. My legs and arms—perhaps my temper—got wooden. Clumsy. I suffered from one undiagnosable ailment after another—serious ones that doctors couldn't treat. "I don't know what's wrong with me, I can't seem to catch my breath . . ." Sickly and odd and in a zone of silence—a human giraffe, so openly a freak with pain—someone half dead and *thinking all the time*—I was in bed one evening, lying there hopelessly, and my dad said, "Don't do this to me." Mom had already said that—she'd shouted it really.

But she and I didn't have that kind of life-and-death alliance.

I thought for a bit. I had one arm behind my head and the other was lying across my stomach.

I said, "All right, I won't."

And I blinked.

And I came out of it then and there.

But that was when I was twelve. Earlier I hadn't done that. Dad said I did it for love, that I was okay, I knew how to be a friend . . . He said I was a Cupid of a guy.

In a sense, after that, everything scary became kind of hopeful, or at least turned into a devil-may-care-ishness—a humor. I thought it was that the three of us—and death made four—that we were all four of us in on this; but on sleepless nights I would feel that with my parents, their deaths were not congruent, were not the same thing, were not the products of the same force; and mine was present and was different from theirs as well: the three deaths in the same house were separate things and were not one thing or in one category even rhetorically. "Us and our shadows," Lila had said once, daringly. Daddy has said, "I'm the daring young man on the flying trapeze—didn't you know?" But he also had said, "The scared old Jew on the dying trapeze . . ."

Nearly everything outside this subject stopped dead—among the six of us. Three people; three deaths. Our deaths preoccupied us and ate our pretensions, ate our jokes, ate the idler aspects of love, the games in our attachments, the cultivated reaches of evasion and of true and false offers to one another; ate us, perhaps, and the love as well. It was not, for me, the failure of eternity in these things and not a fear of nothingness and of the absence of meaning, but, simply, a sense of time having taken this form in my case; and in theirs; and a further sense that too many meanings I had been offered or taught were empty of a sense of time—that one waited for time to correct them but that that was enough. We could only be felt in terms of moments and differences.

One had to understand in a new way—and patiently—that these things did not stop except in death. Or in mad made-up dreamer's obstinacy (as a way of being respectable). Or as trauma.

They existed in a for-a-while-perpetual and flowingishly renewed way, barely renewed, in an animal chamber of complex and motion-filled feeling, a reality of time and of blood—blood-relationship even if we were not related by blood—but blood was a kind of forbidden, private reality of time—and the thing of bad luck was a sense of safety having gone away in the general rainstorm of a massacre. We were, of course, being massacred.

But as Mom pointed out, "Other people have it worse." The massacre was quicker, harsher, more obdurate.

But the reality of momentary escape—or change—flowed in me and in the moments around me at home and in my dreams and would flow still more clearly if I went away to school. The project which made a kind of very shaky blessing of time was to go on without despair . . . I *think* that's what the project was. Maybe it was to stay sane. Or to be afraid of Dad and Mom. How do you know? Our neighbors and teachers—and Nonie's jealousy—voted to approve of what I did as a decency—not the only decency, and not common; but the only one of its kind that was in my power then. It was in what I did; it was my education; it was responsible for what I became.

What I could bring myself to do, what I could bear to do was always physically limited. I did what I did for the sake of the future. But my faith was limited. I never once cleaned Dad when he stained himself. I never once kissed him nobly—I mean, forgetting all proper limits. What I did was faulty and a little sad and egoish and stubborn; what I did was widely admired, though. So, what Lila meant when she talked about it the way she did was: if people commented on our not being sad all the time or on my being an unusually good or generous son or smart kid who was not entirely self-absorbed, she would say, "I keep you honest."

She was a little like the voice of death always at my back. Not metaphorically. Actually.

She'd get sad, though, and she would say, "It's all too much . . . We've gotten too peculiar, you and I . . . and *that one in the other room* . . ." S.L. "Aren't you embarrassed anymore?" she asked me.

"Naw," I said. "It's a real mess."

She stared at me—finally, she laughed, I'd been trying to be comic in a movie-star way. I laughed stupidly, almost happily—perhaps photogenically.

"You're the real mess," she said as she sobered up. "Speak up when you talk . . . If you're saying something, say it so people can hear you. I can't always hear you: I took a pill tonight. I don't blame you for what's happened even if some people think you are a jinx. You think I want YOU to save me? The skeletons are, none of them, in the closet—you think we have a curse on us? I don't want to blame anyone. But, tell me, why are you smiling?"

I intoned, "And you have a hangnail and you need to have your hair washed . . . And you loathe the woe there is in being human."

"I'm human—I was always too human, if you ask me," she said, thinking about it. She became a wearily sincere self—a the-lies-are-done self. "Don't stare at me," she said. "I can do without young eyes looking at me at this time of night."

But, often, truth is loose and is slinking in our house and in the air of a real moment, it might, if you're not being hysterical, strike you as being a form of beauty.

Beauty

Beauty comes in at the window in the breeze and moves among the pieces of our furniture—and not in a simple way stirs Daddy's hair.

"We keep on trying," Lila said. "But maybe it would be better to give up." And she laughed.

"We only more or less keep trying," I said.

"You have an interesting face," she said. I.e., that was an interesting point in her view.

"Visible thought is interesting." Perhaps thoughtlight fills the eyes and rearranges the lips and determines the postures of the neck.

"People, how do you judge them?"

"Me?"

"Well, you're getting older—it's not so hard to talk to you."

What has lured us here? Why do we say yes to going on?

I had a Cousin Trish who was one of the people who loved Nonie back then. Cousin Trish with her terrific legs and her horsy but affecting face, and her extraordinary body—I saw her mostly naked once when she was asleep and all her clothes had become twisted on her long body—she kind of represented health to me.

The truth slinks into me and blows in and out of my breath—and of hers.

"You're not to blame yourself . . ." Trish said.

"But things are REALLY BAD . . ."

"It's okay. It doesn't show on your face."

"Yes it does," I said.

"You're brave," she said.

"Fuck it: I don't know what else to be," I said.

"Do you blame anyone? Do you blame God—the way Dostoyevsky does?" she asked.

She was really good-looking . . . in a literary way.

"Sure," I said. "I have nothing to do with God anymore. It's just us now . . . you, me, Mom, Dad, the neighbors, U. City—you know?"

"No . . . You're really a strange person . . . But sometimes you're A-one, right? Right." Then she kissed me and walked off; her body sort of suddenly and sexually moored, anchored to sexuality; she walked off, ending the conversation. Maybe too impressed . . . Maybe too sickened . . . What's the difference? I'd done it wrong, though, if what I'd wanted was to have her stick around longer and talk to me. But I wasn't real to her. I was out-of-bounds.

Lila, ill with cancer—it started the year S.L. died—said to me, "Listen, Wiley, don't tell me if *you're* upset, okay—is it all right with you? Pretend I did the right thing, all the time, all right? Will you do that for me?"

"Sure. All right." I was thirteen-going-on-fourteen then.

The months and hours . . . the thing of life down the drain . . . the sense that other people are better off . . . are better at living . . . are better . . . and this as a grounds of ambition, of lying really, when the defeat and the terms of the defeat are okay to live with, to build on. I am a shattered guy, a shallow boy, a battered person—and furthermore, I am someone who has not been the center of everything that happened. Big deal. Perhaps I might begin to escape now. Maybe I won't make it. Maybe I will always be sad and mostly silent. It is likely I won't live too long. I gave my childhood and youth away. Still, the main thing is not to show how hurt you are and how hard it is for you to go on at this moment. You don't want to be mainly a structure of blame, of accusation—of exhaustion.

To make my mother laugh—an absurd and probably mean ambition (she said this to me)—I said, "Your having cancer is another down among *my* ups and downs. Boy, is it ever that we're not lucky right now."

She stares at me angrily for a long second or two, my mother-by-adoption; and then she laughs—a little—for starters—and she partly accepts it that her cancer eats me, too, and then between breath noises of repressed laughter, she says, "To tell you the truth, I'm ashamed of being sick."

"Oh no . . . That's a good one," I said, laughing helplessly. "You're a sinner, right?"

"Yes," she said.

That time, too, no one died. The family, in its ashes, stirred itself and rose and was reconstituted as itself yet one more time for another year. The filthy sweetness of an aging face beginning to give up—making ready to die, Jesus, shit, Christ on a crutch—my mother, by adoption, in a nightmare of caring, said, "Family sickness aside, Wiley, on the whole, do all your dreams come true?"

She thought I was an able person, you see. She thought so by then because I'd lived "and stayed out of the loony bin. How do you do it?" Momma asked in scandalous intimacy. She was on morphine and she was pretty strange.

"I don't know," I said.

"I think the ghost of your real mother takes care of you . . . God knows you're not smart enough to come in out of the rain on your own."

The Germans Invade Poland: 1939

The sounds of city noises, trolleys and trucks, became wartime noises. By the time Nonie went to Carolina, I had a head filled with images of horsemen charging tanks in mist-flecked, raw-earthed farmfields and dive-bombers coming out of daytime glare—images of parachutists and spies and of the pinkish-red firing of guns (this was before smokeless powder). Life and death is unchambered, and there is a steady bleating, *bleeding*, a reality of emergency and of ultimate danger at the point of battle and then everywhere. The ultimate overthrow of everything, an ultimacy loose, brutal, and seemingly final—the sole certainty was of new meaning.

Momma said all the deaths made one death seem silly—even if it was your own.

She said as the country started to mobilize, *You have to be selfish if you're a civilian and you want to die with a little decency* . . .

It was *all the death* that changed everything, that made a heat like summer heat, a climate, a form of fire, a summer, a bonfire of murder, a furnace—butcheries and terror, willful terrorization, grimly exultant victories . . .

The infliction of deaths, exultantly, and exultant speeches of threat every day, even in daylight. A black-and-white world was tangibly near us, everything stained by headlines and photographs and newsprint: the rain of events, the reign of war.

Sometimes it seems in the inglorious holiday of this that one has black-and-white blood. And it *is* the heroes versus *The-Stay-at-Homes*. One's heretofore familiar world erupted into urgent unfamiliarity, partly that of a democratic mobilization and the onset through that of undemocratic procedures in the creeping autocracy of emergency.

The permitted deaths of soldiers and the universe of sorrow and the mobilization of ordinary life emptied the world and set women and children free in an odd way, almost impermissibly . . . even so . . . *odd* wartime world. The astounding destruction.

In the Middle West, where we were, a sort of rubble of parenthetically local wartime hours was created in which women and old men and the young wandered alone and unwatched like so many Tarzans in the story. We lived in a different scale of things, so many men were absent. We lived in a hideous-lovely and immoral safety, a parenthesis as I said, unclean, reckless, walled in real time in some obviously dreadful way. It seemed all right as such things went, as nightmares went (at that time)—but what choice did one have? Exalted and practical *local* immorality and thoughts of a universe of carnage (and of grief) and a *reckless* and clumsy and very clearly imperfect good were ranged against wickedness of an unknown dimension and the obvious overturning of everything: a very widespread clear-sightedness was in evidence in everyone in relation to these matters—it was a smoky and collapsing landscape of a *widespread* realism of attitudes, the *reign* of an imprisoning and strange freedom based on the absence of men and the consequent skewing of things. The styles and fates of *the grown-ups* involved reckless and indulgent and often fatal disciplines: death in wartime is a species matter, coarse and constant and a generally recognized presence of awful glory, the pulse of *genius*—it was as if nearly everyone everywhere was in one army or another of those who were dying, artists in that sense—would-be artists, counterfeit artists—*geniuses* . . .

The more successful (more assiduous) death-givers, the blasting, body-tearing, teeth-exploding *joke* of it, Momma said, "I can't think about this war . . . Well, I don't want to be turned into a crazy woman . . . Still, I am so anti-Nazi I can't see straight . . . But I'll tell you, I'd be a pacifist if I knew how." Daddy said he hated the war and was in favor of the Nazis killing us all.

Lila said, "That's a very hard joke to take, S.L."

"I can't help that," Dad said.

The War Further Considered: 1940 The Fall of France, 1941 Pearl Harbor

Even in 1942, *the public-opinion polls* (they were called that then) said that most people did not want an active war. The vast movielike cancellation and rearrangement of everything and the sort of crudely farcical and yet earnest and expensive hurtling into purpose—and, lo, all the speeches, so rhetorically resonant—at least they sounded that way to me when I was ten and eleven years old—led to no unanimity. Nothing was simple then, either. Things are simple because of short sentences, not because of anything in life. The, oh, call it human nature, prostitution, drugs, theft, drunkenness—the wildness of wartime: *No one wants an army camp next door to them . . . not if it's a nice place you live in, Wiley*—that was only a widespread sentiment (it was thought), of ruthlessness, when it first came into existence, came into existence mostly journalistically, some reporters said, mostly among slackers and officers of back-up operations. The real fighting was different from that, they said, had more blundering and accident in it than ruthlessness.

That wasn't quite true either, though. Some sort of wartime spirit came into existence in a variety of tones and manifestations, a strange nudity of human purpose—nationwide—without unanimity.

To govern: to exhort, to tease and allure and bully and persuade: and to lie: one lived in this infinite rearrangement, in the propagandized steeliness of purpose which splintered into individual purposes. One lived at the edge of that steeliness of purpose in action—mistaken generals and *Glory*, wartime money, and various kinds of confusion, *Democracy is on the march*, and the odd true thing of death-and-freedom. The *lies* were clearly lies, and yet everything WAS part of an issue of individual, and national, life-and-death. Everything was changed and serious—serious in the way of life and death—and swallowed up in the thing of it being true that such issues of cultural survival were everywhere and that one's hours were fields of such issues in whatever direction you looked. This was an awful lot of meaning to endure. Not everyone endured it. A lot of wartime was unendurably moving. A lot was endurably moving. A lot was awful and made you hysterical. I was an adolescent then.

One's illicit uncensored private responses to war stuff was maybe a wistful and vicarious viciousness or a heroic unvicarious viciousness. Or one had a wistful steeliness of vicious purpose. Or was a secret peacemonger. Or doubted *The Allies* would win. Or one had an innocence, after all, of a steeliness of vicious purpose, mostly, or off and on, between periods of personal collapse, as part of the curiously enlarged and far-from-unanimous communal consciousness of the community's patriotic aims of a-blatantly-criminal-order-nobly-spoken-of—in a way—and devoted to death and mayhem hardly ever realistically sought with any precision; and this included your own death . . . in a training accident, say, or in combat under a battlefield commander of little merit, or from a bombing run by the others who did not even see you, or a child unregarded in the uproar while you were still a child, or as a Jew later if *The Others* won . . . Well, this far-from-single-souled public consciousness was at times a mass staring at outcomes—at meanings considered in the way of outcomes—and this drafted or coopted one in strange ways, as if in a strange dance to a music inside people's heads and drawn from the more than slightly mad words of wartime urgings and wartime reportings and wartime pathos—an infinity of pathetic bits—until one's spiritual and physical enlistment in the mighty consciousness, such as it was, was part of one's life, of one's very appearance—a wartime adolescent . . . Maybe it was merely a mass membership and loss of self in the meaning available in the *mighty* conflagration which involved so many people, so many bodies, so many souls. But one's private stuff, knowledges and third-and-first-person sense of things, the meat and the shadow, the hallucinations and the gifts of brotherhood (if one had them) had a curiously clear reality as part of their unusual and not entirely changed unclear reality in the main—one has a mathematical nature now; one is a recruit, a member of a faction; the numbers line up for democracy; one votes and votes cipherously and individually.

I read in the paper or heard on the radio more than once that the soldier votes with his blood. Blood and noise, confusion, and a self-erasure not only before death but in the beginning stages of a martial engagement: the way one is a number, a cipher . . . *a piece of cannon fodder* . . . *A citizen*—but only in a special sense: the mathematical citizen and the democratically minor and statistically tiny bit of cannon fodder that one is, that self *keeps the homefires burning* as one's share of the clumsy vastness of the democratic war effort, the democratic effort to make war; one helps as much as one can to preserve and increase the velocity of the national motions toward apocalypse, *another world—win-or-die.*

And one forgets—and has moments in which one *cheats-on-battle-and-lives-on-slyly.* With moments of independence of all of it. One's morale, everyone's *morale,* war nerves, war nerve, the courageous bullying of one's war nerve, one's gambling on this or that public attitude and this or that private one, that stuff goes up and down. I'll become a guerilla fighter. If I get sent to a camp, I'll laugh and work hard in the march to the camp. Maybe what seems strong will, in battle, prove to be weak-nerved, *hysterical,* physically and psychologically . . . if one sees battle. One was tormented by the torture or was tormented by being untormented—shallow, childish, whatever . . . among the killers. In a way, individuality in regard to mass actions is emphasized in the historic moment hereabouts and elsewhere—heroes are pointed out; slackers are named; commanders are appointed—and so on. It is an *absolute* historical moment, since so much death was involved. That is to say, it was a moment that was absolute in biological ways, although it was not absolute in meaning.

It had meaning in terms of one team and its nature over another team of a different nature and it had a meaning of lesser crimes against greater ones; but those are real, not absolute meanings. It was dreamlike it was so almost absolute at times or could be taken as that. And the displacement of meaning onto general issues of victory and *freedom* and onto less general issues but still quite general ones of suffering and dismay and chagrin of *history* replaced all other meanings for some people and supported certain meanings and attacked others. People kept their own counsel then and held off, or held back, if they preferred meanings of a different sort. The weak, huge forcefulness (and lies)—perhaps, relatively, a necessity once a certain sort of challenge is offered—do you know?—seemed to be a test of *absolutes*, as expensive and final as any believer could wish. What other true test of absolutes is there? What is the purpose of absolutes except to lead to this form of proof? Perhaps one can't live without some absolutes, which is to say, illogically in absolute terms, but logically if you grant the idea of some absolutes; and then, since one is using untrue and illogical systems, and most other people are too, it is semi-inevitable the world will go out of kilter. And this choking and burning of itself, our doing this, our obliterating great parts of what we are as a species, moves toward an ashen balance, a postwar awakening, simplified and a bit desperate—it seemed like that, too, when one was, a little blankly, in the midst of it.

Mobilization, Then War

A peacetime army of a hundred thousand men became an array of a million men; and then one of two million men—two million actual men, ta-ra, ta-ra . . . *two million* men, dressed alike, similarly jumpy, and indisputably only momentarily alive in this way, and morally at sea, smiling a lot, most of them, when on leave. Some didn't smile. Ah God, the universal swagger. Which wasn't universal. The slouch, the amble, the guys who slunk around . . . And the outbursts of tears. And the dry-eyed stuff. The sentiment, as I said, of *ruthlessness* . . . The worldwide school of ruthlessness, ruthless cleverness, of ruthless scandal. Actually, often, quite disciplined, oxymoronically—at least in the more successful armies: disciplined limitlessness . . . A calculated and not quite completely messy bloodthirstiness.

Around me, where I was, a jalopy rural society was transfixed into grieving self-surrender inseparable from self-importance and fear. You wrung the suburbs and the farming counties dry and the slums and the expensive parts of the city in order to produce army camps which were small cities really—mostly male cities—and the two million men became I don't know how many finally—four, five, six, seven million men?—until all cities and all empty places everywhere (but in the end, proportionately, only a limited number of neighborhoods) had a different kind of reality, a different social reality, a different order of peace and of violence.

Existences were inundated with new events, military events, often, and with men in a newish form—compared to a few years before—khaki larvae, soldiers, new inhabitants—a new history, a new brutality, new habits, new thoughts, new postures, new affections and sorts of actions, government money splashing noisily in the streets while the living bodies, the thing of being young, the crime everywhere—people robbing the soldiers; the soldiers robbing people; girls hurting soldiers; soldiers hurting girls—the crimes were not all of the same order of criminality. A kind of universality as in a Golden Age or in a Golden Age reversed and become a Brazen Era of Blood, Heroism, and Death, no conversation was without reference to the war. Most decisions were unwise; what a stream of unwise decisions there were. Nothing was empty of content or was outside the context of cultural measurement and rivalry—the bloodbath of cultural measurements and rivalries was terrifying but exhilarating—nothing was entirely well run or well done. Everything was last-ditch, desperate, but bloodiedly interesting. And then the *context* of blundering, the slow music of a national consciousness of national and international *blundering*, of things unthought and badly thought, the human species and its pronouncedly evident trait of *blundering* became a sense of inevitable and unavoidable large-scale blundering, unimaginably worse than peacetime horrors, but, somehow, the major thing, the real determinant of national and cultural rivalrous mutual and heavily bloodied measurements.

The side that blunders least wins. And: *Blunder for blunder, in the end, it is individual morale surviving the blunders and keeping on that decides battles . . .*

And so on.

The journalistically interpreted purposeful murders—the murder on such a mathematically gross plane—the *blundering* deaths that yet mattered, *that yet are piled on the scales of victory and make the difference between whether our children live in freedom or slavery* . . . and I being a child . . . less so each year . . . this meant that I could avoid seeing that people died with the taste of chagrin in their mouths. The blunders and the excitement and the need to fight-and-win was hardly a joke but what could you do about it in the face of the more and more national, more and more *popular* chagrin and vague, hysterically general censorship of *what was too hard to face* and realistic ruthlessness and resigned ruthlessness of approaching victory.

One's complicity in this is, brutally, entire, all at once, and savage. Over and over, the invented thing—perhaps a true thing—was that it was beyond choice—and, in truth, to be beyond choice means one and everyone can be morally absent, morally obtuse, morally absent-minded. Or stylishly and patriotically ruthless. Or ideologically ruthless. For some people, it came to seem that all ruthlessness was suspect. Was paradoxically semi-absolute and therefore, false, and therefore, hysterical. Hallucinatory. One became more ruthlessly ruthless, hoping to be it, to prove one was it, was ruthless. To be in combat—and to be observed so that if one chose to follow out an act of cowardice—bailing out of an airplane or climbing out of range of the dogfight or turning around and barrelling toward home on the full rpm's of the engine, burning out the cylinders—one was then shamed publicly or court-martialled; or officers covered up for you, it depended . . . It depended on which way the issue of ruthlessness bent inside the common ruthlessness of a male group. The measurements of focussed and of successful wills as a nationalistic male thing—and as a rare thing—seemed to be the social anatomy of successful communities. The nation . . . the ethnic group . . . and the politics of a successful war . . . and a kind of secret moral code, not so secret actually, but never publicly worded to any great extent, came into existence in relation to death and the expenditure of time, money, and lives. To have spent so much money, to have come to believe in the national danger—some of which belief was true—to take on the absolute expense of the community and of lives as a serious matter; and then to weasel while urging others on—much of the war writing after 1943 was concerned with a war behind the other war, with this other war between those who inveighed against cowardice and those who governed the movements and weapons of men who had to display bravery and perhaps die—the months of the movement toward *victory* were littered with revelations, exposures, unmaskings of *wartime* identities; more and more generals were named as violent jerks.

So, the slow discretionary processes of evolving personal and national views of what a hero was, what a hero really was, and who had really behaved well and who really had not dwindled into a kind of antiheroic attitude. People praised the war, sort of, but no heroes emerged; I mean none were created. It was quite strange. It may have been ethnic rivalry and then tact that led to that, or social rivalry. Officers had not behaved so well (or so badly), and the men likewise, that any group could claim enough say to name its heroes or to judge who was heroic and who was not. One's views of how much unity we had had actually, or how little, finally changed and were codified. The stage lighting changed; and we were not underdogs or Hamlets—or interested in heroes. The chagrin went away. It came again. We were figures of fate in the world; and we were ciphers and the rest of it. The swollenly semi-adroit military services and militarily productive civilian home front were partners in a silence inside a plenitude, a multitude of stories, all of them mistold. The ideological uproar, the right wing, the left (the right wing hadn't done well in wartime), the sympathizers with this and that, the populists, the old-line upper-echelon government families (such as they were) drowned everything in disagreement. Wartime unions had threatened to strike and to hell with the war. Men had deserted. Generals had been drunk. The fear of personal and of national defeat exacted one thing from the war: no defeat for anyone in America, almost, for a while—perhaps a long while as such things go. Perhaps the most amazing amnesty and the most prolonged and mostly wordless and untheoretical exploration of various actualities of semi-actual Utopias—mental health and money and never being laughed at and so on—began here. Of course, it was merely human.

Songs and editorials pictured us in one or another simplified fashion without much, if any, reference to real things. Our automobiles and our houses, our movies, our psychological claims, our high art, our low art, our hopes became more and more fanciful—more and more like things in children's books. The wartime *simplicities* became peacetime simplicities of an attempted sort, our reparations, our trophies: our nearly universal attribution, politically, of heroism: an extraordinarily disingenuous sentimentality. People did not crack up much. The Utopian thing spread and spread; and then people started cracking up, sort of on a national scale.

But, during the war, people of all sorts cracked up in the pressure of the so-called *absolute* situation—the simplifications (supposedly) of life-and-death stuff—cracked up in the pressure of knowing it was not *absolute*, it was personal, death was, death and the shaming and irreversible consequentiality of actions, of one's life, of one's consciousness in the months of violence, during a violent war, biologically, humanly at the edge of the absolute extinction of some and even all of us.

Surrender protected nothing. *Words fail us.* One's life was already different. After all, what continuity of sense there was had rested on what a writer describing an earlier war had called *a hedge of men bloodily renewed every day.* The reasons and the degree to which men were willing, had to be *willing* to be murdered, to be chewed and pierced and picked and torn apart and ground up—that and the *brilliance* and *honesty* of the weapons, such as it was, those as the determining things, or as things of great importance, if one cared about the war, that ended with the war—as a kind of death of unsentimental realism and as the birth of sentimental brutality and rebelliousness and new definitions of normalcy—as universal—in contradistinction to the actual meaning of the term before the war.

S.L. said, "Shame makes men crooks." It was very strange the crooked ruthlessness and seeming directness of the war, and then the Utopian and avid crooked ruthlessness of will and fantasy, of hallucination, as victory neared.

It was very strange during the war, the events, the absolutions. It was as if the bloodied and essential figures in dreams of adventure and combat were living as images within a terrible rate of change and with a good deal of waiting around and with daily falsity.

But in my dreams, the long gliding crash of an airplane—a long expiring under a bush of a wounded guy in a woods, in battle—the slow appearance of a giant (in the dream) rising as slowly as a sun on a dream horizon to decide the battle: this stuff became for me the curse of the *known* human absolute, the force it takes to shut up all the others once and for all.

And, in my dreams, the secret force had to do with a kitchen in a bombed house where soldiers rape a woman who looks like a movie star and who betrays them to a warplane that then strafes the house . . .

It was too much logic illogically deployed . . . The wrong premises, the wrong sense of reality—my dreams, I mean, and some of the lies about the war.

The scenes disappear when it begins to be light.

*

I named the issue *Subjection to Others' Wills.*

My dad, S.L., laughed at me for my childhood patriotism. He became a pacifist in *The First World War* in the course of fighting in three famous and tremendous battles—all of them unnecessary, he learned *afterwards,* he said. *I know what this stuff is all about . . . You don't know . . . Well, don't be cannon fodder,* he said.

War: we, we Americans, I was, *we were* OPPOSED to careless, greedy, merciless, *foreign* wills. To their statistically massive indifference toward us—impertinence really, and on a very grand scale at that—to our lives, our tempers, our deaths, my death and yours and the deaths of others.

And the massed warplanes overhead on their flyovers and the barges of war matériel on the Mississippi and the weird density of the steel used in armaments were part of one's youth and of one's adolescence. One could measure one's growth against the length and weight of a rifle, for instance. The public displays of weaponry, and the military parades, the thrilling element in the sight of so many men marching, the peculiar and dirty effectuality suggested that it was peculiar and dirty, war was, the majesty and reality of war. The thing, over and over, of being of the lineage of God in order to bear and explain wartime reality, the terms of national and of personal self-worship: this was called *morale.*

But *Fate* concerned with one's self . . . a single dark, or half-lit, service of one's sense of this, of it—and who was there who could have an impersonal sense of fate, who was there who was alive and not alive to think in the way shadows seem to do, convincingly, as if thought was ever not enclosed in flesh-and-blood?

Fate, I was saying, took on a nationally *noble* unselfishness—we all almost loved any number of things more than life itself; or we felt like that for a while when we were led to do so, when we were inspired to do so.

I mean ideals in that sense were present although not always very well worded. But *ideal* meant more-absolute-than-death. Among human absolutes, it meant something even more absolute than death and defeat, I would say.

But, still, there was something almost like a vacuum of selfish will—a nation of women loving its male leaders or its leader, loving him best—and into that vacuum rushed the pressure of Providence and of a sense of Providence, a Presence of Fate, of fatedness, that seemed an echo of an angelic service: meaning, meanings everywhere, purpose and rank, a vicious grayness, or steel, of human service, not fictional at all.

The unreasonable became *reasonable* purpose, in which the vagueness of some conclusions in ordinary life, as when you say, *Are you* REALLY *hurt?* and even to a dead body, *Are you* REALLY *dead, S.L.?*, that vagueness is more and more identified as madness, as a symptom of your breaking down.

War strips away sleep and ordinary wakefulness and becomes a specialized wakefulness among the crotches and butts, the eyes and haircuts, the cripplings and the deaths, not like any other wakefulness one will ever know.

SAINT NONIE

or The War

Forestville
or The History of Envy

Not able to bear our life at home, or for some other reason (or for a number of reasons), Nonie, in 1941, went to live in Forestville, in North Carolina, to live with S.L.'s sister, our Aunt Casey, my aunt by adoption, of course, and with S.L.'s brother-in-law and their three mostly grown children. One said of them that they were quite well off, or that they were "rich people—Southerners"—that is to say, they were not as rich as rich Northerners back then, in those days.

Not long after Nonie left, S.L. and Lila having had a serious fight and living apart, S.L. mostly in the hospital—and Lila's probably taking a lover and having some kind of period of nuttiness—Lila arranged to have me live with her oldest brother, Simon, in Oklahoma City, Oklahoma, a much larger place than Forestville—Forestville had only 44,000 people, 59,000 in the depth (or height: Lila said both things) of wartime when it had a staging depot, an army warehouse, and a large air force base, none of which were in full existence when Nonie went off, or was sent off, husband-hunting, or whatever it was—I mean, a child isn't told everything, or, sometimes, anything; and much of the life at home, and, certainly, a lot of Nonie's life was kept quiet or private or hidden and secret from me, the child, and from the child's opinions of Nonie and her, our, parents, and of the things she did.

It was a form of truce: we had the same parents but our tie to each other was officially unacknowledged. This negotiation did not mean that she and I sat down at the dining-room table, in the shadows or the light there, with pads and pencils, to talk.

Or even that we walked along the street and talked or sat on the couch holding hands and talked: the negotiations were among the grown-ups, on telephones and visits; it was a family compromise; and Lila asked me my opinion of it, if I agreed; I don't really know how much choice I had.

Oklahoma was an unlikely place for me considering the difficulty the local—and very sophisticated—school system already had with me as a student, with me, my grades, my answers in class (I was usually asked not to speak in class as an act of kindness to the teacher) and that there was a local movement, well, three of them, on the part of local Protestants and Catholics separately and enlightened Jews to send me to private school either in Missouri or far away.

Uncle Simon was someone who did not speak to Grandma and who hadn't visited anyone in the family for twenty years at that time; and he knew least about me; and was willing to pay Lila, or to give her a subsidy, of fifteen dollars a week if I went to live with him.

Lila also had the money sent by my real father.

After a few months of my being away, Lila wanted me to come back, partly because she wanted to return to living with S.L. and he would not live with her if I was not there; he would not come out of the hospital. S.L. said Lila was not *nice* and was awful to live with and that she insisted on winning too many fights in such dirty ways that he could not bear it.

I returned to live with her and S.L. who rejoined her after I returned; and I envied Nonie in Forestville, living with rich people—rich enough—especially after Lila, mentally kind of off-balance, began to be physically ill, and then in 1943, was diagnosed as having breast cancer and was operated on.

It is to be understood that Nonie in (North) Carolina is a story I was excluded from—although I will try to tell it—even though, perhaps, for a number of reasons (again), I am excluded from it still; but I am interested in the problems of sympathy and judgment and of morality in actual circumstances. And of the reality of good and evil—in us, in me . . . in everyone, perhaps.

That is, how does comparative sinlessness or bystanderishness or limited involvement, limited in some way, work in terms of a referee, a storyteller, a personal or an impersonal judgment?

Law, of course, implies relativism. One would not need law or ritual, study or theory, theological or scientific, without it. Absolutism, of the sort I saw in governments and in people—and more than occasionally in myself—seemed more a principle of argument and of organization of one's energies, one's allegiances, as in Lila's saying, for instance, of

Simon, *He's a perfect man to be a father*—he was childless—although she also said, *He's a pain in the neck but so are you: the two of you ought to get along like a house on fire.*

I told Simon once—I only spoke seriously to anyone as a test of whether they would accept me or not; this was in the middle of the night when I'd screamed in my sleep; Simon didn't accept this part of me; and, after this, if I yelled, his wife, my Aunt Elizabeth—*big dumb Elizabeth*, Lila, slightly mad off and on, had begun to call her—came to my room.

I was saying I told Simon once that chaos in the world was possible only among people who had a number of absolute notions including a final absolute notion, that relativism engendered law after law, little ones and bigger ones and still bigger ones. And that permissions and licensings, absolutions were always more formal, more practical among relativists than among absolutists and monomaniacs and Single-Idea semi-Führers who *always* practiced politics differently. Uncle Simon owned three hardware stores but his real interests lay in politics; he was the sidekick-adviser of the senior senator from Oklahoma, a considerable figure nationally at that time, a florid, brilliant man, stylistically current still, who had a number of sidekicks. Simon, who had been a very good amateur prizefighter—a bantamweight when he was young—was the local political-public-moralist-go-between-compromiser, more and more a lesser figure to the senator as he, the senator, became famous and an institution.

But real politics was the overt or hidden notion that politics came first and was like the stage—the proscenium—or was like *the basket* that held all the rest . . . Or held it first.

And, therefore, a certain chaos or collapse of meaning, a certain weight, or momentum, of evil was impossible—only another order of evil was possible, a resigned untotality or political level of it was possible, although it must be admitted that language faltered since it is one of the privileges of the absolute that one who believes it can believe in the utter sincerity and accuracy of his or her arguments and purposes: a divine licensing is always dangerous but so is a secular licensing if it is without limits and public examination.

In fact, and in reason, any absolute position can be governed here on earth only by having it cease to be absolute—as among a committee (a comity) of nations or as in public opinion.

The self-importance, the self-assurance, to be derived from absolutes is addictive, intoxicating, blinding—a form of inebriation—of dreaming violently while awake. I believed the Germans had killed Jews and would kill more, too many, perhaps all, partly in the blind licensing of not being part of a community of equals and partly in the dark logic, or willfulness, of an absolute seeking to act itself out, to embody itself as terrestrial fact, which it can never do.

The absolute hierarchy of (supposed) meanings forms a pyramid that dances or a whirling and evolving fir tree that absolutists say is stillness itself.

I mean the one-idea people can never name the idea—it is always a congery of ideas, a political problem in which politics are banished, supposedly, but they always exist; so, the most absolute person rules—that *is* the rule—and, so, there are no moral limits, not by terrestrial terms.

And, so, I dreamed of death dealers even more than of death, and of the madness of purported logics of the third order but claiming to be final. Only Lila had ever listened to me at all, I said to Simon in the middle of the night, and she always laughed at me but said people could be very bad indeed, and that, indeed, there was a tendency to solitude and dreamlike violence, to forms of moral chaos (in which the hope and purpose is always the birth on earth of the actuality of one-idea madly); and so, she and I, in a small way, had brought over German and then European refugees, mostly but not always Jews.

Simon, in Oklahoma, through the senator, had helped.

But Simon said he didn't believe in atrocity stories. He'd been fooled in the First World War by all sorts of atrocity tales about plucky little Belgium and the like, but no more. The German Jews he'd met he didn't like.

I lied and said I'd heard from soldiers who'd dated Nonie that German submarines radioed tales of slaughter and massacre.

"Why is it so important to you?"

"Because I can't sleep!" I said.

It was the free-will, or complicity, element.

He said, "You're a regular little dictator yourself." He said it, not exactly crossly, but dismissively.

He would not listen.

I—I became somewhat fond of him anyway. I gave in and more or less obeyed him and so on but I minded doing it: it hurt, quite a lot.

I am trying to explain my unomniscient curiosity—as well as my dislike even for omissive omniscience in a narrator: it is so immediately a lie, a cruelty to the earth itself and to meaning and to the characters of the story.

The attack on absolutism is, however, to an absolutist, who can, after all, only believe in one truth, that of a lying absolutist—that is, I believe this is a one-way crime . . . Oh, not entirely one-way but, still, mostly a crime engendered by the very nature of acting on, as a premise, any final absolute—even that, supposedly, of art.

But art, even mathematics, although mathematics does not seem so, becomes art only when the variations in the attempts to control the material become, even in the embodiment, as in architecture or music or prose, of geometries, of geometrical notions, practical and human, humane and variable, and when they succeed in embodying the *humane*, as well as the demoniac, real.

Well, as Lila said—often—*Nothing ventured, nothing gained* . . . And the story of envy in a life interests me.

Family History

I know very little of the family history . . . Of any of the family histories, on either side, Lila's, S.L.'s, my real mother's, my real father's. But I made notes of what was said: it was interesting, the trends and fashions of snobbery. Anyway, it is possible that the men of the Silenowicz line, S.L. and his father and brothers, were Frankists, Christianized Jews of a sect that believe in promiscuity and in keeping none of the Jewish laws except in a perverse form: this was in hope of forcing the coming of the Messiah. And, also, it is a comment on the disparity between *The Law* and the actual world, the idea of truth and the reality of wandering minds, in shul and out of it, and of heatedly well-made or heatedly ill-made bodies. This has to do with the palpable torment to the will of actually glimpsed and always, eternally, lost absolutes.

Frankists tend to do well economically and to form rather tightly knit families.

The family came to this country from Lithuania—perhaps. I know that S.L.'s older brother, Raymond, the oldest child in that family, went mad on the battlefield of Château-Thierry in the First World War. Dad told me: *Dead bodies had piled up on him and blood went drip-drip: it dripped in his face and he went mad . . . The Marines retook the position and there he was . . . But it was too late . . . God has some sense of humor: the finest white man I ever knew, my big brother, the poor bastard was as crazy as a loon . . .*

Dad said that he and his big brother, growing up in North Carolina, reasonably *well-to-do,* had been *good-looking* and *a little wild*, and *like fools had enlisted* and they had wanted to see active service.

Mom said—but she was talking about Aunt Casey in Forestville (this was after Mom became ill and was, herself, a violent and violently jealous person, openly so) as *a jealous person*—that *Ray and S.L. were close—very, very,* VERY *close as brothers: you know how it is in a little town . . . When Ray came back crazy, S.L. ran away from them all: he was never someone liked to face things; he was the sensitive type—he wasn't the sensitive type, but he was sensitive all the same when it came to sickness: he'd nurse you like he was part nun—or he'd run away . . . The brother—what a gorgeous guy—and to end like that, just like a little child, eating peanut brittle all day long . . . Remember this, Wiley, every family has its tragedy . . . Nobody understood S.L.: well, I'll tell you what S.L. was like, he was like someone who had a brother who'd ended like that, a brother hurt that bad in the war . . . Monkey see, monkey do . . .*

I think she meant he hated tragedy, the ordinary kind and the wartime kind, that he was wounded by it—wounded and shaky.

Mom said: *It hurt S.L. and drove him away when his mother wouldn't make him his brother's keeper . . . The executor . . . She gave that little plum to Casey who got enough income from it to be financially independent irregardless; the mother was a very difficult person—she didn't like men; she didn't trust them. Well, life is hard: what can you do? Some mothers favor daughters; some favor sons. Not everyone says they're sorry. Casey and her mother was close.*

Then: *Casey never liked me. At every little sign of difficulty between me and S.L., she and that damned screaming hag of a mother wanted me and S.L. to get a divorce. They never got tired of riding* THAT *hobby horse. They had in mind for him someone who took orders from them. Crazy people—absolutely crazy: they threw a fit when we adopted you, as if that was spitting in God's eye. They wouldn't even acknowledge you. We drove all the way to Carolina to show them you. The sight of you would have melted a heart of stone but Casey and her mother refused even to* SEE *you. What do you think that meant? What kind of fetish is it, to be like that about family blood?*

And: *Casey said to me that we had a daughter, what did we need a son for? And why* NOT *get a divorce, why save the marriage by adopting a stranger? Well, when S.L. got sick, she couldn't wait to save Nonie from me. All things being equal, blood is thicker than water, Wileykins. Don't be jealous.*

I WAS jealous. Envious to such an extent that I ached with it.

I also wondered if Momma was a reliable storyteller—a narrator to be trusted. But in life you take the narrators you are given, the voices that are there; or you have to adopt a doctrine or an anti-doctrine, a system, by the use of which, in all its parts, you seem to yourself to be *intelligent*; and you have to give up the real world. If I say it interested me to fail ever to believe Lila quite but that she was one of my favorite authors—and, so, was one of the authors of my being although she was my mother only by adoption—does that make any sense?

Saddened (and despairing), darkened by having to stay at home with Lila in these years when I might have been elsewhere and learned how to be a person, I became, in my mind, almost close to Nonie, first in my mind as I grew taller, since she was my nearest model of such a procedure in nature and in the household, and then with her, with Nonie, when she came home, first to visit, and then, after a serious, and final, fight with Aunt Casey, to live with us again.

Perhaps it was that I was close to her because she was not Lila. And because she and I were children who had a rocky time and who, in the area of feeling and of odd emblems, were weighty-bodied (with sadness and event) and were migratory similarly. So, I could be close to her—if that is what it was that I was to her—without feeling an immanence of solitary grief.

Ah, it's true that I was interested in her, Saint Nonie of *The War*, the daughter of our parents, the daughter of, forgive me, *world events* —my sister by the processes of law.

Nonie When I Grew Taller: 1943

Go ahead, look at her . . .

It is not easy. The figure in my mind stands at a crossing of paths as in a woods.

In real light I am in her room in the apartment; I have just come in from a long walk in Forest Park, *getting some sun*, taking care of myself—a tall, gawky boy with that look.

I don't quite like or trust my sister but I am, in this moment of time, prepared to be a brother-protector (if someone insults her) and I daydream, dream of, and then act out certain *brother-sister* scenarios, realities—but bookish ones or as in Disney full-length cartoons: not clearly, or personally, thought out.

I stand in the doorway half smiling to myself in *a brotherly way* before I settle down on her bed perhaps—she is packing to go back to Casey, to Forestville, after visiting us, Dad and Mom and me. This was during the time Mom was having cobalt treatment. Casey, I know from things Nonie has said, insists on Nonie being a daughter to Lila and a sister to me—remembering my birthdays and the like: "Casey has a lot of rules," Nonie said. See, the mind skates like a room on ice or like a Hans Brinker who is always partly a real flash of mental light moving through subjects cheatingly like light beams that flaringly and silently touch another year, an opinion, a lost dream and return, reflected Einsteinianly from a spaceship or sailing *hither and yon* a bit sarcastically —like Jonathan Swift's floating kingdom-island of Laputa—and one cannot harness it, the mind; one can't make it a healthy and wise horse; it is beaten-up and slavish and sly or it is sly and truly prowly and foxylike or it flicks and is windblown and is a lot of theaters and houses and rooms at once—a thought is a theater, a bit of eyesight, of seeing someone: in the theater of a glance before hurrying on—Gypsyishly—to á dream-laden imagining of her with Casey, *normal,* in a normal life—among rich people, during a war—does that seem strange and incoherent? The coherencies of the mental world begin with self-recognition and self-will in regard to one's discomfort, one's discomfort-in-the-universe. A partial coherency: a discomfort toward her, a wanting-to-be-admired, a wanting the past to be over-and-done-with—an enormous absence of trust toward her, her feelings, her touch—even the odor of her in reality: a jangling, ongoing, genderal music. I start with what I know.

She says, "Mr. Cat-Who-Ate-the-Canary . . . Oh, does that open up your ears? Are you ready to think I'm *interesting* now?"

She's *in good form: she knows how to handle herself*: she is in that mode—I mean her emotions, her hidden quality as she finishes packing . . . *She does a lot of things right* . . . "Are we going to have a little talk? Did you come to say good-bye?"

I blush. I'm a little hot and sweaty saying good-bye to *her,* but I am *socially* (with her) reasonably *cool. Cool* was a term then. But I blush and sweat, *cool* or not; and this makes her laugh very politely in a far-off grown-up hoarse woman-who-has-a-job-and-who-chain-smokes fashion. She "likes" me—thinks I am interesting, to use her phrase (in *The Law of Opposites*), in some new way now that I am grown.

She says, almost intimately, ironically (in incredibly gorgeous grown-up irony), "Don't mind me: I'm just a woman: I don't count—I don't have a husband yet."

She was ruthless in her way, but in a new way; and I am *older* than I was and bigger and almost safe. I am considered to be *attractive* . . . If I mention it again, it is because it came and went, or seemed to me to do that; and it has a different weight, or weightiness, with different people—this thing here, today, with her, is not as it will be with Abe whom I will meet in three months or Daniel whom I will meet in six months or so or as it is with *X* or *Y* at school or with people at any of my jobs, tutoring or working in a shoestore downtown or in the warehouse. A dream come true in real air is wilder than a dream working itself out in your head. It is logical differently in the real sequence of things, in real consequentiality and in coming-and-goingness, if I can say that.

I am, even though I am standing in real air, dimly aware of being made of pipe and lathes in her eyes—her feelings, that is—and having a head almost like a hat with a stuffed bird on it, wings outspread, but this a real bird, smelly, mostly beardless, its chest heaving, its wingspan large—male, I think in her eyes—an albatross: a young male face, boyish.

Dad said at this time—from time to time—*Water, water everywhere—and not a drop to drink*: I don't know how the real words go in "The Rime of the Ancient Mariner." He was ill and becalmed; and an albatross haunted the ill-fated ship . . . Youth, unexamined sexuality as yet—one has glanced at only a page or two.

We are where breath is, where people die—my sister and I are where you are when you are awake; and I think that when you have real space and real time, then perhaps real-world logic is moral no matter how harsh it may seem: to walk across the floor to her or the size and purposes of your voice near *actual sunlight-in-a-window*, the sunlight shifting on the chains and pulleys of the real world; and the smells there, in Nonie's bedroom, mine first surrounding me, and then past or through S.L., the smell of her long, now dyed, now reddish-blond hair, the smells of her cardigan—whatever I said of her before, I am afraid of her illogic or her logic differently now: she has begun to smell to me of the question of what-will-become-of-her; I may have to take care of her when I grow up.

She is partly dressed in that—it is as if her youth has gone into that.

One is aware of her discipline now and of her *interest* in me—perhaps mirroringly—that is real along with her differently brassiered breasts: they are very noticeable; they are pure 1943. Nonie's 'love' (or 'interest') is *realistic*; Nonie's feelings are neatly displayed; her sense of domestic, and proper, theater is much further along than mine; the bits of 'nifty' *ironic* expression on her face and in her lips are truly enviable ribbony highlights of an intelligence-of-the-world that creates a kind of movingly highlit *value* that her powdered and rouged and light-stained and pretty cheeks have.

The *love*—and the no-saying—like the familiarity as knowledge (*ho, ho, ho, I know, know, know*) and not as encyclopedia entries of varieties of affection—her glance—her glances—are so quick that they define the unease, the suspicions we might have of the other's intentions. They flick here and there in machine-gun order, in the new dispensation of her training, and are like cupped hands for me to throw a glance to, or an ironic smile back to, or in; or they are like snapped fingers or like a rubber band snapped at my nose, her glances: they can make me wince —that makes her laugh; as time ticks along; the speed of the abortive dialogue is still that of a dialogue, a peculiarly homegrown *stichomythia*, a thing in Greek plays in olden time, where the exchanges are short and often idiomatic; but it is the short rat-a-tat-ness that defines them; the speeches are bits of a flying moment with all the past contained like bits of ghost-splash of sensations, bits of pictures and of syllables—so that there is no need for a prompter or a book or a continuity expert. Lila often said, *I have to laugh*, meaning something like now when *I have to laugh*, in an aggrieved way.

I am *not* someone no army would ever want to have in it—Nonie, when wanting something from me, has said that of me.

The ribbon-bits of twists of expression of her lips, the slaplike, *loud-voiced* reality of her heartbeat, of her breath, and the feelings in her because of her own business and then those and others that come to exist at-the-sight-of-me—like animals at the doorways of their dens—I guess it is easier for me to *feel* or *suspect* or *sense* (viscerally) that she is cold to me as the predisposing line of the dialogue and not that I am cold toward her first—wary, unloving.

But whether I start it or she does, the issue is that I don't like her very much. This is so now with almost every woman—they are often a bit angry with me. I can only distantly admit what is going on—sexual reality—or economic-and-sexual reality—and the like. A heat, a radiance of *virginity* intervenes. I can have no feelings in me at all—except those that come from the fact of my being in the lee of her life, her age: sexual and economic currents break near her figure—or on it—and I stand, nonplussed by reality (and by my reality) in the shallows sheltered by her life, if not by her.

When I *say* that to myself, not in words but by permitting a sense of that, a music, a dumb show, a bit of a movie, a child's sense of it—of her breasts and behind, her lips, her life and prettiness as buffers between sexual urgency and my existence—that shows on my face: that defines me. I have feelings burning away in me, but turned down low; or, maybe, I back away into thought—as if onto a golf course, an area of ritualized concentration on something. I transfer those feelings; I ascribe those feelings to her; I see myself as innocent.

But not for long. In the space of a heartbeat I am then only as innocent as the reading room of the public library in U. City, as the uninnocent, hardly *innocent* books there. The things I want from her and for her would destroy her as she is if they were to be imposed, whoops, this very second: remorse, charm, concern for others.

I hold back, inwardly and outwardly—I am a theater of almost neutral *innocence* . . . This tempts her: I am *almost* shrewd enough to see that; Mom has told me stuff about this. I am an empty space—I am carefully lifeless: it is as if I have little choice. *Nonie likes to stir still waters, Wiley: she's human* . . .

I fear her too much to be *sensible* or entirely sentimental . . . Or *straightforward* . . . Nonie's *moods*—my *dumb* sister—her fate—in the watery, barely westering Missouri sunlight. But to call it fear is wrong: it is a primal familiarity.

The shifting light and the notion of unalterable law and the human: I prefer alterable law. Nonie has come home briefly from Carolina, having quarrelled with Casey—before I knew Casey, I could not imagine quarrelling with one's money, so to speak; the idea of *quarrels, quarrels everywhere* inside the self and outside it came and went.

As did the idea of *familiarity* as being like the physical sense when, in warm weather, at the end of winter, one sits in the sunlight on grass, or on someone's steps, in front or in back of their house; and the different temperatures and the day are familiarity around the oddity of one's wintered body, time-charged, time-electrified, time-chemicalled.

Stirred blood, the heat, and the recognitions, have a sports element and a sexual component: one's throwing arm becomes limber. The different temperatures of pants and legs inside the pants and feet (sometimes bare) on pavement or on grass and in sunlight.

Now here at home, she has quarrelled with Momma. *The Declaration of Independence* in its various forms tends to be a cry of war. *People are people*, Momma said with a kind of determination to adjust to such a state but with no sign of giving in to it. S.L. said the same words, *People are people*, completely disowned the whole kit and caboodle, the human thing—I mean I had never seen, in real life, such a human mightiness of disgust, a male majesty of abdication, of refusal; he has checked into the Veterans Hospital blaming Nonie and Momma: he saw Nonie rifling Momma's bureau, stealing things: "*She has no use for them!*" Nonie said, flushed but not ashamed. I was standing in my room and saw down the hall and past Dad but I couldn't see what *flashed* or *flared* between the two of them . . . *Nonie won't take a backseat to anyone or to anyone's ideas* . . . Momma, Daddy . . . *She listens to Casey*—now and then . . . Nonie has been able, really a heroine, in her war work: St. Nonie in the war. She has *good* suitcases so that when she travels, she will get a certain kind of treatment.

Nonie is older, more experienced in the world, having lived so far in wartime in this war, Nonie has a theatrical thing, a style of letting her moods buzz and mumble and pop—*formidably*, her feelings come and go. The fluctuations of her softish lips have pebblelike varieties of *hardness* behind them—beanbag-and-pistol lips and eyes, and face: *she's a pistol . . . she's as hot as a pistol* . . . At school, some of the softer-fibered girls scare me and seem almost unreal and to be part of a different order of human being; the homosexual boys and girls, however, don't seem unreal, merely temperamental. Nonie's breath *cackles*—it's a family trait: S.L. had it slightly; and Daniel. I mentioned her dyed reddish-yellow hair: she is a girl of *the free world*, a democratic windblown girl of the era; and her blouse and her bra and its straps and her slightly pudgy, slightly bulgy hips in her pale blue expensive skirt, her really high heels—platform pumps, slingbacks—the pearls and pale beige cardigan she wears—mark her social class. The *peculiarity* of her eye-nests—eyebrows, bone sockets, eyelids, eyelashes and her faintly hectic, well-made-up (or fictional) cheeks and the actualities of her breasts are really her—the true heroine, the saint of her own predicaments, of her stories now: the *who-she-is*—her being as smart and ironic and as tough-and-grown-up as a man her age—well, you have cooler feelings and then time-warmed, hotter, *farmyard* feelings, blood, bloody, mulelike, maybe stupid . . .

But the maybe stupid shrewdness and the quality of both our faces—lovely faces—one male, and briefly, in early adolescence, fragile or ghostly, and the other less amateurishly, less surprised, less helplessly what it is—our moods, almost a mutual flirtatiousness, a distaste—the absurdly straight-postured, rather ugly boy child who is briefly *pretty*, and the young woman, half passing as a girl (democratic windblown girl of *the free world*), her eyes crowded with Nonie-esque stuff, an unveiledness here is a kind of wit of maybe false or artificial *good-fellowship*: I had no words back then for real things. One lives through one's moments without workable captions. Or maps. What I say now, forty-five years later (four and a half decades further on), is that the best map I had came from her at those times when she *put on a show for Casey* or some boy she was seeing, *a show of family feeling, you know what that is, Pisher*—it is a form of perfume or of flowering in order to entice certain feelings.

But I was saying that when she put on a show of that sort, when that theater place was in play, the theatricality would dissolve, perhaps, in her giving me a tennis racquet, a wartime ID bracelet, or the like, things that reminded me of what I *almost* was or could be, a role in a middle-class drawing-room comedy or the like, a momentary costume for the soul.

My parents taught me different things—things from further back and which they thought had lasted or would last, theatrical and domestic elements of traits, attributes, habits, attitudes one ought to manifest and which were part of personal virtue.

Back then I guessed and felt my way along—a halfway transformed animal or a blind beggar-boy in not quite entirely sentimentalized moments.

Vaguely smelly, openmouthed *intimacy—for-no-reason* . . . Momma's nestlings, between them is a sense of her eyes like pieces of deluding, maybe poisoned candy in close-pored milky-and-pink skin . . . ha-ha . . . a fortunate and shocking, and enviable prettiness-as-ordinariness; Momma says: *It is lucky to have that English coloring in wartime, I'll tell the world. Nonie has the luck of* THE DEVIL.

I cannot see my eyes. I do not know, really, how I strike people. This phenomenological ignorance is what gives form to the episodes of my dreams and to most of my thoughts: I am the blank spot, the determining erasure who dreams you: give me a face and a life, a character and a human quality, and perhaps I will not wake but will stay here with you.

She is, of course, enticing but she comes equipped with a face and a life, a character and a human quality as if people have dreamed her quite enough or as if she has turned the dream world of her centrality inside out like a pocket, and she can suffer untold hurt and survive it; she can be a third-person self; she can know who she is—and if that is not true—she can hide the selfsame blankness that is so important a part of me, she can hide her real face: that quality of her is hidden, made-up, dressed, reduced-in-immediacy: she doesn't seem to await definition as I do; she seems to be defining—she seems to be a force of definition. I look into a mirror or a camera—or into her eyes—and I see mostly only how I look when I try to see myself—when I try to wake from that sense of myself-as-blankness. The eyes: I have never seen my eyes except with a foolishly searching or self-defending expression in them: asleep with posing or with peering.

Momma has yelled at her not to smoke in the apartment: *WE'RE SICK HERE* . . . Nonie smokes anyway.

"Hey, Nohns, don't, hey?"

"Ohuhah Christ, I hate you . . . You're a fool . . . It's too late to make a difference to *them* . . . Show some common sense; show some backbone; don't always do what you're told . . ."

Mutual semi-murder, the real, or factual, common sense of it, of rivalry—her tone of *cutting through the shit* and being really reasonable (really *at home*) *in the real world*: "She's going to die anyway, it doesn't matter if I smoke around here or not . . ." As she'd said it to Daddy.

I never quite got it through my head how fixed certain things in the world were for Nonie—facts and tact, untact, love for her, no love toward her—whatever.

She is checking through her strangely large wartime plastic purse with its immense plastic floral clasp. Her skirt has a long fringe on the hem that Mom has advised her not to wear. She is successfully pretty in a somehow ill-judged way: small bones, restlessness, her character: a coed, unconvincingly fluffy, with an unusually piercing manner—and an unusually piercing, very pretty face, disciplined.

The bra is padded; I know from long familiarity with her outlines in various clothes. I am self-conscious when she smokes since I have been wrestling with and spanking her and removing the cigarettes by force. She is testing me, checking to see if I will tear the cigarette from her lips at the last minute before she leaves. *She tests everything everywhere she goes—she gets on people's nerves; she's no fool but she is a fool.*

In the mirror of her actions, I am now a force of law at my own say-so. This echoes what she did in Momma's room, smoking and rifling Mom's bureau.

Is it sexy to be challenged? Nonie's lipsticked, lady-commanding-officer's grinless thing of the shrewd, *mad* soldier—you know—lets her speak.

"Nayow you a'n't so bay-id looking—yuhoor eeeevin uh lit-tell c-you-uuuute . . . so you may as well learn to be ni-eeeeece . . . now when you have a lit-ful time . . . before you're drafted . . ." Spoken like a Southern belle in a popular novel, Southern flattery—a kind of mockery.

She is politicking inside a blood relationship. I practice a *moral* relationship. I slouch in the poisoned honey of self-display, squinting out of uncertainly blond, very youthful features, out of a history of bemused and hallucinatory self-expenditure, sexually and morally. I am inside what I do, which is to say I am largely unknown to myself; and what I do know is of someone crashing and large, thoughtless and assertive. In that persona, *willy-nilly*, I say, "Put out the goddamn cigarette, *Sis*, or go on the goddamn back porch and smoke it."

She laughs—shrilly, a little. It is odd how, at that age, the semiconstant, ill-explained humiliation of everyone reviewing what you do makes each thing a public gamble, more or less, depending on how thick-skinned and past learning-all-the-time you and your character have become. It is not certain that I will survive my youth. Or this moment. My voice breaks a little. She judges my face.

That year my crotch misbehaved *all the time—every goddamned day—practically* EVERY OTHER MINUTE—praise of a rapable world (that could defend itself against me).

Nonie is not kind. My prick really goes at it in my pants when I give orders, when I assert myself, when I get tough. I am so constructed that if I have a real hard-on, it is visible, embarrassing.

Nonie *respects* this inside a frame of realpolitik. She gives credence to the embarrassed but boyishly capable and clumsy and well-lit (not yet tricky) mood of willfulness. After all, I spanked her for what she did to Dad and Mom.

She and I both know she will *never forgive me.* And that she will lie about the story. People who take my side when she complains about me do it because they like the idea of my future or tend to distrust women. I have lived slandered by her ever since I was four years old.

"Don't be a smart aleck—no one likes a smart aleck." She says this and puts one of the bedposts between her and me. She is not actually being comic or like a comedienne. But I am smiling—fixedly, with a rictus; I am forcing the smile to be grim—Frankenstein-monsterish. She says, "Try to be *nice* if you want people to like you or you'll wind up in left field—like a lot of others." That's a threat. I may have set my shoulders to get ready to lunge at her. She says, "You know where you'll wind up? In the hoosegow." She backs around the next corner of her bed, puffing away. "You're the type winds up in the penitentiary . . . So do yourself a real big favor . . . Be smart: keep a sharp lookout on your p's and q's . . . and learn RESTRAINT: WILEY: DON'T! Be nice . . . Be *practical* . . ."

She screams a little. One of the pads in her bra gets knocked to one side. She calls me a son of a bitch. I throw the cigarette out the window. Lila's daughter says then, *dryly*, not extending the scene, "You goddamn smart-aleck little son of a bitch; well, no point throwing good money after bad. You're not worth fighting with, Brother Mine. Is my skirt straight on my heinie? My hind end? Is my tushie straight? Are we all set, Lieutenant? Shall we go downstairs and wait for the cab?"

On the sidewalk she says, "Take my advice." She sighs. "Be smart: don't be a hero." Like upstairs. "Don't throw *your* chances away. I know what I know: I don't live at home like you, Sonny Boy. I'll write you but don't expect too much—don't expect me to gush." She lit a cigarette, she eyed me, she winked *dryly* . . . This is a kind of permission, even a kind of offer of alliance.

Nonie rarely or never squints in sunlight. My hair blows in the warm, sticky St. Louis wind. The sycamore colonnade along the sidewalk, the light, the shadows in it and around it and the thing of being *young*, I suffer a faintly stinging light-headedness, another erection, the same one in the next chapter of itself that day between masturbations.

"All set, *Lieutenant*?" Nonie asks me when the cab comes: that's to impress the cabby. It's a kind of social-class thing—I will protect her against *him* . . .

"All set, Lieutenant," the cabby says to me. He is likely to try to make time with her in the cab—a pretty *girl*, a lyrical and dirty and silent object of thought; he won't go too far, he is saying. It's a swindle; he doesn't know what our wishes are.

From her point of view, hallucinations are useful air.

"Carolina is just heaven, you have no idea," Nonie says to me, cruelly leaving me behind with the sick people I defended. She gets into the cab—she is *famously* pretty; she has a radiant, hidden-eyed smile: a little piggish—overall, she is exuberantly alive by wartime notions, glossily ripe, gross-willed, hiddenly faintly glum and *deep*, not disreputable—not rapable. Almost all comparisons with other people crush her. "Carolina is the bestest place what am, Honeylamb . . ." Nonie said from within the cab. *I was never one to think that if you weren't the Czar of Russia, you were nobody . . . but Nonie always did feel that way: if she wasn't the best, if something wasn't the best, it was cheap, you were cheap . . .* "The BESTEST—and only the best is good enough: you won't go too far wrong with the best. Union Station," she said to the cabby. She moved her head right to the plane of the rolled-down window. She said, "Look at us—we're two heroes; we're ICE CUBES . . . Remember: rich girls are just as good as poor girls and they're rich. Don't let yourself be caught. Don't get trapped. Men aren't good at defending themselves from *women*. Men don't have a chance. So remember: hold your horses; keep your trousers on—you've got time." And she reached for me; her hands touched and held my boyishly scrawny shoulders with their bits of late-childhood muscle. "You're too skinny; you're like a girl," she said, with self-satisfaction. My shoulders had started to widen but were girlish. And Nonie kissed me on the mouth, borderline dirty, exploratory—a bit wooden—and she spoke between parts of the kiss (I didn't like the kiss): "Beware of Cupid," she said. "Learn to have a sense of humor if you want to stay out of the penitentiary . . . And not kill anyone . . . You know what they say: you're only young once—ha ha ha ha . . ." Then she did a mock-French thing: "La, la, la, la . . ."

Momma sometimes said to me, *Accept her. Learn to live in the world she lives in, Wiley, and you won't go too far wrong.* And: *In a way I can't find it in my heart to make houseroom for her, she loves life.*

It isn't only adolescent snobbery that makes me refuse her in the ways I do refuse her. It is that I hardly felt like fighting with her as hard as I would have to fight with her over what I was and over what the world was in order to talk to her or be near her—she had no interest in any but her own opinions—that was as a form of self-respect—and nothing friendly or reasonable could force her to think or feel—or live—in a different way—so, if you weren't like her, and probably if you were, it was an expensive and big-time thing to go near her.

When I am tall, the small bones of her pink fingers, her sweaty palms are smaller in the scale of things for me than they had been when Nonie was going to work on the first day in 1938 or 1939. I half remember the discussions of what she was to wear, what she ought to wear in 1939, 1940, 1943 . . . Voices of collusion discuss these matters. The politics of American sanity back then were scary to me. I remember when it seemed to rip the heart from Nonie to wake up and dress, have coffee, go to work. I would be sent to wake her. She has on a white nightgown. Her breasts are visible among ribbons. She has a nighttime smell. She screams a little, gasps a little when I say, *Nonie, it's time to wake up.*

A marriageable girl—from a polite family (even if there is illness in the family)—Nonie, Nonie's eyes are supposed to show a discretionary nothing, a vague, general, exclusive sociability. The limits of the political and economic availability of her flesh, soul, mind, spirit, will—a sort of romantic *realism*—if you want to have a household you can call your own, some love as well, if you want to have this in a frame of practical good sense, you will do this back then—in St. Louis (and in St. Louis County).

Nonie muttered—or *shouted*, "I don't want to sacrifice myself!"

I remember Nonie saying in the beginning, "Make Wiley walk me to the bus stop. I'm not a working girl." She would look more familied if her smallish brother walked her to Delmar Boulevard.

On the street, even if I refuse to hold her hand, just walking at her side and being short, I can feel her pulse racing in her wrist, which sort of hangs a little below my head and at the level of my chest. I was at that time up to her waist or higher. The hefty swing of her buttocks, girdled and gabardine-skirted, that rear end, its complex side-to-side motions, her high heels—the physical reality of that is part of my childhood (in St. Louis).

She said to Momma one night, "Anyone who wants to can insult me now. You can't protect me, and Daddy's sick—and Wiley doesn't like me."

The family tragedies marked her as not such good *breeding stock*; I heard her and Momma discussing this. I *think* I was supposed to be outwitted by her, by her in her strength, her mightiness, and by her use of her privileges as a woman and by her use of her sufferings and horrors and by their reality—the idea was that it was normal for me to be outwitted by her and it cheered her up and kept her going.

She *told* me I was boring . . . She figured it didn't matter what she said: I ought to help her . . . I was her brother . . . But she wasn't my sister. "I don't earn money for *him* . . ." I had to start paying board and room.

"She feels insulted," Lila said. And: "Why do you hate her so?"

Mom kind of pointed out that the *only* POLITE thing was for me to be heartbroken over her unhappiness . . . Nonie's. At Nonie's say-so. "Men are nice to women," Lila said to me. She instructed me. We wrestled to the death every day really—Nonie and I: my looks, my breathing, my attitudes represent this wrestling. Lila shouted, in a drugged state, "She is not your blood!" That is, I should have adopted her—this was when I was nine. She is a girl and life has wronged her. Mediocre and ferocious and not to be trusted, she can fuck her way to safety—she says so: "I can be a whore"—and I am sexually latent but I kind of know what she means and I kind of wish she would.

Lila whispered to me, "Give her a hand—don't let her throw herself away."

Dad, in his dark moods of hating the world, doted on her in complex fashions; but periods of such doting did not last: he would check himself into the hospital to get away from her—her ego, he said. One time he refused to come out until she had moved out of our apartment; and she moved out and in with a friend, another bachelor girl, for a while. And he came home.

Momma would insult Nonie as if it was a regular mother-daughter thing (which it may have been): "You can't get anyone to like you except second-raters." She said that to Nonie. She apologized: "We're all a little crazy now from the war . . ."

I accepted all of the past in return for being able to live on, to live now.

Nonie kind of evened things out with me (for my being a boy) by inflicting on me personal details about herself: she had a rash under her left breast, she needed a new bra, the Tampax stuff she used once a month was horrible, she was constipated: "You're a brat: you may as well learn what real life is." If I didn't listen, if I made faces and laughed at her, or if I answered her back, Nonie would have trouble breathing—like an asthmatic. If I walk off and leave her on the street, she got into that asthmatic state. At night, sometimes, she had screaming fits, tantrums: shouting and falling on the floor and foaming and dribbling at the mouth. Sometimes then Dad hides in my room. Sometimes he fusses over her. Sometimes Lila sobs dry-eyed. Sometimes she closes her eyes and says, "I feel sorry for her but I won't let her get me down. I have my own troubles."

Nonie learned. Her early despair and heartbreak faded. Relatively soon she was, on the whole, a cool, sort of inhibited young woman of quite apparent competence—and of considerable confidence. When she spoke in temper, or crazily, it was a shock: it was like ghosts gibbering at me—boy, was it weird . . .

What came to be called later in my life *the bottom line* was called in my early years simply *money*. "I want my own MONEY NOW," she said. "I don't want everything to be sickness and just-plain-awful . . . I won't do it all myself." She turned to me: "It's time you learned to pull your own weight. It's time you learned how to pull your oar."

"Leave him alone," Ma said.

"Go to hell, all of you," Nonie cried out. "I'll do what I want . . ."

Lila said to me, "You don't know what's tragic—and what isn't, Wiley . . . Wileykins . . . Nothing is *tragic* for a Wileykins . . . Help her. Help ME . . ."

Mood, privacy, self-will become family matters, matters of family politics.

Nonie went to the school asking for help from them financially. Lila said, "She gave them a whole sob story, she was crazy for a little while—the whole thing backfired—well, she can't say I didn't warn her . . ."

Her predicament was *laughed out of court* by some people. A number of people became anti-Nonie.

(I felt old and stern; I called my parents Mom and Dad often.)

My existing near Nonie worsened things for her. My presence put things that bothered her in a certain light—relatively speaking.

The "smell" of the predator: I remember this: an active will in a persecuted-by-hunger alertness, the sour smells of her neck, the odors of her hair, the often relipsticked, tobacco-y smell of her lips, the smells of her breath caused sudden pit-of-the-stomach misery; I felt, or saw (to use the idiom, to *see*), in how she jabbingly smoked a cigarette or talked about her office—and in her smells—how real her sadness was, how sad she actually was.

"Butter wouldn't melt in her mouth—she has the temper of a rattlesnake." Momma said these things.

In a relatively short time, confident much of the time—on-her-feet, established, Ma said—Nonie preferred her life in the office and the people there, that daylight life, to us, to the life at home. At this time I began to see stories in novels as loonily beautiful, linguistic *corrections* of real life. I used to think Nonie was a great prophet actually, in the world.

She used to say of me, *His life hasn't begun; make him help me.* I thought Nonie was crooked and awful, no-good, second-rate, dull to be around but really smart in a worldly way. I think she is a hero; but her being heroic strikes me as being a pale, raw thing like a nightgown—like moonlight become such a thing as a nightgown over her soul—thoughtlight depicts this sense of things *re* Nonie.

Nonie was promoted soon and often. At the end of six months, she bought herself a small, pretty briefcase and fairly expensive office clothes, a new "office" watch, an "office" necklace. She had new "*friends.*" This exile, with its moments still of real pain, became a life she honored and enjoyed.

"You wouldn't be any good in an office," she said to me.

She sometimes then had an executive look in the mornings. And in the evenings, too. Her posture had executive meanings; she had a look of power-in-the-world. She rose in the world even while she fell in it . . . into it. She rose and fell, not symmetrically. The pale-raw courage I mentioned and her fate were mysterious to me. She seemed to me to know about the reality I might not be able ever to live in but would rot in, go crazy in, become ill in, die in.

Then she went away to Forestville and I grew.

The boy's body hardened and was pale, and it was as if I had entered onto being a member of a new species, pubescent, then postpubic—a boy weedy and shy. Everything was different from before. It was as if, since all the motions of the world had become different, existence had moved into a different range of meaning as in the third movement of a string quartet (of a boy's life); and it was in this range of the quartet, of the instruments generating a four-voiced statement that, now I was taller, I saw when Nonie was home that Daddy and Nonie, the uneasy forgiveness between them was tolerance and affection, not forgiveness, as I'd thought, and was occasional, farfetched occasionally, and changeable; and it was not always tolerant; but occasionally they meant it to be; and perhaps it was a strange model of forgiveness, a next step *further on* if that is possible . . .

Nonie was happy or unhappy, angry—and anger made her more clever. Happiness lay in talking afterward, savoring something: "I was the belle of the ball—" today, metaphorically, or actually, at a country club ball. The afterwards was perhaps fanciful, *propaganda* for the sake of *morale* . . . or as part of the new, newly grown-up irony she used: a lie for those purposes, propaganda, which Dad did not unmask. I think she went on feeling misused or abused, but not so much that she was driven wild; or driven to marry; she had no intention of marrying: she didn't need to escape in that way; her breakdowns were mostly premenstrual; her breakdowns did not last.

In short, she was reasonably functionable, unreasonably bitter. It was *scandalous*, locally, her disposition now; she *snooted* our neighbors and was brightly cheerful and bitter and sharp and snooty-haughty, not the-same-as-always at all. Military cars, olive drab, picked her up some days, brought her home at night; and extraordinary-looking men, heroic pilots, fat purchasing agents with extremely alert faces, came to see her, bringing flowers and to take her out to dinner and to go dancing.

In wartime, her life became again a life of a high-up sort; she was sort of a local vaguely soiled but still mostly *pure* debutante—but a wartime model of that; she had a future, a chance to be rich—almost no one kept track of the thing that she was a Jew . . . the boys she saw, the men . . . the gossip. She was extraordinarily free to "make a move"—Ma's phrase. Nonie's favorite phrase of sexual judgment was "I can't see him for smoke."

She talked about the office differently, about who obstructed her, who helped her, the half-knowable daisy chain of favor-doing, the factions (*taking sides*), the "flirtations," the friendships. She put her work first and did not dissolve into sympathy and fear; she felt that requests for sympathy were made "dishonestly," to subdue her, to control her new-power-in-the-world. "I cannot bear it," she said.

This impermeability had a curious effect on her over time: it enclosed her, her wits, in impermeability. She was an unteachable snail, slowed, boneless, armored. One *understands* the *nifty* consequentiality of things in a *moral* history. The way things turn out—God as success—the success of a kiss, the success one has in a rivalry—has the weight of piety. Office piety, semi-*debutante* piety, social piety. The office thing about stealing pencils: to steal pencils was a privilege; to have others see you do it and then for them to go along with it reflected your civil-service category and a degree of friendly acquaintanceship and human encouragement (of a certain kind). The rank and the alliances, Daddy laughed, in a small bitter way, remembering a lot of this stuff in his own life, when Nonie told him about them and offered him some of the good yellow pencils she'd taken from the office although she and he had no use for them at home.

His laugh and then the little-breathed, *cruel*-girlish, sweet-tricky smile of Nonie in answer: their moments together now have a "depth" of exclusion—they excluded Lila, who had never even once "really worked for a living," and me. She had worked but in a different mood. I worked, but they did not consider that work in the way they considered their own lives. I don't lie much. I play human politics differently from them. Nonie was a kind of artist of middle-class privacies . . . and of exclusions. She and Dad, their kind of excluding, well, to me it was like a *private* darkness in which they met but they handed back and forth a sort of light, a piece of skinny, lighted kindling in a darkness. The absolute heart of the semi-comic and tragic and ultimately *filthy* universe, they shared that in a kind of bemused and final disgust—which made *having-a-good-time* necessary as an explanation of one's will in life, necessary to one's self. And this struck me at the time as *final* and dangerous. But I was jealous of this stuff they did.

I wondered if such moments were what true love and the height of human life were: these kindled states among deprivations.

I suppose what they shared was a "shrewd" ridicule of any actuality, of its failure of justice, its failure to be simple and steady; but also a sense that they "knew" what actuality really was as no one else perhaps in the whole world did.

So, one sees them talk. They have a kind of dress-up of the eyes in private (with each other) so that a *private* costume of knowledgeable sarcasm covers the anatomy of their knowledge of the world in an intimate way not meant to be observed. I remember their posed necks, their dressed-up eyes. Sight becomes thought with them: *I see what you mean . . . ha-ha, oh ha-ha* . . . (The transfer from one sense to another was extensive: judgment arises from how a thing smells; one gets the feel of it—the taste . . . one gets a grip on the dialogue . . . one has a heart for true meaning.) I cannot veer away from a silence of the senses among the transfers, a gray-and-white silence in me, a kind of snowy snobbery of silence in which hurt moves quietly since I know they are experiencing stuff I don't know: they are living in the reality of a blood tie.

In that blood tie, Nonie lights a cigarette and puffs on it. S.L. smiles at her in an experienced, sweet, pseudo-doting way that knowingly and wearily suggests to what extent that smile is paternally edited.

Lila said, "A lot of what he does, Wiley, a lot of what they both do, is they like to make you jealous."

If any of us balk Nonie, if we all do, if we turn against her, her will—fairly or unfairly—she *fights* shrilly, at the top of her lungs, or with considerable other extremism of mood, to have her own way in the understanding that there is no moral consideration of her on the part of the universe so long as other people do as they like toward her.

Little-boned, smooth-skinned, bent-necked, made-up, and combed, she may scream—if something is asked of her—"I have things on my mind—I don't want to hear about you . . . I don't want to hear about your problems—Oh God, another county heard from—LEAVE ME ALONE OR I'LL SCREAM."

Momma said, "These are the best years of her life. It's normal for a girl to want her own way then, Wiley." Then: "It's easy to hate people: who can blame her—are you too young to know how things work, Wiley? Are you too young to understand a pretty young woman, My Old Kiddo?"

It becomes a strangely moral outcry for me to say to her, as she and Dad (and Nonie) sometimes do, "Leave me alone."

I want to be blind to some of what goes on. And I want to know stuff and not be blind. So, I often fail to observe the "innocence" in the engeneralled, the colonelled girl being domineering, the sacrificed, pretty-faced, hard-willed, slightly mad girl with her long hair and remarkable eyes. She is luminous with perhaps justified self-pity. She does not propose that you see her (in a real moment) without her reality being tinged for you by your sense of her as *ideal. A fine girl.*

Nonie: *Did-anyone-fall-in-love-with-her-today? Are* THEY *all sweet on you, Honey? Ha-ha . . .* This pornographic frame around a romance of her chastity and Nonie's speaking of office presents, office graft, sleeping around in the office, romancing someone to get ahead; and of who is a Republican and who is a Democrat; who had recommended whom (in order to get the job, the promotion, the raise); and what the payoffs were; and what companies paid how much to have their office supplies be the ones bought: Momma said with a sigh, "Well, we all have to grow up sometime . . . Hush, here comes the child." *What-did-you-do-today?,* if asked of Nonie now, is a compound sympathy and satire about the loss of innocence, her present state of corruption . . .

Nonie would sometimes shriek at her sick parents: "YOU'RE PUSHING ME INTO THINGS . . . YOU DON'T CARE ABOUT ME! YOU ONLY CARE ABOUT HIM!"

The further whisper of grown-up knowledge: she is jealous in her corrupt state.

"Nonie is still flesh-and-blood," Momma said. Nonie is defiantly big-breasted—padded—lately. It is a girlish buffoonery thing within the dark satiric thing that she is flesh-and-blood plus cotton batting.

She says it is *boring in a suburb.*

Mom's concern for Nonie: "Do you have a headache . . . Do you have a headache again?"

Mom gets satiric: "Do you have hurt feelings *again*?"

Mom says to me, "She's making friends. It's a hard adjustment. She has to fit in: of course, those aren't our sort of people she's fitting in with . . . Wiley, you have to learn to handle her with kid gloves when she's having trouble. I had some hard times in my life but I never had to take orders from anyone . . ."

She did, though, after Daddy became ill.

Nonie says, "Wiley is upsetting me." Or, to Mom: "You are driving me crazy, I'll die, I'll get TB, I'll go on the streets and become a streetwalker." She tells Daddy, "You're getting me down . . . I'll die . . ."

"No," he said. "I'm the one who is dying."

For a while, I was maybe ill in a certain way—in my feelings. In an argument with her, even if she is shrieking in menace or whatnot, I can point out that her chin is slightly off center or that the padding of her left breast is in crooked or that she is gaining weight; and that stops her. Factuality in the face of the ideal is her enemy.

Momma asked me not to fight back too much: "It is Nonie's turn . . . Stand aside . . . These are important years for a girl . . ." She said, "For God's sake, let the girl *have her chance.*"

Perhaps my jealousy of Nonie is the most powerful thing in me. Or is one of the most powerful things, along with grief and other stuff from before I was adopted.

Then am I wrong about what happened? In a family, as in an office, you do a lot of detective work. You chase down who-did-what. You keep track of what you've figured out and what you haven't. Lila pointed out to people she talked to that Nonie was good at that stuff. A good citizen, of use, real use in the real world, good wife material, certain to be important in her community.

Nonie rather good-humoredly, a little sourly, said, "Everyone is all in a rush to get me married."

"Nonie is an accomplished liar," Momma said. "A quite good actress . . . In her way."

In a torrent of new circumstances, Nonie achieves a success: she is of a new sort of wartime woman.

Of office sadism, Nonie said, "I hate cruelty."

Momma said, "To understand Nonie, if you want to appreciate her, you have to know about being a woman, Wiley. In a lot of ways, Nonie was a saint. I know you don't believe it but it is true. I am not joking about this."

Nonie. St. *Not-a-Victim*. It is important.

She says to me, "You're a boy, you'll get everything you want anyway. I'm a good-time Charlie . . . I know how to live . . . Daddy taught me . . . We're philosophers, him and me: we're regular saints of knowing how to have a good time . . ." Nonie said, "I won't go mad no matter what . . . I'm happy-go-lucky—and that's that. I don't have to be a saint—I'm normal."

(Momma said, "She doesn't have to be a saint . . . She doesn't have to give in.")

Before she moved away—and became the person Casey met and liked and "rescued"—Nonie came home at night and mostly complained. Momma said to her, "My God, have a little pity on me—there's only so much sadness I can take." Then, in a shrewd tone: "And there's only so much I can take the blame for . . . I admit I married the wrong man and I didn't leave him to marry for money so you could go to college and join a sorority. Maybe I ruined your life but have a heart, will you? I'm not exactly in the best of fettle in case you haven't noticed."

"Go to HELL," Nonie said. "You can't bear to let anyone have any sympathy."

Mom said to me, "All in all, Nonie and I are not what you'd call good for each other. She holds it all against me . . . every last little thing.

Everything . . . Well, what can I do? I can't do it all over again now . . ."

I listened to as many of Nonie's stories as she was willing to tell me, stuff about tight shoes, an unoiled typewriter, a balky stamp machine, a boss who pinched her. Her stories were never so complete or clear that I could just listen; each of them rested so much on implication that I couldn't follow what she was saying unless I consciously set myself to have a kind of obedience to the will behind the story—you had to share attitudes with her to understand her.

I faked some of that. The discipline thing of making myself listen to Nonie in that way, I had this thing of Nonie and me being a team now among the family disasters. But it was clear Nonie and I were not a team; Nonie was interested in my lying to myself about this—she liked to fool me.

Sometimes I let her think she was fooling me. Sometimes she did fool me. I tried to pay no attention to *the truth*. "She refuses to feed you," Lila said in exasperation. Lila had an income and so did I: so the argument had been over how the money was to be budgeted, allocated. She had tried to raise money from Nonie by playing on her sympathies. "If you want my advice, you can stop being nice to her," Lila said to me. But I thought things over and I decided not to be insulted and not to be fooled by anyone—but not to trust Nonie, either. Nonie was as bad as Mom said, or, at least, was that sometimes. Momma said to Nonie, "I don't care what you do: just take care of yourself and let us all go to hell—be as goddamned selfish as you like! Just don't torture me anymore. Don't try to cut the heart out of MY breast."

She was blaming Nonie for her cancer by then.

"Oh Christ, you make me *SICK*!" Nonie said.

Years later, in California, Nonie started out to cook me dinner in her own kitchen, but she fainted. She was boozed-out; but the thing is, she could not feed me. And never did, not once.

Not once.

Nonie in the early days of her working carried on: "I WON'T WALK TO DELMAR ALONE AND TAKE THE BUS AND HAVE EVERYBODY SEE ME!" Nonie shouted. "MAKE HIM GO WITH ME!" A pair of middle-class kids in a time of war. A fine-faced pair, children of disaster, almost brother and sister.

Oddly, Lila and S.L. and Nonie were in agreement that I should not have new clothes. One way or another, through their scenes and borrowings (of my money), their pleadings (for me not to be fancy and vain), I was not *allowed* to buy new clothes. I wore what relatives sent me. I looked like a fool, maybe a dear, pale fool in one-time expensive and oddly styled and out-of-place and ragged and ill-fitting *knickers* (from the 1930s), knickers and a moth-eaten red sweater from England, too small, with a thin but highly figured band of Greek and pagan motifs on it, on the upper part of the chest, elegant and quite strange in U. City.

I could not bear to notice the faces of people looking at me, skinny as I was, in the clothes I had, what their looks showed, what their faces showed—when they looked at us then.

I walked self-consciously and comically male, as I had when I was littler and more squat, and very cold inwardly and often mean. When I grew tall, I walked self-consciously and comically male like before, but differently because I was so tall and so shy.

After I was tall, she was home only on visits, two of those; and then she returned for good just as Daddy died.

If she was "mean," I would go off and let her walk to Delmar alone, a government stenographer. Some days I would laugh at her. On some days I was disgusted and long-suffering. She liked to scoop up pawpaws or strip leaves off privet hedges and drop them in my hair or throw them at me. She said, "You're a sissy . . . You don't know anything."

If I refused to go with her, she would argue, "He's my brother! He has to walk with me!"

"I get to choose!" I said. "She never says I'm her brother when I want her to do something." I said to her, "You don't treat me like a brother."

"What do you know about it? You're so stupid, it makes me puke."

But she never did treat me like a brother that I know of—not when I was ill, not when we got along, not ever. I suppose I mean I never felt it. What would being-treated-like-a-brother consist of?

She would get a sly, crossways look.

Fooling me is the spine of her self-respect, just about.

At Delmar I helped her into an express car, a dowdy public limousine, but a limousine still, in which, for a quarter (it took a nickel to ride the bus), you rode behind a chauffeur but along with eight or nine other people, two of them on the folding seats, in a crowded limousine, you rode the seven or eight miles downtown. The smells of the automobile upholstery, of cigarettes, of the clothes fabrics then. Nonie discussed, seriously, with me what it would be like for her to become a movie star and what it would be like for her to marry Elliott Roosevelt, the president of the United States' handsomest son. She spoke some of how her soul cringed at the wrong touch—at others brushing against you, others of the wrong sort. When I was thirteen, but earlier too, in a slightly different inward vocabulary, mostly unworded, when I walked her to Delmar, it seemed to me that to know her was a nasty, funny, strangling thing, a *hysterically* funny thing.

It seemed farcically bad for me to have known her, my having known her.

S.L. said to me from time to time that I was a villain.

An idea is a strange thing. An idea in its posture of attention in supposed timelessness. Not posture of attention in real time. But an idea of Nonie. An idea of me. Dad had no one idea of me. Nonie claimed to have only one idea of each of us.

The *moral* cast of a moment: one time when Nonie was home and I had grown tall, S.L. had another stroke; and Nonie came to the U. City public library to find me to tell me I was wanted at the hospital . . . Daddy wanted to see me. She was angrily upset. The librarians, good-looking young women, monied, both of whom wore figured silk scarves and round-necked beige sweaters under pale tweed suit jackets, wouldn't let her interrupt me in the stacks where I was reading. One of them came back to the stacks where I was sitting on a windowsill and reading Stendhal; and she bent over and put her arm around my shoulders and said, "Wiley, your father is ill. They want you." When I walked into the reading room and saw Nonie standing by the book desk, I felt to what seemed to be a suddenly much fuller extent how different our fates were likely to be—and were, already.

Or really that we were different social classes.

I apologized to her. Or, rather, I started to and she cried, "Stop it . . . Stop it . . . I hate this . . ."

I take her literally, her *I hate this.*

One builds *a truth,* scramblingly, in trial and error. It may not be a truth, after all. Momma says, "She has a right to her own life; just leave her alone. Whatever her life is, it's hers, Wiley. *Leave it alone . . . Leave her alone . . . Leave me alone too, while you're about it.*"

I mostly had cast off God—and victory. I mean consciously. I mostly refused God, Whose meaning is *triumph,* if I was going to triumph and Mom and Dad weren't. I refused God for the sake of my ill father, who was among the defeated. I was maybe teasing the universe. It was a complicated thing. I adopted failure as beauty.

But I did not want that stuff to overrun and rule the rest of life.

Sometimes I respected Nonie as a failure and sometimes I respected her as a success and sometimes I did neither.

Nonie claimed victory and dominance so that the thing of individual meaning in the hurt person, the sense of failure as inevitable in the world and as *beautiful*, maybe in a kind of horrible way, that was impossible in relation to her except in a way that was secret. Or that she made use of. She was human. I confess I did not often think of her with respect for her success in being independent, a rebellious woman of will and audacity, somewhat less lucky than I was.

Nonie's reasoning was rarely visible to me except as a form of deep calculation . . . fairly deep. Philosophers have said we are trapped in ourselves. I think that is unlikely to be true. But I admit that finally she is not me—and that it seems wrong to claim that she is.

I don't know how to figure the degree of difference in velocity and spirit between her and me.

The War

Mom said, "I know about damn the torpedoes, full steam ahead. I'll tell you this: war makes me sick. Of course, I can say the same thing of life . . . Well, I suppose the least said, the soonest mended."

But Nonie undertook the moral reality of wartime service. After Pearl Harbor, she began to be nice to me. She sent me things, presents—the tennis racquet that I mentioned, I still have it. The war itself involved her in a curiously taut relation to suspense: *Time will tell* . . . (We wait on the *judgment* of the *God-of-victories* . . . Or we wait out the triumph of the devil.) *Her small pink hands, small-knuckled, nifty-fingered* . . . Nonie was exasperated by evil. "People are bad, Wiley," she said.

Nonie's peculiar seethe and burn of half-hope and her interest in apocalypse and the beauty of her courage: *We're going to bomb and strafe them to kingdom come,* her battle cry, and then she said, "I'm becoming burnt out." In the weird iron festivity of the war . . . (Daddy used to make a joke about Nonie: *I knew her as a child—I know her from the bottom up.*) Nonie was one of an army of Nonies. Every side has an army of Nonies. It was *known* that Nonie slept with no one: *It's just a good time and a little smooching—if they're cute and know how to act —and that's it. I'm window dressing—and it's going to stay that way— for the duration.*

She didn't mind if boys were not Jewish. She broadly admired courage with the proviso that it didn't go with *a swelled head*: she wanted it understood that it didn't *loosen her legs.* She complained about *hotshots*—hotshot pilots, hotshot heroes, high-up hotshots and hotshot *wheeler-dealer big wheels.*

Some of the men were nuts: they were loony boys, blood-*bespattered*—in some cases *still ambitious, tricky as they come* . . . in some cases, *done for.* She described an event: "He was crazy and shaky. He asked me to sit on his knee . . . He said it was good for his shaking. He said, 'I never had malaria but I shake—the trick cyclists LOVE me . . . How about you?' he asked me." She told an anecdote of a manufacturer (who was said to be both folksy and grand, dashingly) who leaned over to her during a military luncheon and said, "Are you intreh-hesteddddd in manuFACTuring, cutie?" She said that when she met him for a drink later, he asked her if she wanted to " 'PUT ON THE FEEDBAG.' I said, 'Goody-goody,' to him," Nonie said in baby-talk. "And he said, 'Okay, sugarbaby.' "

In wartime, the actions of an entire people become a piece of an epic poem of a strained and nervous consciousness.

Mom said in a voice of ironic puzzlement: *She is my daughter . . . she's a wartime doozy . . . an angel of the trenches . . . flesh of my flesh, blood of my blood.* Mom was often drugged by then because of pain. Nonie, of wartime dating, said, "I still can't bear to kiss a silly man—a silly man, ugh, gives me the creeps. You know, someone who likes to be pushed around by *an air force goddess*? I *am* the best there is: I have great morale."

Lila said that Nonie was a hero *like a man.*

How frightened I am of reality . . .

Nonie in a wartime jumble of emergencies was evangelical about violence, the necessity for it if we were to win the war. Lila said that Nonie never thought about the things she said; but I think Nonie thought and failed to satisfy herself with thought. Momma said Nonie calculated once and for all and that was that, systematic Nonie, almost always mad, almost always at least a little bit loony: her mother pictured her as representing one idea; she thought Nonie did that to others because Nonie was of that nature.

To the airmen, when she worked at the airfield in St. Louis and then in Forestville, Nonie was of value. I saw her hardly at all once she was in Carolina; so I know what I know of that part of her life long-distance or from imagination. In those days, not many women, not many men, could be around men troops who were going into combat. Some people choked on the nearness of death, on the brooding fact of wartime loss, the loss of one's right to live; but Nonie could brushingly make her way past that; unsquinting, she could endure the systematized brutality and stupidity, the government of pride, the adroit killers, the *second-raters.* She was quite a strong-willed citizen.

Nonie's moral taste—I don't mean of a goody-goody sort—her open-eyelidded thing toward violence and will, she came to hate what was not like that—*I'm not a naïve girl.* She had always hated in herself any sense of having been fooled. Or wrong. But the destruction wrought by certain *s.o.b.'s,* inept fatality so readily available, the revelation reflected unsteadily from the deaths of others, and grief that *stupid accidents* were unbounded, unpenned, loose in the world—it was like when she was thirteen . . . It *was* Nonie in the storm . . . She was somewhat like that in disposition. She was quite expert on armament and manufacturing and on the cheating manufacturers did in their manufacturing procedures and that of some unions, the cheating, the laziness, the stupidity. The possibility of death because of the actions of dishonest *souls* being *petty* (her word) affected her day by day. *It's all wrong but what can you do about it.* She said, "I feel *whupped . . .*" Momma said Nonie was burnt out. Momma said Nonie refused to give in. Momma said, *Nonie keeps on going.* Death in combat might be death by accident. Or by semi-assassination by your own side. *I know enough to know what's going on*—that meant she knew of death arriving because of an airman's failure of nerve. She knew about death following on the apparently shallow blunders of bad leadership. The reality of uninspired, self-loving officers and the gutting of good units out of malice and the inspiriting of certain other units, the realities of officers and pilots and of maintenance men and of the metal of pieces of equipment: this sort of weight, she wanted to know what this meant.

Or she wanted to ignore it, toss it off; she wants to say it doesn't matter; she has a job to do; everyone has a job to do—well, let's do it.

Men she knew, collapsing, cracking up or being promoted and cracking or being demoted, flunked out, sometimes viciously, the difference in fates and in personal strength, she could not maintain *her* sense of reason . . . She said in a stiff voice, "I am having my ups and downs . . ."

Then, every few months, she went *violently* crazy but only for two or three days. She got mean and careless, moistly loony. She would fight with anyone. The entwining of her sense of things, her perceptions, her systems (her pride), the inside of her flesh, with the outer project of the war and the ways she was instructed in how things happened in the conduct of the war and caused the outcomes of battles and of aerial combats more and more upset her with her own current sense of truth . . . I mean her concern for certain of her own principles of triumph became knotted in a bad way in her. She couldn't separate herself from her moods—she couldn't get the knots undone. In her were reactions and knowledge about the *how-it-works . . . the works, the kit and caboodle*. Those terms, *how-it-works . . . the works, the kit and caboodle*, refer to what-is-involved in real-world stuff over periods of time. They have to do with meaning when time is taken into account.

I don't know how Casey helped in those periods or not—I wasn't there—and I don't know how they taught each other lessons and so on.

The authoritarian and lawless, the extravagantly third-rate and vicious began, briefly, to *get her down. It's burnout, I guess*, she said, finally adopting that term for herself.

It is possible to use that term, but in real moments runaway souls —lying and crying and trying to get away to truth and less pain, mercifully or mercilessly—become different from before—one's troubled minutes are like that; she had entered a different world of resolve—of clarity, but of damaged momentum and perhaps of opacity, after all . . . Lila said, *Nonie made an investment*. Nonie speculated on her youth . . . The speculation tormented her, a certain suspense in it.

Boys: she rarely, never really, let them influence what she thought—so far as I know. And she managed her independence toward women. She was somewhat *brilliant* about those things. Her systems impressed me. Her style: she had a kind of plunging style in sync with certain currents of feeling and thought that placed her in American daily politics as semi-extraordinary in a *normal* way—within a certain social range—a woman, *a nice girl*.

Warlike, competent, competently flexible in the situation of the war and also in the local situations arising from the circumstances of the war, adaptable, successful on the home front at preparing others for fatal combat in war, she came into a certain self-conscious attention of mind. People saw her value. Outsiders admired her. Her more or less self-centered silence and her kind of pain, even her pain about the world, these were *centered* on what was in her own mind, were fixed on her own observations, came from her own life and from her own dreams . . . her new misery.

Not from Casey. Nonie admired Casey and the possibilities in life for a woman that Casey saw and the extremity of self-will, the marvelous drama of that; *I* think these things are so; and let us say Casey was a rival to existence and to my ways of thinking and behaving, but as Nonie grew into someone influenced by Casey, the magnetic orbits changed; and I became a rival of Casey's, although we did not know each other. I mean I am part of what Nonie knew. And used to fight off Casey's influence. Nonie used bits and versions of my ways of reasoning and my sorts of perceiving in order to live.

"I'm a good general—I'm not *a saint*," Nonie said to me . . . We don't have many American *saints* . . .

She was still Nonie, but she would call long-distance, and in the house of the sick people, I would answer the phone.

"Are you still a sucker for stories?" she might begin.

"Sure," I would say, if I was eleven years old or twelve.

Or about her *love life*—she called it that—or some guy's attempted suicide—or a real suicide, a divorce: information about the world.

She would say, "Tell me what you think a real bastard is, first."

Or: "Do you think life is sad? Do the books you read say a lot about sadness?"

It was funny: I could hear her *jealousy*-in-abeyance—it was in her breath, that it was in abeyance, like the sound of nervous running around in the switching tail of a horse, in the dark, a whispery thing.

I would answer her by rote, cautiously, in some politic fashion. And I ran away from her often, even face-to-face, but especially at a distance, in spirit and on the phone, I mean. And I never wrote to her about these things.

"It depends," I said. "It's usually not too smart to have a closed mind on matters like this."

"Is that so? Why is that?"

"A closed mind doesn't win a war."

"Oh? But why? Tell me why."

"Nonie, I can't . . . I *think* that when you close a subject, it's bad . . . Or it turns bad—or conclusions get to be untrue very fast . . . But you don't always get a choice . . . You have to shut down. And go on . . . That's a lot of the time, I mean."

"I'd like to be a nice person," she said vaguely.

In an odd, broken, adolescent voice I said, "You are a nice person . . ."

"No. I'm not. I'm all right, though. Keep your nose clean, Little Brother."

It's in-the-air, it's the zeitgeist—wartime fashion.

"Understanding these things is one of the things we're poor in," I would half shout, a fatuous kid over the phone to her.

None of her wartime friendships lasted. The romances with guys didn't last more than a few years. Casey lasted two and a half years.

Nonie is cracking under the weight of what she now knew . . .

No one she knew from the jobs she had in the earlier parts of the war looked anybody up a year later—she said—after transfers and breakdowns and burnout . . . *Everyone is too ashamed*, she said. Then: "It's all so petty I could spit," she said.

She and I are part of a far harder mathematics than the multiplications and divisions of family emotion are.

Her sadness now means her vocabulary is different: events in life (and this includes love) have a peculiar nature, the number of *lives down the drain . . . cannon fodder . . .* the hierarchy of merit—and of survival—and the hierarchies marking one's being of greater or of less use to the world—and the hierarchies of will, of successful vanity and wickedness . . .

What Casey had seen in Nonie early on, Casey's excitement at seeing a young woman in a state of silence at the beginning of her flowering, was no longer visible.

Nonie said, "We get older, Wiley . . . Not too many people get smarter, I'll tell you . . ."

She has various kinds of absolutism of focus, of narrowness, various *disciplines*, but now each is expanding in a clouded, perhaps harmed and harmful way, into an extended and personal sensibility about the world . . . not more intelligent, but experienced and sad. *Nonie was never tactful, you know. We were all surprised by what she became—it was a surprise party for all of us . . .* "Love" as a surprise party? How educational . . . How trying . . . *A lot of the education you get in this world is what you don't want to know, but you learn to know it anyway.* The SOUL, which is the sum total of what you are, up to this moment, what has been done to you, what you have done in return, that weight in the breast, fogs up the chambers of attention. You have an emergency—of the soul. Her condition of attention and of being able to focus, her degree of concentration has become strange. When *shutting out* becomes the topic, she opens in an oddly oblique way instead. *Shutting out* is a common wartime thing, *shutting out* and then opening out into a situation with concentration is what is meant when you say someone is *good-at-something.* It is what *concentration* is. And *being a nut. She is a nut for working hard, she loves her work . . .* It is called *love-for-one's-work* until one is *burned out.*

Nonie told me that no one can tell being burned out from malingering . . . from having had enough . . . from mere restlessness . . .

The now-unrecognized moments in a mythical and maybe *immortal* way—I mean as in a parable—show me Nonie moving as if *by remote control* at some sort of distance from herself among the deaths, the emotions, the stupidities that *controlled* things in such a way that things become uncontrolled . . .

Nonie said, "The people who do the best are serious but *not too serious* . . ." She wants to find a formula.

She is like a china doll, Momma said. *People expected too much of her . . . You have to be nice at a party, but you have to learn to say no, too* . . . And: "*She's a little cracked, my daughter . . . Well, I'm ill: I hope Casey can take care of her . . . Everything is a battle and a half when you're ill,*" Momma said and sighed.

No one I knew made it through the war without cracking up—at least, they cracked up for a while . . . Some got over it—some got over it a little. Some didn't get over it; not ever.

You have to be as tough as you have to be . . . If people are rough, you have to learn to play rough . . . Everybody and his brother has a hand in what you have to be . . .

It was like one's dreams. In the skull of the dreamer, in these stilted representations of the real, the motions of breath nearby are a stilted attempt to recognize the plausibility that in the Messerschmitt is *Monsieur Smith* with a knife rat-a-tat-tat, the vehicle of every man and of every man's murder—and are not real motions.

"Who am I?" Nonie asked. "I wish someone would tell me . . ."

Some of the early deaths had been unnecessary even as sacrifices. Training became more sophisticated, realer, more concerned with actualities of enmity and topography and weaponry. Ignorance and exhaustion are great forces that shape our lives and determine battles. Everyone she had known had lied to her.

Nonie worked hard—*she worked herself into the ground*—she helped establish the Air Force and Air Force training methods; she helped impart procedures of combat to human minds . . . *The airmen gave her a joke medal.* She fought hard, and she looked so young. *They named twelve planes after her, and streets in two separate camps.* In the streets of tents you would come on signs with her name on them: Nonie Street. N. S. Silenowicz Street . . . *She was as good as any colonel . . . She's my daughter and she does important work . . . She has done very important things . . . It was important work that meant* SOMETHING—*life and death for many, many people . . .*

Perhaps more important than anything I do or can do or will ever do.

Nonie's nerves: two years at that time was a wartime generation. She said her work was two steps from combat.

Willful and a troublemaker, a woman of guile and will—and very good-looking—she accomplished a good deal on a very specific level of accomplishment. The millions and millions of kids who turned eighteen at every instant of that year and then the harvesting of their youth in the shadow realm of minds and then, in reality, and the destruction of the animal world, well, how do you live with that? Perhaps war is the triumph of the exalted ordinary. I really do not know. In the war she eased the way for many and helped preserve the minds of many. Eased the way to murder? The ways one moment props or crowds the next and elusively becomes it, but not clearly, makes it hard to judge these matters. Most outcries of moral insult are incompetent in relation to reality. Surely, we were about to be murdered by enemies.

"Who are you to judge? I don't know why anyone asks you anything," Nonie said to me.

I said, "But YOU asked me."

Who am I to judge? I don't know. Nonie's was an old role, one that women have filled for millennia—a priestess thing of preparing virgins for the sacrifice. She was a true heroine of an old-fashioned kind—expensive for the world.

Also, a lifesaver . . .

She said, "I'm a lot nicer than you are, Wiley, and I count for more in the world, you know . . ."

She faded into illness of soul. Immolation and repentance came when the momentum had turned—and was in our favor. And a different spirit had set in: and even more complicated office procedures and training procedures had to be followed. *The tide of victory* was a phrase back then.

It seemed to me that in war relativism ruled almost everywhere; it was the key to what went on—who is stronger now and where, and to what extent. Everything was comparison. The mind swam in one dangerous comparison after another . . . Death is an absolute of sorts in comparison to life. "*It is my personal absolute,*" a boy said to me once. The mathematics by which a large number of deaths add up to a national fate is part of that flexibility of real-time logic in which relativism becomes wartime merit. One sees, in wartime, that the victors are odd-eyed relativists who measure and weigh real moments and who feel and know and who study the reality of time, its realities; but Nonie could not endure an exile from her sense of having access to the only meaning there was.

Her self as having access to the central truth, her soul's real nature was that of A Single Daydream labelled perhaps *THE LAST LAUGH* for-which-millions-have-to-die. Her hallucination was of a stonily eternal foliage somehow tissue-y but set outside of time in an unchangeably motionless rightness. A bow to her was made by the universe, the world, made to her as a daughter, a citizen. This is the weighty and a shatterable thing of herself as a speculation that did then in wartime shatter . . .

She says, "I don't cry . . . I never cry . . ." She tosses her head. The female will in a girlishly muscular body, really a beauty, a more and more agonized example of a cheerful coed who knows too much, someone *who had the nerve to go out and get her own way and pay the price—and not in her daydreams, either* . . .

These were years in which Nonie felt no envy toward men and only a little toward women . . .

Perhaps she glimpsed, then, barely, how absolute convictions isolate someone, island you . . . the continent of yourself surviving in an ocean of shifting makeshifts . . . it is like the breakdown some people have in college . . .

She wasn't the right type anymore . . . I shouldn't talk like this to you but what the hell . . . the hell with it . . . Everyone had become a patriot by then and she couldn't hold her own with so much competition . . . And, to be honest, she wasn't so young: that goes fast, you know. She needed a rest. She wanted a different kind of life with no news in it . . . You understand that in people, Wiley?

The sadness of a person, not of the highest sort, the person, but a person on our side? Having been chosen by God for this suffering and for all her luck, good and bad, and for the events of her life, Nonie, with a suddenly half-dismissed ego and a profound experience of the deaths and humiliations of numberless others, Nonie was humble and punished. Nonie, bruised and shaken, honestly educated in a severe fashion by then . . . her idea(s) of herself, which had been one of the loonier forms of the conviction of absolute grace, fled from her—leaving her heart-broken, bereft, and mad.

The expression of her eyes—I saw her twice in this period—the expression in her eyes, in those aquariums of somewhat lurid light—her persistent physical health—my sister's purposes—well, Mom said, *Make no mistake, Nonie found herself—too bad it didn't last* . . .

I.e., the moments hadn't stopped . . . They never do . . .

"I get mixed up . . . I have a headache . . ." Nonie said. And: "You do things for a moment and you haven't any time to think but the results last . . . do you know what I mean? Well, if you know, tell me what that means . . . What do philosophers say about that . . ."

I said, "I want the world to go on . . . I don't want an apocalypse . . . And everything to be over . . ."

"Well, you're young," Nonie said. She said it almost absently . . .

"Sure. I know that. But *beyond* that, I want the world to go on . . . After me . . ."

She said, "I get mixed up when you talk . . . I have a headache."

Momma said, *I hate the way things turned out for her.* Momma cried hot tears. *I hate her* . . . Then she got hold of herself and she said, *She was always a mess* . . .

Nonie had her life in wartime because I stayed with her ill parents. I gave part of her youth to her—and then she suffered because of that. I gave up my childhood and early adolescence—this was talked about; it was known and discussed. I wanted my sister Nonie to serve the war effort—I wanted her to have her life . . . I wanted her to be rich and have her daydreams happen. I wanted her to leave me alone.

When Nonie was in Forestville with the Warners and working for the Air Corps, Aunt Casey, or perhaps Cousin Daniel, or Uncle Abe, in their sense of law and of decorum, of appearances and of indebtedness, made her call *me* long-distance every few weeks. Because I'd made her escape possible. And because I was having a drab life.

I heard a voice behind her say, *Ask him what he needs* . . . I never got the clothes or the books I told her I needed. At her saintliest, she was still *practical* in her feelings toward me—*Live and learn,* Momma said to me. She said, *And let live . . . Look at you, you're the home front* . . . And she'd laugh.

It is a kind of spiritual discipline to forbid oneself to wish anyone ill . . . One hides behind words, one says to oneself, almost in an inward whisper, *I want to get away* . . .

Meanwhile, as part of the deal, my parents did not tell me what to do. They could only ask things of me but they couldn't give orders. I got to do what I wanted—in a sense . . . In a sense, I was *the head of the house now* . . .

Time has done this. I am becoming tall . . . And people spoke of that . . . Momma said, *You're beginning to have a face* . . . People talked about that, too.

Momma said, *Nonie's starting to like you a little; you're sort of cute like that guy in the movies with the freckles—and as you know, a girl gets good feelings about people she gets to take advantage of . . . Ha-ha . . .*

Momma had not lost her sharpness . . .

The Telephone Call

"Guess who . . . But don't say who . . . Zip your lip, save a ship . . . Well, let's have our monthly talk—but don't give me a headache this time, okay?"

Black plastic phones . . . If the window of her office at *the air base* was open, I could hear the planes warming up, cooling down, landing and taking off . . . Sometimes I could hear military talk in the background . . . behind her *moody*, heroic-young-woman-in-wartime voice . . . Kindness in rebuke to chance is justly exalted—corrupted—by death, by danger, by the sight of death . . . I have an incurable pale fever: a peculiar ironic fever of patience with anyone's *love* for anything—their love of the actions in not liking me, for instance . . . A fever of impatience, too.

But, first, the kindness: "How are things out there—you still like it out there?"

"Yes." Impatiently.

"Work is okay?"

"Oh, work is *boring* . . . so *boring* . . . I could *die* . . . I put things in cubbyholes . . . that's all I do, *all the time*—I'm *good* at *cubbyholes.* I'm the strong, silent type—I'm one of the big wheels . . . the Colonel wants to run off with me—I'd be a good service wife . . . The more fool him . . . I'm just the girl who *can* say no . . . Well, how are you? How is every little thing? Old U. City, how is it?"

I hardly knew her . . . At a distance, my ignorance about her was a cold thing in my chest . . .

Her voice: *"I don't put things in cubbyholes . . . I'm just teasing you. We're having a real cute* sunset, *Brother, Brother mine . . . Little Brother mine . . . You're not in any trouble, are you? Well, keep it up . . . I'm not talkative today. This isn't a good time for me . . . I'm havin' a reel guhid tyimmm . . . How about you, Little Brother . . . If no one is too fancy, I all-us say, why not have a good time? You'll be glad to know I hev lunned to spell here in sun-sun-sunny Carolina . . . I like fliers; you should be a flier . . . I think fly-boys are special . . . Wiley, they uhr smart and quick—they're small—you know it's better to be small? I don't know if you can be a pilot now . . . I wish you were the pilot type—you want to be a fighter-plane pilot you better cut off your legs, right off at the knees—ha-ha . . . You'll need new eyes: pilots got to have eyes like hawks . . . You'll need to hevv a new head, too . . . I like the men here—they need to talk—they talk to me; I know what's going on—believe me, you have to love guys like these—I hate whiners: what I like are winners . . . I can do without the chisellers . . . And the weaselers . . . The Air Corps is no place for that type, believe you me . . . You have to do what you have to do if you're a real person and that's the end of it. Well, you're not the worst man I know—if you buckle down, there might be some use for you yet . . . No complaining now, you hear—we got to hev a solid home front . . . Well, I called—you've heard from me . . . And I've heard you . . . Another county heard from . . . I've got to get back to work . . . The war is calling me . . ."*

I asked her, "Are you engaged? Are some of the instructors aces? What battles did they see? Tell me before you go . . ."

"I give them their marching orders, Little Brother . . . I don't ask them about the war . . . I know what they have to do and I expect them to do it . . . They don't give me any back talk . . . Live and learn . . . Listen, I have to run. Good-bye . . ."

I say, though, now, she was a different person then, in those moments.

Her voice was different—blandly confident, then shaky, relieved, defensive . . . intimate in the way women's voices were in the movies sometimes.

She said, "You want me to marry a hero?" She asked me.

"A good guy . . . that's all . . ." I said carefully.

She said, "Well, I know one hero—Huddleston—he's Canadian . . . I'm wearing his wings . . . You can take my word for it, Little Brother mine, HE'S A HERO . . ."

"God, Nonie, really . . ." Then: "Does he—does he have nightmares about the war?"

She said, "I tell THEM, *Don't press me too hard*—I'd be no good to anyone if I had a broken heart . . . I like them all. I wear their wings

—I wear my heart on my sleeve. I don't really. I wear three sets of wings on my blouse . . . I let them all photograph me . . . Hi, Marina," she said to someone at the other end. "Hi, Jocko . . . Oh, you're such a devil, Jocko . . ." Then, to me, in a different tone: "I tell them they're all devils . . . Jocko was wounded over Lae . . . He's the funniest man I know: get away from me, you bastard! Stop that . . . Life is funny . . . You believe in *luck*?"

"I don't know . . . I guess so . . . Why? Do you?"

"Well, sure . . . I have a job to do. I happen to care about my work . . . I have someone I love—and he's a REAL hero, Wiley—he's a REAL *gentleman*, Wiley, and not a sorry excuse for a man. I'm sad in my heart . . . Wiley: this awful war . . . But I put a good face on things . . . I have good morale . . ." Then: *"Can you help me?"*

"Does he—does Huddleston—have 'a lovely, lovely family'?" I don't quite know why I thought a little irony semi-smoothed out would calm her but it did . . .

She roused herself for the struggle: "Oh yes—they have a wonderful, wonderful house . . . I'll have a very good life . . . He has real stick-to-it-iveness, he's not a *stick-IN-the mud*, he's not moody . . . The men here are closer to each other and to me than family ever is . . . than it can be . . ."

Mom said, *She went mad for a while* . . .

It felt strange to hear her. I wonder what it's like to feel yourself going mad in a war? A whiz or whisper of dangerous meaning? A sudden suffocating elasticity of one's charity so that you can bear no one's pain at all? Is it a virus perhaps, a virus that expands your sense of things profoundly?

It felt as if she loved me—in a way . . .

Not in any way that was useful to her . . . Or to me . . .

"You get to fly any of the planes?"

"Machines go crazy—it isn't just fun-and-games: planes get metal fatigue . . . I named my typewriter. I don't let anyone else use it: it's a giant-killer; it's full of beans—*Jack*—I have a new friend—Huddleston —he looks like Clark Gable . . . He's blond . . . I think blonds are happy . . . Well, wait 'til you see him. He has the most beautiful, beautiful hair . . . I can't keep my hands off his hair . . . I finally found someone to love—and his name is Roy. Pierson. Huddleston . . . Don't tell Mom. Or Dad. Are you listening? I bring you news from the news fronts of the world. Well, read it and weep: *This dispatch is about a small group of guys who were wiped out to protect the retreat of their buddies.* A lot of what I do *is stupid* here, Little brother mine—it's all catch-as-catch-can.

Luck—you couldn't stand it. You wouldn't be any good here . . . I can't jaw-jaw on the long-distance phone to you all day—the walls have ears . . . I have someone with big ears listening to me right here right now . . . Roy, go 'way . . ."

It was always hard for her to talk to me . . . Always . . .

"I'm getting to be a little crazy, Brother mine . . . I'm going a little crazy, Brother-of-mine . . . I'm not having such a real good time . . . War, war, war, boots, boots, boots . . . You can imagine . . . Children are advised to go to bed early . . . This isn't a good time for children . . . Well, tell it to the Marines . . . I'm a young woman, I'm not a machine. I don't sleep like myself . . . The paperwork is coming out of my ears . . . Well, be a patriotic civilian and don't leave our boys in the lurch . . . Onward, Christian soldiers . . . I do what I can—I think I'm coming down with flu—tell me in twenty-five words or less what's the point of being *holier-than-thou*? Tell me: luck is funny, isn't it? I'd be a good gambler . . . A lot of the guys crack up: the wiseguys and Sir Galahads, they don't last. But I'm not like that . . . Some guys make me sick . . . They drive me mad, if you really want to know . . . You don't know anything yet . . . You don't know anything about anything . . . Well, what would you like for your birthday? . . . Wiley, is what it all is, the main thing in life, what it comes down to, Wiley, tell me your opinion, is it all, all it is, just plain dumb luck?"

"That's a good question . . . A lot of people ask that."

"Well then, tell me . . . what is it, what do you think?"

"I don't think it's ever just one *dumb* thing . . ."

"I always forget what stupid answers you give . . . Talking to you is a pain in my hind end . . . You're a little idiot who thinks he knows it all. Well, don't take any wooden nickels. Well, my time is up. I have to go; I'm going now. I have to clear this line . . . Keep your chin up and your worries down: may you live forever, keep a stiff upper lip, Little Brother mine . . ."

She wasn't crazy often—maybe she was. I often hated her when she was crazy. I don't want to imagine myself her. I don't want to know if she felt guilty or not, and if she did, what she felt guilt for. I don't want to know her. I don't want to know what she was like. Hell, twenty years later, she burned to death. I don't want to imagine her on the long slide inside herself toward the flames . . .

HOMOSEXUALITY

or Two Men on a Train

In Which I Partly Enter a Story from Which I Am Excluded

The train ride: reality sometimes has the feeling of oppression that some of one's dreams have. First, across the great spread of flat Illinois plain, the abomination of vastness of American distances, the train went, crowded and lurching, the view altering daylong in the dirty windows.

In the queer clackety-clack addition of motionful moments, myself a fatherless orphan (and time-ridden and disbelieving), I travelled with my twenty-nine-year-old *rich* cousin.

The other travellers in their individual and momentary travelling states were young soldiers in kepis, with strong, appalled faces, tense, war-readied, khaki'd bodies in most of the seats which had horsehair upholstery. And prosperous, cautious-faced, somewhat shocked-with-travel civilians, sometimes freed-looking, as if drunken, as if having truly drunken-by-travelling selves, an excitement of this . . .

At the time of S.L.'s funeral, Benjie, he had said, "Daniel's a serious person, but me? I'm pure *Gone-with-the-Wind*, honey."

The atmosphere of kindness directed at me—well, it wasn't unknown to me. I was skinny, perhaps a hundred and forty pounds and over six feet tall and rather unthreatening and young-looking, rather strong (from exercise). I was stubbornly ordinary in manner in what I took to be *all the time with lapses*—in short, *some of the time*—and, while I was perhaps odd-looking, people often stared at me, strangers spoke to me, touched me or tried to, and were more often anxious to be helpful than not, quite a bit more often than not.

Daniel's kindness: the story so far: Aunt Casey and Cousin Isobel, her youngest child, came to St. Louis in the spring I was still twelve;

they were considering colleges for Isobel, a tall, poor-skinned, good-looking, angularly postured and quick-talking and comically wild girl, drug-taking, jazz-loving in the style of advanced small-town girls in those years, and very bright and snobbish. Maybe psychologically fragile. A little loony.

I went to some effort to make myself presentable; and Isobel, eighteen, and I, thirteen, were "in love" for three days—necking, going to movies, some petting.

She ended the affair, having met a boy her age, dark, shadowy, very smart, overweight, a troubled, monied bully, also fragile but tremendous in a way, too. They stayed in touch for two years.

Casey was considering social colleges, not too bookish, but good enough in terms of education, and with a reputation of not being anti-Semitic and very cruel to the young women in them.

Casey had an amiably spectacular forward-jutting, very good-looking face and a long, thin body which was encased in tight clothes; and she was very popular in St. Louis with women. She met no men; and she and S.L. did not meet. Nonie at that time was living with Casey in Forestville and with Isobel, Abe, and the sons, Benjie and Daniel. Daniel had already been drafted.

Dad asked me, indirectly, to stay away from Casey; and Casey reacted at once and for all time.

Dad had said she was a liar and a bully and that she did not like men and that he'd thought her okay and that had misled him about Lila, whom he'd thought, also, to be *unlike* Casey . . . It is difficult to explain how I listened and, at the same time, did a lot of not-listening to the same words: I half attended, a tall, vague, hidden boy—with sudden periods of daydreamlike boldness although probably not much like the boldness then in style among boys in St. Louis County and not a boldness much like Dad's.

I don't know how to explain what I heard and didn't hear. Mom said Dad didn't want me to like Casey. Stories were hinted at, family stories, stories partly acted out in a scene or half-scene or two and were referred to, stories I knew a little bit about from other times, the family's version, or S.L.'s version . . . Dad as a narrator was always oblique, allusive, and he fell short of mimicry—he relied on your knowing the story, on everyone's having the same experiences, or on comprehensions being widely and genuinely available.

His stories, when he was ill, were often short of drama; it was bad for his heart for him to be excited. The bits of allusive story he recounted (and which he expected me to understand) were oddly told both as gesture and overall—what ages he and Casey were and what the issues and motives were; or where he sat in the room or what day of the week it was or what time of day—all that was artfully omitted; the texture of comprehension had to do with bits of parable of *masculine* fate, how men were mistreated, used up, damaged, driven mad. He kept sliding into descriptions taken from movies and the effect of movies on him: one was the part of *Tom Sawyer* in which Tom and Becky were lost in the cave, or locked in—I no longer remember—and another chief reference point was a pacifist movie about the First World War called *All Quiet on the Western Front.*

Both of those were useful in describing the cruelty of life to a man. Outside, then, of a wrong Casey had done him, I recognized very little in the stories and speeches and libels or truths he told me. But the oddly grammared way he spoke, underplayed and yet somehow exclamatory and using bits and tags—and accents from all over—and images and dialogue from those two movies and some others, and his discursive or terse dismissal and contempt: he was not bookish at all; and the ways he spoke were not much related to books or even to newspapers very much; but, always, so far as I could guess (feel-and/or-recognize), from living or at one time living men with actual voices who had stood in front of him and spoken in some way he had found of interest and had appropriated for his own later use—for his large vocabulary of common speech.

Lila, Nonie, and I rarely reviewed his stories with one another. We were, ipso facto, confronted with the obvious *problem* that the stories were sheathed in opinion and in mood, often in mood as opinion, and were changeable, accordingly; nor was it clear what the degree of fact was and where and how to grip those facts—he was a fabulist, a liar; and I tended to believe his lies didn't matter—that he essentially spoke the truth.

When I say we, the immediate family, did not often try to discuss his stories, review them, come to a joint conclusion, I mostly mean I did not agree with Mom's approach or with Nonie's.

He judged us as listeners; he had decided Lila was a terrible listener; and Nonie too; and he often walked out of the room unable to finish what he had begun to say.

He often found my reaction—whether it was a spoken one or a gestural one or a facial expression or one of the body, slumping shoulders and the like—inadequate, stupid, not to the point; but he didn't always break off when he spoke to me.

I *think* he told me that Casey's family life was rich and was unclean but okay and well bred but terrible and fancy-schmancy—not at all bad compared to rednecks and trash but not like him, Dad.

Actually, I don't know what *he* meant except that Casey had bested him. He said, *She has no mercy in her* . . . things like that.

Necking with Isobel, I thought she said that her family was weird, but I don't remember Isobel's words. My degrees of consciousness of things and of unconsciousness toward other things meant a kind of staring alternated with unimportant glimpses with not a lot riding on them; and then, as error and self-teasing, when I was jerking off and hallucinating or otherwise daydreaming or inventing scenarios for my life—imagined, partly real, certain-in-outline, authoritarian, omniscient in the way of narratives in books—I throw in my blurred sense of stuff in that family, in that household, with some hope that something would occur to me but nothing did.

Like bicycling very fast past a wire-mesh fence, the velocity, the blur—perhaps that is a kind of *romantic* thing when you're young.

Then Casey's husband, Abe, came that winter when I was thirteen, the winter after I'd met Casey and Isobel. I was anxious to escape from the situation between me and S.L. although the fact that I had held out for so long in that situation probably was the chief reason anyone was interested in me.

That and *my future*. I had perhaps become *the prince in the tower*: Lila muttered this.

I could do research, I could be of use—to *America* and to my *people* (no matter how those two terms were to be construed) and I was *at a cute age*—Gentiles wanted me to stop being Jewish and Jews were concerned about Gentile cruelty to bright Jewish kids—*and people are bored and they like to meddle*, S.L. said—but it was also clear and known that what I did and thought was strange—or *unheard-of*: that was Lila's term: or *mad* or *lunatic* or *hoity-toity* and *impractical: no use to anyone*—so that the bridge or overriding point in those who were *interested* was that I had loved my father, S.L.

I guess they figure enough is enough, Lila said.

A summary does reduce the opacity of one's actual experience to one's own gaze, outward and inward. I had a certain glamour because of various things; and it was almost fashionable to attempt to rescue me—the whole business seemed to me to be mostly a trashy business, although one might be of use in the world, except I thought it was too late for me: I was too odd. I really hadn't lived in the world from the time I was nine; I had to be defended—I couldn't do it myself. My ideas did not strike me as readily useful.

When I did anything, even when I went to sleep, I turned the act over to something other than my worded consciousness; the realest expression of this was that it was like an athlete's thing, practiced maybe, but not talkable and not observable; and one couldn't be self-conscious if one wanted to do whatever it was one was doing.

I mean there was some final part of whatever I did in which whatever I could do or was doing wasn't really in my power but did what it wanted; so you couldn't promise it or sell it or rely on it—it was as likely to go too far as it was to be restrained and on target.

But if, in rebellion or despair, or in despair and curiosity, or in good sense, one gave it up, or destroyed this in oneself and embarked on self-training, long hikes and exposure to the elements, and one grew silent and narrow-cheeked and gave no more answers in class, the books of climate of what I was—well, Lila and S.L. pointed out that I was taking away their positions in the world as ill people, their leverage with others; the chief reason they gave as their being worth so much charity was that they gave this difficult and very loyal boy (me) a home.

Uncle Abe was on his way to California when blizzards out west stopped all train travel for a few days. He was in Chicago and somehow got to us in St. Louis—a hired car, maybe. It was possible he came to look at what I was, to see what the story was—S.L. and Lila said that he had come to take me away from S.L.—he and Casey had made it a lifelong practice to win out over Lila and S.L.

Lila, angry with S.L. in a cold, final way and ill now with cancer herself, wanted to hurt Dad; and S.L. did not bother to make a scene; but, instead, to my semi-amused despair, he grew pale with despair and a kind of guilt and he said something on the order of *Do what you can for yourself, get what you can out of him*—he had never taken an interest in my life apart from him before.

The issue of loyalty and of true love in actual moments is much too strange to be treated realistically. It is always present, it is omnipresent . . . *You're pretty as a girl,* Daddy said . . . That meant he was *really* upset, too angry and sad to be angry, he just wanted me kind of wrecked—you know? He often used literary allusions: *You're a regular Little Tom Sawyer Fauntleroy . . . Tell me, Pretty Maiden, are there any more at home like you?*

He patted my tush—heinie—hind end, rump, behind, ass—and because I was new at being an adolescent and at being tall and so on, this stuff was quite an issue between us—well, for me.

But he liked the finality of the disrespect. He'd get a twisty look on his face—a half-smile I find it hard to place.

I find you hard to get along with, you're a real head-splitting hair-splitter, Dad said humorously.

(Lila overheard and said it too: like some movie stars of the period, she adopted male talk at times.)

He had told me in the middle of the night that I was killing him anyway. He had said it in a dry tone, not decipherable by me then . . . All the terms I am using here are too clear to describe the moments.

That I was *ugly as sin* and quite beautiful in an *American-looking* almost popular way—that the bones and whatever had led to a peculiar result—hardly universally popular—I was aware of . . . I was aware *reasonably* . . . I forgot it . . . I wasn't quite a fool—or quite not a fool. This was an area of translucent opacity—one time when S.L. was in the hospital; and Momma was upset with my arrogance; Lila used pull to get me a job selling women's shoes downtown; I didn't want to do it; she blackmailed me—and in the end the perverse sexuality (and curiosity) drew me: I was thirteen and to work you had to be sixteen; and I had to borrow a suit and ties; but both those things were arranged; and in the store I was placed in the second group of six seats near the front window alongside another guy, twenty-seven and tubercular, who was extraordinarily good-looking; we could be seen from the sidewalk.

But I refused to lie to the women and I sold many fewer shoes than the other guy; and the boss, a corseted, tiny-mustached, very, very tall, silly and very tough man, kept moving me around and haranguing me to get me to be more coldly ambitious.

So, I sort of knew in the translucency and opacity of this stuff, the crowded paradoxes and semi-wonder and discomforts and dangers of it, and a shamed sense of its being trashy and subject to variation as well as to quick death (in time as well as among its own variations or if you grew older with the wrong sense of what to do with yourself) and a sense of doom that attended this condition and then the inner conceit—the thing of knowing stories, of knowing about *romance*—but maybe not enough—all of this is included in the word *okay* and in the term *half-okay* about this stuff—that I never thought about directly or lucidly. I "knew" it was there—and I often forgot. But it would be recalled to me.

Both my parents made it clear it was wasted on me. I was odd and badly dressed; and if I talked, *people pick up their heels and run in the opposite direction, ha-ha-ha,* Mom said.

I was aware that it was considered something, by some people, to look at me—when I was that age; but I ignored this stuff pretty much—

I had no sexual interest in myself or in exploring whether what I looked like was worth something in the world—I *think* that was a modest sense of myself as tinged, tainted really, by sickness and death and by precocity and by any number of things.

I didn't really want to know who I was and I didn't want to translate whatever I was into popular terms. I was pretty sure—in a rather angular, self-possessed, but ignorant way—that my life was unlivable, was unreal, was of no use in the world or to the world or to anyone. Uncle Abe was on his way to San Francisco where he had to do some big-time wartime business. And he was going to Reno to run around with showgirls, Mom said. Dad implied it was boy dancers but Dad was always very bitter about Abe. Mom carried on a bit about how Abe insisted on staying in hotels but would stay in our apartment this trip—she did this over the phone talking to women: *Abe's fan club,* she said. People in town had seen Abe and knew him; but I don't know how that came about.

Often during the war you couldn't get a room no matter how much money you paid as a bribe; even so, he could have stayed with some of our relatives, the richer ones with large houses; but he stayed with us although only for one night; then he moved to a government-run hotel and came to see us once each day.

Abe was in the food industry and, also, in cotton and tobacco; and a little bit in coal—not a tycoon or a major figure but a part of the war effort. S.L. refused to be in the same house with him; and he checked into the hospital. If I put myself-at-thirteen—really, that other boy in the story—into the third person, I would say that the boy's adopted father did not want to see the boy place himself on the auction block.

And the father had no confidence by then that he deserved any further loyalty from the boy—that is to say, he had acted so badly so often toward the boy, not to mention the sexual teasing that was driving me crazy at that point—literally, in long tense nights of pointless disorder: I was strong enough to keep S.L. off me: but some group of perverse elements—that S.L. was dying, that what he was doing kept the books balanced toward me—was as if aroused not by tenderness or his own predicament or by his curiosity at the last minute, but by envy or a wish to tease or a desire to matter, to be the most important influence.

Well, if you're going to have a weird life, then, even though you're in love with normalcy and ordinariness and having a life that's not weird, you might as well enjoy having it. I used to test my nerve by imagining bad things as realistically as I could—even going so far as to ride in freight cars from the local station for the Wabash Railroad out into the country. I wanted to practice laughing and cheering people up and playing the clown on the way to the death camps—also, I wanted to practice getting away. Only a few people I knew believed in the death camps but I believed in them—I believed in the death trains. I took from the Bible the image of throwing Jews into a furnace. And from history and ritual, the war between the emperors at Rome and their claims of being divine and the Jews. Such wars, like a fight over final earthly love, led, if you were on one side or the other (and everyone was), to your having to be humiliated as extremely as possible in order to prove you didn't have *the blessing* or that it didn't matter if you did—this reflected in some way or other the stuff that went on between me and Dad: my sense of historical reality, or whatever, came from that stuff. The school and Dad and Mom somewhat and Nonie all the time said *I* had harmed certain people and slowed or pulled awry the course of their functioning. Or I had blocked their ambition.

Harm was strange stuff. If you're supposedly the brightest kid—brighter-even-than-a-girl—some people take that a whole hell of a lot further than you do and they wonder if you're the smartest person in the world or something; and, then, if you are, who *they* are, by comparison—what hope is there for *them*—like Dad refusing to be in the same house as Abe. In a sense, I was *always* fugitive, but so were a number of other kids. Later, when I met Abe's sons, I noticed they just about never spoke to me about Abe, at least never anecdotally or emotionally—this stuff was as if covered with a fig leaf. I was presented to Uncle Abe in a semi-ceremonial way late one afternoon, in that pale, faded, grayish wintry light; and I saw a man S.L.'s age who was, I saw, with profound shock, the handsomest man I'd seen in my life up until then.

When I saw what he looked like, I *saw* some of the elements of my proposed abduction or rescue. I *saw* the failure of his sons to amuse him, to satisfy him; and I saw elements of his personal power—as a rich man who looked like that. Those elements were like big white birds, albatrosses that had come into the room and were flapping around one's head. Ah, one's concussed response. I have never attempted to reenter that moment. He was concussed, too. The electrically amused-looking, theatrically good-looking man, his treble breath, the queer brightness of the quality of his face, the approval or acknowledgment—something like an enormous neural splash refreshed and startled me until, as in being wet, and swimming and using one's hands to pull one's hair back and smooth, one forgot much of one's life until then—I was willing, at least at that moment, to learn common sense from Abe and to take the risk of putting myself and my future, my mind and my beliefs into his hands. Whatever had prepared him and brought him here, he now nodded . . . He was very tall, very thin, handsome-featured, tensely well-built, strong-looking—as if famously (and professionally and usefully and maddeningly-for-his-soul) irresistible—this man with a backwoods fortune and an odd wife. And the thirteen-year-old weirdo in a breathless moment of physical acceptability invisible to him but useful now. One is part of the grown-up system of love(s)—not all of them consummated: such affections amuse the grown-ups and keep them alive and, to large extent, clumsily explain their lives—this is part of the truly awful scandal of being alive, of being real—the embarrassment, the truly terrible experience of being guilty and not caring, a happy guilt, a happily accepted guilt, uncaringly accepted: *I'll take this path*—my uncle had almost a violence of amorous and personal alertness—nothing ordinary, nothing to be quickly explained—nothing quite public either.

I can see why, in most books, and in life, people want for a hero someone passive and colorless: this bastard stank of privilege and power, of kinds of truth and of ruthlessness of will . . . He was not without conscience but it was a different sort of overshadowing, project-absolved, most-important-person-in-the-room conscience.

It was worth it to be no good around him. Ora in New York, in 1956, felt my disapproval of her and me was bad because it meant I no longer felt her as having this other quality of being worth what she cost. And it was true that Abe was sort of the measure of glamour and of eminence. I was aware from the beginning, as I was in the shoe store, too, where I worked, but not in school, how cheap this stuff was, in a way, how it forced you into a kind of cruelty unless you were obnoxiously pure and nuts. Abe was awful to Lila, idly flirtatious and contemptuously dismissive; he had very little shame—although I knew he prayed every morning; he put on the *tefillin—he's afraid of going to hell in a handbasket*, S.L. had said to me: he's not a good guy.

He was easily as wicked as S.L. and as quick to put women on the defensive and he was as set on living and on triumph as Mom was. It seemed to me he was more expert at being himself than they were, more self-consciously experienced; he was *systematic*, as if on automatic pilot on a bombsight run; and his own feelings were automatically safe—as after castling in chess—but it was nice that he was not sweet. He held my hand too long but not sexually but just to get the say-so between us—to get me off-balance and to show he was not *ordinary*—not predictable. I thought I saw the flicker of *sin* in him, conscious sin—that sense a man has of regularly going too far and doing it expensively, expansively, and not without generosity, but always alertly; and then a world, a sphere of boredom and rage at having to be like that, at running a large business and at what life was and at himself and then an outraged determination to go on.

I was tougher with him and felt easier in my own particular wildness of spirit and I yanked my hand away with the help of my other hand.

He simply took my hand again.

He said, "Don't be difficult," which I didn't understand clearly. I knew it in real life as meaning, *Pay attention to me, you bastard . . .* That's how my Dad talked. And some people in school.

Lila, who was watching us, said, "Don't be shy, Wiley . . ."

Abe said to my mother, with infinite cruelty, "You have to take a backseat to this one now . . . well, live and learn, I guess it's a real bitch, isn't it, Lila?"

He had been rude to her for years—he was one of those men who talk on automatic pilot in echo of earlier speeches. Essentially silent, a man of pained (but excited) action, he spoke only cruelly as a form of giving orders, cruelly and kindly or cruelly with some shade of rushing and automatic judgment—this was a concomitant of rank and power, *part of the weight of the world on his shoulders.* A kind of staleness of language, like a box he was in. I thought Mom would be insulted but she sat there, trickily amiable-faced, fadedly good-looking, and with her arms crossed—over her mauled breast.

She said later, of him, of this trip, lyingly, *We flirted to beat the band, him and me, let me tell you, we waited a lifetime, and even then we never got around to anything with each other.*

She gave up her bedroom to him; she slept in my room. I slept at a friend's.

Perhaps they did *flirt*—or talk. The phone rang a lot, though, with calls for him . . . No: that was the next day. They had a tie together: a child is lied to (and protected) in regard to the sexual realities of the older people near him and is intruded upon and harmed anyway. Abe *took the opportunity to conduct a little business in St. Louis,* Lila said later. That is, a government car and two sailors moved him into one of the hotels run by the War Department on Kingshighway the next day. I looked forward to seeing Abe that afternoon; but I didn't moon over the moments when he was away doing stuff in the snowbound city and I was in school . . . If I did, I refuse to remember it now. Mom found ways to prevent me from going with him on his business rounds. She said she didn't want to spend the money to buy me clothes to go with him on those rounds. But she wasn't a miser. That next day when I came home from school, she was sitting in the living room, waiting: "Kiss me," she said. "Kiss me," she commanded.

God, I hate remembering myself.

She smells of drugs—morphine and gloom—Dad has called her *Madame Schopenhauer, Mrs. Doomsayer* . . . Her physical pain is visible in the way she sits, visible behind the drug surface of almost ease, of hopeful passage from this moment to the next. Let me escape now. She says, "Are you tired of all the lovey-dovey hanky-panky?" Then: "Are you playing hard-to-get? Are you being a big man on campus? Are you too much a big shot to kiss a woman who's gotten to be ugly?"

I hid behind being thirteen—behind being a son—behind being *modest* and shy.

"Come on, *Big Shot*, it won't kill you . . ."

It's like being inside a glove—the long-legged skin—being alive that year—can I say that? Jesus, I'd forgotten how different everything was for me that year . . . what my face felt like on my neck, what it felt like to have that neck . . . My feelings? I don't trust her . . . I'm tired of her methods, her systems of control . . . her ways of having her life.

"I'm not in the first volume for you, am I, Pisher?"

The sense of my body and of my face—high in the air so to speak—and the stuff between my legs, the soft, blobby tangle, and its geometrization all the time that year—and my feet in my shoes, my clothes . . . my mind . . . The shifting inequalities and particularities of rank and specific histories of love and stuff for you as a coward here in this apartment—sexual or erotic stuff as generality for the moment and specific to us—and of my having to learn it over and over—the romantic duty and the mutual contempt—and knowledge of each other—the respect and no respect—the comparison and measurement of lives—me, Wiley in the world of others, starting with my mom . . . I am on the other side of the curtain, among the romances—although *not-with-all-my-wits-about-me*: in Mom's formulation, *You only know what* YOU *know*—well, and who gives a fuck? I'd been seduced by Abe, taken by him, I was taken with him: that was who I would be . . . Mom lies about her romances, her motives, her moods, everything—no, not everything: she lies not totally, not absolutely—to herself and to her confidants, to her lovers and to her husband and to me—she said to me once, *I forget a lot of what went on* . . .

"No," I say vaguely in the scene—a general refusal—as in a book.

"You give nothing away," Mom says.

"No, I don't want to kiss you," I say. "We didn't have to play any of these games," I say.

She didn't have to know.

I turn and look at her before I leave the room in the muted theatricality of this gesture.

But in the theater of the politics of a moment in which I am an active participant, she and I know I will return and kiss her; and I will let her fuck up things for me with Abe, but not if he is determined to go on with his abduction—adoption—whatever . . .

Abe could never stay in anyone's house: the maids, the daughters, the wives—no one was safe when that one was around . . . It takes Casey with a heart of stone and crazy as they come and with an iron disposition to live with a man like Abe. Casey had a lifelong friend, the wife of the doctor in that town where they lived; they kept each other going. I envy Casey, how she managed things . . . She came out a winner and, believe me, Wiley, life is hard—too hard for you. Abe had the confidence of the devil and he was mean—mean as the devil . . . He was no bargain . . . You were well out of it with him—he destroyed everything and everybody . . . He was kind in many, many ways but he was mean as a skunk—he took all the air in the room, he ate everyone up right and left—such a highflier . . . No one rooted for him: you could be mad about him but you [no one] *rooted for him . . . He had his kicks and his kinks—he liked professionals . . . No one could say no to him . . . And he didn't like any excitement in his own house—no sirree—his kids were prisoners—he's a nut: a rake like that being such a fuddy-duddy . . .*

Abe had as part of his extreme personal glamour an *I-know-how-to-do-this* air. Each day or evening, of the three evenings he was there, when I was handed over to him, Lila, she handed me over; I was as if mesmerized . . . or was mesmerized . . . but I was fiercer with him, more disrespectful, than I had ever been with anyone; and it was also like being set free: I felt lost, bitter parts of myself that had vanished, I felt them *return.* Lila said to me privately, *I understand you—you don't want to be a goody-goody . . .* I wanted to learn the odd moral math of a man like that . . . like Abe . . . He wanted me to learn it. If I disliked him after I knew him, there'd be trouble: I mean this was a heavy sacrament—a lifetime promise. Essentially, unapologetically, he gave orders—*Some people like that, Wiley*—and one saw why Mom had said he was *hot stuff but he's a cold fish . . .* The physical effect he made and then his quality of male (and of sexual) focus was as if his eyeing me on first introduction and then on *each and every* reintroduction was a considerable coldness of attention (his, at those moments) that gripped me coldly with a sense of the heat of his opinion—of his regard: a persisting and insistent checking up on *you, your* alertness, and your loyalty, and to see if *you* were worth it—and this, when it came out as *approval, still* was contagious as cold-and-heat, cold and hot excitement, and one shattered stonily or metallically, chattered watchfully, watching one's tongue, one was of use to him . . . even in the so-called tough part of one's heart.

To be personal, if I reenter the moment, more fully as one of the people there—as a character there and then—if I am fully an *I* (and not a *he* or a *one*), what I felt was, I'm sorry to say, a promotion; I was raised in rank, lifted; and I looked down on Lila's luck, on the room, on nearly everyone . . . on S.L., on such elements of our histories together as the things he told me in the middle of the night when he could not sleep . . .

Those things had always the tone and function, the grammar, of nightmare at the busied importance and at the necessities of rank of someone like Abe—no: of important men, women too, the rich ones he'd known and ambitious wives: S.L. felt they hacked up the world and had no conscience, that in the rush of things everyone and everything was cannon fodder for them . . . He, S.L., had spoken of the "harm" Abe had done his children and of Abe being a fiend in the world.

S.L. had proposed a humanity of being overshadowed—both a statistical and a spiritual thing. And, then, more than that a matter of human stuff, of avoiding despair . . . This was in the tone and tempo of how he spoke, usually in my arms, or lying next to me in my bed.

It was a cumulative meaning, put together, pieced together over the years of his illness and of my sticking by him—such as it was.

It wasn't in the words so much; they suffered from elision, omission, from the very *functioning* of his omissive omniscience based on pain, accusation, blame, his sense of the cruelty of fate, of him having been fooled and hurt and needing to be held, of him being *typical,* typically human and important that way, and, as I said, needing to be held, listened to, understood in a *manly* way.

I had held him maybe five hundred times so far while he calmed down from nightmare and lived on.

Abe was one of the models for the causes of S.L.'s nightmares, literally.

Lifted and promoted? I supposed I showed it. Lila said dryly of Abe, *He's a king among men.* He looked at me and chattered some and then he looked at Momma's thickeningly weak-fleshed arms, and it was a judgment on what she and I were that chilled me and scared me, although I wasn't scared—and when he looked out the window, I felt judged by that but not merely disowned but as something equal to the climate itself—to the snow itself.

(Momma said to her friends on the phone, and I overheard her, that he had inherited money and made a great deal more, that he was *a millionaire several times over*, that he checked out what you were, that he compared you to other people, that he estimated what your price was. She said, *If you ask me, I have to say it: he's one hell of a son of a bitch—but he's exciting to be around.*)

He asked me, "Are you the apple of your father's eye? That's what I hear . . ." It interested him (and a lot of men) that I had shown S.L. a certain long-term respect in his illness. "Tell me: is that right, *honey*?" *Honey?* In real life it *was* shocking, that Southern stuff as part of his dark untranslucency of health and standing, personal power, sexual power—and so on. You knew mysteriously what he felt mostly as a dark joke—the honied quality of youth in a real smart bastard . . . Momma has said, at various times: *Casey and Abe have nothing to do with each other but they get along.* Well, he was someone of whom that might be true: he was *at least* that complicated. Momma said, when she spoke of a number of different families at various times, *I can't keep it straight, who loved who* . . . I could imagine people fighting for his regard—that was part of his regard—*I can't stand men like that, who manage it there's a free-for-all for their attention all the time* . . . I wasn't as tall as Abe. He sat in a chair and he took hold of my arm, pulled me over in front of him and said, "You're not a bad-looking kid—and you're not hard to talk to, either." I repeat: a certain automatism attended him when he spoke; a great deal of experience, of conscious choice to say this routine speech and not another: and the free-will part, the tang or savor of the moment's reality, the poisonously inebriating—or honied—part of it was in the tempo of the speech, was the squeezed and narrowed, edited and amended, set of implications in his face—his being pleased or not pleased.

And part of it was him breaking into watch fires, heats, the pleasures of discovery—of double-crossings, of self-protection—the living-body thing of nipples and waist under his clothes and of his visible mouth and nostrils and his moods . . . He threw his body invisibly against his own automatisms of system—as certain movie stars did pratfalls in movies of farce-romance—and it was a trick, he didn't *mean* it, he just did it—with a secular intention—as a practical matter—so that his purposes, for all their heat and manhandling, you had a leaving-you-alone quality except for the practical matters—of taking you over, I mean.

But the words that directed you to give him your attention or to shelter him in your agreement with his purposes—or with your companionship for a moment—they weren't central: "You want a watch? Take mine . . ." He took the watch on his wrist—it had an expandable band; they were new then; I didn't like such bands—and pulled it off and slid it over my hand onto my wrist and he gripped my wrist hard so I couldn't step back and we were physically close, but me standing and him sitting, but eye-to-eye on a slant, chest-to-chest on a slant, and he said, "I'm making you take it as a favor to me—and I have a temper—ha-ha—I'm a hard case: *try me* . . ." And when I grinned fleetingly, nervously, controllably, he laughed some more: almost freely; and he said, "You don't want to look like a charity case . . ." That was a common remark back then. "Always be on top of the world—like on a crapper—hear me: *shittin' on top of the world* . . ." Then: "Listen, I'm going to take care of you—do you know what that means?" He looked past or around me, he moved his head to look at Lila: "The shit is going to stop for you right now . . ."

"Not your shit, Abeleh," Mom said.

He shrugged. "My shit is pure gold, Lila-bet . . . I'm on my feet . . ." She wasn't, obviously. Anyway, it was a negotiation: we talked about my future; and I said I wanted to go into his business—it was like that—and I said I wouldn't leave Dad right away; and he said, well, he understood that.

Then, after that, he sent money each week on top of money that Casey sent—this money was meant for me but I never got it although he telephoned from time to time, checking up, maybe . . . I don't really know. I presume Lila lied about how she spent it. I don't want to be too cynical here—after all, I am guessing at what he meant and at how things happened. I never spoke to him again. He sent cards with greetings and a note, too, one suggesting I come to stay with them; and Lila said, "I'll handle it." Then he fell ill toward the end of that winter and he died the following spring.

Lila said, *How it happens is you go to bed one night, and everything is what it was, it's fine, and you wake the next day and you're sick and everything is over; everything is falling apart—believe me, I know . . . Wiley, Abe got a terrible, terrible thing*—(whisper) *bone cancer: nothing is worse—it's terrible; it was agony; his bones break just with him lying on them; it doesn't matter how thin he gets, his own weight breaks his bones day after day, can you imagine . . . I never gloat over anyone but can you imagine a change in your luck like that; what does it feel like over and over? Casey is loyal and she's nursing him* (Mom hadn't nursed S.L. much)—*it doesn't matter to her about the screaming; she keeps her nerve . . . All the years he bossed her around and she resisted: still, she comes through for him. She's a serious person when it comes to her obligations . . . There's no point your writing him: he's on drugs: believe me, a man going through something like that can't be bothered with letters from you.*

He died; and S.L. died, not long after—I never again felt anything of that sort, even close to it with any man again.

His sons—Abe's sons—Daniel and Benjamin, came to S.L.'s funeral. Not Casey, not S.L.'s sister. Daniel, the elder son, has a good watch with a leather strap; and he says, "My father never wore good watches when he travelled; he lost them or he gave them away. The one he gave you is no good; and he wanted me to bring you a good one. He picked this one out before he was bedridden."

And: "He told me to go take a look at you and see what I could do to help you . . ."

By then, Nonie had returned home to live with us.

One of Abe's Sons

There are so many ways to be homosexual or partly homosexual—or flatly not homosexual—that you'd have to know everyone who was alive and everyone who had ever been alive to know much about it.

Abe's younger son, Benjie, before he died, came to New York; when he was young, he was known for his looks: big-shouldered, square-jawed, blond, with dark brown eyes . . . Lila had said he was *very, very likable* and had *joie de vivre*; he said at the end, "Now I'm old and my face looks like I got it out of the linen closet . . . I need ironing . . ."

He had on lip gloss, pancake makeup, and quite a noticeable thick blond wig. I knew a number of heterosexual men in New York who did that stuff: it has more to do with being considered to be charming at some point and you refuse to go on to the next physical phase: who wants to rethink and redesign everything all the time. Benjie was wry and fluttering, embarrassed, comic and obstinate: and serious—charming, I think . . . Lila had said of him that he was *undemanding—as bright as a penny: he makes no parade of himself which is really something when you think how much money he'll come into. I think he's very, very good-looking—he has bones; it's not just the luck of the Irish* . . . (I.e., his looks were real and not like mine, an accident of mind perhaps.) *He doesn't have willpower, which is a shame—that's a drawback—he'll never be a rock or shield for anyone* . . . He'll never defend anyone. *But he's fun . . .*

He said he wanted to talk to me about "secret lives." I told him I hadn't had a secret life. And he hesitated for a minute, and then he said, "I *loved* you . . ." He said it naughtily, airily, while frowning. "I loved my daddy and I loved Daniel so much I thought it would kee-YILLL ME and I thought you were *nice*: I'm drunk—don't mind me . . . I took a pill or two [as well]: why waste time when you only have a weekend—in the Big Apple—and it's costin' an arm and a leg—a leg and an arm—and another arm if you got it?"

I should say I had been convinced that he'd had an oddly peaceful life—or peaceful in a way—and prosperous; but I hadn't really thought about it. His jocularity, his limited self-licensing to do harm, his semi-overt plea to be allowed to be corrupt in certain ways: when I was young—when I was thirteen and fourteen, in the various uncompleted ways in which I thought about things back then and knew him—I had thought, not condescendingly, that what he was was almost a fairy-tale thing or fairylike in a number of senses and represented that kind of malicious, playful, wee-people sense of things. Boredom, meaninglessness, *meaningless pain*—human things—the flesh-and-blood awful stuff of *the big people*—or some such thing and a gallant and frivolously defiant *excellence* of social manner: these were his insignia, and his social manner in part, and his taste and his metaphysics . . . It was related in him to the stuff that went on in the kind of house Katie Rogers had lived in in U. City. In a certain obvious sense, Benjie is the perfect child still but he is also a rat, a snitch, a plotter; but he is, also, a factual wit and a man with the *gentle* death of the will in him offered to you as a sign of how acceptable as company he is or might be if you are nice to him or can be if you will only help and applaud Tinker Bell—I don't actually mean this snidely but he was extraordinarily devious: he has never been generous, kind, or really good to anyone, never subservient to anyone except his mother, although he has a manner of subservience to everyone; and his manner of sexual subservience partly contains his will and ability to *do shit* to others—his ability to get them to eat shit. I liked him a lot but he double-crossed absolutely everyone in the short time I knew him—he did it purposefully and as a matter of sort of last-ditch self-respect . . . He is laughing at me now and he is pleading and he is entirely unsacramental. He is, in a way, beautiful and brave: his social manner and his beliefs and habits don't stop or alter because of age and the approach of death—he is unrepentant and marvelous and truly awful.

And his sense that his privileges had been deformities or attached to them did not mean he felt inferior in any final way at all . . . Indeed, he had long ago made the moral discovery that you were at fault for minding his faults.

He said, "We shoulda seen MORE uv each other—Wileeeee . . ."

Charm. I had aged, I thought, considerably better than he had—at least as such stuff was to be measured at that moment—and I ploughed through *the shit* and said to dear old Benjie, testingly (I was thinking of Abe and of Benjie's brother, Daniel), "Were you tormented? In your life?"

"Oh shuah but it made me no never mind . . . I'm certainly very glad to see you, Wiley . . ."

"I'm certainly glad to see YOU . . . BUT DID YOU HAVE A BAD TIME?"

He laughed, not in any of his old ways. He laughed with a kind of turgid resentment; and he said with irony: "Oh, I forget just how suh-yus y'ah—you er BIG-TYIM SUH-YUS . . ."

"And you?" I tried not to be cross-examinerish but sort of faux–Oscar (or Ockie) Wilde: "And you, my DEAR . . ."

He blinked—and flinched—at the ways I was being sympathetic and failing to be sympathetic to him—i.e., what he expected. He blinked and flinched, making me—really it was as if he slathered me with makeup and changed the stage lighting—making me villainous . . . But villainous and *cute* . . . "Oh, we're all so interestin' now . . ." he said tactfully. And vaguely. Then he eyed me to suggest we flirt and mean more than our words when we talked. Then brightly (but wearily): "Oh you, you alwez saw right through us . . . You saw right through *everything* . . ."

The last was a fairly devastating attack.

"No, no . . ." Then: "It never occurred to me to be *that* realistic, Benjie . . ."

"Me neither and I lived there!" Benjie said in an incredible shriek, changing the subject, maybe without knowing it—and maybe not for him.

His loud, shrill voice—late *joie de vivre*—can go off like an alarm clock announcing that it is time to wake up.

It is a kind of partial if jabby truth-telling and kinds of evasion and self-will now, too.

"What a *charmer* you always were," I said in pursuit of revelations. Then because I have gotten into the habit of explaining myself: "People have to have some reason to speak; kindness turns quickly into silence and you just commiserate then, and you never stay in that state long . . ."

Benjie said, "Oh, you were always hokey-jokey . . . So suh-yus . . . I was hokey-jokey . . . *too* . . . [Whe] 'N you were *fourteen*—you were *the charmer* . . . weren't you just? I ain't just a-clackin' my gums . . . Wouldn't you just love to go back and do jes' one or two things you didn't do when you had the *figure* for it?"

I felt a kind of agonizing despair at not sharing much with him—at my loss of him, if I can say that. I said, politely blank, "I don't have that kind of science-fiction sense of time . . . Benjie: If I'm working, if I'm writing, I can't play around when I talk or I'll lose my train of thought—in the work . . ."

He said with the old placatory charm, "You know how it is . . . easy come when you're young but it's hard to let go when you're old . . . I'm so glad with how things turned out for you—I'm glad you finally found peace doing work you respect—I know you had a hard life . . ." Then: "Ha-ha . . ."

"It's not exactly peace I found—I don't think it is," I said.

"Oh, I read what you write. You like to talk about the past don't you? And you jes' settle right down in it—"

"The past?"

"You're a regular *Ancient Mariner* when you write—"

Souls like albatrosses flapping around a restaurant table, some of them from the past, in a story . . .

"I like to hear stuff about the past . . ." Benjie said. "I learned a lot, you know . . . I didn't just stand still. I didn't just tell myself, Hold your water, hold your horses—I went to an analyst—I kept my eyes and ears open—I grew up—some . . . Oh, that stuff is crazy, it's just so *scary* . . . you start diggin' around; I just loved all of us, I was a good kid, but it was a difficult household . . . My oh my. My parents couldn't stand each other—I bet you knew that . . . You saw through thet and it took me years of analysis to know I have a much better marriage than my father did . . ." He blinked, a film of tears in his eyes—"Don't mind me: it's just a little emotion and the pills and my contact lenses . . ."

"I remember only a little bit at a time, Benjie," I said. "I don't remember better than you do."

"Oh you DO . . ."

I remembered that Daniel, years before, had characterized Benjie to me once as *someone who thinks my parents loved each other. Well, they had manners* . . . I decided not to repeat it to Benjie. Then I decided that wasn't fair and I told him.

Benjie, in an emotional mood, said charitably, "That's all

right . . . You don't have to tell me things about *my* life . . . Tell me dirty things about your life—I *like* to have a good time . . . I think only *parents* should be allowed to *look* at suh-yus things *anyway* . . . When I'm in New York, I'm not a parent—I'm a travelling salesman and I'm no good seventeen different ways till Tuesday . . . Isn't this a good seafood restaurant?"

"It's fine," I said, meaning it wasn't.

"*Isn't* this a good seafood restaurant?" he said astonished.

I was startled that he didn't know. I suppose he couldn't taste the food.

"Isn't this a good seafood restaurant?" he chanted, making a routine out of the moment . . . People at other tables were looking at us. Benjie said cheerily—but entirely without cheer—"I was always just a weed . . . a bad boy . . ." He expects me to understand what he means by what he is saying, but when he sees I don't quite, he politely asks, "What are you working on now?" He does it with the charm of someone showing he is interested in other people and that he is flexible; he says when I don't answer, "You always wanted to change the world—me, I only wanted to change a tire— Do you have a spare tire? I'm outright fat. I'm so sad I could die. Nothin' ever happened to me; all I ever did was have a good time. No *sad* stuff for me—I can't *deal* with sad stuff. Combin' mah hair—combin' what hair I-uh hevv lef(fi)t—is sad enough for me. I'll tell you the truth: I don't hev enny moh hayir. This is A WIG. And I'll tell you more of the truth, I surely do admire you. I never had the courage to rock the boat. I was selfish but I did a good job of standing by Momma. I had a good time but it was hard—and it was hard on me!" He looked at me with an odd, *human* smile. "I kept a male lover in San Francisco for twenty years."

"Twenty years?"

"A different one every few years," he said boastfully-sweetly—changing the story.

"Casey knew?"

"She was a difficult person, but she could learn new tricks—she wasn't an old dog, you know. Are you as sophisticated as I think? Aren't you very left-wing? Oh, Momma knew how to be difficult with *you*." I was thinking that the trouble with confessions was that they were never true enough. When I asked him about San Francisco, he said shamefacedly, "Oh, I shared the upkeep of one." Then: "Not always the same one . . . Now and then . . ." He muttered the last thing. "It was like Daddy and his show girls," he said defiantly . . . perhaps hopefully. "I stayed married, too . . . I never knew what I was doing—did you know what you were doing? I wish to hell I knew what it meant. Any help you could give me would be surely welcome."

"Was it strange for you? Did you think about the guy all the time?"

"Oh you know me," he said. "Out of sight, out of mind." Then: "I called him from the office; we had a code . . . Them . . . I called them . . . I don't remember . . . It's too much, Wiley-pet . . . too much for my old head to remember: it's all dead and buried—like everyone I knew—and us, you and me, sooner or later—" He leered at me in a friendly and meaningful way: "You know what the doctors say: Too soon old, too late smart."

"S.L. used to say that—sometimes. That and *Monkeys is the cwaziest people* . . ."

The moments of greeting between the lovers—between the kept one and the keeper—Benjie wouldn't want to be met at the airport by a guy . . . were the moments obliterating? Passionate, not clearly individual, stylized, highly dramatic?

"I was always disappointed," he said.

I said, "Homosexual ties aren't necessarily better than heterosexual ones . . ."

Benjie said, "Ohah uh dohinn't tayll me thettt! I heff to hev somethin' tuh dreem uhbut."

The past is not a dream.

Daniel's Kindness

1

DANIEL'S KINDNESS again: Perhaps the boys, Benjie and Danny (as he was called when he was young), took the place of their mother with each other. Their mother had a strong sense of her own life. (Or: Casey being a very cold person perhaps . . .) It is *logical* that the men in that household would share and soothe each other's *unhappiness*—perhaps in dangerously informative ways. Perhaps they adopted modified doctrines of pleasure like their father's—with such changes as made sense to them. I was unclearly aware of such matters.

Perhaps they shielded each other from Abe. Or their parents used them. I don't presume to judge.

Daniel's grandmother was S.L.'s mother—that is the degree of cultural proximity. S.L.'s manners and beliefs—his bedtime kisses—tie me to Daniel in some degree—in an odd way. A family thing is not to be *explained*. I am not unlike Daniel's mother physically: after all, I was adopted in part because of a resemblance to S.L.

Daniel looks like a lesser Abe . . . In some respects this is an easier, *lesser* world than Abe's was.

When it's your own reality, you feel it differently—the story you tell. Momma cannot speak of *herself* when she *speaks* of herself—and I can't either. I don't know what Nonie's version of this was, what it felt like to her to be rescued, to be on her way to Carolina. Daniel looks at me in an intensely familiar way: it is a peculiar familiarity, one without great reason: the shared shape of the noses doesn't explain the familiarity in the staring. We have no humid, sweaty, muscular, and charactero-logical blood-similarity of nerves and senses. Our minds, their acrobatics and flights don't echo with similar tempos. Or vocabularies. Moods, eyelids and breath, are noticeably very different. Postures and hands—fingers and fingernails—are unlike.

He has been described to me as *the brainy one* in the family. He said to me, "Nonie is trash." If he thinks of intelligence (of some kind) and of disliking Nonie as being very tightly formed, absolute categories, I can understand the look of familiar similarity. People do look at me in that way but then they take it back.

Some people think S.L. fathered me on my real mother. If that was what happened, then Daniel and I were actually first cousins; and everything here would be explained.

Everything? Bits of nostalgia echoing and defining something and modifications and bits of information whispering about oneself in a perception, if not of resemblance, then of affectionate semi-twinship—echoing and resonant for someone who might, perhaps, feel lonely.

Perhaps we are sexually alike; and he, in his greater sophistication, sees and knows this. Something about him is familiar: he resembles his father but is not greatly like him; I wouldn't trust him to be, in the sense in which people sometimes mean this, *his father's son*.

My sense of his chances in life may be flecked with ill will—and with a curious potency in my corresponding sense of myself.

In reply to his remark about Nonie which, in its way, offers too much sympathy for the past—his sympathy, expressed even that way, thrums some chord of emotion in me that might dissolve me once and for all—I say, "S.L. said at times I was *trash*—"

"People say things . . ."

"He said—of himself, *Perhaps I got the worst of it the whole goddamn time* . . . I.e., he suffered from knowing me . . ."

"It's a sign you care that you go on about it."

"He wasn't bad to me . . . I was the dangerous one to him. Not all the time . . . He was bad, too, a lot of the time . . . People in the family—people in school—say I talk oddly . . ."

Daniel did not choose to tease me. He said, "I don't seem to mind the way you talk." It was a promise, you know? Not a solid one. The syntactical do-jiggy of *seem to mind* was a social-class thing.

Do you arouse feelings in your life as you go along? Did you when you were young? Do you exist among feelings, yours and those of other people, feelings turned toward you and some turned away from you?

Were people ever a bit on edge and interested? In you?

He is an employer of a couple of thousand people off and on. He owns stuff, cars, properties—he has more attachments, deeper ones, more solid ones to the world than I do. He is moody, self-willed, powerful: *my cousin* Daniel . . .

In our eyes, in our faces, the topic as it develops, *trash*, as well as being called names by one's (now dead) father, is not entirely unromantic; a ground of sympathy, it has a certain heat to it which is not unsexual: *trash* is—threatening: to neatness, to pretensions. Is unserious. *Up-for-grabs.* Who wants it can have it. Value can be bestowed on it or taken away at will. I sit on the horsehair seat on one side of the compartment. Daniel faces me. I am aware of feelings in him directed at me—but perhaps at my momentary physical self mostly: is this a sad thing after S.L.'s death?

"Human things come and go," he says. Human seasons? "You did what you could . . ." He says it intently. I had been for a long time, I had been almost permanently, it seemed, *a consoling child.* Did you ever love someone who helped you? He was helping me, Daniel . . . Daniel says, "You showed a helping spirit."

A blundering brouhaha of innocence and help . . . *Blundering* is clearly involved here. I am willing as a guest and as a charity case to accept the blundering and not show distaste. Patience, tolerance, forbearance in a guest, a young cousin, are also signs of the wildness in the cousin. A wildness of experience is a tacitly admitted thing between us, a knowledge of (male) life, brainy in a sense, for people like us, for him and me, a community of sympathetic relation between us.

"We both like books," he says and smiles.

One is young but is old enough to know someone younger will replace you as being young. But, meanwhile, this is your turn. Your chance—these are (were) Mom's terms. This, too, has a wilderness quality to it, knowing this stuff, half knowing it; the reality of it and of knowing it is *wild.* I have often needed special help but I did not always get it—but perhaps I more often got it than some other people get it, help when they need it . . . Cousin Daniel had come to see if I needed help. And he'd come to see what I looked like; *everyone* that year was *interested* in what I looked like—it was talked about a lot. One is not a child anymore—one can say one is not a child anymore—but one echoes with unfinished, unquenched childhood still. This stuff is partly a chapter of childhood. His face—Daniel's—here in the same compartment with me—surely the interest in it toward me is homosexual . . . The quality of attention . . .

We are alike. We are not alike.

Daniel's attention, if it was not okay, would I know it? Was it noticeably *homosexual*? Big deal . . . The sexual curiosity in him, the nature, the tone of his attention, perhaps the professionalism of his interest, were bad things. His attention as we travel—his being interested *not* in his mood so much and not in the curiously hint-filled large flatness of the landscape outside the train windows, the unrolling skin of American earth, the almost-wilderness of scenic novelty out there—but his interest in a young example of his own gender, a brute, undiagrammatic example, me—I am vague and hardly well informed about this stuff; I am theoretical, young and *obtuse* about it to a considerable extent.

And I am smeared with death, and obtusely and carefully propitiatory toward people who serve in the army; and I am unexploratory except in watchfulness in my grief; I am aware of the *horror* and *strangeness*, the pleasure and the strain of this stuff with a few boys (whom I like) at school.

A boy aglimmer with doubt, then? And a *polite* compartmentalization of his boyish attention, a politely purposeful focus? A boyish manner—a purity of such effort, such compartmentalization?

Boyish pride and the male politics of a moment with an older guy and an ethic—a greatly modified imitation of what other boys did in this matter or about these things *socially* and humanly? Look, I want Dan to like me; the hope that I might manage to grow up and not be mad, not too loony—not suicidal, not burdened with obscene self-explanation as an addiction or as a hobby—that category of wishes makes me reasonable-and-patient inwardly under a boyish blankness, somewhat tense. That plus a need for immediate semi-absolution and a consequent moral politics of *getting along in the world* and then a specific sense—please forgive me—of my nipples and ribs and hands and my legs in my trousers and my eyes and mind and my hair as *something*—making up a social reality of a kind for a boy *of a kind*—that stuff is *flattered*. And I am able to leave Daniel at any minute if I have to, leave him and the compartment and make friends with maybe anyone—male or female, young or old—on that train; I am generally acceptable, says his flattery; and, socially, fairly well protected (maybe). Anyway, mostly not trapped.

I mean that sort of practical absolution holds me here. I don't, beyond any of that, *mind* this stuff. Or I do, but it's not a big deal—is it?

A sort of unwise clearheadedness of definitions hung over the actuality of his feelings as if they were maybe fixed and reliable. But that was a form of lying, one that was a form of *intellectual truth*. He has beliefs about what he is doing. What he is feeling. He is a very specialized observer of a boy.

How odd he is, how much odder than I am he is as an object of attention. His feeling that he is odd shows. No one has ever been *fair* to Daniel . . . Daniel liked to philosophize. He believed in final, clear, and absolute meanings. In certain ways I can rescue *him*, he thinks. He glances at me with a certain austerely insulted and half-hidden delectation. He said for the third time that day, on the train, "We aren't related by blood."

I smiled like a guest—a young guest.

The temperature in the compartment, my sense of it and of sexual (and social) matters, embarrassment, and my feelings of ignorance are mixed in me with sensations, oh, of a hunted arrogance, a dim sort of excitement.

I repeat, this was during one of those times in my life—a month, six weeks—during which *everyone* (or *everyone and his brother*), as when I was two years old, said they loved me. Or seemed to care. Or be *interested*. (That was Lila's term.) Everyone? A lot of people. Everyone who looked at me and did a double take, for instance. For various reasons, this filled me with a regular and rather quick, guiltily glum exhilaration. I knew it was a mode of escape—maybe of expensive escape—and of self-destruction . . . superficiality . . . et cetera. One was primarily ignorant. The ignorance was a blackness, a kind of void of *So?* and of *So what?* and of *What do you mean?* and *What does this mean?* Of *Does this matter to me? If so, how, for how long, how much . . .*

And so on . . . Is it a big deal?

2

He had a certain sort of intellectual hauteur and resignation, an intellectual belief in himself, and an early form of sexual opinionatedness. He was also, as a matter of fact, spiritually and emotionally and sexually haughty. He did, of course, like others, feel his way along in talk and companionship—at least with me. In front of me. The train chugged. He got me to talk about sports stuff; he watched me lightly, with variations of attention; he turned the subject to books. Then we did family gossip, philosophy, and God. I get a glimpse of how different the world is for him from me—it seems as if he is *all other people*. It seems *I come tumbling after*. Nonie did this: left home and went out among other people's feelings. A lot of what I do I can't consciously control. I shudder, I sweat (I glimmer); I play politics. I automatically say no to things. I am guessing about what to do, even about what I *want* to do . . . I want to do a lot of *different* things. Khaki'd Daniel sits in the compartment; he is on compassionate leave from the army—maybe also on business leave—the family company is immersed in *the war effort* . . . His father is dead, too, like mine.

Your banjo is between your knees . . . I am going to Carolina . . .

Daniel says with a certain amount of hope that I will enjoy talking *philosophy* with him: "Objectivity means not being selfish—about what you know—and feel."

Clickety-clack, the train goes.

I say, "Is it an aspect of attention?"

He blinks at me.

"Is it a quality in what certain sorts of attention see as facts?" I said, "It's not separate from attention—is it?"

I did not know at what level of speech I would no longer seem to him to be okay and interesting and he would decide not to like me.

Cousin Daniel said, "Look at it like this: the eye of *God* is objective, Wiley."

"We probably shouldn't talk about the Eye of God . . ."

"The eye of *Elohim* . . ."

"No. I mean, I mean why should God bother to have *eyes?* Or gender? Why would *God* bother with distinctions between objective and subjective?"

"I don't follow you. Are you being enlightened? Are you quoting . . . someone?"

"I doubt it . . . But I can't remember everything I read."

"You shouldn't try to reason about *God* . . ."

"I wasn't. You were ascribing attributes to God . . . I was talking about what you said."

"Well, we Jews do that . . . with God."

"Which Jews? All Jews do that?"

"Well, yes. Wiley, yes. You are being young—very young—your feelings aren't hurt if I say that? Are they hurt? *We* are allowed to address God."

"Allowed? I really don't understand—unless God isn't very much but is only sort of an idea of an Idea you don't really intend to have—why would God *allow* something—do you know what I am trying to say?" Once I press the switch of *not lying*, I can't help myself for a while.

I can't turn on a dime. Maybe he'll like me anyway. Maybe the way he is what he is means he *likes* someone who argues the way I argue. "Objectivity your way seems to mean you think you stop all real connection to ordinary purpose and that you separate yourself from everything in life and attach yourself to God and religion, and you say that is in order to see clearly . . . objectively. But it just means you have a towering absolute that no one can examine—it's a very, very big mental stick you carry."

"Do you think you are smart nationally?" Daniel asks.

"No pillar of fire has sprung up near me," I say wryly. People have asked me stuff like this. I am semi-rehearsed.

"I am thinking," Cousin Daniel told me, "of becoming a big-schmear scientist or else a modern Orthodox rabbi."

This odd lanky-handsome, rich Carolinian, superbly well kempt and smart, didn't hear my ideas. Big deal. But cross-pollination, cross-breeding of ideas, of lives, he resisted that. His was a final faith and an addicted need for absolute statements, absolute truths, in the end, a single truth which encompassed everyone and everything so that his sense of a single truth defined me as a figure in his landscape. Nonie had said he was a *bully*. She had gotten along with Benjie, not with Daniel.

I was determined to like him. Inspired and newly reinspired by thinking Nonie hadn't liked him, I looked at him: he was truly neat, faintly exotic: not a jumble: amazingly self-concerned—more a man of charity than a man of thought or of awareness. He was omnigendered, commanding, a breeder of *exotically and erotically* charged situations of an *intelligent* nature. He was almost certainly not a *lover* . . . I mean, taking that as a category. Not of real people. He was not a thinking scientist. He was not entirely self-concerned: he was in possession of the traits of others as their employer and as a donor or patron. Perhaps the possession, through love and hate, of an intensity of focus *was* narcissistic in him in that it did not involve him in any honest sense of the relative merits of someone else going off into any doctrines other than those set up, predicated, inflecting his rather absolutist daydreaming. So that even if I was *convenient* in some ways for his fantasies, I mean the boy I was those few months, the *fact* was that his sense of absolute things said I was the best person, the ideal kid, the highest form of what was to be admired or felt this way about. They said that that day.

And there was no qualification, nothing of the ideal-for-him in any intellectual limit to his variety of absolutism. There was no way I could "romantically" accept his attentions except by being a conduit for aphorisms and laws and psalms almost about the ideal thing, the boy-I-was;

a truly grand angelic flutter accompanied the image of me in him . . . maybe. I did not disbelieve his feelings so much as I added onto my clouded sense of his feelings, my sense of other men, supplying that default rendition of a male self to him and to me. I was dodge-y. The extent to which he was ironic about himself and the extent to which he was gentle with himself and then the extent to which he was serious in his admiration of the loon kid formed a sort of fingerprint to which I attached the general stuff about flirtations that wouldn't lead to marriage and kids, you know? Mom had flirted with women. Again, one had noticed stuff in school. One now half believes his mother and my sister had flirted in some way or other. I laughed out loud for no reason—not so loudly he had to ask me what I was doing or be surprised or stare.

Of course, years of reading—years of peering at reality through the wrought-iron fence of the alphabet—well-known prose and famous stories (famous at least among most of the English teachers at school)—meant I saw him in a changeably blurred pattern-y way having to do with this stuff as shown in books, those opinions; but the reality of those interpretations, not a story but a person, pretty much amazed me.

As a matter of policy, I disbelieved my teachers. I disbelieved myself whatever I thought. I thought it *contingently*.

Time will tell. My sense of fact includes time. What *factually* occurs will show in some way what "the truth" is, truth perhaps semi-childishly measured. Perhaps eventually, at the moment of death maybe, I will see factually what really went on, see finally, a little anyway, see a little.

A certain fineness in him, a practical narrowness had become a sense of willed limitation that helped limit his pietistic absolutism—he was almost liberal. But the thing of him being a "desirable" older man in the compartment on a train rescuing me, and my being the-most-desirable-boy-in-the-world, the shoving and bumping of that, the inequality of those terms, desirable and the-most-desirable-in-the-world representing "romance" kind of as a-thing-that-was-in-his-favor was not so liberal. Or generous. Him believing, essentially, that there was only one of each good thing, only one form of high example, and everything else was shit or else was an aspect of the high example, of the standard normal high-up great thing, meant that each thing was judged as being close or not to the final point or meaning, or else it was held to be dirt and a dead subject and so on. Ignorant or not ignorant, one has ways of knowing stuff like the above that predict what someone's hands will feel like on you if they touch you, when they touch you.

I don't *know* of what elements my heterosexuality consists. Or my androgyny.

My opinions of him? A few things my senses register include this: that he did not abandon his awareness of his own superbly physically (and socially) well-tended self, at least as far as I could see, for a single second during the hours of his wakefulness. He did not stir beyond that, bulge out and dematerialize or become purely staring or some such thing. Or fly into a sense of the air. I reminded him of himself. Whatever it was that I was, it was reflected back tinglingly, ticklingly, so that you could see stuff about yourself in how he sat. He stared *intelligently*, though . . .

3

If I say that looking a gift horse in the mouth obliges me to rethink something about me, I mean only that I apparently felt I had quite a lot of choice. I did not, even from time to time, grant to myself any particular *beauty* except negatively. I knew I did not have a grinding choicelessness. I knew people reacted to me. So I knew I wasn't someone people *didn't* react to. I knew that what I was, all told, when I spoke commanded allegiance in some people and immediate disgust in others—for a while; and disappointment then, too, or often. But I had no orderly sense of this, no workable theory or hypothesis other than a physical socially political sense of the *unlikely* and *politically obtrusive* thing of arousing feeling, feelings that were undefined in my inner world but which had temperature and tempo. I swear I had no clear idea, and did not day-dream, of any of this—at least not after it became part of my life. I knew I affected people. Not always. Daniel had taken me to an expensive store in St. Louis, and the salesman and manager and the other people had made a fuss and had stared at me—not a great fuss, a discreet but intense enough fuss—one is aware that *this-stuff-might-happen*. People get mad at you . . . Boy-stuff, meanness, the eerie lyricism, the depth or whatever of *teasing*, people trying to figure *what-you-are-made-of*; it happens. I did not think of it as a basic dimension, reliable and unmoving, of my life; or as a given of my adolescent *fate*; it was sometimes there, often there, and sometimes not: it came and went, goddamn it: it was an unreliable matter. To attempt to reproduce it daily or to know it as a sure thing was to invent a form of it and change it, was to invent something new and to change what was there: what was there was accidental, improvisatory—a source of amusement (sometimes) and of trouble (often). Very few people—perhaps only lesbians—leave me alone *as a rule*. They sometimes like me, sometimes attack me. Sometimes they like to flirt with and own me and compete with me with my only half-knowing what is going on. There are few or no photographs from that period that show the boy clearly. The ones that exist show little except the movie-ish thing of being visible and odd among others, *the-one-looked-at* . . . the one teased . . .

What-I-looked-like was often talked about in my hearing but not my looks. My looks were never discussed; my actual looks did not interest anyone. It wasn't symmetry and cheekbones and a good hairline. I was a fork-legged and surprising kind of physical reality or presence, a sort of ambulatory metaphor for comparison with other such metaphors of attention, other collections of similes of attention (eyes, manners, postures), objects of comparative attention. Thoughts were what I evoked, sensations . . .

Mom said, *You have no proportions . . . no bones* . . . I thought she was wrong. I had seen myself in store windows, a vague, erased image, mostly proportion, a lit shadow, flattened but reflecting dimensionality, revealing the bones of the thing. The effect *I* made, or that *it* made—I figured that would last a while . . . Oh, not the *same* effect. That isn't what I mean at all. *It* was a bit like being a bag spilling out packages—wrapped packages. People looked at me suddenly as if they had that sense of me. My friends told me I was ugly—it wasn't *not* true. If the police came anywhere near us, my friends at any given time and me, I was pushed forward to speak. Strange policemen reacted to me at sight—to the *sight* of me. I could expect special treatment . . . most of the time . . . of a highly polite and patient or a highly impolite—and bumptious—sort . . . dangerous. At times, in bars, underage, we'd had to fight because of me. Sometimes a brawl would break out and the brawlers would make an exception of me. *Not you,* some guy would say, and back off. Some people made a point of sparing me things. Lila said often, *It doesn't matter what you look like . . . You're a boy . . . You have a future* . . . Girls at school wrote me notes, propositioned me—often innocently, not sexually, but offering themselves up to a point. When sometimes they saw I had not daydreamed about them, they *hated* me. They got even in all sorts of fairly crude or fairly slick ways. For convenience' sake and in modesty I listened to my mother about this stuff which had entered my life so unexpectedly and which I did not understand. It seemed to me I had not understood her; she did not mean that the surface effect did not matter: she meant that it was not a surface effect but that my life so far, the illness, Dad's I mean, and me sticking around and my unhappiness, that stuff and biology had created an effect.

It may be hard to listen to anyone say such things as this but it is really hard to bear having it happen to you, the adopted child, the adopted-father-lover, the penniless and intelligent anarchist-moralist, the mind, prick—eyes—mouth . . . One ought to try to be simple. One had a skull shaped in a certain way, inherited features, eyes of a certain cast and outline, height and sadness, a proportion of cheerfulness, a degree of self-willed freshness. One had facial expressions. One looks out the window of the compartment, looks down at the upholstery of the seat, looks at the wall, looks into Daniel's eyes, and sees there, as so often in those weeks in the eyes of people, a response, immediate, fairly intense, not really obscure. Not completely obscure.

It is an interest in life . . . because I—because someone who looks like me, someone I am inside of, is there: it is something like that.

4

In the weird world of slithering and suddenly present perceptions, in the interpretation and amendment of interpretations, hypotheses, in having *an idea* (or *ideas*) of or about what-happened-before and in the immediate and near and far-off comparisons of these to now and then one's gamblings in regard to the future, a moralist is someone with hope of meaning.

A moralist, Daniel had that moralistic whorishness that supplies at moments a realistic domination of the world through thoughts already set up, thoughts already there to be verified by existence now; one's will pushes to see that that happens, that one's thoughts are verified—thoughts in their gray-robed immortality, seemingly. And, actually, since thoughts cannot be the same in different minds day after day or in the same mind when they recur, his were thoughts that had a quality of *his* notions of immortality, finality, and moral excellence. They were personal to him but they had elements of a claim to being universal. Their only modification lay in his sense of tactics and his sense of payments, of money, and of actual allure, all of which he saw as absolutes and as moral things, one by one, incoherently; but because of his strength of character and force of personality, he thought he was deeply and even violently *coherent*. I am trying to convey the sense of him one had—the faintly sweaty sense of him.

My wrists in the cuffs of my new shirt and the new veins on my new arms and the curious vein down the center of my forehead . . . I felt him with these newly.

Daniel wasn't essentially a whore. Good-looking and presentable, he wasn't someone people longed after. He was noted and admired and avoided: a somewhat angular, self-spellbound-and-impatient-with-that, handsome and intelligent man . . . *Narcissistic*—convinced one could know the whole truth from knowing him. Some kids used the term *sadistic* for such dispositions, meaning the overall effect of the plunge of the self in real air was cruelly afflicted in the influence of a-burning-meteor-as-a-single thing every hour and in every mood. The terms of a specific encounter, the thing of naming that specific encounter as it is going on, that goes on minute by minute, becomes oppressive near him, the *Oh, what a surprise* and *the twists and turns* and naming things in people as you go—there were wartime programs, *lend-lease* and *pay-as-you-go*, and there was a daily sense of the war, always different a bit—it was like riding a horse, but really, in real time, in the war, people even rewrote the immortal war aims of the democracies all the time—there was a meanness of *The Single Truth* about him.

He was rich—and autocratic . . . good at things . . . *These are bits-and-pieces on the way to a theory, a hypothesis* . . . one's traits, one's looks, one's haircut, one's smiles, these when one is in his presence—well, this was so on that trip—these were judged by him steadily in remarks or in glances, were judged in the light of what he *knows* from the larger world—*feels*, has decided is the *truth*. He *knows* about fashions in men's stuff. One was aware—from one's experience—one was *aware* at moments—one is aware that one is among conscious and unconscious judgments of oneself—not as breeding stock perhaps, but as a *sport*—a special case . . . an oddity . . . a beauty . . . And you kind of have to decide to what extent he *knows what he's talking about*, or if *he's a child still (despite appearances)*, or a *neuroid*—crazy and self-loving and with bad judgment about the world—or if he's been-left-out-of-it (provincial, stubborn), or if he is *loony*-with-*love*—*gaga* (Lila's term; Nonie's term, too—Nonie had categories for guys who liked her: one such was "Momma's-boy-fool" . . . *Well, you have to be the spine for a boy like that—that's not such a bad life—there's money in that family* . . . and so on . . .), or you can make up your mind to be simple. You can consider things to be settled. You can be drunk or just mindless. Or driven by despair. You can adopt the velocity of the visual, the speed of eyesight with no time to think. Or you can hold back. Holding back or holding off is, willy-nilly, a form of thought in real life.

5

"At high school in U. City we have a fad—we go around asking, What kind of gun are you? You don't have to answer . . ."

"A six-shooter," Daniel said after a moment—and wryly.

I knew some of the kids at school who practiced some of the separate disciplines of homosexuality—a group homosexual tone—and some who were temporarily homosexual; and a church group of believers who were *intellectual* and who waved their hands around but who used funny voices and had funny stares they gave people but they were earnest in their religion. Daniel is not part of any group stuff of that sort—he is a rigorous enemy of that stuff. He is rigorous, severe, stern toward loose mannerisms, but he is, as it were, overly musical in a *foreign* way, pleading some sort of special meaning as if la-la-ing it; he offers some sort of special *melodic* humor.

"Are you an opera lover?" I ask as the train goes bumpety-clack over wartime roadbed.

"Yes. What kind of gun are you?"

"People change every day—you get to have moods—I'm a cannon . . . an old-fashioned railway cannon . . . I'm slow . . . I'm a lot of work."

The judging when you partly disapprove of judging and the fencing and the offering(s) and the flags of truce, the lying down and showing one's belly, or the showing one's neck while sitting up, or one's presenting one's hind end—and hiding your mind (under leaves so to speak, or behind systems of chatter or of silence)—mind, will, ambition, calculations, or showing them like a passport—one did those things long before one read about them in anthropologically and biologically slanted pieces in *Reader's Digest.* One is judged as an uncertain anthology of traits—it is like being a horse buyer at a country fair, since, after all, one may be lying or simplifying or simply be in a special state—like being drugged up or having your hide painted, as living horses' pelts were—a smile, some sort of brains, a physical height, a character-as-a-fighter (or not) or as *sweet* or not—the ways one is courteous or not (in terms of male effrontery, impudence, sass, and so on, or not) . . . but not in a naturally pluralistic sense at all. Mostly one measures one's danger from him and one's chances of having him for an ally if one is in danger.

One measures, one makes a finding, a drill sample, of him offering amusement, companionship, good advice, money . . . love, admiration-in-spite-of-doubts, and so on. His decency or indecency . . . his beliefs—his code—one's sense of how many people already usurp his time . . . What is left for friendship, for oneself in this regard, what are the possibilities for one in the offer of attention that he is making . . .

I can't say I was entirely unfamiliar with the sexual idea of *the boy in the* (nearby) *bed* or exactly familiar with it.

One's traits are those of *an available orphan* . . . available for daydreams: that is something Lila said. That is a form of glamour that one has in an underclass way—Gypsyish. Mind, or school abilities, can be looked at in relation to *money and standing.*

Or to originality. Temperament. *Dangerousness . . . Do you have a stomach for this,* or *the stomach for it?* This stuff is resident in one's circumstances—you learn it because it's at your school, it's in the locker room; your brothers and mother teach you it; your father meddlingly teaches it—or an uncle.

And books often teach it . . . *Books, looks, and being a crook* . . . the wavering willow branches, pseudopods, dreamed hands and dreamed lips of others, and others' sense of their own circumstances, often *erotic* or amatory circumstances . . . Sometimes you measure people by how sought after they are or have been: have they known what it is to be romanced and married and divorced and abandoned from early childhood on? How much nerve do they have toward the world? It's true I like some of the openly faggy guys at school, like them quite a lot, because they are so nervy, as tough-nerved, as bold as the high school quarterbacks, varsity and junior varsity. I admire the extraordinary audacity of one guy who says he kisses guys' asses, and other guys say he does. I can't yet bear to think of it, and I would swear it was no desire of mine to have my ass kissed (and it never did become a desire). Back then it is forbidden ground, but I admire that guy for his nerve and energy.

And guys who are bulkily foundations of stability in school, who take boxing lessons and who are good at sports and who are sports fans —who *never fool around* . . . I like them, too.

I was never so thoroughly bought by Lila and S.L., or by the school, that I lyingly hold their opinions as my own.

But at school, everyone, in a way, *picks-on-me,* picks a fight with me sooner or later: I am the guy in school with the best grades (by far), the front-runner in that sense; but it isn't just that . . . It's more that my parents are ill or in trouble and that a number of people like me, that when I guess what to do, it often comes out okay. The *what-I-know* has some of the erotic qualities of a guy's chest. Or of a girl's chest. The *what-I-know*—the life-I've-had—the *life-I'm-having* and the theories I come up with now because of my unowned, unlucky life have a feather-headdress quality, maybe. The school superintendent is a sort of off-again on-again fan or devotee or friend—the tonality of what he is in regard to me wavers and changes, day to day, time to time—he's a little bit anti-Jew, but he's a nice guy, he's nice about it—he assigns bodyguards to me at times when I've done something, made an enemy in an argument or won an award, say, or written something for the school paper or even for the school system and some kids get threatening—or, a couple of times, when I fell in love, was infatuated or whatnot, and some guys said they'd get me then . . . It's funny when someone, a gang, is out to get me, how the politics at school moment-by-moment change. He has a funny attitude toward my *helplessness*. Like my mom, he says I'm going to get killed. See, books are vague in the kinds of *power* they ascribe to a given character, even really good books; but in life you are measured as a magnet and as an-influence-on-others and in all kinds of ways relating to what *powers* you have. I have quite a lot in an odd sense of things. *You still have a crotch, Wiley?* You still got a banjo *between your knees*? I get mocked a lot. But I've been to one or two small parties and two big ones where the chief thing, or one of them, was to get me undressed or partly undressed and see me dance and so on.

I don't know what this means. A life, no matter how eerie or weird, is only a variant—I mean, of life, and then, of species life, an example, unideal as hell, of gender and era and so on. That he and I—Dan, Daniel, *Danny* and I—have lives, minds, purposes, views, *needs* (a popular word back home at that time), and have legs, and pricks between our legs, and nerves and moods—I *think* one is forced to enter onto madness—a segment of the population did that back then at school—or into a certain sort of propriety, into manners—and mental fixity; it depends on the form one's interest in *real life* takes . . . But *other things* go on as well . . .

I am aware of outbursts of anger and even of rage and certainly of curiosity in me, but more oddly than that, of curiosity-and-dismissal at the same time, of a *no thank you* or an *oh no* which is pretty firm, which includes fighting and maybe even death. Death rather than giving in.

To the thing-in-general, to how it is presented, or offered, or is forced on me, physically or through some kind of attempted blackmail.

Of course, I am new at it all—new at this stuff at this size, in this scale of being at this age. When I do stuff now, I am aware of carefulness in me at being *this scale*, this size, this age; I do a balancing thing; I try to keep my balance; but this can shred into wildness pretty quickly—I can make up my mind in advance but I still don't know if I will do a *yes* or a *no* thing, when the moment comes, if it comes, in which people decide to *love* or *not love*. Or to fight or not fight. Or whatever.

I don't fight. I'm a pacifist. I can't help it. Because of all the suffering. But I sort of fight. I don't like being pushed to the sidelines by guys who are willing to be *unpleasant*.

I defend myself by saying that each time such stuff happens it happens in a specific way, with a degree of openness and a variety of meaning and is different . . . Or not . . . Love—or enmity.

With guys who are *fruits* openly and in a group—*fruits* was the word some guys used for themselves back then—depending on how systematized those guys are in what they are, the presence of my *mind* and my judgment, such as it is, seems, in a way, to be opposed to the effrontery of illusion-ridden and absolutist daydreaming, including their sense of whatever it is they like and their sense of being driven to do certain things and of having a right to do them, maybe . . .

6

"Do you believe all is fair in love and war?" I asked Dan.

"Well, I never trust a Gentile epigram," he said with a smile.

"I don't believe in that. I don't think that stuff is so. You're outside the law in some ways but that's all." Outside the law in some ways in love and war. "Maybe I'm wrong . . ."

A lot of people back off; some become, uh, semi-frozen when you talk in certain ways.

He said, "Would you say you were spoiled?" Then: "By what you've become?"

"I would say that this stuff happens at least once, for a while, to everyone, no matter who you are, boy or girl, man or woman, child or grown-up—this is so at some point in your life. I would bet on this. Nonie knows this."

Dan is sweating a little. Clickety-clack-clack-clickety goes the train. The difference in our ages, and all the rest of it—and it's pretty complex-complicated—the teamwork-and-snobbery thing (of cousins), the snobbery-in-abeyance thing (sexually and because of *age*), the forbearance thing (the forbearance which is a sign of infatuation but which passes itself off as social okayness)—one has to ignore it. I mean, you can't discuss it, any of it, without its all coming to a head, and how are you going to manage the consequences then? I want to go to Forestville. That today might not work out makes me quietly *tense*. That, overall, a lot of things might not work out, this becomes on his side a truly stringent, far-out, slightly acrid thing of an *absolutist* courting you (me) with an intensity of feeling varying as his approval goes up and down; but mostly it's okay with him so far; you mostly pass this test; the whole universe (he truly believes this) is being bent for you. But still you're put off—it's not enough: let him bend the universe—he's not really talking to *me*.

Perhaps with this kind of stuff, it's better if you ARE put off. I'm assuming a morality in him but who knows what he's like *in a hug*. The thing on my side of my being alive and grateful and cautious-and-evasive:

well, few people listen to me without fighting with me over what I say; but the stuff with Daniel is different—he does not fight with me over anything. He ignores me while noticing me. If I feel horrified at moments anyway, in spite of the universe-in-a-cone-around-me-as-a-boy, it is a form of being travel sick inside the tense, unhappy thing of someone's infatuation (with you) and your conviction that it might not (will not) work.

I feel, sitting here on the train, *flashes* of escape; and phallic reassurance (of a shaky sort) in mere flashes, seeds of almost involuntary smiles, half-smiles, smiles that form and then hastily are taken back. I feel we have varied and various exercises of contradictory superiorities alternately already, him and me, he and I; and we recognize this in a sort of communal charity, a mutual awareness.

But his charity in this matter is systematized, almost rote. I *think* he will kneel to my prick, to my youth. Guys have. One girl has. But I don't want that: I am young still, for one thing. The reassurance would be in relation to Dad's death and to Dan's money. And it would be insanely disrespectful in itself. To *me*. It would be like being a gas pump and refuelling a car. This is a complex issue for me with most men, whatever they're like as men, or who they are, and with some women, and a few girls.

7

My awareness is more actual than his—is less systematized. This is an intellectual choice and the result of trying to nurse my father for six years; and it comes, largely, from reading. The multiplicity of voices in a book and then the enormous multiplicities of voices of different books, a lot of books, and different sorts of books—those voices in me are not bound together into a chorus of doctrine. A doctrine is something that one applies after the fact in order, mostly, perhaps, to control the voices—I say this. I think a workable unsystematization, a constant improvisation, or *recitativo* (Dan and I talked about some of these things), I think of as forms of *independence*, of rebellion—a *purposeful* superiority-in-inferiority, as in being a frontier scout and having smelly buckskin clothes and being in old St. Louis among the laundered and elaborately coiffed and mustached rich.

Dan is older and is himself rich and he is smart and he is far better looking by most notions than I am, but he is at this moment in his life less attractive than I am; and I did not "know" this. But it emerges minute by minute on the train. One picks it up . . . I catch glimpses, perhaps, of what Lila thought. I catch on, in part—only in part—retroactively to stuff in the past; the now-stuff is fairly mysterious.

Dan asks me questions about Darwin and about revelation. He asks in a voice that hints he is asking *ultimately* and with reference to some superhumanly absolute answer. Now, an answer as a thing is a repellent *idol* to me. As are some images of Jesus, for instance, if they are all thing'd up. But a living-breathing dying-crying-out-and-rising-again God-Jesus is different.

I am not about to be bullied by *Dan's* sense of God, and he would not try to do that (bully me) if he didn't suspect me of being untrapped: I pick this up from how he acts. I *am* impressed by him. He is doing this stuff with *politeness*, not as an ultimatum all the time but as something far out at the edge of behavior as self-surrender in a sort of mirror-occupied nothingness—one is sort of there in a blowsy cloud-riddled nowhere, as before sleep, and it's warm, like under the blankets. This is the kingdom of the great mirror of China—where everything is parodied but with a momentary, hiddenly hysterical sincerity which is a form of thought and then it suddenly shows in the mirror, the as-if-third-person self and its history, the autobiography, the erotic self, chaste or not, whatever is objective because that is how the mirror's attention works, if I can say that—do you know?

All another person can be to him is a thinly cavernous source of echoes of what he already knows, echoes that announce an occasion. And then one is the *meat-and-potatoes* of the occasion. But it is a bitch to know this, one is a bitch to *know* (or notice) this stuff; everything is all bitched-up—you know what I'm talking about *socially*?—but something else is in place, too: he isn't unfamiliar with this stuff; he knows about doing this with guys who are better at this than I am; and two kinds of allowance are present, the sophisticated or organized-and-reorganized systematized kind and the rudely improvisational kind, which is just us, us two, only us—me in my absurd degree of recent loneliness and vast, vastly devouring hope for a friendship and for a cousinly similarity, something to count on, and him, in his degree of experience and in the full armor of his beliefs, making an exception for me, making an exception of me at moments, granting me a permissiveness, not weakly, in my oddities.

Nonie has accused me of needing *queers* because they are the only ones who, under the pressure of things, will accept me even halfway as I am.

My hopes, my ambitions, in a sense, when most of the hopes are of the rude sort, *rude* meaning new and improvised, tentative and uncertain—it embarrasses him in his sophistication and intellectual assurance that I am the way I am and have hopes of a rude sort that he does not have.

And he tends to back off, to change it to the other, to him feeling sorry for me and to patience in him—he tends to choke and kill the self in him that permits or licenses the existence of a territory of companionship in which, without demure self-protection or even commonsense resistance, I feel love when I feel it and am merely (or interestingly to him) what I am.

Some sort of demand is in what he does, is in what he is. He asks questions, I believe, as a whole-life thing, a life's work, him being himself: I am a *potential* (a common word then), foetal, or a cloud—of a boy—something long-leggedly *handsome*, even if not really; and that is what he is; but he sees me as that but as not in the style he is it; that is how he singularizes my life, my identity.

He is quite, quite rich—richer than anyone in school with me in U. City or than the fathers of anyone I knew well. He is polished, finished in that sense; and I am jealous, a jealous dirtier, a jealous and clean-cut virgin cutter-upper of polish and of any high degree of finish—perhaps not purposefully, though. Perhaps I am. Certainly, with some distance thrown in and some privacy as well, I am addicted to courtship. One can be addicted to courtship, to the special behaviors then, the quality of the permissions, the light that such permissions cast and then the actions, the smiles that arise under that licensing of what is almost a patience with what-you-are in real life—the illumination your existence and the existence of emotion bring then: see, the *relativism* of this is of things being changed by this unless you firmly and ironically keep the belief that this is all an illusion and you should not be changed, you should not carry out the rush into a different life, should not go over the falls, should not be swept into the rapids, into the bridal, sun-bitten moments—or whatever.

The different mind, the different history now, the different body (and the *different* sides of one's bodily existence, the *amazingly* different smell or feel of the moment), some people laugh at this; but I am addicted to it, the thing of being someone else who is with someone else now and it is something else now . . .

Sometimes, in real life, sensitivity (and manners) springs from a conceited source in me such that I can, rightly or wrongly, as a bastard or okay guy, feel that what I am here reflects a lousy ripeness of self-love in someone who likes me. The kind of bomb-shelter or trench thing of them liking you, your taking shelter in that, this civilized and intricately coded, or codified, other thing is another person maybe in an extreme narcissism of sophistication, making offers to you, some of which are true and some of which are not.

And which is which is not a fixed matter either. He, or she, often retreats into a bomb shelter and abandons the frontier—and you altogether.

An able guy there, he can only deduce my reality—he cannot feel it directly—I am unassuaged, unfed in the real sense. But I'm half pleased; it's not an either/or thing except in the neighborhood of the yes-or-no of the *suck my cock?* The *suck-my-cock* as a joke order, jocular command. Or just the diddling with each other with hands—or the eyelid game. It's *no* there, in that game, but that makes the kid sad. He is amazed that in Dan—*in such people* as Dan—these things are fixed and yet are breakable. Wiley imitates and absorbs some of Dan's reliance on categories, some of his absolutism: this is part of being with him, part of talking to him—well, such talk as we had—it is part of being *companionable.* It is also theft and spying and perhaps treachery.

But I feel Dan as *wooden*, as a *blindness* (a term of Dan's for the uninitiated, an uninitiate, an outsider), a blindness out of which develops an amazing sensitivity of the *hands.* A woodenness that leads to caution. But to a liveliness of the voice. It is kind of remarkable . . . a sign language among the sophisticated and systematized, a kind of area of pain in which some degree of education takes place.

But unless it is revolutionary, that education, unless it is a complete overturning—through love, say, through my desire to shock him, say, assuming that I could shock him, hour after hour until he was upended, *bouleversé*, remade—if it is not that, then what he learns is promptly applied to what he feels is nobly religious belief. One is attached, he, his mind attaches what he learns about you to what he already knows . . . which is stuff you know, too, or will know soon.

I think of him as Danny, Dan, Daniel depending on the curve of feeling in me toward him in a given moment.

8

Cousin Dan was actually appallingly handsome. His lips were a deep red color. He had sleek, brownish skin with heavy stubble closely shaved, glossy, geometrically stippled *blackness,* ornamental and curiosity-provoking—what causes that effect, compound and orderly, of beauty? He has enormously long, rather structural-and-yet-caterpillary eyebrows that go almost to his hairline over large, big, eyelashed brown eyes of immense yearning, long black lashes, huge eyelids. He has a tiny, very thin nose under a wide brow topped by clustering curls—really too much.

And enormously long, faintly hairy fingers, and fingernails which, although cut short, were on the finger phenomenally long, starting as they did almost at the knuckle. He had a cleft in his chin and a widow's peak and small neat ears. He spoke with a good accent, a good deal of sarcasm (or *irony* in an ideal and educated way), a good deal of sinuous lip curling—he had an extraordinary voice, drawly and Southern, with repressed but still extremely deeply felt vocal postures, operatic, almost beautiful. Perhaps beautiful: it is a matter of taste. Only that, after all. A sense that he must have a sense of his own (stylistic and economic and social) superiority is goading, willy-nilly sexual, if you find struggle and rivalry sexual, if you want to bring him down a peg.

Some of what he feels comes from the thing that while I respect his monomaniacal structures of absolute knowledge and the immense conceit of such things—such claimed lineage from the maker and soul of the universe—I hardly believe in it at all. I do not love God in him or through him—through Daniel—or my own safety through him by order of God, so-to-speak. I love my safety and would like to have it from Daniel if he would negotiate it, but I do not see it as safety under the seeming terms of the *so far with him* which is all that is present in the moment and is all that can be present in the moments. I see it as suffocation of the worst kind—an immense cowardice on my part if I go after it—the falsely offered counterfeit safety here.

I don't know why I am the way I am. My life has led to this. I love the possibility of these things, it is true, and being on the train with Dan, I kind of love that; but mostly I sort of slyly and also a bit purely *love* him—for his kindness, for his audacity, for his wrongness, for his being so slick and yet a klutz or schmuck, after all. I love the amateur thing, the semi-amateur thing of a lot of the stuff, most of the stuff in him.

Well, see, he *feels* that "love" in him for me as a ghost, a kind of blur of heat, a heat mirage in a feelingly inhabited air, a heat of possibility. The self that holds the ideas—the basket, not the genital basket, the human self overall, the secular prow of the soul, of the soul part—the part that is the overall whole—well, he sees *the punished kid, the freed kid,* whom he, Daniel, freed—I see those terms on his face. All the moments until now of him with me his functioning mind sees as a story detached from the moments. To an absolutist such stuff as what is going on in a minute can't exist except maybe pathetically in someone unenlightened, unenlightened and wrong. What truly exists are the conclusions, the ideas.

For me, though, it's a thing like jazz. The moment is real. He is measured by the moments in a *jazz* way. In a warfare-and-battle way as well. War depends on time. He is punishing Nonie. He is taking me to Carolina with him; in having someone there he "likes," in "*loving*" me, of course, other stories are involved. One senses those only vaguely. But *fooling around—diddling around*—at my age certainly—or 'flirting' or making friends, when it is NOT part of the H-group stuff, denies being part of a fixed story and denies being anything but parenthetical, temporary, closed off from ordinary meaning in the passages of middle-class time and attached to jazz meanings, in a way, or emotional ones, or, in my opinion, real and not fake ones.

His "*love*" intellectually includes such a clear and then such an unclear honest estimate of itself, of the emotion in him, of the acts, of who he is in such a state, that it is a wonder to me how he can find terms, all of them empty of time, of time moving—and chugging along. When will his "love" occur? When will it act itself out? It seems to me that my life when he is in this state, we, me, my life, and I hardly exist for him . . . we are expendable—for the sake of a clarity that consists of him snooting time, the universe, and the reality of feelings, the reality of everything.

But maybe he feels the pagan breath of the reality of existence with *love in it*—love in it and unacknowledged. He wavers some: he is drawn to it, or toward it, the pagan existence of *love* as a reality, but maybe only as his own reality, with me omitted, him and his jealousy, his jealousy being an almost living breathing simulacrum, or Frankenstein monster, or shadow thing of me, or not me, but the boy I looked like just then, that day.

But jealousy is him dreaming of me, with him asleep in a state in which he is the universe.

He has no momentum going: I suppose it's not certain, though, if he does or not. *Sometimes if you don't get a word in edgewise, if you don't get an oar in edgewise, you don't know where you are—puppet strings, puppet strings . . . You have to watch out, Wiley . . .* I sit up straight again and lay my sweater across my lap. Lila told me a lot of stuff, advice, before I left home: *Don't show off . . . Be smart: hide how smart you are and hide how dumb you are.* Whew. Tricky. "Beep-beep-a-deep," I say, and look at Daniel. Then I raised my eyebrows. Momma told me cryptic stuff about Daniel. And his mother, Casey. *They're strange, Wiley: they're strange people: they couldn't negotiate their way out of a paper bag: they're religious; they couldn't, neither one, be president of a dog-and-cat society . . . They're people have to have their way.*

She said, *Be patient with him but don't lose your self-respect. And remember that self-respect is not the be-all and end-all—but use your head. Now, listen, Wiley, don't be a fool and think Daniel means it when he says he likes intelligence: what he wants is someone to be nice to him. Take my advice and play dumb: Be reasonable—that's what he thinks* intelligence *is.* And: *Be careful not to show how conceited you are.*

"How conceited am I, Momma?"

Enough . . . Enough that it's a problem, Wiley. No one's prepared for anything . . . You expect too much of people—do me a favor and don't disapprove of anyone this trip . . . Daniel thinks very well of himself . . .

He falls back into being himself—a man who *knows* what he does. He is asserting himself as the ruler of the household-at-this-moment, it's sort of that—him foisting *me* on his family. This is in the air. *He's easily bored is his problem,* Momma told me before I left St. Louis. *Life is very simple, Wiley: be nice to people and they will be nice to you.*

I say to Daniel, "Being *nice to people* isn't simple. Being *nice to people* is not a *simple* matter, no. Since I got to be taller than my mother, she begins talking to me with *Sit down, Wiley,* even if she is standing up—she does this invariably."

As an adopted kid I have no basic language. My language does not originate in the shadows of this family. It is a clear structure of falsity and of deduction—playacting with a more or less good-hearted *sincerity* involved, *playacting* at being part of the family, but it is a bit problematic, questionable.

What I think and feel is mostly unworded. The light from the window plays on the starched and angle-y front of Daniel's khaki shirt. Daniel leans forward, leans back . . . Gusts of *something-or-other* form and blow this way and that, not so much *where they list* as where the geography in me permits passage. The inclinations of a landscape in a person can't easily be talked about.

I permanently have an interior voice talking, even when I am asleep. I used to think that originated in genetic solitude—in being abandoned by the families, both my families, unless I did as they asked. That voice is like a false day, a recent day, the chief yesterday, a family, a mother, a brother, a careful father . . . such voices as those . . . but they become one voice and not willed or full of aim but merely *instructive,* as when you were little and people said things to you while they held your hand and you walked alongside and their minds wandered some and they enjoyed your innocence.

This inner voice only indirectly *explains* things—it may be seven steps off from a translation into words of what has happened, but it tends to cry out, *YOU'RE JEALOUS OF HIM* or *YOU'RE BEING TOO ANALYTICAL, YOU'LL FREEZE HIM TO DEATH.*

But unexpressed-as-yet *thoughts* often exist as feelings and as internal postures of excited attention in a certain direction or a group of directions known almost as if from a list on a treasure map, so many paces here, so many there, then look up at the magic owl, and so on.

"She's okay," Daniel said, eyeing me—rescuingly . . . With overtones.

"She looks seriously upset."

"She's actressy." Then: "She's a ham." Testing me, testing the connections I might have to people . . . At Daddy's funeral, Momma wore no makeup and was a plain-faced and tousled tragedy queen. "A Hecuba," Daniel said, eyeing me and testing my *classical* education as well—not eyeing me sharply, though: he wasn't dominant . . . or dominating: he was *polite* . . . permissive . . . respectful or bribe-y . . . or all of those. Usually, in the U.S., doing antique-classical stuff is a way of making a sort of a pass. He said, "The good times are over for her . . . I feel sorry for her . . . You are the Helen of Troy of the family now."

"She wouldn't agree," I said, starting to laugh, then becoming somber and looking down at my knees.

9

Some people, not many, spoke in that extravagant way to me. Enough did it that it was part of my life.

"I don't know how you stand it," Daniel said, squinting in the light that came so pulsingly and lurchingly through the window of the compartment: he was riding with his back to the engine—for my sake. *You could use a little nursing . . . Use your head and you'll get it*: the reason (one of them) that I am here . . . A sort of middle-class moral reason. The tremor in my nerves was that it was such an uncertain thing what I *really* felt—the moment was improvisational and yet it was habit-ridden, systematized in ways I don't know about. I am maybe not an able saxophonist.

"I think my mother is interesting to talk about, but do me a favor and don't talk about St. Louis." I smiled politely, perhaps youthfully. Then I tested the moment by going pretty far conversationally: "Do me a favor and *shut up* about St. Louis." He said nothing and I went on, not watching him, "Lila talks to me better if I sit on a stool with my head no higher than hers. But if I talk about her I feel funny. I'd just as soon be a different person." I slouched down in my half of the compartment, I cross my legs and tilt my head back and look down my face at him, at my cousin, very vaguely, very shyly—in an abstract or pale version of a kind of metamorphosis because of his interest.

A lot of what I think I know here comes from certain boys at school. I don't know every boy, after all—I know certain boys. "Personal questions are like necking . . . I hate tongue-kissing."

Daniel, on the train, exploded with hooting laughter, staccato, amused, shocked, quickly silent. "You talk in a *very* fancy way"—Daniel on the train, in an exploring tone.

I grin nervously—I can only *think* ahead so far. "I don't want to talk about the stuff at home . . . Nothing real happens the way I think it will . . . I sound weird to myself." If I register reality, I usually realize that I'm proceeding blindly no matter whether I think I see ahead or not. "Things go haywire . . . In me . . . It's a strain—it's okay. Trying to talk is like taking a walk in a minefield—things you don't want to say explode . . . you get exploded, *I* get exploded." *Ha-ha* . . .

"You know about the Scots regiments at El Alamein, walking in kilts and bagpipes skirling, into the minefield? The explosions?" Guys who use good grammar, or girls who do, and guys who talk about kilts—it's flirting, you know? It's a pass. He says, "The Germans called them *the Ladies from Hell*, they were such good soldiers, the kilt wearers." The response to *excitement*—to things at risk in a real moment—means you flash from one of your senses to another—the chattering and clicking and clattering and chugging of the train—to the heat of the window glass—to the sight of a small river in the distance—to a sense of dirt because of the dirt-covered surface of the earth rocketing past the windows on your trembling fingers, trembling because the train vibrates, and the dirt on the windows: another dirt-covered surface. This chokes my throat, so I fly, take refuge in, the feel of new, lightweight pants on my fingertips running up and down the trousers crease past the sweater on my lap.

I can hardly trust him. I have an irritating sense of him sexually. I don't want to explore this stuff—one can't fool around with that stuff and learn about someone without learning too much. Brutal self-risk, amatory self-risk—all that. The desperation that underlay (and might still if he were here in the compartment) this sort of stuff with certain boys when I was pursuing an imbecile, hot mitigation in St. Louis—that stuff might recur here with him, in this compartment. I hoped to avoid that by not discussing St. Louis.

And the associations, the recurrence of old feelings modified now, vestigial, rudimentary, with the fresh edge of now, the fighting with other boys, for instance, and the thing of despising the other person, boy or girl, because you're not sentimental, a thing of being committed in advance because the stuff is not carnal, not really, and involves a different *politeness,* so to speak, this stuff; and the *maybe* stupid courage of the other stuff is not required here, the maybe immoral carelessness (of an immortal kind) of other kinds of *love*—the dexterities of will and of self-forgiveness, of drunkenness while sober, and anger and ironic despair, I want to avoid that stuff . . . Almost certainly love and infatuation are here . . .

But to some extent—changeably.

10

I can see, as I curve through a mental arc inwardly (in an actual moment), the shape of how I sort of kind of *hate* people who make me say no.

11

I can force myself to say yes. I can be enticed. I can be perverse. I bumble along in "what I feel" among possibilities. Of course, it's *interesting* to live through stuff, but it's nerve-racked in the moments when you do it, it's fraught—too fraught for me to be anything but a little hoity-toity toward it as well as overexcited and kind of grinny. We are about the same height, Daniel and I. Daniel's got that look I sometimes arouse, the Wiley's-not-a-real-man-sort-of-boy look that moves back and forth into the opposite thing of *A-REAL-MAN-SORT-OF-BOY*. I'm kind of *a sexual joke,* maybe, a *regular* boy with a serious face.

He leans forward and touches a *regular* boy with *a serious face*—I remember his khaki sleeve, the cuff of it, starched; the button, cracked; his watch—a cheap metal watch with a cheap band—the hairy wrist, its shape, the kind of slanted shadow and dimple of the thin musculature of the wrist; and the ornate human thing of fanned-out tendons and the archipelagic row of knuckles; and the muscle in the bay curve between the thumb and the forefinger—it is the back of a hand, his; he touched me in a carefully *ordinary* way; but if I remember the moment correctly (the moment given to me), the twist of the air then is for me almost like the twist of language in a story I didn't write—I mean at one point; it can be even inside a sentence when a reference to another world of almost entirely other reference offers the wit of relativistic juxtaposition. One's feelings, words, and opinions are not immortal, are not part of an immortal law-and-disobedience thing. They last varying lengths of time—even as art (so-called).

But the twist then of meaning is toward a burden of feeling which is more intensely meaningful as meaning or which is meaning in a grander or more grandly useful state. A cloud is advancing along the ground with something in it—a fox, a swan . . . who knows? Temporary love, a sudden maybe mostly unwanted *knowledge of things*—I knew a girl who said that the sensation of recognizing *feelings* in the touch was like undergoing a test or a fire drill in school; and I agree if you combine it with being hit in the head—a useful amnesia, a useful concussion or enforced moment of dreaming while awake, a startled hallucination not at one's own hand.

And it is like a battlefield, a real one, and it is like an episode in a real war; you are in a blurred and as-if-fatal terrain in which the events have the massive independence from one's will of a battle. Of course, one has one's will anyway—to lie down, to be brave, to keep on. You can immerse yourself in the weird story line, things happening in a sequence in real life. You will encompass what you do although there is force and there is strategy and swindling. The thing is that here is a story very different from any attempt I might make to understand it.

An *Iliad* in him and which includes me—in a way—and which now has become in the chugging and clack-clacking minute part of my innerscape.

That he does not look confident when he does it is manners-of-a-sort and part of the reality that some of the story, while it involves him, is beyond him. He doesn't admit that. The difference between what he is with me and what his manner is with Lila is the difference between his (maybe Jewish male) disrespect toward most things and then the hint in that of the importance of some other things which he doesn't examine because he doesn't want to know their otherness from him. One's importance for him shows in a sort of smelly way—of nerves. His. Because of the blank spaces in this field of maneuver and of onset and so on. Mine because I'm younger and don't clearly want this sort of thing to happen but I'm nosy and because his feelings might be a mistake on his part, now—forever: my importance to him . . . *Maybe you're one of the ones who gets remembered* . . . Oh hell: things move along before you can disentangle them.

Maybe I care more than he does, at least in this way of adolescent wonder at the phenomenology of large feelings in oneself—I hide this from him. Disrespect and *discretion*—mine and Daniel's—echo each other but aren't alike; his lack of confidence and then the war, the physical moment in its historical version, are jammed in blazingly in what I feel flaringly. In the chug-chugging and click-clacking minute, the verb tenses of my mind—the *now's* and *then's* in various forms—in the partly natural daylight in the compartment become disaligned in a school sense but more accurately mine in the curious rolling and alighting and yet unalit present tense.

Dimly present are guys in childhood, older guys even before kindergarten, and moments in school, some of them bad moments since, some of them sentimental; and my sister is here; Nonie is here, and my dad, and the locker room at school, and my real dad. I think that, for me, in a certain way, *negotiation* is the way through the maze of refusal to sexuality even if the drama of certain sexual events for everyone else concerned is of various single-willed acquiescences and single-willed drives. But I am not sure.

It is because I still don't know. I will this or that, I inherit this or that, I believe this or that. What circumstances seem to indicate as *we* go along (in the moments) is the politically *active* thing of my existence as counting for a lot with us (him and me), but he sees things as fixed; he keeps resettling them, reconcluding how things are; and I feel things as a negotiation that is time-riddled and haunted. Not so much that I go mad but enough that my feelings are in spite of him and me not being in sync.

He does not use madness as seduction—or as an excuse—but he did, *maybe*, use a sense of the peculiar human wish to escape from Ordinary Wakefulness—the *ow* . . . He had a funny look that watched stuff and triggered other stuff (in me); the politeness or discretion or whatever, the courtship (if it was that) gives me a sort of quasi-absolute rule of the moments through his character, but only maybe. And it depends on my footwork, my guesswork.

Love as a state of particular attachment—to one person—and a marriage to the present tense as it goes on for as long as the love lasts is a little new to me as an ex-middle-class-child with a lot of people around him and concerned with him: I remember the uproar and unpleasantness when I disowned my parents and my sister. Now the concentration of one's jealous attention shows that one's freedom is riddled, for a moment, with feelings that have to do with another person in the third person: *he*, in this instance—but it could be a child, a girl—and one's sense, my sense of this, is that I know about this stuff—in some ways—and Danny knows it: he knows it from the stories about me with my dad when my dad was well and when he was ill.

Lover's knowledge is like the theft of fire in the myth. You give someone this fire of criminally singular self-knowledge in you as in a myth: they can't, however, necessarily reproduce it. But putting that boastfulness (if that is what it is) aside you are aware that you, or the type or idea that you give rise to, gives birth to a sense of life and of the moments in regard to this subject in the real moment in the hallucinatory whistle of sexual beauty. Sexual play—hallucination in the eerie light of hallucination maybe.

It is very real stupidity to be a virgin in any sense—and ignorance is like a soft or hard club slamming you. I can deny the reality of this stuff and of what I thought and felt, deny any sightedness in me toward this subject: *I am not sloppy about love*: but I am aware off and on that such awareness in me shows as the color of my eyes does and is a large part of the reality—'the historical reality'—of those years, of that month . . . of that particular moment. The reality in me that holds his interest.

In a sense, only a sense, one doesn't have to be clear. One has a feeling that one burns in his sight; one is a shaky and swinging lantern in the moments for him—the moments of his feelings about himself.

Those feelings involve youth, my youthfulness. He is both right and wrong—one is hardly the *perfect* object of romance: what is he doing, being such an idealist? The moments come and press against me fleshily and are a weight on, or in, my lap. One can deny the existence of *love* to oneself but the admission of the existence of emotion within the range of interest called *love* is forced out of you at moments. You *burn* with it wastefully.

I tend to assume that older people and really *all* other people know what they are doing. I often fail to believe that a present moment has a blind edge for everyone . . . The blind man's buff or bluff sense of life or the midnight and drugged dreamers on the dark(ling) plain stuff isn't something I can hold as a steady belief. A moment may make a really fatal demand for your heart. The posture of one's smile, of one's smiles, absentminded, ignoring the touch, yet acknowledging it as someone much younger might, one has been startled into showing one's extravagance in regard to love.

As if sticking to the subject, Daniel says, "We all know you loved your father."

"Did I love my father? I forget. I like to be told that."

"I like you for that," he says. "I like you, period."

"You like me too soon," the boy says stiffly. "I'm a hard person to like." I remember wanting the subject to be adhered to and not changed.

I remember ignoring Daniel's reaction to me and feeling fatuous and uselessly precocious.

HE, Daniel, when I look at him, he sits there blankly, without meaning for me; I say now he was perhaps past meaning anything since what I said and my not wanting to end the exchange have pushed us into a silence.

It may have seemed then that I knew what I was doing or that we might as well act as if I did know because of the way I talked and looked. I was hardly fit to be a leader although I did know some stuff because of things that went on between me and my ill father. I feel myself in memory that day knowing consciously certain medical, smelly, imprisoning things about ties between people—pitiable things maybe—and expensive in terms of one's life. Part of an absurd life. When I decided to be okay with Dad when he came back from the hospital the first time, I was pretty young but I was spoiled and I had guessed it might cost me my life including in this way, oh, not *exactly*, but in that surprised *I told-you-so* way—that *keep-the-child-away-from-sick-people* way. Knowledge of how you see and notice that stuff moment by moment is given you in an absolute way by a smitten absolutist for whom you are, as you are for a lot of people it now seems to you, a special and dangerous taste, impressive and with powers of command and amazingly ignorant and strange. And perhaps violent in any number of hidden ways. The flapping of the technical dead dull diagrams of one's power in the moment becomes one's pulse rate along with the feeling: *I would disappoint him* (if he knew better, if we get into a thing, a friendship or something more elaborate). One is ignorant but one knows his systems and his beliefs permit nothing to be real, so, of course, he will be disappointed.

The sense of oneself as a YOUNGER boy of a certain sort up to a point and then semi-horrifyingly and embarrassingly and a little melodramatically not a sort at all but oneself—and oneself in a certain state—a month further on from the day at the river—so that the *no* in me is like a knot of musculature. Perhaps it is *a moral beauty*. Perhaps a tease—for certain narcissistic fools. And Daniel sits facing this.

Daniel is sunburned, dark-haired; he is wearing tailored khakis; I don't know much about him yet. I am not likely to know much about him—how can I judge his feelings? He is crisply shaped, he is confident and condescending, he is sour-and-bitter (the family says this about him) and he is sweet-and-mannerly—a maybe *spoiled* man (i.e., a *narcissist* in the sense of having a private existence which has *no women* in it, no one loving him with his permission; he has contemplation and companionable but melodramatically sweet and impassioned sex and emotion—I am guessing . . . I am guessing about this. The light that is coming through the windows—I don't mind being brightly lit. Daniel is in a state of tense or as-if-electrified excitement. It is a little as if the moment for him was in a part of a book fairly far along from the beginning. A tense book. I am not reading the same book. Or if I am, not the same part of it.

I don't know him. I don't know my position vis-à-vis this stuff—or him. I know this is some kind of romantic thing but this isn't one of the things I ever focus on—being loved or whatever it is by a grown-up. I am embarrassed. I am middle-class—a kid of the middle class toward this stuff—maybe only wistfully and fantastically so. I am crude—ugly and good-looking both. If I were shorter and had rich parents and we were playing some sort of sport, I would be clearer in my head.

But we have no clear human tie of an ordinary sort: just his feelings which have triggered mine.

I wondered if this stuff was ruinous. I sense each thing he does; and the frame in which I sense his arms, his legs, the tickling hair on his arms, the muscles in his arms, makes that stuff not objects of my regard but subjects for playful and really dangerous male *verb forms* of attachment . . . Childhood stuff. The ceaseless daily exercise of it, a lifetime's experience of it, of attachment, means one knows the danger of it; one hates it, the humiliations, *the ups and downs,* the experience of it. A sense of the neighbors, of people at school, of *the others* as a measure of the factual nature of this stuff. People lie about feelings and moments and they get hysterical because they're lying; and then they chop off *your* head.

An exchange of glances can wipe out the day, wash out the trip, infect the silence for a long time. One's nerves. One's breathing. A drawback to my wanting Daniel to like me. Outside the window, Indiana is turning into Ohio. Shit, here it is, emotion-and-tension—boy, it is as if enormous bedsheets were hung in the light between us, making the compartment theatrical and the air whitish. Feeling outlines me on the bedsheet in some giant or some dear and dwarfish size. And he is a distorted shadow, nightmarish—or comic: maybe it's funny? Is it funny? Jesus.

Nonie often said, *I feel sorry for anyone who gets mixed up with you.*

In part, though, one is in one's own home in these matters—like a snail with its transportable shelter.

But it's also true that one is unroofed, unshelled; one is out in the world. I'm scared.

He isn't off trying to pick up women on the train. He isn't reading a book or a newspaper. HE ISN'T TALKING ABOUT WOMEN.

This is better than being ignored. The excitement of this is *interesting*; this excitement (such as it is) makes life interesting. I'm weird: hate is no amusement for me. What I know may be false and lead to a crash; and I'm tired, often, of being brave and pretending things are okay. His feelings, his attentions to me, his kindness correct defects of my confidence; they correct my vision in my life—they do that for the moment. I'm not a complete dud. I would like friendship and no sex and no complicity—that's my Utopian notion and I know enough to know it's probably not possible. I don't like to admit it's probably not possible—my dad said I was something of a dreamer. He said, though, too, and others have said, I was cynical. I wouldn't mind minor diddling if no love was to be involved. Or knowledge would do. I might do something or other if he really wanted. Fun. Gratitude. You know? But I hoped not to do it. I *wished* I did want to do it. Meanwhile, my youth, my past, my various kinds of heat are being amended as we travel in this sort of *fun*. The clickety-clacks and jolts of the train and excitement of the possibility add up to a morning of amendment, an afternoon of my history edited and maybe wrecked until I sweatily stir inwardly inside with, uh, the *dignity* that his behavior toward me all day long grants me.

By four o'clock, we aren't far from Pennsylvania. The sense of my life as a son, adopted or not, very much like a son in a story, the power of that, the field of mischief granted one, the guarantee of absolution even as a prodigal—at least for a while: real life isn't exactly a parable—the thing of someone on your side, someone predisposed in your favor for good reason, genetic reason such as what you look like and how you carry yourself—it's lasted this long, which means nothing in terms of chaining the future to it, but it means you have a certain weight of possibility in the world because other people have feelings about you. The mysterious thing of sexual force, of romantic coercion: who bends to it? Who is tortured by it? Some people are. That sense of things, that such stuff is concerned with you for a few hours, is itself a form of seduction—more so, on some level, once it becomes a topic that a living consciousness feels a lot about in the moments. It involves some plane of reality on which I live and which *he sees* and which becomes real to me in his attentions, real to both of us but differently. Real although not directly worded. It is part of the knot, part that is partly hidden, of how things are. When others walk past the compartment—and our door is open to let air circulate at this time before there was air-conditioning—when they walk past, they recognize in the scene something, oh, like a brother and a younger brother perhaps. I am recognizably under his patronage here. But what I really am is unrecognizable: who can imagine *me*? I know it's hard to imagine anyone—I mean in such a way it's really someone else and not you—but in the locker room, in the games in the locker room, when someone touches your genitalia, you feel *known* suddenly; and perhaps you are, not in words, but under the shadow of the fig leaf—pre-sin, ready for sin—or whatever. That may be an ancient thing in the world. Or only in the self from one's time in the nursery when people played with your body; and now here, in this stuff—but this stuff is more daylit than the locker room. I believe and I don't believe in the stuff today, the present-tense day, the present-tense day today as it goes along. I don't believe in love after S.L., in this stuff with Daniel, but I feel real to myself and recognized although a bit secretly; and I am excited and interested but just in the moments, in friendship, not really in this stuff. The stuff *is* there. I am polite at the boundary of the field of mischief I mentioned—from Dad to here is present in my mind although some of this is an antidote to Dad's death. The unreality here of what is real and my living through it anyway as through something unreal but real, sort of, this is my form of daydreaming—maybe a result, maybe an end of grief.

I think it was like this for Nonie.

12

On the train, I do not want to start in on the fairly awful struggle to *know* what one finally thinks the *reality* here is. The sense of unreality ends at moments in a kind of thump at whatever comes along next in the line of action: that thump brings mostly a sinking sense of realpolitik. Let us say I am a sort of time-knotted (Jewish) grotesquerie—or not truly Jewish but actually pagan—a pagan grotesquerie, then; a knottedly odd, deeply angry, much vandalized boy; anyway, a grotesque version of a boy, a grotesquerie of a boy, actually thirteen and eight months who says he is fourteen, that age of steadily, minutely altering sexuality day by day—almost a holy grotesquerie of phallic torment. Then the thing of being *chosen*—not lastingly or in legend and yet somewhat like Joseph or David or Ganymede or one of those—the astounded realizations, half-realizations, the disbeliefs, the self-protective meager half-awareness of it is faced *realistically*, as realpolitik in the moment, breathingly . . . The stuff here is due to my mother's complicity and my sister's actions over the years and my own wish to see the place where Nonie was *saved*—and it is due to my own cleverness . . . such as it is. This particular part of the moments forms, I think, a kind of kinship for Daniel and me—I think everyone has been through this at some point: blackmailed, coerced by desire of some sort, even if not sexual desire, but partly sexual no doubt, desire uncertainly placed in the people involved, desire when the sense of privacy and of having money at one's disposal, the sense that it is biologically universal, that stuff one has read about is part of one's life, that beyond people's lies it is here in this sort of moment. I mean, one has been a tutor to kids and one has gone as a friend into kids' families—the worrisome *burden* of realpolitik operates there; and one runs, perhaps one runs *away*, into some form of shapelessness, not exactly *wait-and-see*, not exactly *resignation*, but from earlier versions of this moment, in their *sweet* stickiness, their horribleness, their heartbreakingness, their quality of being an opening into caverns and caverns of shadows and of dim light.

But one is half experienced. Somehow one allows him to hurt one; one allows him to make the next move but one doesn't accede hintingly—it is politeness, it is virtue. One keeps one's nerve and begins to practice the various, very odd, very hurtful disciplines of the unbearably complicated thing of the rumored or momentarily granted responsibility of the possession of a not entirely androgynous, no-longer-childhood ability to arouse, or be the cause of, feeling: it is a kind of *beauty*. And one practices the *discipline* of wanting something that is not entirely necessary to one: this trip to Forestville, a month or two as a kid in this other setting, this paradise, this Utopia . . .

The soldiers in the corridor, *guys*, their *eerie* cuteness—in being young and uprooted—by war—and their strength and niceness (often), their degrees of training, the kind of training depending on the service and their particular assigned role in it, their gentlemanliness—as the mask of death and as the sharpened or honed and polished face of the real self separate from domestic reality . . . it is a wartime matter, not an aesthetic matter in a usual sense; a moral aesthetics is involved in service, but it is a separate aesthetics, the aesthetics of battle, of conflict—a *male* moral aesthetics shared by a great many women. In my case, my merely adolescent version of that, my version of their manner, is a matter of ambition oddly reproducing the circumstances of my first abduction, my being adopted. It isn't entirely separate from domestic reality but it mostly is. And it is, to an odd degree, an aesthetic matter; a moral aesthetics is involved—not in a simple form. I am aware I have a secular (and sexual) right to *escape* my circumstances.

But it seemed to me a misuse of the term *soldier* to be a soldier in one's own service. Of course, one might be an officer: an Alexander the Great or an Antinous in service to the gods of escape, of rising in the world—the gods of one's rumored beauty, of personal beauty in terms of arousing feeling, a destiny; one can do this in service to the *romance* of events and the gaiety of nations—so to speak.

I had been courted at school by a girl who was an educated socialist who already knew Greek and was studying Latin and Roman history—our high school was a good school in a lot of ways, really—and then I was *courted* by two queer guys whom I liked but had no sympathy toward. I learned *intellectual* things from them. A sensitivity, a self-absorption which I'd learned to see in them, I saw in Daniel now: I imitated it to a slight degree so that Dan would understand me as we talked—one did this theoretically. It included a sense of Daniel, a sense of being scissored out and distinct now in outline from anyone else on the train—even from Daniel—I got this from him, from his absolutist mind, in which an ALL was the major thing; I got this vacation aspect. The *All* was the only thing—but with a lot of parts, I guess. I never quite knew what was going on except I *felt* the images involved as, oddly, passed on to me from my life with my adoptive parents. I mean the images and patterns from real things moved on to something internal and not easily or readily glimpsed in regular time. Lila has said that the ghost of my dead mother whisperingly summons angels and kinds of help for me. Or I am merely my real mother's son and that "saves" me and things I do work out on their own. And this maternal inheritance like a thread in a labyrinth (this is what I think Lila meant; I mean the Greek tale was like the thing Lila meant with her ghost of my mother) led me back through the darkness from the evil places where I fought and won (I guess), led me away from the stench of defeat and domination, maiming, and I don't know what. Now a heroism through genetic and ghostly intervention perhaps whispered to you by a long-dead real mother you haven't seen in actual presence since you were two years old is pretty damn strange. But reality is such that I felt it in ways. Well, as being hunted by an albatross-octopus—this stuff flew after me along the railroad tracks and then crowded itself into the compartment. It landed on my head; and its tentacles and beak engulfed me; I had a mad Achillean and space traveller's helmet of invisibility and self-loss. Thought of a kind entered me through my eyes, pierced my brain, and in some ways ate my usual sense of things. Part of the reason reality can be complicated is that it has so many moments. But a moment of emotional attraction isn't simple anyway. And isn't just a moment. The hollow resonance, the auditorium thing inside me, was perhaps stirred merely by restless motions of the mind patterned by the past. I *feel* her: the ghost. I feel *her* moods. The moods of someone else, not me. I feel the true history of *love* of a kind. And of a kind of mathematical destiny in these matters. A depth of love. A pattern of what is emotionally compelling in the most complete way.

13

Alongside the house where I was born and running at a diagonal to it is a single-track railroad set on a causeway six feet high. When a train was approaching, the house would begin to shake; it would shake with an amazing faint steadiness until, as if in an arithmetical theater, the house begins to slide and shimmy in a quickening rhythm that is not human. It is as if a few pebbles in a shaking drum become four, then eight larger pebbles, then a great many, and then they become rocks perhaps like numbers made of brass and placed in a tin cylinder, antic and clattering—almost like birds—but more logically. In lunacy, the sound increases mathematically, with a vigor that is nothing at all like the beating of a pulse or the rhythms of rain. It is loud and real and unpicturable. The clapboards and nails, glass panes and furniture, and wooden and tin objects in drawers tap and whine and scratch with an unremitting increase in noise so steadily that there is nothing you can do to resist or shut off these signals of approach. The noise becomes a yawning thing, as if the walls had been torn off the house and we were flip-flopping in chaos. My mother and I. All of us. The noise and echoes came from all directions. The almost unbearable bass of the large interior timbers of the house has no discernible pattern but throbs in an aching shapelessness, isolated. At night, the light on the locomotive comes sweeping past the trembling window shades and a blind glare pours on us an unstable and intangible milk in the middle of the noise. The rolling and rollicking thing that rides partway in the sky among its battering waves of air does this to me: noise is all over me and then it dwindles; the shaking and noise and lift flow off, trickle down and away, and the smell of the grass and of the night that was there before is mixed with the smell of ozone, traces of burnt metal, a stink of vanished sparks, bits of smoke from the engine if it was a night without wind. The train withdraws and moves over the fields, over the corn. The house and one's senses tick and thump, ting and subside. The trains move south toward St. Louis . . . my life-to-come.

Here, too, is the wooden-odored shade of a porch, the slightly acid smell of the house: soap and wood—a country smell. My mother's torso in a flowered print dress. A summer, an autumn, a winter—those that I had with my first mother, my real mother. She vanished. For once and all. She went to the hospital; she was carried from the house to an ambulance; she never came back.

The house had very large windows that went down quite close to the floor. Those windows had drawn shades that were an inhumanly dun-yellow color, a color like that of the pelt of an old lion in a zoo, or the color of old corn tassels, of cottonwood leaves after they have lain on the ground for a while—that bleached and earthen clayey white-yellow. My mother's happiness was not the concern of the world. She may have loved women, at least by the time she was in her thirties—perhaps always. I believe my mother had a woman as a lover, a very, very pretty woman, an immigrant, a peasant from the Tyrol, a soubrette sort: she worked for my mother and was perhaps why my mother agreed to marry my father and to go live in such a small town, to be near her and to employ her, that woman. Of course, I don't know. I half remember going with my mother on a train to escape from the lover—the day had the tone of redemption. I think my mother wept a little bit and made jokes to me. My hand marks and nose marks and breath marks on the window glass of the train, I remember those and the automatic way my mother's hand wiped the marks away. I see wheeling rows of corn, occasional trees, windmills, farmhouses. Two years after I met Daniel, Lila told me my mother loved women—not men. Lila said, *She had more character than any woman I ever knew, but a lot of good it did her.* She said, *My brother, who was no slouch at making a buck, said she was a genius at business.* She said, *You know, all things considered, I feel sorry for anyone who falls in love with your pretty face.*

14

The patterns you see: as opposed to the ones in you that you can't see: for my tastes then Daniel has mostly the wrong look. And I get to choose. I don't know. I don't have a *pretty* face. Maybe I did for a while. A boy at school, Bill Gill, newly grown, abruptly after being a kid, in him when he was newly sexual I saw a fierce, temporary sort of new *beauty*—I saw it when other kids talked about it in him . . . Bill's newly silvery skin, dark eyebrows, reddish lips, and aghast, staring, and shy and almost horrified eyes. An unsinging—and temporary—Orpheus already half-dismembered. I don't know by what or whom. Then he got used to it all. He forgot the other stuff, of having been a kid. He woke to his new life; and his eyes became *amused,* startled, sweet, then sullen. Then snobbish.

Then the moment of him being *pretty* was over; he was a good-looking *older boy* with a lot of brothers.

He and I had been good friends. His mother had been a real friend. For a couple of years she *saved* my life.

I remember his prophetic and lunatic eyes during his pretty period when guys and girls started following him, pantsing him, courting him. He was not so tall and gawky with such frozenly careful movements as I'd been a few months before. He'd felt some appalled rejection of orphan's *whorishness* that I hadn't felt and some heat of carelessness in the middle of his being so careful in this temporary masquerade of the flesh that I hadn't indulged.

His mother came to the schoolyard one morning to apologize to me for what Bill had become. Lying in my bunk, in the lower bunk, the night I spent on the train, as the train clattered, I heard Daniel stirring above me. At school we'd sort of had *the cute boy of the month*—the next boy to go through this phase of initiation to this stuff.

It lasts only for a short while, that prettiness, that view of another world. If you forget it and then remember it, it seems very strange, as if it had no real duration. People who come near you at that time *are* shocked. Jolted. Not everyone. Some days it *is* everyone. It feels like a ticket to the loony bin. Dan at moments had been averted and yet staring or peering or aware—remembering? Was it that you are like a scene in a movie that is too harsh or something, too reminiscent, and children and some nice people hide their eyes? Some absurdity or other colors your outline with glare—a boy is burning at his edges. I rush along sleddingly on my breath.

Is everything foreordained? If it is, why do *I* have to decide anything? One laughs silently—*for no reason*. If one laughs aloud, Dan will say, *Are you all right, Wiley?*

In the dark, the window of the compartment still holds a dulled reflection. One remembers drawing, oh, whistles of derisive interest in the shower after football and track. One remembers people showing you an oddly intrusive indulgence. One feels rigidly uncaring. Sometimes it feels like when a friend is driving you in his car too fast: one endures the moment: your youth—your crotch suddenly a prize, in no simple way. To be uncaring is a *glamourous* thing especially after you've lived with someone sick whom you did care about, often dutifully. Along the edge of the whisper and rush of actual distances between cities and in the lurching clatter of the train at night—minutes whirring and galloping and trotting by, and one's new crotch in the dark of one's pajamas—one lives on. I'd counted in February and March eighty-two people who tousled my hair, fifty-eight men (including boys), twenty-four women (and girls). On the train so far, eighteen people have spoken to me. And most of those touched me.

Being touched makes me nervous. I follow Lila's advice: *Don't give a hint you know what's going on or you'll be asking for it . . . Don't show* ANYONE *you know* ANYTHING.

I don't know what's going on, Momma: tell me. Tell me in simple terms—am I a special case? What am I, Momma?

She decided to answer: *You're cute, you're cute this year. It's wartime. You have a fresh look. People will never say you're pretty. Wiley, I will say it is interesting how you aren't like me.*

But most likely none of this means anything. I whisper inwardly, *I wish I knew more . . .* And attempting to measure possibilities, *Don't touch me . . .* And: *Touch me.*

Lila said: *People who care about you—I want you to try to be grown-up about these things—they don't mind using you and throwing you away . . . Like a Kleenex. I will say this: I don't envy you.*

She does but not all the time.

When you listen to someone talk, do you listen more to the words or do you mostly look at the momentary stagecraft of it? What part of what she says really concerns *me*? She makes some sort of exception of me. I knew the spy-ey feeling you get sometimes at how you were treated when people were *interested* in you.

Lila said, *Daniel respects you. He's good-looking and smart and he can be counted on.*

I doubt it. I doubt that he can be trusted. *He is what he is. Don't expect too much of people.*

15

If I introduce the idea here that Daniel expects actual *sex* of a kind unheard of by me so far and not easily guessed at by me—me taking off my clothes and not in a locker room, and him taking off his, even if the two of us are with a B-girl or a whore—well, I feel it as a kind of unsacramental marriage that is being proposed—like being asked to be seriously on a team. Or like being initiated into a club or into a fraternity you're expected to take seriously—and which I haven't taken seriously so far. And like a mysterious secret thing that maybe could belong to me and might have no outward consequences, or none worth thinking about, except, of course, for the metamorphosis of the self into someone who has had that experience. This moment exists and is like a roadway into moments unlived so far. If you do certain things the moments ahead of you for a while are slain—are as fixed as consequences as if they were corpses—except you can sort of run away or die or go crazy. You have to guess what will kill your future and make the moments seem dead. Or semi-dead. Or worthless. If we proceed, Dan and I, won't I be semi-helpless then, the rest of my life? Angry or limp? Maybe just human. And he will be consoled. By the sacrifice. The robbery. But I don't know anything here for sure. *What do I know?* I have a friend in U. City who tells me to forget things and just be myself. He means: *Be a zero . . .* Naked—like Tarzan—pretend only to a simple identity. Life is scary. *Be a hero-zero, Wiley . . .*

The idea of an intrinsic identity and of difference is hateful to the guy I was just talking about. Like everyone else I know, he has more rage in him than I have. He's way to the left politically; he ascribes identity to money and family—and to athletic stuff. Sometimes to sexual stuff but not really: that stuff can all be settled *medically*. The whole thing of being hetero for him is to get even for every single advantage that every other identity has. I think he learned that in psychoanalysis, the guy I'm talking about.

A bit of sexual do-jiggery buys a truce or a half-truce. But if you kind of whore around, you may turn into a frog. It would be *interesting* to try whatever Dan wants and see if one froze up and was sickened or could manage, say, as Nonie couldn't with any of the rich guys she hadn't been able to manage with.

Again, I know a little about this stuff because of the locker room at school and because of my sick dad.

Dan doesn't know that I know anything. A series of yeses or no's, flashingly, like flicking light switches or the gauges of machinery—that's what he sees. Maybe he sees that.

A dozen times or so, I decide to say yes to anything he offers, but part of me *knows* I won't say it. I can't. I know that nothing will happen.

Was it like this for Nonie? Did it happen like this for Nonie? Are we really brother-and-sister in lots of ways?

16

As a rule, one can't guess the nutty direction individuality in someone will go in. A sweaty moisture in one's crotch—one is young. Being unchanged is a myth—even if you say no to everything, that admits you've changed. One can be less changed or more changed. I know some of what is true for me. I half know . . .

Dan is, I think, *homosexual, realistic, and moral*; but he never said so; we never had it out. He is apologetic *on the edge* of being triumphant—my observations of him are that the moments now irritate and excite him into an unwise love. I don't know how this happened. I won't gamble on it—that's for sure.

A real moment of almost unbearable exoticism, not without its attractions, sexual reality, secret stuff, and the immanence of something, the weight of that in me: and something is now *tormented* in him almost every single moment while we get dressed in the morning. The whole thing of charity is reversed—is two-sided, anyway. If-you-love-me-you-find-the-aroma-of-my-torment-in-what-you-see-in-what-you-sense-in-a-touch-over-a-period-of-time. It is cruel to be relieved, in my pride, at his torment.

My mother said, *You don't always have to be so sensitive.* I can get drunk, *toute suite.* I can have a morning Scotch with Daniel. We have a kind of malely sinful openness to event; plausibility has changed. I can insist on The Old Plausibility, though. It seems to me I feel each moment in its own lighted frame in its momentariness with emphases of dutiful worry about what ought to happen next, about what one ought to do, and with frivolous not-caring, with unaccustomed *mischief* and with the sense of his new torment and of the new *plausibility* between us.

The train goes clickety-clack, and so do my feelings; and the train and its motions are intensely and pulsingly and unclearly present in *his* chest, his shoulders, his *skull* this morning—my cousin's—in my cousin's heart: that man and his faulty love—if it is love. I have to wait and see. I am half overwhelmed, half merely amused that the train's motions have become my feelings. I suppose I mean the train's motions carry that meaning—is it a meaning? I am an exile from yesterday here in the lurchingly tormented morning. It's his torment. I eye him obliquely getting dressed in the compartment, shirtlessly shaving. Perhaps one way or another I will die, castaway, derelict. Frivolously thrown away. Plausible *sexuality* sucks at my balance and makes me giddy as in a play about warriors and *girls.* Dan's feelings are directed at a boy—at the boy he sees, skin and eyes, not at the boy he does not yet know, the compendium-and-anthological boy of days and days and days—the one my mother suspects of too much *conceit.*

I half know that a *dirty* social merit consists of pretending to submit to the blackmail arrangements in human goings-on (as Lila understands these things). Lila has taught me what she knows. She has taught me what she wanted to teach me. S.L., too, has taught me, differently from Momma. Looking back into the morning light in the compartment, I think I see that Dan expects to be disappointed but doesn't quite believe it. I think the boy knows how limited he (the boy) would be in a hug. And he guesses at how Dan would make use of that. I think I see why Benjie usually *pretended* to confidence and knowledge of *my* sexuality. Daniel is being cheerful; he is prepared. *People are realists, Wiley, more than you are.* Daniel is puffy-eyed, rosy-cheeked, respectful, and full of trespass in embryo and a kind of very decent half-hidden resentment. Is he far along in his spiritual death? Is he moving toward rebirth? Does it depend on me? What will it cost me?

I mean either way.

Nothing is ideal when you get right down to it. The hours spent together nonstop in the overstrained *precocity* of emotion cloudily overlaid with stratagem. *People make use of you is all anything is.* Nonie said that in 1943 when she was deeply unhappy. The *you* she meant was partly a general thing, everyone, reflections of her. Does Daniel want a son? *Someone bright? Do me a favor and learn to wait to see what happens.*

17

I feel I am being rifled *spiritually*. I am afraid of *my* savagery, my own sense of justice, of what I might do. My father when he was dying asked me again and again to kiss him in a certain way because he had never kissed a boy or a man that way, but I could not, would not do it. I don't know. I had taken care of him all those years in a lot of ways—why wasn't that enough? But why not do more? He wanted in part to tease me. He wanted me to prove I *loved* him. He wanted still to have sexual power and command even at the end. I am partly stifled with resentment toward men.

An entire life of thousands and thousands of moments is there in the compartment with Daniel. I want to tell him honestly what I think, but I can't. The unwordedness of nearly everything for me in the moments with Daniel on that trip and my efforts later in life to become articulate are related to the phenomenal and entirely not-credible richness of reality.

I am being slammed back and forth in the oddity of being on the train. Locker-room talk is: *Don't get your hopes up; don't get your balls in an uproar; don't think so well of yourself.* Guys said, *I'm not your slave.* Girls said it, and grown women. Some people did get slavish—some get slavish meanly, upsettingly. Some do it in a way that breaks your heart. People indulge you threateningly. *Life's at the boil, hunh,*

Kiddo? You like your life now, Pisherkins? S.L. said that before he died when things were tense between us.

It's interesting some of the time to live. I feel alive.

"Do you cheat at games, Dan?" I ask him. He is buttoning his shirt.

"No . . . . I don't like games." A small smile.

Beginning to get an erection, I ask, "But everything is fair in love and war?"

"No . . . Yes . . . Sometimes . . ."

(Well, I certainly won't trust *him* . . .)

(Lila said, *One thing I'll say for Daniel is, he is certainly trustworthy.*)

The electrical thing of the flirtation—of the question—is like being overdressed. I understand that I have an odd look now because of this stuff at breakfast in the dining car. People stare at us. (I am *amused.*) I know in the onrush of ordinary time that hour-by-hour in the real world I have no protector and that I am a woods of Dan's nocturnal hunting. I know that I mostly don't know what is in the woods—even if the woods is me. The part of me that is prey is not known to me as identity. I don't entirely mind bad stuff when it happens to me, because then, when that stuff happens, you get to spy on the world in a new way. Am I *incredibly* BAD? WOW. POW. KAZOW. It depends on who you ask.

Is it a tactic, a hope, a blindness TO ACCEPT THIS SHIT AS *NORMAL*? I become deadpan, since each thing that I show brings about a responding thing in him, and the number of his responses—he echoes with me—begins to be like babble. God knows what Daniel sees when he looks at me. Moment by moment. Well, I don't want to be a victim. In any way. Dense, stiff-souled, prickly—me—and *then* that is the story then.

Ten percent of the world is made up of overt practitioners of the special disciplines of self-consciously semi-public homosexuality. Homosexuality is in part a way of modelling the world—one can spy on men and on women and on language, using your own life and love as specialized versions of the rest. It's like electric-train stuff (in part). I thought, *I'm sorry.* I did then think that homosexual love wasn't real love but was a model of love, well-thought-out and functional. I do now think it is real love. But then I thought any homosexual flirtation must collapse under the weight of any other actuality of love, must fail to outweigh the world. Loss and longing are actuality, though. Love of the second rank is still love. Maybe another ten percent of the world's population is made up of covert practitioners and of part-time partakers and of people who tried it and chose not to go on with it much or often but who retain a kind of interest. And five percent of the world is uncertain and wavers or pretends to. So, by my estimates, twenty-five percent of everybody is directly implicated. Everyone is familiar with it no matter what they say. A fistfight and then the afterward of such a fight, a wrestling match, anything you do with *a brother*, the thing of being yelled at by a lesbian teacher who doesn't like boys: our own feelings off and on: we all know a lot. Or some. We react differently though, each one of us.

What Nonie maybe went through when she got away from our house and the illness in it, the emotional color of her moments when she was rescued, well, the emotional color of my moments were like this. The compartment is khaki-ish or dun, the color of a certain countryside sunlight at this time of day, a travelling light unfamiliar to me. Sand-colored, changeable. The shifting room, swaying, bouncing, moving above the wheels—*light is never still*—nowhere in the universe is light ever still. It is supposed to be in heaven and it is slowed in black holes maybe. I get a sense, for whatever it's worth, of a release for Daniel from the inexplicable narcissistic loneliness of the self through infatuation. I mean, the difficult thing for him is to be interested in the world; he has an aching, partial freedom; I suspect him of sudden, capriciously tyrannical reversals, changes of mood, him casting you off morally. His *personality*. I'm wrong often about life but I think he blurs his drama even when he means to make it sharp and *Biblical*.

So: is he *vain and creepy*—a bit reptilian? Gorgeously lizardlike? In courtship? The quick coldness of posture, the perceptible longing for heat? Is he easily affronted?

Lila has pointed out, *The world consists of number one's; people who put themselves second is in short supply*.

The hooves of milling and racing horses of heartbeat—a *hallucination—What's the big idea?*

What's the big deal?

I could be completely wrong about everything.

18

The next morning.

Is Daniel a creep? Is he *IN LOVE* in an unquieted, wild way—I mean a later-than-in-high-school way or a more-uncontrolled-than-a-good-but-emotional-teacher way?

Objective means you are not inside the story. *Subjective* means you are. The existence of a reader sets up a race between the writer and him or her to see who is more outside the tale. It is the opposite of what the technology of an advertisement does to a product, the opposite of setting up an ideal fantasy, the evaporation of reality.

19

At dawn.

On the rocking-rickety train, the compartment smells of night.

It is barely light, fresh and shadowy, smelly but clement here behind the half-drawn, odorous window shade. The strangeness of travel and of the moment makes me feel myself to be a skinny balloon—that fragile—and that I am proceeding and being carried along in what is essentially *a fairy tale*, the nowhere-somehow-somewhere of the mental space of a dimensional tale set among objects foreign to my actual experience.

It is *bright and early* but it is not bright. I sit up in my bunk and see the shadows here, in this shadowy light, the fur left here by struggling and circling night-wolves—the melodrama of boys' books affects my wits.

Then, in the already slightly sweaty heat of the morning, I hear Daniel stirring above me in his bunk. He is awake.

Daniel, invisible, a voice near the roof—and the train is noisy—tells me he prays in the mornings, as his father had before him; he puts on the *tefillin*; but not this morning.

He swings himself down. I look out the window, I lift the side of the shade, and see an immense dew-glittering field and a farmhouse and a running and silent dog far off and small on the field.

Daniel is in white shorts and a khaki T-shirt and has a couple of dog tags. He has too powerful muscles in his legs; they embarrass me; I don't like them.

But, otherwise, he is thin, almost spidery, handsome and admirable—admirably in condition—and this is noble to my youthful vision.

But not him asking, "And what were you up to all night?"

He goes into the small bathroom in the corner and he lathers his bony jaw and the strong-looking stubble of his face and neck. I stay in my bunk. If I stood up, me being the size I am and him being the size he is, we would crowd the compartment.

His reflecting-me eyes, the periscope-mirror eyes of someone-who-likes-me, that male interest, should be, by my lights, masked. Well, reality is unreal.

He begins to talk about driving lessons he will give me. He does this while he shaves. He is bargaining. Learning to drive is important to me; but his talking about it has the itchy aura of too much feeling; and his body is too near me although it is maybe three feet away. Yet, this is almost standard male wartime camaraderie.

He asks me if I am having a good time on the train; and I say, not knowing why I am saying this complicated and far-out thing, "I don't know if I'm having a good time but I'm not in pain."

Then I see it is again a way of seeing if he can bear me and for how long or if I am a shadow image—with adolescent coloring—for him.

I register that *he doesn't listen* when he says, "Tell me . . . Tell me what your dreams were . . ."

I feel I am like a child, or almost-a-child, at the foot of a wall around a place he, the child, wants to enter. I don't know if this is *sexual* longing or not.

I would like to bump against him and wrestle symbolically but not as if one were on an escalator, an elevator, or a train, a single track of action, but in a field with everything possible including a No.

Or an event that is really a No.

To drive him away—at least I think that is what it was—although I was aware that I would *do things* with him if that is what he wanted, if he showed signs of knowing how limited those actions would have to be and if he could bear me, my reality, at least somewhat.

"Well, Daniel," I said, "in the mornings I don't pray the way you do, I contemplate the presence in the world of something near me that suggests the possibility of the actuality of me having luck-in-the-long-run . . . A favorable outcome—you know? And as for short-term luck, I think about masturbation—".

His face grew smooth. "Yes?" Now he's listening to me.

"I think about luck and sin, I guess. I think about luck and sin as being like a peony preparing itself for the day's commerce with insects, you know? A peony wind-rubbed and fluffed early in the morning?"

No one can bear the way I talk. It isn't all that plausible. I have my hands behind my head in what now seems the warm gloom of the train compartment. Daniel didn't say, *You're crazy.* He merely edited the look in his eyes—his eyes were full of the reality and the pretense of judgments.

I went on, alternately watching him and staring into the air—and at the bottom of the upper berth: "Well, prayer is getting what you want; it has to do with winning out; so it's funny for a Jew or for a Christian, at least one who loves Christ, a Christ-lover, unless they turn the feeling into the pursuit of vengeance. Prayer mostly has to do with being on top of the world—success, a favorable outcome. I can't do that. I guess I think God is omnipresent, inside and outside everyone, so that you have no need to address *Divinity* ever, except for your own sake, for the sake of stuff in you, to exercise it. I think that prayer takes me back toward sleep and dreaming, when my skull seems to contain the whole, real universe and hours of time and millions of inhabitants. Anyway, I like a lot of crappy things: people who lose out and ideas that are no good, you know? And dead flowers? I'm not exactly on the side of nature. Or of sleep. Or of superpeople. I practice a kind of thing of going outward; I focus outside myself and see how long I can hold it: you know—I just stare—it's no big deal; I vaguely pass out and I feel the presence of God. He's pissed with me usually—presumably, that's how *I* feel. That *It's* pissed. The *All* is pissed. Now that S.L.'s dead, we are kind of negotiating my return, the *All* and me—I chose S.L. over God. I chose him over everything. I respected my earth-father—the one down here. But it's not a real negotiation if you do both voices—then it's just free will playing around. I do both voices, so I don't know really what the terms are. Anyway, short of that, I just stare at the world and then I think, well, I *feel* I saw God, sort of, which is hard to make sense of if God is everywhere and is you, whoever you are, among all the others who, and which, are also God, you know? I think it's just sort of a messy glimpse—maybe a sissy glimpse. Maybe a glimpse for a tough guy—I don't really know: the feeling is realer than anything I can say about it. Then my eyes—and my hope—get out of hand; they go apeshit. My hopes. Plural. It's okay. I can hack it. It's kind of grand and stupid—grand and imbecile—very grand and terrible when you admit how stupid you're being and how the truth is like seventy thousand infinitudes greater and bigger and more serious and funnier and more everything: you get a glimpse of awe. That doesn't sober you up; you just fall into this giddy expectation of psychological, maybe spiritual, favor, you know? Love instead of only pain? It's not just, you know—it's like being the favorite child—for a moment. You have to sober up but it's okay so far. *See*, then I have to disbelieve it, all of it: ALL: *Oh what a load of bullshit*, right? But it runs in my family—my real family. Another thing I do is I count to seventeen slowly—well, don't laugh—a vision *always* comes before I get to seventeen. I don't believe that vision either. I never *believe* it. But I like it . . . It appears usually between the numbers 11 and 14—I think I'm afraid of the number *15*. It's not always visual—it's more a sense of presence, a further thing, a kind of lion stink of not entire invisibility. A breathing-almost-visibility and a stink of that—maybe a cryptic formula, too: *Let go* . . . *Let go* . . . It's probably just a genetic tic, anyway. It's there now . . . But I know I'm not a prophet. It's just me. Tick-tock. So it doesn't *mean* anything—except it means something to *me*, just to me, so it's a team-and-ego thing after all . . . Us versus them . . ."

Although Dan's told me that he is lonely and would like not to be, I think that is soft soap, and that in real life, he does most of the talking near him and perhaps even all of it.

If he didn't do all the talking with someone he liked—if *all* the speeches weren't to his taste—then it wasn't a dream come true.

I'm lonely when I talk but I'd met Casey in St. Louis and I really believe it wasn't paradise for Daniel if Daniel didn't do all the talking.

If he admitted Casey was real, he would probably explode into brightly burning pieces of who-knows-what.

I think Daniel in his daydreams imagined a dialogue *without* a second voice, a dialogue between him and someone without his having to listen to the other person; he calculated that someone might want him—his money, his discipline, his looks . . . his body, chest, chest hair, strong legs, dick—throat—enough that that wanting would be the equivalent of a good speech in a book making sense—all that. Then Daniel would *make love* to that person, making the other person *happy*—i.e., the other person would make that perfect speech; that would be the other person's speech, the other's share of the dialogue, the happiness or at least the release, or the relief, the lovemaking would be for her, him, it.

I think he ejaculatingly calculated that in him being wanted a dialogue was occurring in a *better* way than it could happen in words.

I believe he conveyed this to me over the next several years: this mystically absolute view of sex and of possible happiness within it.

I don't say he wasn't right; but I saw something early on when I knew him, even on the train, and I pitied him; he made me frantic and tense—with pity and with silence. I mean it was so unworded that it felt as if I had been excluded from my own story except as the *NO* that put me into his story and which held his attention.

Nothing was *identified* or footnoted on the train. The moment was just there; it was just itself—cryptic—and with us in it—a boundaried and not-naked moment.

Anyway, now I knew he would kiss me—I hoped it would be on my hair—him kissing me, unless I made a scene, would be my real speech to take the place of the interior meaning of what I'd just said.

That is, its interior meaning was that it elicited feeling from him.

He was shaving still; he rinses his face and launched into a lecture on Jewish morning prayers—as if I were a Catholic. I sighed at being not all that honestly or accurately lectured—it was propaganda mostly—and then, his face and hair wet, he walked over to me, paused, and he put on his khaki pants, and then, lecturing still, his lips, loosened—

sinuous, longish, brick-red—his large brown eyes (with their black centers)—came near me where I lay in the bunk; it was his whole face, his skull; but it was out of focus. He breathed a little noisily; he didn't hold his breath tactfully; he didn't tiptoe in approaching me; he seemed almost to semi-roaringly whistle and hiss—and to smack his lips and watch—as he kissed my hair, then my ear.

In a natty and gentle way—lingering, a bit feminine—not male roughhousing—not with contempt although it was a bit *don't-fool-with-me* (*I'm-sensitive-and-rich*) and it was also *YOU can't judge me.*

I was amazed though—he is a different soul from me; it's not just the distance between our ages; it's an incredible extent of *Difference*—as if he were another species, or was a dancing thing, a rock that came alive in the mornings, say. It was that amazing—*It was nothing, don't make a big song-and-dance out of it*—it was affection and of the sort I'd seen dozens and hundreds of times but it was aimed at me *differently*—across some *other* gulf.

It had a sort of inelegant elegance—as if he felt a lot—one way or the other—disapproval or shock, shocked liking—and, so, he walked off physically (a step or two) and mentally further than that while he was standing there: his mind went some distance away; his feelings did too. Well, what happened in the kiss and after was that he was daydreaming. I should have been a blond toy with good legs and all that—all that shit of being malleable—toward a limber and lithe monkey wrench of a kind of *iron* man—but I wasn't of that sort.

And he was glad I wasn't—this was maybe my first recognition of sexual taste as oddity—as a perversity in itself and toward oneself, him feeling it, and me feeling it as it emanated from him.

I laughed. Sometimes I think I want to write about love as envy—as *Let me harm you and ruin your life* . . .

Or as *I envy the grown-ups* . . .

Or *I envy the pederasts.*

And then the inebriation of this—partly in its allowing me a deep silence to rest in from speech. The thing of being *chosen* or settled for—or idealized and yet seen clearly enough all in all to have your faults on the list—is oddly secretive and unsettling.

Also, if he says nothing and if I don't look at him but down at the railway blanket covering me—*What the fuck am I going to do now?*—it's possible I'm loony tunes bar none all by my lonesome, that I'm making all this up.

I kind of hear his heartbeat—perhaps not really in the noise of the train in the compartment.

A stiffness of focus in me means what? That his body, his peculiar chest, narrow from front to back and not wide, but large-muscled—and a peculiar tense *rigidity* of his hips—oh, I *half* recognize the basic derrick with the cantilevered or upright lever thing of an erection—but I am too shy and I lack style (and humanity) and do not realize it with any fullness . . .

I mean I don't hear his speech delivered that way—it is like his not hearing my speeches, the ones I make in words.

The long-legged possessing thing of a man you feel as spidery and as not inwardly generous but as caught in the singular ego thing of the dream-of-romance—a peculiar disorderliness of loneliness and of his experience search for companionship—this isn't at all like the disorder of being suckered or sucked in by a woman or a girl: you enter nowhere—you enter yourself with the curious quality of *logic* of a dream—or of a hallucination while jerking off—and this distorts the air with some sense in that state of a power that I have (over his blood? over his prick?) and which I dislike but which makes me grin inwardly and sweatily—in an odd way—and which sets me free to *think* . . .

I mean it: it has the quality of reverie.

"Uh," I say. "Well, hey." I have already begun to sit up in the complicated way enforced by the presence of the upper bunk; I sit at the edge of my bunk, in my underwear but with the blanket pulled over me, in part, not too unpleasantly I hope . . . But, see, it is absolute, unbearable hell to be touched physically by an absolutist . . . The feeling, the what-it-feels-like, the meaning is piercing—and really horrible.

It isn't homosexuality that I mind. It's the trespassed-on self-reverie thing and a sense of being clumsily looted while one is semi-pseudo-blissfully *silent* . . . This is me, not a general principle.

He touches the nape of my neck. What I felt then, what I knew I was feeling, was that I didn't want to blame him or have *tragedies* or scenes come about. And I didn't want the spermatic-milk derrick to release—or discharge anything—and that, contradictorily, I liked, in a blackened, despairing, semi-amused way, having power over *his* body.

Well, when things get *complex* (*complex* was a term of disapprobation in U. City among adolescents), I just sort of say to myself, *Just pay no attention* . . .

And: *I don't want anyone to talk to me about this* . . . (That meant Daniel, too. I wanted no description, no advice—no witnesses.)

I wanted, in an odd meaning of the term, to be innocent—on examination, not necessarily at sight—and I wanted that *in the worst way*—not like a child but like a guy in a locker room or like the character in some famous love stories who is a visitor and hears or sees the story but isn't in it; the guy is taking shelter in a haunted house in a storm or something; and he will survive the attack or the seduction by the blood-sucking vampire in his (or her) promiscuous love of *gore*: but he won't *hate* the vampire—or the lovers if it is a different type of story—or himself if things work out that this, too, is love.

The thing of wanting *not* to be a part of a maybe *mean* story is a peculiar thing in life, upperish or ordinary, super-potent or cowardly. A brave guy is clearly *not cowardly*—do you know what I mean? A nose is not an eye. An eye is not a cheek. The iris is not the white of the eye. Bravery is often a really obvious, habitual thing. What I do is maybe cowardly. It's possibly brave. I don't know. He has chosen me to be in a story, and I don't want to be in it in the way he proposes—this isn't final but he's not a flexible guy. He's spoiled.

But he had maybe a certain amount of trouble when he was young: pain can train you, can lead you to try changing unless you have a thing against changing and think it's awful.

In real life he maybe *felt* this as part of my *youth* and as a ground for him feeling stuff: that I hoped, kind of, that pain would change him, that I felt nothing *favorable* about his sexual nature, and not a lot about him.

He touched the nape of my neck as I said. Then I think he touched the nape of his own neck, the back of his neck. Mine, then his. Like he was planning a decapitation—of a sort. I couldn't see this except out of the corner of my eye as he walked to the corner where the tiny bathroom was. I looked up into the air and then at the partly shaded window and the motionful stuff under the bottom of the partly lifted shade. I didn't sigh; I had some kind of feeling or other—what would happen if I made a face now and muttered, *Don't do that . . .* ?

So, I muttered it. Well, everyone gets a shock now and then—mine was that it seemed, weirdly and *terribly*, that I, tired and semi-ill as I was from stuff at home in St. Louis, was stronger in some way than he was. What the fuck. He came back out of the john almost right away, he had his toilet kit in one hand; his razor was in his other hand; both hands held things. He dropped the stuff in my lap. His hands were scratched, blood-flecked—the nails were bitten and bleeding here and there along the cuticles.

Add it up? I can't.

It was a moment leery of itself. The moment is, for me, my realer dress, my clothes: it blows or moves or stirs in some overly passionate silent storminess of electric power . . . I have a huge amount of shyness about myself. A moral shyness? A feminine one? A fear of scandal? No. Yes. One can throw off the blanket, see what happens—and one can say it was all a joke. One might get sent to college . . .

It is the offer of one life curling itself like a wind, an image in a mind, toward another life, a body and an image in a mind, toward an eventual, disillusioned, further passionate, often hate-filled closeness. I know what happens for me with people. To know someone well, to be permeated with them when you have had a history: this stuff can make you shy.

The prick is an unlikely structure. As is any finger but especially the thumb. And so is a neck *unlikely*. The *prick* is elongated, changeable, and boneless, tethered, full of feeling, pallid in color—willful—a willful elephant trunk, a guy's own *sensitive* puppy-or-puppet sausage, dead meat, a mysterious and unopposed thumb for the grasp of sensation—it is small flesh, proud, white and shy; it is shy and meaty; shyly meaty whenever I say no and the no is listened to.

The power in me laughably fills the wind sock—and feels the air currents, images, and hallucinations here.

Its connections to people and to events are wrapped in shyness. All discussions of force are oddly obscene. Who and what is infatuated with *it* with any *force* of feeling now? Who and what is *it* infatuated with? Am I the policeman here—me, my strength, my luck, some mysterious element of what I am?

Am I in love with my own dominance or domineering chances, even if such dominance is a lie? Or with the force of money? Bridling it? Being a bride of it—or a groom?

The force of being *normal*—plus or minus a few events?

Or with the defeat of the Nazis—myself as an officer in the army (in a few years)?

The Germans are nowhere near the train. The Japanese hold no fields outside the moving window. The names of war-torn cities—Rangoon, Stalingrad, Salonika—offers a kind of license? Who would suspect a bony, thin-armed adolescent of having a sexually anonymous soul? (Actually, anyone would; but no soul is anonymous in this world . . . How strange that is.)

I was dealing with the readiness with which absolution is given, almost without exception, to someone like me. In a few minutes a decision will appear and time will go on.

Nonie has exclaimed in my hearing, *Things don't have to be named!*

They're not what you say they are! And: *It's a lot easier to talk about marrying a rich man than it is to live it out.*

You swing out and around and back and up and then off into the dark of not-knowing only a little. Of course, I did love Daniel (off and on) and at that moment: with juvenile exasperation and impatience. He knew. It wasn't unfamiliar. He expects this. To be liked in this way. Love, so to speak, comes out of the corridor—or out of the sunlit air outside. In the perspective in the compartment, Daniel's deep-socketed, unmildly-colored-by-feeling eyes wear a mask of shadow. Do we start guiltily? Does Daniel? I am not guilty yet, so far as I know. I am glad to think he knows that if I *love* him, I have to spare him knowing me; I have to forgo the interruption of the sensual-and-personal dialogue which is paradise for him (if it is). I am glad to say I would never permit or allow nor can I live out his fantasy.

The agony of loving *the wrong person . . .* Well, Jeest, that's *not* uncommon—is it?

Still, it feels uncommon and secretive and privileged to say no while saying nothing in words, merely by sitting in a stiffened way.

The intensity of this particular moment fades into something which is echoed in the stridently ironic cast his version of fraternity (or maternity) and of hospitality takes—at the sight of me in the next moment over, plus one. An outburst-in-a-glance—that's disciplined, kind of—his look of being well-mannered and driven to the breaking point. A rich man's *martyrdom* is not necessarily a joke but it is free of pathos. Daniel is not innocent or sweet, quite. Or a victim. One doesn't suspect him of molesting a child—just of being careless toward me, whom his father chose for him, sort of—or told him to take a look at—perhaps in opposition to his mother's liking Nonie, which may have irritated both men. I will never know. Here we are in this curve of the story and I don't know the terms of the account on his side, the factors of the other plot that pertain here.

Generalizations are unreal to me; I can see why Nonie might be effectual and useful and me not.

I sort of gawp—inwardly. Outwardly I am mannerly.

20

Dan is tautly built, as taut as a trout, but politer. The sun was bright on flat farm fields and on rolling wooded hills—*Oh-here-you-are's, oh-here-*

he-is's, and *ha-ha*'s and *tee-hee*'s (take that), the inner *babble*, the letdowns, the resurgences of *tension*.

"What do you think of Lloyd C. Douglas?" Daniel asked me in the khaki light, with a kind of kindliness on top of a sourness that scared the bejesus out of me.

"I like religious best-sellers," I said with tactful hopefulness.

"Isn't it a waste of time to read them?" He is being tricky or pious . . . Or both.

Or he wants to stop being pious for a while. "I read fast: two hundred and fifty pages an hour, three hundred if I skip the descriptions. I like Pearl Buck and Hervey Allen better than Lloyd Douglas." I looked at him and showed I was willing to talk. People who refuse to talk refuse you a certain *amount* of stuff, but silence helps you stay maybe within the category of being young. I say, "I like reading about women in bestsellers."

"I like Khalil Gibran," he said. "Do you know a book of poetry called *This Is My Beloved*?"

"Is that the one with pubic hair like lettuce leaves?"

"Yes."

"Yeah. Some guys were reading that in the locker room."

He closed his eyes. "It's trash," he said. "My sister reads it." I knew. She'd been in St. Louis and we'd flirted; she'd quoted some of it to me.

He's real; he's not my opinion of him. I am real, too.

Daniel's saddened face shows that my remark about women affects him while his taut posture shows, though, that he allows callowness, callow playing around. Callow cruelty. At least he does if I do it. I slouch where I sit, a form of self-display.

"I'm a slow and steady *serious* reader," he said. "I like Sholem Aleichem: I read Yiddish . . . Yiddish, French, Hebrew, German, a little Latin, Greek . . ." He waits for a response.

"I read only in English. I like James Joyce—the family stuff and the dirty stuff he does. I like Tolstoy. I'm saving Dostoyevsky for college."

"That's a good idea. You don't look like a reader," Cousin Daniel said. I am deadpan then. It's funny how in everything you need training and luck—and courage.

I *don't care if you like me or not, but I like you if you can accept me as I am.*

Bribes, pleasantries . . . Money . . . Looks . . .

His leg sort of slid until his knee was alongside mine itchily not touching. I twitched—involuntarily—and he moved his knee away. I never make the *first* move in sexual matters. But to behave well *is asking for trouble*. I feel embarrassed and apologetic, and I feel a grimly embarrassed *hilarity*.

"Do you like simple things?"

"I am simple," I say.

With someone closer to me in age, we might match dirty words; we might show each other ourselves pantingly if it didn't mean anything, if it was literal information and not part of another sort of personal purpose—such as for the purposes in a perhaps real and perhaps lasting feeling. I mean you settle for it and for the memory of it and for the recurrence of it.

If Daniel was *a regular guy* we'd be wrestling or something. It would be who gives orders and to what extent the other obeys for a while, erotically or not erotically, sort of . . . Who likes who, who runs the thing in the compartment. The taking turns. Or whatever.

The glare outside makes me squint. The train curves on bent stretches of track and exposes our windows to direct light. I tell Daniel in answer to a question: "I am a better wrestler than a boxer; a better pitcher than a first baseman; a better batter than some guys who are really better batters because I can place-hit. I can swing for the fence. I know how."

The questionnaires of social life . . . The train passes through the cold shade among very tall trees in an *allée* in a run-down stretch of countryside. These moments of *almost* and *deeply* and *not deeply* and *glancingly* and *holding back*. I strike myself as being contemptible. Even selfish passion is more of a sacrament than the stuff I do. But passion is pretty bad stuff. I maybe teasingly—and sadistically—"*love*" him . . . just not passionately. Anyway, it was masculine youth that was an object of deeply sacramental feeling for him, not me—or only partly me. The study of *furtherness* in male reality is what he's doing. I think this is part of an adolescent tradition of meaning, but I don't really know. To move, to change into that . . .

Meanwhile, the dragon-breath of his attention as we joggle and vibrate and chug rapidly along is sort of as if he was affected by the sight of me as if I were a girl. I have a light of conferred importance—maybe. Two flies buzz in the heat and jostle each other at a corner of the dirty window. I don't know if this train ride matches the experiences of my dead mother or S.L.'s when he was young. I think so. I don't know for sure—is the world sexual or not?

The immoderate occasions of youth are common.

Toward noon, Daniel said, "We're Jews . . ."

"I find it *interesting* to be Jewish."

He said, "That's a bad thing to say." He says metaphorically, "I will be a door to proper Jewish instruction for you."

I say, "*Torah-door* . . . You—right?" And then bite my tongue, but then I started humming the song from *Carmen* anyway; being out of control, I found myself doing that.

He looked shocked, and briefly sulky, and then *interested. Carmen* is a story of fatal passion . . . *Lolita* had not yet been written as a sort of gloss or commentary on *Carmen*, as another *Carmen*, sadder and purposefully sillier about this stuff.

"We play Three-thirds of a Ghost when we travel: you ever play that?" he asks.

"S.L. doesn't like that game. We never played that. S.L. couldn't spell."

After we flip coins to see who begins Three-thirds of a Ghost—Daniel was to match me, and he did—he says, "O . . ."

"P," I say.

A faint aura of scandal attends every moment.

"E," he says.

" ' 'OPE,' " I say. "The cockney fyth, ope, un chariteeee. R."

The differences in our ages. His money. His looks. The oddity of his self-possession . . .

"A."

"Opera. You lose."

"You like opera?"

"I don't know—do you?"

"Yes. Too much . . ."

"Why do you say *too much*?"

"There are other things to do—and opera is very, very—I don't know . . . It sets you apart from people."

"Oh . . . B . . . If you want to go on . . ."

Winning means you're not flirting.

The conceited thing in him is that *love* in him in general is a monologue—in tones of excited sulkiness and reflecting a spoiled young man's power. But I can see that we are having an oddly exposed, almost semi-blazing, good-bad time—a struggle.

I realize again that it is a sort of scandal to be alive.

He is showy and secretive. I have a *think-no-evil* smile and a snobbishly arrogant-humble look—*like a rich boy*—not a rich boy's smile but *like* it: a poor boy's conceit.

Daniel says, "B? I don't understand you." Then, in a dry tone: "I don't want to understand you."

"Why?"

"It would be bad for me. B? You're not mistaken?"

"I don't think so."

"Tell me, do you believe in God or not? You want to be barmitzvahed?"

"I'll tell you. I believe in God but not in a God that can be talked about. I can't imagine an omnipotent God who would bother with gender or speech—even as amusement. I can't imagine a God that knows the future, but I don't think what I can imagine matters. I imagine revelation as springing from the efforts of certain people . . . It's like piling up books and stones higher and higher . . . I can imagine a final, single truth, but not as a knowable frame for here. I think it's cheap and wrong and really dangerous to pull that single-notion stuff down into stuff that goes on with us. It's what you move toward in your mind and in a moment; and you can talk about it; but not seriously—you can't ever use that stuff as a public premise without condoning murder. A single truth means other stuff is lying and is treacherous and is evilly wrong. The us-them shit is a trap. I happen to believe murder ought to be secular. I can't believe God is more present or is less present. I happen to think the Bible, which I truly admire, is mostly a history of consciousness—the breath moving on the waters and the appearance of the separation between the firmament and the waters and *David* is about being young, and Christ on the Cross is about a lot of stuff. And so is the Koran. It isn't that God doesn't will that you commit murder: how would *I* know what God wills or doesn't will? But I believe that *God* has shown a kind of predilection for wide webbings of interests—democratic Protestant national states . . . In the beginning was the Word, and the Word was God. Or was with God. Sure. So? I can see that language tends to the condition of prayer—it is a spire of meaning—language is—and a final meaning is a thing of being *really* right: but you won't know except at apocalypse. I mean, if you believe a *doctrine* is right—any doctrine—you are essentially gambling in such a way that only apocalypse can mean you throw in your hand and the pot gets awarded. Anyway, I don't want to be part of an us-them thing . . ."

"Jews can't help it . . ."

"I know. But everyone gets *some* of that. It's in everyone—that's why seducers get shot. Is it sexual jealousy? Is it racial? I sort of blunder along. Circumstances set up more circumstances—I accept that as a given. My favorite prayer is *I don't know, help me to have enough strength to go on a while longer.* Daniel, I just don't know. Whether or not something is there, I can't manage the conceit of thinking anyone human can know what It is . . ."

He said, shocking me into silence, in a certain way for the rest of my life: "It's rare: a pretty boy who likes to talk about serious things. What's your word? I've already lost." In the game.

"Operable."

"Is that a real word?" Then: "God would not let me suffer without a message . . ."

"That's pretty conceited." Then, about the game: "Come on: don't cheat . . . You know it's a word." Then: "No one says I'm pretty," I said. The vanity of a semi-comprehension of him—no, of something like a privilege—is a particular shape of silence. The privilege—such as it is—in real time. And the power, changeable, negotiable . . . in real time . . . The *politics* of this thing, I'm not human *that* way. He *almost* shivers downward into being young in response to my *inhuman* closed-off-ness. The plush upholstery covering of the seats, the dead bugs and the dust on the window, the live flies in the compartment, the repetitive bangings and clacking of the train as it advances over the curve of the earth are real, too.

22

"I don't ever win at chess," I offered. "I have a portable chessboard . . . I found it in an ashpit. It's short a knight and a bishop."

"Why don't you win at chess? Why not?" he said.

Is he still interested? Do I have his protection? I care enough to keep track. "I don't know—is that okay?" I said. My heart broke, perversely, literally, in the poisoned increment of opportunity moment by moment. *I'm a jerk.* I have been called names a lot. I don't know how to figure the proportions and ratios—some kinds of refusal are maybe too much of an acknowledgment. I half acknowledge my own perversity. I don't want to know what I am saying no to. To say no can be a game. One can be a problem—steal things, make scenes, cause jealousy. Pure—ghostly, stare-y—hallucinatory moment of the racing mind flinging itself this way or that against the bone as against the walls of the compartment. His breathing makes me fearful.

These moments in a kind of moral lesserness of history—history being one's father—"I can't keep the whole game in my head," I say—*earnestly*.

How much innocence does anyone have in a real moment? This is as innocent as I ever got.

HOMOSEXUALITY 2

After the Train Ride

On Winning and Being Normal Up to a Point

The Soliloquy

At night in that house, in my bedroom, among the sights available in that room by lamplight, and then in the dark the sounds from outside —the summer giggle of the wild grass in the fields beyond the lawns, the ones near the foothills, the rustle of the weedy grassheads, through the window—and the stars dit-dotting the partly silver-bluelit night sky, lit by a crescent moon above the torn tin sheet of the not-very-distant mountains, the Blue Ridge, I was aware in my recurrent nervous sleeplessness of the great whale of this other landscape, partly white with moonlight, with dark moonlight-bordered shadows, swimming with night motions.

One is sleepless. A ceiling fan turns indifferently and with a grinding noise. A wind sprang up, and the house seemed to be shuddering and stirring. I always slept soundly for a while at home . . . This torment was new; I hadn't expected it as part of the obvious fact of rescue.

I feel I am caught in *nervous* sleeplessness as in a web of personal history.

Daniel, later, will tell me he can never sleep in anyone else's house and not well in hotels. He suggested I read Proust on sleeping in strange rooms—but the foreignness of the walls, the misplaced windows, the ceaselessly original rumble of physical reality, while recognizable—and dear and attractive—did not seem to be what so savagely cut into the feeling of escape and of things being, at least in large part, *all right now.*

More, in my case, I suspected the presence of an unsuitability of sleep—of a kind of reproduction in the—comparative—stillness of the room and of the night world at that hour of the thing of being a visitor in this house, of being me, but not really: but being *first and foremost* a visitor—and unlike, in too many ways, the people here.

The unsuitability of my former sleep and previous dreams here, if they were to show up, if I were to have them here, kept me awake the first night I was there—this unsuitability of what I was and had been was the measure of the distance I had crossed to come here—the long landscape of a sentence which now must be followed by another one. The measure of some reality of time or other. The unmoored patterns of earlier kinds of sleep seemed to drift by, out of reach on the black, oily surface of consciousness at night. Old nighttime soliloquies recurred, memories of other circumstances, of questions concerning duties at home and at school—back home, back at school; a dozer's dreams now, the ones I woke from to find insomnia here, were inhabited by people in St. Louis, by friends, by Lila and Nonie: they were together that summer; they were *back* in St. Louis—far to the west.

I refused to think about St. Louis and sum up, study, emend and judge my *opinions* of life there, of my life there, and of my leaving it now—that was both cowardice and anesthesia. *Logic* is presumed to be emotionless but, of course, what is meant is that it is comparatively so —it is supposedly less greedy than most things. I mean the real thing. In real life, a *vacuum* is comparative; and the attempt to stop the motions of thought and to substitute one kind of logic for another—dream logic for a sense of things in wakefulness—a *You don't have too many worries here* for one's past logic, a *moral* emptiness, very sweet, a vacationer's vacuum in which real obligations and one's true history and one's long lists of duties fulfilled and others evaded or faked, one's chronicle of emergencies and one's responses are not there, are supposed not to be there: no list of old and accumulated thoughts: a listlessness . . . The playboy kept playing—but not so lightly. The odd misery I felt was new but was partly worry about Daniel, partly worry at refusing to worry about Daniel—*He's rich; he's young* . . . The stuff of what things meant socially was present. How you talk reflected who you are speaking to and why, now, you are speaking at all; and it is related—not in a fixed way but in a way peculiar to the tie, to the proximity—to the odd factor of near-meaninglessness and, indirectly, a sense of one's purposes and of one's *authority*—one's charm or social standing—one's right to determine what is said and how it is taken, as wise or as foolish. The rules of that are new—I mean who decides or how do the two of you or all of you as in this new family decide what makes sense and what sanity is like and how you're supposed to talk when alone or at dinner or with Aunt Casey? And what is eccentric and what is boring and where the limits of meanness are—and so on.

In a certain way, I spoke *better* than most people, than anyone I had yet met, but not all the time, and not to everyone's taste—and that didn't mean jokes or wit or logically—at least, all the time—but it meant some of those things some of the time; but that gave me too much authority . . . Nonie insisted all her life that I made no sense and I talked like a book—and like a fool . . . *No one likes the way you talk* . . . And she, like Aunt Casey, insisted I must talk *her* way if I was to talk to her: she, they refused to let *me* talk; I did it anyway—but not often. Silence and smiles offered a kind of no-man's-land of not-head-on confrontation or truce-by-default that was what most of the smart boys back home did, practiced a kind of useful silence—somewhat worried and often self-conscious, with a kind of quality of rebellious delinquency and at the edge of scenes related to the ones I went through but expressed differently.

This was part of the speech of *intelligent* women, young or old, that rebellious delinquency in their manner, in their talking, as such—so earnestly, so mockingly and allusively, that war with the rules of polite talk, that admission of the presence of difficulties almost not to be borne except among sophisticatedly troubling people, of multiplicities, diversities, novelties of opinion and of hypothesis.

To adopt the pidgin of decency here—a *decent* pidgin, this—this talk-the-way-others-talk discourse, that of these monied people, to live, to live well—I was tired and more than a bit anxious and I was somewhat angry and a bit fierce about being judged in these ways—but I want to give what I am rather than to be forever alone in this world with a peculiar seriousness for company: Jesus: think of it . . .

Almost the smallest thought woke me, yanked me from the path into sleep. Starved thoughts, hobo, derelict . . . Logic hates motion: people invent things that have more stillness in them than natural things do: iron and gold . . . I wish this was a gold-walled bedroom, as anchored in place as that. The stillness of gold in one's breath—a ballast, a keel. An armor against males grabbing me—ha-ha. Nothing that occurred here among these people was part of my past—had Nonie enjoyed her historylessness? She was cleverer than I was and more sensible, Mom said, and knew more about *winning* and losing. I supposed she had enjoyed having *a clean slate*—was that term too lawyery, too smart-alecky? Probably. Too much like something a newspaperman would say: it would upset Casey.

For me it was a little like trying to sleep on top of the slow evolution at night of my sense of things into a mood of sadness-floored, darkness-chuted dancing tautness of a personal reality of trying to prune myself and costume myself, exercise my will to try for the large prizes visible in the distance, rewards detached from the paragraphs of self-description of their destinies by anyone else I knew . . .

The nervous unwillingness to sleep was an inability—just as a privilege was a deformity (and a deformity was a privilege if you knew how to see it that way), an inability to dream or rest or hope just yet.

Something like an appalled sense of identity at having no identity during *this period of transition*, not different in kind from part of a night I'd spent in jail once, the dangerous claustrophobia that overtook me in the stinkingly close air of an excursus into the nothingness of being imprisoned, of being unable to choose to leave, of having no duties, of being, literally, no one for a few hours.

I hadn't given my name. The boy I was with and with whom I'd been in the brawl in the dirty bar, his uncle came and got us out. It was not that an angel might not hear me or know my voice and protect me but that no one human from the past would: they had all failed. They were all dead or dying. Or bent elaborately on simplifying me, making me working-class, say, or rabbinical, or shy. Personal freedom and personal doom smell alike; they have the same structure, the nearness of death one-way-or-the-other and a sense of being parenthetical, not important to the main line of the sentence but being a note of testimony, a pool or cairn of language—of articulated consciousness.

If it is like being locked in a coffin, rather than a cell, to be alone with yourself and your *destiny* (if I might say that), then it follows that it is sensible for the senses to bulk up so in one's consciousness that every fragment of color and bit of smell registers and not nostalgically but as a blur of clarity of something largely not to be explored here, merely experienced and to be thought about later and known then if it is to be known.

Everything is filtered through the uninformed senses and hidden inside the eyes in the dark and is closed in, in moments known as both wadded and fluttering, caught and held, stifling me, or as outspread and moving like breath or like the outer skin and bony top of my nippled and tucked-and-skinny chest teasing me, the faintly heaving, semi-moored reality, folded, wadded, known . . . A moment here is an extraordinarily odd shape, *sleeved*, or like a sleeve, and the rest of the coat or caftan is the house, a now, sleepless and unsettled and extending in the sleepless minutes. Penniless. To my dismay I am unamused by linen sheets. I was as startled to be me as if my awareness of it was like a whirring owl descending toward me or as if my spirit was like a porcupine on the tree branch, its quills erected, guarding it against me, against my eyes and appetites, the creature in the forest. How strange the independent-of-others effort to stay alive is—and then it seems strange that it is like that in you but is secret. Or shy. *Let me be happy, do you mind?*

I come by blood from an unreasonable family—known for doing as they liked, men and women both.

My grandfather said that he spoke to God every day and that he expected his children to honor this. They hated him instead and he said they were no good. He obeyed no one human and didn't mind their hatred.

As for my father: *Give him an order and he hits you . . .* S.L. said, *Trash like that, they wind up in the gutter . . . What else can become of them?*

Insomnia

I am afraid. I am afraid and I prefer not to dream and if I dream, I prefer not to remember my dreams and the dramas in them, the messages, the jumble of images in their ominous and sweet grammars unknown in any spoken language. One sleeps among the omens and among one's opinions of things named as objective and shown as objects and as dramas, each an example of clarity of vision convincingly; and this goes on for a while if no one interrupts your sleep and wakes you.

A clarity interfered with. Fear and horror in the dark, the dreams of life and death, the thing of wanting in the ways I want it, to be like other people. Of course, one can go to someone's bedroom for company. A number of times I went to the door of my room and I stood there, waiting for a wish, for some automatism to guide me; and I turned back each time. One can rob the house. I am governed by moral distaste, perhaps by fear. The nomadic *zero* among the spaces of the night—I scream silently in the dark. I do. I am adopted and odd. Crazy.

The reality of that, of a zero risking his life and everyone else's, it seemed ill-advised in a moral sense. I hadn't the *genetic* self-respect to go about gambling everything sexually. Or socially. I am too afraid of what one might lose. As it is, I am at best a collection of shadows, of a lot of shadowy things, a false name, a temporary look of youth, a reputation as a young guy who had stood by his dying father. An anthology of shadows and not an encyclopedia of real things—like richer kids. In my borrowed bathrobe, a recipient of charity, I stood by the door of my room. *You don't love anyone enough to ask for help.*

I have never been real; no one is as unreal as I am.

If I let myself believe that I am real, my heart races around and my breath gets funny and my nerves twang and jump like wires or grasshoppers set on fire or beams of light but ones that ache. My reality, minute by minute, actual minute by minute, is inset with a flickering madness of joyous self-will and carelessness of which I am deeply ashamed, violently proud. Madness is near. To murder someone's pride or to pass into social catatonia, these are the common terms of conscious existence for me.

Rage or quasi-pietistic acceptance, I distrust the wavering tick-tock-ishness of the shrinking and of the dangerous enlargement of the self.

I often masturbate in order to sleep. I am ashamed of what I think of when I jerk off. The mood and the life's history that has led to this dark and devious grandeur—this grandeur of lowness—is linked to self-disgust, self-admiration. Help against the temptation is summoned and found in the various incantations of the radio turned on low until that low mutter of distant voices and what is said in that mutter, the cheapness of it, the fantastic folly and uselessness—not the folly of breath but a cruel brainlessness—I prefer, after a while, a silly motionlessness of almost simple pain, the simpleminded and unmoving staring at the dark to distraction and to masturbation.

Please let the pain stop. I don't know if the pain is grief or loneliness or envy of others. The odd formation of thought then holds this credo: *If I can find the right thing to think, I will be set free to fall asleep.* Thought, placated then, will let me sleep.

In order to sleep, one does *mad* things: I measure my *happiness*: I slap a label on it as if I were going to mail it, or a description of it, somewhere. I go bravely into *unhappiness*: I think about wretched injustices—the deaths of others, my own predicaments, my clearly marked dissolution into merely trying to get along inside my peculiar life, my not being able to live here—until then it is all a mode of torture: an inquisition by an unhappiness so great that I Must Answer It in Its Brutal Pursuit of Correction or I Must Die. What feels like bravery and happiness may be a trap: only victory counts, after all. For me everything *interesting* lies in a territory not in the pain continuum. *I lie about this* to myself, to others. I don't quite truly ever feel *unhappy*. I feel real pain: and everything else is a state of *happiness*. The insomnia moves step by step, sometimes into the humiliation of not having a fate like anyone else's. One came here to enter, with luck, a statistical category.

They are rich enough to be able to bear you.

In the daytime, I can pass for real. At moments even—and what bliss it was—for a moment or two here and there, without *nonsense*. Sometimes my reality to some extent matches that of other souls.

Some people can bear me as long as I am this age.

What I am to others is often primarily an idea taken from books and movies, from talk and various things current in the world (at that time) and from a classroom idea of what someone is and of what life is for a boy, and what sort of boy I might be and what I am as a sample boy.

In a football game or at a track meet, running in front of an audience, me, for me a sense of unreality marks the heightened reality, the adrenaline stuff, and the rest of it. To be insomniac erases that. This is the flat thing . . . To be here has the unreality of a major game, and to be good-looking, to be considered it, and to be smart: that's something that confers a sense of unreality. One is not ungrateful, but those things solve nothing: they merely mean you can enter or leave the game.

I have not left the game here. I expect Casey to relent toward me. And Daniel to be sensible. Neither will ever happen but I did not know that.

To be smarter than someone less smart, or to be less smart (than Nonie, say, than Nonie was with Casey), what significance could that possibly have in real life? I knew of no poem on the subject and of no play by Shakespeare that would inform me and no tradition that speaks of this: Is *Hamlet* a tragedy about degrees of intelligence? And of moral intelligence? *The Tempest* and *Macbeth* and *Othello* and *Antony and Cleopatra*—each is in part a study of being more intelligent and then less intelligent than the people around you . . . But what in the world could *intelligence* mean? Or be? A mental attribute that wavers and does not matter much, much of the time? Something without real existence as itself but having to flesh itself in terms of the world and others?

I had no money. I had no power— That's not quite true; I had power in a limited way; but I had no language derived from a relation to the world other than that of my entire life in this world. *Success*: power and language: money. The essence and privation for an organically real thing is that it is not possible for anyone, for everyone to accept it. It has to struggle. Lila had said in a curious sibylline voice: *You had better be a doctor . . . You don't mind sick people.* And people will leave you alone if they're scared for themselves . . .

To be destroyed meant what eventually? A poem? Seventeen finally worthwhile hours in all the hours of one's life?

You're not so smart . . . You're too smart for what ails you . . .

Look where you're going . . . You're dreaming . . . You don't know what you're doing . . .

Everyone has fallen in love with me. The agony of such imposture is like being locked in a barrel—the stiffness of crouching. And the *oddity*: it is all *grotesque*.

The bones hurt; the heart hurts; one cannot sleep.

An uneasily fulfilled nothingness, a temporarily melodramatic fate—it is easily taken as the nothingness of everything.

Madness

Awareness in the dark. Not nothingness—time is something . . . Am I ill? I know that the first enclosing paradise was the human belly of my mother. It was so changeable that I encountered the passage of time in the paradise there, the salt birthplace of my spirit, in my awareness (a dim confidence) that one would feel better, one would be all right: that was the loose evidence: that was the measure of paradise from the beginning. Amphibious state. The unreturn that time is includes the mechanical thing that awareness has always an element of resistance to time itself in it. It refuses the identity that time proposes to bestow on minutes, on everything. It is a force of resistance, resistant even to those forces that constitute it. The force of individuality in a particle, since it is time-ridden, would vary and weaken not entirely mechanically and give birth to the world and to anomalies. A balance, a situation has to have a form of awareness, or knowledge, of itself as *a balance* or how could it exist as moments pass? The urge in time itself is to exist—and it names and individuates everything in a mystic electricity—and force—in eerily always renewed individuation—until it fails for this or that thing—the hurried dawns and semi-sleeplessness of matter and its nakedness to the brushing formation and anatomical trespass of the creation of existence—and then the lapse, the letting go, the decay—the restlessness of amendment—in that, I drown, waking-and-sleeping, fluke-attentioned in ways that jeer in the mental light in the dark at really crippling fear until thoughtlight becomes a dance in mental darkness of fear and beyond-fear, a little natural chemical fire in the skull, a little buzz of hellfire—and resistance—in the skull, beneath the hair.

Without cure or remission, the flickers of memory and the present-tense sense of merely-a-room alternate.

And in resignation to the crawling, wormy, maggoty minutes and breaths, the tiny, transparent monkeys of my breath, the snake-flutters of eyelashes and of lungs, I endure my punishment.

In the alternations, it seems to me, my shadow eats the world and drags me in its belly (in the mind of my mind) into a moment of eclipse. My darkened self proposes and manages an awful kind of marriage and filial thing with darkness itself, with awful matter. An infant patience, seemingly infinite, inside the night, preserves me as I straddle the alternations and twists and moment-by-moment prolongation of this condition of loneliness and of predicament in amphibian contradiction of everything I have been taught about simplicity and ideas.

Clapping a mind on top of a mind, an observing consciousness, another placement of awareness on top of the one before, and then piling body on mind, on minds, and superimposing a giddily aerial (and sad) form of mind on all of that, and still another form of mind to watch, to judge and observe, I rise to a kind of a glimpse of the nighttime room.

People say, *I know all about it . . .* And: *We know nothing about* that . . .

I am not tired of God—but the idea of God is so much simpler than the sense of presence in the passage of moments that I can't ask for anything but merely wait for mercy, here, so long after my birth into the immorality of sheer existence: one rises with a heavy beating of wings into a condition of migration. Thought and recognition of the motions of thought, the most elaborate imaginable collection of simultaneous rifflings of predatory exercises of worded will, stories and whatnot, made of stiff letters erected in a phallic one, a single quill sufficient, or insufficient, for warding off despair. I want to be like a book in its powers of survival, me in my powers of survival. I feel the whispering inside and outside of me—strange primal stories: *Would you like to speak the language of the atoms, Wiley?* The formation of the cosmos? The first war cries on the shore? If you fail to sleep, you can hear the howling of the electrons in the black spaces in you; and a kind of Troy arises—and falls then—the nothing with its peculiar motions stitching it, seamed nothingness, into borders, until it is me—factual and predicted light of awareness, like light, a form of time (maybe), weight and counterweight, weight of attraction, weight of heaviness and of speed. Lila allows me a lot of freedom—because she is ill. We worked this out over the years.

One's democratic sleeplessness . . . I won't sleep with Daniel . . . I won't touch him . . . Reality is instructing me in itself—it is like a courtship: fucking reality breeding a subsidiary reality on the body of what is real in me. That this state is *deprivation*, or zero, I recognize because time now whispers, *Know me.*

If everything is possible to belief, then one might throw oneself from the porch in the conviction that one might fly. We have only small laboratories of time and limited abilities and we have large wonders and great horrors to deal with; and often a vastly unconquerable unhappiness stands in our way—so we had better be limited—limited in terms of knowing anything—limited in terms of fidelity to abstract truth since, then, lying has special importance.

Because then the *truth* is testified to by the lie, by its, the truth's, not being what the lie is. It exists then.

It doesn't though. A possibility. An immediacy. Are unlike. This is among my comparatively absolute truths, this is there inside the torment of them, the insistence that time is a curtain; and on the other side of it is a God with a bellying paradise or a scientific simplification, something mechanically reliable—as nothing is; and the lie representing human will then—human cleverness, Promethean, willful, sly—the lie as the only possibility of representation of truth, in its capacity to startle and freeze me and make me wait in patience and in terror—I choose to stake my life, my sanity on immediacy. It moves in the moments, immediacy and truth: it does, like a lion in an old story, with a rippling pelt and bony ribs: the truth is made of moments and holds or carries or pushes or pulls me now and scatters my wits and eats me, eats my shadow. I had never had an image of stillness no matter how I pressed myself to—or one of *timelessness*; I have never had an image of *eternity*—only of *this-stuff-going-on* a while longer. I think people lie about what they think they see. Nature sets it up that we must be important or we have no reason to be alive in real time.

To go to sleep is to launch a canoe on the dark of liquid noises, and the forces of the currents carry you into a merciless transience of light that proposes itself as stillness and absolute meaning and as theater in a display of such plausibility I believe it is real and am afraid to wake, thinking that waking might be death or lunacy. *That is how I go to sleep.* The nursery rhymes I was told persuaded me I was part of the family of everyone. That is how *I* go to sleep, among the biological absolutes and into a brotherhood and sisterhood of sleep that can be taken from me. My sight and the light it sees by cannot travel in stillness, in stilled air, among eternally unchanging particles. I can't in true stillness know I was separate from the air or that I was, in such a state of stilled, or dissolved, identity, unlike what I saw. I *feel* it as error. I have to lie to myself if I am to manage to escape from a sense of the motion of everything. And when I do, as I said, I have no sense of motionlessness—I have only a sense of universal motion which means I am awake and not dead, which means that I exist and that imperfect consciousness is not all I am. I do not necessarily die when someone else dies or when I sleep. I will die, though. *It*—the death in me—tugs and pulls at me, a kind of unamphibious, unambiguous ascent to a kind of realization about myself: it is that sort of *thought* that keeps me awake; it is like being a bare-legged and barefooted child of seven or eight and sitting in a doorway; the vestibule is the vestibule of death. Mine. Only mine. The unifying node in me, the pinprick of personal light in the universal rush of time, will, when I finish my treading water and my swimming in the realities of present moments, that pellet of light on the cathedral floor (sort of) will be extinguished. I don't want to foresee my death. I doubt that I can, anyway. I think Benjie and Casey and Daniel and Isobel will have lousy lives. But they will have lives. I want to do no harm but I want to live, too. I want to have as much life as they have.

I am buried here in an Egyptian tomb with gold ornaments, a Scythian tumulus, a Red Indian mound.

And it is a Chinese burial chamber with terra-cotta armaments, and terra-cotta soldiers, my army of the dead. My own army.

In this room in the house of quite rich people, one is sleepless differently from those rare times one was sleepless in St. Louis. I am rarely sleepless at home. There, if one suffers—and sweats—at night, it is mostly because of others' sufferings—my father's, or people in the war; suffering that is theirs, that impinges and becomes one's own suffering without ever being equivalent or the same. I don't mean a contagion of ill luck. I don't mean a contagious sympathy. I mean the forearm bone of certain actions affecting others then twists your arm or hits you in the forehead, or whatever, like an atom jumping in quantum mechanics.

The nighttime air has its own noticeable reality such that it seems to me obvious that everything is realer than I am or is less compounded of errors-of-will and of accidents of circumstance. If I do not blame the world, I cannot find myself, but I blame the world and money; and then here I am; I think, The air in here is too warm. I hear the ceiling fan creak and I see in the dark it bends on its stalk with its own turning; familiar and bodiless fingers of air from the motion of the fan touch me—this is like my morning prayer. I have stripped myself, the sleepless orphan among the changes in this tail end from my waking life, in the half-thought that this sort of prayer might happen. Benjie has said, *You-all are a villain, honey.* That was one time in a conversation which included talk about my genitals. *And I ain'ta just clacking my gums.* If I set the switches and gauges and valves in myself to stay here, and if I set them after that to rescue Daniel or to placate Casey, it is as if I am two trains or as if I contain two trains rushing toward a collision. Nothing will quite work out. Save Daniel by letting him find some sort of sexual triumph on my skimpy body? My genitals are here . . . And so am I. In this moment of turning outward in the dark in the hope of a useful thought, in the hope of sleep, in the hope of having a *destiny* that will make the events of my life seem WORTHWHILE.

The Conclusion of the Soliloquy

The differences in lives—whoof. Whuh. Ahhh. To say a life is the SAME as another tends to be an absolute to replace the ancient rhetorics of God and the state. The cipherization. The statisticization of the soul. People get really odd and emotional about it: *You are like us . . . You are not different from us . . .* mean *Our absolutes hold for you, too*; people get violent about that. But the differences in lives becomes truly painful until the sense that this is my body and not Daniel's (he has a better body anyway) and that his money and his attention are not mine is like being whacked over and over—ow, it hurts.

The naked boy in bed is somehow also among a grayish diffused light among clouds. Ah, he is asleep. The thought of differences in lives freed him. Exhaustion came . . . In his dreams, the differences in lives—and his theories about these matters involve the police and a woman he loves in *Czecho*slovakia—the country of money (of checks) and of sanity (checks and balances)—and of slow vac(ation)s—i.e., Slovaks. The *secret* police are hunting me. I cross a very large piazza in quite grand yellow-and-white sunlight. An enormous cathedral is lit in an immense way. It is set in an immensity of light—as if thoughtlight encompassed it (rather than that nature held a pellet of light which was the central node of my consciousness). Now I am on the curving dome of the cathedral. Men are chasing me, other lives, they have guns, he, I have a gun, we all fire; I kill many; they will kill me soon; I *am* wounded; a small plane is coming angelically to spirit me away; but I am shot dead and the immense crowd shouts in the grandeur of light in the piazza; and the naked body screams, mildly, into his pillow, shy about his terror, shy in his terror, and is wide-awake again in the strange house of the rich relations (by adoption) who might save him yet.

Stay with your mouth in the pillow, he tells himself. The bed is shaking so much from my convulsions that it rattles on the wall. Benjie, in the next room, who spies on me—and why not?—came to the door of my room and said, jocularly, and not without kindness, "Are you jerking off, Wiley?" Then: "Is every little thing okay?"

"My dad used to say that." (He must have gotten it from his mother.)

He took a step nearer the bed and held out his arms and said: "What the hell—are you having a bad time? Honey, we're your people."

"Don't put your arm around me—please. Benjie, go away . . . GO AWAY."

A real self, phallic and oppressed, might use and hurt him in some way that we will not easily recover from.

"Don't be oversensitive," he says.

Partly to amuse him and partly knowing he would back away and not wanting to say, *I would like to tell SOMEONE,* I said: "God, I am tired of people loving me."

He backed off and said, "Oh, you are *FEROCIOUS* . . ."

All at once, I am far more crazed than Casey was in the garden. I say to Benjie—without warning—"You cocksucking piece of shit, you momma's boy; asshole; you'd double-cross anybody without thinking twice about it—"

Convulsions rack me with dry sobs. I hate this shit. I'd rather die almost than endure it.

"You're a rough, harsh, thorny *person,*" Benjie says, somewhere on the other side of my seizure. He may have said something else; this is what I thought I heard.

He offers comfort: "You're pretty: you don't have to suffer: you-all'll get to go to a good college: ev'y one'll like you'air."

"Christ, what bullshit," I say, shakingly gored by the pain of my blood running cold at the edge of my ribs near my heart—at what he is as a person, how far I am from caring about him, how far he is from what I need in a world in which bad things happen to me at fairly regular intervals. He is what Casey needs. She's a rich woman.

Naked, I manage to get to my feet. Without shame. And with my back to him, I bend over the sink made of china and flowered, which is in the room, and I splash my face with hot water and use the towel there, and then I wrap the towel around my waist and cover my nakedness. I was, actually, sexually innocent. I was shaking inwardly. I no longer remembered the dream; and I didn't remember the thinking from before during the bout of insomnia. I didn't much care to what extent I had been damaged by my past—or whether Benjie was moved by my youth or not. What embarrasses me is the extent of my own now uncontrollable sadness. Benjie is breathing oddly . . . I turned to him and said, "I still am very young for my age emotionally."

I have no interest in his sins or in my own; they hardly matter in wartime—except when they are being committed. I have some trouble walking and breathing but I get to that door of my room which leads to a very small porch set in a slope on the roof. The porch is high off the ground. I get the screen door open and I held on to the jamb of the wooden door and shivered and shuddered and tried not to breathe too melodramatically—I was blacking out off and on; and I felt recurrent bursts of grief, I think, but pain in the mind; and I expected it to kill me—if not then, in a day or two from the strain of enduring it now. I could not admit to the pain to Benjie since I did not want his comfort . . . I can imagine him saying, *Well, if you're going to be like that, you're welcome to your agony, bubba* . . . In the doorway to the porch, with the screen door open, the outdoors begins. The scale of the freshness out there is helpful. The fear of violence includes the fear of it in me and then the dream fact of the return of the dead and the differences among bodies and lives and destinies and nature choosing among us, and this stuff set in time, in the onrushing nature of time: my life horrifies me.

It need not have been what it had been. What pulled me together was a *sense* of the triumph of other people if I did go mad here: that competitive stuff is present here *shamefully*.

Benjie cannot read this in me; it is not a defect in him that he prefers not to read people's feelings—it is merely part of the *differences* between us. The pain of this is eased to the point of being bearable by a sense of the outdoors. And my being able to kill myself—I can throw myself from the roof. S.L. is dead. I am free. I can choose to go out and lie in the greatly massive extent of dark *out-of-doors* and I can tell Benjie to leave me alone.

"See, you-all on your feet: you got nothing to be afraid of. Did you-all hev a bed dream?" He sees I'm coming out of the spasm.

"I don't remember," I said.

The stars and the dark trees on the lawn—the Boy Scout conformations of identifiable trees, the Boy Scout points of restless light of the stars, the constellations, the *Milky Way*—the silent corporeality of the darkness: it is, of course, unlike the racing oppression of noon heat. The as-if-muscular body of darkness, the shattered lamp of clouds and starlight suggest a kind of ordinariness in everything I have undergone in my life and everything I have done. A singular nurture is in the sense of one's own ordinariness. A singular nurture is in the dark.

"Your peepee's ready for night baseball," Benjie says.

"Go to hell," I say—not angrily—moving out onto the porch. The towel starts to slip. Benjie and Isobel, using the peephole through Benjie's closet wall, have spoken of my genitalia *jokingly* and of my rear end in some sort of unmasking and owning-me way that I know from high school. I know it, too, from my father. My father liked me *differently* from whatever way it is Benjie likes or half likes me. The separate differences curl like the warmish Carolina summer night breeze around me when I stand on the porch.

Benjie says, "You got a hell of a pecker, you got a hell of a cute little pecker."

If I hold him in (spiritual and sexual) contempt, do I then despise Casey? And money?

"Shut up, Benjie," I said. Then: "Like a bird's beak, peckerwood . . . You ever fuck a tree? I had a teacher last year who muttered 'Peckerwood' *all the time*. Daniel has been using the word 'pecker.' " I speak with difficulty—I am trying to be polite.

"He gets it from me, honey."

The thing about privation—of being stripped of identity and having no home and not finding conventions of attitude to be *useful*—the thing is not to let yourself be denied access to the terms that are the first step of the comparisons which are the chief furnishings and work of the mind. The comparisons that make identification possible. What too great a change in your circumstances does is force you to see in a general way—at least for a while you live in more than one room at a time then, generally, unrootedly—you live only vaguely, may I say that? And you lose the power to distinguish between one moment and another and a lesser kindness and a greater one. The larger number of the comparisons I make (which are often reasons for patience) have to do with my real history. With reality. One has a pain-riddled sense of the difference between the lightlessness in the air now outdoors and the lightlessness earlier in the room when one first tried to sleep, but one has this as my real mother's son and as S.L.'s son. One has been educated and not stripped of one's education, one's experiences as oneself.

But to be stubborn about one's past is to be freed—only to bleakness. One is not barren and new, not sleek—is this bearable? It seems so. One shivers in one's new, thin nakedness among the memories of this event-so-far and at the nearness of the night and its extent of air and one's own naked completeness of history in it. On the ranch of transparency, among the herd of winds, the cowed boy (the thin boy is suddenly soaking wet with fear that films his body with a kind of *easy* terror, a mental recurrence, physical as well, of the nightmare) has a theory about the power to be gained by banishing all this from one's daily self.

The convulsions: I am only shakily in the present tense, but I am a king in the present tense, *a major figure for Benjie*: "BENJIE, GO AWAY," I say to distract myself from this goddamn revelation. Then, STRUGGLING to get hold of myself, struggling to get hold of the regular moment: "I want to be alone."

"Listen, Garbo, I'm the head nurse and chief bottlewasher here, so let's just make sure you don't get pneumonia—while you're staying in my mother's house—she's had QUITE ENOUGH ILLNESS FOR ONE YEAR, THANK YOU, THANK YOU VERY MUCH. What you look like isn't going to turn up in any *message to García* . . . I've seen better peepees before."

I am soaking wet—I have no real idea what he is talking about. He may be making sense. But it's not my sense. What does sense matter? I doubt that my life matters. Why does that comfort me? I am bound to the hidden voice, so wordless and clear, of what *I* have known so far; and he has no clear sense of that—perhaps he doesn't care. But I want my pain, my luck, my life for *my* purposes, not his—surely this is common.

Perhaps it is more common among women—he avoids women.

Benjie's assertions of innocence, his protestations of harmlessness, his actions that are meant to be kind have little to do with the consequences that follow on the acts he has in his head that he thinks he wants to do or that follow on the ones he actually does. The way things turn out: he's not responsible for that. In America, morality is an open question, an issue open still, and it has to stay open—that is a political given—and then there is the human freedom of the reality of the acceptance as a general thing in citizens of seeing what you can get away with—and then the guilt, the hypocrisy of living with that.

"I'll be all right in a minute, in five minutes."

Will, projected and trained, still cannot exist consecutively: it blinks and reverses itself: it is a complex of yes-no's, a range of them. He knows this. He is courting me. I don't really know why.

"Let me help you," he says, having come to the doorway of the porch.

"No."

"You don't want to hurt my feelings, do you?"

"I don't want to hurt anyone—not you, not your mother, not Daniel. Not myself. A lot of times, *Daniel*"—I forgot it was Benjie; I forgot I was talking to *him*—"Lila said to me, 'You don't need to know how to box; you don't need boxing lessons; all you have to do is just walk over to someone and say in your nice little sincere way, "I'm smarter than you are," and you can ruin their whole lives.' " I had found my bathing suit on the railing. "This bathing suit is dry." I pulled it on and I put the damp towel around my neck. I moved toward the door of the room in the dark; I moved into the half-light that came from the door; and I said, "I'm smarter than you are, Benjie."

After a kind of *dry* silence, he grinned and said, "Well, honey, THAT makes me no never mind. Honey, I'm the kind that accepts all kinds of bullshit . . . I like *everyone* . . . What you say makes me no-never-mind; I take whatever comes my way and I'm as happy as a little ol' clam at high tide . . ."

I said, "I'll be all right soon—and, no shit, Benjie, I have to be alone now."

His face did something; I don't know what it meant . . . It wasn't ordinary comprehension—I think it was fear of *scandal.* I think he saw me as being a lot like Nonie—or his mother—as someone on the make . . . and tough. I'm pretty sure he was scared of me in a way that he was used to being scared. Fear entered him. Blew inside and around his eyes and puffed at his eyelids. And cheeks. He said, "Call if you want something. If you need me . . ." And he skedaddled.

In love—in a way . . .

You move into the world somewhat explosively—whoever you are —no matter how flaccidly you pretend to be a sort of semi-no-one-good-guy . . . I have my potencies . . . I can do things . . . In the real world, I mean. Maybe not as a writer. Not as an operator.

I was alone on the porch, where I lay down on the porch glider—fourteen, unhoused . . . *unhouseled*—that means outside the range of Communion. I am under the American sky; I am a tenant here; I see the stars overhead. I am in the open air, which will dissolve my outcries if I wake screaming again. Out here my presence is not a trespass. I am a nervous and able boy in a bathing suit, a towel around my neck which I draw up over my mouth and which I bite and keep between my teeth at one side of my mouth silencingly as I try to sleep.

I wonder if it was like this for Nonie . . . I wonder in what ways I share the world with her . . .

HOMOSEXUALITY 3

or Second Sight

I Study What Is Normal (Up to a Point)

In a story, a major character back then was supposed to know the degree of Benjie's loyalty to Danny—preparing the ground, being influenced by him, or double-crossing him and being a rival—and how this affected me, whether it made me sadder and crazier—and, often, in a story the teller used riddles and a cold consciousness of mystification and of paradox to suggest "reality"—but, in life, you may not know enough even to begin to ask (or feel) such important narrative questions much; or your life doesn't go on that way; those questions don't matter except as part of everything else—how much and why Casey disliked me—you're relieved to know anything at all.

Or you're upset but are determined not to show it; or repelled and want to escape from here, too—as if escape were, at once, an addiction and a universal.

For me, the formal element—or knowledge or point—was that under a fit of despair or nerves and semi-madness, at least in a way, was the possibility of a homosexual, or male, flirtation . . . a kind of identity of success, something in a parenthesis and not really part of your destiny (or mine).

And a sense that this was true of "everyone"—men and women—and was how alliances were formed and business concerns and friendships; and the sexual part was unexpressed, not done . . . whatever . . .

The main thing, day to day, was the thing of fitting in, of having a loosely-jointed, flexibly articulated personality—an easy impostorship. Mom and Dad had "understood" the difficulties of "fitting in"—after all, both of them had been kicked out of college (never to return) and both complained about the world and what it cost to live in it.

Fitting in: predictability was abandoned. Obvious safety was gone —since you could fail. Your capacity to feel—as yourself—your having a history, your having attributes separate from this—survived if you rebelled inwardly, if you continued in this birth-rebirth on the hateful quest, genetic, genetically given, world-and-time-tormented, to be yourself and to continue to grasp your own fate.

Surely, Nonie refused, or failed, to become Caseylike but change was not perhaps asked of her to the same extent or much at all. Change is not a light matter. A bend in time around light beams can't really come—only sometimes glimpses and conclusions, theories and (logical) constructions of the past can be reached blindly around the dogleg in the corridor, the grubby but monolithically sincere (it seemed) and monotheistic past.

Mom (and Dad) had been right: I had not realized what would be asked of me, what love would consist of—lies and illusions, while life was real, was corrective, but the illusions came first—the ripping away of the self, the substitution of making-things-work and more in your case as a visitor than in theirs.

It was advisable not to read—not to hold to ideas, the sorts of ideas there were in books. Written reasoning consists of a self, an intimate voice (in a way) addressing one's selves separately from one's life: that is bearable if you are a bedouin-spirit or if your sense of home and of others is solid or if it includes such oddities as what becomes of you if you read (and believe what you read, or experiment with the ideas offered there).

A soliloquy in a moment of rescue can end as an unspoken anathema toward memory, bedrooms, rivers, selves, and ideas; and becomes a song of metamorphosis, maybe an unwilling one, in which, as I said before, you give up your language, and its meanings, in order to live, the decent pidgin, the pidgin of decency—and you adopt talk-the-way-the-others-talk so that you are not alone in the world.

The inadequacy of conversation—and of essays and of theory—in any sense of being of use to oneself in this matter of metamorphoses, physical and year by year and mental, in terms of what one learns, and spiritual, and in terms of grief or guilt or both, or in terms of happiness of some kind—the uselessness of philosophy and of imaginary dialogues when you cannot know of what use you will be in the world ever: one is left with indirection and narrative, with sentimentality and its hidden, always falsely sexual base.

Starting in kindergarten, at recurrent intervals, at my school, people would get upset and say I was *a genius . . . Big deal,* Momma said of that often enough: *Is there money in it? Will people take care of him for the sake of that?*

Actually, yes—which hurt her. It was an odd form of rivalry with what *she* was.

You don't know how things work, she said. *Wait and see what your father does when he hears about* THIS . . .

I said, *He'll be proud of me; he's not mean like you—he likes me . . .*

He doesn't like books—he likes to have the upper hand, Pisher . . . He wants to have you dependent—like the rest of us . . .

The free will of his kindness?

I did not believe her. I thought I owned his affection. S.L.'s, I mean. I thought it was something I could count on completely.

I went out onto our large screened porch and I lay at an angle on the glider, on the pillows on it, and I pushed it with one leg on the rattan rug and while the glider glided back and forth creakingly, I held a third-grade textbook over my head and looked up into it and read it aloud to myself . . . I had taught myself to read that day—actually, within a few seconds; well, chiefly in a few seconds, at a glance; and then I worked out the details over the next half-hour; and then I could read magazines and newspapers—the more and more upset teacher had *tested* me . . . Miss Chatterton, who disliked boys, who was a famous battle-ax, kept testing me; and then she grabbed me and shook me and said, "*You little Jew, your parents are pushing you, aren't they? They trained you at home to do these things . . .*"

No. I learned to read just now, sitting in the class.

She hit me. And I said, with sudden, quite abrupt self-importance, *Stop that . . . You better not do it . . .*

We went to the principal's office, and I saw that when I described what happened, it was clearer and closer to truth than when Miss Chatterton talked.

And the principal, Mr. McClure, saw it, too; he had a funny look but then he pulled me onto his lap and he said, *Well, well, what do we have here?*

The ability to read was oddly like having a moon inside one—it was that way for me that day.

When Daddy came home, he, S.L., sat on the glider in his suit and tie and in his fedora and he hugged me—*as per usual,* he said while I resisted—as per usual lately—*What got into you, Pisher?*—and he kissed my face, my cheek, a number of times, passionately, really; and

I said, *Stop, listen to me. I can read . . . The school said I was* A GENIUS . . .

I read to him and he got up and left the porch and came back to the door to the porch and said, *You little show-off . . . you goddamned little snot—you don't have a modest bone in your body:* YOU HAVE BAD BLOOD IN YOU . . .

His temper was real enough to me but it had never been shown as directed at me before, only at Lila in front of me and at my nurse. I was amazed, enraged, curious, and yet bored: his raised, cold voice, his hurt, his dislike—really, the first dislike he'd showed me so far as I knew—DON'T BE SNOTTY! he cried.

I said—I was not quite five years old—*I will too, if I want to.*

He doesn't like books. He liked me for a while—he will always like a part of me . . . These are things Momma said, and which, clumsily, I accept as part of myself without understanding them: they are not to be understood by me. They are not common things. Actually, they are if you think of them differently—if you think of them as being about *unlikeness* and varieties and differences of *being.* And about *love*—the nature of love . . .

Hide what you know; keep a civil tongue in your head . . .

For a while Dad tried to beat that into me.

I was rescued from that.

But whatever I was "rescued" *for* this last time, that is not the main thing *on my plate,* at least not yet; that lies, so to speak, on the other side of the mountain—as in a folk song—and the now, which is not the sweet by-and-by, but in the here-and-now, one has to fit in—one has to be touching—or honored. *Don't think: sleep . . .* Politics makes strange bedfellows—having sex helps.

An Imaginary Dialogue (Not of Much Help) On Winning and Being Normal Up-to-a-Point

Self A (sixteen and at Harvard but really largely the fourteen-year-old in Carolina modified by further isolation and more complete escape): Is escaping 'winning'?

Self B (in his Harvard room is a mentor, of sorts, his real self ten years later, from New York—his real self with all manner of new and half-new and semi-new parts, some stolen, some having grown): It depends on how you set things up for yourself.

Self A: In a story? Or in life?

Self B: In life . . . A story helps you with your life: life comes first—not to the writer-saint, of course, but as the foundation or guide to where truth is.

Self A: Who the hell are you? I don't recognize you.

Self B: An impossibility, actually. I have to be unindependent and imagined by you, a mere projection of yours with some surprising minerlike quality of being able to illumine thoughts you have but can't get at; I have to be a visitor, someone you desire because you chiefly own him, before I am possible: as an independent will, I can't exist in the same room with you ever.

Self A: Are you homosexual? Are you making a pass at me?

Self B: Not in a real way but yes, if I have to be, to find you in me enough that I can project you and can visit you and can comprehend some of what you are.

Self A: So this is not happening—we can't be doing this . . .

Self B: No. But if I become sixty years old—years and years further on—I can *project* such a meeting among selves I was as a kind of mental fairy tale—or as an image: the way selves merge during utterance—the younger self speaks in the older one and the older one is foreshadowed in the younger self's grammar and knowledge of things; and self-congratulation—and worry—and regret emerge . . . You see, in my view, you never "won"—at best, you "escaped," you never quite understood what was at stake or what was happening.

Self A: It didn't feel like a *victory*—it wasn't a triumph as it had been for Nonie. It felt like a relief—and, to some extent, like a victory over her but only in my head: not in real life: a relief column in an old movie of the 1930s coming to the beleaguered garrison in the desert: your kindness to me, is it homosexual?

Self B: I would think any relationship to oneself was *homosexual*, in part, and androgynous in part—so that one might go looking for outer versions of parts of oneself or similars or even twins—but perhaps not exact twins: I mean I project you as not being so smart but as being quite smart enough, more like what I have come to think people are. A woman entirely different from you might hold in herself a whisper of who you are more clearly heard—or seen, if I can say that—than if you start off being alike. If you start off being alike, then ritual is needed to support the tie, to veil the self-love and the dramas of the love of others and the failure to love others.

Self A: I don't dislike you.

Self B: That would be a great relief if you were not a projection . . . You see, even talking to yourself is a corruption. That is why contemplation is recommended as a spiritual exercise.

Self A: On the other side of the barbed wire were more moments —Daniel was like S.L. and Casey was like Nonie. Like doesn't mean *the same as*: it means your mind goes in that direction and casts about among present possibilities like a hunting dog—or like a light from a flashlight . . .

Self B: I did, you know, want to understand my life, to consider it as important even compared to the war and to the deaths of my parents—just my ordinary life, just breathing and eating and sleeping—and loving and flirting. I wanted to be useful if it turned out that mind could be useful: I had such doubts of it . . . Such doubts about it that I was quite strange . . . See, I am imitating, somewhat, my unconscious memories of you.

Self A: I really didn't want to be isolated anymore . . . I really was scared of having no mind except a specialized one . . . I didn't think I was smart; I thought I had certain very limited possibilities—but never without cost. I didn't see how to exert will without doing damage. I was afraid of falling into a condemnation of life—and of my life—and not ever being able to escape from those postures, that actual imprisonment of blame . . . I think that adolescent *fear* (and oddity) represent a sort of truth of blamelessness: I was not a prince or the head of the family. I wasn't scared to be cannon fodder—it really wasn't conceit. It was a matter of *logic*—well, not of school logic. But the thing of winning—the thing of *winning out*—I'd wanted to have what Nonie had; I'd wanted to get to Forestville; I wanted to leave home—I would rather have gone away to school—Forestville was second or third choice—Lila picked it out; one saw her planning away, figuring things out, making sure that *number one* was represented . . . See, S.L. had lost—he'd gotten ill and had gone under; and when I didn't run away from him, I was stained with that—like a priest or like a doctor. You get away; people sort of like you; things happen—but who are you then, really? An old self? From childhood, from before any trouble arose? The intervening steps are gone. You're plunked down without a thread and without a logical structure to the self. You're a sort of glitter-mirror *No one* who has, at best, a glitter shape, light in a mirror . . . An image-shape—I mean your shadow is the truest thing about you . . . I'll tell you something you've forgotten: all shadows are perfect . . . Not to themselves: they are full of longing for dimension; they are appetite in the sun. I used to sit in the sun in Carolina and I would see my extraordinary shadow, narrow and tucked under me if I was lying on a towel, or flying outward, like a shaped sheet without any blemish, without any feeling really except flight and a significant reference to feeling in posture—or to sexuality—and to youth when I sat up or stood up, the evidence of proportion and even of scientific rationality: I have a shadow. I have a mind. Nonie-Nora, as a twenty-two-year-old, coming down the steps of the house to the pool, bodied, strange, and her fine shadow flying ahead of her or flying backwards toward the house; and I see that I see her as a Nike—she, like Casey, like Lila, knew how to win; Nonie and Casey had not been savaged by illness and some defeat. Nonie and Casey, like Abe, knew that stuff although not perhaps on the same immense, immensely lunatic and life-shortening and incremental scale that Abe did; but they outlasted him; they won actually . . . My victories, such as they were, were always of an odd sort: a rank, a confession or two, a thing of being a focus of feeling for someone or for a number of people, the finding of an opportunity to think and of evidence of life, of actuality, for the thinking that might very well be useless or half-useless but would certainly be flawed. One could see the greed as a kind of light from a window at the top of the stairs, a greed to propound a system, to speak, or to appear to speak, to God—to finality. A real victory is never actually minor, is never actually unevil. A rank, a confession, always partly unearned, always partly projected toward a higher point of the imaginary steps and toward the absolute thing. Mine were never equivalent to others' victories, never actually rectifications of the past, never were a form of true or adequate revenge; but were something much more terrible and much, much weaker—they had almost the charm of babies—or of an adopted child at the age of four beginning to speak again or mute still: a sort of shadow triumph—without life—not actually part of any worldliness. And others die, go mad, snap and fight; and they see the shadow triumph as real but they never acknowledge it and they go to great lengths to keep it from turning real . . . This can't be helped mostly. Most people fight in order to live; most people, most of the time, fight on the wrong side. I, of course, think I am right—and not just the people who already have similar ideas—of limited victories. It is my set of ideas on the subject that I prefer. I have a shadow set of steps right next to the real imaginary steps of system and of doctrine: it is a scene in a ballet: the shadows clash with real life in duels that matter. Perhaps the shadow backs off, Utopianly, semi-absolutely . . . And then one leaves life to the others—the ones who know how to win and how to hate—and one becomes a master, in a way, of impostorships that fool no one. One is this rather tired, sweet, overmental, perhaps pretentious person—a shadow with parts of a body attached—do you know what I mean?

Self B: Yes.

* * *

Escape was not escape. I won nothing—except some access to time, some bits of drama—*some moments of irritating other people the way you irritate me—and everybody else*—(Lila)—some sunlight and moonlight taken as itself and detached from emergency.

But I enjoyed my shadow life. I was important in that house for a while.

* * *

Listen, I was never a *good* soul—no one ever said I was *that.* Important—or smart—useful or well-intentioned . . . But never *good* . . .

This is not about saintliness versus the Nonie-esque. This is about the comparison within a time-harried frame of always greatly unexplained lives but accurately modelled on what is possible and always in relation to one another.

And I am the better person—and the better talker and thinker—but not always, not in all circumstances, not for every purpose.

She has realer victories, realer defeats. She doubts this. Casey doubts it of herself. They are more assured in their comparisons if I am dead.

Meanwhile, they have as grounds to know themselves in comparison to me as possessors of evident superiority in that they are *effectually evil* . . . Bad. Real. NORMAL. But normal women. Whatever.

* *

Lila: *You have to learn to live among people—you have to learn to defend yourself—you can't go around offering yourself as a target* . . .

You can. But that is not the chief part of the story.

Truth, more thoroughly evoked than heretofore, is a weapon of a kind. I really don't know. I offer it as a theory, one that I believe: and others, other people more assured of their competence in regard to life, can judge it.

* *

In a grammar of impersonality: my cousins *treated* me after a while as someone who lived in their house and was acceptable and fine-and-reliable (meant realistically) but troubling because he was odd and who troublingly did a swindler's thing involving a faked and theatrical presentation of second sight.

Our daily life—no: mine—was something like a *dangerous* festival in a comic or serious horror movie or a spy movie or like a masquerade ball in a movie. To be away from home and in another household, among its rules, the party brilliance of each day, as I felt it, was like, well, a form of *dancing around* inside an echoing glass bell, breakable and set up to encourage dramatic dénouements, discoveries, confrontations, a glass bell of *GOINGS ON*—a bell of (in a phrase I never used) SERIOUS *relationships*, somewhat in embryo or old . . . Theirs to one another, theirs to their lives—they were strained in their family ties and needed distraction—some new subjects and terms: me.

I avoided thoughts of melodramatic outcomes, melodramatic moments, stolen bits of love—analysis, opinion. My mind was empty. I did not notice how much the three "kids" drank—really a lot—and Benjie and Isobel were cranked up on coffee and sweets and some drugs much of the time; or I did; but I wanted to stay.

Or how they, the younger ones, double-cross Daniel all the time as a form of identity or how gravely bitter, how responsibly (oddly), with what clear longing-to-escape-from-all-of-them (longing carefully edited to show the presence of love and patience, some love, some patience) Daniel regarded their "forgivable" self-assertion. That he was "trapped" or "caught" like another youngish man of an Episcopalian family down the road, that such a pinioning was A Terrible Thing for a Man was something he and the other youngish man made clear enough that I understood (family) insult and "horrible ways to love" and "unacceptability" in new ways that I resented knowing about: I wanted to be a naïve visitor . . . You can't live with people you don't approve of—except horribly . . . So this house had only a temporary visibility.

Anyway, I *rigorously* paid NO ATTENTION (AS A POLITE VISITOR SHOULD) (rather than sympathetic, or side-taking, attention as a lover should); I was a recipient of CHARITY and of HOSPITALITY . . . This was submission on my part although it was not exactly the fitting-in they had in mind. I was submissive while being in essence UNBOSSED, uncaught—independent-eyed, independent-necked, with a guy's free person's shoulders—which Casey eyed with disapproval and then she would start in with justifiable complaint couched in words that were untrue: *HE'S SHOWING OFF!* But if I was, it was only in the haphazard sense that the (odd) mixture of freed kid and of being *independent* and of being a scarred and scared penniless coward (and orphan) and something of a fool was seductive.

I told fortunes—with cards mostly. The "kids" in the house decided I had *second sight*—this was a fad with them: a tentative solution.

If I lay out the cards after Isobel, maybe sexily, asks me a question, things I thought and had seen and had refused to admit to consciousness would suddenly form and jump into my speech and I would hear what I thought while I struggled to edit it, to keep it polite. I made predictions like a talking dog. Predictions and warnings did no good, I noticed. I noticed that curiosity and a protective-tariff attitude toward their own systems rule the Warners.

Anyway, my telling fortunes and being of some use that way was part of what might be called a "quotidianization" of charity-and-affection toward ME—up to a point.

The wobble of the limits, of the politics and comparative certainties of fitting in—the idealisms and the realities, the daydreams and Utopian moments—and a kind of ruthlessness of seeing things in a fairly real way—myself as complicated, for instance, and other people as being that complicated but with different words and gestures plus the added complications of real wins, real losses, so that I seem simple, simpleminded, and yet not purely so since I have an ego and want certain things—such as peacefulness, peaceful pleasures, a real identity, a real knowledge of how to win and lose, and the like—this stuff becomes a contingent and temporary shelter for the new inhabitant.

To be politically sensible was to be more than charming—was to be normal and unevil since you're easy to handle. The weird foreign-planet aspect of every day with the fatal combat aspect because you're placed out there somewhere in new moments all-the-time . . . although you don't have to admit it . . . We're all combat generals in the course of the often politely unadmitted irreversibility of the moments on the territory of one's own feelings and of the feelings of others—a perverse fever of acts and language and of will—an excitement of not being sent home—this is in a shifting and unnourishing, perhaps *alienated* landscape, of lovely iciness and snowiness of illusions, more or less polite, semi-illusions, ignoring things, semi-struggles, semi-forbearance, nervousness, and novelty.

This is expressed as a fever of contentment, of Eden. I felt real gratitude when I was allowed to be me and I faked happiness at being in the house at other times: that was perversity itself—unadmitted in such phrases as *waste time* and *get nowhere* and *do nothing*—but truth is in our inflections and in our fortune-telling—*You'll like so-and-so, you'll like such and such a movie*—it is present phallically and cuntedly, present in actuality, not symbolically only.

The love of the absolute, the fascism of dreams makes you a pain in the ass as the visitor or as the host but you have to have some of that stuff. The centrality of one's well-being in waking life which cannot ever quite be the case except when love has gone wild and even then only weirdly, seems almost to be true—it is the center of hospitality as such.

Centrality means that all meanings, all, are available to one—to your hostess, say; indeed, they are resident in one's language, one's manners, one's logic, one's position in the house: mannerly *reality* operates under various spoken terms: a good hostess, good people, a good kid, a good student, a good American, a good Jew. Nothing is forbidden but don't test this. No one is stupid but don't be serious about this: don't test this either.

I was openly in pursuit of no one and of nothing. You had to stage a thing before you could say no to me—and own me that way for a scene, a drama.

This stuff rested on paradox in the domestic or democratic pretty-much-tyrannical style of *The Normal* of the household.

The kids protected me. They did it by laughing at me before Casey did, by not protecting me from each other—by getting Casey to avoid me, which meant my being okay (and not sent home) but it also meant my being powerless and on tenterhooks since in the hierarchy of that house, all real power stemmed from Casey and Casey's favor and her knowledge of real victories.

She was the pasha and she permitted harem-y infidelities although you couldn't count on her not becoming furious: this maddened them—they took this, though, to be normal and humane . . . this permitted stuff that they suffered over, the suffering representing an abrasive entrapment between the shells of two paradoxes—normalcy and sexual existence and purity and between the reality of oneself and the reality of others.

That these things might be simple for some people was a daydream of normalcy and inspired sexual desire, I think.

But the function of desire is to extinguish itself. Life here is meant to last a while. Sex isn't so bad if it doesn't lead to *changes* . . . And if no one much knows it is going on. Casey practices *live and let live* but she spies, using the laundry; now she makes sudden hard-breathing descents on us; her standing in the doorway of a room and eyeing us temperamentally, in an abnormally normally-temperamental way is disconcerting but we take it as *normal enough*.

I had been chosen by her dead husband, who'd been a difficult man, chosen because of what I looked like but that included character, as in what a horse looks like—and the sense of the machinery of the household that I had is part of why he chose me or contingently chose me. This sense of *the machinery* is different emotionally (although it has some emotion) from the reactions I had to the house—some of which were faked. I don't know. You say, *It looks like rain.* The real boy is a local case of the normal comparatively, arbitrarily, among the paradoxes in Quite a Nice House.

Among such realities, I could, up to a point, find my way as a visitor better than they could as Old Inhabitants—since they had blinded-blinding notions of how things were at home and clear notions of how things worked there. So, I could predict things they would do at home or outside—I could tell their fortunes, imperfectly.

Momma had told me often, *It's always the same wherever you go . . . Learn to keep some things to yourself—learn to keep your mouth closed—don't even show with your eyes that you notice nothing . . .*

So, I am the resident *fool*—the asshole.

Benjie called me *Sherlock Sure-shot Not-all-there . . . Not entirely at home . . .*

I belong to the what-is-there . . . Simply that.

In the garden, in the heat, earlier that week, I was swimming my late-afternoon laps—a hundred and fifty . . .

Daniel says about Casey: "I hope you don't blame her. She can't help the way she is. She's going through a bad time of life . . ." He had begun to use the tactic of scaring and praising me. He was setting out the grounds of his emotion, the feeling that he wanted me to feel emotion. I understood him in a young way.

I had climbed out of the water; I was gasping; and I lay on the cool-and-hot stones alongside the tiled edge of the pool. I was dripping on the stones; spears of grass among the flagstones tickled me.

"After all, she is not a villain—we are not villains," Daniel says.

Lila is a villain, he has said. I am innocent and not-innocent. I am the villain—the newcomer. The moral dimension in each thing done

—and said—widens breathingly into a question—imperfection: the moral question does exist more strongly in what-is-imperfect; or, rather, there is no moral question otherwise.

What is inescapably present in Daniel—he is an absolutist—is that he avoids the reality of imperfection by choosing to see immediacy as borderline apocalypse—the war, bankruptcy, personal ugliness toward each other. In the light of moral and spiritual apocalypse, then he is the most moral one here—the one nearest being absolutely right. His decisions are final—mostly. His comparisons are of one absolute moment to another. What may be most horrible about most real crime is that it wrecks the reality of everyone blundering along and lying within not-exactly-okay limits but not with the extreme limitlessness of massacre or of robbery, of economic massacre (and rape).

Daniel was no villain. But I am a villain. That is ironic and affectionate. But if he is sexually available, then he is the villain—in a way. The weight of real things as a crime is uncertain.

"I can't help the way I am, either." Morality's pet imbecile.

I judge his intentions in regard to A Ghost Boy and to A Real Boy in whom, actually, I expect him to have no interest. A kid my age would want to know me, if he did, in order to steal some of the structures of what I was and can do; but Dan has a different theft or thing in mind. I am lit only dimly and distantly and can't see myself in the third person.

He studies my back—my backside—if we are rich, other things are not supposed to matter so much. Or if you have a studiable backside, sympathy and envy flow lopsidedly.

"It is *de luxe* here . . . It is *luxy* . . ."

"What are you up to?" Daniel asks.

"I don't *know*."

"What does that mean?"

I have been rescued and it's eating me up—without mercy or remorse or absolving explanation. I don't want him to fuck things up between us. I want things to work.

"I think saying *I don't know* is pious . . ."

Then he is quiet. Among the diversities of weird, unstoppable motions is the one of loving just being silent and stupid in the human wreckage of partial and time-dissolved, temporary submission for one reason or another.

All crimes do not have the same weight. One uses books as other lives one has had. One simplicity, *time*, is not simple at all if you look at it—time has been called a crime for thousands of years.

What I am he does not want—he wants the aura, the envelope—he wants to do something to it, for it. I don't know what. Love supposedly excuses greed.

"You have a knobby spine," he says. Then he says (as nearly everyone says to me sooner or later): "I don't believe a word you say."

"I don't know," I say, adolescent, desperate.

"Are you telling me to shut up?" he asks, sadly amused.

"You never taught me to drive," I say trying to enter onto being human the way other kids are.

I imagine him *talking*-to-me. The other breath, the other voice that I imagine is always time speaking without error to me but then I have to correct it to someone speaking to me with error above the hushed whisper of time in its forcefulness, carrying, pushing, pulling, sweeping us, me into the next moments. You have to understand *time* is on the verge of becoming a voice at each of its advancing corners, inwardly and outwardly; each of its elements is, like it, essentially syllabic—time occurs as a sentence does . . .

"I'll teach you to drive—we could take a trip through the Blue Ridge . . ."

I try to say yes . . . I hear myself in my imagination say yes.

"No," I say without knowing the reason I don't want to be near him in that way.

He looked suddenly terrible, wan or pallid, twisted, hurt—the villainy I am suspected of now exists and if I defend myself by saying to myself that Daniel is dignified and fine, fine enough if you don't look at him too closely, if you don't have to embrace him spiritually or sexually and touch his balls or accept his soul and take his credo into your mind, then the outline of the villainy is clear.

"You play by different rules," Daniel says.

The same ones—differently considered. I say, "Should I go back to St. Louis now . . ."

"No: don't be silly . . ."

It is to my advantage that he regards life in a boy as superior to life-in-him. But he is still utterly the emperor. The inconsistency—and wrongness—of that is amazing.

I say, "Don't take any wooden nickels." I really hope he won't.

I was sick with fear for myself—and him—at my saying no. At what-life-is. I don't know what-all.

He says, "Don't *you* take any wooden nickels." Then, since it doesn't at all sound the same—or even seem to have a similar meaning—he says, "I don't understand you."

I say, again, but smiling hard now, hard but privately, while my eyes and face are turned to him, but I turn away while I speak—turn to my own privacy, "Don't take any wooden nickels *now*—"

He mutters defeatedly—lecturingly—"Stupid . . ."

And he gets up from the pool chair and walks toward the house, pausing only to say, "I hope *you* don't take any wooden nickels . . ."

"I-uh thee-unk we-uh should treat him as a Gypsy pree-ince—" Benjie said.

He hems and haws and fetches from odd points within him bits of what he will say—and he descends-and-rises into manner, into delivery. Daniel says with contempt that Benjie *gives forth*, he *spouts*. What Benjie meant, in part, was that my homelessness, my being a wild boy—my wild *worthlessness*—freed me to journey in mystic worlds and to see things and to be a *sexy* performer.

A half-sad, half-snobbish thing of *I* had nothing to lose by being truthful and being amused by truth—by actual life . . .

Between and among intensities, Benjie—*you don't have to get the point but I expect you to laugh*—in Utopian upper-middle-class moments—moves awed by power and in regard to physical sensation and freedom (mostly of phallic confrontation, watchfulness, and voyeurism, and phallic intrusion)—and he moves breathing an oxygen of ambition from a mask of education and of art in a sense. His thought-out notion of sanity is to do nothing for once and for all.

"Snobbishness goeth before a fall, Benjie," Isobel said. Isobel is Rita-Hayworth-and-Carole-Lombard-irresistible tonight—she isn't really; she's a bit drunk—charming, lackadaisical, and with a certain audacity of a local sort—a swindle usually leading to moments of confession: *I like to pretend but I'm really quite simple* . . . But a swindle suggests the real thing. Isobel says, "We're simple people—too simple—we're *provincial*—nothing happens . . ."

"It's great when nothing happens," says the gawky Gypsy prince.

"Ooh, you're young . . ."

"If people don't want to listen to you—maybe you're doing something wrong in the way you talk," Daniel said.

"I don't like to fight over *ideas*," I say. "Nothing is settled as it is in books—it just gets down to complicity . . ."

Benjie said, "Our Little Gypsy Boy's got every fault in the book but he ain't ugly and he ain't a mouse . . ." Then: "But he never thinks how to treat *people*. Speaks first, thinks later . . . Thinks *never*."

Then I say, "That's just a lot of shit . . ." Then: "It's such a lot of shit, it's a joke."

Benjie repeats it but when he does it it sounds different: it has a different meaning—anti-me.

Daniel—hurt—strained—"passionately" *tormented*—spurned—says, "Swearing is lip filth." Then: "I hate the way we trample on *everything* . . ."

The summery and rustling masses of motion and *hot breath* and particles of unclear, camellia-ghost moonlight and the eight citronella candles burning in the various areas of the porch, smelly, uneven, changeable . . . And light from the bedroom and from Benjie's and Isobel's cigarettes. Bits of such illumination on arms, on noses.

"Wiley, we'll make Coral Emma-Jean give us lunch and you tell us if Coral Emma-Jean is *normal*—or not."

Daniel said, "I'm not coming. Count me out."

"Pretty please—with sugar on it," Isobel said.

"Drama, drama, drama!" Benjie said, almost shrieking.

Isobel leans forward: "Do you *like* me, Wiley? Wiley, am I your favorite cousin? Oh, it's *boring* when you're not devastatingly in love with someone really devastating. Wiley . . . I can't wait to hear a fresh impression of Emma-Jean . . . My trouble is I'm too blasé."

I saw why Daniel wanted people to be roles and codified virtues and that was all.

Daniel said disgustedly and with resignation, "I can't make small talk."

"You want heavy conversation, we'll have to all go into training for they-it," Benjie said.

"It wouldn't hurt you," Daniel said.

I said, "Things ought to mean something," meaning to take his side.

The day of the luncheon, in the dissolving atmosphere of *further information*—in the registry of truth—and the social lies, the imbecile boy asked: "How do you talk to Coral Emma-Jean Marie?"

Daniel said, "You don't. Coral Emma-Jean Marie does all the talking." Daniel said, "You don't have to do *anything*."

Isobel said, "She's *socially prominent. Her* house is A SHOWPLACE."

Her house: A tall, decorative iron gate painted green in a nine-foot-high red brick wall with a white coping was opened by a big guy in coveralls and a straw hat. A pink gravel road went up and down and around past small ponds and willows and flower borders among very large trees. The house was pink brick and had black shutters, seventeen chimneys, a severe white-columned portico and a pediment with a coat of arms on it.

We left the car in a big, beshrubbed gravel oval that opened onto the gravel turnaround in front of the portico. We walked up the steps and through a big hall and then through a smaller, narrower hall that opened off the large. We walked through the smaller hall past gold-framed pictures on the walls and small half-tables set against the same wall—the other wall was empty except for a pictorial wallpaper of a colonial town and countryside and seaport—until we came to a pillared side verandah almost as large as the portico and with similar white pillars.

And there we sat in wicker and in metal chairs. A one-lane gravel continuation of the driveway wound past us, directly in front of the porch; on the other side of it three trellised walks and pollarded trees and topiary shrubs radiated from a dowdy fountain with two half-life-sized figures among flower beds of a big, bloomy sort and then willows and hillocks of grass to a small stone wall over which one could see not terribly distant green and brown foothills and blue mountains showing off a sub-Alpine profile not very far away. From a trio of old oaks at the corner of the scene—and bounding it, closing it in—where the driveway came around from the front of the house, came an almost *limitless* squawking and caroling and whistling of calls and songs of small birds; the leaves rustled continuously here and there with inner motions, and various birds, an oriole, a bluebird, a robin would fly out and return later. The air stirred lightly and touched one's face where one sat in the creaky wicker chair with the floral cushion one sat in. It was superlatively fancy—at least in an American way and *pretty* or *lovely* and surpassingly beautiful in a moderate way but ungeometrical and a little stiff.

Two maids passed around lemonade and cookies; a butler served hard booze.

"I like it—but it *is* showy," Isobel said to me; she sat in a wicker love seat which she made rock slightly. Then she said to me, "Gross, isn't it?"

Suspecting an Isobellian trap—that thing of using conversation as a sort of combination gym class and labyrinth testing you that some women did—I said, "No . . ."

Then, without any sign of duplicity, Isobel said, "I love it. I think it has real *class.*" Time permits unadmitted changes of mind, sequential relativism, compromises, inconsistencies, incoherencies. Traps. Duplicities. Compromises. As normal. Or ordinary—within some social arrangement.

"So do I," I said, happy, relieved, filled with a loosened ease or satisfaction at being in some sort of ultimate setting, the ruling class, rewarded people.

"Forestville is not famous house country," Isobel went on, displaying the sense of hierarchy, of nuances and flat things of rank, that bring real life into an arrangement of clarities. "Most of *this* house was built *after* the Civil War. But"—I could see—I mean this—a lesser *beauty* here then. Isobel went on in a louder, porch-open-air voice—"I love it, I just love it. It has such class, don't you think?"

"It's pretty nice."

Whatever its faults—whatever its realities, whatever the elements of its reality were that were shabby or ill-proportioned or in need of modification, amendment, correction—it was far too *nice*—that is to say, beautiful and lovely with the effort, which was perhaps gigantic, that went into its existence, effort and taste, taste such as it was—I mean one knew it wasn't one of the famous gardens in the state, let alone in the world—it was junior and perhaps ascending to such radiance or it was in decline and would not ever rise so high—but in its mêlée (or medley) of colors, in its vegetable zooish displayishness, and in the soft cleanness of the air, the privacy, the claim of rank, the instruction because the place was empty except for us and people working to make the place habitable and, so, was dream*like*—I mean, obviously *real* and yet it was walled in, not as much as a skull, and was silent: a garden for waking or awake sleepers, for the *woken* ones, to use a Southernism.

And such instruction in dreaming and in dreamed-up, trumped-up reality—in swindling such privilege from rank nature and a semi-raw continent—suggested a largeness of soul—airy, gardeny, unlike that of sick people—such that one understood the *pride* finally of people of rank and of money to be not just that they were so courted and pursued, because of the power of money to be turned like a magic metaphor into all sorts of reality, maybe into every sort (and maybe not); but because of their efforts and abilities—that is to say, their possession of beauty.

I said to Daniel—since he sometimes listened to me, "The *prettiness* here"—i.e., the *beauty*—"might be tainted, might be really ugly at bottom, but on your way to the bottom you feel really good about things—some things," I amended it to, seeing his face. Just at that moment a small-boned, kind of pudgy woman with an interesting but very moderate, very self-contained *intelligent* owner's manner, and with an odd face, a little coarse and unreal looking and heavily made-up, came out wearing jodhpurs and a really big shirt and boots. "Well, hi, you, all," she said mingling automatism of address with some curlicue of acknowledgment almost one by one of all of us and of those members of her family who were on the porch and who'd already been introduced—I skipped that part: they *did* look like people who lived here. There was a kind of proof of effect in their faces—and in their hair—the category of people who lived dulcetly, in a high-up American way, among spaces and servants and various kinds of power which they were allotted and which were not truly rooted in them at all, at least not yet. "Well, hi, you," the owning woman said to me. "It's just real nice to meet you. Randall," she said to the butler-guy, "did y'all remembuh Beefeater gin with the tonic for Mrs. Wahnuh?" (Casey.) "Hi, you . . . Casey, you didin tayll mee he uh looked jus' lyuk Errol Flynn and my father . . ." I looked nothing like Errol Flynn; that was such a joke that Isobel tittered and Benjie laughed outright.

But it placed my looks as marketable, as talkable-about. It touched me somewhat scaldingly, like a heated towel at the barber's. The precocity rests on ignorance and only partial knowledge, after all.

Isobel had gotten big-eyed in a way which hinted that she didn't like Coral Emma-Jean Marie—it hadn't occurred to me that Isobel *hated* Coral Emma-Jean Marie. *I* hadn't really blamed Casey and didn't care that others did for things. But I didn't see that a lifelong friendship, sentimental or not, between Casey and this powerful woman could be *innocent* enough in any reasonable terms to console Isobel.

Casey's actions toward me and toward Daniel took on a tentative dimension of a cast of light—as did Daniel's actions—maybe falsely registered now.

I don't mean I *blamed* them. In U. City, where I grew up, homosexuality among women was really okay, even admired. And among boys it was mostly accepted if it didn't make them too crazy. Furthermore, it was held that it granted on its practitioners access to time and thought enough to be more cultured and stronger-fibered morally than *ordinary people*. Not only that: they were not the enemy at all. You didn't tell some men this, however. An idea that Casey *loved* Daniel now or liked him and hadn't long ago and had made him distrust her and now she was sorry but she refused to think about the past, and so, her rudeness now—or her dislike—could be seen, in part, as her attempt to get on some footing with him too late—all that had a different meaning; and his responding to her would be a certain sort of bad fate—*maybe* . . . I didn't really know; but as a fortune-teller, I got to judge things . . . Not always and not seriously. But I was a reporter or a journalist giving an account from a war zone of a situation; and I had my opinions, my abilities . . . my wildness . . .

"Whale now . . . Uh, Casey keeping you amused?"

At second sight, Coral Emma-Jean Marie was not what you saw at first sight: she was, in some ways, ordinary-looking—smallish clear gray eyes, little nose—but past the first impression her face resolved itself into *the face of a Christian and a melodramatic person.* This was my opinion.

Her somber face on second sight (like rehearing a sonata) was, perhaps, hauntedly conscience-driven, perhaps capricious as a form of denying what she felt to be too-much *conscience.* Her drunkenness permitted will and action beyond ordinary calculations—*an odd duck*, maybe *a great soul.* An owner.

The *wild* unchartedness of a kiss in a territory of untraditional and equivalent response. Originally a truancy—a blasphemous *going-too-far*—a youthful sentimentality or a rhyming sexual diction that somehow became tied to or combined with a sense of hell and of lawlessness—such a kiss rehearsed, repeated, echoed, and growing into a history of such kisses, that kiss might take any shape at all and might be felt in the air as a weight of, oh, *Southern* air, heat waiting for rain—guilt and passion in a story and the capacity for action becoming, in that story, a real-life thing of superiority in an escape-of-a-kind, ruling certain lives . . . Again, I did not know that—and do not know it now. But it seems likely in the light of reality, this hidden structure becoming built-in to pretty much successful lives and those lives become structurally part of everything around me, of how everyone lives—it is no mean achievement to shape a local world. But human feeling is often mean. A kiss which is not given a predictable aim, a kiss not patently romantic or maternal but which is now surrenderingly naughty-maternal, then footnote-y, then oddly mirroring, then an exploration of odd dissimilarities in someone anatomically semi-equivalent to you—like the terms of an equation on the other side of an equals sign—but naughtily so, seriously naughtily—like the elements of a simile or of a metaphor to some such poet as Baudelaire or Rimbaud—greedy-hearted, subterranean, a kiss of the resistance: such a kiss might be outright wicked or driftingly a bad thing wishing everyone ill and it might still leave a lot of *virtue* in place, might permit a lot of well-behaved mindliness, a lot of decent or semi-decent madness. I can *imagine* the interest of a kiss of that sort. But I would imagine that the call of badness, madness, and self-assertion would be more interesting, both in the daydreaming and in the whipping control of the maybe otherwise too tame hallucinations of an erotic moment. Pull down the world? In a kiss that goes on for a lifetime in its variations? Much of the time, only success, success only, only that will free you. Sometimes only failure will. If you doctor your own soul, you have to guess; you do it alone. Casey was a brute in a lot of ways—I didn't mind that; I liked her cool unintelligence and then her being intelligent anyway and having character. She is a sort of laughing knife of a woman, quick to react, to respond—not a good person. I don't mind that. I don't judge that. But I imagine a kiss too aimed, too knowledgeable: it becomes a *shall-we-go-on* kiss; an astounding fluster of implications and hints accruing in the gestural elements of such a kiss—brainy and shrewd and with character—and danger in it—and with an animal *intelligence* that might be like the cooing of a pigeon, then and there in the past and then and there on the porch, Venus's bird, or the soft whoosh in high air of a hawk gliding, or the thin breath of a transparently camouflaged, waitful, then almost silently wing-whirring owl advancing among the resinous-stinking trunks in an airless pinewoods—I felt them in the world of effectual actions, each of them differently, being discreet and feeling, Lila would say (as Ora did), *her oats.*

I can imagine the actions springing from such a lifelong, often interrupted kiss might haunt Daniel—or the kiss itself as the mysterious particle-cum-wave of alliance—might haunt him partly in admiration, partly in mystery and in mystification as the blasphemously knowable center of *the secrets of the universe* . . .

But not necessarily. What is *political* and personal and sinful for Coral Emma-Jean Marie is angrily rebellious and anathematized for Casey and purified in various personally moral distilleries, so to speak, for both of them by loyalties and kinds of social intelligence in each of them—stuff beyond me and of which I am jealous, I believe. This purified and anathematized liquor pleases Casey and Abe—in different ways, maybe in related ways—and Daniel sees it, or feels it, feels his ma's disapproval of parts of him guide him into being something that doesn't interest him but which has glamour: his father's approval and disapproval similarly—so, it was not a simple *equation*.

It is a weight perhaps not weighty enough, and perhaps, only, in the end, a kind of force of love. Perhaps he approves of himself being passed over or struggles to learn how not to be or struggles to solve the why-he-feels-that-way, struggles repetitively; he does it over and over . . . He is looking for the why?

But among the secrets—among the secret things: physical laws and amounts of money, theological principles and body parts, the actions and moral quandaries and moral filth and moral compromises in the power of childhood and in the power of being rich, in the power of looks and in the power of being the oldest child—Daniel forcibly amalgamates the bottles and flasks, the flashing machines and oddly cooled poles of electricities-in-the-flesh until they are trained to merge everything into a single tree, a channel, a spire, a system with a single final secret—a lie, of course; Daniel can't summon God or ascend to heaven at will—even in hallucination as it happens—or love, or find such a kiss, the time-stretched center of a not-bad childhood—or perhaps a bad one. I judge but not in every way; and Casey is more of a person—Daniel is a better one.

Below the stars-and-moons and movie screens and Sinai and potent words of such a sense of wholeness, of light and of shadow as one thing, of a kiss of a certain sort holding the light and shadow of the great chief-one-thing, is Daniel's actual stuff of infatuation and mood and of judging people (and even genders) and of mooded finaglings and power-things until, for me, the orphan, who was taken into another house, another family, the fleshly (or meaty) boy with his needy mind, such kisses in their permutations having in them the hope or claim of singleness rather than the admission of singularity and of my presence in the dialogue, such kisses have no personal recognition for me if they are given to me. Daniel kissed me three or four times—on the forehead, on the ear, on the hair. One can *read* the history of such kisses as *those*—such a kiss—before the history has occurred. One sees the denial of actuality—and of history—in such a kiss and in such a history of a kiss. Denial is what I see, I am a voice that took on a shadow reality as a boy, denial is what I see if I see others kissing in that style—denial of the moments, of the heart, of the child, of the music of their kiss itself. It has no pornographic draw for me. I do not dare generalize in the light of theology or of Darwin about myself about this. The subject of the comparative absoluteness of sexual response, sexual wish, and the banishing or disciplining of sexual terror, sexual horror, sexual no-saying, the supremacy of the romantic ins-and-outs if they are separate from gender. The appetite is not aroused but is quenched in time as if time did not exist. Dangers sprout and branch and flower from what one resists—which is time. One engages in the other, in the time stuff, because of one's hopes. Time will tell which thing works out.

I mean I made one comparison, one test, one experiment having to do with my embarrassment toward actual life. When Casey saw Ora, seven years further on, not long after my first meeting Ora, Casey, after saying, *How do you do*, did not say another word in the meeting except to say, *I have to leave now*.

And she said that within a few minutes: she did not stay and talk or admire Ora—it was nothing like that. Daniel was not there. Isobel and Benjie were. And a month later Dan came to New York and telephoned and came to dinner, which Ora and I made; I thought then, watching him, that he and Casey had by then spoken to each other of their respective sexual adventures, spoken to some extent, and in some way—it was pointless to try to guess—they had a treaty and they did not like each other. The moment for rapprochement for them had been lost.

I bet Casey and Isobel and Benjie had spoken of Ora. I didn't really like Daniel (or Dan or Danny) and he was not *a friend* to me. Whatever his love was, his interest in me, was both boring and dangerous—but dangerous without any flush of adrenaline—an offered kiss in a moment called *In the Castle in a Stables*, a moment in which the echo of similarity of scale, the possible *clarities* of touch—glances, statements made by the eyes—as between two women—defines mostly only a theft, mostly a truncated lesson—desirable whether truncated or not—mostly only the putative and temporary evidence of one's *superiority* to something, Mother or me, his parents' secrets, the general populace—it matters and it doesn't matter since all superiority in the light of the one-direction nature of time and the dream-ridden intelligence of someone like Daniel, of someone so romantic and so pure and so classical as Daniel-who-is-dear-because-he-liked-me-once, is part of what seems to him, what feels to him to be an entire course of superiority which must, in the nature of things, take him, as if on a flight in space, as an angel or as in a spaceship, or in one's head sitting at the dinner table with one's family, at first up to and then past the person you are with or the people and on toward starry—and starring—revelations of a hateful and yet blessèd order, vile with the promises of ugly history to come and with intimations of salvation. These are the things one hears in hearing someone's breath—the peculiar *similarity* in a reality of there being two people of almost a single type of somewhat interchangeable existence can begin a procedure so mightily, if you take the scale of things to be Greek and to be centered on individuals, that it becomes a story of fate and of fatedness . . . Daniel will act out, I believe, over and over his dramas with his mother and his father—kindness to the male and exploitation of and rivalry with it; and he will give parts of himself—but mostly hold back. I want to cry. One doesn't know that life can be better or that it should be—one sees him as self-righteous and a carrier of destruction. In slightly mad moments, I hear the *Odyssey* and its sense of multiplicities crash into the slaughter at the end as when I wake from a dream and all the figures and characters in the dream have been obliterated and I am home.

Or I see a man carrying his father on his shoulders from a burning city. It isn't blame. It isn't the thought that one can escape fate or being unideal. It is a mad and fairly giddy grief—something intrinsic to my character, I bet. In a dream once I came on an owl the name of which was *Fate-maker* and it grabbed me in . . .

You go in and out of the strange-to-you sounds: no: the novel syllables swell and bubble and fly into your ear—wasps and clouds of enunciation, culture, and purpose.

A voice heard for the first time is almost a monstrous thing.

The rules, or *laws*, that I use in regard to speech are: (1) No one is without will so long as she or he is alive. (2) No one is humble or defeated for real, short of death. (3) Part of speech is accidental, and part is cultural, inheritance and education but those things taken as genderal and individual, but most of it is the immediate sense of emergency.

The main *theory* of talk that I use (desperately but amusedly) is that whether or not it is intimate or wandering (or maundering) you (one, I, or really you) can enter it somewhat if you think of it as occurring in a book with a plot—a murder mystery or a murder novel or a war novel (like the Russian ones) or a sailing-ship novel—in which an adventure and an emergency are concerned.

With a woman, if she speaks, any of a whole lot of social categories become the ground of emergency. She is taking a measure of my breeding, of how freely and naturally I respond, whether I answer like a swindler, from the lower reaches of the prep-school class or even lower—or with grandeur and ease or whatever, like some accomplished black kid or the kid of a sharecropper—those are the aggressive elements, the shadow-boxing elements, the bossy ones.

The passive ones are the poetry of soul and then of her sense of language—mother-tongue and father-tongue—and of fame and of ideas—and of social class.

Coral Emma-Jean Marie was not ladylike in a European way. She was American of the *to-hell-with-you* Southern variety, hooty-voiced and assertive in spite of her calm face—and her kindness, such as it was; she was kind of ladylike but overwhelming, not classical, not anxious to pass herself off as *typical* except insofar as she needed it to have her rank and her position function here. Ora had a kind of geometry of wanting to pass herself off as the general rule and public truth and not as someone social: she had caught on from the movies the thing of a woman being successful but not so enviable that one hated her on-screen. Coral Emma-

Jean Marie sure as shit wasn't pitiable or *warm* or a nobody risen to fame. For one thing her children were here, three of them. She was careless in a real-life way—or like a movie star giving a performance that will end her career—but, see, for Coral Emma-Jean it wasn't a *career*; it was her inherited and earned life.

Then too, even while she was going *full steam ahead*, and *not giving a damn for anyone or for what they think*, while she was being socially high-up in that way, she was careful toward Casey—little glances and checking up to make sure Casey was okay.

Too much went on between them—also too little for there to be ordinary meaning or no meaning between them. They were experienced . . . And they were a pair; those two were *those two*: those two people had that quality. Casey as *a landowner*, first and last a defender of family, God, patriotism and the state of Carolina—that came from this house, from Coral Emma-Jean.

Coral Emma-Jean's confidence in its final, *absolute* and (unpolitical) form—its therapeutic form, keeping C.E.-J. alive—that was from Casey. That was a disguise and a bluff. She was a person pretending to be, and dressed as, a collection of semi-absolutes, local, and coming to a point of the put-upon final absolute. She was too proudly unconquerable when, as a matter of course, as a matter of Protestant upbringing, everyone is, of course, conquerable, is conquerable *anyway*, and is protected by favor and grace—by luck, politics, and American armament.

She had that in her, uneasily, jiggling along with the other.

Both women would, I bet, give up each her inner life to preserve her outer one, to keep things going in the way they were going: they agreed on that.

While being absolutists.

Daniel had opposed himself to *them* and was apocalyptic . . . ready to end their world; and he was apoplectic—dangerously romantic in social-life-sacrificing ways they wouldn't go near. Sex for him was a tearing-everything-down—a revolutionary act—a twisting of the world off its axis, a way of mounting furniture on the ceiling . . . He insisted on his inner life; and his outer life was ascetic inside a baroque degree of inheritance. I'm on Casey's—and Coral Emma-Jean Marie's—side to a certain degree; I am more of their faction than I am of his.

But I'm not of their faction either. I'm a know-it-all. Coral Emma-Jean Marie gave an impression of having an emotional range of two degrees of liking and seventeen of controllable dislike and a thousand of uncontrollable dislike: this was effective with dogs and horses and a lot of people; and she had the air of a monarch—absolute and loony, of course—with a lot of property; she had that thing of being a model for others: someone who shaped fashion; she was a democratic, aged tomboy, all shrewdness and anxiety, "drunkenly" wanting to let her hair down and to be deep in front of *children* and everybody like an artist or like a performer onstage while being *a lady*. She wanted this for the hell of it—because it was a hell of a thing to want—and because of a wish, maybe arrogant, to rule the shadow kingdom—the shadow kingdoms of everyone reduced to the single thing of an audience for an art thing or a piece of written declamation—and she wanted to do it *absolutely* and without limit: she didn't understand how relatively open art was to the mind's wandering and to casual erections and to capricious intrusion. She wanted a final *kingdom* on the grounds of her merit—perhaps as a dreamer, perhaps as an heiress, perhaps as a representative of a bloodline, a people, a specific childhood among people she honored unduly and had come greatly to dislike but had no intention of abandoning.

And she had some sort of spiritual merit—and a profundity—of perdition, if you ask me. She was no two-bit ordinary sinner.

But Daniel was at once more logical and more open; he *wished* to enter the shadow kingdoms—and perhaps to rule there—but he granted those kingdoms independent existence, independent of him.

He did not go as far into pretense and into making real versions and actualities for the pretenses as the women in his mind do. His disapprobation, while constant and controlling, had a side of sheer appreciation and of simple, almost courteous dismissal and contempt: you *could* say no to *him*. He'd hate you—and dismiss you, perhaps to barbarism—he was as conceited as they were—but he recognized sin and the mind's wandering and he knew himself to be a child in a number of ways. And he wanted a final kingdom but he was humble in his viciousness (such as it was) and he wanted the finality to be bestowed or to happen logically: he was most reluctantly an *evil*-doer, as he understood the term.

Coral Emma-Jean's husband, *she was way, way over* HIS *head*. And over Daniel's—and the other kids' heads—and she was over the heads of her ministers and doctors: she behaved but just barely; she often did what she liked—but slyly—within a woman's framework, inside the walls of being rich, a kind of maddening, fraudulent, unideal Eden.

If she had operated by the same rules as Daniel, I would have *felt* her to be, truly, his superior. As it was, I liked her a lot better than I did him; but I thought he was more in the right.

And I didn't say to myself, *Pay no attention to yourself* or *Don't believe this horseshit of yours . . .* I took on a kind of authority inwardly—to gamble, to proceed.

It was because of *liking* her—or loving her in some way—at sight. I decided she was a lot beyond but not over my head . . . Not over mine. I'm not sure that that is ever any more than an ambitious and an erotic gamble . . . I mean by that that it is an awful sort of compliment. We squared off as equals.

She permitted it. Licensed it. Had encouraged it—a form of seduction.

Of course, she hadn't expected me to be me. Life tended to surprise her, too, but she was spoiled and would stamp her foot and drink too much in order to trample the surprises underfoot.

Flirtation with her was rough stuff—the combat led to death, death of the ego, death of your life in this place: what happened to you was your business.

At the same time she was charitable although not necessarily toward *you*. This can be said geometrically or sexually, sexually or socially, intellectually and piously about her as *a woman*; it can be treated as a gender do-jigger—a tough woman but she lived in the world everyone lived in, the world of breath—the common world.

My assumption of equality-of-a-kind with Coral Emma-Jean Marie and my not showing fear, was, I *think*, a matter of my having a kind of social freedom because of those factors in my life that had led Benjie to call me *a Gypsy prince* . . . This mimicked and mirrored—muddily—her degree of monied freedom.

Daniel was more purely what-he-was than Coral and I were what we were. For instance, Coral had an utterly remarkable don't-touch-me-ish kind of sexual shame that invited trespass (such as mine) no matter what the details of refusal of oneself in it were—by gender or age or class; Coral's *shame* was a form of a desire to speak and to live in this world in the sense that freedom of speech and freedom of life is held to be a *shamelessness* . . .

Coral openly wanted to fight with me, test me—she was like a shameless tomboy still, one with a rich woman's cosmopolitan and provincial *low-life* glamour: Emma-Jean had seceded from the world of Southern propriety—Dan had not. But then he was a Jew.

I went nuts—berserk—and started in on the real stuff, hacking away.

Confidence—like being silenced—represents a form of *love-at-first-sight*.

"Hi, you," I said in instant mockery and realized at once that I had gone too far.

She peered at me: her potato-face and her potato-or-watermelon-tits kind of stilled, then welcoming: she was no fool—she knew, from glancing at me, that I "loved" her.

She said—I won't transcribe the sounds—she encouraged me, maybe setting me up as some teachers at school had, she said ironically (but not crushingly so far as I could tell: in my judgment, this is), "I'm sure as shit *anxious* that *you* feel right at home, honey—I heard you're a handful . . . I hope you don't mind the way I talk: we talk this way around here . . ."

That is, I could talk if I knew I was eccentric and troublesome. "No, I don't mind," I said naïvely—as if it mattered to her what I thought. Everybody was watching by then. "I say shit quite a lot, myself, actually. My mother uses it every other word." Casey gaped since she knew I was lying—I hadn't *lied* at all to Casey.

"Well, I sure as shit am glad to see you when I've heard so much about you," Coral said stubbornly but not so stubbornly that she didn't become girlish and give up the matriarchal queen-of-everything tone after glancing two or three times at the rigid and faintly frowning Casey.

Political savvy is relativism in action, in an impure form, of course, with touches of absolutism and hypocritical acknowledgments of it along the line.

But Coral Emma-Jean Marie intended to punish my effrontery or to instruct me: as Daniel wanted to do: she was lying in wait. Everybody kind of had bated breath; I was tense myself. Coral was capricious and did as she liked: "I love poetry, don't you?" Coral demanded, really like a friend, but not one my age, but one who had grown-up ideas and money-and-say in the grown-up world.

"Naw. It's too pretentious," I lied. "I like it when it's written by people from St. Louis. And Ireland maybe. A love 'begotten by despair/ Upon impossibility . . .' What good is a line like that? Who wants to be haunted by *shit* like that?"

Daniel knew something was up but it was far from his own experience: he knew what I was doing to be rudeness—which, of course, it was, if you look at it like that. He was watching Emma-Jean and me—and he was *jealous* . . . Sick with jealousy, actually . . . One had a sense in one's mind of nervous and strong and blood-flecked hands. And Casey. I glanced at Daniel but mostly I half-kept-track of him in the periphery of my vision because he had been my sponsor and because now, with Coral Emma-Jean, I could somehow *feel* myself dragging him along; but, also, I forgot him, too.

I glance, though, fairly openly at Casey . . . At that moment, her face was kind of all twisted and filthy with dumb *feelings* . . . It occurred to me finally, in battle excitement (if I might be allowed to say that), that just possibly maybe Casey hated all *serious* talkers and word-minded people except for Coral and to a lesser extent Daniel—and I mean really hated them, as abominations. And S.L. had, too. Hatred in them didn't wipe out other feelings always. You glimpse this—and then you forget. You hold the more childish sense that she was left out. Or that she felt left out. And that you can fix it by means of politeness—I often feel that way and I mind it when I do it to someone and when it is done to me; but there is maybe a more serious level on which you feel it and do it and it is not a joke but is life and death—you can kill something, some spring or mechanism of life in someone, and they die—like savages; the heart is torn from you; or you say the heart is broken.

What you have in your favor is not enough to balance this other penury.

This strange, embittered bankruptcy of the self has degrees and modes—as in psychoanalysis or as in Gestapo torture or as in married life or between brothers or between sisters. Later that night, in bed, I was inwardly writhing with pain and dismay and trying to think out what had happened and to edit and change it when, all at once, I had a sense, and only a sense, that matched one I'd had at a certain point at Coral's—of *the otherness* of someone's life, of a lot of lives, as not like mine, and as having almost at their center a sense of similarity to other lives and of give-and-take as the grounds of a negotiated and partly swindled superiority and sense of *perfection* and of the ideal and the final . . .

I mean, as the superintendent of schools in U. City had tried to tell me, that that stuff in a form of existence as true-because-it-wasn't-true matched and masked the stuff of *I am not the other person and what I know to be true is not what is true for her, or for him, entirely* . . . The beyondness of another life—such as it was, biologically and in terms of salvation possibly—could be matched by the beyondness of a claimed absolutism which is to say perfection of idea—and, furthermore, of idea embodied in actuality—in ritual, say, and in social stuff, and in manners . . .

And people had always killed because of this. If a kind of unabsolute (in terms of killing each other) but universal (in terms of being in everyone) rivalry exists—if it exists *genetically*—then how are we to live if someone is the one the others love best?

By my rules, or laws, of language, true submission is impossible:

you can, at best, get enslavement, zombie stuff, living-death stuff. Which, if you are one of the robots, you can claim is life by being shrill. Or cruel—to someone.

So, then, what do you about the up-and-down thing of *X* doing better than you?

You invent means of coercion—laws and so on, police forces, force of various kinds—to protect certain forms of rank. You invent spiritual forms of modesty-while-being-superior. You inflict death.

Rule is rule. Things collapse. One has an emotional history, which is to say., a history of emotions; and a separate mind, an independent part of the mind, which recalls emotions: that burning linkage may be part of a pain continuum. People die. People are unable to live. Sometimes. Casey with Coral Emma-Jean Marie—the romantic stuff, the assertions, the humilities, the specialized assertions.

Then the spoiled boy. Was there. She saw him. And she knew. What she'd never had with Coral Emma-Jean as a Jewess confronted by the texts and partly obedient and partly rebellious, as someone effectual but passionately silent she saw someone else having.

What if, then, it is natural and logical, to struggle? You can't submit; life and time don't allow that—they permit only an appearance of submission and certain lies told to oneself.

Did I see *true love* on Casey's enraged, unenraptured face?

Yes.

I saw what Daniel—and the other kids (Benjie and Isobel)—were scared of—I mean compared to Casey. I *saw* how some of the stuff worked in the Warner house, Casey's house—Daniel's by law.

I doubt that Casey slept a night through while I was in Forestville. I had seen her walking the corridors of her enormous house at two in the morning when I had insomnia and was wandering myself on my way to the kitchen or just to the lawn to be out in the darkness in fear and some trembling and in no-fear and the shock of the escape from grief. I saw Casey sitting on her second-floor porch—I saw this from the lawn: she was in a fancy gray overthing and a nightgown in the moonlight; I hid.

She sat staring at nothing. A creature of motion looks at stillness, an opinion, or perhaps into it, seeing a concluding notion move as the sky does when you stare into it, moves in the attention: it shatters as you become aware of it.

You bear or do not bear your *jealousy*. People give up things in order to lessen the jealous-attention-of-the-gods—an English teacher told me this; they give up parts of themselves; they tear their children apart to make them *normal*—in the sense of not-too-noticeable . . .

Ambition, however, remains; it is the stuff of breath. Something like a sea of ambitiousness exists among those who have given up a lot or almost everything—some people are nice about this. Disciplines exist.

But in the emotional history, the linked episodes, the being equal to and the same as had hurt her how often? Had *shaped* her life how? One imagines eras in a friendship. Dramas. Coral evoked, earned, *deserved*—this sounds weird—a devoted *effeminacy*: Casey's femininely male manner. She had become what Coral most needed. People grew tired of being used by Coral—but, in the end, Casey hadn't (so far as I know: this is theory).

The question of what would turn out well in the way of a human being in the *role* of mother was always open but did Daniel *see* who his mother *loved* best—loved best in a way? This was just the beginning of the argument—nothing was *proved*. In the moments on the verandah, I sailed along, glimpsing and knowing things, being overexcited at being tested by such an intelligent *person* and was, at best, symbolically, quickly, efficiently (and boyishly) aware of meanings to the right and left and ahead of me and people's feelings and the like.

I did what I did under the flag of doing it for the sake of the future—to exercise my willful reality—a thematically disciplined capriciousness in front of someone who understood caprice—I did it for the sake of the lives of the younger people there.

Not as Julius Caesar. Not as Christ. Not as Antichrist. I had a system from my life at school in U. City—you did stuff in the moment for yourself but you broke off and took nothing for yourself but you preserved the ability to do the stuff *again* or next time: you didn't enter a certain line of history; a certain current of time; you didn't become *human* in that way . . . I don't know if it worked.

I don't know that it worked at all. It may have worked some, a little—my system, such as it was. And that's it: I did it for Daniel—in order to get free of him. To show him. To be finished with him and with my indebtedness to him and with his suffering—God, there is so much suffering that has to be factored in: how in hell does one do with*out* an image of *perfection* and of *real escape*, without belief in a real yet ideal and perfect *escape*? How do you bend your neck to the yoke of the actual?

Oh, fuck, *the Gypsy prince* can do anything—that's an absolute formulation. Unless my system breaks down—or someone *rescues* me

—or God (perhaps in the shape of an illness) intervenes, I will have to leave here if I keep on doing what I'm doing: one's afternoon freedom, one moment's freedom, things hanging by a hair and falling in a second's wildness. In the future, at moments, I will have forgotten this afternoon; and the past will semi-recur in me thinking of Daniel; but the sight of him was so curative, so mindful—and remindful—that, in time, he, noticing that, and insulted by it, came to the point of forbidding us to meet, to see each other ever again, even when he was dying.

What did I do for him that blew everything apart? Well, first of all, *everything* wasn't blown apart. Some things loosened is all that happened. *I* was blown apart.

Coral Emma-Jean said—offering me a drink—"We all know the kids smoke and drink and do a little naughty-naughty: so let's just be open about it—here, you want a real drink, pretty little lamb?"

Casey, now settled in a wicker chair, with her handbag beside her on the chair, next to her thigh, and her long legs crossed, laughed scornfully in the near-distance, off-key.

An untuneful (and pitiful?) rendition of being a good sport? Impatient? Pissed?

Then Isobel—affected by the tension—went into a spasm of coughing—a hacking cough.

I said to Coral Emma-Jean, "You like the movies and *true love*—you think that's close to real life?"

"What?"

"You believe in true love?" I asked.

Coral Emma-Jean Marie said, "I love my garden and my dog with true love but everybody else damn well better watch out." Then: "I love true love in the movies—I don't know about real life—ha-ha-ha . . ."

I said in a boyishly trumpeting, and trumping-her voice (an attempt at being better than *her*, than she was), "Movies are too goddamned sentimental for me—that sentimentality is really a farce . . . I mean that crap about everyone coming *first* with everyone . . . so that there's no pain. Or everyone gets killed at the end: so the pain is over that way . . . I read in a book that if you don't come first, you're invisible—you're like a ghost whether you know it or not: this has to do with true love . . ."

Oh boy.

The silence into which the moment on the verandah moved, the as-if-naïve moment, the denial of its meaning, the refusal even to see its meaning, the admission of the sight anyway of some meaning in it in the silence, was terrific in ordinary life.

Coral Etcetera said, "Well, that's an *interesting* question—if you like interesting questions . . . Me, ha-ha, ah do without interestin' questions . . . Ah lyuk uh qui-utt lyiff en-duh eeezy questions . . . You huntin' for bear, darlin'? Honeylamb . . . you're really somethin'. I niver had a serious talk about love before with a boy—not at lunch—while drinkin' . . ."

I couldn't talk for a second. I felt the full force of the unreality—the novelty of what I had done. I said slowly: "Uh. No. I was sincere: I wasn't out to make a fuss—ah wuz jus' talkin' . . ."

I don't know what the fake accent was supposed to mean.

Casey erupted then and said, "Oh you, don't talk—just smile . . ."

Danny said "She's not kidding, Wiley . . . Take her advice . . ." He had kind of full-time turned against me anyway and now he was anti-me in an infatuated way. Of course, he was right, as well.

I said, "I don't know what I think about coming first . . ."

"Well, you're being fairly *intense*," Coral Emma-Jean Marie said in a not very bossy voice. She said to Casey, "I like him." Which astounded Casey but seemed also to substantiate her fears. Coral turned back to me, sort of like a big animal settling itself; and she said in a smallish voice, "*I* think we should aid and abet one another when it comes to love . . . as good Christians—" Then half in that voice, half in a different one: "Take that, you snot . . ." I laughed in a strangled way. She said—before I took a breath, she cut me off so that I'd made only a foolish breathing sound—"We Southerners hev manners. We can't stand each other but we stand by each other: we know how to do thet. We know how to get along. We know how to *love*; we don't have to think about who comes first with us, who's first with who—that's for Northerners . . ."

In the moment's weirdness, I said, "You're just trying to score a point: you don't mean what you just said . . ."

"Honey, I'm telling you God's own truth: families know how to do this . . ."

"Well, I'll accept the claim of *breeding* on this topic but I have my doubts if the claim of *breeding* works in regard to true love—with real people and not just in an argument—"

Emma-Jean said *oddly*—in a vocal inflection that meant she would, at whatever price, enter this argument: I had never heard anyone before do this so completely: "But we've been doing the same sort of thing for so many years we might as well call it a habit. We're *Southerners.* Does love matter if someone doesn't love you BEST?" Emma-Jean tossed her head and her hair flew around and she said, "I don't know. *I* want always to be loved best. I kin manage it." She turned and looked at some of the people there, Casey. Her own children. And then back to me. She said—dangerously—"Is this fun?" She asked me somberly, charmingly, ridiculingly, seriously—*outrageously*—"You think not being loved best causes cancer?"

Isobel said out of nowhere, said to me, "Oh, you're such a child."

Casey's *jealousy*—if she was *jealous* and not disgusted or bored: the inner boiling and sinking, the unwellness are unlabelled (Casey saw the whole thing as rude and wild, *unnecessary*)—was that Coral Emma-Jean liked this sort of talk; she was interested, anyway.

Daniel said stiffly, intelligently (in that kind of voice), "Coral Emma-Jean is a lot more *agreeable* than I am."

"*Agreeable?* You mean brave?" I was out for bear whether I admitted it or not. I was drunk from having given myself some kind of licensing to go wild, be rude, barbaric, whatever.

"I don't always want to be loved best," Benjie said, dramatically, placatively.

I looked at him—he never had been loved *best.*

That he hadn't been, this animated the silence then with a sense of oppression and of danger and heat—it was like a large animal was pressing against us and might lie on us and crush some of us . . . Its litter. US.

I mean none of us quite understood what was being said, admitted to, denied, lied about, modified.

But if a vote had been taken, I think the majority of responses wouldn't have been as much unlike my views of what was going on as they would have been unlike anyone else's views.

I mean people sort of did follow the subject.

"But it doesn't feel like love, then, does it?" Isobel said. "Then it's a friendship." She sounded aimlessly, idly *tragic* . . . "I'm not a big reader—and I'm *crazy,* to boot—but isn't love *the world well-lost?*"

"Well, Wiley, what do you think?" This was Coral Emma-Jean looking at me demandingly—bored but she was *interested.* I can't hope for much more than that, although I would like more.

"I don't know . . . How do you define *best* or *love—or* ANY of these things . . . Or *matter . . . matter* how?"

"Oh that's a *Jewish* way out!" Coral Emma-Jean said. "Par'n me: I am *not* anti-Semitic."

"Sure you are," I said, grinning nuttily—you know? Mad?

"Does love *die* or is it still love in your breast when you are NOT THE MOST IMPORTANT THING?" Coral Emma-Jean's second daughter asked; she cried out, she was *letting the cat out of the bag*—it was something she did a lot.

"We're all falling through the air in a parachute jump," Coral Emma-Jean said. Then *she* said, manipulating the talk now: "I mean it doesn't matter if you're all important in different ways—FIRST IS FIRST."

"Oh God," Daniel said, disgustedly—not politely, uncivilly.

I said, confident and exhilarant—and hurt—"I see everyone here has thought about this more than *I* have." I tried to sound envious but I felt triumphant, not yet having realized what would happen.

Casey said dryly, with real disapproval, "Is everyone having fun? I prefer good manners, myself. Is this what people think is *fun* nowadays? I don't like *serious* conversation; I prefer good manners but then I'm not an intellectual myself." She had no fear of repeating things. Or she showed no fear of it, anyway.

I saw the extent of Aunt Casey's stupidity, maybe for the first time, as *painful*—as in the phrase *painfully stupid* . . . Maybe I felt how it affected her successful life—maybe this was the beginning of the collapse.

The extent of Casey's style: her bold systems of self-assertion, her courage made up for the *stupidity*, maybe. Maybe they proved she wasn't stupid.

"A lot of movies are like this," Benjie said in his Southern limp way. "All this talk meanin' so much . . ."

Daniel explained to his mother: "People sitting around talking about one theme, one thing—it's in a lot of movies, Mother." He said it with affectionate boredom even while he glanced excitedly and disgustedly around the porch. You could see why Casey preferred Coral Emma-Jean to him, if she did.

Benjie said to me curiously, "Why y'all doin' this, honey?"

I said, "I can't help it . . ." Then: "You can hate me . . . People pay attention oddly; sometimes everything you say counts and sometimes it doesn't . . ." Then: "I *want* to say these things . . ."

It had become clear to me that I thought it was best—the thing to do then, whatever.

That was even though and because these people were so used to one another and were so much not amateur at stuff and were blood children of their parents so that a lot of what they took in and a lot of what they did and a lot of what they misused or ignored was over my head but it struck me as lovely, even *beautiful* whatever anyone else there thought—even if it all was stale and weird in another sense and a waste of time and self-destructive, pure kamikaze—"It's *beautiful* in my view . . . I'm not entirely alone in my reaction," I said to Benjie and looked at him until he felt part of the reality of his own isolation and his difference from Coral Emma-Jean for instance, and the freedom she had, the libertarian brilliance of the motions of her mind onward.

"Is being *the most important* how you manage to enjoy yourself?" Mocking, Emma-Jean Etcetera said that. To me.

Casey said, loonily—sort of in the background—"Your poor sister."

"Your poor sister," Coral Emma-Jean repeated (it's easier to repeat something someone else says than it is to think up your own things) but she said it *gravely*.

"I didn't do anything to her. I don't like her," I said boldly.

"God," Daniel said.

Pause. Emma-Jean said, "Boy, you're really somethin'."

"People have to fight back!" Daniel said.

"Maybe she shouldn't fight back—if we're talking *moral stuff* . . . You ever hear of *taking turns*?" I said.

"That would be a fine kettle of fish, that would be some world—that would be a horror-show-and-half, [if] you *could* film that one . . ." Coral Emma-Jean Marie said.

"Coming out on top?" Benjie asked me snidely, feeling my isolation.

"Taking turns?" I said to Coral Emma-Jean.

"Not fightin' back," Coral Emma-Jean said with infinite common sense—American common sense . . . "I'm tellin' you somethin', boy . . ." Then: "Benjie is the sweetest person here . . ." Marking him as the traitor. Everybody on the verandah was attentive. Coral Emma-Jean then said: "Men are just hell on women . . ." That is, you had to fight back. She said, "I'm Gemini—I'm afraid of fire . . . If YOU weren't *the most* important thing in your house, would YOU be invisible?"

"Anonymous," I said.

Isobel said gaily, "I feel we're talking *very* intelligently. I hope Daniel likes it—he's the one hates small talk . . ."

Coral Emma-Jean said, "I see us all in a special light . . . I do . . . Well, I don't know—" preparing to shut the talk down: "I've hed three martinis—and I swear I'm the greatest woman of the day-and-age—and of any age: ever'body jest has to love me BEST—it's my gin you all are drinkin'—ha-ha—Casey brought the vermouth—I was low on vermouth."

I pushed on with the other subject—it was like pushing the *conversation* like a wheelbarrow with heavy feelings in it: "Oh, it's a farce:

people pretending it's not an issue, that it's easy." Then: "*Everyone* coming first, that's a good one."

Coral Emma-Jean said, half-warningly, but interested all over again—a fair-minded bully: "I'm going to get good and blotto before I think about any of this *anymore*." And then, because she was a fair-minded bully—or an intelligent one—or free-minded—like an aging princess—she said, "Well, being loved more than anything else by someone you want to love you, by someone who interests you, that's *a dream come true* . . ." Emma-Jean said it with her eyes odd with thought (in my view) but her face alight with combat, with thought truncated, which cut me down to size; while she took over, while she was the one the muses loved best . . . She went on, not shrewdly, shockingly: "Being loved second-best: everyone laughs at you then . . ." Then she became shrewd and sort of notably evasive: "Everyone laughs—and knows what's what . . . Only a nut would uh'int mind THAT . . . Well, they're wrong: some of us know and some of us don't know horse manure—well, we all have to live . . . We do what we hev tuh do," she said vaguely but overweeningly—a little like Lila: I arouse this in people. Then, with a wild shrewdness, perhaps not shrewd, with political savvy maybe unwise, even *crazy*, she gave in to me—as Lila sometimes did—she handed me my turn, so to speak: "This is your big moment, i'n't it, honeylamb?"

The butler stood there listening and forgot to serve people—he looked *thoughtful*.

Before I could answer Coral's stuff, while I was still shocked and unbreathing, Benjie said, "Well, I'd be a man about it—being loved second-best. I'd try—I'd put up a good fight." At not being wicked. At being peaceful.

Daniel said, "I will give anyone who cares a piece of advice: Don't listen to anybody who says something is first, second, or third: that's just idolatry . . . On the other hand, I'm an odd duck; and I don't want to *be a man* about *these* things."

I stared at him, not certain what he was saying, but surprised to think that he was thinking.

Benjie said, still following his train of thought and determined to interrupt Daniel, "I don't know: if you have to come first, if a lot of people are like that, if everyone is like that, life just i'n't worth a plugged nickel, it just isn't worth *sheee-it*, it'd be SO dictatorial: I don't think life is that *terrible*, do YOU?"

"Why is this my moment?" I asked Coral Emma-Jean.

"Oh you; you're not a nice person. I like you but you're not nice.

What a mess you make. I had an Irish setter just like you—we had to have him shot—you *are AWFUL*—"

See, the whole thing was disintegrating into *personalities*—that's what we said in U. City at that time.

It always hurt and amazed me—the way that ideas dissipate their reality in the moments and the way a common concentration on a topic disappears into lives plunging on, not in a repetitive surf, but in the kind of mad surf of God heading on out into the infinity of the pretty-much-unknown future.

I mean, the power and dreadful beauty of time, or part of it, is that you can't get anywhere in it—except as hallucination and prayer—it takes *you* with it, an eternal father, with you aloft but you're dissolving in its arms, too.

You just arrive in further moments without having gotten there so much as scrambled and lasted and floated and swung—like Tarzan maybe or like a band singer or a popular singer back then during the war—and *life goes on* and not in-the-same-way unless you mean *in the same way* grandly: if you're awake and not inward in your thoughts, all the other lives are scrambling near you, alongside you . . . Maybe people move differently in time now in a way you like a little better.

One of Coral's kids half ignored his mother; he turned his head sideways and made a squished-up face; and said, "This is really *really* stupid." Then: "It's silly." Then: "I like what *he* says . . ."

Me?

Me.

Coral says, "My daughter Isobel"—a different Isobel—"has this thing where she says: *Why not both?* If you have a choice, take all that you're offered . . . I love greed. I have to come first—there—that's the end of it."

One of her daughters said, "But then that means it is *JUST impossible* around *you*, Ma . . ."

Coral's daughter, *Isobel*, a bold, very tall, young woman, with a coldly hot manner of extreme discretion and distinction, said, not sharply enough to start a fight, "I didn't come first for her in any *way, shape or degree, EVER.*"

"Not in any form?" Daniel asked her.

Coral said *sharply* to him, "Daniel, that's not important." She said, "No one comes first with me—I play fair . . . I have my pride as a woman . . ." Starting on yet another martini but blandly: it was a wearied slyness, a laying down of the law: "No one here comes first with anyone else here."

"Oh my," Benjie said in a narrowed, looking-inward way—now he saw the power thing and the lies—he glimpsed it flying—and came to see me years later when he was ill, as I said.

Daniel kept looking at me as if to say none of this was true for him except as a victim. You have to be responsible for your acts before I trust and like you.

Daniel said, "Well, if we all want to come first . . . it's a horse race . . . It's a crap shoot . . ."

I said, "Benjie, do you play favorites?"

I couldn't bear to address Daniel directly.

I thought I heard someone say: "Then the so-called heart breaks . . ."

Someone said, "Well, try to enjoy yourself *anyway* . . ."

Coral said, with *narrowed*, drunken, responsible-to-truth, irresponsible-to-power eyes, "If you open a can a worms, it's real chaos. Real—reeeeeeeeeeeeeeeeeeeeeeeel. We all have good reason to think well of ourselves: we did reeeeeeeeeeeeeel well today—how much do you think those people could learn from Socrates? I'd'a given him a good swift kick—right in his sit-upon . . . You learn zero, crap from Socrates. You really learn from your parents—ask me: I'm the expert here. And your dogs, you learn from your dogs—do you like dogs? Is that why you brought this subject up? Are we your laboratory dogs? So you threw us this question? Is that why you asked?"

"We don't have to know everything. Enough is enough," Casey said.

This is and isn't an accurate transcription. What happened is hard to describe: nothing in life, especially voices and motives and actions, is as clear as it is in a narrative.

Casey was obscurely drunk. Her somewhat mean look was blankly mean in line with a system of organized thought somewhat independent of speech and of perceptibly organized study.

My cousin Isobel had a pointed air of it's all being *common sense*. I had never guessed that at the center of what she was was something in her that as part of her free will forbade mystery—as a *rule*. I hadn't looked at her hard enough before—it's not easy to know about the lesser figures. Ever.

In the almost imaginary dialogue, the conversation not with Lila or Nonie, one shortened, cleaned up in regard to the past, to the moments, and so on, Coral Emma-Jean Marie put on a determinedly *ordinary* look and said, "We don't tock about feelings all theeee tyimmmm in theee Sow-youth." Then as if sober: "What this country needs is a good five-cent *czar* and a little ol'-fashioned censorship . . . Ah'm very very right-wing in my liberal way . . ." She'd turned against her earlier interest in the subject. In abrupt Christian despair, and in real feeling, she said, "What torments me is that when God came to earth, it ended in torture and death, and it's just like Dostoyevsky said: and it would be the same thing over again if He came back to us." She was speaking with intense and primary even if probably momentary love of what, perhaps, she loved best. "So, let's not take ourselves too serious: we're all just trash . . . I have enough on my plate as it is . . . I just idealized my parents. I do still, ever' day of my life. They were just the most *brilliant* people—ev'ybody loved *them* . . . But they had their little faults. They taught me *walk quietly and carry a big stick.* You carry a big stick, honey? I don't know about the rest of you but I am a quite wretched woman who needs her nap. I hev ensirred tooooo minny questshuns, and I am sleepy. I em jest wuyin beeigg *snore* in spirit—sore all over. I throw things at my dawgs and hev to be put in a home I don't get a nap. I neeeed my nap. I am jist wohn ow-itt. I em just about ready to cash in my chips. If all of you don't jes' go down and stay at the pool and swim and drink in my honuh and for the sake of the old true-blue stars and stripes foreveh while I lie down and refresh myself, I will *die*. Really. Well, it's been interestin'. Really. It's all interestin' . . . You come back and see me. You know somethin', little pretty boy: you got to tease us all a little bit, but the afternoon is over and you're still poor and I'm still rich. I'll come later and watch y'all swim—hear? I hope you hev pretty legs; your sis, Nonie, had real piano legs. I hate pyanna ligs. See you in a hour."

Grimly twinkling at first, she sobered up a lot as she talked and brought in Dostoyevsky, her parents, and Christ, Theodore Roosevelt (the big stick), exhaustion, hospitality and the flag, and death. I would like to write a play some day and I would have in it a character who had a dog called *Meaning-and-kindness*. I'd have a woman character who said, "Watch your manners!" all the time, even to *The Angel of Her Own Death*. And I'd have a character like Casey but who would keep on weeping all the time saying, "Oh don't let us talk about *that now*!" and one like Coral Emma-Jean who keeps saying, *I'm tired of thet, I'm tired of thet*, and then who says, *I'll talk about thet* . . . And I'd have a character like Daniel in the pronounced statement of a well-tended naked body of someone his age—an actor pretending to be Daniel's age would have a naked body that would be a pale whisper in the shadows out of which he speaks and acts.

And I will have no character in it like me at all.

"I'm going back to St. Louis," I said suddenly as we were changing into our bathing suits. I had no energy to be phallic and this or that or to be not phallic and this and that. I knew then a certain amount about myself in reaction to the day—to the mere presence of time in real life so that what you do causes stuff that is over your head and beyond the range of your sight; and you have to lie and be remorseless to some extent or you can't exist and you can't help anyone at all. I wanted someone to say something to stop me. No one said anything. Daniel drained his drink. "I'm going back to St. Louis," I said again. I said, "I'm sorry. I give up. I don't want to bother you all any more. I want no money for college."

Benjie said, "Pooh-pooh, angel, y'all a bee-ig such-siss . . ."

"I'm going back to St. Louis . . . I can't bear any more shit, my own included . . ."

The reality of the harm I do and of what is done to me.

I mean you act and you can't possibly know why, at least with any assurance, and you can't keep track of what happens as it happens, not only at a party or in a battle, but just if you're alone; and you can't know how things will go in the moments after you've done what you've done. The moments open out—like the playground at school when the kids were released at recess and ran into the macadam- and dirt-floored spaces. It takes an incredible amount of courage to live even if you lie about it a lot, to yourself, to others.

No one really knows what they're doing . . . They only sort of know . . . You have to keep guessing . . . I told some of this to Daniel but he didn't noticeably listen—why should he? I try to help or be nice but I don't know enough; and if I'm cautious, I start to go mad with inaction. I'm going to go mad soon if I don't go home. A lifetime of speech, a lifetime of information is at home. My guesses are better there. I can imagine things more clearly from there.

Benjie, in bathing trunks, said, palping his own body: "I'm getting love handles. Nobody's nice to me. I manage though, I get along with crumbs just like a little sparrow. You ain't a-goin' home, are you, Sonny Boy, ol' friend, you little ol' troublemaker, ah you?"

Daniel said in the gloom in the bathhouse, "It's not a good idea . . ."

I said, "I said it three times—like in a fairy tale . . ." I was trying consciously only to sound young and normal.

I realized too late that the word *fairy* had set me free, had silenced Daniel.

It was an accident, more or less. But I let it stand.

*

I don't know what would have happened if he'd asked me to stay but one truth is that he was too impressed; he said, "We can't keep you amused around here . . . You're too smart for us by half . . ." Daniel at the train station, when I left, put his arm over my shoulder; but he withdrew it, having felt the strain in the tendons and bones and skimpy muscles of overexcited *refusal* and tensed-up permission in the boy whom, in a lot of ways, he was sending off or sending back, refusing—almost as if in a courtship mode. He said, "Mr. *Noli-me-tangere*, you have the most impossible mother in North America. You don't know how to act. I want you to know I don't blame my mother—she's old, she's aging, she has a right to her old habits. You are very, very wild: you're a *baby* . . . A real know-it-all . . . I have an income of forty thousand dollars a year and I spend only ten of it: ask me for what you need to go to Exeter . . ."

"No, thank you," I said in a Southern accent.

He persisted and I said, "I'll write you if I need anything."

Years later, in Boston, Johnno said at South Station—he was disgusted and nervous a little—"Do you believe in kissing someone good-bye?"

"No," I said, squinting in a confused light of recollection. Then: "Anyway, not you, Johnno . . ."

On the train, I said under my breath, watching my reflection in the train window: "Leave me alone . . ."

But I was sorry he had.

Do you try to understand people according to books or plays? Johnno asked me in college. "I use movies and fan magazines . . ." He said, *Do you believe movies* AT ALL?

Movies scare me; it is like dreaming in which you breathe in one world and seem to be living in an entirely other one of false but significant plausibility.

Daniel said on the phone, "Ha-ha, I was just thinking about you: so I'd thought I'd call."

Daniel asked me on the telephone, "You don't even know how rude my mother thought you, do you?"

"I guess. I don't know. Whatever you say," I said. It made me really happy, euphoric, that he did not offer to come and see me.

Casey did not say good-bye to me in Forestville. She never wrote to me that I can recall.

*

I used to like to think of myself as a cold person.

I made it to our apartment from the train station. Nonie was at home. Momma looked strained and drawn. I said when Mom and I were alone in her room, "I had a good time on the train—I talked to people—Daniel will send me to Exeter, Mom."

She said, "Don't look at me like I'm an ogre or something, but I can't let you go . . . I can't let you go, Wiley."

I said, "I don't know how much more I can take, Mom."

She said, "Well, let's just play it by ear—can we do that and just be sensible and hold our horses and wait to see how things turn out: can we do that?"

"No," I said.

She started to cry. "Don't leave me alone with Nonie. I promise you I'll die soon. You won't have to stay with me long. Just tell me you won't leave me, Wiley."

I didn't say anything and she took the next step: "Well, it's just you and me now, Kiddo, and what the future brings forth."

Poor Nonie.

In late 1943, Nonie home on a visit, if I remember Nonie's actual face I get a sense of somewhat hardworking *nobility* which wasn't entirely façade, and of political *savvy* and of a savagery of lazied and enraged corruption and a competence she's tired of . . .

She is kind of a shredded person, infinitely touching while being fairly rotten to an extent hard to describe—she is fragilely temperamental and very mean and cold; and she has surrendered to deadened unawareness in order to survive; but she is nervously aware anyway . . . She is having a maybe common-garden-variety wartime breakdown . . . "It's time for her to get married," Momma said. Nonie managed to get dressed every day, and when she had on lipstick and eye makeup and had combed her hair, it would suddenly be a question of how loony she was, maybe in just a regular way of someone who'd been through really a lot of very rough episodes . . .

Momma was careful of Nonie but a little thorny toward her; and she said of her, "She's not at her best but she's got her nose in the air as per usual . . . She's been running around with pilots who are nobodies . . . She lost her social sense of things."

When I saw Nonie with Daddy, I saw that, not androgynously, just flatly, she was as much a man as he was; she was a man *like* him, almost; she hadn't seen battle but she almost had. Sitting there, the two of them in the apartment, a toughened small-town upper-middle-class girl and a dying man, Nonie and Daddy, they were, both of them, strongly anti-Lila. Lila had to have her second operation for cancer at this time. Her cancer has recurred. Daddy and Nonie sit in the dining room; and Nonie smokes avidly, addictedly, lost, cold, an oddly gleaming and exotic and knowing personage, shaky and yet determined and weird. Daddy is gray, is lightless. He sparks with life, or light, now and then, though. The two of them, somberly, yet gigglingly (even laughingly), with the cold-hot ruthlessness of their pasts, say now, right out loud, how great it would be if Lila would die now, how great it would be if Lila were dead.

"Come in, sit in on this," Daddy said to the boy. "We're thinking how *nice* it will be around here if your mother would die on the operating table . . ." Nonie laughed a little, spikily, at the *grown-upness* of this. "We might have a little silence then. Silence—she is wonderful," Daddy said, in a serious way although jocularly. Part of it was said as mock-prayer, eyes cast upward.

Then he stared into my eyes, Daddy, a wartime hero from an earlier war, that said once he was someone who learned and that he'd become too heroic to be *a hero.*

Nonie, deadpan-ishly, darkly very serious, very grown-up, is watching me. I start to breathe rapidly. It is like being in a pit of animals . . .

Affronted, I told them they were being revolting. Dad leaned over the table and sort of half punched me, but not really; it was sort of a slap: he kind of slapped at my face. Then he and Nonie shifted their chairs, closing me out.

"Maybe I'll stay sane for a week or two, maybe I can stop smoking once she's dead," Nonie said to Dad. They, both of them, pointedly ignored me. Nonie gave her brassiere a hitch and looked at Daddy in a sort of foxily conspiratorial way.

Dad was still smoldering. "Let's ignore the oversensitive little son of a bitch," Dad said, although they already were doing that.

Lila didn't die. Nonie went back to Carolina. I am not certain that Daddy and Nonie were friendly with each other after that. I think this was the last time they were friends.

When Daddy was in the last six weeks of his life, Nonie came home from Carolina for good, but S.L. did not want to see or talk to Nonie at that time, when he was dying. He put himself in the hospital. He said dryly that he wanted to spare her.

So, Nonie went East to see a rich guy she'd known when she was nineteen—Ted Prexiter.

"He's a draft dodger is what he is, but he's also *a catch*," Mom said with a sigh. Mom said yet again that Nonie had grown up—she said Nonie had become serious (at last) . . .

The Prexiters were real money. It would be a nationally recognized career to have (married into) so much money. "Nonie could be as *rich* as John D. Rockefeller yet," Mom said. Dad said, "I don't want to hear about it . . ." I remembered the drama when Nonie was nineteen—the really big carryings-on—when Ted Prexiter had asked Nonie to be engaged to marry him. He'd been twenty-two. Nonie had wanted to live and not marry, at least not then when she was so young. "I don't want to marry someone so rich and that short," she said. The family was mostly unhappy at losing the connection to the Prexiters . . . Mom had borrowed money for Nonie's clothes during the courtship . . . Nonie, giggling obstinately between moments of collapse, or of near-collapse, under the pressure, said she wanted someone she loved . . . Momma said, "It was an uphill battle but, in the end, no one interfered, Nonie got to make up her mind, she did what she wanted, she got away with it . . ."

Nonie wrote Ted, then telephoned him, "and he's interested—or he wants revenge," Momma said. Nonie flew East. The Prexiters had a place in New York, on Fifth Avenue, and a place in tidewater Virginia. The weekend Nonie was in Virginia, she said, "they had a cabinet officer there and some other people and 'a movie guy,' Ted's father called him . . . Ted's father talks that way, very down to earth, I'd marry *him* in a minute, he's no creep . . ." Momma said, "Nonie knows how to put a good face on things. She's finally in the mood to be smart about marriage but it looks like it's another case of too little, too late . . ." And: "No one in the family has ever done *that* well but she doesn't really give a damn . . ."

Nonie's wartime *ruthlessness*, her dishevelled and bitter state, her disobedient and clever and commanding wartime disposition, and then her nervousness and oddity now, and her pride "in herself and her accomplishments" and, then, her woundedness: "She isn't the young girl Ted'd been crazy about . . . She's not Betty Coed anymore . . ."

Nonie's wartime glamour, her sexuality at that point, her being responsibly tough: "Those people took her measure and they found her wanting . . . That's what happens if you don't strike while the iron is hot: it is a different ball game. She isn't nineteen."

She doesn't touch one's nerves with her comparative innocence and the perhaps dreadful extent of her coed's will—she doesn't stir emotions as she did. "People like Nonie come into bloom once and that's it for them. It's over. I know when to cut my losses. I'll stand by her and I won't say *I told you so* to her, but she had a chance to be somebody for the rest of her life and she made a mess of it. I have to say it: all the sacrifices, and a fat lot she did, in the end . . . She just laughed at me and said I was a bad person . . . I suppose this isn't like me getting the last laugh. This isn't a laugh. Well, who cares? There's no rest for the wicked . . . Pisher, your sister's not going to be the Queen of England —she's not the Lord High Priestess of soft soap: she can't get the ones she wants to like her; she's not so clever in the end. I don't blame her. I'm not going to let it break *my* heart." And so on.

Momma called the Prexiters to reach Nonie to tell her Daddy was dying. Mom said Dad wouldn't see her if she came back right away; so she might as well stay: "First things first: let's get all that can get settled *be* settled." But Nonie came home and laughed some, in a harsh tone, at the expectations she said I'd had, and she laughed, harshly, at Momma. I had had quite a few expectations. Nonie didn't weep at S.L.'s funeral. She said, "He always saw to it that I was happy . . . I wanted him to die . . . He wanted to die and I wouldn't contradict *him* . . ."

Daniel and Benjie showed up at S.L.'s funeral; and they mostly ignored Nonie: there'd been some sort of quarrel. Nonie said she wanted someone "more of a man" than Ted. She said to me that *Ted* had "gotten very self-important over the years—all he knows is who and what he is —and all he is is just a stick—I can't stand that in a man: a nasty little rich boy—and I mean *boy*. I can't take conceit in a man— Well, I'll tell you something, I went through no hoops . . . not for a conceited little *no one* . . ."

She was still maybe a little crazy. Or ruined by the war. Or by *her* (or our) *hard luck*. Benjie said that of her. Momma said it. Benjie didn't like Nonie much but he never quite broke off with her. Daniel said Nonie made up everything she ever said—I believe he disliked her a lot.

When I think that he was The Real Daniel and Mom was The Real Lila and Nonie was The Real Nonie, then I see a kind of inevitability in things but it makes me sad.

The year after Ted, the next year, Nonie married a Hank Appleberg "from Chicago but his family moved to California and he's much much more California than Chicago . . . He's tall and good-looking, and he's got a medal from the war . . . He's real smart. And he's real brave. And he's A Real Man—and I love him lots and lots—ha-ha—more than is good for me." Nonie and I weren't really in touch—things were formal between us. I have no idea what sort of shape she was in or what the story of that courtship was. I never got to know Hank. Momma, resignedly, said, "He's dumb, she's dumb." But I had become cynical about Lila's accounts by then and did think she had harmed Nonie quite a lot. And reared her, too. Lila said of Hank, she said, "He has no chin . . ." I wasn't asked to Nonie's wedding. Momma said, "Take it as a compliment . . . You're a Harvard man . . ." The wedding was held the first week of classes so that there would be no talk about my being there . . . "You draw too much attention . . . Be understanding . . . with human nature . . ." Nonie and I hadn't fought.

I saw Hank a few times over the years; he said each time, "You can always tell a Harvard man but you can't tell him anything . . ."

"That's right," I said each time. We never got beyond that. I didn't want to. And he had little interest in me—or my reality, although one time he asked, "What is it that makes people say you're smart and me not?"

After a lot of back-and-forth stuff, when I tried not to answer, I said, "If it's true that people say that, then it means that people think I can think what you think but you can't think what I think . . ."

"Shit," he said; and it was as if I'd made a scene—it was like Forestville.

Merely being human and inadequate—and somewhat vicious—I started to smile at him. We'd been drinking—beer. Nonie wouldn't let me drink in her house unless I brought my own booze. And all at once I couldn't stop grinning; and I said, "The brain has a right lobe and a left lobe; and Loeb and Leopold were thrill-killers, you know; and the right *Loeb* is a real thrill-killer in the head—which you probably don't have, *old friend* . . ."

But he didn't laugh. Or unbend. I never knew him except as a human presence in the particular jealous mode.

The Harvard thing wasn't a joke for Lila either, it turned out, although she had decided I should go there. I was called to Lila's deathbed from Harvard. She was in a hospital in Los Angeles. Hank and Nonie lived at that time twenty miles outside San Diego. Lila's nurse called me, not Nonie. We didn't write each other. Or telephone each other. I'd spanked her unjocularly for cursing Mom out when Mom was recovering from the anesthetic after the second cancer operation. Momma, who flunked out of Louisiana State University her sophomore year, kept rearing up in bed and saying, *"Serpent's tooth! Serpent's tooth!"* I held no brief for Lila's treatment of Nonie—I just didn't want Lila to be punished by Nonie. Nonie said, when I got to L.A., that I had no place there—she meant with the dying Lila; I wasn't a real child of Lila's; I wasn't part of the family. She went on and on, dribbling a little with upset. She said, "You're too fancy for us." It got pretty tiresome. Momma's nurse took me down the hall—no one on the staff was speaking to Nonie. But the nurse—well, Momma had promised I'd date the nurse. Momma spent the last three days of her life mostly talking and really only talking to me. She wouldn't let the doctor in her room except once. She said she wanted to talk to me on her deathbed . . . And she wanted everyone else *to stay put. I'm sick of all of them . . . And I'm sick of being sick . . .*

To me she said, "I'm afraid of you—you know fancy people now . . . Tell me about Harvard . . . Tell me about the rich people who go there—how do the girls dress? Tell me some of the things they say when they're stringing you along . . . How do they talk to you when they're trying to be nice, Pisher?"

I told her Harvard was a cold place and that the *girls* were *ambitious* and that it was not fashionable there to be pretty "except sometimes, as a surprise . . ."

"I think you're overly picky about too many things . . ."

"Nonie's having a fit," I said. "Aren't you going to say good-bye to her?"

Momma, on morphine, said, "There's something they don't tell you in school—Freud never taught it, either: Don't be too boring with your parents or there'll be hell to pay . . . Well, enough is enough. Tell me, Pisherkin, you think there is a heaven or not?"

Nonie's marrying Ted Prexiter would have been a bigger thing than my being at Harvard. Or maybe not—worldly stuff is peculiar. Lila said on her deathbed that I'd tricked *everyone* into forcing me to do what I wanted to do anyway. *You're smarter than you look, Pisher . . . kins* . . ." It seemed premature to consider Harvard a step up in the world—I told her—since a lot of the guys I knew were having serious breakdowns, flunking out, fucking themselves to death, becoming alcoholic. A lot of people, a whole hell of a lot of kids, got eaten alive there. By the sharks there. By pride. I had been told there I owed it to society to become a Jew scientist.

Lila said, "Oh, I don't want to hear *your* sad stories . . ."

Well, identity being an uncertain thing, perhaps it is time I tried to imagine myself Nonie.

Imagining Myself Nonie

I can't do this.

Saying I can't is an incantation that often shakes me into seeing that I might, after all, do it, shows me how to cross into the moments of doing it, shows me the border so clearly (if briefly) that, as if teetering on my toes, at the moment I say I can't be Nonie I then perversely and snottily see (or think I do) into the territory (I think) she familiarly sees.

She is physically farsighted. Insensitive to nuances of color and line but she is aware, almost supernaturally prophetic about movement, stirrings, flutters in shadow or in glare behind her back, behind tree trunks, and anywhere around her vision and beyond it, ill-defined or well-defined . . . I *feel* that as her vision: I feel the mind-given self-righteousness of what I can and can't do and what I won't do as her, if she is me, if I have that body, if I am that old . . .

When I say I can't be her, I enter, or the part of me I think of as one's self enters, an empty space; *one* enters her body: the body is below (and rises into) one's editing and explaining self . . . as Nonie . . . I am half present as myself inside this Trojan Horse thing of being her . . .

I imagine I see her territory of vision—I imagine myself asserting I see *everything* . . . What is this? An editorial thing? A preparation for a role. At the border I am an escaping male self, somewhat thievish.

Unescaped, I am a hugely shocking vastness of awareness of nearby movements—of all sorts . . . Imagine a nervous frontier of that sort around you. One has quite a lot of boneless flesh here and there, hips and breasts. And one is partly a perched lemur . . . partly a cat. I never dreamed of such alertness for myself—Wiley—and never fully doubted an almost supernatural extent of that in her . . . As an *actor* doing this, one is a child spying on the women and pretending to be them in order to learn about men.

To be Lila is to be darker: more amused. Not a lemur-cat—more a fat-thighed sphinx reared up . . . But how would I know what a lemur-cat or a sphinx, reared up or not, is like? What do I know of my mother, of my sister? To imagine a state in which one is preparing a show and one asks oneself, *Is my mother like this?*—how strange that would be for me . . .

As Nonie, the skin is young—so is the mind—and the *mind* feels different inside my skull (from Wiley's mind) and the skin feels different on me. The familiarity of the ground of idea toward women vanishes entirely when one hopes to present the reality of one . . . The *imagination* of a woman, the image, the imagined thing, is not likely to be guesswork or a heretofore unworded *mass* of perceptions of them from alongside them but is likely to have something to do with hallucination . . . hallucination and theft . . . The structures of purported psychological indecencies in knowing women and then the joke-work transvestitism (in a brotherly mode—maybe it's that), the connection(s) of the parts of those things to each other has to do with memory—and daydream-reverie—the curious thing of: *What does she think of you . . .*

Why should it matter?

One moves out into darkness on the pendulum-swing of this attempt and returns and tries the incantatory doubt—*I can't* becomes, perversely, *Let me see, let me see*, before the momentary identity fades too much. The medium of actual air imagined in airlike investigation in the mind—blowy, eccentric, as on a windy spring day with clouds skating with perilous speed across the pale blue landscape of the almost spring sky—holds a landscape and a face in it, quickened with life—a face I *can't* bear to imagine myself having. Her actual presence in a real moment, her as viewer and asker—if I divorce her from any purposes of meaning, of use or of instruction to me, then, in memory, it might be real enough, I might become Nonie briefly, my thoughts of my younger brother broken into by my disgust with him—he is disgusting and selfish . . . [Breathe, breathe . . .] He's no one important . . . He's not broken and defeated, he's merely nowhere. What I am is *real. I-may-want-him-to-take-care-of-me-yet.* [Breathe, breathe . . .] [*I bet I could hurt him if I wanted . . .*]

On my head is (dyed, strawish) long, reddish hair. Its weight, its dependent fixity mean a permanent wave. The breasts—the thighs—the butt . . . Inhale. Exhale. My legs, large, powerfully dwindle into small feet, thicken into my hips. My biggish girl's rump drives my oddly pendulumatory walk. In my walking, my small-ribbed and as-if-weightless torso—my *chest*—floats like a different mind beneath the casually *other*-motored, more *intellectual* face . . . Nonie? It is me. I am dressed in a *pendular* papier-mâché costume or an entire float as this splendor-of-myself-as-her. To be her in mood, I must be quieter inwardly and outwardly, with a filigree of motions stirring here and there around me . . . Mine is quieter breathing than I am used to as a boy—my breathing as Nonie is very loud when I am upset. It is noisy in my long neck to me: I am a long-necked, oddish, *pendular*, swift, frighteningly alert girl: I feel it; I feel I am an intruder in her skin, then in my own skin, in the weightedness and heat in her. Her heat—as herself. I feel that to be in her is to be a runaway force—all speediness and deftness and worry and force-of-will and willfulness . . . Conscience and knowledge, the walls of confidence, the flapping of worry, the terrible *alertness*—that sensitivity—the *psychological* sense of other people and my memory, patently, patiently uninspired, then impatiently and marvelously *inspired*, a *quick-wittedness* in a real-life sense . . . formal arrangements of opinion shaded by real-life obstinacy—and resignation—scenes, outcomes, near-presences of actual opinions of me, of things, of clothes, and pain and no-pain, I (Nonie) remember pictorially and I remember in my legs and back with gooseflesh and feeling, real feelings . . . I am differently awake from Wiley. I am the chief example, the best example of anything I choose to pronounce an opinion about. I am the basic measure of truth and of courtesy in this civilization. If I say to someone in the office—or to my brother—*You animal*, it means it was not recognized that the treatment of me is the measure of the degree of civilization in someone. In my peculiar degree of inner silence, practical memory, hard-edged promises, commitments (contracts), and bad dreams question my memory, my confidence, my safety. Voices in me do not talk in words but they give away their secrets and impart information as *animals* speak, with their whole beings, circumstances and glances. Other people utter promises which contain hidden-or-open views of me, of *my* power: they fill the air with reviews of me all day long, all night long. For me, a face is a rapid, nearly worded gesture of immediate moment which sweeps along toward a judgment of me . . . Death (accident, inequity) I am immortally superior to: I am very pretty . . . I know what I know . . . I am *practical* . . . Here's a for instance:

(At the airfield, a guy was killed in a car accident on day leave the same day a mechanic stabbed a pilot who had been berating him . . .) Everyone was buzzing around. They leaned on me. I said, *Let's localize the damage and worry about the afterwards later . . . I mean afterward . . . And I was right: everyone listened to me . . .*

Me, I know what end is up. If I am upset, if I am in trouble at night, I go to Aunt Casey's room and she will pity me; her friend Emma-Jean's husband is a doctor; Casey will give me some of her codeine. The man killed in the car accident was from Columbus, Georgia. (The small-bodied corpse was twisted, partly mangled, charred—it was hideously pretty pink and red and burnt black; and it was yellow and pustulant.) I can bear things.

(At the airfield, planes taking off, planes landing, other planes practicing in the clear air, the sound of the motors echoed off the rocky fence of the pretty and fallen-sideways jumble of mountains.)

I do not give up. I do not give in. I do not give anything away . . .

Ha-ha.

I turn away if I have to. I know how to hide . . . in the whitish tent of the lady-warmth of her body . . .

The one who got killed was a no-good rowdy, an off-again, on-again drunk—he was a coward—he was a poor flight candidate . . . (A peculiar human substance as a candidate-apprentice to be a fighter pilot.)

Then in silence, in silent gesture: *I worry that I have been damaged in my being a woman by what I know.*

The mechanic stabbed a show-off Swedish guy from North Dakota—*he just hated him—you know how it is?*

Truths emerge in the queer spreading *republic* of death. The skewed mathematics of her logic, her sense of the behavior of aluminum-skinned actual fighter planes—slim fuselages, upright tails, slender, metal wings—she knows which of the planes at the airfield are tricky and are better avoided; her advice is good—is close to being life-and-death.

The twitches of a pilot, his reflexes and the certain oddities of his eyesight, the variety of versions, the variations in his will to live, his carelessness . . . I am, she is, the sister of such matters as that. Her—my—senses are so sharp I feel no man can *feel a thing.* My unworded, exclamatorily captioned thoughts are a *mumbled-jumbled* spirit of me being driven round the bend. Other people make me tired. I am as sourly fragile and as quick as a vixen—I am as powerful, in some ways, as Samson, but I don't want to be trapped, captured, caged, even if only a little bit. I am not really an amateur of consolation; grown to this age, I am a *professional* of consolation. I will be the most famous woman in the world. I know this. I have claws. I represent what-is-bearable. I am an emblem for a man of *what-is-not-bearable.* If I can't stand something or if he can't, he says I can't, and then it is forbidden: I inspire men this way—ha-ha. They save themselves this way. The rhythmical *mumbo-jumbo* (the wit or the rhythms) of my breath marks my sense of humor: I breathe and smile my humor—I don't make jokes . . . I pass judgment—with my liking, my moods: I review everything . . .

And then my inward accompanying semi-comic-and-sad soprano screech at each of my initiations into horror in the stench of the present reality of *animal things* . . . I don't know this other self . . . in me . . .

I am strained here, among the grown-ups . . . Among the grown-ups, I am a seriously pretty girl. I am watched because people want to see what I do, what I do with my life. They want to laugh. And the immensity of the truth of this lies around my thoughts like some entangling thing that sometimes forces me almost to my knees. So much has to be sneered at if I am to be a *pretty* girl that I am overweighted by my having to ignore things.

I have my proud, sly belief that I am stronger than the Devil himself.

If I don't feel that way, I look haggard.

My biographical terror, my conceit, I am who I am, and I am in motion at the corners of my own eyes, running for safety's sake . . . with my terror in my breasts and in my *things*—I have to laugh—the enlarged mouth, the big-eyed pretty face that some people stare at—I dive and twist and run, mad girl among mad boys . . .

And my crazedly aging but still young soul, youthfully instructed, I was an athlete before the war taught me what truth is made of, I have a sense now of being overmatched—of injustice being no joke, you know—*it's-more-than-enough-thank-you-very-much* . . . I am inhabited by scrambling little-footed hens pecking, pecking . . . or by fleas and lice scrambling and ticking away in me—I am so nervous I will die of the nerves . . .

Let it all go to hell; you can all go to hell; I want them all to go to hell . . . My hands flutter: *KINDNESS TO WOMEN, KINDNESS TO WOMEN* . . . I ask for good manners—that's not so much to ask: *I'm just a simple person, I'm a nice girl, I'm sorry, I apologize, but you know what that is, don't you . . . THEY DON'T HAVE ANY MANNERS!* I'm not like my mother . . . I have no real brother . . . I pull a lock of my hair toughly-jauntily and I smile at you, and if I flatter you you will dream about me for nights. I know this. Listen to my breath: look into my eyes: I am alive . . . Jaunty *gentille alouette* . . . Alive, alive-o . . . OH . . . An almost giggly rabbity promptness in me knows it isn't wise to be *always* in trouble—I say I was *always* happy—you know? I don't like people to keep track of every little thing I say . . . I don't like to fight with people . . . I don't like to be fought with . . . I like a rainbow and a smile; I'm like my dad . . .

Damp days ruin my hair. The damp air coagulates into necklaces of opals, my favorite stone . . . motes of prismatic light, prismatic particles, the circular bits of colored light—but what good does it do me if I look like death warmed over . . . In the dark of my bedroom a car's headlights move: myself sweating, myself heavyish below the waist, pinioned by myself down there . . . the tense silence in me is the crumpling and at this moment excruciatingly highly regarded glamour of my youth—as it thickens . . . My luck. Me, myself, and I? Me, my luck, and I. The chief music of my soul . . . I'm not badly off. But I am in steep trouble . . .

Oh, I won't crack up . . . I'm stubborn . . .
I'll crack up over my dead body: I'm not a man . . .

Nonie said that out loud once, seriously . . . And once in a semi-comic, partly serious speech. Bits of dust in the air have colored edges —so do oil slicks on the runways—I do a job. The F.B.I. talks to me twice a month. Men love me . . . often. It makes me giggle when men or women talk about fucking. I am always afraid . . . I am never afraid . . . Who here is bitter? . . . Not I, said the sugar cube . . . Not I, said the lemon. Not I, said the good little pretty girl. I am not greedy and sly . . . I am full of hate but I can't help that. I am not a nice young woman—yes I am. My mother says I am blind and I am giving my life away *stupidly*. Not me, damn her, not me . . . I am as pure as the driven snow . . . It's a joke . . . But I really am. Try to corrupt me: see what happens . . . I'll have your head cut off. I do an A-number-one bang-up job when I set out to do anything. The truth is, around here the psychiatrist has to take a back seat TO ME—I am good with the boys . . . I am *not a whore* . . . War is no blessing . . . I keep my nerve . . . I do my work . . . Men can't boast, but a girl can . . . ha-ha. I'd rather be a girl than a stupid smelly boy with hairy armpits any day. If I have lost my nerve, still I am not a coward. Areas of *sin* . . . cowardice . . . and the flames of nervous heat . . . actual flames . . . people looking on . . .

And personal merit and actual courage, as in dying for someone, a woman—who here is able to tell me about these things? I call on you to speak, silence-in-the-corner-of-the-room, molecular glimmers, the sweetly edged and tiny asteroids (that dust motes are) in the open French doors of my room in the early dawn in midsummer . . . Headlights in my room—decks of playing cards—daisies for me to dismember . . . I call on you, and on the lines of my hand, to tell me about myself . . . My fate . . . My luck . . . I am a woman drowning in silence . . . Listen, kiddo, I am all wool and a yard wide . . . These are not my last words . . . I have secret images in me . . . I keep my own counsel . . . I am the best . . . I do the best of anyone . . . I do the best I can . . . I can be mean: try me . . . I have put the fear of God into a few slackers now and sons of bitches now and then . . . I'm a handful in my time . . . This goddamned airfield is a butcher shop . . . I want to sit on my ass in a sunny place and drink daiquiris . . . I'll manage a while longer but I could use a nice engagement ring and a long rest in a pretty place . . . I know about the graft, I don't take graft . . . I am not intimidated . . . The corrupt guys and senior men threaten me but so what—I have the F.B.I. And Army Intelligence . . . And I have the Warners . . . I pooh-pooh a lot of things . . . I'm not a no one . . . But everything is expensive . . . you know how it is . . . I know my limits . . . I don't know anything and neither does anyone else . . . I don't want to go to hell but I'm not going to take crap from people who are nobodies-shit while I'm young, either . . . Believe me . . . I get even . . . We're all just human beings, we all have to go to bed, we all have to go to the john, we take our pants off one leg at a time . . . Ha-ha . . . Talk to me and you'll hear true things—keep that in mind. I'm a well-known girl, as bright as they make them . . . My name is Puddintame . . . *We move at an insane speed above the ground . . . Paul lets me fly his plane . . . I take the joystick in my hand . . . While we flew, he wanted me* TO TOUCH HIM *. . . I can be persuaded but I know how to say no . . . I hate the shit that's in most books . . . I have a gift for not being a goody-goody* . . . You want to kiss me? Don't: it's my *time* . . . and I smell. It's bad luck to talk ABOUT SOME THINGS . . . Like this . . . LISTEN TO ME, YOU SNOT-NOSED PIECE OF SHIT—oh, did I scare you? I meant to scare you . . . I scared you, did I? Are you all right . . . BUT YOU'RE LISTENING NOW I BET.

See, I'm not helpless.

Sometimes I am. How much more can I stand? My nerves, I'm a big shot around here, I mind my p's and q's. I'm the queen of the air base, I have my own bailiwick, I have a nickname: Old Ironcunt: I don't get sloppy. You know what else I've been told? This: *You're a good girl—that means a lot to us. You are an example for us of a lot that's good in this country. Honey, you're a real sweetheart—I think a lot of the songs are about you.*

I'm as smart as you are . . .

LOVE STORY

Casey and Nonie

In the story I am excluded from, Nonie arrives in Forestville and is met by Aunt Casey, then a tall, rangy, fine-looking woman ("she had good bones") with one of those skating-along, far-off Southern voices—musically noisy, friendly but fairly acid all the time . . . all the same . . . Perhaps sexually aggressive . . .

Casey is not yet old. She strides along the platform. One of the men who works for her will carry Nonie's suitcases. Isobel, Casey's daughter, four years younger than Nonie, is there. No. Omissions improve the text when you don't have good information. Nonie looks terrible. Her heart has been broken; her father's ill; she has undergone an eerie descent in social status. But I saw her before she left—she looked excited, a little sad-eyed, but not much. She wasn't greatly marred.

Aunt Casey's *cold glance*—which was famous in the family, actually—a rich woman's glance . . . Nonie returns her aunt's glance, *innocently*: "Well: you're here—are you all right? Was it a hard train ride?"

The professionalism in each of being a good-looking woman—the skin around their mouths, the quality of their eyes, the discretion of their smiles—the two women greet each other with a suffocating and labyrinthine falsity that yet signals a tentative sincerity and which is not effeminate or awful. The slightly moist feminine tact of their kisses when each woman has her own brand of such tact is like speech—it is as contractually informative.

Aunt and niece . . . Lila has said, *Love comes first in a life* . . .

Porters or Aunt Casey's guy carry the suitcases to a twelve-cylinder 1939 Packard convertible.

Nonie in the close spaces in the car—the guy in the rumble seat; Casey driving—Nonie's fingers on window glass—her face shows the pressure she is under to arouse love. Ah: I feel her unhappiness-happiness—one's own jealousies and abruptness force an ideal notion of the reality of others' lives on us.

(Momma said, *What can I tell you: it is never easy to live in a rich man's house* . . . Momma is kind of the voice of God in domestic literature around here.)

I think that at one time I choked on jealousy of this—not of this, of a more simply imagined thing. The burning in me was like being filled with woodsmoke.

In my exiling Nonie from life and into being a two-dimensional shade (one that lived well) I clearly murdered her.

One finds no traces in one's own life of such a state of affairs as I imagined for her. One edits one's senses and one's mind in regard to her. One's mind is on a chain like a pet in regard to her. (Momma said, *You was always crazy where Nonie was concerned.*)

Nonie's speech to Aunt Casey, "Oh, I'm someone nothing has ever happened to. I'm sad but it's not deep. I wish Momma and Wiley would leave Daddy alone. But my life is fine—there never is, are bad things in *my* life . . . I'm real easy to have around . . ."

Then a glance accompanies her sweet smile with a particular further meaning of innocent affection and the pursuit of Aunt Casey's liking . . .

She says, "Momma drives me crazy . . ."

"Let's think only of cheerful things," Casey says. "You're here now . . . One thing at a time . . ." In the bright sunlight.

Women don't have it easy, Wiley. Neither one of them was a talker . . . Give Nonie credit: she knew how to walk into a house and make the people there feel right at home with her . . .

The suspense in a real life story: a *young girl* is an object of special attention . . . Before I romanticize it, though, I can remember something like that in men directed at boys, that sense of youth, that extraordinary pain of admiration, a thing of being burned by an acid; then the way the scarred person gets even and runs things . . .

I have often been drawn to people who lead homosexual lives—Lila told me that my real mother was homosexual.

I have never been accepted in any part of that other world, however.

Well, did Nonie feel that stuff like something squeezing her? Did it make her laugh? Did she refuse to be *bought*? Was she wooden but okay in the politics of the *carrying on* that would not have been the case if Nonie had been thirty years old? Aunt Casey: What is it like to be expert in *buying* people?

Nonie, a little sweatily, inwardly exaggerating being *happy* or *a little happy* or relieved, is putting on a show: is she being 'clever'? Will it work? Are her feelings those of a conniving 'heroine' in *Vanity Fair*, Thackeray, a book I've read, or of Scarlett O'Hara?

Does she feel she's A MOVIE STAR? Johnno, in college, said of a woman star, an ingenue: *She doesn't live in a book, she lives in Hollywood, which is Heaven-on-earth, U.S.A.*

A heroine and movie star, a victim—Mom said, *Nonie had nerves—her nerves gave out* . . . Nonie, this young woman of circumstance—with bitten fingernails and a quite astonishing prettiness and a bold if troubled spirit and a certain obduracy of heart . . . this young woman outside my range of vision . . .

I'm her mother, Lila said, *but if I do say so myself, Nonie has her days when the sight of her would melt a heart of stone* . . .

The singular quality of her courage gives off a whiff of perfume, a whirr as of a sunny day; the proximity of courage in someone, its motions and its heat, are heartening. The womanly *flavor* in her physically of an excellent coolness under stress—for a while—and the bedrock directness of her purposes impart to her smiles and to the movements of her eyebrows a dictionarylike quality of no-mystery. Cousin Isobel imitated Nonie in this—the terribly pretty girl with bitten fingernails offering no-mystery as a quality of romance atop her perhaps monumental sort of darkness of spirit.

And the much, much older woman: they love for a while . . . Well, why not? Why hasn't this been written about more? These casually found loves, the codified festivity and unmasculinity of them? Silence. Silence. I don't trust confessions. Or hope. No one human can *properly* judge anything—one judges legally or personally, that's all. If you rescue Nonie, it is Nonie you rescue.

Did Nonie long to be loved best? Perhaps love has very little difference in how it exists, person to person, type by type of feeling, circumstance by circumstance; but I would doubt it.

How then do you find the will to generalize honestly about someone else's unobserved life? Casey that year and Nonie in that year of Nonie's life, was it *good luck* in all or part for both of them? Lila said, *It was good luck for both of them*, and then in contradiction, *I got even with both of them by sending Nonie off to Forestville that time* . . . It might be either thing, both things. Had Nonie longed for years in her spirit for such a festivity with a woman not Lila? Had she had such a thing with an aunt, with a grandmother? Was this a further step toward a codified pleasure?

They liked each other . . . Casey is not my cup of tea . . . But I have to be obliged to her: that was certainly a load off my mind she took on her own two shoulders . . . Everything was all lovey-dovey between the two of them . . .

Love as lawless and as new law for two such disparate women—such oddity in a new flood of feelings, new arrangements: someone else is important now—it is a flood of relief after all. I am guessing, of course.

I imagine boredom eased; and personal power having the leverage, the fulcrum and platform of the exercise of feeling and of gratitude toward life . . .

Love, love, love . . . Happiness? Was it happiness? Nonie's self-conscious gestures before she had her new command of irony—was she a girl who had seen too much?

Had she seen too little?

Her vulnerability, her availability: she smoked, she chattered—in her office voice?

I imagine a tense, softened, musical, very personal voice that I never heard her use. Or heard without remembering or perhaps even noticing it—is the moment like a test she can pass?

Nonie can always run away with some guy if Casey gets her down; I'm not worried about Nonie, believe me . . .

I am sure that Nonie did *love* Casey—I saw it in her in later years; she *loved* her, no one as much, perhaps not even her children—or, at least, if I was there to see.

I don't know what was included in that love. Were they *evenly matched*? Did Nonie eat Aunt Casey up? *Casey was a selfish bitch but fascinating as a woman—do you know* . . . The classless availability: *She's not weighed down with what you'd call a whole lot of culture and brains* . . . The discretion of a photograph, sepia, from the 1920s, how pretty Casey is, how rigorous in posture, how separate from everyone else . . .

A still photograph without the melodrama of real moments in it.

In an unphotographed, unreal moment, Nonie's aunt rests her hand on Nonie's back while Nonie leans forward in the Packard to use the cigarette lighter in the wooden dashboard. The touch was welcoming and virtuous and had no hint in it whatsoever of any further meaning except that, of course, in reality, as a real touch, it hinted at things and was real and was not like anything in a movie or in a novel or in any book. Issues are focussed in the faint trembling of Casey's hand . . .

If you are sensitive, Wiley, a touch can be enough for you on some days—a touch can change your life . . .

And so on.

Nonie and Casey

I can imagine Casey saying to Nonie, *No news is good news,* and Nonie responding, in a triumphant and happily not witty way, *No news is no news.*

Nonie sits up straighter and turns her face to her aunt, her face, *Love* with a certain explanatory heat of attention on it—chastity and romance, a physically sensitive caution with the flavor of inclination in it, the delight, the delight and the deliciousness of unfailed *love*—the fastidious pornography of a sort in it . . .

And the two women, Casey and Nonie, having piercing moments of comprehension, secret from everyone else . . .

Such comprehension, and something else too, incomprehension or doubt can be revised by a kiss . . . or can go unrevised punitively . . . Or the teasing absence of kisses can enliven as well as darken a day.

Here we have the flutter of an eyelid. And the meaning of the flutter . . . companionable affection . . . yesses spread over minutes and contingent . . . both earnest and teasing, appalled and on occasion desperate, a little grovelling, at times they are menacing . . . The creation of a state of affairs, an affair, or merely a closeness, a thing of being *a favorite* . . . I only know Nonie from when she was in front of me.

Nonie said of herself and Casey: "We know how to laugh, we laugh and laugh, we laugh together, we're just like twins . . ."

A pair of talkative clowns? Comediennes? *I was never bored in Forestville,* Nonie said—a laugh like the flickering of muscles behind the hide of an animal? "We had a real good time." If she had been so happy, why didn't she love *me* for a while?

Lila said, *They drove each other crazy, if you ask me . . .*

But also: *I have to hand it to Casey, she always had the last laugh over me . . . She got the best there was in Nonie—I don't know why her daughter Isobel wasn't enough for her . . . Maybe it was me . . . Maybe Casey just wanted to show me up . . . Casey was very worldly—the first day Nonie was there, Casey took her shopping . . . Casey used to keep seventy-five thousand dollars in cash in her bank accounts . . .*

That was for emergencies . . . And to go shopping on the spur of the moment—for excitement in that one-horse burg . . . Casey was a good shopper for a woman from a little town . . . She'd shopped all over the country . . . She knew her way around and she knew how to settle for things, she was a very, very practical person—that's the highest sort of person there is—if you ask me . . .

One of them smiles at the other. Or blows a kiss.

"I'd give that skirt an A plus . . ."

Or: "Well, cashmere was never the main thing in my life . . ."

Or: "I'm too old for cheap cotton."

And the light savor of *confessions*: "I hate red . . ."

And advice: "What's your view on black? In wartime?"

"I don't think it's nice. What do you think?"

And the *passionate* comparisons: "I have ugly legs—you have *perfect* legs . . ."

And: "You are perfect . . . Your hair is just perfect."

The *touch* of each other's eyes in a glance and fingertips touching in the drama now of handling things, handing them to each other. The thing of straightening the back of a crooked blouse. The *intelligence* at work in each story-riddled moment is at *best-seller level* . . . in terms of romance.

Nonie smoking in a section of a department store devoted to chic clothes (by local standards) and the salesgirl coming near and Nonie lying to her about a burn mark in the sleeve of a dress—the way one tells a lie, one's style of lying, marks one's degree of intelligence in the real world—and the judgments and corrections of each other being *placed on hold* and the terms of derision and of melancholy toward shopping, toward people who don't know the shibboleths: "Black and white socks, they're just too-too . . ." And: "I can't wear rayon . . . But I love those shiny, awful pinks . . ." And: "I'm getting tired . . . Let's take a break . . ."

"I smoke too much—you got the Sen-sen?"

A store called Roth's, a purple dress, and Casey says brusquely, "They trampled out the purple grapes of Roth . . . I got that joke from Emma-Jean . . . It's such an old joke, she must keep it in mothballs . . . Ha-ha . . ."

Perhaps Nonie says, "Ha-ha, everyone knows moths don't have balls . . ."

Nonie says, "Oh don't make me laugh, I'm trying to zip up . . . I love this blue . . . I wish I had the color skin to wear blue under electric light . . . Maybe if I lighten my hair . . ."

"Oh, don't do that—you have perfect hair . . . Mine is too wavy; I love fine hair like yours . . . I love YOUR hair . . ."

Style is fate. Sometimes . . .

Headaches . . . Changes of mind . . . *If you have a mind . . . But you don't have a mind . . .*

Nonie says to Casey, "I wish I had your body."

Casey said, dryly, in her high little voice, "Oh I'm old . . ."

"I'll trade for it as is . . . ha-ha . . ."

Casey, nearing fifty, feels a certain charity toward herself . . . Nonie, heavy-rumped and tremendously pretty, feels her way along in the dark . . .

The colors of the era, and the women's lipsticked lips; if black and white are the colors of most dreams, then this stuff is not *dreamlike* . . . The olive drabs, the simple blues of wartime.

"This is so nice . . . You're being so nice to me . . . I'm having a real good time . . . I'm probably making a fool of myself, I like everything so much . . . The decor here is so nice. I don't usually like to shop . . . It's superficial . . ."

Momma said, *Life is more work than you can ever imagine . . . People earn what they get—in the long run . . .*

"Now you need a bathing suit—and a sweater . . ." Casey says in *her* bossy way . . .

Nonie had her poetry . . . and her *prettiness* . . . "It's paradise here . . ."

The adverbs of flirtation—the diluted or distilled terms and aura of permissiveness . . . Or of restraint . . .

I imagine Casey saying to Nonie about a low-cut dress Nonie is looking at, "People around here wear more extreme things when they finally do get around to dressing up . . . You look like a dream in that . . ."

Shopping is at the edge of hallucination anyway.

Nonie told me that Casey liked tight clothes for herself even at her age . . . *And she looks good in them, too.*

Capricious meanness, as a savory thing, almost a *toy* meanness: "I hate this dress . . . I hate this red . . ."

And: "How many mirrors do you suppose are in this store? You ever count all the mirrors?"

"You're buying me too much . . . Don't throw your money a-way—"

"I want to give you this belt: I like patent leather . . ." A smile. "I'm not throwing my money away . . ."

The face, the *eyes*, the breath of *sensitive* gratitude . . .

"You look so nice in that sweater . . . Sweetheart."

Then later at the house, someone says of them: "It's a conspiracy of you two against the rest of us . . ."

Is the honeymoon over? Do they get the prize?

Nonie said to me, "Dad and Casey and me, we're nicer than other people . . ." But then: "We spend half our time laughing at people . . ."

(Lila told me my real mother had been *very funny—she did imitations—I hate to tell you but she could be very mean, you could die laughing, the mean imitations she could do of people* . . .)

I imagine Nonie saying to Casey, "Well, I don't count my chickens—you never know what's really going to happen . . . I keep a trick or two up my sleeve. I'm a Boy Scout . . ."

Certain kinds of *love* are the consolation of ambition, others are ambition. Some are ambitious make-believe and yet are sweet, but think of the ambition then.

How much courage does it take? To be unlike me?

Is there no justice in love? Is there some justice in love?

In the serious *stink* of life, in the serious stench of real events, a half-known story with a hint to it of the breath of love's madness, well, no dream can instruct you in such a thing . . . No dream or act of the imagination can have actual breath in it, or actual death, or even a small part of the reality of love . . .

Love Story

Momma said, *Travelling broadens people . . . You have to learn to understand people and it helps to do it in a new place. Of course, no one ever learns enough . . . What do you ever* understand*?*

I hear her being *truthful*—inspired—a woman of *God-given* intelligence—revelatory in her analyses, and accurate and just in her anathemas, a daydream perhaps but an actual style . . . a style she uses maybe especially when she talks about love . . .

Her style then is that she is hardworking . . . a genius . . . experienced . . . An element, always, in the claim of knowledge, is that a daydream has come true for the speaker—this is an actual style a number of women use and some men. It is not universal.

She said, in a version of that style when she was dying and I was a sophomore at Harvard called to her deathbed: this was when I was eighteen: "You always was a good listener—are you that sort still? Are you that sort of sweetheart still?"

I had been told she would die within twenty-four hours and I took a night flight across the country and then a taxi and I got to her bedside at three in the morning. She was asleep or barely; but she woke and began to talk; she talked and slept for nearly three days—talking to me the whole time.

The doctor said, a little dryly, that it was a miracle.

Lila told me stories, she monologued, correcting the past, emending old statements, old tactics. She did it somewhat nervously, ignoring whoever it was that I was then in her room, the guy I had become—not my presence; she flattered that and was aware of it to a terrible degree.

But she addressed my odd presence scattered over a number of years and present to her now in the form of an older adolescent, eighteen, who was chiefly a compendium of memories similar to hers—that wasn't true, of course. It affected her in a certain way, that matter of my present-tense presence and the distance between it and her sense of me in multiple moments in the past, down to me ill and diapered and nuts when I was adopted. The stranger there now in her hospital room was tied to her through mental stuff (and various mysteries) and to stuff that was in her head, in her spirit; and, I suppose, in her body, too, although we were really only cousins and not mother and son; but the years we'd spent together had become a mental blood with certain attributes and had become physical knowledge like and unlike the inherited sort.

It's funny about love—and about people who want to talk about it with you—I mean it shows a certain liking to start with. She had left me what money she had in her will, but Nonie had gotten hold of a copy of the will, or Lila had teased her, and Nonie had been upset and Lila had backed down and left me two-thirds of her estate: her estate was too little to matter all that much—*But Nonie says money is money and she has a point*—but she apologized and she said she would like me to know *the truth* about some things to make up for the lost money.

When she woke up at three while I was sitting there, arms folded and trying to breathe in Los Angeles after the weird propeller-aircraft flight, she said, "Wiley, is that you? Have you come? I want to tell you some things."

Some things? What things? Save your voice. Let's just sit.

"No, I want to talk to you . . . This is a legacy: don't be a fool. . . . A legacy is a good thing: listen, one thing I'll say for myself is I never was a liar . . . Everyone else in the family lied, you know that? People always lie. Lie, lie, lie . . . What else is new?" Then, all at once: "You blame yourself too much . . . Casey and Nonie was sweet on one another."

At first I had no idea what she meant. I had forgotten the Warners as any sort of frequent memory and my early adolescence, Nonie's life, the whole thing. The idea of it, even the aura of it, wasn't close enough to the surface of my mind for the memory of those days to be present as important to me.

But then, all at once, I remembered. I remembered, too, that I had sort of known or guessed some such thing—but vaguely.

"Your mother had someone like that, too . . . Casey had an old sweetheart from childhood: they always stuck together—Casey couldn't've lived in that small town otherwise . . . And kept her wits . . ." Casey and Emma-Jean Marie . . . At best I only half woke to what Lila was telling me: the reality of it that she hinted at: the real moments of the women. I had no opinions, no overall view, no interest in the subject that I knew of—yet, when she spoke, after a time lag of a second or two, first the memory but sort of akimbo and askew and then my sense of the past as partly hidden from me and of my not being old enough to deal with it, turned into interest, screwy, collegiate: I didn't want to be a fool anymore. Still, I cannot begin to tell you how strange the sentences with their riders and enclosures of information were to me, how blank they seemed, and then as if blankness were dehiscent in some mind garden, the blankness split open and was vague with not quite credible scenes: puzzling me: how would Momma know these things? What forms of knowledge would lead to such information being *fact*? A good deal, a great deal of my sense of someone's meaning when they talk consists of their purposes—toward themselves, toward you, toward the subject—starting usually with what they intend toward *me*. I can't know everything that is intended; a topographical oddity intervenes: a hill is between us; she is disguised by her existence, the difference between us of when we lived.

But one can see a trajectory. And the trajectory can be simple—with sincerity or with pain—but, usually, it is at least triple in intention—toward the past and toward me now and toward the future: Lila wanted to impress me—or she wanted to impress what she thought was mind-at-Harvard . . . Or what she thought a boy's collegiate mind was: the present tense is awfully sexual—is so inescapably. My looks, such as they were, hadn't vanished entirely; and some other people did what she was doing—a few. But it is hardly ever a simple matter, or not ever, being talked to. Here, in a hospital room in L.A., in a Catholic hospital, what I was aware of first, with a kind of male-finicky bridling, hidden, I hoped, from her (you know about tact at deathbeds?), was that she meant to affect what I thought about women, what I knew, and that this would go on long after she was dead . . . The seeds, eggs—bits of her talk . . . in me, deposited now and with a deathbed weight. She meant to color my attitude toward Nonie. And toward Casey, who would live on after Momma for nearly thirty years more, and whom Nonie would all her life be fonder of and more admiring toward in a profound way and closer to in her thoughts than she was to Momma. Or to the thought of her. Momma meant to help me. She pushed other women aside—ones that she knew about. She was telling me that she was alone—orphaned, too, Momma was, that she was like me—she was saying that since the world was what it was, I was okay. By comparison.

At least now. Now that I was in college. At Harvard.

She was saying as well, by implication and tacitly, that she and Nonie had cared so much about each other, that she and Nonie had talked, had hinted and spied, that she, Momma, had cared so much that she had pried and poked and thought about things a lot and knew-what-she-knew—and Nonie had wanted her to know, had wanted her to find out these things . . . Or to think them. Had wanted it off and on, changeably.

But a spy system, her having ways of finding out things and of seeing things and of deciding *what was going on*, I mean how could Mom have done that, how could Lila have *known* any of this stuff if she hadn't loved the others—and the *awful truth* about them, too?

I think the fact began with knowledge among some people that this stuff was engaged in, known, talked about, and was a fact in a certain ordinary, social sense, not in a school sense, however.

Perhaps, too, Mom meant that Nonie—and my real mother—had talked to her in sensible ways, partly divulging this and that, partly teasing her, lording it over her, getting even, or pursuing her—and she had kept track.

She had loved this stuff and them enough to study them—and they had been interested in her—not in the way Daniel had been interested-in-me—but in some other way.

Was she bitter and editorial—and vicious?

"When they were downtown shopping, they would duck into ladies' rooms to kiss . . . They was romantic—but they was careful . . ." In her voice hoarse with drugs and death, in her face, worn and pretty, exhausted, were signs of mood: a forgiving and yet remorseless bitterness and then the staled beneficence of her inclusion with them widening, shocking to include further her half-betrayal of them now, so late in her life, with me.

But then it was hard to picture Nonie and Casey together in a story without forgetting Mom—it was risqué of Ma to interpose the imagery of such a story on herself dying.

Were the two women in Forestville stringently romantic? Doctrinaire in their affections and in their acts? Was it *half-a-joke* to Nonie—an ironic do-jigger to Casey? A toy thing? Did Momma make it up? Did she piece it together later?

Did they each have a humor, Caseyan, Nonie-esque—a sense of humor, they would call it—in their various defiant, lawless, pretty (and unpretty) banditries, degrees of personal and seductive force—or did they mislead people, partly idly?

Do secrets actually have power—over particles of the mind and of the eyes, a form of no-light or of watery refraction or a blur of only half shape, a queer definition of reality?

My real mother—well, Lila told me a confused story—*tact* restrained *her*, the second mother: so did my *shyness*, if I can call it that —something restrained my responses and constrained my hearing—was Lila right, did I hear correctly, did my real mother, tall, Indian squaw-faced *Ceil* have *a tortured love* for a "pretty-maid-of-hers, she led her a real song and dance, that maid was an awful woman, it went on for years between the two of them . . ." Did it? Lila liked to impute murder to women—she was sure Aunt Henrietta had yelled at Uncle Henry when he had a heart attack and saw to it that he died. She often, or off and on, believed herself about Nonie and the infant princes in the tower. She said her own mother had bullied her older sister and caused her death—caused her to get cancer. She almost always suspected women of having infinite will. She said of *the pretty maid*: "She was jealous of you, and she helped bring on your mother's death—believe me, you don't know what jealousy can do . . ." Perhaps I don't. A dozen years after Lila's death—I was a better listener and observer then—when all my parents were dead, I came back from a stay in England and I went to see the small town where my mother had lived at the end of her life, not knowing she had so small a part of her lifetime left, and where she died—where she lived in the last eight years of her life and died and where I had been born. Driving in a white Chevrolet around the streets of the place, I found I thought I remembered one house in particular. An oldish woman on the street, when I asked her if I could talk to her, said, "Are you from around here? Are you Aaron Weintrub?" She told me where the maid lived; she lived still; it was the house I remembered. The house where I was born I had driven past without recognizing—I recognized it only from its side yard. It is strange how, when objects from the past are actually present, memory doesn't seem to be inside you but to be outside in the air . . . *The place speaks to me*: I had a friend who spoke that way . . . I recognized things from my infancy; the problem of scale and of later experiences tugged at me—I mean, the fact that I knew the wrong things.

I said, *I can't remember*, and then, I saw at the boundary of my failure the mental thing, the thing of impulse and will, of steeping oneself in boundarylessness; and then I did remember—my mother's smell, her clothes, her *bust*, her breasts . . . I remembered the quality of life in her: she had a lover, an interest of that sort—and me: she had me . . . *You were easy for her; you didn't torment her* . . . The ebb and flow of the tension of actual presences—the absence of *emptiness* . . . In that other house, the maid lived still—such faithfulness, really. In the first instant when she came to the door, I—no, she—no: In the first instant when she came to the door, I saw someone *méchant*, terribly pretty still, as an old woman—as pretty as a movie star in a dark-mooded soubrette way: I knew how much was possible with her, for her.

Her husband was as handsome in old age as she was pretty but he was simple and kind-smiled and yet he looked murderous to me, too. People do, well, *odd* things to each other. I said to the woman, "This is going to be very strange." She said, "Aaron?" in an Austrian peasant mountain accent, Tyrolese I think. "I knew you'd come to see me," and she opened the door wide and tried to look naïve and bland, and perhaps she succeeded, who knows: I saw a very dark-souled woman racked and a bit scared and resigned, awful, mirthless, flirtatious, and defiant.

All the while I was with her, she called me by my old name—the one I had first. She described my mother's death in such falsity of detail, let alone in tone, and while touching me and smiling with her truly amazing ancient prettiness, and staring out of movie-star eyes in a puzzled, pretty, scary way; and then this mountain-peasant with no limits in her at all (I felt) gave me a few sideways glances as she lied, glances of such wicked shame and apology, such chagrinned, long-enduring *naughtiness*, that I became ill, *knowing* in an illicit way, unproven, what the truth was.

In the middle of lying she paused and said, with that sly, charming, shameless, chagrinned nightmare look of aged, stained, stale, inflexible naughtiness: "I knew you'd come talk to me someday . . ."

Love. And the things a woman thinks. Lila said on her deathbed, "Was it all right and proper? Was it just talk? I never asked; I never had the nerve to ask: I didn't want to know the truth about them . . ." Casey. Nonie. My mother. Her maid. "Once your mother was ill, Max would never let that other woman near you . . ."

"He knew?"

"You never know with a man like Max—someone could tell him to teach your mother a thing or two: she was a cold, proud woman, very successful—and in the Depression too. Your mother was a scary woman . . . She was smart but in a lot of ways she wasn't too sensible. She'd say what she felt like saying to anyone—she was no cream puff, let me tell you . . . not even by comparison to a mean man . . . A tiger—tigers: they was . . . those women . . . I couldn't've lived in that town." But her tone was that she, Lila, was in luck, talking to the callow boy, tall and recently masculinely silent—Harvard-trained—male—having adopted a long-legged version of that manner most of the time.

I had hoped the maid would have *loved* or enjoyed my mother—or me as an infant—and would reminisce.

But what I felt was the presence of *murder* and of foulness and of passion and thousands on thousands of phony absolutions—Catholic confession, but it hadn't taken in her; she came from a part of the world where people feuded for generations.

Just as in Lila I felt something unmurderous at the end.

But it is a *feeling*.

Lila said, "Both your mothers died young, Pisher . . . You have no luck . . . Watch out for women . . . I tell you, nothing they did, none of it was disgusting to *me*. A woman has a right to love someone who loves back. A different hell isn't always such hell, you know. I hope you're sensible. I'll tell you something, I'll tell you a lot, I'll tell you everything I can if my strength holds out: I don't know about you; but a woman can never tell a man what he doesn't want to hear—he hasn't the ears for it; he can't make hide nor hair of it; and words don't always come when you want to talk to a woman—not everything brings out words in people, Wiley . . . I talk to you but I've been talking to you in my mind for weeks now . . . The ghost of your mother told me to tell you everything. When I was young, I wanted to try anything . . . I wanted to be everyone and get a taste of what they were like for *them* but I got used to being me . . . And I don't want to be anyone else even now; I'd as soon die as not be me. I don't mind dying; I'm used to the idea. But I don't want to be anyone else . . . I don't want to be sent someplace I don't want to go—I don't want to be treated like a wife, Wiley . . . WHO I loved I loved. Wiley. That was how I did things . . . that was how I measured things . . . Are you small-minded? Or can you live in a world where things is the way they are? I don't say it's easy. I don't want to do it again and I don't want to do it over . . . But I don't mind that I did it once and that it came out the way it did. That took some doing—but I did it—and I don't mind telling you I don't care who knows it I'm proud of myself for coming out with a head on my shoulders . . . And no ill feelings for one and all . . ."

The unstill particles and restless waves were mostly already stilled for her or were quieting into a painted surface of memory and summation that she had a certain use for, part of an intention: Lila said, "I've been saving up things to talk to you about. I have the nerve still to say anything . . ." As a form of friendliness, of a friendly laugh, she almost laughed hoarsely. "I'll tell you how I feel sometimes: I see someone, I like them, and it's the straw that breaks the camel's back: I go head over heels for a while: you think I'm funny? I don't always think it's so smart but what are you going to do? Dry up like a prune? I always liked to have an iron or two on the fire—don't blame me, Wiley—I did everything wrong and I'm paying for it but I'm tired of thinking of things that way—look: you're still around; you're the cat's meow, if you ask me. Well, now I'm on your side—I get some credit for how things turned out no matter how many mistakes I made—you do me credit, Pisher, and I want to talk to you as if you was really my son, really my daughter maybe: you think that's funny? You think I'm funny? You think it's all funny business? Well, I don't know what I think—I don't know that I think that's funny . . . I like to think about things; I like to see what happens when you put your bet on a horse—money always came second to me: laugh if you want: I'm not sensitive anymore: so, listen, I never had a harsh thought about some things—oh you think that's funny? You're not very grown-up; Harvard's not teaching you much. You never knew what I was really thinking," she said outraged. "I put on a damned good show as a mother—some of the time . . . When you remember me, will you be silly? I want you to remember I was always funny and not so easy to read, personal that way . . . A serious person. Where was I? Oh yes. I remember. Money was never enough for me—it never is for anyone, Wiley, remember that—I want you to know I had a good time, first, last, and always. I never had to be jealous of everything—of course, I was a terror; I had my self-respect: it was an experiment. I didn't starve . . . This isn't something you talk about to your children but I was always interested in love. I was really something—I liked it even when it happened to other people. Daniel paid for S.L.'s funeral: money didn't come second with him—I knew he cared: he was in deep; he could be relied upon; he was always someone who was serious . . . You would want for nothing and how foolish you are wouldn't show. Maybe that's what a smart mother *should* do—stand aside and make sure her child wants for nothing and is protected. I'm smart, Wiley, but I'll tell you something: I never liked to read in my whole life—you want to laugh? You want a joke? Reading used to give me gas . . . I'm not joking . . . I hated it, I hated it, it made me sick, I had to do my thinking for myself . . . Well, Daniel read as much as you did. He *liked* books. Who wouldn't want to see a child safe? Maybe I can't say all I want to say? Maybe I'm not confessing the right things—how should *I* know? Emily Post wasn't here to advise me . . . Well, live and learn . . . Daniel shamed me for the way I was with you—you always was too soft—I never liked him—he had to have the upper hand; that kind never comes to no good. He had the upper hand with me, I'll tell you—I always hated what people did with money: they got no imagination but they sure manage to have their way sometimes . . . They have imagination in that . . . I hate meanness . . . I like people who give in now and then . . . I didn't want to let you go—I thought you were cute at last . . . You was the one I wanted to talk to: I wanted to get to know you—that's one of my secrets. You was the only one I could talk to. But I let go. Maybe he wasn't so nice, you came back in two months," Momma said hoarsely. "But I let you go and I never got you back—you never really came back to me: did you know that? You were standoffish . . . Do you remember? Did the summer go so bad you blamed me? I think you got conceited: admit it: you was scared of yourself . . . Well, listen, Pisher, I let you learn too much, I always did, and I was too rough: listen to me, Pisher, I want to say I'm sorry . . . I am sorry and I'm scared now . . . I know I often was too shameless with you—the ghost of your mother comes here and scares me, Wiley; Pisher, Pisher, I'm sorry—come hell or high water, I'm sorry—I wasn't a good mother . . .

"But I was the only mother you had—no one tried but me . . ."

The cold audacity back then of formally acknowledged mystification in me at Mom's quasi-formal deathbed narratives, confessions, and the like—a distance between me and the stories, a disbelief—drew her attention: "Oh, you're a handful—you're going to pretend you don't know what it's like to be the favorite son? You don't know what Nonie did to get out of the shade? You going to pretend no one chased you? We all took turns hating you, Pisherkins . . . Tell me, Wiley, how much of a child are you still?"

"I don't know," I said, smiling like a Harvard man—a pale, genteel, humble superiority . . .

"I have a lot to say I'm sorry for but if you're not going to pay attention, I'm not going to do it . . . I like to be appreciated, Wiley . . . I don't do these things just for my health. I'll say it all to you, as much as I can: you can understand it later, when you're older—if you ever get to be sensible. A lot of the time you was the one we fought over: people cared about who you loved best. We wanted to see who it was. Then we didn't want to know."

A listener's inattention: the mind wanders among the puzzles; minds wander: it is what minds do. In real life, you surreptitiously and *politely* scratch your ear while a riddle opens. At times, my parents had been affectionate. If the self-conscious ambiguity of a riddle eats you, if it eats the sense of time in you, then you can experiment in the puzzled dark in which time is obscure to you and in which your mother was always kind and your father had only the character of *father* . . . You can fool around with time . . . I mean lie about it with answers, riddle-ridden: the whizzing spaceship light-beam eye—with its slanted feet like real light—and the flutter of that other time in which one breathes and will die while one pretends time has these other measurements in it, dimensions of mystification, diaphanous and purportedly instructive—the two of them define how compound one's awareness is because one's awareness exists in time and only in time. *The truth is* . . . The *other* time of one's wandering attention mixes and jumbles and wads things and gets mixed up about things that Lila said: it skates right past comprehension—this glorification of the ghostly mind—and scants the body. The mind has no true body—it plays Nonie to the body.

But I believe in the mind, Momma.

Momma, dying, was not Momma so much as some sort of last chapter of Momma, or, rather, of a voice doing a certain sort of something purposeful—purposeful, semi-maternal.

Human at the last minute—as in other minutes.

"Momma!"

"Let me catch my breath—I need a little shut-eye . . ."

I waited out the dying woman's drug doze.

If you have no future, or not much; if time is merely two-sided and is fading as an element of things, what then? Lila tried to tell me about life—at the last minute—about one of the important factors: the ways in which women, some women, care for women. Favoritisms, loyalties—kisses in nightgowns, souls in bodies in pajamas and nightgowns, bedtime cocoa . . . Brief lunatic caresses . . . excitable and loony narratives and *secrets* . . . The secrets go from soul to soul like flung red ants that bite or cockroaches that make you scream—and perhaps laugh: OH NO, NO, NO—UHHH . . . OH, I'M GOING TO DIE . . .

Sitting in her hospital room, I supposed her first impulse was to be the one truly heterosexual woman I'd known in childhood—the only one who preferred men—the one who was the fairest one of all, the fairest to me . . . In a way. Some women sometimes adopt a solitarily heroic aspect of that for themselves in order to be loved best. I don't know. She meant to shock—and to be important; she'd told me of a world in which I would never be important and in which she was important.

She'd said once, "Get a woman—find a smart woman who can fight—only a woman can defend you from women, Wiley . . ."

She meant to explain and warn, to warn and entertain, to entertain and instruct. It is very odd how people assume those two are *mild* things. Momma meant to rend and affect and to alter the structures of the mind—entertainingly . . . She meant to be remembered—to have earned her way. She was a fatal, mortal Scheherazade, a Morgan Le What's-it, *fatale* to the end—innocent by virtue of death, virtuous chiefly as a come-on—how startling she was for me. And how purposefully *dense* and out-of-reach of her I'd been for years—a defense. I purposefully missed the point of her after my fourteenth year.

She meant to tell me certain truths, she meant to do that as a gift on her deathbed, to matter strenuously and rigorously right up to the end. I had pretty much always (often) said I wanted to know *the truth*. And I had minded the puzzles, the puzzling elements, of the incomplete stories I had been told.

She had forgotten my ability to evade her and to draw her interest then. It was like Rogers and Astaire, but Rogers is chasing me; and she is also whirling around on her own, divulging *secrets right and left*.

"Men are no good," she said. "Women want their own way." I'd read that in Chaucer, I said. (In a lot of ways, of course, I'd *always* known it—since before birth although I hadn't known the enclosing shell was barn-and-oceanic woman.) She gazed at me. I hadn't used her liking for me as a premise for understanding something in a long time. Souls dream: lives shift. One pretends but one knows that the realest knowledge is of motions observed. Momma is dying and is telling me things and she is listening to her own stories—not to me, of course. It was always secret that *she* ever listened to me. What she believes is true has changed and is changed further by the words she uses now; she struggles with the mechanics of speech, with linguistics, in the partly ashen, hard-breathed, and bedraggled moments. She is affected by the accidents of her own speech which become the half-accidents of her thoughts surprising her among the knowledges that have come to her while she is dying. The formal geometry of her usual constraint is twisted by life and by death now; and how she came to know the stuff and what I look like to her now (like a horse, the character and all, or like it's-going-to-rain, to bring that up again) and what I act like now (a general principle, sort of, of that) and the accidents of pulse rate and of the idioms and associations in her head—and of her showing off to me—and to herself: it seems to be a different part of her life, a different category of life, a far-out order of *life-at-the-last-minute* . . .

It is true that she is uplifted in a low-down way: "I said a lot of things, too, in my time," she said, "to a lot of people; and I'm sorrier than the chow, sir . . ." She'd misheard and thought it was a dining-hall joke. Or I misheard her now—it was hard for her to talk. Or she is making a dumb joke in a locally Midwestern way although we are in

California, a joke for a boy from the Midwest. The peculiar sense of assured fact for her means that in reality she cannot be for me now an omniscient narrator. Or for her, either. My belief in (part of) what she says falls back into quoting her to myself . . . Absorbing some of what she says . . . The facts for her being these at the moment, the ones in the room—and her and me—me so changed and her dying now—the chief fact being that she is *talking* to me, not quite a real me, but one present to her; and her feeling of rivalry with Chaucer and her sense of death and her rivalry with other women and even with what she will not know, with what will happen for me after she dies, and further and further—she is aware of this maybe unbelievingly or achingly or rackingly—I think she is working inside a rivalry with my sort of (Harvard) truth, her own usefulness, with this form of *pride* . . . She doesn't quite feel *defeat* approaching . . . I am impressed and I can see why I liked her best a lot of the time when I was young; I am moved by the seemingly palpable sense of *truth*—actually, fronds and leaves of a lot of different sorts of truth; but none of it is stuff I can accept as *omniscience* . . . Truth, sure, truth-and-error, and she is *dying* . . . If no blazing chariot is in the room and no mystic light, then the truth, yes, without omniscience, her wanting to be right, more right than me, her wanting to know something I could not *know*, her wanting to be right to such an extent at the end. Truth, yes, but still not *omniscience*. But better than I could do. I doubted that hers was the form of pride that was forbidden, but if it was, I didn't care. I believed her and I disbelieved part but I was proud of her for dying with so much verve—and in a way so much unlike the ways in which, in his last days, S.L., refusing to talk, and to forgive or to accept death, life, the living, the dead, had been kind of epic and darkly satiric and a silent and maybe lying or swindling or self-convinced know-it-all. I didn't love him less now or her more, either, not at all; but I preferred her and the way she did things—this was disconcerting. Also, she wasn't so old she had abandoned the issues and realities of gender—that seemed strange to me—but true, on her part . . . I was kind of shattered but I meant to dance with her up to the edge of the grave if she wanted—to be polite in that way, to that extent, at the end.

The thinking and remembering she has done is sifted and *purified* now by one of her purposes, to treat me as her own flesh-and-blood, that is a point of the exercise—one of the points of the exercise. All the times she has thought of this stuff and of telling me, the thinking and remembering—and the decision to speak—the way it leaves me out, doesn't leave me out: it includes her sense of me which includes her sense that if I talk all this will be wrecked; but my listening is a form of talk; she talks for me, as when I was mute; she steals my speech—but for the sake of doing-good-at-last—her thoughts having occurred over a period of time: the ways I am left out: this tempers the story she tells. Outer time in its unending consequentiality and inner time in its inconsecutive, snotty willfulness (and dictatorial and aestheticized jumble) have brought her to a point of clarity and truth (and last-minute verve in speech) in which things are almost as clear to her at last as laundry of various sizes that she is straightening which the maid or the laundress arranged foolishly, not having Momma's brains, at least as far as Momma is concerned. But this is, as I said, *truth*, and not omniscience. Truth, at last, death being here. Things from a drawer—as in clearing out a desk at the end, things she is putting in stacks, not in a carton, but in me; she will bring order—to the mind, to one's sense of an often cruel past. But I have romanticized the past and made it as ordinary as Nonie did: I don't want to be bothered by it. Or with a sense of reality derived from it. So, some of her storytelling is really quite strange in the moment because of truth and death and my attitude, maybe scared, maybe reasonable, maybe half-cold, that everything was fine in me now in regard to the past—childhood had been Eden. Some of it is strange because of aesthetic and intellectual differences between us that she has an idea of, her idea of, and which she has, in her view, bridged now.

Of the lovers, she cannot say, she doesn't use such terms as *Truly-and-intelligently-they-loved-each-other-as-no-one-else-could-love-them* . . . (as-only-women-can-understand-love). Or that they loved in arrogance and in defiance and in blasphemy, shocking each other as in saying *I shit on war* in wartime to each other, in secrecy of that sort (as in a famous book). Momma, although she is sure of what she knows and is relaying scandal on her deathbed, Momma did not say those sentences about love.

She said, "They were shameless but they were smart." She said, "Listen, I don't say it was bad—who's to say? I say no one is to blame; I don't throw stones. But it's worth your while to know what's what, isn't it, Boychick?"

Yes, but I *don't know* what she *really* means—or if it's true by, uh, *serious* standards.

I thought she meant something like the stuff I just said about love, meant it not in an embryonic form but in one like the one that came to full growth in me for a while much later, and then, beyond that, judged it at the last minute . . . "Love?" I said. "Did Casey *love* Nonie?"

"You think that's so impossible? Who knows. They were a pair of cold fish. *They carried on*—Wiley don't ask me questions—I can't talk and answer questions . . . I'm Jewish . . ." (Something of an absolutist.) "I'm dying—" This parade of *absolute* factors was sort of aerially, and ontologically, dizzying: so many last things, each one total, you know? It's really hard to know what to do.

"I want to understand what you're telling me, Momma . . ."

She hemmed and hawed and sputtered: "Well, it's not so hard if you're not a fool." She said, "Women like to prove they're not men—you prove you're not the son of a man . . . You don't need to bother with the folderol men put out . . . You're not dumb—you're not stuck . . ." I had no real idea what she was talking about except I had some feelings like that for women. "You like your freedom," she said in a tone and in a sequence that meant she was talking about women—women she knew. An initiation occurs? Gender is mocked and the role-playing that women do in ordinary society? Here, everything is will? Will and *escape*? That sort of thing? "It can be a breath of fresh air," Momma said, hurrying on. "It can teach you how to handle yourself . . ." An *ace* negotiator attacks and attacks and gives you nothing, attacks you until you are willing to settle reasonably despite what your power (such as it is) might give you. But doesn't give you if you're not clever and strong. "You have to be a match for Casey . . . What Nonie is—look, Nonie is the same way . . ."

Private, tissue-y, mysteriously throat-and-lip-stippled unabrasive voices: I've noticed them, remarked them, lived with them.

Momma says, "They kissed . . ."

If you see, or know, two people kiss, what do you think you know about them or about yourself, about what you're able to see? What knowledge do you bring to it? Can you see if they're faking it? Can you see the anti-other-kinds-of-kissing-in-their-lives it is? The elements of resistance to time? Or its specialness—as *love*? Momma used a manner that was like an open term of reasoned contempt—but it was to her credit—as an intelligence, as a knower, as a woman who'd seen life—that you had to assume supplied the reason.

I did not imagine the two of them, I did not imagine any part of it, I was not affected by it, I did not feel left out, teased, or excited; I did not picture it as an *example* as if for some enigmatic textbook—I did not feel left out or *initiated*: I have a thing I do, I call it, unwisely, *deadness* or *feeling nothing*, a kind of life-y entombment—as in a fight when someone rains blows on you, and you wait it out.

You refused to be affected but not after you've been pierced but before. So, you don't just play dead, you actually go dead—or into a mood of waiting, a sleeping-prince sort of thing, or a winter storage in a bin . . . You can refuse a movie—I never liked *Tom Sawyer*, the movie that so influenced Dad—or *All Quiet on the Western Front*, either: I don't want to be pushed and pulled and have my emotions touched even in negation; I don't want to be shrill and masculinized and distant—so I am as if really dead, deadened, damaged, done in, a zombie, or a ghost: something belonging to the night, something unpublic.

For something to be a movie or a subject in a talk, for it to be a public subject is already to license it. All the ways I love Lila, or care about her, and trust her, don't include *trust* . . . I know she is psychologically astute. You bury something in silence. Or set it free to be wild. Perhaps if I believed she was helpless, I would have listened—but maybe not. You listen harder usually if you're uneasy. The heart of what I know about Nonie in Forestville is some such thing as this.

"Do you want me to have to explain everything to your dissatisfaction, your royal highness," Momma said impatiently reading my posture in my chair—my male size, my current opinions of things, and getting the word wrong: she meant *satisfaction*—maybe she was being witty; people have weird ideas about wit.

Anyway, beyond that, she was saying she was on my side.

Well, the way someone is on your side depends on what they take reality and the politics there to be: the betrayal here of Casey and of Nonie, the betrayal of women's secrets in a sense, the way the room was closed to intrusion—and Nonie, specifically, was kept out—only two nuns, specific nuns, and one young nurse (whom Mom expected me to date and sleep with, I think) and I were allowed in.

Well, it's confusing but you can *feel* something is HEARTFELT even when it's only one heart—a real person's . . . . You can *feel* the extent —and ferocity—of the adoption at the last minute; and that the kingdom is being turned over to you, to you after all; and, still, it's only Momma, Momma huge maybe if you let her touch your feelings; or if some automatism or dark thing in you that decides such matters lets her.

You can be closed down, watchful, discreet, distinguishedly polite, affectionate and respectful—and this can be a teasing thing: Rogers-and-Astaire-ish.

And all of it out-of-control with feeling and with death being near and with a yet more intense affection—with hidden smiles, smiles of the tomb, sort of, summing up smiles, while on the surface Mom is giving the Harvard guy a serious deathbed visit . . .

So, it is the feelings through the intellect that she addresses: a knowledge of *this* love will "solve" the problem of knowing about these people and of why they do what they do toward us. It gives an answer. Answers that you believe, even really false ones, strengthen you or seem to—do you see? Does your jealousy require a conviction that what you now see contains all meaning?

Momma can *read* me: "*Fuh* [If] you errn't there, you can still know. You have to make a choice: you choose what you think; about things; choose like a fool, you're a fool; Wiley, I mean it. Listen this time. I don't care if you're going to Harvard or not—maybe you're the cat's pajamas and maybe you're not, maybe you're what the cat dragged, ahuh, ahuh [a kind of laugh], you're a fool if you don't know the whereofs and thereas's of what you think you know . . ." This is why what happened happened. I will lessen the mystery in your world. I will strengthen your footing as best I can . . . She said that in various ways. To say it was clear is to beg the question—yet it was humanly clear.

So, too, was the maybe overawing degree of sincerity at last . . .

But it was not a sincerity carried on in cross-examination—it wasn't a case of two voices. It was her speaking to what she thought, or imagined, my voice to be: "Listen, it also happened as a result of what happens—so, live and learn, Pisher . . . This is deathbed advice . . ."

You always have to translate the truth of one kind of thing if it is to be a truth in other moments or in you and not in the book. A kiss, when you are doing it, is rarely seriously what a storyteller was (or is) referring to if he or she refers to a kiss . . .

Even if someone sees you and takes a drug or a lot of drinks and babbles on about your kiss—even if it is the other person in the kiss. It does translate, the thing said does have carrying power, but you have to do some work or you have to undergo the arrival of the weight of revelation—of *Oh so that's what that was* . . . The promotion from silence, so to speak, to your being among the figures in other people's puzzle-dreams as well as among your own often fraudulent clarities is a relative clarity. In reality, the promotion to being an important *lover* and sinner (of course) is tangible enough to feel even if you can't testify to it in chatter—the thing of being much higher on the (pagan) tree of others' attention—you and the remembered kiss come much closer to being an absolute thing in someone's mind than any kiss is when it occurs—in your mind, too, this happens.

I can try to imagine the epistemology, the truth of how I know what I know about a kiss, or I can now imagine the kiss importantly and only importantly affected—but I'd rather not: I was only eighteen. At twenty-six, knowing Ora's women suitors—the monocle-wearing countess; the for-a-while-monocle-wearing actress (who imitated the monocle-wearing countess); a show business agent who also wanted to sleep with *me* or with us . . . I don't know that the *voice*—the deathbed voice—was much help. A lot seems pardonable if you are willing, piously, to be a fool. A lot seems unpardonable. If you don't fool or overpower others what good is there in anything? What good can exist in the world?

I rarely understood much. I know that Momma chose to die among nuns: "They're nice, Wiley, and they leave me alone because I'm a Jew. But they're good—they don't hurt . . . It's like we all go on tiptoe, hand in hand, like in school—are you still a bad Jew?"

"Yes, Momma . . ."

Lila, Lila talking about these things, Lila dying, is the second of my mothers to die; and I was prepared to have die and vanish—to let me be free, free in a way, free to learn and to be bad and free to do things without thinking if those things did her credit, free to follow out the course of mind—as I saw and imagined mind to be—and life and lust and money . . . I really don't know . . . She was dying; I was preoccupied. With that as much or more than with her. I was grateful but I resisted inwardly hearing or noticing or being fully and feelingly aware that she was telling me these *other truths*, such as they were: the scandal which is a truth and which explains a great deal.

And embarrassment and a strong feeling that Lila wasn't so bad had hold of me in my passive-bystander role—I should explain that I am not trying to save her or keep her alive longer—and that we are both aware of this—and that she is *noble* in not laughing at me or mentioning it. We are, both of us, embarrassed and going very fast, faster and faster, even while much of her is slowing down—vacuums and black spaces form. She has the starring role and she is immense in comparison to me, so immense I could not follow what she was saying, to any great extent . . . I *think* I saw that just as one time when I was young and had to have an operation—I was seven years old or so and something had gone fairly drastically wrong—and coming out of the anesthesia I had gone into convulsions and Lila was sitting in the room with me, all dressed up, and she had been unable to help me; interns and nurses had saved my life—I think I knew, as a half son might, what she meant in seeing women as murderers and men, too: the omission of something is seen as a murder, or a foretaste of it, the beginning of it.

I could not join her in her perceptions . . . In one of the famous texts I'd read at college that year it said (and I misquote): *They kissed shamelessly, one soul embracing itself in two bodies.* One can see a kiss that way if one is not one of the people doing it, not one of the people in the embrace; that's a watcher's thing . . . Mom, very oddly, was telling me this. If one is doing the kissing, isn't it true that a kiss can't be felt that way? I mean, first, *can* you kiss *shamelessly* and unself-consciously? I mean can someone who is not me do it? And a kiss never feels shameless . . . That is a part of a tag you put on a certain effort to achieve a certain style or *osculant* reality.

But it can describe a passage past morality and stuff about murder and shame to suicide stuff—to lovers dying, Romeo-and-Julietishly.

Or a passage to madness.

But women—with no admixture of men . . . Of male cowardice . . . I can't convey outward what she conveyed to me, the size, among the constellations, among the elements of a constellation, the hard-to-see figure of Cassiopeia in a chair or of the dragon of a story, the images of truth.

Is it true that two people can have one will, one soul? Isn't that remark only saying one person gives in to the other? *Two people agree on* NIENTE, a guy at Harvard said to me disgustedly, sadly. On nothing. I think that remark about one soul, two bodies is about bossy longing and is an example of immensely true rhetoric of feeling that you know how to interpret (or should know) but the truth is more like what Mom and I had—the *truth* about something that did happen. Love and hurt. One soul—if you wanted to be rhetorical—or a dying woman at some sort of height of her powers (if I can say that) and an awed and unawed bystander, partly a fool.

"You, you've always liked my stories . . . I always told you stories even when you were little . . . You always complain you don't know what goes on . . . Okay, listen, I'm trying to tell you a story now that you're a college man I wouldn't tell you when you was little . . ." She is *noble* in her reasons now—although not quite in the way one would be to a child and not easily to be interrupted or turned into another self, as one would be with a lover—even in the last minutes before suicide.

She was never quite like this in the past. I *felt* with some conviction, too much conviction to talk about it, that she had, somehow, come to love ME at the end.

I suppose I was startled at how things changed for her if she had no reason anymore to protect herself since she wasn't going to continue to go on.

I saw a certain course of illusion.

And how people might use such a thing.

*

I still wanted her to die, though, so I could live in my way . . . The sensation of being loved at last didn't change me—I was geared or set or fixed in a certain course—I was sad, though, and impressed. She always wins to some extent—that's one reason she cares to the extent she does care.

I had always known *that.* And used it sometimes.

But the deepest thing, maybe, for me was the sense of my swinging outward, as on a playground swing, or in some more complicated way —as in flying out a window but actually flying—I'd had this dream— into dark spaces, starlit (to be sentimental about it), into times and realities toward which she had lost hope and was no longer competitive.

I would swear she was having a good time—exasperated some—and *noble*—as such things go.

She saw much of this; she saw something; I think she saw what was the case and that she turned aside from it even while facing it: "Promise me you'll remember me . . . Promise you'll remember what I say here . . . I always preferred you but it didn't always matter . . . What's the use: you're not a good listener anymore . . . You have your own mind now, and how, don't you, Poopchick? Pisher? In life."

She stops and starts; she starts again; she veers; she moves in spirals. She plummets (toward death and silence) . . . Listening, I *know* she will not tell me the details—I *know* that this is an edited *truth.* I know it— and only half listen (in a way). "I know what I know . . ." she says with that towering immensity—or sincerity of death—and with the conviction that I will, in a way, listen. She prefers to be noble because the *nobility*—both the elevated part and the ignoble, low kind—are *love*— love of different kinds and felt with a self-interest different from any when she was not dying, with a *noble* self-interest . . .

She'd seen some of this in S.L., alongside me: he'd died five or six times and had come back to life or been brought back—sort of temporarily.

But she'd seen stuff in the hospital; she'd been *noble* and had gone around in a wheelchair even, dispensing company and help: she had studied actual death, real dying.

"I'm not a writer," she says. "You have to catch on . . ." She almost certainly will not get the meaning right—how can she?

But isn't it that way with writers, too?

It is partly that she was the enemy or rival and a partial cause of events—no one is ever entirely out of the story or is objective: me, I mimic being a dying man. Or woman, I guess—I don't actually know. It is forbidden to bear false witness—it is forbidden even to try to write and to avoid bearing false witness: it is beyond human agency to know the truth sufficiently in these matters.

But she will do it for me. "I was always a bad person," she says complacently.

Then she says it fiercely, hurtling onward.

It is forbidden to write journalism or fiction but I do it—I try to do it. I dedicate some of it to her, not because she taught me—she didn't; she is doing it in the end in my honor, in my style as best she can. It is forbidden to deal in scandal because of the primary unknowability of one's own motives and because one's judgment of one's own judgment is subject to fault but she will do it—at the last minute . . . And I do it as if at the last minute . . . Dad used to say of us, *What a pair* . . .

Truth requires a sense of life and of character—an acquaintance with those things in their real forms, an acquaintance with society. Who Nonie was the first year she went away and then in the other years. And who Casey was and what her life was like—not as a victim only but the interplay between her and circumstances—and without ideality or the false apothegms of false knowledge, of dismissal of knowledge. So, too, Mom's death and Momma's powers of unideal truth at the end. And semi-sort-of one-souled love. At the last minute—the end . . . Whatever . . . And ME, as the listener. Lila with the help of death can shame herself into not bearing as much false witness as before and into bearing some and the weight of punishment ever after—if there is an ever after—and the unappreciative adopted son, as unappreciative as she'd always said people were, *so why bother* . . .

But she is noble and is willing to propagate some truth for the sake of truth—and sometimes, at this or that moment, for a while, to mock, not death exactly, but me and a lifetime's words—and to show me *how it was done*—being intelligent—she mocked all of me really.

Nobly. With immense love.

And I wasn't unappreciative—even though it was only human . . . Even though angels with trumpets and wings and made of wild colors didn't fill the room and stand along the walls in ranks, on stepped platforms, in utter emotional and entirely timeless significance. I was simply keeping my distance from the deathbed scene and the promises she would extort (and which she did extort). My guess is she would still partly (and sighingly) lie, sometimes in order to suggest a fuller range of maybe approximate truth—as in standing in a wide field in the rain.

You have to break yourself as if by torture; you do it in certain ways, tame yourself, instill an awful humility, kind of a death-camp scandalous thing, scandalous submission—scandalous crimes—scandal—such humility —if you are to be driven and goaded by truth and not by pride and disrespect—a poor, pure ox of narrative—gelded, too—perhaps this is true for her when she is dying. Perhaps nothing broke her entirely. I was not shocked by her—or by the stories. I was pleased and I felt she praised me and I thought it was love and I was enormously, enormously, enormously grateful, but I could do and say nothing. She wanders in a field of purposeful, persisted-in language on the three days of her postponed and then arriving death. In the syllabic windings and unwindings of her breaths, she self-consciously refers to events, people, moments, and to other actual moments. She speaks in a jolly and terrific and really scary nerve-scratchy last-minute breathlessness, lost and daily . . . I cannot interrupt her with what I know and have learned or once thought—or with any sense of how she misread or misestimated or misguessed at me long ago or at my mind or what I read and what I guessed at from my reading and what I knew since I left her, since I went to college, and what I know and have read, and what girls and instructors and some guys have told me, and what I have done. She has said in the past, *Wait until I die, I want to talk to you* . . . She didn't mean as a ghost: she meant she wanted me to be available for a last-minute scene.

In which she would double-cross Nonie? Well, tell me the truth as she, Lila, saw it—that maternal weight of specialized truth and the rebellious universalization or half-universalization of it—the usurpation of law. The lawlessness.

The whispers and pits and the gravel sluices and dirty shores of chilly and dark-shadowed rivers (of what she says in the depths of feeling and the heights of attempt here on her part) take on awful implications of a seemingness-of-truth. For me. A seemingness of life-and-beauty in death-and-ugliness. And in a woman's knowledge of things. Scandal. I was and am often held to be scandalous because of my mind and degree of (hardly universally admired) beauty but I have never been vivifyingly scandalous in my actions . . . Human . . . If I had been, I would assume the right to forgive or to blame, consciously and easily. Maybe not. Still, Casey and Nonie were, in my view, genuinely evil, more so than me and Momma, and Momma more than me; but more than them if you turn the hourglass upside down, although we were not all that guilty, although we were plenty guilty, but even so we were hardly as evil as some others,

S.L. and Abe, and me in 1956, and, of course, a million others, millions. Casey and Nonie were in the acceptable communal range—but so were Nazis—but not in any serious group and they were not acceptable for all types of love: only the dark, maybe violent, *death-camp* and *realpolitik* and lose-all-the-wars kind of love . . .

I see. I see it then. It half works as a hypothesis—a story is a hypothesis about human events or one event—a bit, a model, for some part of life: hearing or living or kissing or whatever. What I think of as my death in me, as one's death, the disbanding, the abandon of the congress of one's selves, the committees of one's selves, that stuff is listening (even when I was speaking) to Momma, the near and far isolations in my mother, the spaces of listening—hell, Lila even said, "Is there an echo in here? . . . The morphine does funny things to me—I hear an echo . . ."—and the trial and error of the effort to find outward terms, those combine; and then the suspense starts of *what-next* but as truth, as thought first and then of acts, or as truth-at-last—maybe only half-truth in the comparisons made by the listener—Momma is not Aristotle; Momma *is* Aristotle here—up to a point—the listener, the reader, compares other deathbed truths to this one. "Will you make use of what I say, Wiley?" The thing of you to her is just that for the first time she is sending me off on my own—this stuff, once she has my attention, once it is past the getting hold of me for now, is a thing that has to do with letting me go—she has to—but she is doing it with a certain *respect*—as if some of my notions about myself were, after all, true—in her view.

If the world is not absolute, then I am mostly right—just not absolutely right. If the world is not the least bit (or not at all) absolute, then I am okay—just not absolute okay. The different ways one hears and grasps a story, grasps the things said, the study of that in the light of time and the unideal—in the light, too, of love (and death)—would my mother have truly spoken if she had truly known me? "I was always unfair to you and I apologize—I always knew what you was but I didn't want you to make use of that with me; I thought I was pretty special—I thought I had my rights . . . Listen, Pooperkins, I know what you're like . . . I know this speech isn't *final* . . ." She said that. Lila? I think she did know me in part.

No, I thought, she would not speak if she knew me better . . . She feels better if I am silent. If I am silenced and overcome with death.

Actually, I think I was wrong.

She wanted to talk at the end.

Belatedly, inadequately, as a young man, I can pretend it is final

—a final scandal—although I hadn't any desire or impulse to think it was scandal: what mattered was how it unfolded in time, the map or chart it became, the force it exerted, the moral dimension and heat that time arouses like a magic matchbox-cattle-car-immensity of garden in which we flame up, now this way, now that. It is not an easy thing to try to grant finality. To listen and comprehend what a woman says, to believe a woman is hard, Lila said, to do such a thing you have to know the lives of women—the real moments of them. One knows the lives of women, though, maybe. I can check on what I hear now against memories that reappear, that, in this case, re*occur*, shocking—and a bit comic—and which are, say, ah, it's me, I know a little, it's not just from Mom that I know stuff—this other stuff was from when I was small, six years old say, and among the giant women, those women took me everywhere (and they, gigantic and blowsy, return nightly in my dreams), everywhere unembarrassedly: they undressed and peed and talked. They sometimes touched each other. Until I was seven. In front of me. Women spoke in front of me—I can almost guess at their words . . . They laughed at me . . . Nicely often . . . They took me on their laps . . . They let me stare at their bodies—at parts of their bodies . . . The odors. The garters. Their legs and skirts and eyes—and what was in their eyes and their clothes . . .

And what was in their *minds*. And in the ways they touched you. I can use the sense of women-among-women from back then—more and more, I heard as she spoke in these last days odd little snippets of things: by association: weird sorts of memory-producing voices as if the voices were ignited by what was said and became visibly audible: she or Nonie saying—back in time, a long time ago, and then perhaps mockingly recently, perhaps even now in the hospital: *Sssh, here he comes . . . Little pitchers have big ears . . .*

The words the women use, the way they touch each other are like whirring, fluttering moths on my skin, large, whitish moths: *Little Pitchers have big eyes too . . . Well, it's time for a change—you go to the boy's room from now on . . .*

What does it mean? what does it mean?

That returns.

Perhaps one should pretend to be a baby and to lie there quietly and be infantile—will *they* talk then in front of you?

Momma is dying. She is the woman I knew best in the world. I listen to her, when I do listen, with the most comprehension of a certain kind that I can manage with anyone.

Love . . . Is It Love?

You want to know what went wrong? Everything always goes wrong—what do you think? You think people are reasonable? The trouble started early: Nonie would let anyone come to see her in their house who wanted to; they came in groups, four or five soldiers—sometimes a hundred . . . People took photographs of her . . . It was a patriotic time; she was a patriotic girl. War is hard on people; you have no idea the sacrifices people made—you have no idea what people are capable of when the chips are down—blood, sweat, and tears—but people who have some life in them, there are laughs along the way, they don't just roll over and die, Wiley . . . Well, how do you think Casey felt? Proud? You can look for reasons if you want to—Casey had a nice house, she didn't like having strangers come to it wholesale, she was house-proud . . . You can say Casey liked to run things, you know . . . You can say, Well, Nonie is Nonie: you know Nonie: she took over the house . . . She has to be the star of everything. She'll fight with you and say it's all your idea or you have to do this but it's just Nonie . . . You can imagine . . . She didn't pick and choose: once the ball was rolling, she went along with the war; she wasn't a good sport, you know, but she could go along with it. You think the army was made up of nice boys? Who do you think does the killing? You think people are sweet? Don't put your head in the sand. A lot of them are no better than they should be and that's being wishy-washy about the subject . . . Casey carried on like they were dirt—maybe they were—some of them stole things . . . They wanted souvenirs . . . War makes people wild. What do you think it should do? Casey was in favor of winning the war but not this way; and I'll tell you something:

the way Casey acted makes no sense [if] you leave out the other, unless she loved Nonie and lost her to the war . . . Well wouldn't you be jealous of that kind of excitement? Talk about being belle of the ball . . . She was Queen of the Whole War in that town . . . in that state . . . I tell you it nearly killed Casey; I heard about her carryings on all the way out here. Abe never could stand Nonie; he flirted with her and dropped her; but he let fly a few things that got to me out here . . . I can tell you what I use to measure by; I can tell you how I acted—and believe you me, Nonie always said I was jealous of her being young; and I had moments of that. But I told my momma, it was worth it, her coming to America, Nonie had a moment in the sun . . . You don't know what it's like to be given a reason for your being who you are—it's like a breath of spring after a bad winter. Women's lives are hard, Wiley . . . and a lot of what's hardest is the bad reasons and the no-reasons people give you . . . It's in the Bible or it's this or that . . . It gets so that if you think for yourself you expect to get struck by lightning . . . Nonie was never independent to the same degree I was but she had a mind of her own. She had a sense of what she looked like—she looked like the girl next door but she had better features. She was a little on the pudgy side on the rump and arms but she was thin, too, but she didn't scare anybody, not unless they were terrible-looking. And whatever YOU *think, Nonie wasn't shallow: she'd been around S.L.; he'd been sick . . . She'd fought with you all her life: she could make sense—a lot of people thought she was interesting . . . And she didn't make them feel like lowlifes. What I'm saying is scratch her and you'd see she wasn't just another pretty girl: she knew that people could pass away . . . She knew about being over-shadowed. She knew what it was like to feel terrible—to lose everything overnight. She knew about books, not from reading them, but she disliked them; she struck people as being funny but she wasn't silly: she was someone who knew there were cemeteries in the world . . . She knew how smart people talked . . . I don't care what you think—all in all, she is a deep person. I don't take the credit. She rose to the occasion and she was deep for a while and I was very, very proud of her. I knew she had no staying power—you think I'm a fool . . . I know her faults backwards, forwards, sidewards, and up and down. I'm proud of her still—I'll say a terrible thing: it's too bad for Nonie the war didn't go on forever. What she was then—and it doesn't matter what you think—and I never liked her—she never fooled me once, not when she was a child, not when she was in Carolina either—what Casey did was she loved somebody, Nonie was a somebody, Nonie was the rage in the state of Carolina, North Carolina, Casey was silly for a while . . .*

One time at a war-bond rally in the First War, I got up onstage and several thousand men looked at me and I felt it—it was like a hot blast of air: I could read their minds . . . I started to smile but you know what? I remembered seeing women get a silly look onstage, and I didn't want to be undesirable*; and I drew myself up and looked, oh you know, like a vamp—and the way people clapped their hands and whistled, I knew I was just a girl, I wasn't an actress, but it was at that moment I knew I was an outstanding person . . . In my way . . . for a while . . . I was never conceited like you are—the way Nonie is . . . I'm smart, Wiley: I'm telling you a thousand men at a time cared what Nonie did and said—she was the mascot, the belle—I don't know what-all . . . A lot of things depended on her—the way people felt. I'm not talking nonsense, I'm talking about a* WAR*. I'm not a child; I may not be a Harvard professor; but I know what's what. She was* important*. You don't know what that's like. What really goes on is people want a piece of you. A lot depends on whether people are nice people—or not. Not too many are. You don't know how jealous a woman like Casey can be . . . of what she thinks she wants, of what she thinks her position is; she starts fighting right away . . .*

I barely half know.

But Nonie starts before you have time to say hello to her . . . The things men say—a lot of it isn't nice . . . Nonie wanted a little world to call her own: she wanted something Casey couldn't touch—that Casey couldn't tell her what was good manners and what was bad, and smack her fingers, and make it clear she was giving her a good life . . . If Casey had known what was good for her, she would have learned to give Nonie her head . . . I'm saying Casey shouldn't have listened in . . . People get hurt. War is war. It was what you might expect if you weren't going to be a fool about it . . . Of course, men came in droves: Nonie had the looks for the war; and she caught on how to act; and she was nosy—and she was happy—she was happy in her way . . . So, let her play: it's not a sandbox but so what. I'll hand it to Casey about one thing—she was trying to save feelings . . . She didn't want the wartime spirit to ruin the people she cared about; but Casey lost her head if you ask me: she wouldn't let Isobel have anything to do with soldiers and she wouldn't let the boys swear: I'm telling you she lost her head . . . Maybe I'm a bad person and she's a good person . . . The soldiers trampled dirt everywhere, they broke everything—Casey has a thing about people having big feet anyway—they took a dislike to her—well, that happens . . . But it's a case of what do you think the story was? Was Nonie teasing her? Was they sweet on each other? It's only human . . . A colonel wanted to leave his wife for Nonie . . . It doesn't make sense how Casey carried on—that kind of thing happens all the time; it happened to me more times than I can shake a stick at—you have a nice smile, someone's gloomy, and the next think you know you're the Mahatma Gandhi for them . . . The Messiah, the Second Coming, but you're a woman and you don't scare him like you're going to change the whole world and drop a bomb or send people to hell. So someone chases you, and there's a little drama—it's not the end of the world . . . Unless your smile is the Messiah for someone. Ask me: I spent a lifetime keeping my eyes open. I know you, Wiley: you don't want to listen. You want to play Little Lord Fauntleroy and think everything is hunky-dory when it's not. Well, I can't tell the story to suit you. I would but I thought about it and I won't. The F.B.I. and Army Intelligence, they came too; Nonie kept an eye on things for them: she was smart; no one knew for sure; everyone knew a little. She told me what she did; she threatened me. It was a stick she could hold. Casey couldn't stand it. Nonie did it for the war effort—Nonie wasn't the type who balked at things like that—hard things—she made trouble for people . . . Those other people protected her—I think she needed people to protect her—how could she trust Casey? She would have if Casey had been on the up-and-up—Casey was honest about money matters, you know; so why didn't Nonie trust her? I tell you Nonie's no devil; she's just an ordinary person, as dumb as they make them. You have to know who you can call on for help and she liked to give orders, Nonie did—she often needed help—was she such a fool? All right, all right. It could be religion. It could be politics. Maybe it was social. I'm telling you it won't make good sense unless you think of them both as women tired of usual things. All right, I'm being mean. Why shouldn't they be tired of things? Why didn't Casey stand by her? Why? Don't tell me it was principle—Casey stood by Abe his whole life; she stood by her friend lifelong—and they were a pair, those two.

It was for me, she told the story to me; but her solitude—her *solipsism*—was like someone attempting to write a novel. She wanted to know the story herself; she was examining things—humanly balancing the fact that she had banned everyone from her room. She said to me when I got there that she was glad to see me, she meant to die in my arms, she said. But now this was something else: this was the anger, the rage of the dying I'd seen sometimes when I worked in hospitals and that I'd seen some of in S.L.—the logical madness of the dying, of the genius in them. The rage and shock which like someone driving a car she crashed into me with inside the other stuff that was going on. Gleams and splatters of light on the window screen are like tiny match flares. Or, seriously now, like reflections of distant gunfire. I am trying to sound sane and above-it-all and I tried to be it then, too. Justice in real life, short of apocalypse, has to do with cleaning a situation up as well as you can under whatever circumstances are present—and it hurts—and assault and anathema then have to do with injustice and are tactics that refer to justice in the face of apocalypse—the threat of entire violence . . . Do you want to understand the world—this world—our world—ours in some sense? Then you have to know about this. You have to admit it. You sit and hear the California wind stir outside, warm, laden with heat, and Mom's anguished, laboring, laboringly angry breath—sure, I wanted to be somewhere else; yes, I didn't want to see this; but this was what shocked and hurt and harmed and sheltered (at times) and helped shape me. I will confess now that I was never to be in the presence of such rage again—I have managed to be evasive, private, and powerful enough to have an effect on what people dare. Anonymous letters, sure, and hints of this.

Even with Mom I was pretty sure that if I drew in my breath noisily—and warningly—that she would change how she spoke.

Or if she insisted on it, we could manage as equals. It was the combination of pathos, pitiability and willful ugliness and rage that was pretty much beside the point that was unpleasant, that seemed humanly wasteful, although one couldn't *judge* such things in someone who was dying.

She and I had long ago agreed that she would spare me this reality. We had agreed that this reality harmed her health.

But just as the absence of the future freed her for a kind of display of feeling that warmed me and, in a way, straightened and firmed the floor of my existence, so it freed her for this; and this stuff supplied a sense of shadowy walls at night—an enclosure in which, in a half-spoiled way, I lived.

I didn't *blame* her—it wasn't that at all: I swear it. I did blame her; and I didn't want to hear this crap; but I "understood" it was part of the other—part? It followed along in the curve of the moments' reality: it was why I hadn't wanted to be with her when she died.

It was like looking into a pit of hell—not that she was really so hellish directly as it was a matter of the implications: *ordinariness*, to use that term again, the enraged days of embittered or hardworking or of liberal people: I don't know. Hell is having not done something? And hating someone who did it? I don't know. I'm not even sure it was hate, that it wasn't comedy, or a form for speaking of an attraction something has for you when, really, you're quite modest—oh, not modest so much as enraged and sour, or not sour, but commonsense-smart-ass: bitter . . . Do you regret your life? Do you fester?

I don't know under what circumstances one can speak of the limitations of real voices. Or of the law of compensation. Or of reality as a dark thing. Surely, one is fortunate to hear a voice at all. To be loved. One doesn't feel that way, though, always.

One speaks of *what I was given*. It is not autobiographical: it is a way of dealing with actuality, perhaps responsibly.

But one lies in just that way, too, not always but sometimes: *given?* In what sense.

Mom moved into a comedy aspect of her story: *Upsy-daisy . . . round and round: a lot of what happens, people deserve; a lot not even a dog deserves, Wiley*, she said self-righteously.

Then she said it again, in a warm depth of feeling, without anathema: *A lot not even a dog deserves, Wileykins . . .*

I think I felt that she cheated on feelings and on discipline and felt alive and stayed alive for an hour or two more: you know how it is?

She even said, *It feels like a straitjacket . . .* Dying does. Telling a story. *You have no idea how ugly people can be—I knew Gentile women who said they knew people were worse even than the Devil was—even than God was when He was angry . . .*

But, Mom, how can that be: it's a matter of comparable and of incomparable powers; you have to show some care toward the comparisons.

I don't have to do anything: I'm dying and I have a little money in the bank; and I can cover my expenses. I'm not scared of God—He's smart; He knows how to listen—I'm scared of what I feel . . . People get hurt: you get ashamed—you get nervous . . . I never meant for her to come home and interrupt us, Wiley . . . I know you went off to college and left us. You left us to go have a good time. You left me because I wouldn't let Nonie go . . . I blame myself, Wiley . . . There's something wrong with Casey: there's something wrong with the way she's mean . . .

It's one person talking about another.

Wiley, put a nice look back on your face . . . I'm telling you what I know: you always wanted to know . . .

Momma, Nonie used to complain that your stories were mean. And not true.

About the undercover stuff which Mom had hinted at, with despair before, when I asked Nonie, Nonie said: *I was a big shot, I kept an eye on everyone . . .* That was verification maybe . . . She said, *No one tells me what to do . . .*

I suppose someone did.

Don't be a smart aleck . . . Mostly it is my sense of Nonie later that forms the ideas I had of Nonie back then as I am putting it together now . . . I asked Nonie when she came back to St. Louis—this was from war novels about serious stuff—*Did your conscience hurt?* In the war. Among the things you had to do.

You talk like a baby, she said.

I've read a lot of books—[I know that] it's hard on a person . . . War . . .

She said, *War is hell . . . You read too much—sticking your nose in a book is a good way to ruin your looks.*

For a while, she acknowledged as real about me only what I looked like, how I looked.

Different emotional realities: a story of popularity (in wartime), a girl's success, the competition for her daughter's attention, the control you have over your own life—even as you die: she said, Momma said:

I don't mind it anymore what happened. Maybe it was all life-and-death for them. I'm dying young and I'm getting tolerant, I can manage to be tolerant . . . Well, I want to make a good impression—She was, again. *If there's a lot of carryings-on after you die, if they're all standing there, my momma and your mother, poor Ceil, and my poppa, if you ask me, it's time to be a nice person—you have funny tastes—well, what can you do? Both of them disliked me*—Casey and Nonie—*they thought I had bees in my bonnet—they thought I was bad news;* THEY WENT TOO FAR—THEY WERE THAT KIND OF PEOPLE *. . . So they got together, there they were, two of a kind, one with the other and they were better than me, they laughed at me, got even with me, you think I didn't care? I didn't. I'm having the last laugh—it's not much of a laugh but what can you do? I had more brains than both of them put together; I had better legs; I had more life in one half of my rear end than they had, put together . . . But put two heads together and it feels good, a lot better than one, but there was a string attached, ha-ha: they were stuck with each other . . . It doesn't do you any good to be too smart . . . It's good to be nice now and again: you don't turn so sour; you don't end up looking like a battle-ax. I'll tell you about me: I got thrown out of college for having too many men buzzing around but I always kept an eye on women; I get along with women; but Casey was one of those who had to outdo the* *men—she had to outfox them; she was a good liar; she kept her end of bargains unless she had good reason. I'm someone who can see a little ways ahead—Casey couldn't. But she was lucky. She played it by ear—moment by moment—and it all worked for her. I still think I knew what was going to happen . . . I had bad luck . . . I got surprised . . . Bad luck came along and took me for a ride: you feel sorry for me, Pisherkins . . . But I wasn't bad . . . I wasn't even half bad, ha-ha . . . People had respect for my opinions—I saw to it they did . . . I have no faith in you, Pisher, but you did all right so far, and that's something—that's something to write home about. It wouldn't hurt you to wake up and see what's going on—you should try a little of it, of real life. You know what they say about Harvard men, you can always tell one, but you can't tell him anything . . . My mind is a little of this, a little of that . . . I hope you can take care of yourself . . . I wasn't the world's best mother to you but I would like to have an easy mind at the end in case I have to meet your mother; she comes to this room and talks to me. The root of evil is it's monkey see, monkey do—that was always my downfall. What's the point of doing something because someone else does it? It's a trap. Do what you can do. I had too much ambition. I still do. Casey was always so calm: she's cold; well, she's not sick . . . She has feelings; she's crazy, you know. People say they have no feelings but they do it just to get your goat—it takes a lot of feeling to have no feelings. It's a way you are to get things done—you can't draw breath without feelings . . . Men don't care about lies; they care about results: why should women care? What happens happens . . . Women do what they can . . . I'm not someone who gives up but I'm dying young, so what do I know? I like to talk to you but I think you're the wrong one to talk to. You ought to have some respect for what happens to people . . . And you, you give up too soon. No one's life is perfect—you can't hold that against someone . . . Something or somebody comes along and a person thinks, Maybe this will be nice—it's time I learned something worth my while about the sunny side of the street—you think that and you get involved and then where are you? I'll tell you: you're in never-never land is where you are and I wouldn't wish that on a dog . . .* Mockingly-seriously-shyly, almost catching herself up: *Are you fascinated? Do I talk as well as the people you know at Harvard? I'm a little on the ignorant side but I always had some fire in me . . . Nobody ever said I was somebody with nothing to hide. I'm somebody who has a little something to her . . . I'll take a look—you say . . . you say it to yourself . . . and then you're in deep . . . and you know what? you don't care . . . It's a horse race: it's a case of what the other person puts first as what's most important and can you get them* to change it before you go mad and upsetting things right and left. People have their pride in odd corners . . . S.L. and I was a mismatch but it wasn't a bad marriage: I was interested in what became of him; I could get him to change his mind—it always hurt me, what he thought of me . . . I never got him out of my system . . . Of course, HE said he never had a chance against me, but who knows what that meant? I'm dying and don't shake your polite little head. Casey and Nonie—those were two peas in a pod—and Nonie held her own: not an ounce of fear in either one of THEM . . . They each had a vocabulary of about two words . . . Well, I don't have to tell you . . . But you don't have to talk to be smart in this life . . . Look at me on my deathbed—with my tall, silent cutie pie . . . Don't be self-conscious: it doesn't suit me . . . Then softening: Well, what's so bad about feeling a little something for a change? I think that's how everybody stays alive. I think that's why people come to America in the first place—to have a little time and money to flirt around in on their own—I don't mean just one thing: anything that interests you: charities, the P.T.A., a dog, you can flirt around with a smart idea someone has once you get it in your own head—did you know I was a skeptic—did you know I was skeptical? I hid it from you. Did you forget me at Harvard? I'm cynical—did you know that about me? I'm a cynic who believes that being foolish about someone or something is what makes the world go round or you put a bullet in your head. Or you get sick and drop dead. I mean it. I'm a generous woman in my way—I love you, Wiley, but I lost out, didn't I? I lost out. In a lot of ways. I hoped they wouldn't find out about each other too soon; I hoped they would be happy in their crush on each other; they both let me know right away what was going on: Casey upped the amount of money she sent; and a new bed jacket, a new bedside lamp for the sick woman, painted china, the lamp, with pleated silk shade: you think I'm ungenerous? You think I didn't know what she was telling me? She was taking care of her rear end, she was covering her flank, covering herself. She wanted no enemies. I don't know . . . And Nonie on the phone, all icky-drippy—Casey wanted her to call: Let's make up, she said: I KNEW what that meant . . . She wanted me to know . . .

Well, what can you do? They got on each other's nerves. That happens, you know? That was bound to happen—Casey saw through Nonie—Nonie is selfish—Nonie saw through Casey—Casey is crazy and has to have her foot on your neck . . . Well, so what: is it life and death? I was the peacemaker, believe me . . . Don't believe me . . . I don't care . . . I didn't make trouble between them . . . And if I did, well, that was nasty of me; I slipped up—I'll tell you the truth now: I saw it was *life-and-death stuff . . . I was left out and I had life-and-death stuff of my own—but not like that—and the least said, the sooner mended . . . Isn't that what they say? I behaved well, Wiley,* she said but her voice wavered and was bold and pleading; she said it pleadingly: *What more can you ask of a woman like me? What's unendurable is always being a little wrong about everything and not knowing how it's going to add up . . .*

Listen: knowing Casey is no bed of roses for anyone . . . Everyone in that family [who] wanted to meet people to romance with, went out of town to do it: that's how things were around Casey, she was such a know-it-all do-it-all run-it-all. General of the armies. When you're that rich, you can get an exaggerated idea of yourself—an exaggerated idea of what you can make people put up with—Casey treated Nonie like a poor relation . . . NEVER, NEVER treat Nonie like a poor relation . . . if you value your sleep . . . She's a real Robin Hood that girl . . . Well, well, what do you know, Nonie had learned a thing or two: she had her own army: she had her own secret service: it went to her head—she forgot to be scared of Casey . . . She wasn't scared of the future . . . You don't laugh but I laughed . . . Listen to me: it was FUNNY, the two of them . . . Everyone got hurt . . . Even you, Pisher . . . The soldiers came and went; they used to serenade Nonie. Some drunken officer candidates drove a jeep through Casey's azaleas . . . People react—and there's no end to it: you learn something; and how do you unlearn it? Well, monkey see, monkey do . . . Nonie had to be Casey. Casey had to be King of the Hill. They fought over it without raising their voices—they wanted to be well-bred. Isobel was so scared, she stuck to boys—of course, I'm guessing. I don't mean it was a fight you'd know about . . . It was only women . . . She was being ironic. *No man stands a chance in that cross fire . . . Here's a simple truth: a lot of life is you fight over people . . . And people don't catch on to what's happening . . .*

Then they made up. Who knows how it went. Then when Abe got sick, you know something?—there's a man went to his grave as secret as the tomb, taking his secrets with him . . . Do you think he had a good time and died young? He was bored by the thought of going on? I might not want to see myself old. Like Momma. Maybe I'd rather die, Pisher . . . I'll be honest with you, Pisher, I'm bored lately. I lose my nerve now and then. But in many many ways I'm content it's over . . . My doctor is sweet on me and look at you staring at me . . . It's funny: you learn to take things as they come but you don't want them anymore; you say no and then you change your mind but it's too late; and that's the end of it . . . It's all as strange as a moon full of green cheese . . . I'll tell you about Abe: he never found the miracle, he never got to the real top, he laughed at people and it went bad for him . . . Well, but he was smart: Casey knew he was; she gets some credit . . . Well, the day Abe was diagnosed, cancer of the bones, well, Casey wasn't close to her old friend what's-her-name at that time, or she was, her old friend, Whosits, Emma-Jean whatever, but Casey's life changed and she didn't turn to Nonie; she turned to the other one; and I'll tell you something you won't hardly believe: Nonie who hated sickness was so jealous she went a little crazy from that day on . . .

She was jealous that Abe was sick and that it mattered to people . . . She was jealous of Abe . . . She was jealous of Casey's attention . . . Nonie was under a strain, and after S.L., it was too much. And I'm sick. Casey can't take craziness. She's patient but she runs away, not from the person, but from the feelings. So, there you are, that was the end of it whether they knew it or not; there was no for better or for worse between THEM *. . . Casey was a faithful nurse to Abe—I got to hand it to her . . . Of course, some people said she enjoyed it—she lorded it over everybody as Queen-Saint Florence Nightingale. Abe was helpless . . . He mostly screamed: Wiley, it was a terrible thing. Casey and her friend, the two old friends stood by each other—and guess who was out in the cold? Nonie said there was a war on. She pish-tushed everything. Her life came first—maybe it did. Casey said at first she understood that Nonie was scared of illness. But the soldiers kept coming . . . That was too crazy . . . You know how it gets, things go from bad to worse . . .*

Mom, stop. NO more of the scary story. Let it alone. Leave me alone.

Casey called me: listen: it was interesting—she asked me if Nonie had sold her soul to the Devil—isn't that interesting?

Well, I told her, you can't ask a mother that . . .

I don't know what it really was with Nonie . . . I'm her mother and I don't know . . . I think maybe it was she couldn't feel sorry for anyone or for anything and that it drove her crazy in the long run . . . She tried to be sophisticated but what good is it to be a smarty-pants when you're crazy? Nothing worked . . . She would listen only to herself—like she was The Second Coming . . . She couldn't trust anyone . . . She was like S.L. all over again . . . Mahatma Gandhi Leo Tolstoy Man o' War Franklin Roosevelt Gary Cooper Babe Ruth rolled into one . . . Those two were too proud for their own good . . .

Momma, stop.

What can I tell you? Nonie had her ups and downs . . . She wasn't sensible . . . She was a moron in some ways . . . I suppose that's what psychology is, that's what a lot of things are for, to make morons smart, smart enough . . .

I DIDN'T WANT HER TO GO ON . . . I sat there patiently, however.

So Casey, Casey called me . . . ME *. . . You could have knocked me over with a feather . . . We were friends again: I had to get Nonie to leave Forestville and come home . . . I spoke to Nonie but the two of them had a scene: Nonie had held her tongue all that time—I tell you she liked Casey a lot. Nonie spoke her mind—well, she blew off steam and Casey threw Nonie out of the house . . . I mean it: she had her put on the train back to St. Louis . . . Nonie was outright crazy but she could manage okay in front of people . . . I have a lot to answer for. I'm sorry she had to be in your life but* (and this was in a mean voice, this was in a tone of attack) *I'm sorry for how I treated her more . . .*

I'm her mother . . . Now, in my last days, I don't have to be a mother anymore and I'm relieved—and I don't want her in here . . . I don't want you blaming yourself; I don't want you hiding behind the fact she's the blood child and you aren't. But I want you to take care of her after I'm gone. For now, I don't want her in here. Promise me you'll help her so we can get back to talking: I want to talk to you; I want to say I'm sorry; I want you to forgive me . . . I never meant for things to happen the way they did . . . I meant well . . . If I didn't, I kept it to myself—I certainly didn't make a big song and dance out of it. Casey won't forgive and forget, she won't let bygones by bygones, she never let Nonie come back, she's sent her cards and presents, but she won't see her . . . Casey plays for keeps . . . That's how she got ahead in the world . . . She's always been afraid Nonie's told me things, but I will say this for Nonie: she can keep a civil tongue in her head—she can keep a secret. She has a mind of her own . . . She has stamina . . . She said she didn't care. But she did care. Nonie always loses out. Who doesn't. She thinks she can fool people—and she can some of the time . . . She thinks she sounds okay—she doesn't know when she's crazy . . . She hardly had one bad word to say about Casey . . . How does that make me feel, do you think?

Maybe everything's terrible: maybe it's for the best if you're tough about atonement . . .

I admire Casey. She's come out a winner in her life. I like cold people—the fewer feelings the better, I always say . . . People can be too cold: enough's enough . . . Poor Nonie . . . She's no different from anyone else but she ruins things for herself—why do you suppose that is? I want you to take care of her after I'm dead . . . Wiley, I know she won't listen to you, I know there's bad blood, I know you get bored . . . I know you can say I wouldn't let her in my room even to say good-bye to; but so what, you lived as brother and sister, you have a head on your shoulders, take care of her, help her, don't let go, do for her what I never did for her . . . please? I ask you this from my deathbed . . . Don't lie to me . . . Lie to me if you have to . . . You always look good compared to Nonie . . .

What I hear happened is they had a scene; Casey can't stand scenes; everyone heard everything; and Nonie was so horrible, they all decided a year later they loved you . . . Ha-ha . . . No ha-ha . . . Some things it's better not to think about. You have your own road to hoe. Nonie knew how to play her cards short-term but she never knew how to do the long haul . . . Maybe no one does . . . Maybe it's our family . . . She makes a little home for herself among people who are mad at me: that's how she does it. She's like a little animal in a book . . . I want you to forgive her and help her . . . I failed and I want you to take over . . . I have a little pride and faith in you . . . I have a lot . . .

The other range of voice and manner was back—the other mode, or method for dying, unenraged—or enraged with tenderness—enflamed with affection.

Sometimes I think she hasn't a grain of sense in her head. Too much of everything she's done has been a mistake for her to stop covering up now—that's a mistake a lot of people make. You'd think they'd be more logical. Nonie wants things her way, she doesn't like sadness: help her. There's a lot I don't know . . . I don't understand you at all but you get along somehow . . . I can't leave her alone in the world now, Wiley, and just prefer you at the end and let it go . . . I don't like her but I have a conscience . . . You have a conscience . . . Have you lost your conscience at Harvard? Have you learned to bend like a reed? Nonie, something knocked her down, she got up again . . . What else can you ask from a daughter? What else do you want from a daughter you don't love enough anymore? But you were always different. Knock you down and you'd lie there, ha-ha, or you wouldn't be knocked down. I wanted her to have what I didn't have but you were the one who wound up different. I gave her what I could but you're the one who's like me. We had a hard time of it sometimes but, well, I'm the one you should blame, not her . . . You can't force yourself to love someone . . . She was always just a child. Be big, be nice to her. Good. Take care of me now. It's your turn: tell me a story—tell me about a girl you met, you liked . . . No: wait: I want you to go and get the nurse . . . Don't let Nonie see you. Don't let her in here. I can't take it anymore, any of it, from her

—get the nurse and tell her it's time for my shot . . . I want to talk about something else but I have to have a little rest . . . I want to talk about you and me—me and you . . . I'll tell you a terrible thing about me: I'd like to enjoy my dying if I can . . . When I wake up, I'll tell you some serious things . . . I'll tell you about all sorts of things I thought of to tell you—much better things than I've told you so far. Trust me. I'll be serious—you'll see . . . Just don't leave me: just sit here by the bed so I can find my way back when I'm dozing . . . My dreams take me far from here and I get lost; I feel young and that I can do what I want; and it's hard to come back . . . But I know what you're like. You don't like people to die. You're a softy. I promise I'll come back to you at least one more time. GET THE NURSE. AH, AH . . .

The pain she felt was extraordinary.

We talked for two more days . . . Well, mostly she talked. She talked and slept. She mentioned Nonie once each time she, my mother Lila, was awake; she wanted to see if I still would tell her I would take care of Nonie.

But she and I never spoke about Nonie again or about what she was like or what the world was like with her in it.

We talked about the past and my adventures at Harvard and about the hospital as if they were worlds in which no one and nothing like Nonie existed.

And we had a damned good time. Mother said so—in various surprised and gentle ways. I made her laugh a couple of times and she smiled now and then; and she made me laugh twice. It really was okay. She said, *I'm holding my end up . . . We're not doing so badly, are we, Pisher? Are you okay?*

Sure, I said, *Sure if you say I am . . .*

She said, *You're nuts through and through but I like you . . .*

She said, then: *Things didn't always go so well . . . Tell me you forgive me . . .*

I suppose I had known before then that the sympathy and closeness in one—in me, in her—had a limit. I suppose I remembered from when S.L. died that someone died and you lived on—the separation was that acute (like a rock and a stone in a row of stones) even if the person who was gone lived on as a presence and as a voice in your mind; still one rock in the row tumbled over and vanished out of sight, and the other stayed. I suppose I thought or believed one could go beyond that to other fields or levels of feeling and of attachment: earlier, when Lila had talked to me about my real mother and how she'd died, perhaps of a bungled abortion after having been mistreated by my real father (Lila told me nothing optimistic except for sentences of praise for life and for the people in the stories), she'd said my first mother, in her life in such a small town, had invested everything—emotionally—in the baby, me at that other time; and the baby had seemed attached to his mother so strongly that she, Lila, felt it was strange, even remarkable that the baby had lived, that I had lived. *No one expected you to live but here you are,* she said.

I said, *Maybe I didn't really live—maybe it's just a shadow thing . . .*

Lila said, *No, it was your mother: she didn't want her effort wasted . . . she kept you alive . . .*

But having said that, Lila then did want to explore the subject of life-after-death and of limitlessness of emotion between people—of things that were beyond ordinary discipline and that were beyond calculation—attachments of one soul to another on one hand and then sizable sins on the other—but she did believe me, or so she said, when I pointed out that to give yourself over to one emotion or to one goal had no limit in terms of how far you went but it had limits to either side of itself in that it didn't turn into another feeling or let itself be deflected or diluted. And that maybe you shouldn't call it *calculation* if it was done warmly—or hotly—(*Ha-ha,* Lila said hoarsely)—but it required will or *heart* in the sense you used the word *heart* of athletes, of boxers, and of horses who *ran-their-hearts-out.*

Lila said, *Well,* YOU'RE *still alive—will wonders never cease . . . I swear you've been* PROTECTED . . . [in a whisper] *by a ghost . . . Your* MOTHER . . .

I knew Mom was a little jealous—and competitive—toward other deathbed scenes and toward things in operas and toward S.L. and, generally, toward what other people had. And I had, a bit, been keeping things shallower than she intended—mostly so I could keep on going and not be horrified and upset; and she'd been keeping track, I think—keeping score. When she asked for forgiveness, I was a little startled, first, because it seemed un-Jewish—of course you *forgive* the dying; you forgive everyone—but, more, because it suggested something existed between her and me that did not exist: we'd never, even in my infancy, been sentimental with each other—Lila had little or no gift for sentimentality. I thought she meant something hackneyed as in a movie scene—fabricated, fictitious life, envy solved for a while: she didn't like candy and she had no talent for sentiment but she had a weakness for doing famous scenes in real life—they made life seem unordinary: they opened into history.

But I disbelieved myself—I didn't think I could be right. But I thought I could read her somewhat. So, I tried a movie scene anyway: *There's nothing to forgive—you were always open with me . . . pretty open . . . You played fair: we were always pretty close, Mom . . . Forgiveness isn't an issue for* US *. . . not for us, Momma . . .*

I want it, she said. *I want it from you*—WILL YOU GIVE ME YOUR FORGIVENESS!

Well, do you forgive me*?* Isn't this all beyond question? You and me? Isn't it just here? Don't we take it for granted between us—you and me?

It's different between you and me; it's different for me; I'm not you; I'm nobody and I'm dying—you was a child: I didn't keep the promises I made your mother; I didn't do the things she wanted me to do—I thought I could get away with doing what I wanted to do—I need you to forgive *ME . . .*

Ma . . . I don't care that you didn't keep all your promises . . . I'm not my other mother . . . I don't even remember her . . .

You are her . . .

Ma . . . you're making it too serious—really, what do you need MY *forgiveness for? What did you do that's so bad? I'm alive, I'm here, I'm in school; I sleep at night; I have girls now; some people like me . . .*

It's a hard world, Wiley. I know what went on. I won out when I shouldn't of won out. I did things I regret. I want your forgiveness. Don't just be polite: I'm talking seriously. I am serious. I've thought about this. I've thought about you every day for months now. This is what I want from you.

Mom, you have it—you always had it—here's my forgiveness: I sure as hell forgive you: you saved my life . . . I'm glad I'm alive—I never blamed you for anything you did, I never blamed you for what you did . . .

I WANT YOU TO SAY IT WITH YOUR WHOLE HEART AND SOUL . . .

For almost a moment, I couldn't go on. I couldn't get my lips and throat and lungs to do anything. Or my soul. Or my heart. Except breathe—and, finally, to blink.

It was astonishment first, astonishment as a passional form of bitterness over the past; I didn't feel bitter about the past; I just didn't want to think about it or take it seriously now when I had to face it that she was dying; I wasn't dying; I didn't feel any bitterness toward *her*; it was a matter of not wanting to be *sincere* now and feeling a lot and admitting things just because she felt like it. Or needed it.

It was a form of agonized astonishment at how real, maybe, and how deep her feelings went, and how unsentimental and how real they were. It was the presence of real feeling in the room.

Not mine. Not only mine. My astonished silence lifted me for a moment into being someone who could perceive or glimpse the size of something larger than himself. This was an ashy feeling I glimpsed, largely lightless. I maybe made up the form in which I saw it but its presence was unmistakable. She hadn't asked for forgiveness in any real way before except only of a light sort, that and forgetfulness, some of which was automatic, and she'd asked me not to harm myself and punish her that way but to go on—I mean in the past—and that was all that we'd ever rehearsed. I'd never thought she would be scared and *guilty*—not toward me anyway—I was flattered. I was enormously moved. I was overawed. But I couldn't match her tone, produce a response as a partner. I couldn't face it that her feelings were real or that I couldn't face them. Hell, I was inwardly angry—not burningly so—but scared as hell, she seemed so huge with feeling—and brimstony—made of ashes and clay: almost a golem: and I seemed petty and minor to myself—and she liked that although wearily, only wearily.

But I was pissed at her not knowing how tricky it was for me to manage to go on day by day; I lived fairly completely but within limits, aestheticized, and with a lot of stuff, most stuff, *turned-over-to-the-mind*. It is hardly complete or hardly even a majority of parts of myself that I use—hell, or can use without becoming violent and weird: isolated and in a certain kind of danger and in a certain kind of dance or boxing match with people and with moments as they pass and with life. My past is explosive for me—it's the presence of the reality of so much difficulty, it's the difficulty of understanding and of guessing all along at things. I believe I hardly knew anyone who wanted not to remember as much as I wanted not to have to remember *anything* . . . Nonie, Dad, and Mom, for all their gassing about never looking back, reminisced a lot, the whole time; they did memory-lane stuff right and left . . . I had by then in my life a built-in sense of when I was near the point (my limit) and how, if I went on—if I went past this point—I would be inconsolable, uncontrollable, ill or dead, in half a hundred ways—Mom used to call it *losing my head* and I am afraid of the rearoused pain in it. And then, too, this was in L.A. where I knew only a few people . . . I knew my relatives would not help me . . . The doctor would. I mean I had a long history of no-*kindness*-from-my-family—and some kindness from outsiders. Any automatism of forgiveness would have been okay for me with her—I'd have just this upheaval of a sense of danger in me, but the real thing, real forgiveness person-to-person, from deep down, us having sort of like equal lives and rights and being in the same room, with me being the wronged and important one, the one pushed around, though, was impossible if I was to survive her death.

Forget about kinds of *murder*—it was murderous but on both sides and the murderous stuff went in all directions and as it often is, it's a sign of stuff being ultimate. Then if you think of maybe *carelessness* and *curiosity* and love-of-a-kind—not for a child but of your own body and not for a synopsis of what is in you but for a Casanova-Romeo-Francis-Bacon-Caesar *coward* or for a false, local, really powerful, though, *Cleopatra*—maybe someone you don't think is so alive or is tough enough to live anyway: or someone who doesn't *love* in a way you really understand; or you do but that's all buried under the blankets; and one of you sees maybe a *murderously* lovely kind of male doll you want to take with you, half-gently, emotionally into the shades; and the other sees vanished breasts, pain, giant pride at the last minute—a kind of humor—even of sincerity . . . Or you do think Little Lord Casanova is *tough* . . . or *lucky* . . . and you want to measure this, see this . . . and you think the failing *Cleopatra* isn't so lucky or so tough after all . . . but she has some surprises in her still . . . some unreadability . . . Then think of a feeling shaded with its opposite, with a wish to save the other creature all along its boundaries and your own and all along the boundaries of the other feelings in you, a wish to be close and to say farewell in this way maybe and maybe not, to say it on your own terms and from within your own life and will.

And that is partly because you don't, and can't, excuse the other life, the other life's continuing, the other life's luck of whatever sort. It isn't you. And the bridge out is too new. Imagine feelings not tightly edited, not dedicated, and moving along second by second. Imagine generosity itself as ungenerous and so what but maybe so-a-lot. And a curious measure a parent takes of a child who is not hers but who has lived with her in often stunning degrees of intimacy, a measurement now acted out and not at all clear to me—what the shit do you *do*? It was enormously flattering and utterly dismantling and it suggested an at least comparative innocence and personal worth and one that required no further protection. And in its truth it denies any real sort of lying to you or about you then or in the past. It was impossible for me to understand that she was dying and then not to comprehend her feelings somewhat. So to fail to comprehend her request and to fail to be generous, openly, boldly, had a certain implication. Not consciously at first. But consciously then—an element of judgment I could not bear to have. I could not bear to know this, *too*. On top of the rest I could not bear to know. I could not bear even to begin to know I could not bear to know something here. Blame, regret, not only regret, horror, filled me: and resistance—an insomniac griever's swirl of independent time, of independence of thought and feeling in the moments, independent motions going off to one side, veeringly resistant, and perilous: words, an outburst formed—I evaded them. I sidestepped the monstrous (or the angelic) scene. I used boyish and shallow mastery—and the *flirtation*, if I might be allowed to say it like this—and obstinacy. Life, a continuing of life, a continuing of whatever line of half-life and quarter-thought I had, a continuing of history—those were my chief premise, my chief concern—nothing apocalyptic . . . Nothing absolute. Not even her death. I had died, or cooled emotionally toward her years before. Certainly not her death now. I had a wish to ask her questions and to haggle over her answers. But I avoided the *upheaval* of personality, the redeeming thing she wanted, the salvationary metamorphosis (into being *a real boy* and into having straightforward ambitions and rages).

But the *no* in me—the years of refusing her entry into my moods and the continuing of *that* into this last scene with her—ah, I stink still as I did then of sudden sweat at her wanting to save both of us, at how wrong she thought I was, at how wrong she thought the tie between us was, or pretended to think it was in order to have her will now on the vestibule of her exiting from *the* world. I denied her a triumph. I forswore the past of her triumphs. And sins. Over me. In regard to me. The *no* won out—as it often had before. It had its way. The past summed itself up in me as *No-I-CAN'T-do-this*. I can writhe and be in pain but I can't do some things . . . I can die. I can die and be jealous but I can't do these things.

I love you, I always loved you, we're fine, Mom—I forgive you, there—is that okay?

No . . . But it will have to do . . .

Then she said: *I hope you can learn to take care of yourself . . .*

Later she went back to the forgiveness motif and I tried to fake a sincerity and even to be a little sincere but without remembering and without tearing myself open and being sort of pieces lying around waiting to be put together in some grotesquely torn way, in some original form, in some *after-my-second-mother's-death* sort of way.

This stuff went on for an hour and then recurred for another two hours: I said, *Mom, look at me: I'm doing okay . . . How can I blame you without throwing away every single thing that I have now; and if I don't blame you, will you tell me how the fuck I can* forgive *you the way you're talking about?*

I guess they teach you to argue at Harvard, she said. *No: you was always good at it. Do as you like—you will anyway . . . I think that, after death, I'm going to meet your real mother and I wanted to feel clean about things; but I know you're a thoughtful boy, a thoughtful person, I know you always liked me, you always had a soft spot for me . . . But love, you're careful about love . . . Maybe, in the end, you're the kind that lasts . . .*

And she said: *I'll tell you the truth now: I loved you. I always loved you. I went in circles maybe. I didn't do the right thing—I'll tell you here and now I didn't always want to do the right thing . . . I lie here and think about it and I regret it: tell me you forgive me for that . . .*

I forgive you, sure—that's not so bad, Mom . . .

I loved you and I took advantage of you and I didn't always take care of you and it didn't come out like love . . .

Yes, it did . . . It's just that things get different—some times . . .

And she thought and she gathered herself together and then she said mightily (or so I thought): *You mean at the end when there's no time ahead of you—and having to take care of things as they go along isn't the be-all and the end-all . . . ?*

That's right—that's what I think, Momma . . .

Well, live and learn—see, I can still joke. Kiss me and say you forgive me and we can change the subject then . . .

So I did.

And she said, *I shouldn't have made you live with Nonie . . .*

Then, the last day, a half-hour before she died: *You've been very nice, Wiley—you made dying seem almost nice . . . Now go a little bit away; go sit in the corner where I can't see you clearly—I'll know you're there but it won't distract me . . . The next part is hard. The next part is serious. The next part is something I don't want you to see—you won't approve of me if you look at my face up close. And I can't take any more; I'm ready; it's time; and I don't want your opinions pulling at me the whole time—I don't want to be saved. I don't want you to see my face up close while I'm dying. I don't want to have to think about any of that while I die . . . I don't want you to go away, though: don't leave me alone until I'm gone; but let me do what I have to do . . .*

She closed her eyes and her breath labored—I thought, almost idly, she would change her mind and live. I could see her face from where I was. I realized within a short while that she was letting go and then grabbing on to breath and then letting go . . . I did not have thoughts encouraging her to live. She died laboringly—by that I mean that it sounded from her breath and it seemed from her face and neck that it was some kind of dirty thing—letting go—dirty and of interest to her: she did it with determination—as if she'd learned how almost to let go in the five years she was sick and as if now she did let go, rehearsed step by rehearsed step and was not appalled by the novelty or by the immensity, either one, or by the intelligence and bitterness and grave luminosity of meaning.

Or if she was, she went ahead anyway and did it, not all that differently from the way she had described Daddy doing it when she came home the day he died and said, *I want to talk about it—can I talk about it with you, Pisher? . . . You ought to know a little about death, about S.L., don't you think?*

No, I said.

Well, listen anyway . . .

I'd covered my ears. I'd been lying on the couch reading a novel and she sat on the edge of the couch.

She'd said, *I can't tell it like a story—I know you two loved each other . . . Yours was the only name he mentioned; I won't tell you what he said—I'll spare you that . . . He wouldn't talk to anyone at the end; he turned his face to the wall and he made himself die. I asked him not to but he wouldn't listen to me . . . I guess you were the only one he really loved, Pisher . . . It certainly is funny how things turned out . . .*

Her death rattle was small and final. Some wet came out of her mouth. Not a lot. She looked ugly. The only sound in the room was my breath and then I got up and went over and closed her eyelids and kissed each one and her cheeks on either side of her lips. The movements of my eyelids sounded truly loud, a terrible intrusion, like a storm of insects, or like a weird, quiet clapping for me on the part of time which she had, in her way, nurtured, off and on.

I said *Good-bye, Mom* out loud but I suddenly realized it was what I wanted that mattered now. So I straightened her hair a little and lay my cheek on her forehead as if tenderness was the chief force in the world or had been for us—as perhaps, comparatively, it had been—and then I thought to myself, letting myself be honest, *I'm through* (with a lot of stuff) *and I'm glad*; and I went to find a doctor or a nurse, someone to tell that Lila was dead.

The doctor said, "Yes, well it's been a miracle . . ."

I went to the waiting room where Nonie and Lila's younger sister and one of her brothers had been waiting for three days, and I told them, but I mostly looked at Nonie, who said, "I don't believe you . . . I'll wait to hear it from the doctor . . ."

And that was really the only time I made any real effort to keep my deathbed promise to my mother (by adoption).

I was ill off and on for a year after her death and then I resumed my life. I experimented with homosexuality—partly because I could not bear the sadness of women or the memories in trying to be strong and to be a partner, partly because I couldn't bear to saddle them with me or with my thoughts; and the silence then when I was with them suffocated me and made me cruel—and evasive . . . I saw some women, though, always. Perhaps they were the main part of my life. I set about building some trust for myself in myself so that I might become a scientist or a writer. The approximations in science which then were taken as *facts* when they were only slightly better than squinting guesses—and my failure to be able to bear the eyes of an audience on me if I tried to be an actor—drove me to try to write.

But I'd always known I would try.

Daniel sold the family business and became a painter, failed, and went back to school and studied various useful things and led a useful and charitable life among the poor but sometimes among tough pioneers in various countries, ending piously in Israel, a pious man and a pioneer working hard in a number of agricultural settlements and vacationing in Paris, Rome, and, on occasion, Berlin. I believe he did a considerable amount of good but then I want to think it: I don't really know. Summaries are not ever really true enough genuinely to matter.

LEONIE

or The History of a Kiss

On Almost Getting Laid

But, see, inside a present moment, among the enormous eyelids of the unfinal and sailing rose, a gangling boy comes and sits on a couch. Under my shirt is a hairless chest—there is this mad thing some older girls do, Nonie's friends, that year, when I was fifteen, the year Nonie was almost engaged to Tom, and the next year, when I was sixteen, Nonie's friends, they poke their fingers between the buttons of the shirt—*Well, it's wartime: I guess I do wild things*—and they stroke their own and yours to see how much yours is like or unlike theirs, the skin, the reality of touching it.

Sometimes then I find it hard to breathe. Often they keep their heads turned away or their eyes are unfocussed while they talk and giggle and chatter and do that. But sometimes, though, they look at you, at me, while they do it, and you try to look back at them, I do, their equal; I'm bluffing; sometimes it works. And the two of you stare at each other unblinkingly-and-as-if-sophisticatedly and it gets *hot*—a wartime term for combat or for sex—it is an intense and an unblessèd moment.

I get this kind of immense and frightening-to-me feeling then, when their fingers are on me, perhaps a demonic rush of a lot of feelings—me, still gawky, different-faced, almost used to things, and yet, one did formally change almost every day, and certainly, with every event—sometimes when you're looking right at a girl and trying to be tough-for-your-age and she's touching you, your eyes fade as existent entities; they become dim marble things like the eyes of a statue. And you feel the hot, blurry, milk-hazy, statue-y eyes in your face when they're in that form as some absence of fragility and some presence of metamorphosis.

What makes fooling around possible is being made of stone—I think some guy I know said that; maybe it was my mother. Wistfully-toughly made of stone—not too humanly serious—not too frail—this might be me in Carolina—this is something I learned early on—I'm a bad guy—trash of a certain kind—girls can fool with me. *It's not like it's walking on eggshells, Wiley . . .* The world loses nothing if I'm ruined—or silly—here, in this moment, if I'm obsessed and stupid for a while—or always.

I'm not talking about love you daydream of but it's love—sometimes . . . here and there . . . for a moment . . .

In the moment are oddly opposed and yet simultaneous things. In my half-blindness, I sort of half see the girl's eyes are woodland sharp—in a story—blindness and taking this risk having eyes anyway—in this woodland dusk. Your skin, your arms, your cock are staring—and the odors, the sexual style of the moment, the fox eyes—the owl's eyes, the goggling fish eyes . . . the seaweed hair—or hair-in-a-windstorm, blizzard-white at its edges where the lamplight is like snow glare on dark threadiness—sometimes their teeth show, and mine: mermaid and ferret shit. Momma has accused me of wildness; she is dying: *This isn't one of your good years, Wiley . . . one of the years when you're good to me; if you ask me, you're out of control . . . You don't care what happens to you.*

My uncaution. My being Nonie's *goat* . . . or under Nonie's influence was what she talked to me about.

A good time in the shadows . . . It depends on the girl, my degree of danger . . . so to speak. Tonight the girl is Leonie Sminship Midder—I am *ready and willing* to sacrifice others to my intention to live—but that includes other selves within me, other than the one that wants to live.

You know that reaching, unhappy, restless thing some girls have about flirting? The thing of because it's you it's *nothing serious . . .* Nonie said Leonie was *kinky . . .* a joke, not a joke—I had no clear notion of *kinky* except it was what Nonie said of anyone who liked me.

Puberty sometimes produces amazing effects using you. Fresh and glistening, barely unwrapped, I knew some things from experience and about some things in obscene comics and in some *great* books—*The Decameron* and Ovid's stuff and *The Golden Ass* and James Joyce. I took a couple of breaths and I found myself staring at Leonie because of what she'd said when we were introduced by Nonie: "Ooooh, cute . . ." Something like that. "So tall . . ." Then I probably misheard: "Pretty spaghetti . . ." Because I was so thin and had such weird posture . . . *A boy* . . . an idea.

I start to laugh—comedy takes the place of some kinds of modesty —but the buttock-deep shivers and the partly involuntary shrugs of the upper back are kind of anguished foolishly, hideously, with early amusement and toughness—as in football. She grinned, more or less sightlessly staring at *the idea*—a fresh-faced boy—in wartime.

She laughed, too, a short, high-pitched yelp: "I *am* kinky, I guess." The mid-body Midwestern *restlessness*, deep-dirty, semi-doomed, stupid —you know what I mean—*older* women show that a lot.

Nonie said, "Well, why don't you two neck . . . ha-ha." Nonie's using her old chirping voice—the legs-tied-together, cloud-of-small-birds, fixed-in-tone voice—sometimes she does that at home, but mostly it was gone. Mostly her will, nowadays, was dressed in a wholly other voice, another range, fastidious-wartime-lady-manly-(lighting-a-cigarette) brutal feminine-au*thoritative*. In some ways, the voice of an unsuccessful athlete: a *serious* person. Was she a serious person now?

She said that, and Leonie and I didn't start guiltily and didn't, either one of us, take a step backward.

"I have to go change my shoes," Nonie said. "Ha-ha," she said to herself.

Leonie puts her tongue in her cheek, which then really sticks out —this is all wartime stuff: you can see it in movies that came out that year.

She moves her head and then says, "How old are you?"

"*Let's sit down*," I said dirtily. I was amazed, always, at this point, that nearly everything said in English can be dirty. I had much more nerve that year than maybe I've ever had since. We made room for each other on the couch.

She said, amusedly and sympathetic, too, "You're breathing funny."

"Dirty breathlessness . . . I talk fancy . . . Wanna mess around?"

The fragments of a second of the encroaching *messing around* . . . the players (us) being *good sports*—or maybe not . . . our torsos self-consciously separated by air . . . are temple-precinct time—but then Leonie says, "You are old enough to take care of yourself?" Then: "You're funny-looking, you're all legs." Her head has moved a little toward me.

"What does that mean?" I ask, already slightly tousled—and with obscenely readied breathing—I'm ready to hold my breath in a kiss.

"It doesn't mean a thing if you haven't got that swing," she says.

I remember Leonie's smeared face and my hot nervous guilt—and my exhilaration—when we are really close together, our heads, but then she licks my nose and backs away; she glances at me superiorly, down her nose a little—she has a small nose—*authoritatively*, a superior officer. What does this mean?

Leonie says to the air, "*He's* a cross between Gary Cooper and Bud Abbott . . ." It's not true. That's not true. What does it mean, her saying an untrue thing? Then she says, of me and Nonie, "You look like brother and sister."

"Tweet-tweet," I say.

"What's that?"

"Lovebirds . . ." Then: "Everything pretty much is a joke on me . . ."

"Poor you," Leonie said. Leonie had long legs . . . In those days I rarely noticed things in such a way that I could give form to what I noticed. I was not clearly aware what I looked like—I had some pride in the matter but no clear or cogent reason or sense—but merely a historical sense of how other people acted—and so I had little sense of other people's looks formally but mostly of how people acted toward them . . . including me. The odd tonality of sexual flirtation—the immanence of the idea and physical sense of real, if limited sex—the antagonism and fear at the start of the lesser story of *dirty* romance—a tragicomedy —my comparative innocence, even as a *sharp* boy: that was a term back then that meant *astute*—it smelled scarily, some, and even a lot, of metamorphosis in the woods.

I looked and saw that Leonie had a boy's face and coarse hair the color of bronze and dully brown-yellow dead leaves in autumn—and some kinds of sexual cowardice in her are visible even to me when I was fifteen—and I can see some sexual snobbery peering out from below the dead-leaf coloring . . . at me. I hadn't heard or read the phrase *sexual terror*. I thought of my nervy and nerved-up state as *smelly* or as *a smelloid deal*. I didn't use deodorant . . . I trusted to virtue and some sort of honesty toward nervousness to prevent stench. It is a matter of eyes to show you mean it—that you value the pleasure . . . and then it is a matter of luck.

"Oh you, you're too young to have bedroom eyes." Pause. "But you have them." She *kissed* me on my nose—then licked me again. My lips slip up onto hers.

Shyness and weakness, and some slyness and some not-weakness . . . She pulls away: "I like truthful people," she says.

"I'm fairly truthful," I say.

Each of us straightens ourselves slightly.

She says, "Do you like me or do you think I'm an old hag?" Then: "Let's swear we will never lie to each other—don't lie to me now." The rural now, *Be good now, you hear* . . . The *Don't laugh at me* . . .

"I'm honestly attracted to you . . ."

"I'm honestly attracted to you, but let's not get into trouble."

"We won't get into trouble . . ."

"I'll tell you about me . . . I'm a little bit wild: I like to kiss. Don't be mad . . . Don't be mad at me." For putting this on an impersonal level: I'm just there, it isn't *me* she is chasing—don't be angry because of that.

"I don't take anything seriously," I said.

"Oh. Well, contact, roger, over and out," she said. Then, breaking the first touch of our lips: "You confess something: it's your turn: I confessed about myself."

"I confess I want . . ." I put my lips back on hers and we breathed. She rubbed me with her foot with *her shoe on*.

She pulled away and said, "I'm a kind of foot freak . . ."

I kiss clumsily. I am too shocked by how real-seeming, except it's not just *seeming*, how real lips and minds and the whole person are. I'm too far into a state of shock to kiss well . . . or easily. For instance, I feel in her mouth her sadness at not being a boy.

I kissed her—i.e., I moved my lips—with a vague sense of familiarity with her since that thing of her stroking me with her foot with her shoe on. I remembered that as a little-boy thing I had used my shod foot as a fist in fights with people bigger, or in fights with a lot of kids in the then physically comic world of heroic changeability, weird odds, and bits of patience toward me as a little kid. I think I feel in the hot movements of her breath, as our lips maneuver on each other, her *amusement* at my sissy hairlessness and at my beginner's shoulders. At my height cum inexperience. The clumsiness of the way I am phallic.

Early phallicism.

It was *locally* conceivable—as dirty—with underneath stuff about death and war (around here) influencing people's lives. I was interested in this stuff. I was someone half-girlish now but at a crossroads and about to be a man—maybe. So to whatever extent she was like me, she could *imagine* a man's reality sprouting from her . . . her becoming a man . . . sort of . . .

This between her and me was a success thing but dark—and it felt deep and drowny, exhilarating, weird . . . like being in waves . . . *deep water*. I'm in deep—no safety—silent feelings. The kind of *tone* her lips had—what was conveyed in the touch of her lips in the so-called kiss—was that she was thinking about herself and she was kissing me.

She placated the boy with a certain notable potency of temporary affection . . . not an overwhelming weight of it. She wasn't the testing kind—the kind that tested you with finality and huge hints of fucking. The first kisses only lightly—tactfully, cutely—touched on the scandal of my being *male*, if I can say it like that. I felt a little bit *kidnapped* by feelings. My lips and her lips, her voice and my voice were silenced except in kissing and in the feelings aroused by kissing—you crawl into the small, damp, shadowy tunnel of *this stuff* . . . the conduit of other stuff that moves toward you and in you until, in a sense, you are professionally male although as a beginner in the black tunnel of the moment at the edge of an obscure future . . .

I knew myself as male largely through sports—most other things were shared. Not sports or clothes . . . Not clothes entirely . . . A person not remotely phallic but held by the phallic compass point—a young man—an apprentice and a bit obscure as to character. One is being tested and one is not allowed to look at the answers at the back of the book. I am rewarded ahead of time even if she backs out at any moment. She wants me not to be rambunctious.

We are giving *birth* to one another—I am giving birth merely to an element in her—but it is a pair of stories.

I don't want her to *know* me. Except as what I pretend to be. I don't want her to know what I really feel. I don't want a final attachment. But I do, inevitably, love somewhat when these things happen. I lied in my account about Carolina: how much I loved the house, the sunlight, the people . . .

In a sexual moment one is partly wooden—a puppet—the genetic and social power of sexual event is greater than one's own powers: the webby framework of that.

Isobel said boys, "*The mean boys—their bodies are like, oh, I don't know—big toys . . .*"

I think she wanted *a man* to be as strange as she felt life to be—a man represented life-outside-the-house, maybe. She wanted partly an automaton paralyzed in mood or with a set mood, a painted one. The absence of visible will—no, the absence of idiosyncratic will—an obedience to acting out having a general will—the thing of *free* volition in her is *pity*, a voluntarism. Neural helplessness—no display of physical power—a *mean* boy—a *collusive* toy . . . an ambition of hers.

I guess Leonie reminds me of that.

"Oh, we're mad, this is so *mad*," Leonie said, brushing her coarse dead-leaf hair back from her faintly moist forehead.

"I like this a lot—" Then: "A very great deal," I said, attempting to be droll and mannerly—serious.

It is hard to describe sexual style honestly and not be sarcastic or else do it as an advertisement for sex and purity and for yourself.

But what it is is a posture and a velocity in a moment of attention to entering in on the lax gaiety of a submission to sexual reality—whatever that is for you.

And whatever that is, it is important in nature. The segments of those moments, marked by breath and the excruciating melodramas of changes of posture—her pushing back your hair or hers and your resettling yourself on the couch—make up a section of your life of flutters of modest and immodest dilutions of scariness in a wilderness of possibilities. Knowing yourself here is like knowing yourself in the permutations of a baseball game or mountain climbing—the structures of suspense are fraught—lip to lip. Of course, you can be cool. The difference of the bodily structures—breast, chest, prick, cunt—is the key to the thrills moment to moment and the way stuff is fraught, all of it blurred with actions and meanings and with the guy attempting to ignore things and the woman paying attention.

But both of you are lying: she's not really paying attention and you're not ignoring things . . . The real tonality of a kiss and of an undone button in this situation *is* melodramatically unsayable in terms of who is paying attention and who is thinking, sometimes willfully, of something else. Too much momentum spoils the possibilities of absolute stuff and of any simple nature of the flight from the absolute to the mind-wandering stuff. The course of the event, the blurred thing, the biological rehearsal, the decency (or indecency) and the lunatic individuality of it cannot be exemplified in any single action or term—this is of the thing unlied about—the actual intensity or unintensity of the touch of her *five* fingers or her *ten* fingers if both hands cup my obstinately trembling chin—I mean this is the most startling, and astounding, form of counting that I know of, more astonishing than when you bet hits and slaps and someone coldcocks your deltoid twenty-five times and you grunt and groan and half laugh and count argumentatively, loudly, to hurry them up, to measure the comic horror or whatever it is—but how are you going to symbolize this touch? It's her and you, it's one moment, it's specialized and personal, temporary (and even skidding), an electric thing, sparks, a gateway of sparks defining dead and undead passages of one's arcs of motion among all the motions.

I don't understand the emotions. The range of her attentions and the unimportance of some of them and the importance of some others are a kind of careless grandeur of will, nervous and reluctant, with a power of attraction like that of some shapes of bone under pretty skin: her nervousness, her boldness—her "*boldeur*"—her touch, the spirit in it, and what I knew. What she intends I half know from a general report from before we started: she is a friend of Nonie's; she is older than I am . . . She is not a whore . . . She is not a stranger on a train. But the ceaselessly stirring electric feel of her touch is a little as if I had been taken prisoner by some primitive people and I was being overrun by small mammals and nudged by their snouts and nipped by their little teeth and tickled insanely and inwardly by their dirty disease-carrying little paws, their gentle and maddened and wild gnawing as in some book about being inhibited and then being a prisoner dirtily of sexual event.

One is *young-and-romantic* . . . at least in this sense. Is this an awful sense? Not romantic as in a book that trafficks in such matters, but young-and-eaten, young-and-*dirty*, knowingly conceited but contingently, depending on how things come out, half-instructed, scared-and-fearless, YOUNG-DIRTIED with this reflecting certain possibilities—of sexual ambition outside of what books say about the matter. The moment's factuality is restlessness and odd resistance (and contempt) toward time, that foliate fusillade of sensation, blows and trespasses—one's existence lurks and leaks a bit—the blindness in the motion of the thing—the story of trespassed-on nerves, the ripples of the passion of blond childhood extended to here. "Oh wow . . . Oh my," the boy says, startled and somewhat in control of himself and wanting to be droll.

The relative nature of an embrace—of really kissing—lies in the *relative imprisonment* in a change of scale when you come close to someone.

Then the exclamatory explosions and bursts of response—milkweed pods of feelings—are bits of neural light and enormities of heat. One's larger bones and this other flesh are me, and they shudder in close proximity to other bones even more unfamiliar and exciting and unknown and scary *other* flesh in this new scale. My mother is dying but childhood curiosity, that staring from outside grown-up moments into them, exists now as a sense of new and as yet uncommonly-experimented-with capacities of feeling where one was in the midst of horrors or not—war, illness, greedy whoredoms. The stalky, semi-towering, blond (perhaps sensually stupid) kid hopes for a charitable representation of one of the styles of local affection from her, measured and focussed, not foreign, not bookish, not *overdone*.

It's just her and me—it's just me and her . . . And social caution and psychological wariness and then a thing of looking askance at the nudity of immanent chagrin—this wholly new area of struggle in which one is judged and beaten or neutral or something of a winner—this exists in the distanced attention of that part of me not trembling in the actual moment. The kid is a huge newborn except for a bookishly worded tribunal part of myself, a lunatic, would-be sane but mad owl-clock-and-huffing-judge part—the God's-child part—which is not fully grown.

It judges the part of me that reaches out a real hand to touch the curly hair of the girl alongside her cheek—judges like a kid at the movies. *Is that a good idea, is that a good version of a good idea . . .* Her mouth opens and eats air waiting near my mouth, moves into a heated nearness and toward the savor of what is left of her lipstick and the rudely uneven grooves of her lips.

An erection, one eye—1 I—a branch of flesh—during the kiss—I am off and on aware of the as-if-heavy weight of my *spine* and of the torsion and twist of muscles of my back and side with my arms around her, and of the other complication—in my lap. I transfer my attention to this state, from the kiss, from her: I sometimes think transformations of states is a horror. Other times it seems okay. I laugh and resist inside the kiss, the joined lips, inside the technique, the peculiar matter of the suburban technique of *kissing*—which, in my case, includes no-calculation . . . no attempt at manipulation . . . no ordinary surprise: nothing grabs you as in a darkened hallway or as in a joke but, rather, it approaches, barefoot, and is there, in the *silence* of being new to you.

I mean to me.

She says, "We aim to please . . . Ha-ha."

The twitchingly shifting reality is utterly all that surrounds me and it sucks at my heart as if a mouth were inside my chest. My enlarged, swollen, oddly rhythmic heart—life has this in it, the attention blinkingly *filled*. I realized bit by bit from my sensations of her too active other mouth that she dominates me—I can't bear to be dominated, at all. The thrill of my near-virginity is of not being dominated. My burdened studious *attention* has a fresh and misty but also a burned quality of airy hallucinations—as if by accepting an accompaniment of music on a piano for a show that you have to put on—the physical realities of kissing. Some of the hallucinations are slants and beams of memory, bits of motionful memories coming and going, oneself and other women and oneself alone (masturbating) and guys talking dirty and boasting . . . maybe flattering me, encouraging me. A time when I ran for a touchdown and then the stuff afterward in the locker room. The *sensitive*, ill-defended reaches of the face-mouth and of the almost hidden palate and of the mind and of one's confidence: the tongue crosses the teeth and the invasive excitement is displeasing; it gutters; so, one is odd; but her pulse can be felt and mine and my prick pulse and the pulse in her belly—electric or mechanical—a warehouse roar of a weighty thing (like a stack of filled cartons) being shifted and an auditorium sense of hollowness make it that I am uneasily *happy* in a curious reflexiveness—or openness—my interior self is a place of laboring toughness. I grip her arms probably too hard and am astonished and scared how my erectile velocity strengthens and becomes more assured with sadism and toughness and sweat. I am upset at being, as it were, perpendicularly mounted on *sinful event* . . . a violent attitude . . . Partly undefended—and unaccused—her *female* (cunted) reality makes me *a villain*—and this erects the boy *finally*—the axiom of this fleshly geometry resting on theorems of undomination as clear-cut law, for a while.

Accident and nature provoke a sense of fateful individuality. The boy is of a size such that degrees of full erection, perhaps five stages of it, exist for him. The erection has become sufficiently *involving* among its stages at the present time—if *I* can say this—that it is almost inviolate in regard to my will: but whether this is Genetic Nature or merely mine, or even more merely mine at this age or even just at this moment; I was in speculative and also skeptical awe of it, as of a train chugging and hooting without noise and proceeding down the tracks toward me.

My own erection has a mind of its own. I keep muttering *yeah, yes, yeah, yeah, yes,* as I kiss her and I laugh inside the motions of tongues, in there, in order to act out the thing of being undominated, but I am as if locked in the curtains of the stage at school in the auditorium . . .

My sense of time—of motion—shows when I pull back from her and mutter, "The History of a Kiss . . ."

"Ha-ha," she says.

Another arc of sensation—of feeling in motion—involves the somewhat intrusive arrow movements of the recurring and always odd and oddly new actuality of the couch. Love and pleasure and then idea and the study of truth—the show of feeling has in it two chief currents, the current of steamy reality, the mob scene of the now, the mob of sensations—and then the tribunal thing, the blink of judgment. Doubt, shyness, nerves—heat and the attempt of judgment, blinkingly as I said, form a stained piece of biography: one loves the history of one's St. Louis kisses, the kisses of Western Man—and Woman—for a moment.

And for a moment nothing is stale, or if that is too strong, what was in the air, to use an old and sentimental term, was not so much the possibility of sexual pleasure in a grown-up way, not the possibility of distraction in such a way, but, rather, this hot, imbecile mitigation.

Comfort for Ma's briefly nelly son—the *dirty* kiss, tonguingly, lippily, prowlingly—me passive in the mouth toward her and my hand on her breast a little cruelly: I never kissed Nonie on the mouth once I began to speak—words permitted no possible feeling of that sort in me for Nonie. Leonie's breast: part of a program of escape. I want Nonie to respect me sexually. The Air Corps girl's kiss. I don't want Nonie to laugh at me.

Leonie ends the kiss. I as-if-wake to her—Leonie, a smoker, is coughing a little; she puts two fingers on my cheek and says—coughingly—"Not bad."

I had ignored her, lost sight of her, hadn't known how she condescended to kiss me—how unpierced, how unthreatened by me she was. I associate this moment in which I woke to my sexual existence with her, I associate it with childhood ripening. A ripeness in an appetite for her fear? Nonie watches from the archway. One would have spit in the face of *reality* to abjure all this. Nonie did not fuck before marriage that I know of—some, maybe even much, of her sexual experience lay in watching me. And others. She said of sex to people sometimes, *Why settle for what's less good when you can wait and have the best?* Tom, one of Nonie's almost-fiancés, had said to me that Nonie was *a clean girl* (i.e., it was *easy* for him to be with me, to meet her family). What does *honest* mean in real time? The reality of companionship is not like some fictional or metaphysical *example* of companionship. The clear colors of great speed require cloudless light. Time moves differently in the spaceship . . . In school, lab experiments never come out exactly. A teacher—it is not vanity that says this—a woman who wanted to flirt with me—said of students who claimed their experiments had come out exactly, *They are lying.*

Ah, how shocking is a memory of specific sunlight—and heat—at a swimming pool—inside the new-boned and adolescent skull of the boy in University City.

Behind the newishly older, not entirely honest eyes is a polite thing, a sense of old chastities—and of substitutions now.

"Let's smile and kiss," I said. "Keep the smile on your face."

God, the look of patience on her face . . . With my youth . . . Like my dad, sometimes, in the last year before he died.

She tousles my hair and says, "I know how to arm wrestle . . . I've watched my brothers do it."

"From up close?"

Pallid, *phallic* arms . . . one imagines this abruptly . . . harsh with effort.

"Life is just too sexy," I say in a falsetto, imitating no one but pretending I am imitating someone. The possession of male beauty . . . it is realer and yet unactual in lovemaking . . . curiously *veiled* in the sequence of phenomena . . . an emotional-*technical* basis for grudging and lie-torn, persecutory *approval*.

"Kiss me, my fool," she says. It is a joke from her mother's day. Reactions . . . Be tough or die . . . *A leader* . . . Nonie in the shadows in the hallway . . . I fuck for the household—do you?

Leonie says, "You have a nice mouth." She is being older. Invulnerable. Invulnerably she says, "Pretty, pretty, pretty . . ." making it all a baby-talking joke about how much nerve she has . . . *cutely* denying the actual and palpable intimacy—removing it from its place in the arc of having a settled-on sexual future—then to stare at someone's *lips*—to stare at someone's lips *unsmilingly* and then to smile willfully—at him—that's bold.

Reality does not have to be plausible. It's not a dream. It goes its own way. You can yell, *HEY WAIT FOR MY CONSCIOUSNESS*, but hearing you isn't its business . . . reality's. In the shadows, fingertips are braced against the rise of the couch and the other set of fingertips touch the faintly gritty waxed floor. My shirt is partly unbuttoned.

I say, "It hurts . . ."

She says, topping that, "It's *scary*." Then turning her face upward: "You have to wonder—*is this* real?" A kind of automatic tone . . . It is a line. She touches my chest—*flutteringly*. Her mind is elsewhere. She is thinking about her own desires. And I fight not to breathe or smile *flutteringly*. I fight to be deadpan—the most sexual thing for me is to be in a territory of phallic will—not necessarily active but active in the sense that *embarrassment* is constrained—it is a territory where I can presume. I poke and push against her. Readiness—*good-sized* . . . I don't *know* —locker-room randiness—a thing of being a *strong, silent type*? It is not a settled matter. Because of rivalries—with all other men sexually—my masculinity maybe is emblematic . . . Perverse . . . "I wish we were drunk . . . It *HURTS* to be wide awake." My line: an automatism of sorts, like hers. What is it we want? "Lila keeps no liquor in the house. She checks my bureau to see if I hide any. A lot of kids at school are drunks." Nonie drinks too much—and passes out—and claims to be a teetotaller and unused to liquor.

If I am undominated, am I then dominant? If I am free and she is not—I don't mean in relation to me—am I dominant by *comparison*?

Cruelty here is to be inwardly absent, busy differently from the other person. The just-getting-it-to-happen—that other stuff—doesn't mean you're there.

To be there is a little like bartering your soul in some kind of anxious and maybe overfull drunkenness for pottage . . . for sex. I want my soul for later—*Socratically*. Who cares what *I* want? I'm not rich. *You have to fit in, Wiley* . . . If *I* give off some sense—some aura—of being *endowed* with abilities, having a future, and of regular (and irregular) *naïve* merit and humor—if I give off some sense of being lucky—or blessed—*endowed* that way, it might have the effect of my being *rich*—or princely—and then it would matter to Leonie what I wanted. It would matter what became of me. That might make her perverse and kind of violent—I might not be able to manage. I often couldn't manage.

The gestures of fate, sexual fate, how these things work is that then I really looked at *her*.

But a lot of what I feel is fear and unease, curiosity and desire and envy, and some confidence. The male-female equity-inequity is lawful within the illegality of her being so old—proud-chested, fine-necked, exhibitionist Leonie—she is cleverer than I am: I am outmanned, outgunned . . . I don't feel guilty. She is all concealed and all exhibited—I am as if all exhibited like a kid on a porch with older girls or with women observing his maleness—caution seems suicidal and is *suicidally* present. An athletic-and-spoiled-rich-boy's and tough-lower-class-kid's and little kid's alternation of roles, gimmicks, spyings, self-displayings, submissions, independences, assertions? I am a spy on my own life. In the war years, to be lecherous was to be *a wolf*.

Leonie knows I have waked to her.

Leonie says—in what is a local high style in a certain milieu—"I'm not sure I like liking you. I'm not sure you're as sweet as you look. Are you likable?"

This is compliment-sugar in reverse . . . I am *dangerous* and not entirely sweet.

It also has the other meaning of: she isn't afraid and has room to play in . . .

Am I likable? "Is that just a line or do you mean it?"

She says, "Don't hate me . . ."

"I don't *hate* you . . . Ha-ha . . ." Then: "Guys lie about sex."

"What do they say?" she asked.

She was too interested. I said, "They lie like rugs . . . You like *madmen*?"

"Do you talk like this all the time?"

"I talk a lot of crapola . . . A lot of it is malarkey. It's *blarney* . . ."

"You have a big vocabulary."

"I don't know . . . When you fuck older men, do they make weird faces?"

"I don't want to talk about that . . ."

"*Real Men* are the most important people in wartime."

"Don't ask too much of me, Wiley."

The persiflage section of getting to know each other while necking . . .

The skin of her face—faint fuzz and bits of makeup—and her neck and the parts of her body, a bit sweaty, jointedly *melty*, amused and heated—a little—there is a limited (and semi-domestic) fire in her . . . Like a coal grate with a low fire. I wasn't completely ashamed. I didn't know enough to be consciously flattered, either.

I said, stiffly, leaning back and covering my forehead with my forearm—but my other hand was around her back and emerged on her waist on her far side, which it lightly, a little loonily, palped—just her waist—"I'm sorry."

"What are you up to?" she said, laughing.

"I *know* what I do is *young*," I said. I said gloomily, "I'm a child."

"So what?" Then: "What are you trying to say?"

"I'm afraid we're not going to go on."

"Whew . . . You speak right up and you're so *pretty*." The tone was of a milieu unknown to me.

I made a face—I felt endearingly and familiarly tormentedly grotesque to myself. "Are you a turtle?" I said. It was a semi-secret remark at high school: some of the kids in fraternities and sororities, Gentile kids, made it at school, high school: it was a fad.

She looked at me blinkingly. "I'm out of my shell—I'm turned over and can't get a move on . . . what is it?"

"I don't know . . . It's just a thing to say . . . Like mairzy doats . . ."

She blinked some more. Then she said, "I . . . like . . . you."

"What a hero," I said—still jealous of *real men*.

"You're nice. I hate to be part of a *score*—of *scoring*," she said; and I sighed. She said, "Huff, huff, puff, puff, you want me to blow your house down."

I didn't know until a year afterward that she might mean *blow* with the meaning of oral sex. She meant for me to laugh.

"I want to fuck . . ."

"Oh. Babe, don't try so hard." Her body lay oddly, as if pecked and struck by a horny bill. Bruised. "You have *perfect health* . . ."

"Hunh? *That* doesn't matter."

"It does if someone's tastes run in that direction," she said.

"Oh," I said, thoughtfully. I got carried away with a notion of excited, and exotic, parody of the flattery she put out: "Well, *you're* terrific," I said sadly.

My heart and pulse, *my* heatedness, there is a whole up-and-down thing as in a costumed amusement park in a surreal dream—free-willed automatism—so to speak—means you pick the ride you go on. Pick your terror and your scream. I hear a kind of clicking in her breath . . .

"Can I unbutton your blouse . . ."

She just breathed as I unbuttoned one button . . . I am dry-mouthed. And my body bucks a little. "I seem like a fool," I said, fumbling idiotically with the next button.

"Will you go to a good college? I think you're smart." Her odor is faintly working-class . . . the soap, her underwear. She says as I palp her brassiere, her breast in it, "Are you a Communist?"

"No. I don't know. Maybe. I wouldn't mind."

She says, "Sometimes I say no to things because I really don't care, I just say no, but sometimes it's part of a line. Do you do that? Do you understand what I am saying?"

I didn't, no. But "Yes," I said.

"You're very sure of yourself." She *lightly* clambers up on top of me: she says, "*Oof* . . . Am I like a sister to you?"

"No . . . Unnnh . . ." A grunt. I touch her . . . down there. My more or less *sore* erection seems to whirl with light—itchy, hot: a hallucination but eerily actual heat . . .

She says, "Isn't this French? You like *French* stuff?"

I unbutton my pants, I undo my pants from the top—only a few pants had zippers in those days—I unbutton while looking at her; I assert myself in this local way—conventional. A lot of the sphinx shit of the *veering* and slippery reality of *before-a-fuck* is snapping at me and offering puzzles you solve or you have to die. I mean it was hardly certain that she'd fuck . . . I mean only that the feelings in me were a tensed leaning of a juvenile and giddy and a bit grim . . . boyish . . . *readiness* . . .

"It is Leonie here," she said. "Over and out . . ."

"It is Wiley here," I said—gently *wild-man*-smart-ass-*fresh* . . . ?

She partly gives in. We do, she does a tongue-and-lip kiss with me

. . . I attempt a little toothplay—some mild lip-biting. I bite her lip . . . like a big shot . . .

Nothing. Nihil. Nil.

I become orally passive. I have found that my being passive lures people—their curiosity. I am passive and bossy . . . She was carrying out local wartime sexual practices—in a wartime style, curt and self-conscious, folkishly studious, and argumentatively challenging, high-morale-triumphant—a bit dishonest. A still-unexpressed obscene self lurks: dirty older girl. She has a good deal of physical discipline—she is athletic—I *feel* her nervous half-amusement and wish to hurt me to prove how relatively strong she is. I don't know if that is different from my wish to prove how strong I am in comparison or not . . . She is engaged to a fighter-plane pilot who has flown a number of missions—all that fear and adrenaline . . . I believe he had three kills to his credit at this time.

She said, giggling some: "I think you're *very* French—oh, you make me wild." It was sort of like a joke—you know? She meant almost the opposite of what she said. If I were strong, clever, and beautiful, I could wreck her life.

I looked at her out of sad, dumb eyes—kind of alive.

She had a density of being *jam-packed* with a psychological carelessness of some sort. I could hear it buzzing in her, dirtied and *treacherous* and unkind—authoritative, unguardedly so, a kind of final, i.e., *devilish* ambition in her. But I am rescued *from-the-ashes* . . . By this sphinx-gnawing-at-you-and-snapping-(and-whispering)-at-you and careless almost-sex. Glory may lie in the *passionate* criminality of me twisting this stuff and swindling her into a fuck while not being in earnest about my own feelings.

Leonie, smacking her lips, says, contemptuously-admiringly-*condescendingly*, "You're a wonder . . . Oh, we're in trouble."

If it was true, she would be silent and amused in a deep way.

I touched both her breasts.

I took off her barrette and said with apology, "I have a small tongue."

"Yes? I think that's all right," she said in a grown-up voice; she had a local accent. "You're very *sensitive* . . ."

"Sorry," I said.

"Do you have a hard life?"

"Oh, you know . . ."

She said, "I bet you've had a good time with girls . . ."

I didn't know what was smart to say—I said, "Sometimes I do . . . In a lot of ways . . ."

Her slightly swollen lips—fluffed—had a kind of oral erectility. She touched my underpants with one finger, her finger touched my erect, aching thing under the white cotton behind the ship's wake thing of the parted pants. I was *sincere* . . . And hopeful. Much of the time, sexually, that year. It is not a dream. One is awake. A boy in his shocked, slightly self-awed-and-female-awed readiness . . . There is no justice if you want to be grand about it, but there is some justice. Here is some justice. By comparison. *Some* acceptable logic was here. One continues into the moment by invitation or by really strenuous and abrasive will. You laugh doubtingly, mockingly; but, then, as feeling arches itself, one's self is no longer interested in one's own story but takes on a natural abnegation and is focussed on her soul, her eyes, her sense of this stuff here, the *fooling around*. Your heart starts to pound and you get literally *hot*, sweaty—a woman's liking you enough for this intimacy kind of changes the light; and the falcon heart (and mind), the predator nurses her. You want to protect her from yourself.

"You reeeeally are something," I say to her.

"You're something, too," she shoots right back, but kind of whooshily, with an oddity of the eyelids that is encouraging *in re* going on.

"Momma, Momma, pin a rose on me," I say and kiss her now odd-acting eyelids.

Her body inside some of its entrances and her skin studies the evidence that accident-and-hallucination here have become reliable delusion. That is one measure of sex. It is remarkable, and maybe one should despise it, the amount of measurement that goes on in a sexual moment. The ambition . . . The hope . . . In the cage of splashingly unstopping, heat-ridden, shuddering air. The ins-and-outs of sexual privacies are unfolded and glimpsed. I don't know how general this is . . . I think it's common. The bedouin *mind*—and the sandy moment . . . nameless crimes—nameless virtues. I gamble with my conscience and with her judgment of things. The lion in the treetops screams at this as juvenile. Leonie's tongue past a certain shallow point in my mouth chokes me. She stroked the back of my neck while we kissed but I choked on her tongue anyway. I rub her invisibility with various powders in microscopic and semi-shattered attentiveness until she is dimly visible. As a body . . . She rubs me with one hand and she held me at the neck with her other hand—I am in a void of her owl-darkness . . . *depths* and heights in a woods and above the woods.

"Is this what you do with men?" I asked.

She didn't answer.

Then, after a while, she lifted her head, moved it to move her hair, and she said, "I like you, Wiley . . ." I.e., she didn't *love* me. She said, "I am a wise old owl . . . Wiley . . ."

She took the shoe off one foot, using her other foot, and she stroked me with her stockinged foot—which irritated me—and I kneaded her breast, which I was too young to know was beautiful; but I handled it as if I wasn't as young as all that.

Still, I thought it was a *typical* breast. I liked it a lot but I thought my liking it came from my naïveté. I wanted to be *a real man* (who knew which breasts were great and which were not). The somewhat flattish-planed but globular breast—beauty has an odd quality . . . It is almost a stupidity to recognize it. If you recognize it, you kowtow to it. I rubbed my skimpily muscled, boyishly pink (I guess) chest against her *breasts* . . . I don't know . . .

She generalizingly says, "Boys your age are interesting." Then: "You smell good."

I say, "What do you know about boys my age?"

She says, "Touché." Then: "You're nice."

"No. It's you," I said. She looked as if she understood—her vanity was conceited about her *English*.

The poetry of hallucination asks for orgasm—it is a formal command in the bent universe among miracles of racing bits of light.

"Here, I'll lick the back of *your* neck," she said. She said it to stop me from licking the back of hers. I stopped. "Why do you say that?" she said, suddenly leaning back and not licking me after the first second.

"I didn't say anything," I said. Her movements weren't sudden—she was talented motionally. I lay still and said, "I don't know—why would I say anything? Are we going to go on?" Then: "Ha-ha," I added to cover up the ways in which I was young.

"Ha-ha," she said agreeably. Then, putting her head back, she said, "Ha-ha," some more.

She was LISTENING, actually, to *something*. She had an air of *brave doom*. The rushing kind of inventories you do cause an injection of shopkeeper's cunning into the affection overall but *it* (the moment) is mostly lazy in regard to cunning—who gives a fuck really? So it's like a cliff's edge. It's like kissing underwater. Affection—at the edge of love.

The issue is of *going too far . . . over the edge*.

"Wheeeeeee," I murmured.

Sometimes I know that what I am saying doesn't make sense to the other person. If they're absolutists, they say, *Speak up* . . . If someone likes you, it can *feel* to them that you've stolen the narrow path to God . . . My dad used to say to me, *You're the absolute McCoy*, and then, often, he would walk away from me. (Sometimes he would tickle me and make me kiss him, though.) Do you ever get the feeling that it's not too smart to turn against your own fate? I was pleased shitless that things were going *so well* and I felt that a lot of my earlier failures in the world hadn't been my fault.

This making and not-making love—sort of avoiding love—look, she is more male than I am at the moment. I know that. I am more *sincere* and less deathish than her fiancé. She and I look at each other and we almost understand and the gaze is warm babble—us lying to each other. It is *a matter of feelings*. We avoid scandal. I am half lost, half okay here. What was love to Leonie as a child? A dirty and intense ha-ha silence, two-sided, so that neither her parents nor she could picture love and event as continuous in the generations and inside one's life?

Will her sexual rage become religiosity? A secular silence? Her boyfriend perhaps is humiliated by his own odor of fear in the cockpit of the noisy plane—he pisses on himself each time he goes into combat. Perhaps he quietly weeps most of the time he is aloft. Perhaps his sphincter shames him—pilots have told me about this stuff.

A slantedly romantic sympathy, erotic and with a heavy smell of death, is this sympathy? Reality goes too far. I hurry after it—like a child after a nurse. Tenderness and the crushing guilt of desire—*Eat me, suck my prick*—one is overly human—I sit up, and pull her up into a thin-ribbed kiss—thin-ribbed on both sides—holding her, I topple sideways in play but I make fuck motions as we fall. "This is like sports," I explain to her. It is like *friendship* and alliance in sports.

One slips her panties down . . .

"No, no," she says. Then: "You're barely in high school."

"I'm college material."

She laughs—it is illogically *valuable*, that laugh.

Leonie says something but I don't hear her—I am fingering her cunt. *The glorious horror of it* . . .

"Oh, you are *delicious*!" she says, removing my hand from down there. "Someday someone is going to just kill you . . . And eat you right up . . . How come no one has killed you yet?"

A field of nowhere-silence: a male blossoming of breath: I say, "*Ding-dong dingdong bell.*" I push up her blouse and shove her bra up and nuzzle her left breast.

"Hunh, you're some little brother," she says.

In terms of my "behaving" in order to preserve *the status quo* (a big-time term that year), I was as female as she and Nonie were.

One's breathing—and hers—and the colors of her face—and the

heat of mine—and the heat in my abdomen—and my breath-laden weird sense of my *arched* back—me being this guy—and my complaisance and hers—and my erection—a boy's erection—I collapse into sudden *listening* . . . I am like her as she was earlier.

This is a minor pleasurable happiness for her, not a goring excitement, not a gorgeous darkness—it's not part of the deaths of the self. We are like our lying notions of *other people*.

She says, "Our feet are getting muddy . . . Let's slow down."

I lay down beside her. "That's what a mother says."

"I know," she says. The pride of the lioness. Leonie established an automatic rivalry, a looking for insult and a lesson at the hands of the universe . . . A Lutheran truthfulness.

Her clothes are rumpled. She says, "This is heaven . . . *You're* heaven."

I say—idly (my arm over my face)—"You're the world to me."

"You're laughing at me."

"Yeah," I said, holding one arm up toward the ceiling of the living room. "You're right."

"Ha-ha . . . Are you *funny*, too? Umm." She rolled over and kissed me wetly and condescendingly.

"You have pretty hair," I said, afraid, and *affronted* by her mood.

"Oh, I have problem hair," she said. Taking away my right to talk. "My hair is difficult and requires *a lot of work: it is too straight and too off a brown and too fine.*"

She has her wit, her body . . . she is standing thigh-deep, so to speak, in the blood river of the feminine. She is not particularly *happy*. The conscious attempt at growing up by an adolescent boy perhaps, wisely, lacks a sense of individuation. One crawls through women's depths—the depths of nearby women—toward the almost inconceivable pain of the realized individuality of one's fate. I am scared of being of no value. Of her being of no value. Me, me on the couch, bleary-faced me, touched and praised, fourteen-year-old-eyed, fire-chested . . . Youth: I am grateful to be included, an apprentice in sexual reality.

Then Nonie's footsteps, the sounds of clothes. Here comes zeroness. I am startled truly and stilled. I hide myself with a couch cushion. Momentum and dark life—and gradations of feeling when she enters the room: "I'd thought I'd see how the two of you are coming along . . . Are you behaving yourselves . . . ?"

Nonie pretty much claimed to have absolute knowledge of the world. In that knowledge, she wasn't *so crazy* (her term) as to be *self-sacrificing*.

Part of her knowledge was knowledge of me—and through me, through my existence . . . Nonie's overall sense of knowledge was that it was omniscient, and that it was a piece of Omniscience. It was all and part at the same time. Her contempt for her own looks as she got older—she wasn't sexually excited by her own flesh. A term of brightness had ended in disdain for her own eyes and for her hair. Her pride went on, though—a nearly unhoused omniscience. Her sexuality always seemed to me to be exploding in a vacant place—not unseen quite but in a walled and mostly empty place.

She emanates feelings—an air of conscious *cleverness* and tolerance toward us while being wearily oppressed by what we do. The emptiness of her methods disperses any sense of a plentitude in her. I glance at Leonie to see what way she is going in the bleakness and general bleariness of the sad focus of being in her presence—and a kind of familiar *excitement* that I feel. I don't have to be just to Nonie. I'm not her judge—I'm her brother.

She has a *civilized* and *commanding* air. She smokes a long cigarette—it is an excited but sad, even gloomy dismissal of excitement, tragicomic, semi-tragic, living-room-enormous, the *depression*, the defeat . . . the she-is-betrayed—this stuff plays about her wonderfully pretty, tired face . . . perhaps a bit leaden-set.

"I'm in a bad mood tonight. Well, what can you do: easy come, easy go . . ."

"Yeah," Leonie said.

Is it *traditional* that I have little sense of Nonie, little sense of her story, I mean beyond my knowledge of her capacity to lie? It is common enough in novels—and in movies—to know a woman only to that extent. Love. Lovelessness. Loneliness. Nonie liked being persuaded that happiness existed. She liked happy-go-lucky movies. Her existence lies beyond and around and under and over that stuff—amusement and acceptance, hers, the other motions of her consciousness—an almost marriageable girl. I had a lesbian teacher whom I liked a lot who said, *What is the game here?* She would say, *You see that is an interesting and subtle question.*

Nonie puffed at her cigarette—a pretty empress and her piercing gaze—is the game for keeps now?

"You've got really big boobs tonight," I said. She padded them.

Leonie kicked me and murmured, "Oh, Wiley . . ."

On a scale of one to a hundred for people being dangerous, how dangerous was Nonie? Two? Seventy-two?

Nonie said, "Wiley, you have more imagination than is good for you . . . He's the bucket that went once too often to the well. I hate it when he talks about me . . . The two of you are a sight for sore eyes . . . Pretty funny: I have to laugh—you make me laugh, ha-ha."

We laugh some, too.

She's not young anymore. She is a girlish Lear. She says, "Oh, Wiley, do up your pants; no one cares about a little brother."

"I like him," Leonie says in a tone that comes from the office probably.

"He and I are *close*—this month," Nonie says. The thickened, hardened softness of an aging *girl* . . . "Monkey see, monkey sees too much," Nonie said and laughed—she was laughing at me. She placed an arm over her padded breasts. "Don't try to know everything: don't be a know-it-all: a little human nature is nice in a little brother." She is chattering.

"I support myself, I'm self-supporting," I boast to Leonie; I say to Nonie: "I pay board and room—more than you do . . ."

Nonie said dryly, "I'm no fool . . . I don't make money to help you."

"No. You borrow money from me . . . Well, don't expect me to make money to help you . . ."

"You're a sucker, who knows where you'll wind up," Nonie said. "I can always get around you . . . You'll see . . ."

"I don't know why she talks like that," I said—wearily—to Leonie.

Nonie says, "Oh you, you're wrong all the time, no one listens to you . . . Well, what have you two no-goods been up to? Were you being bad people: don't lie to Mama Bear. I know all about it. I know, I know. You ought to be shot."

"Ha-ha," Leonie says. She straightens her clothes some more.

I say, "Ha-ha," too. But I am hurt . . .

Living-room lamplight in an early-darkening month: yellow and orange and a bit of blue-white reflected light on the glass that covers the paintings . . . and shadows, ununiform shadows: Nonie looks famous and smeary. Her photograph is on two recruiting brochures. One brochure cover showed her alone in sunlight upright but as if tilted back from the camera, which is at her knees and at which she smiles in nervous alarm and with a certain boldness anyway; and, in the other, she is the middle one, with two fliers on either side of her—she is in a polka-dot dress blowing in the wind: she is tossing her head; she has a faintly clenched, bold-brave smile different from the other smile. (Lila told me, *The idea is that women of Nonie's sort like men in the air force and pilots have a good time before they get killed—whether they're poor in peacetime or not.*) Windblown and sunlit in the photographs . . . *she is a great girl* . . . a sunnily wartime sun-and-wind-touched girl . . . Here she is approximately lit by electric light and her pretty face has an unfinal look. Her eyebrows are plucked in an artificially *natural* curve, a wartime style. Her pointed bra is padded. She has long, red, celluloid fingernails . . . false. Her straight hair is combed and set—it has long, full, loosely flowing *glamour.* It was thickened: a wartime hairdo; and its color has been tampered with: it's red-blond. She is an ad come true—a soldier's dream actually present.

She is in the same room with me, and her will and mood and the low murmur of her breath—and my chagrin toward her (Who wants to placate her *night and day*?) and the girdled weight of her selfhood, an *anchoring-and-unanchored* prettiness floating shiftingly in the shadows. *High-moralled, high-moraled girl.* Omniscient. *Imprisoned.* Cheerful and slanderous. Impatient. Indomitable. The reality of plotting and of slander are part of a girl's career. "He's a liar, like all men." Nonie is here. This enforces an absence of charity. God is that which wins.

The air and light in the room, and my sister's fine, pale skin—her small features are agonizingly sweet inside the twisted postures of her smoking a Pall Mall—I am promised to the war—I am a fiancé, a bridegroom of the war.

"You're just loco—just plain loony [*puff, puff*], but there's a time and a place for everything . . ." Is she a deep person? Her appearance, its falsity, says, *Dream me.* The bird-skulled, thin-torsoed girl—in her wartime form—and me, six feet, two and a quarter inches tall, fourteen years old, and I weigh a hundred and forty-two pounds. Nonie has bitten nails under the false ones. She wears a tailored jacket with wide shoulders and a nipped waist, a longish pleated skirt, and bedroom slippers. A glamourous scarf is wound around her long neck; the ends are tucked into the lapels of her jacket.

"He's as pretty as a girl," Nonie says, puffing on her cigarette. She rises. Now the scarf is around my neck above my skinny (and unbuttoned) chest. She casually did it. I started to fight her off but the heel of my hand hit Leonie in the temple and Nonie said, "BE CAREFUL . . ."

So the scarf is around my neck, serpentine, mauvish-gray, green-figured chiffon. Does she mean me well? I don't think that is a major issue. It is for me but not for the world. I will go ahead with the evening anyway.

Nonie says, "Here, try my earrings—show Leonie." I am an affliction, a decoy . . .

I say, "No. I have a headache."

"You *are* a headache . . . He is a headache," Nonie says to Leonie. She says, "I can manage him . . . I'm not ever *depressed*—I'm a realist. I can handle him. You want a cigaboo?" she says to Leonie.

Nonie, not in high heels, is a bit squat. So far as I know I don't want sympathy. It is a sad, satisfying joy, an explanation of much of my childhood for me to be with her. Nonie is amused by what I am. I am incautious: my mind takes continuous time and creases and folds it and smothers most memories then—this is part of the folly of oneself in an actual moment.

The dust, the upholstery—*This Moment's Loneliness*—do you know? My pitying contempt for myself happens to me more strongly in Nonie's presence than anywhere. The agitation of her small hands—pale sparrow flicker—she and I, her face and mine—we have a shared vocabulary of facial stuff. She knows my feelings and remembers them better than I do. Her *ordinariness* is not ordinary to me. Or is so ordinary it is truth itself. She says to me and to Leonie, "*Now, don't move* . . ." and she pretends to be taking a photograph of us, using her hands as if they held a camera to her eye.

You're supposed to be fooled by women . . . It is *the ne plus ultra* of sophistication. When I go to war, I will commit murder and be treacherous.

"You want to pray for us? Have you prayed for us?" Nonie asks me mockingly—as if I were dressed as a nun and not in her scarf. Her mockery, which my friends think is coarse and badly judged, is subtle and sad if you have known her for a long time. It is subtle and sad to me. She is *lovely*: provincial . . . Not young. I move and twist and follow her as if I were a radar screen in *The Battle of Britain*. Nonie stands by the couch and pushes and moves my head—now she is showing to her friend whom I have necked with (a little) my profile. It is small-town politeness to let her do this.

Leonie is not pretty, she's attractive . . . Her hair, bunched up, roughly bouffant, tops an athletic, *sensual* presence. Hers is a wide face with shallow insets and no deep recession to the jaw. Shadows on her face are summary and move in youthful thrust when she moves her head. A slightly predatory maskiness—like a wolf's: a degree of costume of a face. I am in an unbuttoned shirt and I have my sister's scarf around my neck—it is a confused moment, erotic and funnily, excitedly at some boundary or other.

Nonie says, "You be nice to Leonie. I want her to see you at your best—I told her about you. Put on my earrings . . . Show her."

"No . . . I don't want to . . ." *Naw . . . I dun wannuh* . . .

"Be fair . . ." There is no audience. There is only us. Nonie wrestlingly labors to get an earring on me. Abruptly I submit. Why? Hell, I want to be bad . . . I want to know these two women . . . I want to collaborate in a moment with the *slick*, uncertainty-tinged surfaces on which you might slide into getting laid . . . My face with earrings on aches as the palms of my hand do when I open my hands wide and hold the palms up with my fingers stretched out as hard as I can stretch them. The muscular spreading of my face—*I don't know what I'm doing . . . Well, hell, fuck, shit . . . My* eyes are as if splashed on my face. Hotly splashed . . . I practice a willed unclenchedness in travesty. A twitch of the moistly stilled, somewhat swollen genital. Ah. The feel of the scarf, the weight of the earrings . . . the attention of the women . . . I avoid for a second or two and let out the outraged laugh, the violated noise in me—the eerie pleasure and the boredom: not a pleasure—the being made much of and little of. "Is this *kinkiness*?" I ask. Leonie laughs—a little shocked.

I want to be funny. Nonie and I are testing each other's intelligence in regard to Leonie. I am illuminated, humiliated, available, *engaged in funny business*. For all I know, I am contemptibly male, dirty, dirtied . . . *awful*.

Set right . . . *teased* . . . Instructed in secrets.

Is Nonie mistaken? She says, "Isn't he sweet?" Then: "Bad is the word for us—it *is* what is wrong with us." Nonie, hysterically bold, speaks in a faintly whispered bird-tone of considerable audacity—a girl hero: "I ought to be shot. I ought to go outside and stand in the street and let a policeman shoot me . . . I ought to be shot like a policeman." She is smoothing my hair.

"Oh, it's true—you're terrible," Leonie says.

Then I repeat it: "Oh, it's true—you're pretty damn terrible." A mocking imitation, sternly baritone. But I am dressed in the scarf and earrings. Leonie laughs—loudly—but within social bounds—she is startled. *Blasé* was an important word back then. Nonie says, "You're not blasé . . ."

I say in a yet deeper voice that cracks some: "Yeah—remember your etiquette . . ."

I see by their faces that I am inside a thing of being displayed that I do not know much (if anything) about. A lack of tact here is almost like a quality of the skin: Here is the burning-skinned *young* male face, the delicately aimed and spilled and sparking eyes, the splashes, spilled and readable. The readable splashing from interior springs of the *What-I-think*, now a *raw* ocular joke . . . perhaps like an actorly beauty . . .

I don't know. But now I see what *dignity* is for. A *raw* availability for transgressions is an orphan-politician's thing. This is a moment of magic bureaucracy for me. Nonie's manner is *a little official* (*She's too official*—Momma says this of her sometimes). This is official *woman*-good-bad-girl stuff on the fire stairs—badness as part of romantic authority. It is a strain to keep track of what you're supposed to know. It is an animal thing to show knowledge. You put some of your knowledge on display to show you are suitable for being a friend . . . Or whatever . . . Nonie the loonily commanding quality of a wartime virgin—*Fight for me.* An erotic command . . . *A flicker of muscle* under the skin: an experiment. In that year of my life I saw nothing wrong yet in the destiny of a girl. I don't understand very much. The nature of female disgust and fear and longing, for instance: those are beyond me.

"Smile for *Leonie*," Nonie wheedles.

Clutch-clench . . . *I look like a girl . . . But I am okay. It is like the Trojan horse* . . . Curiosity and heat crowd me and I breathe in a half-suffocated way. Nonie has fooled me before so badly I spent months recovering but this doesn't seem bad like those times—so far, I feel only a little ashamed. I hang on to my will.

Nonie sings, "I am so bad tee-hee . . . Don't make silly faces—be pretty . . . Be nice." Then: "Wiley, please . . . I saw the casualty lists today . . ." Weekly lists.

I find Nonie repulsive for using that. But I'll bet that Leonie will make up to me for this stuff.

Nonie says in *sensitive* angry wheedling: "Don't be *serious*, be nice." She laughs disapprovingly—encouragingly: a sister. She has a light, bird-like look. She often plays the game of being pitiable and yet the boss—it is a technique.

Scarfed and earringed, an impostor-boy, a semi-party thing, his heart pounding, in my stifled-breathed sadness—and curiosity—in a shameful and private way, I smile like a guy in the movies dressed like this to please two women. It is complicated what Nonie does. What Nonie and I are. The earrings are fake rubies set in fake gold.

Nonie says to Leonie, "He won't *relax* . . ." To me she says, "Relax and enjoy it . . . We think you're cute. We're flattering you . . . Be patient: we like you . . . Wiley doesn't know about *family life* . . ." I don't know what she is talking about.

Her walk, oddly clumsy, is that of a fattening girl athlete . . . In its unskilled reluctances of movement—its girlish massiness and self-announcement. The will in her is *Let me have my way in the world* . . . Her life shames me . . . Nonie said scornfully-intently to Leonie, in front of her, to the air in front of Leonie, "He's young: *he* doesn't have to think." I have risen from the seat of the couch and am staying on it in one shoe and one foot barefoot and evading her and fending her off with one hand: she wants to put lipstick on my mouth. "HE doesn't have to think about marrying—well, you have to enjoy him while he's nice. He is *pretty*—like a girl—it won't last long—" She aims the lipstick while I dodge. "Hold still . . . I like you like this . . . It can't hurt you: I won't hurt you." Nonie half forces lipstick on one of my lips.

"No . . . That stuff feels terrible."

"Hold still, be nice, let me . . ."

I'm skinny but I'm on the football team. I'm skinny and pretty and owl-eyed—I'm a grotesque person to start with and now I am eerily decorated and silent. The odd, shapeless equation of middle-class, *shapeless* personal beauty . . .

Leonie says, "PLEASE . . . let her put the lipstick on you." Then staring at Nonie working, saying this to quiet me: "You have a beautiful mouth . . ."

Nonie says, "It's a shame to waste it on a boy." And: "He's got funny coloring: the lipstick will help."

I said with pursed-up lips, "I know men with better mouths." Then: "This is dumb . . ."

Curiosity is a trumping thing that abridges certain impulses. I am not apocalyptic. I want the world to go on. I am a fan of duration. Nonie and Leonie labor—Leonie uses her little finger to straighten the edge of lipstick on my upper lip. I perseveringly *submit* with a kind of angular amusement. Feeling pools up . . . My skin is itself a pored eye . . . I feel Leonie's and Nonie's movements in my skin and in the veins and tendons, muscles and smallish bones of my *neck*. Nonie mutters, "Hold still—you know me, Al." Now she is sighing, half-laughing: "Oh, I'm a bad person, I ought to be shot. You know me, Al."

Dislike, sharp friendliness—busy and maybe *practical* sexiness: Nonie . . .

"You're childish," Nonie says. I have no names inside me for things. For a moment—an actor—a spy—I wonder will *things here* turn out badly. That concern is in the small of my back. And in my *knees*. Am I *ruined* yet? Have I been *ruined*? *What will happen next?* I manage not to be too alert. In the straw flutter of the light in the room . . .

"Hold still—you *overreact to everything*," Nonie said.

I grab Leonie and pull her to me, like a hostage. "No more of this shit!" I say. Leonie moved the back of her body tightly against me—the ornate boy. "Oh, Wiley," my sister says, "we are just playing around

. . . What's the matter with you? Are you a sissy?" Speech from a school-playground-recess speech: If you're not, hold still—you know what they say—put up or shut up . . .

Communal Meaning, soldierly-dirty . . . Unexplained . . . Any verb: *like, dislike, tease, love, loathe, desire*—it's funny they all fit. I pose in the scarf and one earring—the other has fallen off—and with lipsticked lips. Nonie says, "Look, I missed one whole part . . ." Leonie titteringly laughs. I tilt my head like a movie star and I have my hands in my pockets. "No. Don't fix it," I say. "I like it like this . . ."

I grope for the fallen earring inside the line of my pants—it is wedged there. I toss it to Nonie, who gruntingly catches it. A potency . . .

I had seen old movies where the men wore lipstick. I do a sword fight: I stand on the couch and fence with my shadow. "That's dumb," Nonie said. I towered, made-up and scarfed, over the girls. Leonie says, "Oh, you're so funny . . ."

Nonie says, "Come on, be a trooper—be a good soldier . . . sit down and be a girl now . . ."

A heroine. Of theirs. I smell of sweat. Of adolescent rut. Of lipstick. My head is full of leftover images of petting: I smell of *petting* and of running around the room—and of youth. Leonie has an unvirgin look: her tight skirt is wrinkled across the triangle of her abdomen.

"Stop that," Leonie says.

She reaches up and pulls my face to her and kisses me on the mouth. In front of Nonie. She says as if to Nonie, "You didn't finish the lipstick on him—here I'll do it . . ." Nonie tosses the lipstick to her.

In harem glamour gone a little wild she leans toward me and I lean back on the couch; and Nonie sits next to me while Leonie correctingly paints my mouth.

"The lipstick tastes funny—it's gloppy."

"It's cherry red. Helena Rubinstein." That's Nonie.

Leonie is panting and concentrating. *She is really something, that new friend of Nonie's* . . . (Lila.) I am agonizedly watchful—lazy, *spoiled*, sexed-up. I am an advertisement for my sister (and my mother). Fragments of social caste ornament us—Leonie and me and Nonie—differently. *It's small-town money* . . . (Lila.) Leonie, looking at me, so pitches her voice it's clear she is talking to Nonie—the tension and posture of her neck are as if that flesh was erected and the sight of it scalds and as-if-scars me. Leonie says, "Oh, he's adorable . . ."

It concerns them if I am; it's not *my* business, she means.

Nonie said, "Well, you and I are like sisters and, ha-ha ha-ha—now [*sigh*]—we're all TWINS!"

Leonie said, "Oh, I don't know . . ." To Nonie she said, "You think he'll scare the cattle . . ."

I said suddenly, "I like to gallop!" and I jumped off the couch and cantered around the room, striking the floor with my feet and making hoof noises with my heels and with my mouth.

"Don't wake Momma," Nonie said.

The mild pornography, slightly daring, took on a different tonality then, the pornography that I was included in the girls' world—if I can say that. I was included with them in some category or other for a moment or two.

"Giddyap," Leonie said to me.

Nonie laughingly said, "Oh, those two . . ." as if to herself. Nonie's laugh—her open and sounding mouth—the moment has in it the extreme force of the *wild* streaming of love anyway . . . A local creek in flood . . . No possible acceptable relativism is here. Nonie has her claim of omniscience and of primacy of appetite: real death gives her status—and accreditation. She laughs because I am not a convincing girl . . . Is it funny that I am not? Is it eerie and funny? I don't *know* what it *costs* me to be agreeable. I carry around *feelingly* the newly incised (visible) muscles of my forearms . . . Nonie laughs and says, "He's like a lamb—for the slaughter . . ."

Nonie's laugh, at times, its sound, its reality could make Lila say, "I give up," and she would rise from her chair and leave the room.

Nonie said to Leonie—intimately—"We won't make good mothers."

(Lila said of Nonie to me, *Her secret weapon is she's in charge of herself: no one* HAS *to take care of her—and that's attractive in somebody* . . .)

Tomboy . . . freed girl . . . Legs. Cunt. Breasts. Mouth.

Inside me, my jolted sense of things is sportive—and hard-willed—vain and physically aware—*cleverly* docile. I am part of a motionful photograph—some pix—this is memory. Nonie's nighttime, not-on-a-date face, her manner with Leonie, I bear all this, I enjoy it, but it is not actually particularly bearable for me.

It may be that this is just before her period. She has not been denied the reality of love stories. She says to Leonie—I think of me and Momma—"They want me to save them . . ."

"I will do what I want—you shut up . . ." I imitate her.

"Tom ought to marry Wiley. *Tom* could be a politician—you'd be surprised . . . But I don't know who would elect him . . . Ask me no questions, I'll tell you no lies."

"Nonie, you are *never* nice," Leonie says.

"I am too. Yes, I am, to nice people. I am a very nice person to you . . ." The reality of prettiness—*she is perhaps too proud* . . . "I am famished . . . I am starving to death like in India . . ."

Nonie had an angrily pathetic look. She has a feeling of waiting—it shows in her face now. "I have to go watch Momma take her medication . . ." Already drugged, Momma needed a witness to make sure that she didn't take too much more morphine in her grogginess. Nonie said to me and Leonie, "Busy, busy, busy. Why don't you two neck and see if you like it? Ha-ha . . ."

She is a sensible virgin—superior to us: the lipsticked boy, the vaguely wolfish twenty-year-old girl.

"She's *nifty*—she has really a lot of common sense," Leonie says.

Lipsticked–sticky-lipped, I say, "Oh you two are good at a lot of things . . ."

She brought her face to maybe within six inches of mine. In the moment, snub-boned (wolflike), her sharply jutting-nosed central face, the tightly-fitted-to-her slicked, competent movements, the showy teeth when she grins—a striking and likable girl—*a nobody*, Lila says.

Of course, I don't know the worst about her. Strong-lipped, she places a *pretty* kiss on the mouth . . . She says, "I don't know. I suppose it's not important what becomes of you if you live in St. Louis . . ." I see the top of her head when I hold her close. I swing back and forth. "Ha-ha," I murmur. Our feet are way down there . . . The nerve, the toughness in her: *you* know that physical whisper of a strong female body—of a strongly boned spirit of a young woman who is partly *male in spirit* . . . Possibly a whore-to-be . . . Or a-girl-who-will-be-a-suicide . . . A doing-things-at-the-last-minute girl . . .

I sat on the couch. Leonie sat in my lap, put her arms around my neck, and said, "Please talk to me with that pretty mouth . . ." Then, eyeing me, she bends backwards and sideways—nuttily—she is in motion—with the help of me holding her—my strained arms hold her and let her down slowly—she topples back slowly to being horizontal on the couch . . .

I say, "QUIZ: Do you feel your palms getting clammy when you are alone with her? Did you feel lucky? Do you feel superior to other people? Her breasty-poos are the meaning of the occasion. Take a look at the world." Addressing her nipples . . . "For God's sake, whoopee . . . It's mostly really okay . . . Tell me if she likes me: she likes me, she likes me not . . ."

"Ow," she said. I was biting her, first on one breast, then the other.

"She loves me not. Tell me," the boy said breathlessly, lying mostly on top of her, "is this meaningless? Are you ashamed of us? Are you ashamed of yourself?" I ask from on top of her.

"I have thought about it backwards and forwards for the last six years and I've been engaged since I was seventeen and I just haven't time to be ashamed of myself, Wiley . . ."

She had a mussed mouth and cluttered (but shrewd) eyes and a Vacation-with-Me-from-the-Grimness-of-War quality.

"Well, it *is* the END-OF-THE-WORLD—*you should see the photographs,*" I say. The almost post-hallucinatory judgment of the milky and light-smitten applause—of the pulse in a state of desire—is that I am lucky to know Leonie . . . "Madam, my pulse greets you"—showing her the erection: a greeting (a return after interruption) covered over by underpants except for some of the head and some of the balls.

The daily, vulgar whisper of history; I am being ill with history—with wartime. I am so lonely that I don't use the word *lonely* at all anymore. Everyone in the world is busy . . . I am lipsticked, earringed, and erect.

We are half safe.

Leonie whispers in my ear, "I call Nonie *The Dragon Lady—*" Then: "Don't tell her . . . Don't wipe your mouth: leave a little for me to taste. Do you like your sister, Tiger-brother?"

"My dad has said: *Don't be a fool . . . don't be cannon fodder* . . . Lipstick and earrings and this stupid scarf—for CANNON FODDER . . ."

Leonie says, "I don't understand," and tongues my cheek . . . The illogical, weird amusement . . . My internal oohs, ohs, ughs, ihs . . .

The words, the terms *first, at first sight, at once, right away, right now, now*—those are hers. The hurry in her is *at-the-last-minute.* She is loose-faced, erotic-tactical. Procedural: *speedy* . . . a word in style among us that year. She kisses me briskly, wetly on the side of the nose . . . A small tickled snort . . . God . . . My *love* such as it is—agonized, sensational, *sensationally* present—personal and tinted and cooled and brought to a flood by an agony of half-comprehension—I want to feel less . . . Time flowers into the recognition on my part of my mood as painful—and manipulated—infatuation . . . an *amusement.*

She probably senses this . . . She loves me for a moment . . . I think I *recognize* the odd curvature of that heat—that peculiar wit . . . the lovely girl-woman propped, spread—but not available. I tug lippily at her breasts. The minute like a wasp buzzes in my sweaty nose . . . June bugs of appetite itchily hop outside and inside my throat . . . My cheek is against hers. "Our hair marries each other," I say. She is silent.

Then she repeats it, a joke in the hoarse, hurried voice of hers which I as-if-hear for the first time: "Our hair marries each other, does it?"

My breath spills at my lips already different and stained by *love*—the escaped, pale, dragonfly-monkey's-paw breath tugs at her hair, at her eyelids . . . *Escaped* breath . . .

She says, "Do you swear a lot?"

"Fuck-a-dee-fuck-fuck, camel turd . . ."

"Kiss me . . ."

"Fun-tongue," I say. "Fuun-tongue soup . . ."

"You're so corny—"

"Corned beef. I have a short tongue . . ."

"I have a big one," she said.

"Don't show me," I say, pulling back.

"I love your lipstick—I like you in lipstick—it's very flattering," she said with "intellectual" hysteria—a shyness toward words . . . Push her away and hack and haw-hiccckkk . . . And cough some . . .

The physical sense I have of her: a girl-woman with a lyingly abandoned loosened face and a fast or rushed and businesslike and commonsensical, shrewd, undoomed heat. Her skin smells of cigarettes. You see why I sort of love her and half wish this wasn't happening?

I confess I have an emptied smile, a drooping smile. It is a sexual compliment to her, semi-grinning insignia of a sergeancy of the enlistee-recruit. The *corporeality* of the moment, the motion of sensation: is it of moral consequence that she is five seven and has a wide rib cage (one narrow from front to back), has small breasts like sachets (or quilted pockets), and that she is not rich? Her neck is luscious—strong, throbby. In her is a range of shadows—hidden stuff. Hidden stuff shows, but I cannot read it. Me: in one earring and with the scarf on, I hold her in my skinny arms. She strokes me—like a pet . . . Truth is godawful. Shadows listen at the walls of the skins for each other's whispers. Pulling back, she says something that she has heard: "You know who the great pornographer is? God is . . . God's a pornographer." She said it madly-sanely, explanatorily, to my nearby face.

The odd flooring of limitlessness in a moment: *what-the-hell* . . . My stomach: I have a kiddy's belly. A boy's death-loving stomach . . . In wartime . . .

"We're all home-front soldiers here," she says, making a joke. Then: "Nonie says you're not the good-provider type. You're a good-time Charlie . . ."

"I don't know . . ."

"I think you're an ace." Leonie repeats, "You're an ace."

My chest burned with the accidental reality of events . . .

"Yeah, well . . . Who knows?" I said to Leonie.

Leonie said with the impoliteness of no-marriage—said to the walls of the room, "Stick this in your pipe and smoke it . . ." And she stuck her big tongue, grossly and suffocatingly, chokingly into my mouth. I didn't choke for a second or two. She is *not* looking for a proper man just now. I am guessing. She is looking into the darkness in a stuffy closet.

I am weighted suddenly with heat and blood; it is phallic *weightedness* and an appetite for finality . . . with infatuated flashes of translation toward sheltering in it.

A degree of love . . .

She pulls away and is smiling and nodding her head. "You're so clean!—look/uh/kccck/ng," she says: her mouth is strained—and strange—from *the necking*. I get the sense that she is so far along in having a grown-up life that she has *already* become *mental* about being a woman. That is, ideas command her. I say, "Ha-ha," scared-excited . . . A little forceful. Leonie's face is heat and gaudy parts, and gooshy parts and *bone* . . . Et cetera. She said in the third person to my shoulder, "Why isn't he ten years older? And horny from being overseas? And mad for me . . ."

"I am mad for you . . . ha-ha," I say. "Why is this called necking?" And I kiss her neck.

She kisses *my* neck boringly . . .

The heavy persuasiveness and allure of sexual sensation is a separate consciousness. I kiss her coarsely. I let my tongue rest like a strange flexible small rib on her lower lip. I began to write her name across her face with my tongue sweatily—high-schoolishly-dirtily . . . My sweaty *please-think-I'm-trash* face kissingly rode in the various milieus of this stuff—the membranous smell of the (delicate) skin of her neck—these are kisses in bad faith . . . She wasn't laughing at me in a superior way. The fragility of the self here explained itself as the fragility of events in the present tense, in the only actuality there is. I said, "I'm on my *good behavior*"—not meaning it as I put two fingers on her down there and groped my way into her . . .

"You're on your bad beHAVIOR," she said. She wasn't really startled. Something like a bird-flutter down there and a kind of slimy stickiness came to her mouth in a set of tremors . . . The surprisingly hurtful aggression of sensation—nothing can defend ignorance . . . I know better than to say to her that necking is a friendly grief with babies-and-grown-men's inner cries and urgencies in it . . . the noble trashiness thing of throwing your life away because of meaninglessness or some sort of mistake in you about meanings . . . The availability of animal faith—eyelids, hearts, bared chests—one is hopelessly excited.

"I'm out, I'm out of my mind, I'm out of my head, I'm far out," she said, politely.

I want to say, *Oh, thank you,* but I don't.

In her breath and eyelids and in the odd, faintly glaucous spill of opacity over the irises of her eyes—and over mine—in those circumstances, the stench is almost of bearskin—sweat and rut and mussed clothes . . . And the wrinkled couch . . . I am in a true rage of private velocity in a moment of intimacy with someone else who is modest-and-immodest *complicatedly.* The kind of tragic intimacy of sexual confessions . . . a dirty and intimate deliciousness—also, a bit sickening . . . We do this in silence: among soft breaths—*neighborhood* sexual bullies—people blackmailingly tacitly saying to the other person, *You better cooperate* . . . She is not thinking.

"Are you scared?" she asks.

"I am scared shitless—I can barely *hold my water* . . ."

"Oh you . . ."

We will fuck . . . That is what her mood means. I gaze at her . . . Attention is dear—is love of a kind. Nothing has vanished, not our feet, not our shoes, not our ages or odors, but *attention* edits and presents, stages and permits pure-seeming meaning for a second or two, here and there. The sensible reality vanishes in blinks and she is somehow *ideal*: this is called back home *not thinking* . . . The poetry of hallucination is of shrewdness being hidden. Leonie's spirit has withdrawn . . . Then she is there, she returns—her conscious attention returns to her mouth and eyes like birds to the openings of a birdhouse . . .

She sighs. One is found to be okay in a real verdict in a real court, *romantic enough anyway* . . . A provincial and skeletal approximation of physical flirtation . . . Maybe I can live in the real world . . . I said to her, "I bet your father liked you . . ."

The lashes and lids of her eyes . . . sanely . . . real. *We are fooling around* . . .

I felt gazingly but behind my suddenly lowered eyelids, *I Love You* . . . I said to myself, *BOY, DON'T SAY* THAT *OUT LOUD* . . . One is being transformed, for better or worse, into someone who has now done these things. Veeringly, I began to hate myself and to be more urgent physically.

She said, "How do you know that about my father?"

"I don't know . . ."

I hold her arms with my hands and I show her my face. Nonie's scarf is sloppily every which way over my shoulders.

"Oh God, you're the limit," Leonie said stiffly. She said, "If you were older, I'd make you marry me." Then: "WOULD you marry me?"

"Sure," I said. The hand (or fin) of boyish casualness, the thing of not being serious about the possibility—I felt only pain suddenly—she is superior again . . . out of reach . . .

"You're a devil," she said—tactically—tactfully undoing the excitement.

"I'm no pussyfooter," I said. *Another nail in my coffin* . . .

"Oh, kiss me," she said wildly and strangely, impatiently—being sorry—who knows, who can tell me what it was? The world is faulty and crowded and full of lousy teachers and inept confessions that don't tell you much of anything.

"Are you, kind of, a bad person?" she asked me.

"Oh yes," I said impatiently.

"Tell me how . . ."

Ah: I shake my head now.

She moves her head forward, through the intervening air . . . But it is an automaton's thing. I make a face—I pull away—*sloppily*—and lean back against the back of the couch. I see the appeal of simple onrushingness . . .

Oh God . . .

"Talking to you is so interesting," she said—she is sort of someone else. She says, "You're fifteen."

She smiled.

A kind of bustling noise in the hall is Nonie. "Am I interrupting?" she says. She is in a blue bathrobe.

Leonie says to Nonie, "Your brother is a devil . . ." Leonie kind of jokingly says to me in front of Nonie: "Is it all over between us, Wiley?" She sighs and looks at Nonie and shrugs her shoulders; she doesn't really straighten her clothes much, but she covers herself up with her blouse and skirt. "I should've been loyal to the air force . . . He's a killer-diller . . . He's just a heartbreaker . . ."

Nonie's a smoker; she has loud panting breathing.

Nonie said, "Watch out . . . He bites."

"Oh shut up," I said stiffly.

Leonie said to me, "Do you bite?"

"No . . ." The two of them have a private speech. I don't really know what they are talking about. "No," I say again. Then: "Am I supposed to?"

"No . . ."

I look at Nonie, and then I put my head in Leonie's lap. Leonie puts her hand on my chest inside my shirt . . .

Saying, "Uh," Nonie got up, stood still a half second, and left the room . . .

Leonie's hand waitfully sits on the almost idle heat of the new skin of my chest. I was as if covered with kisses as when you're a child and hide in a pile of raked leaves and the leaves touch and tickle and poke and smother you. I am more odorous and staler than a child.

"Is it a good thing if you *bite*?" I ask, looking up.

Leonie said to me, "Oh, you're YOUNG . . ."

Her blouse, now again open, shows thin ribs and the smallish cotton brassiere crookedly placed on the unevenly globular breasts.

I free her breasts—and feel their presence—and that of the fierce liveliness of her hair.

Leonie takes hold of my hands, stopping me. She says, almost defeatedly, "I'm getting to be an old person. It's nice to be with you . . . I like the way you look at things."

Close-pressed body parts. Damp . . .

"What's your fiancé like?"

"Oh . . . This isn't a time for hard questions . . ." Then Leonie sighingly said, "Nonie said you were a know-it-all." Then, shifting her weight, a bit heavily: "Nonie said you read a lot of books—do you?"

I don't answer.

She leaned forward, somewhat moisty-bodied, and she tickled my skinny ribs. "Talk to me—don't sulk . . ."

"Am I being stupid?" I asked her.

"Well, how do you mean that?"

"With you . . ."

She gave up straightening out what I meant. "No," she said alertly. "You're interesting." Then: "Nonie says she can't understand you half the time . . . People say you have tragedy in your background . . ."

"Yeah. I guess." Then: "People get bored and say anything—so it gets all very, very funny—know what I mean?"

"Do you think you're an important person somehow, someday . . . Down the road?"

I shrugged.

"No. Let's be serious? Do you feel you'll be important someday?"

"It depends on you—if you ruin me . . ." I said, moving my hand on her leg.

"Don't be funny . . . I'd like to be important," Leonie said. "Are you going to be a doctor, do you think? Some people think Jewish doctors are the best . . . I like Jewish comedians, too."

"I don't know," I said. "I'd like to be a fighter pilot first."

"How are your eyes? You're too tall, anyway. It won't make me silly or mad, but tell me the truth: you think you're really important—maybe—and I'm not?"

After a while: "No." Then: "When you were little, you ever kill a fly and ask God to bring it back to life if there was a God and if He cared what you thought?"

"No." Then: "Yes . . ."

"Did it ever happen?"

"Oh, Silly," she said, tweaking my nose. "But sometimes I prayed and things happened . . ."

"Me too . . . But it wasn't clear-cut."

"Ummm . . . ?"

"It was never a clear sign . . ."

"I know what you mean . . ."

"It's hard to figure out. I like your mole." She had a mole on her cheek.

"Say something really *intelligent* . . . really logical—and let's see if I can follow it . . ."

"If you think I'm interesting, can't we fuck?"

"What a strange boy you are . . . You *are* a devil . . ."

"Well?"

"A well is a hole in the ground . . ."

"Do you think life is crazy?"

"Sometimes. Off and on. Maybe yes and no. I get very sad about it. You have nice lips."

"You're only being half serious—you want your own way," I accused her.

She said, "I like nutty men—that's my weakness. You talk like a book. I think the things you say are pretty."

"KISS ME! MY BALLS HURT!"

The air between us shrinks in the odd shapes of us being nearer, until films and fingers of warm air and semi-sweat half glue us. The shapes of her hair surround the carnival lights of bits of her skin so near my eyes . . . Condescension, curiosity: her posture in the lightly huffing closeness, in the deranged coherence of no space between our bodies. Closeness is ungeographically blurred, is casually spendthrift sensually . . . She lacks the power of melodrama which would include me. She says snidely-charmingly (a local kind of charm): "You talk so pretty. Really, you're sweet—I bet you turn into a really bad person: what are we doing? A pair of idiots is what we are . . . Oh well, who cares? What else is there to do on a weeknight . . . ?"

"You like it when people tell you what to do?" I asked. Snidely, in a high-school form. "So you can do the opposite—and they can go to hell?"

"You're partly Gypsy, you're psychic: ha-ha . . . Come on . . . kiss me the way you did at the beginning . . . Don't look at me like that . . ."

"I hurt," I said, holding my testicles in a pantomime, only partly faked, but it was too fake the way I did it. "More porridge please," I asked. Then: "Forget it . . ."

"Try to bear up. Let it hurt you," she said dryly. "Better you than me."

"I don't want to hurt you . . . I don't like to play with feelings."

"God, you're going to be hard for a woman," she said. Then: "You're too moody . . . You're too much to handle: what a handful. Do you care about scoring? Do you keep score? Don't get too hot . . . I like cool men."

The fabric of my unbuttoned shirt touches my mostly exposed and skimpy chest in a lonely, pretty way . . .

The lonely self-love of that flows into my thinking that maybe that is how her blouse feels on her.

Does she feel alive and potent? Is her potency a corruption . . . of the world?

"You tell too many lies," I say.

"Nice lies," she says. "They're nice lies . . . Kisses are nice lies, too."

If I *go along with her* (as we used to say back home), if I smile (as I do at her), then it is as if we were in the imagery produced by one skull.

She's Nonie's buddy. In erotic artfulness, the boy whispers, "No."

"I'm a fake, Wiley," she says. "I'm an old woman. If you're thirsty, you learn to drink from a dirty fountain. I've learned to compromise . . . How about you?"

"I don't know."

Hers is a small breast. Her mouth is filled with absentmindedness

. . . One hollow ballroom-cave breathes into another . . . I keep thinking I love her . . . I already know most of the time that I just like her some.

She says, "Pardon my dirty talk . . . Do you know a lot of girls as sensitive as you?"

I leaned as if into a white fire of memory of her as I felt toward her a while ago. Her face is tethered to her neck, to being shrewd and *moody*. She is a bit wild. There's stuff in her to like.

"You get better and better," she said, pulling away from a kiss. What she is saying is part of her line . . .

"Well, it's simpler now . . ."

Her mouth is a bit raw. Her breath is short and quick. In her eyes is what seems to me to be her twenty-year-old completeness. I imagine a moral quality in her having lived that long. She says, "You're sweet . . ."

"I don't want to be *sweet.*" I ask her, "Do you play movies in your head when you kiss?"

"I haven't led you on, have I? I'm sorry if I've been a pain . . ."

She's not of the same social class as before . . . Boy, you really do get fooled . . . Maybe, in some sense, you don't. Heat rises from her skin. She tickles my bare foot with hers. It is a complicated intelligence test here . . . In her nice self's voice or whatever, she says in a certain *dirty*, really scary way, "I'm certainly making myself right at home . . ."

"Mmmm," I say cautiously, wondering what the hell is going on . . .

"Your hospitality is real nice," she said appreciatively but not *sincerely*. Then: "You aren't talkative . . . ."

She is, by virtue of her age in relation to me, somewhat. I cringe inwardly, frightened at how sincerity affects me sexually and what insincerity makes me feel . . . how cruel. Leonie is unphallic—and naïve—in some ways. Someone smarter and more experienced than I am and the leader for the moment isn't *perfectly* smart or comprehensively more experienced but is a failed leader: Leonie . . .

In a fit of sane madness, I say in a certain lunatic tone: "You don't know a lot about getting fucked, do you?"

Leonie bristles. She closes her legs on my hand, which was on her thigh. Her tissues moisten, though . . . An interest in sexual victory isn't the same as sexual interest.

She says, "I liked you because I thought you were sensitive . . . But I was wrong . . . You're insensitive . . . Oh you're too much—you're impossible . . . Never mind: I'm just an old woman . . ." Her breath, squeakingly-bassoish, is that of a good sport. She hasn't a wide choice of men tonight . . . My breath is hoarse, too . . . She says, not exactly wearily, not exactly entirely the good self either, and in a fairly deft way that makes me stare at her: "You're too big: it would matter—even though you're a kid . . . I can't take it inside me . . ."

I said, I exclaimed, with a terrible broken heart, maybe in a childish voice: I was out of control and I didn't listen to myself or aim my voice: "That's not FAIR . . ."

"It would matter . . . Isn't this all right?"

"It's all nothing, nothing, nothing . . . It's all the same . . . It's nothing." I put my arm over my eyes.

She said, "You're too young. Nonie would kill me." She placed her hand on my cheek: "When you're famous, will you remember me? Be nice, okay?"

"I won't be famous . . ." Then, when she stared off into air, I said, "There's too much wrong with me . . . I don't want to be famous: I want to get laid . . ."

"Hih . . ." An odd noise, maybe a grim laugh. "You're not a bad boy—that's awfully nice. Oh I have to give you a squee-eeze . . . You're going to be hell on the ladies . . . Oh *hi*, there . . . I wish I had a brother like you." Then, leaning back: "But you are spoiled . . . You're so young and you're spoiled already: Nonie's right about you . . . Lord have mercy on us. Let's close down the shop, okay?"

"Shit," I muttered, and took one of her hands in both of mine . . . My head danced with hallucinations . . . Maybe with *vanity*—absurd, electrical. The tribunal thing of meaning for me hovers at its own madness of distance. Islanded and surrounded by one's own breath, by one's eyelashes, by one's hair, among a plethora of *distances* . . . alone, anonymous, not widely loved, I hear her speak.

"Are you honest, Wiley?" Leonie asks.

"Hoo, hoo, hoo," I say. Then: "More than you . . ." Then: "I'm honest sometimes."

"Hoo, hoo, hoo," Leonie says.

"Sometimes you have to be dishonest." Spent-and-expended time is black-space-and-loss, a night shroud, a robe of created spaces of dreams in which you deal with the gleaming bludgeon of emotion . . . *Nonie is here* . . . She comes silently into the room this time. The kissed boy echoes in his crotch and butt the way a wooden vat echoes if you shout into it . . . from the embraces before. The echoes are tickling, prickled, ticking along. The heart seems to sweat now. The dashing and maddening clatter of one's pulse: the whispery room.

Real light, not symbolic light: nighttime: electric light—the lamps in the room, *powdery* white light floating spikily in ovals on the ceiling, light reflections on skin, and on the china bases of table lamps, and on *waxed and polished wood*—and light floating on the fibers of the deep red Persian carpet. And the light of the mind and the light, shockingly, of eyes. Suburban privacy and the comparative silence of the neighborhood: the day and month: the state of one's nerves—greed, a modern moment: memory in its motions eerily, merrily, plays in me a thing of the past—it is over now. Hallucinations and the pain of waiting are commonsense elements of *love: understand me at your danger*; we are the only survivors of the night so far. Oldish stuff, the hidden air is full of childhood sleep: suburban-amorous, nosy: poetry in a suburb is nuttiness—a boy's *sense* of the situation, him and the two women: the most complicated imaginable *forgiveness*-love-and-sex: belated and informed: is that what it is to be redeemed?

Lit and ill-lit and unlit, semi-light, half-light, quarter-light, light as if borrowed from a fuller light and partly broken and smeared and smudged: the nerve-rending and ordinary shadows . . . The light and dark variations of the air: this tiny and unstable community of three: a sense of brownness and a breast freckle. Gradation, graduation, calibration—an idiocy about pain, me in my sister's presence in this way . . . "What's your favorite line of poetry?" Leonie asks although Nonie is there.

"I don't know."

"Tell me . . ."

"Aw . . ."

"Please . . ."

"You think I'm crazy?" That I would talk like this in front of Nonie.

"I certainly do," Leonie said in a flirty way.

Nonie is smoking.

"Think of w-o-u-l-d spelled w-o-o-d—would that be crazy or not?"

"You're not making sense . . ."

"Mmmm," Nonie says.

I blush and say, "Well, so what? I am strong for my size."

"You—you aren't making sense."

Clear Thought and PURE DELIGHT . . . time—and ordinary romantic sexual thought, an unbothered, burning speed, inept, interruptible thoughtlight, curled, blackish . . .

"Hey there," Nonie says, "ain't we got fun? ARE WE HAPPY?" (A famous bandleader used to say that back then.) "You two just *flying* along? Well, any wood will burn in an oven."

"Nonie, you're no help . . ."

"You know about garbage? Garbage ends as garbage . . . You know what garbage is?" Bureaucrat's tautologies—the wit of a friendly bureaucrat's *affectionate* tautology.

"Coffee grounds, old newspapers, orange peels . . ."

"Oh that's very funny . . . You *are* a child," Nonie says. To Leonie: "He's a nice kid if you like baby billy goats . . . He'll be buried with the garbage . . . Be careful: he's the devil . . ." She is strong-speeched . . . In a woman that is like a man's having a strong back.

Then Leonie says to me, "Oooh, move your arm—the hairs on it tickle me." Then: "Arf, arf . . . It's a dog's life."

"You'll never take Bob Hope's place—you're just not a national laugh riot," Nonie said to her.

I said to Leonie, "I'm in the category of *Everyone-and-HER-brother.*" Leonie looked blank.

Nonie said, "I think very little of puns."

"God loves his garbage," I say to Nonie. "That wasn't a pun, Slowpoke."

"I don't know what you're talking about . . . I never know what *you're* talking about. Bad feelings are a luxury I don't let myself have." The untranslatable tangents of ego in Nonie's eyes are a stirrable murk, a *sociable* mud, a shallows subject to what I do—smile, say.

Nonie's authoritative and strange office voice, grubby with tension, with the absence of real-life courtesies in it, says to me, "See, I told you, you have to like a woman if she goes after you. Learn it now, Little Boy Wonder . . . But no man can protect himself . . . Women are too smart for men: learn it now," she said scornfully, "Wileykins . . ."

"I HATE this war," Leonie says.

"I do, too," Nonie says, shaking her head as if in sadness.

The utterly motionful reality, the most complex medium of a glowing lumber in a rapids—or lumber falling off a lumber truck—an accidental actuality—or the clapping wings of geese—or of a pulse—*fate* here—Nonie crosses her legs and straightens her bathrobe . . . And a boy partly rebuttoning his shirt . . .

"He has a nice profile," Leonie says to Nonie.

Is life evil? Is life evil and *sweet*? The soul's smell is what? A quality of attraction—as if to moths? A dark-and-light *sexual* or *social* murmur or whisper, can the bones and look—the mood—of a face do that? The ordinary is on fire . . . *We are mad tonight* . . . However, she is present in her own moments. A sheen of watery and powerful reflections. I sit there, breathing a little loudly.

Nonie says, "He doesn't act like a normal person." Normill purrrsinnnnnn. "He ought to be put away—he's disgusting! Ha-ha . . ." A bureaucrat-sister's joke. It is a locally *sophisticated* face she has at this moment. The robe, her hair, her look . . . She says, "The awful ones are easy to love but hard to live with—ask me, I know . . . I know . . . Who knows it better?" Then: "I don't like to think about myself." Nonie said, "Have you been a good boy?"

I suddenly start in imitating Lila, my mother, in a way: "What is the point of letting people laugh at you? It makes good sense to know how to be funny, but only a fool thinks that's all there is to it . . . Be funny if you want—but know what you're doing—be careful about what you really want—there are other ways to skin a cat—there are always other ways. Being popular isn't what people think it is." Then: *"I have the anger of The Beauty of the Family . . . Ha-ha . . . I've had to learn how to take a joke . . . ha-ha . . . Take a leaf from my book—learn to laugh at yourself. A lot of it when people pick on you is that people want to get close to you. Anyone can be bought but some of us are too inexpensive—I was never someone you could pull my pigtail—I was always too proud to live but I lived. I was someone people were jealous of—go ahead, you want people to think you had a bad person for a mother. Wiley, you have to stop saying* YOU-KNOW-WHAT-I-MEAN *all the time . . ."*

Nonie said, "I don't want you ever to imitate me . . ."

"Then be nice to me."

"He's not so big in the shoulders," Nonie said to Leonie.

"He's not so big in the shoulders," I said, two-edgedly, dismissively and thoughtfully. Then I said, looking at the pretty oval, clunkily made-up, of my sister's face: "No-no: OW AND HOW . . ."

She threw her lighter at me. Then a slipper.

I said, "She offers *feud for fought* . . . It would be better to say *feud for thought* . . . I'm not a pawn," I said to her.

"Goddamned little know-it-all," she said. Nonie in her klutzy bathrobe . . . ungirdled . . .

"Are you getting fat?" I ask her. I said to Leonie, "She never forgets . . . not one little-bitty eentsy tiny teeny *bit* . . ."

How much can someone like her forgive or forget?

Being a boy, you live as a spy and liar. Among menaces.

"He's like this all the time," Nonie said. "What can you do? He's like a machine. He's just a robot . . . You can't do anything to him."

"I think he's nice," Leonie said.

I say, "Am I olly, olly, oxen free?"

Leonie said, "We might let you live . . . You want to leave home, you can come live with me—I'm a lousy cook and you have to do the cleaning but you'd be welcome. You won't like it, but there's space for you."

Nonie said to me, "I need a fresh pack of cigs—can you take a hint? Don't be the sort of fool who always has to have everything clear." To Leonie, Nonie says, "Doesn't he have the damnedest attitude? He has a damned funny attitude . . . Do me a favor, Wiley, and keep your mouth shut some of the time."

"What a joke . . . This is all a joke . . . That's all it is—a joke."

Nonie said, "Just be human and it'll be okay. I hate this war. It's all so awful. I *hate* Hitler . . . I wish I had a good brother—I know a lot of girls who have brothers they can be proud of . . . People are just people," she said, looking at me.

"I don't understand—what is the war for? What are the laws about . . . ?"

"Oh Wiley," Leonie said wearily.

I say to Leonie, "I don't understand. I really don't. All the meaning of civilization is that we can't say we're all good people here—aren't we?"

"No one's good—they're just courting you. A lot of people are afraid," Nonie said.

I had a posture of listening, almost an air of complicity—that complicity of comprehension of long familiarity—or of the truth of something.

I say to the voices in my head, *Silence in the courtroom: monkey wants to speak* . . . Then, for no reason clear to me, I say it out loud, "Silence in the courtroom: monkey wants to speak . . ."

Nonie said, "This is enough; I've had enough from a smart aleck. It's cruel to make a tired civil-service rank three listen to a baby's bull."

Leonie said to me, "Be nice." Then: "I'm not tired." It took me a while to realize she meant she'd stay up after Nonie went to bed. She said to Nonie, "He's impossible but he has bedroom eyes . . . I think I like your pest of a brother, Nonie."

"Life, life, life," I say, imitating everyone—sort of. I say, "We're not flirty—we're enemies."

Nonie says, "You think you have a mind of your own but what it is is you're crazy . . . I'm going to the kitchen: anyone want a glass of milk and a graham cracker?"

"A Happy Ending . . . A Certain Joy on a Quiet Occasion for Chosen Protagonists . . . Nonie leaves the room," I say to Leonie. "What now? Do I get to choose?"

"Say something fancy. Let me hear how you talk . . ."

"The ghost machine wants you, gobble, gobble, gobble . . . Bits of fate for the geese subdue the sense of wartime alarm. Avoid the ancient forms of wishes."

"Does that mean anything? You didn't make that up."

Nonie reenters the room. "Here comes the milkman . . ."

Leonie says to Nonie, "I feel so old in relation to him."

"Well, I'm not old," Nonie says. "He doesn't deserve special treatment for being young. You could lift my morale if you treated him with a little *caution*."

"I'm a caution . . ."

Leonie blinks. "Well, I'm not in the middle . . . I'm a neutral party."

On Nonie's earnestly pretty face—at this moment—contempt flickers, and then is quickly held back. "Isn't he funny-looking? He's all legs." She said it in her chirping voice, the legs-tied-together, cloud-of-small-birds, fixed-in-tone voice—an underdog. She is tired . . .

"Well, hi," Leonie says—guiltily—to me. Peacemaker—sexy Leonie. "Hi, hi, hi," Leonie says a little acidly, charmingly, smartly-nervously bossy.

"Hi," I say. *Hu(h)-eye . . .*

In a sudden as-if-cawing silence—a drama of some sort is in it—Nonie's careless, to-hell-with-things look—a look of knowingness—is squelching and arrogant. I am the parvenu omniscience in her world, a small example of junior observation.

It is soon after childhood for me.

My sister: I've known her all along.

Leonie's Fiancé

I know about him . . . When I kiss her, I kiss stuff from him in her—stuff about being a young man in combat. His hairy chest—I know it approximately, not in its singularity, in how she reacts to me being hairless. His solitude, his silliness, his horrors . . . His kinds of response to her and how she, in turn, responds and feels lousy or great, like a great person . . . I don't know . . . How can you get near someone without getting the shadowy stuff of a lot of other people and interrupting nearly everything. It's like becoming a historical figure in the world, isn't it, but it's in someone's life . . . I'm an orphan; and, in a way, I'm clearer, clearer-outlined, less rooted than most men, and a lot more like a bandit you might meet in a woods; but if you come near me, you come near my history . . . I can see where it would be advisable to lie about one's history in order to think certain things of oneself—things about, oh, the absence of evil or why one should shut up.

I know this stuff viscerally and not in words. But later in one's life, one might transfer this knowledge of the viscera to the strings-in-the-labyrinth mind and then, slowly, into the words of a given era, of a given profession . . . What one knows . . .

And you might be teased by the omissiveness in that stuff, by the jiggy-jogging of memory itself; you might want to make sense of something; and you start to make fictional constructions—things that never happened, people you never knew—and they interfere, interrupt things that go on in language—or so to speak—and come near other histories; and sometimes they seem true and sometimes they don't.

I say now that what I *felt* in her as well as what she was partly was him—you educate yourself, you are educated by other people—and gray-mooded and ruthless (in a girl's way); one has to shift that only some to imagine him in his perpetual male strategy, man at rest and on leave, a fighting man at play so to speak, and scared in the world and somewhat obedient—how strange he is to her!

And his sense of how strange he is, his control over his emotions —incomplete but complete enough for him to fly and go into combat —him sweatily befouled with feelings and wanting to live, him *fighting* and maybe beyond comfort and capable only of distractions—the chemical electricity states of those things—he is aware: and *he kills and remembers* . . . How strange the realities of life are . . . How unhappy he is . . . That exists in her, contagion, spillage, stain, echoes, imprinting —like me and Nonie. Her defiant sense of independence—the mix of blasphemy and faith—the grubby and yet almost sublime inconsistencies bordering on loony incoherence—her defiant sense of *sin* and of herself and of you . . .

The hidden man is realer in my view than I am. In his duties, in his life, he is sternly unclean—he is not everyone, *not* a general male, although I tend to feel it (him, his presence in her, in me through my episodes with Leonie) that way. I know I'm not him and, still, I am him in part. I bet he has a repertoire of phrases—an armament . . . I bet . . . *Fuck 'em, fuck 'em all, punch 'em, pinch 'em, pitch 'em into jail, Pardon-me, make way for little boy* Death . . . *Now you die, you fucker* . . . as a real statement in combat and as a joke. And so on . . .

A lot of life consists of *paying-no-attention* even while you pay some . . . The self as like a cast stone dancing from area to area of a lake . . . but not really. You turn into an I-spy, a peekaboo, an I-will-learn . . .

Fighting a war means everyone is infected one way or another. I can't see this guy as a separate person but I am stained by him, and in wanting to get along with Leonie, I suppose I vaguely imitate the ghostly presence of him in her; and, so, I am older than I was earlier in the evening.

At this point, Leonie and I have smeared faces and nervously guilty-and-guiltless *attitudes* . . .

Nonie—a threatening but *acceptable* soul—I am better than she is: it is important to me that this is somewhat so: isn't this important to me? Embarrassment and *charity*—Nonie *is* trying to live, of course . . . I get a sense of a real moment in memory when what is going on seems crazily guessed at by the figures in the scene, even while it is partly clear that being assured—like someone in a book or in a movie—the thing of being *absolutely* certain is *nice*—or horrible—the way it works in reality. The body's sense of things—the guessed-at in actual time in an immediate stillness of the mind blinking away from watchfulness and recapitulating—or calculating—the moment—is of embarrassed and charitable or hardened and berserker *herohood* . . . "Well, what happened—or shouldn't I ask? What's been going on, the two of you . . ." Nonie asks.

"Nonie is impressed by stuff in ads. You can scare her by saying we had a perfectly good time—like in an ad. Or in a musical show."

Happiness is a frightened obsession with her, although maybe what she maybe likes best in people as an emotion reflecting her reality: a frightened obsession in them toward her forming a kind of steel web like that stuff in suspension bridges. She is practical about how people act; and when I said that thing, her face got odd: she was thinking about the reality of me and Leonie, not as a taunt or as a sad exposé, but just as that: a reality . . . If she fails with you, to get that frightened obsession in you with what she'll say and do next and with what she feels, how can she be a boss in her office or a mother and run a household? You laugh about this—as you might at a creepy ad—and you can feel her as being raw and cold in temperament, but she is also hot and goaded—in the end it is the compounded complexity of stuff with her for me that drives me away from her. I am not as a narrator necessarily an honorable or discreet judge of character—I do what I can in the tribunal of prose narrative, but my voice is not without elements of hers and of elements inherently opposed to hers in it . . .

Just so, I hear elements of Nonie in what Leonie says and I see elements of her in what Leonie does—not just imitation but human overlap.

It is partly a matter of the blessing who is listened to.

Nonie was the hand of *The Absolute* for me—this was a casual idolatry and not a matter of making her into an emblem, although it meant that when I thought about her, part of what thought ascribed to her—like giving an *x* or a *y* a mathematical quantity or a real-world or classic reality—was emblematic . . .

I mean the emblematic thing called up a memory of Nonie and a memory of Nonie called up a certain opinion of reality, of the universe. Some of what she is is in everyone. Nonie believes in God frantically at times. Some people love her. Love tends to be an off-and-on-again thing: "Oh shut up: you talk like a boy . . . Shut up and make a song out of it." Her motions are gooselike—in flight or waddling—the movements of her mind and of her emotions. *I think she stinks* of staleness . . . because she loves systems and methods so much: God is what wins . . . She has all these triumphant *methods,* you know . . . I want to leave this house and her, and have since I was ten years old. But maybe not purely. I want to love and embrace her and in so doing accept the world and myself and my life and the war and the deaths of my parents. A cage fits over her but leaves her weeping head *free,* and I want to enter that cage with her and I want to kiss her weeping head but I am afraid and sickened and I am tired: I am fearful—like the pilot. In frightened hatred, she comes alive a little—that is when she comes alive and feels her own excellence—her own adequacy. What she is determines my politics. I said to Lila: *You want me to throw my life away for her the way you did?*

Don't do this to me, Wiley. Don't ever speak of these things to me—or to other people: promise me . . .

Nonie is saying, "What a person is matters . . . You should get some manners, oh Brother Mine."

"Thank you, Nonie . . . That explains the world . . ."

"Oh, leave me alone—you're no fun. You're too big for your britches."

"What's wrong with that?"

"You think too well of yourself—do me a favor and don't answer any more questions until I ask you."

"I don't take orders from you, in case you hadn't noticed . . ."

Nonie, Lila's daughter, says: "You've ruined your face—you look like something the cat dragged in—ha-ha: you've been thinking again . . . Fix the scarf: you're ruining it . . ."

I listen to her with a sort of wildness. I risk comprehending all sorts of things—up to a point.

It actually is quite a risk.

Nonie says—gently—"I hope the way you are turns out well for you, I really do . . ."

"If I'm worthless, don't ever ask me to help you," I say coldly—angrily—justice-mad.

"Oh you're logical, aren't you? Well, you fool a lot of people, Wiley, but you don't fool me. I'm *practical* . . ."

"You're civil-service *three* . . ."

She sighed: "He likes everyone more than he likes me. There isn't anything I can do about it . . ."

I can't establish the value of anything with Nonie except through the most strenuous imaginable warfare. My experience of language—of truces during the unfolding of sentences, the thing of being a herald under a flag of truce—is worthless. My mother has said that if a stranger was struck by gunfire in front of me, I would rescue him—or her—and not Nonie. I have talked about this some (incoherently) with boys my age—and with Lila: *But what is she worth? Goddamn, Momma, look what she manages to cost* ME. And Lila said, *DON'T talk like that! Have a heart when you talk! It's like you're hitting me with a club when you talk like that. She's my child . . . Like her for my sake . . . Please . . . I haven't been a good mother: help me, Wiley. I feel terrible . . .* Help me die and feel I was all right in the end . . . *Tell me you'll stand by her—family is family . . .*

The hell it is. The fuck it is. *You don't want to live because of her and you said you would never die for Nonie and—*

No one means everything they say, Wiley.

What do they mean, then? I don't like her . . .

Be fair to her . . .

That won't work out in her favor.

Oh my God, what sort of person are you? You share many things with her, Wiley . . .

Not enough, Momma, she lies—Momma, there would be no problem if she was halfway fair to me . . . I can't afford her . . .

YOU CAN . . .

I can't . . .

A lot of people say you're selfish, Wiley.

A lot of people say it of everyone.

You're not the only who knows what the true story is—you should learn to make room for other people—people don't have to be careful of your feelings all the time for them to have rights, Wiley, or to be worth a lot of kindness in the world . . .

But I have rights too . . .

I love you, Wiley . . . I.e., you have no rights compared to the rights of those I don't love in this manner . . . *You think I don't know what Nonie's like? She's not a good sister—but don't think about it—do this for me—you've been good to me . . .*

She wants that dutiful part of me to continue after her death—I mean she wants it to be part of her estate. She liked having me to fool around with in the sense of dispensing *my* favors.

Well, the hell with it. *Sure, Momma . . . okay . . . Whatever you say . . . And I will try . . . I won't be like the bad brother in books that women write . . . But it won't work . . . She'll want to own me. She lies and steals* . . . She would steal from Momma's deathbed. And insulted Momma: which is why Momma had ordered her to be kept from the room. She never said good-bye to Nonie . . . She wouldn't have her at her deathbed. Momma said, "I'm sorry but enough is enough."

But she didn't want me to say it . . . And, dying, Momma wanted to give orders . . . She wanted to be potent up to *the last minute* . . .

Nonie'll manage it that I can't afford her—you'll see . . .

You have a trick, Wiley . . . *You encourage people to go too far and be awful and then you walk out on them and leave them to stew in their own juices* . . . She burst out into a deathbed gurgle, a laugh, kind of: *You taking care of her will be no picnic for her, I* CAN *assure you* . . .

When I was little, S.L. shouted at me more than once about Nonie, *LOVE HER, DAMN YOU, LOVE HER! SHE'S YOUR SISTER!*

I said more than once—when I was little—"I wish you'd put Nonie in a home."

The gangling boy on the couch—the flaming, half-grown child—sees Nonie's eyes as alive and secretive: she does not intend to be visible in the war between us . . . Look and look, you will never see her. In a sense, you mustn't ever see her. "Oh, look-at-there . . . Mr. Good Guy, Mr. Tom Mix . . ."

I hate her—help me . . .

It's just brother-and-sister stuff . . .

The boy's memory is sporadic in its operation—it comes and goes and what it deals in are fragments, not of reality, but of long-ago opinions of what had taken place still earlier: it flies from hilltop to hilltop in that sense, imaginary hilltop to hilltop, across England, like the heliograph system in the days of Napoleon. The boy's sense of now is based on a closed-off sense of evidence and opinion in a cabinet and behind a closed door and now reduced to an odor so that his muscles, the fibers of his identity react. *It*, his reactions have to do with something like *someone's meaning him no harm* . . . or *someone's meaning him well* . . . or *someone's meaning him nothing good, I can assure you* . . . And *you never know* how mild or how strong those feelings are . . .

I have at least fifteen feelings—twenty, thirty, a thousand . . . A bureaucrat is halfway a voyeur. By profession. I always more or less *forgive* her, whatever that means, up to a point. Sometimes when I am unhappy, my unhappiness binds me to her and some kinds of *pain* make me a star in regard to her wanting things from me. But I don't want to be drawn into being in pain in order to be free of her importunities.

She knows I am useless, worthless for her when I am ill, and she doesn't nurse me, she taunts me. *I want you to die*, she's said. I think she means it. I don't know if she has other feelings down the chutes and past the crossroads. It is not clear where she will wind up in attitude toward me, or, rather, I think it is clear and I don't intend to test it. She is tied to wishing me harm.

And that wish will keep her afloat—or will sink her.

I had the sense that my eyelids were thickening into stone—do you ever get that? You come to a *final* opinion—not as in logic or as in geometry—but as in life: you close off a subject; you dream about it even when you are awake and even when you are in its presence: you use an emblem of an emblem; someone real and emblematic for you like a mother or a sister or a girl you know becomes a flag . . . Not just momentarily but *eternally* now . . . that is, for a long campaign . . .

Disliking her, fearing her, protective toward her in a way, hating her underlyingly, loving her, I perhaps paralyzingly am the same way toward mostly everybody underneath all the *chitchat, geegaws,* and *frou-frou* (my cousin Benjie . . .) as I am toward her. And perhaps I am this way toward much of what goes on in the world . . . The mood (of the soul) stretches and flaps its wings and squawks—or sings—as in an Irishman's poem. But moral neutrality-cum-complicity—a complicitous *appeasement*—a negotiated affection . . . not quite a human acceptance, not quite a warmly felt charity . . . that defines her and her life and makes her unhappy enough and with such a profound implication of meaning that, see, it perhaps pushes her over some edge or other . . . *You don't really wish her well,* Momma says. *Not deep down. It was always a war between the two of you . . . Which one of you was worse I can't say, I can't begin to think about it. You're a cold, mean player —no: it was the ghost of your mother* [that] *did it . . .*

See, I have gone astray. Too much of my life is explained in Momma's saying, *Don't* you *throw rocks at her, too; it won't hurt you to have a heart for once where she's concerned . . .* It's Nonie's youth-plumaged lump of a brother . . . An undercurrent of the agonized semi-loony rapturous is in his *youth* at the moment, a wasp-mass of the unsettling foreignness of him—she cares about me in her hatred-and-love, in her cold passion of that, more than I care about her . . . Lila has said, *That puts you in the wrong, Wiley . . . You're too cold . . .*

Her ghost is here: no, it is her body, her settled-on rump, the fated girl, the faded and altered and magically reworked *potency*. The silent creatures of feelings scamper in me—in the attic of the antic, Attic self . . . The silence of the *winglike* motions of sensation—of silent emotion—testify: *The world is difficult to live in* . . . The boy laughs and Nonie says, "Look at him: he does things for no good reason . . ."

" 'The empty laugh that bespeaks the vacant mind . . .' "

"Ask him if he likes to kiss . . . He's just my long-lost heart's desire is all": this is Leonie mixing poetic-sounding stuff with a kind of moistly soft semi-peacemaking—semi-incoherently. She's *nice* . . . Not entirely . . . Leonie is a fierce-mooded girl, *humbly* nervous, complicated—complicatedly many-humored, interesting-willed, unvirtuous . . . partly reliable . . .

"He read about kissing in a book," Nonie says.

"That's true," I said.

Leonie smiles: my nerves flutter in hallucination—a howling hallucination actually, an elucidation of the nerves in a state of desire, in a flaring of sexual *opinion* untranslated into power . . . But not entirely impotent . . . The neurally lit-up boy . . . The breasts of the women and his own sexual self—a common matter of command and study—are areas of mood and of ignorance—are a class and gender matter—the boy's mind defends itself with a sense of cunt, but the polemical *thrust* of that fades and becomes a real sense of the sensitively muscular, sensitively furred thing, fragile and garbage-y (in a way) and fastidious and the source of *beauty* and of *truth* as I know it . . .

Leave well enough alone . . . You're just like everyone else, you want your own way, you want to be in the spotlight . . . Well, everyone wants it . . . I want it on me, too, Mr. Too-Big-for-His-Britches Wiley Silenowicz . . . Little Big-Shot Dream Romeo . . . Learn to like us and you'll learn to live in the world. You'll have a home just like everyone else—a home is not a bad thing to have . . .

I tremble a little. *Nonie's reality* . . . the assault of comparison—the question how to act: an all-purpose, or omnibus, shame: it is a monkey velocity—I feel *a kind of wonder*, and shame, and distaste and disgust . . .

Nonie is as if rigorously calm among her purposes, her realisms—her pieties, her stonewall pieties . . .

You ruined her life, Wiley; it was an accident but you did it . . . [But] I [Lila] *did the best I could . . .*

Nonie does not feel her life has been *ruined* . . .

"Wiley," Nonie says—with mocking, unjocular *distaste* . . . It is dreamlike. I often have bad dreams. I have died in her dreams—she has told me. In the real air I live still . . . She wants me to be tied to her and comprehensibly defeated—*like a real man* . . . We are enemies in real life . . . Not entirely—it is not an absolute thing. It is fairly steady, steady enough—she has enough character for that. That enmity has a certain recurrent poetry to it: *She's human,* Lila says, *and so are you . . . Well, I give up. I give up on both of you . . . I'm tired. You go figure it out on your own . . .*

At the moment we are living in *comparative* peace. This is the most peaceful we've ever been . . . She bores me . . . Much of this stuff between me and her is in my voice . . . it is the posture of my neck . . . it shapes the expressions on my face . . .

She says, "I'm nervous tonight. Let me sit on your lap . . . Let me sit on your lap, Wiley . . ."

I think a bit. Then: "Okay . . ." Then: "But be nice. Let's try to make things work: let's show off for Leonie . . ."

Leonie has already begun to move, to make room on the couch, she so much wants the *tone* of things here to change . . . *Everybody is creative one way or the other,* Momma used to say. Nonie sat on my lap and leaned back, against me, in the curious silence of this act—Leonie and me watching: we are the audience—and then Nonie said, "I'm scared. Sometimes I wonder if I can manage . . . I don't know . . ."

A true thing . . . Partly true . . . She spoke like this in front of me so rarely that I felt, and noted, the moment as important, and it was not ever one of the memories I forgot, even for a day. It always springs to mind at the thought or sound of the name *Nonie* . . . My life squeezed hers—and so did I, uninnocently. To speak hurts and exasperates her: "I don't like to talk. Wiley's the one who talks—he's nothing but a talker . . . Leonie likes to talk: she barely gets her work done . . ." Nonie's attitude toward love is governed in part by her "dislike" for it occurring in others. This is her pride . . . These feelings are unnamed, are dismissed *Utopianly.* I would have liked her to marry some guy who would want to help me in my life, with money, or if not money, then in spirit . . . She meant that she didn't intend to let anyone help me go to school . . . This, of course, is a *very* selfish interpretation of what she is saying. From the point of view of Nonie's squeezed soul, she is asking me to be reasonable—and to die to my own life . . .

Momma said with a sigh of a new boy Nonie was seeing: *He meets Nonie's requirements: He goes through hoops. He's nothing special. He's respectable. He has a mother problem: he's all set for Nonie . . . I don't know how she's going to deal with a lifetime of it, how can anyone last in that kind of life for a lifetime . . .*

I put my arms around her. "Are you really sad?" *Is this genuine—you're not trying to lead me around by the nose . . .*

She said, "I'm scared of what it's going to be like . . . If it's really no good [down the road a pace, or a piece], can I count on you? Will you help me?"

"Sure," I said. I didn't mean it—except contingently. I was willing to mean it if she was *nice to me . . .*

"Can I?" she asked. "Say it . . ."

Go to hell, I thought. I mean, her body was rubbery and repellent to me but effectively sexual which I resented: the highly evolved antagonistic rule-i-ness in it, in her body, meant that she didn't mean to be *nice to me . . .*

"Maybe," I said. "Sure . . . I'll see . . . Yes," I said. A lie.

She wriggled her fairly big, hardish butt—on me—a girdled biggish thing . . .

She said with a little sigh: "I can manage you like Momma can."

Leonie coughed—her smoker's cough.

Nonie said in a mock-childish way to me—I think it was to me—"Give me a kiss."

My body twisted in *a Get-off-me way* but I went, "Ha-ha-ha," in a *this-is-friendly* way . . . In a democracy you're not supposed to be appalled by other people . . . And I started scooting around to kiss her if she wanted.

On the cheek, I thought. She presented her mouth, though.

Lila said to me before she died, *I never knew why you two hated each other so much. It must've been something I did . . .* And: *You could be patient with her—she's not so different from everyone else . . .* But flesh has a serious memory. *A little humor would help you with her . . .* Male humorous meanness? But her will, her wishes are unacceptable to my *flesh.* Lila, dying, said: *Dying's not so bad . . . I'll be glad to get away from her myself . . . Oh, it's terrible but what can you do—it's six of one, half a dozen of the other if you ask me: if you have a life, you have to eat what's on your plate . . . I won't blame you if you drop her but if you can, do what you can for her . . .*

Nonie says to Leonie, or to the air, I can't quite see since Nonie is on my lap, "I wonder if a woman's life is better if she's a streetwalker . . . I'd like to go on the streets and be a STREETWALKER for a while and find out . . . I guess I'm not the type though . . . The thing about me is my parents always loved me. I'm normal: I know who I am. I had a happy childhood . . . I don't know about you—I have always been happy . . . I'm sorry if you're different from me . . . I'm sorry for you . . . Sometimes when people talk about unhappiness, I just don't know what they're talking about. I just feel sorry for them . . ."

I respect her as a fighter—I half respect her. I don't know. She expects a regularity of response which is hardly more than an automatism but which she can count on and use. She moves in a dream of matchless freedom, her own really, but she is *political* . . .

"I wish what I had on everybody—I wish everybody could have what I have had—then the world would be a better place . . . I don't know why everybody just can't be honest and do an honest day's work and be *nice* to people . . ."

(Lila said before she died, *At least no one can say I didn't give her her confidence . . . She's confident, isn't she? I did a good job with her in one respect at least . . .*)

Nonie said, "I don't have enough money; if I had enough money and position, I would have a perfect life . . . Ha-ha . . . I'm young, I'm pretty, I'm smart—even if I have to be the one to say so: I know how to live . . . I know how to have a good time . . . I'm lucky—I'm a lucky person . . . My parents taught me how to be happy . . . I'm a very special, very, very, very, very, very lucky person . . ."

I don't think so. I think it is a tactic on her part to say so.

I say out loud, "I think we should all learn to think . . ."

"Oh he talks," Nonie said, "but he never makes any sense . . ."

She has an absence of humility among her motions . . . I DON'T THINK NONIE'S MUCH GOOD.

Nonie, on my lap, says to Leonie, "I wish I had his eyelashes . . . He's selfish but he has nice eyelashes . . ." Then: "He's selfish, he's not so smart. He does everything by the numbers. He has to memorize how to pee or he can't go to the bathroom . . . He's too spoiled—the air force would straighten him out fast, in no time—whoo-hoo, wouldn't that be something?"

"Are you interested in the air force?" Leonie asks me: her bold eyes have less boldness when Nonie is there, but something else is in place in her. She promises not to flinch. To endure what happens. You know that kind of promise of the reality of courage in a young woman? In a young woman's face and manner?

Having seen it, I was, then, ever after, attracted by it whenever it appeared and only by it and never by anything else . . .

LIES! LIES! LIES! TRUTH! TRUTH! TRUTH!—that kind of exclamation, that kind of exclaimed would-be explanation rings silently in the air.

Leonie on the assumption that heroism is a good idea says to Nonie, she asks, "Should I move to a chair?"

Nonie says—knowing she is being odd—"I mind my own business: if you ask me, well, I'm not, I'm not a worrier . . . I'm finishing my cigarette and I'm going beddy-beddy . . ." Then, in a kind of good nature so shocking to me that I feel old and tough all at once and without warning, she grins—she really *knew* she was in the wrong: "I'll leave you two lovebirds alone . . ."

No one says anything then. Then we see her flowing hair and body in her blue bathrobe from behind, Leonie and I, as we, Leonie and I, breathe in unison as we watch Nonie leave.

When Nonie is out of sight, down the back hallway, Leonie says, "She's a great person—we became friends fast but we're real friends . . ."

My eyes feel slightly blurred. I am always surprised by what people do, by what they say. I look down my body to see how close to me she is: it is nothing much, a sexual sight to me. I don't know what she will do. The moment is like hiding in the shrubbery, a moment of seclusion, of spying, but I am partly what I am spying on. I am no good as a regular person; I sense Leonie more than I see her; and because of my youth, I sense her as if with my forehead and ears and hair—it's all crazy—sensorily. When I touch her with my hands, it feels strange and crazy. She is *patient*, though . . . I have no worded vocabulary for any of this. I *get an impression* of Leonie as quickened amnesia, judge-y, getting ready to play the game here in a useful (and somewhat sensational) half-forgetfulness—an opinion of Nonie, then some contrary sexual stuff . . .

I turn to her with a kind of revealed sleepiness, an ache, an achy carelessness: a thing of having no past where she is concerned. I even say out loud—trying to be smart and attractive but it probably comes across as dumb—"Who am I?"

I feel a sort of new alertness in Leonie but one partly aimed against me, too, now—*a who-are-you-after-all*—I mean Nonie defines part of what human reality is. Perhaps because of what Nonie said about me—perhaps because of feeling a lot of things including that I hid some of myself—a lot of myself—from her, from Leonie before . . . Perhaps we're at that place now in sexual whuh'sit of truth-mongering . . .

Leonie has become the oldest person in the room. A moment without Nonie in the room . . .

Leonie looked at me. In the real world, it is as if one were screen-tested for a kiss. I am innocent—I lower my eyelids . . .

Leonie says, "Don't put ideas in my head."

I am somewhat always in error. There is an undercurrent of enmity here, too, now . . . A home-y distrust of the world. A sexual regime in which under-the-surface things flick at me with their heat-steam . . . Lila used to advise me: *You want something to happen with people? Let them make a fool of you . . . I* am dutifully a fool—now—and I like her; I am interested—with slightly louder breath suddenly, *listening* to hidden but also really quite visible things if you look hard . . . my dutifulness reeks of free will.

Leonie thinks that she is maybe a *champion* in knowing what feelings are. She-uh-ahh-rub-a-dubs my chest using two fingers only. Then she uses her palm and leans toward me and says—playing by rules—"Women start by bidding high but they don't intend to stick to it . . ."

"And men are bastards?" I murmur—youthfully asking . . .

The permissions in her face, her parted lips, had not included the permission to talk. She hadn't expected me to talk. She braces herself now as if her bones were wing struts on biplanes.

The thing here is of us being like really drunk but undrunkenly—we are outside grown-up police-i-ness, of dirty policing . . . Of course, I don't believe this is *truly* happening—I don't want a scandal and I don't trust Nonie's effect on Leonie. It is like a removed echo.

"I give up. Who are you?" she says in a local way. "I want to know you . . . I know who you are . . ."

Her line. She went to Lutheran college for six months and switched to the University of Indiana for two more years and then she gave up and went to work for the army.

This is remarkable: us on the couch. In language, being young can be made to seem absolute, but in life it doesn't seem *absolute* at all and isn't: it's reliable, though, as a biographical fact for a while, for an evening.

For instance, in my case, Leonie's glance was veiled or muzzy in terms of superiority. What I am—physically—she isn't overwhelmed—she likes me—so far, unofficially—but it is the other thing, my being, in some ways, not exactly young . . . *Sweet* wasn't a term of sexual praise. It was supposed to be lousy—spineless. But a *trenchant* sweetness is in Leonie . . . The honied whatevers of an ear-kiss—I tongue the whorls of her ear . . . I say, "May I?" A lawn moment but wild like a moment in a dream, limitless and imprisoned anyway.

She bears it and then moves and says, "No . . . I hate that." Like Nonie, but with Leonie I understand it is because I am in some ways amateurishly, and with juvenility, formidable.

She shakes her head to clear it of the tickle.

She says an unpolicing-policing thing of "I don't want us to hate each other . . ."

I say, "I'm not trying to get us into trouble . . ."

She gazes at me until I move my head so near hers that she closes her eyes. Then I kiss the frail curve of her eyelid and the small bristling flutter of her unmade-up and unsoft eyelashes. A precocious and privileged use of her face.

She stirringly withdraws her presence . . . A clattering and flattered and maybe nervous loudness of breath in me means I have no idea of her degree of amusement as I persist. The flutter of her eyelids, the eyelashes, the quirk of her lips: a short way of saying that *we* don't deal in *real* approval.

In the motion of the moment, courtesy and co-conspiracy and a degree of specific wit in each of us became the felt shock of courtship collusion: a dirty approval with possibilities of sudden absolution if it widens into devotion, say, or some sort of love, not any sort of love, though. It is incessantly uninnocent and yet *romantic*: one is asking nothing: one is expressing a hope . . . You don't have to go on. Or be practical.

When a thing has no price, it has a chance to be taken as priceless—so Lila told me . . . *The Diamond as Big as the Sky* . . . Clear but stylized megalomania and greed in this matter, the amusement quotient of that, well, no one is being RESCUED. I get up on one knee on the couch, then—as a joke sort of—on both knees—a somewhat spaghettilike boy—and I dive, or keel over, forward onto her, boylike—but not heavily, not asking for major patience in her. She jerks—and braces herself again. I find her mouth. The other tongue of mine, the tonguelike meat-staff, still pantsed, is against her side, not squirmingly but tickingly—involuntarily so, complimenting her (except I am young . . .). Stupid, nearly blissful, crude pantomime . . . This echoes from body to body, but I don't know what sounds the echoes have in her. And her hands and arms go partway *haywire*, sexily-sweetly (i.e., far down the hierarchy of strongly sexual responses), petting me, patting me. She says, into my mouth, "Ha-ha." Then she grunts and moves away from me and then back again. Leonie strokes the back of my head with electric worms, skinny fingers . . . She says in a pause, "You're so crazy." She says it sweetly, abandonedly, submissively to life and whatnot, and rulingly . . .

In a fifteen-year-old way, I feel at home. We're lollygagging along, wasting time mostly. I am set about inside, all around the chest cavity, with bits of broken music. In a way, for me, it is as if we were inside a wheel of music—cacophonous and loud off and on—a neural and *trenchant sweetness* almost the same as harshness, the weird toughness of the grammar of what I recognize as a kind of *ruthlessness* in the procedures of orgasm. Inexplicable and inexpressible principles, uncataloguable, in the category of without-sacrament: standing around: this is in me, the wobbly sexual plane of discourse of that. She kisses in a way that shows she likes me *still*, even while the question exists of Do-I-like-to-kiss-this-way? Do I like to kiss *her*? An older *woman*? Actually I don't much; it is a substitute, *sloppy* and not *purely* anything. That's my sexual opinion . . . I am a stupid boy whom novelty blinds and caresses. Everything is blurred and fresh, stupid and frustrating—but it is *new*.

"Sure," I say, extending to myself no credit for youth but attempting to use it with her. I can feel in her the interest and tie and imprint of *the real man*, as I said. I mean, the masculine stuff that is not me. "Are you an expert in what is crazy? I'm not," I said.

"Me neither," Leonie said in a kind of madness of complicated meaning in the light of the reality. She says: "You have clean lips—no stubble . . ."

"You too," I say, madly grinning.

I half know her social caste. She isn't *social* . . . I can *smell* it that her dad's partly a crook: it's that sort of moniedness that she comes from. The girl has her breasts against me and, well, I'm close to her dad, her boyfriend, her boyfriend-before-last—there's a kind of stink of other men in a woman that I mostly ignore. I don't want to know those men through her . . .

The good wicked stink of real life embracings—I am half mad with the flattery of it. And, true to my type, am somewhat sickened.

"Is this real?" she asks—a line. It's okay.

"Let's see," I say, kissing her harder—not with skill. I ask, "*IS* THIS REAL?" The kiss—blindingly—was not skillful—but it was blinding. "Let's see how we kiss," I persist, guessing wrong. "Ha-ha," I say. The sheer electric wash of the sea of airy meaning of the justice and reward . . . Justice is reward, and without reward the animal will die of sexual permission, hers toward me because of how Nonie was . . . The boyish-lipped, driving, diving clumsiness of my kissing . . . The intimacy of a head near one's own is like the lights and doorway of a house. The lights and doorway that my kissing presence is, the large, oppressive head of the clumsy kisser, the spaceship-acropolis of the mind, the true sting in an actual moment of candles of sensation, stilled flesh and god-beams, a crazedness . . . the closeness in the sudden jags and jigs and jogs of the kiss mean one will not wake from this event ever: it will be part of my continuing character in a large way . . . This will be partly the example of the tremendous importance of consolatory presence. The specific moment, the real moment, is terrifying and outlines no generality except a biological finality unless you exile yourself from the moment while you are in it . . . I did not ever want to believe in God. I did not want to be a good person . . . The bones of her face and the hair of her head, the moment forms an isthmus thing, with winds and seas on either side. Me, I am peninsular. A committee of selves with an extremity of purpose. An ambition . . .

She is careful and giddy both—an oddly compounded style—sort of femininely cruel by means of a certain daring in her, cruel toward the obvious fragility of the animal in her and in me. We could have been thrown into being civilized—this was in parts of the episodes in her kissing.

She issues a mutual, anti-parental dare, tender, sloppy, and appalled—not exactly sweet—and then she takes it back: fear makes her like a parent. Like a goody-goody in regard to the seas, the dignity and storminess, and the wallow of sexual stuff—well, this is so for her with me, well, that time, in those minutes.

I have half an idea what to do in response; I have an idea of a harshly mannerly assertion while being overwhelmed—do you know? I got the idea of it from books and from watching football. I can't say I ever executed it even in pretend . . . I have a sense of a broken heart mostly—because I am untrained and not well armed—but I am still glad that this stuff is happening. Memories afterward change stuff: books really are mostly about memories afterward and not about what happened so much—they just pretend to that—but they are made of events changed for the sake of the convenience of someone now, for the convenience of memory and in order to have some halfway convincing sense of success. Or it's for apology maybe. It takes nerve to go near real moments—are other people like that or is it just me?—the feel of the air; the nearness of her lips: my blank, maybe blankly vile desires. I was so young. I wasn't certain what I was excluding among my desires in my wish to be sane. Leonie offers a partnering sense to this. She is, by my notions (back then), *peculiarly* free of guilt—she is escaping it moment by moment—a feminine blasphemy, perhaps. An audacity—this is part of how she is interesting sexually. Her being interesting to me sexually is all tilted and propped up on what has already happened and it is temporary and changeable. She is not afraid of me—of what might happen . . . She really is pretty interesting sexually. If the idea of *charming* means kind of strugglingly half-magical, partly logical wit, and whatever, then Leonie was *really charming* sexually. She is genuinely not broken, or not yet; and she is more grim than sad, but sensibly sad—*things-being-what-they-are*—whereas my state is absurd-high-pitched, high-flown—kind of horrified and trapped-in-quicksand, guilty, exasperatedly grief-stricken, too happy, a lot of *too* things . . . I know Leonie *almost* in the terrible way of knowing someone in actuality in the huge scale and sensual clarities and heat of regard and of ignorance and of innocence in childhood, but I know her sexually. Still, it is like in childhood when you know someone (for your purposes) entirely and at once from the way they smell and from the feel of their hands: you know the merit of their touch, so you know them. You know them from how their clothes are ironed—that stiffness: this isn't sensible; it is more sensible than just being sensible—this acting on the immediate evidence of nerves. I know her from her lips and from the texture of the skin and I know the men she has known. Really.

Immense, intense, frightening, partly unthwarted, partly unfailed intimacy, *early* intimacy even now, and the end of *loneliness* (when it still is loneliness contingently) is a sort of death—a dirty death, you bite the dust, all that—and yet it is a good thing, grown-up, a good-bad thing—heartbreaking—you know? And I want it: it's desirable. I hugged her in the silly-seeming dirtied, gritty-grotty *grace* of the business-deal-like trafficking just about entirely in present-tense stuff, in the rolling, skin-inflected happening moment, and doing it with some connivance at the appearance of ease—a dirty childhood ease: it is almost that.

But it is also childhood rectified. Is it a genetic swindle? Do I have to be clever, lucky, blessèd to handle this, or can I just go ahead without thought?

"Wah, wah, wah," I say out loud, stupidly, catching my breath; her eyes, then, look at me—my imitation of the infantile—her eyes hold a fogged-over thing of light in them: there are limits even in the momentary heat of our almost passionate agreement to do this stuff. Those limits, though, border, almost thrillingly, the almost fieldlike, oddly lit thing of *we-are-about-to-kiss* . . .

"Pwease keeisss me," I say in baby talk.

Her eyes do loosen a bit at the baby talk.

So, our lips come together in the mutual oddity of something like being retarded or having regressed. They touch, a little moistly, chapped. We pause without parting from each other: we listen at our lips to each other's *stuff* in the caves of our mouths. I think I hear a buzz of parts of her mind—like schoolchildren—or like the self decomposed in a tomb —the smell of death is here. I am oddly phallically well instructed in my own requirements, although specifically a fool as a Casanova that way. My feelings are an odd pressure, like a muscular pressure, or clenching, and yet some quality in the feeling, like an edge (as if the feeling were a butterfly wing or a moth wing of a man-moth), rots the surfaces of the lips and into the rot her rot pours and oozes until my eyelids fly open and I look into her eyes and she is there . . . I don't know who she is but this is an uncontingent end of loneliness—oddly sportive— and yet a fatality. It is like bleeding to death, but that is not what is happening. How odd the world is. I know her. How odd. How odd. How odd. I hold my mouth rottingly to hers and bleed to death emotionally into a ghoulishly after-everything-is-over sense of intimacy. But nothing is over. I intensely mind intimacy—and I wrap myself in it. It scares me. Revenant creatures walk then: the dead. Love and its griefs—you know that shit? The skulls, with the hair and features, of the two deadishly living *kids* are like lanterns half buried where some sort of breath of wind blows them in such a way that—if I may say this—it is as if the burning stuff inside each skull—sexual hallucination, sexual calculation, sexual wit, sexual selfishness, sexual stupidity, whatever—moves weirdly, dirtily, effectually, from skull to skull and burns each soul up in the magnetisms that arise from such motions.

Stormlike passages then *arise* in the mind, and one senses this is so in the other person's mind . . . I must say it hurts to an extraordinary degree to care. And it is *dirty* . . . the drool and all. It does seem like vice, the chemicaled slop of echo and of *taste*—the taste of the other person, who is merely human, after all—and . . . It seems rigid unversatility is more informative than I would like.

In the slippery heat and feast of information (as if of a king) it is embarrassing—and wicked—and *sportive*—and effective (sometimes)— to say, "Suck my dick . . ."

I say it but it is, after all, really a question.

She likes to kiss; she likes to touch; but this is a little different—she pauses now to think. She doesn't say yes or no: she says, "You have nice arms . . ."

"I'm sorry," I say. I rushed the other and I intend to be unclear—

poetic; sexual poetry is rougher and more political than I would have expected.

Actually, I'm crushed.

She says again, "You have nice arms," but you know how saying something can be not saying it? By not responding to what I said, she says an unsaid thing more than forgivingly. The liking and dismissal are odd: she is not commanded or overwhelmed and she is not afraid of having things go badly; she is not afraid about losing me—she is not bullied; she enjoys my stupidity. Also, she doesn't mind it—my not kissing well . . . Or my saying that thing I said.

But she also means, *Why go on—you're not good enough. You're not someone with traits successful enough in the world for me to breed with* . . . Or it's something complicated like that.

So, I straighten up, kind of, and with my back off the couch, and my muscles all stretched and twisted in this posture, I do kiss her well—speakingly and kind of honestly—accepting the badness in things in general and my own bloodcurdling, wadded-up, cruddy sexual will and putting her in a special category.

But I don't want her to think ill of me and just *dally*. I want and need the intimacy I mind. Now the earthen stench and the horror and ghosts I have and which show in intimacy, that interests her as an apartment or weird poem or stuff about menstruation might interest her.

Bringing my head near hers, my whole taut body nearing hers, eyes and crotch, skinny and taut torso—I can see this whole thing affects her in a favorable way. But I don't know why. Is it all luck? Do I have grown-up character? Her breath quickens on my skin around my lips and in my nostrils. The silk of her femininity . . . I remember thinking with a kind of desperation that I probably liked men more than she did, as *things*. I didn't intend a euphemism. The search, or reach, *through her* exotically to the private shadow of personally manly stuff (and of *unmanly* stuff)—this part may be *over her head* but I doubt it—and to distant men, that scared me—and seemed wrong—not exciting—but so did any sort of looking for her. I don't want to be feminine. I am offered no safety here and no really acceptable naming of sexual stuff: I'm a boy and not all that eligible . . .

Anyway, I feel it, I am wronging a *man* . . . It matters who you wrong.

Tongues and breath. My skinny arms and hesitations—for her I am almost a version of her. My age, my body, my desires. She likes *them* in some way that is not like the way I *like HER* . . . I feel picked at, lightly bitten—it is like someone taking the stitches out of a football or a basketball with a cuticle scissors and stabbing me and slowly deflating me: not the erection but some myth about the sexual brouhaha. Inflation. Deflation. Humiliatingly (hallucinatorily) momentary . . . The *assertive* orphan is moving his hips against her . . . Does her body read me like a book? Does she?

I wasn't *following* her lead, I realized glumly.

She said, "You're *wild* . . ."

Her tone meant that I was "impossible . . . No one owns you," which was something Ora said.

"That's a compliment," I say, hoping to be reassured it was a compliment, that, at last, I was *normal* . . .

Her eyes flash—sort of maybe lyingly—and she says, "Oh YES . . ."

Even so, I *hate* being judged. It burns and stings . . .

In the hollow spaces of the moment, though, despite the burning-shyness stuff and stinging stuff and what-all, the ripe outdoors thing of the permissiveness of a woman moves me until my motions in time, if I can say that, are happy without being at all like childhood . . . It is *PERSONAL* . . . Or whatever, this unsmiling, lightly sweaty *happiness*—it is as if a white searchlight was turned on inside me and illuminated my time on earth, my life, in this way, false stillness and time, anyway—a geography of it.

But it is a geography that is not sitting still.

This sucks at my balance so that I am a force right at the edge of being forceless in an ocean of off-again, on-again white light, illuminating what is essentially a matter of the tissues but which somehow affects the soul deeply. This is supposedly one of the major mysteries of life: I've read about it. And here it is. It is in me. And a version is in her. I laugh suffocatedly silently and her body brightens. Can I say these things? She may like sexual seriousness but she has her doubts about it, too. Sexuality is not necessarily amusing: it is not necessarily amusing in an amusing way. My body and my soul are suffocated in the convulsions of laughter and by a kind of stillness—I am an observer and a captain and an actor and a recruit—having a good time thrillingly and darkly while about to be sincere about life and death maybe.

Maybe I am already *sincere*. Maybe it's already too late to pretend I'm not sincere. She feels maybe like *a star*—I am guessing. Her breath bends; it oozes; and then is boardlike and then supple. Seconds pass. Her body is bony, ribby, and strong—*this way, that way*. What am I going to do next? It's not as if I wasn't shocked to be doing this at all. I start to sweat. I am aware that nothing in my movements or in my breathing controls her—I am on sufferance unless I have scared her in some way. She is cheating on a *hero*.

It's all choice here. It's choice stuff: wicked.

God. I am shocked. I am juvenile. I slow down. I am as if frozen with stagefright. I am as if too honorable to go on. *Wickedly*, she takes over. Sighingly, she releases the imprisoned boy. She kisses me—with a lot of tongue, *sloppily* but speakingly—nobly and obscenely. It's a little diagrammatic, but I am not about to look a gift kiss in the mouth . . . ha-ha. I am happy, excited, overexcited, desperate, despairing, aware that I am on trial—and I don't give a damn . . . This is all partly in sequence and is partly an as-good-as-simultaneous meteoric arc of this stuff, harmonic or clashing simultaneity—pulse, breath, feelings, her moods—this is sexy for me but I distrust her and I try to mislead her about what is happening to me.

I don't want to comment on my feelings to her, and I don't want her to go on reconnaissance and see my *real* feelings.

She fools with me—here is further darkness, further light. I am aware from her smell that she feels this stuff. You are played on. She *intends* a partial betrayal of everyone who is not here. That's how I feel the compliment of sex in the withholding of tacit mocking. I have my hands on the halves of her behind. Is she going to fuck with a kid whether she wants to or not? She expects to laugh at me if I don't overcome her—she's a friend of Nonie's . . . I don't give a fuck if she laughs at me: she is sad and reasonable and she has a great body. I don't know. I move my hand in her cleft behind and then I do it with my hand as a fist and then I do it—slide back and forth—touching her mostly with one finger . . . Then I just let my thumb ride on some of the curves of her buttocks while she considers the feelings . . . I feel alone, almost a deathly grown-upness of an irrevocable male rage at being alone . . . Male loneliness is not a joke. The erection, not in one of its states of final fullness, is semirigid *fluff*. The fooling around sets the warm fluff on restless and nervous muscular fire, kind of . . . Meanwhile, my emotional heat is like that of a stinking mattress . . .

I want to belong to the action but I can feel Leonie's holding back in that no fucking is promised or is included in what is going on, if you know what I mean. Her tight abdomen, its front, the sense of the hollow in it, it's private there.

But it is a moment of rare and mostly unspeakable interest to us . . . THIS SURPRISES BOTH OF US. THIS ISN'T HAPPENING IS IT? SHE IS RESENTFUL. And surprised. I *feel* it in her. I don't want to be in love with her . . . The hallucinatory is a weird playground of the soul—I see that—I start to imagine pleasures . . . My guess is that sexually I was *daring-and-lonely*, a certain high-school type, a *chump* of a local variety.

The cunt: smelly tepee, warm . . . You put your finger in . . . You goosh around . . . You pull your finger out . . . puritanically . . . out of the home of *distraction*. I prefer this to being with a boy but I am more scared here. I don't want to love her but the erectile beauty of the moment and its blasphemously sacramental nature—horsing around in relation to *Nonie*—is a form of wakefulness more dreamlike—more attractive to the ego—than most things in my life. Men dream their lives. Leonie might discuss sexual stuff with Nonie—ah, Jesus . . . "Yah, yah, yah," you whisper—stupid jokes in bed are sexy depending on your taste: "The Tour of Bauble," the boy said, gripping, a little inanely, one of her breasts while moving himself against her leg.

She was quiet. Maybe she is phallically daydreaming. Who knows. Her mind flits, flies: then is here, it lies here. I say then: "I want to learn to fuck."

She doesn't answer but masturbatorily pumps at me, reducing my too great success with her—at my age—to a dry fuck. Still, a lovely gift. I buck back, lightly, self-consciously, then in a rhythm (partly rubbing) of as-if-sleeping presumptuousness . . . as if I were doing it in my sleep . . .

She said, "You have a nice throat: you don't have an ugly Adam's apple . . ." I swallow noisily foolishly. If she talks that much, this won't become a fuck. She speaks in pretend mindlessness, supposed sleepiness, though.

She is a little in love with me—though—but not much, I guess.

She says, as if my posturing had shown what I was thinking, "I'm a little in love with you . . ."

It becomes a fact of a sort, not a secret. One has to move on. Someone phallically vain may be disgusting—or interesting.

"I'd kind of like to fuck . . ." Then: "Hey, I WANT TO FUCK . . ."

She didn't say anything. I kissed her *inconsolably*, fiercely. She stiffened in unsubstantively relative ratio to the ferocity.

How many times in the course of a year do you give in? Does it have a religious aura, the giving in? Had there been a big scene in her life of force and argument and her being forced to give in?

Would she hope to be the victorious one? I guess so.

Her eyelids flutter. "Please don't," she says.

I get the creepy feeling that she sees ME morally. As I said, she loves me some . . . But without hope. I now spurn her love. With my face. With my hurt. Her inner eyes in this landscape recognize the brooding adolescent grief. It is grief: I can't bear reality. I think, *This is only necking* . . . Villain-fool, the boy says, "Have it your way—you're a guest . . ."

Handsome-eyed, sexually-forward Leonie pushed or moved my lips with hers until I kissed her back—a little—and then she let my lips nestle, or alight, or perch, on hers. And then her hardened lips parted slowly; and parchingly we breathed and touched at the mouth—and she licked slowly—I understood the terms—and limits—of her apology . . . I don't lick—in a nestled way within some rule of it's-less-pain-this-way . . . We spoke in this way into each other's mouths . . . This stuff is from the flier—or from her brother: it is deep, sincere, tender, truly dirty stuff: Leonie wiggles and fits her midsection against my belly, against the head of the prick inside my clothes more than the shaft, and then she settles some of her legs' weight along the underside of the erect shaft where a lot of feeling flutters and moves because of her movements. The sensation for me from the weight of her body of my being almost enclosed is as heavy as the weight of the water in a large river against me. Willful, insolent, and *sad, I know* this is the real sexual thing, a little stale but stalely magnificent and a gift with some holding back *still* but way over my head. On both sides, we *see* our limits . . . Oh, the mutual sadness . . . But you can't argue that sex doesn't matter—or that it doesn't change you—it changes a lot of definitions—such as of the motions of the moments and of the self, of the selves . . . It would be a betrayal to do this easily. I suppose you could close yourself off. I never kissed this way again.

Betrayal? Oh, of physical closeness and privacies and intimacies with a mother, say, unless your mother was cold and careful, but of childhood, always, and of complaints . . . a betrayal of complaints. If one is truthful, one has few rights here. One is set free, as trash-shit; it's too hard to talk about.

I start to buck, mostly just to be ugly in a restless urge to lessen the progressive weight of evidence and of instruction of *The Moment*, which has a certain tone hardly less emotionally serious than a kind of seeing what is likely to matter to one the rest of one's life. A young man in pain—lyingly: truthfully—and Leonie—Madame Polygraph—and her listening and semi-acrobatic and surging and weighing-on-me body, and the inner body hollowly murmuring of truth, untruth, worth and unworth . . . This is awful. And it is interesting, too. Beauty of any sort has an immense kind of fleshiness and an even more immense shadow or conviction or burriness, it sticks to you, and the obscenity, the obscene beauty, the judgments, the holding back, the *toying*-with-infatuation—

Do you love me at all, lover boy? And: *Will you die for me or at least destroy your life for me, nice lady* . . . I proceed, we proceed, alternately ignoring the beauty, going on, since that is what, in reality, you do. I am bucking, but now I am doing it openly in the light of the beauty—a kind of ugliness, if you can imagine it, half-dissolved, converted, illuminated, and half-resistant and willful—and trying to persuade the inner sight of hers to approve of me and to like this catchy mix of stuff and me, and to bend it, her inner vision, into that of a *thrilled* I-don't-know-what—partner-audience, mother-sister giving in? Not thrilled by me exactly but by obscenity itself or by her wish to harm others—I can be fairly ruthless in a way—I wanted her thrilled by what was happening with me. That is too much to hope for. She is reasonably attentive—past the point of just being indulgent and not at a point of older-girl-storminess—or of a hooked boy, hooked on this stuff, either.

This part of us being together was done slowly with small sections of quietness. The avoidance of nightmare is our guide along with our proceeding in a kind of morality of curiosity—in the avoidance of nightmare, I repeat—blindly and with heat toward *Let's-go-over-the-edge*—this is as if in stares and blinks—more than blinks, tightly closed eyes and then stares that aren't regular, aren't the regular kind from wakefulness but mostly a kind of *social* madness—loon-eyed, loony-eyed, a politeness in the madhouse—loosened and dirtily and in a way tentatively sexual—as if one was merely being logically mad. As if this stuff was always there. And one had stopped fighting to hide it and control it. And one wasn't pushing it, either. Manliness, maleness, by permission, in a suspension of doubt, well, I am crossly on a stage, in a proscenium frame being looked at while I stroke her thighs, her belly. I am now proceeding in a style of half swindle, part antagonism, part wishful sexuality in relation to her *morality*, such as it is, and her judgment, and part love with a secret hidden inner joke in it of male *ruthlessness* and male tenderness—favoritism—indulgence—toward that considerable beauty which was her spirit here "in bed" and which was also that of *her* body—that body which was, in part, listening to me, inwardly and outwardly.

"It's easy to get all fucked up," she said. "Time out."

"I don't know," I said.

"No. I mean it. I need a time out . . ." She put her head back against the couch and coughed into her hand. "Am I the worst person you have ever known?"

"Yeah. Sure. No. Who knows?"

She semi-half-laughed, quarter-laughed, and tousled my hair—she kissed one of my eyelids. "You're cute. Everything you think you are, well, just double it by four," she said unmathematically. "You can make someone lose their head, Honey . . ." Then: "Honey Bear . . ."

"Really?"

"You don't want to do that . . . I might scratch your eyes out," she said, almost contentedly in regard to her madness of ferocities and to scenes hidden from me.

And she said it shamedly—dirtily—her eyelids fluttering, her lips oddly alive and independent in her face in regard to language—*dirtily* . . . "Go and read about it, you pretty little devil of a brain . . ."

"Dig it out of you?"

"Oh you can't . . . My lips are sealed . . . It's all so different with you . . ."

"You're not afraid of me . . ."

She barely smiled. She moistened her lips. She said—her lips sticking, her enunciation sluggish—"No, that's God's honest truth, I am not afraid of you."

Maybe I was a daydream, entirely a daydream . . . Maybe a daydream semi-horror from a radio play she'd heard. Or something. As an orphaned kid I was glad (and maybe even arrogant) to have this evidence that I would not be left out of all these stories—certain sorts of sentimental comedy and certain so-called *dramas* (of those days) and certain sorts of dreams and wishes turned into silly actions as if in a silly play.

She leaned forward archingly—self-lovingly I see now—warm and so bleak: a rocky hotness: and Leonie's eyes, as we hold each other and nuzzle—and only that—her eyes are old and stony and architectural with experience and practice—this is when they open, when she is present in them—her eyes are architectural structures of murk and light as a permissiveness not entirely true and as a sad *gaiety*, a somewhat giddy thing of forbiddenness. I think she intends to make up for this: expiate it. She is not *finer* than I am but she is more worthwhile at this moment—this is something Nonie wants me to admit about her, Nonie, and me. I tickle Leonie faintly, stroke her near her crotch—but I don't really presume—then, in our lives, this moment is the only real one just now. I know from a residual tension in the long muscles of her thighs and hips and in a kind of cleanliness-toward-me atmosphere in her that *going-all-the-way* is real to her but is a counterfeit possibility toward me because she *is loyal* to various things and will have to *atone* if anything happens.

I mean I am really closed out and can go along for the ride—and try to change things—but it will cost too much. She might do it because

I am of a higher social rank than she is—but then she'll be screwing for the experience of the social rank—do you see? And I am *pretty* . . . which is useful up to this point but is a bore now . . . Or she might screw me because I am Nonie's brother . . . I don't know. If she decides to have a drink and to *get* really drunk, really truly family-shaming drunk, that might be a kind of usable, shameful, almost neutral fuck—both of us out of our skulls . . .

For me, to see into a moment, and to trust or half trust my judgment, is like when I let go and push myself to run so hard that I know I will pass out of my own control and enter on an appeal to *grace* in the darkness of will—grace of will if nothing else—grace and, ultimately, *forgiveness* for the thing of being ambitiously present in the universe, alive in terms of partly willed, partly inescapable motion—and out of control. She isn't urging me to this or hinting *welcomingly* or being tricky. But she has, in part, a kind of trash-soul, in which she is "offering" me the madness of her realism.

I am *learning* about her—and a little about sex and about me from a limited point of view: SHE IS NONIE'S FRIEND. I don't know that I want to be normal . . . I have a kind of destiny. If I live. Through the war. And the rest of it. She is maybe a *quarter theoretically* interested in a-man-like-me sexually in love with her, but she is not finally interested in *me* . . . If she is I don't want to know it.

Chiefly, though, she can't picture me. She is less well guarded than before: this is an *intelligent* and dangerously loony thing some women back home did—offer themselves as bait or lure. Of course, it is a compliment—but it is perhaps an ambush, a trap. The thing is, she is really likable and maybe okay and maybe not, but she is not *good* . . . She may be good to me. Or good at this stuff . . . I doubt both those things. She and I are approaching—as in an allegory—a poverty of the soul that would make us need each other—that would remove all trace of luxurious playfulness and swindling and setting traps from what we are doing in regard to each other now and would replace it with a reality of need that might erase conscious individuality—and moral judgment—for a while. You can twist your mind and ignite it so that it gives light of a sort in a world of loosened moral effects just beyond your knowledge, just out of the range of your usual sight, but who are you then? Half loosened, a quarter loosened? The same boy as before? An Impostor? To be *sexually* admired is real hell if you are troubled by a sense of truth, is sexually dull if it limits you and her, and it is a kind of heaven . . . One isn't in love—or is, or is in love with one's privileged whatever here. It is hateful, the mess of desire and some love. It gouges me. The half-light in the room in this moment of motion and of steamy necking and streamy feeling—and sensation—is part of a sighing air of the poetry of the time—leopards and emeralds and phonographs and cynicism and other shit: I am choked by her, by styles, by youth, by privilege, by sexual heat, by adolescent maundering. Truly emotions are part of an extraordinary realm of power, which is to say, love, which one, as with any other power, can avoid, can escape from, to some extent. I feel that I have found in this cocoonish closeness with her the evidence of my own sexual invalidity and my future validity—the thing and its boundary—and this is (maybe) *a crushing weight* of *a kind of* understanding of Lila and Nonie—of a maybe not exactly distant kinship . . .

At the same time, the *physical* possibility in one's bodily reality—this does confer a truly eerie sense of happiness . . . of a kind.

"It's too risky . . . You're good at this," Leonie says, defining me as out to get something—defining me as a force. She is breaking off and breathing but not pulling away from me any farther than necessary to suck in air—air heated by our skins. We are pressed so close we breathe our own heat. Gouged and garrotted and boyish in that—as in a game of volleyball inside the maybe airless gym in late winter—and as if looted—but I have *some say*—I know her. I know her (and stuff) crazedly: self-judgment and self-ridicule—well, the folly of the erect prick—and the cruelty and bitterness about gradations of sexual merit . . . *Well, you didn't get laid this time either, fuckface* . . . And: *Leonie is a real dirty ferret of a woman* . . . A wolf-ferret-owl? One *knows* in one's heart and mind, it depends on the moment, but one tries to be absolute and final. One *knows* genetically certain shit about this *dirty* stuff: I am acceptable to Leonie as *breeding stock*. The gradations of response in her don't register her as a sexual star of my life or me as a *movie lover* or worldly gigolo or *real Casanova* or saint or whatever for her, but, nevertheless, a *thing* of flickering hairs and maddened muscles and (a wartime phrase) *mad lips*—she can say she had *a thing* for me . . . and I was *a thing in her life* . . . but what she does gives certain hopes of mine credence and defines certain pains (as in being a *romantic* [or a sexual] *object*: an adolescent daydream), as my being ungrateful and jealous of life, of nearly everyone in a kind of easiness of spiritual grace which is, axiomatically, a form of loving the world and respecting it . . . This is in conscious knowledge of Nonie but without knowledge of Nonie as emblematic of anything except certain human qualities and contemporary aspects of existence I would like not to be a party to. A sense of evil being inescapably present in anything imperfect, in everything terrestrial, my own feelings seem evil, whether they have a youthful grace of spirit in Leonie's eyes or not. She looks and listens through various holes and through the vibrations of various thinnesses of skin and various animallike nerves and so on: it is not just possible, it is likely she will *kill me* (as in saying, *You kill me, you really do,* when it is true) by enforcing a law of loneliness on me again. I can tell she is kissing *a pretty boy, a Romeo, a godforsaken trap for a sensible woman* . . . (S.L. said those things.) She is kissing Nonie's brother, a young imbecile, a bookish boy.

I say aloud to her: "A pretty boy, a Romeo, a godforsaken trap for a sensible woman . . . Nonie's brother . . ." I was embarrassed and unembarrassed: a boasting kind of *exhibitionism* I saw with Leonie was to some extent basically sexual . . . a flaunting as part of an obscure contemporary ritual. "See my muscle," I said, flexing my arm. "It's thin. See my other muscle," I said, pointing. "It's not so thin."

My father, before he died, had flirted with me some. I had thought S.L. was joking . . . No, I hadn't . . . I had believed him in a very diluted semi-childish way and had failed to understand much but had taken it in as *information*.

I had been afraid to be sensually amused, hopeful, *stuff* like that . . .

Leonie said, "You're a terror . . . You're not what Mother ordered."

"You guessed it . . . You're really big-time—you know that? My father tried sometimes to kiss me on the mouth . . ." She stares at me from close to my eyes. I stare back. "I *know* I scare people sometimes . . . I'm supposed to keep my mouth shut . . . People say they don't know what I'm going to say next. Big deal. Then they get obnoxious, though—it's competitive if you ask me."

"Your *father*?"

"I made a big deal out of it but it wasn't exactly a big deal," I said bravely. "It was part of life."

"Oh . . . Wiley . . ." My name didn't exactly spring to her lips. She kissed me as if to erase the pain.

"There's a lot of life I don't want—I don't want war or death or pain either. I'm *a difficult* BOY . . . The Greeks were crazy: you can't know yourself." Then I go way too far: "And my sexual clumsiness is an enticement—to me, too—almost a perverse virtue."

Her eyes have a foxy peering like something in a pagan story—their architecture of murk-and-light is pagan—she is self-consciously-hiding-stuff-from-me . . . We stare at each other peeringly . . . She wriggled her mid-body on the new drawing-compass (and bludgeon) of the erection and she showed her teeth, devouring my self-possession, but I closed and pursed my lips—and touched her lips with one of my fingers to show it wasn't working. Then, next, she moves her hand down *there* as if in great good humor . . . Ooh, oh, ah . . . "How does anybody live?" the boy says, squinting.

Well, we all die—is that an answer?

No.

I need a specific phallic meaning. *I will trade you for it* . . . I'm not sure she's not a little sick with vertigo and resistant toward her own power. The license to live is not, in my experience, a promise of silent ease.

I get a fix on us as a pair: I'm not sure she finds all this *exciting* so much as—*idly alluring*. "It's not an even-steven kettle of fish," I say. She cannot be bothered with that. I was in a boyish state as of being shattered—that sense of oneself sexually as grief-stricken and ragged and poverty-stricken while being contrarily rich and perhaps winged and light-struck and inordinately, superhumanly willed and yet, in the end, resigned. I feel my state as real and as something I will not escape from. It is factual—as is the structure of the loose mammary flesh of her breast and her bony hips and the taut flesh of the thigh and of her thigh muscle as I clumsily, earnestly caress her there. Feelings are part of her . . . Men are dry.

I am barely breathing, I am pierced airlessly in my immersion in the medium of motionful saltiness—her victim.

But, for me, isn't it self-love that starts the progress toward orgasm?

Now I am noisily breathing in the realities of too much kinship with actuality itself. Actuality is everywhere. Is time-riddled. Is humiliation, death, courage, and good sense. But nothing is marked with a contractual description of what it will do to you. I don't like her specific rhythms but I don't mean to be ungrateful. I'm not wild about the textures of her skin. If I weren't an orphan, I'd back off now. One of the great resources of chastity is to compare and rate people sexually without knowing a lot about the matter—the real comparison tears you apart, really rends you, no shit. The difficulty of love is that love is, of course, earned, given, cruelly coerced—the animal thing—and is time-ridden as everything else so that the thing of being not-in-agony-for-a moment is agony anyway. I long for my own rhythms; I will nurse myself. No. I impose them by grabbing her hand and *moving* her hand on me . . .

This sudden as-if-*neat* rearrangement of momentums changes everything.

She goes along for a second or two and then halts. She leans back.

"You're a little doggy in the manger," she says.

"Sorry," I said from within an inner spasm of quite real agony.

She says, "You're-a-dirty-book . . ."

"SHUT UP!" I say. Then: "Sorry . . ."

Thank God, she thinks I didn't mean it.

I took her into my arms. "I'm not someone who knows the right thing to do. Are you?" She nestled against me—the matter of rights—and of personal merit—is unstable when you're in motion unless you're an *Alexander the Great* type, all-conquering.

"Don't," she whispered. *"Please don't . . ."* She has the upper hand. I had been lifting her skirt and pulling at her underpants—I hadn't only taken her in my arms: *"Please don't," I* whispered ironically as if, by saying it, I could erase her will—and find my way . . . I started to laugh, a minor jerky noise, kiddish enough or odd enough to scare her. She stared, thinking deeply: you know that state in a woman? In one you're physically courting right at that instant? Testing and measuring and you don't know what she's saying to herself in the chief chambers of her mind: a field of summoned problems, wishes, images, freakish and private . . . like lying in the leaves.

What is love to her? Death? I mean the real experience of it—an uncle dying of cancer, guys at an airfield, whatever . . . Motherhood? I know she knows about being young and competitive. I figure her ego isn't much different from mine. Her degree of violence maybe is different.

I started to laugh some more with less noise but in the uncontrolled manner of no speech but this shivering, half with sexual heat (a coldness) in a sexual situation, a sexual landscape. In a place, or in a story, afflicting and blessing me.

"You aren't going to fuck me," I said.

"It wouldn't be a real fuck *here.*" In the apartment: she said it reasonably. "We'd just be carrying on . . . You're weird . . . I like you." Then, "I like you so much . . ."

Then, abruptly, angrily—with huge regret—I *loved* her.

I wrestled with it. I tried to get it out of me . . . Speech sounds stupid—it is stupid. It is risky to talk about anything you care about. Buttock-deep wrestling, then a shrugging—then moving it all against her. And she is, uh, *touched,* and she moves back . . . Well, that's where we are . . .

I hold her butt and move her back and forth in my rhythm: she joins in, in a halfway manner . . . She doesn't exactly catch on. Even if it doesn't happen *the right way*—the way it does in books—the body sort of explodes—and so does the will—and one *feels* bigger and realer—maybe one is bigger and realer than one usually feels—and the flopping of one's hair on one's head and the motions of one's breath mark the rhythm of this further rage (of action of a kind): one really is not a child anymore . . . But one won't win the way one wants to, this time either. I won't.

She grinned—Leonie. Americans try out a lot of girls—easy come, easy go . . . A kind of leatheriness—a toughness—is in place. Her grin wasn't sightless: her eyes had a wildly sweet wolfishness. The posture of her neck and shoulders was wolfish, too. It all hurt a lot but it was fun.

Femininity and nerves: triumph and condescension: I suffered pleasurably in some living-through-something way. I wanted a girl and a situation that would be easier—simpler—than this . . . I took her by the ears and held her close in a kiss—as in the movies—demeaningly—and she yelped in a mean way, scary, a short, high-pitched noise . . . But there was satisfaction here, atonement on her part and on mine a kind of sense of command of a moistly limitless thing. Her response was not male. Weird amusement and silliness-cum-threat with a kind of sense of direction to it, having to do with me . . . She did a real fucking motion down below, not just rubbing, not a fobbing-off, and it scared the bejesus shit out of me . . . "The real thing"—the resonance of—"actual fucking is really something . . . Nature sets it up that way, hunh?"

"Are you scared? We don't dare," she said.

I said, "Shit . . ."

She said, grinningly, on my level, or I was on hers for a minute or two, "That's right."

We're having a good time in a way, aren't we? Isn't that right? A *still and yet* good time, really-a-good-time; it was touch and go and it changed but it was good, wasn't it? I guess so. I don't really know, obviously. Lila said to me more than once, *I love to swindle you, Wileykins . . .*

Leonie's hand moves on me. Leonie's face is *false-sisterly* inside the strains of her coarse sex-dampened hair. The sexual charge in the grinding thing, the bone and lip mix-up, the blood-mass and flesh-gooeyness and bumpy-collision stuff—my longing to be intelligent about the world is perverse . . . Sexual hallucination here—of her going down on me—is hardly a matter of clarity. A sense of strained something or other might be what a grown man who was intellectual would call sexual terror but I just felt strained. Time was real, had brought me through childhood and past it, as if out of Egypt, and to this. Leonie has devices and talents, tricks, patterns of sexual stuff—bodily emotional speech. She whispers something and I put a prefix on it: *This isn't anything much but* "I will never forget you, Wiley . . ."

"You're so nice off and on," I say. I am sadly happy—you know what I'm talking about? You know what I mean?

"I will never forget you," I said.

"Yes you will," she said; and she kissed me; we kissed some more; it was all mixed up: I surrounded her lips with mine and sucked both her lips with my short tongue in her; and then she ate my whole mouth with her biggish, choky tongue in my mouth, which jolted me and made me a little ill . . . I am shocked and charred, transformed: we lay still briefly, like worms after our mock worm-in-the-earth cohabitation in the dusty body of the immediate air.

Young and nuts, that kind of thing, we weren't *sloppily* serious—although we were off and on—but we didn't care what we did, although we did care, but we didn't mind it that we were cheating each other and bothering each other in deep ways. We weren't serious to the point we were really scared—*Oh, this is scary . . . you make me feel so much—I feel so much* . . . My lips, my throat, my heartbeat, my muscles felt mushy.

She said, "We're attracted to each other . . . I see *that* . . ." Then: "This is terrible . . ."

"Yeah. We should fuck . . ."

"You feel that way because you're young. It will just make things *worse*. It's not right for you . . . Not yet."

"I'm not exactly a virgin," I said sourly.

"Ssh," she said. Then: "You're remarkable, Honey . . ."

"Prove it," I said.

The transformation that has come is a heat perhaps as in a tightly wound chrysalis. The strange machinery of change, the actuality of transformation is a darkness of actual time with states of utter otherness in it that you resist: "It's the same as always," I say in the deep motionfulness of a new self that moves on chains or tethers or swings at these extraordinary addresses of imprisonment and of repetitive rapture. Or galling capture . . .

A rehearsal for eligibility . . . You know what I mean? You traverse the new medium, a sad, flirting, undocile *boy* in a form of personal existence he had not foreseen in any reality for himself. The cagey boy says, "I don't know where I am with you . . ." Throwing myself backward against the arm of the couch: "Am I here? Am I anywhere? God . . . I don't know where I am . . ." The jerky movements of awareness have attached to them an odd sense of foreign color which then becomes pictorial, breeding the shape of the ceiling. The somewhat heavy delight (and disorientation) in the protest is facetted, and aerial to boot, with *privileged* youth, whether the youth is mad or not. And one *knows,* not in words, that this is romance and mimicry . . . a throb of rivalry. The sudden truth is that the glistening and blurred and reddened (from necking and petting) selves (of the self) toughen and grow both bony and filmy —overtly sexual, vague and horny—courtly and showy. She has not *cut me down to size* . . . Ah, the *uncertain* absence of despair, the hope the world is a *nice* place, at least in your case . . . None of this is like pain in childhood. The motion of thought is slowed—and feels seriously beautiful-and-hideous in a sexual trance and spell that radiated from her. Tall, thin, slightly pinkened, *sweaty,* partly undressed *American* girl—no, Jesus, it's me, the boy, bare feet, bare ankles, bare chest inside an open shirt—do you remember how *liquid* it was who was who and which was which?

I looked at her—I hoped fuckworthily . . . "Isn't this wonderful?" I said.

"Unh," she said, not looking at me.

I remembered feeling thin and meager. "All right," I said aloud. Strangely tropical, rotting heat and nakedness of not being selfish more than this. I felt dead and strange, rotted really, but okay. The sense of loss was so bad I thought I wanted to die—I'm not joking—but I decided it was essentially okay. She did a thing then of touching me with just one finger and then with a sudden partly laughing clutch of her legs on one of my legs along with ritual breaths that she produced she tried to suggest an orthodoxy—or conventionality—of *liking* . . . "You're cuckoo," I said. I had the feeling that I'd made it possible for her to be *nice.* Leonie laughed apologetically in the social-class-absolution way of her class—this was back in those years back there, back home, that confession of being a girl and guilty and not rich and daring. She wasn't being *a goody-goody* but she was staying okay, not Lutheranly, but ex-Lutheranly and middle-classishly-during-the-war.

She wasn't a sweet little nothing (Lila) except in part: disguised . . . a habit. She is really sincere for a moment.

I am a kind of weightlessness, aerial—I guess I have some weight but not as a *last-minute-thing* for her to grab at. Leonie is capable of ruining the world for a dumb idea. She is a real person, all shit aside. Here it is the pleasure of her being a boss and more open about my transformation—men always are transformed, leering monsters or into *sweetness,* or dead-and-limp or manic-and-showy. She has a kind of commonsense seriousness, and then, underlying that, is a kind of crazed-romp thing in her.

Then there is a kind of little stench of all sorts of madness and pain and she is capable of making a lot of different kinds of threats. The truth is that she is supple-spined and knows a lot and is aware she's dumb and we are bumbling and improvising and discovering stuff—we are not completely ignorant. I bet she's seeing (among other things) how much she can control things. "You are a real treat—a boy and a half . . ." She says that, giving absolution . . . She and Nonie talk to each other every day—she sounds like a *fake* member of a social class the two of them invented.

I say to myself that this isn't real love—this is practice. I feel truly rotten. But I was glad, too. She seems weakened behind the softly fluctuating walls of her skin. Hidden electricities flutter—time doesn't need wings, but it often takes the form of winged creatures in me. I am in love with her, of course. With me, too. With time and adolescence. With our living room. "You are as slick as water," she says in a local accent, a local ruralese.

"There's a lot to you," I say, thinking she wants to be reassured *intellectually*. Then: "Yeah . . . hhhhhhhhhhhhhhhhh . . . ooh-buhhhhhhh . . . ubbbbbba . . ." Wartime noisemaking . . . A breath . . .

She is talking and kissing-in-a-picky-pecking way—a lot of girls back home did that back then—"Oh you, you're *sweet*—now *behave* . . ."

She is, maybe, an iron soul. And the rubble of war and American-front-porch-wild-and-untamed-and-independent woman—and religious discipline and psychological stuff of sexual pride in her body and in her eyes and in her wit, such as it was. She smells of war, lady-of-war, war perceived. She has gradations of shadow of that. She can half understand death . . . war deaths . . . And male *malice* . . . rebellion . . . She is slapping herself in the face, sort of, constantly, reducing her hysteria . . . I mean it . . . She really does want to shine with goodness—not all the time: all-the-time would be villainous. She's sophisticated that much.

What degree of harm can she inflict?

"What a brother you would be . . . I'd like to have . . . a brother like you . . . You for a brother? No . . . I take that back . . . Not *you* for a brother . . . Ha-ha." She didn't nuzzle me.

"You're *cute*," I say with a twisted upper lip—and a raised eyebrow.

Her breath—as she watches me—her breasts—faint gusts of stale but moist air . . . The *Temple of the Cleft Between the Legs . . . (and the dark future and its citizens therein)* . . . She says—abruptly—"Are you pussy-whipped? I'm sorry. I didn't mean for that to happen . . ."

"No . . . Yes . . . I don't know . . ."

She pulls her blouse more closely over her breasts and partly openly judges me . . . Partly *sentimentally* . . . "Are you more bad than good?"

"I am said to be a demon . . . *The Wild Man from Borneo* and *the Devil* . . ." I say this *elegantly* (in a local way). What I am here is emergent as a youngish man, half-formed, frailly, fragilely *instructed* . . . new . . .

Leonie will tell Nonie "all" about what happens here but it won't seem like this narration.

And what Nonie learns will be part of her armory, her treasury, of knowledge.

Leonie was a "responsible" person—only in real life, not in a book. The chief responsibility for meaning here in a bookish way is mine. She says *coarsely*, not exactly fending me off, just rewarding me and fending me off *a little bit*, "You're . . . mmm . . . *hot*—you're too hot to handle—you must be Rory Calhoun's younger brother . . ." An untamed movie star—not a great star or anything like that . . .

It's a form of wit to run things and it's witty to ruin things *slightly* —it's grown-up.

"You don't know anything," the tentatively transformed, newly older boy says recklessly. (She quoted that to me twenty years later on the phone.)

"Don't be a prick," she says.

He smiles—and the prick is there—he smiles with a certain *dirty* glamour—not *boastfully*, just actively—with a certain male primacy of drama—a silent orator in an oddly congressional moment—at the edge of congress. Of course, it is a sexual moment for him and he is handicapped by the realities of desire, desires and their weird breaking quality of onrushing hallucinatory, mostly extreme, romantic extremism.

"I can't have you . . . Oh, I'm so sad," she said tactfully.

I say out loud, struttingly bitter, "So I lose it all . . . It is *really* scary, how completely I get nothing but compliments . . ."

She said, "Wiley, *no one* talks like this . . ."

She is staring at me.

"I love this stuff," I say. Then: "Never mind . . . It makes me no-never-mind . . ." The fullness of feeling and the depth of liking are as pungent and as poignantly affecting as the stink of *rotten loneliness*, the pain—well, nature is extravagant . . . I rock back and forth, my arms wrapped around my own waist.

The omnipresence of danger in life, the sense of something dreadful in sexuality, too—actually—like a vast haunted estate of sudden inheritance—the duties, the self-sacrifices that go with the new title—increasing staleness and rigidity of torment—deathbound fear, the conviction of being minor, the advisability of dying now—among the sins—I turned my face to her . . . I am newborn from this chrysalis—big deal. I am half a man through her doing. This stuns her and she is *flabbergasted* . . . Then she says aloud, misusing a certain wartime journalistic term, "No more gobbledygook?" I don't know what she means.

"I'm in *agony* . . ."

"Oh," she murmured. What I am, what we are commands her feelings—but not entirely. The slipperiness of the slope is the extent to which we are in *agreement*—more at her say-so than at mine . . . It is not war.

"Lover's nuts . . ."

She is pitying—and a little angry, too. Lila says it costs a lot to know me . . . Whitely, heatedly flustered, balked, unclean . . . useless . . . unsimple: it won't simplify—what I am.

I start it; she jumps in—I'm tense and *nutty*; she is out to persuade; her laugh is swindly. We amuse each other? We laugh, nervously bold, not quite in synchrony—I think with clear audacity until we have a simplicity I said I don't have in myself; I wriggle my bedraggled, abandoned, *useless*, clownish-courtly dragonfly abdomen which has failed to implant anything in her. I am cautious, a newborn male—sexually—sort of as if in the trenches, in a foxhole, in the stench of *normalcy* . . . that is what is here, maybe. Newborn, sincere . . . This may have a kind of airy beauty compared to the darker stuff she has of her fiancé, who has seen real combat and who is a real man to start with, willy-nilly.

She stops laughing, leans back, and says, "It's almost as if you're slapping me." She says it almost crossly, sighingly—from behind her arm.

I lean back similarly. Similarly but in a grossly male way—a *sincere* imitation of *guys*—and I say, "Yeah? So what: none of it matters—*probably* . . ." Then: "My heart is broken—" She and I look at each other and start to laugh again—not all that explicably. "Life is really hell," I say.

"Life is such hell," she says, correcting me—clichéward, I feel.

I scowl—scathingly, really. "I see my whole life: it is a dumb life—it is not typical—it is all no good—it is not even all that friendly . . ."

With my fingers I smooth her pretty ass's, horse's skull below the hairline, the broad forehead, the hair at the edge . . . She smiles sleepily. She has an exclamatory smile—her smile switches to that. I feel goaded.

When Nonie introduced us, Leonie, not like an older woman, but laughing and teasing, said, "Oh, he is good-looking . . ." She says it now, pityingly, "Oh, he is good-looking . . ." I think she means it would be better if I were a different *type*, she would go further. What I am is, in a practical sense here-and-now, unfortunate—ill-starred—not the most appropriate thing. I get the quick sense, confusingly, that if I made faces and grunted and was appalling, stuff would be easier, better.

I ask her, "Why can't I get what I want?"

She says to this very young guy which I also am and who she has permitted all sorts of liberties—she says to the privileged libertine kid and not to the denied boy—she says condescendingly pitying (in another tone or class of pitying me), "Wiley, that's a *selfish* question . . ."

"I can't handle this glass-half-full and not the glass-half-empty stuff, and then you're nice to the other, then you talk to the glass-half-empty guy and I'm lost . . ."

"Don't talk like that! Those are awful things you're saying."

I lower my head. Not looking at her, I feel suddenly and deeply that she and I are not exactly talking to each other—it hurts.

She says then to my lowered head, "You can knock me over with a feather . . . You're not what I expected . . . Nonie is not what you'd call a good describer . . ."

I look up, smiling, in a sickly way, and yet in a weird sense I'm pleased: "I'm a disappointment?" I say.

"Yes and no," she says with a smile of a friendly sort—it's steeply friendly.

All at once a different mood is back. I am at her side: I cover my face with her hair; her hair and mine mix and tangle. "Should I be homosexual . . . ?" I ask. I've heard that sometimes works with sensitive older girls.

Leonie is maybe ALL sexual comparison where *men* are concerned —and then behind that she is ignorant, she is maybe ignorance itself, as I am, but I feel, in my heated blood, I feel it coldly in my heated blood, that the ignorances don't match—at all.

That is really scary, really steep: that is arroyo-and-gun-at-my-head stuff—that kind of fear. But then on top of *that* she is brilliance and total recall of an older person's experiences of tough moments like this one, and of body tissues and of flesh and of other lives. The bright light of insight in her may be a constant light and not unsettled and jumpy and off-and-on, as it is in me.

And now the total of what I am—by her measurement—is reflected in her body and face and lidded eyes—is the shadow there, in the light and paler shadow of what she is. I am too naïve and too palely odd and too clever—too young in that fashion—and I am different socially—so she cares too much to care at all: I mean to the extent that she has curiosity in her, social and sexual about guys, she cares: her curiosity cares about me; her eyes care about me; her mouth half cares—it is balked and wicked. Her hands emerged as if from under blankets—that's her inner distance. I am a monster—a petty monster—and must fare ill among larger monsters—I am not *a champion*—but I am dear to her. But the *overall* thing is that that is *too much* for her to care about—and it is the wrong thing for her to care about—and she is sorry and she does care but she doesn't care—and then something malicious steps in, at that point in her feelings, and she would just as soon have me dead and not her and not her real boyfriend and so on . . . What a description for a feeling—painstaking and stupid.

Anyway, how in hell can I be supposed to *understand* this stuff in her—but I can see in her face, she does expect it because of all the reasons why she is too sharp to care about me—unless I swindle her and am morally pathetic—morally *piteous*—like other men—in the way she is used to.

So, I am staring at her and she is *gazing* back, but I don't *do* anything; and, so, she says: "You're so smart and you're so dumb."

"FUCK OFF!" I cry in this complicated whisper—of sorts. And I turn away from her; and then I turn right back: she is not specifically interested in *me* but she is interested in what I do and in stuff I know—in what I *represent?*—and I turn back into that: it's like a neural surf. "Flood alarm," I say. Then: "It's three days and three nights away by choo-choo train—the ocean . . . Little turtles—of *feeling* . . ." Then: "This stuff I'm saying," I say as I walk my fingers over her right breast and part of her collarbone, "is all from audio-visual aids—at school."

"I know," she says sagely. She says, "Never force me, never force a woman: women hate you for that."

"I know. I have a sister," I say with a kind of courtly condescension. Then, sadly (because who knows what this means?): "If I don't force you, nothing will happen." I don't mean rape: but, rather, pushing at certain barriers and tetherings—judgments, stuff like that. I say, "I don't mean rape . . ."

"That's still rape," she says. Then: "And so on . . ." She partly loves me. Loves, though—not *wants* . . . She can *forgive* certain things, and be patient or *tolerant*, but she can't *want* those things . . .

I can feel her body withdraw, harden a bit. It would be better to say the neural aura is of a kind of ebbing away of approval and of permission and, so, a rockiness emerges. A living death.

It is a mindly moment—I mean I die into consciousness and am a mechanical, or bodiless, robot of it—periscope-binoculars, an array of metal eyes—metal to avoid the impact of the fear of what nature has fashioned as the kind of open-ended destiny of darkness we are faced with . . . Or I am.

And it is in my face, on my face, this stuff . . . Hers shows she sees this. She cleans the space between us of the filaments of hair. She uses one finger—in a sage way. She shifts her head. She blows at the remaining hair. Miserable as I am in my robot state and with her being like a rocky shore, I am glad to be here. I love it, all of it—even though I hurt like hell; I am hurt and I feel a lifetime of starvation ahead of me. But I am glad to be here. In a way. Her head—and all that is in it—rises; it stirs on her long, strong neck: that bony *Colosseum contemplates* me . . .

With a start, I realize that this moment is *set* on the moment before: it has evolved from it—like one room from another through an open archway. The burning "*immediate*" memory of the recent past is sort of as if from the lawn and woods—the more physical moments—but (or *so*) the woods and lawns have lighthouses and flaming buoys and lightning in them—discontinuously: sexual memory is even more discontinuous, even more disjunct and incoherent than physical memories of being tackled or of wrestling or of fighting. The phosphorescent bursting into life at hot distances is unsteady and rhythmic but not sexually rhythmic—more askingly or remindingly. Anyway, it is the demarcation of desire . . . of desires . . . as, some of them, being too real . . . outdoorsy . . . too male . . . too given over to danger—and to self-assertion.

The use of unlikelihood, of implausibility—here, in the hallucinatory reaches of a sexual reality where one is the newborn one and frivolously sexual, not serious; and one's not-newborn soul hurts—here one sees it is a dream that one will ever fully understand other people—or one other person . . . She may get there, a woman, through some intensity of focus and of mind—and safety of a kind—and through pregnancy, the other life actually living in her. She may escape loneliness. I am sincere and I am passionate and I will never escape it—it will always be like this; I will return again and again to this crossroads.

And I am not well defended toward life. I shatter in a way—and turn to metal. I have sincerity at a readiness—a readiness of sexual stuff—of a *nudity*—a readied spirit that way and an almost obedient (but really truly reluctant) body. And I have a great deal of stupidity; and an absence of thought—I am a monster accompanied by the silence and confronted by the rage and curiosity that accompanies the newness of anything when it appears to the sensoria and arouses the reactions of another (but related) species.

Still, I am not entirely sincere—you know? I am, was, a boy.

"Wiley, you want me to jack you off?" She knows a lot.

"No. You know I don't—that would be boring." I was hoping for more.

"Please don't be childish—please be considerate of me . . ."

"That's what my mother says . . . Are you dying of cancer?"

"You are so petty—and just think, a person like you, even you, you have to be petty . . ."

"Now you sound like my biology teacher . . ."

She paused, she swallowed. "I don't want to fuck up the good stuff . . . I had a good time with you—I really do like you—let's round things off and be nice to one an*other* . . ."

"A good time? I'm glad. But a lot of good it does me."

"Don't try to do everything by TALK!" she said in a muted, compressed-lip, almost exclamatory way. And she kissed me.

What was the identity of that kiss? It started out like a pair of typewriter do-jiggies locked together—her lips were sort of locked together or were toughly muscular or some such thing—and then they strike the white paper—that's me—me? lips and breath: I become a platen, dark, and white and flat with reception.

Then, see, this is where being *athletic* comes in—and young: I can feel freshly soon after her lips part and her tongue touches me that I can feel the texture of her tongue and sort of rollick in the dirtiness or I can go, flashingly, down *the other path* into startled feeling: the heat there is in light and the atoms of the flesh—the summer-foliage thing of some woods (in the Midwest)—or the light at the window of a summer house at a lake where I went to stand, half-undressed, feeling myself at the edge of puberty—at the window where the light and heat have a kind of precocity of meaning . . . a kind of precocity of something or other —reciprocal affection, *quasi*-suicidal things . . . of *We will die* . . . and: *It is real* . . . I.e., we're not kids.

And then, beyond that, her limits—at the moment—the edge of the woods, the lawns, the house—so to speak—and the meanness in it and the self-preservation as the absence of strong love—it's all just glimpsed—painfully—and it's burning: no, it's felt *burningly* . . . "I'm okay. I'll do what you want: you don't have to do anything: I'm okay—you want me to go into the john and cheer up?"

It seemed like fate was undone, was sidestepped. It seemed nice. I resented it all, but I was relieved, too.

She smiled. "I don't mind helping—I've gotten a lot out of today," she said.

But something had happened: I think it was that I had begun to reflect her feelings; I was less good at knowing about this than she was about her reflecting feelings in other people: she was almost pondlike—or puddlelike—in that way—but I felt it was too dangerous to owe her real pleasure: I might not ever get over it; I felt it was dangerous to do anything with her—to feel too much or too little—to be sincere or to be insincere—and what we now felt was haphazardly a kind of unison but more really, a shared vote—two ponds voting, or a pond and a glassy pool—except that the atmosphere of us was so uproarious and dense—with desires and holding-back, and with tactics and liking and dislike and curses and anathemas toward each other kept at bay, and threats, overt and oblique and haplessly there—and yet it was, no matter its compoundness, still this side of *major*: it was maybe so *minor* that good wishes still, at this moment, mattered more than temper, realism, doubt, desire, or sin (or whatever you want to call it)—good wishes mattered more than the uproar . . . a *pleasant* outcome more than really fucking . . . even to me.

I was maybe lying about that: I will never know. I was trying to be *subtle*, but part of the joke was that the wishes of good temper and a happy ending were also bribes, lies, demonic courtship shit . . .

Maybe it was all okay—maybe it was all really flattering . . . Maybe it was no good but maybe it was all I would ever get and so I'd better *adjust* to it, *rapido*.

The balance of things is tricky—you don't ever know for sure quite what is going on in you or in someone else. In the wallowing tumult of feeling, among the elements of self-defense—of realism—in this realm of interchange—light seemed to be here in *not* proceeding and *darkness* in going on; but there were no captions—no footnotes—only feelings and the tacit or ocularly overt agreement between us . . . audible, visible in our breathing, in the *semi*-permissions and holding-back (as described above) of our bodies. I had no sense of its being immortal light, immortal goodness—or a blessing to *not* go on—or that it was a manifestation of some giant principle that showed that *God's* will or nature's *intentions* were here. I wasn't that malely spiritual about fucking—and begetting children: I was a sort of beggar-orphan in a musical dream—but among real odors, too. I had a sense of wanting her to love me on her own, if only for this, and to feel sorry for me or whatever, and to give herself to me but with everything being *clear* if we did fuck that I wasn't *guilty*. And this other thing where you break each other's hearts and shatter each other's lives and control memory and its motions later . . . And the evanescent limitlessness, of giving in, and of revenges, and of forgiveness and of no forgiveness at all, that scared me and was not what I wanted, but it seemed the realer landscape behind the scrim or thin copse of woods or behind the walls of the room where we were and where we were *catching our breath* (a local phrase).

"Don't help," I said.

She laughed because the implication was that she was dangerous to me because she was so attractive to me.

She said with real satisfaction, "Oh, you're so hot . . ."

Because she was so attractive to me and because I seemed to her to be what I wasn't, a hot young kid.

I walked self-consciously into the bathroom, feeling her watch my back, feeling her as aware of me. She whispered, "You don't have to do this," but she didn't sound to me as if she meant it; she sounded as if she preferred it. I felt *tragic* and ashamed of that. *What the hell* . . . And: *Jesus Christ, show a little perspective, will ya?* CHRIST ON A CRUTCH . . .

But shortly after beginning, I did not think of her much or have daydreams—or hallucinations—or of anything unreal or real or recognizable except the *pain* of it, the *rawness* of sensation, the initial resistance and then almost sensationless *ease*—and then the quivering and sudden materialization of as-if-tall, gawky SENSATION, AND I MEAN IT WAS QUIVERING, IT WAS QUIVERING WIND, wind on a sandy plain . . . I had all I could manage then in not yelping so loudly and sharply it would have been *funny* and then *a scandal*.

O life . . . I more or less enunciatorily thought, regarding the toilet bowl and the cloudy stuff in it, in the water, and on the seat and the back and on the porcelain of the bowl above the water. I wasn't consciously addressing it—the spermatic life: I was thinking of the overall situation, the white tile, the phallic nature of consciousness—some consciousness—sins, stupidities, me: it really was like I was beginning on a soliloquy.

I tend to forget how much of masturbation is tied to hallucination —my friend Remsen collects stuff to use, hot stuff, goading stuff. I have a friend. Leonie is in the other room.

I'm not asleep. I move without moving. *Je suis* in motion—it's a genital thing—I'm *hallucinating* and remembering (girls, guys, books, whatever); I'm *hallucinating* among the physical facts—*Leonie is in the other room*—but I'M HERE . . . It's me in the world: moving along: *fate* has given me this: this isn't a good one—*hallelujah* and a dulled *Wowee*—

But here is a moment flashingly taut—*as* all *hell* (the sensation[s]). Wow—all charged-up . . . half-unbridled, boy-bridal, partly loathsome, partly lost, racking.

It's of a puzzling *enormous* interest (to me), my inner stuff, the fluctuations of attention—and of judgment—at getting that sensation—that sensation, heated and mercurial and yet also, in part, cool, cold, deadened—the touch of my own hand on me, the hintful *indication* of the non-hallucinatory act . . .

I am unsheltered, deathless in a glumly exhilarating triumph of shadows—a feely-movie of *hallucination*—with a girl (woman) in the next room—this is painful morally.

Among *the facts of existence* is that no one is here but me. It is amazingly foolish, the peculiar wonder of this circumstance, the bathroom drama of it—a *local insanity*—a sanity if I don't cry out.

Boy, the insanity of pleasure in this form—moored, unmoored. Sexual pleasure, sexual reality, the momentarily overripe thing of sensual reality—a silliness kind of—it tugs and pushes: me: strongly: sensations, rhythm, workmanlike-sensational rhythm, images passionately almost present, the blurred now in the white-tiled bathroom, the time-out thing, actual but not in the usual sense of idleness or of sleep or of napping: it is like and not like dreaming—I guess one's consciousness blinks from this to the world and then back again: concentrate, concentration: a camp thing—like making a lanyard.

Part of the world is a commerce deal in sensations. There is a commerce in this stuff among us . . . maybe all the time.

This seems a hurtful, really agonized, dimly pleasurable, wowee-pleasurable sort of suicide: *Leonie is in the other room* . . .

I feel my consciousness deepen with a dull *contrapuntal* glow of self-use and of wordliness: it is a deeper, wider, more *carpentered* sense of something I knew in childhood: an attentiveness—as if to the air—while one is aware of the drifting heat of one's own childish skin and of your nurse's skin nearby . . .

I feel tissue-y and real—and like warm cloth—limply heated, fabric-y—I am cooking myself—sexually—ho, hi, can I ball? I am fried and twisting—*like bacon in a pan*—oh, oh, hot, agonized sensation: weeeee—*whoop*EEEEEEEEE . . .

Perhaps this is the heat of hellfire and damnation . . . Then, all at once, it is human—unmetaphorically so: the heat is like the neck heat of someone you kiss on the neck. It is all over me: it has spilled and it sticks to me: it is me; neck heat; necking did it; the boy is watched by the night shadows in the window screens . . . *Ooooh God and Christ,* now it's this mattress-stuffing heat—ticklingly suffocating me—I can't breathe as the dampish darkness of ebbed sensation crests—with light and heat, a little like lightning—I am hellishly sweaty and blotched with the fake presence of the hallucinations—the piety of my own body, erect, erected, yet kneeling to sensory reality, in this white-tiled and absurd bathroom solitude.

In the recent past, jacking off with another boy—the hand goes like an automobile jack: *quelle levitation,* Remsen said—I am startled when the other boy shouts, IT'S HOT! or I'M GETTING HOT! If he shouts that . . . Jass says it in a twisty way . . . Oooh, shit, I am twisted, too: bacon-twist . . . Bacon's reality is that of well-judged experiment and of reasonable expectation of successful repetition . . . I see, *confusedly, how to rub two sticks together* (prick and woodenishly curved hand) to get to *my* own *heat* . . . I sense the rhythms *jazzily* as I go along—not clearly.

The incomplete unleashedness of the moment makes me a ventriloquist of unleashedness: *I'm hot, I'm hot* . . . I sing jazzily under my breath: scat syllables. Then it all turns dull—my skills at marshalling sexual stuff are limited, and so is my concentration. Then the dullness is blown apart: a certain rhythmical touch, slidingly done, is blowsily explosive—oh wow, nice, I'm glad—i.e., experienced, even semi-expert, *yet withal, my Lord, in the matters of the hallucinatory theater here, I am* amateurish . . .

An old sensation illustrates this—the old sensation comes and is present and is gone: it's me as a little kid, my bathing suit coming off me: I'm on a table in a changing room, in a pool house maybe: the bareness and helplessness, kind of, and the hurtful readiness of the self—bare feet, nude chest, ribs, arms, nerves—for the bareness and helplessness—the truly *peculiar* recognition of the bareness and helplessness from before and the smells now: damp concrete: Daddy—is it Daddy? Sure: the chest, the abdomen, the thing there, the legs—the smell, blondish, salty—we must be at the ocean, no, the Gulf of Mexico—that complicated odor, *odors,* of his: he smells of eyes, eyes and new baldness and worry: a kind of glamour of major tissues and size . . . Oh *who will love me?* Will I ever know love? Be buried in it . . . Be cruel in the *lordship* or ownership of it? The past is, in part, *ignorantly* rectified: I am my own father here, I am my son, my lover: the entire act is one of editing—editorial rectification—in a moment of semi-potency after a childhood, much of it extensive with enigmatic longing and amazement with people—as if with numberless corridors.

That is tied to a flashing-flaring history in brief segments of how good at sports I have been at the different sizes I've been so far . . . Capacities of the body. And of the will . . . *Do you yearn to shine, Wiley? Do you want to be a star in THE HEAVENS*? (Daddy said it.)

Then those two sections are cupped in *a moment* that is a trance of exaggerations—all the matters of scale, of relative scale, become instead matters of giantisms and of elfishness: giant breasts on a giant woman, giant prick, giant hands, tiny hands, tiny self among leaves . . .

Then the world returns and bits of judgment—tribunal shit—toward the masturbation here, toward masturbation in general, toward Leonie, toward me now and as a child, at various ages, toward my dad, toward the toilet bowl and the Bible . . .

This segment of failure and dullness gives way to bolts and batterings of *pleasure* such that I push my pants down and shrug my shirt off: I am so sweaty suddenly, so closed in, so much a prisoner. Pleasure is not knowable by memory: it can only be glanced at; or it can sting you—then it vanishes: this is so even in immediate memory, of just a second ago. The jagged zigzaggings and moonings of memory are really palpable loss and ego . . . Grim. But this stuff . . . the good stuff . . . it is only knowable here. Reality has a monopoly of it. Nature. It owns, it has a patent on, you have to come here to this puzzle-ridden and sometimes large-scale light-struck *area* of maybe *general illumination* . . .

Leonie won't share this with me . . . This is the third time in twenty-four hours that I've done this . . . This passage of it is palely redlit, the redlit adolescent trek among rhythms, among fantastic imaginings—among hand movements—and their speed and *emotion*—like a carpenter with an adze or a tree guy with an ax, chop and chop, hands on the handle—for a minute, I do this stuff just physically—without any thought and without images: you can (at this age) do this.

Hey, Wiley, do you pay other people for your thinking about them when you jerk off? That's Jass Nolloquot. The first voice in the darkness. I hadn't thought about it until he mentioned it. He said, *Do you think we ought to pay people if we use them for jerking off?* Royalties? *Sure.* One mounts, grandly and humbly from that, in something like *familiarity* with the phenomenon, and this despite the always great novelty of the intensity; one stirs like a ruthless hobo on heavy, just barely workable, illicit wings. At that time. *A boyish, ragged, shabby Piece of Thievish Fire*—I don't know how to punctuate the terms of the action—through whitelit, *quivering* distances, and unsteadily through what seem like immense elevations, to a *quivering* ache of altitude, tormenting, into an alluring and aerial and wicked, and banned, and uncalibrated and imaginarily dimensioned dementia of *meaning*, one comes to a stage of *feeling* in which duration and pungency are shown to be dimensions of the universe—as true as width and length, which one feels in one's hands —in them and in what one of them holds—and in one's feet, bare, and the floor. And one sees then the animal bribe: the seeming reality of a favorable apocalypse . . . You can fight it off still; it's not quite irrevocable . . . But it's here, in this elevation, that you are falsely persuaded that the conclusion is everything and its brother.

To ripen toward the false apocalypse is real easy—the hand and bent knees and a dirty picture in your mind—a leering girl spread-legged in the leaves, sly-eyed, moist and witless or worldly and filthy with sexual wit—these are bits of sun in this caverned planet: it's here—and only here—that the Platonic shit is true. And here it's really true. Here, boy, you lived before. And here are the caverns measureless to man . . . (Poetry, ageless, matchless, et cetera.) And here are chained prisoners—I love holding slaves in my dreams . . .

When you see this, you giggle. I do. Mostly not out loud. My mouth gets twisty and full of feeling; and mostly my body giggles, thin bones, attenuated height, weird-weirdly craning neck all of a sudden . . .

Ooh shit, here comes a big one: *Do-I-want-to-come-and-then-go-back-(quickly, all things considered)-to-Leonie?* The boy *sees* and is inwardly silent as if in the face of a tidal wave, a cyclone, a huge grown-up appearing suddenly—or a god in the old sense, or faith in the new —he is violently affected and silent and dense and steady and not twisty and moving: he sees big red, convulsed zeroes and pallid ones that moo or mow at him—it is so interesting that some of the stitches of the self-in-relation-to-the-sensation—staring, feeling, containing, inflicting—break into near-orgasm, which is to say, into a kind of Homeric and later death, sword strokes, arrow piercings, hand grenades, bullets, explosions. *Do I want to come?* NO—N-O—NO, UNH-UNH, GO AWAY, I'LL COME SOME OTHER DAY . . .

The sensation does retreat, but incompletely: it leaves behind corpses that jump up or minefields that go off: its echoing is present and has receded; it passes and burbles and bumbles on—the sinewless hand—the staring boy . . . *Hey, this is me* . . . Is life interesting? In a horrible way? Yeah. Sure. Well, why not? A surf and then a web or net of quick thought—almost as of a shark or of a turtle or of a school of gleaming mackerel attempting to break free of the waves and to climb—amphibiously—into the air: that stuff, in this second wave of wavelets of the stuff, breaks him at certain odd other seams, memory here being a killing half-illusion of your knowing the stuff now so that it is happening now as well as then, less really now, but more known or something . . .

Then that announces itself as not present: this is all within a few half-seconds; it strains you; you can feel this stuff is bad for you if you want a long life.

I proceed cautiously and sighingly—it hasn't been more than three minutes or so in the john, the loo, the head—I proceed cautiously in a greeting-to-death way, so to speak, wide awake in a way, but then the silence and slippage of feeling—becomes in the motion—a bunch of wordless, unsyllabled, but elevated and babbling voices, a neural chorale: one is half-tranced, witless, witty, contrapuntal—with breathing: with echoes among the tile: with memory and the present tense; with the present tense and the future locked into place if you pump yourself right—with pleasure and no pleasure and with highly nuanced comparisons of pleasure resulting in unworded judgments which are moods, actions, tempos really—and with the throbbing and twitching sweetness, motionful but seeming to be static, the honied *pricklings* and bursts of eerie self-lightedness—as if one were buried in the dirt—the sporty, odd, and loony light, and then the lapses, now so incomplete, into troughs of failure—one is almost beyond failure—this crazed stuff has a set kind of glamour to it: an irresistibility: it starts—a kind of abandonable wisdom —a *ripeness is all* thing—you can see where advertisements and art and certain pieties come from. *Why-am-I-doing-this-jerkhole-asinine-thing? It's not really dirty: it's educational . . . Oh God . . . Oh God . . . I'm coming . . .* The rhythmic accretions and the pungency of the fanatic-of-desire hallucinations go into the jerking dance of coming and the boy backs off—mentally and physically: he raises his hands until they are waist-high: he stares with exaggerated innocence into the whitish air—he looks withered and bursting with blossoming both. He likes this world of sensation whether he trusts it or believes in it or not. Also, the boy is something of *a prude* and is embarrassed often, even in solitude, by sensation . . . by *pleasure* in the lurching and shoving half-breathless gauntlet-labyrinth of the *sensationalism* and puzzle-ridden semi-somnambulism of nearly coming.

The attention and inattention of backing off—look: no hands: I'm a cripple—and the not-stayingness of the pleasure hurt in combination and separately oracularly and intimately—they testify to some feebleness or other.

But it's as if your skin is ripped off. Mine, I mean. Now would I do this with Leonie? Would I trust her? I'm ripped, flayed, stripped—I mean this is the real nakedness that the boy knows—I am down to the burning *inner skin*, heats and oils, exudations and flares, *consolation*, BRILLIANT renderings of this peculiar crossroads in one's life in nature. I know something here; I half know it; I know that I know stuff here that I don't with her; and I *know* that this is shallower for me . . . It has rooms to it, though, where I stand and watch . . .

But *pleasure* as a coalescing conviction that pleasure exists, that it has been invented or found, or carried off from the garden or was given after the expulsion, this thing that is the world and that other people showed me, sort of—Christ, God, the beauty of what some people know: I know that nothing can undo your life—so, it is safer here, less of a roll down into the ravine, into the darkness of the not-yet-unbudded future; there is less feeling and more sensation: it is okay to be alone. Except it is minor. One half wakes. This chimpanzee reality and light. Lord. I am in love with Tarzan doings—animal carryings-on . . . Is it all right with YOU, OLD YAH? The cheapness of sexual images? This gambling and sport and rehearsal? It is irreligious but true here that lazy easiness and lies rule everything (here). Simple thoughts (here) are okay. They are good enough *here* to grip and alter the crude obstinacy of daily pleasurelessness.

But if I resume—*If I presume to resume* is what I used to sing to myself when I was in college—I am, all at once, on a higher plane of feeling, with great space all around and below me, and above me: I am in the middle of emptiness and I am the eye, the human eye, the sole source of pious deference in the universe. I accede to this nomination —this election . . . I accede to being chosen here. On this different level of reality . . . I agree to be sincere and driven. (This is practice for breeding children—to be *sincere and driven*.) This is on the edge of a gulf of waste.

Here I am: homemade flesh. But I have risen to this plane of identity—whatever it is worth.

I make a small noise in a dream of (genital) *happiness* and I move against the mock-mocking *cuntflesh* of my unfortunately bony hands (one hand holds the balls crushingly a little, a little the way a girl has) —the *head* of the cock sticks out of its knuckly nest in what seems full memory of pleasures and difficulties in the past—and in anxiously flinching recklessness, it and the boy, in a kind of pathos, blindly—the boy does fuck motions with his hips—he persists in these partly, mostly involuntarily—the warm-hot clasp of the false cunt—*of a sort*—this homemade fucking, oh God oh God God—the intoxication—the foolishness—the shamefulness—the distance from the actual air—in an unwilled, unwieldy semi-sobriety of an early acquaintance with masculinity, I laugh out loud, under my breath . . . I feel *normal* and part of the world's history as it is commonly known among boys . . . What a mess: hoo-ha—okay? I keep my mind on this matter. I pay it such scandalous attention that *if the house caught on fire, I don't think you'd even notice*. Holding myself and fucking my hand, I say, *"I love you, Leoneeeee, I love you, good old right hand . . ."* I laugh—ha-ha—*hotly* under my breath in this scandal of imbecile close attention and scandalous absence from here—from real life—and from the presence in that scandalously unperpetual otherwhere of the whitelit shock. I mutter, *Oh you* DARLING—to pleasure? To the white light? To nature? To my cleverness and heroism in coming here? This is while I am hallucinating *rhythmically* mostly about having sexual power with people . . . over people. To reward myself a little, I spit on the palm and fingers of my hand and I start being tender with little motions of the spittle-dampened fingers. My concentration is good but I am dimly awake, aware in a satiric way of the brute romanticism. I wouldn't want anyone to see me like this. Certainly not a girl unless I loved and trusted her A LOT. The unsystematic mad twisty jerking of the lips and of the mid-body and the blurred eyes and the grunts—the acrobatic, pantomimic, aromatic, *grotesque* nakedness, weird and chanty—there is a necessary absence here of anyone else in their real existence. I could not write this until I was quite old. I am romping here in a mental reality of the real existence elsewhere of people and their sexual realities, their sexual momentums . . . But no one is here. I'm *not* here. Pleasure and astonishment and shame and curiosity become the blabbery pseudo-bonelessness of the as-if-coerced and final writhing devotion to the sensations here and the final light . . . *OH FUCK FUCK* FUCK *OH YOU DARLING* (*INNNNNNGGGGGGGgggg*) and *KAZOW, KAZOWIE* . . . I fail to semi-control things here with words and exclamations. Substitutions and apings and compensations be damned: this is REAL, THIS *mental* light. Money and power and personal beauty and some truths are like this—are a kind of explanation of the world. This is a corner of the world common to boys. No one is more beautiful or commanding than oneself in this light. It is dreamlike and ambitious. The self-enclosed irreversible alteration in one's knowledge here happens ridiculously, I grant you, but with a tentative and dirty (and changeable) glory. One is a bore-whore, a dull jerk . . . *A jerk-off* . . . Uh-oh . . . Duhhh . . . The grammar of childhood, which I learned from other (mostly older) boys in fear and attention—and in supposed wickedness and ruthlessness toward one's destiny—sheathed in that as in the tinctures of different sorts of sweat, I am afraid I might be broken—that I am more child-y or more womanly than other boys and cannot do this stuff and live. Just before the lurch into irreversibility of coming, I always think it is scandalous to be a real person and I am *always*—truly, really always—*consoled* for the scandal. It's okay. And that it is scandalous to be alone, that is consoled, too.

The *scandalous* excitement of the pulsating hemorrhage, the *scandalously* coerced attentiveness as you come, the hallucination of having all your wonderings answered and you yourself validated. S.L. said when he was terminally ill, *I swear to God dreams can kill a man: they have no mercy: ask me what I want and I'll tell you: I want a woman's dreams—I want to dream like a woman: I want to live a little longer yet* . . . He wanted a woman's dreams at the end of his life. He didn't want this stuff anymore.

The boy's head—as if in a pointless wartime accident, as bumping onto a land mine while doing a cartwheel, say—explodes in a baffling noise of breath. The operative, tensely cooperative will, the hallucinatory white physical consciousness, the slowed, elevated, inspired state, the flaring up of heat, the woundedness, the violence of the sensation—its *limitlessness*: it's like being hit; nothing matters but this . . . Life is a cheat but not this part . . . I feel this about other things when I do them or feel them, sports and friendship, good books, good weather, real wind . . . Here, the body in its duplicitousness takes up a reversed stance: it is not only oddly illuminated flesh; it is passionately committed to nothingness (and impotence-of-a-kind), except toward this—it commits itself, it enlists itself in service to the echoes and the liar's sense of certainty: the stupid king of electricity . . . The head bows forward; the lips loosen drastically; then the head jerks upward and the neck tightens; sexual sensation felt as a large jolting heat-and-visibility of inner light becomes a beautiful whitish light outspread in the neural marvelousness that a slowed and pulse-ridden and *kindly* lightning would be, a heartbeat-and-pulse-ridden-but-silent furnace of seemingly explanatory consolation. It is all metamorphosis.

The boy loved the bleached, hiddenly ocular pleasure.

One is not allowed to persist in this flaring light. *Well, plod plod, you clod.* One has fathered a strand, a small torrent of this different sort of time. To pause in astounded denial of *this shit* is *second nature* . . .

This supplies a thin-ribbed breath to the throbbing which then replaces it. The thing of being split stops; and then the thing is of being under a roof: time to be respectable. That's what pays the rent.

And the soul's *readiness* to die (in the adventures and explorings of this stuff—as into being a *father* or a son—or as into being a hero and having *balls* . . . or into love and all its clauses and unjocular sacraments), it goes away.

I feel unsheltered but *dry*. How can one feel sheltered in being shelterless like this? It's a shrewdness that comes over you, a modern shrewdness. This stuff is said to be sin. Apple-eating. But among boys I know, practicing this stuff is a virtue—is to be human and friendly. Well, we'll see.

A dry memory of a *laughter* of a denial of lots of things, the memory of it spreads over and through the buttocks, neck, fingers, to the instep of the feet—to my bare toes on the tile floor. The being *a slave* to things: the tuneless physical hilarity—I guessed back then that *a lot of guys* felt this—I felt men and boys, women too, and girls, and children had better lives than I did, better experiences.

They had a different tie to this *nowhere*-somewhere of explanatory light.

I am *drunk* with dryness. With sobriety. You know that state? I scowlingly pump myself: I hate this part—the anticlimax. I am chaste for considerable periods of time, I hate this part so much: it is as if I stood on a kitchen chair and faced its back and bent over and held the back of the chair and made the chair hop across a room and into and out of light—a spotlight, a sunrise—me and my new grip, my long back bent, and *MY BIG FEET* braced on the chair seat . . . the half-educated jerks of the torso . . . the stringent tics of the abdomen . . . into and out of the light, into and out of a kind of system of ordinary moments and torture . . .

After another torture.

Dick and hands—eyes and forebrain—will and sweat glands—unnatural and clownish multiplicity. To be grown is a groan thing: *Be smart, don't overdo, you'll live longer* . . . A scene, really fragmented, really whizzing, goes by, the compressing and wheezing self, a nozzle of coming . . . This isn't the way it is with girls when they come. Are you a citizen of the real? Are you an idealist?

Then, all at once, I bend over and constrainingly and partly surrenderingly, using my forearms and my elbows, hug *my dick* to my stomach, my abdomen. I murmur *tactfully* under my breath: *It's okay*

. . . *it's okay* . . . *Old Kiddo* . . . I parent myself often. It's a little SCARY . . . But then real life is scary.

What I had done was MASTURBATORY.

Well, plod plod, you clod. Stupid king of electricity . . . off and on—an agony reveals itself here. *God*—a memory comes so that I am a cup (of flesh) holding feeling-flecked but fadingly immediate white sparks; I am a vat of fading attention to a hallucination-memory that has considerable power *anyway*—I am all longing and distaste: I am fretful *now* and dangerous—cheated . . . I associate this tone with passing for *normal.*

Dry and exacerbating as this state is, it is part of, like a back porch to a house of, delirium thrillingly endured . . . and *Oh fuck it* . . . It feels strange to be alive. One is mostly unworded even if inwardly talkative—or ready to be talkative. It is all sort of ironic—faintly angry, worried, resigned—a thing of *what-my-life-is* . . . This is a private image. You can dream of sharing it with someone. It is momentarily solidified and glistening, but it has vague edges of a sad and nervous dream, but it is about one's life: *Nobody wants you when you're old and gray* . . . No: that's not it . . . Maybe that's it . . .

Nobody wants to make you happy—that's not the point of anyone's life, Wiley . . .

One's clumsy hands—knuckly and calloused and pink and nervous . . . and familiar . . . not strange—are redressing oneself. My clothes are, in a way, a true vote for phallic reality . . . I looked at my fingers. I flexed them. I kept on saying for a few seconds, Okay . . . okay . . . *It's okay* . . . This is so I can go back to the living room and be in public again. I am trying for Daddy's tone from when he was young and well of *Can't complain* . . .

It's sad inside me . . .

You probably wouldn't like me if you knew me closely.

Some people like me.

I don't want to be shallow.

In the dim somehow dark-whitish *blur* of the room, in the compromised dark of the air, when I turn the light off, I shake in the return, distortedly, *sadly*, of the memory, undefined, mind you, of childhood catatonia, of grief and madness: the preliminary stuff of my life now. I tremble—or shudder—and am very still. The tiny amount of belated dribble is a convulsion that is past my strength to bear suddenly; and I vibrate with dryness, with winding down when winding down might not work and might be carrying me in the direction of dead madness. The tight-balled postcoital grief and the ashen ache and the brief sociability of the fucked-out orphan's lost-boy *readiness* for the world—the rictus-smile on my pale and cooling-off but still sweaty face—the way it actually HURTS—muscularly, electrically—spiritually—in the *heart and soul*—*Well, maybe-I'll-live-with-it* for now. *Let's act as if this were me* . . . It burns. Daddy sometimes said when he was alive and I came out of the bathroom after doing this stuff, *JESUS GOD LOOK AT YOU*—

I would blush palely-hotly on top of the semi-exhausted heat of the other, which I did now in memory and association or maybe out of habit as if the other (momentary) blaze of supreme heat behind my eyes, now juiceless and cold—ironic-*lunatic* (by comparison)—spills itself, too . . . seed . . . Johnny Appleseed, Johnny Apple-eater on the loose in the *bandit* territories behind my eyes where the mind is: I have changed my mind . . . I am of a different mind . . . Peekaboo . . .

My fear is of going unslaked all my life . . .

I guess, though, I am scared, too, of being wild in the world and *shot down like a dog*.

Air flutters at the edge of my lips. This part is over. I am less safe for a while.

An internal soliloquy isn't necessarily in words. Coming was as if it had been dug out of me by a cruel spoon . . . I saw a tin kitchen spoon, dirty with wear, not with dirt, a ten-cent spoon of that era. I cleaned up the john, cleaned up myself; and each motion was like a piece of a speech to myself. When I noticed the light in the john, that was like a piece of a speech. The sound of flushing made me grin but *painfully* at first, no, second, and then more painfully: it was sort of dry-eyed tears but of the angles of the lips, of the mouth.

I sloped back toward the living room, anxious to get away from *that stuff* of one's actual singularity of being. Scoured and filthy although cleaned up and filthy with will and standoffish (suddenly) and kind of organized, or conditioned to protect oneself now—from her now—and I felt myself to be really a dangerously stupid but (if you can forgive me for this) a forsakenly and unappreciatedly *beautiful* THING . . .

Then her, too: I saw her as that.

"I understand the line about one touch of nature making the whole world kin," I said, lying down, facedown. Well, first I was propped on my extended arms, then they retracted and then they were folded under me and my feet were pressed against the arm of the sofa and my face was buried. I sighingly said, "It wasn't *all* kiddy stuff, was it?"

"No," she said *intelligently.* I felt dominated and constrained by some big, biggish sense of MIND in her. Her voice had liquid in it, not tears—something tearful, maybe. I wriggled a bit, reached over and touched her cheek with my lower lip . . .

"No! Do nothing!"

"You want to come?" I asked. I knew next to nothing about this part of things but I'd read in books about men not doing this being no good, unlikable, and so on.

"No." Then: "You don't know how to do that."

"You could teach me . . ."

"*Shut up, Wiley,*" she said—really intensely.

I paid no attention—maybe I was being hysterical—I wasn't paying attention to her anymore in that other *sexual* way: "Let's start a kiss we haven't seen in any movie," I said.

"I WANT YOU TO SHUT UP FOR A WHILE AND I WANT YOU TO DO IT NOW," and now tears were apparent in her voice. But not on her face—I felt with my fingers and I looked. She sounded genuinely angry. Minutes passed and I thought of various things—worriedly, then contentedly, then I don't know what I thought, it was so mixed up. She raised herself and she leaned over and she kissed me in a kind of sticky version of how I had kissed her when I was most in rut—if you will pardon me: she was deep and speechful but it was *a lecture.*

"We aren't synchronized," I said, guessing. I didn't care but I used an especially naïve tone so she wouldn't know I was being wicked; and I goaded her in how I kissed her back; but I wasn't confident—I didn't feel I tempted her: I felt I tempted her into invention—only that: of course, I was a young kid, I had privileges of stupidity—maybe not as much as grown men had but, still, quite a few, or to quite an extent.

But she was irked. I might not like her or what she did . . . you know? I'd set the pitch of a kind of dangerous high-school game—it was dangerously high for kids—and she remembered it and returned to it, visited it, or she recognized it in its male form and she showed me the mechanics of a *sincere* kiss—for her—now that I had come and we were in this other context. She descended through murky levels back to a nursery-nursy thing of neediness and power and letting go—she let go of self-defense—briefly: she let go blackly and sloppily. But briefly.

And I didn't like it.

I went, "Ugh, aargh," softly, kindly, but still, judgingly—you know? And she was dumbly enraged and self-righteous because she *knew* that was real sexy. And she had flattered me by doing it with me and I hadn't known *what it was all about*—I had failed in sophistication (one) and in sensitivity (two). But I really had. I had wanted her to let me be dominant, but I was like *this* . . .

"See, you can't trust me," I said almost inaudibly—to her cheek, a little in front of the shallow whorls of her ear.

I said it so she would trust me some and go on even though I had failed. I was being sensitive-and-good kind of shamefacedly because I couldn't be truly MALE or whatever the hell it was I wasn't being.

Her mood in relation to her engagement, which had been set in regard to I-don't-know-what—her half-approval of my unmanly maleness —now was whirringly reset to my *voice* . . . not to my *body*.

And this was tied to *how she* looked. She had odd good looks and a very, very good body—so good it couldn't last in this form past childbirth—but this was quite a high rank she had—some of this (maybe all of it) was tied to its being wartime . . . And *I* was invisible to her once again—a mere figment of corporeality realer as *a voice*—that's what she liked me for . . . now.

So she is kidding THE VOICE—more for her sake in a kind of ghostly romance story than for my sake. I mean I'd been taken care of, so to speak—and she was showing me something, anti-patriotically; she re-started the self-invented kiss; she said, "Here, you're sweet, this is my own patented kiss . . ." Her own patented kiss? Firm-lipped up to a point but not-quite-closed-mouthed, and soon, almost at once, openmouthed because of the nestling-and-nursing-and-nursy-wrestling stuff she liked —the kiss as dominant, the odd meanings and fluctuations of *the kiss* . . .

"Sort of kiss my kiss," I said, like a smart-ass.

She ignored that—or didn't get it—she was busy showing me what she liked . . . or what it was like for her. She didn't like that . . . doing that . . . But she liked not liking it . . . the uncoerced *confession* in a sense: *telling Wiley* . . . I don't know. My view of it was that in her (Lutheran) mind she wanted to tempt me then-and-there *at the edge of hell* . . .

She thought I knew a lot. She thought what she knew was knowable easily by others. She moved further into her system, her ritual—there was no way for me to know this but I knew she was unshielded, as much as I had been: I *felt* the echo thing in it—the equality do-jigger—but I did not know what to do about it.

Her kiss got directionless and nowhereish. I happen to be good at taking tests, at answering questions, as I've said probably a dozen times by now. On oral tests, you answer questions in any number of ways but the first way is you look at the questioner and you try to read the mind of the questioner. If you really engage with the question, you lose all confidence: the world dissolves into atoms and rays; all your own lights are turned off. All light, *all*, is elsewhere—well, on that basis, I thought maybe that she wanted something, me to *do* something, something *masculine*, and I closed my lips over hers, drew hers into a kind of pout like before, but this time I bit them gently-sharply in syllables of a sincerity of condescension to her wish that I be smarter and older and richer and tougher and yet not too much—it shocked me that I felt superior to her—and yet I *knew* that coming did that.

I thought I *felt* sincere rage and hatred in her and sincere wonder and attachment—for a moment—alternating with childish nothingness and half-lying directionlessness—I mean a bit of how rocky she was and how she set limits, or more than a bit, that showed, too. It was kind of monstrous.

I licked the outside of her mouth and her nostrils and said, "Monster loves monster."

She ignored that, too.

Licking her had a salt taste and I saw red and purple behind my eyelids: I was partly open-eyed for some of the seconds as they passed: it turned into a "deep" kiss, a lot of tongue, but it was like being eaten by a sea anemone while you were holding your breath underwater. I hate being bossed; and she reacted to the kiss so that, as usual, when someone reacts to something and you're there, what you do is like your being an angel or a Cupid or a man or a bad boy to them, in their view of things—and it is in order to rule that that you do it and go on, but they judge and so they have the upper hand. To impose a notion of the universe that was in me and which was anxious to enclose her, as in a net, I proceeded to respond—to be me and not just a figure she could judge. I did it until she pushed me away and then she turned onto her back and she breathed—she took a loud breath and then a few little ones—and she may have farted. She said, "You're hot stuff . . . You're bad . . ."

"You don't mean it . . . You're just saying it."

"Shut up and kiss me," she said; she covered her mouth with her arm, though, and looked at me—that line was in a lot of movies at that time.

I was embarrassed—and a little happy—since being bad in this way is altogether part of being *intimate*. And your whole background—and your body—are being said to be acceptable at least to this extent. It may be that you and the other person respect each other as sinners and co-

conspirators or as opposites and magnetic even if you really don't respect each other overall.

And I was trying again to get seduced or to get her to be seduced-and-ruled (by an amateur).

One of the things you feel in a kiss is the degree of susceptibility and resistance of the other person to being ruled and how nice (and submissive) you are each being now or not. I could feel in her that she was a death-or-freedom girl . . . No one to joke with.

And all the acceptance stuff of me was just honey-and-delusion. Cross-pollination time. Not only that: it's really hard to describe . . . You pile on sloppy kisses, filler kisses, fuller kisses, nursery-amoeba kisses inside the one big continuing (and often interrupted) kiss even while you both know the real sexual stuff is not in *kisses.* And yet it is for now. She is learning things. And she is the judge and I'm just a kid . . . a spoiled kid. *Spoiled kid with judgment-handing-out harlot*—sort of.

I tried to make it that each individual kiss inside the big kiss had individual meaning but she bit me and went sloppy and kept generalizing things and distracting me; and then when I would heat up, she would pause and comb her hair with her fingers and look at me and sigh . . . affectionately. Meanly. In a homelike way.

It was and was not *kissing-in-general.* It was clear that I was being eaten up alive. She's going to loll here in the surf and roll back and forth and she is going to fuck me over but that's it . . .

But she's given me a lot already. I am laughing at her in a way by not respecting my own defeat too much—by being cynical in the face of her soul which is using my *defeat* sort of—my *defeat* such as it is. And she rebels against all sorts of shadows, not just against me. She asserts herself *generally,* although specifically, she is here with me. She reveals who is the lost queen of local paradise around here. She says, "No. Don't kiss me like that . . . Do it like this . . ."

I am very sweaty (in a youthful way: a damp blond) with all this. We weren't lying so much anymore although we were lying a lot. We had come out of the cavern into a shallow bit of lighted territory. Sexual truth? I could say we were lying enough to be credible but were naked enough that it was sort of a truth where we were, what we were doing. I had a sense I was of more value than she was, not privately or as a mother, and not overall or across-the-board, but in-the-world. She kept receding somehow, for some reason, inside her mischief, her will, her honor, her courage, her whatever-it-is, her what-she-was. I was stringently consequential and *took a broad view* and saw, maybe falsely, her and her religious stuff, her father and him being of another generation, and her job and her knowing Nonie, and AMERRRRRICA and the pilot she was engaged to and her being young in relation to him and her becoming a mother soon or maybe she was even pregnant now and pissed about it . . . That would explain me. I knew it wasn't *love* for *me* in any case—it was love off and on, sort of, that she felt. And I didn't want to die to protect her. She wasn't the most important thing in the world to me at that moment. (That was the system I used for telling whether I *loved* someone or not.)

And considering her feelings, and the grounds for them, there was no way she could be the most important thing in the world to me, short of being willing to give up her life and concentrating on me . . . And that was not what she had in mind.

This wasn't vanity on my part; or not exactly: this was the truth inside a certain mood. I would die for her—her giving up the importance of other things in relation to me. A peculiarly wrongheaded truth inside some *steeply* shadowy feelings of respectable life as *hard work* . . . Meanwhile, I loved her *anyway*—obviously. But don't ask too much of me . . . okay, Leonie?

Was that lousy? Sure it was.

But that becomes *fair* if she is doing it, too, even if she is doing it more *deeply* and more wholeheartedly and *wildly* than I am and, also, more cold-bloodedly and more intelligently.

I am selfishly whole-skinned with *reason* . . . with the help of reason and for the sake of the *future* of my family (and of me).

I am selfish but not completely if I am also unselfish, passionate, spendthrift, and glorious with stupid onrushing into love and whatever—isn't that what she is imitating in this phase of the necking-and-petting?

Something here is unfair and evil—Nonie-esque . . . but what is it? The horrible extravagance of totality—the all or nothing of what is not ambiguous as time rushes on? The rending thing in real life of any form of almost unarguable emotional clarity of gesture—of a giving of the self to *a thing*, if not to a person, and then the holding back or the implicit limits of it at the moment and then in the next moment and how those can be broken through . . . And then your responsibility, your guilt, your being joined to the other person through the acts you both have engaged in, Leonie's kisses and actions in this part of what we did, the abortive, adolescent, thinly fleshed-out and thinly experienced reality, even of her completeness (compared to my boyishness), it is off-putting, upsetting, hideously real—truly scary . . . The self is too skimpy for truth. *Nothingness* is easier—much easier.

But what kind of murder of the world is it to say that this stuff is *nothing*? Nothing much? Another example of nothingness?

"Shit and crap," I said from the depths of these feelings—which were quite blurred in me—as if by rain, long slanting lines, dot-and-dashed, like a field of weeds to an ant. I hoped I sounded older and *deep* and sensitive.

"I'm a cradle-robber and you're a heartbreaker," she murmured.

I grimaced: I respected her soul . . . I did love her. I loved her as much as I loved myself—just not more than myself.

She knew it, I bet; I bet she felt her "love" deeper than mine was for her—she wasn't just protecting herself as I was protecting myself: she was protecting her fiancé and her father . . . I started feeling I was protecting Lila and Nonie: I sort of squared my shoulders and was self-sacrificial and sort of a family kind of guy, or familied.

She didn't say anything, not this that I claim was implicit in her sigh then: *HAVE YOU NEVER BEEN LOVED BEFORE, YOU COLD SLIPPERY (BOY-) MAN?*

The sexual stuff was incomplete! I was sulky—and astonished by her sigh. The next moment, in the peculiarities of the skinny boy—and of emotions and time—I'd forgotten that and was *at sea*—aimless and warm—lost in a fog on *the Indian Ocean*—one of two souls—licking, groping, fondling the seaborne, sea-y destiny—two souls ocean-tossed, moved along, castaway, disparate—and ill suited to this adventure.

This may not matter very much . . .

Leonie was a foot freak—it reminded me of the little-boy thing of using a foot as a fist—A Great Warlike Phallus, maybe. She bent her leg at an impossible angle and she was stroking me *there* with her foot—toed phallus to underpanted and sated-but-refreshing-itself phallus . . . sort of.

Jesus! People really do live like contortionists.

I kind of kept remembering (as I said) by association and so I felt as a memory the sadness of a child sometimes at not being bigger and more powerful, the sadness at not being a flying thing (so to speak), the sadness at not being everything conceivable . . . bird, flower, snake, whale . . .

Man.

Now, though, for me, everything but being a boy was inconceivably *dirty*. Everything tested you—everything was a test. Reality in its flattery was a horse kicking you to death. I liked people who *understood* this. A lot of women's interest in women is a kind of unspoken thing in them of being sickened by failure in men and at their own not having grown into a man and done things without failing all the time. Of course, if they are defeated by men, that stuff takes on a different cast in them. Sometimes women are men of a sort. All the velocities: our clothes and the couch are fondling us . . . The evening is a pimp. The finality of the sexual terrain is terror-cum-outcry in the scandal of being male, not as a preliminary, as in my experience so far, but at being given a huge white world, whitelit, brief, briefly comprehensible, in regard to others' destiny—a gambler's intrusion on further time—and on life . . . Romantic distances are not real distances—not like time or like going out into a river. Romantic distances ache with their breakability. There's something unwilling to be looked at in me, then comes a *half*-willingness to be loved. This is a malleable masculinity—momentary—absurd. Then comes the as-if-simple (or merely simplified) pleasure at being liked, at being played with: like light captured in interlocked fingers over my eyes not in a *grim* way. The childish part of me, the leftover blondness of what I am, is a dirtiable, naughty sunlight warmingly touching her. She was supple—some girls I'd fooled around with had collapsed after a while into woodenness and fluster, into being rooted and heaving twigs and leaves in a wind, sexually. The clumsy intimations of how anarchic and ungeneral the power is in love in each person—love in regard to one's own self, which is all one can know from immediate experience—one's own powers and defenselessness in regard to that interfere with one's perceptions: the sickening and deliciously sticky sense of guilt and innocence fixes one's eyes, inward and outward—not everyone can bear this stuff . . . It is now a little as if we were jammed into a dovecote, a pigeonhole thing; in her *sexual*, aimlessly sexual—partly sexless—explorations, we are as if in a flock of fluttering birds, that smell and the cooings . . . I am not a genius of sexual touch or of sensual, or of sexual or of sensual momentum. Or if I was (or am), it is only at moments of being in love with the person I was with. I was good at registry. The question for her of all-that-I-am is present in the intimacy, such as it is. The question is as it is in sports: What is she worth—on a team? What am I worth—in the world? What are our opponents like? How are we going to end up? This includes a sense of *moral* possibility . . . how much forgiveness we will require and what degree of banditry we will share or turn against each other. Real self-sacrifice for each other . . . for the team . . . how much? This is in the fluttering kisses.

Or something like that gets mixed up with the uncensoredly fluttering famous amusement—of this sport. The deeply amused, scared thing, mystically, semi-mutually hysterical: THIS IS GOOD! she whispers. And I say, half-meaninglessly: ENOUGH IS ENOUGH! And she says: THIS IS NO GOOD . . . meaning almost the same as when she said it was good: it was good *but* . . . An active wolverine sniffs at you in ferocity and with a capacity for loyalty, and it sniffs at your crotch and growls at it and then at its own crotch and then yours again and so on . . . *Voici les animaux* . . . The whole funny and stinking sexual-excess feeling is of a sense of the future *given away*. And I think one feels the oddity of death then, the little sexual death that people have written about and that I have read about—and one's becoming a genius here although not at this but in this isolation . . . And this is stinking and comic, too, and it is too much . . . The fragile, sneaky moments . . . I whispered that I found unloving people interesting. Well, what I said is "Too much, too much . . . enough, too much . . ." This was more pecking than necking—that was a joke a guy I know used—a form of wit, I thought it. What I said I didn't really mean. I didn't intend for her to listen. I guess I was asking to know less about her—to be allowed my lies in my sense of things—especially there, on the couch. It was true that I found unloving people interesting—"like a recess," I said out loud. She still doesn't have to hear me. My purposes are unclear to me. I think one hears purposes more than words. The withdrawal from the use of power in the light of what Leonie was doing and maybe of what she felt—her feelings at her not being a boy, at her fiancé not being a boy—my retreat into that recurring *neutrality* of mine—was a coital-postcoital sadness, maybe a form of cowardice, gendered, maybe an attempt at virtuously seductive behavior . . . I DON'T KNOW . . . A lot of what I am is hidden from me. She can tell at once, or pretty soon; and something creeps into her manner: I think she is relieved somewhat in that lax gaiety, that it is only a little intense.

In order not to be a fool—and in a kind of anxiety to dominate in part—and because of its being wartime—I stopped being good while I went on with the *lax gaiety* part—I was a sort of evil, limp boy—oh, I had it up; but it was rawly and sorely up; I was sort of mental-and-perverse sexually: a bad guy: and I would bet that it showed in my breath and face—a dark flicker of the eyes—and a kind of pinching grip of the lips. Somehow this suggests a near-equality of fate in men and women, or in one guy and one woman, not equal and well-matched *stupidities* and metamorphoses but an equality of hellishness and of punishments and of guilts and of lesser and larger pleasures for a while.

And she is startled and *her* face flickers and she falls in love, but not permanently, for a moment . . . contingently, if I am young and largely simple but then have this evil side as well.

I don't know what Leonie was *As A Person* in that I don't know how her life came out. I can't compare it to other lives. Her *magnificence*—her sexual quality that so impressed and imprisoned me—was like a mixture of common sense—of coldness—with an unfrightened depth and width of (and curiosity about) lawlessness in her—it was that lawlessness which was favorable to me, sort of *bandit-to-bandit* . . . and which set limits to what she felt: *He's only a kid* . . . She said it out loud, "You're only a kid . . ." She said it mysteriously. It had depths. She had a generosity toward living with a completeness and a fullness in the moments that was way beyond me. The rushing reality of that girl.

The evening. The boy. We are gamblers and guessers.

She said, "I'd like to get to know you. I'd like to spend more time with you." And she lay back, ending that passage of her sexual aggressiveness.

"I'm not very special," I said grouchily. Then I said, "I'd like to get to know *you*: I'd like to spend *a lot more* time with *you* . . ."

"I'm not very special," she said, not with mockery either.

It is possibly the case that maybe I am half in love with *everything* to start with . . . that year. She hid her competitive self, her criticizing self, her destroying self. She was being a courtship marvel, "nice" and "bad": *nice-and-bad*: wonderful. And she credited me with inspiring her to want to do it and to do it. And me with her: it was personal: it wasn't just adolescent horniness and her being acceptable-looking.

The other, *darker* stuff shows in her lips and on her shadowy and semi-gouged and slightly used and puffy *face* and in the way her head sits inside the tousled, coarse hair and on her long neck.

Evilly, I wonder if she cut the *kissing* short before the other stuff could be found out for certain about her . . . The way she loosens and spreads and gets sly-eyed . . . "You know too much," she says to the air. "I want a cigarette." She felt me looking and *noticing* . . .

I wasn't *realistic* . . . I didn't want any Nonie stuff . . .

She may have felt I thought her to be old and dirty. The sexual wish for orgasm is as if, for me, we stand in a mouth of flame, and kiss and quench the sense of being attacked by flames which then, when we stop, is worse—you know that sense of being burned and stung by *flames*? You can call it jealousy if you want. It is like that, a kind of anguish toward otherness—other outcomes, other folks' minds and feelings . . . knowledges . . . experiences.

The agonized and amazing succession of kisses and touches they might know.

Immediate memory was growing too painful. A careless and semi-ceaseless (because of memory) and semi-causeless (*we-were-only-fooling-around-so-how-did-this-happen*) sexual grandeur forms. This seems *typical.* "I don't know about you but I find all this *agonizing,*" I said.

"But you came," she said.

"That doesn't help one whole hell of lot."

"You want to come again?" she said, interested. Then a moment or so later—her arm over her head again—"Kids . . ." Then, still another moment further on, or in, or more deeply in, "You run with the ball for a while . . ."

Heaving myself up on my elbows, semi-lightly, I said, "With the blue balls . . ." Then: "I run . . ." I guess it was for the first time in my life, this next kiss, my full will in it, my full-willedness, and in this moment of touching her breast, the slightly *prickled* areola, the foreign-to-me *nipple* . . . I say it out loud: "*Nipple* . . ." and something in me explodes, not *nicely,* at me naming it . . . A lot of linguistic theories are very sexual, I bet.

But I am in a full regalia of will—I might as well have been wearing an Indian chief's headdress of turkey feathers with a long tail: that's how I was holding my head. The core of it at that time was not that I was kissing her, but it lay in an extreme but tortured pleasure at my being, for a while, a boy like any other of the bossy, nakedly-an-Indian-chieftain type.

I took her wrist and moved it so it and the heel of her hand went down the front of my still-fastened pants. And touched the head of my hidden prick. I said—unforgivably (I was saying no to her)—"I have no money; I have to be careful . . ." I had a coldly chagrinned sense of my own loony momentums. I didn't care if she loved me or not.

A ritualized freedom, a partly predictable terror, a restless and careless animal prowling—a dirty heroism, a championship matter: reality is where you die for real, where the killer air is too weak to hold me and the resistant cry of "*Please, let's not—*" I hear and obey and—at the same time—bury in a flood of hallucinations. In her this causes a form of enraged humor felt oddly, in her breasts as I touch them and lie, shirt opened, atop them (skin to skin), and in the roof of her mouth as I kiss her, and it is visible in her eyes and in the changed odor of her heat and in the mischief (and kindness) of her giving in and going on a while longer in spite of this distancing of rage and humor in her.

But it makes her feel dry. Something abrasive slows the boy. Thereupon, a sense of her importance, sexual-maternal, whorish, rests in part on my *seeing* that she is NOT in the presence of someone stronger-willed—or more powerful—than she is. It is only me. I am the one who is there. She loved me in that way . . . With that dismissiveness . . .

Her moods are less strong than mine but deeper—she was not so remote or so immediate or so ruthless or absolute in mood as I was. She did not gamble so much in order to be or seem *typical* for a while. She was, within reason, *typical* in whatever state she found herself. She was not unselfish. But she avoided too much selfishness—I don't know why. If I say I *felt* she knew me as someone smelly (from sweat and rut in parlor sex) and anarchic and difficult—someone no good in certain ways—then what I feel is her presence as *a star's glow* after all—an actress's quality of doing this stuff for effect—and doing it to good effect.

In this fashion she *felt-up* the dick. She wasn't theatrical but she was boyishly female. He felt a *priced* generosity in her, an American thing: I remember it . . . I remember that he felt his prick ran him. He felt happy—cured—silly—endangered. There was no way to escape morally by that point. He is pawing her—and he is dry-fucking her legs—and he wants to enter her now a lot so that he can say he did. Really, how can meaning be concentrated, obliteratingly, on this? And if it is like that for you, what the fuck kind of philosopher are you? In the animal sense of things?

The strained, thin, early-adolescent body of the boy knows this ghastly—blowsy—comfort—this comfort of a sort.

Whatever happens, one resists it, at least a little, in order to name it, except maybe in the moments of a rush of love or of hate (as in combat). In the near-infinity of details (of structure) of the self is the thing that the self has so many complex balances that it, or part of it, is insulted by anything that happens, insulted at least for a little. Whatever it is that happens doesn't matter. Somebody by nature insulting, somebody by nature often insulted, sometimes has an air of action and of suitability for going first—it's odd. The quilt of purposes being torn by complicitous stupidity—by this animal permission based on a complete lack of claims, a sort of equality of lowness, lowness and villainy of a kind—can be *lovely* as well as insulting. Moments take on a structural reality of a sexuality of fingers, dick, stomach, of one's breath, known in this way. One is horrified and excited—by life—and consoled: what a trio, horror and excitement and consolation: it's like certain murder mysteries, some horror movies, some suspense and adventure movies, some public football games. It *feels* like a recurrence of mercy . . . And like a joke . . . This intimacy in the light of, oh, I would say *ordinariness*, but I am kind of a freak . . . Another part of me—sort of from deeper down, farther in, floatingly higher up but in a glade or on a planet farther away inside me—sees it as a kind of communal breakfast of corruption: *See, I'm alive* . . . And: *See, I've lived this long* . . . And: *I've lived this long with Nonie and Lila—and S.L. and the world-as-it-is* . . . In some intimacy, you lie too much—as with a parent—or with a child you're tutoring: you have *a play world.* But this moment, even as a moment in *a play world*, it is a definition of something kind of real—but it is private. You turn your back on *her* and see her as THE WOMAN or as HOW I FIRST HAD THAT SORT OF SEX (sexual carryings-on) . . . or you choose a theme: *betrayal-of-the-male—of the guy*—or: *the role of the demure in the life of a girl her age and of her social class* (*in wartime*): to know her by. I really mean to not know her while being with her, while being familiar, while being intimate. In this secret way (as in being in a closet and hiding when you are a child) of *good-and-bad* mixed. Us: we're not being *pure* in relation to *ordinary* things—or even to things in the house. And her fiancé-lover: what of him? I didn't know about things like screwing in the ass and the woman-as-animal or cow yet. Or, if I did, it was semi-conscious. We had a thing back home, at home and in school, of *Don't give it houseroom* or *Don't give it houseroom in your head* . . . It's not like repressing it: you just don't look at it: you *don't take it home with you* . . . But the violence, if I might be allowed to use that word, of the contact, the sexual contact between the two of them, and what he required of her, or what she was bent on doing, or aroused to by him, the nursing abasement, for instance, or the awe at the raw pain, or the flagellation and rending of her for her by her being in the presence of such extreme cowardice and bravery, such pain as that—none of the fliers I knew was lighthearted about going into combat or about having been in it—the weird realities of experience blended with the weirder actualities of identity, of sexual identity—but I am omitting the *will*—the onrush of the self: the black and violent streams of that, and the plunging boulders and logs, the upset and the overset, or the tentative but willful tendernesses, silences, collusions, complicities—and, above all maybe, the way the heroic includes murder, murder and acceptance of it, killing and ignoring —I mean as well as *not giving it houseroom,* we had a thing of *Open up, open up a little bit, it won't hurt you to open up for once*; and drinking was supposed to help you do that—you open up rooms in the head and doors into the rooms; and you also leave yourself and float disembodied among moods and similarities, translations, bridges, isthmuses in and out. It's scary and lost, you're lost as in a woods, a woods set in the middle of your life, and people come and go, in you really, or you're flayed and sensitive to them . . . I don't know. Sometimes, back home, people said, *Be big* . . . Like being pregnant with someone else's life-and-feelings—for a moment—or with the whole community. Of course, a lot of that is fake; you can hide behind mottoes. But you can also *feel*, in a kind of hidden anguish, with a kind of hideousness—as if there really was a deformity of the self in comparison to how you passed yourself off during the day—what you comforted your parents with in yourself when you were a little kid, the ways in which you were another world, or a flag of *innocence*, of innocence and purpose, really, and how that partly continued into this moment but in this hopelessly other *impure* way—I guess I mean the way this part of her life compares to the rest of her life, and then what that life is—as darkness and smell—as what I don't know—and as what I must put my arms around. Must? Well, it's like that if you *open up* . . . if you *loosen up* . . . And you feel her astonished *pain* and the rushing thing of her—wind in the leaves of olive trees turning over the silver undersides: her breath—the wings and bird odors—of the female? of the *feminine*? is that it—some *horrid* sense of deformity and death, submission, humiliation—monsters in the street—Nazis, gangsters, things like dragons, HUGE ILL LUCK—or guys like you if you're cold and don't *open up*—I DON'T KNOW—and the *safety* or the *decency*, the thing of providing a home or protection—and the way guys hate that and tear it apart to get at you, to get even with them—or the death-tinged, death-dealing, shot-at, shot-up pilot *scoffing*—and me making use of her and then her making use of me: as of arbors, crawling into arbors, leafy nooks—I DON'T KNOW—the absence of a sacrament—of permission—the logical realities of merely personal permission to be *bad to this extent*—to describe it perhaps psychologically (and morally—or theoretically), the mutual, or shared, *rudeness* of the now undone pants, of the sight of *the thing*, of the boy stilled, of the older girl *toying* effectually with it, her having a comparatively simple power over it compared to her relation, goddamn it, to the prick of the crazed and maybe sexually overwrought or sexually feeble or sexually great but overweening pilot—or of Leonie's boss in the office, or her dad—or the spiritual whatever of Nonie—or of the shadows of the world—what anguished semi-irony in the counterfeit presence of me feeling her as a pirate and me as a bandit on this queerly astronomical voyage around a world—a world in place, existent and seemingly stilled, while I move, but actually it moves, too, it whirls and dances and slides, kind of menacingly, kind of meanly—this stuff happens . . . The integrity of the mind's connections to certain of its lies and some of its truths is lost in the yo-yo-joke-not-a-joke of the not greatly adroit but pretty god-damn effectual up-and-down of Leonie's after all amateur hand.

But, truly, it is a world, an inner room—a nook—of an entirely different order of distinctions.

"Oh God . . . Oh *God* . . . Leonie . . ."

Villain. Dier. Tyrant. Tyrant-hero . . . Winter-of-discontent guy —Crookback—with his back crooked—that is, *arched*—someone's brother, someone's child . . . letting judgments go—among the blowingly weedy black richness of the tolerant brutalities of the sexual world—you know?

"I'm sorry if I'm not a nice person," she says idly . . . sitting up: not quite sitting up: she is going to stop—or not stop. She stops. She says, leaning back, gazing off into the air after looking at my prick—which leaps, salmonishly, at being *looked at*—at being *looked at by her*—she says somewhat mysteriously, "It matters . . . how much money a girl has."

"Mmmm?" I am staring at her. I am with her among the shadows—sort of with her—and I am only partly among the lamps or among my own shadows—and lightedness—or memories of it—and expectations, wishes, anxieties for her to go on . . .

I *know* she is comparing us—our lives—our skins, our minds—I *know* she is occupied with *knowing* us and herself and herself-in-her-life—and I know it is a matter of comparisons slidingly, a slide-rule thing, in her head, *relatively-we-are* or *you-are*—it is that stuff in some sort of *violent* and limitless and as-if-coldly-rational vocabulary in her: "What she can do, what she will do, what she wants to do, she can do what she wants to do," she says owlishly. "Well . . . I like that . . ." Again she says it *owlishly*—but it's a different owl, I guess. I *know* it is a compliment but I don't know on what terms: I would like to pound a hole in her head and put in a glass window and make her think in visible words that I could read. I'd like to tie her up and chain her to the couch as in a laboratory experiment so she'd be thinking something I could logically guess: so her mind and her associations would be *limited* . . . One breast peers idly out of her partly undone blouse. Her hand, her princely hand is stilled. Does she want me to *ask* her to do it some more? WHAT THE CHRIST FUCK DOES SHE WANT? I would like to say inwardly it doesn't matter but it does matter, it matters to me, and it colors the universe; the tinted glassy dust of this will go flying off into space and become a big datum that changes the weight of *everything-there-is* . . .

Taking time to think, half think, think a little, I say, "I have a good friend who believes meaninglessness is the only meaning. He's ambitious. He's a Nihilist-Marxist. He doesn't enjoy sex but he has a lot of it—by hand."

She takes my remark as indicating an *obsession* with sex, the sex we were having; and she resumes her hand movement, but she is still sitting up and the hand movement is without concentration. Even so, her hand in its postures and its motions as mock-cunt or whatever does bring on in me the neural light of sexuality, until I then see the untinted splotches of light inside me and then the tinted and real ones on either side of her nose in the half-light of the room. I see the mock graves and tubes of her nostrils and of her mouth past her shiny teeth while I sort of rock and roll up a silvery ladder or off-and-on whitelit *flight* of stairs —or tilted sea—toward those seconds of sexual wakefulness . . . if I can put it like that. Here is her animal smell—I am in her hand(s). Oh, it is all actual. *It is real and all of them are dead.* It is arousal and burial . . . or lightedness and lapse-into-darkness . . . up, up, sink back—I want her lap. She is *specifically* repelled by this aspect of me and amused at herself for being here. And she wants her power and I want her to have more power—to thrill me, that is. Oh, the twisted geographies and the gravity, the weight, the weightedness, oh, the higher purposes . . . look at what is here . . . I LOVE HER NOW! She says—why does she say this?—why does she continue her conversation with me?—"I know it matters how much money a woman has—I wasn't born yesterday." Then: "If I were rich, we could run off for a day or two and everybody would keep it hushed up." Why must she make me feel how minor and sociable this fucking around is. Oh . . . . Oh oh . . . OH . . .

Her eyes, her mouth reject me. I am as if gouged at in the middle. Harried. I say to you, Carry me. The line of hair on the boyish abdomen—the cone of it—hairy? hairy'd . . . Hurry? Do you care for me? If you say it fast, it comes out *care-eee* . . . The rhythm is too slow, too unsteady: *hurry care-eee* . . . If I am rendered helpless—as when I'm tackled in football practice and a half-dozen guys leave their weight on me—I laugh, I laugh loonily; I cry, too, I cry overshadowingly. I am loose in her own life—as an image—but I am tied down, weighted, floored by the surf and the light, I am moored to her erratic movements.

I am a specific size and shape phallically and of a specific order neurally and psychologically in relation to rhythms—and her touch is a little general . . . There is a gender thing . . . I mean she won't be cross in the way I would enter her if I could. I am privileged wildly-vividly in this imparted suicide. It hurts and is apparent that she has no overriding wish to fill her spaces, her mouths—the mouths in herself—with *me.*

The dance of no's and yeses, the almost numberless *sorts* of inner doors, the steps and the lights in the boy—*sexually*—and the veilings and willow branches and sheets that the sexual-spiritual light comes through, and her will, erected but not phallic; in fact, it is unanimal largely and likes its bleakness and its self-consciously visible, rehearsed, common and already familiar-from-other-times nakedness and its *ordinary* bravery more than the natural sexual treacheries toward the world and the entirety of depths and the transparent limitlessness toward the future of the more literal sexuality of real fucking—the *weird* mixture of gaiety-ungaiety, the grudging novelty of it—she persists . . . Leonie's *limited* beauty is more than I can bear . . . *You asshole . . . Love her.* Actually, the spirit hasn't a lot of choice, even knowing this is a scarring, scary thing. She was surprised, not surprised, lackadaisical—not weary —well, a little weary—hardworking, knowing—and dubious—an employee of some company that showed you this sexual courtesy—*you know?* Everything, infuriatingly—infatuatingly—having to do with my prick in her hand is grounds for vengeance of some sort and is reason to forgive the moment and everything else and is a pretty good reason for gratitude—for affection, tolerance, what-have-you.

Brotherhood. She leans over and puts her lips on it—on the head: she feels really guilty toward me . . . She doesn't suck it . . . I once went down on a boy at YMCA camp after the five other guys had gone down on me, they having lost to me at poker: but then they had sort of ganged up on me in complaint and then in wrestling: so I went down on one guy—the biggest one . . . *You're snotty and biting,* he said . . . She's being a little nice to the poor, blue-balled boy . . . And she's being snotty-and-a-little-biting . . . Memory tries to repress this. Or the mind tries to repress memory and to assign this to some other part of myself —to my wicked banditry . . . I've tricked her into this . . . I'VE TRICKED HER! HOT SHIT! I can boast to guys, maybe.

I try to assign to all this *another* weight . . . not its present weight.

She stops. She is sitting up. She says, "I admire men who are sensible about money. Well, I have some. If you got me pregnant, I have enough: I could send you to college: I would make you marry me in spite of your age." Then she said, "Whoop-de-doo . . ." She said this in a not very playful voice. She knew she had scared the living shit out of me. I didn't want to be *stuck* with her for the duration of the rest of my life . . . I didn't know enough . . . She wasn't too sane.

Neither was I—maybe . . .

She *breathed*—she breathed in that offering way—and then when I said, "I don't want to go to college," she breathed in a cutting and mean tone; it had a dismissive quality—she didn't take no lightly.

I hadn't said no clearly, had I? She was *jumping-the-gun* . . . Well, never mind. It's all right to be scared. It's even all right to run away . . . I started to do up my pants—even back then, I was tired of fake, pathetic moralists. I say that out loud, bookishly: "I'm tired of fake, pathetic moralists," in the inner, dry rattle and inner unitariness of longing for orgasm—you know? But I'm telling her to go to hell: I don't feel *guilty*. I don't feel I owe her my life from now on. Or any masculine-slavery-to-principle-for-her-sake, either . . . Then I said, "No. You wouldn't marry *me*." She made a face. "You wouldn't either—unless it was a good thing socially." Hell, she was a friend of *Nonie's*, wasn't she?

"You're a bastard," she said idly—in these knowingly bandit reaches of our *little get-together*.

"I was saying you were a *nice* person . . . too *nice* to do that stuff for *me*." I pinched her behind: I didn't want to seem to be *angelic*.

She bit my ear. "You're terrible," she said.

"You don't want *me*," I said—it started out okay but it went fast into another mood—a mode: sincerity in the bandit territories? It's kind of a *terrorist* moment: back then, the word was German, from Hitler's panzer tactics: *Schrecklichkeit*—the infliction of terror through being terrible.

But here the terrible thing—the slash with an old-fashioned beheading sword—the whistle of the descending bomb—was the honesty, or, if you like, the sudden sincerity—of a boy, sure, but of me, a specific guy: a voice stripped of generality. So, *slash, slash* . . .

Faint pause. Breath. You know how the sound of a girl's breathing can be like the drip, drip, drip of blood? "You want me to feel sorry for you?" she said, and she laughed dryly and sort of idly almost patted my dick which was mostly back in my pants which I hadn't fully fastened but had, with a certain loony style, left partly undone—*insultingly*.

I did and didn't know what I was doing. I knew what was going on in the sense that I had a very good sense of the history of the last several moments and then of larger blotches and splotches and splashes of time and then all the way back to my opening the front door for her and Nonie when they arrived at the house. The apartment.

But I knew it within the framework, the limitations of what I knew at that age plus—if you will forgive me—the sexual inspiration—or even inspirations—of the moment.

This is a kind of trumpery assurance.

But, still, it *is* assurance and it has the glamour of sequins and glittery stuff and black paint: semi-knowledgeability.

She *stared* at me.

I said in a really gravelly and grown-up voice—it, uh, thrilled me to hear anything so real and old coming out of me—"I'm no good. I am not *a regular guy*. People would laugh at you." Then: "Stop making me feel like an asshole, okay?"

She gazes at me in a way that shows that beyond the shit she is a little like me. I am an orphan who joined a circus but most of the people in the circus are ghosts—are ideas. She is sort of a runaway soul of that type, too. But as a girl of that type.

She said, in a funny voice, *"Do you want to finish, Wiley?"*

She wants me to say no—to snub her. She half *respects* me—you know what I mean?

I stroke the back of her hand—coolly, a little madly—"Do it some more," I say, not as someone bribed, or like a kid, or in any way that's possible, but as if I were sitting on a stool and was really handsome and huge-pricked—and was laughing at her. I wasn't clear in my head about those things—those *details*—of the scene: I felt I was like a truly *great* bomber pilot—or fighter pilot—or outfielder—or a truly great, great quarterback.

I didn't really think I would get away with it.

Which of us is the madder? The meaner? How could we characterize what we would feel or do next?

The *runaway soul* goes groping—and plunging—flying and lying —and trying—and dying . . .

"Oh, I'm not afraid of people," she says; i.e., she is attracted by the nature of my soul, which she now, sort of as if *finally* for the moment, for the occasion, sees: I feel strained and sweaty and like I've been acting this part, posing or whatever—for her liking me this way which has in it a quota, a modicum, a soupçon of sexual *respect*. See: watch: she is reaching nicely for the prick . . .

Hot shit.

"OH . . ."

She wants access to my soul: she talks: she runs this exchange: "I'm a hateful person—very shallow. My mother says I'll change when I have children . . . You're very young, but I'm shallow." It is insulting—and noble—in a world of insult and of ignobility.

I wanted something else.

She insulted us both in that she meant: *You don't really matter yet—and I don't matter as your girlfriend.*

She was omniscient and stupid now. I SAW IT.

"My *eyes* hurt!" I was too angrily potent in my *pain* (and it was a complex and compound pain) not to say, "Nothing has happened to *me* yet!"

She bounded a little in place as if struck by an arrow or a flaming coal.

"Should I go faster? Show me . . . Show me what to do . . ." My complaints didn't make her *sexual*—they made her nervous—and pliable.

"Is there a Kleenex around?" I asked . . . wearily . . . an as-if-sophisticated kid (of the sort my cousin Isobel admired: I wasn't that sort, even in the slightest).

"Everything has happened to me today," she said. "I had an attack of allergy . . . I used my Kleenex up." It was scarce anyway. She got hers from the PX. "Use the inside of my coat sleeve . . ." Her jacket on another chair.

"Okeydokey," I said, nuttily giving up all my feelings and my rank: *God knows why* . . . It was her having a runny nose all day. "I really like health," I say out loud, getting up, holding my partly fastened pants with one hand. "My sick parents and all . . ." I am partly back into my role—my rank. The hand I'm playing. It is *all* eerily jocular . . . a comedy with sexual music.

"Show me," she said as I returned to the couch. Then: "Think of me 'n . . ." Think of her while I showed her? I asked her with my face, with my eyebrows, what she meant. "Keep it romantic," she said—as if from an inferior position.

I shook my head no.

She pursed her lips. "Show me," she said.

I showed her.

By the way, if Nonie said of a boy that he had *a ghetto look,* she meant he would be unfair to women.

Leonie would sleep with Nonie that night in a double bed.

"Here." I put her hand on me and, holding her wrist, set the rhythm . . .

It hurt at first . . . Then the light started up but rawly and kind of selflessly, the way it does when you've already come once. Then all at once I was horrified. Why? I had no power to withstand the *horror* or the reality or to comprehend it: I had no comprehension at all and I had acres, a whole ranchful of will—fanciful will? Kind of. But realistic, too.

The lust maybe, the burning actuality of lust, the boyishly shocked exercise moving toward satisfaction . . . me being bossy and yet being more and more tied down, more and more vulnerable, to the slash-flash of lighted sensation—the magnesium flare . . . "The bouncing balls," I said: in the movies, sometimes they had short films with songs you sang: you followed the bouncing ball. The absence of unhappiness is incomplete . . . The incomplete absence of unhappiness is a queer state. A practical one, I guess. Leonie and I for now *disliked* each other, but it was affectionate—kind of—and we pretended we didn't dislike each other but the pretense didn't go deep . . . But we, er, had *a lot of respect for each other* . . . Or maybe not. The pain and thwartings and the half-love and the indifference—and the passion behind the indifference—and the real burningness of the pain—the weird toppling-icity of *feeling good* . . . "FEELING GOOD, GEELING FOOD, FEELING BETTER . . ." How do people stand it? I didn't know at that time, at that moment, if I would survive that stuff or not.

Nonie is in the hall—a strange presence—I feel her suddenly. She can't see us: maybe she is listening to us. Did you ever feel that putting your clothes to rights was like a sarcastic speech or a poem of mockery of someone? I mean, if I got us, Leonie and me, ready for Nonie's entry, who would be mocked? I felt guilty-as-hell—really as if I represented hell and hellfire and a lurid light in the living room—or as if I had come from hell and smelled of inward screams—of pain, of rage—but, fuck it, I didn't care. I felt a big *So what?* Now, though, writing this, I ask, what could she hear or understand?

Leonie is laughing. I am more fastened than before but still not entirely.

And I am full of damning her . . . Of a kind of nudity of defiance—not as the visiting lieutenant from hell but as someone *entirely* innocent—compared to her.

It is a ruse. I never felt *entirely* innocent in my life except under questioning as a device to get through the period of being questioned.

Nonie says, entering the dim, now slightly smelly room, although the windows are open, "How are you two coming along?"

That dried up Leonie's jollity or embarrassment. I grew both stern and lyrical—you know? Nonie had a sense of humor; it showed at times: you couldn't be sure when she was joking and when she was being insensitive—or dumb. As I said, my pants were mostly fastened: she took a good sighting; she checked them out. I was real to her—that is what is *hardest* for me to admit: the other ghost book that she wrote about herself being there, and me on the couch with Leonie. Leonie knew that book better than she knew anything at all about me.

With Nonie in the room, very little in Leonie has to do with me —it is all carom shots and rebounds, reactions . . .

She gets up and pats my hair and moves to a chair and puts her legs over the arm of the chair and she addresses her attention to Nonie. I start to laugh under my breath—then I can't stop . . . I am unwell . . .

Something I left out from earlier when my dick was in the open air: I said, "Now-now . . ." It could have meant Now? Now? or Now, now, laughingly, don't do that but do it, or Oh my God, now it's real—do you see? After I said that, Leonie said, "You have a funny face." Aw. Oh. Ow. Not now. Now now, I said. "Are you being a good boy?" Leonie asked. I said, "My mother and father have said that to me and I never know what it means." She said, "I feel—I'm talking to you—I'm kissing you—when I do this to your *thing* . . ." I said, "I feel—but I don't want to tell you this—I feel that you are taking my picture . . ." Then I look at her, I hear her intent breathing: I say, ". . . our picture . . ."

"IT TAKES SO MUCH ENERGY TO BE ALIVE I DON'T THINK I CAN STAY AWAKE ANOTHER *MINUTE*." Nonie says this.

"Why not just die and get it over with?" Leonie says in a grown-up way, lighting a Lucky Strike from the big lighter that Nonie hands her.

They talk this way at the office. The office—and the war—get them down.

A *flash*, a *flare* of MEMORY: My hand crawls onto the back of her neck. My hand (the other one) crawls onto her butt—her buttocks. Beautiful semi-hard—tense—sloppy—there, and sweaty—sweatily present—

power and helplessness—

"I wish we had instructions for things written on our bodies," I said earlier and saw (in the third person almost but also felt it in immediacy) and heard it now . . . Ooooh shit, the pain, the pang, the SHOOTS *OF WILD MATTER OF LOST SENSATION RETURNED* . . . in a way . . . hallucinatorily, historically . . . without rhythmic force . . .

Shit . . .

Well, it doesn't matter.

It does though.

*

It was frightening to have been born of her, of Leonie, *as a man*; and then to have her turn to Nonie, and Nonie being so much more important to her than I was: frightening and truly painful—even though the pain had been foreseen. The ballooning of it, the shifting of the ground of one's being until one is in what is at first a sharp, semi-silly pain, then into more pain—that is, it isn't trivial (to the boy); he is in the pain continuum—he is on the other side of the living border of life as a history, more or less, of more or less pain . . . He sees things grayly. It may very well be minor: he may go crazy . . . this pain—the shifting as of smoke of its curling patterns, the shifting-around shittiness of the pain of being in their hands—in terms of pain—and ultimately in Nonie's hands, as a human matter, as the given order of things in this moment —the thing of being born by her, Leonie, and, so, by them, Leonie-and-Nonie, *as a man*, and then the rhythms, hidden or overt, of them in their lives, the *hidden* reality of their moods, the bodies, sexual realities in the room at the moment, mine, too, my sexual reality for them, the reality of my life—of my *spirit* . . . the muscles of my hands . . . my arms . . . my legs . . . the birdlike flutter of ideas around my head and in their talk . . . I button my shirt. I whistle under my breath: that's as if to say they bore me—those two. Those two mothers . . . *I will not let them see my pain* . . . Fuck them . . . Do I cause *them* pain? Have I given birth to them in their moments now? To the sense of *inferiority* in each one of them—and to the sense of compensation—of them managing themselves and their lives—and what I have caused them to feel . . . I smile and whistle Beethoven, from one of the late quartets—music that is over their heads, maybe, maybe not—Nonie is at times profoundly musical: she likes Brahms and early Stravinsky . . . Meanwhile, the pain ebbs and flows and floods in me—vile cramps . . . Burning bile in me . . . I am in the neighborhood of *hell* . . . Hell-and-death . . . I know why pilots paint devils on their planes . . . Or why some troops, the Scots for instance, call themselves *The Ladies from Hell* . . . The mad unobstinacy of battle when it has gone on so long no one can stay sane—no one . . . The few surviving nearly sane judges are two-eyed and everyone else is blinded—more or less. It is foolish to keep on being torn . . . By battle. By women—the Harpies—mad goddesses . . . It is stupid to go on being born into being *a man* . . . But what can you do? I want it. In the departure of sexual light and in its replacement, trainingly, purposefully—unknowably—by a kind of gentlemanly, adolescent *exhibitionism*, and then by a somewhat slyer shyness—slyer than the *ex-*

hibitionism and less friendly—in this is wartime *survival* and *obstinate* malice (a common thing) and hellishness.

But malice mixed resentfully with *forgiveness*, with an acceptance of things, *of life*, one's being *a sport*, a *good sport*—ah, you know this evokes love, even among those hell-bent on constraining you and your influence and your powers.

Perhaps one remembers Nonie saying, *I don't know about you but I am happy* . . . Or perhaps she said that because you had done it to her when you were little, and that was quite a weapon. If *X* is happy, is Y visited by envious recollections of bits of lost *happiness*? Or by a sense of X's happiness as being beyond Y's luck? His—or *her*—possibilities? "This is all so so-to-speak. I'm going to bed," the boy says—i.e., watching them, being in the presence of their hips and eyes and hair is no pleasure—isn't pleasure enough.

I am destroyed. And I am made of fragmentary recollections of *grace*—this is in a bile-ridden, torturingly regretful way. But I am *ONE HELL OF A GOOD SPORT* . . . No: I am it quietly: one hell of a good sport . . . And I get up quietly—and stretch—male, a male creature, tall, skinny, young—you know? Not entirely fastened. Or buttoned. It is as if I wear laborers' *overalls* in A State of (Masculine, Endurance-riddled) Grace for a while . . .

Kind of . . .

And they—the two middle-class *girls*—are punished in a way . . .

But I am *innocent* of punishing them—practically speaking . . .

How do you set the value of one moment? In a story or in life?

Do you consciously choose one moment and exalt it? By the choice of it for the role of measure and example or of watershed? Are you skeptical and ruthless as some kids are with their air of a shadowy and squinting *Here we are* . . . *What are YOU going to do?* I mean, in the moments.

"It's okay," I said to Leonie with a half-smile in the darkness of the back hall. It is hard to admit how unforgivingly I forgive people. Leonie is spending the night, Leonie in her bathrobe, me in mine—a hand-me-down from a cousin . . . My face is bent backward out of her reach . . . A smile boyishly recopying the incomplete momentum of earlier . . . an uneasy, unevenly partial momentum, forgiveness, dismissal—a persistent lifeliness: I pinch her butt through the robe—trying for humanity . . .

She looks at me with angry, jocular, pitying feeling: with a twisted affection . . . I have failed her. She is older and differently forgiving from me—*very* forgiving . . . I am pretty sure she is lying . . .

In the darkness in the hall:

"It was perfect . . . you're just PERFECT," she says with a sort of touchingly smart-assed enthusiasm, almost a well-judged kindness.

Leonie had a slow, half-bored, kind of sick tonguing system of kissing sometimes. Why not forget that? My tongue moves reminiscently in my mouth. When I speak, the speech is blurred although I try for exact enunciation—unexpected at my age: "No, *you're* perfect . . . ." Then: "I'd say everything was perfect but what purpose would that lie serve?" I said this, using my *intellectual potential*—to put her in the category of momentary things. Her face brightens and darkens *oddly*. "Anyway, I have to get my sleep—I'm in training . . ."

"You don't need any more training," she said.

I shake my head wearily—delightedly—like some seventeen-year-old boys at school, the better athletes . . . I am being *old for my age . . . You can't catch me that way* is part of what that gesture of the head means. I am bare-legged, long-legged. I move past her in the hallway and feel the sting of her watching me and waiting for yet more evidence of what I am as someone she did not sleep with.

I feel this with all the nerves of my back—perhaps with all my heart and all my soul such as they are.

Leonie in memory does not speak in real words but in rather precise, almost enclosed speeches, suddenly heard with a clarity unlike anything during the actual hearing: "It's a snafu—a real fuck-up—we're a real pair of real fuck-ups . . ."

She talked sort of accidentally; she slid and skidded in speech and sort of fell into what she was saying—I saw it now.

"You don't love me—you're excitable in a nice way." Her wolf eyes shone with her accepting what she said: devourer's eyes she had . . . Moral disorderliness . . . The reality of the tiny street or sheath of air—sweat-flecked (on eyelashes) between us, warmed, spiky, shiftingly curtained *friendliness* . . . "I shouldn't do this . . ."

I wish memories of her would leave me alone but they erect me and tug at my skin and shoulders and eyes . . . *I guess you're going to be my torment of the month* . . . The prick ticked, moved against her upper leg, tickingly.

Memory is a hot-lantern thing, spilling burning, sticky stuff on you . . .

"Go to hell," I said, maybe only in an amendment of reality: the memory is emended, edited . . . Too much feeling ruins things . . . *I wish you were easygoing as a person* . . . I see that. I wish you were.

Borrrrrrrrrrrrrrrrr-ingggggggggggggggggggg.

"Leonie knows what's what: I hope you didn't let your feelings get out of hand . . ." Nonie, able-willed in the flicker of the seconds, speaks . . . Or Nonie in a premenstrual fit pointing her finger at me screams: I DON'T WANT HIM TO SLEEP. I DON'T WANT HIM TO GO TO SCHOOL. EVERYONE OUGHT TO HATE HIM. HE'S A TERRIBLE PERSON . . .

What happens if she doesn't calm down?

Oh, don't be LOGICAL *now—just help me: I have all I can handle as it is* . . .

Nonie feels contempt for things and remains herself and is unseduced . . . Lila said, *Nonie wants her chance to live—it's her turn—I don't blame her* . . . The contempt Nonie felt for her looks as she got older led to her saying: *People are fooled by me, ha-ha* . . . She could not breathe. Nonie said she had no regrets of any sort ever—*I'm a good person; I don't have regrets* . . . Whenever I said I was sad about the past, or things now, she said harshly, *I don't have those feelings; you're a fool—you're crazy—you're a crazy person—everyone knows you're crazy, ugly in the ways you act, ugly and crazy—people hope you die, they'd like it if you were dead* . . . Reality has a kind of stink to it. How much harm does Nonie intend as an average, respectable, morally harmless thing?

In bathroom mirrors at home and at school, the face is older—with a faintly abraded mouth, worn-out, reddened eyes . . . A woundedness . . . Leonie is in one's mind: the afterwards like a pitch, a tar stuck to one's feet in summer, the impersistencies and the insistent recurrences of sexual memory: nothing consecutive—nothing exact. The extent of the loss and the extent of presence is maddening. One is nude in bed but is on the living-room couch but is suddenly the site of vanished sexual recollection: the *stuff with Leonie* . . . Then one is in class, in class after class, *obscene boy with a familied look of clean clothes*: his eyes are marked up and smeared: I am marked up and smeared, long-boned, achingly *obscene* . . . long-eyelashed Middle Western American boy's obscene and tremendously fragmented recall. I misheard her, surely: "Your veins are people—" Oh it's purple—purple—purple— Royal? Bruised? Twilit—like the sea in Homer—the teacher was talking about Homer: I half heard her say some of it: four-bagger. I sharply tumble—or dive—into slanted flickings of heated recurrence of sensation—flicks of mental flukes, sexual memory: *"I think* YOU'RE *French . . ."* Or something like that. *You know what? I'll get into trouble if you don't keep your sense of humor* . . . God, what a complicated idea. *Wiley—Wiley—Wiley-dear—Wiley—OOPS-EE-DOOPS* . . . The music of sexuality as nonsense that wartime year of jive talk? *In real life, I don't know who loves me and who does not . . . who laughs at me and who doesn't . . .*

Maybe you're a weak person . . .

Eyes, balls, head of the dong, stomach, and brain hurt—I have sad, dumb, dreary staring eyes—and a girl named Sally Brown who is pretty and pale and who has big breasts suddenly starts liking me that day and I am fatally jumpy and odd: she cries . . . Many-eyed, I consider the hurt Sally and Leonie's minor necking-orgasms . . . pre-orgasms . . . my own dribbling some . . . Facts of life: plumbing the depths: suffocation: death: escape. And the return of excited terror. *I presume. I presume.* To a certain common order of infatuation and a leftover heat . . .

If I try to imagine myself Nonie, oh my God, how much more vivid but scattered is her sense of the war than mine was; how much more intelligently and vividly she looks at other women; how sharp and active and actual are the envy and contempt and warmth-and-coldness in my breast . . . in *my breasts* . . . how strong I am . . . I move *solidly* (and deep inside horrifiedly) among *the thought* of sweet girls, of sweet young women, shy, willful, pretty-haired, as a thing in me separate from their presence even when they are present—ah, how tragically warm I am—how close to care-torn. Deeply felt invective, hysteria: *the contented bitches . . . Girls . . .*

How free of observation I am if I am masked as Nonie is. The feeling of angry risk and nobility in me, no one had better thwart it—better not . . . A shadow but real, I have a kind of slick proud sense of my body —and its movements, a sense of privacy—like being inside a fur coat. The feet, the ankles, the girlish womanliness: the boyishness: the greed: the plotting sociability—the intense silvery-shadowy *sweetness*—of—my be*cunted* physical reality . . . I think I remember this.

Myself, as Nonie. When I am her, my fear of someone else's reality and ambitions—as real people—I have a recklessness in me of opposition—as if at the approach of horsemen—those *Mongols*, those *barbarians*—and then the unembarrassed, uninhibited thing of the practice of bravery: my ambition explodes outward, explodes inward, too, omnisciently, ubiquitously . . . I am a fighter like her, ruled by chance events, strategic audacity and the like. I pray. I have courage. I am pretty.

Nonie says, "I expect to be present at *the end of the world . . .*"

*

When I oppose my full will, my full presence, as tyrant-dreamer to Leonie or to anything, I become, essentially, an enclosing universe in which only one mind remembers. Only one mind moves the elements of destiny.

I can remember presenting myself to girls in my head as hard wish and then as sweet wish and as madness and even in my own head, as part of the hallucinatory parleying with this power, being turned down and my suffering then and the further suffering that the suffering was real and went on and lasted. I have a real and defective life now.

The landscape, crushed and vaginally centered, of the boy's new, ill-informed sexual sensibility has a weird hot, even burning light. A sense of girls in a flurry of transgressions brings on a faint sweat and then a contradictory coolness: rebellious delectation . . . In an odd moment of one's personal history. I closed down parts of myself—so that they wouldn't burn—closed down so many I saw chastity as a device to improve one's intellect because one would have more of one's mind at one's disposal . . . One was like a warship this way, with closed bulkheads, with sexuality continuing illegally in me . . . a heavy milk-water of unwanted memory, snakelike lengths of current . . . I choke . . . My shoulders and my butt *embarrass* me. Lonely, brute, true ground. An ordinary day of indifferent madness—of moments of the fire-torn nausea of sexual recall—*sexy boy*, Sally Brown said—it requires some technique to get through it.

Still, much of me is enfolded, budded—power, of amusement, of *prettiness* tightly hidden . . . of the insobriety of sex which could not be *known* except by living it—so that much of what went on, much of what went on between people might have occasions, might have reality, but might not have a name.

THE

END MUSIC

Remsen

I am in Remsen's bedroom with Remsen. Outside the windows (of one wall) two Lombardy poplars utter their green exclamations at the boundary of a good-sized suburban backyard; and one sees the red tiled roof of a three-car garage; while outside the windows of another wall, a well-trimmed privet hedge separates a side yard from the tar-paved aisle of the St. Louis street, practicing some tactic or other of recession under a sky in which the moving clouds, very fat, King Cole–ish and very white, seem to be seated above a city of low-lying buildings which moves faintly in a shadow-tinted procession, roof by roof, in a queerly powdery light of considerable beauty before the seated and reviewing and as-if-overfed and stupendous and sovereign vapors in the air.

I do not know why, to my eyes, the cloud shadows are still and the street and the roofs seem to float to the east. Or why, from the cloud-occupied reviewing stand above the house, light descends to surround the house I am in with Remsen with cloudless and unchanging near-brilliance.

Remsen has pale blue eyes, brightish-colored lips—rosy and curly—to go with his thick and tousled, very dark hair. A tousled soul? Suburban-Byronic?

And then a look—more than a look, the somewhat startling young man's reality of what is to me an almost searing athleticism: he is so powerfully shaped and so tall—and so young—seventeen—that remembering it I am restless, whereas at the time it seemed heated of him but not disturbing: the gym-inflected physical proportions: the physical smartness—the thick, pulsing neck, the adolescent but wide chest, the big (or biggish) arms: the youthful thick and new hairness of him—a precocity of physical existence.

He is precocious, too, in his reading, his scholarship, his schooled mind. Above the abysses of the physical and intellectual self—sensations, recognitions, outcries—moves the rather fancy raft of willful measurement—the vanity here is restrained by a sense of scientific measurement: I get better grades; X has larger arms. Y is handsomer.

It is as if he has a seagoing nature—or a seagoing mathematical code of reality, of danger and courage, and a seagoing mathematical version of himself that he has grown into—legs and mouth, tousled hair, all of him—and so his vanity, a psychological thing, and his ambition, which is a given but which is riddled in his case with large, rotten sports of surrender, have to do with being seaworthy.

But the eyes, a spiritual thing—uncorrupt and not like my eyes—his considerable, warmly frozen good looks—*it (he)* is entirely isolated: only a single ship moves on his ocean except for fragments from a shipwreck, fragments, measurements . . .

Careful, willful—not discreetly restrained—not entirely effective on dry land or even on his solitary sea—he is not considered *attractive* in spite of the above, in spite of his parents having money: he is standoffish—well, to extend the image, he sails in his solitary way, and he is shy, even recessive, but a captain of the ship, spoiled, assertive, abruptly unshy, demanding, demandingly talkative, too talkative, too bold, too conceited, too assertive—a spoiled child hotly enclosed in the freezing clasp of demons—stumbling on the pile of new money (up *from the slums*: Lila said)—he is so difficult, so deeply mooded that only I like him. The measurement thing in him—it is like a menu (or some other list) which, if he courts you—me, I mean to say—he casually tosses it down in front of me and I can choose, wisely to know him, foolishly to escape him—that is what his courtship seems like or that is what enters my mind when he courts me.

A late-in-adolescence masculine self that is not me and, furthermore, which has grown in milieus and locales and sites unlike those I have known, and which is physically differently placed and socially and economically.

The mind, the Marxism (of that era in a smart seventeen-year-old mind: he was two years older than I was), the Freudianism—he had three sessions with a refugee analyst—a rigid (rigidly programmatic) mind doctor, physically repellent and yet a man assured of his ultimate charm and his power over your imagination and my extraordinarily alone, vain friend: this other doctor that he'd had since he was thirteen he used as an example of error in regard to Freudian doctrine and to neurological science (in 1944), and the surviving (and worsened) American vanity, the spirit of rivalry, the sense of *pain* in him—he was an unhappy young man. The almost incredible extent to which he was spoiled, self-deferential, closed off, and full of longing—the extent of his knowledge of the world and his absence from it even while he was wrestling in it—he was a wrestler, mountain climber, restless athlete of an irregular sort: contemptuous of *it* (the reality of himself as an athlete or of athleticism or of the world: almost a tantrum of seeing *it all* as *a joke*)—his only admitted current inferiority being to the corruption of the school and of grades—that is, his moral superiority—his pride was such that one cannot call it *Luciferian* so much as a sort of totality—the pride of an absolutist: the four corners of the universe are in it in a carpentry of willful comprehension but not entirely true.

His comprehension proved its accuracy in terms of the navigation on the sea on which he was the only ship, the only captain, a sea he had brought into being by some sort of demand his existence made on reality; this accuracy of placement worked directly in regard to the *utter* corruption of anything that would argue any falsity in the setup of his totality.

I mean, imagine the *contempt* in which he held anything that was part of an un-Freudian capitalism.

He has *a brain*, Remsen—it is inaccurately placed (although he thinks he has navigated accurately) and it is tossed up and down. Remsen is, actually, a superior sort: a lonely, agonized, very handsome and somewhat appalling-looking creature, of phenomenal shyness, superior ability, and wry, ruthless and cold and nervous awareness, alternately half-panicked and sublimely superior, grimly amused in his superiority.

He is coldly aware that his looks are arbitrary and not entirely successful, but he does not quite believe it all the time: that alternates with periods of daydreaming in which he is wistfully and coldly, oddly, full of longing for Utopian sex and *perfect* good times and *perfect* looks and so on, all of which, somehow, he believes are possible here on earth, for lucky people.

That daydreaming coincides, in peculiar *symbiosis* (one of his favorite words), with hallucination-tinged periods of strenuously physical practicality—trips and treks or gym stuff, wrestling meets, and the like. His physical strength and his being rich don't make him humble: perhaps they exist in some irregularity and in terms of comparisons. In courtship, he is very humble, pleased to want something, perhaps, and perhaps, then, even a little crawly-crawly and defiant—or deviant—it's odd . . .

And then he's given to ownership claims and to quick retreats from that: he owns your attention—and then he is sarcastic and produces sort of would-be withering *critiques* of your (and others') capacity for friendship and he does oddly cold betrayals of you—he walks by you even though you say hello—but more frequently these are betrayals of himself, since he is the only ship on the sea . . .

He does not talk seriously. He and I have '*intelligent* talks' but not '*serious* talks'—he has an elaborate code in these matters, some of it from his reading, some from his analysis, from his thinking about how things ought to be, Utopianly or, at least, under circumstances in which he is *happy*, or happy enough.

Grinning, his handsome eyes curiously alight, oblique, or slanted with a kind of observance—of masculinity and of you and of himself, of his pulse, and of the pulse of the moment as it moves in the curious ways time does move—he says *lightly*—it is a matter of attitude, clearly—that we are not homosexual and that we do not fiddle with anything homosexual . . . This seems arbitrary and a matter of naming, but it is also true in another sense in that it sets the pitch for feelings.

But if you do not have some sense of male attachment as *romantic* and you go off without regard to *jealousy*, say, or to someone's, his need to see you, then he becomes enraged, pitiable, and lonely. He comes to you in the lunchroom and tells you of his betrayals of you—with a doctor or with someone you never heard of: a temporary friend to upset you: a betrayal you never noticed; I hadn't known that our friendship, his and mine, extended that far; then he flashes with feeling, his eyes take on a burning glow, almost a reddish illumination—a smouldering—and his mouth glitters—not just the teeth between the savagely healthy lips but the curls of the lips themselves in a sort of salivary thing that perhaps, if you are older, suggests what he will like when he is older if he lives; and he flushes, a reddening of himself, a confession of a sort; and, in real life, a passage of glamour—he is betrayed by it—by life, into life. He has access to a handsome car; you go out in it with false ID and go to a rough bar where there are whores, something like that—and feeling, and feelings roil and boom; and you discuss them with him—intelligently but not seriously . . .

He is a good friend and a fine companion—at times (when he feels like it or when the spirit moves him—or when I have seduced him or elicited it), or it is for long stretches of time because it is a fashion among intellectuals in wartime, or his mind doctor is influenced by that and feels that is good, and Remsen fills with that; the doctor eggs him on to be a good guy with me. Or his parents love him in such a way that he cares for me—or 'loves' me openly—or one of his parents does it, or eggs him on. Remsen is unmusical, unaffectionate, essentially untalented but very intelligent, a sad boy whose grief is concentrated on himself in a form of, I think, depressive rage, not a diagnosis I would have made back then or known how to make, but I had a sense of him that I say now was of someone self-autopsied—a little as if a tulip could tear itself apart in a spiritual wind.

If I take simple terms—again, not terms I commonly used when I was young, but terms such as *ambition* and *love* and *the infant discovery of the world* and *the child's discovery of language and of human hours* and of *the course of light*—I feel in him a vastness—well, let me avoid the image of the sea and use the actual river and a boy there, grieving over a father, but not the father's death so much as the father's reality—and the reality of the father's life—and let me place this in the varied onrushes, flowerings and flowings, exfoliations, acrobatic swirls and tricks of time, in the universal restlessness, the unending motion, himself made of related motions, cousin motions—this other male self, perhaps of mine—since perhaps I only imagine I see him—the vastness or completeness of things, certain things—birth, say, or the restlessness of an hour as it shudders, shimmers, glides, flaps its wings, alights, crawls, scurries and scutters—the unending curved (like a wing) universe of an hour stretching here, there, to Saturn, to the Milky Way, to night on the other side of the globe—this is attached to the self, like fingers, the bone-length and tendon-sewn and muscle-inflected and skin-wrapped fingers of the mysteriously childlike, then boylike hand—but to the mind as an absolute idea, an idea of absolute things, including the self, so that, in a sense, one feels the universe, the entire truth murmuring in one—as if *time*, all unknown to oneself, were God—or this is known but denied since it cannot be controlled.

And the effort to control this—to bring this under the rule of one's moods, as one's moods constrain the feelings and attentions of one's parents, one's nurse, one's self, and under the rule of one's logic, as one's logic constrains the mechanisms and comprehensions of things, and under the rule of one's prayers as one's prayers, and wishes and dreams, constrain and control the attention of the all, of the great curved, brooding, onrushing universe—brings him to such games as, like Jass's—or Nonie's—or like mine but differently—try to effect the conquest of this last finality of entirety: to emerge from and to fly, despite the contradiction of having motion in the midst of motionlessness—it is not logic now for him, it is mooded prayer and he is the solitary pray-er, the captain of address to meaning—to fly in timelessness which he controls and in which, to use a term I would hardly have used *back* then, down the corridors of time, or along the river, or through the interlaced and superimposed tulips and cups of various now's to then, he rides and overrides and cancels by a personal motionlessness, a contradictory rage of stillness, like a child's stubbornness, a writing-of-reality—so that he is a very, very handsome suicidal depressive—in a tantrum of God-defiance, time-hatred, often barely able to find a reason to go on with things, to go on, to continue to live in the rush and bumble and buzz and self-willed, other-willed relentlessness of motions of time.

But his mind is like an octopus of hands, some of them as vast as the river, and some of them articulated like skeletons with theory, and all them driven by will to grasp this and that—as if in a fairy tale or in an audiovisual film at school of nature lore—but not exactly theoretically but in accordance with birth-and-identity—his, of course—and his flowering flight toward death, with the narrow personal meaning seen as a true width taken as the first term, the plane of argument, so he is holding a great many workable ideas, almost truths—sexuality, for instance, and historical, or dialectical, analysis, Marxist notions of justice and of social class, a Freudian sense of personal reality—but everything is distorted by his personal existence, by the infant ambition, tantrum, trauma of pursuing limitlessness in an actual light.

Now, it is understood—as it was then—that to spend so much time on description, to expend words and thoughts in such drawn-out and complex metaphors means you love someone. His attempt to command truth and to make *time* be obedient—the powers of the will seem to be elements more of a science than of any practice of wizardry nowadays—ends in his being able to manage me, my feelings: he can seduce me somewhat; he can command my love—not endlessly or timelessly or even tirelessly, but often and recurringly—it is unlikely that this can take the place of the command of the universe but it does sometimes . . . which is to say, you see, that he, in a way, loved me.

In a way.

This stuff, these things—this that I have spoken about, these elements of the mind and these bent-back corners of the real world—are vaguely curative, temporarily, are therapeutic—life preservers . . .

But I think we all knew that when we were adolescent. To him, with his cast of mind—him as an intellectual creation partly of absolute language, of a sense of language locally permitted—him in his inevitable sense of failure in regard to time, real time with a witness, ideas that interest him also sadden him, they excite him—a depressive—with a sense of happy ending, of final power; and they are interesting in themselves—works of genius—and, then, bewilderingly, bitterly regarded toys, items of furniture of a nursery of a world—I don't remember the phrases common among people like us for such things then except the slighting ones: *too brainy for his own good . . . moody, very smart . . . not an easygoing, happy person . . .*

But my father was in that last category and he was not easygoing or particularly happy: he was in motion toward and around and above and below those things: they were each an axis, each a summit, a lawn, sunlit or dark: I *always* felt he had chosen that category. And then I felt that elements of the category, *naturally*, had chosen him, had exerted their wills, their rules: the earthen gravity had caught him now and then.

Because of my father's manner of speech, and because of lawns and backyards back then, I had mixed in my mind—a little like photographs of paintings of the three Graces, or like an erotic notion of the Muses—the words *suckle* and *sucker* and *honeysuckle* . . . Folly or error, nourishment, and the mad, and maddening, vine of God and its intoxicating scent enticing you to breed.

I remember Remsen's bitter dependence on a kind of kindness to an infant, a suckling element—or a merchandising one—in such ideas as the ones he admired: *But that's just because it makes you feel good,* I would say; and he would say, *This idea is pure torture, Wiley—I am tortured by it*—and I would say, *Oh you just want to win the argument; you don't care [if] what you're saying is true or not.*

And in the books he read, he pursued this sucker's comfort—often, he entered onto a kind of swindler's pact with the writers or philosophers: he would cheat as they did, merchandise comfort (and command of the universe) as they did. What was so different about him was that, unlike Jass, a Protestant, and me, adopted and all that shit, he never was puritan: hardworking but not puritan. This part of him—comforted, in part, seductively comforting—as a swindle—but in a pact—the ideas of *greatness*—and of sexy indulgence now—as if sex were separate from time and death—like our odd, or very odd friendship—or half-and-half on again, off again love affair—not homosexual but a bit on the freed side—this part of him was utterly extraordinary to me—even if suddenly at times it grew stale for me, and when it seemed *familiar* and boring when he passed out of reach and when the whole thing, him, his mind, his looks, his will, his theories, his affection, all of it seemed unworkable then, so that one felt him as *suicidal* even if one didn't put that name on it or use that word much, if at all, except in jokes.

The menu—the program—he offered (of comfort, of comfort withdrawn, of cruelty, of obedience, of mockery, and so on) is that which someone might offer who had the curious exoticism of his background in that he grew up in a slum and had very handsome parents whose sexual and social reality was never particularly real to him—he never saw himself as an appendage of their lives, or them as foliage rustling with time and being rushed onward by time and rushing further, by their will, into and through time—he had then lived in a semi-slum and then his parents became 'rich' and moved here, to the suburbs—to University City. He still goes back from time to time to the slum and the semi-slum to visit people: perhaps he reroots himself—he goes back—he has mentioned it but he hasn't described it to me—he has no intellectual or emotional gift for description—he keeps too tight a grip on his sense of his possible off-again, on-again command of the universe—he doesn't tell me about his trips back, but he gets sexy right after. From somewhere—in his past, in the slums, and from analysis now and his doctor, and from his reading, and from what he sees in school—he has a notion, an idea of actual love-and-friendship between men, something necessary, but something obscure to him—he is as eyeless as Samson in Gaza—he is something of a hero, he is partly a man (a young man)—sublimely strong, half-captured, sublimely dangerous—and subject to holy messages (so to speak)—and he had an idea of loneliness—alienation rethought and placed in a suburb—and of despair, *acedy*—modern and not necessarily Christian but firmly affixed to an idea of God's absence in some physical sense which involved there being just two of them, as on the river—or as in a dream—anyway, as I go rushing on—like me on my bike—among trees, in the perspective of the suburb's streets, under the vast, colossally beautiful, truly immense Middle Western sky—because of all this, intimacy was easily and piercingly possible with him—even on the phone—but more so in his presence and much more so if it was somewhere such as his own house or his father's car which he was allowed to use: if he owned it; if we were as if inside his head and he was wakefully thinking—dreaming us, permitting us, but allowing some independent will in the figures in the dream.

This intimacy was not contractual—or a matter of private sacrament. It was not intently conspiratorial, us against the world. It was not truly intense as in operas or staged readings of *Romeo and Juliet* or in books about boys at English private schools (called *public*) . . . But that may have been me.

Much of what I am is someone who is—and he partly knew this but he often forgot it or did not any longer notice—like a hunter or a scientist in a duck blind, interested in finding out what is true that is not me: what the ant does if the shadow of my head does not fall on it; or what happens in the woods if I am like a fallen and partly rotted tree trunk . . . I am interested in what in him I can command through my intelligence, my role(s) at school, my looks now, my social standing (such as it is), and my socio-sexual masculine-friendship wit—or wit in regard to those things—but I am also interested in the world behind the not entirely glass bell of my existence, beyond the glass smudged with my breath, or opaque with inscriptions or with hope and will; and I presume to a passivity of observation and to odd moments of presence in which I dream but dream myself into a kind of knittedness, or holes-in-it or holiness and trellislikeness of the skull so that real light, of the moment, and the natural light cast by the artificial light of the mind of the other, leafily and shade-spotted, enters where I am, in here.

But I often slip up—I slide not merely into jealousy and selfishness, self-will and private ambition, and not merely as a given or baseline, but I do it as conscious revenge on the other; and, often, I presume to ascribe to myself a too large amount of innocence because of the passivity, forgetting that one's reputation and one's physical existence—and not only that but one's physical existence *moment-by-moment*—that my time-riddled reality continues with all the traces and actualities of my will and of my purposes, even while being passive, being heartily present . . .

That is, I *religiously* (unrealistically, stubbornly, almost as a matter of principle) refuse to see myself as *temptation* and as eliciting behavior and truth (of a kind and limited) in that role.

So I am inclined to announce that Remsen had such-and-such a program of friendship, when I ought to pull myself up short and let me be my mind and heart where he is concerned and say I do not know of him caring for anyone as he did for me and that I persisted in ignoring that and taking it as ordinary, as ordinary neighborliness (of minds-in-school).

Again, so, if I leave abstraction to one side and remember his eyes in a specific moment when he was talking to me—lecturing me really —on friendship in a universe of absolute meaning—absolute meaning having no great interest in friendship—absolute meaning having great interest in love, in primacy, in jealousy, in the fate of the self (and of the universe), in supernal (superior?) love, and in revelation . . . "Friendship is secular and belongs to us," he said . . . He had a *perfectly* enormous vocabulary which he thought was an absolute vocabulary and, so, unless I was irritated or playing a game with him, I never used words in ways foreign to him, so far as I could tell, or words new to him or that referred to social and emotional realities he was, with his slum background and his present state of being monied and his analyst and his reading and his handsomeness, unfamiliar with . . . If I remember his eyes at such a moment—well, then I am hurled into a novel of such moments—of the variations on that theme—or that stuff moving onward in time because of him and his sisters and him and his parents and analyst and him at school and because of me, him at me, because of him observing *me*—because of what he learned, I mean—because of a whole, semi-vast story I choose to hint at.

So, it must be a *scene* and it must be a scene in which the one writing it is not too artificial in his use of time, or, if artificial, is truly brilliant, or inspired, or lyrical in the false (and editorial and amended) sense of time. That is, if we want him to be real. If we want him not to be animated statuary, mere symbol, only a fleshly flag—flesh-as-a-flag—OF *MY YOUTH*—if we want a picture of youth, male youth, with the truth in it, of more than one male will—not a multiplicity of gods, not insulting final meaning in that sense—but multiple gods anyway, his, mine, the different aspects of God, not only in what we thought but in what we embodied, the differently onrushing opacities of separate bags of time, the bags themselves being time, handiwork—I don't know what.

But I am perverse, too—like him—and in his honor—or in male imitation; or I was it from early in my childhood, as he was—and I foreshorten the scene, *viz.*, the front seat of a car, well-kept, the car, in wartime, dashboard, leather of the seats, horn steering wheel: I am large and skinny over here—oh, it cannot be done—all that I am in his eyes cannot be shown: let me say it was the *boy* who had the session with Leonie, him plus the boy who read so many books—he used to start at one end of a shelf in the local library and read through the entire shelf, more or less murmuring to himself, *Imagine that* . . . The boy at the river: his face, his shoulders—the shirt, the odors—the cigarettes we smoked to show we could do as we liked—the odors of fabric, then of armpits; it is night; the car is halted at a stoplight; we do not have just his eyes, we have the eyes of the other boy, a boy who, or whom, at the moment I do not claim relation to; we are following, and perhaps terrifying, another car . . . Remsen is going to lecture me on loyalty, sexual permissiveness within that loyalty, tolerance, and the nearly automatic absolution of each other as friends—I do not know all the terms of the negotiation; I do not really know what he is going to say; I know approximately what the power is in the car. It is a matter of *balls* although not, in my view, as that was shown in books that year (and for a decade after). In some respects, we have here rank based on the balls of the mind—if I might be allowed to say that—and that rank tested, denied, toyed with, fought over in various ways.

Remsen will say, or I will point out to him, to his unflinching and handsome face—but his eyes will be roiled and threatening—or placative—and to his chest, so to speak, and to his hands on the steering wheel: his hands are already hairy and mine are not—that you don't necessarily share money, or moods, unless you felt like it.

So the whole contract as he outlined it was worthless: I would argue this—lightly enough. You were just boys (*we* were) or, I suppose, *men*; of course he was more a man than I was, being older and larger and so on—we were companions, drinking buddies. Explorers of the world. *We-do-not-love-one-another* was his formulation, but it was a form of love—*agape*, maybe; something sophisticated, though . . . I could tear his calm up by saying it was *love*. I'd done that, accidentally, not knowing what would happen, only once—and then, once to test it, to see if it was so—and, then, never again.

I would have to care about him more than I mostly did to risk such an upheaval . . . You (one can) love to one degree or another and varyingly. And besides the tumult of degrees is the noise of tones. And throbbing under all of that is sexuality—curiosity mostly—but that takes various forms. And the urge to *know* someone? That can be carnal—that can concern the penetration or sexual exploration of each other. But the main thing about it, in the unmendable relativism of reality, is the way it consists of mutual measurement, of attributes not always consciously known as velocities, or unideal, and not always accepted as given in the terms of the moments; but felt as the grounds of warfare, almost that, as part of the bloodbath of measurements.

Of course, like my dad, one hopes one can know peace and know peacefully, and that *things will settle down* and so on.

Remsen and I—now it is my aged eyes that speak—did not love one another as friends or romantically or sexually—or as souls—or in the romantic tradition—but in that other romance, as cousins, which we were not, and as neighbors, with the other elements being present—we play around, as if with fire, sometimes with love, love without limit but from within the bounds of truce: we play with sexuality but inhibitedly: it is not serious.

But it is real and final in its way—and absolute. I mean it is *absolute* in that we carved and shaped each other: I had other people, many of them; he had fewer . . . I would not presume to propose here an equality, an equivalence, or a justice. In the male world Nonie can never enter and will not, except in wartime, with fliers, glimpse, in the moral sink-hole, or moral primacy, in the freedom, in the murderous freedom and intellectual fires, in the nothingness—take your pick, choose all of them if you like—Remsen is not smart enough to know he wills a kind of shapelessness, like that from which beauty comes into existence—he wills a blurred buddedness, that comic punctuation at the end of winter on empty, windswept branches and withes. This shapeless semi-shapeliness, although affectionate, and even though affectionately representing a form of closeness, is dismissed as a prior boyishness even while it is happening—prior to Freudian maturity.

And one sees this on his face—the flinching and budded rush of how determinedly he has named (and placed) his feelings which exist, in spite of that in him, in other terms, quite other terms, terms entirely other from those within the rush of emptied eggs his breathing becomes in the car. Or in his house. That sort of comedy—of his face and feelings—the enormous passion of it—the aerial view of that is outside the range of fashions in intelligence, a range to which he, in his worldly ambition and his corruption, limits himself—he has given himself to this—the comedy then of feelings, of *his* feelings, is outside that range and is outside the range of his mind.

I see this only in terms of my own nonexistence—a kind of death, a very frail opacity, nearly a transparency, in the actual moment. He nearly comprehends me—and to such an extent that it is like a long description or a passage of love. He abjures the comedy because I am so *aerial*—so given to flight, flights of mind, and to evasion, in hiding myself, in being unlike myself with him when I am at school, in going off to nurse my parents—or some such thing—but also flights of mind, soft, heavy-bodied, predatory flights as of an owl-body: I mean I think, now that I am old, it was true then that my eyes flew with heavy, nearly silent wingbeats toward him in a perpetual dark shouting visually WHO-WHO . . . I can escape the difficulties of this by proposing myself as unloved, but then he vanishes as a presence in my memories. I do not know if this is a flaw or lapse or absence of mind. A repellent vanity. Or a fine thing. My father, dying, said, *You think you are like David . . .* In the Bible, I think. I was said to cheer him, and we were said to be a David-and-Saul sort of story . . . It is painful to me to admit to myself that perhaps I danced in my life or sang—with my eyes, so to speak—even though I *feel* it is true as I say it. But then it is clearer—to me—what it was like in the moments back then that he—Remsen—whom I at times preferred to my father and at times ignored in favor of my father—feels he has a better but less appreciated mind than I have.

Nonie—and my dad and mom—felt that way, too—I guess a number of people feel that way toward me as the primary thing they consciously feel where I am concerned. But that is the school's fault for insisting that I am smart. Remsen and my father blame me for this stuff; they say I am a politician who arranges the above, cleverly. And Nonie and Mom blame me as unloving and male, and they blame the world for misseeing things where women are concerned . . . I half know *The Law of Opposites* is in operation in many of the uses of language. My father, when he was alive, and Remsen did try to arrange the above. And Nonie and my mom are, in different ways, and out of pride, unloving and female—defiant, you know?—and create intensely as-if-perfumed corners of the world, harem-realities, in which *I* am mis-seen as a (phallic?) prop of their lives . . . And so on.

Whatever Remsen says, or confesses, and he says and confesses a lot at times—and often he is silent—and whatever he does or professes, for a certain number of years, in school or in his car, or if we are walking along a street toward his house, in a rich part of the suburb, I think he watches me with the infatuated attention of ambition, various ambitions including those of love, love immediate, love ultimate—like hawks sitting on his wrists and on top of his head, a raw helmet of sheer life, absolute in the moment, and waiting on further evidence—as real-life absolutes always do and always must—a stirring of animate meaning—final in my life if in no one else's, his love, if it is love, *his* love such as it is, and him being, presumably, of the same species, and yet foreign to me and unlike me, as unlike me as a hawk. Or as an angel—a boy with his own parents, the different moral principles from his past and from his sessions, talkative or silent, with his doctor, moral principles derived differently and applied to a far different world, different in terms of how time flowers in it—we might, if we love each other enough, die almost in the same moment, but we can never make the actual time we contain congruent with the time in the other.

Or intellectually and economically, and in terms of the processes he sees as running *things* (or as adequately symbolizing the procedures of the world, in the way chemical formulas might represent the real-life steps and sweat for making this or that)—and his principles or no, what I am aware of is his *beauty*—such as it is—of the storylike aspects of this moment (its treasure, its being a treasure house of that stuff for me)—and of a distance from Nonie here—her guilt, my guilt—and it is like smelly feathers and a fire of will and of opposition, burning in a hawk —a hawk lazy or in flight and busy—and this is, at times, as if apparent along his *edges*, the forward shape of his legs, each one when it moves forward as he walks, or of his stomach—or of his chest—inside his shirt—or at the crown of his handsome head and its tousled hair . . .

But if one enters into-the-moment—if one tries to approach the *meat*, or the *meat-and-potatoes*, as a teacher I had named Gangtinney said about a lot of topics—if as a human duty or as an act of conceit or a moment's *boyish* daring, one goes further into reality—if one invades Russia, if one crawls, or walks, scratched and stung, toward the center of the as-if-thorny thicket—those last are my private terms—then the shapes and blinking of the *other boy's* intelligent eyelids and the broad cheekbones of his bonily handsome but boring but brightly health-tinctured face which somehow yet has in its pallor of thought and its melodrama of egoistic occasions its occasional spurts of glamour . . . If I love him in this way—or maybe it should be stated as when I love him—he astounds me, he is so lithe—so strong, so sad, so smart. So at the end of his rope. So firmly and fiercely there. And so frail and deathbound—and in a way absent. He is a ferocious presence. And he is barely alive at all . . . It is as if I hold a rifle to the hawk's head. He has a raw helmet and visor of hungry identity—it is his identity, so to speak, which loves me, if I am not in error about his feelings in that regard—and he has an extreme physical validity which bores him—it is not just looks but it is an exceptional vitality and an exceptionally strong physical will: but it is contradicted by something, his restless vitality, by a sense of death as meaning—and as genius—by himself as fully alive only for a final second or two: that is what I suspect of him: some unabsolvable childhood thing of limitlessness, a final cry, a truly un-sleepy, undaily thing of the proposal of oneself as the child of the entire universe and the bearer of the sole important meaning: anger and guilt-lessness: a thing from being a younger child, a Jew, and not quite of the social class he is in now—he is not really of any social class anymore. He is mobile and unabsolved and modern. He commands love and silence, sympathy and the stages of the moments on which he appears with what he is with this fatality of sadness . . . But this is for himself, too. He cannot set up the mirrors in such a way that he, too, is not misled. His looks are of that sort: I mean the would-be sly king—or David—but he is merely ultimately truthful about the nature of his own will. He is tremendous but not valuable at our school in wartime . . . But he will be in the next war—if there is a next war, and if he lives . . .

He is not a symbol to other boys . . . Not a local idol. So far as I know, no one loves him but me. His parents fear his finality. They dote on him and are wounded and fragile in how they perchingly live. And I love him only at times, mostly when his solipsistic dramas and fatalities permit me room—to matter, too . . . That isn't often. It rests on sex, on the transmission of ideas—on the importance of ideas, our skeletons for the bodies of what we know, the corpus of knowledge—and it rests on power and on cruelties, because sentimental measurements are not only incomplete, they are not measurements, they are lies; they exist as statements, as aspects of one's politics; but they do not exist as realities.

And when my love for him exists it has the curious form in real moments of being primarily intellectual—intelligent, intelligently admiring, not a folly, except perhaps morally, of course—I love him for good reason: he has established the reasons, with his exercises and his reading and his courtesies—such as they are—but he permits my love for him to exist only erotically—in the prior state to his loving women in that fashion, the fashion I show him by loving him . . . as if he were girlish and struggling to become male . . . within some mad chrysalis of boys' companionship . . . and whatever.

My guess is that he knows himself to be circumstantially so much better looking than I am and so much richer (in terms of cash and inheritance and of possessions now, of things he can pay for) that he is willing to court me dishonestly—honestly as an erotic object—and he is not homosexual—rather than for the real reasons he cares about me. He will never admit that I know of to his intellectual dependence on me or to his actual liking for me in my faintly opaque transparency and unhappiness and various oddities—he will never admit to his obsession-for-a-while or schoolboy crush or neediness-toward-me, or, if one is incautious, his obvious love, lifelong, tireless, cool and bitter, rivalrous, ill-informed, perhaps accursed, perhaps okay.

His parents show little feeling about him—he scares them too much. He is this way: I mean as someone who frightens feeling in others so that it remains in burrows; and he cannot see it run or feel its silken haunches near him or on him. He is unreachable largely. Is it intelligent of me to say this of him? To see this in him? Am I being intelligent now? Perhaps I should love him simply and more or less madly . . . *Love him, you damn fool, love him* . . . He picks on me for not being intelligent—for not having read and believed and used the books he has read and believed and used—he blames me for having conned the school to think I'm smart—he has blamed me for my being merely local . . . Not universal . . . Not great . . . At college in a few years a dean will tell me that I am "nationally smart" and I will literally go crazy then, in front of him, screaming inside my head because of Jass and Remsen and another boy named Jimbo, and for Leonie and Nonie, and for my parents. The screaming didn't stop for six months. I hid this from people and went about my daily stuff; and so no one put me away. In a bin. In a home. But I was desperate and unbelieving.

And every once in a while, I would break down further. I'd go to a tiny nearby park even if it was cold, merely to be away from the carpentered geometries of an indoors, and I'd rub my face with snow or with leaves or with oily buds later, and say to myself, *Wake up Come out of it Snap out of it It's no big deal They're just guessing They're probably wrong* . . .

Or if I used my other, private—perhaps more honest—voice, I would think unwordedly but just this side of wordedness that it was in the nature of the world that whatever happened—the stuff that happened—was shocking. Or astounding. Astonishing, if you like. Cruel and ordinary. Before he died in his thirties, Remsen had a far more distinguished life than I had . . . No: that's not true. He did distinguished work as a doctor. He was murdered by a patient who, it is my guess, was affronted by Remsen's merits and his inner distances, his being out of reach.

The question arises for me with Remsen a lot—so often—I mean it is so frequent in its recurrence, it recurred over so many months and years that it had the duration of knowing and being impressed by him and of caring about him that it is almost its theme—that I liked him because it was so difficult. It was part of getting along with him for me, to admit that in getting along with him I was comparing myself to others who could not—and not just to him. It is a cat's cradle of comparisons, this way and that. He irritates me—more than *X* does? Sometimes. But the difficult defines me: I am he-who-does-this . . . He is, in part, armored against that: he defines me—or he is suicidal—really. That strength in him—and it is a strength—is a recurring horror—male, flexible, dynamic, extensive—that he inflicts. And my patience with it—which is part of what he likes—or needs—or is familiar with—and addicted to—permits him to live more easily than he would otherwise.

This *sounds* noble, but in real life, walking along a street past lawns and shrubs and houses in a real place and not in a story where characters and a story are limited for a while—but here the question is why not walk with someone else, why not do something else—the above thing seems stupid, vaguely shameful, collusive, grown-up in a way and boyish (and amateur) in another way.

A woman should do it.

Imagine Nonie doing it for him . . .

To live with this stuff, to be me—to be a boy in my circumstances—it is faintly spiritual in tone, middle-classy, with a spine to it of my being strongly ambitious in a worldly sense as a matter of faith. I mean that as a matter of faith *my life means something, I bet*—it is a gamble. This stuff, familiar to me as a boy, allows a considerable looseness of attachment and demands no discipline of tones toward him day after day—I can explore and be forgetful and careless and even brutal—but not in every circumstance. No fixed crudity of response that you become furtively expert in is allowed short of more obsessive love than this.

Perhaps this is part of what holds him, and Ora later—the way in which I am not Nonie but was her *rival* in the house for attention and money. For love, say. And to be the one whose sadness and anger was feared most or second or third . . .

At any rate, this is not exactly a crudity: it is adolescent and not entirely amateurish, which is to say that in the sense I was *prior* for him, then, in my own terms, what happened here was *a curable fate*.

But what if I am wrong and he and I—or me alone, without him—are trapped in a crudity of incurable fate because of my past plus my knowing him plus my acting in this way until all the components are mixed for *an incurable fate*.

Remsen was *a reciter* . . . someone who claimed, and who had, no authority underived from someone else. He can't have his own life as the grounds for his authority—as I can. So he is a *natural* thief of styles and of time and of attention—a crow-and-a-hawk.

Even so, he is stubbornly alive . . . It is obstinately real to me, him walking beside me along the street, his size, his voice—his view of things. I laugh at him and fail to be amused. Or truly mocking. He says—quotingly—"You jape at me . . ." I did not, truly, love him—I did not cross any of the lines of *loyalty* or of private sacrament—or of obligation—that I, rightly or wrongly, regard as true love (those lines at which, when I cross them, Ora exclaims, *Oh you love me*—and Leonie exclaimed, *You are a little devil, you're going to be a devil with women* . . .). I did not cross those lines with him; without remembering every moment I spent with him, I cannot be certain I did not even stand (so to speak) at such lines, or at one of them; but he saw me in the locker room waltzing naked with Jass in front of the naked other boys; he saw me with my father; he saw me staring at the sky—so he knew; or he could have known . . . No, I am certain he knew all along what I did not do. He is aware that I am not a hero with him—at least in that sense. I tell him, "I don't accept your *stupid* views on things no matter how many times you tell me it's from Freud or Marx or Schopenhauer—okay?" I *know* he gets a lot of his quotes wrong—a lot of this is on purpose: he claims the authority of the famous name and puts his own thought in to see if his own thought is as good. He says something and he says it is Marx, and I say, "Shit, Rem, that isn't Marx, that's you in University City being a shit-poor *liar* . . ."

He pretty much grovellingly comes after me so long as I don't plan it and don't want it. He is incredibly aware of such matters in me.

So, I give up on him. I have him by not wanting me. He comes after me and after me, day after day after day, to my astonished and *irritated* amusement . . . My mother says, *That's a scalp you have . . .* And some teachers and Caulkins, the school superintendent, my particular protector, who watches over my education and is concerned about my future and is interested whether I am to be heterosexual or homosexual or more a public or a private person—he, I, and a good many kids kept track of Remsen's pursuit of me—kids who kept track of such things as that . . . It would be *nice* (worth a lot, maybe everything) to be anonymous, no matter what Milton said about fame being the spur, anonymous in order to think as an unwatched nobody, as no one unabominably concerned with the course of one's thoughts and concerned only with that . . .

Remsen sees to it that I do not greatly profit from his attachment. Or from his pursuit of me. That isn't just haggling . . . it is something odd, it is haggling-cum-romance . . . Jass, the Protestant, insists that we risk death and maiming—everything with him (everything) is the exercise of courage. Ora demands that I "love" her enough not to care if the love harms her—or whatever it is: I can't think about her now. I don't humiliate him or try to set things up to show off his doglike thing toward me—and he is cautious and shrewd about it.

But when I walk home, he sometimes literally pops out from behind a tree along the route I take and where he was hiding so no one will see how much he wants to see me. He won't lend me his car, he won't lend me books, he doesn't offer to lend me clothes. One winter when I knew him I had no coat. Lila thought the pathos would bring me a coat fast. And Remsen's mother nervously—and prettily—offered me a coat; a lot of people did; I always refused in order to shame Lila and to stay out of debt. But Remsen didn't offer. I had the sense he wanted me to become ill. I went through the winter being cold and wearing a lot of sweaters, often four or five at the same time, one over the other, which some kids, some of the poorer kids, then some of the very rich kids, turned into a school style that winter, for a number of months.

Remsen has said I am a freak, a phenomenon, but not a real mind. I have a better-judged memory than he does—that is, it presents things with more judgment in the presentation and in the caption or footnote aspects (*this was yesterday*) than his memory can manage—he just remembers things and hopes there is meaning in that memory, but my memory aligns itself with its purposes and then admits that it does that. He is a kind of blind but determined and fairly smart gambler on his own limitations—I am, too, but in a different style. It is hard to talk about such things as this. I have a far better sense of consequences and, therefore, am almost infinitely better at induction and deduction than he is; and he is sometimes humble and sometimes murderous toward me because of this. His mind is better-stocked, more conventional—he is a Marxist-Freudian Positivist—well, you can't be that and be *logical*, but you can be it and be *conventional*, conventionally intellectual, and that is what he is. At moments, when he is a bit drunk, or when he has been sniffing glue, partly as a duty—to be "fast," to be *radical*, to be young-and-intelligent, et cetera, he says it is *magical* (to sniff glue) and his weird background shows through, not directly then, but by opposition to what he pretends is his being logical and reasonable at other times. Some primitive mess of semi-inspired superstition that yet is accurately enough placed in regard to life is what he is rooted in. This comes roaring through as indicating a kind of intellect and one of a certain rank; and sometimes that frightens me and I retreat into being a single ship alone on a vast ocean and am as isolated as he is—if he is the world, or if he is closer to being it than I am. Mostly, he is a dying or at least strangled rationalist, incapable of reason in the traditional Western sense; but since he is so hardworking and can be rational by rote and watchfully and out of a gray and ambitious despair, and since he is incapable of life, except erotically (he is too absolutist to live: living is political, *unmendably* political or relativist, as I said), and is incapable of feeling life to any great extent except as his doctor and his books and his body force him to—and except, at the moment, through me—he is pretty much an okay mind by almost all standards but mine. And will be—if he lives . . . And he was, as long as he lived. But I always laughed at his mind—and was fond of him . . .

But his mind really is an expanse of curiously ashen deadness, a dullness: it is strange to *see* this in someone so clearly spectacular and so bright. Maybe it comes from a partly misguided idea of being young (and spectacular) and has only a crooked and suffocating connection to his reality.

So that he is a sort of unembraceable hero, marvelous flesh that is a field of skipping ashes that fly into my grasp if I touch him—he is a shadow among the shades in an epic of ambition, but willfully; it is self-willed, much of what he is. What he calls 'neurotic' or 'unfavorable circumstances' is his romantic anxiousness not to pay the price for what he is as he goes along but to pay only afterwards, in a subsequent hell. He is truly alive at moments in terms of his escaping from reality and logic as into the hallucinatory stuff of sex—not the reality part but the accompaniment, as if the hallucination were music and he was a musician. Much of what he calls logic is like fingers clinging to a ledge which he then blithely releases from their intent desperation, and they, and he, as-if-scutter lithely away inside the music. So that if I did, for a while, hold, or earn, his 'love' as a boy of a certain kind and in relation to him, it was, in part, or so I say, a storm of ashes and of hallucination in him and of humiliation among shades, shadows, mental constructs. The physical thing, or the strongly emotional thing, when it comes near him, the ash breaks into finer and finer fragments, pitiably, us, us as shadows and ashes at the end of the world. He grovels some—it is as if playful and on a dreary plain; it is sexually polite, vaguely working-class, odd. It is not contractual. It is not a swindle. It does not mean much—but nothing does when it is momentary if you do not believe the moments are real or that time is or that moments and time matter. He grovels toward destiny as well as toward whoever he wants to engage with him in shadowy acts—that does not mean much either, his attitude toward destiny. He is brave but the grovelling makes him vengeful—toward what his ambition gains him; he grovels with immense, immense pride, on his way to a higher position in the world (higher than he has now), but he keeps score and he has his resentment toward this.

We walk. He wears a pale blue polo shirt that shows his muscles—or the shadows of them in this light. He is close to being physically beautiful. His face is coldly focussed with the wish to have me join him in his study of sex—sex among the shades, not our real selves but our mental selves, autonomous in regard to most physical rules—or at least it feels that way to the mind: the tender membranes and flying sparks and chemical whizzlings feel they are armor-and-rock. People write about this, how powerful and bronzelike and long-lived a mind is, not ruled by physical law exactly but stained, so to speak, by it, or if the physical is pure, then stained by the will: the mind, the mind in the shape of a long-legged, almost brilliant, quite handsome, nearly beautiful boy—him . . . Remsen . . . I am not responsive and yet I am so deeply flattered, so profoundly moved I am crazy with it. The cold focus of his face is to hide the grovelling. Is to undo it. Is to see to it that it doesn't occur as it did the last time. I try to hide in my behavior, in a ceramiclike surface of myself that he has not grovelled at all. He has gone to a school in the slums and he has lived in neighborhoods *where boys fooled around—naturally* (he has said this and does not need to say it again)—and he is being natural-natural and boyish at a different site, commanding, different-handed, gang-leaderish, gang-followerish—naturally but artificially . . .

A book review of this stuff—an analysis of it—is that I think he has been an object of this stuff and relives it from various angles—but the other experiences are, some of them, too shadowy, and others are too clear. I don't know what he is repeating or studying—or what his desires are. I know he cares about me some and that I do not care to know more about him. He has older sisters—three of them. He has a *very* pretty, youngish mother . . . All my friends and the girls I saw something of had pretty mothers . . . His father is handsome, polite, very oddly mannerly—not the manners of a sect or of a social class. His father is unusually good-looking but nervous (or fearful) and wet-lipped, shy—*a gangster* maybe—or so Lila theorized.

He had become proper. Perhaps, he had been unable to bear his life until now—who knows what lives people have . . . Sins. Crimes.

But one can theorize, too, that there had been in Remsen's life, in other neighborhoods, neighborhoods in the sexual world, older boys larger and tougher than he was; there he was—in all that physical fear—and the desire—and he is smart . . . But anyway, I suspect the presence of the streets and storefronts of his childhood. Protectors. Gangs. Danger. It is as if I seemed to him to be more valuable than he was, and at the same time he believed that he came first . . . I haven't the power, or the will, to interrogate him.

You can tell, sort of, what's going on, but not clearly . . . He might want to move up in the world, measure himself in this way, demean the suburbs. I do not know. This topic—he is supremely, almost sublimely orderly in a *down-to-earth* way during our time together, on this topic, he cannot make the effort to understand me—he *wins* my admiration, my adherence, but without addressing me, without me, so to speak, but with the factual stuff of the bribes—a certain number of compliments, a degree of *niceness* in his tone, a kind of obeisance or acceptance of my school rank—without bitterness—a certain display of humor—a certain kind of offer of sexual pleasures a little beyond my desserts, beyond my sexual merits . . . But this is done without reference to me. It has some reference to what my tastes must be according to the rules of psychoanalysis and of his 'brilliant' perceptions of the political realities of this world. That includes his social analysis as well. His neural sense—and his genital sense—of things. These qualities of friendship *plus* a kind of sexual intimacy—as boys, that is to say without kinkiness—all of it has everything to do with him, with what he is, what he knows, what he has learned. He opens a cabinet door, and there on the shelves is nothing physical but is everything learned and known, is the sort of proudly housekept household of the self. I cannot do that. I *must* tell him nothing—it gives him a headache; he must discuss what I say with his doctor. He spends a day or two in bed. He demands clarity: that is, what he already knows, delicately modified—if modified at all. In discussing a wrestling meet—or a mountain climb—he somehow mixes mountains with boys he has wrestled with: massive topographical difficulties he has wrestled with, plodded through, or upward, or sprinted upward. One of the problems with symbolic representation of things is that then things can be represented by images which are imagined equivalences, piles of money, degrees of triumph, one's own responses. But the mountain exists beyond my own response to it and beyond my father's response and my family's sense of it as does Remsen whom, in spite of it all, I love. He asks me what I read and he reads the same books in a kind of powerful rivalry, to *win* them from me—him keeping his balance, him doing his schoolwork, him as an athlete: it is him winning out over forces of disorder outside him and inside him—he is a walking *Trojan War* of neural and intellectual *forces*, oddments really, all of them accepted by him as *general*, and yet no one is like him: I am more widely understood, in my oddities, than he is; and he invariably dismisses with abuse the books I care about, so that I do not tell him anymore what I like. I lie to him and joke, or half joke, rather than duel with scorn, innuendo, summonings of rank, quotations about literary excellence, and so on. Depending on the judge, on who referees us, I win most of such exchanges, but then I have the dying Gaul, the wounded Remsen—young man in despair. In his courtship, in his peculiar affection, as he marches toward me—so to speak—or walks alongside me, talking sidelong about preparations for a match and tactics—how to prepare the legs—and how a love of Marx and Lenin helps in this . . . how Jack London understands and so on—is both a command, a logical progression of lawgiving, and also a human request for sympathy—the two arms of the seduction, of the nutcracker (a feminization in a sense, but only in a sense) of which he is enormously proud—that he is so *normal*—as to be able to elicit and command and to ask for sympathy *humanly*—but none of this is mutual. We do not take turns. What is *understood*, or silent, is that I am more normal, more successful, stronger, or some such thing, or all those things at the moment, because the world is hideous and wrong.

The compliment, or obeisance, is tacit, is in a tone, is to be understood. Lila used to say of certain things—of such things as this—human bargains, people acting out their dreams—*It makes me laugh* . . . And then she would not laugh except in certain stage-y often ironically-scoffing ways just this side of an outbreak of wild behavior—telling her mother to leave her alone: that sort of thing.

Or Daddy would say it, not necessarily about me, but I never saw Daddy doing business for a whole day: I never saw the negotiations or knew the terms of his dealings. But certain swindles, certain counterfeit things, claims, pretensions, certain claims of legitimacy (of claims) and of equivalency (for a trade, in order to establish justice or merely parity) would lead him to say, *It makes me laugh*, and he would take on a truly tragic air and he would snort and whinny a bit: a tragic horse in a tale or a sad king in a famous play . . . It was something like that.

On the sidewalk Remsen says, "Let me show you the arm lock I used on Willy Boston."

"Not on your life," I say. "Don't make me laugh . . ." And I twist away, or threaten to kick him in the nuts if he already has taken hold of my arm.

But much of the meaning lies even beyond that—beyond the voices—and, as with Nonie, who always says, *Don't make me laugh*, within a negotiation or progression toward her own kingdom of triumphs and some defeats, it lies in the relation of the kingdoms and of their comparative value: it is a relative shortcut to measurement by means of a *certain* kind of force he is trained in and I am not trained in.

"Don't be an asshole," I say; and then it depends on the set of my shoulders, on the degree of anger in my eyes, on the posture of my lips whether I am calling him a creep, or a slum child, or a truly inadequate lover . . .

My powers—those of scorn and of school popularity of a sort (my opinions are well regarded, partly because I don't lie or use the opinions merely politically) and the consequent spread, the contagious spread of the scorn—control him, bridle him somewhat, although he passes that off mostly as his *affection*, his knowing about friendship-in-the-real-world . . . the real give-and-take. He and Nonie do occupy similarly constructed worlds, or cities, of winning and losing, of rank, of position. They are similarly aware of sharing a household with other children, citizens dependent on parental dispensations, in uneasy and quarrelsome—and heartbreaking—sharing.

His mouth twists—scornfully: it is not powerful scorn, not powerfully abusing. The most relative thing he does, the thing that most includes me, or permits me to be there, is a kind of weakness that he parades—it is a real thing, however. I am perhaps mischievous, and I parade a counterfeit, polite, paper-thin similar weakness, or matching one. He grows still then, suspecting, half seeing a truth—as one might see a deer or a deer scut in the pinewoods on one's ascent of a mountain. He suspects me of some sort of emotional sleight-of-hand—of some slight of his *things*—the elements of his reality—so much so, moment after moment, that I am driven to experiment: "You *are* an asshole . . ." He may be so hurt, so angry, so whatever that he will now march off. I am *forced*—FORCED—to smile and grab his shoulder if I am at all interested in the sort of *sexual* intimacy possible with him.

Then, because he has been so hurt, I follow along where he leads—he has shortcuts from here to his house, and for us to take them means going mostly in single file with me following him. He cannot follow me at any time. He has told me he has a proud soul.

I see in him the world Nonie inhabits—the one Lila speaks of—but I see it more clearly and with less shock of immediacy when it is freed from gender (and family matters) and is set in a boy . . . an older boy . . . powerfully built, as I said . . . and monied, and not pathetic. I see that he feels, feels and thinks, that time will not change us, that, in justice, we will not take turns since there is no justice yet, and that what changes occur in our standing will come about from his efforts—his will, his cleverness—but even as I follow him through backyards and across the back part of a farm field where a farmer has not yet sold to developers, I believe that he is cluttered with timelessness and with stillnesses and that he is without the will to be any other way and that I can evade him endlessly because I move and exist in time . . . Ahead of me, his back: his buttocks in motion, the literal façades of his vanity, embodiments of the *men*, the elements of reality he plays with in the board game of his sense of things: is he safe from me? I am phallically larger than he is, cleverer in the few ways I am cleverer: I am often hurt, often resentful of my life compared to his, and of him and of what he is: I am often tired of being patient: I often long to commit a terrible and private and hidden crime and then to *laugh* about it: I am often tired of him, always tired of him in a way—he is not what I desire. Lately, I have thought I must learn to accept what is given me, but sometimes I want to overturn everything in my life: it is an immense disrespect, even a contempt in me—that is what *Don't make me laugh* refers to when I say it, or think it, that next state, that quality of soul that one might enter on, through a door, willfully . . .

But that does not mean I do not care for him. I repeat, he is *an older boy* . . . two and a half years older than I am. We are the same height; he outweighs me by nearly twenty-five well-organized pounds. To be near him is to be near the humiliation imposed by the stone face of a cliff or the fear-inflicting chest and forelegs—and hooves—of a horse. Trampled and buried, overwhelmed, thrown to the ground, conquered: it is present here. Would I then try to kill him? Beat his skull in with a rock? Humiliate him so in school he would never forget it? Some days he haplessly imitates my postures and the motions of my face—that sickens me—bores me. To see him at a distance—the posture, the physical power, the clothes, the motions—to feel at a distance that he is imitating me—it sometimes gives me a frisson . . . Of power? Strings leading from me to him *physically*? Morally? Immorally? Things inside me have no labels. He and I have secrets from the school. What does it mean I accept his love such as it is, accept it sometimes, perhaps mostly to punish my family. And then I resist being like that. I try to like him for what he is in the middle of the starvation of him being courtly out of his own feelings and in line with his judgment and without reference to my reality. He is very truthful—in his way—very fine—but he has never seen me. I love, I think, the capacity of his chest, the actual muscular and spread-rib capaciousness of the chamber of breath and of the faintly audible heartbeat when I lie near him on the bed in his bedroom.

And the backs of his thighs, the outline of his buttocks, but not the actual things: they are too real, too real as *organized* masses of muscle, as sources of accomplishment: they are youthfully hairy and singularly his. They are him. I never, or very rarely, tell him any truth from my side of the bones and tissues and skin and skimpy muscle which is me. I dislike his face. I dislike the shapes his courage takes—perhaps I am jealous . . . I mimic him: I long for the ideal thing, as in a dream, when the world, the sky, the liner among the leaves of the treetops are within my head: the *ideal* means my nearness to God—or to ultimate truth: the suicidal murderer's platform. Ultimates are near-death. I have never kissed him. Never touched him tenderly. Part of me never stops laughing at him—the streams of time, the committees of selves, which are me rush along in regard to him like a brook or a laughably rattling wagon. In his presence—me as a male nymph—I refer to *truth* only from doctrines or to no truth: it is a chamber to lies to be near him, a stage; it is as if we wear makeup in order to simulate the dream things of the theater, of his own mind, of his sense of the ideal. I rarely use words other than his own when I talk to him, but when I do, it shatters him—momentarily; and often, he shows temper, temper or grief. If I were a doctor of the mind, I would say that *ideas* underlie pain and that *ideals* generate actions and are useful in private as pellets of solace, but that they must never be used as premises and one must realize, ipso facto, they cannot be used for human measurements.

I have been longer settled in University City than he has. I know people here and am known. The aura of how I am known, the accumulation of forgetfulness and of memory, that *plus* what I am physically now and mentally, that has *hooked* him to me . . . Boyhood romances: *Do you know how to hold someone's interest? Be rich*, my mother has said.

I do it differently, Mom . . .

I have lived in this suburb for nine years and I want to live here for the rest of my life in that pulsating and changeable aura—that nest . . . That brief-time thing, that small matter is the center of my being able to sleep, to bear my dreaming, to walk in the streets, to be *seen*. He, Remsen, *my beloved*, ha-ha-ha, don't make me laugh, sees this as a matter of social rank in the U.S.

Remsen says, "You're all right for a *bourgeois* . . . But history will chew you up in little bits and spit you out . . ."

"And what if you are wrong?"

"Wrong?"

"What if history approves of me more than it does of you?"

"You think you are smarter than Marx?"

We are walking side by side down an alley in the late-afternoon shadows . . . Here and there, the sun, from the west, is suddenly nakedly brilliant.

"You think you are smarter than Freud? Than Schopenhauer?"

"You're sure you *know* what Freud was saying . . ."

"I am brilliant," he says, which is charming. In front of me, in some internal exhibition of recent memory becoming less recent second by second and serving more and more different purposes, in front of me but inside my head his exceedingly powerful and shapely butt wiggles like a mockery of a face—or like a mockery of breasts. The two mounds suckle nothing, at least in terms of actual food: it is the other face of food: the hinder end, *the hind end* . . .

"Me too—I'm brilliant," I say in the flooding western light, the extraordinarily huge, hugely bright flare of blinding illumination (if one can say that) in the alley.

It is immodest to say this, but it was all right for him to say it: the claim was of a certain sort. His heart was in it. I was joking—I was laughing at him—*as per usual* was a local idiom back then—my heart was not in it; and it was a horror . . . The school does consider me brilliant and him of a good but lesser rank in those areas.

I cannot see him in the glare but I feel him slapped by the horror and I *feel* my own solecism: whether or not I am right or half right or a quarter right about the ways he is walled in and is self-concerned and self-referential, his reality is still one of awareness. The warriors and the abruptly dead are there.

"That was a socially decadent remark," I say. In the bright blindness I can make out his shoulders, not as a complete sight or even as a complete line, and his neck, and the line of his jaw. "Mine. You are everything and everything is you . . ."

I am so sickened at making peace that, without warning, I start to jog, but then I half turn and now I see him illuminated and obliterated both, and I say, "Come on, set the pace for me . . ."

He hesitates for a second—murderously?—and then he takes off: he runs past me and ahead. "Come on, asshole," he says . . . We are without fixed rank, he and I—egalitarian, democratic. His egalitarian-democratic would-be socialist absolutist and universe-comprehending buttocks move ahead of me in a shadow in which, as I run, lopingly, I see him as a physical fineness, as, clearly, in shadow, fineness enough for me.

Now we are in his backyard, having talked dirty while we passed through his garage, panting from the run. It was odd talk, odd in its *dirtiness* . . . semi-medical.

"You know what a fistula is?"

"No. Do you?"

"No. I just like the sound of cunt fistula . . . Oh my God, it's a form of Count Dracula!"

"You're afraid of being vampirized . . . Your prick falls off . . ."

"Your prick does *not* fall off if you're vampirized: Dracula was a great lover . . ."

"You like the smell of sperm?"

"No! Ugh . . . Do you?"

"You're supposed to like it—you're supposed to accept all your natural oils and stuff . . ."

"Jesus, Remsen! I don't know if I can do that . . . When you dream of fucking—well, first, you dream of it lately?"

A little suspiciously, since he hates Socratic dialogues: "Yeah?"

"Did you dream of motions on your part and not on *hers*? Was it a specific cunt?"

"I don't know: why?"

"Because the last three times I got caught in one of those dreams, it started as me seeing someone else fucking someone, and I got jealous and then it was me, sort of wrestlingly, but it was just me: there was so little trace of the other, the plausibility was no good and I woke up and I was, you know, fucking the mattress . . ."

"You're very sick . . . You ought to see a doctor."

"Yeah? You want to play doctor? Is that what you're going to say next?"

His father had a lot of free time, and in their backyard was a sundial that said *Carpe Diem* and spokes of garden beds filled with neatly tended rosebushes, all of them in shades of red. White ones lined the yard. And yellow ones in half-oval beds were along the sides of the house.

"You're of no interest to me sexually, *buddy*," Remsen said. "You're a human Kleenex."

"Right."

"You have no sense of humor," he told me. "You're *social-and-decadent* . . . You are truly *bourgeois* . . ."

I stop walking. The anger—or the flirtatiousness in that tone—stops then: his face and his breathing change. "I got hold of a new dirty book . . ."

"You refuse to believe in my real family, which is working-class . . ."

"I bet they have money . . ."

"They are crude and violent, Remsen . . ."

"But you live with people with country-club connections . . ."

"Jesus, am I ever highly ranked . . . Me, the bourgeois desirable one . . . It must really drive you crazy . . ." He was so much better built . . . If I refer to that, he, almost gently, blossoms. "I am a more *acceptable local form* . . . You're too much a body. You're too educated—and sensual . . ." It's odd about lies in real life, when you're talking, how they slant and curve and shine like some kinds of metal, and they reflect something glancingly, something real and unexplained. I hesitated and then I said that to him; I heard the words *glancingly*, or the meanings, shades of meaning: the sentence moved like a dog, almost, or an otter—or like an armada of flaming otters shatteringly, meltingly . . .

At times, the language I use, the way it curves—like a stocking on a girl's leg, Remsen said once—stirs him physically—the way he is a mind-become-a-boy . . .

"Tell me again about your real family?" he says askingly, with his chest and arms so thrust into the glare-surrounded shadow where we stand among the spokes of rosebushes that it is a familiar signal, a variant of when he is sexually needy or curious or whatever it is in him toward me . . .

"I am working-class by blood—unless you count my real uncles—and of a far, far lower-ranked class than any you can be from. My real father lives on a street where there are only a few houses and it's not in a neighborhood and mostly prison guards live in those houses. Do you see what I mean?"

He doesn't answer. He is in motion—like a thought—among the bushes, past the many-lipped silence of the rose into the glare where the shadow of the garage stops near the back door of his house. My rearranged face, my *disarranged* face, my hair flip-flopping as I settle creakingly on the bed—in his bedroom—me: I am clothed, buttoned, I am in a long-sleeved shirt—*jeune homme fatal*, although you would hardly believe it at first sight. If I am honest, I should say that some people do believe it: some days, when I go to the grocery store for my mother and sister, I count the number of people who react to me. It gets *intense* . . .

As I settle on Remsen's bed—gangling, conceited-humble—reasonably glad to be here compared to being at home—I am, on this occasion, so glad to be not ignored that my posture is of my unrefused *friendship* for him—with some quite noticeable distances in it—in the end I am not really here except as a mind-cum-an-excitable-substance neural-physical but mostly neural, since he bores me with his determination-to-be-a-fixed-quantity-as-a-man-who-will-win-out-in-the-universe. I say out loud, "Losing now and then is not *such* a bad idea . . ." And he is not honest about absolutist and relativist matters, although he has read two of Einstein's papers in German (he has completely misunderstood them, I think). I have no real political franchise here: merely power: it is a *very fragile* love, not as an emotion inside me, but as a color and a territory in which I move and act. It is inward, messy, approximate . . . unideal . . . But it is love.

He asks—well, he has fondled himself but not elaborately and he has put his hand over the muscle of his chest; that the context is sexuality interests my blood, so to speak, and my nerves, which become shadowy in their pulsing sense of meanings—he asks as part of an ongoing conversation about dominance and a Utopian escape from any sexual cruelty: this is supposed to get me *excited* and to represent a modern attitude, a modern attitude as absolution—"Well, would *you* hit a woman to stop her from making a scene with you?"

"I WOULDn't hit her . . ."

"Would you THINK about hitting her?"

I have an erection and so does he . . . I have a part of an erection, a specific erection, a cast of excitement.

"No," I say.

"Are you saying this to make me feel lower-class again?"

"Christ, I don't know . . ." He has asked me not to mention to him anything about analysis and not to ask him about his analysis or about the psychoanalyst he sees: this is part of what it is forbidden me to say. I am grist-for-a-mill, the ground on which he will find his balance in order to proceed, heroically, from there to another and, of course, deeper affair. An attitude: *We are failures here together*: as part of a seduction, of a seduction of a kind, a move toward collusion which he rules absolutely, in a way, but not quite. Perhaps competing with that or rather measuring myself against it is one of the things that amuses me, although perhaps not enough.

Judging from his actions in high school, I believe that he knows very little about social rank and social rankings in this country (and in other societies) but that he bends all his worries, all his pain until he feels it can be explained because of his social rank and the corruptions in it.

It is symbolic representation based on ignorance and a personally skewed perspective—an aesthetic matter posing as an ultimate secular truth, which is okay—except there is a sense in which, in a corrupt tradition, if one wants to be loyal to it, or if one has to be loyal to it, psychologically, in order to breathe, then ignorance of certain things becomes the mark of that loyalty, ignorance, unawareness, a kind of doom.

Which then relegates you to a fierce and lower and doomed rank. It is not what being of family or part of a valuable tradition is about. Remsen simply has not even the beginnings of a sense of the merits, denials, willfulnesses, braveries, offers of amusement and of human absolution that go with class things. Although he counts on such absolution sexually . . . Or he is aware of it, I should say, and he does not count on it for himself.

"Are you saying this to make me feel lower-class again?"

"Christ, I don't know . . ." is what we have just said. "No," I say. Then, in deadpan naughtiness, maybe in boredom: "Yes—"

He is too remarkable-looking and too powerful and too well read not to be irritating when he gets onto the social-class thing so stupidly-slyly. He wants to save himself only a little.

With that savoir faire as someone older and huger than I am, he says, "So, uh, tell . . . uh . . . me the uh ah huh the uh trooooooithhhhh . . ." He believes that he speaks normative English. His accent and his manner are not pleasing. But they're not *repulsive*—a term in local use back then. They're not so bad, but he makes no real effort to please, either. When I don't speak, he—after eyeing my pants, my crotch as I recline on the bed catty-cornered and at a distance from him but within the intimacy of being on the same bed—he, after irritating me out of the sexual mood I was in, comes to the point, at the wrong time, and says, "Will you uh uhwahtchu(h) meeeee—uh mahhssss-tuhr-bayyyyyte(h) . . . ?" When I don't answer—I am hesitating—he adds, "Layturrrr . . . ?"

I raise my eyebrows without focussing my eyes, so that it is as if the hairs in those crescent shapes look at him . . .

At any rate, another kind of sightedness is suggested. I don't have to be honest with myself around him. Lies, within a certain range of untruth, on a certain plane of reference, are okay here—they are all that is possible here. He breathes in a way that is not a sigh: he will make an effort to see that I am aroused . . . My erections, which, after all, do have a factual nature, like my turn running the 440 and my grade average (101+ to show I do unexpectedly good schoolwork), are realer to him than I am. "You said you had a dirty book . . ."

"It's not obscene: it's dirty . . ." He hands it to me from a drawer in a bedside table in which are dirty books, dirty photographs loosely spread.

"They been like that all day?"

"My mother never cleans in here—only Sarah cleans. And she thinks I'm going to hell, but she won't tell on me . . ."

"Does Sarah like it that you're going to hell?"

"She doesn't read the books," he said. "I leave stuff in them so that I can tell."

He makes mistakes about what affects me, but he often understands how to have an effect and how these things operate with and touch me. As a matter of fact, he knows that better than I know myself. I learn each time, learn a little bit, about myself. Within the ambit of a casual and skipping *dirtiness*, he won't discuss his social class or matters of social class endlessly, which leaves room for me to exist—a little room—and he won't irritate me in the next few moments—if he can help it—which also leaves room: it is a form of obscene truce.

His looks, the pale eyes, dark, firm, profuse lashes, strong eyelids, the in-a-way *glare* of his reality—the burning eastern-and-morning shine, almost blinding, of fresh health, an effulgence in his skin—it is more than acceptable if I don't think about the life inside the haylike heat and summer smelliness of his looks: the sheaf of optical and tactile details of human surfaces—of this one person—in the fragments and torn sheets and showers and rags of the light, the brilliantly outflung afternoon light and its shadows (as of the window sash) in the room and some solitary rays revolving like solitary glances from the sky and the glare around the house and under our cloudless part of the sky are warming and enticing: one *plays around*—sins—inside the light as one looks at a dirty picture and reads in the silly book which proposes truly perfect, blinding, blindingly obliterating pleasures.

For a moment, one resents his somewhat too juicy presence. But what if he is the soul of mankind—or something? Or Nonie is? What if I am, in the end, a mistake, or am as momentary, and as bodiless, and as hurried in the end, as the light in the room is? What if he is a true reflection of some ultimately absolute thing in the universe? And I am to be punished in the end—on the way to Lethe?

I say—carefully not sighing, hedging my bets—"You want to do this in socialist brotherhood?" Then: "Or not?"

He considers for a moment whether to let me tease him—whether my rights extend that far—or my power . . . Or my powers . . . He doesn't know my mood, my state, with any precision.

"Yes," he says, "let me see your prick . . ." He says it with different inflections and with just a touch of a tone of cleverness to show he's *on top of the situation* . . . heroically. He claims too much: that he can read everything I feel, that he's not the fool here. It's a disaster, socially (or sexually)—to be beyond someone's comprehension; so that people who claim to comprehend you are forcing you into a bind. You have to agree or else insult them.

Also, if you're spending a couple of hours with some kid who believes in clichés, you have to be clichéd or the whole thing turns into a nightmare of overt struggle—often really violent, as if you were a demon, a goblin, a hobgoblin, as if your being unlike him, or her, meant you were part of an army of unseen powers. And that it is not all linguistic . . . I mean linguistic snobbery, like genital snobbery, seems to be demonic . . . bile and brimstone. But it *irritates* me to pretend he understands me . . . Of course, in a way he does. His stuff, based on that pretension, partly works. I feel I am all bent over, bent together, as if we were locked in a toy chest, he and I, or something, but his stuff partly *works*. It is not like being with a helpless girl. It works and some of it doesn't work and I am not really the demon here. In my irritation with his claims of absolute truth—and of absolute understanding—I speak in a way familiar to him—I mean it is a way he feels that *people* speak except for some girls: "Socialism is bullshit," I say. "What control is there of the governors? Power corrupts. Real power really corrupts . . . Absolute power corrupts absolutely . . . The claim of absolute thought corrupts. You have to have electoral socialism—and, probably, you can't. That's what's wrong with your Stalin . . ."

"You [are] bullshit[ting]," he says. I am, too, but I also mean that what I say is pretty much correct—in part. Remsen goes on: "He [Stalin] has to guard a great new idea from killers . . . from the dead men of the old regimes."

Very few people accuse you of what is not true of them and which scares them in themselves.

"Oh, what bullshit . . . Anyone who does that with power, well, power is power, my friend . . ."

"That's not a famous epigram," he said almost humbly in his triumph (at this reply). I look at him, though, and his eyes are glaring masterfully. He has one hand stroking his crotch. Disgusting . . .

I smile patiently.

Affection in me toward him humbles him . . . sort of.

"Don't handle yourself . . . Your mother thinks we're talking intellectually . . ."

"This is intellectual," he said masterfully-slyly-argumentatively (meaning that sex of this sort *was* intellectual). I hear his zipper; I am not looking at him. I know from experience he gets sleepy-eyed and weird when he shows himself to the air—I think that is like some boy or boys he knew earlier, but maybe it is natural to him—it is foreign and creepy to me.

Then, usually, after a long few seconds of that, he wakes to himself and then to me . . . which moves me if I look . . . I wasn't looking. I meant not to look today or be moved by him, but I did and was moved; and, then, grinning in a shadowy way with raised eyebrows, I looked away—calmly—into the middle of the reality here as he has defined it over and over, which is to say, I look into the middle of the lightlessness of *We are not in love* . . . He had a firmer—and more sensible—sense of lying than I did, a more excitable and doom-laden sense of untruth —by that I don't mean lies; I mean the failure of an absolute . . . of the absolute . . . A truth he believes is invariably a total and unchanging truth. His face darkened and lightened whatever he did with a kind of dense illumination of his forms of logic by the action he was doing as he went along—by a pragmatic relativism somewhat beyond me physically. I was jealous of him, of the ways he was, in a lot of ways. "I like to imagine things," he says. Then he says, "I like to lie . . ." A kind of innocence as he *toys* with himself . . .

"*My mother* says that . . ." I can't, at the moment, remember the term *free will* . . . "No one likes to be coerced by truth . . ."

He reaches over to stroke my skinny chest between the buttons of my shirt—he does it with one long, knuckly, gently hairy finger. Like my mother, he is a cold lover of mine—if he is a lover of mine—cold except for the excitement of the ups and downs of *who's-the-boss, who-loves-who-more-at-the-moment*: a weird historicism of this stuff, they both like that—in different ways.

"I am using my left hand," he says. It is kind of a cold moment. "I'm ambidextrous sexually now: I've trained myself . . . God, the woman who gets me will be lucky . . ."

He touches flesh—my flesh—to get himself going. Perhaps he touches me in the hope of his being able to get me going. It is a *cold* business—hot in some ways, hot as a byproduct, a leftover and amateur heat.

"Bad sex is an earnest of *normalcy* . . ."

"What does *earnest* mean?" he asks.

"A sign, a promise . . . a token . . ."

"You and the dictionary," he says. He says, "You want to read out loud from the Marquis de Sade?"

"I'm all right," I say. That means *Leave me alone* . . .

My assurance, my half-assurance—the half-bumptious thing of perception, often semi-worded close to its origination as perception in a boy—and the way that that shows that I am allied to suburban words and some secret words and to words for secret things—that is a lot of what about me excites him . . . the real world and emotions and moments known in words and inflections, in hints and the like, and then that *knowledge* is seen, somewhat foolishly, as a sign of *social caste*.

The longer he knows me the more like me he becomes in some mannerisms—and some skills—and often he shows his feelings of superiority at having learned what I learned, at his having *mastered* it.

"No one is all right," he corrects me. "People are immature or they are mature." He comes to the correction of others almost like a porpoise bringing its blowhole to the surface of the sea—it is a necessity of breath, death-and-life really, something like that.

I move away slightly, only slightly, from his finger—actually by then two absentminded knuckly fingers. I turn partly onto my side, out of his reach. I sigh and start in on a sort of dryly strained pantomimic jousting, a jostling with him but made of silence and distancing—a resistance to the somewhat sexy maneuverings, fluctuations, pulsings of the bed (those go with the movements of his right hand on himself), and to the thoughts, the meanings. In this oceanic set of seconds I am inert despite the movements of his left hand—and of his mood—inert toward the eroticism in me which reflects or answers to or echoes his. Or is rivalrous with it. Pride. And a different sense of what is sexual? Or virtue? A moral cowardice? A bravery? The circling, semi-startled nature of my mood, the comparative ease of sexuality at that age, a sense of the difficulty of continuing in my life—and then sexuality itself, cumulatively—accumulatingly—and, looking ahead, crescendoingly, unprotectedly, unshieldingly interesting.

My style is to be inert . . . an indolent insolence. Remsen named it (on other occasions) *an insolent indolence*—a phrase from some book, or perhaps his own, with the help of a thesaurus. The phrases don't mean the same thing. He wants to have a vocabulary like mine but he is careless about usage and connotation—or uncaring or thoughtless—and he believes meaning has been established: he sees universal and absolute meanings everywhere. I am erotically inert, indolent—whatever—and that indolent inertia—or suburban virtue—is part of how I talk to people: it is an unsettling discarding of erotic ambition—*hence* (*hence* is a show-off word) an odd claim to victory-and-defeat both, a sense of superiority in terms of foresight and in regard to not being tricky, an offer of a truce, an implication of some rank in regard to a bleak acceptance of the moment.

This sex—between boys—at the edge of a blossoming into some sort of social existence has in it an acceptance of failure as a principal thing: it is a field of effort without further purpose here: it is directed elsewhere in its purposes. Procreation is not its goal; and pride is only oddly involved, as in the grunting sweatiness of wrestling.

Remsen said, calmly ignoring my mood of resistance while categorizing it—you know that tone in someone your age when you're young—"You're bloodless. Doesn't your blood ever boil?"

The loneliness of being unspoken to even though someone is speaking, it's like being a cavern—and being turned into a monster—the terms of your monsterhood, deformity or scales or that you breathe fire and are a devourer; the terms, I say, are unclear . . .

"You're the cold one," I say from my odd posture, but then I lean back; I roll onto my back again. I say it with inflection but not with a recognizable music. "You're the one who *always* says you have the heart of a lizard . . ."

He ignores that. Too. He speaks aloud from within the breathing whelk shell of his hallucinatory moment: "She is spreading her legs," he intones. "The soft fur of her muff is—"

"—braided to spell *For Remsen* . . ."

"Why-are-you-a-cold-fish?" he asks as he works.

He is mostly really talking to himself—perhaps he is talking about himself. So it is a bid for attention. I want to insert myself in his daydreams; I say, "Miss Gangtinney says *I* am a cold poached fish . . . a carp. I am provincial and sarcastic . . ."

Confession as a sort of solicitous rape of attention: he says orderingly: "Unbutton your shirt . . ."

I think giving sexual orders was his favorite sexual daydream. Remsen was scared of Miss Gangtinney. He was scholastically ambitious, and she was *social*, wellborn (by St. Louis standards, not at the top but okay), and very bright and had a lot of say with good colleges. And she was on record as disliking boys in general and bright Jews with pretty sisters in particular, bright Jewish girls who were, in general, much brighter than their brothers, Miss Gangtinney said; the brothers she derided as pushy and Christless—i.e., without mercy or a true sense of values—without a sense of the value of the nothingness of the worldly mind: they (the brothers of the girls she preferred) were too entranced at the *profits* (she was egregiously anti-Semitic but not Nazi) to be made in the newly discovered world . . . The profit the mind can find in the world. And they, the brothers, were unaware of the very real beauty of drunkenness and defeat . . . And of the power of women, the private primacy of breasts . . . And so on . . .

She is a loon—*brilliant* and vital—but a loon—an important woman, a person: a necessary person if you want to learn anything at our school. She does like (and deride) me. But she breaks a lot of her rules for me—and, bitchily and troublemakingly, says so in class, even in classes that I am not in.

"I hate that sor-did bih-bee-bi(h)itch," Remsen says.

I unbutton only one button. "She hates you, too." I sigh and am inert. She can't stand anything about him—except his eyes. She has said, "His eyes make me nervous."

"She doesn't pick on you," Remsen says in an eerily new, sexually tinted, far-off voice.

"She picks on me with *an ax* . . . She's a battle-ax." When I am in trouble in my life, he comes close and is there, not quite as a help, but mostly, maybe, only to look at the wounded beloved, the hatefully beloved—whatever . . . I feel in his breathing that he is returning and is nearer.

He says, "Are you in trouble with her?"

"She makes *room* for me," I said finally, too stirred—too agitated—by the sex he was having to manage much more in the way of speech. Propping my head up with my hand, I turn onto my other side so that he is visible to me. We are visible to each other. Then, perversely, I close my eyes and begin. I remember how well built he is—I am flattered. My elbow digs into the mattress. Do some boys escape this? Are they let alone? Is it a matter of plainness? Of disguise? I open my eyes and I look across him so that his physical reality lies under the whizzing and yet stilled glacier of my pointless staring . . . The meaning here is blurry—as if it were physically hesitant; I am uninstructed and instruction does not shape itself genetically here.

But in this reluctance—the time lag of it, so to speak—one has a stronger sense of the progress of sensation, of the opening of the sexual whatever, of the initial hallucination and of how it warms up and then loses its power to affect me. The loneliness here, like the peculiar lurchingness of the physical reality, seems to be of immense value and yet to be valueless. *He* says, "Hunh? What's that me[an]?" Gangtinney making room for me. I have to ponder and work back in the seconds to find in my memory what I said. He says again, "Let's see your prick . . ." He said it in a kind of nasal voice that made language seem to be a backyard part of his spirit—and of his *body* . . . He is *always* looking for a way to feel he's smarter than I am in the actual moment . . .

I say, "I don't feel like it . . ." But I turn myself, I angle my back slightly. My blood tingles at this exercise of genital fact. We are in touch with each other *oddly*, Remsen and I, in this *odd* way. Abruptly I say, "*I* haven't seen it in hours . . ." And I look down at it and angle myself further and for a moment it is real as heft and length and as sensation, too, but the sensation itself is different and the mind is infinitely more present in this kind of display with a different sort of comparison or struggle hinted at or dealt with.

I tended when I was in his company to drop vowels and hit *n*'s—*navint n'eeN (N)it nowers* . . . Masculine talk. Locker-room jazz. A senseless pretense to yet another style . . .

He knows different things. He feels different things. He breaks off his motion and yet he continues in a sexual arc—I could not do that—he has some information, or some myth, about genitalia that I know little about and can't feel (sensually) except when I am with him. "Jesus," he says. Then, in a mounting arc of feeling that I cannot share but am partly pleased to see: "Let's arm wrestle . . ." That is part of his sensual daydream, his fantasy, of being Hercules—or Samson . . . Unfearful . . . Huge . . . Betrayed, blinded . . . But able to destroy everything nearby—not everything in sight . . . It is an oddly physical semi-hallucination, a symbolic whatever: he likes that a lot.

I say, "Anything to touch flesh in a fighting way . . ." Combative. "No . . ." I said it and heard myself, heard that my breath was quilled with some possibility that included him. Perhaps only as a semi-demi-dominated watcher . . . A minor moment. A major one would be if booze and drugs or some other sort of finality entered in, the drugs of those days being benzedrine, ether, opium, morphine, chloral hydrate, aspirin with brandy, I forget the other ones—I tried the above ones; so did Remsen. *Major* is when you can be *destroyed* . . . I can harm him . . . He can harm me . . . This bothers me a lot. I stop. I am exposed but I lie on my back and put my arm over my eyes.

The bed shudders slightly with *his* movements. "Would your mind doctor think I was crazy?" His doctor has forbidden him to talk seriously with people his own age, he has said. Then I say: "Hit a woman? Twist her wrist? Spank her? Under what circumstances? In what tone? If you do that stuff, who gets the most mileage out of it—you know? It has to be part of a whole shebang—I mean the episode doesn't just stop *there*: it goes on . . ."

"Smash her—smash her to smithereens," he said, sort of roiling semi-demi-mightily on the bed: he is speaking of a difficult woman or of his sisters or of some sort of male heroism perhaps. He jerks off so much that this stuff in the afternoons which doesn't happen all the time partly ends, when it does happen, sometimes, in a dry come.

And the difficulty for him in getting past that point where coming is not certain is not emotionally moving. He curls around on the bed so that his extended arm can touch and start to stroke my leg, not lecherously toward me—he is partly a gentleman—he is in pursuit of a flesh-fiery *idea* of sexuality. It is a gesture for himself, part of an imagined (or actual) sexual ruthlessness, his sexual actuality.

"I don't want to be sad," I said. Postcoital.

Or guilty.

I found what he did on the whole to be repellent but to be acceptable because it was fake—it did not really involve me even in conspiracy. I thought it did not involve any real responsibility for me . . . I thought it was like a tutorial.

"My sisters are shrews," he said. "They're all shrewd enough. I'd like to run over and over them with the car . . . Ah . . ." He is trying for an exciting idea. I may have misheard him. An idea verging on shocked hallucination. Removing my arm from my eyes, looking at him, I see that he is not bold and clear in mood but is *blurry* and lost, half there sexually—faintly shocked by himself, tired, unorgasmic, unsatisfied and already knowing it. You can't talk to someone about what he hasn't done—you cannot teach him to feel sexually. He must protect his sense of the centrality of his life.

"I am rich," he says. "I am rich and I am *handsome* . . . A stiff prick is like a pylon . . . POWER *on* . . . ZZZZZ . . . BZZZZ . . . IZZZ . . ." He was erect in a way that seemed boring and minor to me . . . "Get yours hard—I want to see it," he said.

Guys did that in the locker room for each other sometimes. It wasn't something I liked but I thought it was *normal*, that I ought to do it now. Sometimes when I am *fatuous*, it makes some people like me with an admixture of contempt . . . Remsen liked to lean his head on my bared shoulder if I would bare it and then my stomach would be visible, would be right in front of his eyes, while he jerked off preferably but not necessarily with me *seriously* erect and kind of jerking off, too, but only half seriously. If I was serious, he stopped what he was doing and he stared. I was bigger than he was and I was more sincere when I did it . . . when *I* did anything. And he lost track of himself in curiosity sometimes . . . That was in the past. But right after I came—or he would ask me to wait for him and to come when he did—he would come then, dryly, or not dry but dryly in tone, sort of all mind and relief and study: a playfulness, serious and overweening . . . And I would be struck with grief postcoitally . . . At any rate, we don't do that anymore. Originally I dodged it, prevented it, refused to do it; the original refusal is what I am talking about. But now it has become his taste: I have outgrown my girlish phase; I am now repellent to him, he sometimes says. I know better than to say aloud, "You *won't leave me alone* if I get an erection." One time he called it *Napoleonic artillery, pure Clausewitz, bim, bam, boom*, but he would not explain any part of what he meant and he would not hint; and the way he acted showed nothing. He says now: "Unbutton your shirt . . . please . . . I'll just look and think of Jean . . ." Look and remember being younger and think of a girl he sees now? One pursues a certain tact in these matters . . . One doesn't *say* no. One is merely unmoving . . . unloving . . . inert . . . It is a confusing *subject* . . . a peculiar suburban moment . . .

Who is more unkind here—he or I; he for asking, me for refusing? Is fate or destiny unkind? Genital fate? Sexual destiny—with every man, every woman with an individual sexual character, a singular sexual life? One ought to be stricken with fear and trembling, with a sickness of the soul, of the nerves—of one's soul? This is part of the world. Nonie—and Remsen's sisters—live in the world of men hinted at here in a small corner of the afternoon of two boys . . .

The Last for Now About Nonie

Back when I was a little kid, when we were all sincere that day—in the lightning storm—Nonie was suffering and it was pleasure and no pleasure at all to see her like that.

Daddy's not insincere exactly, but what fantasy-and-reality of his is he instructing her in as a truth when he says, "Nonie, Nonie darling, you have to stop"? *Have to* means what? The *or else* is what? (*He's not* simple—*he was always too much for me*, Lila said.)

"Nonie, it's killing me—you're killing me. Oh, Hon, what can I do to help?" he says.

It used to be that before there were painkillers people went mad from toothache sometimes. He means she will destroy him and who will take care of her then? Isn't that the threat?

She can kill him this way and he won't fight back, but he won't die to help her first. She tries to figure it out without words: you can see it on her face, that she's trying to figure it out, the cathedral child, our cathedral virgin, she wants to comprehend the stained-glass devotion of the man while she is in a state of unsubdued terror, but I don't think she can do it; it makes her suffer more; it makes her crazier to try . . . These are some of the politics of actual love, actual terror.

Her safety, her well-being, is a mark of our excellence and refinement. In Nonie, in her eyes, in her ideals, in her touch, is a bleakness, a bleak area—a distance, a landscape, a wordlessness that still is human . . . Nonie is well within the species' limits. I guess she reads Daddy's attitude as indifference. Indifference to her invites her violence, the girl in the rainstorm—her prettiness, her bitten fingernails.

She knocks a doll off a longish wooden rack on a bookcase; but then she's afraid right away and she says, "I DIDN'T DO THAT. IT JUST BROKE. IT JUST BROKE!"

It was rubberoid and it tore; she says it *broke*.

She looks sly, then woodenly innocent. Nonie defeated me often over the years. Even now her shadow threatens me in a number of ways. I kind of sincerely mean it when I say, *God damn her to hell.*

The silver-gray-white lightning pushes a dark tree trunk racingly onto, into the window, into the room. It flies into my eyes, my mind, where it shivers, vibrates, is stilled.

Nonie stands in the passionate thin albino reality of the light. Leapingly it recedes—across her glaring eye sockets as well. Across Daddy's white-shirted chest, too.

"GO TALK TO IT, YOU SON OF A BITCH. MAKE IT STOP. IT'S A BAD LIGHT, DADDY." Then to Anne Marie: "GO STAND BY THE WINDOW. YOU'RE FAT; WE PAY YOU MONEY—LET IT GET YOU!"

Nonie knows herself to be the cheated one—she's not an able lawyer, not proficient at contention in words and principles, at least in today's tribunal. Whosoever's lightning it is, why doesn't Daddy help her? Shadows like those that mar the face of the moon are in her mouth: "MAKE IT GO KILL MOMMA! MOMMA TELLS LIES. MAKE IT GO KILL MOMMA, BURN HER UP. IT CAN TURN *HER* BLACK."

Sins are those acts that guarantee defeat. Nonie was sinless for all practical purposes until the damned lightning started.

"For God's sake, Hon—"

The child—me—laughs at Nonie's stricken and illumined and knotted face.

"I DON'T LIKE IT!" Nonie shouts.

She's given up inside herself, given up to some extent . . . momentarily.

She faces blinkingly the maybe Holy Beast . . . outside . . . that is in the room suddenly . . . the Angelic Flutter of This Injustice, the paw of the Beast of Interrogation . . . the loss of her citizenship now.

Then she grabs the doll she knocked off the rack; she stoops, grabs—swiftly—and throws it—a gesture of unmaternal shamelessness.

The seriousness of The Onslaught: she wants to supply a recent minor, childish crime in this cruelly unfavoring context, a mock sacrifice, a display of ritual temper by a flat-chested girl who is the soul of quick logic and respectability and who has just done something *not-so-bad* . . . It's a kind of weird combination of things passionate and harshly shrewd but childlike in her, and *pure* . . .

Spittle is on her chin, and Daddy is crying.

Forgiveness is easy if the moment is not particularly real . . .

Short of her death, and not even then, in a way, she doesn't *have* to feel inferior. As a fighter, she was, on occasion, happy. She could feel triumphant, pure, well loved, well taken care of, whether in much of a true way she was or not, whenever it seemed necessary or advisable to her.

The pain for me after the session with Leonie, the pain of not being liked enough, of Nonie's knowing the world better than I did, was so horrific—so biting and long-lasting—that I vowed never to do *that* to anyone, the thing that Leonie and Nonie did, or that Nonie did, and never to be *agreeable* in the way I had been, to that stuff, never to struggle sexually or in any other way with women at all . . .

But a dozen years before that night, when I was little, I watched Nonie suffer. And, here, inside that night, Nonie in her terror looks innocent again, innocent in a way: it's Nonie still in the little openings when her terror lets up. She is riddled by thoughts, her kind of thoughts; she has her kind of thoughtful terror. Is there such a thing as a lesser soul? What if she really is as good as me?

Jesus!

Don't hurt me, God, for judging her.

The doll she threw is one she never liked; that useful (or placatory) sin was witty . . . She is panting and outraged—and full of waiting . . . A ghost appears at the window, through a glass veil; the veil is running with water; howling gutturally, it ignores the offering, it runs toward Nonie . . . And she screams. She makes a movement of terror. Bent over, she clutches her own thigh. The intruding light swells and ebbs. Nonie spits and dribbles—she cowers, rouses herself; she perseveres and is brave—that is to say, she is impenitent. Impenitence is remarkable in her here.

I want Nonie broken and penitent and saved. The ammoniac smell of her pee and the frenzy of her resistance afflict me. Can someone make her penitent, short of violence and horror stronger than her own?

I don't want things to be like this.

Is it wrong to see her in this way, when she is like this?

Nonie's open mouth and soldiering eyes and the walls of the room and Anne Marie's face and breast are covered with wrecked light. The fleeting shadow-films of the rain—the rain's shadows—are a sort of terrible ruin . . . Come on, gang, let's all pitch in and SAVE our Nonie now. My NONIE. The rain noises are like a horse snuffling, a lynx breathing in my ear—in a dream. Nonie is looking at Daddy: "YOU DON'T CARE

ABOUT ME. YOU DON'T TAKE MY SIDE EVER. YOU HATE ME. YOU WANT ME DEAD. I KNOW YOU. GOD DAMN YOU. I WON'T LOVE *YOU* ANYMORE—GET OUT ON THE LAWN. LET THE LIGHTNING GET YOU. I'M NOT BAD. LET IT GET YOU, DADDY." Christ, it's almost funny—it's funny if you have no heart. Let's save her . . . "YOU'RE BAD. YOU HATE ME." She kicks at Anne Marie: "YOU FAT BITCH, GOD DOESN'T LIKE YOU AT ALL. YOU PLAY WITH YOURSELF AND YOU LIE. YOU GET OVER, YOU GET OVER BY THE WINDOW: LET IT BURN *YOU* . . ." Nonie means, surely, doesn't she, that only *evil* meets evil head-on?

I can't imagine life experienced as blamelessness. Yes I can.

Nonie is a distraught child.

Daddy says, "Nonie, you're breaking my heart." He wants to save her. He doesn't want to touch her while she's sweaty with emergency and craziness and whatever, while she's undulating and spitting, and is hot and fat and cold with terror and a kind of soul's starvation and bitterness. Daddy's gentleness is unreliable. He doesn't want to learn *anything* today: he knows enough, he feels . . . He does feel that way. He often says Nonie's perfect; and he avoids her—he avoids modifying his *sweet* view that Nonie's sweet, she's perfect, she is sinless, she will never die, that with luck she will never suffer: "Nonie honey, my head hurts. Please, Honey. Nonie—that's enough, that's enough of this *filth* . . . You don't want to do this, you don't want to do this to me. My heart is breaking, Nonie."

"DON'T TOUCH ME. YOU LIE. FUCK YOU, DADDY. I WANT TO GET AWAY FROM YOU. I WANT TO KNOW NICE PEOPLE."

"Nonie, you don't know what you're saying. You like your home. The bluebird is right here. You'll find I'm right. People here care about you, be assured of that, Hon. Be smart, Honey."

"I READ YOUR LETTERS IN YOUR DESK. I KNOW ABOUT YOU. I KNOW THE THINGS YOU DO WITH ANGELA." Angela Martin runs his office.

He shouldn't tell Nonie to be smart in a voice that's sad and that has longing in it. It scrapes on her nerves and her sensibility, her sense of things.

"Nonie . . ." he says.

"YOU DON'T KNOW ANY-THING," she says. "YOU NEVER KNOW ANYTHING—EVERYBODY SAYS YOU'RE A FOOL . . ."

She is frantic. It's clear that she does love him, even if mostly in this way of accusation and request.

I don't think I understand *love* as the right to ask too much of someone.

"Nonie, please: forgive and forget. We are who we are; everybody has to learn to put up with what they can get. We can't keep track of every little thing or we'll wind up on the rubbish heap."

Nonie shouts, "GO AWAY!" to him. Then, as if to a ghost (she is addressing a confusion, Lila maybe—maybe me): "HE'S *MY* FATHER. HE LOVES *ME*. HE WANTS TO DO THINGS FOR ME. YOU WANT HIM TO DO THINGS ONLY FOR YOU. YOU'RE SELFISH AND I HATE YOU. YOU SHOULD BE DEAD . . ."

"We know it's a bad time for you, Honey," Daddy says in a mournful voice. He's no longer listening to her.

Nonie *soldiers* away still in a swift and eerie light. The great round noise comes rolling in; it smoothly shrinks away. She cringes and straightens up again: "THAT FUCKING LIGHT IS BAD . . ."

Daddy doesn't mind what she does as much as I do because he *loves and forgives and forgets*—he does: he forgets.

Also, he doesn't care the same way I do. Sometimes he does, but he can take up and drop fatherhood, he can take up and drop his romance with her . . . She's a child—*what does she know?* I am more involved with her—more implicated in what she is than he is . . .

Nonie has something tough in her bulging and toughly outward-focussed eyes—even when she is in extreme terror. Even then. Even then you can't see into her eyes: she doesn't want you to.

If Nonie were finally to come to harm today, if she were to change now in any way that would be disapproved of widely, or if she were to become miserable for a long time—if she stops fighting and takes a risk of being another sort of person (or child), a sad or hurt child, even if a sweet one, easily defeated, always ashamed and unhappy—S.L. would be as if emasculated . . . He would not be comfortable if she became more sexual—and less mean. He would like her more but he would suffer then, too. Nonie knows that—she will try at times to shame him willfully, in revenge, as his lover tidying up the past and making it fair—I mean *just*. Honestly sexless in a sense, after the fact. She is maybe angrily defeated—without hope, but she intends to continue . . . Her state is jumbled. For a moment, she is pure, although in a jumbled state . . . But she attaches the change in her not to being threatened by justice but to being unfairly cut off from having-a-good-life, joyous and comfortable—the sort of life Daddy wants for her. I don't want to sound like a nag but how free of judgment can *anyone* be—man, woman, or child? At what point does injustice begin? But if you start with a sense of human evil, then justice is what begins, with an effort, and troubledly—isn't that so? Nonie will be fiercer than she is here—much more fierce—and more desperately unrepentant—more hysterical and mad if she is permanently defeated today but not *hurt* enough for-once-and-all to move into that other state of gentleness and civilization.

I don't want the world to be essentially different—I think that is a stupid thing to wish for: who would ever be smart enough to know what a world should be, let alone this world—but I want *her* to be different.

Daddy has to dodge Nonie and the nature of her disasters—or this one disaster, here—or he can't live. He's running away even as he sort of tends to her and is present.

Maybe he thinks Momma will see to it that this isn't a *disaster*; Momma is gambling at this moment that Nonie won't throw herself out the window, that Nonie won't have *serious hysterics* or a breakdown, upstairs, today, et cetera. Momma is keeping her nerve, downstairs with the company . . . Momma and Nonie each blame the other's character and the other's being nerve-racking for S.L.'s erraticisms of attachment to them.

Daddy is holding me; I start to wriggle and he bends to put me down rather than risk squeezing or juggling me. I want to give Nonie my hope and my contentment with things—such as it is, that contentment. I want her penitent—and saved . . . No one will do this, only me.

Momma said once, *I want to go for six months without telling a single lie. You know, it takes real nerve to lie in front of the whole world and then wait and see what happens to you.*

In Daddy's grip—held by his hands at the end of his outstretched arms—I press one foot down on the carpet. In Nonie's room. In this house. I want to go to Nonie—my other self . . .

"Go to Anne Marie," Daddy says to the stretched-out, spinally contorted kid.

My heartbeat is a mass of knocking pulsations in me. The rainlight in the room is darkish-brown and gray-blue. And a lot of wet is in the air. Nonie's hands are the same color as a puddle.

The grown-ups' speeches are the differently weighted branches of a tree. I am a child; I am intent on Nonie, one child to another—I join myself to her now in the separate sect.

When I start toward Nonie, Anne Marie shouts, "*NEIN!*" and Daddy drags me back.

See, here is Nonie as a marvel—her reality is part of the lied-about, filthy sweetness of childhood. I remember Nonie—this-girl-here, the one in pain, the one I want to help—not Nonie-of-other-times much. I'm about to do something; I'm about to go and hug mad, ammoniacal Nonie. Daddy and Anne Marie think Nonie is very bad or they would not try to prevent me. But in my mind they are *quiet*. I have a steamy chaos in me. All order is concentrated in my will—my concentration. They don't matter—Nonie's in pain. I tear, I pierce the *badness* in the room. I move toward her legs, the reachable legs below the terrified and stony *face* of the shouting girl. In her anger and piteous prettiness and ferocity and blindness, Nonie is here. I hug her smelly leg. I preferred having her be calm to having her sacrificed in order to have a world with less evil in it. Nonie raises her hand. Her hand is moving—*swattingly.* Pay no attention. Blink. Squint. See the pewter-and-peony-skinned child's face pucker. *If you ask me, it's a shame.*

"HE'S BOTHERING ME."

The slap rocked me. I can't find the nerve connections to my eyes.

She damaged my eyes.

Maybe I exaggerate.

This isn't EVIL—this is just something that happened. This is just something that happens.

The child's cry—that upward fluster, that ascent of a noise of pain, and then the sound of the slap—change the face of the girl. The girl is wild-eyed but shrewd. She looks like Lila for a moment. She gazes around measuringly; then she glares madly again . . .

The child's outcry in the rain-dark, in the wet air, and the smell on Nonie, and Nonie's face, its multiple expressions, are gruesome, crawly—also sympathetically childhoodlike . . .

"I DIDN'T MEAN ANYTHING. IT WAS AN ACCIDENT. I DON'T HATE MYSELF, DADDY."

Anne Marie and Daddy said things and tried to pull me away from Nonie, but I clung to her, to Nonie.

You'll survive.

She *feels* the stupidity of having shown such a quick automatism of temper in front of DADDY. She feels her terror still—the storm is weighty outside—and now she is anguished and chagrined: is that guilt? For a few seconds, Nonie blacks out. She hopes to return from her terror to some more central space. She says, "HE WAS BOTHERING ME, DADDY." She squints as if she were being beaten on—in what is, she feels, her own vast innocence. With one hand, in a gesture of pudgy unanger, while she stares at Daddy, she clubs the kid with blows of erratic trajectory, some quite brief, a cover-up, a risk to make her accusation look true—her nerves are strung tight—she's embarrassed now . . .

The child, in a way, expected this. He has an odd childhood sense of futurity—and of the rightness of his life—he clings to her on and on . . . He feels very little pain . . . He is intent on erasing her wildness . . .

Because he doesn't cry out, Anne Marie stops pulling at him, she stops trying to rescue him.

The child's choked, hurried breath, near his sister, is as if around a hollowing and echoing pit in him of devastations, from long before now, from before Nonie, an old grief, the dead matter of a literal silence in him, the once almost dead child. I have *some* knowledge of what pain is. Nothing has granted Nonie such a silence; she never goes inward; she has no silence in her; everything in her is a living voice, a chorus of live voices: the child hugging her leg and squinting and making no noise except for his breath is inexpressibly foreign to her, his mind—his presence. She did not expect to have such a presence in her life. His silence is *unreal,* the silence of that male child—but he is physically real to her even if only as an emotional pressure bound up in certain gestures—perhaps as a ghost—another ghost evoked by the rain . . .

Demons take her and hide her, and I want her here. Presence is an absolute in real life for many of us.

If you are here, you matter to me.

Daddy moves forward, takes Nonie's hair, and pulls and jerks her head so that she stops hitting the kid. She glares at him . . . Then merely stares . . . He is embarrassed and backs away while she stares at him . . . *His* silence mixes sexual and paternal shock and a sense of justice and a surging but suffocated relief—all of us now are tangled in will and shame . . .

Nonie, testing him, returns to wildness—she persists—she grabs my arm and yanks it, as she did her doll's. *(She has the devil in her.)*

I doubted the pain I felt then . . .

The pain fluttered and slid—slid away for a while, to some extent: do you remember the anesthesia childhood could summon up, the thick blanketing, the psychic musculature? I moved into inward angled places and into sturdy postures in them over an emptiness, postures of the mind meant for accepting hurtful blows while at the same time bouncing (in slow ways) away from such blows without affect—this was in a childhood reality of hurt, forgiveness, folly, and lunatic willfulness, at that age when one is important as a child for whose sake grown-ups indulge in restraint and calm and in special faces and even redemption . . .

It's easy enough to think the kid deserves to be hit—he's so odd, so stupid, so alert.

He is so much in another place in the story.

Daddy has released her. I haven't—I mean my presence and my purposes haven't released her.

"THERE'S TOO MUCH LIGHTNING. DADDY, I HATE THE LIGHTNING!"

She is explaining things to S.L. Nonie shouts, "IT WAS AN ACCIDENT!" She is trying to push me away from her legs—what use does she have for penitence?

Daddy says, "She's so upset she doesn't know what she's doing. Nonie—oh, Nonie, look how he likes you."

His eyes aren't focussed—if S.L. doesn't look at her, he's not concerned about what she might do, although it seems that her mind, her soul weren't geared to abhor accidents.

Also, Wiley is a small creature, an accusing ghost perhaps sent by caterpillars and other small creatures that she's put or beaten to death, for instance. His circumstances undermine her position as a wronged and pure child. She is *exasperated,* as if to say that everyone has the right to some jealousy, some violence—the right, the habit of those things, the right, the habit of normality: these habits . . .

It is harder for me to believe in Nonie's mind as worth respect, it is harder for me to believe in her right to live, in this fashion, in *her* fashion than it is for me to accept the fact of my own future death. I have tested myself to see.

I was given this girl to love, I was given this girl as a companion in my childhood—our childhood, I guess.

Nonie's eyes aren't blind; she's a little crazy. I see her eyes; they're wretched. I forget my own feelings at the sight of so much drama and expressiveness as I awedly see in her eyes . . .

"He *wants* to help her—look, he took his punishment, he's standing his ground—he's a real ace, he's a *trouper.*"

Anne Marie says strangely, in her deeply accented English, "*He does not melt . . .*"

I see uncertain malice in Nonie's eyes—a shapeless rage of childhood, its helplessness half-and-half mixed with *I-won't-be-helpless-anymore.* Her malice is not actually focussed on *me* but on my not being as upset by the lightning as she was. I saw it. She hated my (temporary) guiltlessness. I saw it. I'm sure that she excepted me from her really serious rage that day—not later. Things changed later. But she only hated me a little that day. It was a momentary exemption. But still, my innocent kindness, selfish and childish as it was, sickened her.

The partly privileged child embraced Nonie's smelly legs.

Her angled body, her face are—a fist. Her face is a fist. Her whole body is a fist. Sweat ripples the already uncertain planes of her clayey cheeks—above me, at that *not grown-up* height. The sweat further dissolves the already uncertain outlines of her anger, her malice, her capacity for doing harm, for harming me . . . I remember her face from other moments. I piece her together inside myself, where I am oppressed by the reality of the presence of her grief and terror, and mine on occasion as a measure and a consequence or parallel or half-twin of hers. I see her as a malicious child—she maybe will be less rambunctious when she is prettier, or maybe not. I see her in small, ejaculatory spurts of surprise. I see a bad face on a pretty girl. Then I see a wolf, a solitary cat the size of a girl, a creature from down the street, not from here. That is, I see the animal meanness of her eyes, my sister's eyes . . . Look, my sister is a secret thing from a dream, not otherwise admitted to, save as marriageable flesh, breeding fodder for nephews. Otherwise, she is completely hidden from me, she is only her name plus an epithet, *Nonie, my sister* . . . Even to myself, she is as secret as that. How much is she going to hurt me today? How much will she insist on seeing to it that my suffering is *the same as* (equal to) hers?

It takes nerve to live—Momma says so. She has said, *The thing is to be quick on your feet and not a coward.* S.L. says to Anne Marie, "Stop it—let him be nice to her: what do you think? That she's a mad person? She won't hurt him—she wouldn't hurt a flea."

Is that true? Or will she hurt me so badly today I will live with it for the rest of my life, suffer one way and another in who I am and in what I do, because of her—is that what is going to happen?

Nonie is looking at Daddy. She is staring at him. She is trembling. She moved her hand—Nonie struck me on the forehead without looking.

"It's only her hand!" Daddy shouted at Anne Marie.

Her hand, then her elbow, as a matter of fact.

"IT WAS AN ACCIDENT. HE BUMPED INTO ME."

That was partly true.

"*Ach, Gott,*" fat Anne Marie said in her *accent.* Her facial posture said we all knew, everyone knew, Nonie *always* lied.

Anne Marie reached for me with a fat, indignant snort of dislike for Nonie . . .

"YOU HATE ME, *YOU* SHOULD BE KILLED," Nonie said to her. Nonie swung at her.

Daddy, partly at an averted angle—as if shyly—pushed Nonie back from me and away from Anne Marie; Nonie stumbled—but I went on clinging to her.

"We all feel bad. Don't say that, Sweetie," Daddy said while he reached, almost idly, *almost* effectually for me.

My forehead hurts. So what?

The immediacy of Nonie's pain, her loneliness goad me—I'm in the shadow of her emotions—the emotions of a child in this family—

in this house, this air, this rain, among these people . . . I am an often bored child; when she's in trouble, she often plays with me—it's like that now; we're in limbo. She and I.

I tug at her arm—silently. Nonie's pain, mine—in the moment—burn me. My pain is from loneliness in my sympathy, as if I'd embarked on something that held contractually a kind of paralyzed or stilled or dead sense of myself—my inner deadness and old grief are stirring in me, monsters beneath their wrappings of my conceit in the supposed goodness of my life and in my supposed powers of consolation and rescue as a (male and monied) child . . . I am a someone-not-me at the moment; I have to be hugged by a special Nonie who hugs *The Sympathizer*—then, the child expects, we will be freed from this moment, she and I, and we will *play* then—and history will be different then.

Nonie emits a funny cry when I press my head against her belly—she's partly bent over, because of a bolt of lightning outside. Nonie's noise draws from S.L. a gasp of intractable emptiness, his form of being gentlemanly, a purposeless will—no self, no selfish will, that emptiness, a formal thing.

DADDY. Daddy.

DO YOU SEE NONIE'S EYES?

Nonie presses her hands over my eyes, over my mouth, those of the child, to be honest—not me but just *a child* who was there.

Daddy says to Anne Marie, "Don't be a second-guesser. Stand back. That child knows. He's got a good heart. He knows what he's doing. Let him do what he wants to do."

Nonie shoved, she pushed, she almost lifted the child, pushed him toward the window. The disappearing light had drawn back, as if it had been poured out by tilting our house toward that window. The light flowed down rainy perspectives—the fading light of the beast. The thunder was big, thunderous and threatening, wooden and empty, mere bulges of sound now, sturdy and fat. I was joggled, I tottered. I was thrown to block it, to dam the sound, the huge, bodiless gavelling.

It is possible I never knew Nonie well.

The child, at Nonie's shove, plays S.L.'s old role, when he used to go stand on the lawn, or the torn doll perhaps—a sacrifice, a feint—a Golden Apple—an experiment to distract the beast.

Daddy can't go to her. My father's illicit, hapless, shamed excitement, automatic and sad, means he can't go to her.

Then abruptly, with squinting eyes, she stumbles forward, grabs me, and she turns in an overburdened circle. She's hugging and carrying me now—like a dog, a captured dog, a doll. Are you frightened? Will the horror be that she will put out my eyes? This is *an environment* in which few come to actual harm, this suburb, isn't that so? Her movements, our sorrow, are a cumulative muffling, a sort of special silence. She turns in a clumsy circle, like a walker in a snowstorm. I disappear in the white.

Lila has said, *Don't be a fool, S.L. You know the things that happen.*

She means: Be cautious. Don't trust people.

If Nonie is an ordinary woman and if, as an ordinary person, she doesn't matter, what am I to forgive her for? If she does matter, forgiving her is a spiritual thing that occurs in relation to her continuing repentance, which never occurs. And so my forgiveness is never quite apt, never quite real, never quite there. Only my *folly* (my being fooled) is there. She's a fighter. Of what spiritual use is my forgiveness to her? It has only a tactical value for her. I can only just bear to admit that she causes me pain and has shaped my life day by day, every day for most of my life —no: all my life. Indifferent forgiveness is a vile concept: *Your sins don't matter; shut up; go away; they don't matter; you're not in trouble; go away.*

Indifference is a sort of pragmatic absolution. And a mode of destruction of the mind by disregarding the potency of others . . . I spent years with Nonie; and indifference to her means losing huge chunks of myself, and distrusting my own darkness. It means losing my sense of why certain kinds of lousiness occur. That might be absolution, but it's also blindness and stench. I'm not a pope, a saint, a prophet . . .

Nonie is experiencing the direct intrusion of God in her vicinity.

Carrying me in that burdened and clumsily staggering way, she says, "TAKE AWAY THE FAT ONE THERE. LOCK HER IN A TRUNK—IN THE DARK, DADDY . . ."

Us—against outsiders . . .

Nonie keeps moving in a trapped circle, joggling and resettling me constantly. Nonie wants God to go away. We can't live together much longer if Nonie continues to shame me with my inability to console her, my inability to keep her from her violence and her undoing herself or whatever this is.

What Nonie is is truer over a longer period of time and more complex as truth than almost anything I later studied in school.

But because of what she was, and I was, she became minor for me, despite the extent to which she is a conduit for Evil entering my world in my presence, minor because I had no choice but to love her to some extent for a while and little choice except to dislike—and ignore—her later . . . But she is not minor. Still, I cannot imagine myself *punishing* her—only competing with her—and not face-to-face, once I have the power to live as I choose. Also, I wear out, my nerves wear out—*they* forget her. The changeability of my nerves applies a disguise to evil in my world.

Or is she merely ordinary and a common type?

And then, of course, I am like her in some ways. I am complementary to her, and Daddy is like her, and other men and women I know are like her.

I must live with her, she enjoys attacking me, and I want someone to attack her for me—she's a girl—and so the part of me that's like Nonie becomes more a part of me: I hold back like some girls, although if I could catch Nonie in an act of foulness, I might be able to kill her—I don't know. She likes it that I loathe her; she's addicted to it. It excites her—it soothes her some when I *hate* her: maybe she will be tough and famous in the world. I don't know. When I pause and listen to my own breathing and sort of firmly want her dead, I then abruptly half laugh.

I really do truly want someone else to kill her.

I don't want to be guilty of her death—this is a kind of inhibition; maybe it's despicable.

We're still fighting away—against the dark, against the light. All at once, the adopted child is shoved into black, wet, breaking window glass—is this in a dream? My eye is gone, my eye is put out, my face is bleeding, the facial nerves are cut: and my vision will be uncertain all my life now.

WATCH OUT.

She doesn't want to be sacrificed for my sake. It is a dream . . . She did not push me through the window. (She did on another occasion, and I was cut on my chin and forehead and eyelid, and my vision was tampered with by the wound and by the nervous fear that affected the muscles of my eyes after that.) Today, she shoved me toward the window and then grabbed me back before I plowed into the windowsill.

She doesn't want an *unhappy* life—she's *normal*.

The child, the boy, is a locus of powers she hasn't recognized yet. Maybe I'm more resigned about things in my life than I should be . . . than I would have been if it hadn't been for watching her and thinking her bad and distasteful . . . But still I went on living with her heat, the suggestion of excitement and of shelter for me in it, and the strength of it. Of course, no protection exists for me in her except as it suits her. A number of my definitions of things start with her, here, in her room. I am not a god. I am, for her, supremely not-God: I am a brother. Nonie's is the nearest childhood, the most accessible portion of the world to me. We are the most explicable beings for each other, the most handily available for inspection, for some experiments, sources of a lot of further information close by when things are obscure and we are singly too narrow to have a satisfactory view of the mystery.

In her voice and body she keeps up her manner of defiance, of courage—the claim of her herohood in what she does is her true vocation. "YOU'RE DISGUSTING AND I'M NOT"—to Daddy. "YOU'RE NO GOOD. I DON'T LOVE YOU . . ."

Her affection is incurably strange to me. It smells of disorder. Her skin is hot; her breath peppery and foul.

"LISTEN TO ME. YOU DON'T LISTEN. I'M A GOOD PERSON—"

But I listen; I hear her; I want to know what she's saying—she is familiar and lunatic and bad—look at her mouth, look at her eyes—no, don't. No one studies Nonie except me. I'm the best student of what Nonie is at this moment.

Nonie is struggling to walk, carrying me in front of her—she is choking me. Ha-ha. It is a farce. I am partly unconscious; I'm unhurtable; I'm a dear child; I'm an innocent—I'm the elaborate semi-existence of something remarkable in her eyes. If she can hurt someone unhurtable, a dear child, but innocently, then that's evidence that she is not hellish but potent-and-misunderstood—this is a dear ambition of hers. Then she can confront the lightning and be innocent and wronged.

I am nearly unconscious in her arms. She's scared of the lightning but she has a dulled—and pretty—child in her arms whom she has not *meanly* hurt; it is a maternal posture but boyish, maybe strange, that she has. This moment is giving her strength; it is a pattern from which strength is derived; she has an animal obstinacy. It's all right if I love her—isn't it? This is worth it, that we do this, that I have to live having been through this with her? Isn't it? The ecstatic fear and dauntlessness in her shout, "MAKE IT GO AWAY, YOU BASTARDS. MAKE IT GO AWAY. WILEY'S NOT MAD AT ME. I'M NOT DOING ANYTHING TO HIM." Nonie's voice: I never understood the utter sincerity of will and rigor of her voice and the falseness and obviousness of her tone, the way she lied—the limited sagacity.

What a bold thing it is to shrink and then harden one's entire self and never be able to have the rest of one's self, or one's other self, for the entire period of one's life on earth. She did that, and if I stop loving her I'll be doing it. If I can't love her at all, if I can't figure a way to do it, to risk loving her, I'll become at least a sort of bastard.

I mean, we know I have to forgive her—don't we?

Even if she is monstrous. Anyway, I can't tell if she is monstrous—right? I am a corrupt and inadequate judge—isn't that so?

If she is *ordinary and like everyone else,* it will be terrible for me not to love her—bad consequences will follow me all my life. Maybe.

If I had been angry, her rage would have been cold and settled against me for accusing her at such a time as this. My life would have been easier if she hadn't admired and liked the child in between the times of hating what he'd done to her life, what his existence had done to her life. I mean her reaction to his traits and moods and deeds was natural and particular to her, not typical, but hers: that's okay. She loved him, pursued him from time to time—the smaller child is fascinating and strange and peripheral to *Nonie*—and he arouses jealousy and other feelings on an uncomfortable scale—sometimes a gigantic scale: she is shrieking inside with temporary hope . . . "I WANT TO BE ALONE . . . I WANT TO BE ALONE WITH WILEY . . ."

She takes me into the closet—her closet . . . Now we are in Nonie's closet, with the door closed. Daddy is outside the door; he is in the room with the rain noises. Nonie and I are closed off in here . . . Ah, the suspense of real life. It smells of clothes and of Nonie here. She bites me shakingly on the side of my jaw—she quiets her mouth that way, maybe. She drags her teeth over my chin . . . I quiver. I feel her hot breath, I am suffocated against her quivering neck. I lean against the vibrating tissues and bones of that girl's shoulder and chest. She's squatting in the close, dark air in here. In the uproar of human heat and childish temperament and evil and fear we were in, I kissed the wet pulp of the chewed corners of Nonie's mouth.

Outside the closet, Daddy said, "Nonie, do you feel any better in there? I think the storm is getting lighter. Are you any better yet?"

He can't see us in here, in the dark.

He says, "See, Wiley's not afraid of the lightning." He says it in that funny, less intense way of someone talking through a door; he claims to see in a way: he's worried. Has she observed that her fear is not universal? He is less interested and more defeated in speech under these circumstances, when he can't see our faces. It's as if only the *side* of his voice, the part that's like a beam of wood, falls inside where we are; his voice is sawed and shortened, is deprived of the authority it has when it is attached to his face: he likes his own face; he likes his own voice less. "Wiley knows no one here is a bad person, he knows no one's going to be hit by the lightning today," he said with the disinterest and obliquity of being on the other side of the door.

Nonie pants. She hates him for saying I was a good judge—she shouts at him: "YOU'RE DISGUSTING. YOU SPY ON ME WHEN I UNDRESS."

(Momma used to ask me, *Why do you hate Nonie so much?*)

Nonie's indignation is crumpled in here but large and dark anyway. We have no light in here.

Daddy did sometimes wander down the hall in his pajamas to get a look at Nonie. He would do that when he was undressed and warm-fleshed—in his pants, say, and no shirt, or in shorts or naked or in pajamas or a robe. Daddy didn't think about things like this—he sort of lived them, offering his body for contemplation, for regard, and his feelings as well: *The Father's Body*, a grown man's; The Father's Feelings, a grown man's. Momma said he had *the gift of not thinking*—she meant the gift of conviction that he was moral in what he did, at least according to his own lights, on the ground that he was *a real man* and could rely on his reactions, on his innate decency—all his innate decencies—and that what was moral was obvious and he could be expected just regularly and automatically to do it.

Nonie burned to death; I said that, didn't I? A portable heater shorted out—this is what I was told. And she was drunk.

Her fear of being burned by lightning was prescient, I guess. She said often, at various ages of her life, that she was going to be a rich woman. But she never did become rich. She owned some buildings at one time; she ruled over her tenants probably in a foul way—I can't believe she ever stopped assaulting people's lives. I don't know what moral authority she ever gained in her community, but my guess is none. I used to hope something favorable would happen to her that would validate our childhood—mine with her, I mean: that she would become rich—rich even if foul—or moral and fine: then all the meanings would be there, wouldn't they? It's different if she's nobody. All the meanings are different. All. One wouldn't have to look back and wonder if silence was essential if one was to go on living now . . .

Wishing aside, if Nonie had opened her mind and become brave on a larger scale and become rich or moral, it would still have been dangerous for me to know her unless some great miracle occurred in her of *generosity*—over and beyond the possibility of moral generosity, I mean. And I can't imagine it, her making room for me generously. Maybe one of Nonie's sons—she had five—will accomplish something extraordinary, world-shaking, big-time, and be admirable—wouldn't that be good? And he might like me. I'd be surprised, though. But I'd think differently, and better, passionately well then, of Nonie. I'd blame myself for not having had the sense to *love* her, *anyway*. For not having taken the world as it was and being warm, *anyway*.

She's dead. I'm glad. Her sons, I'm told, are litigious, rigid, competitive, black-mooded, difficult, detestable—not successful—or religious. "They are to be avoided," I was told. "It's sad how regrettable they are." And: "They're mean the way she was—they're not good people." I suppose I ought to go West and see them for myself, but I don't want to know if they are not fine-nerved and obstinate; I don't want to know they are not bringing up fine children. I don't want to face any more than I have to.

For the moment, I am with Nonie in the closet, and she is a young girl with some sort of halfway-promising future and I'm a little kid and in her company, within the range of her prowess; and I know I am like her and I am aware that she can be happier than she is. We're all trash but in different ways. In the dark, in the closet, among Nonie's clothes—they rustle and rub me and smell—the child wriggles in Nonie's grasp; Nonie is silent except for protracted mutterings and whimperings and threats toward the grown-ups and the storm—and me, too, but vaguely—and at the center of her mêlée she's strangely still . . . she's in pain . . .

She does things to me—trespasses, sexual, hurried . . . Farcical . . . Faintly tender . . . Overly abrupt . . . Then she starts to push my hand into my own stomach while she tightens her arm on my throat as if to choke me into forgetfulness—or whatever . . .

Anne Marie and Daddy on the other side of the door: Anne Marie calls out at the sound the choked child makes. Nonie screams too.

She screams, "LET HIM HELP ME!"

"Es is nicht gut."

She always loved you, Wiley; it's just that it was Nonie [who loved you]—she was a handful and you weren't so easy yourself.

"No!" Anne Marie says to Nonie's plea. Anne Marie is out in the bedroom, in the big cube of air where the rain sounds are and where the rainlight quivers on and on. Her voice is large and has a room shape—but at a distance. When it enters my ears, it is partly muffled and partly wrinkled, like the sleeve of Nonie's middy coat lying against my forehead.

A line of light becomes a thick pole of light growing to be a torso of light and then a doorway. Of gray light. I see Nonie's bedroom and Daddy and Anne Marie. Anne Marie has wrenched the door open. Our shelter—Nonie's, mine, I guess—and our darkness are gone. Anne Marie knew. Nonie's fingers are in my mouth as if I might cry out otherwise. She has partly undressed me. Her fingers are digging into my waist. I can't breathe because of Nonie's hand and fingers on my mouth and nose. Anne Marie says in her heavily accented voice—as she hauls us out of the closet—"Let go of him, look at his lips . . ." The purpling lips.

Maybe we're just a trashy family.

"THE LIGHTNING SHOULDN'T GET ME. I'M GOOD," Nonie says from the half-darkness near the shoes from which Anne Marie is dragging her . . . And me . . .

"You? La-la-la—*don't make me laugh.*"

"Oh, my God," Daddy said, "this is no time to be hard on her."

Still set on my earlier purposes—obstinate and unlearned child—I reach, I grasp, I lean out from Anne Marie's grasp, and I grasp *Nonie* as Anne Marie lifts me—I hug Nonie's *head.*

Nonie is surprised; she stiffens; I hug the rumpled hair and the hard bone inside the rumpled hair. Nonie began to hug me back. She hugs my torso, my ribs, sliding her pink arms around me and avoiding Anne Marie's fat, yellowy-skinned arms. Nonie hugs the small body, the small-ribbed child's body. Nonie in her physical proficiency, her marred grace—her hugs can be vile; this one is, but it is also startlingly adept, knowing, athletically tender, smooth. She pokes me hurtingly and with one finger for fear she is making a mistake—it was like a curl of irony, a small, localized physical brutality, a curl of affection in her language, and a matter of safety first. And it was a piece of brutality of spirit to mix with so expert and in its way so wonderful and still so vile and so personal and so well remembered a hug. A confession. Nonie smelled of the closet and of stale sweat and pee, and she was scattered in her wits, and she was alert, blinkingly; her mind is on a number of things: this is Nonie's hug.

My childhood had a lot of tricky things in it.

What-I-am amazes me: this is when I was a child . . .

Daddy said, "Anne Marie, you think well of yourself, but look at that—look at those two—I ask you seriously; open your eyes and admit you were wrong and I'll say you were a big person. Here is something worth remembering right in front of your very eyes."

He is ironic in style, but he's mostly serious—no, not serious, truly dismissive, truly uninterested, truly confused morally—he doesn't care at the moment *what the truth is*—he's *relieved.*

Well, why not? Nonie's *his own flesh-and-blood.* I'm legally his son nowadays . . . We're a family, of sorts . . . *She's* one of us. We have our styles of morbid aggression, of death-dealing. We all have them. Nonie spits at Anne Marie. "LEAVE ME ALONE." Anne Marie was trying to lever her off me. But it's clear Nonie's not hurting me, and when Daddy says—more sharply—"Leave the kids alone," Anne Marie releases me to Nonie's grasp. Daddy says to Nonie, "Be lovable, Honey . . ."

The monstrous girl, Evil or not, problematically Evil or not, is of course, of a certainty, innocent to *some* extent.

The questions are: What harm will she do? How far will she go? Is her judgment all right? What will happen to me with her today? What will save her *today*? What is the right thing to do now? These are only some of the questions while the summer rain tumbles weightily outside.

She holds me backwards; my back is to her. She lugs me out of Anne Marie's reach. I'm a bulky weight for Nonie although she's strong. My legs are like pillows filled with dirt, I am that heavy for her. My rear end is a sack of weight. My neck, the back of my head bounce and slide against the girl's pudgy chest, the ribs, the ligaments and little muscles, childy smooth, bulgy with the little pockets and outpushes of the fat of her girlishness. It is almost shapeless what the back of my head bangs against. Her elbows dig into me, into my ribs and waist, my sides, unevenly, joltingly—a by-product of motion and whatever. She has physical acumen and can spare me some of this discomfort if she wants—no: she's too upset, maybe. I see her in the mirror on the closet door, the distorted and almost terrifying lynx mask of glare formed by the light on the bones of the upper part of her face—in the gray rainlight, in the flickering shadows of raindrops. She shouts, "I'M ALL RIGHT," and lugs me through the quivering air . . .

She puts me on the carpet—standing. I turn—at once—and reach up, to embrace her. I want her to be okay. I want her to be reliably present. I want *her* to love me. I want her to be *saved*. I can smell her damp neck in the rainy air. Her face is near mine but is higher. I see Nonie's chin, I see Nonie's terror-wet lips, her eyes, the lopsided lynx mask—I am determined to affect her. I'm not much bruised. The casual standards of harm in early childhood (unless you have some sensitive, thin standard—usually a lie) mean that some stuff about being hurt is up in the air. At the moment, Nonie's ability to hurt, and her attractions, and her character are an abstract matter of other occasions—of a multitude of occasions—moments of our being in the house with each other again and again over a number of years, over a period of years—an abstract matter of physical change, itself the cause of quarrels, spread over weeks and then years, the various bodies and shapes and sizes and attributes we had, while what is present now is her simple nearness as she becomes less caught in terror. Then the reality of her proximity at the moment is as if a sponge is cleaning away heat and dismay—disorder, too—or as if she is walking toward him even while she is standing still . . .

I am involved in the emotional reality, to me, of her life moment-to-moment during the time that I knew her. Nonie's being evil is not always important to me—that's all there is to that—but that some *evil* exists in everyone, the logic of that is important to me.

Anne Marie, whom I thought well of, thought (or *thinks* in a present-tense moment) that Nonie is pretty foul. Momma gets depressed at what parts of Nonie's character are. What things add up to bothers Daddy more than it does me, but he is dead and now it bothers me. Daddy doesn't face any of it except when he walks out on Momma. Except when he withdraws. He is dead. What people are and do gets on his nerves. She drives him crazy. So have I—driven him crazy. He avoids thinking about that—*He's a very, very, very affectionate man—in his way . . .*

Anne Marie, as part of her politics, her culture, and her church, has a sense of Evil. Daddy denies that Evil exists. Momma says, *Yes-and-no, I play it by ear . . .* Daddy denies its existence (*evil's*) for the sake of women (and children), even while feeling superior because of his superior knowledge and experience of it in wartime and among men—criminal politics, crimes and politics. Lila hates him for this and is as dark as he is when he is dark—and he tries not-to-*give-houseroom* (his phrase) to his real feelings or thoughts or memories of that stuff when he is near her or us.

He prefers to take shelter in women, in his forbearance, in theirs, in innocence as it exists—in sunsets and by will, by programmatic *goodness.*

Lila's sense of evil is really dark, but it is changeable—sometimes amused, relentless, and female: not steady. She's not serious about fighting it *until I'm good and ready, just wait until I get my war paint on, will you*—she says she will lie down with *it* (with whatever evil comes her way) and approve of it if it will be good to her and to her children—does she love us that much?

Much of the time when I was young, a lot of this stuff didn't matter to me. I lived from *day to day and ate my cereal*—S.L.'s words. Nonie's life, her actual life and not my view of it, well, a lot depended on how seductive her life was for me and how interesting she was as a playmate.

She is a serious person in her way—middle-class with brown hair is her as a child: not really a child: but young for her age.

She can be described in all sorts of ways. And like that. If Nonie frightens or saddens me enough, what will become of me? If she feels the possibility of such a victory, of some ease, of the murder of possibility in me, will she back off? Console me? She consoles no one. She's alone. If she does win out, then no matter how I lie, or what I do, my story will be secondary to hers—to Nonie's—my life will matter less than her life does—in real time, this is. I would think she would find it hard to choose to be secondary in her life to mine, to my luck, my ill luck or my good luck.

No matter what she might learn or gain, she'd lose a lot of her momentum. But maybe for a while she should have tried to be secondary, anyway. We could have taken turns—is that too Utopian? She chose to compete all out, not for equality—how was that to be measured?—but to be the one who was the most important, whose pain mattered most of anyone's . . . And whose pleasures were the most important—the most praiseworthy—the most typical—in the world.

Any extreme lawfulness was a defeat for her. Under the actual rule of law, she'd have to share and not punish—and not win. She went not just for victory but for the taking over and absorption of qualities, opportunities, virtues from her opponent. Her fear was that she'd lose out in the end otherwise and prove to have been wrong, all along, in her pride. She comforted herself by being a rival in everything and appropriating everything, such comfort as there was, by inventing absolute terms—one goodness, one mode of justice, which she administered, and so on—and she called that love for a while.

It was love in her sense. But after a while she simply was unrelentingly out to get what she could—I suppose that came from the pain of defeat or was what adulthood was for her: that sour. It seemed to me that after a certain point it never let up: the sour appetite of acquisition—that immense game.

When we were both grown, she was so afraid of me and so bitter that she would not agree with me about anything. She would not remember anything jointly with me—not picnics, not Christmases, not anything. One time she had access to some money and I was ill (I was maybe eight years old) and she said, "Let him die."

I'd said things like that about her, but not when she was ill.

I mean, I didn't take harming her so directly into my own hands: but then I was not a girl. There were intervening powers to filter and censor and limit the stuff I might do in my state, state of emotion or of unreason.

She said it again when I was older and had been in a car crash: "I can't help him—let him die."

It wasn't even interesting that she hated me.

One time, Lila and S.L. were broke; I wanted to go away to prep school and they wanted to borrow some money from Nonie. She screamed and screamed: *NOT HIM, HE'S HAD ENOUGH, I'VE HAD NOTHING . . .*

Anyway, I stayed home and did not go away to school—her money was hers. I guess I was twelve at that point.

She was never ashamed of what she did when I was there to see her. She "talked about" me—Lila meant Nonie *lied* about me so that "if the truth comes out she won't look so bad—no one will believe your half of the story is the whole story."

I don't know. S.L. was ill and difficult. After a set-to with Nonie, he had his first stroke, and after another set-to, his second stroke. Those strokes didn't kill him, though. Nonie said that she *loved* S.L. but that she didn't care if he died now and that he would understand that feeling in her. She said it would be good for him to die, that he was tired of living and that he wanted to die. I didn't pay a whole lot of attention, since I was afraid her blood tie to him gave her secret (and reliable) insight, information, knowledge about him. I wasn't given to indignation at that point. I didn't want to lose my grip on things. I couldn't afford to.

I figured Nonie hated Lila—and S.L.—it's a silly thing to try to measure: someone's emotions.

She used to tell people she was helping in my education when she wasn't helping: she was actively hindering it, or, often, trying to prevent it. In my adolescence, when I was at my meanest, I was sort of *sympathetic*—understanding-of-her—even in this. She was such a murderous and competitive clunker. A loser. A real competitor . . . I didn't think time would be good to her. I hoped time would be kind to her. I didn't always care. Or care much.

On occasion, after I was grown up, to preserve some outward fiction or other (such as that she wasn't a disaster, as far as I was concerned), I'd arrange to see her when she came to the town where I was living. I have this sloppy habit of trying to make talk to conceal the realities of a situation and not blaming or loathing something or someone I really do loathe or am revolted by and think is foul—her, in this case, Nonie. I go leaning into the situation to conceal what would be shown if I stayed stiff and antagonistic—or merely distant or bored. I don't say I'm right in this. I do it, that's all. I hope to stop being like this someday but I am getting old and I am still like that.

The last time I saw her, it bothered me that it was just as on the day of the rainstorm, that I became, in some perverse and perverted and twistedly ill-advised way, concerned with her mood. Why the hell should

I care what *her* mood is? That's fine in stories but that's stupid in real life. You know who the hell cares what *her* mood is? Anyone who's scared of her. The thing to care about is fending her off. Concern for Nonie is a trait for someone not at all disciplined by sadness, someone spoiled—someone stupid, in a way. *A clown* . . .

Daddy called me that when I worried about Nonie. My being like that makes Nonie crazed—in the present tense, but in the past. Coldly, hotly. But she's addicted to it: this is long, long ago. She died nearly twenty years ago, burned to death—*burned to death*. My God, imagine that . . . My Nonie—dead. Dead in that way . . . Hush, be silent . . . Be silent . . . You're not a child anymore.

She has asked to see me. She has come to see me. The one-time colossally pretty girl, the one-time *older* child, now fat, hard-eyed, obese actually, she sits in a chair and is nervous and far-off in a grimacing way, disapproving, menacing as a general tactic—like an angry business-woman. She never referred to me in my hearing as her *brother* on any grown-up occasion that I know of . . .

She wants favors. She means, hopes, aims to elicit favors from me—a dozen of them: she wants money, information, to meet some people I know. She wants to stay with some people I know and whom she has never met but who she has heard about, including that they are *friends* of mine. She asks of me that I arrange this and she makes faces as if I were mad and a beggar and not someone who can say no to her if I change the subject or try to weasel out of it.

Or if I simply, flatly, say no.

It doesn't much matter to her who I am or what I am—she hates it all—I mean as a *natural* thing. It is her right. And my physical quality is more foreign, more monstrous to her than when we were young. It is worse for her that I exist than it is for anyone else.

Lila said *I* destroyed Nonie—I won out—but it was Lila who told me the story of the infant sons.

Nonie says, "Well, you are conceited as ever . . ."

I say, "Yes? You think so? Well, but I try not to be a hero . . . I think it is important *nowadays* not to be a hero . . . even in your own mind."

"I don't know what you're talking about; I never know what you're talking about . . ."

I start to feel around me the closet smells, the pressure of hot flesh that earlier day.

I say, "Well, here we are again; we're an odd pair. Just like old times."

She says, "I don't like to talk about the past, I don't like that sort of talk, I don't have to talk about water under the bridge. I have no interest in it. I don't like those things. I don't know about you but I had a happy childhood—a very happy childhood—and that's all I know. That's all anyone needs to know if you ask me, if I know anything about it. I loved everybody and everybody loved me—that's enough for anyone—that's what I think. That's all I want to know. I don't know about you. You had problems."

She burned to death when she was forty-two years old.

"Nonie, the bedroom, your bedroom on Vista Drive—that color was nice: a watery-pale-green. Really."

She said, "That's really boring—that's too boring for me to talk about."

But I think she remembers.

If I don't dislike her, I can't have characters in what I write—I can't attempt to make them come alive if they don't have a shadow of her in them.

"Well, what do you suggest we talk about?"

"Tell me, do you have any money *now* or not?"

"At times, I do. Right now, no." For you, always no.

It's the truth in my voice, in my manner that upsets her. In the truth is the offer of a truce if she will allow me to live.

I mean, I will have money then.

She suddenly said, tauntingly, "Hank and I are very happy. I have five wonderful sons and everything I want." She went on for a while in that fashion; and then she said, "I have no interest in people I don't know. I don't know how people stand it who have to read a lot of books and take themselves seriously and just talk, talk, talk all the time." She began to discuss some of her friends—how rich they were, how much they liked her, how awful they were. "She has just awful brighty-bright eyes—" Then she said, "You think you're smart, but we're pretty smart out West now, you know." It was in California that she died. Then she asked me to set it up for her and her family to visit people I knew and whom she had never met.

That was the last time I saw her. Other people disliked me then and still others do so now. *I am not an angel.* Lila used to say that. One grows from having merely human curators in childhood to having outright enemies in one's adult life, and they prevent certain actions; they propose limits to one's will—one's rewards—they want a cut of whatever you have—and so on.

That last meeting, her rage—she's not smart enough to hide it. And she's afraid of me. She has energy. She does her part forcefully, with a will. She denies us a past, and she pursues me anyway with her malice and her uneasiness and her anxiety about the past, an anxiety to make use of me, to keep the past going, to have it be continuous with now and herself and her life being not so foul—perhaps they aren't so foul: I am a snob and I have old scores, I suppose—not conscious ones, not mostly. She wants to have this meaning, too, in her life, of my attachment to her, but one-sidedly. I am reasonably certain I would do it if it was to be two-sided. She allows me little or no reality—which is what kills me, of course. She's human; *SHE'S ONE OF US;* I remember one time when I was six or seven and she was seventeen or eighteen, and she was being amiable, even flirtatious—on a porch. She taught me some tricks on a yo-yo. She hated me the worst at that time and, contrarily, had periods of being nicer than ever. She laughed at me and was sweet, but she became angry—even murderous—when I proved dextrous. She said, "You have a filthy mean streak." She threw hot coffee at me—in my eyes, naturally. "Don't make a big fuss over him!" she yelled when the grown-ups showed up. She complained to the grown-ups stubbornly on that occasion that they babied me. She did it as a pretty girl who would not speak reasonably or allow herself to be dealt with unless it was admitted to as an assumption around our house that I had a mean streak in me that made me show off and made people want to kill me and no one could be blamed for wanting to hurt me—and for doing it. No one could help hurting me or could be considered guilty for doing it.

That was a clearer occasion than some—I mean people saw it the way I saw it—but just the year before then, something like that happened and Momma had been sympathetic to her, to Nonie.

In those days, and perhaps still, if she's "normal," if she's what people are, then who—and what—am I?

Her bedroom. She is still being a soldier. But nothing and no one instructs Nonie or instructed her ever in the victories she hungers for—I mean, she has mostly the wrong victories, ones she doesn't want, that Momma and Daddy, one way and another, taught her about. But she wants them anyway, to soothe herself because she feels others' victories as pain for her . . . My real mother is not present to vote for me here in Nonie's bedroom. It's grim that a lot of people won't grant you the moral authority to defend yourself—you're defending too much and calling it yourself—*and we want you limited now.* You have to be cold and obstinate and tricky—I mean, so many people want you undone; and some people who are on your side are really worthless. The flux of

Nonie's temper gives *houseroom* to her sorts of emotion; I mean, toward actualities of the monstrous; life includes special areas of the monstrous aimed at her: life happens to her in her style—not entirely, but a lot. She perceives it that way; she sets it up, too, sometimes as a perversion of judgment and of mood that just barely fails to be comic—this shapeless-souled girl, perhaps misunderstood, perhaps destroyed, who has me in her keeping . . . I have embraced her and now she kisses me, sobs faintly. Lightning glows distantly a good ten miles to the east. In that glow, enormous reaches of hollow, gray-blue, rainy sky are visible. Then the brownish, darker areas of rain reemerge from the glow, return, the vista is removed, and we are inside the repetitive and mufflingly domestic, somehow amorous noise of the rain.

Nonie touches me with a wan, vaguely athletic coolness, a tenderness poised, not deadened—partly hysterical, though; but it's real, it's between us, it's been gained. And one's appetite for consolation can rest here—or mourn its inevitable loss-to-come or simply observe it for a moment, at this moment of existence, a truce of wills, of breath.

Comfortable, in a way, we are with each other, hands and bodies childishly in touch—she has a lasting tact about some of the pragmatic realities of childhood.

But that tact turns outward and is clearly part of a case of Nonie's being the center of decency in her system, the central repository of civilization: she is a young girl of suffering semi-equilibrium now, a consciousness stretched taut over certain inadequacies, of consciousness. She has for a moment a quality of sweetness, nerve-ridden, luminous—she's comfortable, to a degree, too guilt-ridden, too naked to persist in it wholeheartedly; but if I bother to remember this moment clearly, what is clearest is her affection for the child and the *intelligence* of that affection in that time and in that household . . . A faint light in the mirror—a smallish after-flicker of nearby lightning, that's all—cheats her of immediate escape. At once, Nonie flings herself, holding me, to the floor, and the rubbery weight of her body and its thrashing, at her gasping and twitching, are crows' wings, and her breath's cawing is all over me, all around me—I'm in the darkness under her body, in the gasps and thrashings, in the shadow of all that she was; I get banged around by that. Completely used, completely ignored, I'm there—it means too much that *I'm* there—I'll just put myself there and forget meaning, but still, the meaning exists whether I ignore it or not. Where I am, under her body, *it's like the end of the world*, as Daddy said—rhetorically—then and there it is an odd childhood apocalypse . . .

Nonie's grunting and twisting. Nonie rolls back and forth.

S.L.: "Oh, Christ, why doesn't it stop? It's killing me. It's like the end of the world . . ."

(Lila: "*She doesn't like to stop. You have to stop her. Be a realist:* IT'S THAT SIMPLE.")

No, it's not.

"DADDY, THE THUNDER IS TERRIBLE. YOU BASTARD . . . OH, YOU BASTARD . . ."

It was a small thunder.

On the floor, under her body, where I am, it's warm and roiling and breath-torn and dark and smelly.

It's okay.

Daddy stoops and puts his arm around us—her and me; and he scoops us up at an angle. "Nonie, that's not bad thunder—now, come on. That's not real close, Hon. Come on."

She's gagging more than she's crying in the rubbery bleakness of this almost-an-afterward.

A gray-green light is at the windows and is in the room, watery and flickering. Nonie's sweaty neck is a river of light. The light pulses on her concise neck—an illuminated rhythm unexplained as beauty but still beauty whether it is explained or not, this symptom of life—of her life . . . It glows and grows steadier in speed and assurance but is not very steady for all that—the pulse, her life. The sputter and jerk of her skin continue. Her pulse is scared. It isn't exactly calm. I hear it, I see it, I'm close to her.

The thunder shakes the floor a little. Inside the warm interlacings and smells, I feel Nonie shake. Nonie is shaking a lot. I cover her with myself.

Her face.

My belly's bent over her. Her face.

I do and don't care what this means.

I don't care what has happened.

Besides the other things I do is this: I embrace her will and shame, her being Evil . . . It's okay with me so far . . . Maybe only in a family sense . . . But I doubt that . . .

Nonie was right to think that lightning lay in wait for her and she was right to think I did not ever have her interest at heart in a way she could really like . . .

But something was there in me, and concerned with her.

For instance, I think that to the best of my knowledge—maybe this is just stupidity—I would prefer to have had Nonie go crazy on this occasion, for good, and for her to say crazed things, and to become mistaken in the names of things and then to die young and nice and pitiable than for her to live out the life she had in the way she did, in fact, live it. I wish she'd died and been satisfactorily dead for most of my life.

And I would have the memory of having *loved her madly*—even if such terms are beyond using, they are so sentimental.

Yet that's not entirely true . . . I wish that I'd been as clever as she was, and that while I hugged her I'd hurt her mortally . . . What I'm getting at is that I'm not much glad that the gesture stands, my hugging her—my accommodation, my fearless embrace and affection with Evil, my shy hatred, my being conned into and out of equality, superiority, inferiority, favors, reparations, all of it—all that. I'm not glad . . . But it stands . . . I stand behind the act.

I partly do accept my life. Her. Possibilities of willed goodness. Jesus, I did love her at times—I loved that mess of putrefaction . . . Also, the girl in her . . .

The fire that killed her—in California, in her bedroom—it wound up burning through a wall, it set the lawn on fire, then shrubs; the trees were blazing on the lawn as in a disaster of a war—and then the house—the house she lived in—burned up . . .

A cousin called to tell me. "Nonie's dead," said the long-distance voice; then, in a whisper, "Goody-goody."

In Nonie's room, in the increasing light—the rain is letting up—in Daddy's funny grip, I hold her in my short, bony, childish arms in a kind of ecstatic sternness of possession. Of my protection of her. Me, not the demons, not Daddy or Anne Marie, I'm the most powerful one here, in the end, sort of—maybe it is an illusion. My sweetness rules here—one way and another. And I'm scared—I'm not an *invincible* conqueror. I kiss her. She kisses my hair—in a slow, webbed, maybe drying-her-terror way. Nonie and I rule here. An intelligence in each of us about the other and about such an embrace as this strips and informs us, it is a childish knowledge, a vulnerability. We weren't clumsy with each other always. We were clumsy and sometimes skillful . . . sometimes in order to hurt each other in certain ways. We were maybe clumsy at life, but we did all right with each other as enemies and during truces, too, and in some rivalries, too, we had real skills about each other.

I embraced demon-filth Nonie. She had her arms around killer-trash Wiley. We are insiders. The enmity, the hate, is real. It is very real. We twine arms and legs and *necks.* These childish hugs of differing creatures, the sense of two lives being present—I remember the considerable excellence of how mutual it all was despite the disparities in size and mind and state of mind and in the passions and degrees of violence between us . . . at that time. We know this about each other at this moment of the child's peculiar victory–half-victory; we know this, *too.* Among the knowledges that were there . . . We huddle and combine. At this moment, we are lives and heat in a knot, in a sickening real marriage, a combination of souls. Her arm snakes and then tightens on the small of my back. For a lifetime. Her chin presses into my shoulder. Her breath moves on my skinny back, familiarly. She is family . . . Well, that term is sentimental: for eternity . . . .

The Preparation for the Eulogy

Our attachment, our embrace: I see the point of lying, *for eternity,* changing all connections, all meaning. Lila said to me before she died: *I tell you, Wiley, people felt sorry for her: she had to live with you—you would try the patience of a saint—anyone human would have felt sorry for her . . . You hurt her all the time; you judged her . . .* This stuff hurts: Ma—being blamed. I judged her. I judge her now. So what. Big deal.

Lila, S.L., when in battle with me, often would impose her on me: *Goddamn it, don't act like she disgusts you . . . You're going to have to live your life with people, Wiley . . . She loves you . . . You ought to love her . . . .*

Are hatred and jealousy, dislike and will, cleverer than sweetness? Does that remain to be proved? *You have to learn to get along with her* . . . In the familiarity of half-concealed, mostly concealed enmity? *You have to learn to live in the real world,* I was told.

To which I replied, *So does she.* But no one understood me. She is the world . . . She is a definition of the world . . . I am not. But what if I am? What if some people who said I am not are wrong? Nonie is not my definition of the entire world. But she is an inescapable presence and a necessary part of the reality of everyone, in my view. She is what *I* look for in someone, traces of her reality—the shadow of that reality is largely how I judge people. Lila, in the last seventy hours of her life, had the nurses and nuns keep Nonie out of her room—away from the deathbed. *It has been a lesson to know her,* Momma said, dying: *I learned it the hard way.* But Momma told me Nonie wasn't worse than other people: she asked me to take care of her. Nonie said to me once, *Take my side or else* . . . That didn't seem strange. Most of the people I knew in New York tried that, did that. I partly didn't understand, even if I expected it, the echo of this crooked experiment, this genetic crusader, this agent of disappointment, the enraged child, the pink-legged girl . . . Perhaps sweetly and *normally* wronged, a rivalrous person—a rivalrous girl. Daddy used to say, *We're not such good people, we're not such bad people* . . . He was trying for a reasonable moral assessment in real time, outside of books. He hoped for a daily basis of *good judgment.* How curious *the* forms of civilization are . . .

When Nonie went to live with Aunt Casey, Lila said to me, *It serves you right—you're stuck with us now* . . .

I want to say I don't understand it, any of it. I want to be an okay-seeming narrator, not one so implicated that he is hardly better than someone you would know in life. Nonie's jealous rivalries, her maybe extraordinary, maybe ordinary hopes for herself: I cannot be her accomplice, her friend, her brother without my taking part in some conscious or unconscious cruelty of large dimension in some direction, toward her, toward others . . . Lila said to me, *You are oversensitive and spoiled. I hate to tell you this and ruin your day but you are naïve, you are very naïve, Wiley* . . . I am afraid. I am afraid. Lila said, *She's better when you're not around, you should see it sometimes; you should try to put yourself in her place sometimes—it wouldn't hurt you* . . . And: *Wiley, she* LOVES *you—*

Love's like that? Big deal . . . I don't care . . . I DON'T CARE . . . CHRIST . . .

I said, *I don't care if she loves me or not: just keep her away from me* . . .

On her deathbed, Lila said, *We did a bad thing; we treated Nonie as if she was okay. I'm sorry you had to go through it; I'm sorry what you had to go through with her, all of it; I apologize; I apologize to you . . . At first, I was on my guard, but you know how it is: things wear out; things wear down* . . . Lila had lived long enough that I was at college—a good college. Harvard, a tall boy, neurotic and easygoing: she thought I had risen to the moral simplicities, the purities and law-abidingness of a much higher social standing than she had achieved in her life. From inside my new life, I saw her die, you know? She said, *I'm a little afraid of what you think of me—I confess . . . Besides, the ghost of your real mother comes to see me here, on my deathbed. I'm everything of everything now that I'm sick—I'm my old self once I get a little steam up: then I'm not afraid of anything—just of you now that you're a Harvard man . . .*

She thought I could be sentimental and aloof toward hatred and ordinariness from then on. I said, "Yeah, sure, but I'm still on your side, Mother . . ."

I know of no neutral judge.

Lila may have lied in what she said to me about Nonie. Or it was a mood. A deathbed statement has a kind of brilliance to it that makes it not like an easy truth. When Nonie tried to force her way into the room, Lila screamed, *KEEP HER OUT! KEEP THAT ONE OUT!*

She said, *I'm no shrinking violet but that one takes the cake . . .*

The promise at the end, Lila making me promise to be good to Nonie—I broke that promise. I never even tried to keep it. I remember Daddy shouting, *Why can't you two love each other? I want a home with some love and peace in it, Goddamn it: is that too much to ask? You think that's abnormal? You think I'm strange? I want you two to learn to get along . . .*

Fat chance. Lila said, *S.L. maybe was wrong now and then but he* really *loved you—you should forgive him*—he *wasn't the type to be a policeman all day long. What can you do? People aren't mirages—if you don't like real people, you wind up with no one; you know that, don't you? That's true even at Harvard, isn't it?* She meant was the truth the same there. *Is it all the same when you're lucky or do you see things in a different light? Sickness makes me see things in a different light—and that's* God's *ordinary truth, Sonny Boy . . . Forgive me if I talk too much. It's the morphine. It makes me like the way I sound. I love you, Wiley. Be nice to her, if you can . . .*

A Eulogy (of sorts)

Nonie's death I take as a generous absence on her part—I mean this. I wake up sometimes and think with a rush of warmth that it is *nice* that I cannot possibly hear from her except from among the shadows as a revenant ghost or as a memory speaking. I like the feel of the moments that don't have her in them—or her voice, or the dread unreason of her ambitious pain—or the grimacingly painful-funny stuff—of her reality: I like the moments to be empty of that although, often then, the moments have the presence of someone else being that way in them. I don't bother with blame much. I feel shame, grief, giddiness, relief—pity for people: each of those things is different from liking . . . I'm glad to be done with her. But just below that as-if-painless gladness, as if down shadowy wooden stairs into a basement, is a further gladness, like further shadows: a heat of sympathy and disdain, pity and, actually, horror—and self-recognition, a sense of being like her. And here it is painful and real. Here is my brute acceptance of her death and my isolation. But down the as-if-basement steps into further darkness and silence and self-judgment, down there stands a shadowy, shamed boy: all the while that she was alive he kept quiet about her. He sheltered her with his silence . . . *She has to live, too* . . . Yes, I know. But now that I am old, well, I don't know . . .

My feelings don't fit any grammatical or syntactical model. They do not suggest a requiem. I imagine in my eulogy a moment of my being prepared for the loneliness that comes to me at her absence and *real love* sort of floating in a void since she is the object of it and old feelings, daydreams, hotly desirous, of her and me making peace. *I* want her to become generous, to be made it by discipline—or to be generous through success. Or so educated by death, illness, love, money, by the pain of being deceived, if that is necessary, that she knows what kindness is, in real moments, existing second after second and being interrupted by a telephone or a fire or an air raid. I am sorry I wish this. I would have liked to have been a different man. Standing on the basement floor, near the drain, I feel pity, charity, forgetfulness . . . But it is because she is dead. It is because she is not present in reality with her shadowy eyelids and her as-if-innocent malice. Romance as truth—as unromantic, ordinary *truth* . . . how different it would be for her. The romances in her life were ironic and fantastic tactics of greatness, of perfection, of something she felt to be universal and absolute, total and perfect. She is a girlish Samson, a fierce David. Kindness and charity hurt and erase her and tempt her to wrestle with them as with demons. They are demonic in some forms. For me not to hate her—for me to love her *charitably* at my own will insulted her. She had to *force* people to feel what they felt—otherwise, she felt their feelings to be valueless and that she was a valueless and dead object in relation to those feelings—that was how it worked for her. Feelings we had on our own about her were like found objects, a kind of trash, without merit: she felt she could do as she liked with them . . . This is what I think she felt, that we could do as we liked with such feelings: it did not matter to her—all of that was only trash. She would have liked a more common sort of eulogy than this.

If I summon her physical presence—breasts, skin, dyed hair at an adult age—I feel in her huffy breath and in her gaze at me how *I* hurt her when I was not coerced and edgy in her presence. *I* can feel how hints are to her liking and outright statements of rage and clever or stupid actions are to her liking—and how it scares *her* that she is the way she is—she is doubly scared because of me—I exist and I do fairly well in the world. That I am, in sum, a truth, a something that is the case, this widens her eyes: this makes her ill . . .

If I imagine us meeting after death, *for eternity*, as souls were thought to do, maybe, by some poets, I imagine the slow reconciliation in limbo in the slow alteration of souls, the spiritual education.

How much pain those old poets proposed as part of one's instruction. I cannot imagine her greeting me with pleasure at seeing someone of a nearly common history in the great unchanging light of ***HEAVEN*** . . . History would not matter then, of course . . . All sentiment aside, no one could break off from the searing final bliss for a sentimental moment. But if I allow myself, unseriously, then to imagine a meeting after death, I see in my imagined *moments* a stiffness. I doubt that even in a pliable and sentimental *Heaven* that she would address me in such a way that what we meant to one another would fill her with heavenly warmth and a wish to share any of it with each other.

So, if we meet, if we are to speak, I suppose it will have to be in Hell.

But when I imagine us meeting in Hell, there I think she would turn her back on me—even there, then, too—unless I could do her a favor there, among the flames, the ashes . . . I think I mean to say that hatred and balked ambition are serious and final.

Ah, my pretty and complex and difficult and violent sister, ah, my long-lost, clear-eyed Nonie, I don't care if you forgive me or not . . . What do you suppose *that* means?

If I step out of the frames of narrative, out of all such frames, and enter the present actual moment, I see that while I bear a floating kind of forgiveness toward her (and why should she want my forgiveness: what were her crimes?), all this is ultimately beside the point for me. It is only in leaps and spasms of will that I can make myself see that if I had been as bad to her as I think she was to me, I would forgive her now. I would be close to her in spirit. I would not, even if only idly, think ill of the dead.

Perhaps this story should be continued by other means . . . As time was, once she was dead.

But, for a moment, let us pause. Let us be still. Or, rather, let me be quiet in her memory—and in memory of me—for a little while.